Willa Cather
Collected works:
The Troll Garden,
O Pioneers!
The Song of the Lark,
and My Antonia

By Willa Cather

CONTENTS

BOOK ONE.

THE TROLL GARDEN

AND

SELECTED STORIES

ON THE DIVIDE

Near Rattlesnake Creek, on the side of a little draw stood Canute's shanty. North, east, south, stretched the level Nebraska plain of long rust-red grass that undulated constantly in the wind. To the west the ground was broken and rough, and a narrow strip of timber wound along the turbid, muddy little stream that had scarcely ambition enough to crawl over its black bottom. If it had not been for the few stunted cottonwoods and elms that grew along its banks, Canute would have shot himself years ago. The Norwegians are a timber-loving people, and if there is even a turtle pond with a few plum bushes around it they seem irresistibly drawn toward it.

As to the shanty itself, Canute had built it without aid of any kind, for when he first squatted along the banks of Rattlesnake Creek there was not a human being within twenty miles. It was built of logs split in halves, the chinks stopped with mud and plaster. The roof was covered with earth and was supported by one gigantic beam curved in the shape of a round arch. It was almost impossible that any tree had ever grown in that shape. The Norwegians used to say that Canute had taken the log across his knee and bent it into the shape he wished. There were two rooms, or rather there was one room with a partition made of ash saplings interwoven and bound together like big straw basket work. In one corner there was a cook stove, rusted and broken. In the other a bed made of unplaned planks and poles. It was fully eight feet long, and upon it was a heap of dark bed clothing. There was a chair and a bench of colossal proportions. There was an ordinary kitchen cupboard with a few cracked dirty dishes in it, and beside it on a tall box a tin washbasin. Under the bed was a pile of pint flasks, some broken, some whole, all empty. On the wood box lay a pair of shoes of almost incredible dimensions. On the wall hung a saddle, a gun, and some ragged clothing, conspicuous among which was a suit of dark cloth, apparently new, with a paper collar carefully wrapped in a red silk handkerchief and pinned to the sleeve. Over the door hung a wolf and a badger skin, and on the door itself a brace of thirty or forty snake skins whose noisy tails rattled ominously every time it opened. The strangest things in the shanty were the wide windowsills. At first glance they looked as though they had been ruthlessly hacked and mutilated with a hatchet, but on closer inspection all the notches and holes in the wood took form and shape. There seemed to be a series of pictures. They were, in a rough way, artistic, but the figures were heavy and labored, as though they had been cut very slowly and with very awkward instruments. There were men plowing with little horned imps sitting on their shoulders and on their horses' heads. There were men praying with a skull hanging over their heads and little demons behind them mocking their attitudes. There were men fighting with big serpents, and skeletons dancing together. All about these pictures were blooming vines and foliage such as never grew in this world, and coiled among the branches of the vines there was always the scaly body of a serpent, and behind every flower there was a serpent's head. It was a veritable Dance of Death by one who had felt its sting. In the wood box lay some boards, and every inch of them was cut up in the same manner. Sometimes the work was very rude and careless, and looked as though the hand of the workman had trembled. It would sometimes have been hard to distinguish the men from their evil geniuses but for one fact, the men were always grave and were either toiling or praying, while the devils were always smiling and dancing. Several of these boards had been split for kindling and it was evident that the artist did not value his work highly.

It was the first day of winter on the Divide. Canute stumbled into his shanty carrying a basket of cobs, and after filling the stove, sat down on a stool and crouched his seven foot frame over the fire, staring drearily out of the window at the wide gray sky. He knew by heart every individual clump of bunch grass in the miles of red shaggy prairie that stretched before his cabin. He knew it in all the deceitful loveliness of its early summer, in all the bitter barrenness of its autumn. He had seen it smitten by all the plagues of Egypt. He had seen it parched by drought, and sogged by rain, beaten by hail, and swept by fire, and in the grasshopper years he had seen it eaten as bare and clean as bones that the vultures have left. After the great fires he had seen it stretch for miles and miles, black and smoking as the floor of hell.

He rose slowly and crossed the room, dragging his big feet heavily as though they were burdens to him. He looked out of the window into the hog corral and saw the pigs burying themselves in the straw before the shed. The leaden gray clouds were beginning to spill themselves, and the snow flakes were settling down over the white leprous patches of frozen earth where the hogs had gnawed even the sod away. He shuddered and began to walk, trampling heavily with his ungainly feet. He was the wreck of ten winters on the Divide and he knew what that meant. Men fear the winters of the Divide as a child fears night or as men in the North Seas fear the still dark cold of the polar twilight. His eyes fell upon his gun, and he took it down from the wall and looked it over. He sat down on the edge of his bed and held the barrel towards his face, letting his forehead rest upon it, and laid his finger on the trigger. He was perfectly calm, there was neither passion nor despair in his face, but the thoughtful look of a man who is considering. Presently he laid down the gun, and reaching into the cupboard, drew out a pint bottle of raw white alcohol. Lifting it to his lips, he drank greedily. He washed his face in the tin basin and combed his rough hair and shaggy blond beard. Then he stood in uncertainty before the suit of dark clothes that hung on the wall. For the fiftieth time he took them in his hands and tried to summon courage to put them on. He took the paper collar that was pinned to the sleeve of the coat and cautiously slipped it under his rough beard, looking with timid expectancy into the cracked, splashed glass that hung over the bench. With a short laugh he threw it down on the bed, and pulling on his old black hat, he went out, striking off across the level.

It was a physical necessity for him to get away from his cabin once in a while. He had been there for ten years, digging and plowing and sowing, and reaping what little the hail and the hot winds and the frosts left him to reap. Insanity and suicide are very common things on the Divide. They come on like an epidemic in the hot wind season. Those scorching dusty winds that blow up over the bluffs from Kansas seem to dry up the blood in men's veins as they do the sap in the corn leaves. Whenever the yellow scorch creeps down over the tender inside leaves about the ear, then the coroners prepare for active duty; for the oil of the country is burned out and it does not take long for the flame to eat up the wick. It causes no great sensation there when a Dane is found swinging to his own windmill tower, and most of the Poles after they have become too careless and discouraged to shave themselves keep their razors to cut their throats with.

It may be that the next generation on the Divide will be very happy, but the present one came too late in life. It is useless for men that have cut hemlocks among the mountains of Sweden for forty years to try to be happy in a country as flat and gray and naked as the sea. It is not easy for men that have spent their youth fishing in the Northern seas to be content with following a plow, and men that have served in the Austrian army hate hard work and coarse clothing on the loneliness of the plains, and long for marches and excitement and tavern company and pretty barmaids. After a man has passed his fortieth birthday it is not easy for him to change the habits and conditions of his life. Most men bring with them to the Divide only the dregs of the lives that they have squandered in other lands and among other peoples.

Canute Canuteson was as mad as any of them, but his madness did not take the form of suicide or religion but of alcohol. He had always taken liquor when he wanted it, as all Norwegians do, but after his first year of solitary life he settled down to it steadily. He exhausted whisky after a while, and went to alcohol, because its effects were speedier and surer. He was a big man and with a terrible amount of resistant force, and it took a great deal of alcohol even to move him. After nine years of drinking, the quantities he could take would seem fabulous to an ordinary drinking man. He never let it interfere with his work, he generally drank at night and on Sundays. Every night, as soon as his chores were done, he began to drink. While he was able to sit up he would play on his mouth harp or hack away at his window sills with his jackknife. When the liquor went to his head he would lie down on his bed and stare out of the window until he went to sleep. He drank alone and in solitude not for pleasure or good cheer, but to forget the awful loneliness and level of the Divide. Milton made a sad blunder when he put mountains in hell. Mountains postulate faith and aspiration. All mountain peoples are religious. It was the cities of the plains that, because of their utter lack of spirituality and the mad caprice of their vice, were cursed of God.

Alcohol is perfectly consistent in its effects upon man. Drunkenness is merely an exaggeration. A foolish man drunk becomes maudlin; a bloody man, vicious; a coarse man, vulgar. Canute was none of these, but he was morose and gloomy, and liquor took him through all the hells of Dante. As he lay on his giant's bed all the horrors of this world and every other were laid bare to his chilled senses. He was a man who knew no joy, a man who toiled in silence and bitterness. The skull and the serpent were always before him, the symbols of eternal futileness and of eternal hate.

When the first Norwegians near enough to be called neighbors came, Canute rejoiced, and planned to escape from his bosom vice. But he was not a social man by nature and had not the power of drawing out the social side of other people. His new neighbors rather feared him because of his great strength and size, his silence and his lowering brows. Perhaps, too, they knew that he was mad, mad from the eternal treachery of the plains, which every spring stretch green and rustle with the promises of Eden, showing long grassy lagoons full of clear water and cattle whose hoofs are stained with wild roses. Before autumn the lagoons are dried up, and the ground is burnt dry and hard until it blisters and cracks open.

So instead of becoming a friend and neighbor to the men that settled about him, Canute became a mystery and a terror. They told awful stories of his size and strength and of the alcohol he drank.

They said that one night, when he went out to see to his horses just before he went to bed, his steps were unsteady and the rotten planks of the floor gave way and threw him behind the feet of a fiery young stallion. His foot was caught fast in the floor, and the nervous horse began kicking frantically. When Canute felt the blood trickling down into his eyes from a scalp wound in his head, he roused himself from his kingly indifference, and with the quiet stoical courage of a drunken man leaned forward and wound his arms about the horse's hind legs and held them against his breast with crushing embrace. All through the darkness and cold of the night he lay there, matching strength against strength. When little Jim Peterson went over the next morning at four o'clock to go with him to the Blue to cut wood, he found him so, and the horse was on its fore knees, trembling and whinnying with fear. This is the story the Norwegians tell of him, and if it is true it is no wonder that they feared and hated this Holder of the Heels of Horses.

One spring there moved to the next "eighty" a family that made a great change in Canute's life. Ole Yensen was too drunk most of the time to be afraid of any one, and his wife Mary was too garrulous to be afraid of any one who listened to her talk, and Lena, their pretty daughter, was not afraid of man nor devil. So it came about that Canute went over to take his alcohol with Ole oftener than he took it alone, After a while the report spread that he was going to marry Yensen's daughter, and the Norwegian girls began to tease Lena about the great bear she was going to keep house for. No one could quite see how the affair had come about, for Canute's tactics of courtship were somewhat peculiar. He apparently never spoke to her at all: he would sit for hours with Mary chattering on one side of him and Ole drinking on the other and watch Lena at her work. She teased him, and threw flour in his face and put vinegar in his coffee, but he took her rough jokes with silent wonder, never even smiling. He took her to church occasionally, but the most watchful and curious people never saw him speak to her. He would sit staring at her while she giggled and flirted with the other men.

Next spring Mary Lee went to town to work in a steam laundry. She came home every Sunday, and always ran across to Yensens to startle Lena with stories of ten cent theaters, firemen's dances, and all the other esthetic delights of metropolitan life. In a few weeks Lena's head was completely turned, and she gave her father no rest until he let her go to town to seek her fortune at the ironing board. From the time she came home on her first visit she began to treat Canute with contempt. She had bought a plush cloak and kid gloves, had her clothes made by the dress maker, and assumed airs and graces that made the other women of the neighborhood cordially detest her. She generally brought with her a young man from town who waxed his mustache and wore a red necktie, and she did not even introduce him to Canute.

The neighbors teased Canute a good deal until he knocked one of them down. He gave no sign of suffering from her neglect except that he drank more and avoided the other Norwegians more carefully than ever, He lay around in his den and no one knew what he felt or thought, but little Jim Peterson, who had seen him glowering at Lena in church one Sunday when she was there with the town man, said that he would not give an acre of his wheat for Lena's life or the town chap's either; and Jim's wheat was so wondrously worthless that the statement was an exceedingly strong one.

Canute had bought a new suit of clothes that looked as nearly like the town man as possible. They had cost him half a millet crop; for tailors are not accustomed to fitting giants and they charge for it. He had hung those clothes in his shanty two months ago and had never put them on, partly from fear of ridicule, partly from discouragement, and partly because there was something in his own soul that revolted at the littleness of the device.

Lena was at home just at this time. Work was slack in the laundry and Mary had not been well, so Lena stayed at home, glad enough to get an opportunity to torment Canute once more.

She was washing in the side kitchen, singing loudly as she worked. Mary was on her knees, blacking the stove and scolding violently about the young man who was coming out from town that night. The young man had committed the fatal error of laughing at Mary's ceaseless babble and had never been forgiven.

"He is no good, and you will come to a bad end by running with him! I do not see why a daughter of mine should act so. I do not see why the Lord should visit such a punishment upon me as to give me such a daughter. There are plenty of good men you can marry."

Lena tossed her head and answered curtly, "I don't happen to want to marry any man right away, and so long as Dick dresses nice and has plenty of money to spend, there is no harm in my going with him."

"Money to spend? Yes, and that is all he does with it I'll be bound. You think it very fine now, but you will change your tune when you have been married five years and see your children running naked and your cupboard empty. Did Anne Hermanson come to any good end by marrying a town man?"

"I don't know anything about Anne Hermanson, but I know any of the laundry girls would have Dick quick enough if they could get him."

"Yes, and a nice lot of store clothes huzzies you are too. Now there is Canuteson who has an 'eighty' proved up and fifty head of cattle and—"

"And hair that ain't been cut since he was a baby, and a big dirty beard, and he wears overalls on Sundays, and drinks like a pig. Besides he will keep. I can have all the fun I want, and when I am old and ugly like you he can have me and take care of me. The Lord knows there ain't nobody else going to marry him."

Canute drew his hand back from the latch as though it were red hot. He was not the kind of man to make a good eavesdropper, and he wished he had knocked sooner. He pulled himself together and struck the door like a battering ram. Mary jumped and opened it with a screech.

"God! Canute, how you scared us! I thought it was crazy Lou—he has been tearing around the neighborhood trying to convert folks. I am afraid as death of him. He ought to be sent off, I think. He is just as liable as not to kill us all, or burn the barn, or poison the dogs. He has been worrying even the poor minister to death, and he laid up with the rheumatism, too! Did you notice that he was too sick to preach last Sunday? But don't stand there in the cold, come in. Yensen isn't here, but he just went over to Sorenson's for the mail; he won't be gone long. Walk right in the other room and sit down."

Canute followed her, looking steadily in front of him and not noticing Lena as he passed her. But Lena's vanity would not allow him to pass unmolested. She took the wet sheet she was wringing out and cracked him across the face with it, and ran giggling to the other side of the room. The blow stung his cheeks and the soapy water flew in his eyes, and he involuntarily began rubbing them with his hands. Lena giggled with delight at his discomfiture, and the wrath in Canute's face grew blacker than ever. A big man humiliated is vastly more undignified than a little one. He forgot the sting of his face in the bitter consciousness that he had made a fool of himself He stumbled blindly into the living room, knocking his head against the door jamb because he forgot to stoop. He dropped into a chair behind the stove, thrusting his big feet back helplessly on either side of him.

Ole was a long time in coming, and Canute sat there, still and silent, with his hands clenched on his knees, and the skin of his face seemed to have shriveled up into little wrinkles that trembled when he lowered his brows. His life had been one long lethargy of solitude and alcohol, but now he was awakening, and it was as when the dumb stagnant heat of summer breaks out into thunder.

When Ole came staggering in, heavy with liquor, Canute rose at once.

"Yensen," he said quietly, "I have come to see if you will let me marry your daughter today."

"Today!" gasped Ole.

"Yes, I will not wait until tomorrow. I am tired of living alone."

Ole braced his staggering knees against the bedstead, and stammered eloquently: "Do you think I will marry my daughter to a drunkard? a man who drinks raw alcohol? a man who sleeps with rattle snakes? Get out of my house or I will kick you out for your impudence." And Ole began looking anxiously for his feet.

Canute answered not a word, but he put on his hat and went out into the kitchen. He went up to Lena and said without looking at her, "Get your things on and come with me!"

The tones of his voice startled her, and she said angrily, dropping the soap, "Are you drunk?"

"If you do not come with me, I will take you—you had better come," said Canute quietly.

She lifted a sheet to strike him, but he caught her arm roughly and wrenched the sheet from her. He turned to the wall and took down a hood and shawl that hung there, and began wrapping her up. Lena scratched and fought like a wild thing. Ole stood in the door, cursing, and Mary howled and screeched at the top of her voice. As for Canute, he lifted the girl in his arms and went out of the house. She kicked and struggled, but the helpless wailing of Mary and Ole soon died away in the distance, and her face was held down tightly on Canute's shoulder so that she could not see whither he was taking her. She was conscious only of the north wind whistling in her ears, and of rapid steady motion and of a great breast that heaved beneath her in quick, irregular breaths. The harder she struggled the tighter those iron arms that had held the heels of horses crushed about her, until she felt as if they would crush the breath from her, and lay still with fear. Canute was striding across the level fields at a pace at which man never went before, drawing the stinging north winds into his lungs in great gulps. He walked with his eyes half closed and looking straight in front of him, only lowering them when he bent his head to blow away the snow flakes that settled on her hair. So it was that Canute took her to his home, even as his bearded barbarian ancestors took the fair frivolous women of the South in their hairy arms and bore them down to their war ships. For ever and anon the soul becomes weary of the conventions that are not of it, and with a single stroke shatters the civilized lies with which it is unable to cope, and the strong arm reaches out and takes by force what it cannot win by cunning.

When Canute reached his shanty he placed the girl upon a chair, where she sat sobbing. He stayed only a few minutes. He filled the stove with wood and lit the lamp, drank a huge swallow of alcohol and put the bottle in his pocket. He paused a moment, staring heavily at the weeping girl, then he went off and locked the door and disappeared in the gathering gloom of the night.

Wrapped in flannels and soaked with turpentine, the little Norwegian preacher sat reading his Bible, when he heard a thundering knock at his door, and Canute entered, covered with snow and his beard frozen fast to his coat.

"Come in, Canute, you must be frozen," said the little man, shoving a chair towards his visitor.

Canute remained standing with his hat on and said quietly, "I want you to come over to my house tonight to marry me to Lena Yensen."

"Have you got a license, Canute?"

"No, I don't want a license. I want to be married."

"But I can't marry you without a license, man, it would not be legal."

A dangerous light came in the big Norwegian's eye. "I want you to come over to my house to marry me to Lena Yensen."

"No, I can't, it would kill an ox to go out in a storm like this, and my rheumatism is bad tonight."

"Then if you will not go I must take you," said Canute with a sigh.

He took down the preacher's bearskin coat and bade him put it on while he hitched up his buggy. He went out and closed the door softly after him. Presently he returned and found the frightened minister crouching before the fire with his coat lying beside him. Canute helped him put it on and gently wrapped his head in his big muffler. Then he picked him up and carried him out and placed him in his buggy. As he tucked the buffalo robes around him he said: "Your horse is old, he might flounder or lose his way in this storm. I will lead him."

The minister took the reins feebly in his hands and sat shivering with the cold. Sometimes when there was a lull in the wind, he could see the horse struggling through the snow with the man plodding steadily beside him. Again the blowing snow would hide them from him altogether. He had no idea where they were or what direction they were going. He felt as though he were being whirled away in the heart of the storm, and he said all the prayers he knew. But at last the long four miles were over, and Canute set him down in the snow while he unlocked the door. He saw the bride sitting by the fire with her eyes red and swollen as though she had been weeping. Canute placed a huge chair for him, and said roughly,—

"Warm yourself."

Lena began to cry and moan afresh, begging the minister to take her home. He looked helplessly at Canute. Canute said simply,

"If you are warm now, you can marry us."

"My daughter, do you take this step of your own free will?" asked the minister in a trembling voice.

"No, sir, I don't, and it is disgraceful he should force me into it! I won't marry him."

"Then, Canute, I cannot marry you," said the minister, standing as straight as his rheumatic limbs would let him.

"Are you ready to marry us now, sir?" said Canute, laying one iron hand on his stooped shoulder. The little preacher was a good man, but like most men of weak body he was a coward and had a horror of physical suffering, although he had known so much of it. So with many qualms of conscience he began to repeat the marriage service. Lena sat sullenly in her chair, staring at the fire. Canute stood beside her, listening with his head bent reverently and his hands folded on his breast. When the little man had prayed and said amen, Canute began bundling him up again.

"I will take you home, now," he said as he carried him out and placed him in his buggy, and started off with him through the fury of the storm, floundering among the snow drifts that brought even the giant himself to his knees.

After she was left alone, Lena soon ceased weeping. She was not of a particularly sensitive temperament, and had little pride beyond that of vanity. After the first bitter anger wore itself out, she felt nothing more than a healthy sense of humiliation and defeat. She had no inclination to run away, for she was married now, and in her eyes that was final and all rebellion was useless. She knew nothing about a license, but she knew that a preacher married folks. She consoled herself by thinking that she had always intended to marry Canute someday, anyway.

She grew tired of crying and looking into the fire, so she got up and began to look about her. She had heard queer tales about the inside of Canute's shanty, and her curiosity soon got the better of her rage. One of the first things she noticed was the new black suit of clothes hanging on the wall. She was dull, but it did not take a vain woman long to interpret anything so decidedly flattering, and she was pleased in spite of herself. As she looked through the cupboard, the general air of neglect and discomfort made her pity the man who lived there.

"Poor fellow, no wonder he wants to get married to get somebody to wash up his dishes. Batchin's pretty hard on a man."

It is easy to pity when once one's vanity has been tickled. She looked at the windowsill and gave a little shudder and wondered if the man were crazy. Then she sat down again and sat a long time wondering what her Dick and Ole would do.

"It is queer Dick didn't come right over after me. He surely came, for he would have left town before the storm began and he might just as well come right on as go back. If he'd hurried he would have gotten here before the preacher came. I suppose he was afraid to come, for he knew Canuteson could pound him to jelly, the coward!" Her eyes flashed angrily.

The weary hours wore on and Lena began to grow horribly lonesome. It was an uncanny night and this was an uncanny place to be in. She could hear the coyotes howling hungrily a little way from the cabin, and more terrible still were all the unknown noises of the storm. She remembered the tales they told of the big log overhead and she was afraid of those snaky things on the windowsills. She remembered the man who had been killed in the draw, and she wondered what she would do if she saw crazy Lou's white face glaring into the window. The rattling of the door became unbearable, she thought the latch must be loose and took the lamp to look at it. Then for the first time she saw the ugly brown snake skins whose death rattle sounded every time the wind jarred the door.

"Canute, Canute!" she screamed in terror.

Outside the door she heard a heavy sound as of a big dog getting up and shaking himself. The door opened and Canute stood before her, white as a snow drift.

"What is it?" he asked kindly.

"I am cold," she faltered.

He went out and got an armful of wood and a basket of cobs and filled the stove. Then he went out and lay in the snow before the door. Presently he heard her calling again.

"What is it?" he said, sitting up.

"I'm so lonesome, I'm afraid to stay in here all alone."

"I will go over and get your mother." And he got up.

"She won't come."

"I'll bring her," said Canute grimly.

"No, no. I don't want her, she will scold all the time."

"Well, I will bring your father."

She spoke again and it seemed as though her mouth was close up to the key-hole. She spoke lower than he had ever heard her speak before, so low that he had to put his ear up to the lock to hear her.

"I don't want him either, Canute,—I'd rather have you."

For a moment she heard no noise at all, then something like a groan. With a cry of fear she opened the door, and saw Canute stretched in the snow at her feet, his face in his hands, sobbing on the doorstep.

ERIC HERMANNSON'S SOUL

It was a great night at the Lone Star schoolhouse—a night when the Spirit was present with power and when God was very near to man. So it seemed to Asa Skinner, servant of God and Free Gospeller. The schoolhouse was crowded with the saved and sanctified, robust men and women, trembling and quailing before the power of some mysterious psychic force. Here and there among this cowering, sweating multitude crouched some poor wretch who had felt the pangs of an awakened conscience, but had not yet experienced that complete divestment of reason, that frenzy born of a convulsion of the mind, which, in the parlance of the Free Gospellers, is termed "the Light." On the floor before the mourners' bench lay the unconscious figure of a man in whom outraged nature had sought her last resort. This "trance" state is the highest evidence of grace among the Free Gospellers, and indicates a close walking with God.

Before the desk stood Asa Skinner, shouting of the mercy and vengeance of God, and in his eyes shone a terrible earnestness, an almost prophetic flame. Asa was a converted train gambler who used to run between Omaha and Denver. He was a man made for the extremes of life; from the most debauched of men he had become the most ascetic. His was a bestial face, a face that bore the stamp of Nature's eternal injustice. The forehead was low, projecting over the eyes, and the sandy hair was plastered down over it and then brushed back at an abrupt right angle. The chin was heavy, the nostrils were low and wide, and the lower lip hung loosely except in his moments of spasmodic earnestness, when it shut like a steel trap. Yet about those coarse features there were deep, rugged furrows, the scars of many a hand-to-hand struggle with the weakness of the flesh, and about that drooping lip were sharp, strenuous lines that had conquered it and taught it to pray. Over those seamed cheeks there was a certain pallor, a greyness caught from many a vigil. It was as though, after Nature had done her worst with that face, some fine chisel had gone over it, chastening and almost transfiguring it. Tonight, as his muscles twitched with emotion, and the perspiration dropped from his hair and chin, there was a certain convincing power in the man. For Asa Skinner was a man possessed of a belief, of that sentiment of the sublime before which all inequalities are leveled, that transport of conviction which seems superior to all laws of condition, under which debauchees have become martyrs; which made a tinker an artist and a camel-driver the founder of an empire. This was with Asa Skinner tonight, as he stood proclaiming the vengeance of God.

It might have occurred to an impartial observer that Asa Skinner's God was indeed a vengeful God if he could reserve vengeance for those of his creatures who were packed into the Lone Star schoolhouse that night. Poor exiles of all nations; men from the south and the north, peasants from almost every country of Europe, most of them from the mountainous, night-bound coast of Norway. Honest men for the most part, but men with whom the world had dealt hardly; the failures of all countries, men sobered by toil and saddened by exile, who had been driven to fight for the dominion of an untoward soil, to sow where others should gather, the advance guard of a mighty civilization to be.

Never had Asa Skinner spoken more earnestly than now. He felt that the Lord had this night a special work for him to do. Tonight Eric Hermannson, the wildest lad on all the Divide, sat in his audience with a fiddle on his knee, just as he had dropped in on his way to play for some dance. The violin is an object of particular abhorrence to the Free Gospellers. Their antagonism to the church organ is bitter enough, but the fiddle they regard as a very incarnation of evil desires, singing forever of worldly pleasures and inseparably associated with all forbidden things.

Eric Hermannson had long been the object of the prayers of the revivalists. His mother had felt the power of the Spirit weeks ago, and special prayer-meetings had been held at her house for her son. But Eric had only gone his ways laughing, the ways of youth, which are short enough at best, and none too flowery on the Divide.

He slipped away from the prayer-meetings to meet the Campbell boys in Genereau's saloon, or hug the plump little French girls at Chevalier's dances, and sometimes, of a summer night, he even went across the dewy cornfields and through the wild-plum thicket to play the fiddle for Lena Hanson, whose name was a reproach through all the Divide country, where the women are usually too plain and too busy and too tired to depart from the ways of virtue. On such occasions Lena, attired in a pink wrapper and silk stockings and tiny pink slippers, would sing to him, accompanying herself on a battered guitar. It gave him a delicious sense of freedom and experience to be with a woman who, no matter how, had lived in big cities and knew the ways of town folk, who had never worked in the fields and had kept her hands white and soft, her throat fair and tender, who had heard great singers in Denver and Salt Lake, and who knew the strange language of flattery and idleness and mirth.

Yet, careless as he seemed, the frantic prayers of his mother were not altogether without their effect upon Eric. For days he had been fleeing before them as a criminal from his pursuers, and over his pleasures had fallen the shadow of something dark and terrible that dogged his steps. The harder he danced, the louder he sang, the more was he conscious that this phantom was gaining upon him, that in time it would track him down. One Sunday afternoon, late in the fall, when he had been drinking beer with Lena Hanson and listening to a song which made his cheeks burn, a rattlesnake had crawled out of the side of the sod house and thrust its ugly head in under the screen door. He was not afraid of snakes, but he knew enough of Gospellism to feel the significance of the reptile lying coiled there upon her doorstep. His lips were cold when he kissed Lena goodbye, and he went there no more.

The final barrier between Eric and his mother's faith was his violin, and to that he clung as a man sometimes will cling to his dearest sin, to the weakness more precious to him than all his strength, In the great world beauty comes to men in many guises, and art in a hundred forms, but for Eric there was only his violin.

It stood, to him, for all the manifestations of art; it was his only bridge into the kingdom of the soul.

It was to Eric Hermannson that the evangelist directed his impassioned pleading that night.

"*Saul, Saul, why persecutest thou me?* Is there a Saul here tonight who has stopped his ears to that gentle pleading, who has thrust a spear into that bleeding side? Think of it, my brother; you are offered this wonderful love and you prefer the worm that dieth not and the fire which will not be quenched. What right have you to lose one of God's precious souls? *Saul, Saul, why persecutest thou me?*"

A great joy dawned in Asa Skinner's pale face, for he saw that Eric Hermannson was swaying to and fro in his seat. The minister fell upon his knees and threw his long arms up over his head.

"O my brothers! I feel it coming, the blessing we have prayed for. I tell you the Spirit is coming! just a little more prayer, brothers, a little more zeal, and he will be here. I can feel his cooling wing upon my brow. Glory be to God forever and ever, amen!"

The whole congregation groaned under the pressure of this spiritual panic. Shouts and hallelujahs went up from every lip. Another figure fell prostrate upon the floor. From the mourners' bench rose a chant of terror and rapture:

"Eating honey and drinking wine,
Glory to the bleeding Lamb!
I am my Lord's and he is mine,
Glory to the bleeding Lamb!"

The hymn was sung in a dozen dialects and voiced all the vague yearning of these hungry lives, of these people who had starved all the passions so long, only to fall victims to the barest of them all, fear.

A groan of ultimate anguish rose from Eric Hermannson's bowed head, and the sound was like the groan of a great tree when it falls in the forest.

The minister rose suddenly to his feet and threw back his head, crying in a loud voice:

"*Lazarus, come forth!* Eric Hermannson, you are lost, going down at sea. In the name of God, and Jesus Christ his Son, I throw you the life line. Take hold! Almighty God, my soul for his!" The minister threw his arms out and lifted his quivering face.

Eric Hermannson rose to his feet; his lips were set and the lightning was in his eyes. He took his violin by the neck and crushed it to splinters across his knee, and to Asa Skinner the sound was like the shackles of sin broken audibly asunder.

II

For more than two years Eric Hermannson kept the austere faith to which he had sworn himself, kept it until a girl from the East came to spend a week on the Nebraska Divide. She was a girl of other manners and conditions, and there were greater distances between her life and Eric's than all the miles which separated Rattlesnake Creek from New York City. Indeed, she had no business to be in the West at all; but ah! across what leagues of land and sea, by what improbable chances, do the unrelenting gods bring to us our fate!

It was in a year of financial depression that Wyllis Elliot came to Nebraska to buy cheap land and revisit the country where he had spent a year of his youth. When he had graduated from Harvard it was still customary for moneyed gentlemen to send their scapegrace sons to rough it on ranches in the wilds of Nebraska or Dakota, or to consign them to a living death in the sagebrush of the Black Hills. These young men did not always return to the ways of civilized life. But Wyllis Elliot had not married a half-breed, nor been shot in a cowpunchers' brawl, nor wrecked by bad whisky, nor appropriated by a smirched adventuress. He had been saved from these things by a girl, his sister, who had been very near to his life ever since the days when they read fairy tales together and dreamed the dreams that never come true. On this, his first visit to his father's ranch since he left it six years before, he brought her with him. She had been laid up half the winter from a sprain received while skating, and had had too much time for reflection during those months. She was restless and filled with a desire to see something of the wild country of which her brother had told her so much. She was to be married the next winter, and Wyllis understood her when she begged him to take her with him on this long, aimless jaunt across the continent, to taste the last of their freedom together. It comes to all women of her type—that desire to taste the unknown which allures and terrifies, to run one's whole soul's length out to the wind—just once.

It had been an eventful journey. Wyllis somehow understood that strain of gypsy blood in his sister, and he knew where to take her. They had slept in sod houses on the Platte River, made the acquaintance of the personnel of a third-rate opera company on the train to Deadwood, dined in a camp of railroad constructors at the world's end beyond New Castle, gone through the Black Hills on horseback, fished for trout in Dome Lake, watched a dance at Cripple Creek, where the lost souls who hide in the hills gathered for their besotted revelry. And now, last of all, before the return to thraldom, there was this little shack, anchored on the windy crest of the Divide, a little black dot against the flaming sunsets, a scented sea of cornland bathed in opalescent air and blinding sunlight.

Margaret Elliot was one of those women of whom there are so many in this day, when old order, passing, giveth place to new; beautiful, talented, critical, unsatisfied, tired of the world at twenty-four. For the moment the life and people of the Divide interested her. She was there but a week; perhaps had she stayed longer, that inexorable ennui which travels faster even than the Vestibule Limited would have overtaken her. The week she tarried there was the week that Eric Hermannson was helping Jerry Lockhart thresh; a week earlier or a week later, and there would have been no story to write.

It was on Thursday and they were to leave on Saturday. Wyllis and his sister were sitting on the wide piazza of the ranchhouse, staring out into the afternoon sunlight and protesting against the gusts of hot wind that blew up from the sandy riverbottom twenty miles to the southward.

The young man pulled his cap lower over his eyes and remarked:

"This wind is the real thing; you don't strike it anywhere else. You remember we had a touch of it in Algiers and I told you it came from Kansas. It's the keynote of this country."

Wyllis touched her hand that lay on the hammock and continued gently:

"I hope it's paid you, Sis. Roughing it's dangerous business; it takes the taste out of things."

She shut her fingers firmly over the brown hand that was so like her own.

"Paid? Why, Wyllis, I haven't been so happy since we were children and were going to discover the ruins of Troy together some day. Do you know, I believe I could just stay on here forever and let the world go on its own gait. It seems as though the tension and strain we used to talk of last winter were gone for good, as though one could never give one's strength out to such petty things any more."

Wyllis brushed the ashes of his pipe away from the silk handkerchief that was knotted about his neck and stared moodily off at the skyline.

"No, you're mistaken. This would bore you after a while. You can't shake the fever of the other life. I've tried it. There was a time when the gay fellows of Rome could trot down into the Thebaid and burrow into the sandhills and get rid of it. But it's all too complex now. You see we've made our dissipations so dainty and respectable that they've gone further in than the flesh, and taken hold of the ego proper. You couldn't rest, even here. The war cry would follow you."

"You don't waste words, Wyllis, but you never miss fire. I talk more than you do, without saying half so much. You must have learned the art of silence from these taciturn Norwegians. I think I like silent men."

"Naturally," said Wyllis, "since you have decided to marry the most brilliant talker you know."

Both were silent for a time, listening to the sighing of the hot wind through the parched morning-glory vines. Margaret spoke first.

"Tell me, Wyllis, were many of the Norwegians you used to know as interesting as Eric Hermannson?"

"Who, Siegfried? Well, no. He used to be the flower of the Norwegian youth in my day, and he's rather an exception, even now. He has retrograded, though. The bonds of the soil have tightened on him, I fancy."

"Siegfried? Come, that's rather good, Wyllis. He looks like a dragon-slayer. What is it that makes him so different from the others? I can talk to him; he seems quite like a human being."

"Well," said Wyllis, meditatively, "I don't read Bourget as much as my cultured sister, and I'm not so well up in analysis, but I fancy it's because one keeps cherishing a perfectly unwarranted suspicion that under that big, hulking anatomy of his, he may conceal a soul somewhere. Nicht wahr?"

"Something like that," said Margaret, thoughtfully, "except that it's more than a suspicion, and it isn't groundless. He has one, and he makes it known, somehow, without speaking."

"I always have my doubts about loquacious souls," Wyllis remarked, with the unbelieving smile that had grown habitual with him.

Margaret went on, not heeding the interruption. "I knew it from the first, when he told me about the suicide of his cousin, the Bernstein boy. That kind of blunt pathos can't be summoned at will in anybody. The earlier novelists rose to it, sometimes, unconsciously. But last night when I sang for him I was doubly sure. Oh, I haven't told you about that yet! Better light your pipe again. You see, he stumbled in on me in the dark when I was pumping away at that old parlour organ to please Mrs. Lockhart It's her household fetish and I've forgotten how many pounds of butter she made and sold to buy it. Well, Eric stumbled in, and in some inarticulate manner made me understand that he wanted me to sing for him. I sang just the old things, of course. It's queer to sing familiar things here at the world's end. It makes one think how the hearts of men have carried them around the world, into the wastes of Iceland and the jungles of Africa and the islands of the Pacific. I think if one lived here long enough one would quite forget how to be trivial, and would read only the great books that we never get time to read in the world, and would remember only the great music, and the things that are really worth while would stand out clearly against that horizon over there. And of course I played the intermezzo from *Cavalleria Rusticana* for him; it goes rather better on an organ than most things do. He shuffled his feet and twisted his big hands up into knots and blurted out that he didn't know there was any music like that in the world. Why, there were tears in his voice, Wyllis! Yes, like Rossetti, I *heard* his tears. Then it dawned upon me that it was probably the first good music he had ever heard in all his life. Think of it, to care for music as he does and never to hear it, never to know that it exists on earth! To long for it as we long for other perfect experiences that never come. I can't tell you what music means to that man. I never saw any one so susceptible to it. It gave him speech, he became alive. When I had finished the intermezzo, he began telling me about a little crippled brother who died and whom he loved and used to carry everywhere in his arms. He did not wait for encouragement. He took up the story and told it slowly, as if to himself, just sort of rose up and told his own woe to answer Mascagni's. It overcame me."

"Poor devil," said Wyllis, looking at her with mysterious eyes, "and so you've given him a new woe. Now he'll go on wanting Grieg and Schubert the rest of his days and never getting them. That's a girl's philanthropy for you!"

Jerry Lockhart came out of the house screwing his chin over the unusual luxury of a stiff white collar, which his wife insisted upon as a necessary article of toilet while Miss Elliot was at the house. Jerry sat down on the step and smiled his broad, red smile at Margaret.

"Well, I've got the music for your dance, Miss Elliot. Olaf Oleson will bring his accordion and Mollie will play the organ, when she isn't lookin' after the grub, and a little chap from Frenchtown will bring his fiddle—though the French don't mix with the Norwegians much."

"Delightful! Mr. Lockhart, that dance will be the feature of our trip, and it's so nice of you to get it up for us. We'll see the Norwegians in character at last," cried Margaret, cordially.

"See here, Lockhart, I'll settle with you for backing her in this scheme," said Wyllis, sitting up and knocking the ashes out of his pipe. "She's done crazy things enough on this trip, but to talk of dancing all night with a gang of half-mad Norwegians and taking the carriage at four to catch the six o'clock train out of Riverton—well, it's tommyrot, that's what it is!"

"Wyllis, I leave it to your sovereign power of reason to decide whether it isn't easier to stay up all night than to get up at three in the morning. To get up at three, think what that means! No, sir, I prefer to keep my vigil and then get into a sleeper."

"But what do you want with the Norwegians? I thought you were tired of dancing."

"So I am, with some people. But I want to see a Norwegian dance, and I intend to. Come, Wyllis, you know how seldom it is that one really wants to do anything nowadays. I wonder when I have really wanted to go to a party before. It will be something to remember next month at Newport, when we have to and don't want to. Remember your own theory that contrast is about the only thing that makes life endurable. This is my party and Mr. Lockhart's; your whole duty tomorrow night will consist in being nice to the Norwegian girls. I'll warrant you were adept enough at it once. And you'd better be very nice indeed, for if there are many such young Valkyries as Eric's sister among them, they would simply tie you up in a knot if they suspected you were guying them."

Wyllis groaned and sank back into the hammock to consider his fate, while his sister went on.

"And the guests, Mr. Lockhart, did they accept?"

Lockhart took out his knife and began sharpening it on the sole of his plowshoe.

"Well, I guess we'll have a couple dozen. You see it's pretty hard to get a crowd together here any more. Most of 'em have gone over to the Free Gospellers, and they'd rather put their feet in the fire than shake 'em to a fiddle."

Margaret made a gesture of impatience. "Those Free Gospellers have just cast an evil spell over this country, haven't they?"

"Well," said Lockhart, cautiously, "I don't just like to pass judgment on any Christian sect, but if you're to know the chosen by their works, the Gospellers can't make a very proud showin', an' that's a fact. They're responsible for a few suicides, and they've sent a good-sized delegation to the state insane asylum, an' I don't see as they've made the rest of us much better than we were before. I had a little herdboy last spring, as square a little Dane as I want to work for me, but after the Gospellers got hold of him and sanctified him, the little beggar used to get down on his knees out on the prairie and pray by the hour and let the cattle get into the corn, an' I had to fire him. That's about the way it goes. Now there's Eric; that chap used to be a hustler and the spryest dancer in all this section-called all the dances. Now he's got no ambition and he's glum as a preacher. I don't suppose we can even get him to come in tomorrow night."

"Eric? Why, he must dance, we can't let him off," said Margaret, quickly. "Why, I intend to dance with him myself."

"I'm afraid he won't dance. I asked him this morning if he'd help us out and he said, 'I don't dance now, any more,'" said Lockhart, imitating the laboured English of the Norwegian.

"'The Miller of Hofbau, the Miller of Hofbau, O my Princess!'" chirped Wyllis, cheerfully, from his hammock.

The red on his sister's cheek deepened a little, and she laughed mischievously. "We'll see about that, sir. I'll not admit that I am beaten until I have asked him myself."

Every night Eric rode over to St. Anne, a little village in the heart of the French settlement, for the mail. As the road lay through the most attractive part of the Divide country, on several occasions Margaret Elliot and her brother had accompanied him. Tonight Wyllis had business with Lockhart, and Margaret rode with Eric, mounted on a frisky little mustang that Mrs. Lockhart had broken to the sidesaddle. Margaret regarded her escort very much as she did the servant who always accompanied her on long rides at home, and the ride to the village was a silent one. She was occupied with thoughts of another world, and Eric was wrestling with more thoughts than had ever been crowded into his head before.

He rode with his eyes riveted on that slight figure before him, as though he wished to absorb it through the optic nerves and hold it in his brain forever. He understood the situation perfectly. His brain worked slowly, but he had a keen sense of the values of things. This girl represented an entirely new species of humanity to him, but he knew where to place her. The prophets of old, when an angel first appeared unto them, never doubted its high origin.

Eric was patient under the adverse conditions of his life, but he was not servile. The Norse blood in him had not entirely lost its self-reliance. He came of a proud fisher line, men who were not afraid of anything but the ice and the devil, and he had prospects before him when his father went down off the North Cape in the long Arctic night, and his mother, seized by a violent horror of seafaring life, had followed her brother to America. Eric was eighteen then, handsome as young Siegfried, a giant in stature, with a skin singularly pure and delicate, like a Swede's; hair as yellow as the locks of Tennyson's amorous Prince, and eyes of a fierce, burning blue, whose flash was most dangerous to women.

He had in those days a certain pride of bearing, a certain confidence of approach, that usually accompanies physical perfection. It was even said of him then that he was in love with life, and inclined to levity, a vice most unusual on the Divide. But the sad history of those Norwegian exiles, transplanted in an arid soil and under a scorching sun, had repeated itself in his case. Toil and isolation had sobered him, and he grew more and more like the clods among which he laboured. It was as though some red-hot instrument had touched for a moment those delicate fibers of the brain which respond to acute pain or pleasure, in which lies the power of exquisite sensation, and had seared them quite away. It is a painful thing to watch the light die out of the eyes of those Norsemen, leaving an expression of impenetrable sadness, quite passive, quite hopeless, a shadow that is never lifted. With some this change comes almost at once, in the first bitterness of homesickness, with others it comes more slowly, according to the time it takes each man's heart to die.

Oh, those poor Northmen of the Divide! They are dead many a year before they are put to rest in the little graveyard on the windy hill where exiles of all nations grow akin.

The peculiar species of hypochondria to which the exiles of his people sooner or later succumb had not developed in Eric until that night at the Lone Star schoolhouse, when he had broken his violin across his knee. After that, the gloom of his people settled down upon him, and the gospel of maceration began its work.

"If thine eye offend thee, pluck it out," et cetera. The pagan smile that once hovered about his lips was gone, and he was one with sorrow. Religion heals a hundred hearts for one that it embitters, but when it destroys, its work is quick and deadly, and where the agony of the cross has been, joy will not come again. This man understood things literally: one must live without pleasure to die without fear; to save the soul, it was necessary to starve the soul.

The sun hung low above the cornfields when Margaret and her cavalier left St. Anne. South of the town there is a stretch of road that runs for some three miles through the French settlement, where the prairie is as level as the surface of a lake. There the fields of flax and wheat and rye are bordered by precise rows of slender, tapering Lombard poplars. It was a yellow world that Margaret Elliot saw under the wide light of the setting sun.

The girl gathered up her reins and called back to Eric, "It will be safe to run the horses here, won't it?"

"Yes, I think so, now," he answered, touching his spur to his pony's flank. They were off like the wind. It is an old saying in the West that newcomers always ride a horse or two to death before they get broken in to the country. They are tempted by the great open spaces and try to outride the horizon, to get to the end of something. Margaret galloped over the level road, and Eric, from behind, saw her long veil fluttering in the wind. It had fluttered just so in his dreams last night and the night before. With a sudden inspiration of courage he overtook her and rode beside her, looking intently at her half-averted face. Before, he had only stolen occasional glances at it, seen it in blinding flashes, always with more or less embarrassment, but now he determined to let every line of it sink into his memory. Men of the world would have said that it was an unusual face, nervous, finely cut, with clear, elegant lines that betokened ancestry. Men of letters would have called it a historic face, and would have conjectured at what old passions, long asleep, what old sorrows forgotten time out of mind, doing battle together in ages gone, had curved those delicate nostrils, left their unconscious memory in those eyes. But Eric read no meaning in these details. To him this beauty was something more than colour and line; it was a flash of white light, in which one cannot distinguish colour because all colours are there. To him it was a complete revelation, an embodiment of those dreams of impossible loveliness that linger by a young man's pillow on midsummer nights; yet, because it held something more than the attraction of health and youth and shapeliness, it troubled him, and in its presence he felt as the Goths before the white marbles in the Roman Capitol, not knowing whether they were men or gods. At times he felt like uncovering his head before it, again the fury seized him to break and despoil, to find the clay in this spirit-thing and stamp upon it. Away from her, he longed to strike out with his arms, and take and hold; it maddened him that this woman whom he could break in his hands should be so much stronger than he. But near her, he never questioned this strength; he admitted its potentiality as he admitted the miracles of the Bible; it enervated and conquered him.

Tonight, when he rode so close to her that he could have touched her, he knew that he might as well reach out his hand to take a star.

Margaret stirred uneasily under his gaze and turned questioningly in her saddle.

"This wind puts me a little out of breath when we ride fast," she said.

Eric turned his eyes away.

"I want to ask you if I go to New York to work, if I maybe hear music like you sang last night? I been a purty good hand to work," he asked, timidly.

Margaret looked at him with surprise, and then, as she studied the outline of his face, pityingly.

"Well, you might—but you'd lose a good deal else. I shouldn't like you to go to New York—and be poor, you'd be out of atmosphere, some way," she said, slowly. Inwardly she was thinking: *There he would be altogether sordid, impossible—a machine who would carry one's trunks upstairs, perhaps. Here he is every inch a man, rather picturesque; why is it?* "No," she added aloud, "I shouldn't like that."

"Then I not go," said Eric, decidedly.

Margaret turned her face to hide a smile. She was a trifle amused and a trifle annoyed. Suddenly she spoke again.

"But I'll tell you what I do want you to do, Eric. I want you to dance with us tomorrow night and teach me some of the Norwegian dances; they say you know them all. Won't you?"

Eric straightened himself in his saddle and his eyes flashed as they had done in the Lone Star schoolhouse when he broke his violin across his knee.

"Yes, I will," he said, quietly, and he believed that he delivered his soul to hell as he said it.

They had reached the rougher country now, where the road wound through a narrow cut in one of the bluffs along the creek, when a beat of hoofs ahead and the sharp neighing of horses made the ponies start and Eric rose in his stirrups. Then down the gulch in front of them and over the steep clay banks thundered a herd of wild ponies, nimble as monkeys and wild as rabbits, such as horse-traders drive east from the plains of Montana to sell in the farming country. Margaret's pony made a shrill sound, a neigh that was almost a scream, and started up the clay bank to meet them, all the wild blood of the range breaking out in an instant. Margaret called to Eric just as he threw himself out of the saddle and caught her pony's bit. But the wiry little animal had gone mad and was kicking and biting like a devil. Her wild brothers of the range were all about her, neighing, and pawing the earth, and striking her with their forefeet and snapping at her flanks. It was the old liberty of the range that the little beast fought for.

"Drop the reins and hold tight, tight!" Eric called, throwing all his weight upon the bit, struggling under those frantic forefeet that now beat at his breast, and now kicked at the wild mustangs that surged and tossed about him. He succeeded in wrenching the pony's head toward him and crowding her withers against the clay bank, so that she could not roll.

"Hold tight, tight!" he shouted again, launching a kick at a snorting animal that reared back against Margaret's saddle. If she should lose her courage and fall now, under those hoofs—He struck out again and again, kicking right and left with all his might. Already the negligent drivers had galloped into the cut, and their long quirts were whistling over the heads of the herd. As suddenly as it had come, the struggling, frantic wave of wild life swept up out of the gulch and on across the open prairie, and with a long despairing whinny of farewell the pony dropped her head and stood trembling in her sweat, shaking the foam and blood from her bit.

Eric stepped close to Margaret's side and laid his hand on her saddle. "You are not hurt?" he asked, hoarsely. As he raised his face in the soft starlight she saw that it was white and drawn and that his lips were working nervously.

"No, no, not at all. But you, you are suffering; they struck you!" she cried in sharp alarm.

He stepped back and drew his hand across his brow.

"No, it is not that," he spoke rapidly now, with his hands clenched at his side. "But if they had hurt you, I would beat their brains out with my hands. I would kill them all. I was never afraid before. You are the only beautiful thing that has ever come close to me. You came like an angel out of the sky. You are like the music you sing, you are like the stars and the snow on the mountains where I played when I was a little boy. You are like all that I wanted once and never had, you are all that they have killed in me. I die for you tonight, tomorrow, for all eternity. I am not a coward; I was afraid because I love you more than Christ who died for me, more than I am afraid of hell, or hope for heaven. I was never afraid before. If you had fallen—oh, my God!" He threw his arms out blindly and dropped his head upon the pony's mane, leaning limply against the animal like a man struck by some sickness. His shoulders rose and fell perceptibly with his laboured breathing. The horse stood cowed with exhaustion and fear. Presently Margaret laid her hand on Eric's head and said gently:

"You are better now, shall we go on? Can you get your horse?"

"No, he has gone with the herd. I will lead yours, she is not safe. I will not frighten you again." His voice was still husky, but it was steady now. He took hold of the bit and tramped home in silence.

When they reached the house, Eric stood stolidly by the pony's head until Wyllis came to lift his sister from the saddle.

"The horses were badly frightened, Wyllis. I think I was pretty thoroughly scared myself," she said as she took her brother's arm and went slowly up the hill toward the house. "No, I'm not hurt, thanks to Eric. You must thank him for taking such good care of me. He's a mighty fine fellow. I'll tell you all about it in the morning, dear. I was pretty well shaken up and I'm going right to bed now. Good night."

When she reached the low room in which she slept, she sank upon the bed in her riding dress, face downward.

"Oh, I pity him! I pity him!" she murmured, with a long sigh of exhaustion. She must have slept a little. When she rose again, she took from her dress a letter that had been waiting for her at the village post-office. It was closely written in a long, angular hand, covering a dozen pages of foreign note-paper, and began:

My Dearest Margaret: if I should attempt to say *how like a winter hath thine absence been*, I should incur the risk of being tedious. Really, it takes the sparkle out of everything. Having nothing better to do, and not caring to go anywhere in particular without you, I remained in the city until Jack Courtwell noted my general despondency and brought me down here to his place on the sound to manage some open-air theatricals he is getting up. *As You Like It* is of course the piece selected. Miss Harrison plays Rosalind. I wish you had been here to take the part. Miss Harrison reads her lines well, but she is either a maiden-all-forlorn or a tomboy; insists on reading into the part all sorts of deeper meanings and highly coloured suggestions wholly out of harmony with the pastoral setting. Like most of the professionals, she exaggerates the emotional element and quite fails to do justice to Rosalind's facile wit and really brilliant mental qualities. Gerard will do Orlando, but rumor says he is *epris* of your sometime friend, Miss Meredith, and his memory is treacherous and his interest fitful.

My new pictures arrived last week on the *Gascogne*. The Puvis de Chavannes is even more beautiful than I thought it in Paris. A pale dream-maiden sits by a pale dream-cow and a stream of anemic water flows at her feet. The Constant, you will remember, I got because you admired it. It is here in all its florid splendour, the whole dominated by a glowing sensuosity. The drapery of the female figure is as wonderful as you said; the fabric all barbaric pearl and gold, painted with an easy, effortless voluptuousness, and that white, gleaming line of African coast in the background recalls memories of you very precious to me. But it is useless to deny that Constant irritates me. Though I cannot prove the charge against him, his brilliancy always makes me suspect him of cheapness.

Here Margaret stopped and glanced at the remaining pages of this strange love-letter. They seemed to be filled chiefly with discussions of pictures and books, and with a slow smile she laid them by.

She rose and began undressing. Before she lay down she went to open the window. With her hand on the sill, she hesitated, feeling suddenly as though some danger were lurking outside, some inordinate desire waiting to spring upon her in the darkness. She stood there for a long time, gazing at the infinite sweep of the sky.

"Oh, it is all so little, so little there," she murmured. "When everything else is so dwarfed, why should one expect love to be great? Why should one try to read highly coloured suggestions into a life like that? If only I could find one thing in it all that mattered greatly, one thing that would warm me when I am alone! Will life never give me that one great moment?"

As she raised the window, she heard a sound in the plum bushes outside. It was only the house-dog roused from his sleep, but Margaret started violently and trembled so that she caught the foot of the bed for support. Again she felt herself pursued by some overwhelming longing, some desperate necessity for herself, like the outstretching of helpless, unseen arms in the darkness, and the air seemed heavy with sighs of yearning. She fled to her bed with the words, "I love you more than Christ who died for me!" ringing in her ears.

III

About midnight the dance at Lockhart's was at its height. Even the old men who had come to "look on" caught the spirit of revelry and stamped the floor with the vigor of old Silenus. Eric took the violin from the Frenchmen, and Minna Oleson sat at the organ, and the music grew more and more characteristic—rude, half mournful music, made up of the folksongs of the North, that the villagers sing through the long night in hamlets by the sea, when they are thinking of the sun, and the spring, and the fishermen so long away. To Margaret some of it sounded like Grieg's *Peer Gynt* music. She found something irresistibly infectious in the mirth of these people who were so seldom merry, and she felt almost one of them. Something seemed struggling for freedom in them tonight, something of the joyous childhood of the nations which exile had not killed. The girls were all boisterous with delight. Pleasure came to them but rarely, and when it came, they caught at it wildly and crushed its fluttering wings in their strong brown fingers. They had a hard life enough, most of them. Torrid summers and freezing winters, labour and drudgery and ignorance, were the portion of their girlhood; a short wooing, a hasty, loveless marriage, unlimited maternity, thankless sons, premature age and ugliness, were the dower of their womanhood. But what matter? Tonight there was hot liquor in the glass and hot blood in the heart; tonight they danced.

Tonight Eric Hermannson had renewed his youth. He was no longer the big, silent Norwegian who had sat at Margaret's feet and looked hopelessly into her eyes. Tonight he was a man, with a man's rights and a man's power. Tonight he was Siegfried indeed. His hair was yellow as the heavy wheat in the ripe of summer, and his eyes flashed like the blue water between the ice packs in the north seas. He was not afraid of Margaret tonight, and when he danced with her he held her firmly. She was tired and dragged on his arm a little, but the strength of the man was like an all-pervading fluid, stealing through her veins, awakening under her heart some nameless, unsuspected existence that had slumbered there all these years and that went out through her throbbing fingertips to his that answered. She wondered if the hoydenish blood of some lawless ancestor, long asleep, were calling out in her tonight, some drop of a hotter fluid that the centuries had failed to cool, and why, if this curse were in her, it had not spoken before. But was it a curse, this awakening, this wealth before undiscovered, this music set free? For the first time in her life her heart held something stronger than herself, was not this worthwhile? Then she ceased to wonder. She lost sight of the lights and the faces and the music was drowned by the beating of her own arteries. She saw only the blue eyes that flashed above her, felt only the warmth of that throbbing hand which held hers and which the blood of his heart fed. Dimly, as in a dream, she saw the drooping shoulders, high white forehead and tight, cynical mouth of the man she was to marry in December. For an hour she had been crowding back the memory of that face with all her strength.

"Let us stop, this is enough," she whispered. His only answer was to tighten the arm behind her. She sighed and let that masterful strength bear her where it would. She forgot that this man was little more than a savage, that they would part at dawn. The blood has no memories, no reflections, no regrets for the past, no consideration of the future.

"Let us go out where it is cooler," she said when the music stopped; thinking, *I am growing faint here, I shall be all right in the open air*. They stepped out into the cool, blue air of the night.

Since the older folk had begun dancing, the young Norwegians had been slipping out in couples to climb the windmill tower into the cooler atmosphere, as is their custom.

"You like to go up?" asked Eric, close to her ear.

She turned and looked at him with suppressed amusement. "How high is it?"

"Forty feet, about. I not let you fall." There was a note of irresistible pleading in his voice, and she felt that he tremendously wished her to go. Well, why not? This was a night of the unusual, when she was not herself at all, but was living an unreality. Tomorrow, yes, in a few hours, there would be the Vestibule Limited and the world.

"Well, if you'll take good care of me. I used to be able to climb, when I was a little girl."

Once at the top and seated on the platform, they were silent. Margaret wondered if she would not hunger for that scene all her life, through all the routine of the days to come. Above them stretched the great Western sky, serenely blue, even in the night, with its big, burning stars, never so cold and dead and far away as in denser atmospheres. The moon would not be up for twenty minutes yet, and all about the horizon, that wide horizon, which seemed to reach around the world, lingered a pale white light, as of a universal dawn. The weary wind brought up to them the heavy odours of the cornfields. The music of the dance sounded faintly from below. Eric leaned on his elbow beside her, his legs swinging down on the ladder. His great shoulders looked more than ever like those of the stone Doryphorus, who stands in his perfect, reposeful strength in the Louvre, and had often made her wonder if such men died forever with the youth of Greece.

"How sweet the corn smells at night," said Margaret nervously.

"Yes, like the flowers that grow in paradise, I think."

She was somewhat startled by this reply, and more startled when this taciturn man spoke again.

"You go away tomorrow?"

"Yes, we have stayed longer than we thought to now."

"You not come back any more?"

"No, I expect not. You see, it is a long trip halfway across the continent."

"You soon forget about this country, I guess." It seemed to him now a little thing to lose his soul for this woman, but that she should utterly forget this night into which he threw all his life and all his eternity, that was a bitter thought.

"No, Eric, I will not forget. You have all been too kind to me for that. And you won't be sorry you danced this one night, will you?"

"I never be sorry. I have not been so happy before. I not be so happy again, ever. You will be happy many nights yet, I only this one. I will dream sometimes, maybe."

The mighty resignation of his tone alarmed and touched her. It was as when some great animal composes itself for death, as when a great ship goes down at sea.

She sighed, but did not answer him. He drew a little closer and looked into her eyes.

"You are not always happy, too?" he asked.

"No, not always, Eric; not very often, I think."

"You have a trouble?"

"Yes, but I cannot put it into words. Perhaps if I could do that, I could cure it."

He clasped his hands together over his heart, as children do when they pray, and said falteringly, "If I own all the world, I give him you."

Margaret felt a sudden moisture in her eyes, and laid her hand on his.

"Thank you, Eric; I believe you would. But perhaps even then I should not be happy. Perhaps I have too much of it already."

She did not take her hand away from him; she did not dare. She sat still and waited for the traditions in which she had always believed to speak and save her. But they were dumb. She belonged to an ultra-refined civilization which tries to cheat nature with elegant sophistries. Cheat nature? Bah! One generation may do it, perhaps two, but the third—Can we ever rise above nature or sink below her? Did she not turn on Jerusalem as upon Sodom, upon St. Anthony in his desert as upon Nero in his seraglio? Does she not always cry in brutal triumph: "I am here still, at the bottom of things, warming the roots of life; you cannot starve me nor tame me nor thwart me; I made the world, I rule it, and I am its destiny."

This woman, on a windmill tower at the world's end with a giant barbarian, heard that cry tonight, and she was afraid! Ah! the terror and the delight of that moment when first we fear ourselves! Until then we have not lived.

"Come, Eric, let us go down; the moon is up and the music has begun again," she said.

He rose silently and stepped down upon the ladder, putting his arm about her to help her. That arm could have thrown Thor's hammer out in the cornfields yonder, yet it scarcely touched her, and his hand trembled as it had done in the dance. His face was level with hers now and the moonlight fell sharply upon it. All her life she had searched the faces of men for the look that lay in his eyes. She knew that that look had never shone for her before, would never shine for her on earth again, that such love comes to one only in dreams or in impossible places like this, unattainable always. This was Love's self, in a moment it would die. Stung by the agonized appeal that emanated from the man's whole being, she leaned forward and laid her lips on his. Once, twice and again she heard the deep respirations rattle in his throat while she held them there, and the riotous force under her head became an engulfing weakness. He drew her up to him until he felt all the resistance go out of her body, until every nerve relaxed and yielded. When she drew her face back from his, it was white with fear.

"Let us go down, oh, my God! let us go down!" she muttered. And the drunken stars up yonder seemed reeling to some appointed doom as she clung to the rounds of the ladder. All that she was to know of love she had left upon his lips.

"The devil is loose again," whispered Olaf Oleson, as he saw Eric dancing a moment later, his eyes blazing.

But Eric was thinking with an almost savage exultation of the time when he should pay for this. Ah, there would be no quailing then! if ever a soul went fearlessly, proudly down to the gates infernal, his should go. For a moment he fancied he was there already, treading down the tempest of flame, hugging the fiery hurricane to his breast. He wondered whether in ages gone, all the countless years of sinning in which men had sold and lost and flung their souls away, any man had ever so cheated Satan, had ever bartered his soul for so great a price.

It seemed but a little while till dawn.

The carriage was brought to the door and Wyllis Elliot and his sister said goodbye. She could not meet Eric's eyes as she gave him her hand, but as he stood by the horse's head, just as the carriage moved off, she gave him one swift glance that said, "I will not forget." In a moment the carriage was gone.

Eric changed his coat and plunged his head into the water tank and went to the barn to hook up his team. As he led his horses to the door, a shadow fell across his path, and he saw Skinner rising in his stirrups. His rugged face was pale and worn with looking after his wayward flock, with dragging men into the way of salvation.

"Good morning, Eric. There was a dance here last night?" he asked, sternly.

"A dance? Oh, yes, a dance," replied Eric, cheerfully.

"Certainly you did not dance, Eric?"

"Yes, I danced. I danced all the time."

The minister's shoulders drooped, and an expression of profound discouragement settled over his haggard face. There was almost anguish in the yearning he felt for this soul.

"Eric, I didn't look for this from you. I thought God had set his mark on you if he ever had on any man. And it is for things like this that you set your soul back a thousand years from God. O foolish and perverse generation!"

Eric drew himself up to his full height and looked off to where the new day was gilding the corn-tassels and flooding the uplands with light. As his nostrils drew in the breath of the dew and the morning, something from the only poetry he had ever read flashed across his mind, and he murmured, half to himself, with dreamy exultation:

"'And a day shall be as a thousand years, and a thousand years as a day.'"

THE ENCHANTED BLUFF

We had our swim before sundown, and while we were cooking our supper the oblique rays of light made a dazzling glare on the white sand about us. The translucent red ball itself sank behind the brown stretches of cornfield as we sat down to eat, and the warm layer of air that had rested over the water and our clean sand bar grew fresher and smelled of the rank ironweed and sunflowers growing on the flatter shore. The river was brown and sluggish, like any other of the half-dozen streams that water the Nebraska corn lands. On one shore was an irregular line of bald clay bluffs where a few scrub oaks with thick trunks and flat, twisted tops threw light shadows on the long grass. The western shore was low and level, with cornfields that stretched to the skyline, and all along the water's edge were little sandy coves and beaches where slim cottonwoods and willow saplings flickered.

The turbulence of the river in springtime discouraged milling, and, beyond keeping the old red bridge in repair, the busy farmers did not concern themselves with the stream; so the Sandtown boys were left in undisputed possession. In the autumn we hunted quail through the miles of stubble and fodder land along the flat shore, and, after the winter skating season was over and the ice had gone out, the spring freshets and flooded bottoms gave us our great excitement of the year. The channel was never the same for two successive seasons. Every spring the swollen stream undermined a bluff to the east, or bit out a few acres of cornfield to the west and whirled the soil away, to deposit it in spumy mud banks somewhere else. When the water fell low in midsummer, new sand bars were thus exposed to dry and whiten in the August sun. Sometimes these were banked so firmly that the fury of the next freshet failed to unseat them; the little willow seedlings emerged triumphantly from the yellow froth, broke into spring leaf, shot up into summer growth, and with their mesh of roots bound together the moist sand beneath them against the batterings of another April. Here and there a cottonwood soon glittered among them, quivering in the low current of air that, even on breathless days when the dust hung like smoke above the wagon road, trembled along the face of the water.

It was on such an island, in the third summer of its yellow green, that we built our watch fire; not in the thicket of dancing willow wands, but on the level terrace of fine sand which had been added that spring; a little new bit of world, beautifully ridged with ripple marks, and strewn with the tiny skeletons of turtles and fish, all as white and dry as if they had been expertly cured. We had been careful not to mar the freshness of the place, although we often swam to it on summer evenings and lay on the sand to rest.

This was our last watch fire of the year, and there were reasons why I should remember it better than any of the others. Next week the other boys were to file back to their old places in the Sandtown High School, but I was to go up to the Divide to teach my first country school in the Norwegian district. I was already homesick at the thought of quitting the boys with whom I had always played; of leaving the river, and going up into a windy plain that was all windmills and cornfields and big pastures; where there was nothing wilful or unmanageable in the landscape, no new islands, and no chance of unfamiliar birds—such as often followed the watercourses.

Other boys came and went and used the river for fishing or skating, but we six were sworn to the spirit of the stream, and we were friends mainly because of the river. There were the two Hassler boys, Fritz and Otto, sons of the little German tailor. They were the youngest of us; ragged boys of ten and twelve, with sunburned hair, weather-stained faces, and pale blue eyes. Otto, the elder, was the best mathematician in school, and clever at his books, but he always dropped out in the spring term as if the river could not get on without him. He and Fritz caught the fat, horned catfish and sold them about the town, and they lived so much in the water that they were as brown and sandy as the river itself.

There was Percy Pound, a fat, freckled boy with chubby cheeks, who took half a dozen boys' story-papers and was always being kept in for reading detective stories behind his desk. There was Tip Smith, destined by his freckles and red hair to be the buffoon in all our games, though he walked like a timid little old man and had a funny, cracked laugh. Tip worked hard in his father's grocery store every afternoon, and swept it out before school in the morning. Even his recreations were laborious. He collected cigarette cards and tin tobacco-tags indefatigably, and would sit for hours humped up over a snarling little scroll-saw which he kept in his attic. His dearest possessions were some little pill bottles that purported to contain grains of wheat from the Holy Land, water from the Jordan and the Dead Sea, and earth from the Mount of Olives. His father had bought these dull things from a Baptist missionary who peddled them, and Tip seemed to derive great satisfaction from their remote origin.

The tall boy was Arthur Adams. He had fine hazel eyes that were almost too reflective and sympathetic for a boy, and such a pleasant voice that we all loved to hear him read aloud. Even when he had to read poetry aloud at school, no one ever thought of laughing. To be sure, he was not at school very much of the time. He was seventeen and should have finished the High School the year before, but he was always off somewhere with his gun. Arthur's mother was dead, and his father, who was feverishly absorbed in promoting schemes, wanted to send the boy away to school and get him off his hands; but Arthur always begged off for another year and promised to study. I remember him as a tall, brown boy with an intelligent face, always lounging among a lot of us little fellows, laughing at us oftener than with us, but such a soft, satisfied laugh that we felt rather flattered when we provoked it. In after-years people said that Arthur had been given to evil ways as a lad, and it is true that we often saw him with the gambler's sons and with old Spanish Fanny's boy, but if he learned anything ugly in their company he never betrayed it to us. We would have followed Arthur anywhere, and I am bound to say that he led us into no worse places than the cattail marshes and the stubble fields. These, then, were the boys who camped with me that summer night upon the sand bar.

After we finished our supper we beat the willow thicket for driftwood. By the time we had collected enough, night had fallen, and the pungent, weedy smell from the shore increased with the coolness. We threw ourselves down about the fire and made another futile effort to show Percy Pound the Little Dipper. We had tried it often before, but he could never be got past the big one.

"You see those three big stars just below the handle, with the bright one in the middle?" said Otto Hassler; "that's Orion's belt, and the bright one is the clasp." I crawled behind Otto's shoulder and sighted up his arm to the star that seemed perched upon the tip of his steady forefinger. The Hassler boys did seine-fishing at night, and they knew a good many stars.

Percy gave up the Little Dipper and lay back on the sand, his hands clasped under his head. "I can see the North Star," he announced, contentedly, pointing toward it with his big toe. "Anyone might get lost and need to know that."

We all looked up at it.

"How do you suppose Columbus felt when his compass didn't point north any more?" Tip asked.

Otto shook his head. "My father says that there was another North Star once, and that maybe this one won't last always. I wonder what would happen to us down here if anything went wrong with it?"

Arthur chuckled. "I wouldn't worry, Ott. Nothing's apt to happen to it in your time. Look at the Milky Way! There must be lots of good dead Indians."

We lay back and looked, meditating, at the dark cover of the world. The gurgle of the water had become heavier. We had often noticed a mutinous, complaining note in it at night, quite different from its cheerful daytime chuckle, and seeming like the voice of a much deeper and more powerful stream. Our water had always these two moods: the one of sunny complaisance, the other of inconsolable, passionate regret.

"Queer how the stars are all in sort of diagrams," remarked Otto. "You could do most any proposition in geometry with 'em. They always look as if they meant something. Some folks say everybody's fortune is all written out in the stars, don't they?"

"They believe so in the old country," Fritz affirmed.

But Arthur only laughed at him. "You're thinking of Napoleon, Fritzey. He had a star that went out when he began to lose battles. I guess the stars don't keep any close tally on Sandtown folks."

We were speculating on how many times we could count a hundred before the evening star went down behind the cornfields, when someone cried, "There comes the moon, and it's as big as a cart wheel!"

We all jumped up to greet it as it swam over the bluffs behind us. It came up like a galleon in full sail; an enormous, barbaric thing, red as an angry heathen god.

"When the moon came up red like that, the Aztecs used to sacrifice their prisoners on the temple top," Percy announced.

"Go on, Perce. You got that out of *Golden Days*. Do you believe that, Arthur?" I appealed.

Arthur answered, quite seriously: "Like as not. The moon was one of their gods. When my father was in Mexico City he saw the stone where they used to sacrifice their prisoners."

As we dropped down by the fire again some one asked whether the Mound-Builders were older than the Aztecs. When we once got upon the Mound-Builders we never willingly got away from them, and we were still conjecturing when we heard a loud splash in the water.

"Must have been a big cat jumping," said Fritz. "They do sometimes. They must see bugs in the dark. Look what a track the moon makes!"

There was a long, silvery streak on the water, and where the current fretted over a big log it boiled up like gold pieces.

"Suppose there ever *was* any gold hid away in this old river?" Fritz asked. He lay like a little brown Indian, close to the fire, his chin on his hand and his bare feet in the air. His brother laughed at him, but Arthur took his suggestion seriously.

"Some of the Spaniards thought there was gold up here somewhere. Seven cities chuck full of gold, they had it, and

Coronado and his men came up to hunt it. The Spaniards were all over this country once."

Percy looked interested. "Was that before the Mormons went through?"

We all laughed at this.

"Long enough before. Before the Pilgrim Fathers, Perce. Maybe they came along this very river. They always followed the watercourses."

"I wonder where this river really does begin?" Tip mused. That was an old and a favorite mystery which the map did not clearly explain. On the map the little black line stopped somewhere in western Kansas; but since rivers generally rose in mountains, it was only reasonable to suppose that ours came from the Rockies. Its destination, we knew, was the Missouri, and the Hassler boys always maintained that we could embark at Sandtown in floodtime, follow our noses, and eventually arrive at New Orleans. Now they took up their old argument. "If us boys had grit enough to try it, it wouldn't take no time to get to Kansas City and St. Joe."

We began to talk about the places we wanted to go to. The Hassler boys wanted to see the stockyards in Kansas City, and Percy wanted to see a big store in Chicago. Arthur was interlocutor and did not betray himself.

"Now it's your turn, Tip."

Tip rolled over on his elbow and poked the fire, and his eyes looked shyly out of his queer, tight little face. "My place is awful far away. My Uncle Bill told me about it."

Tip's Uncle Bill was a wanderer, bitten with mining fever, who had drifted into Sandtown with a broken arm, and when it was well had drifted out again.

"Where is it?"

"Aw, it's down in New Mexico somewheres. There aren't no railroads or anything. You have to go on mules, and you run out of water before you get there and have to drink canned tomatoes."

"Well, go on, kid. What's it like when you do get there?"

Tip sat up and excitedly began his story.

"There's a big red rock there that goes right up out of the sand for about nine hundred feet. The country's flat all around it, and this here rock goes up all by itself, like a monument. They call it the Enchanted Bluff down there, because no white man has ever been on top of it. The sides are smooth rock, and straight up, like a wall. The Indians say that hundreds of years ago, before the Spaniards came, there was a village away up there in the air. The tribe that lived there had some sort of steps, made out of wood and bark, hung down over the face of the bluff, and the braves went down to hunt and carried water up in big jars swung on their backs. They kept a big supply of water and dried meat up there, and never went down except to hunt. They were a peaceful tribe that made cloth and pottery, and they went up there to get out of the wars. You see, they could pick off any war party that tried to get up their little steps. The Indians say they were a handsome people, and they had some sort of queer religion. Uncle Bill thinks they were Cliff-Dwellers who had got into trouble and left home. They weren't fighters, anyhow.

"One time the braves were down hunting and an awful storm came up—a kind of waterspout—and when they got back to their rock they found their little staircase had been all broken to pieces, and only a few steps were left hanging away up in the air. While they were camped at the foot of the rock, wondering what to do, a war party from the north came along and massacred 'em to a man, with all the old folks and women looking on from the rock. Then the war party went on south and left the village to get down the best way they could. Of course they never got down. They starved to death up there, and when the war party came back on their way north, they could hear the children crying from the edge of the bluff where they had crawled out, but they didn't see a sign of a grown Indian, and nobody has ever been up there since."

We exclaimed at this dolorous legend and sat up.

"There couldn't have been many people up there," Percy demurred. "How big is the top, Tip?"

"Oh, pretty big. Big enough so that the rock doesn't look nearly as tall as it is. The top's bigger than the base. The bluff is sort of worn away for several hundred feet up. That's one reason it's so hard to climb."

I asked how the Indians got up, in the first place.

"Nobody knows how they got up or when. A hunting party came along once and saw that there was a town up there, and that was all."

Otto rubbed his chin and looked thoughtful. "Of course there must be some way to get up there. Couldn't people get a rope over someway and pull a ladder up?"

Tip's little eyes were shining with excitement. "I know a way. Me and Uncle Bill talked it over. There's a kind of rocket that would take a rope over—lifesavers use 'em—and then you could hoist a rope ladder and peg it down at the bottom and make it tight with guy ropes on the other side. I'm going to climb that there bluff, and I've got it all planned out."

Fritz asked what he expected to find when he got up there.

"Bones, maybe, or the ruins of their town, or pottery, or some of their idols. There might be 'most anything up there. Anyhow, I want to see."

"Sure nobody else has been up there, Tip?" Arthur asked.

"Dead sure. Hardly anybody ever goes down there. Some hunters tried to cut steps in the rock once, but they didn't get higher than a man can reach. The Bluff's all red granite, and Uncle Bill thinks it's a boulder the glaciers left. It's a queer place, anyhow. Nothing but cactus and desert for hundreds of miles, and yet right under the Bluff there's good water and plenty of grass. That's why the bison used to go down there."

Suddenly we heard a scream above our fire, and jumped up to see a dark, slim bird floating southward far above us— a whooping crane, we knew by her cry and her long neck. We ran to the edge of the island, hoping we might see her alight, but she wavered southward along the rivercourse until we lost her. The Hassler boys declared that by the look of the heavens it must be after midnight, so we threw more wood on our fire, put on our jackets, and curled down in the warm sand. Several of us pretended to doze, but I fancy we were really thinking about Tip's Bluff and the extinct people. Over in the wood the ring doves were calling mournfully to one another, and once we heard a dog bark, far away. "Somebody getting into old Tommy's melon patch," Fritz murmured sleepily, but nobody answered him. By and by Percy spoke out of the shadows.

"Say, Tip, when you go down there will you take me with you?"

"Maybe."

"Suppose one of us beats you down there, Tip?"

"Whoever gets to the Bluff first has got to promise to tell the rest of us exactly what he finds," remarked one of the Hassler boys, and to this we all readily assented.

Somewhat reassured, I dropped off to sleep. I must have dreamed about a race for the Bluff, for I awoke in a kind of fear that other people were getting ahead of me and that I was losing my chance. I sat up in my damp clothes and looked at the other boys, who lay tumbled in uneasy attitudes about the dead fire. It was still dark, but the sky was blue with the last wonderful azure of night. The stars glistened like crystal globes, and trembled as if they shone through a depth of clear water. Even as I watched, they began to pale and the sky brightened. Day came suddenly, almost instantaneously. I turned for another look at the blue night, and it was gone. Everywhere the birds began to call, and all manner of little insects began to chirp and hop about in the willows. A breeze sprang up from the west and brought the heavy smell of ripened corn. The boys rolled over and shook themselves. We stripped and plunged into the river just as the sun came up over the windy bluffs.

When I came home to Sandtown at Christmas time, we skated out to our island and talked over the whole project of the Enchanted Bluff, renewing our resolution to find it.

Although that was twenty years ago, none of us have ever climbed the Enchanted Bluff. Percy Pound is a stockbroker in Kansas City and will go nowhere that his red touring car cannot carry him. Otto Hassler went on the railroad and lost his foot braking; after which he and Fritz succeeded their father as the town tailors.

Arthur sat about the sleepy little town all his life—he died before he was twenty-five. The last time I saw him, when I was home on one of my college vacations, he was sitting in a steamer chair under a cottonwood tree in the little yard behind one of the two Sandtown saloons. He was very untidy and his hand was not steady, but when he rose, unabashed, to greet me, his eyes were as clear and warm as ever. When I had talked with him for an hour and heard him laugh again, I wondered how it was that when Nature had taken such pains with a man, from his hands to the arch of his long foot, she had ever lost him in Sandtown. He joked about Tip Smith's Bluff, and declared he was going down there just as soon as the weather got cooler; he thought the Grand Canyon might be worth while, too.

I was perfectly sure when I left him that he would never get beyond the high plank fence and the comfortable shade of the cottonwood. And, indeed, it was under that very tree that he died one summer morning.

Tip Smith still talks about going to New Mexico. He married a slatternly, unthrifty country girl, has been much tied to a perambulator, and has grown stooped and grey from irregular meals and broken sleep. But the worst of his difficulties are now over, and he has, as he says, come into easy water. When I was last in Sandtown I walked home with him late one moonlight night, after he had balanced his cash and shut up his store. We took the long way around and sat down on the schoolhouse steps, and between us we quite revived the romance of the lone red rock and the extinct people. Tip insists that he still means to go down there, but he thinks now he will wait until his boy Bert is old enough to go with him. Bert has been let into the story, and thinks of nothing but the Enchanted Bluff.

THE BOHEMIAN GIRL

The transcontinental express swung along the windings of the Sand River Valley, and in the rear seat of the observation car a young man sat greatly at his ease, not in the least discomfited by the fierce sunlight which beat in upon his brown face and neck and strong back. There was a look of relaxation and of great passivity about his broad shoulders, which seemed almost too heavy until he stood up and squared them. He wore a pale flannel shirt and a blue silk necktie with loose ends. His trousers were wide and belted at the waist, and his short sack coat hung open. His heavy shoes had seen good service. His reddish-brown hair, like his clothes, had a foreign cut. He had deep-set, dark blue eyes under heavy reddish eyebrows. His face was kept clean only by close shaving, and even the sharpest razor left a glint of yellow in the smooth brown of his skin. His teeth and the palms of his hands were very white. His head, which looked hard and stubborn, lay indolently in the green cushion of the wicker chair, and as he looked out at the ripe summer country a teasing, not unkindly smile played over his lips. Once, as he basked thus comfortably, a quick light flashed in his eyes, curiously dilating the pupils, and his mouth became a hard, straight line, gradually relaxing into its former smile of rather kindly mockery. He told himself, apparently, that there was no point in getting excited; and he seemed a master hand at taking his ease when he could. Neither the sharp whistle of the locomotive nor the brakeman's call disturbed him. It was not until after the train had stopped that he rose, put on a Panama hat, took from the rack a small valise and a flute case, and stepped deliberately to the station platform. The baggage was already unloaded, and the stranger presented a check for a battered sole-leather steamer trunk.

"Can you keep it here for a day or two?" he asked the agent. "I may send for it, and I may not."

"Depends on whether you like the country, I suppose?" demanded the agent in a challenging tone.

"Just so."

The agent shrugged his shoulders, looked scornfully at the small trunk, which was marked "N.E.," and handed out a claim check without further comment. The stranger watched him as he caught one end of the trunk and dragged it into the express room. The agent's manner seemed to remind him of something amusing. "Doesn't seem to be a very big place," he remarked, looking about.

"It's big enough for us," snapped the agent, as he banged the trunk into a corner.

That remark, apparently, was what Nils Ericson had wanted. He chuckled quietly as he took a leather strap from his pocket and swung his valise around his shoulder. Then he settled his Panama securely on his head, turned up his trousers, tucked the flute case under his arm, and started off across the fields. He gave the town, as he would have said, a wide berth, and cut through a great fenced pasture, emerging, when he rolled under the barbed wire at the farther corner, upon a white dusty road which ran straight up from the river valley to the high prairies, where the ripe wheat stood yellow and the tin roofs and weathercocks were twinkling in the fierce sunlight. By the time Nils had done three miles, the sun was sinking and the farm wagons on their way home from town came rattling by, covering him with dust and making him sneeze. When one of the farmers pulled up and offered to give him a lift, he clambered in willingly. The driver was a thin, grizzled old man with a long lean neck and a foolish sort of beard, like a goat's. "How fur ye goin'?" he asked, as he clucked to his horses and started off.

"Do you go by the Ericson place?"

"Which Ericson?" The old man drew in his reins as if he expected to stop again.

"Preacher Ericson's."

"Oh, the Old Lady Ericson's!" He turned and looked at Nils. "La, me! If you're goin' out there you might a' rid out in the automobile. That's a pity, now. The Old Lady Ericson was in town with her auto. You might 'a' heard it snortin' anywhere about the post-office er the butcher shop."

"Has she a motor?" asked the stranger absently.

"'Deed an' she has! She runs into town every night about this time for her mail and meat for supper. Some folks say she's afraid her auto won't get exercise enough, but I say that's jealousy."

"Aren't there any other motors about here?"

"Oh, yes! we have fourteen in all. But nobody else gets around like the Old Lady Ericson. She's out, rain er shine, over the whole county, chargin' into town and out amongst her farms, an' up to her sons' places. Sure you ain't goin' to the wrong place?" He craned his neck and looked at Nils' flute case with eager curiosity. "The old woman ain't got any piany that I knows on. Olaf, he has a grand. His wife's musical: took lessons in Chicago."

"I'm going up there tomorrow," said Nils imperturbably. He saw that the driver took him for a piano tuner.

"Oh, I see!" The old man screwed up his eyes mysteriously. He was a little dashed by the stranger's noncommunicativeness, but he soon broke out again.

"I'm one o' Miss Ericson's tenants. Look after one of her places. I did own the place myself once, but I lost it a while back, in the bad years just after the World's Fair. Just as well, too, I say. Lets you out o' payin' taxes. The Ericsons do own most of the county now. I remember the old preacher's favorite text used to be, 'To them that hath shall be given.' They've spread something wonderful—run over this here country like bindweed. But I ain't one that begretches it to 'em. Folks is entitled to what they kin git; and they're hustlers. Olaf, he's in the Legislature now, and a likely man fur Congress. Listen, if that ain't the old woman comin' now. Want I should stop her?"

Nils shook his head. He heard the deep chug-chug of a motor vibrating steadily in the clear twilight behind them. The pale lights of the car swam over the hill, and the old man slapped his reins and turned clear out of the road, ducking his head at the first of three angry snorts from behind. The motor was running at a hot, even speed, and passed without turning an inch from its course. The driver was a stalwart woman who sat at ease in the front seat and drove her car bareheaded. She left a cloud of dust and a trail of gasoline behind her. Her tenant threw back his head and sneezed.

"Whew! I sometimes say I'd as lief be *before* Mrs. Ericson as behind her. She does beat all! Nearly seventy, and never lets another soul touch that car. Puts it into commission herself every morning, and keeps it tuned up by the hitch-bar all day. I never stop work for a drink o' water that I don't hear her a-churnin' up the road. I reckon her darter-in-laws never sets down easy nowadays. Never know when she'll pop in. Mis' Otto, she says to me: 'We're so afraid that thing'll blow up and do Ma some injury yet, she's so turrible venturesome.' Says I: 'I wouldn't stew, Mis' Otto; the old lady'll drive that car to the funeral of every darter-in-law she's got.' That was after the old woman had jumped a turrible bad culvert."

The stranger heard vaguely what the old man was saying. Just now he was experiencing something very much like homesickness, and he was wondering what had brought it about. The mention of a name or two, perhaps; the rattle of a wagon along a dusty road; the rank, resinous smell of sunflowers and ironweed, which the night damp brought up from the draws and low places; perhaps, more than all, the dancing lights of the motor that had plunged by. He squared his shoulders with a comfortable sense of strength.

The wagon, as it jolted westward, climbed a pretty steady up-grade. The country, receding from the rough river valley, swelled more and more gently, as if it had been smoothed out by the wind. On one of the last of the rugged ridges, at the end of a branch road, stood a grim square house with a tin roof and double porches. Behind the house stretched a row of broken, wind-racked poplars, and down the hill slope to the left straggled the sheds and stables. The old man stopped his horses where the Ericsons' road branched across a dry sand creek that wound about the foot of the hill.

"That's the old lady's place. Want I should drive in?" "No, thank you. I'll roll out here. Much obliged to you. Good night."

His passenger stepped down over the front wheel, and the old man drove on reluctantly, looking back as if he would like to see how the stranger would be received.

As Nils was crossing the dry creek he heard the restive tramp of a horse coming toward him down the hill. Instantly he flashed out of the road and stood behind a thicket of wild plum bushes that grew in the sandy bed. Peering through the dusk, he saw a light horse, under tight rein, descending the hill at a sharp walk. The rider was a slender woman— barely visible against the dark hillside—wearing an old-fashioned derby hat and a long riding skirt. She sat lightly in the saddle, with her chin high, and seemed to be looking into the distance. As she passed the plum thicket her horse snuffed the air and shied. She struck him, pulling him in sharply, with an angry exclamation, *"Blazne!"* in Bohemian. Once in the main road, she let him out into a lope, and they soon emerged upon the crest of high land, where they moved along the skyline, silhouetted against the band of faint colour that lingered in the west. This horse and rider, with their free, rhythmical gallop, were the only moving things to be seen on the face of the flat country. They seemed, in the last sad light of evening, not to be there accidentally, but as an inevitable detail of the landscape.

Nils watched them until they had shrunk to a mere moving speck against the sky, then he crossed the sand creek and climbed the hill. When he reached the gate the front of the house was dark, but a light was shining from the side windows. The pigs were squealing in the hog corral, and Nils could see a tall boy, who carried two big wooden buckets, moving about among them. Halfway between the barn and the house, the windmill wheezed lazily. Following the path that ran around to the back porch, Nils stopped to look through the screen door into the lamplit kitchen. The kitchen was the largest room in the house; Nils remembered that his older brothers used to give dances there when he was a boy. Beside the stove stood a little girl with two light yellow braids and a broad, flushed face, peering anxiously into a frying pan. In the dining-room beyond, a large, broad-shouldered woman was moving about the table. She walked with an active, springy step. Her face was heavy and florid, almost without wrinkles, and her hair was black at seventy. Nils felt proud of her as he watched her deliberate activity; never a momentary hesitation, or a movement that did not tell. He waited until she came out into the kitchen and, brushing the child aside, took her place at the stove. Then he tapped on the screen door and entered.

"It's nobody but Nils, Mother. I expect you weren't looking for me."

Mrs. Ericson turned away from the stove and stood staring at him. "Bring the lamp, Hilda, and let me look."

Nils laughed and unslung his valise. "What's the matter, Mother? Don't you know me?"

Mrs. Ericson put down the lamp. "You must be Nils. You don't look very different, anyway."

"Nor you, Mother. You hold your own. Don't you wear glasses yet?"

"Only to read by. Where's your trunk, Nils?"

"Oh, I left that in town. I thought it might not be convenient for you to have company so near threshing-time."

"Don't be foolish, Nils." Mrs. Ericson turned back to the stove. "I don't thresh now. I hitched the wheat land onto the next farm and have a tenant. Hilda, take some hot water up to the company room, and go call little Eric."

The tow-haired child, who had been standing in mute amazement, took up the tea-kettle and withdrew, giving Nils a long, admiring look from the door of the kitchen stairs.

"Who's the youngster?" Nils asked, dropping down on the bench behind the kitchen stove.

"One of your Cousin Henrik's."

"How long has Cousin Henrik been dead?"

"Six years. There are two boys. One stays with Peter and one with Anders. Olaf is their guardeen."

There was a clatter of pails on the porch, and a tall, lanky boy peered wonderingly in through the screen door. He had a fair, gentle face and big grey eyes, and wisps of soft yellow hair hung down under his cap. Nils sprang up and pulled him into the kitchen, hugging him and slapping him on the shoulders. "Well, if it isn't my kid! Look at the size of him! Don't you know me, Eric?"

The boy reddened tinder his sunburn and freckles, and hung his head. "I guess it's Nils," he said shyly.

"You're a good guesser," laughed Nils giving the lad's hand a swing. To himself he was thinking: "That's why the little girl looked so friendly. He's taught her to like me. He was only six when I went away, and he's remembered for twelve years."

Eric stood fumbling with his cap and smiling. "You look just like I thought you would," he ventured.

"Go wash your hands, Eric," called Mrs. Ericson. "I've got cob corn for supper, Nils. You used to like it. I guess you don't get much of that in the old country. Here's Hilda; she'll take you up to your room. You'll want to get the dust off you before you eat."

Mrs. Ericson went into the dining-room to lay another plate, and the little girl came up and nodded to Nils as if to let him know that his room was ready. He put out his hand and she took it, with a startled glance up at his face. Little Eric dropped his towel, threw an arm about Nils and one about Hilda, gave them a clumsy squeeze, and then stumbled out to the porch.

During supper Nils heard exactly how much land each of his eight grown brothers farmed, how their crops were coming on, and how much livestock they were feeding. His mother watched him narrowly as she talked. "You've got better looking, Nils," she remarked abruptly, whereupon he grinned and the children giggled. Eric, although he was eighteen and as tall as Nils, was always accounted a child, being the last of so many sons. His face seemed childlike, too, Nils thought, and he had the open, wandering eyes of a little boy. All the others had been men at his age.

After supper Nils went out to the front porch and sat down on the step to smoke a pipe. Mrs. Ericson drew a rocking-chair up near him and began to knit busily. It was one of the few Old World customs she had kept up, for she could not bear to sit with idle hands.

"Where's little Eric, Mother?"

"He's helping Hilda with the dishes. He does it of his own will; I don't like a boy to be too handy about the house."

"He seems like a nice kid."

"He's very obedient."

Nils smiled a little in the dark. It was just as well to shift the line of conversation. "What are you knitting there, Mother?"

"Baby stockings. The boys keep me busy." Mrs. Ericson chuckled and clicked her needles.

"How many grandchildren have you?"

"Only thirty-one now. Olaf lost his three. They were sickly, like their mother."

"I supposed he had a second crop by this time!"

"His second wife has no children. She's too proud. She tears about on horseback all the time. But she'll get caught up with, yet. She sets herself very high, though nobody knows what for. They were low enough Bohemians she came of. I never thought much of Bohemians; always drinking."

Nils puffed away at his pipe in silence, and Mrs. Ericson knitted on. In a few moments she added grimly: "She was down here tonight, just before you came. She'd like to quarrel with me and come between me and Olaf, but I don't give her the chance. I suppose you'll be bringing a wife home some day."

"I don't know. I've never thought much about it."

"Well, perhaps it's best as it is," suggested Mrs. Ericson hopefully. "You'd never be contented tied down to the land. There was roving blood in your father's family, and it's come out in you. I expect your own way of life suits you best." Mrs. Ericson had dropped into a blandly agreeable tone which Nils well remembered. It seemed to amuse him a good deal and his white teeth flashed behind his pipe. His mother's strategies had always diverted him, even when he was a boy—they were so flimsy and patent, so illy proportioned to her vigor and force. "They've been waiting to see which way I'd jump," he reflected. He felt that Mrs. Ericson was pondering his case deeply as she sat clicking her needles.

"I don't suppose you've ever got used to steady work," she went on presently. "Men ain't apt to if they roam around too long. It's a pity you didn't come back the year after the World's Fair. Your father picked up a good bit of land cheap then, in the hard times, and I expect maybe he'd have give you a farm, it's too bad you put off comin' back so long, for I always thought he meant to do something by you."

Nils laughed and shook the ashes out of his pipe. "I'd have missed a lot if I had come back then. But I'm sorry I didn't get back to see father."

"Well, I suppose we have to miss things at one end or the other. Perhaps you are as well satisfied with your own doings, now, as you'd have been with a farm," said Mrs. Ericson reassuringly.

"Land's a good thing to have," Nils commented, as he lit another match and sheltered it with his hand.

His mother looked sharply at his face until the match burned out. "Only when you stay on it!" she hastened to say.

Eric came round the house by the path just then, and Nils rose, with a yawn. "Mother, if you don't mind, Eric and I will take a little tramp before bedtime. It will make me sleep."

"Very well; only don't stay long. I'll sit up and wait for you. I like to lock up myself."

Nils put his hand on Eric's shoulder, and the two tramped down the hill and across the sand creek into the dusty highroad beyond. Neither spoke. They swung along at an even gait, Nils puffing at his pipe. There was no moon, and the white road and the wide fields lay faint in the starlight. Over everything was darkness and thick silence, and the smell of dust and sunflowers. The brothers followed the road for a mile or more without finding a place to sit down. Finally, Nils perched on a stile over the wire fence, and Eric sat on the lower step.

"I began to think you never would come back, Nils," said the boy softly.

"Didn't I promise you I would?"

"Yes; but people don't bother about promises they make to babies. Did you really know you were going away for good when you went to Chicago with the cattle that time?"

"I thought it very likely, if I could make my way."

"I don't see how you did it, Nils. Not many fellows could." Eric rubbed his shoulder against his brother's knee.

"The hard thing was leaving home you and father. It was easy enough, once I got beyond Chicago. Of course I got awful homesick; used to cry myself to sleep. But I'd burned my bridges."

"You had always wanted to go, hadn't you?"

"Always. Do you still sleep in our little room? Is that cottonwood still by the window?"

Eric nodded eagerly and smiled up at his brother in the grey darkness.

"You remember how we always said the leaves were whispering when they rustled at night? Well, they always whispered to me about the sea. Sometimes they said names out of the geography books. In a high wind they had a desperate sound, like someone trying to tear loose."

"How funny, Nils," said Eric dreamily, resting his chin on his hand. "That tree still talks like that, and 'most always it talks to me about you."

They sat a while longer, watching the stars. At last Eric whispered anxiously: "Hadn't we better go back now? Mother will get tired waiting for us." They rose and took a short cut home, through the pasture.

II

The next morning Nils woke with the first flood of light that came with dawn. The white-plastered walls of his room reflected the glare that shone through the thin window shades, and he found it impossible to sleep. He dressed hurriedly and slipped down the hall and up the back stairs to the half-story room which he used to share with his little brother. Eric, in a skimpy nightshirt, was sitting on the edge of the bed, rubbing his eyes, his pale yellow hair standing up in tufts all over his head. When he saw Nils, he murmured something confusedly and hustled his long legs into his trousers. "I didn't expect you'd be up so early, Nils," he said, as his head emerged from his blue shirt.

"Oh, you thought I was a dude, did you?" Nils gave him a playful tap which bent the tall boy up like a clasp knife. "See here: I must teach you to box." Nils thrust his hands into his pockets and walked about. "You haven't changed things much up here. Got most of my old traps, haven't you?"

He took down a bent, withered piece of sapling that hung over the dresser. "If this isn't the stick Lou Sandberg killed himself with!"

The boy looked up from his shoe-lacing.

"Yes; you never used to let me play with that. Just how did he do it, Nils? You were with father when he found Lou, weren't you?"

"Yes. Father was going off to preach somewhere, and, as we drove along, Lou's place looked sort of forlorn, and we thought we'd stop and cheer him up. When we found him father said he'd been dead a couple days. He'd tied a piece of binding twine round his neck, made a noose in each end, fixed the nooses over the ends of a bent stick, and let the stick spring straight; strangled himself."

"What made him kill himself such a silly way?"

The simplicity of the boy's question set Nils laughing. He clapped little Eric on the shoulder. "What made him such a silly as to kill himself at all, I should say!"

"Oh, well! But his hogs had the cholera, and all up and died on him, didn't they?"

"Sure they did; but he didn't have cholera; and there were plenty of hogs left in the world, weren't there?"

"Well, but, if they weren't his, how could they do him any good?" Eric asked, in astonishment.

"Oh, scat! He could have had lots of fun with other people's hogs. He was a chump, Lou Sandberg. To kill yourself for a pig—think of that, now!" Nils laughed all the way downstairs, and quite embarrassed little Eric, who fell to scrubbing his face and hands at the tin basin. While he was parting his wet hair at the kitchen looking glass, a heavy tread sounded on the stairs. The boy dropped his comb. "Gracious, there's Mother. We must have talked too long." He hurried out to the shed, slipped on his overalls, and disappeared with the milking pails.

Mrs. Ericson came in, wearing a clean white apron, her black hair shining from the application of a wet brush.

"Good morning, Mother. Can't I make the fire for you?"

"No, thank you, Nils. It's no trouble to make a cob fire, and I like to manage the kitchen stove myself" Mrs. Ericson paused with a shovel full of ashes in her hand. "I expect you will be wanting to see your brothers as soon as possible. I'll take you up to Anders' place this morning. He's threshing, and most of our boys are over there."

"Will Olaf be there?"

Mrs. Ericson went on taking out the ashes, and spoke between shovels. "No; Olaf's wheat is all in, put away in his new barn. He got six thousand bushel this year. He's going to town today to get men to finish roofing his barn."

"So Olaf is building a new barn?" Nils asked absently.

"Biggest one in the county, and almost done. You'll likely be here for the barn-raising. He's going to have a supper and a dance as soon as everybody's done threshing. Says it keeps the voters in good humour. I tell him that's all nonsense; but Olaf has a head for politics."

"Does Olaf farm all Cousin Henrik's land?"

Mrs. Ericson frowned as she blew into the faint smoke curling up about the cobs. "Yes; he holds it in trust for the children, Hilda and her brothers. He keeps strict account of everything he raises on it, and puts the proceeds out at compound interest for them."

Nils smiled as he watched the little flames shoot up. The door of the back stairs opened, and Hilda emerged, her arms behind her, buttoning up her long gingham apron as she came. He nodded to her gaily, and she twinkled at him out of her little blue eyes, set far apart over her wide cheekbones.

"There, Hilda, you grind the coffee—and just put in an extra handful; I expect your Cousin Nils likes his strong," said Mrs. Ericson, as she went out to the shed.

Nils turned to look at the little girl, who gripped the coffee grinder between her knees and ground so hard that her two braids bobbed and her face flushed under its broad spattering of freckles. He noticed on her middle finger something that had not been there last night, and that had evidently been put on for company: a tiny gold ring with a clumsily set garnet stone. As her hand went round and round he touched the ring with the tip of his finger, smiling.

Hilda glanced toward the shed door through which Mrs. Ericson had disappeared. "My Cousin Clara gave me that," she whispered bashfully. "She's Cousin Olaf's wife."

III

Mrs. Olaf Ericson—Clara Vavrika, as many people still called her—was moving restlessly about her big bare house that morning. Her husband had left for the county town before his wife was out of bed—her lateness in rising was one of the many things the Ericson family had against her. Clara seldom came downstairs before eight o'clock, and this

33

morning she was even later, for she had dressed with unusual care. She put on, however, only a tight-fitting black dress, which people thereabouts thought very plain. She was a tall, dark woman of thirty, with a rather sallow complexion and a touch of dull salmon red in her cheeks, where the blood seemed to burn under her brown skin. Her hair, parted evenly above her low forehead, was so black that there were distinctly blue lights in it. Her black eyebrows were delicate half-moons and her lashes were long and heavy. Her eyes slanted a little, as if she had a strain of Tartar or gypsy blood, and were sometimes full of fiery determination and sometimes dull and opaque. Her expression was never altogether amiable; was often, indeed, distinctly sullen, or, when she was animated, sarcastic. She was most attractive in profile, for then one saw to advantage her small, well-shaped head and delicate ears, and felt at once that here was a very positive, if not an altogether pleasing, personality.

The entire management of Mrs. Olaf's household devolved upon her aunt, Johanna Vavrika, a superstitious, doting woman of fifty. When Clara was a little girl her mother died, and Johanna's life had been spent in ungrudging service to her niece. Clara, like many self-willed and discontented persons, was really very apt, without knowing it, to do as other people told her, and to let her destiny be decided for her by intelligences much below her own. It was her Aunt Johanna who had humoured and spoiled her in her girlhood, who had got her off to Chicago to study piano, and who had finally persuaded her to marry Olaf Ericson as the best match she would be likely to make in that part of the country. Johanna Vavrika had been deeply scarred by smallpox in the old country. She was short and fat, homely and jolly and sentimental. She was so broad, and took such short steps when she walked, that her brother, Joe Vavrika, always called her his duck. She adored her niece because of her talent, because of her good looks and masterful ways, but most of all because of her selfishness.

Clara's marriage with Olaf Ericson was Johanna's particular triumph. She was inordinately proud of Olaf's position, and she found a sufficiently exciting career in managing Clara's house, in keeping it above the criticism of the Ericsons, in pampering Olaf to keep him from finding fault with his wife, and in concealing from every one Clara's domestic infelicities. While Clara slept of a morning, Johanna Vavrika was bustling about, seeing that Olaf and the men had their breakfast, and that the cleaning or the butter-making or the washing was properly begun by the two girls in the kitchen. Then, at about eight o'clock, she would take Clara's coffee up to her, and chat with her while she drank it, telling her what was going on in the house. Old Mrs. Ericson frequently said that her daughter-in-law would not know what day of the week it was if Johanna did not tell her every morning. Mrs. Ericson despised and pitied Johanna, but did not wholly dislike her. The one thing she hated in her daughter-in-law above everything else was the way in which Clara could come it over people. It enraged her that the affairs of her son's big, barnlike house went on as well as they did, and she used to feel that in this world we have to wait overlong to see the guilty punished. "Suppose Johanna Vavrika died or got sick?" the old lady used to say to Olaf. "Your wife wouldn't know where to look for her own dish-cloth." Olaf only shrugged his shoulders. The fact remained that Johanna did not die, and, although Mrs. Ericson often told her she was looking poorly, she was never ill. She seldom left the house, and she slept in a little room off the kitchen. No Ericson, by night or day, could come prying about there to find fault without her knowing it. Her one weakness was that she was an incurable talker, and she sometimes made trouble without meaning to.

This morning Clara was tying a wine-coloured ribbon about her throat when Johanna appeared with her coffee. After putting the tray on a sewing table, she began to make Clara's bed, chattering the while in Bohemian.

"Well, Olaf got off early, and the girls are baking. I'm going down presently to make some poppy-seed bread for Olaf. He asked for prune preserves at breakfast, and I told him I was out of them, and to bring some prunes and honey and cloves from town."

Clara poured her coffee. "Ugh! I don't see how men can eat so much sweet stuff. In the morning, too!"

Her aunt chuckled knowingly. "Bait a bear with honey, as we say in the old country."

"Was he cross?" her niece asked indifferently.

"Olaf? Oh, no! He was in fine spirits. He's never cross if you know how to take him. I never knew a man to make so little fuss about bills. I gave him a list of things to get a yard long, and he didn't say a word; just folded it up and put it in his pocket."

"I can well believe he didn't say a word," Clara remarked with a shrug. "Some day he'll forget how to talk."

"Oh, but they say he's a grand speaker in the Legislature. He knows when to keep quiet. That's why he's got such influence in politics. The people have confidence in him." Johanna beat up a pillow and held it under her fat chin while she slipped on the case. Her niece laughed.

"Maybe we could make people believe we were wise, Aunty, if we held our tongues. Why did you tell Mrs. Ericson that Norman threw me again last Saturday and turned my foot? She's been talking to Olaf."

Johanna fell into great confusion. "Oh, but, my precious, the old lady asked for you, and she's always so angry if I can't give an excuse. Anyhow, she needn't talk; she's always tearing up something with that motor of hers."

When her aunt clattered down to the kitchen, Clara went to dust the parlour. Since there was not much there to dust, this did not take very long. Olaf had built the house new for her before their marriage, but her interest in furnishing it had been short-lived. It went, indeed, little beyond a bathtub and her piano. They had disagreed about almost every other article of furniture, and Clara had said she would rather have her house empty than full of things she didn't want. The house was set in a hillside, and the west windows of the parlour looked out above the kitchen yard thirty feet below. The east windows opened directly into the front yard. At one of the latter, Clara, while she was dusting, heard a low whistle. She did not turn at once, but listened intently as she drew her cloth slowly along the round of a chair. Yes, there it was:

I dreamt that I dwelt in ma-a-arble halls.

She turned and saw Nils Ericson laughing in the sunlight, his hat in his hand, just outside the window. As she crossed the room he leaned against the wire screen. "Aren't you at all surprised to see me, Clara Vavrika?"

"No; I was expecting to see you. Mother Ericson telephoned Olaf last night that you were here."

Nils squinted and gave a long whistle. "Telephoned? That must have been while Eric and I were out walking. Isn't she enterprising? Lift this screen, won't you?"

Clara lifted the screen, and Nils swung his leg across the window-sill. As he stepped into the room she said: "You didn't think you were going to get ahead of your mother, did you?"

He threw his hat on the piano. "Oh, I do sometimes. You see, I'm ahead of her now. I'm supposed to be in Anders' wheat-field. But, as we were leaving, Mother ran her car into a soft place beside the road and sank up to the hubs. While they were going for the horses to pull her out, I cut away behind the stacks and escaped." Nils chuckled. Clara's dull eyes lit up as she looked at him admiringly.

"You've got them guessing already. I don't know what your mother said to Olaf over the telephone, but be came back looking as if he'd seen a ghost, and he didn't go to bed until a dreadful hour—ten o'clock, I should think. He sat out on the porch in the dark like a graven image. It had been one of his talkative days, too." They both laughed, easily and lightly, like people who have laughed a great deal together; but they remained standing.

"Anders and Otto and Peter looked as if they had seen ghosts, too, over in the threshing field. What's the matter with them all?"

Clara gave him a quick, searching look. "Well, for one thing, they've always been afraid you have the other will."

Nils looked interested. "The other will?"

"Yes. A later one. They knew your father made another, but they never knew what he did with it. They almost tore the old house to pieces looking for it. They always suspected that he carried on a clandestine correspondence with you, for the one thing he would do was to get his own mail himself. So they thought he might have sent the new will to you for safekeeping. The old one, leaving everything to your mother, was made long before you went away, and it's understood among them that it cuts you out—that she will leave all the property to the others. Your father made the second will to prevent that. I've been hoping you had it. It would be such fun to spring it on them." Clara laughed mirthfully, a thing she did not often do now.

Nils shook his head reprovingly. "Come, now, you're malicious."

"No, I'm not. But I'd like something to happen to stir them all up, just for once. There never was such a family for having nothing ever happen to them but dinner and threshing. I'd almost be willing to die, just to have a funeral. *You* wouldn't stand it for three weeks."

Nils bent over the piano and began pecking at the keys with the finger of one hand. "I wouldn't? My dear young lady, how do you know what I can stand? *You* wouldn't wait to find out."

Clara flushed darkly and frowned. "I didn't believe you would ever come back—" she said defiantly.

"Eric believed I would, and he was only a baby when I went away. However, all's well that ends well, and I haven't come back to be a skeleton at the feast. We mustn't quarrel. Mother will be here with a search warrant pretty soon." He swung round and faced her, thrusting his hands into his coat pockets. "Come, you ought to be glad to see me, if you want something to happen. I'm something, even without a will. We can have a little fun, can't we? I think we can!"

She echoed him, "I think we can!" They both laughed and their eyes sparkled. Clara Vavrika looked ten years younger than when she had put the velvet ribbon about her throat that morning.

"You know, I'm so tickled to see mother," Nils went on. "I didn't know I was so proud of her. A regular pile driver. How about little pigtails, down at the house? Is Olaf doing the square thing by those children?"

Clara frowned pensively. "Olaf has to do something that looks like the square thing, now that he's a public man!" She glanced drolly at Nils. "But he makes a good commission out of it. On Sundays they all get together here and figure. He lets Peter and Anders put in big bills for the keep of the two boys, and he pays them out of the estate. They are always having what they call accountings. Olaf gets something out of it, too. I don't know just how they do it, but it's entirely a family matter, as they say. And when the Ericsons say that—" Clara lifted her eyebrows.

Just then the angry *honk-honk* of an approaching motor sounded from down the road. Their eyes met and they began to laugh. They laughed as children do when they can not contain themselves, and can not explain the cause of their mirth to grown people, but share it perfectly together. When Clara Vavrika sat down at the piano after he was gone, she felt that she had laughed away a dozen years. She practised as if the house were burning over her head.

When Nils greeted his mother and climbed into the front seat of the motor beside her, Mrs. Ericson looked grim, but she made no comment upon his truancy until she had turned her car and was retracing her revolutions along the road that ran by Olaf's big pasture. Then she remarked dryly:

"If I were you I wouldn't see too much of Olaf's wife while you are here. She's the kind of woman who can't see much of men without getting herself talked about. She was a good deal talked about before he married her."

"Hasn't Olaf tamed her?" Nils asked indifferently.

Mrs. Ericson shrugged her massive shoulders. "Olaf don't seem to have much luck, when it comes to wives. The first one was meek enough, but she was always ailing. And this one has her own way. He says if he quarreled with her she'd go back to her father, and then he'd lose the Bohemian vote. There are a great many Bohunks in this district. But when you find a man under his wife's thumb you can always be sure there's a soft spot in him somewhere."

Nils thought of his own father, and smiled. "She brought him a good deal of money, didn't she, besides the Bohemian vote?"

Mrs. Ericson sniffed. "Well, she has a fair half section in her own name, but I can't see as that does Olaf much good. She will have a good deal of property some day, if old Vavrika don't marry again. But I don't consider a saloonkeeper's money as good as other people's money."

Nils laughed outright. "Come, Mother, don't let your prejudices carry you that far. Money's money. Old Vavrika's a mighty decent sort of saloonkeeper. Nothing rowdy about him."

Mrs. Ericson spoke up angrily. "Oh, I know you always stood up for them! But hanging around there when you were a boy never did you any good, Nils, nor any of the other boys who went there. There weren't so many after her when she married Olaf, let me tell you. She knew enough to grab her chance."

Nils settled back in his seat. "Of course I liked to go there, Mother, and you were always cross about it. You never took the trouble to find out that it was the one jolly house in this country for a boy to go to. All the rest of you were working yourselves to death, and the houses were mostly a mess, full of babies and washing and flies. Oh, it was all right—I understand that; but you are young only once, and I happened to be young then. Now, Vavrika's was always jolly. He played the violin, and I used to take my flute, and Clara played the piano, and Johanna used to sing Bohemian songs. She always had a big supper for us—herrings and pickles and poppy-seed bread, and lots of cake and preserves. Old Joe had been in the army in the old country, and he could tell lots of good stories. I can see him cutting bread, at the head of the table, now. I don't know what I'd have done when I was a kid if it hadn't been for the Vavrikas, really."

"And all the time he was taking money that other people had worked hard in the fields for," Mrs. Ericson observed.

"So do the circuses, Mother, and they're a good thing. People ought to get fun for some of their money. Even father liked old Joe."

"Your father," Mrs. Ericson said grimly, "liked everybody."

As they crossed the sand creek and turned into her own place, Mrs. Ericson observed, "There's Olaf's buggy. He's stopped on his way from town." Nils shook himself and prepared to greet his brother, who was waiting on the porch.

Olaf was a big, heavy Norwegian, slow of speech and movement. His head was large and square, like a block of wood. When Nils, at a distance, tried to remember what his brother looked like, he could recall only his heavy head, high forehead, large nostrils, and pale blue eyes, set far apart. Olaf's features were rudimentary: the thing one noticed was the face itself, wide and flat and pale; devoid of any expression, betraying his fifty years as little as it betrayed anything else, and powerful by reason of its very stolidness. When Olaf shook hands with Nils he looked at him from under his light eyebrows, but Nils felt that no one could ever say what that pale look might mean. The one thing he had always felt in Olaf was a heavy stubbornness, like the unyielding stickiness of wet loam against the plow. He had always found Olaf the most difficult of his brothers.

"How do you do, Nils? Expect to stay with us long?"

"Oh, I may stay forever," Nils answered gaily. "I like this country better than I used to."

"There's been some work put into it since you left," Olaf remarked.

"Exactly. I think it's about ready to live in now—and I'm about ready to settle down." Nils saw his brother lower his big head ("Exactly like a bull," he thought.) "Mother's been persuading me to slow down now, and go in for farming," he went on lightly.

Olaf made a deep sound in his throat. "Farming ain't learned in a day," he brought out, still looking at the ground.

"Oh, I know! But I pick things up quickly." Nils had not meant to antagonize his brother, and he did not know now why he was doing it. "Of course," he went on, "I shouldn't expect to make a big success, as you fellows have done. But then, I'm not ambitious. I won't want much. A little land, and some cattle, maybe."

Olaf still stared at the ground, his head down. He wanted to ask Nils what he had been doing all these years, that he didn't have a business somewhere he couldn't afford to leave; why he hadn't more pride than to come back with only a little sole-leather trunk to show for himself, and to present himself as the only failure in the family. He did not ask one of these questions, but he made them all felt distinctly.

"Humph!" Nils thought. "No wonder the man never talks, when he can butt his ideas into you like that without ever saying a word. I suppose he uses that kind of smokeless powder on his wife all the time. But I guess she has her innings." He chuckled, and Olaf looked up. "Never mind me, Olaf. I laugh without knowing why, like little Eric. He's another cheerful dog."

"Eric," said Olaf slowly, "is a spoiled kid. He's just let his mother's best cow go dry because he don't milk her right. I was hoping you'd take him away somewhere and put him into business. If he don't do any good among strangers, he never will." This was a long speech for Olaf, and as he finished it he climbed into his buggy.

Nils shrugged his shoulders. "Same old tricks," he thought. "Hits from behind you every time. What a whale of a man!" He turned and went round to the kitchen, where his mother was scolding little Eric for letting the gasoline get low.

IV

Joe Vavrika's saloon was not in the county seat, where Olaf and Mrs. Ericson did their trading, but in a cheerfuller place, a little Bohemian settlement which lay at the other end of the county, ten level miles north of Olaf's farm. Clara rode up to see her father almost every day. Vavrika's house was, so to speak, in the back yard of his saloon. The garden between the two buildings was inclosed by a high board fence as tight as a partition, and in summer Joe kept beer tables and wooden benches among the gooseberry bushes under his little cherry tree. At one of these tables Nils Ericson was seated in the late afternoon, three days after his return home. Joe had gone in to serve a customer, and Nils was lounging on his elbows, looking rather mournfully into his half-emptied pitcher, when he heard a laugh across the little garden. Clara, in her riding habit, was standing at the back door of the house, under the grapevine trellis that old Joe had grown there long ago. Nils rose.

"Come out and keep your father and me company. We've been gossiping all afternoon. Nobody to bother us but the flies."

She shook her head. "No, I never come out here any more. Olaf doesn't like it. I must live up to my position, you know."

"You mean to tell me you never come out and chat with the boys, as you used to? He *has* tamed you! Who keeps up these flower-beds?"

"I come out on Sundays, when father is alone, and read the Bohemian papers to him. But I am never here when the bar is open. What have you two been doing?"

"Talking, as I told you. I've been telling him about my travels. I find I can't talk much at home, not even to Eric."

Clara reached up and poked with her riding-whip at a white moth that was fluttering in the sunlight among the vine leaves. "I suppose you will never tell me about all those things."

"Where can I tell them? Not in Olaf's house, certainly. What's the matter with our talking here?" He pointed persuasively with his hat to the bushes and the green table, where the flies were singing lazily above the empty beer glasses.

Clara shook her head weakly. "No, it wouldn't do. Besides, I am going now."

"I'm on Eric's mare. Would you be angry if I overtook you?"

Clara looked back and laughed. "You might try and see. I can leave you if I don't want you. Eric's mare can't keep up with Norman."

Nils went into the bar and attempted to pay his score. Big Joe, six feet four, with curly yellow hair and mustache, clapped him on the shoulder. "Not a Goddamn a your money go in my drawer, you hear? Only next time you bring your flute, te-te-te-te-te-ty." Joe wagged his fingers in imitation of the flute player's position.

"My Clara, she come all-a-time Sundays an' play for me. She not like to play at Ericson's place." He shook his yellow curls and laughed. "Not a Goddamn a fun at Ericson's. You come a Sunday. You like-a fun. No forget de flute." Joe talked very rapidly and always tumbled over his English. He seldom spoke it to his customers, and had never learned much.

Nils swung himself into the saddle and trotted to the west of the village, where the houses and gardens scattered into prairie land and the road turned south. Far ahead of him, in the declining light, he saw Clara Vavrika's slender figure, loitering on horseback. He touched his mare with the whip, and shot along the white, level road, under the reddening sky.

When he overtook Olaf's wife he saw that she had been crying. "What's the matter, Clara Vavrika?" he asked kindly.

"Oh, I get blue sometimes. It was awfully jolly living there with father. I wonder why I ever went away."

Nils spoke in a low, kind tone that he sometimes used with women: "That's what I've been wondering these many years. You were the last girl in the country I'd have picked for a wife for Olaf. What made you do it, Clara?"

"I suppose I really did it to oblige the neighbours"—Clara tossed her head. "People were beginning to wonder."

"To wonder?"

"Yes—why I didn't get married. I suppose I didn't like to keep them in suspense. I've discovered that most girls marry out of consideration for the neighbourhood."

Nils bent his head toward her and his white teeth flashed. "I'd have gambled that one girl I knew would say, 'Let the neighbourhood be damned.'"

Clara shook her head mournfully. "You see, they have it on you, Nils; that is, if you're a woman. They say you're beginning to go off. That's what makes us get married: we can't stand the laugh."

Nils looked sidewise at her. He had never seen her head droop before. Resignation was the last thing he would have expected of her. "In your case, there wasn't something else?"

"Something else?"

"I mean, you didn't do it to spite somebody? Somebody who didn't come back?"

Clara drew herself up. "Oh, I never thought you'd come back. Not after I stopped writing to you, at least. *That* was all over, long before I married Olaf."

"It never occurred to you, then, that the meanest thing you could do to me was to marry Olaf?"

Clara laughed. "No; I didn't know you were so fond of Olaf."

Nils smoothed his horse's mane with his glove. "You know, Clara Vavrika, you are never going to stick it out. You'll cut away some day, and I've been thinking you might as well cut away with me."

Clara threw up her chin. "Oh, you don't know me as well as you think. I won't cut away. Sometimes, when I'm with father, I feel like it. But I can hold out as long as the Ericsons can. They've never got the best of me yet, and one can live, so long as one isn't beaten. If I go back to father, it's all up with Olaf in politics. He knows that, and he never goes much beyond sulking. I've as much wit as the Ericsons. I'll never leave them unless I can show them a thing or two."

"You mean unless you can come it over them?"

"Yes—unless I go away with a man who is cleverer than they are, and who has more money."

Nils whistled. "Dear me, you are demanding a good deal. The Ericsons, take the lot of them, are a bunch to beat. But I should think the excitement of tormenting them would have worn off by this time."

"It has, I'm afraid," Clara admitted mournfully.

"Then why don't you cut away? There are more amusing games than this in the world. When I came home I thought it might amuse me to bully a few quarter sections out of the Ericsons; but I've almost decided I can get more fun for my money somewhere else."

Clara took in her breath sharply. "Ah, you have got the other will! That was why you came home!"

"No, it wasn't. I came home to see how you were getting on with Olaf."

Clara struck her horse with the whip, and in a bound she was far ahead of him. Nils dropped one word, "Damn!" and whipped after her; but she leaned forward in her saddle and fairly cut the wind. Her long riding skirt rippled in the still air behind her. The sun was just sinking behind the stubble in a vast, clear sky, and the shadows drew across the fields so rapidly that Nils could scarcely keep in sight the dark figure on the road. When he overtook her he caught her horse by the bridle. Norman reared, and Nils was frightened for her; but Clara kept her seat.

"Let me go, Nils Ericson!" she cried. "I hate you more than any of them. You were created to torture me, the whole tribe of you—to make me suffer in every possible way."

She struck her horse again and galloped away from him. Nils set his teeth and looked thoughtful. He rode slowly home along the deserted road, watching the stars come out in the clear violet sky.

They flashed softly into the limpid heavens, like jewels let fall into clear water. They were a reproach, he felt, to a sordid world. As he turned across the sand creek, he looked up at the North Star and smiled, as if there were an understanding between them. His mother scolded him for being late for supper.

V

On Sunday afternoon Joe Vavrika, in his shirt sleeves and carpet slippers, was sitting in his garden, smoking a long-tasseled porcelain pipe with a hunting scene painted on the bowl. Clara sat under the cherry tree, reading aloud to him from the weekly Bohemian papers. She had worn a white muslin dress under her riding habit, and the leaves of the cherry tree threw a pattern of sharp shadows over her skirt. The black cat was dozing in the sunlight at her feet, and Joe's dachshund was scratching a hole under the scarlet geraniums and dreaming of badgers. Joe was filling his pipe for the third time since dinner, when he heard a knocking on the fence. He broke into a loud guffaw and unlatched the little door that led into the street. He did not call Nils by name, but caught him by the hand and dragged him in. Clara stiffened and the colour deepened under her dark skin. Nils, too, felt a little awkward. He had not seen her since the night when she rode away from him and left him alone on the level road between the fields. Joe dragged him to the wooden bench beside the green table.

"You bring de flute," he cried, tapping the leather case under Nils' arm. "Ah, das-a good' Now we have some liddle fun like old times. I got somet'ing good for you." Joe shook his finger at Nils and winked his blue eye, a bright clear eye, full of fire, though the tiny bloodvessels on the ball were always a little distended. "I got somet'ing for you from"—he paused and waved his hand—"Hongarie. You know Hongarie? You wait!" He pushed Nils down on the bench, and went through the back door of his saloon.

Nils looked at Clara, who sat frigidly with her white skirts drawn tight about her. "He didn't tell you he had asked me to come, did he? He wanted a party and proceeded to arrange it. Isn't he fun? Don't be cross; let's give him a good time."

Clara smiled and shook out her skirt. "Isn't that like Father? And he has sat here so meekly all day. Well, I won't pout. I'm glad you came. He doesn't have very many good times now any more. There are so few of his kind left. The second generation are a tame lot."

Joe came back with a flask in one hand and three wine glasses caught by the stems between the fingers of the other. These he placed on the table with an air of ceremony, and, going behind Nils, held the flask between him and the sun, squinting into it admiringly. "You know dis, Tokai? A great friend of mine, he bring dis to me, a present out of Hongarie. You know how much it cost, dis wine? Chust so much what it weigh in gold. Nobody but de nobles drink him in Bohemie. Many, many years I save him up, dis Tokai." Joe whipped out his official corkscrew and delicately removed the cork. "De old man die what bring him to me, an' dis wine he lay on his belly in my cellar an' sleep. An' now," carefully pouring out the heavy yellow wine, "an' now he wake up; and maybe he wake us up, too!" He carried one of the glasses to his daughter and presented it with great gallantry.

Clara shook her head, but, seeing her father's disappointment, relented. "You taste it first. I don't want so much."

Joe sampled it with a beatific expression, and turned to Nils. "You drink him slow, dis wine. He very soft, but he go down hot. You see!"

After a second glass Nils declared that he couldn't take any more without getting sleepy. "Now get your fiddle, Vavrika," he said as he opened his flute case.

But Joe settled back in his wooden rocker and wagged his big carpet slipper. "No-no-no-no-no-no-no! No play fiddle now any more: too much ache in de finger," waving them, "all-a-time rheumatic. You play de flute, te-tety-tetety-te. Bohemie songs."

"I've forgotten all the Bohemian songs I used to play with you and Johanna. But here's one that will make Clara pout. You remember how her eyes used to snap when we called her the Bohemian Girl?" Nils lifted his flute and began "When Other Lips and Other Hearts," and Joe hummed the air in a husky baritone, waving his carpet slipper. "Oh-h-h, das-a fine music," he cried, clapping his hands as Nils finished. "Now 'Marble Halls, Marble Halls'! Clara, you sing him."

Clara smiled and leaned back in her chair, beginning softly:

"I dreamt that I dwelt in ma-a-arble halls,
With vassals and serfs at my knee,"

and Joe hummed like a big bumblebee.

"There's one more you always played," Clara said quietly, "I remember that best." She locked her hands over her knee and began "The Heart Bowed Down," and sang it through without groping for the words. She was singing with a good deal of warmth when she came to the end of the old song:

"For memory is the only friend
That grief can call its own."

Joe flashed out his red silk handkerchief and blew his nose, shaking his head. "No-no-no-no-no-no-no! Too sad, too sad! I not like-a dat. Play quick somet'ing gay now."

Nils put his lips to the instrument, and Joe lay back in his chair, laughing and singing, "Oh, Evelina, Sweet Evelina!" Clara laughed, too. Long ago, when she and Nils went to high school, the model student of their class was a very homely girl in thick spectacles. Her name was Evelina Oleson; she had a long, swinging walk which somehow suggested the measure of that song, and they used mercilessly to sing it at her.

"Dat ugly Oleson girl, she teach in de school," Joe gasped, "an' she still walks chust like dat, yup-a, yup-a, yup-a, chust like a camel she go! Now, Nils, we have some more li'l drink. Oh, yes-yes-yes-yes-yes-yes-*yes*! Dis time you haf to drink, and Clara she haf to, so she show she not jealous. So, we all drink to your girl. You not tell her name, eh? No-no-no, I no make you tell. She pretty, eh? She make good sweetheart? I bet!" Joe winked and lifted his glass. "How soon you get married?"

Nils screwed up his eyes. "That I don't know. When she says."

Joe threw out his chest. "Das-a way boys talks. No way for mans. Mans say, 'You come to de church, an' get a hurry on you.' Das-a way mans talks."

"Maybe Nils hasn't got enough to keep a wife," put in Clara ironically. "How about that, Nils?" she asked him frankly, as if she wanted to know.

Nils looked at her coolly, raising one eyebrow. "Oh, I can keep her, all right."

"The way she wants to be kept?"

"With my wife, I'll decide that," replied Nils calmly. "I'll give her what's good for her."

Clara made a wry face. "You'll give her the strap, I expect, like old Peter Oleson gave his wife."

"When she needs it," said Nils lazily, locking his hands behind his head and squinting up through the leaves of the cherry tree. "Do you remember the time I squeezed the cherries all over your clean dress, and Aunt Johanna boxed my ears for me? My gracious, weren't you mad! You had both hands full of cherries, and I squeezed 'em and made the juice fly all over you. I liked to have fun with you; you'd get so mad."

"We *did* have fun, didn't we? None of the other kids ever had so much fun. We knew how to play."

Nils dropped his elbows on the table and looked steadily across at her. "I've played with lots of girls since, but I haven't found one who was such good fun."

Clara laughed. The late afternoon sun was shining full in her face, and deep in the back of her eyes there shone something fiery, like the yellow drops of Tokai in the brown glass bottle. "Can you still play, or are you only pretending?"

"I can play better than I used to, and harder."

"Don't you ever work, then?" She had not intended to say it. It slipped out because she was confused enough to say just the wrong thing.

"I work between times." Nils' steady gaze still beat upon her. "Don't you worry about my working, Mrs. Ericson. You're getting like all the rest of them." He reached his brown, warm hand across the table and dropped it on Clara's, which was cold as an icicle. "Last call for play, Mrs. Ericson!" Clara shivered, and suddenly her hands and cheeks grew warm. Her fingers lingered in his a moment, and they looked at each other earnestly. Joe Vavrika had put the mouth of the bottle to his lips and was swallowing the last drops of the Tokai, standing. The sun, just about to sink behind his shop, glistened on the bright glass, on his flushed face and curly yellow hair. "Look," Clara whispered, "that's the way I want to grow old."

VI

On the day of Olaf Ericson's barn-raising, his wife, for once in a way, rose early. Johanna Vavrika had been baking cakes and frying and boiling and spicing meats for a week beforehand, but it was not until the day before the party was to take place that Clara showed any interest in it. Then she was seized with one of her fitful spasms of energy, and took the wagon and little Eric and spent the day on Plum Creek, gathering vines and swamp goldenrod to decorate the barn.

By four o'clock in the afternoon buggies and wagons began to arrive at the big unpainted building in front of Olaf's house. When Nils and his mother came at five, there were more than fifty people in the barn, and a great drove of children. On the ground floor stood six long tables, set with the crockery of seven flourishing Ericson families, lent for the occasion. In the middle of each table was a big yellow pumpkin, hollowed out and filled with woodbine. In one corner of the barn, behind a pile of green-and-white striped watermelons, was a circle of chairs for the old people; the younger guests sat on bushel measures or barbed-wire spools, and the children tumbled about in the haymow. The box stalls Clara had converted into booths. The framework was hidden by goldenrod and sheaves of wheat, and the partitions were covered 'With wild grapevines full of fruit. At one of these Johanna Vavrika watched over her cooked meats, enough to provision an army; and at the next her kitchen girls had ranged the ice-cream freezers, and Clara was already cutting pies and cakes against the hour of serving. At the third stall, little Hilda, in a bright pink lawn dress, dispensed lemonade throughout the afternoon. Olaf, as a public man, had thought it inadvisable to serve beer in his barn; but Joe Vavrika had come over with two demijohns concealed in his buggy, and after his arrival the wagon shed was much frequented by the men.

"Hasn't Cousin Clara fixed things lovely?" little Hilda whispered, when Nils went up to her stall and asked for lemonade.

Nils leaned against the booth, talking to the excited little girl and watching the people. The barn faced the west, and the sun, pouring in at the big doors, filled the whole interior with a golden light, through which filtered fine particles of dust from the haymow, where the children were romping. There was a great chattering from the stall where Johanna Vavrika exhibited to the admiring women her platters heaped with fried chicken, her roasts of beef, boiled tongues, and baked hams with cloves stuck in the crisp brown fat and garnished with tansy and parsley. The older women, having assured themselves that there were twenty kinds of cake, not counting cookies, and three dozen fat pies, repaired to the corner behind the pile of watermelons, put on their white aprons, and fell to their knitting and fancywork. They were a fine company of old women, and a Dutch painter would have loved to find them there together, where the sun made bright patches on the floor and sent long, quivering shafts of gold through the dusky shade up among the rafters. There were fat, rosy old women who looked hot in their best black dresses; spare, alert old women with brown, dark-veined hands; and several of almost heroic frame, not less massive than old Mrs. Ericson herself. Few of them wore glasses, and old Mrs. Svendsen, a Danish woman, who was quite bald, wore the only cap among them. Mrs. Oleson, who had twelve big grandchildren, could still show two braids of yellow hair as thick as her own wrists. Among all these grandmothers there were more brown heads than white. They all had a pleased, prosperous air, as if they were more than satisfied with themselves and with life. Nils, leaning against Hilda's lemonade stand, watched them as they sat chattering in four languages, their fingers never lagging behind their tongues.

"Look at them over there," he whispered, detaining Clara as she passed him. "Aren't they the Old Guard? I've just counted thirty hands. I guess they've wrung many a chicken's neck and warmed many a boy's jacket for him in their time."

In reality he fell into amazement when he thought of the Herculean labours those fifteen pairs of hands had performed: of the cows they had milked, the butter they had made, the gardens they had planted, the children and grandchildren they had tended, the brooms they had worn out, the mountains of food they had cooked. It made him dizzy. Clara Vavrika smiled a hard, enigmatical smile at him and walked rapidly away. Nils' eyes followed her white figure as she went toward the house. He watched her walking alone in the sunlight, looked at her slender, defiant shoulders and her little hard-set head with its coils of blue-black hair. "No," he reflected; "she'd never be like them, not if she lived here a hundred years. She'd only grow more bitter. You can't tame a wild thing; you can only chain it. People aren't all alike. I mustn't lose my nerve." He gave Hilda's pigtail a parting tweak and set out after Clara. "Where to?" he asked, as he came upon her in the kitchen.

"I'm going to the cellar for preserves."

"Let me go with you. I never get a moment alone with you. Why do you keep out of my way?"

Clara laughed. "I don't usually get in anybody's way."

Nils followed her down the stairs and to the far corner of the cellar, where a basement window let in a stream of light. From a swinging shelf Clara selected several glass jars, each labeled in Johanna's careful hand. Nils took up a brown flask. "What's this? It looks good."

"It is. It's some French brandy father gave me when I was married. Would you like some? Have you a corkscrew? I'll get glasses."

When she brought them, Nils took them from her and put them down on the window-sill. "Clara Vavrika, do you remember how crazy I used to be about you?"

Clara shrugged her shoulders. "Boys are always crazy about somebody or another. I dare say some silly has been crazy about Evelina Oleson. You got over it in a hurry."

"Because I didn't come back, you mean? I had to get on, you know, and it was hard sledding at first. Then I heard you'd married Olaf."

"And then you stayed away from a broken heart," Clara laughed.

"And then I began to think about you more than I had since I first went away. I began to wonder if you were really as you had seemed to me when I was a boy. I thought I'd like to see. I've had lots of girls, but no one ever pulled me the same way. The more I thought about you, the more I remembered how it used to be—like hearing a wild tune you can't resist, calling you out at night. It had been a long while since anything had pulled me out of my boots, and I wondered whether anything ever could again." Nils thrust his hands into his coat pockets and squared his shoulders, as his mother sometimes squared hers, as Olaf, in a clumsier manner, squared his. "So I thought I'd come back and see. Of course the family have tried to do me, and I rather thought I'd bring out father's will and make a fuss. But they can have their old land; they've put enough sweat into it." He took the flask and filled the two glasses carefully to the brim. "I've found out what I want from the Ericsons. Drink *skoal*, Clara." He lifted his glass, and Clara took hers with downcast eyes. "Look at me, Clara Vavrika. *Skoal!*"

She raised her burning eyes and answered fiercely: "*Skoal!*"

The barn supper began at six o'clock and lasted for two hilarious hours. Yense Nelson had made a wager that he could eat two whole fried chickens, and he did. Eli Swanson stowed away two whole custard pies, and Nick Hermanson ate a chocolate layer cake to the last crumb. There was even a cooky contest among the children, and one thin, slablike Bohemian boy consumed sixteen and won the prize, a gingerbread pig which Johanna Vavrika had carefully decorated with red candies and burnt sugar. Fritz Sweiheart, the German carpenter, won in the pickle contest, but he disappeared soon after supper and was not seen for the rest of the evening. Joe Vavrika said that Fritz could have managed the pickles all right, but he had sampled the demijohn in his buggy too often before sitting down to the table.

While the supper was being cleared away the two fiddlers began to tune up for the dance. Clara was to accompany them on her old upright piano, which had been brought down from her father's. By this time Nils had renewed old acquaintances. Since his interview with Clara in the cellar, he had been busy telling all the old women how young they looked, and all the young ones how pretty they were, and assuring the men that they had here the best farmland in the world. He had made himself so agreeable that old Mrs. Ericson's friends began to come up to her and tell how lucky she was to get her smart son back again, and please to get him to play his flute. Joe Vavrika, who could still play very well when he forgot that he had rheumatism, caught up a fiddle from Johnny Oleson and played a crazy Bohemian dance tune that set the wheels going. When he dropped the bow every one was ready to dance.

Olaf, in a frock coat and a solemn made-up necktie, led the grand march with his mother. Clara had kept well out of *that* by sticking to the piano. She played the march with a pompous solemnity which greatly amused the prodigal son, who went over and stood behind her.

"Oh, aren't you rubbing it into them, Clara Vavrika? And aren't you lucky to have me here, or all your wit would be thrown away."

"I'm used to being witty for myself. It saves my life."

The fiddles struck up a polka, and Nils convulsed Joe Vavrika by leading out Evelina Oleson, the homely schoolteacher. His next partner was a very fat Swedish girl, who, although she was an heiress, had not been asked for the first dance, but had stood against the wall in her tight, high-heeled shoes, nervously fingering a lace handkerchief. She was soon out of breath, so Nils led her, pleased and panting, to her seat, and went over to the piano, from which Clara had been watching his gallantry. "Ask Olena Yenson," she whispered. "She waltzes beautifully."

Olena, too, was rather inconveniently plump, handsome in a smooth, heavy way, with a fine colour and good-natured, sleepy eyes. She was redolent of violet sachet powder, and had warm, soft, white hands, but she danced divinely, moving as smoothly as the tide coming in. "There, that's something like," Nils said as he released her. "You'll give me the next waltz, won't you? Now I must go and dance with my little cousin."

Hilda was greatly excited when Nils went up to her stall and held out his arm. Her little eyes sparkled, but she declared that she could not leave her lemonade. Old Mrs. Ericson, who happened along at this moment, said she would attend to that, and Hilda came out, as pink as her pink dress. The dance was a schottische, and in a moment her yellow braids were fairly standing on end. "Bravo!" Nils cried encouragingly. "Where did you learn to dance so nicely?"

"My Cousin Clara taught me," the little girl panted.

Nils found Eric sitting with a group of boys who were too awkward or too shy to dance, and told him that he must dance the next waltz with Hilda.

The boy screwed up his shoulders. "Aw, Nils, I can't dance. My feet are too big; I look silly."

"Don't be thinking about yourself. It doesn't matter how boys look."

Nils had never spoken to him so sharply before, and Eric made haste to scramble out of his corner and brush the straw from his coat.

Clara nodded approvingly. "Good for you, Nils. I've been trying to get hold of him. They dance very nicely together; I sometimes play for them."

"I'm obliged to you for teaching him. There's no reason why he should grow up to be a lout."

"He'll never be that. He's more like you than any of them. Only he hasn't your courage." From her slanting eyes Clara shot forth one of those keen glances, admiring and at the same time challenging, which she seldom bestowed on any one, and which seemed to say, "Yes, I admire you, but I am your equal."

Clara was proving a much better host than Olaf, who, once the supper was over, seemed to feel no interest in anything but the lanterns. He had brought a locomotive headlight from town to light the revels, and he kept skulking about as if he feared the mere light from it might set his new barn on fire. His wife, on the contrary, was cordial to every one, was animated and even gay. The deep salmon colour in her cheeks burned vividly, and her eyes were full of life. She gave the piano over to the fat Swedish heiress, pulled her father away from the corner where he sat gossiping with his cronies, and made him dance a Bohemian dance with her. In his youth Joe had been a famous dancer, and his daughter got him so limbered up that every one sat around and applauded them. The old ladies were particularly delighted, and made them go through the dance again. From their corner where they watched and commented, the old women kept time with their feet and hands, and whenever the fiddles struck up a new air old Mrs. Svendsen's white cap would begin to bob.

Clara was waltzing with little Eric when Nils came up to them, brushed his brother aside, and swung her out among the dancers. "Remember how we used to waltz on rollers at the old skating rink in town? I suppose people don't do that any more. We used to keep it up for hours. You know, we never did moon around as other boys and girls did. It was dead serious with us from the beginning. When we were most in love with each other, we used to fight. You were always pinching people; your fingers were like little nippers. A regular snapping turtle, you were. Lord, how you'd like Stockholm! Sit out in the streets in front of cafes and talk all night in summer, just like a reception—officers and ladies and funny English people. Jolliest people in the world, the Swedes, once you get them going. Always drinking things—champagne and stout mixed, half-and-half, serve it out of big pitchers, and serve plenty. Slow pulse, you know; they can stand a lot. Once they light up, they're glowworms, I can tell you."

"All the same, you don't really like gay people."

"*I* don't?"

"No; I could tell that when you were looking at the old women there this afternoon. They're the kind you really admire, after all; women like your mother. And that's the kind you'll marry."

"Is it, Miss Wisdom? You'll see who I'll marry, and she won't have a domestic virtue to bless herself with. She'll be a snapping turtle, and she'll be a match for me. All the same, they're a fine bunch of old dames over there. You admire them yourself.

"No, I don't; I detest them."

"You won't, when you look back on them from Stockholm or Budapest. Freedom settles all that. Oh, but you're the real Bohemian Girl, Clara Vavrika!" Nils laughed down at her sullen frown and began mockingly to sing:

"Oh, how could a poor gypsy maiden like me
Expect the proud bride of a baron to be?"

Clara clutched his shoulder. "Hush, Nils; every one is looking at you."

"I don't care. They can't gossip. It's all in the family, as the Ericsons say when they divide up little Hilda's patrimony amongst them. Besides, we'll give them something to talk about when we hit the trail. Lord, it will be a godsend to them! They haven't had anything so interesting to chatter about since the grasshopper year. It'll give them a new lease of life. And Olaf won't lose the Bohemian vote, either. They'll have the laugh on him so that they'll vote two apiece. They'll send him to Congress. They'll never forget his barn party, or us. They'll always remember us as we're dancing together now. We're making a legend. Where's my waltz, boys?" he called as they whirled past the fiddlers.

The musicians grinned, looked at each other, hesitated, and began a new air; and Nils sang with them, as the couples fell from a quick waltz to a long, slow glide:

"When other lips and other hearts
Their tale of love shall tell,
In language whose excess imparts
The power they feel so well."

The old women applauded vigorously. "What a gay one he is, that Nils!" And old Mrs. Svendsen's cap lurched dreamily from side to side to the flowing measure of the dance.

"Of days that have as ha-a-p-py been,
And you'll remember me."

VII

The moonlight flooded that great, silent land. The reaped fields lay yellow in it. The straw stacks and poplar windbreaks threw sharp black shadows. The roads were white rivers of dust. The sky was a deep, crystalline blue, and the stars were few and faint. Everything seemed to have succumbed, to have sunk to sleep, under the great, golden, tender, midsummer moon. The splendour of it seemed to transcend human life and human fate. The senses were too feeble to take it in, and every time one looked up at the sky one felt unequal to it, as if one were sitting deaf under the waves of a great river of melody. Near the road, Nils Ericson was lying against a straw stack in Olaf's wheat field. His own life seemed strange and unfamiliar to him, as if it were something he had read about, or dreamed, and forgotten. He lay very still, watching the white road that ran in front of him, lost itself among the fields, and then, at a distance, reappeared over a little hill. At last, against this white band he saw something moving rapidly, and he got up and walked to the edge of the field. "She is passing the row of poplars now," he thought. He heard the padded beat of hoofs along the dusty road, and as she came into sight he stepped out and waved his arms. Then, for fear of frightening the horse, he drew back and waited. Clara had seen him, and she came up at a walk. Nils took the horse by the bit and stroked his neck.

"What are you doing out so late, Clara Vavrika? I went to the house, but Johanna told me you had gone to your father's."

"Who can stay in the house on a night like this? Aren't you out yourself?"

"Ah, but that's another matter."

Nils turned the horse into the field.

"What are you doing? Where are you taking Norman?"

"Not far, but I want to talk to you tonight; I have something to say to you. I can't talk to you at the house, with Olaf sitting there on the porch, weighing a thousand tons."

Clara laughed. "He won't be sitting there now. He's in bed by this time, and asleep—weighing a thousand tons."

Nils plodded on across the stubble. "Are you really going to spend the rest of your life like this, night after night, summer after summer? Haven't you anything better to do on a night like this than to wear yourself and Norman out tearing across the country to your father's and back? Besides, your father won't live forever, you know. His little place will be shut up or sold, and then you'll have nobody but the Ericsons. You'll have to fasten down the hatches for the winter then."

Clara moved her head restlessly. "Don't talk about that. I try never to think of it. If I lost Father I'd lose everything, even my hold over the Ericsons."

"Bah! You'd lose a good deal more than that. You'd lose your race, everything that makes you yourself. You've lost a good deal of it now."

"Of what?"

"Of your love of life, your capacity for delight."

Clara put her hands up to her face. "I haven't, Nils Ericson, I haven't! Say anything to me but that. I won't have it!" she declared vehemently.

Nils led the horse up to a straw stack, and turned to Clara, looking at her intently, as he had looked at her that Sunday afternoon at Vavrika's. "But why do you fight for that so? What good is the power to enjoy, if you never enjoy? Your hands are cold again; what are you afraid of all the time? Ah, you're afraid of losing it; that's what's the matter with you! And you will, Clara Vavrika, you will! When I used to know you—listen; you've caught a wild bird in your hand, haven't you, and felt its heart beat so hard that you were afraid it would shatter its little body to pieces? Well, you used to be just like that, a slender, eager thing with a wild delight inside you. That is how I remembered you. And I come back and find you—a bitter woman. This is a perfect ferret fight here; you live by biting and being bitten. Can't you remember what life used to be? Can't you remember that old delight? I've never forgotten it, or known its like, on land or sea."

He drew the horse under the shadow of the straw stack. Clara felt him take her foot out of the stirrup, and she slid softly down into his arms. He kissed her slowly. He was a deliberate man, but his nerves were steel when he wanted anything. Something flashed out from him like a knife out of a sheath. Clara felt everything slipping away from her; she was flooded by the summer night. He thrust his hand into his pocket, and then held it out at arm's length. "Look," he said. The shadow of the straw stack fell sharp across his wrist, and in the palm of his hand she saw a silver dollar shining. "That's my pile," he muttered; "will you go with me?"

Clara nodded, and dropped her forehead on his shoulder.

Nils took a deep breath. "Will you go with me tonight?"

"Where?" she whispered softly.

"To town, to catch the midnight flyer."

Clara lifted her head and pulled herself together. "Are you crazy, Nils? We couldn't go away like that."

"That's the only way we ever will go. You can't sit on the bank and think about it. You have to plunge. That's the way I've always done, and it's the right way for people like you and me. There's nothing so dangerous as sitting still. You've only got one life, one youth, and you can let it slip through your fingers if you want to; nothing easier. Most people do that. You'd be better off tramping the roads with me than you are here." Nils held back her head and looked into her eyes. "But I'm not that kind of a tramp, Clara. You won't have to take in sewing. I'm with a Norwegian shipping line; came over on business with the New York offices, but now I'm going straight back to Bergen. I expect I've got as much money as the Ericsons. Father sent me a little to get started. They never knew about that. There, I hadn't meant to tell you; I wanted you to come on your own nerve."

Clara looked off across the fields. "It isn't that, Nils, but something seems to hold me. I'm afraid to pull against it. It comes out of the ground, I think."

"I know all about that. One has to tear loose. You're not needed here. Your father will understand; he's made like us.

As for Olaf, Johanna will take better care of him than ever you could. It's now or never, Clara Vavrika. My bag's at the station; I smuggled it there yesterday."

Clara clung to him and hid her face against his shoulder. "Not tonight," she whispered. "Sit here and talk to me tonight. I don't want to go anywhere tonight. I may never love you like this again."

Nils laughed through his teeth. "You can't come that on me. That's not my way, Clara Vavrika. Eric's mare is over there behind the stacks, and I'm off on the midnight. It's goodbye, or off across the world with me. My carriage won't wait. I've written a letter to Olaf, I'll mail it in town. When he reads it he won't bother us—not if I know him. He'd rather have the land. Besides, I could demand an investigation of his administration of Cousin Henrik's estate, and that would be bad for a public man. You've no clothes, I know; but you can sit up tonight, and we can get everything on the way. Where's your old dash, Clara Vavrika? What's become of your Bohemian blood? I used to think you had courage enough for anything. Where's your nerve—what are you waiting for?"

Clara drew back her head, and he saw the slumberous fire in her eyes. "For you to say one thing, Nils Ericson."

"I never say that thing to any woman, Clara Vavrika." He leaned back, lifted her gently from the ground, and whispered through his teeth: "But I'll never, never let you go, not to any man on earth but me! Do you understand me? Now, wait here."

Clara sank down on a sheaf of wheat and covered her face with her hands. She did not know what she was going to do—whether she would go or stay. The great, silent country seemed to lay a spell upon her. The ground seemed to hold her as if by roots. Her knees were soft under her. She felt as if she could not bear separation from her old sorrows, from her old discontent. They were dear to her, they had kept her alive, they were a part of her. There would be nothing left of her if she were wrenched away from them. Never could she pass beyond that skyline against which her restlessness had beat so many times. She felt as if her soul had built itself a nest there on that horizon at which she looked every morning and every evening, and it was dear to her, inexpressibly dear. She pressed her fingers against her eyeballs to shut it out. Beside her she heard the tramping of horses in the soft earth. Nils said nothing to her. He put his hands under her arms and lifted her lightly to her saddle. Then he swung himself into his own.

"We shall have to ride fast to catch the midnight train. A last gallop, Clara Vavrika. Forward!"

There was a start, a thud of hoofs along the moonlit road, two dark shadows going over the hill; and then the great, still land stretched untroubled under the azure night. Two shadows had passed.

VII

A year after the flight of Olaf Ericson's wife, the night train was steaming across the plains of Iowa. The conductor was hurrying through one of the day coaches, his lantern on his arm, when a lank, fair-haired boy sat up in one of the plush seats and tweaked him by the coat.

"What is the next stop, please, sir?"

"Red Oak, Iowa. But you go through to Chicago, don't you?" He looked down, and noticed that the boy's eyes were red and his face was drawn, as if he were in trouble.

"Yes. But I was wondering whether I could get off at the next place and get a train back to Omaha."

"Well, I suppose you could. Live in Omaha?"

"No. In the western part of the State. How soon do we get to Red Oak?"

"Forty minutes. You'd better make up your mind, so I can tell the baggageman to put your trunk off."

"Oh, never mind about that! I mean, I haven't got any," the boy added, blushing.

"Run away," the conductor thought, as he slammed the coach door behind him.

Eric Ericson crumpled down in his seat and put his brown hand to his forehead. He had been crying, and he had had no supper, and his head was aching violently. "Oh, what shall I do?" he thought, as he looked dully down at his big shoes. "Nils will be ashamed of me; I haven't got any spunk."

Ever since Nils had run away with his brother's wife, life at home had been hard for little Eric. His mother and Olaf both suspected him of complicity. Mrs. Ericson was harsh and faultfinding, constantly wounding the boy's pride; and Olaf was always setting her against him.

Joe Vavrika heard often from his daughter. Clara had always been fond of her father, and happiness made her kinder. She wrote him long accounts of the voyage to Bergen, and of the trip she and Nils took through Bohemia to the little town where her father had grown up and where she herself was born. She visited all her kinsmen there, and sent her father news of his brother, who was a priest; of his sister, who had married a horse-breeder—of their big farm and their many children. These letters Joe always managed to read to little Eric. They contained messages for Eric and Hilda. Clara sent presents, too, which Eric never dared to take home and which poor little Hilda never even saw, though she loved to hear Eric tell about them when they were out getting the eggs together. But Olaf once saw Eric coming out of Vavrika's

45

house—the old man had never asked the boy to come into his saloon—and Olaf went straight to his mother and told her. That night Mrs. Ericson came to Eric's room after he was in bed and made a terrible scene. She could be very terrifying when she was really angry. She forbade him ever to speak to Vavrika again, and after that night she would not allow him to go to town alone. So it was a long while before Eric got any more news of his brother. But old Joe suspected what was going on, and he carried Clara's letters about in his pocket. One Sunday he drove out to see a German friend of his, and chanced to catch sight of Eric, sitting by the cattle pond in the big pasture. They went together into Fritz Oberlies' barn, and read the letters and talked things over. Eric admitted that things were getting hard for him at home. That very night old Joe sat down and laboriously penned a statement of the case to his daughter.

Things got no better for Eric. His mother and Olaf felt that, however closely he was watched, he still, as they said, "heard." Mrs. Ericson could not admit neutrality. She had sent Johanna Vavrika packing back to her brother's, though Olaf would much rather have kept her than Anders' eldest daughter, whom Mrs. Ericson installed in her place. He was not so highhanded as his mother, and he once sulkily told her that she might better have taught her granddaughter to cook before she sent Johanna away. Olaf could have borne a good deal for the sake of prunes spiced in honey, the secret of which Johanna had taken away with her.

At last two letters came to Joe Vavrika: one from Nils, enclosing a postal order for money to pay Eric's passage to Bergen, and one from Clara, saying that Nils had a place for Eric in the offices of his company, that he was to live with them, and that they were only waiting for him to come. He was to leave New York on one of the boats of Nils' own line; the captain was one of their friends, and Eric was to make himself known at once.

Nils' directions were so explicit that a baby could have followed them, Eric felt. And here he was, nearing Red Oak, Iowa, and rocking backward and forward in despair. Never had he loved his brother so much, and never had the big world called to him so hard. But there was a lump in his throat which would not go down. Ever since nightfall he had been tormented by the thought of his mother, alone in that big house that had sent forth so many men. Her unkindness now seemed so little, and her loneliness so great. He remembered everything she had ever done for him: how frightened she had been when he tore his hand in the corn-sheller, and how she wouldn't let Olaf scold him. When Nils went away he didn't leave his mother all alone, or he would never have gone. Eric felt sure of that.

The train whistled. The conductor came in, smiling not unkindly. "Well, young man, what are you going to do? We stop at Red Oak in three minutes."

"Yes, thank you. I'll let you know." The conductor went out, and the boy doubled up with misery. He couldn't let his one chance go like this. He felt for his breast pocket and crackled Nils' letter to give him courage. He didn't want Nils to be ashamed of him. The train stopped. Suddenly he remembered his brother's kind, twinkling eyes, that always looked at you as if from far away. The lump in his throat softened. "Ah, but Nils, Nils would *understand*!" he thought. "That's just it about Nils; he always understands."

A lank, pale boy with a canvas telescope stumbled off the train to the Red Oak siding, just as the conductor called, "All aboard!"

The next night Mrs. Ericson was sitting alone in her wooden rocking-chair on the front porch. Little Hilda had been sent to bed and had cried herself to sleep. The old woman's knitting was on her lap, but her hands lay motionless on top of it. For more than an hour she had not moved a muscle. She simply sat, as only the Ericsons and the mountains can sit. The house was dark, and there was no sound but the croaking of the frogs down in the pond of the little pasture.

Eric did not come home by the road, but across the fields, where no one could see him. He set his telescope down softly in the kitchen shed, and slipped noiselessly along the path to the front porch. He sat down on the step without saying anything. Mrs. Ericson made no sign, and the frogs croaked on. At last the boy spoke timidly.

"I've come back, Mother."

"Very well," said Mrs. Ericson.

Eric leaned over and picked up a little stick out of the grass.

"How about the milking?" he faltered.

"That's been done, hours ago."

"Who did you get?"

"Get? I did it myself. I can milk as good as any of you."

Eric slid along the step nearer to her. "Oh, Mother, why did you?" he asked sorrowfully. "Why didn't you get one of Otto's boys?"

"I didn't want anybody to know I was in need of a boy," said Mrs. Ericson bitterly. She looked straight in front of her and her mouth tightened. "I always meant to give you the home farm," she added.

The boy stared and slid closer. "Oh, Mother," he faltered, "I don't care about the farm. I came back because I thought you might be needing me, maybe." He hung his head and got no further.

"Very well," said Mrs. Ericson. Her hand went out from her suddenly and rested on his head. Her fingers twined themselves in his soft, pale hair. His tears splashed down on the boards; happiness filled his heart.

THE TROLL GARDEN

FLAVIA AND HER ARTISTS

As the train neared Tarrytown, Imogen Willard began to wonder why she had consented to be one of Flavia's house party at all. She had not felt enthusiastic about it since leaving the city, and was experiencing a prolonged ebb of purpose, a current of chilling indecision, under which she vainly sought for the motive which had induced her to accept Flavia's invitation.

Perhaps it was a vague curiosity to see Flavia's husband, who had been the magician of her childhood and the hero of innumerable Arabian fairy tales. Perhaps it was a desire to see M. Roux, whom Flavia had announced as the especial attraction of the occasion. Perhaps it was a wish to study that remarkable woman in her own setting.

Imogen admitted a mild curiosity concerning Flavia. She was in the habit of taking people rather seriously, but somehow found it impossible to take Flavia so, because of the very vehemence and insistence with which Flavia demanded it. Submerged in her studies, Imogen had, of late years, seen very little of Flavia; but Flavia, in her hurried visits to New York, between her excursions from studio to studio—her luncheons with this lady who had to play at a matinee, and her dinners with that singer who had an evening concert—had seen enough of her friend's handsome daughter to conceive for her an inclination of such violence and assurance as only Flavia could afford. The fact that Imogen had shown rather marked capacity in certain esoteric lines of scholarship, and had decided to specialize in a well-sounding branch of philology at the Ecole des Chartes, had fairly placed her in that category of "interesting people" whom Flavia considered her natural affinities, and lawful prey.

When Imogen stepped upon the station platform she was immediately appropriated by her hostess, whose commanding figure and assurance of attire she had recognized from a distance. She was hurried into a high tilbury and Flavia, taking the driver's cushion beside her, gathered up the reins with an experienced hand.

"My dear girl," she remarked, as she turned the horses up the street, "I was afraid the train might be late. M. Roux insisted upon coming up by boat and did not arrive until after seven."

"To think of M. Roux's being in this part of the world at all, and subject to the vicissitudes of river boats! Why in the world did he come over?" queried Imogen with lively interest. "He is the sort of man who must dissolve and become a shadow outside of Paris."

"Oh, we have a houseful of the most interesting people," said Flavia, professionally. "We have actually managed to get Ivan Schemetzkin. He was ill in California at the close of his concert tour, you know, and he is recuperating with us, after his wearing journey from the coast. Then there is Jules Martel, the painter; Signor Donati, the tenor; Professor Schotte, who has dug up Assyria, you know; Restzhoff, the Russian chemist; Alcee Buisson, the philologist; Frank Wellington, the novelist; and Will Maidenwood, the editor of *Woman*. Then there is my second cousin, Jemima Broadwood, who made such a hit in Pinero's comedy last winter, and Frau Lichtenfeld. *Have* you read her?"

Imogen confessed her utter ignorance of Frau Lichtenfeld, and Flavia went on.

"Well, she is a most remarkable person; one of those advanced German women, a militant iconoclast, and this drive will not be long enough to permit of my telling you her history. Such a story! Her novels were the talk of all Germany when I was there last, and several of them have been suppressed—an honor in Germany, I understand. 'At Whose Door' has been translated. I am so unfortunate as not to read German."

"I'm all excitement at the prospect of meeting Miss Broadwood," said Imogen. "I've seen her in nearly everything she does. Her stage personality is delightful. She always reminds me of a nice, clean, pink-and-white boy who has just had his cold bath, and come down all aglow for a run before breakfast."

"Yes, but isn't it unfortunate that she will limit herself to those minor comedy parts that are so little appreciated in this country? One ought to be satisfied with nothing less than the best, ought one?" The peculiar, breathy tone in which Flavia always uttered that word "best," the most worn in her vocabulary, always jarred on Imogen and always made her obdurate.

"I don't at all agree with you," she said reservedly. "I thought everyone admitted that the most remarkable thing about Miss Broadwood is her admirable sense of fitness, which is rare enough in her profession."

Flavia could not endure being contradicted; she always seemed to regard it in the light of a defeat, and usually colored unbecomingly. Now she changed the subject.

"Look, my dear," she cried, "there is Frau Lichtenfeld now, coming to meet us. Doesn't she look as if she had just escaped out of Valhalla? She is actually over six feet."

Imogen saw a woman of immense stature, in a very short skirt and a broad, flapping sun hat, striding down the hillside at a long, swinging gait. The refugee from Valhalla approached, panting. Her heavy, Teutonic features were scarlet from the rigor of her exercise, and her hair, under her flapping sun hat, was tightly befrizzled about her brow. She fixed her sharp little eyes upon Imogen and extended both her hands.

"So this is the little friend?" she cried, in a rolling baritone.

Imogen was quite as tall as her hostess; but everything, she reflected, is comparative. After the introduction Flavia apologized.

"I wish I could ask you to drive up with us, Frau Lichtenfeld."

"Ah, no!" cried the giantess, drooping her head in humorous caricature of a time-honored pose of the heroines of sentimental romances. "It has never been my fate to be fitted into corners. I have never known the sweet privileges of the tiny."

Laughing, Flavia started the ponies, and the colossal woman, standing in the middle of the dusty road, took off her wide hat and waved them a farewell which, in scope of gesture, recalled the salute of a plumed cavalier.

When they arrived at the house, Imogen looked about her with keen curiosity, for this was veritably the work of Flavia's hands, the materialization of hopes long deferred. They passed directly into a large, square hall with a gallery on three sides, studio fashion. This opened at one end into a Dutch breakfast room, beyond which was the large dining room. At the other end of the hall was the music room. There was a smoking room, which one entered through the library behind the staircase. On the second floor there was the same general arrangement: a square hall, and, opening from it, the guest chambers, or, as Miss Broadwood termed them, the "cages."

When Imogen went to her room, the guests had begun to return from their various afternoon excursions. Boys were gliding through the halls with ice water, covered trays, and flowers, colliding with maids and valets who carried shoes and other articles of wearing apparel. Yet, all this was done in response to inaudible bells, on felt soles, and in hushed voices, so that there was very little confusion about it.

Flavia had at last built her house and hewn out her seven pillars; there could be no doubt, now, that the asylum for talent, the sanatorium of the arts, so long projected, was an accomplished fact. Her ambition had long ago outgrown the dimensions of her house on Prairie Avenue; besides, she had bitterly complained that in Chicago traditions were against her. Her project had been delayed by Arthur's doggedly standing out for the Michigan woods, but Flavia knew well enough that certain of the *rarae aves*—"the best"—could not be lured so far away from the seaport, so she declared herself for the historic Hudson and knew no retreat. The establishing of a New York office had at length overthrown Arthur's last valid objection to quitting the lake country for three months of the year; and Arthur could be wearied into anything, as those who knew him knew.

Flavia's house was the mirror of her exultation; it was a temple to the gods of Victory, a sort of triumphal arch. In her earlier days she had swallowed experiences that would have unmanned one of less torrential enthusiasm or blind pertinacity. But, of late years, her determination had told; she saw less and less of those mysterious persons with mysterious obstacles in their path and mysterious grievances against the world, who had once frequented her house on Prairie Avenue. In the stead of this multitude of the unarrived, she had now the few, the select, "the best." Of all that band of indigent retainers who had once fed at her board like the suitors in the halls of Penelope, only Alcee Buisson still retained his right of entree. He alone had remembered that ambition hath a knapsack at his back, wherein he puts alms to oblivion, and he alone had been considerate enough to do what Flavia had expected of him, and give his name a current value in the world. Then, as Miss Broadwood put it, "he was her first real one,"—and Flavia, like Mohammed, could remember her first believer.

"The House of Song," as Miss Broadwood had called it, was the outcome of Flavia's more exalted strategies. A woman who made less a point of sympathizing with their delicate organisms, might have sought to plunge these phosphorescent pieces into the tepid bath of domestic life; but Flavia's discernment was deeper. This must be a refuge where the shrinking soul, the sensitive brain, should be unconstrained; where the caprice of fancy should outweigh the civil code, if necessary. She considered that this much Arthur owed her; for she, in her turn, had made concessions. Flavia had, indeed, quite an equipment of epigrams to the effect that our century creates the iron genii which evolve its fairy tales: but the fact that her husband's name was annually painted upon some ten thousand threshing machines in reality contributed very little to her happiness.

Arthur Hamilton was born and had spent his boyhood in the West Indies, and physically he had never lost the brand of the tropics. His father, after inventing the machine which bore his name, had returned to the States to patent and manufacture it. After leaving college, Arthur had spent five years ranching in the West and traveling abroad. Upon his father's death he had returned to Chicago and, to the astonishment of all his friends, had taken up the business—without any demonstration of enthusiasm, but with quiet perseverance, marked ability, and amazing industry. Why or how a self-sufficient, rather ascetic man of thirty, indifferent in manner, wholly negative in all other personal relations, should have doggedly wooed and finally married Flavia Malcolm was a problem that had vexed older heads than Imogen's.

While Imogen was dressing she heard a knock at her door, and a young woman entered whom she at once recognized as Jemima Broadwood—"Jimmy" Broadwood she was called by people in her own profession. While there was something unmistakably professional in her frank *savoir-faire*, "Jimmy's" was one of those faces to which the rouge never seems to stick. Her eyes were keen and gray as a windy April sky, and so far from having been seared by calcium lights, you might have fancied they had never looked on anything less bucolic than growing fields and country fairs. She wore her thick, brown hair short and parted at the side; and, rather than hinting at freakishness, this seemed admirably in keeping with her fresh, boyish countenance. She extended to Imogen a large, well-shaped hand which it was a pleasure to clasp.

"Ah! You are Miss Willard, and I see I need not introduce myself. Flavia said you were kind enough to express a wish to meet me, and I preferred to meet you alone. Do you mind if I smoke?"

"Why, certainly not," said Imogen, somewhat disconcerted and looking hurriedly about for matches.

"There, be calm, I'm always prepared," said Miss Broadwood, checking Imogen's flurry with a soothing gesture, and producing an oddly fashioned silver match-case from some mysterious recess in her dinner gown. She sat down in a deep chair, crossed her patent-leather Oxfords, and lit her cigarette. "This matchbox," she went on meditatively, "once belonged to a Prussian officer. He shot himself in his bathtub, and I bought it at the sale of his effects."

Imogen had not yet found any suitable reply to make to this rather irrelevant confidence, when Miss Broadwood turned to her cordially: "I'm awfully glad you've come, Miss Willard, though I've not quite decided why you did it. I wanted very much to meet you. Flavia gave me your thesis to read."

"Why, how funny!" ejaculated Imogen.

"On the contrary," remarked Miss Broadwood. "I thought it decidedly lacked humor."

"I meant," stammered Imogen, beginning to feel very much like Alice in Wonderland, "I meant that I thought it rather strange Mrs. Hamilton should fancy you would be interested."

Miss Broadwood laughed heartily. "Now, don't let my rudeness frighten you. Really, I found it very interesting, and no end impressive. You see, most people in my profession are good for absolutely nothing else, and, therefore, they have a deep and abiding conviction that in some other line they might have shone. Strange to say, scholarship is the object of our envious and particular admiration. Anything in type impresses us greatly; that's why so many of us marry authors or newspapermen and lead miserable lives." Miss Broadwood saw that she had rather disconcerted Imogen, and blithely tacked in another direction. "You see," she went on, tossing aside her half-consumed cigarette, "some years ago Flavia would not have deemed me worthy to open the pages of your thesis—nor to be one of her house party of the chosen, for that matter. I've Pinero to thank for both pleasures. It all depends on the class of business I'm playing whether I'm in favor or not. Flavia is my second cousin, you know, so I can say whatever disagreeable things I choose with perfect good grace. I'm quite desperate for someone to laugh with, so I'm going to fasten myself upon you—for, of course, one can't expect any of these gypsy-dago people to see anything funny. I don't intend you shall lose the humor of the situation. What do you think of Flavia's infirmary for the arts, anyway?"

"Well, it's rather too soon for me to have any opinion at all," said Imogen, as she again turned to her dressing. "So far, you are the only one of the artists I've met."

"One of them?" echoed Miss Broadwood. "One of the *artists*? My offense may be rank, my dear, but I really don't deserve that. Come, now, whatever badges of my tribe I may bear upon me, just let me divest you of any notion that I take myself seriously."

Imogen turned from the mirror in blank astonishment and sat down on the arm of a chair, facing her visitor. "I can't fathom you at all, Miss Broadwood," she said frankly. "Why shouldn't you take yourself seriously? What's the use of beating about the bush? Surely you know that you are one of the few players on this side of the water who have at all the spirit of natural or ingenuous comedy?"

"Thank you, my dear. Now we are quite even about the thesis, aren't we? Oh, did you mean it? Well, you *are* a clever girl. But you see it doesn't do to permit oneself to look at it in that light. If we do, we always go to pieces and waste our substance astarring as the unhappy daughter of the Capulets. But there, I hear Flavia coming to take you down; and just remember I'm not one of them—the artists, I mean."

Flavia conducted Imogen and Miss Broadwood downstairs. As they reached the lower hall they heard voices from the music room, and dim figures were lurking in the shadows under the gallery, but their hostess led straight to the smoking room. The June evening was chilly, and a fire had been lighted in the fireplace. Through the deepening dusk, the firelight flickered upon the pipes and curious weapons on the wall and threw an orange glow over the Turkish hangings. One side of the smoking room was entirely of glass, separating it from the conservatory, which was flooded with white light from the electric bulbs. There was about the darkened room some suggestion of certain chambers in the Arabian Nights, opening on a court of palms. Perhaps it was partially this memory-evoking suggestion that caused Imogen to start so violently when she saw dimly, in a blur of shadow, the figure of a man, who sat smoking in a low, deep chair before the fire. He was long, and thin, and brown. His long, nerveless hands drooped from the arms of his chair. A brown mustache shaded his mouth, and his eyes were sleepy and apathetic. When Imogen entered he rose indolently and gave her his hand, his manner barely courteous.

"I am glad you arrived promptly, Miss Willard," he said with an indifferent drawl. "Flavia was afraid you might be late. You had a pleasant ride up, I hope?"

"Oh, very, thank you, Mr. Hamilton," she replied, feeling that he did not particularly care whether she replied at all.

Flavia explained that she had not yet had time to dress for dinner, as she had been attending to Mr. Will Maidenwood, who had become faint after hurting his finger in an obdurate window, and immediately excused herself As she left, Hamilton turned to Miss Broadwood with a rather spiritless smile.

"Well, Jimmy," he remarked, "I brought up a piano box full of fireworks for the boys. How do you suppose we'll manage to keep them until the Fourth?"

"We can't, unless we steel ourselves to deny there are any on the premises," said Miss Broadwood, seating herself on a low stool by Hamilton's chair and leaning back against the mantel. "Have you seen Helen, and has she told you the tragedy of the tooth?"

"She met me at the station, with her tooth wrapped up in tissue paper. I had tea with her an hour ago. Better sit down, Miss Willard;" he rose and pushed a chair toward Imogen, who was standing peering into the conservatory. "We are scheduled to dine at seven, but they seldom get around before eight."

By this time Imogen had made out that here the plural pronoun, third person, always referred to the artists. As Hamilton's manner did not spur one to cordial intercourse, and as his attention seemed directed to Miss Broadwood, insofar as it could be said to be directed to anyone, she sat down facing the conservatory and watched him, unable to decide in how far he was identical with the man who had first met Flavia Malcolm in her mother's house, twelve years ago. Did he at all remember having known her as a little girl, and why did his indifference hurt her so, after all these years? Had some remnant of her childish affection for him gone on living, somewhere down in the sealed caves of her consciousness, and had she really expected to find it possible to be fond of him again? Suddenly she saw a light in the man's sleepy eyes, an unmistakable expression of interest and pleasure that fairly startled her. She turned quickly in the direction of his glance, and saw Flavia, just entering, dressed for dinner and lit by the effulgence of her most radiant manner. Most people considered Flavia handsome, and there was no gainsaying that she carried her five-and-thirty years splendidly. Her figure had never grown matronly, and her face was of the sort that does not show wear. Its blond tints were as fresh and enduring as enamel—and quite as hard. Its usual expression was one of tense, often strained, animation, which compressed her lips nervously. A perfect scream of animation, Miss Broadwood had called it, created and maintained by sheer, indomitable force of will. Flavia's appearance on any scene whatever made a ripple, caused a certain agitation and recognition, and, among impressionable people, a certain uneasiness, For all her sparkling assurance of manner, Flavia was certainly always ill at ease and, even more certainly, anxious. She seemed not convinced of the established order of material things, seemed always trying to conceal her feeling that walls might crumble, chasms open, or the fabric of her life fly to the winds in irretrievable entanglement. At least this was the impression Imogen got from that note in Flavia which was so manifestly false.

Hamilton's keen, quick, satisfied glance at his wife had recalled to Imogen all her inventory of speculations about them. She looked at him with compassionate surprise. As a child she had never permitted herself to believe that Hamilton cared at all for the woman who had taken him away from her; and since she had begun to think about them again, it had never occurred to her that anyone could become attached to Flavia in that deeply personal and exclusive sense. It seemed quite as irrational as trying to possess oneself of Broadway at noon.

When they went out to dinner Imogen realized the completeness of Flavia's triumph. They were people of one name, mostly, like kings; people whose names stirred the imagination like a romance or a melody. With the notable exception of M. Roux, Imogen had seen most of them before, either in concert halls or lecture rooms; but they looked noticeably older and dimmer than she remembered them.

Opposite her sat Schemetzkin, the Russian pianist, a short, corpulent man, with an apoplectic face and purplish skin, his thick, iron-gray hair tossed back from his forehead. Next to the German giantess sat the Italian tenor—the tiniest of men—pale, with soft, light hair, much in disorder, very red lips, and fingers yellowed by cigarettes. Frau Lichtenfeld shone in a gown of emerald green, fitting so closely as to enhance her natural floridness. However, to do the good lady justice, let her attire be never so modest, it gave an effect of barbaric splendor. At her left sat Herr Schotte, the Assyriologist, whose features were effectually concealed by the convergence of his hair and beard, and whose glasses were continually falling into his plate. This gentleman had removed more tons of earth in the course of his explorations than had any of his confreres, and his vigorous attack upon his food seemed to suggest the strenuous nature of his accustomed toil. His eyes were small and deeply set, and his forehead bulged fiercely above his eyes in a bony ridge. His heavy brows completed the leonine suggestion of his face. Even to Imogen, who knew something of his work and greatly respected it, he was entirely too reminiscent of the Stone Age to be altogether an agreeable dinner companion. He seemed, indeed, to have absorbed something of the savagery of those early types of life which he continually studied.

Frank Wellington, the young Kansas man who had been two years out of Harvard and had published three historical novels, sat next to Mr. Will Maidenwood, who was still pale from his recent sufferings and carried his hand bandaged. They took little part in the general conversation, but, like the lion and the unicorn, were always at it, discussing, every time they met, whether there were or were not passages in Mr. Wellington's works which should be eliminated, out of consideration for the Young Person. Wellington had fallen into the hands of a great American syndicate which most effectually befriended struggling authors whose struggles were in the right direction, and which had guaranteed to make him famous before he was thirty. Feeling the security of his position he stoutly defended those passages which jarred upon the sensitive nerves of the young editor of *Woman*. Maidenwood, in the smoothest of voices, urged the necessity of the author's recognizing certain restrictions at the outset, and Miss Broadwood, who joined the argument quite without invitation or encouragement, seconded him with pointed and malicious remarks which caused the young editor manifest discomfort. Restzhoff, the chemist, demanded the attention of the entire company for his exposition of his devices for manufacturing ice cream from vegetable oils and for administering drugs in bonbons.

Flavia, always noticeably restless at dinner, was somewhat apathetic toward the advocate of peptonized chocolate and was plainly concerned about the sudden departure of M. Roux, who had announced that it would be necessary for him to leave tomorrow. M. Emile Roux, who sat at Flavia's right, was a man in middle life and quite bald, clearly without personal vanity, though his publishers preferred to circulate only those of his portraits taken in his ambrosial youth. Imogen was considerably shocked at his unlikeness to the slender, black-stocked Rolla he had looked at twenty. He had declined into the florid, settled heaviness of indifference and approaching age. There was, however, a certain look of durability and solidity about him; the look of a man who has earned the right to be fat and bald, and even silent at dinner if he chooses.

Throughout the discussion between Wellington and Will Maidenwood, though they invited his participation, he remained silent, betraying no sign either of interest or contempt. Since his arrival he had directed most of his conversation to Hamilton, who had never read one of his twelve great novels. This perplexed and troubled Flavia. On the night of his arrival Jules Martel had enthusiastically declared, "There are schools and schools, manners and manners; but Roux is Roux, and Paris sets its watches by his clock." Flavia had already repeated this remark to Imogen. It haunted her, and each time she quoted it she was impressed anew.

Flavia shifted the conversation uneasily, evidently exasperated and excited by her repeated failures to draw the novelist out. "Monsieur Roux," she began abruptly, with her most animated smile, "I remember so well a statement I read some years ago in your 'Mes Etudes des Femmes' to the effect that you had never met a really intellectual woman. May I ask, without being impertinent, whether that assertion still represents your experience?"

"I meant, madam," said the novelist conservatively, "intellectual in a sense very special, as we say of men in whom the purely intellectual functions seem almost independent."

"And you still think a woman so constituted a mythical personage?" persisted Flavia, nodding her head encouragingly.

"*Une Meduse*, madam, who, if she were discovered, would transmute us all into stone," said the novelist, bowing gravely. "If she existed at all," he added deliberately, "it was my business to find her, and she has cost me many a vain pilgrimage. Like Rudel of Tripoli, I have crossed seas and penetrated deserts to seek her out. I have, indeed, encountered women of learning whose industry I have been compelled to respect; many who have possessed beauty and charm and perplexing cleverness; a few with remarkable information and a sort of fatal facility."

"And Mrs. Browning, George Eliot, and your own Mme. Dudevant?" queried Flavia with that fervid enthusiasm with which she could, on occasion, utter things simply incomprehensible for their banality—at her feats of this sort Miss Broadwood was wont to sit breathless with admiration.

"Madam, while the intellect was undeniably present in the performances of those women, it was only the stick of the rocket. Although this woman has eluded me I have studied her conditions and perturbances as astronomers conjecture the orbits of planets they have never seen. if she exists, she is probably neither an artist nor a woman with a mission, but an obscure personage, with imperative intellectual needs, who absorbs rather than produces."

Flavia, still nodding nervously, fixed a strained glance of interrogation upon M. Roux. "Then you think she would be a woman whose first necessity would be to know, whose instincts would be satisfied only with the best, who could draw from others; appreciative, merely?"

The novelist lifted his dull eyes to his interlocutress with an untranslatable smile and a slight inclination of his shoulders. "Exactly so; you are really remarkable, madam," he added, in a tone of cold astonishment.

After dinner the guests took their coffee in the music room, where Schemetzkin sat down at the piano to drum ragtime, and give his celebrated imitation of the boardingschool girl's execution of Chopin. He flatly refused to play anything more serious, and would practice only in the morning, when he had the music room to himself. Hamilton and M. Roux repaired to the smoking room to discuss the necessity of extending the tax on manufactured articles in France—one of those conversations which particularly exasperated Flavia.

After Schemetzkin had grimaced and tortured the keyboard with malicious vulgarities for half an hour, Signor Donati, to put an end to his torture, consented to sing, and Flavia and Imogen went to fetch Arthur to play his accompaniments. Hamilton rose with an annoyed look and placed his cigarette on the mantel. "Why yes, Flavia, I'll accompany him, provided he sings something with a melody, Italian arias or ballads, and provided the recital is not interminable."

"You will join us, M. Roux?"

"Thank you, but I have some letters to write," replied the novelist, bowing.

As Flavia had remarked to Imogen, "Arthur really played accompaniments remarkably well." To hear him recalled vividly the days of her childhood, when he always used to spend his business vacations at her mother's home in Maine. He had possessed for her that almost hypnotic influence which young men sometimes exert upon little girls. It was a sort of phantom love affair, subjective and fanciful, a precocity of instinct, like that tender and maternal concern which some little girls feel for their dolls. Yet this childish infatuation is capable of all the depressions and exaltations of love itself, it has its bitter jealousies, cruel disappointments, its exacting caprices.

Summer after summer she had awaited his coming and wept at his departure, indifferent to the gayer young men who had called her their sweetheart and laughed at everything she said. Although Hamilton never said so, she had been always quite sure that he was fond of her. When he pulled her up the river to hunt for fairy knolls shut about by low, hanging willows, he was often silent for an hour at a time, yet she never felt he was bored or was neglecting her. He would lie in the sand smoking, his eyes half-closed, watching her play, and she was always conscious that she was entertaining him. Sometimes he would take a copy of "Alice in Wonderland" in his pocket, and no one could read it as he could, laughing at her with his dark eyes, when anything amused him. No one else could laugh so, with just their eyes, and without moving a muscle of their face. Though he usually smiled at passages that seemed not at all funny to the child, she always laughed gleefully, because he was so seldom moved to mirth that any such demonstration delighted her and she took the credit of it entirely to herself Her own inclination had been for serious stories, with sad endings, like the Little Mermaid, which he had once told her in an unguarded moment when she had a cold, and was put to bed early on her birthday night and cried because she could not have her party. But he highly disapproved of this preference, and had called it a morbid taste, and always shook his finger at her when she asked for the story. When she had been particularly good, or particularly neglected by other people, then he would sometimes melt and tell her the story, and never laugh at her if she enjoyed the "sad ending" even to tears. When Flavia had taken him away and he came no more, she wept inconsolably for the space of two weeks, and refused to learn her lessons. Then she found the story of the Little Mermaid herself, and forgot him.

Imogen had discovered at dinner that he could still smile at one secretly, out of his eyes, and that he had the old manner of outwardly seeming bored, but letting you know that he was not. She was intensely curious about his exact state of feeling toward his wife, and more curious still to catch a sense of his final adjustment to the conditions of life in general. This, she could not help feeling, she might get again—if she could have him alone for an hour, in some place where there was a little river and a sandy cove bordered by drooping willows, and a blue sky seen through white sycamore boughs.

That evening, before retiring, Flavia entered her husband's room, where he sat in his smoking jacket, in one of his favorite low chairs.

"I suppose it's a grave responsibility to bring an ardent, serious young thing like Imogen here among all these fascinating personages," she remarked reflectively. "But, after all, one can never tell. These grave, silent girls have their own charm, even for facile people."

"Oh, so that is your plan?" queried her husband dryly. "I was wondering why you got her up here. She doesn't seem to mix well with the faciles. At least, so it struck me."

Flavia paid no heed to this jeering remark, but repeated, "No, after all, it may not be a bad thing."

"Then do consign her to that shaken reed, the tenor," said her husband yawning. "I remember she used to have a taste for the pathetic."

"And then," remarked Flavia coquettishly, "after all, I owe her mother a return in kind. She was not afraid to trifle with destiny."

But Hamilton was asleep in his chair.

Next morning Imogen found only Miss Broadwood in the breakfast room.

"Good morning, my dear girl, whatever are you doing up so early? They never breakfast before eleven. Most of them take their coffee in their room. Take this place by me."

Miss Broadwood looked particularly fresh and encouraging in her blue serge walking skirt, her open jacket displaying an expanse of stiff, white shirt bosom, dotted with some almost imperceptible figure, and a dark blue-and-white necktie, neatly knotted under her wide, rolling collar. She wore a white rosebud in the lapel of her coat, and decidedly she seemed more than ever like a nice, clean boy on his holiday. Imogen was just hoping that they would breakfast alone when Miss Broadwood exclaimed, "Ah, there comes Arthur with the children. That's the reward of early rising in this house; you never get to see the youngsters at any other time."

Hamilton entered, followed by two dark, handsome little boys. The girl, who was very tiny, blonde like her mother, and exceedingly frail, he carried in his arms. The boys came up and said good morning with an ease and cheerfulness uncommon, even in well-bred children, but the little girl hid her face on her father's shoulder.

"She's a shy little lady," he explained as he put her gently down in her chair. "I'm afraid she's like her father; she can't seem to get used to meeting people. And you, Miss Willard, did you dream of the White Rabbit or the Little Mermaid?"

"Oh, I dreamed of them all! All the personages of that buried civilization," cried Imogen, delighted that his estranged manner of the night before had entirely vanished and feeling that, somehow, the old confidential relations had been restored during the night.

"Come, William," said Miss Broadwood, turning to the younger of the two boys, "and what did you dream about?"

"We dreamed," said William gravely—he was the more assertive of the two and always spoke for both—"we dreamed that there were fireworks hidden in the basement of the carriage house; lots and lots of fireworks."

His elder brother looked up at him with apprehensive astonishment, while Miss Broadwood hastily put her napkin to her lips and Hamilton dropped his eyes. "If little boys dream things, they are so apt not to come true," he reflected sadly. This shook even the redoubtable William, and he glanced nervously at his brother. "But do things vanish just because they have been dreamed?" he objected.

"Generally that is the very best reason for their vanishing," said Arthur gravely.

"But, Father, people can't help what they dream," remonstrated Edward gently.

"Oh, come! You're making these children talk like a Maeterlinck dialogue," laughed Miss Broadwood.

Flavia presently entered, a book in her hand, and bade them all good morning. "Come, little people, which story shall it be this morning?" she asked winningly. Greatly excited, the children followed her into the garden. "She does then, sometimes," murmured Imogen as they left the breakfast room.

"Oh, yes, to be sure," said Miss Broadwood cheerfully. "She reads a story to them every morning in the most picturesque part of the garden. The mother of the Gracchi, you know. She does so long, she says, for the time when they will be intellectual companions for her. What do you say to a walk over the hills?"

As they left the house they met Frau Lichtenfeld and the bushy Herr Schotte—the professor cut an astonishing figure in golf stockings—returning from a walk and engaged in an animated conversation on the tendencies of German fiction.

"Aren't they the most attractive little children," exclaimed Imogen as they wound down the road toward the river.

"Yes, and you must not fail to tell Flavia that you think so. She will look at you in a sort of startled way and say, 'Yes, aren't they?' and maybe she will go off and hunt them up and have tea with them, to fully appreciate them. She is awfully afraid of missing anything good, is Flavia. The way those youngsters manage to conceal their guilty presence in the House of Song is a wonder."

"But don't any of the artist-folk fancy children?" asked Imogen.

"Yes, they just fancy them and no more. The chemist remarked the other day that children are like certain salts which need not be actualized because the formulae are quite sufficient for practical purposes. I don't see how even Flavia can endure to have that man about."

"I have always been rather curious to know what Arthur thinks of it all," remarked Imogen cautiously.

"Thinks of it!" ejaculated Miss Broadwood. "Why, my dear, what would any man think of having his house turned into an hotel, habited by freaks who discharge his servants, borrow his money, and insult his neighbors? This place is shunned like a lazaretto!"

"Well, then, why does he—why does he—" persisted Imogen.

"Bah!" interrupted Miss Broadwood impatiently, "why did he in the first place? That's the question."

"Marry her, you mean?" said Imogen coloring.

"Exactly so," said Miss Broadwood sharply, as she snapped the lid of her matchbox.

"I suppose that is a question rather beyond us, and certainly one which we cannot discuss," said Imogen. "But his toleration on this one point puzzles me, quite apart from other complications."

"Toleration? Why this point, as you call it, simply is Flavia. Who could conceive of her without it? I don't know where it's all going to end, I'm sure, and I'm equally sure that, if it were not for Arthur, I shouldn't care," declared Miss Broadwood, drawing her shoulders together.

"But will it end at all, now?"

"Such an absurd state of things can't go on indefinitely. A man isn't going to see his wife make a guy of herself forever, is he? Chaos has already begun in the servants' quarters. There are six different languages spoken there now. You see, it's all on an entirely false basis. Flavia hasn't the slightest notion of what these people are really like, their good and their bad alike escape her. They, on the other hand, can't imagine what she is driving at. Now, Arthur is worse off than either faction; he is not in the fairy story in that he sees these people exactly as they are, *but* he is utterly unable to see Flavia as they see her. There you have the situation. Why can't he see her as we do? My dear, that has kept me awake o' nights. This man who has thought so much and lived so much, who is naturally a critic, really takes Flavia at very nearly her own estimate. But now I am entering upon a wilderness. From a brief acquaintance with her you can know nothing of the icy fastnesses of Flavia's self-esteem. It's like St. Peter's; you can't realize its magnitude at once. You have to grow into a sense of it by living under its shadow. It has perplexed even Emile Roux, that merciless dissector of egoism. She has puzzled him the more because he saw at a glance what some of them do not perceive at once, and what will be mercifully concealed from Arthur until the trump sounds; namely, that all Flavia's artists have done or ever will do means exactly as much to her as a symphony means to an oyster; that there is no bridge by which the significance of any work of art could be conveyed to her."

"Then, in the name of goodness, why does she bother?" gasped Imogen. "She is pretty, wealthy, well-established; why should she bother?"

"That's what M. Roux has kept asking himself. I can't pretend to analyze it. She reads papers on the Literary Landmarks of Paris, the Loves of the Poets, and that sort of thing, to clubs out in Chicago. To Flavia it is more necessary to be called clever than to breathe. I would give a good deal to know that glum Frenchman's diagnosis. He has been watching her out of those fishy eyes of his as a biologist watches a hemisphereless frog."

For several days after M. Roux's departure Flavia gave an embarrassing share of her attention to Imogen. Embarrassing, because Imogen had the feeling of being energetically and futilely explored, she knew not for what. She felt herself under the globe of an air pump, expected to yield up something. When she confined the conversation to matters of general interest Flavia conveyed to her with some pique that her one endeavor in life had been to fit herself to converse with her friends upon those things which vitally interested them. "One has no right to accept their best from people unless one gives, isn't it so? I want to be able to give—!" she declared vaguely. Yet whenever Imogen strove to pay her tithes and plunged bravely into her plans for study next winter, Flavia grew absent-minded and interrupted her by amazing generalizations or by such embarrassing questions as, "And these grim studies really have charm for you; you are quite buried in them; they make other things seem light and ephemeral?"

"I rather feel as though I had got in here under false pretenses," Imogen confided to Miss Broadwood. "I'm sure I don't know what it is that she wants of me."

"Ah," chuckled Jemima, "you are not equal to these heart to heart talks with Flavia. You utterly fail to communicate to her the atmosphere of that untroubled joy in which you dwell. You must remember that she gets no feeling out of things herself, and she demands that you impart yours to her by some process of psychic transmission. I once met a blind girl, blind from birth, who could discuss the peculiarities of the Barbizon school with just Flavia's glibness and enthusiasm. Ordinarily Flavia knows how to get what she wants from people, and her memory is wonderful. One evening I heard her giving Frau Lichtenfeld some random impressions about Hedda Gabler which she extracted from me five years ago; giving them with an impassioned conviction of which I was never guilty. But I have known other people who could appropriate your stories and opinions; Flavia is infinitely more subtle than that; she can soak up the very thrash and drift of your daydreams, and take the very thrills off your back, as it were."

After some days of unsuccessful effort, Flavia withdrew herself, and Imogen found Hamilton ready to catch her when she was tossed afield. He seemed only to have been awaiting this crisis, and at once their old intimacy reestablished itself as a thing inevitable and beautifully prepared for. She convinced herself that she had not been mistaken in him, despite all the doubts that had come up in later years, and this renewal of faith set more than one question thumping in her brain. "How did he, how can he?" she kept repeating with a tinge of her childish resentment, "what right had he to waste anything so fine?"

When Imogen and Arthur were returning from a walk before luncheon one morning about a week after M. Roux's departure, they noticed an absorbed group before one of the hall windows. Herr Schotte and Restzhoff sat on the window seat with a newspaper between them, while Wellington, Schemetzkin, and Will Maidenwood looked over their shoulders. They seemed intensely interested, Herr Schotte occasionally pounding his knees with his fists in ebullitions of barbaric glee. When imogen entered the hall, however, the men were all sauntering toward the breakfast room and the paper was lying innocently on the divan. During luncheon the personnel of that window group were unwontedly animated and agreeable all save Schemetzkin, whose stare was blanker than ever, as though Roux's mantle of insulting indifference had fallen upon him, in addition to his own oblivious self-absorption. Will Maidenwood seemed embarrassed and annoyed; the chemist employed himself with making polite speeches to Hamilton. Flavia did not come down to lunch—and there was a malicious gleam under Herr Schotte's eyebrows. Frank Wellington announced nervously that an imperative letter from his protecting syndicate summoned him to the city.

After luncheon the men went to the golf links, and Imogen, at the first opportunity, possessed herself of the newspaper which had been left on the divan. One of the first things that caught her eye was an article headed "Roux on Tuft Hunters; The Advanced American Woman as He Sees Her; Aggressive, Superficial, and Insincere." The entire interview was nothing more nor less than a satiric characterization of Flavia, aquiver with irritation and vitriolic malice. No one could mistake it; it was done with all his deftness of portraiture. Imogen had not finished the article when she heard a footstep, and clutching the paper she started precipitately toward the stairway as Arthur entered. He put out his hand, looking critically at her distressed face.

"Wait a moment, Miss Willard," he said peremptorily, "I want to see whether we can find what it was that so interested our friends this morning. Give me the paper, please."

Imogen grew quite white as he opened the journal. She reached forward and crumpled it with her hands. "Please don't, please don't," she pleaded; "it's something I don't want you to see. Oh, why will you? it's just something low and despicable that you can't notice."

Arthur had gently loosed her hands, and he pointed her to a chair. He lit a cigar and read the article through without comment. When he had finished it he walked to the fireplace, struck a match, and tossed the flaming journal between the brass andirons.

"You are right," he remarked as he came back, dusting his hands with his handkerchief. "It's quite impossible to comment. There are extremes of blackguardism for which we have no name. The only thing necessary is to see that Flavia gets no wind of this. This seems to be my cue to act; poor girl."

Imogen looked at him tearfully; she could only murmur, "Oh, why did you read it!"

Hamilton laughed spiritlessly. "Come, don't you worry about it. You always took other people's troubles too seriously. When you were little and all the world was gay and everybody happy, you must needs get the Little Mermaid's troubles to grieve over. Come with me into the music room. You remember the musical setting I once made you for the Lay of the Jabberwock? I was trying it over the other night, long after you were in bed, and I decided it was quite as fine as the Erl-King music. How I wish I could give you some of the cake that Alice ate and make you a little girl again. Then, when you had got through the glass door into the little garden, you could call to me, perhaps, and tell me all the fine things that were going on there. What a pity it is that you ever grew up!" he added, laughing; and Imogen, too, was thinking just that.

At dinner that evening, Flavia, with fatal persistence, insisted upon turning the conversation to M. Roux. She had been reading one of his novels and had remembered anew that Paris set its watches by his clock. Imogen surmised that she was tortured by a feeling that she had not sufficiently appreciated him while she had had him. When she first mentioned his name she was answered only by the pall of silence that fell over the company. Then everyone began to talk at once, as though to correct a false position. They spoke of him with a fervid, defiant admiration, with the sort of hot praise that covers a double purpose. Imogen fancied she could see that they felt a kind of relief at what the man had done, even those who despised him for doing it; that they felt a spiteful hate against Flavia, as though she had tricked them, and a certain contempt for themselves that they had been beguiled. She was reminded of the fury of the crowd in the fairy tale, when once the child had called out that the king was in his night clothes. Surely these people knew no more about Flavia than they had known before, but the mere fact that the thing had been said altered the situation. Flavia, meanwhile, sat chattering amiably, pathetically unconscious of her nakedness.

Hamilton lounged, fingering the stem of his wineglass, gazing down the table at one face after another and studying the various degrees of self-consciousness they exhibited. Imogen's eyes followed his, fearfully. When a lull came in the spasmodic flow of conversation, Arthur, leaning back in his chair, remarked deliberately, "As for M. Roux, his very profession places him in that class of men whom society has never been able to accept unconditionally because it has never been able to assume that they have any ordered notion of taste. He and his ilk remain, with the mountebanks and snake charmers, people indispensable to our civilization, but wholly unreclaimed by it; people whom we receive, but whose invitations we do not accept."

Fortunately for Flavia, this mine was not exploded until just before the coffee was brought. Her laughter was pitiful to hear; it echoed through the silent room as in a vault, while she made some tremulously light remark about her husband's drollery, grim as a jest from the dying. No one responded and she sat nodding her head like a mechanical toy and smiling her white, set smile through her teeth, until Alcee Buisson and Frau Lichtenfeld came to her support.

After dinner the guests retired immediately to their rooms, and Imogen went upstairs on tiptoe, feeling the echo of breakage and the dust of crumbling in the air. She wondered whether Flavia's habitual note of uneasiness were not, in a manner, prophetic, and a sort of unconscious premonition, after all. She sat down to write a letter, but she found herself so nervous, her head so hot and her hands so cold, that she soon abandoned the effort, just as she was about to seek Miss Broadwood, Flavia entered and embraced her hysterically.

"My dearest girl," she began, "was there ever such an unfortunate and incomprehensible speech made before? Of course it is scarcely necessary to explain to you poor Arthur's lack of tact, and that he meant nothing. But they! Can they be expected to understand? He will feel wretchedly about it when he realizes what he has done, but in the meantime? And M. Roux, of all men! When we were so fortunate as to get him, and he made himself so unreservedly agreeable, and I fancied that, in his way, Arthur quite admired him. My dear, you have no idea what that speech has done. Schemetzkin and Herr Schotte have already sent me word that they must leave us tomorrow. Such a thing from a host!" Flavia paused, choked by tears of vexation and despair.

Imogen was thoroughly disconcerted; this was the first time she had ever seen Flavia betray any personal emotion which was indubitably genuine. She replied with what consolation she could. "Need they take it personally at all? It was a mere observation upon a class of people—"

"Which he knows nothing whatever about, and with whom he has no sympathy," interrupted Flavia. "Ah, my dear, you could not be *expected* to understand. You can't realize, knowing Arthur as you do, his entire lack of any aesthetic sense whatever. He is absolutely *nil*, stone deaf and stark blind, on that side. He doesn't mean to be brutal, it is just the brutality of utter ignorance. They always feel it—they are so sensitive to unsympathetic influences, you know; they know it the moment they come into the house. I have spent my life apologizing for him and struggling to conceal it; but in spite of me, he wounds them; his very attitude, even in silence, offends them. Heavens! Do I not know? Is it not perpetually and forever wounding me? But there has never been anything so dreadful as this—never! If I could conceive of any possible motive, even!"

"But, surely, Mrs. Hamilton, it was, after all, a mere expression of opinion, such as we are any of us likely to venture upon any subject whatever. It was neither more personal nor more extravagant than many of M. Roux's remarks."

"But, Imogen, certainly M. Roux has the right. It is a part of his art, and that is altogether another matter. Oh, this is not the only instance!" continued Flavia passionately, "I've always had that narrow, bigoted prejudice to contend with. It has always held me back. But this—!"

"I think you mistake his attitude," replied Imogen, feeling a flush that made her ears tingle. "That is, I fancy he is more appreciative than he seems. A man can't be very demonstrative about those things—not if he is a real man. I should not think you would care much about saving the feelings of people who are too narrow to admit of any other point of view than their own." She stopped, finding herself in the impossible position of attempting to explain Hamilton to his wife; a task which, if once begun, would necessitate an entire course of enlightenment which she doubted Flavia's ability to receive, and which she could offer only with very poor grace.

"That's just where it stings most"—here Flavia began pacing the floor—"it is just because they have all shown such tolerance and have treated Arthur with such unfailing consideration that I can find no reasonable pretext for his rancor. How can he fail to see the value of such friendships on the children's account, if for nothing else! What an advantage for them to grow up among such associations! Even though he cares nothing about these things himself he might realize that. Is there nothing I could say by way of explanation? To them, I mean? If someone were to explain to them how unfortunately limited he is in these things—"

"I'm afraid I cannot advise you," said Imogen decidedly, "but that, at least, seems to me impossible."

Flavia took her hand and glanced at her affectionately, nodding nervously. "Of course, dear girl, I can't ask you to be quite frank with me. Poor child, you are trembling and your hands are icy. Poor Arthur! But you must not judge him by this altogether; think how much he misses in life. What a cruel shock you've had. I'll send you some sherry, Good night, my dear."

When Flavia shut the door Imogen burst into a fit of nervous weeping.

Next morning she awoke after a troubled and restless night. At eight o'clock Miss Broadwood entered in a red and white striped bathrobe.

"Up, up, and see the great doom's image!" she cried, her eyes sparkling with excitement. "The hall is full of trunks, they are packing. What bolt has fallen? It's you, *ma cherie*, you've brought Ulysses home again and the slaughter has begun!" she blew a cloud of smoke triumphantly from her lips and threw herself into a chair beside the bed.

Imogen, rising on her elbow, plunged excitedly into the story of the Roux interview, which Miss Broadwood heard with the keenest interest, frequently interrupting her with exclamations of delight. When Imogen reached the dramatic scene which terminated in the destruction of the newspaper, Miss Broadwood rose and took a turn about the room, violently switching the tasselled cords of her bathrobe.

"Stop a moment," she cried, "you mean to tell me that he had such a heaven-sent means to bring her to her senses and didn't use it—that he held such a weapon and threw it away?"

"Use it?" cried Imogen unsteadily. "Of course he didn't! He bared his back to the tormentor, signed himself over to punishment in that speech he made at dinner, which everyone understands but Flavia. She was here for an hour last night and disregarded every limit of taste in her maledictions."

"My dear!" cried Miss Broadwood, catching her hand in inordinate delight at the situation, "do you see what he has done? There'll be no end to it. Why he has sacrificed himself to spare the very vanity that devours him, put rancors in the vessels of his peace, and his eternal jewel given to the common enemy of man, to make them kings, the seed of Banquo kings! He is magnificent!"

"Isn't he always that?" cried Imogen hotly. "He's like a pillar of sanity and law in this house of shams and swollen vanities, where people stalk about with a sort of madhouse dignity, each one fancying himself a king or a pope. If you could have heard that woman talk of him! Why, she thinks him stupid, bigoted, blinded by middleclass prejudices. She talked about his having no aesthetic sense and insisted that her artists had always shown him tolerance. I don't know why it should get on my nerves so, I'm sure, but her stupidity and assurance are enough to drive one to the brink of collapse."

"Yes, as opposed to his singular fineness, they are calculated to do just that," said Miss Broadwood gravely, wisely ignoring Imogen's tears. "But what has been is nothing to what will be. Just wait until Flavia's black swans have flown! You ought not to try to stick it out; that would only make it harder for everyone. Suppose you let me telephone your mother to wire you to come home by the evening train?"

"Anything, rather than have her come at me like that again. It puts me in a perfectly impossible position, and he *is* so fine!"

"Of course it does," said Miss Broadwood sympathetically, "and there is no good to be got from facing it. I will stay because such things interest me, and Frau Lichtenfeld will stay because she has no money to get away, and Buisson will stay because he feels somewhat responsible. These complications are interesting enough to cold-blooded folk like myself who have an eye for the dramatic element, but they are distracting and demoralizing to young people with any serious purpose in life."

Miss Broadwood's counsel was all the more generous seeing that, for her, the most interesting element of this denouement would be eliminated by Imogen's departure. "If she goes now, she'll get over it," soliloquized Miss Broadwood. "If she stays, she'll be wrung for him and the hurt may go deep enough to last. I haven't the heart to see her spoiling things for herself." She telephoned Mrs. Willard and helped Imogen to pack. She even took it upon herself to break the news of Imogen's going to Arthur, who remarked, as he rolled a cigarette in his nerveless fingers:

"Right enough, too. What should she do here with old cynics like you and me, Jimmy? Seeing that she is brim full of dates and formulae and other positivisms, and is so girt about with illusions that she still casts a shadow in the sun. You've been very tender of her, haven't you? I've watched you. And to think it may all be gone when we see her next. 'The common fate of all things rare,' you know. What a good fellow you are, anyway, Jimmy," he added, putting his hands affectionately on her shoulders.

Arthur went with them to the station. Flavia was so prostrated by the concerted action of her guests that she was able to see Imogen only for a moment in her darkened sleeping chamber, where she kissed her hysterically, without lifting her head, bandaged in aromatic vinegar. On the way to the station both Arthur and Imogen threw the burden of keeping up appearances entirely upon Miss Broadwood, who blithely rose to the occasion. When Hamilton carried Imogen's bag into the car, Miss Broadwood detained her for a moment, whispering as she gave her a large, warm handclasp, "I'll come to see you when I get back to town; and, in the meantime, if you meet any of our artists, tell them you have left Caius Marius among the ruins of Carthage."

THE SCULPTOR'S FUNERAL

A group of the townspeople stood on the station siding of a little Kansas town, awaiting the coming of the night train, which was already twenty minutes overdue. The snow had fallen thick over everything; in the pale starlight the line of bluffs across the wide, white meadows south of the town made soft, smoke-colored curves against the clear sky. The men on the siding stood first on one foot and then on the other, their hands thrust deep into their trousers pockets, their overcoats open, their shoulders screwed up with the cold; and they glanced from time to time toward the southeast, where the railroad track wound along the river shore. They conversed in low tones and moved about restlessly, seeming uncertain as to what was expected of them. There was but one of the company who looked as though he knew exactly why he was there; and he kept conspicuously apart; walking to the far end of the platform, returning to the station door, then pacing up the track again, his chin sunk in the high collar of his overcoat, his burly shoulders drooping forward, his gait heavy and dogged. Presently he was approached by a tall, spare, grizzled man clad in a faded Grand Army suit, who shuffled out from the group and advanced with a certain deference, craning his neck forward until his back made the angle of a jackknife three-quarters open.

"I reckon she's agoin' to be pretty late ag'in tonight, Jim," he remarked in a squeaky falsetto. "S'pose it's the snow?"

"I don't know," responded the other man with a shade of annoyance, speaking from out an astonishing cataract of red beard that grew fiercely and thickly in all directions.

The spare man shifted the quill toothpick he was chewing to the other side of his mouth. "It ain't likely that anybody from the East will come with the corpse, I s'pose," he went on reflectively.

"I don't know," responded the other, more curtly than before.

"It's too bad he didn't belong to some lodge or other. I like an order funeral myself. They seem more appropriate for people of some reputation," the spare man continued, with an ingratiating concession in his shrill voice, as he carefully placed his toothpick in his vest pocket. He always carried the flag at the G. A. R. funerals in the town.

The heavy man turned on his heel, without replying, and walked up the siding. The spare man shuffled back to the uneasy group. "Jim's ez full ez a tick, ez ushel," he commented commiseratingly.

Just then a distant whistle sounded, and there was a shuffling of feet on the platform. A number of lanky boys of all ages appeared as suddenly and slimily as eels wakened by the crack of thunder; some came from the waiting room, where they had been warming themselves by the red stove, or half-asleep on the slat benches; others uncoiled themselves from baggage trucks or slid out of express wagons. Two clambered down from the driver's seat of a hearse that stood backed up against the siding. They straightened their stooping shoulders and lifted their heads, and a flash of momentary animation kindled their dull eyes at that cold, vibrant scream, the world-wide call for men. It stirred them like the note of a trumpet; just as it had often stirred the man who was coming home tonight, in his boyhood.

The night express shot, red as a rocket, from out the eastward marsh lands and wound along the river shore under the long lines of shivering poplars that sentineled the meadows, the escaping steam hanging in gray masses against the pale sky and blotting out the Milky Way. In a moment the red glare from the headlight streamed up the snow-covered track before the siding and glittered on the wet, black rails. The burly man with the disheveled red beard walked swiftly up the platform toward the approaching train, uncovering his head as he went. The group of men behind him hesitated, glanced questioningly at one another, and awkwardly followed his example. The train stopped, and the crowd shuffled up to the express car just as the door was thrown open, the spare man in the G. A. B. suit thrusting his head forward with curiosity. The express messenger appeared in the doorway, accompanied by a young man in a long ulster and traveling cap.

"Are Mr. Merrick's friends here?" inquired the young man.

The group on the platform swayed and shuffled uneasily. Philip Phelps, the banker, responded with dignity: "We have come to take charge of the body. Mr. Merrick's father is very feeble and can't be about."

"Send the agent out here," growled the express messenger, "and tell the operator to lend a hand."

The coffin was got out of its rough box and down on the snowy platform. The townspeople drew back enough to make room for it and then formed a close semicircle about it, looking curiously at the palm leaf which lay across the black cover. No one said anything. The baggage man stood by his truck, waiting to get at the trunks. The engine panted heavily, and the fireman dodged in and out among the wheels with his yellow torch and long oilcan, snapping the spindle boxes. The young Bostonian, one of the dead sculptor's pupils who had come with the body, looked about him helplessly. He turned to the banker, the only one of that black, uneasy, stoop-shouldered group who seemed enough of an individual to be addressed.

"None of Mr. Merrick's brothers are here?" he asked uncertainly.

The man with the red heard for the first time stepped up and joined the group. "No, they have not come yet; the family is scattered. The body will be taken directly to the house." He stooped and took hold of one of the handles of the coffin.

"Take the long hill road up, Thompson—it will be easier on the horses," called the liveryman as the undertaker snapped the door of the hearse and prepared to mount to the driver's seat.

Laird, the red-bearded lawyer, turned again to the stranger: "We didn't know whether there would be anyone with him or not," he explained. "It's a long walk, so you'd better go up in the hack." He pointed to a single, battered conveyance, but the young man replied stiffly: "Thank you, but I think I will go up with the hearse. If you don't object," turning to the undertaker, "I'll ride with you."

They clambered up over the wheels and drove off in the starlight tip the long, white hill toward the town. The lamps in the still village were shining from under the low, snow-burdened roofs; and beyond, on every side, the plains reached out into emptiness, peaceful and wide as the soft sky itself, and wrapped in a tangible, white silence.

When the hearse backed up to a wooden sidewalk before a naked, weatherbeaten frame house, the same composite,

59

ill-defined group that had stood upon the station siding was huddled about the gate. The front yard was an icy swamp, and a couple of warped planks, extending from the sidewalk to the door, made a sort of rickety footbridge. The gate hung on one hinge and was opened wide with difficulty. Steavens, the young stranger, noticed that something black was tied to the knob of the front door.

The grating sound made by the casket, as it was drawn from the hearse, was answered by a scream from the house; the front door was wrenched open, and a tall, corpulent woman rushed out bareheaded into the snow and flung herself upon the coffin, shrieking: "My boy, my boy! And this is how you've come home to me!"

As Steavens turned away and closed his eyes with a shudder of unutterable repulsion, another woman, also tall, but flat and angular, dressed entirely in black, darted out of the house and caught Mrs. Merrick by the shoulders, crying sharply: "Come, come, Mother; you mustn't go on like this!" Her tone changed to one of obsequious solemnity as she turned to the banker: "The parlor is ready, Mr. Phelps."

The bearers carried the coffin along the narrow boards, while the undertaker ran ahead with the coffin-rests. They bore it into a large, unheated room that smelled of dampness and disuse and furniture polish, and set it down under a hanging lamp ornamented with jingling glass prisms and before a "Rogers group" of John Alden and Priscilla, wreathed with smilax. Henry Steavens stared about him with the sickening conviction that there had been some horrible mistake, and that he had somehow arrived at the wrong destination. He looked painfully about over the clover-green Brussels, the fat plush upholstery, among the hand-painted china plaques and panels, and vases, for some mark of identification, for something that might once conceivably have belonged to Harvey Merrick. It was not until he recognized his friend in the crayon portrait of a little boy in kilts and curls hanging above the piano that he felt willing to let any of these people approach the coffin.

"Take the lid off, Mr. Thompson; let me see my boy's face," wailed the elder woman between her sobs. This time Steavens looked fearfully, almost beseechingly into her face, red and swollen under its masses of strong, black, shiny hair. He flushed, dropped his eyes, and then, almost incredulously, looked again. There was a kind of power about her face— a kind of brutal handsomeness, even, but it was scarred and furrowed by violence, and so colored and coarsened by fiercer passions that grief seemed never to have laid a gentle finger there. The long nose was distended and knobbed at the end, and there were deep lines on either side of it; her heavy, black brows almost met across her forehead; her teeth were large and square and set far apart—teeth that could tear. She filled the room; the men were obliterated, seemed tossed about like twigs in an angry water, and even Steavens felt himself being drawn into the whirlpool.

The daughter—the tall, rawboned woman in crepe, with a mourning comb in her hair which curiously lengthened her long face sat stiffly upon the sofa, her hands, conspicuous for their large knuckles, folded in her lap, her mouth and eyes drawn down, solemnly awaiting the opening of the coffin. Near the door stood a mulatto woman, evidently a servant in the house, with a timid bearing and an emaciated face pitifully sad and gentle. She was weeping silently, the corner of her calico apron lifted to her eyes, occasionally suppressing a long, quivering sob. Steavens walked over and stood beside her.

Feeble steps were heard on the stairs, and an old man, tall and frail, odorous of pipe smoke, with shaggy, unkept gray hair and a dingy beard, tobacco stained about the mouth, entered uncertainly. He went slowly up to the coffin and stood, rolling a blue cotton handkerchief between his hands, seeming so pained and embarrassed by his wife's orgy of grief that he had no consciousness of anything else.

"There, there, Annie, dear, don't take on so," he quavered timidly, putting out a shaking hand and awkwardly patting her elbow. She turned with a cry and sank upon his shoulder with such violence that he tottered a little. He did not even glance toward the coffin, but continued to look at her with a dull, frightened, appealing expression, as a spaniel looks at the whip. His sunken cheeks slowly reddened and burned with miserable shame. When his wife rushed from the room her daughter strode after her with set lips. The servant stole up to the coffin, bent over it for a moment, and then slipped away to the kitchen, leaving Steavens, the lawyer, and the father to themselves. The old man stood trembling and looking down at his dead son's face. The sculptor's splendid head seemed even more noble in its rigid stillness than in life. The dark hair had crept down upon the wide forehead; the face seemed strangely long, but in it there was not that beautiful and chaste repose which we expect to find in the faces of the dead. The brows were so drawn that there were two deep lines above the beaked nose, and the chin was thrust forward defiantly. It was as though the strain of life had been so sharp and bitter that death could not at once wholly relax the tension and smooth the countenance into perfect peace— as though he were still guarding something precious and holy, which might even yet be wrested from him.

The old man's lips were working under his stained beard. He turned to the lawyer with timid deference: "Phelps and the rest are comin' back to set up with Harve, ain't they?" he asked. "Thank 'ee, Jim, thank 'ee." He brushed the hair back gently from his son's forehead. "He was a good boy, Jim; always a good boy. He was ez gentle ez a child and the kindest of 'em all—only we didn't none of us ever onderstand him." The tears trickled slowly down his beard and dropped upon the sculptor's coat.

"Martin, Martin. Oh, Martin! come here," his wife wailed from the top of the stairs. The old man started timorously: "Yes, Annie, I'm coming." He turned away, hesitated stood for a moment in miserable indecision; then he reached back and patted the dead man's hair softly, and stumbled from the room.

"Poor old man, I didn't think he had any tears left. Seems as if his eyes would have gone dry long ago. At his age nothing cuts very deep," remarked the lawyer.

Something in his tone made Steavens glance up. While the mother had been in the room the young man had scarcely seen anyone else; but now, from the moment he first glanced into Jim Laird's florid face and bloodshot eyes, he knew that he had found what he had been heartsick at not finding before—the feeling, the understanding, that must exist in someone, even here.

The man was red as his beard, with features swollen and blurred by dissipation, and a hot, blazing blue eye. His face was strained—that of a man who is controlling himself with difficulty—and he kept plucking at his beard with a sort of fierce resentment. Steavens, sitting by the window, watched him turn down the glaring lamp, still its jangling pendants with an angry gesture, and then stand with his hands locked behind him, staring down into the master's face. He could not help wondering what link there could have been between the porcelain vessel and so sooty a lump of potter's clay.

From the kitchen an uproar was sounding; when the dining-room door opened the import of it was clear. The mother was abusing the maid for having forgotten to make the dressing for the chicken salad which had been prepared for the watchers. Steavens had never heard anything in the least like it; it was injured, emotional, dramatic abuse, unique and masterly in its excruciating cruelty, as violent and unrestrained as had been her grief of twenty minutes before. With a shudder of disgust the lawyer went into the dining room and closed the door into the kitchen.

"Poor Roxy's getting it now," he remarked when he came back. "The Merricks took her out of the poorhouse years ago; and if her loyalty would let her, I guess the poor old thing could tell tales that would curdle your blood. She's the mulatto woman who was standing in here a while ago, with her apron to her eyes. The old woman is a fury; there never was anybody like her for demonstrative piety and ingenious cruelty. She made Harvey's life a hell for him when he lived at home; he was so sick ashamed of it. I never could see how he kept himself so sweet."

"He was wonderful," said Steavens slowly, "wonderful; but until tonight I have never known how wonderful."

"That is the true and eternal wonder of it, anyway; that it can come even from such a dung heap as this," the lawyer cried, with a sweeping gesture which seemed to indicate much more than the four walls within which they stood.

"I think I'll see whether I can get a little air. The room is so close I am beginning to feel rather faint," murmured Steavens, struggling with one of the windows. The sash was stuck, however, and would not yield, so he sat down dejectedly and began pulling at his collar. The lawyer came over, loosened the sash with one blow of his red fist, and sent the window up a few inches. Steavens thanked him, but the nausea which had been gradually climbing into his throat for the last half-hour left him with but one desire—a desperate feeling that he must get away from this place with what was left of Harvey Merrick. Oh, he comprehended well enough now the quiet bitterness of the smile that he had seen so often on his master's lips!

He remembered that once, when Merrick returned from a visit home, he brought with him a singularly feeling and suggestive bas-relief of a thin, faded old woman, sitting and sewing something pinned to her knee; while a full-lipped, full-blooded little urchin, his trousers held up by a single gallows, stood beside her, impatiently twitching her gown to call her attention to a butterfly he had caught. Steavens, impressed by the tender and delicate modeling of the thin, tired face, had asked him if it were his mother. He remembered the dull flush that had burned up in the sculptor's face.

The lawyer was sitting in a rocking chair beside the coffin, his head thrown back and his eyes closed. Steavens looked at him earnestly, puzzled at the line of the chin, and wondering why a man should conceal a feature of such distinction under that disfiguring shock of beard. Suddenly, as though he felt the young sculptor's keen glance, he opened his eyes.

"Was he always a good deal of an oyster?" he asked abruptly. "He was terribly shy as a boy."

"Yes, he was an oyster, since you put it so," rejoined Steavens. "Although he could be very fond of people, he always gave one the impression of being detached. He disliked violent emotion; he was reflective, and rather distrustful of himself—except, of course, as regarded his work. He was surefooted enough there. He distrusted men pretty thoroughly and women even more, yet somehow without believing ill of them. He was determined, indeed, to believe the best, but he seemed afraid to investigate."

"A burnt dog dreads the fire," said the lawyer grimly, and closed his eyes.

Steavens went on and on, reconstructing that whole miserable boyhood. All this raw, biting ugliness had been the portion of the man whose tastes were refined beyond the limits of the reasonable—whose mind was an exhaustless gallery of beautiful impressions, and so sensitive that the mere shadow of a poplar leaf flickering against a sunny wall would be etched and held there forever. Surely, if ever a man had the magic word in his fingertips, it was Merrick. Whatever he touched, he revealed its holiest secret; liberated it from enchantment and restored it to its pristine loveliness, like the Arabian prince who fought the enchantress spell for spell. Upon whatever he had come in contact with, he had left a beautiful record of the experience—a sort of ethereal signature; a scent, a sound, a color that was his own.

Steavens understood now the real tragedy of his master's life; neither love nor wine, as many had conjectured, but a blow which had fallen earlier and cut deeper than these could have done—a shame not his, and yet so unescapably his, to bide in his heart from his very boyhood. And without—the frontier warfare; the yearning of a boy, cast ashore upon a desert of newness and ugliness and sordidness, for all that is chastened and old, and noble with traditions.

At eleven o'clock the tall, flat woman in black crepe entered, announced that the watchers were arriving, and asked them "to step into the dining room." As Steavens rose the lawyer said dryly: "You go on—it'll be a good experience for you, doubtless; as for me, I'm not equal to that crowd tonight; I've had twenty years of them."

As Steavens closed the door after him be glanced back at the lawyer, sitting by the coffin in the dim light, with his chin resting on his hand.

The same misty group that had stood before the door of the express car shuffled into the dining room. In the light of the kerosene lamp they separated and became individuals. The minister, a pale, feeble-looking man with white hair and blond chin-whiskers, took his seat beside a small side table and placed his Bible upon it. The Grand Army man sat down behind the stove and tilted his chair back comfortably against the wall, fishing his quill toothpick from his waistcoat pocket. The two bankers, Phelps and Elder, sat off in a corner behind the dinner table, where they could finish their discussion of the new usury law and its effect on chattel security loans. The real estate agent, an old man with a smiling, hypocritical face, soon joined them. The coal-and-lumber dealer and the cattle shipper sat on opposite sides of the hard coal-burner, their feet on the nickelwork. Steavens took a book from his pocket and began to read. The talk around him ranged through various topics of local interest while the house was quieting down. When it was clear that the members of the family were in bed the Grand Army man hitched his shoulders and, untangling his long legs, caught his heels on the rounds of his chair.

"S'pose there'll be a will, Phelps?" he queried in his weak falsetto.

The banker laughed disagreeably and began trimming his nails with a pearl-handled pocketknife.

"There'll scarcely be any need for one, will there?" he queried in his turn.

The restless Grand Army man shifted his position again, getting his knees still nearer his chin. "Why, the ole man says Harve's done right well lately," he chirped.

The other banker spoke up. "I reckon he means by that Harve ain't asked him to mortgage any more farms lately, so as he could go on with his education."

"Seems like my mind don't reach back to a time when Harve wasn't bein' edycated," tittered the Grand Army man.

There was a general chuckle. The minister took out his handkerchief and blew his nose sonorously. Banker Phelps closed his knife with a snap. "It's too bad the old man's sons didn't turn out better," he remarked with reflective authority. "They never hung together. He spent money enough on Harve to stock a dozen cattle farms and he might as well have poured it into Sand Creek. If Harve had stayed at home and helped nurse what little they had, and gone into stock on the old man's bottom farm, they might all have been well fixed. But the old man had to trust everything to tenants and was cheated right and left."

"Harve never could have handled stock none," interposed the cattleman. "He hadn't it in him to be sharp. Do you remember when he bought Sander's mules for eight-year-olds, when everybody in town knew that Sander's father-in-law give 'em to his wife for a wedding present eighteen years before, an' they was full-grown mules then."

Everyone chuckled, and the Grand Army man rubbed his knees with a spasm of childish delight.

"Harve never was much account for anything practical, and he shore was never fond of work," began the coal-and-lumber dealer. "I mind the last time he was home; the day he left, when the old man was out to the barn helpin' his hand hitch up to take Harve to the train, and Cal Moots was patchin' up the fence, Harve, he come out on the step and sings out, in his ladylike voice: 'Cal Moots, Cal Moots! please come cord my trunk.'"

"That's Harve for you," approved the Grand Army man gleefully. "I kin hear him howlin' yet when he was a big feller in long pants and his mother used to whale him with a rawhide in the barn for lettin' the cows git foundered in the cornfield when he was drivin' 'em home from pasture. He killed a cow of mine that-a-way onc't—a pure Jersey and the best milker I had, an' the ole man had to put up for her. Harve, he was watchin' the sun set acros't the marshes when the anamile got away; he argued that sunset was oncommon fine."

"Where the old man made his mistake was in sending the boy East to school," said Phelps, stroking his goatee and speaking in a deliberate, judicial tone. "There was where he got his head full of traipsing to Paris and all such folly. What Harve needed, of all people, was a course in some first-class Kansas City business college."

The letters were swimming before Steavens's eyes. Was it possible that these men did not understand, that the palm on the coffin meant nothing to them? The very name of their town would have remained forever buried in the postal guide had it not been now and again mentioned in the world in connection with Harvey Merrick's. He remembered what his master had said to him on the day of his death, after the congestion of both lungs had shut off any probability of recovery, and the sculptor had asked his pupil to send his body home. "It's not a pleasant place to be lying while the world is moving and doing and bettering," he had said with a feeble smile, "but it rather seems as though we ought to go back to the place we came from in the end. The townspeople will come in for a look at me; and after they have had their say I shan't have much to fear from the judgment of God. The wings of the Victory, in there"—with a weak gesture toward his studio—"will not shelter me."

The cattleman took up the comment. "Forty's young for a Merrick to cash in; they usually hang on pretty well. Probably he helped it along with whisky."

"His mother's people were not long-lived, and Harvey never had a robust constitution," said the minister mildly. He would have liked to say more. He had been the boy's Sunday-school teacher, and had been fond of him; but he felt that he was not in a position to speak. His own sons had turned out badly, and it was not a year since one of them had made his last trip home in the express car, shot in a gambling house in the Black Hills.

"Nevertheless, there is no disputin' that Harve frequently looked upon the wine when it was red, also variegated, and it shore made an oncommon fool of him," moralized the cattleman.

Just then the door leading into the parlor rattled loudly, and everyone started involuntarily, looking relieved when only Jim Laird came out. His red face was convulsed with anger, and the Grand Army man ducked his head when he saw the spark in his blue, bloodshot eye. They were all afraid of Jim; he was a drunkard, but he could twist the law to suit his client's needs as no other man in all western Kansas could do; and there were many who tried. The lawyer closed the door gently behind him, leaned back against it and folded his arms, cocking his head a little to one side. When he assumed this attitude in the courtroom, ears were always pricked up, as it usually foretold a flood of withering sarcasm.

"I've been with you gentlemen before," he began in a dry, even tone, "when you've sat by the coffins of boys born and raised in this town; and, if I remember rightly, you were never any too well satisfied when you checked them up. What's the matter, anyhow? Why is it that reputable young men are as scarce as millionaires in Sand City? It might almost seem to a stranger that there was some way something the matter with your progressive town. Why did Ruben Sayer, the brightest young lawyer you ever turned out, after he had come home from the university as straight as a die, take to drinking and forge a check and shoot himself? Why did Bill Merrit's son die of the shakes in a saloon in Omaha? Why was Mr. Thomas's son, here, shot in a gambling house? Why did young Adams burn his mill to beat the insurance companies and go to the pen?"

The lawyer paused and unfolded his arms, laying one clenched fist quietly on the table. "I'll tell you why. Because you drummed nothing but money and knavery into their ears from the time they wore knickerbockers; because you carped away at them as you've been carping here tonight, holding our friends Phelps and Elder up to them for their models, as our grandfathers held up George Washington and John Adams. But the boys, worse luck, were young and raw at the business you put them to; and how could they match coppers with such artists as Phelps and Elder? You wanted them to be successful rascals; they were only unsuccessful ones—that's all the difference. There was only one boy ever raised in this borderland between ruffianism and civilization who didn't come to grief, and you hated Harvey Merrick more for winning out than you hated all the other boys who got under the wheels. Lord, Lord, how you did hate him! Phelps, here, is fond of saying that he could buy and sell us all out any time he's a mind to; but he knew Harve wouldn't have given a tinker's damn for his bank and all his cattle farms put together; and a lack of appreciation, that way, goes hard with Phelps.

"Old Nimrod, here, thinks Harve drank too much; and this from such as Nimrod and me!"

"Brother Elder says Harve was too free with the old man's money—fell short in filial consideration, maybe. Well, we can all remember the very tone in which brother Elder swore his own father was a liar, in the county court; and we all know that the old man came out of that partnership with his son as bare as a sheared lamb. But maybe I'm getting personal, and I'd better be driving ahead at what I want to say."

The lawyer paused a moment, squared his heavy shoulders, and went on: "Harvey Merrick and I went to school together, back East. We were dead in earnest, and we wanted you all to be proud of us some day. We meant to be great men. Even I, and I haven't lost my sense of humor, gentlemen, I meant to be a great man. I came back here to practice, and I found you didn't in the least want me to be a great man. You wanted me to be a shrewd lawyer—oh, yes! Our veteran here wanted me to get him an increase of pension, because he had dyspepsia; Phelps wanted a new county survey that would put the widow Wilson's little bottom farm inside his south line; Elder wanted to lend money at 5 per cent a month and get it collected; old Stark here wanted to wheedle old women up in Vermont into investing their annuities in real estate mortgages that are not worth the paper they are written on. Oh, you needed me hard enough, and you'll go on needing me; and that's why I'm not afraid to plug the truth home to you this once.

"Well, I came back here and became the damned shyster you wanted me to be. You pretend to have some sort of respect for me; and yet you'll stand up and throw mud at Harvey Merrick, whose soul you couldn't dirty and whose hands you couldn't tie. Oh, you're a discriminating lot of Christians! There have been times when the sight of Harvey's name in some Eastern paper has made me hang my head like a whipped dog; and, again, times when I liked to think of him off there in the world, away from all this hog wallow, doing his great work and climbing the big, clean upgrade he'd set for himself.

"And we? Now that we've fought and lied and sweated and stolen, and hated as only the disappointed strugglers in a bitter, dead little Western town know how to do, what have we got to show for it? Harvey Merrick wouldn't have given one sunset over your marshes for all you've got put together, and you know it. It's not for me to say why, in the inscrutable wisdom of God, a genius should ever have been called from this place of hatred and bitter waters; but I want this Boston man to know that the drivel he's been hearing here tonight is the only tribute any truly great man could ever have from such a lot of sick, side-tracked, burnt-dog, land-poor sharks as the here-present financiers of Sand City—upon which town may God have mercy!"

The lawyer thrust out his hand to Steavens as he passed him, caught up his overcoat in the hall, and had left the house before the Grand Army man had had time to lift his ducked head and crane his long neck about at his fellows.

Next day Jim Laird was drunk and unable to attend the funeral services. Steavens called twice at his office, but was compelled to start East without seeing him. He had a presentiment that he would hear from him again, and left his address on the lawyer's table; but if Laird found it, he never acknowledged it. The thing in him that Harvey Merrick had loved must have gone underground with Harvey Merrick's coffin; for it never spoke again, and Jim got the cold he died of driving across the Colorado mountains to defend one of Phelps's sons, who had got into trouble out there by cutting government timber.

"A DEATH IN THE DESERT"

Everett Hilgarde was conscious that the man in the seat across the aisle was looking at him intently. He was a large, florid man, wore a conspicuous diamond solitaire upon his third finger, and Everett judged him to be a traveling salesman of some sort. He had the air of an adaptable fellow who had been about the world and who could keep cool and clean under almost any circumstances.

The "High Line Flyer," as this train was derisively called among railroad men, was jerking along through the hot afternoon over the monotonous country between Holdridge and Cheyenne. Besides the blond man and himself the only occupants of the car were two dusty, bedraggled-looking girls who had been to the Exposition at Chicago, and who were earnestly discussing the cost of their first trip out of Colorado. The four uncomfortable passengers were covered with a sediment of fine, yellow dust which clung to their hair and eyebrows like gold powder. It blew up in clouds from the bleak, lifeless country through which they passed, until they were one color with the sagebrush and sandhills. The gray-and-yellow desert was varied only by occasional ruins of deserted towns, and the little red boxes of station houses, where the spindling trees and sickly vines in the bluegrass yards made little green reserves fenced off in that confusing wilderness of sand.

As the slanting rays of the sun beat in stronger and stronger through the car windows, the blond gentleman asked the ladies' permission to remove his coat, and sat in his lavender striped shirt sleeves, with a black silk handkerchief tucked carefully about his collar. He had seemed interested in Everett since they had boarded the train at Holdridge, and kept glancing at him curiously and then looking reflectively out of the window, as though he were trying to recall something. But wherever Everett went someone was almost sure to look at him with that curious interest, and it had ceased to embarrass or annoy him. Presently the stranger, seeming satisfied with his observation, leaned back in his seat, half-closed his eyes, and began softly to whistle the "Spring Song" from *Proserpine*, the cantata that a dozen years before had made its young composer famous in a night. Everett had heard that air on guitars in Old Mexico, on mandolins at college glees, on cottage organs in New England hamlets, and only two weeks ago he had heard it played on sleighbells at a variety theater in Denver. There was literally no way of escaping his brother's precocity. Adriance could live on the other side of the Atlantic, where his youthful indiscretions were forgotten in his mature achievements, but his brother had never been able to outrun *Proserpine*, and here he found it again in the Colorado sand hills. Not that Everett was exactly ashamed of *Proserpine*; only a man of genius could have written it, but it was the sort of thing that a man of genius outgrows as soon as he can.

Everett unbent a trifle and smiled at his neighbor across the aisle. Immediately the large man rose and, coming over, dropped into the seat facing Hilgarde, extending his card.

"Dusty ride, isn't it? I don't mind it myself; I'm used to it. Born and bred in de briar patch, like Br'er Rabbit. I've been trying to place you for a long time; I think I must have met you before."

"Thank you," said Everett, taking the card; "my name is Hilgarde. You've probably met my brother, Adriance; people often mistake me for him."

The traveling man brought his hand down upon his knee with such vehemence that the solitaire blazed.

"So I was right after all, and if you're not Adriance Hilgarde, you're his double. I thought I couldn't be mistaken. Seen him? Well, I guess! I never missed one of his recitals at the Auditorium, and he played the piano score of *Proserpine* through to us once at the Chicago Press Club. I used to be on the *Commercial* there before I began to travel for the publishing department of the concern. So you're Hilgarde's brother, and here I've run into you at the jumping-off place. Sounds like a newspaper yarn, doesn't it?"

The traveling man laughed and offered Everett a cigar, and plied him with questions on the only subject that people ever seemed to care to talk to Everett about. At length the salesman and the two girls alighted at a Colorado way station, and Everett went on to Cheyenne alone.

The train pulled into Cheyenne at nine o'clock, late by a matter of four hours or so; but no one seemed particularly concerned at its tardiness except the station agent, who grumbled at being kept in the office overtime on a summer night. When Everett alighted from the train he walked down the platform and stopped at the track crossing, uncertain as to what direction he should take to reach a hotel. A phaeton stood near the crossing, and a woman held the reins. She was dressed in white, and her figure was clearly silhouetted against the cushions, though it was too dark to see her face. Everett had scarcely noticed her, when the switch engine came puffing up from the opposite direction, and the headlight threw a strong glare of light on his face. Suddenly the woman in the phaeton uttered a low cry and dropped the reins. Everett started forward and caught the horse's head, but the animal only lifted its ears and whisked its tail in impatient surprise. The woman sat perfectly still, her head sunk between her shoulders and her handkerchief pressed to her face. Another woman came out of the depot and hurried toward the phaeton, crying, "Katharine, dear, what is the matter?"

Everett hesitated a moment in painful embarrassment, then lifted his hat and passed on. He was accustomed to sudden recognitions in the most impossible places, especially by women, but this cry out of the night had shaken him.

While Everett was breakfasting the next morning, the headwaiter leaned over his chair to murmur that there was a gentleman waiting to see him in the parlor. Everett finished his coffee and went in the direction indicated, where he found his visitor restlessly pacing the floor. His whole manner betrayed a high degree of agitation, though his physique was not that of a man whose nerves lie near the surface. He was something below medium height, square-shouldered and solidly built. His thick, closely cut hair was beginning to show gray about the ears, and his bronzed face was heavily lined. His square brown hands were locked behind him, and he held his shoulders like a man conscious of responsibilities; yet, as he turned to greet Everett, there was an incongruous diffidence in his address.

"Good morning, Mr. Hilgarde," he said, extending his hand; "I found your name on the hotel register. My name is Gaylord. I'm afraid my sister startled you at the station last night, Mr. Hilgarde, and I've come around to apologize."

"Ah! The young lady in the phaeton? I'm sure I didn't know whether I had anything to do with her alarm or not. If I did, it is I who owe the apology."

The man colored a little under the dark brown of his face.

"Oh, it's nothing you could help, sir, I fully understand that. You see, my sister used to be a pupil of your brother's, and it seems you favor him; and when the switch engine threw a light on your face it startled her."

Everett wheeled about in his chair. "Oh! *Katharine* Gaylord! Is it possible! Now it's you who have given me a turn. Why, I used to know her when I was a boy. What on earth—"

"Is she doing here?" said Gaylord, grimly filling out the pause. "You've got at the heart of the matter. You knew my sister had been in bad health for a long time?"

"No, I had never heard a word of that. The last I knew of her she was singing in London. My brother and I correspond infrequently and seldom get beyond family matters. I am deeply sorry to hear this. There are more reasons why I am concerned than I can tell you."

The lines in Charley Gaylord's brow relaxed a little.

"What I'm trying to say, Mr. Hilgarde, is that she wants to see you. I hate to ask you, but she's so set on it. We live several miles out of town, but my rig's below, and I can take you out anytime you can go."

"I can go now, and it will give me real pleasure to do so," said Everett, quickly. "I'll get my hat and be with you in a moment."

When he came downstairs Everett found a cart at the door, and Charley Gaylord drew a long sigh of relief as he gathered up the reins and settled back into his own element.

"You see, I think I'd better tell you something about my sister before you see her, and I don't know just where to begin. She traveled in Europe with your brother and his wife, and sang at a lot of his concerts; but I don't know just how much you know about her."

"Very little, except that my brother always thought her the most gifted of his pupils, and that when I knew her she was very young and very beautiful and turned my head sadly for a while."

Everett saw that Gaylord's mind was quite engrossed by his grief. He was wrought up to the point where his reserve and sense of proportion had quite left him, and his trouble was the one vital thing in the world. "That's the whole thing," he went on, flicking his horses with the whip.

"She was a great woman, as you say, and she didn't come of a great family. She had to fight her own way from the first. She got to Chicago, and then to New York, and then to Europe, where she went up like lightning, and got a taste for it all; and now she's dying here like a rat in a hole, out of her own world, and she can't fall back into ours. We've grown apart, some way—miles and miles apart—and I'm afraid she's fearfully unhappy."

"It's a very tragic story that you are telling me, Gaylord," said Everett. They were well out into the country now, spinning along over the dusty plains of red grass, with the ragged-blue outline of the mountains before them.

"Tragic!" cried Gaylord, starting up in his seat, "my God, man, nobody will ever know how tragic. It's a tragedy I live with and eat with and sleep with, until I've lost my grip on everything. You see she had made a good bit of money, but she spent it all going to health resorts. It's her lungs, you know. I've got money enough to send her anywhere, but the doctors all say it's no use. She hasn't the ghost of a chance. It's just getting through the days now. I had no notion she was half so bad before she came to me. She just wrote that she was all run down. Now that she's here, I think she'd be happier anywhere under the sun, but she won't leave. She says it's easier to let go of life here, and that to go East would be dying twice. There was a time when I was a brakeman with a run out of Bird City, Iowa, and she was a little thing I could carry on my shoulder, when I could get her everything on earth she wanted, and she hadn't a wish my $80 a month didn't cover; and now, when I've got a little property together, I can't buy her a night's sleep!"

Everett saw that, whatever Charley Gaylord's present status in the world might be, he had brought the brakeman's heart up the ladder with him, and the brakeman's frank avowal of sentiment. Presently Gaylord went on:

"You can understand how she has outgrown her family. We're all a pretty common sort, railroaders from away back. My father was a conductor. He died when we were kids. Maggie, my other sister, who lives with me, was a telegraph operator here while I was getting my grip on things. We had no education to speak of. I have to hire a stenographer because I can't spell straight—the Almighty couldn't teach me to spell. The things that make up life to Kate are all Greek to me, and there's scarcely a point where we touch any more, except in our recollections of the old times when we were all young and happy together, and Kate sang in a church choir in Bird City. But I believe, Mr. Hilgarde, that if she can see just one person like you, who knows about the things and people she's interested in, it will give her about the only comfort she can have now."

The reins slackened in Charley Gaylord's hand as they drew up before a showily painted house with many gables and a round tower. "Here we are," he said, turning to Everett, "and I guess we understand each other."

They were met at the door by a thin, colorless woman, whom Gaylord introduced as "my sister, Maggie." She asked her brother to show Mr. Hilgarde into the music room, where Katharine wished to see him alone.

When Everett entered the music room he gave a little start of surprise, feeling that he had stepped from the glaring Wyoming sunlight into some New York studio that he had always known. He wondered which it was of those countless studios, high up under the roofs, over banks and shops and wholesale houses, that this room resembled, and he looked incredulously out of the window at the gray plain that ended in the great upheaval of the Rockies.

The haunting air of familiarity about the room perplexed him. Was it a copy of some particular studio he knew, or was it merely the studio atmosphere that seemed so individual and poignantly reminiscent here in Wyoming? He sat down in a reading chair and looked keenly about him. Suddenly his eye fell upon a large photograph of his brother above the piano. Then it all became clear to him: this was veritably his brother's room. If it were not an exact copy of one of the many studios that Adriance had fitted up in various parts of the world, wearying of them and leaving almost before the renovator's varnish had dried, it was at least in the same tone. In every detail Adriance's taste was so manifest that the room seemed to exhale his personality.

Among the photographs on the wall there was one of Katharine Gaylord, taken in the days when Everett had known her, and when the flash of her eye or the flutter of her skirt was enough to set his boyish heart in a tumult. Even now, he stood before the portrait with a certain degree of embarrassment. It was the face of a woman already old in her first youth, thoroughly sophisticated and a trifle hard, and it told of what her brother had called her fight. The camaraderie of her frank, confident eyes was qualified by the deep lines about her mouth and the curve of the lips, which was both sad and cynical. Certainly she had more good will than confidence toward the world, and the bravado of her smile could not conceal the shadow of an unrest that was almost discontent. The chief charm of the woman, as Everett had known her, lay in her superb figure and in her eyes, which possessed a warm, lifegiving quality like the sunlight; eyes which glowed with a sort of perpetual *salutat* to the world. Her head, Everett remembered as peculiarly well-shaped and proudly poised. There had been always a little of the imperatrix about her, and her pose in the photograph revived all his old impressions of her unattachedness, of how absolutely and valiantly she stood alone.

Everett was still standing before the picture, his hands behind him and his head inclined, when he heard the door open. A very tall woman advanced toward him, holding out her hand. As she started to speak, she coughed slightly; then, laughing, said, in a low, rich voice, a trifle husky: "You see I make the traditional Camille entrance—with the cough. How good of you to come, Mr. Hilgarde."

Everett was acutely conscious that while addressing him she was not looking at him at all, and, as he assured her of his pleasure in coming, he was glad to have an opportunity to collect himself. He had not reckoned upon the ravages of a long illness. The long, loose folds of her white gown had been especially designed to conceal the sharp outlines of her emaciated body, but the stamp of her disease was there; simple and ugly and obtrusive, a pitiless fact that could not be disguised or evaded. The splendid shoulders were stooped, there was a swaying unevenness in her gait, her arms seemed disproportionately long, and her hands were transparently white and cold to the touch. The changes in her face were less obvious; the proud carriage of the head, the warm, clear eyes, even the delicate flush of color in her cheeks, all defiantly remained, though they were all in a lower key—older, sadder, softer.

She sat down upon the divan and began nervously to arrange the pillows. "I know I'm not an inspiring object to look upon, but you must be quite frank and sensible about that and get used to it at once, for we've no time to lose. And if I'm a trifle irritable you won't mind?—for I'm more than usually nervous."

"Don't bother with me this morning, if you are tired," urged Everett. "I can come quite as well tomorrow."

"Gracious, no!" she protested, with a flash of that quick, keen humor that he remembered as a part of her. "It's solitude that I'm tired to death of—solitude and the wrong kind of people. You see, the minister, not content with reading the prayers for the sick, called on me this morning. He happened to be riding by on his bicycle and felt it his duty to stop. Of course, he disapproves of my profession, and I think he takes it for granted that I have a dark past. The funniest feature of his conversation is that he is always excusing my own vocation to me—condoning it, you know—and trying to patch up my peace with my conscience by suggesting possible noble uses for what he kindly calls my talent."

Everett laughed. "Oh! I'm afraid I'm not the person to call after such a serious gentleman—I can't sustain the situation. At my best I don't reach higher than low comedy. Have you decided to which one of the noble uses you will devote yourself?"

Katharine lifted her hands in a gesture of renunciation and exclaimed: "I'm not equal to any of them, not even the least noble. I didn't study that method."

She laughed and went on nervously: "The parson's not so bad. His English never offends me, and he has read Gibbon's *Decline and Fall*, all five volumes, and that's something. Then, he has been to New York, and that's a great deal. But how we are losing time! Do tell me about New York; Charley says you're just on from there. How does it look and taste and smell just now? I think a whiff of the Jersey ferry would be as flagons of cod-liver oil to me. Who conspicuously walks the Rialto now, and what does he or she wear? Are the trees still green in Madison Square, or have they grown brown and dusty? Does the chaste Diana on the Garden Theatre still keep her vestal vows through all the exasperating changes of weather? Who has your brother's old studio now, and what misguided aspirants practice their scales in the rookeries about Carnegie Hall? What do people go to see at the theaters, and what do they eat and drink there in the world nowadays? You see, I'm homesick for it all, from the Battery to Riverside. Oh, let me die in Harlem!" She was interrupted by a violent attack of coughing, and Everett, embarrassed by her discomfort, plunged into gossip about the professional people he had met in town during the summer and the musical outlook for the winter. He was diagraming with his pencil, on the back of an old envelope he found in his pocket, some new mechanical device to be used at the Metropolitan in the production of the *Rheingold*, when he became conscious that she was looking at him intently, and that he was talking to the four walls.

Katharine was lying back among the pillows, watching him through half-closed eyes, as a painter looks at a picture. He finished his explanation vaguely enough and put the envelope back in his pocket. As he did so she said, quietly: "How wonderfully like Adriance you are!" and he felt as though a crisis of some sort had been met and tided over.

He laughed, looking up at her with a touch of pride in his eyes that made them seem quite boyish. "Yes, isn't it absurd? It's almost as awkward as looking like Napoleon—but, after all, there are some advantages. It has made some of his friends like me, and I hope it will make you."

Katharine smiled and gave him a quick, meaning glance from under her lashes. "Oh, it did that long ago. What a haughty, reserved youth you were then, and how you used to stare at people and then blush and look cross if they paid you back in your own coin. Do you remember that night when you took me home from a rehearsal and scarcely spoke a word to me?"

"It was the silence of admiration," protested Everett, "very crude and boyish, but very sincere and not a little painful. Perhaps you suspected something of the sort? I remember you saw fit to be very grown-up and worldly.

"I believe I suspected a pose; the one that college boys usually affect with singers—'an earthen vessel in love with a star,' you know. But it rather surprised me in you, for you must have seen a good deal of your brother's pupils. Or had you an omnivorous capacity, and elasticity that always met the occasion?"

"Don't ask a man to confess the follies of his youth," said Everett, smiling a little sadly; "I am sensitive about some of them even now. But I was not so sophisticated as you imagined. I saw my brother's pupils come and go, but that was about all. Sometimes I was called on to play accompaniments, or to fill out a vacancy at a rehearsal, or to order a carriage for an infuriated soprano who had thrown up her part. But they never spent any time on me, unless it was to notice the resemblance you speak of."

"Yes", observed Katharine, thoughtfully, "I noticed it then, too; but it has grown as you have grown older. That is rather strange, when you have lived such different lives. It's not merely an ordinary family likeness of feature, you know, but a sort of interchangeable individuality; the suggestion of the other man's personality in your face like an air transposed to another key. But I'm not attempting to define it; it's beyond me; something altogether unusual and a trifle—well, uncanny," she finished, laughing.

"I remember," Everett said seriously, twirling the pencil between his fingers and looking, as he sat with his head thrown back, out under the red window blind which was raised just a little, and as it swung back and forth in the wind revealed the glaring panorama of the desert—a blinding stretch of yellow, flat as the sea in dead calm, splotched here and there with deep purple shadows; and, beyond, the ragged-blue outline of the mountains and the peaks of snow, white as the white clouds—"I remember, when I was a little fellow I used to be very sensitive about it. I don't think it exactly displeased me, or that I would have had it otherwise if I could, but it seemed to me like a birthmark, or something not to be lightly spoken of. People were naturally always fonder of Ad than of me, and I used to feel the chill of reflected light pretty often. It came into even my relations with my mother. Ad went abroad to study when he was absurdly young, you know, and mother was all broken up over it. She did her whole duty by each of us, but it was sort of generally understood among us that she'd have made burnt offerings of us all for Ad any day. I was a little fellow then, and when she sat alone on the porch in the summer dusk she used sometimes to call me to her and turn my face up in the light that streamed out through the shutters and kiss me, and then I always knew she was thinking of Adriance."

"Poor little chap," said Katharine, and her tone was a trifle huskier than usual. "How fond people have always been of Adriance! Now tell me the latest news of him. I haven't heard, except through the press, for a year or more. He was in Algeria then, in the valley of the Chelif, riding horseback night and day in an Arabian costume, and in his usual enthusiastic fashion he had quite made up his mind to adopt the Mohammedan faith and become as nearly an Arab as possible. How many countries and faiths has he adopted, I wonder? Probably he was playing Arab to himself all the time. I remember he was a sixteenth-century duke in Florence once for weeks together."

"Oh, that's Adriance," chuckled Everett. "He is himself barely long enough to write checks and be measured for his clothes. I didn't hear from him while he was an Arab; I missed that."

"He was writing an Algerian suite for the piano then; it must be in the publisher's hands by this time. I have been too ill to answer his letter, and have lost touch with him."

Everett drew a letter from his pocket. "This came about a month ago. It's chiefly about his new opera, which is to be brought out in London next winter. Read it at your leisure."

"I think I shall keep it as a hostage, so that I may be sure you will come again. Now I want you to play for me. Whatever you like; but if there is anything new in the world, in mercy let me hear it. For nine months I have heard nothing but 'The Baggage Coach Ahead' and 'She Is My Baby's Mother.'"

He sat down at the piano, and Katharine sat near him, absorbed in his remarkable physical likeness to his brother and trying to discover in just what it consisted. She told herself that it was very much as though a sculptor's finished work had been rudely copied in wood. He was of a larger build than Adriance, and his shoulders were broad and heavy, while those of his brother were slender and rather girlish. His face was of the same oval mold, but it was gray and darkened about the mouth by continual shaving. His eyes were of the same inconstant April color, but they were reflective and rather dull; while Adriance's were always points of highlight, and always meaning another thing than the thing they meant yesterday. But it was hard to see why this earnest man should so continually suggest that lyric, youthful face that was as gay as his was grave. For Adriance, though he was ten years the elder, and though his hair was streaked with silver, had the face of a boy of twenty, so mobile that it told his thoughts before he could put them into words. A contralto, famous for the extravagance of her vocal methods and of her affections, had once said to him that the shepherd boys who sang in the Vale of Tempe must certainly have looked like young Hilgarde; and the comparison had been appropriated by a hundred shyer women who preferred to quote.

As Everett sat smoking on the veranda of the Inter-Ocean House that night, he was a victim to random recollections. His infatuation for Katharine Gaylord, visionary as it was, had been the most serious of his boyish love affairs, and had long disturbed his bachelor dreams. He was painfully timid in everything relating to the emotions, and his hurt had withdrawn him from the society of women. The fact that it was all so done and dead and far behind him, and that the woman had lived her life out since then, gave him an oppressive sense of age and loss. He bethought himself of something he had read about "sitting by the hearth and remembering the faces of women without desire," and felt himself an octogenarian.

He remembered how bitter and morose he had grown during his stay at his brother's studio when Katharine Gaylord was working there, and how he had wounded Adriance on the night of his last concert in New York. He had sat there in the box while his brother and Katharine were called back again and again after the last number, watching the roses go up over the footlights until they were stacked half as high as the piano, brooding, in his sullen boy's heart, upon the pride those two felt in each other's work—spurring each other to their best and beautifully contending in song. The footlights had seemed a hard, glittering line drawn sharply between their life and his; a circle of flame set about those splendid children of genius. He walked back to his hotel alone and sat in his window staring out on Madison Square until long after midnight, resolving to beat no more at doors that he could never enter and realizing more keenly than ever before how far this glorious world of beautiful creations lay from the paths of men like himself. He told himself that he had in common with this woman only the baser uses of life.

Everett's week in Cheyenne stretched to three, and he saw no prospect of release except through the thing he dreaded. The bright, windy days of the Wyoming autumn passed swiftly. Letters and telegrams came urging him to hasten his trip to the coast, but he resolutely postponed his business engagements. The mornings he spent on one of Charley Gaylord's ponies, or fishing in the mountains, and in the evenings he sat in his room writing letters or reading. In the afternoon he was usually at his post of duty. Destiny, he reflected, seems to have very positive notions about the sort of parts we are fitted to play. The scene changes and the compensation varies, but in the end we usually find that we have played the same class of business from first to last. Everett had been a stopgap all his life. He remembered going through a looking glass labyrinth when he was a boy and trying gallery after gallery, only at every turn to bump his nose against his own face—which, indeed, was not his own, but his brother's. No matter what his mission, east or west, by land or sea, he was sure to find himself employed in his brother's business, one of the tributary lives which helped to swell the shining current of Adriance Hilgarde's. It was not the first time that his duty had been to comfort, as best he could, one of the broken things his brother's imperious speed had cast aside and forgotten. He made no attempt to analyze the situation or to state it in exact terms; but he felt Katharine Gaylord's need for him, and he accepted it as a commission from his brother to help this woman to die. Day by day he felt her demands on him grow more imperious, her need for him grow more acute and positive; and day by day he felt that in his peculiar relation to her his own individuality played a smaller and smaller part. His power to minister to her comfort, he saw, lay solely in his link with his brother's life. He understood all that his physical resemblance meant to her. He knew that she sat by him always watching for some common trick of gesture, some familiar play of expression, some illusion of light and shadow, in which he should seem wholly Adriance. He knew that she lived upon this and that her disease fed upon it; that it sent shudders of remembrance through her and that in the exhaustion which followed this turmoil of her dying senses, she slept deep and sweet and dreamed of youth and art and days in a certain old Florentine garden, and not of bitterness and death.

The question which most perplexed him was, "How much shall I know? How much does she wish me to know?" A few days after his first meeting with Katharine Gaylord, he had cabled his brother to write her. He had merely said that she was mortally ill; he could depend on Adriance to say the right thing—that was a part of his gift. Adriance always said not only the right thing, but the opportune, graceful, exquisite thing. His phrases took the color of the moment and the then-present condition, so that they never savored of perfunctory compliment or frequent usage. He always caught the lyric essence of the moment, the poetic suggestion of every situation. Moreover, he usually did the right thing, the opportune, graceful, exquisite thing—except, when he did very cruel things—bent upon making people happy when their existence touched his, just as he insisted that his material environment should be beautiful; lavishing upon those near him all the warmth and radiance of his rich nature, all the homage of the poet and troubadour, and, when they were no longer near, forgetting—for that also was a part of Adriance's gift.

Three weeks after Everett had sent his cable, when he made his daily call at the gaily painted ranch house, he found Katharine laughing like a schoolgirl. "Have you ever thought," she said, as he entered the music room, "how much these seances of ours are like Heine's 'Florentine Nights,' except that I don't give you an opportunity to monopolize the conversation as Heine did?" She held his hand longer than usual, as she greeted him, and looked searchingly up into his face. "You are the kindest man living; the kindest," she added, softly.

Everett's gray face colored faintly as he drew his hand away, for he felt that this time she was looking at him and not at a whimsical caricature of his brother. "Why, what have I done now?" he asked, lamely. "I can't remember having sent you any stale candy or champagne since yesterday."

She drew a letter with a foreign postmark from between the leaves of a book and held it out, smiling. "You got him to write it. Don't say you didn't, for it came direct, you see, and the last address I gave him was a place in Florida. This deed shall be remembered of you when I am with the just in Paradise. But one thing you did not ask him to do, for you didn't know about it. He has sent me his latest work, the new sonata, the most ambitious thing he has ever done, and you are to play it for me directly, though it looks horribly intricate. But first for the letter; I think you would better read it aloud to me."

Everett sat down in a low chair facing the window seat in which she reclined with a barricade of pillows behind her. He opened the letter, his lashes half-veiling his kind eyes, and saw to his satisfaction that it was a long one—wonderfully tactful and tender, even for Adriance, who was tender with his valet and his stable boy, with his old gondolier and the beggar-women who prayed to the saints for him.

The letter was from Granada, written in the Alhambra, as he sat by the fountain of the Patio di Lindaraxa. The air was heavy, with the warm fragrance of the South and full of the sound of splashing, running water, as it had been in a certain old garden in Florence, long ago. The sky was one great turquoise, heated until it glowed. The wonderful Moorish arches threw graceful blue shadows all about him. He had sketched an outline of them on the margin of his notepaper. The subtleties of Arabic decoration had cast an unholy spell over him, and the brutal exaggerations of Gothic art were a bad dream, easily forgotten. The Alhambra itself had, from the first, seemed perfectly familiar to him, and he knew that he must have trod that court, sleek and brown and obsequious, centuries before Ferdinand rode into Andalusia. The letter was full of confidences about his work, and delicate allusions to their old happy days of study and comradeship, and of her own work, still so warmly remembered and appreciatively discussed everywhere he went.

As Everett folded the letter he felt that Adriance had divined the thing needed and had risen to it in his own wonderful way. The letter was consistently egotistical and seemed to him even a trifle patronizing, yet it was just what she had wanted. A strong realization of his brother's charm and intensity and power came over him; he felt the breath of that whirlwind of flame in which Adriance passed, consuming all in his path, and himself even more resolutely than he consumed others. Then he looked down at this white, burnt-out brand that lay before him. "Like him, isn't it?" she said, quietly.

"I think I can scarcely answer his letter, but when you see him next you can do that for me. I want you to tell him many things for me, yet they can all be summed up in this: I want him to grow wholly into his best and greatest self, even at the cost of the dear boyishness that is half his charm to you and me. Do you understand me?"

"I know perfectly well what you mean," answered Everett, thoughtfully. "I have often felt so about him myself. And yet it's difficult to prescribe for those fellows; so little makes, so little mars."

Katharine raised herself upon her elbow, and her face flushed with feverish earnestness. "Ah, but it is the waste of himself that I mean; his lashing himself out on stupid and uncomprehending people until they take him at their own estimate. He can kindle marble, strike fire from putty, but is it worth what it costs him?"

"Come, come," expostulated Everett, alarmed at her excitement. "Where is the new sonata? Let him speak for himself."

He sat down at the piano and began playing the first movement, which was indeed the voice of Adriance, his proper speech. The sonata was the most ambitious work he had done up to that time and marked the transition from his purely lyric vein to a deeper and nobler style. Everett played intelligently and with that sympathetic comprehension which seems peculiar to a certain lovable class of men who never accomplish anything in particular. When he had finished he turned to Katharine.

"How he has grown!" she cried. "What the three last years have done for him! He used to write only the tragedies of passion; but this is the tragedy of the soul, the shadow coexistent with the soul. This is the tragedy of effort and failure, the thing Keats called hell. This is my tragedy, as I lie here spent by the racecourse, listening to the feet of the runners as they pass me. Ah, God! The swift feet of the runners!"

She turned her face away and covered it with her straining hands. Everett crossed over to her quickly and knelt beside her. In all the days he had known her she had never before, beyond an occasional ironical jest, given voice to the bitterness of her own defeat. Her courage had become a point of pride with him, and to see it going sickened him.

"Don't do it," he gasped. "I can't stand it, I really can't, I feel it too much. We mustn't speak of that; it's too tragic and too vast."

When she turned her face back to him there was a ghost of the old, brave, cynical smile on it, more bitter than the tears she could not shed. "No, I won't be so ungenerous; I will save that for the watches of the night when I have no better company. Now you may mix me another drink of some sort. Formerly, when it was not *if* I should ever sing Brunnhilde, but quite simply when I *should* sing Brunnhilde, I was always starving myself and thinking what I might drink and what I might not. But broken music boxes may drink whatsoever they list, and no one cares whether they lose their figure. Run over that theme at the beginning again. That, at least, is not new. It was running in his head when we were in Venice years ago, and he used to drum it on his glass at the dinner table. He had just begun to work it out when the late autumn came on, and the paleness of the Adriatic oppressed him, and he decided to go to Florence for the winter, and lost touch with the theme during his illness. Do you remember those frightful days? All the people who have loved him are not strong enough to save him from himself! When I got word from Florence that he had been ill I was in Nice filling a concert engagement. His wife was hurrying to him from Paris, but I reached him first. I arrived at dusk, in a terrific storm. They had taken an old palace there for the winter, and I found him in the library—a long, dark room full of old Latin books and heavy furniture and bronzes. He was sitting by a wood fire at one end of the room, looking, oh, so worn and pale!—as he always does when he is ill, you know. Ah, it is so good that you *do* know! Even his red smoking jacket lent no color to his face. His first words were not to tell me how ill he had been, but that that morning he had been well enough to put the last strokes to the score of his *Souvenirs d'Automne*. He was as I most like to remember him: so calm and happy and tired; not gay, as he usually is, but just contented and tired with that heavenly tiredness that comes after a good work done at last. Outside, the rain poured down in torrents, and the wind moaned for the pain of all the world and sobbed in the branches of the shivering olives and about the walls of that desolated old palace. How that night comes back to me! There were no lights in the room, only the wood fire which glowed upon the hard features of the bronze Dante, like the reflection of purgatorial flames, and threw long black shadows about us; beyond us it scarcely penetrated the gloom at all, Adriance sat staring at the fire with the weariness of all his life in his eyes, and of all the other lives that must aspire and suffer to make up one such life as his. Somehow the wind with all its world-pain had got into the room, and the cold rain was in our eyes, and the wave came up in both of us at once—that awful, vague, universal pain, that cold fear of life and death and God and hope—and we were like two clinging together on a spar in midocean after the shipwreck of everything. Then we heard the front door open with a great gust of wind that shook even the walls, and the servants came running with lights, announcing that Madam had returned, *'and in the book we read no more that night.'*"

She gave the old line with a certain bitter humor, and with the hard, bright smile in which of old she had wrapped her weakness as in a glittering garment. That ironical smile, worn like a mask through so many years, had gradually changed even the lines of her face completely, and when she looked in the mirror she saw not herself, but the scathing critic, the amused observer and satirist of herself. Everett dropped his head upon his hand and sat looking at the rug. "How much you have cared!" he said.

"Ah, yes, I cared," she replied, closing her eyes with a long-drawn sigh of relief; and lying perfectly still, she went on: "You can't imagine what a comfort it is to have you know how I cared, what a relief it is to be able to tell it to someone. I used to want to shriek it out to the world in the long nights when I could not sleep. It seemed to me that I could not die with it. It demanded some sort of expression. And now that you know, you would scarcely believe how much less sharp the anguish of it is."

Everett continued to look helplessly at the floor. "I was not sure how much you wanted me to know," he said.

"Oh, I intended you should know from the first time I looked into your face, when you came that day with Charley. I flatter myself that I have been able to conceal it when I chose, though I suppose women always think that. The more observing ones may have seen, but discerning people are usually discreet and often kind, for we usually bleed a little before we begin to discern. But I wanted you to know; you are so like him that it is almost like telling him himself. At least, I feel now that he will know some day, and then I will be quite sacred from his compassion, for we none of us dare pity the dead. Since it was what my life has chiefly meant, I should like him to know. On the whole I am not ashamed of it. I have fought a good fight."

"And has he never known at all?" asked Everett, in a thick voice.

"Oh! Never at all in the way that you mean. Of course, he is accustomed to looking into the eyes of women and finding love there; when he doesn't find it there he thinks he must have been guilty of some discourtesy and is miserable about it. He has a genuine fondness for everyone who is not stupid or gloomy, or old or preternaturally ugly. Granted youth and cheerfulness, and a moderate amount of wit and some tact, and Adriance will always be glad to see you coming around the corner. I shared with the rest; shared the smiles and the gallantries and the droll little sermons. It was quite like a Sunday-school picnic; we wore our best clothes and a smile and took our turns. It was his kindness that was hardest. I have pretty well used my life up at standing punishment."

"Don't; you'll make me hate him," groaned Everett.

Katharine laughed and began to play nervously with her fan. "It wasn't in the slightest degree his fault; that is the most grotesque part of it. Why, it had really begun before I ever met him. I fought my way to him, and I drank my doom greedily enough."

Everett rose and stood hesitating. "I think I must go. You ought to be quiet, and I don't think I can hear any more just now."

She put out her hand and took his playfully. "You've put in three weeks at this sort of thing, haven't you? Well, it may never be to your glory in this world, perhaps, but it's been the mercy of heaven to me, and it ought to square accounts for a much worse life than yours will ever be."

Everett knelt beside her, saying, brokenly: "I stayed because I wanted to be with you, that's all. I have never cared about other women since I met you in New York when I was a lad. You are a part of my destiny, and I could not leave you if I would."

She put her hands on his shoulders and shook her head. "No, no; don't tell me that. I have seen enough of tragedy,

God knows. Don't show me any more just as the curtain is going down. No, no, it was only a boy's fancy, and your divine pity and my utter pitiableness have recalled it for a moment. One does not love the dying, dear friend. If some fancy of that sort had been left over from boyhood, this would rid you of it, and that were well. Now go, and you will come again tomorrow, as long as there are tomorrows, will you not?" She took his hand with a smile that lifted the mask from her soul, that was both courage and despair, and full of infinite loyalty and tenderness, as she said softly:

For ever and for ever, farewell, Cassius;
If we do meet again, why, we shall smile;
If not, why then, this parting was well made.

The courage in her eyes was like the clear light of a star to him as he went out.

On the night of Adriance Hilgarde's opening concert in Paris Everett sat by the bed in the ranch house in Wyoming, watching over the last battle that we have with the flesh before we are done with it and free of it forever. At times it seemed that the serene soul of her must have left already and found some refuge from the storm, and only the tenacious animal life were left to do battle with death. She labored under a delusion at once pitiful and merciful, thinking that she was in the Pullman on her way to New York, going back to her life and her work. When she aroused from her stupor it was only to ask the porter to waken her half an hour out of Jersey City, or to remonstrate with him about the delays and the roughness of the road. At midnight Everett and the nurse were left alone with her. Poor Charley Gaylord had lain down on a couch outside the door. Everett sat looking at the sputtering night lamp until it made his eyes ache. His head dropped forward on the foot of the bed, and he sank into a heavy, distressful slumber. He was dreaming of Adriance's concert in Paris, and of Adriance, the troubadour, smiling and debonair, with his boyish face and the touch of silver gray in his hair. He heard the applause and he saw the roses going up over the footlights until they were stacked half as high as the piano, and the petals fell and scattered, making crimson splotches on the floor. Down this crimson pathway came Adriance with his youthful step, leading his prima donna by the hand; a dark woman this time, with Spanish eyes.

The nurse touched him on the shoulder; he started and awoke. She screened the lamp with her hand. Everett saw that Katharine was awake and conscious, and struggling a little. He lifted her gently on his arm and began to fan her. She laid her hands lightly on his hair and looked into his face with eyes that seemed never to have wept or doubted. "Ah, dear Adriance, dear, dear," she whispered.

Everett went to call her brother, but when they came back the madness of art was over for Katharine.

Two days later Everett was pacing the station siding, waiting for the westbound train. Charley Gaylord walked beside him, but the two men had nothing to say to each other. Everett's bags were piled on the truck, and his step was hurried and his eyes were full of impatience, as he gazed again and again up the track, watching for the train. Gaylord's impatience was not less than his own; these two, who had grown so close, had now become painful and impossible to each other, and longed for the wrench of farewell.

As the train pulled in Everett wrung Gaylord's hand among the crowd of alighting passengers. The people of a German opera company, en route to the coast, rushed by them in frantic haste to snatch their breakfast during the stop. Everett heard an exclamation in a broad German dialect, and a massive woman whose figure persistently escaped from her stays in the most improbable places rushed up to him, her blond hair disordered by the wind, and glowing with joyful surprise she caught his coat sleeve with her tightly gloved hands.

"*Herr Gott*, Adriance, *lieber Freund*," she cried, emotionally.

Everett quickly withdrew his arm and lifted his hat, blushing. "Pardon me, madam, but I see that you have mistaken me for Adriance Hilgarde. I am his brother," he said quietly, and turning from the crestfallen singer, he hurried into the car.

THE GARDEN LODGE

When Caroline Noble's friends learned that Raymond d'Esquerre was to spend a month at her place on the Sound before he sailed to fill his engagement for the London opera season, they considered it another striking instance of the perversity of things. That the month was May, and the most mild and florescent of all the blue-and-white Mays the middle coast had known in years, but added to their sense of wrong. D'Esquerre, they learned, was ensconced in the lodge in the apple orchard, just beyond Caroline's glorious garden, and report went that at almost any hour the sound of the tenor's voice and of Caroline's crashing accompaniment could be heard floating through the open windows, out among the snowy apple boughs. The Sound, steel-blue and dotted with white sails, was splendidly seen from the windows of the lodge. The garden to the left and the orchard to the right had never been so riotous with spring, and had burst into impassioned bloom, as if to accommodate Caroline, though she was certainly the last woman to whom the witchery of Freya could be attributed; the last woman, as her friends affirmed, to at all adequately appreciate and make the most of such a setting for the great tenor.

Of course, they admitted, Caroline was musical—well, she ought to be!—but in that, as in everything, she was paramountly cool-headed, slow of impulse, and disgustingly practical; in that, as in everything else, she had herself so provokingly well in hand. Of course, it would be she, always mistress of herself in any situation, she, who would never be lifted one inch from the ground by it, and who would go on superintending her gardeners and workmen as usual—it would be she who got him. Perhaps some of them suspected that this was exactly why she did get him, and it but nettled them the more.

Caroline's coolness, her capableness, her general success, especially exasperated people because they felt that, for the most part, she had made herself what she was; that she had cold-bloodedly set about complying with the demands of life and making her position comfortable and masterful. That was why, everyone said, she had married Howard Noble. Women who did not get through life so well as Caroline, who could not make such good terms either with fortune or their husbands, who did not find their health so unfailingly good, or hold their looks so well, or manage their children so easily, or give such distinction to all they did, were fond of stamping Caroline as a materialist, and called her hard.

The impression of cold calculation, of having a definite policy, which Caroline gave, was far from a false one; but there was this to be said for her—that there were extenuating circumstances which her friends could not know.

If Caroline held determinedly to the middle course, if she was apt to regard with distrust everything which inclined toward extravagance, it was not because she was unacquainted with other standards than her own, or had never seen another side of life. She had grown up in Brooklyn, in a shabby little house under the vacillating administration of her father, a music teacher who usually neglected his duties to write orchestral compositions for which the world seemed to have no especial need. His spirit was warped by bitter vindictiveness and puerile self-commiseration, and he spent his days in scorn of the labor that brought him bread and in pitiful devotion to the labor that brought him only disappointment, writing interminable scores which demanded of the orchestra everything under heaven except melody.

It was not a cheerful home for a girl to grow up in. The mother, who idolized her husband as the music lord of the future, was left to a lifelong battle with broom and dustpan, to neverending conciliatory overtures to the butcher and grocer, to the making of her own gowns and of Caroline's, and to the delicate task of mollifying Auguste's neglected pupils.

The son, Heinrich, a painter, Caroline's only brother, had inherited all his father's vindictive sensitiveness without his capacity for slavish application. His little studio on the third floor had been much frequented by young men as unsuccessful as himself, who met there to give themselves over to contemptuous derision of this or that artist whose industry and stupidity had won him recognition. Heinrich, when he worked at all, did newspaper sketches at twenty-five dollars a week. He was too indolent and vacillating to set himself seriously to his art, too irascible and poignantly self-conscious to make a living, too much addicted to lying late in bed, to the incontinent reading of poetry, and to the use of chloral to be anything very positive except painful. At twenty-six he shot himself in a frenzy, and the whole wretched affair had effectually shattered his mother's health and brought on the decline of which she died. Caroline had been fond of him, but she felt a certain relief when he no longer wandered about the little house, commenting ironically upon its shabbiness, a Turkish cap on his head and a cigarette hanging from between his long, tremulous fingers.

After her mother's death Caroline assumed the management of that bankrupt establishment. The funeral expenses were unpaid, and Auguste's pupils had been frightened away by the shock of successive disasters and the general atmosphere of wretchedness that pervaded the house. Auguste himself was writing a symphonic poem, Icarus, dedicated to the memory of his son. Caroline was barely twenty when she was called upon to face this tangle of difficulties, but she reviewed the situation candidly. The house had served its time at the shrine of idealism; vague, distressing, unsatisfied yearnings had brought it low enough. Her mother, thirty years before, had eloped and left Germany with her music teacher, to give herself over to lifelong, drudging bondage at the kitchen range. Ever since Caroline could remember, the law in the house had been a sort of mystic worship of things distant, intangible and unattainable. The family had lived in successive ebullitions of generous enthusiasm, in talk of masters and masterpieces, only to come down to the cold facts in the case; to boiled mutton and to the necessity of turning the dining-room carpet. All these emotional pyrotechnics had ended in petty jealousies, in neglected duties, and in cowardly fear of the little grocer on the corner.

From her childhood she had hated it, that humiliating and uncertain existence, with its glib tongue and empty pockets, its poetic ideals and sordid realities, its indolence and poverty tricked out in paper roses. Even as a little girl, when vague dreams beset her, when she wanted to lie late in bed and commune with visions, or to leap and sing because the sooty little trees along the street were putting out their first pale leaves in the sunshine, she would clench her hands and go to help her mother sponge the spots from her father's waistcoat or press Heinrich's trousers. Her mother never permitted the slightest question concerning anything Auguste or Heinrich saw fit to do, but from the time Caroline could reason at all she could not help thinking that many things went wrong at home. She knew, for example, that her father's pupils ought not to be kept waiting half an hour while he discussed Schopenhauer with some bearded socialist over a dish of herrings and a spotted tablecloth. She knew that Heinrich ought not to give a dinner on Heine's birthday, when the laundress had not been paid for a month and when he frequently had to ask his mother for carfare. Certainly Caroline had served her apprenticeship to idealism and to all the embarrassing inconsistencies which it sometimes entails, and she decided to deny herself this diffuse, ineffectual answer to the sharp questions of life.

When she came into the control of herself and the house she refused to proceed any further with her musical education. Her father, who had intended to make a concert pianist of her, set this down as another item in his long list of disappointments and his grievances against the world. She was young and pretty, and she had worn turned gowns and soiled gloves and improvised hats all her life. She wanted the luxury of being like other people, of being honest from her hat to her boots, of having nothing to hide, not even in the matter of stockings, and she was willing to work for it. She rented a little studio away from that house of misfortune and began to give lessons. She managed well and was the sort of girl people liked to help. The bills were paid and Auguste went on composing, growing indignant only when she refused to insist that her pupils should study his compositions for the piano. She began to get engagements in New York to play accompaniments at song recitals. She dressed well, made herself agreeable, and gave herself a chance. She never permitted herself to look further than a step ahead, and set herself with all the strength of her will to see things as they are and meet them squarely in the broad day. There were two things she feared even more than poverty: the part of one that sets up an idol and the part of one that bows down and worships it.

When Caroline was twenty-four she married Howard Noble, then a widower of forty, who had been for ten years a power in Wall Street. Then, for the first time, she had paused to take breath. It took a substantialness as unquestionable as his; his money, his position, his energy, the big vigor of his robust person, to satisfy her that she was entirely safe. Then she relaxed a little, feeling that there was a barrier to be counted upon between her and that world of visions and quagmires and failure.

Caroline had been married for six years when Raymond d'Esquerre came to stay with them. He came chiefly because Caroline was what she was; because he, too, felt occasionally the need of getting out of Klingsor's garden, of dropping down somewhere for a time near a quiet nature, a cool head, a strong hand. The hours he had spent in the garden lodge were hours of such concentrated study as, in his fevered life, he seldom got in anywhere. She had, as he told Noble, a fine appreciation of the seriousness of work.

One evening two weeks after d'Esquerre had sailed, Caroline was in the library giving her husband an account of the work she had laid out for the gardeners. She superintended the care of the grounds herself. Her garden, indeed, had become quite a part of her; a sort of beautiful adjunct, like gowns or jewels. It was a famous spot, and Noble was very proud of it.

"What do you think, Caroline, of having the garden lodge torn down and putting a new summer house there at the end of the arbor; a big rustic affair where you could have tea served in midsummer?" he asked.

"The lodge?" repeated Caroline looking at him quickly. "Why, that seems almost a shame, doesn't it, after d'Esquerre has used it?"

Noble put down his book with a smile of amusement.

"Are you going to be sentimental about it? Why, I'd sacrifice the whole place to see that come to pass. But I don't believe you could do it for an hour together."

"I don't believe so, either," said his wife, smiling.

Noble took up his book again and Caroline went into the music room to practice. She was not ready to have the lodge torn down. She had gone there for a quiet hour every day during the two weeks since d'Esquerre had left them. It was the sheerest sentiment she had ever permitted herself. She was ashamed of it, but she was childishly unwilling to let it go.

Caroline went to bed soon after her husband, but she was not able to sleep. The night was close and warm, presaging storm. The wind had fallen, and the water slept, fixed and motionless as the sand. She rose and thrust her feet into slippers and, putting a dressing gown over her shoulders, opened the door of her husband's room; he was sleeping soundly. She went into the hall and down the stairs; then, leaving the house through a side door, stepped into the vine-covered arbor that led to the garden lodge. The scent of the June roses was heavy in the still air, and the stones that paved the path felt pleasantly cool through the thin soles of her slippers. Heat-lightning flashed continuously from the bank of clouds that had gathered over the sea, but the shore was flooded with moonlight and, beyond, the rim of the Sound lay smooth and shining. Caroline had the key of the lodge, and the door creaked as she opened it. She stepped into the long, low room radiant with the moonlight which streamed through the bow window and lay in a silvery pool along the waxed floor. Even that part of the room which lay in the shadow was vaguely illuminated; the piano, the tall candlesticks, the picture frames and white casts standing out as clearly in the half-light as did the sycamores and black poplars of the garden against the still, expectant night sky. Caroline sat down to think it all over. She had come here to do just that every day of the two weeks since d'Esquerre's departure, but, far from ever having reached a conclusion, she had succeeded only in losing her way in a maze of memories—sometimes bewilderingly confused, sometimes too acutely distinct—where there was neither path, nor clue, nor any hope of finality. She had, she realized, defeated a lifelong regimen; completely confounded herself by falling unaware and incontinently into that luxury of reverie which, even as a little girl, she had so determinedly denied herself, she had been developing with alarming celerity that part of one which sets up an idol and that part of one which bows down and worships it.

It was a mistake, she felt, ever to have asked d'Esquerre to come at all. She had an angry feeling that she had done it rather in self-defiance, to rid herself finally of that instinctive fear of him which had always troubled and perplexed her. She knew that she had reckoned with herself before he came; but she had been equal to so much that she had never really doubted she would be equal to this. She had come to believe, indeed, almost arrogantly in her own malleability and endurance; she had done so much with herself that she had come to think that there was nothing which she could not do; like swimmers, overbold, who reckon upon their strength and their power to hoard it, forgetting the ever-changing moods of their adversary, the sea.

And d'Esquerre was a man to reckon with. Caroline did not deceive herself now upon that score. She admitted it humbly enough, and since she had said good-by to him she had not been free for a moment from the sense of his formidable power. It formed the undercurrent of her consciousness; whatever she might be doing or thinking, it went on, involuntarily, like her breathing, sometimes welling up until suddenly she found herself suffocating. There was a moment of this tonight, and Caroline rose and stood shuddering, looking about her in the blue duskiness of the silent room. She had not been here at night before, and the spirit of the place seemed more troubled and insistent than ever it had in the quiet of the afternoons. Caroline brushed her hair back from her damp forehead and went over to the bow window. After raising it she sat down upon the low seat. Leaning her head against the sill, and loosening her nightgown at the throat, she half-closed her eyes and looked off into the troubled night, watching the play of the heat-lightning upon the massing clouds between the pointed tops of the poplars.

Yes, she knew, she knew well enough, of what absurdities this spell was woven; she mocked, even while she winced. His power, she knew, lay not so much in anything that he actually had—though he had so much—or in anything that he actually was, but in what he suggested, in what he seemed picturesque enough to have or be and that was just anything that one chose to believe or to desire. His appeal was all the more persuasive and alluring in that it was to the imagination alone, in that it was as indefinite and impersonal as those cults of idealism which so have their way with women. What he had was that, in his mere personality, he quickened and in a measure gratified that something without which—to women—life is no better than sawdust, and to the desire for which most of their mistakes and tragedies and astonishingly poor bargains are due.

D'Esquerre had become the center of a movement, and the Metropolitan had become the temple of a cult. When he could be induced to cross the Atlantic, the opera season in New York was successful; when he could not, the management lost money; so much everyone knew. It was understood, too, that his superb art had disproportionately little to do with his peculiar position. Women swayed the balance this way or that; the opera, the orchestra, even his own glorious art, achieved at such a cost, were but the accessories of himself; like the scenery and costumes and even the soprano, they all went to produce atmosphere, were the mere mechanics of the beautiful illusion.

Caroline understood all this; tonight was not the first time that she had put it to herself so. She had seen the same feeling in other people, watched for it in her friends, studied it in the house night after night when he sang, candidly putting herself among a thousand others.

D'Esquerre's arrival in the early winter was the signal for a feminine hegira toward New York. On the nights when he sang women flocked to the Metropolitan from mansions and hotels, from typewriter desks, schoolrooms, shops, and fitting rooms. They were of all conditions and complexions. Women of the world who accepted him knowingly as they sometimes took champagne for its agreeable effect; sisters of charity and overworked shopgirls, who received him devoutly; withered women who had taken doctorate degrees and who worshipped furtively through prism spectacles; business women and women of affairs, the Amazons who dwelt afar from men in the stony fastnesses of apartment houses. They all entered into the same romance; dreamed, in terms as various as the hues of fantasy, the same dream; drew the same quick breath when he stepped upon the stage, and, at his exit, felt the same dull pain of shouldering the pack again.

There were the maimed, even; those who came on crutches, who were pitted by smallpox or grotesquely painted by cruel birth stains. These, too, entered with him into enchantment. Stout matrons became slender girls again; worn spinsters felt their cheeks flush with the tenderness of their lost youth. Young and old, however hideous, however fair, they yielded up their heat—whether quick or latent—sat hungering for the mystic bread wherewith he fed them at this eucharist of sentiment.

Sometimes, when the house was crowded from the orchestra to the last row of the gallery, when the air was charged with this ecstasy of fancy, he himself was the victim of the burning reflection of his power. They acted upon him in turn; he felt their fervent and despairing appeal to him; it stirred him as the spring drives the sap up into an old tree; he, too, burst into bloom. For the moment he, too, believed again, desired again, he knew not what, but something.

But it was not in these exalted moments that Caroline had learned to fear him most. It was in the quiet, tired reserve, the dullness, even, that kept him company between these outbursts that she found that exhausting drain upon her sympathies which was the very pith and substance of their alliance. It was the tacit admission of disappointment under all this glamour of success—the helplessness of the enchanter to at all enchant himself—that awoke in her an illogical, womanish desire to in some way compensate, to make it up to him.

She had observed drastically to herself that it was her eighteenth year he awoke in her—those hard years she had spent in turning gowns and placating tradesmen, and which she had never had time to live. After all, she reflected, it was better to allow one's self a little youth—to dance a little at the carnival and to live these things when they are natural and lovely, not to have them coming back on one and demanding arrears when they are humiliating and impossible. She went over tonight all the catalogue of her self-deprivations; recalled how, in the light of her father's example, she had even refused to humor her innocent taste for improvising at the piano; how, when she began to teach, after her mother's death, she had struck out one little indulgence after another, reducing her life to a relentless routine, unvarying as clockwork. It seemed to her that ever since d'Esquerre first came into the house she had been haunted by an imploring little girlish ghost that followed her about, wringing its hands and entreating for an hour of life.

The storm had held off unconscionably long; the air within the lodge was stifling, and without the garden waited, breathless. Everything seemed pervaded by a poignant distress; the hush of feverish, intolerable expectation. The still earth, the heavy flowers, even the growing darkness, breathed the exhaustion of protracted waiting. Caroline felt that she ought to go; that it was wrong to stay; that the hour and the place were as treacherous as her own reflections. She rose and began to pace the floor, stepping softly, as though in fear of awakening someone, her figure, in its thin drapery, diaphanously vague and white. Still unable to shake off the obsession of the intense stillness, she sat down at the piano and began to run over the first act of the *Walküre*, the last of his roles they had practiced together; playing listlessly and absently at first, but with gradually increasing seriousness. Perhaps it was the still heat of the summer night, perhaps it was the heavy odors from the garden that came in through the open windows; but as she played there grew and grew the feeling that he was there, beside her, standing in his accustomed place. In the duet at the end of the first act she heard him clearly: *"Thou art the Spring for which I sighed in Winter's cold embraces."* Once as he sang it, he had put his arm about her, his one hand under her heart, while with the other he took her right from the keyboard, holding her as he always held *Sieglinde* when he drew her toward the window. She had been wonderfully the mistress of herself at the time; neither repellent nor acquiescent. She remembered that she had rather exulted, then, in her self-control—which he had seemed to take for granted, though there was perhaps the whisper of a question from the hand under her heart. *"Thou art the Spring for which I sighed in Winter's cold embraces."* Caroline lifted her hands quickly from the keyboard, and she bowed her head in them, sobbing.

The storm broke and the rain beat in, spattering her nightdress until she rose and lowered the windows. She dropped upon the couch and began fighting over again the battles of other days, while the ghosts of the slain rose as from a sowing of dragon's teeth, The shadows of things, always so scorned and flouted, bore down upon her merciless and triumphant. It was not enough; this happy, useful, well-ordered life was not enough. It did not satisfy, it was not even real. No, the other things, the shadows—they were the realities. Her father, poor Heinrich, even her mother, who had been able to sustain her poor romance and keep her little illusions amid the tasks of a scullion, were nearer happiness than she. Her sure foundation was but made ground, after all, and the people in Klingsor's garden were more fortunate, however barren the sands from which they conjured their paradise.

The lodge was still and silent; her fit of weeping over, Caroline made no sound, and within the room, as without in the garden, was the blackness of storm. Only now and then a flash of lightning showed a woman's slender figure rigid on the couch, her face buried in her hands.

Toward morning, when the occasional rumbling of thunder was heard no more and the beat of the raindrops upon the orchard leaves was steadier, she fell asleep and did not waken until the first red streaks of dawn shone through the twisted boughs of the apple trees. There was a moment between world and world, when, neither asleep nor awake, she felt her dream grow thin, melting away from her, felt the warmth under her heart growing cold. Something seemed to slip from the clinging hold of her arms, and she groaned protestingly through her parted lips, following it a little way with fluttering hands. Then her eyes opened wide and she sprang up and sat holding dizzily to the cushions of the couch, staring down at her bare, cold feet, at her laboring breast, rising and falling under her open nightdress.

The dream was gone, but the feverish reality of it still pervaded her and she held it as the vibrating string holds a tone. In the last hour the shadows had had their way with Caroline. They had shown her the nothingness of time and space, of system and discipline, of closed doors and broad waters. Shuddering, she thought of the Arabian fairy tale in which the genie brought the princess of China to the sleeping prince of Damascus and carried her through the air back to her palace at dawn. Caroline closed her eyes and dropped her elbows weakly upon her knees, her shoulders sinking together. The horror was that it had not come from without, but from within. The dream was no blind chance; it was the expression of something she had kept so close a prisoner that she had never seen it herself, it was the wail from the donjon deeps when the watch slept. Only as the outcome of such a night of sorcery could the thing have been loosed to straighten its limbs and measure itself with her; so heavy were the chains upon it, so many a fathom deep, it was crushed down into darkness. The fact that d'Esquerre happened to be on the other side of the world meant nothing; had he been here, beside her, it could scarcely have hurt her self-respect so much. As it was, she was without even the extenuation of an outer impulse, and she could scarcely have despised herself more had she come to him here in the night three weeks ago and thrown herself down upon the stone slab at the door there.

Caroline rose unsteadily and crept guiltily from the lodge and along the path under the arbor, terrified lest the servants should be stirring, trembling with the chill air, while the wet shrubbery, brushing against her, drenched her nightdress until it clung about her limbs.

At breakfast her husband looked across the table at her with concern. "It seems to me that you are looking rather fagged, Caroline. It was a beastly night to sleep. Why don't you go up to the mountains until this hot weather is over? By the way, were you in earnest about letting the lodge stand?"

Caroline laughed quietly. "No, I find I was not very serious. I haven't sentiment enough to forego a summer house. Will you tell Baker to come tomorrow to talk it over with me? If we are to have a house party, I should like to put him to work on it at once."

Noble gave her a glance, half-humorous, half-vexed. "Do you know I am rather disappointed?" he said. "I had almost hoped that, just for once, you know, you would be a little bit foolish."

"Not now that I've slept over it," replied Caroline, and they both rose from the table, laughing.

THE MARRIAGE OF PHAEDRA

The sequence of events was such that MacMaster did not make his pilgrimage to Hugh Treffinger's studio until three years after that painter's death. MacMaster was himself a painter, an American of the Gallicized type, who spent his winters in New York, his summers in Paris, and no inconsiderable amount of time on the broad waters between. He had often contemplated stopping in London on one of his return trips in the late autumn, but he had always deferred leaving Paris until the prick of necessity drove him home by the quickest and shortest route.

Treffinger was a comparatively young man at the time of his death, and there had seemed no occasion for haste until haste was of no avail. Then, possibly, though there had been some correspondence between them, MacMaster felt certain qualms about meeting in the flesh a man who in the flesh was so diversely reported. His intercourse with Treffinger's work had been so deep and satisfying, so apart from other appreciations, that he rather dreaded a critical juncture of any sort. He had always felt himself singularly inept in personal relations, and in this case he had avoided the issue until it was no longer to be feared or hoped for. There still remained, however, Treffinger's great unfinished picture, the *Marriage of Phaedra*, which had never left his studio, and of which MacMaster's friends had now and again brought report that it was the painter's most characteristic production.

The young man arrived in London in the evening, and the next morning went out to Kensington to find Treffinger's studio. It lay in one of the perplexing bystreets off Holland Road, and the number he found on a door set in a high garden wall, the top of which was covered with broken green glass and over which a budding lilac bush nodded. Treffinger's plate was still there, and a card requesting visitors to ring for the attendant. In response to MacMaster's ring, the door was opened by a cleanly built little man, clad in a shooting jacket and trousers that had been made for an ampler figure. He had a fresh complexion, eyes of that common uncertain shade of gray, and was closely shaven except for the incipient muttonchops on his ruddy cheeks. He bore himself in a manner strikingly capable, and there was a sort of trimness and alertness about him, despite the too-generous shoulders of his coat. In one hand he held a bulldog pipe, and in the other a copy of *Sporting Life*. While MacMaster was explaining the purpose of his call he noticed that the man surveyed him critically, though not impertinently. He was admitted into a little tank of a lodge made of whitewashed stone, the back door and windows opening upon a garden. A visitor's book and a pile of catalogues lay on a deal table, together with a bottle of ink and some rusty pens. The wall was ornamented with photographs and colored prints of racing favorites.

"The studio is h'only open to the public on Saturdays and Sundays," explained the man—he referred to himself as "Jymes"—"but of course we make exceptions in the case of pynters. Lydy Elling Treffinger 'erself is on the Continent, but Sir 'Ugh's orders was that pynters was to 'ave the run of the place." He selected a key from his pocket and threw open the door into the studio which, like the lodge, was built against the wall of the garden.

MacMaster entered a long, narrow room, built of smoothed planks, painted a light green; cold and damp even on that fine May morning. The room was utterly bare of furniture—unless a stepladder, a model throne, and a rack laden with large leather portfolios could be accounted such—and was windowless, without other openings than the door and the skylight, under which hung the unfinished picture itself. MacMaster had never seen so many of Treffinger's paintings together. He knew the painter had married a woman with money and had been able to keep such of his pictures as he wished. These, with all of his replicas and studies, he had left as a sort of common legacy to the younger men of the school he had originated.

As soon as he was left alone MacMaster sat down on the edge of the model throne before the unfinished picture. Here indeed was what he had come for; it rather paralyzed his receptivity for the moment, but gradually the thing found its way to him.

At one o'clock he was standing before the collection of studies done for *Boccaccio's Garden* when he heard a voice at his elbow.

"Pardon, sir, but I was just about to lock up and go to lunch. Are you lookin' for the figure study of Boccaccio 'imself?" James queried respectfully. "Lydy Elling Treffinger give it to Mr. Rossiter to take down to Oxford for some lectures he's been agiving there."

"Did he never paint out his studies, then?" asked MacMaster with perplexity. "Here are two completed ones for this picture. Why did he keep them?"

"I don't know as I could say as to that, sir," replied James, smiling indulgently, "but that was 'is way. That is to say, 'e pynted out very frequent, but 'e always made two studies to stand; one in watercolors and one in oils, before 'e went at the final picture—to say nothink of all the pose studies 'e made in pencil before he begun on the composition proper at all. He was that particular. You see, 'e wasn't so keen for the final effect as for the proper pyntin' of 'is pictures. 'E used to say they ought to be well made, the same as any other h'article of trade. I can lay my 'and on the pose studies for you, sir." He rummaged in one of the portfolios and produced half a dozen drawings, "These three," he continued, "was discarded; these two was the pose he finally accepted; this one without alteration, as it were."

"That's in Paris, as I remember," James continued reflectively. "It went with the *Saint Cecilia* into the Baron H——'s collection. Could you tell me, sir, 'as 'e it still? I don't like to lose account of them, but some 'as changed 'ands since Sir 'Ugh's death."

"H——'s collection is still intact, I believe," replied MacMaster. "You were with Treffinger long?"

"From my boyhood, sir," replied James with gravity. "I was a stable boy when 'e took me."

"You were his man, then?"

"That's it, sir. Nobody else ever done anything around the studio. I always mixed 'is colors and 'e taught me to do a share of the varnishin'; 'e said as 'ow there wasn't a 'ouse in England as could do it proper. You ayn't looked at the *Marriage* yet, sir?" he asked abruptly, glancing doubtfully at MacMaster, and indicating with his thumb the picture under the north light.

"Not very closely. I prefer to begin with something simpler; that's rather appalling, at first glance," replied MacMaster.

"Well may you say that, sir," said James warmly. "That one regular killed Sir 'Ugh; it regular broke 'im up, and nothink will ever convince me as 'ow it didn't bring on 'is second stroke."

When MacMaster walked back to High Street to take his bus his mind was divided between two exultant convictions. He felt that he had not only found Treffinger's greatest picture, but that, in James, he had discovered a kind of cryptic index to the painter's personality—a clue which, if tactfully followed, might lead to much.

Several days after his first visit to the studio, MacMaster wrote to Lady Mary Percy, telling her that he would be in London for some time and asking her if he might call. Lady Mary was an only sister of Lady Ellen Treffinger, the painter's widow, and MacMaster had known her during one winter he spent at Nice. He had known her, indeed, very well, and Lady Mary, who was astonishingly frank and communicative upon all subjects, had been no less so upon the matter of her sister's unfortunate marriage.

In her reply to his note Lady Mary named an afternoon when she would be alone. She was as good as her word, and when MacMaster arrived he found the drawing room empty. Lady Mary entered shortly after he was announced. She was a tall woman, thin and stiffly jointed, and her body stood out under the folds of her gown with the rigor of cast iron. This rather metallic suggestion was further carried out in her heavily knuckled hands, her stiff gray hair, and her long, bold-featured face, which was saved from freakishness only by her alert eyes.

"Really," said Lady Mary, taking a seat beside him and giving him a sort of military inspection through her nose glasses, "really, I had begun to fear that I had lost you altogether. It's four years since I saw you at Nice, isn't it? I was in Paris last winter, but I heard nothing from you."

"I was in New York then."

"It occurred to me that you might be. And why are you in London?"

"Can you ask?" replied MacMaster gallantly.

Lady Mary smiled ironically. "But for what else, incidentally?"

"Well, incidentally, I came to see Treffinger's studio and his unfinished picture. Since I've been here, I've decided to stay the summer. I'm even thinking of attempting to do a biography of him."

"So that is what brought you to London?"

"Not exactly. I had really no intention of anything so serious when I came. It's his last picture, I fancy, that has rather thrust it upon me. The notion has settled down on me like a thing destined."

"You'll not be offended if I question the clemency of such a destiny," remarked Lady Mary dryly. "Isn't there rather a surplus of books on that subject already?"

"Such as they are. Oh, I've read them all"—here MacMaster faced Lady Mary triumphantly. "He has quite escaped your amiable critics," he added, smiling.

"I know well enough what you think, and I daresay we are not much on art," said Lady Mary with tolerant good humor. "We leave that to peoples who have no physique. Treffinger made a stir for a time, but it seems that we are not capable of a sustained appreciation of such extraordinary methods. In the end we go back to the pictures we find agreeable and unperplexing. He was regarded as an experiment, I fancy; and now it seems that he was rather an unsuccessful one. If you've come to us in a missionary spirit, we'll tolerate you politely, but we'll laugh in our sleeve, I warn you."

"That really doesn't daunt me, Lady Mary," declared MacMaster blandly. "As I told you, I'm a man with a mission."

Lady Mary laughed her hoarse, baritone laugh. "Bravo! And you've come to me for inspiration for your panegyric?"

MacMaster smiled with some embarrassment. "Not altogether for that purpose. But I want to consult you, Lady Mary, about the advisability of troubling Lady Ellen Treffinger in the matter. It seems scarcely legitimate to go on without asking her to give some sort of grace to my proceedings, yet I feared the whole subject might be painful to her. I shall rely wholly upon your discretion."

"I think she would prefer to be consulted," replied Lady Mary judicially. "I can't understand how she endures to have the wretched affair continually raked up, but she does. She seems to feel a sort of moral responsibility. Ellen has always been singularly conscientious about this matter, insofar as her light goes,—which rather puzzles me, as hers is not exactly a magnanimous nature. She is certainly trying to do what she believes to be the right thing. I shall write to her, and you can see her when she returns from Italy."

"I want very much to meet her. She is, I hope, quite recovered in every way," queried MacMaster, hesitatingly.

"No, I can't say that she is. She has remained in much the same condition she sank to before his death. He trampled over pretty much whatever there was in her, I fancy. Women don't recover from wounds of that sort—at least, not women of Ellen's grain. They go on bleeding inwardly."

"You, at any rate, have not grown more reconciled," MacMaster ventured.

"Oh I give him his dues. He was a colorist, I grant you; but that is a vague and unsatisfactory quality to marry to; Lady Ellen Treffinger found it so."

"But, my dear Lady Mary," expostulated MacMaster, "and just repress me if I'm becoming too personal—but it must, in the first place, have been a marriage of choice on her part as well as on his."

Lady Mary poised her glasses on her large forefinger and assumed an attitude suggestive of the clinical lecture room as she replied. "Ellen, my dear boy, is an essentially romantic person. She is quiet about it, but she runs deep. I never knew how deep until I came against her on the issue of that marriage. She was always discontented as a girl; she found things dull and prosaic, and the ardor of his courtship was agreeable to her. He met her during her first season in town. She is handsome, and there were plenty of other men, but I grant you your scowling brigand was the most picturesque of the lot. In his courtship, as in everything else, he was theatrical to the point of being ridiculous, but Ellen's sense of humor is not her strongest quality. He had the charm of celebrity, the air of a man who could storm his way through anything to get what he wanted. That sort of vehemence is particularly effective with women like Ellen, who can be warmed only by reflected heat, and she couldn't at all stand out against it. He convinced her of his necessity; and that done, all's done."

"I can't help thinking that, even on such a basis, the marriage should have turned out better," MacMaster remarked reflectively.

"The marriage," Lady Mary continued with a shrug, "was made on the basis of a mutual misunderstanding. Ellen, in the nature of the case, believed that she was doing something quite out of the ordinary in accepting him, and expected concessions which, apparently, it never occurred to him to make. After his marriage he relapsed into his old habits of incessant work, broken by violent and often brutal relaxations. He insulted her friends and foisted his own upon her— many of them well calculated to arouse aversion in any well-bred girl. He had Ghillini constantly at the house—a homeless vagabond, whose conversation was impossible. I don't say, mind you, that he had not grievances on his side. He had probably overrated the girl's possibilities, and he let her see that he was disappointed in her. Only a large and generous nature could have borne with him, and Ellen's is not that. She could not at all understand that odious strain of plebeian pride which plumes itself upon not having risen above its sources."

As MacMaster drove back to his hotel he reflected that Lady Mary Percy had probably had good cause for dissatisfaction with her brother-in-law. Treffinger was, indeed, the last man who should have married into the Percy family. The son of a small tobacconist, he had grown up a sign-painter's apprentice; idle, lawless, and practically letterless until he had drifted into the night classes of the Albert League, where Ghillini sometimes lectured. From the moment he came under the eye and influence of that erratic Italian, then a political exile, his life had swerved sharply from its old channel. This man had been at once incentive and guide, friend and master, to his pupil. He had taken the raw clay out of the London streets and molded it anew. Seemingly he had divined at once where the boy's possibilities lay, and had thrown aside every canon of orthodox instruction in the training of him. Under him Treffinger acquired his superficial, yet facile, knowledge of the classics; had steeped himself in the monkish Latin and medieval romances which later gave his work so naive and remote a quality. That was the beginning of the wattle fences, the cobble pave, the brown roof beams, the cunningly wrought fabrics that gave to his pictures such a richness of decorative effect.

As he had told Lady Mary Percy, MacMaster had found the imperative inspiration of his purpose in Treffinger's unfinished picture, the *Marriage of Phaedra*. He had always believed that the key to Treffinger's individuality lay in his singular education; in the *Roman de la Rose*, in Boccaccio, and Amadis, those works which had literally transcribed themselves upon the blank soul of the London street boy, and through which he had been born into the world of spiritual things. Treffinger had been a man who lived after his imagination; and his mind, his ideals and, as MacMaster believed, even his personal ethics, had to the last been colored by the trend of his early training. There was in him alike the freshness and spontaneity, the frank brutality and the religious mysticism, which lay well back of the fifteenth century. In the *Marriage of Phaedra* MacMaster found the ultimate expression of this spirit, the final word as to Treffinger's point of view.

As in all Treffinger's classical subjects, the conception was wholly medieval. This Phaedra, just turning from her husband and maidens to greet her husband's son, giving him her first fearsome glance from under her half-lifted veil, was no daughter of Minos. The daughter of *heathenesse* and the early church she was; doomed to torturing visions and scourgings, and the wrangling of soul with flesh. The venerable Theseus might have been victorious Charlemagne, and Phaedra's maidens belonged rather in the train of Blanche of Castile than at the Cretan court. In the earlier studies Hippolytus had been done with a more pagan suggestion; but in each successive drawing the glorious figure had been deflowered of something of its serene unconsciousness, until, in the canvas under the skylight, he appeared a very Christian knight. This male figure, and the face of Phaedra, painted with such magical preservation of tone under the heavy shadow of the veil, were plainly Treffinger's highest achievements of craftsmanship. By what labor he had reached the seemingly inevitable composition of the picture—with its twenty figures, its plenitude of light and air, its restful distances seen through white porticoes—countless studies bore witness.

From James's attitude toward the picture MacMaster could well conjecture what the painter's had been. This picture was always uppermost in James's mind; its custodianship formed, in his eyes, his occupation. He was manifestly apprehensive when visitors—not many came nowadays—lingered near it. "It was the *Marriage* as killed 'im," he would often say, "and for the matter 'o that, it did like to 'av been the death of all of us."

By the end of his second week in London MacMaster had begun the notes for his study of Hugh Treffinger and his work. When his researches led him occasionally to visit the studios of Treffinger's friends and erstwhile disciples, he found their Treffinger manner fading as the ring of Treffinger's personality died out in them. One by one they were stealing back into the fold of national British art; the hand that had wound them up was still. MacMaster despaired of them and confined himself more and more exclusively to the studio, to such of Treffinger's letters as were available— they were for the most part singularly negative and colorless—and to his interrogation of Treffinger's man.

He could not himself have traced the successive steps by which he was gradually admitted into James's confidence. Certainly most of his adroit strategies to that end failed humiliatingly, and whatever it was that built up an understanding between them must have been instinctive and intuitive on both sides. When at last James became anecdotal, personal, there was that in every word he let fall which put breath and blood into MacMaster's book. James had so long been steeped in that penetrating personality that he fairly exuded it. Many of his very phrases, mannerisms, and opinions were impressions that he had taken on like wet plaster in his daily contact with Treffinger. Inwardly he was lined with cast-off epitheliums, as outwardly he was clad in the painter's discarded coats. If the painter's letters were formal and perfunctory, if his expressions to his friends had been extravagant, contradictory, and often apparently insincere—still, MacMaster felt himself not entirely without authentic sources. It was James who possessed Treffinger's legend; it was with James that he had laid aside his pose. Only in his studio, alone, and face to face with his work, as it seemed, had the man invariably been himself. James had known him in the one attitude in which he was entirely honest; their relation had fallen well within the painter's only indubitable integrity. James's report of Treffinger was distorted by no hallucination of artistic insight, colored by no interpretation of his own. He merely held what he had heard and seen; his mind was a sort of camera obscura. His very limitations made him the more literal and minutely accurate.

One morning, when MacMaster was seated before the *Marriage of Phaedra*, James entered on his usual round of dusting.

"I've 'eard from Lydy Elling by the post, sir," he remarked, "an' she's give h'orders to 'ave the 'ouse put in readiness. I doubt she'll be 'ere by Thursday or Friday next."

"She spends most of her time abroad?" queried MacMaster; on the subject of Lady Treffinger James consistently maintained a very delicate reserve.

"Well, you could 'ardly say she does that, sir. She finds the 'ouse a bit dull, I daresay, so durin' the season she stops mostly with Lydy Mary Percy, at Grosvenor Square. Lydy Mary's a h'only sister." After a few moments he continued, speaking in jerks governed by the rigor of his dusting: "H'only this morning I come upon this scarfpin," exhibiting a very striking instance of that article, "an' I recalled as 'ow Sir 'Ugh give it me when 'e was acourting of Lydy Elling. Blowed if I ever see a man go in for a 'oman like 'im! 'E was that gone, sir. 'E never went in on anythink so 'ard before nor since, till 'e went in on the *Marriage* there—though 'e mostly went in on things pretty keen; 'ad the measles when 'e was thirty, strong as cholera, an' come close to dyin' of 'em. 'E wasn't strong for Lydy Elling's set; they was a bit too stiff for 'im. A free an' easy gentleman, 'e was; 'e liked 'is dinner with a few friends an' them jolly, but 'e wasn't much on what you might call big affairs. But once 'e went in for Lydy Elling 'e broke 'imself to new paces; He give away 'is rings an' pins, an' the tylor's man an' the 'aberdasher's man was at 'is rooms continual. 'E got 'imself put up for a club in Piccadilly; 'e starved 'imself thin, an' worrited 'imself white, an' ironed 'imself out, an' drawed 'imself tight as a bow string. It was a good job 'e come a winner, or I don't know w'at'd 'a been to pay."

The next week, in consequence of an invitation from Lady Ellen Treffinger, MacMaster went one afternoon to take tea with her. He was shown into the garden that lay between the residence and the studio, where the tea table was set under a gnarled pear tree. Lady Ellen rose as he approached—he was astonished to note how tall she was—and greeted him graciously, saying that she already knew him through her sister. MacMaster felt a certain satisfaction in her; in her reassuring poise and repose, in the charming modulations of her voice and the indolent reserve of her full, almond eyes. He was even delighted to find her face so inscrutable, though it chilled his own warmth and made the open frankness he had wished to permit himself impossible. It was a long face, narrow at the chin, very delicately featured, yet steeled by an impassive mask of self-control. It was behind just such finely cut, close-sealed faces, MacMaster reflected, that nature sometimes hid astonishing secrets. But in spite of this suggestion of hardness he felt that the unerring taste that Treffinger had always shown in larger matters had not deserted him when he came to the choosing of a wife, and he admitted that he could not himself have selected a woman who looked more as Treffinger's wife should look.

While he was explaining the purpose of his frequent visits to the studio she heard him with courteous interest. "I have read, I think, everything that has been published on Sir Hugh Treffinger's work, and it seems to me that there is much left to be said," he concluded.

"I believe they are rather inadequate," she remarked vaguely. She hesitated a moment, absently fingering the ribbons of her gown, then continued, without raising her eyes; "I hope you will not think me too exacting if I ask to see the proofs of such chapters of your work as have to do with Sir Hugh's personal life. I have always asked that privilege."

MacMaster hastily assured her as to this, adding, "I mean to touch on only such facts in his personal life as have to do directly with his work—such as his monkish education under Ghillini."

"I see your meaning, I think," said Lady Ellen, looking at him with wide, uncomprehending eyes.

When MacMaster stopped at the studio on leaving the house he stood for some time before Treffinger's one portrait of himself, that brigand of a picture, with its full throat and square head; the short upper lip blackened by the close-clipped mustache, the wiry hair tossed down over the forehead, the strong white teeth set hard on a short pipestem. He could well understand what manifold tortures the mere grain of the man's strong red and brown flesh might have inflicted upon a woman like Lady Ellen. He could conjecture, too, Treffinger's impotent revolt against that very repose which had so dazzled him when it first defied his daring; and how once possessed of it, his first instinct had been to crush it, since he could not melt it.

Toward the close of the season Lady Ellen Treffinger left town. MacMaster's work was progressing rapidly, and he and James wore away the days in their peculiar relation, which by this time had much of friendliness. Excepting for the regular visits of a Jewish picture dealer, there were few intrusions upon their solitude. Occasionally a party of Americans rang at the little door in the garden wall, but usually they departed speedily for the Moorish hall and tinkling fountain of the great show studio of London, not far away.

This Jew, an Austrian by birth, who had a large business in Melbourne, Australia, was a man of considerable discrimination, and at once selected the *Marriage of Phaedra* as the object of his especial interest. When, upon his first visit, Lichtenstein had declared the picture one of the things done for time, MacMaster had rather warmed toward him and had talked to him very freely. Later, however, the man's repulsive personality and innate vulgarity so wore upon him that, the more genuine the Jew's appreciation, the more he resented it and the more base he somehow felt it to be. It annoyed him to see Lichtenstein walking up and down before the picture, shaking his head and blinking his watery eyes over his nose glasses, ejaculating: "Dot is a chem, a chem! It is wordt to gome den dousant miles for such a bainting, eh? To make Eurobe abbreciate such a work of ardt it is necessary to take it away while she is napping. She has never abbreciated until she has lost, but," knowingly, "she will buy back."

James had, from the first, felt such a distrust of the man that he would never leave him alone in the studio for a moment. When Lichtenstein insisted upon having Lady Ellen Treffinger's address James rose to the point of insolence. "It ayn't no use to give it, noway. Lydy Treffinger never has nothink to do with dealers." MacMaster quietly repented his rash confidences, fearing that he might indirectly cause Lady Ellen annoyance from this merciless speculator, and he recalled with chagrin that Lichtenstein had extorted from him, little by little, pretty much the entire plan of his book, and especially the place in it which the *Marriage of Phaedra* was to occupy.

By this time the first chapters of MacMaster's book were in the hands of his publisher, and his visits to the studio were necessarily less frequent. The greater part of his time was now employed with the engravers who were to reproduce such of Treffinger's pictures as he intended to use as illustrations.

He returned to his hotel late one evening after a long and vexing day at the engravers to find James in his room, seated on his steamer trunk by the window, with the outline of a great square draped in sheets resting against his knee.

"Why, James, what's up?" he cried in astonishment, glancing inquiringly at the sheeted object.

"Ayn't you seen the pypers, sir?" jerked out the man.

"No, now I think of it, I haven't even looked at a paper. I've been at the engravers' plant all day. I haven't seen anything."

James drew a copy of the *Times* from his pocket and handed it to him, pointing with a tragic finger to a paragraph in the social column. It was merely the announcement of Lady Ellen Treffinger's engagement to Captain Alexander Gresham.

"Well, what of it, my man? That surely is her privilege."

James took the paper, turned to another page, and silently pointed to a paragraph in the art notes which stated that Lady Treffinger had presented to the X—gallery the entire collection of paintings and sketches now in her late husband's studio, with the exception of his unfinished picture, the *Marriage Of Phaedra*, which she had sold for a large sum to an Australian dealer who had come to London purposely to secure some of Treffinger's paintings.

MacMaster pursed up his lips and sat down, his overcoat still on. "Well, James, this is something of a—something of a jolt, eh? It never occurred to me she'd really do it."

"Lord, you don't know 'er, sir," said James bitterly, still staring at the floor in an attitude of abandoned dejection.

MacMaster started up in a flash of enlightenment, "What on earth have you got there, James? It's not-surely it's not—"

"Yes, it is, sir," broke in the man excitedly. "It's the *Marriage* itself. It ayn't agoing to H'Australia, no'ow!"

"But man, what are you going to do with it? It's Lichtenstein's property now, as it seems."

"It ayn't, sir, that it ayn't. No, by Gawd, it ayn't!" shouted James, breaking into a choking fury. He controlled himself with an effort and added supplicatingly: "Oh, sir, you ayn't agoing to see it go to H'Australia, w'ere they send convic's?" He unpinned and flung aside the sheets as though to let *Phaedra* plead for herself.

MacMaster sat down again and looked sadly at the doomed masterpiece. The notion of James having carried it across London that night rather appealed to his fancy. There was certainly a flavor about such a highhanded proceeding. "However did you get it here?" he queried.

"I got a four-wheeler and come over direct, sir. Good job I 'appened to 'ave the chaynge about me."

"You came up High Street, up Piccadilly, through the Haymarket and Trafalgar Square, and into the Strand?" queried MacMaster with a relish.

"Yes, sir. Of course, sir," assented James with surprise.

MacMaster laughed delightedly. "It was a beautiful idea, James, but I'm afraid we can't carry it any further."

"I was thinkin' as 'ow it would be a rare chance to get you to take the *Marriage* over to Paris for a year or two, sir, until the thing blows over?" suggested James blandly.

"I'm afraid that's out of the question, James. I haven't the right stuff in me for a pirate, or even a vulgar smuggler, I'm afraid." MacMaster found it surprisingly difficult to say this, and he busied himself with the lamp as he said it. He heard James's hand fall heavily on the trunk top, and he discovered that he very much disliked sinking in the man's estimation.

"Well, sir," remarked James in a more formal tone, after a protracted silence; "then there's nothink for it but as 'ow I'll 'ave to make way with it myself."

"And how about your character, James? The evidence would be heavy against you, and even if Lady Treffinger didn't prosecute you'd be done for."

"Blow my character!—your pardon, sir," cried James, starting to his feet. "W'at do I want of a character? I'll chuck the 'ole thing, and damned lively, too. The shop's to be sold out, an' my place is gone any'ow. I'm agoing to enlist, or try the gold fields. I've lived too long with h'artists; I'd never give satisfaction in livery now. You know 'ow it is yourself, sir; there ayn't no life like it, no'ow."

For a moment MacMaster was almost equal to abetting James in his theft. He reflected that pictures had been whitewashed, or hidden in the crypts of churches, or under the floors of palaces from meaner motives, and to save them from a fate less ignominious. But presently, with a sigh, he shook his head.

"No, James, it won't do at all. It has been tried over and over again, ever since the world has been agoing and pictures amaking. It was tried in Florence and in Venice, but the pictures were always carried away in the end. You see, the difficulty is that although Treffinger told you what was not to be done with the picture, he did not say definitely what was to be done with it. Do you think Lady Treffinger really understands that he did not want it to be sold?"

"Well, sir, it was like this, sir," said James, resuming his seat on the trunk and again resting the picture against his knee. "My memory is as clear as glass about it. After Sir 'Ugh got up from 'is first stroke, 'e took a fresh start at the *Marriage*. Before that 'e 'ad been working at it only at night for a while back; the *Legend* was the big picture then, an' was under the north light w'ere 'e worked of a morning. But one day 'e bid me take the *Legend* down an' put the *Marriage* in its place, an' 'e says, dashin' on 'is jacket, 'Jymes, this is a start for the finish, this time.'

"From that on 'e worked at the night picture in the mornin'—a thing contrary to 'is custom. The *Marriage* went wrong, and wrong—an' Sir 'Ugh agettin' seedier an' seedier every day. 'E tried models an' models, an' smudged an' pynted out on account of 'er face goin' wrong in the shadow. Sometimes 'e layed it on the colors, an' swore at me an' things in general. He got that discouraged about 'imself that on 'is low days 'e used to say to me: 'Jymes, remember one thing; if anythink 'appens to me, the *Marriage* is not to go out of 'ere unfinished. It's worth the lot of 'em, my boy, an' it's not agoing to go shabby for lack of pains.' 'E said things to that effect repeated.

"He was workin' at the picture the last day, before 'e went to 'is club. 'E kept the carriage waitin' near an hour while 'e put on a stroke an' then drawed back for to look at it, an' then put on another, careful like. After 'e 'ad 'is gloves on, 'e come back an' took away the brushes I was startin' to clean, an' put in another touch or two. 'It's acomin', Jymes,' 'e says, 'by gad if it ayn't.' An' with that 'e goes out. It was cruel sudden, w'at come after.

"That night I was lookin' to 'is clothes at the 'ouse when they brought 'im 'ome. He was conscious, but w'en I ran downstairs for to 'elp lift 'im up, I knowed 'e was a finished man. After we got 'im into bed 'e kept lookin' restless at me and then at Lydy Elling and ajerkin' of 'is 'and. Finally 'e quite raised it an' shot 'is thumb out toward the wall. 'He wants water; ring, Jymes,' says Lydy Elling, placid. But I knowed 'e was pointin' to the shop.

"'Lydy Treffinger,' says I, bold, 'he's pointin' to the studio. He means about the *Marriage*; 'e told me today as 'ow 'e never wanted it sold unfinished. Is that it, Sir 'Ugh?'

"He smiled an' nodded slight an' closed 'is eyes. 'Thank you, Jymes,' says Lydy Elling, placid. Then 'e opened 'is eyes an' looked long and 'ard at Lydy Elling.

"'Of course I'll try to do as you'd wish about the picture, 'Ugh, if that's w'at's troublin' you,' she says quiet. With that 'e closed 'is eyes and 'e never opened 'em. He died unconscious at four that mornin'.

"You see, sir, Lydy Elling was always cruel 'ard on the *Marriage*. From the first it went wrong, an' Sir 'Ugh was out of temper pretty constant. She came into the studio one day and looked at the picture an 'asked 'im why 'e didn't throw it up an' quit aworriting 'imself. He answered sharp, an' with that she said as 'ow she didn't see w'at there was to make such a row about, no'ow. She spoke 'er mind about that picture, free; an' Sir 'Ugh swore 'ot an' let a 'andful of brushes fly at 'is study, an' Lydy Elling picked up 'er skirts careful an' chill, an' drifted out of the studio with 'er eyes calm and 'er chin 'igh. If there was one thing Lydy Elling 'ad no comprehension of, it was the usefulness of swearin'. So the *Marriage* was a sore thing between 'em. She is uncommon calm, but uncommon bitter, is Lydy Elling. She's never come anear the studio since that day she went out 'oldin' up of 'er skirts. W'en 'er friends goes over she excuses 'erself along o' the strain. Strain—Gawd!" James ground his wrath short in his teeth.

"I'll tell you what I'll do, James, and it's our only hope. I'll see Lady Ellen tomorrow. The *Times* says she returned today. You take the picture back to its place, and I'll do what I can for it. If anything is done to save it, it must be done through Lady Ellen Treffinger herself, that much is clear. I can't think that she fully understands the situation. If she did, you know, she really couldn't have any motive—" He stopped suddenly. Somehow, in the dusky lamplight, her small, close-sealed face came ominously back to him. He rubbed his forehead and knitted his brows thoughtfully. After a moment he shook his head and went on: "I am positive that nothing can be gained by highhanded methods, James. Captain Gresham is one of the most popular men in London, and his friends would tear up Treffinger's bones if he were annoyed by any scandal of our making—and this scheme you propose would inevitably result in scandal. Lady Ellen has, of course, every legal right to sell the picture. Treffinger made considerable inroads upon her estate, and, as she is about to marry a man without income, she doubtless feels that she has a right to replenish her patrimony."

He found James amenable, though doggedly skeptical. He went down into the street, called a carriage, and saw James and his burden into it. Standing in the doorway, he watched the carriage roll away through the drizzling mist, weave in and out among the wet, black vehicles and darting cab lights, until it was swallowed up in the glare and confusion of the Strand. "It is rather a fine touch of irony," he reflected, "that he, who is so out of it, should be the one to really care. Poor Treffinger," he murmured as, with a rather spiritless smile, he turned back into his hotel. "Poor Treffinger; *sic transit gloria.*"

The next afternoon MacMaster kept his promise. When he arrived at Lady Mary Percy's house he saw preparations for a function of some sort, but he went resolutely up the steps, telling the footman that his business was urgent. Lady Ellen came down alone, excusing her sister. She was dressed for receiving, and MacMaster had never seen one so beautiful. The color in her cheeks sent a softening glow over her small, delicately cut features.

MacMaster apologized for his intrusion and came unflinchingly to the object of his call. He had come, he said, not only to offer her his warmest congratulations, but to express his regret that a great work of art was to leave England.

Lady Treffinger looked at him in wide-eyed astonishment. Surely, she said, she had been careful to select the best of the pictures for the X— gallery, in accordance with Sir Hugh Treffinger's wishes.

"And did he—pardon me, Lady Treffinger, but in mercy set my mind at rest—did he or did he not express any definite wish concerning this one picture, which to me seems worth all the others, unfinished as it is?"

Lady Treffinger paled perceptibly, but it was not the pallor of confusion. When she spoke there was a sharp tremor in her smooth voice, the edge of a resentment that tore her like pain. "I think his man has some such impression, but I believe it to be utterly unfounded. I cannot find that he ever expressed any wish concerning the disposition of the picture to any of his friends. Unfortunately, Sir Hugh was not always discreet in his remarks to his servants."

"Captain Gresham, Lady Ellingham, and Miss Ellingham," announced a servant, appearing at the door.

There was a murmur in the hall, and MacMaster greeted the smiling Captain and his aunt as he bowed himself out.

To all intents and purposes the *Marriage of Phaedra* was already entombed in a vague continent in the Pacific, somewhere on the other side of the world.

A WAGNER MATINEE

I received one morning a letter, written in pale ink on glassy, blue-lined notepaper, and bearing the postmark of a little Nebraska village. This communication, worn and rubbed, looking as though it had been carried for some days in a coat pocket that was none too clean, was from my Uncle Howard and informed me that his wife had been left a small legacy by a bachelor relative who had recently died, and that it would be necessary for her to go to Boston to attend to the settling of the estate. He requested me to meet her at the station and render her whatever services might be necessary. On examining the date indicated as that of her arrival I found it no later than tomorrow. He had characteristically delayed writing until, had I been away from home for a day, I must have missed the good woman altogether.

The name of my Aunt Georgiana called up not alone her own figure, at once pathetic and grotesque, but opened before my feet a gulf of recollection so wide and deep that, as the letter dropped from my hand, I felt suddenly a stranger to all the present conditions of my existence, wholly ill at ease and out of place amid the familiar surroundings of my study. I became, in short, the gangling farm boy my aunt had known, scourged with chilblains and bashfulness, my hands cracked and sore from the corn husking. I felt the knuckles of my thumb tentatively, as though they were raw again. I sat again before her parlor organ, fumbling the scales with my stiff, red hands, while she, beside me, made canvas mittens for the huskers.

The next morning, after preparing my landlady somewhat, I set out for the station. When the train arrived I had some difficulty in finding my aunt. She was the last of the passengers to alight, and it was not until I got her into the carriage that she seemed really to recognize me. She had come all the way in a day coach; her linen duster had become black with soot, and her black bonnet gray with dust, during the journey. When we arrived at my boardinghouse the landlady put her to bed at once and I did not see her again until the next morning.

Whatever shock Mrs. Springer experienced at my aunt's appearance she considerably concealed. As for myself, I saw my aunt's misshapen figure with that feeling of awe and respect with which we behold explorers who have left their ears and fingers north of Franz Josef Land, or their health somewhere along the Upper Congo. My Aunt Georgiana had been a music teacher at the Boston Conservatory, somewhere back in the latter sixties. One summer, while visiting in the little village among the Green Mountains where her ancestors had dwelt for generations, she had kindled the callow fancy of the most idle and shiftless of all the village lads, and had conceived for this Howard Carpenter one of those extravagant passions which a handsome country boy of twenty-one sometimes inspires in an angular, spectacled woman of thirty. When she returned to her duties in Boston, Howard followed her, and the upshot of this inexplicable infatuation was that she eloped with him, eluding the reproaches of her family and the criticisms of her friends by going with him to the Nebraska frontier. Carpenter, who, of course, had no money, had taken a homestead in Red Willow County, fifty miles from the railroad. There they had measured off their quarter section themselves by driving across the prairie in a wagon, to the wheel of which they had tied a red cotton handkerchief, and counting off its revolutions. They built a dugout in the red hillside, one of those cave dwellings whose inmates so often reverted to primitive conditions. Their water they got from the lagoons where the buffalo drank, and their slender stock of provisions was always at the mercy of bands of roving Indians. For thirty years my aunt had not been further than fifty miles from the homestead.

But Mrs. Springer knew nothing of all this, and must have been considerably shocked at what was left of my kinswoman. Beneath the soiled linen duster which, on her arrival, was the most conspicuous feature of her costume, she wore a black stuff dress, whose ornamentation showed that she had surrendered herself unquestioningly into the hands of a country dressmaker. My poor aunt's figure, however, would have presented astonishing difficulties to any dressmaker. Originally stooped, her shoulders were now almost bent together over her sunken chest. She wore no stays, and her gown, which trailed unevenly behind, rose in a sort of peak over her abdomen. She wore ill-fitting false teeth, and her skin was as yellow as a Mongolian's from constant exposure to a pitiless wind and to the alkaline water which hardens the most transparent cuticle into a sort of flexible leather.

I owed to this woman most of the good that ever came my way in my boyhood, and had a reverential affection for her. During the years when I was riding herd for my uncle, my aunt, after cooking the three meals—the first of which was ready at six o'clock in the morning-and putting the six children to bed, would often stand until midnight at her ironing board, with me at the kitchen table beside her, hearing me recite Latin declensions and conjugations, gently shaking me when my drowsy head sank down over a page of irregular verbs. It was to her, at her ironing or mending, that I read my first Shakespeare', and her old textbook on mythology was the first that ever came into my empty hands. She taught me my scales and exercises, too—on the little parlor organ, which her husband had bought her after fifteen years, during which she had not so much as seen any instrument, but an accordion that belonged to one of the Norwegian farmhands. She would sit beside me by the hour, darning and counting while I struggled with the "Joyous Farmer," but she seldom talked to me about music, and I understood why. She was a pious woman; she had the consolations of religion and, to her at least, her martyrdom was not wholly sordid. Once when I had been doggedly beating out some easy passages from an old score of *Euryanthe* I had found among her music books, she came up to me and, putting her hands over my eyes, gently drew my head back upon her shoulder, saying tremulously, "Don't love it so well, Clark, or it may be taken from you. Oh, dear boy, pray that whatever your sacrifice may be, it be not that."

When my aunt appeared on the morning after her arrival she was still in a semi-somnambulant state. She seemed not to realize that she was in the city where she had spent her youth, the place longed for hungrily half a lifetime. She had been so wretchedly train-sick throughout the journey that she had no recollection of anything but her discomfort, and, to all intents and purposes, there were but a few hours of nightmare between the farm in Red Willow County and my study on Newbury Street. I had planned a little pleasure for her that afternoon, to repay her for some of the glorious moments she had given me when we used to milk together in the straw-thatched cowshed and she, because I was more than usually tired, or because her husband had spoken sharply to me, would tell me of the splendid performance of the *Huguenots* she had seen in Paris, in her youth. At two o'clock the Symphony Orchestra was to give a Wagner program, and I intended to take my aunt; though, as I conversed with her I grew doubtful about her enjoyment of it. Indeed, for her own sake, I could only wish her taste for such things quite dead, and the long struggle mercifully ended at last. I suggested our visiting the Conservatory and the Common before lunch, but she seemed altogether too timid to wish to venture out. She questioned me absently about various changes in the city, but she was chiefly concerned that she had forgotten to leave instructions about feeding half-skimmed milk to a certain weakling calf, "old Maggie's calf, you know, Clark," she explained, evidently having forgotten how long I had been away. She was further troubled because she had neglected to tell her daughter about the freshly opened kit of mackerel in the cellar, which would spoil if it were not used directly.

I asked her whether she had ever heard any of the Wagnerian operas and found that she had not, though she was perfectly familiar with their respective situations, and had once possessed the piano score of *The Flying Dutchman*. I began to think it would have been best to get her back to Red Willow County without waking her, and regretted having suggested the concert.

From the time we entered the concert hall, however, she was a trifle less passive and inert, and for the first time seemed to perceive her surroundings. I had felt some trepidation lest she might become aware of the absurdities of her attire, or might experience some painful embarrassment at stepping suddenly into the world to which she had been dead for a quarter of a century. But, again, I found how superficially I had judged her. She sat looking about her with eyes as impersonal, almost as stony, as those with which the granite Rameses in a museum watches the froth and fret that ebbs and flows about his pedestal-separated from it by the lonely stretch of centuries. I have seen this same aloofness in old miners who drift into the Brown Hotel at Denver, their pockets full of bullion, their linen soiled, their haggard faces unshaven; standing in the thronged corridors as solitary as though they were still in a frozen camp on the Yukon, conscious that certain experiences have isolated them from their fellows by a gulf no haberdasher could bridge.

We sat at the extreme left of the first balcony, facing the arch of our own and the balcony above us, veritable hanging gardens, brilliant as tulip beds. The matinee audience was made up chiefly of women. One lost the contour of faces and figures—indeed, any effect of line whatever—and there was only the color of bodices past counting, the shimmer of fabrics soft and firm, silky and sheer: red, mauve, pink, blue, lilac, purple, ecru, rose, yellow, cream, and white, all the colors that an impressionist finds in a sunlit landscape, with here and there the dead shadow of a frock coat. My Aunt Georgiana regarded them as though they had been so many daubs of tube-paint on a palette.

When the musicians came out and took their places, she gave a little stir of anticipation and looked with quickening interest down over the rail at that invariable grouping, perhaps the first wholly familiar thing that had greeted her eye since she had left old Maggie and her weakling calf. I could feel how all those details sank into her soul, for I had not forgotten how they had sunk into mine when I came fresh from plowing forever and forever between green aisles of corn, where, as in a treadmill, one might walk from daybreak to dusk without perceiving a shadow of change. The clean profiles of the musicians, the gloss of their linen, the dull black of their coats, the beloved shapes of the instruments, the patches of yellow light thrown by the green-shaded lamps on the smooth, varnished bellies of the cellos and the bass viols in the rear, the restless, wind-tossed forest of fiddle necks and bows—I recalled how, in the first orchestra I had ever heard, those long bow strokes seemed to draw the heart out of me, as a conjurer's stick reels out yards of paper ribbon from a hat.

The first number was the *Tannhauser* overture. When the horns drew out the first strain of the Pilgrim's chorus my Aunt Georgiana clutched my coat sleeve. Then it was I first realized that for her this broke a silence of thirty years; the inconceivable silence of the plains. With the battle between the two motives, with the frenzy of the Venusberg theme and its ripping of strings, there came to me an overwhelming sense of the waste and wear we are so powerless to combat; and I saw again the tall, naked house on the prairie, black and grim as a wooden fortress; the black pond where I had learned to swim, its margin pitted with sun-dried cattle tracks; the rain-gullied clay banks about the naked house, the four dwarf ash seedlings where the dishcloths were always hung to dry before the kitchen door. The world there was the flat world of the ancients; to the east, a cornfield that stretched to daybreak; to the west, a corral that reached to sunset; between, the conquests of peace, dearer bought than those of war.

The overture closed; my aunt released my coat sleeve, but she said nothing. She sat staring at the orchestra through a dullness of thirty years, through the films made little by little by each of the three hundred and sixty-five days in every one of them. What, I wondered, did she get from it? She had been a good pianist in her day I knew, and her musical education had been broader than that of most music teachers of a quarter of a century ago. She had often told me of Mozart's operas and Meyerbeer's, and I could remember hearing her sing, years ago, certain melodies of Verdi's. When I had fallen ill with a fever in her house she used to sit by my cot in the evening—when the cool, night wind blew in through the faded mosquito netting tacked over the window, and I lay watching a certain bright star that burned red above the cornfield—and sing "Home to our mountains, O, let us return!" in a way fit to break the heart of a Vermont boy near dead of homesickness already.

I watched her closely through the prelude to *Tristan and Isolde*, trying vainly to conjecture what that seething turmoil of strings and winds might mean to her, but she sat mutely staring at the violin bows that drove obliquely downward, like the pelting streaks of rain in a summer shower. Had this music any message for her? Had she enough left to at all comprehend this power which had kindled the world since she had left it? I was in a fever of curiosity, but Aunt Georgiana sat silent upon her peak in Darien. She preserved this utter immobility throughout the number from *The Flying Dutchman*, though her fingers worked mechanically upon her black dress, as though, of themselves, they were recalling the piano score they had once played. Poor old hands! They had been stretched and twisted into mere tentacles to hold and lift and knead with; the palms unduly swollen, the fingers bent and knotted—on one of them a thin, worn band that had once been a wedding ring. As I pressed and gently quieted one of those groping hands I remembered with quivering eyelids their services for me in other days.

Soon after the tenor began the "Prize Song," I heard a quick drawn breath and turned to my aunt. Her eyes were closed, but the tears were glistening on her cheeks, and I think, in a moment more, they were in my eyes as well. It never really died, then—the soul that can suffer so excruciatingly and so interminably; it withers to the outward eye only; like that strange moss which can lie on a dusty shelf half a century and yet, if placed in water, grows green again. She wept so throughout the development and elaboration of the melody.

During the intermission before the second half of the concert, I questioned my aunt and found that the "Prize Song" was not new to her. Some years before there had drifted to the farm in Red Willow County a young German, a tramp cowpuncher, who had sung the chorus at Bayreuth, when he was a boy, along with the other peasant boys and girls. Of a Sunday morning he used to sit on his gingham-sheeted bed in the hands' bedroom which opened off the kitchen, cleaning the leather of his boots and saddle, singing the "Prize Song," while my aunt went about her work in the kitchen. She had hovered about him until she had prevailed upon him to join the country church, though his sole fitness for this step, insofar as I could gather, lay in his boyish face and his possession of this divine melody. Shortly afterward he had gone to town on the Fourth of July, been drunk for several days, lost his money at a faro table, ridden a saddled Texan steer on a bet, and disappeared with a fractured collarbone. All this my aunt told me huskily, wanderingly, as though she were talking in the weak lapses of illness.

"Well, we have come to better things than the old *Trovatore* at any rate, Aunt Georgie?" I queried, with a well-meant effort at jocularity.

Her lip quivered and she hastily put her handkerchief up to her mouth. From behind it she murmured, "And you have been hearing this ever since you left me, Clark?" Her question was the gentlest and saddest of reproaches.

The second half of the program consisted of four numbers from the *Ring*, and closed with Siegfried's funeral march. My aunt wept quietly, but almost continuously, as a shallow vessel overflows in a rainstorm. From time to time her dim eyes looked up at the lights which studded the ceiling, burning softly under their dull glass globes; doubtless they were stars in truth to her. I was still perplexed as to what measure of musical comprehension was left to her, she who had heard nothing but the singing of gospel hymns at Methodist services in the square frame schoolhouse on Section Thirteen for so many years. I was wholly unable to gauge how much of it had been dissolved in soapsuds, or worked into bread, or milked into the bottom of a pail.

The deluge of sound poured on and on; I never knew what she found in the shining current of it; I never knew how far it bore her, or past what happy islands. From the trembling of her face I could well believe that before the last numbers she had been carried out where the myriad graves are, into the gray, nameless burying grounds of the sea; or into some world of death vaster yet, where, from the beginning of the world, hope has lain down with hope and dream with dream and, renouncing, slept.

The concert was over; the people filed out of the hall chattering and laughing, glad to relax and find the living level again, but my kinswoman made no effort to rise. The harpist slipped its green felt cover over his instrument; the flute players shook the water from their mouthpieces; the men of the orchestra went out one by one, leaving the stage to the chairs and music stands, empty as a winter cornfield.

I spoke to my aunt. She burst into tears and sobbed pleadingly. "I don't want to go, Clark, I don't want to go!"

I understood. For her, just outside the door of the concert hall, lay the black pond with the cattle-tracked bluffs; the tall, unpainted house, with weather-curled boards; naked as a tower, the crook-backed ash seedlings where the dishcloths hung to dry; the gaunt, molting turkeys picking up refuse about the kitchen door.

PAUL'S CASE

A Study in Temperament

It was Paul's afternoon to appear before the faculty of the Pittsburgh High School to account for his various misdemeanors. He had been suspended a week ago, and his father had called at the Principal's office and confessed his perplexity about his son. Paul entered the faculty room suave and smiling. His clothes were a trifle outgrown, and the tan velvet on the collar of his open overcoat was frayed and worn; but for all that there was something of the dandy about him, and he wore an opal pin in his neatly knotted black four-in-hand, and a red carnation in his buttonhole. This latter adornment the faculty somehow felt was not properly significant of the contrite spirit befitting a boy under the ban of suspension.

Paul was tall for his age and very thin, with high, cramped shoulders and a narrow chest. His eyes were remarkable for a certain hysterical brilliancy, and he continually used them in a conscious, theatrical sort of way, peculiarly offensive in a boy. The pupils were abnormally large, as though he were addicted to belladonna, but there was a glassy glitter about them which that drug does not produce.

When questioned by the Principal as to why he was there Paul stated, politely enough, that he wanted to come back to school. This was a lie, but Paul was quite accustomed to lying; found it, indeed, indispensable for overcoming friction. His teachers were asked to state their respective charges against him, which they did with such a rancor and aggrievedness as evinced that this was not a usual case, Disorder and impertinence were among the offenses named, yet each of his instructors felt that it was scarcely possible to put into words the real cause of the trouble, which lay in a sort of hysterically defiant manner of the boy's; in the contempt which they all knew he felt for them, and which he seemingly made not the least effort to conceal. Once, when he had been making a synopsis of a paragraph at the blackboard, his English teacher had stepped to his side and attempted to guide his hand. Paul had started back with a shudder and thrust his hands violently behind him. The astonished woman could scarcely have been more hurt and embarrassed had he struck at her. The insult was so involuntary and definitely personal as to be unforgettable. In one way and another he had made all his teachers, men and women alike, conscious of the same feeling of physical aversion. In one class he habitually sat with his hand shading his eyes; in another he always looked out of the window during the recitation; in another he made a running commentary on the lecture, with humorous intention.

His teachers felt this afternoon that his whole attitude was symbolized by his shrug and his flippantly red carnation flower, and they fell upon him without mercy, his English teacher leading the pack. He stood through it smiling, his pale lips parted over his white teeth. (His lips were continually twitching, and he had a habit of raising his eyebrows that was contemptuous and irritating to the last degree.) Older boys than Paul had broken down and shed tears under that baptism of fire, but his set smile did not once desert him, and his only sign of discomfort was the nervous trembling of the fingers that toyed with the buttons of his overcoat, and an occasional jerking of the other hand that held his hat. Paul was always smiling, always glancing about him, seeming to feel that people might be watching him and trying to detect something. This conscious expression, since it was as far as possible from boyish mirthfulness, was usually attributed to insolence or "smartness."

As the inquisition proceeded one of his instructors repeated an impertinent remark of the boy's, and the Principal asked him whether he thought that a courteous speech to have made a woman. Paul shrugged his shoulders slightly and his eyebrows twitched.

"I don't know," he replied. "I didn't mean to be polite or impolite, either. I guess it's a sort of way I have of saying things regardless."

The Principal, who was a sympathetic man, asked him whether he didn't think that a way it would be well to get rid of. Paul grinned and said he guessed so. When he was told that he could go he bowed gracefully and went out. His bow was but a repetition of the scandalous red carnation.

His teachers were in despair, and his drawing master voiced the feeling of them all when he declared there was something about the boy which none of them understood. He added: "I don't really believe that smile of his comes altogether from insolence; there's something sort of haunted about it. The boy is not strong, for one thing. I happen to know that he was born in Colorado, only a few months before his mother died out there of a long illness. There is something wrong about the fellow."

The drawing master had come to realize that, in looking at Paul, one saw only his white teeth and the forced animation of his eyes. One warm afternoon the boy had gone to sleep at his drawing board, and his master had noted with amazement what a white, blue-veined face it was; drawn and wrinkled like an old man's about the eyes, the lips twitching even in his sleep, and stiff with a nervous tension that drew them back from his teeth.

His teachers left the building dissatisfied and unhappy; humiliated to have felt so vindictive toward a mere boy, to have uttered this feeling in cutting terms, and to have set each other on, as it were, in the gruesome game of intemperate reproach. Some of them remembered having seen a miserable street cat set at bay by a ring of tormentors.

As for Paul, he ran down the hill whistling the "Soldiers' Chorus" from *Faust*, looking wildly behind him now and then to see whether some of his teachers were not there to writhe under his lightheartedness. As it was now late in the afternoon and Paul was on duty that evening as usher at Carnegie Hall, he decided that he would not go home to supper. When he reached the concert hall the doors were not yet open and, as it was chilly outside, he decided to go up into the picture gallery—always deserted at this hour—where there were some of Raffelli's gay studies of Paris streets and an airy blue Venetian scene or two that always exhilarated him. He was delighted to find no one in the gallery but the old guard, who sat in one corner, a newspaper on his knee, a black patch over one eye and the other closed. Paul possessed himself of the peace and walked confidently up and down, whistling under his breath. After a while he sat down before a blue Rico and lost himself. When he bethought him to look at his watch, it was after seven o'clock, and he rose with a start and ran downstairs, making a face at Augustus, peering out from the cast room, and an evil gesture at the Venus de Milo as he passed her on the stairway.

When Paul reached the ushers' dressing room half a dozen boys were there already, and he began excitedly to tumble into his uniform. It was one of the few that at all approached fitting, and Paul thought it very becoming—though he knew that the tight, straight coat accentuated his narrow chest, about which he was exceedingly sensitive. He was always considerably excited while he dressed, twanging all over to the tuning of the strings and the preliminary flourishes of the horns in the music room; but tonight he seemed quite beside himself, and he teased and plagued the boys until, telling him that he was crazy, they put him down on the floor and sat on him.

Somewhat calmed by his suppression, Paul dashed out to the front of the house to seat the early comers. He was a model usher; gracious and smiling he ran up and down the aisles; nothing was too much trouble for him; he carried messages and brought programs as though it were his greatest pleasure in life, and all the people in his section thought him a charming boy, feeling that he remembered and admired them. As the house filled, he grew more and more vivacious and animated, and the color came to his cheeks and lips. It was very much as though this were a great reception and Paul were the host. Just as the musicians came out to take their places, his English teacher arrived with checks for the seats which a prominent manufacturer had taken for the season. She betrayed some embarrassment when she handed Paul the tickets, and a hauteur which subsequently made her feel very foolish. Paul was startled for a moment, and had the feeling of wanting to put her out; what business had she here among all these fine people and gay colors? He looked her over and decided that she was not appropriately dressed and must be a fool to sit downstairs in such togs. The tickets had probably been sent her out of kindness, he reflected as he put down a seat for her, and she had about as much right to sit there as he had.

When the symphony began Paul sank into one of the rear seats with a long sigh of relief, and lost himself as he had done before the Rico. It was not that symphonies, as such, meant anything in particular to Paul, but the first sigh of the instruments seemed to free some hilarious and potent spirit within him; something that struggled there like the genie in the bottle found by the Arab fisherman. He felt a sudden zest of life; the lights danced before his eyes and the concert hall blazed into unimaginable splendor. When the soprano soloist came on Paul forgot even the nastiness of his teacher's being there and gave himself up to the peculiar stimulus such personages always had for him. The soloist chanced to be a German woman, by no means in her first youth, and the mother of many children; but she wore an elaborate gown and a tiara, and above all she had that indefinable air of achievement, that world-shine upon her, which, in Paul's eyes, made her a veritable queen of Romance.

After a concert was over Paul was always irritable and wretched until he got to sleep, and tonight he was even more than usually restless. He had the feeling of not being able to let down, of its being impossible to give up this delicious excitement which was the only thing that could be called living at all. During the last number he withdrew and, after hastily changing his clothes in the dressing room, slipped out to the side door where the soprano's carriage stood. Here he began pacing rapidly up and down the walk, waiting to see her come out.

Over yonder, the Schenley, in its vacant stretch, loomed big and square through the fine rain, the windows of its twelve stories glowing like those of a lighted cardboard house under a Christmas tree. All the actors and singers of the better class stayed there when they were in the city, and a number of the big manufacturers of the place lived there in the winter. Paul had often hung about the hotel, watching the people go in and out, longing to enter and leave schoolmasters and dull care behind him forever.

At last the singer came out, accompanied by the conductor, who helped her into her carriage and closed the door with a cordial *auf wiedersehen* which set Paul to wondering whether she were not an old sweetheart of his. Paul followed the carriage over to the hotel, walking so rapidly as not to be far from the entrance when the singer alighted, and disappeared behind the swinging glass doors that were opened by a Negro in a tall hat and a long coat. In the moment that the door was ajar it seemed to Paul that he, too, entered. He seemed to feel himself go after her up the steps, into the warm, lighted building, into an exotic, tropical world of shiny, glistening surfaces and basking ease. He reflected upon the mysterious dishes that were brought into the dining room, the green bottles in buckets of ice, as he had seen them in the supper party pictures of the *Sunday World* supplement. A quick gust of wind brought the rain down with sudden vehemence, and Paul was startled to find that he was still outside in the slush of the gravel driveway; that his boots were letting in the water and his scanty overcoat was clinging wet about him; that the lights in front of the concert hall were out and that the rain was driving in sheets between him and the orange glow of the windows above him. There it was, what he wanted— tangibly before him, like the fairy world of a Christmas pantomime—but mocking spirits stood guard at the doors, and, as the rain beat in his face, Paul wondered whether he were destined always to shiver in the black night outside, looking up at it.

He turned and walked reluctantly toward the car tracks. The end had to come sometime; his father in his nightclothes at the top of the stairs, explanations that did not explain, hastily improvised fictions that were forever tripping him up, his upstairs room and its horrible yellow wallpaper, the creaking bureau with the greasy plush collarbox, and over his painted wooden bed the pictures of George Washington and John Calvin, and the framed motto, "Feed my Lambs," which had been worked in red worsted by his mother.

Half an hour later Paul alighted from his car and went slowly down one of the side streets off the main thoroughfare. It was a highly respectable street, where all the houses were exactly alike, and where businessmen of moderate means begot and reared large families of children, all of whom went to Sabbath school and learned the shorter catechism, and were interested in arithmetic; all of whom were as exactly alike as their homes, and of a piece with the monotony in which they lived. Paul never went up Cordelia Street without a shudder of loathing. His home was next to the house of the Cumberland minister. He approached it tonight with the nerveless sense of defeat, the hopeless feeling of sinking back forever into ugliness and commonness that he had always had when he came home. The moment he turned into Cordelia Street he felt the waters close above his head. After each of these orgies of living he experienced all the physical depression which follows a debauch; the loathing of respectable beds, of common food, of a house penetrated by kitchen odors; a shuddering repulsion for the flavorless, colorless mass of everyday existence; a morbid desire for cool things and soft lights and fresh flowers.

The nearer he approached the house, the more absolutely unequal Paul felt to the sight of it all: his ugly sleeping chamber; the cold bathroom with the grimy zinc tub, the cracked mirror, the dripping spiggots; his father, at the top of the stairs, his hairy legs sticking out from his nightshirt, his feet thrust into carpet slippers. He was so much later than usual that there would certainly be inquiries and reproaches. Paul stopped short before the door. He felt that he could not be accosted by his father tonight; that he could not toss again on that miserable bed. He would not go in. He would tell his father that he had no carfare and it was raining so hard he had gone home with one of the boys and stayed all night.

Meanwhile, he was wet and cold. He went around to the back of the house and tried one of the basement windows, found it open, raised it cautiously, and scrambled down the cellar wall to the floor. There he stood, holding his breath, terrified by the noise he had made, but the floor above him was silent, and there was no creak on the stairs. He found a soapbox, and carried it over to the soft ring of light that streamed from the furnace door, and sat down. He was horribly afraid of rats, so he did not try to sleep, but sat looking distrustfully at the dark, still terrified lest he might have awakened his father. In such reactions, after one of the experiences which made days and nights out of the dreary blanks of the calendar, when his senses were deadened, Paul's head was always singularly clear. Suppose his father had heard him getting in at the window and had come down and shot him for a burglar? Then, again, suppose his father had come down, pistol in hand, and he had cried out in time to save himself, and his father had been horrified to think how nearly he had killed him? Then, again, suppose a day should come when his father would remember that night, and wish there had been no warning cry to stay his hand? With this last supposition Paul entertained himself until daybreak.

The following Sunday was fine; the sodden November chill was broken by the last flash of autumnal summer. In the morning Paul had to go to church and Sabbath school, as always. On seasonable Sunday afternoons the burghers of Cordelia Street always sat out on their front stoops and talked to their neighbors on the next stoop, or called to those across the street in neighborly fashion. The men usually sat on gay cushions placed upon the steps that led down to the sidewalk, while the women, in their Sunday "waists," sat in rockers on the cramped porches, pretending to be greatly at their ease. The children played in the streets; there were so many of them that the place resembled the recreation grounds of a kindergarten. The men on the steps—all in their shirt sleeves, their vests unbuttoned—sat with their legs well apart, their stomachs comfortably protruding, and talked of the prices of things, or told anecdotes of the sagacity of their various chiefs and overlords. They occasionally looked over the multitude of squabbling children, listened affectionately to their high-pitched, nasal voices, smiling to see their own proclivities reproduced in their offspring, and interspersed their legends of the iron kings with remarks about their sons' progress at school, their grades in arithmetic, and the amounts they had saved in their toy banks.

On this last Sunday of November Paul sat all the afternoon on the lowest step of his stoop, staring into the street, while his sisters, in their rockers, were talking to the minister's daughters next door about how many shirtwaists they had made in the last week, and how many waffles someone had eaten at the last church supper. When the weather was warm, and his father was in a particularly jovial frame of mind, the girls made lemonade, which was always brought out in a red-glass pitcher, ornamented with forget-me-nots in blue enamel. This the girls thought very fine, and the neighbors always joked about the suspicious color of the pitcher.

Today Paul's father sat on the top step, talking to a young man who shifted a restless baby from knee to knee. He happened to be the young man who was daily held up to Paul as a model, and after whom it was his father's dearest hope that he would pattern. This young man was of a ruddy complexion, with a compressed, red mouth, and faded, nearsighted eyes, over which he wore thick spectacles, with gold bows that curved about his ears. He was clerk to one of the magnates of a great steel corporation, and was looked upon in Cordelia Street as a young man with a future. There was a story that, some five years ago—he was now barely twenty-six—he had been a trifle dissipated, but in order to curb his appetites and save the loss of time and strength that a sowing of wild oats might have entailed, he had taken his chief's advice, oft reiterated to his employees, and at twenty-one had married the first woman whom he could persuade to share his fortunes. She happened to be an angular schoolmistress, much older than he, who also wore thick glasses, and who had now borne him four children, all nearsighted, like herself.

The young man was relating how his chief, now cruising in the Mediterranean, kept in touch with all the details of the business, arranging his office hours on his yacht just as though he were at home, and "knocking off work enough to keep two stenographers busy." His father told, in turn, the plan his corporation was considering, of putting in an electric railway plant in Cairo. Paul snapped his teeth; he had an awful apprehension that they might spoil it all before he got there. Yet he rather liked to hear these legends of the iron kings that were told and retold on Sundays and holidays; these stories of palaces in Venice, yachts on the Mediterranean, and high play at Monte Carlo appealed to his fancy, and he was interested in the triumphs of these cash boys who had become famous, though he had no mind for the cash-boy stage.

After supper was over and he had helped to dry the dishes, Paul nervously asked his father whether he could go to George's to get some help in his geometry, and still more nervously asked for carfare. This latter request he had to repeat, as his father, on principle, did not like to hear requests for money, whether much or little. He asked Paul whether he could not go to some boy who lived nearer, and told him that he ought not to leave his schoolwork until Sunday; but he gave him the dime. He was not a poor man, but he had a worthy ambition to come up in the world. His only reason for allowing Paul to usher was that he thought a boy ought to be earning a little.

Paul bounded upstairs, scrubbed the greasy odor of the dishwater from his hands with the ill-smelling soap he hated, and then shook over his fingers a few drops of violet water from the bottle he kept hidden in his drawer. He left the house with his geometry conspicuously under his arm, and the moment he got out of Cordelia Street and boarded a downtown car, he shook off the lethargy of two deadening days and began to live again.

The leading juvenile of the permanent stock company which played at one of the downtown theaters was an acquaintance of Paul's, and the boy had been invited to drop in at the Sunday-night rehearsals whenever he could. For more than a year Paul had spent every available moment loitering about Charley Edwards's dressing room. He had won a place among Edwards's following not only because the young actor, who could not afford to employ a dresser, often found him useful, but because he recognized in Paul something akin to what churchmen term "vocation."

It was at the theater and at Carnegie Hall that Paul really lived; the rest was but a sleep and a forgetting. This was Paul's fairy tale, and it had for him all the allurement of a secret love. The moment he inhaled the gassy, painty, dusty odor behind the scenes, he breathed like a prisoner set free, and felt within him the possibility of doing or saying splendid, brilliant, poetic things. The moment the cracked orchestra beat out the overture from *Martha*, or jerked at the serenade from *Rigoletto*, all stupid and ugly things slid from him, and his senses were deliciously, yet delicately fired.

Perhaps it was because, in Paul's world, the natural nearly always wore the guise of ugliness, that a certain element of artificiality seemed to him necessary in beauty. Perhaps it was because his experience of life elsewhere was so full of Sabbath-school picnics, petty economies, wholesome advice as to how to succeed in life, and the inescapable odors of cooking, that he found this existence so alluring, these smartly clad men and women so attractive, that he was so moved by these starry apple orchards that bloomed perennially under the limelight.

It would be difficult to put it strongly enough how convincingly the stage entrance of that theater was for Paul the actual portal of Romance. Certainly none of the company ever suspected it, least of all Charley Edwards. It was very like the old stories that used to float about London of fabulously rich Jews, who had subterranean halls there, with palms, and fountains, and soft lamps and richly appareled women who never saw the disenchanting light of London day. So, in the midst of that smoke-palled city, enamored of figures and grimy toil, Paul had his secret temple, his wishing carpet, his bit of blue-and-white Mediterranean shore bathed in perpetual sunshine.

Several of Paul's teachers had a theory that his imagination had been perverted by garish fiction, but the truth was that he scarcely ever read at all. The books at home were not such as would either tempt or corrupt a youthful mind, and as for reading the novels that some of his friends urged upon him—well, he got what he wanted much more quickly from music; any sort of music, from an orchestra to a barrel organ. He needed only the spark, the indescribable thrill that made his imagination master of his senses, and he could make plots and pictures enough of his own. It was equally true that he was not stagestruck—not, at any rate, in the usual acceptation of that expression. He had no desire to become an actor, any more than he had to become a musician. He felt no necessity to do any of these things; what he wanted was to see, to be in the atmosphere, float on the wave of it, to be carried out, blue league after blue league, away from everything.

After a night behind the scenes Paul found the schoolroom more than ever repulsive; the bare floors and naked walls; the prosy men who never wore frock coats, or violets in their buttonholes; the women with their dull gowns, shrill voices, and pitiful seriousness about prepositions that govern the dative. He could not bear to have the other pupils think, for a moment, that he took these people seriously; he must convey to them that he considered it all trivial, and was there only by way of a jest, anyway. He had autographed pictures of all the members of the stock company which he showed his classmates, telling them the most incredible stories of his familiarity with these people, of his acquaintance with the soloists who came to Carnegie Hall, his suppers with them and the flowers he sent them. When these stories lost their effect, and his audience grew listless, he became desperate and would bid all the boys good-by, announcing that he was going to travel for a while; going to Naples, to Venice, to Egypt. Then, next Monday, he would slip back, conscious and nervously smiling; his sister was ill, and he should have to defer his voyage until spring.

Matters went steadily worse with Paul at school. In the itch to let his instructors know how heartily he despised them and their homilies, and how thoroughly he was appreciated elsewhere, he mentioned once or twice that he had no time to fool with theorems; adding—with a twitch of the eyebrows and a touch of that nervous bravado which so perplexed them—that he was helping the people down at the stock company; they were old friends of his.

The upshot of the matter was that the Principal went to Paul's father, and Paul was taken out of school and put to work. The manager at Carnegie Hall was told to get another usher in his stead; the doorkeeper at the theater was warned not to admit him to the house; and Charley Edwards remorsefully promised the boy's father not to see him again.

The members of the stock company were vastly amused when some of Paul's stories reached them—especially the women. They were hardworking women, most of them supporting indigent husbands or brothers, and they laughed rather bitterly at having stirred the boy to such fervid and florid inventions. They agreed with the faculty and with his father that Paul's was a bad case.

The eastbound train was plowing through a January snowstorm; the dull dawn was beginning to show gray when the engine whistled a mile out of Newark. Paul started up from the seat where he had lain curled in uneasy slumber, rubbed the breath-misted window glass with his hand, and peered out. The snow was whirling in curling eddies above the white bottom lands, and the drifts lay already deep in the fields and along the fences, while here and there the long dead grass and dried weed stalks protruded black above it. Lights shone from the scattered houses, and a gang of laborers who stood beside the track waved their lanterns.

Paul had slept very little, and he felt grimy and uncomfortable. He had made the all-night journey in a day coach, partly because he was ashamed, dressed as he was, to go into a Pullman, and partly because he was afraid of being seen there by some Pittsburgh businessman, who might have noticed him in Denny & Carson's office. When the whistle awoke him, he clutched quickly at his breast pocket, glancing about him with an uncertain smile. But the little, clay-bespattered Italians were still sleeping, the slatternly women across the aisle were in open-mouthed oblivion, and even the crumby, crying babies were for the nonce stilled. Paul settled back to struggle with his impatience as best he could.

When he arrived at the Jersey City station he hurried through his breakfast, manifestly ill at ease and keeping a sharp eye about him. After he reached the Twenty-third Street station, he consulted a cabman and had himself driven to a men's-furnishings establishment that was just opening for the day. He spent upward of two hours there, buying with endless reconsidering and great care. His new street suit he put on in the fitting room; the frock coat and dress clothes he had bundled into the cab with his linen. Then he drove to a hatter's and a shoe house. His next errand was at Tiffany's, where he selected his silver and a new scarf pin. He would not wait to have his silver marked, he said. Lastly, he stopped at a trunk shop on Broadway and had his purchases packed into various traveling bags.

It was a little after one o'clock when he drove up to the Waldorf, and after settling with the cabman, went into the office. He registered from Washington; said his mother and father had been abroad, and that he had come down to await the arrival of their steamer. He told his story plausibly and had no trouble, since he volunteered to pay for them in advance, in engaging his rooms; a sleeping room, sitting room, and bath.

Not once, but a hundred times, Paul had planned this entry into New York. He had gone over every detail of it with Charley Edwards, and in his scrapbook at home there were pages of description about New York hotels, cut from the Sunday papers. When he was shown to his sitting room on the eighth floor he saw at a glance that everything was as it should be; there was but one detail in his mental picture that the place did not realize, so he rang for the bellboy and sent him down for flowers. He moved about nervously until the boy returned, putting away his new linen and fingering it delightedly as he did so. When the flowers came he put them hastily into water, and then tumbled into a hot bath. Presently he came out of his white bathroom, resplendent in his new silk underwear, and playing with the tassels of his red robe. The snow was whirling so fiercely outside his windows that he could scarcely see across the street, but within the air was deliciously soft and fragrant. He put the violets and jonquils on the taboret beside the couch, and threw himself down, with a long sigh, covering himself with a Roman blanket. He was thoroughly tired; he had been in such haste, he had stood up to such a strain, covered so much ground in the last twenty-four hours, that he wanted to think how it had all come about. Lulled by the sound of the wind, the warm air, and the cool fragrance of the flowers, he sank into deep, drowsy retrospection.

It had been wonderfully simple; when they had shut him out of the theater and concert hall, when they had taken away his bone, the whole thing was virtually determined. The rest was a mere matter of opportunity. The only thing that at all surprised him was his own courage—for he realized well enough that he had always been tormented by fear, a sort of apprehensive dread that, of late years, as the meshes of the lies he had told closed about him, had been pulling the muscles of his body tighter and tighter. Until now he could not remember the time when he had not been dreading something. Even when he was a little boy it was always there—behind him, or before, or on either side. There had always been the shadowed corner, the dark place into which he dared not look, but from which something seemed always to be watching him—and Paul had done things that were not pretty to watch, he knew.

But now he had a curious sense of relief, as though he had at last thrown down the gauntlet to the thing in the corner.

Yet it was but a day since he had been sulking in the traces; but yesterday afternoon that he had been sent to the bank with Denny & Carson's deposit, as usual—but this time he was instructed to leave the book to be balanced. There was above two thousand dollars in checks, and nearly a thousand in the bank notes which he had taken from the book and quietly transferred to his pocket. At the bank he had made out a new deposit slip. His nerves had been steady enough to permit of his returning to the office, where he had finished his work and asked for a full day's holiday tomorrow, Saturday, giving a perfectly reasonable pretext. The bankbook, he knew, would not be returned before Monday or Tuesday, and his father would be out of town for the next week. From the time he slipped the bank notes into his pocket until he boarded the night train for New York, he had not known a moment's hesitation. It was not the first time Paul had steered through treacherous waters.

How astonishingly easy it had all been; here he was, the thing done; and this time there would be no awakening, no figure at the top of the stairs. He watched the snowflakes whirling by his window until he fell asleep.

When he awoke, it was three o'clock in the afternoon. He bounded up with a start; half of one of his precious days gone already! He spent more than an hour in dressing, watching every stage of his toilet carefully in the mirror. Everything was quite perfect; he was exactly the kind of boy he had always wanted to be.

When he went downstairs Paul took a carriage and drove up Fifth Avenue toward the Park. The snow had somewhat abated; carriages and tradesmen's wagons were hurrying soundlessly to and fro in the winter twilight; boys in woolen mufflers were shoveling off the doorsteps; the avenue stages made fine spots of color against the white street. Here and there on the corners were stands, with whole flower gardens blooming under glass cases, against the sides of which the snowflakes stuck and melted; violets, roses, carnations, lilies of the valley—somehow vastly more lovely and alluring that they blossomed thus unnaturally in the snow. The Park itself was a wonderful stage winterpiece.

When he returned, the pause of the twilight had ceased and the tune of the streets had changed. The snow was falling faster, lights streamed from the hotels that reared their dozen stories fearlessly up into the storm, defying the raging Atlantic winds. A long, black stream of carriages poured down the avenue, intersected here and there by other streams, tending horizontally. There were a score of cabs about the entrance of his hotel, and his driver had to wait. Boys in livery were running in and out of the awning stretched across the sidewalk, up and down the red velvet carpet laid from the door to the street. Above, about, within it all was the rumble and roar, the hurry and toss of thousands of human beings as hot for pleasure as himself, and on every side of him towered the glaring affirmation of the omnipotence of wealth.

The boy set his teeth and drew his shoulders together in a spasm of realization; the plot of all dramas, the text of all romances, the nerve-stuff of all sensations was whirling about him like the snowflakes. He burnt like a faggot in a tempest.

When Paul went down to dinner the music of the orchestra came floating up the elevator shaft to greet him. His head whirled as he stepped into the thronged corridor, and he sank back into one of the chairs against the wall to get his breath. The lights, the chatter, the perfumes, the bewildering medley of color—he had, for a moment, the feeling of not being able to stand it. But only for a moment; these were his own people, he told himself. He went slowly about the corridors, through the writing rooms, smoking rooms, reception rooms, as though he were exploring the chambers of an enchanted palace, built and peopled for him alone.

When he reached the dining room he sat down at a table near a window. The flowers, the white linen, the many-colored wineglasses, the gay toilettes of the women, the low popping of corks, the undulating repetitions of the *Blue Danube* from the orchestra, all flooded Paul's dream with bewildering radiance. When the roseate tinge of his champagne was added—that cold, precious, bubbling stuff that creamed and foamed in his glass—Paul wondered that there were honest men in the world at all. This was what all the world was fighting for, he reflected; this was what all the struggle was about. He doubted the reality of his past. Had he ever known a place called Cordelia Street, a place where fagged-looking businessmen got on the early car; mere rivets in a machine they seemed to Paul,—sickening men, with combings of children's hair always hanging to their coats, and the smell of cooking in their clothes. Cordelia Street—Ah, that belonged to another time and country; had he not always been thus, had he not sat here night after night, from as far back as he could remember, looking pensively over just such shimmering textures and slowly twirling the stem of a glass like this one between his thumb and middle finger? He rather thought he had.

He was not in the least abashed or lonely. He had no especial desire to meet or to know any of these people; all he demanded was the right to look on and conjecture, to watch the pageant. The mere stage properties were all he contended for. Nor was he lonely later in the evening, in his lodge at the Metropolitan. He was now entirely rid of his nervous misgivings, of his forced aggressiveness, of the imperative desire to show himself different from his surroundings. He felt now that his surroundings explained him. Nobody questioned the purple; he had only to wear it passively. He had only to glance down at his attire to reassure himself that here it would be impossible for anyone to humiliate him.

He found it hard to leave his beautiful sitting room to go to bed that night, and sat long watching the raging storm from his turret window. When he went to sleep it was with the lights turned on in his bedroom; partly because of his old timidity, and partly so that, if he should wake in the night, there would be no wretched moment of doubt, no horrible suspicion of yellow wallpaper, or of Washington and Calvin above his bed.

Sunday morning the city was practically snowbound. Paul breakfasted late, and in the afternoon he fell in with a wild

San Francisco boy, a freshman at Yale, who said he had run down for a "little flyer" over Sunday. The young man offered to show Paul the night side of the town, and the two boys went out together after dinner, not returning to the hotel until seven o'clock the next morning. They had started out in the confiding warmth of a champagne friendship, but their parting in the elevator was singularly cool. The freshman pulled himself together to make his train, and Paul went to bed. He awoke at two o'clock in the afternoon, very thirsty and dizzy, and rang for icewater, coffee, and the Pittsburgh papers.

On the part of the hotel management, Paul excited no suspicion. There was this to be said for him, that he wore his spoils with dignity and in no way made himself conspicuous. Even under the glow of his wine he was never boisterous, though he found the stuff like a magician's wand for wonder-building. His chief greediness lay in his ears and eyes, and his excesses were not offensive ones. His dearest pleasures were the gray winter twilights in his sitting room; his quiet enjoyment of his flowers, his clothes, his wide divan, his cigarette, and his sense of power. He could not remember a time when he had felt so at peace with himself. The mere release from the necessity of petty lying, lying every day and every day, restored his self-respect. He had never lied for pleasure, even at school; but to be noticed and admired, to assert his difference from other Cordelia Street boys; and he felt a good deal more manly, more honest, even, now that he had no need for boastful pretensions, now that he could, as his actor friends used to say, "dress the part." It was characteristic that remorse did not occur to him. His golden days went by without a shadow, and he made each as perfect as he could.

On the eighth day after his arrival in New York he found the whole affair exploited in the Pittsburgh papers, exploited with a wealth of detail which indicated that local news of a sensational nature was at a low ebb. The firm of Denny & Carson announced that the boy's father had refunded the full amount of the theft and that they had no intention of prosecuting. The Cumberland minister had been interviewed, and expressed his hope of yet reclaiming the motherless lad, and his Sabbath-school teacher declared that she would spare no effort to that end. The rumor had reached Pittsburgh that the boy had been seen in a New York hotel, and his father had gone East to find him and bring him home.

Paul had just come in to dress for dinner; he sank into a chair, weak to the knees, and clasped his head in his hands. It was to be worse than jail, even; the tepid waters of Cordelia Street were to close over him finally and forever. The gray monotony stretched before him in hopeless, unrelieved years; Sabbath school, Young People's Meeting, the yellow-papered room, the damp dishtowels; it all rushed back upon him with a sickening vividness. He had the old feeling that the orchestra had suddenly stopped, the sinking sensation that the play was over. The sweat broke out on his face, and he sprang to his feet, looked about him with his white, conscious smile, and winked at himself in the mirror, With something of the old childish belief in miracles with which he had so often gone to class, all his lessons unlearned, Paul dressed and dashed whistling down the corridor to the elevator.

He had no sooner entered the dining room and caught the measure of the music than his remembrance was lightened by his old elastic power of claiming the moment, mounting with it, and finding it all-sufficient. The glare and glitter about him, the mere scenic accessories had again, and for the last time, their old potency. He would show himself that he was game, he would finish the thing splendidly. He doubted, more than ever, the existence of Cordelia Street, and for the first time he drank his wine recklessly. Was he not, after all, one of those fortunate beings born to the purple, was he not still himself and in his own place? He drummed a nervous accompaniment to the Pagliacci music and looked about him, telling himself over and over that it had paid.

He reflected drowsily, to the swell of the music and the chill sweetness of his wine, that he might have done it more wisely. He might have caught an outbound steamer and been well out of their clutches before now. But the other side of the world had seemed too far away and too uncertain then; he could not have waited for it; his need had been too sharp. If he had to choose over again, he would do the same thing tomorrow. He looked affectionately about the dining room, now gilded with a soft mist. Ah, it had paid indeed!

Paul was awakened next morning by a painful throbbing in his head and feet. He had thrown himself across the bed without undressing, and had slept with his shoes on. His limbs and hands were lead heavy, and his tongue and throat were parched and burnt. There came upon him one of those fateful attacks of clearheadedness that never occurred except when he was physically exhausted and his nerves hung loose. He lay still, closed his eyes, and let the tide of things wash over him.

His father was in New York; "stopping at some joint or other," he told himself. The memory of successive summers on the front stoop fell upon him like a weight of black water. He had not a hundred dollars left; and he knew now, more than ever, that money was everything, the wall that stood between all he loathed and all he wanted. The thing was winding itself up; he had thought of that on his first glorious day in New York, and had even provided a way to snap the thread. It lay on his dressing table now; he had got it out last night when he came blindly up from dinner, but the shiny metal hurt his eyes, and he disliked the looks of it.

He rose and moved about with a painful effort, succumbing now and again to attacks of nausea. It was the old depression exaggerated; all the world had become Cordelia Street. Yet somehow he was not afraid of anything, was absolutely calm; perhaps because he had looked into the dark corner at last and knew. It was bad enough, what he saw there, but somehow not so bad as his long fear of it had been. He saw everything clearly now. He had a feeling that he had made the best of it, that he had lived the sort of life he was meant to live, and for half an hour he sat staring at the revolver. But he told himself that was not the way, so he went downstairs and took a cab to the ferry.

When Paul arrived in Newark he got off the train and took another cab, directing the driver to follow the Pennsylvania tracks out of the town. The snow lay heavy on the roadways and had drifted deep in the open fields. Only here and there the dead grass or dried weed stalks projected, singularly black, above it. Once well into the country, Paul dismissed the carriage and walked, floundering along the tracks, his mind a medley of irrelevant things. He seemed to hold in his brain an actual picture of everything he had seen that morning. He remembered every feature of both his drivers, of the toothless old woman from whom he had bought the red flowers in his coat, the agent from whom he had got his ticket, and all of his fellow passengers on the ferry. His mind, unable to cope with vital matters near at hand, worked feverishly and deftly at sorting and grouping these images. They made for him a part of the ugliness of the world, of the ache in his head, and the bitter burning on his tongue. He stooped and put a handful of snow into his mouth as he walked, but that, too, seemed hot. When he reached a little hillside, where the tracks ran through a cut some twenty feet below him, he stopped and sat down.

The carnations in his coat were drooping with the cold, he noticed, their red glory all over. It occurred to him that all the flowers he had seen in the glass cases that first night must have gone the same way, long before this. It was only one splendid breath they had, in spite of their brave mockery at the winter outside the glass; and it was a losing game in the end, it seemed, this revolt against the homilies by which the world is run. Paul took one of the blossoms carefully from his coat and scooped a little hole in the snow, where he covered it up. Then he dozed awhile, from his weak condition, seemingly insensible to the cold.

The sound of an approaching train awoke him, and he started to his feet, remembering only his resolution, and afraid lest he should be too late. He stood watching the approaching locomotive, his teeth chattering, his lips drawn away from them in a frightened smile; once or twice he glanced nervously sidewise, as though he were being watched. When the right moment came, he jumped. As he fell, the folly of his haste occurred to him with merciless clearness, the vastness of what he had left undone. There flashed through his brain, clearer than ever before, the blue of Adriatic water, the yellow of Algerian sands.

He felt something strike his chest, and that his body was being thrown swiftly through the air, on and on, immeasurably far and fast, while his limbs were gently relaxed. Then, because the picture-making mechanism was crushed, the disturbing visions flashed into black, and Paul dropped back into the immense design of things.

BOOK TWO
O PIONEERS!

PART I. THE WILD LAND

I

One January day, thirty years ago, the little town of Hanover, anchored on a windy Nebraska tableland, was trying not to be blown away. A mist of fine snowflakes was curling and eddying about the cluster of low drab buildings huddled on the gray prairie, under a gray sky. The dwelling-houses were set about haphazard on the tough prairie sod; some of them looked as if they had been moved in overnight, and others as if they were straying off by themselves, headed straight for the open plain. None of them had any appearance of permanence, and the howling wind blew under them as well as over them. The main street was a deeply rutted road, now frozen hard, which ran from the squat red railway station and the grain "elevator" at the north end of the town to the lumber yard and the horse pond at the south end. On either side of this road straggled two uneven rows of wooden buildings; the general merchandise stores, the two banks, the drug store, the feed store, the saloon, the post-office. The board sidewalks were gray with trampled snow, but at two o'clock in the afternoon the shopkeepers, having come back from dinner, were keeping well behind their frosty windows. The children were all in school, and there was nobody abroad in the streets but a few rough-looking countrymen in coarse overcoats, with their long caps pulled down to their noses. Some of them had brought their wives to town, and now and then a red or a plaid shawl flashed out of one store into the shelter of another. At the hitch-bars along the street a few heavy work-horses, harnessed to farm wagons, shivered under their blankets. About the station everything was quiet, for there would not be another train in until night.

On the sidewalk in front of one of the stores sat a little Swede boy, crying bitterly. He was about five years old. His black cloth coat was much too big for him and made him look like a little old man. His shrunken brown flannel dress had been washed many times and left a long stretch of stocking between the hem of his skirt and the tops of his clumsy, copper-toed shoes. His cap was pulled down over his ears; his nose and his chubby cheeks were chapped and red with cold. He cried quietly, and the few people who hurried by did not notice him. He was afraid to stop any one, afraid to go into the store and ask for help, so he sat wringing his long sleeves and looking up a telegraph pole beside him, whimpering, "My kitten, oh, my kitten! Her will fweeze!" At the top of the pole crouched a shivering gray kitten, mewing faintly and clinging desperately to the wood with her claws. The boy had been left at the store while his sister went to the doctor's office, and in her absence a dog had chased his kitten up the pole. The little creature had never been so high before, and she was too frightened to move. Her master was sunk in despair. He was a little country boy, and this village was to him a very strange and perplexing place, where people wore fine clothes and had hard hearts. He always felt shy and awkward here, and wanted to hide behind things for fear some one might laugh at him. Just now, he was too unhappy to care who laughed. At last he seemed to see a ray of hope: his sister was coming, and he got up and ran toward her in his heavy shoes.

His sister was a tall, strong girl, and she walked rapidly and resolutely, as if she knew exactly where she was going and what she was going to do next. She wore a man's long ulster (not as if it were an affliction, but as if it were very comfortable and belonged to her; carried it like a young soldier), and a round plush cap, tied down with a thick veil. She had a serious, thoughtful face, and her clear, deep blue eyes were fixed intently on the distance, without seeming to see anything, as if she were in trouble. She did not notice the little boy until he pulled her by the coat. Then she stopped short and stooped down to wipe his wet face.

"Why, Emil! I told you to stay in the store and not to come out. What is the matter with you?"

"My kitten, sister, my kitten! A man put her out, and a dog chased her up there." His forefinger, projecting from the sleeve of his coat, pointed up to the wretched little creature on the pole.

"Oh, Emil! Didn't I tell you she'd get us into trouble of some kind, if you brought her? What made you tease me so? But there, I ought to have known better myself." She went to the foot of the pole and held out her arms, crying, "Kitty, kitty, kitty," but the kitten only mewed and faintly waved its tail. Alexandra turned away decidedly. "No, she won't come down. Somebody will have to go up after her. I saw the Linstrums' wagon in town. I'll go and see if I can find Carl. Maybe he can do something. Only you must stop crying, or I won't go a step. Where's your comforter? Did you leave it in the store? Never mind. Hold still, till I put this on you."

She unwound the brown veil from her head and tied it about his throat. A shabby little traveling man, who was just then coming out of the store on his way to the saloon, stopped and gazed stupidly at the shining mass of hair she bared when she took off her veil; two thick braids, pinned about her head in the German way, with a fringe of reddish-yellow curls blowing out from under her cap. He took his cigar out of his mouth and held the wet end between the fingers of his woolen glove. "My God, girl, what a head of hair!" he exclaimed, quite innocently and foolishly. She stabbed him with a glance of Amazonian fierceness and drew in her lower lip--most unnecessary severity. It gave the little clothing drummer such a start that he actually let his cigar fall to the sidewalk and went off weakly in the teeth of the wind to the saloon. His hand was still unsteady when he took his glass from the bartender. His feeble flirtatious instincts had been crushed before, but never so mercilessly. He felt cheap and ill-used, as if some one had taken advantage of him. When a drummer had been knocking about in little drab towns and crawling across the wintry country in dirty smokingcars, was he to be blamed if, when he chanced upon a fine human creature, he suddenly wished himself more of a man?

While the little drummer was drinking to recover his nerve, Alexandra hurried to the drug store as the most likely place to find Carl Linstrum. There he was, turning over a portfolio of chromo "studies" which the druggist sold to the Hanover women who did chinapainting. Alexandra explained her predicament, and the boy followed her to the corner, where Emil still sat by the pole.

"I'll have to go up after her, Alexandra. I think at the depot they have some spikes I can strap on my feet. Wait a minute." Carl thrust his hands into his pockets, lowered his head, and darted up the street against the north wind. He was a tall boy of fifteen, slight and narrow-chested. When he came back with the spikes, Alexandra asked him what he had done with his overcoat.

"I left it in the drug store. I couldn't climb in it, anyhow. Catch me if I fall, Emil," he called back as he began his ascent. Alexandra watched him anxiously; the cold was bitter enough on the ground. The kitten would not budge an inch. Carl had to go to the very top of the pole, and then had some difficulty in tearing her from her hold. When he reached the ground, he handed the cat to her tearful little master. "Now go into the store with her, Emil, and get warm." He opened the door for the child. "Wait a minute, Alexandra. Why can't I drive for you as far as our place? It's getting colder every minute. Have you seen the doctor?"

"Yes. He is coming over to-morrow. But he says father can't get better; can't get well." The girl's lip trembled. She looked fixedly up the bleak street as if she were gathering her strength to face something, as if she were trying with all her might to grasp a situation which, no matter how painful, must be met and dealt with somehow. The wind flapped the skirts of her heavy coat about her.

Carl did not say anything, but she felt his sympathy. He, too, was lonely. He was a thin, frail boy, with brooding dark eyes, very quiet in all his movements. There was a delicate pallor in his thin face, and his mouth was too sensitive for a boy's. The lips had already a little curl of bitterness and skepticism. The two friends stood for a few moments on the windy street corner, not speaking a word, as two travelers, who have lost their way, sometimes stand and admit their perplexity in silence. When Carl turned away he said, "I'll see to your team." Alexandra went into the store to have her purchases packed in the egg-boxes, and to get warm before she set out on her long cold drive.

When she looked for Emil, she found him sitting on a step of the staircase that led up to the clothing and carpet department. He was playing with a little Bohemian girl, Marie Tovesky, who was tying her handkerchief over the kitten's head for a bonnet. Marie was a stranger in the country, having come from Omaha with her mother to visit her uncle, Joe Tovesky. She was a dark child, with brown curly hair, like a brunette doll's, a coaxing little red mouth, and round, yellow-brown eyes. Every one noticed her eyes; the brown iris had golden glints that made them look like gold-stone, or, in softer lights, like that Colorado mineral called tiger-eye.

The country children thereabouts wore their dresses to their shoe-tops, but this city child was dressed in what was then called the "Kate Greenaway" manner, and her red cashmere frock, gathered full from the yoke, came almost to the floor. This, with her poke bonnet, gave her the look of a quaint little woman. She had a white fur tippet about her neck and made no fussy objections when Emil fingered it admiringly. Alexandra had not the heart to take him away from so pretty a playfellow, and she let them tease the kitten together until Joe Tovesky came in noisily and picked up his little niece, setting her on his shoulder for every one to see. His children were all boys, and he adored this little creature. His cronies formed a circle about him, admiring and teasing the little girl, who took their jokes with great good nature. They were all delighted with her, for they seldom saw so pretty and carefully nurtured a child. They told her that she must choose one of them for a sweetheart, and each began pressing his suit and offering her bribes; candy, and little pigs, and spotted calves. She looked archly into the big, brown, mustached faces, smelling of spirits and tobacco, then she ran her tiny forefinger delicately over Joe's bristly chin and said, "Here is my sweetheart."

The Bohemians roared with laughter, and Marie's uncle hugged her until she cried, "Please don't, Uncle Joe! You hurt me." Each of Joe's friends gave her a bag of candy, and she kissed them all around, though she did not like country candy very well. Perhaps that was why she bethought herself of Emil. "Let me down, Uncle Joe," she said, "I want to give some of my candy to that nice little boy I found." She walked graciously over to Emil, followed by her lusty admirers, who formed a new circle and teased the little boy until he hid his face in his sister's skirts, and she had to scold him for being such a baby.

The farm people were making preparations to start for home. The women were checking over their groceries and pinning their big red shawls about their heads. The men were buying tobacco and candy with what money they had left, were showing each other new boots and gloves and blue flannel shirts. Three big Bohemians were drinking raw alcohol, tinctured with oil of cinnamon. This was said to fortify one effectually against the cold, and they smacked their lips after each pull at the flask. Their volubility drowned every other noise in the place, and the overheated store sounded of their spirited language as it reeked of pipe smoke, damp woolens, and kerosene.

Carl came in, wearing his overcoat and carrying a wooden box with a brass handle. "Come," he said, "I've fed and watered your team, and the wagon is ready." He carried Emil out and tucked him down in the straw in the wagonbox. The heat had made the little boy sleepy, but he still clung to his kitten.

"You were awful good to climb so high and get my kitten, Carl. When I get big I'll climb and get little boys' kittens for them," he murmured drowsily. Before the horses were over the first hill, Emil and his cat were both fast asleep.

Although it was only four o'clock, the winter day was fading. The road led southwest, toward the streak of pale, watery light that glimmered in the leaden sky. The light fell upon the two sad young faces that were turned mutely toward it: upon the eyes of the girl, who seemed to be looking with such anguished perplexity into the future; upon the sombre eyes of the boy, who seemed already to be looking into the past. The little town behind them had vanished as if it had never been, had fallen behind the swell of the prairie, and the stern frozen country received them into its bosom. The homesteads were few and far apart; here and there a windmill gaunt against the sky, a sod house crouching in a hollow. But the great fact was the land itself, which seemed to overwhelm the little beginnings of human society that struggled in its sombre wastes. It was from facing this vast hardness that the boy's mouth had become so bitter; because he felt that men were too weak to make any mark here, that the land wanted to be let alone, to preserve its own fierce strength, its peculiar, savage kind of beauty, its uninterrupted mournfulness.

The wagon jolted along over the frozen road. The two friends had less to say to each other than usual, as if the cold had somehow penetrated to their hearts.

"Did Lou and Oscar go to the Blue to cut wood to-day?" Carl asked.

"Yes. I'm almost sorry I let them go, it's turned so cold. But mother frets if the wood gets low." She stopped and put her hand to her forehead, brushing back her hair. "I don't know what is to become of us, Carl, if father has to die. I don't dare to think about it. I wish we could all go with him and let the grass grow back over everything."

Carl made no reply. Just ahead of them was the Norwegian graveyard, where the grass had, indeed, grown back over everything, shaggy and red, hiding even the wire fence. Carl realized that he was not a very helpful companion, but there was nothing he could say.

"Of course," Alexandra went on, steadying her voice a little, "the boys are strong and work hard, but we've always depended so on father that I don't see how we can go ahead. I almost feel as if there were nothing to go ahead for."

"Does your father know?"

"Yes, I think he does. He lies and counts on his fingers all day. I think he is trying to count up what he is leaving for us. It's a comfort to him that my chickens are laying right on through the cold weather and bringing in a little money. I wish we could keep his mind off such things, but I don't have much time to be with him now."

"I wonder if he'd like to have me bring my magic lantern over some evening?"

Alexandra turned her face toward him. "Oh, Carl! Have you got it?"

"Yes. It's back there in the straw. Didn't you notice the box I was carrying? I tried it all morning in the drug-store cellar, and it worked ever so well, makes fine big pictures."

"What are they about?"

"Oh, hunting pictures in Germany, and Robinson Crusoe and funny pictures about cannibals. I'm going to paint some slides for it on glass, out of the Hans Andersen book."

Alexandra seemed actually cheered. There is often a good deal of the child left in people who have had to grow up too soon. "Do bring it over, Carl. I can hardly wait to see it, and I'm sure it will please father. Are the pictures colored? Then I know he'll like them. He likes the calendars I get him in town. I wish I could get more. You must leave me here, mustn't you? It's been nice to have company."

Carl stopped the horses and looked dubiously up at the black sky. "It's pretty dark. Of course the horses will take you home, but I think I'd better light your lantern, in case you should need it."

He gave her the reins and climbed back into the wagon-box, where he crouched down and made a tent of his overcoat. After a dozen trials he succeeded in lighting the lantern, which he placed in front of Alexandra, half covering it with a blanket so that the light would not shine in her eyes. "Now, wait until I find my box. Yes, here it is. Good-night, Alexandra. Try not to worry." Carl sprang to the ground and ran off across the fields toward the Linstrum homestead. "Hoo, hoo-o-o-o!" he called back as he disappeared over a ridge and dropped into a sand gully. The wind answered him like an echo, "Hoo, hoo-o-o-o-o-o!" Alexandra drove off alone. The rattle of her wagon was lost in the howling of the wind, but her lantern, held firmly between her feet, made a moving point of light along the highway, going deeper and deeper into the dark country.

II

On one of the ridges of that wintry waste stood the low log house in which John Bergson was dying. The Bergson homestead was easier to find than many another, because it overlooked Norway Creek, a shallow, muddy stream that sometimes flowed, and sometimes stood still, at the bottom of a winding ravine with steep, shelving sides overgrown with brush and cottonwoods and dwarf ash. This creek gave a sort of identity to the farms that bordered upon it. Of all the bewildering things about a new country, the absence of human landmarks is one of the most depressing and disheartening. The houses on the Divide were small and were usually tucked away in low places; you did not see them until you came directly upon them. Most of them were built of the sod itself, and were only the unescapable ground in another form. The roads were but faint tracks in the grass, and the fields were scarcely noticeable. The record of the plow was insignificant, like the feeble scratches on stone left by prehistoric races, so indeterminate that they may, after all, be only the markings of glaciers, and not a record of human strivings.

In eleven long years John Bergson had made but little impression upon the wild land he had come to tame. It was still a wild thing that had its ugly moods; and no one knew when they were likely to come, or why. Mischance hung over it. Its Genius was unfriendly to man. The sick man was feeling this as he lay looking out of the window, after the doctor had left him, on the day following Alexandra's trip to town. There it lay outside his door, the same land, the same lead-colored miles. He knew every ridge and draw and gully between him and the horizon. To the south, his plowed fields; to the east, the sod stables, the cattle corral, the pond,--and then the grass.

Bergson went over in his mind the things that had held him back. One winter his cattle had perished in a blizzard. The next summer one of his plow horses broke its leg in a prairiedog hole and had to be shot. Another summer he lost his hogs from cholera, and a valuable stallion died from a rattlesnake bite. Time and again his crops had failed. He had lost two children, boys, that came between Lou and Emil, and there had been the cost of sickness and death. Now, when he had at last struggled out of debt, he was going to die himself. He was only forty-six, and had, of course, counted upon more time.

Bergson had spent his first five years on the Divide getting into debt, and the last six getting out. He had paid off his mortgages and had ended pretty much where he began, with the land. He owned exactly six hundred and forty acres of what stretched outside his door; his own original homestead and timber claim, making three hundred and twenty acres, and the half-section adjoining, the homestead of a younger brother who had given up the fight, gone back to Chicago to work in a fancy bakery and distinguish himself in a Swedish athletic club. So far John had not attempted to cultivate the second half-section, but used it for pasture land, and one of his sons rode herd there in open weather.

John Bergson had the Old-World belief that land, in itself, is desirable. But this land was an enigma. It was like a horse that no one knows how to break to harness, that runs wild and kicks things to pieces. He had an idea that no one understood how to farm it properly, and this he often discussed with Alexandra. Their neighbors, certainly, knew even less about farming than he did. Many of them had never worked on a farm until they took up their homesteads. They had been HANDWERKERS at home; tailors, locksmiths, joiners, cigar-makers, etc. Bergson himself had worked in a shipyard.

For weeks, John Bergson had been thinking about these things. His bed stood in the sitting-room, next to the kitchen. Through the day, while the baking and washing and ironing were going on, the father lay and looked up at the roof beams that he himself had hewn, or out at the cattle in the corral. He counted the cattle over and over. It diverted him to speculate as to how much weight each of the steers would probably put on by spring. He often called his daughter in to talk to her about this. Before Alexandra was twelve years old she had begun to be a help to him, and as she grew older he had come to depend more and more upon her resourcefulness and good judgment. His boys were willing enough to work, but when he talked with them they usually irritated him. It was Alexandra who read the papers and followed the markets, and who learned by the mistakes of their neighbors. It was Alexandra who could always tell about what it had cost to fatten each steer, and who could guess the weight of a hog before it went on the scales closer than John Bergson himself. Lou and Oscar were industrious, but he could never teach them to use their heads about their work.

Alexandra, her father often said to himself, was like her grandfather; which was his way of saying that she was intelligent. John Bergson's father had been a shipbuilder, a man of considerable force and of some fortune. Late in life he married a second time, a Stockholm woman of questionable character, much younger than he, who goaded him into every sort of extravagance. On the shipbuilder's part, this marriage was an infatuation, the despairing folly of a powerful man who cannot bear to grow old. In a few years his unprincipled wife warped the probity of a lifetime. He speculated, lost his own fortune and funds entrusted to him by poor seafaring men, and died disgraced, leaving his children nothing. But when all was said, he had come up from the sea himself, had built up a proud little business with no capital but his own skill and foresight, and had proved himself a man. In his daughter, John Bergson recognized the strength of will, and the simple direct way of thinking things out, that had characterized his father in his better days. He would much rather, of course, have seen this likeness in one of his sons, but it was not a question of choice. As he lay there day after day he had to accept the situation as it was, and to be thankful that there was one among his children to whom he could entrust the future of his family and the possibilities of his hard-won land.

The winter twilight was fading. The sick man heard his wife strike a match in the kitchen, and the light of a lamp glimmered through the cracks of the door. It seemed like a light shining far away. He turned painfully in his bed and looked at his white hands, with all the work gone out of them. He was ready to give up, he felt. He did not know how it had come about, but he was quite willing to go deep under his fields and rest, where the plow could not find him. He was tired of making mistakes. He was content to leave the tangle to other hands; he thought of his Alexandra's strong ones.

"DOTTER," he called feebly, "DOTTER!" He heard her quick step and saw her tall figure appear in the doorway, with the light of the lamp behind her. He felt her youth and strength, how easily she moved and stooped and lifted. But he would not have had it again if he could, not he! He knew the end too well to wish to begin again. He knew where it all went to, what it all became.

His daughter came and lifted him up on his pillows. She called him by an old Swedish name that she used to call him when she was little and took his dinner to him in the shipyard.

"Tell the boys to come here, daughter. I want to speak to them."

"They are feeding the horses, father. They have just come back from the Blue. Shall I call them?"

He sighed. "No, no. Wait until they come in. Alexandra, you will have to do the best you can for your brothers. Everything will come on you."

"I will do all I can, father."

"Don't let them get discouraged and go off like Uncle Otto. I want them to keep the land."

"We will, father. We will never lose the land."

There was a sound of heavy feet in the kitchen. Alexandra went to the door and beckoned to her brothers, two strapping boys of seventeen and nineteen. They came in and stood at the foot of the bed. Their father looked at them searchingly, though it was too dark to see their faces; they were just the same boys, he told himself, he had not been mistaken in them. The square head and heavy shoulders belonged to Oscar, the elder. The younger boy was quicker, but vacillating.

"Boys," said the father wearily, "I want you to keep the land together and to be guided by your sister. I have talked to her since I have been sick, and she knows all my wishes. I want no quarrels among my children, and so long as there is one house there must be one head. Alexandra is the oldest, and she knows my wishes. She will do the best she can. If she makes mistakes, she will not make so many as I have made. When you marry, and want a house of your own, the land will be divided fairly, according to the courts. But for the next few years you will have it hard, and you must all keep together. Alexandra will manage the best she can."

Oscar, who was usually the last to speak, replied because he was the older, "Yes, father. It would be so anyway, without your speaking. We will all work the place together."

"And you will be guided by your sister, boys, and be good brothers to her, and good sons to your mother? That is good. And Alexandra must not work in the fields any more. There is no necessity now. Hire a man when you need help. She can make much more with her eggs and butter than the wages of a man. It was one of my mistakes that I did not find that out sooner. Try to break a little more land every year; sod corn is good for fodder. Keep turning the land, and always put up more hay than you need. Don't grudge your mother a little time for plowing her garden and setting out fruit trees, even if it comes in a busy season. She has been a good mother to you, and she has always missed the old country."

When they went back to the kitchen the boys sat down silently at the table. Throughout the meal they looked down at their plates and did not lift their red eyes. They did not eat much, although they had been working in the cold all day, and there was a rabbit stewed in gravy for supper, and prune pies.

John Bergson had married beneath him, but he had married a good housewife. Mrs. Bergson was a fair-skinned, corpulent woman, heavy and placid like her son, Oscar, but there was something comfortable about her; perhaps it was her own love of comfort. For eleven years she had worthily striven to maintain some semblance of household order amid conditions that made order very difficult. Habit was very strong with Mrs. Bergson, and her unremitting efforts to repeat the routine of her old life among new surroundings had done a great deal to keep the family from disintegrating morally and getting careless in their ways. The Bergsons had a log house, for instance, only because Mrs. Bergson would not live in a sod house. She missed the fish diet of her own country, and twice every summer she sent the boys to the river, twenty miles to the southward, to fish for channel cat. When the children were little she used to load them all into the wagon, the baby in its crib, and go fishing herself.

Alexandra often said that if her mother were cast upon a desert island, she would thank God for her deliverance, make a garden, and find something to preserve. Preserving was almost a mania with Mrs. Bergson. Stout as she was, she roamed the scrubby banks of Norway Creek looking for fox grapes and goose plums, like a wild creature in search of prey. She made a yellow jam of the insipid ground-cherries that grew on the prairie, flavoring it with lemon peel; and she made a sticky dark conserve of garden tomatoes. She had experimented even with the rank buffalo-pea, and she could not see a fine bronze cluster of them without shaking her head and murmuring, "What a pity!" When there was nothing more to preserve, she began to pickle. The amount of sugar she used in these processes was sometimes a serious drain upon the family resources. She was a good mother, but she was glad when her children were old enough not to be in her way in the kitchen. She had never quite forgiven John Bergson for bringing her to the end of the earth; but, now that she was there, she wanted to be let alone to reconstruct her old life in so far as that was possible. She could still take some comfort in the world if she had bacon in the cave, glass jars on the shelves, and sheets in the press. She disapproved of all her neighbors because of their slovenly housekeeping, and the women thought her very proud. Once when Mrs. Bergson, on her way to Norway Creek, stopped to see old Mrs. Lee, the old woman hid in the haymow "for fear Mis' Bergson would catch her barefoot."

III

One Sunday afternoon in July, six months after John Bergson's death, Carl was sitting in the doorway of the Linstrum kitchen, dreaming over an illustrated paper, when he heard the rattle of a wagon along the hill road. Looking up he recognized the Bergsons' team, with two seats in the wagon, which meant they were off for a pleasure excursion. Oscar and Lou, on the front seat, wore their cloth hats and coats, never worn except on Sundays, and Emil, on the second seat with Alexandra, sat proudly in his new trousers, made from a pair of his father's, and a pink-striped shirt, with a wide ruffled collar. Oscar stopped the horses and waved to Carl, who caught up his hat and ran through the melon patch to join them.

"Want to go with us?" Lou called. "We're going to Crazy Ivar's to buy a hammock."

"Sure." Carl ran up panting, and clambering over the wheel sat down beside Emil. "I've always wanted to see Ivar's pond. They say it's the biggest in all the country. Aren't you afraid to go to Ivar's in that new shirt, Emil? He might want it and take it right off your back."

Emil grinned. "I'd be awful scared to go," he admitted, "if you big boys weren't along to take care of me. Did you ever hear him howl, Carl? People say sometimes he runs about the country howling at night because he is afraid the Lord will destroy him. Mother thinks he must have done something awful wicked."

Lou looked back and winked at Carl. "What would you do, Emil, if you was out on the prairie by yourself and seen him coming?"

Emil stared. "Maybe I could hide in a badger-hole," he suggested doubtfully.

"But suppose there wasn't any badger-hole," Lou persisted. "Would you run?"

"No, I'd be too scared to run," Emil admitted mournfully, twisting his fingers. "I guess I'd sit right down on the ground and say my prayers."

The big boys laughed, and Oscar brandished his whip over the broad backs of the horses.

"He wouldn't hurt you, Emil," said Carl persuasively. "He came to doctor our mare when she ate green corn and swelled up most as big as the water-tank. He petted her just like you do your cats. I couldn't understand much he said, for he don't talk any English, but he kept patting her and groaning as if he had the pain himself, and saying, 'There now, sister, that's easier, that's better!'"

Lou and Oscar laughed, and Emil giggled delightedly and looked up at his sister.

"I don't think he knows anything at all about doctoring," said Oscar scornfully. "They say when horses have distemper he takes the medicine himself, and then prays over the horses."

Alexandra spoke up. "That's what the Crows said, but he cured their horses, all the same. Some days his mind is cloudy, like. But if you can get him on a clear day, you can learn a great deal from him. He understands animals. Didn't I see him take the horn off the Berquist's cow when she had torn it loose and went crazy? She was tearing all over the place, knocking herself against things. And at last she ran out on the roof of the old dugout and her legs went through and there she stuck, bellowing. Ivar came running with his white bag, and the moment he got to her she was quiet and let him saw her horn off and daub the place with tar."

Emil had been watching his sister, his face reflecting the sufferings of the cow. "And then didn't it hurt her any more?" he asked.

Alexandra patted him. "No, not any more. And in two days they could use her milk again."

The road to Ivar's homestead was a very poor one. He had settled in the rough country across the county line, where no one lived but some Russians,--half a dozen families who dwelt together in one long house, divided off like barracks. Ivar had explained his choice by saying that the fewer neighbors he had, the fewer temptations. Nevertheless, when one considered that his chief business was horsedoctoring, it seemed rather short-sighted of him to live in the most inaccessible place he could find. The Bergson wagon lurched along over the rough hummocks and grass banks, followed the bottom of winding draws, or skirted the margin of wide lagoons, where the golden coreopsis grew up out of the clear water and the wild ducks rose with a whirr of wings.

Lou looked after them helplessly. "I wish I'd brought my gun, anyway, Alexandra," he said fretfully. "I could have hidden it under the straw in the bottom of the wagon."

"Then we'd have had to lie to Ivar. Besides, they say he can smell dead birds. And if he knew, we wouldn't get anything out of him, not even a hammock. I want to talk to him, and he won't talk sense if he's angry. It makes him foolish."

Lou sniffed. "Whoever heard of him talking sense, anyhow! I'd rather have ducks for supper than Crazy Ivar's tongue."

Emil was alarmed. "Oh, but, Lou, you don't want to make him mad! He might howl!"

They all laughed again, and Oscar urged the horses up the crumbling side of a clay bank. They had left the lagoons and the red grass behind them. In Crazy Ivar's country the grass was short and gray, the draws deeper than they were in the Bergsons' neighborhood, and the land was all broken up into hillocks and clay ridges. The wild flowers disappeared, and only in the bottom of the draws and gullies grew a few of the very toughest and hardiest: shoestring, and ironweed, and snow-on-the-mountain.

"Look, look, Emil, there's Ivar's big pond!" Alexandra pointed to a shining sheet of water that lay at the bottom of a shallow draw. At one end of the pond was an earthen dam, planted with green willow bushes, and above it a door and a single window were set into the hillside. You would not have seen them at all but for the reflection of the sunlight upon the four panes of window-glass. And that was all you saw. Not a shed, not a corral, not a well, not even a path broken in the curly grass. But for the piece of rusty stovepipe sticking up through the sod, you could have walked over the roof of Ivar's dwelling without dreaming that you were near a human habitation. Ivar had lived for three years in the clay bank, without defiling the face of nature any more than the coyote that had lived there before him had done.

When the Bergsons drove over the hill, Ivar was sitting in the doorway of his house, reading the Norwegian Bible. He was a queerly shaped old man, with a thick, powerful body set on short bow-legs. His shaggy white hair, falling in a thick mane about his ruddy cheeks, made him look older than he was. He was barefoot, but he wore a clean shirt of unbleached cotton, open at the neck. He always put on a clean shirt when Sunday morning came round, though he never went to church. He had a peculiar religion of his own and could not get on with any of the denominations. Often he did not see anybody from one week's end to another. He kept a calendar, and every morning he checked off a day, so that he was never in any doubt as to which day of the week it was. Ivar hired himself out in threshing and corn-husking time, and he doctored sick animals when he was sent for. When he was at home, he made hammocks out of twine and committed chapters of the Bible to memory.

Ivar found contentment in the solitude he had sought out for himself. He disliked the litter of human dwellings: the broken food, the bits of broken china, the old wash-boilers and tea-kettles thrown into the sunflower patch. He preferred the cleanness and tidiness of the wild sod. He always said that the badgers had cleaner houses than people, and that when he took a housekeeper her name would be Mrs. Badger. He best expressed his preference for his wild homestead by saying that his Bible seemed truer to him there. If one stood in the doorway of his cave, and looked off at the rough land, the smiling sky, the curly grass white in the hot sunlight; if one listened to the rapturous song of the lark, the drumming of the quail, the burr of the locust against that vast silence, one understood what Ivar meant.

On this Sunday afternoon his face shone with happiness. He closed the book on his knee, keeping the place with his horny finger, and repeated softly:--

He sendeth the springs into the valleys, which run among the hills;

They give drink to every beast of the field; the wild asses quench their thirst.

The trees of the Lord are full of sap; the cedars of Lebanon which he hath planted;

Where the birds make their nests: as for the stork, the fir trees are her house.

The high hills are a refuge for the wild goats; and the rocks for the conies.

Before he opened his Bible again, Ivar heard the Bergsons' wagon approaching, and he sprang up and ran toward it.

"No guns, no guns!" he shouted, waving his arms distractedly.

"No, Ivar, no guns," Alexandra called reassuringly.

He dropped his arms and went up to the wagon, smiling amiably and looking at them out of his pale blue eyes.

"We want to buy a hammock, if you have one," Alexandra explained, "and my little brother, here, wants to see your big pond, where so many birds come."

Ivar smiled foolishly, and began rubbing the horses' noses and feeling about their mouths behind the bits. "Not many birds just now. A few ducks this morning; and some snipe come to drink. But there was a crane last week. She spent one night and came back the next evening. I don't know why. It is not her season, of course. Many of them go over in the fall. Then the pond is full of strange voices every night."

Alexandra translated for Carl, who looked thoughtful. "Ask him, Alexandra, if it is true that a sea gull came here once. I have heard so."

She had some difficulty in making the old man understand.

He looked puzzled at first, then smote his hands together as he remembered. "Oh, yes, yes! A big white bird with long wings and pink feet. My! what a voice she had! She came in the afternoon and kept flying about the pond and screaming until dark. She was in trouble of some sort, but I could not understand her. She was going over to the other ocean, maybe, and did not know how far it was. She was afraid of never getting there. She was more mournful than our birds here; she cried in the night. She saw the light from my window and darted up to it. Maybe she thought my house was a boat, she was such a wild thing. Next morning, when the sun rose, I went out to take her food, but she flew up into the sky and went on her way." Ivar ran his fingers through his thick hair. "I have many strange birds stop with me here. They come from very far away and are great company. I hope you boys never shoot wild birds?"

Lou and Oscar grinned, and Ivar shook his bushy head. "Yes, I know boys are thoughtless. But these wild things are God's birds. He watches over them and counts them, as we do our cattle; Christ says so in the New Testament."

"Now, Ivar," Lou asked, "may we water our horses at your pond and give them some feed? It's a bad road to your place."

"Yes, yes, it is." The old man scrambled about and began to loose the tugs. "A bad road, eh, girls? And the bay with a colt at home!"

Oscar brushed the old man aside. "We'll take care of the horses, Ivar. You'll be finding some disease on them. Alexandra wants to see your hammocks."

Ivar led Alexandra and Emil to his little cave house. He had but one room, neatly plastered and whitewashed, and there was a wooden floor. There was a kitchen stove, a table covered with oilcloth, two chairs, a clock, a calendar, a few books on the window-shelf; nothing more. But the place was as clean as a cupboard.

"But where do you sleep, Ivar?" Emil asked, looking about.

Ivar unslung a hammock from a hook on the wall; in it was rolled a buffalo robe. "There, my son. A hammock is a good bed, and in winter I wrap up in this skin. Where I go to work, the beds are not half so easy as this."

By this time Emil had lost all his timidity. He thought a cave a very superior kind of house. There was something pleasantly unusual about it and about Ivar. "Do the birds know you will be kind to them, Ivar? Is that why so many come?" he asked.

Ivar sat down on the floor and tucked his feet under him. "See, little brother, they have come from a long way, and they are very tired. From up there where they are flying, our country looks dark and flat. They must have water to drink and to bathe in before they can go on with their journey. They look this way and that, and far below them they see something shining, like a piece of glass set in the dark earth. That is my pond. They come to it and are not disturbed. Maybe I sprinkle a little corn. They tell the other birds, and next year more come this way. They have their roads up there, as we have down here."

Emil rubbed his knees thoughtfully. "And is that true, Ivar, about the head ducks falling back when they are tired, and the hind ones taking their place?"

"Yes. The point of the wedge gets the worst of it; they cut the wind. They can only stand it there a little while--half an hour, maybe. Then they fall back and the wedge splits a little, while the rear ones come up the middle to the front.

Then it closes up and they fly on, with a new edge. They are always changing like that, up in the air. Never any confusion; just like soldiers who have been drilled."

Alexandra had selected her hammock by the time the boys came up from the pond. They would not come in, but sat in the shade of the bank outside while Alexandra and Ivar talked about the birds and about his housekeeping, and why he never ate meat, fresh or salt.

Alexandra was sitting on one of the wooden chairs, her arms resting on the table. Ivar was sitting on the floor at her feet. "Ivar," she said suddenly, beginning to trace the pattern on the oilcloth with her forefinger, "I came to-day more because I wanted to talk to you than because I wanted to buy a hammock."

"Yes?" The old man scraped his bare feet on the plank floor.

"We have a big bunch of hogs, Ivar. I wouldn't sell in the spring, when everybody advised me to, and now so many people are losing their hogs that I am frightened. What can be done?"

Ivar's little eyes began to shine. They lost their vagueness.

"You feed them swill and such stuff? Of course! And sour milk? Oh, yes! And keep them in a stinking pen? I tell you, sister, the hogs of this country are put upon! They become unclean, like the hogs in the Bible. If you kept your chickens like that, what would happen? You have a little sorghum patch, maybe? Put a fence around it, and turn the hogs in. Build a shed to give them shade, a thatch on poles. Let the boys haul water to them in barrels, clean water, and plenty. Get them off the old stinking ground, and do not let them go back there until winter. Give them only grain and clean feed, such as you would give horses or cattle. Hogs do not like to be filthy."

The boys outside the door had been listening. Lou nudged his brother. "Come, the horses are done eating. Let's hitch up and get out of here. He'll fill her full of notions. She'll be for having the pigs sleep with us, next."

Oscar grunted and got up. Carl, who could not understand what Ivar said, saw that the two boys were displeased. They did not mind hard work, but they hated experiments and could never see the use of taking pains. Even Lou, who was more elastic than his older brother, disliked to do anything different from their neighbors. He felt that it made them conspicuous and gave people a chance to talk about them.

Once they were on the homeward road, the boys forgot their ill-humor and joked about Ivar and his birds. Alexandra did not propose any reforms in the care of the pigs, and they hoped she had forgotten Ivar's talk. They agreed that he was crazier than ever, and would never be able to prove up on his land because he worked it so little. Alexandra privately resolved that she would have a talk with Ivar about this and stir him up. The boys persuaded Carl to stay for supper and go swimming in the pasture pond after dark.

That evening, after she had washed the supper dishes, Alexandra sat down on the kitchen doorstep, while her mother was mixing the bread. It was a still, deep-breathing summer night, full of the smell of the hay fields. Sounds of laughter and splashing came up from the pasture, and when the moon rose rapidly above the bare rim of the prairie, the pond glittered like polished metal, and she could see the flash of white bodies as the boys ran about the edge, or jumped into the water. Alexandra watched the shimmering pool dreamily, but eventually her eyes went back to the sorghum patch south of the barn, where she was planning to make her new pig corral.

IV

For the first three years after John Bergson's death, the affairs of his family prospered. Then came the hard times that brought every one on the Divide to the brink of despair; three years of drouth and failure, the last struggle of a wild soil against the encroaching plowshare. The first of these fruitless summers the Bergson boys bore courageously. The failure of the corn crop made labor cheap. Lou and Oscar hired two men and put in bigger crops than ever before. They lost everything they spent. The whole country was discouraged. Farmers who were already in debt had to give up their land. A few foreclosures demoralized the county. The settlers sat about on the wooden sidewalks in the little town and told each other that the country was never meant for men to live in; the thing to do was to get back to Iowa, to Illinois, to any place that had been proved habitable. The Bergson boys, certainly, would have been happier with their uncle Otto, in the bakery shop in Chicago. Like most of their neighbors, they were meant to follow in paths already marked out for them, not to break trails in a new country. A steady job, a few holidays, nothing to think about, and they would have been very happy. It was no fault of theirs that they had been dragged into the wilderness when they were little boys. A pioneer should have imagination, should be able to enjoy the idea of things more than the things themselves.

The second of these barren summers was passing. One September afternoon Alexandra had gone over to the garden across the draw to dig sweet potatoes--they had been thriving upon the weather that was fatal to everything else. But when Carl Linstrum came up the garden rows to find her, she was not working. She was standing lost in thought, leaning upon her pitchfork, her sunbonnet lying beside her on the ground. The dry garden patch smelled of drying vines and was strewn with yellow seed-cucumbers and pumpkins and citrons. At one end, next the rhubarb, grew feathery asparagus, with red berries. Down the middle of the garden was a row of gooseberry and currant bushes. A few tough zenias and marigolds and a row of scarlet sage bore witness to the buckets of water that Mrs. Bergson had carried there after sundown, against the prohibition of her sons. Carl came quietly and slowly up the garden path, looking intently at Alexandra. She did not hear him. She was standing perfectly still, with that serious ease so characteristic of her. Her thick, reddish braids, twisted about her head, fairly burned in the sunlight. The air was cool enough to make the warm sun pleasant on one's back and shoulders, and so clear that the eye could follow a hawk up and up, into the blazing blue depths of the sky. Even Carl, never a very cheerful boy, and considerably darkened by these last two bitter years, loved the country on days like this, felt something strong and young and wild come out of it, that laughed at care.

"Alexandra," he said as he approached her, "I want to talk to you. Let's sit down by the gooseberry bushes." He picked up her sack of potatoes and they crossed the garden. "Boys gone to town?" he asked as he sank down on the warm, sun-baked earth. "Well, we have made up our minds at last, Alexandra. We are really going away."

She looked at him as if she were a little frightened. "Really, Carl? Is it settled?"

"Yes, father has heard from St. Louis, and they will give him back his old job in the cigar factory. He must be there by the first of November. They are taking on new men then. We will sell the place for whatever we can get, and auction the stock. We haven't enough to ship. I am going to learn engraving with a German engraver there, and then try to get work in Chicago."

Alexandra's hands dropped in her lap. Her eyes became dreamy and filled with tears.

Carl's sensitive lower lip trembled. He scratched in the soft earth beside him with a stick. "That's all I hate about it, Alexandra," he said slowly. "You've stood by us through so much and helped father out so many times, and now it seems as if we were running off and leaving you to face the worst of it. But it isn't as if we could really ever be of any help to you. We are only one more drag, one more thing you look out for and feel responsible for. Father was never meant for a farmer, you know that. And I hate it. We'd only get in deeper and deeper."

"Yes, yes, Carl, I know. You are wasting your life here. You are able to do much better things. You are nearly nineteen now, and I wouldn't have you stay. I've always hoped you would get away. But I can't help feeling scared when I think how I will miss you--more than you will ever know." She brushed the tears from her cheeks, not trying to hide them.

"But, Alexandra," he said sadly and wistfully, "I've never been any real help to you, beyond sometimes trying to keep the boys in a good humor."

Alexandra smiled and shook her head. "Oh, it's not that. Nothing like that. It's by understanding me, and the boys, and mother, that you've helped me. I expect that is the only way one person ever really can help another. I think you are about the only one that ever helped me. Somehow it will take more courage to bear your going than everything that has happened before."

Carl looked at the ground. "You see, we've all depended so on you," he said, "even father. He makes me laugh. When anything comes up he always says, 'I wonder what the Bergsons are going to do about that? I guess I'll go and ask her.' I'll never forget that time, when we first came here, and our horse had the colic, and I ran over to your place--your father was away, and you came home with me and showed father how to let the wind out of the horse. You were only a little girl then, but you knew ever so much more about farm work than poor father. You remember how homesick I used to get, and what long talks we used to have coming from school? We've someway always felt alike about things."

"Yes, that's it; we've liked the same things and we've liked them together, without anybody else knowing. And we've had good times, hunting for Christmas trees and going for ducks and making our plum wine together every year. We've never either of us had any other close friend. And now--" Alexandra wiped her eyes with the corner of her apron, "and now I must remember that you are going where you will have many friends, and will find the work you were meant to do. But you'll write to me, Carl? That will mean a great deal to me here."

"I'll write as long as I live," cried the boy impetuously. "And I'll be working for you as much as for myself, Alexandra. I want to do something you'll like and be proud of. I'm a fool here, but I know I can do something!" He sat up and frowned at the red grass.

Alexandra sighed. "How discouraged the boys will be when they hear. They always come home from town discouraged, anyway. So many people are trying to leave the country, and they talk to our boys and make them low-spirited. I'm afraid they are beginning to feel hard toward me because I won't listen to any talk about going. Sometimes I feel like I'm getting tired of standing up for this country."

"I won't tell the boys yet, if you'd rather not."

"Oh, I'll tell them myself, to-night, when they come home. They'll be talking wild, anyway, and no good comes of keeping bad news. It's all harder on them than it is on me. Lou wants to get married, poor boy, and he can't until times are better. See, there goes the sun, Carl. I must be getting back. Mother will want her potatoes. It's chilly already, the moment the light goes."

Alexandra rose and looked about. A golden afterglow throbbed in the west, but the country already looked empty and mournful. A dark moving mass came over the western hill, the Lee boy was bringing in the herd from the other half-section. Emil ran from the windmill to open the corral gate. From the log house, on the little rise across the draw, the smoke was curling. The cattle lowed and bellowed. In the sky the pale half-moon was slowly silvering. Alexandra and Carl walked together down the potato rows. "I have to keep telling myself what is going to happen," she said softly. "Since you have been here, ten years now, I have never really been lonely. But I can remember what it was like before. Now I shall have nobody but Emil. But he is my boy, and he is tender-hearted."

That night, when the boys were called to supper, they sat down moodily. They had worn their coats to town, but they ate in their striped shirts and suspenders. They were grown men now, and, as Alexandra said, for the last few years they had been growing more and more like themselves. Lou was still the slighter of the two, the quicker and more intelligent, but apt to go off at half-cock. He had a lively blue eye, a thin, fair skin (always burned red to the neckband of his shirt in summer), stiff, yellow hair that would not lie down on his head, and a bristly little yellow mustache, of which he was very proud. Oscar could not grow a mustache; his pale face was as bare as an egg, and his white eyebrows gave it an empty look. He was a man of powerful body and unusual endurance; the sort of man you could attach to a corn-sheller as you would an engine. He would turn it all day, without hurrying, without slowing down. But he was as indolent of mind as he was unsparing of his body. His love of routine amounted to a vice. He worked like an insect, always doing the same thing over in the same way, regardless of whether it was best or no. He felt that there was a sovereign virtue in mere bodily toil, and he rather liked to do things in the hardest way. If a field had once been in corn, he couldn't bear to put it into wheat. He liked to begin his corn-planting at the same time every year, whether the season were backward or forward. He seemed to feel that by his own irreproachable regularity he would clear himself of blame and reprove the weather. When the wheat crop failed, he threshed the straw at a dead loss to demonstrate how little grain there was, and thus prove his case against Providence.

Lou, on the other hand, was fussy and flighty; always planned to get through two days' work in one, and often got only the least important things done. He liked to keep the place up, but he never got round to doing odd jobs until he had to neglect more pressing work to attend to them. In the middle of the wheat harvest, when the grain was over-ripe and every hand was needed, he would stop to mend fences or to patch the harness; then dash down to the field and overwork and be laid up in bed for a week. The two boys balanced each other, and they pulled well together. They had been good friends since they were children. One seldom went anywhere, even to town, without the other.

To-night, after they sat down to supper, Oscar kept looking at Lou as if he expected him to say something, and Lou blinked his eyes and frowned at his plate. It was Alexandra herself who at last opened the discussion.

"The Linstrums," she said calmly, as she put another plate of hot biscuit on the table, "are going back to St. Louis. The old man is going to work in the cigar factory again."

At this Lou plunged in. "You see, Alexandra, everybody who can crawl out is going away. There's no use of us trying to stick it out, just to be stubborn. There's something in knowing when to quit."

"Where do you want to go, Lou?"

"Any place where things will grow," said Oscar grimly.

Lou reached for a potato. "Chris Arnson has traded his half-section for a place down on the river."

"Who did he trade with?"

"Charley Fuller, in town."

"Fuller the real estate man? You see, Lou, that Fuller has a head on him. He's buying and trading for every bit of land he can get up here. It'll make him a rich man, some day."

"He's rich now, that's why he can take a chance."

"Why can't we? We'll live longer than he will. Some day the land itself will be worth more than all we can ever raise on it."

Lou laughed. "It could be worth that, and still not be worth much. Why, Alexandra, you don't know what you're talking about. Our place wouldn't bring now what it would six years ago. The fellows that settled up here just made a mistake. Now they're beginning to see this high land wasn't never meant to grow nothing on, and everybody who ain't fixed to graze cattle is trying to crawl out. It's too high to farm up here. All the Americans are skinning out. That man Percy Adams, north of town, told me that he was going to let Fuller take his land and stuff for four hundred dollars and a ticket to Chicago."

"There's Fuller again!" Alexandra exclaimed. "I wish that man would take me for a partner. He's feathering his nest! If only poor people could learn a little from rich people! But all these fellows who are running off are bad farmers, like poor Mr. Linstrum. They couldn't get ahead even in good years, and they all got into debt while father was getting out. I think we ought to hold on as long as we can on father's account. He was so set on keeping this land. He must have seen harder times than this, here. How was it in the early days, mother?"

Mrs. Bergson was weeping quietly. These family discussions always depressed her, and made her remember all that she had been torn away from. "I don't see why the boys are always taking on about going away," she said, wiping her eyes. "I don't want to move again; out to some raw place, maybe, where we'd be worse off than we are here, and all to do over again. I won't move! If the rest of you go, I will ask some of the neighbors to take me in, and stay and be buried by father. I'm not going to leave him by himself on the prairie, for cattle to run over." She began to cry more bitterly.

The boys looked angry. Alexandra put a soothing hand on her mother's shoulder. "There's no question of that, mother. You don't have to go if you don't want to. A third of the place belongs to you by American law, and we can't sell without your consent. We only want you to advise us. How did it use to be when you and father first came? Was it really as bad as this, or not?"

"Oh, worse! Much worse," moaned Mrs. Bergson. "Drouth, chince-bugs, hail, everything! My garden all cut to pieces like sauerkraut. No grapes on the creek, no nothing. The people all lived just like coyotes."

Oscar got up and tramped out of the kitchen. Lou followed him. They felt that Alexandra had taken an unfair advantage in turning their mother loose on them. The next morning they were silent and reserved. They did not offer to take the women to church, but went down to the barn immediately after breakfast and stayed there all day. When Carl Linstrum came over in the afternoon, Alexandra winked to him and pointed toward the barn. He understood her and went down to play cards with the boys. They believed that a very wicked thing to do on Sunday, and it relieved their feelings.

Alexandra stayed in the house. On Sunday afternoon Mrs. Bergson always took a nap, and Alexandra read. During the week she read only the newspaper, but on Sunday, and in the long evenings of winter, she read a good deal; read a few things over a great many times. She knew long portions of the "Frithjof Saga" by heart, and, like most Swedes who read at all, she was fond of Longfellow's verse,--the ballads and the "Golden Legend" and "The Spanish Student." To-day she sat in the wooden rocking-chair with the Swedish Bible open on her knees, but she was not reading. She was looking thoughtfully away at the point where the upland road disappeared over the rim of the prairie. Her body was in an attitude of perfect repose, such as it was apt to take when she was thinking earnestly. Her mind was slow, truthful, steadfast. She had not the least spark of cleverness.

All afternoon the sitting-room was full of quiet and sunlight. Emil was making rabbit traps in the kitchen shed. The hens were clucking and scratching brown holes in the flower beds, and the wind was teasing the prince's feather by the door.

That evening Carl came in with the boys to supper.

"Emil," said Alexandra, when they were all seated at the table, "how would you like to go traveling? Because I am going to take a trip, and you can go with me if you want to."

The boys looked up in amazement; they were always afraid of Alexandra's schemes. Carl was interested.

"I've been thinking, boys," she went on, "that maybe I am too set against making a change. I'm going to take Brigham and the buckboard to-morrow and drive down to the river country and spend a few days looking over what they've got down there. If I find anything good, you boys can go down and make a trade."

"Nobody down there will trade for anything up here," said Oscar gloomily.

"That's just what I want to find out. Maybe they are just as discontented down there as we are up here. Things away from home often look better than they are. You know what your Hans Andersen book says, Carl, about the Swedes liking to buy Danish bread and the Danes liking to buy Swedish bread, because people always think the bread of another country is better than their own. Anyway, I've heard so much about the river farms, I won't be satisfied till I've seen for myself."

Lou fidgeted. "Look out! Don't agree to anything. Don't let them fool you."

Lou was apt to be fooled himself. He had not yet learned to keep away from the shell-game wagons that followed the circus.

After supper Lou put on a necktie and went across the fields to court Annie Lee, and Carl and Oscar sat down to a game of checkers, while Alexandra read "The Swiss Family Robinson" aloud to her mother and Emil. It was not long before the two boys at the table neglected their game to listen. They were all big children together, and they found the adventures of the family in the tree house so absorbing that they gave them their undivided attention.

V

Alexandra and Emil spent five days down among the river farms, driving up and down the valley. Alexandra talked to the men about their crops and to the women about their poultry. She spent a whole day with one young farmer who had been away at school, and who was experimenting with a new kind of clover hay. She learned a great deal. As they drove along, she and Emil talked and planned. At last, on the sixth day, Alexandra turned Brigham's head northward and left the river behind.

"There's nothing in it for us down there, Emil. There are a few fine farms, but they are owned by the rich men in town, and couldn't be bought. Most of the land is rough and hilly. They can always scrape along down there, but they can never do anything big. Down there they have a little certainty, but up with us there is a big chance. We must have faith in the high land, Emil. I want to hold on harder than ever, and when you're a man you'll thank me." She urged Brigham forward.

When the road began to climb the first long swells of the Divide, Alexandra hummed an old Swedish hymn, and Emil wondered why his sister looked so happy. Her face was so radiant that he felt shy about asking her. For the first time, perhaps, since that land emerged from the waters of geologic ages, a human face was set toward it with love and yearning. It seemed beautiful to her, rich and strong and glorious. Her eyes drank in the breadth of it, until her tears blinded her. Then the Genius of the Divide, the great, free spirit which breathes across it, must have bent lower than it ever bent to a human will before. The history of every country begins in the heart of a man or a woman.

Alexandra reached home in the afternoon. That evening she held a family council and told her brothers all that she had seen and heard.

"I want you boys to go down yourselves and look it over. Nothing will convince you like seeing with your own eyes. The river land was settled before this, and so they are a few years ahead of us, and have learned more about farming. The land sells for three times as much as this, but in five years we will double it. The rich men down there own all the best land, and they are buying all they can get. The thing to do is to sell our cattle and what little old corn we have, and buy the Linstrum place. Then the next thing to do is to take out two loans on our half-sections, and buy Peter Crow's place; raise every dollar we can, and buy every acre we can."

"Mortgage the homestead again?" Lou cried. He sprang up and began to wind the clock furiously. "I won't slave to pay off another mortgage. I'll never do it. You'd just as soon kill us all, Alexandra, to carry out some scheme!"

Oscar rubbed his high, pale forehead. "How do you propose to pay off your mortgages?"

Alexandra looked from one to the other and bit her lip. They had never seen her so nervous. "See here," she brought out at last. "We borrow the money for six years. Well, with the money we buy a half-section from Linstrum and a half from Crow, and a quarter from Struble, maybe. That will give us upwards of fourteen hundred acres, won't it? You won't have to pay off your mortgages for six years. By that time, any of this land will be worth thirty dollars an acre--it will be worth fifty, but we'll say thirty; then you can sell a garden patch anywhere, and pay off a debt of sixteen hundred dollars. It's not the principal I'm worried about, it's the interest and taxes. We'll have to strain to meet the payments. But as sure as we are sitting here to-night, we can sit down here ten years from now independent landowners, not struggling farmers any longer. The chance that father was always looking for has come."

Lou was pacing the floor. "But how do you KNOW that land is going to go up enough to pay the mortgages and--"

"And make us rich besides?" Alexandra put in firmly. "I can't explain that, Lou. You'll have to take my word for it. I KNOW, that's all. When you drive about over the country you can feel it coming."

Oscar had been sitting with his head lowered, his hands hanging between his knees. "But we can't work so much land," he said dully, as if he were talking to himself. "We can't even try. It would just lie there and we'd work ourselves to death." He sighed, and laid his calloused fist on the table.

Alexandra's eyes filled with tears. She put her hand on his shoulder. "You poor boy, you won't have to work it. The men in town who are buying up other people's land don't try to farm it. They are the men to watch, in a new country. Let's try to do like the shrewd ones, and not like these stupid fellows. I don't want you boys always to have to work like this. I want you to be independent, and Emil to go to school."

Lou held his head as if it were splitting. "Everybody will say we are crazy. It must be crazy, or everybody would be doing it."

"If they were, we wouldn't have much chance. No, Lou, I was talking about that with the smart young man who is raising the new kind of clover. He says the right thing is usually just what everybody don't do. Why are we better fixed than any of our neighbors? Because father had more brains. Our people were better people than these in the old country. We OUGHT to do more than they do, and see further ahead. Yes, mother, I'm going to clear the table now."

Alexandra rose. The boys went to the stable to see to the stock, and they were gone a long while. When they came back Lou played on his DRAGHARMONIKA and Oscar sat figuring at his father's secretary all evening. They said nothing more about Alexandra's project, but she felt sure now that they would consent to it. Just before bedtime Oscar went out for a pail of water. When he did not come back, Alexandra threw a shawl over her head and ran down the path to the windmill. She found him sitting there with his head in his hands, and she sat down beside him.

"Don't do anything you don't want to do, Oscar," she whispered. She waited a moment, but he did not stir. "I won't say any more about it, if you'd rather not. What makes you so discouraged?"

"I dread signing my name to them pieces of paper," he said slowly. "All the time I was a boy we had a mortgage hanging over us."

"Then don't sign one. I don't want you to, if you feel that way."

Oscar shook his head. "No, I can see there's a chance that way. I've thought a good while there might be. We're in so deep now, we might as well go deeper. But it's hard work pulling out of debt. Like pulling a threshingmachine out of the mud; breaks your back. Me and Lou's worked hard, and I can't see it's got us ahead much."

"Nobody knows about that as well as I do, Oscar. That's why I want to try an easier way. I don't want you to have to grub for every dollar."

"Yes, I know what you mean. Maybe it'll come out right. But signing papers is signing papers. There ain't no maybe about that." He took his pail and trudged up the path to the house.

Alexandra drew her shawl closer about her and stood leaning against the frame of the mill, looking at the stars which glittered so keenly through the frosty autumn air. She always loved to watch them, to think of their vastness and distance, and of their ordered march. It fortified her to reflect upon the great operations of nature, and when she thought of the law that lay behind them, she felt a sense of personal security. That night she had a new consciousness of the country, felt almost a new relation to it. Even her talk with the boys had not taken away the feeling that had overwhelmed her when she drove back to the Divide that afternoon. She had never known before how much the country meant to her. The chirping of the insects down in the long grass had been like the sweetest music. She had felt as if her heart were hiding down there, somewhere, with the quail and the plover and all the little wild things that crooned or buzzed in the sun. Under the long shaggy ridges, she felt the future stirring.

PART II. NEIGHBORING FIELDS

I

IT is sixteen years since John Bergson died. His wife now lies beside him, and the white shaft that marks their graves gleams across the wheat-fields. Could he rise from beneath it, he would not know the country under which he has been asleep. The shaggy coat of the prairie, which they lifted to make him a bed, has vanished forever. From the Norwegian graveyard one looks out over a vast checker-board, marked off in squares of wheat and corn; light and dark, dark and light. Telephone wires hum along the white roads, which always run at right angles. From the graveyard gate one can count a dozen gayly painted farmhouses; the gilded weather-vanes on the big red barns wink at each other across the green and brown and yellow fields. The light steel windmills tremble throughout their frames and tug at their moorings, as they vibrate in the wind that often blows from one week's end to another across that high, active, resolute stretch of country.

The Divide is now thickly populated. The rich soil yields heavy harvests; the dry, bracing climate and the smoothness of the land make labor easy for men and beasts. There are few scenes more gratifying than a spring plowing in that country, where the furrows of a single field often lie a mile in length, and the brown earth, with such a strong, clean smell, and such a power of growth and fertility in it, yields itself eagerly to the plow; rolls away from the shear, not even dimming the brightness of the metal, with a soft, deep sigh of happiness. The wheatcutting sometimes goes on all night as well as all day, and in good seasons there are scarcely men and horses enough to do the harvesting. The grain is so heavy that it bends toward the blade and cuts like velvet.

There is something frank and joyous and young in the open face of the country. It gives itself ungrudgingly to the moods of the season, holding nothing back. Like the plains of Lombardy, it seems to rise a little to meet the sun. The air and the earth are curiously mated and intermingled, as if the one were the breath of the other. You feel in the atmosphere the same tonic, puissant quality that is in the tilth, the same strength and resoluteness.

One June morning a young man stood at the gate of the Norwegian graveyard, sharpening his scythe in strokes unconsciously timed to the tune he was whistling. He wore a flannel cap and duck trousers, and the sleeves of his white flannel shirt were rolled back to the elbow. When he was satisfied with the edge of his blade, he slipped the whetstone into his hip pocket and began to swing his scythe, still whistling, but softly, out of respect to the quiet folk about him. Unconscious respect, probably, for he seemed intent upon his own thoughts, and, like the Gladiator's, they were far away. He was a splendid figure of a boy, tall and straight as a young pine tree, with a handsome head, and stormy gray eyes, deeply set under a serious brow. The space between his two front teeth, which were unusually far apart, gave him the proficiency in whistling for which he was distinguished at college. (He also played the cornet in the University band.)

When the grass required his close attention, or when he had to stoop to cut about a head-stone, he paused in his lively air,--the "Jewel" song,--taking it up where he had left it when his scythe swung free again. He was not thinking about the tired pioneers over whom his blade glittered. The old wild country, the struggle in which his sister was destined to succeed while so many men broke their hearts and died, he can scarcely remember. That is all among the dim things of childhood and has been forgotten in the brighter pattern life weaves to-day, in the bright facts of being captain of the track team, and holding the interstate record for the high jump, in the all-suffusing brightness of being twenty-one. Yet sometimes, in the pauses of his work, the young man frowned and looked at the ground with an intentness which suggested that even twenty-one might have its problems.

When he had been mowing the better part of an hour, he heard the rattle of a light cart on the road behind him. Supposing that it was his sister coming back from one of her farms, he kept on with his work. The cart stopped at the gate and a merry contralto voice called, "Almost through, Emil?" He dropped his scythe and went toward the fence, wiping his face and neck with his handkerchief. In the cart sat a young woman who wore driving gauntlets and a wide shade hat, trimmed with red poppies. Her face, too, was rather like a poppy, round and brown, with rich color in her cheeks and lips, and her dancing yellow-brown eyes bubbled with gayety. The wind was flapping her big hat and teasing a curl of her chestnut-colored hair. She shook her head at the tall youth.

"What time did you get over here? That's not much of a job for an athlete. Here I've been to town and back. Alexandra lets you sleep late. Oh, I know! Lou's wife was telling me about the way she spoils you. I was going to give you a lift, if you were done." She gathered up her reins.

"But I will be, in a minute. Please wait for me, Marie," Emil coaxed. "Alexandra sent me to mow our lot, but I've done half a dozen others, you see. Just wait till I finish off the Kourdnas'. By the way, they were Bohemians. Why aren't they up in the Catholic graveyard?"

"Free-thinkers," replied the young woman laconically.

"Lots of the Bohemian boys at the University are," said Emil, taking up his scythe again. "What did you ever burn John Huss for, anyway? It's made an awful row. They still jaw about it in history classes."

"We'd do it right over again, most of us," said the young woman hotly. "Don't they ever teach you in your history classes that you'd all be heathen Turks if it hadn't been for the Bohemians?"

Emil had fallen to mowing. "Oh, there's no denying you're a spunky little bunch, you Czechs," he called back over his shoulder.

Marie Shabata settled herself in her seat and watched the rhythmical movement of the young man's long arms, swinging her foot as if in time to some air that was going through her mind. The minutes passed. Emil mowed vigorously and Marie sat sunning herself and watching the long grass fall. She sat with the ease that belongs to persons of an essentially happy nature, who can find a comfortable spot almost anywhere; who are supple, and quick in adapting themselves to circumstances. After a final swish, Emil snapped the gate and sprang into the cart, holding his scythe well out over the wheel. "There," he sighed. "I gave old man Lee a cut or so, too. Lou's wife needn't talk. I never see Lou's scythe over here."

Marie clucked to her horse. "Oh, you know Annie!" She looked at the young man's bare arms. "How brown you've got since you came home. I wish I had an athlete to mow my orchard. I get wet to my knees when I go down to pick cherries."

"You can have one, any time you want him. Better wait until after it rains." Emil squinted off at the horizon as if he were looking for clouds.

"Will you? Oh, there's a good boy!" She turned her head to him with a quick, bright smile. He felt it rather than saw it. Indeed, he had looked away with the purpose of not seeing it. "I've been up looking at Angelique's wedding clothes," Marie went on, "and I'm so excited I can hardly wait until Sunday. Amedee will be a handsome bridegroom. Is anybody but you going to stand up with him? Well, then it will be a handsome wedding party." She made a droll face at Emil, who flushed. "Frank," Marie continued, flicking her horse, "is cranky at me because I loaned his saddle to Jan Smirka, and I'm terribly afraid he won't take me to the dance in the evening. Maybe the supper will tempt him. All Angelique's folks are baking for it, and all Amedee's twenty cousins. There will be barrels of beer. If once I get Frank to the supper, I'll see that I stay for the dance. And by the way, Emil, you mustn't dance with me but once or twice. You must dance with all the French girls. It hurts their feelings if you don't. They think you're proud because you've been away to school or something."

Emil sniffed. "How do you know they think that?"

"Well, you didn't dance with them much at Raoul Marcel's party, and I could tell how they took it by the way they looked at you--and at me."

"All right," said Emil shortly, studying the glittering blade of his scythe.

112

They drove westward toward Norway Creek, and toward a big white house that stood on a hill, several miles across the fields. There were so many sheds and outbuildings grouped about it that the place looked not unlike a tiny village. A stranger, approaching it, could not help noticing the beauty and fruitfulness of the outlying fields. There was something individual about the great farm, a most unusual trimness and care for detail. On either side of the road, for a mile before you reached the foot of the hill, stood tall osage orange hedges, their glossy green marking off the yellow fields. South of the hill, in a low, sheltered swale, surrounded by a mulberry hedge, was the orchard, its fruit trees knee-deep in timothy grass. Any one thereabouts would have told you that this was one of the richest farms on the Divide, and that the farmer was a woman, Alexandra Bergson.

If you go up the hill and enter Alexandra's big house, you will find that it is curiously unfinished and uneven in comfort. One room is papered, carpeted, over-furnished; the next is almost bare. The pleasantest rooms in the house are the kitchen--where Alexandra's three young Swedish girls chatter and cook and pickle and preserve all summer long--and the sitting-room, in which Alexandra has brought together the old homely furniture that the Bergsons used in their first log house, the family portraits, and the few things her mother brought from Sweden.

When you go out of the house into the flower garden, there you feel again the order and fine arrangement manifest all over the great farm; in the fencing and hedging, in the windbreaks and sheds, in the symmetrical pasture ponds, planted with scrub willows to give shade to the cattle in fly-time. There is even a white row of beehives in the orchard, under the walnut trees. You feel that, properly, Alexandra's house is the big out-of-doors, and that it is in the soil that she expresses herself best.

II

Emil reached home a little past noon, and when he went into the kitchen Alexandra was already seated at the head of the long table, having dinner with her men, as she always did unless there were visitors. He slipped into his empty place at his sister's right. The three pretty young Swedish girls who did Alexandra's housework were cutting pies, refilling coffeecups, placing platters of bread and meat and potatoes upon the red tablecloth, and continually getting in each other's way between the table and the stove. To be sure they always wasted a good deal of time getting in each other's way and giggling at each other's mistakes. But, as Alexandra had pointedly told her sisters-in-law, it was to hear them giggle that she kept three young things in her kitchen; the work she could do herself, if it were necessary. These girls, with their long letters from home, their finery, and their love-affairs, afforded her a great deal of entertainment, and they were company for her when Emil was away at school.

Of the youngest girl, Signa, who has a pretty figure, mottled pink cheeks, and yellow hair, Alexandra is very fond, though she keeps a sharp eye upon her. Signa is apt to be skittish at mealtime, when the men are about, and to spill the coffee or upset the cream. It is supposed that Nelse Jensen, one of the six men at the dinner-table, is courting Signa, though he has been so careful not to commit himself that no one in the house, least of all Signa, can tell just how far the matter has progressed. Nelse watches her glumly as she waits upon the table, and in the evening he sits on a bench behind the stove with his DRAGHARMONIKA, playing mournful airs and watching her as she goes about her work. When Alexandra asked Signa whether she thought Nelse was in earnest, the poor child hid her hands under her apron and murmured, "I don't know, ma'm. But he scolds me about everything, like as if he wanted to have me!"

At Alexandra's left sat a very old man, barefoot and wearing a long blue blouse, open at the neck. His shaggy head is scarcely whiter than it was sixteen years ago, but his little blue eyes have become pale and watery, and his ruddy face is withered, like an apple that has clung all winter to the tree. When Ivar lost his land through mismanagement a dozen years ago, Alexandra took him in, and he has been a member of her household ever since. He is too old to work in the fields, but he hitches and unhitches the work-teams and looks after the health of the stock. Sometimes of a winter evening Alexandra calls him into the sitting-room to read the Bible aloud to her, for he still reads very well. He dislikes human habitations, so Alexandra has fitted him up a room in the barn, where he is very comfortable, being near the horses and, as he says, further from temptations. No one has ever found out what his temptations are. In cold weather he sits by the kitchen fire and makes hammocks or mends harness until it is time to go to bed. Then he says his prayers at great length behind the stove, puts on his buffalo-skin coat and goes out to his room in the barn.

Alexandra herself has changed very little. Her figure is fuller, and she has more color. She seems sunnier and more vigorous than she did as a young girl. But she still has the same calmness and deliberation of manner, the same clear eyes, and she still wears her hair in two braids wound round her head. It is so curly that fiery ends escape from the braids and make her head look like one of the big double sunflowers that fringe her vegetable garden. Her face is always tanned in summer, for her sunbonnet is oftener on her arm than on her head. But where her collar falls away from her neck, or where her sleeves are pushed back from her wrist, the skin is of such smoothness and whiteness as none but Swedish women ever possess; skin with the freshness of the snow itself.

Alexandra did not talk much at the table, but she encouraged her men to talk, and she always listened attentively, even when they seemed to be talking foolishly.

To-day Barney Flinn, the big red-headed Irishman who had been with Alexandra for five years and who was actually her foreman, though he had no such title, was grumbling about the new silo she had put up that spring. It happened to be the first silo on the Divide, and Alexandra's neighbors and her men were skeptical about it. "To be sure, if the thing don't work, we'll have plenty of feed without it, indeed," Barney conceded.

Nelse Jensen, Signa's gloomy suitor, had his word. "Lou, he says he wouldn't have no silo on his place if you'd give it to him. He says the feed outen it gives the stock the bloat. He heard of somebody lost four head of horses, feedin' 'em that stuff."

Alexandra looked down the table from one to another. "Well, the only way we can find out is to try. Lou and I have different notions about feeding stock, and that's a good thing. It's bad if all the members of a family think alike. They never get anywhere. Lou can learn by my mistakes and I can learn by his. Isn't that fair, Barney?"

The Irishman laughed. He had no love for Lou, who was always uppish with him and who said that Alexandra paid her hands too much. "I've no thought but to give the thing an honest try, mum. 'T would be only right, after puttin' so much expense into it. Maybe Emil will come out an' have a look at it wid me." He pushed back his chair, took his hat from the nail, and marched out with Emil, who, with his university ideas, was supposed to have instigated the silo. The other hands followed them, all except old Ivar. He had been depressed throughout the meal and had paid no heed to the talk of the men, even when they mentioned cornstalk bloat, upon which he was sure to have opinions.

"Did you want to speak to me, Ivar?" Alexandra asked as she rose from the table. "Come into the sitting-room."

The old man followed Alexandra, but when she motioned him to a chair he shook his head. She took up her workbasket and waited for him to speak. He stood looking at the carpet, his bushy head bowed, his hands clasped in front of him. Ivar's bandy legs seemed to have grown shorter with years, and they were completely misfitted to his broad, thick body and heavy shoulders.

"Well, Ivar, what is it?" Alexandra asked after she had waited longer than usual.

Ivar had never learned to speak English and his Norwegian was quaint and grave, like the speech of the more old-fashioned people. He always addressed Alexandra in terms of the deepest respect, hoping to set a good example to the kitchen girls, whom he thought too familiar in their manners.

"Mistress," he began faintly, without raising his eyes, "the folk have been looking coldly at me of late. You know there has been talk."

"Talk about what, Ivar?"

"About sending me away; to the asylum."

Alexandra put down her sewing-basket. "Nobody has come to me with such talk," she said decidedly. "Why need you listen? You know I would never consent to such a thing."

Ivar lifted his shaggy head and looked at her out of his little eyes. "They say that you cannot prevent it if the folk complain of me, if your brothers complain to the authorities. They say that your brothers are afraid--God forbid!--that I may do you some injury when my spells are on me. Mistress, how can any one think that?--that I could bite the hand that fed me!" The tears trickled down on the old man's beard.

Alexandra frowned. "Ivar, I wonder at you, that you should come bothering me with such nonsense. I am still running my own house, and other people have nothing to do with either you or me. So long as I am suited with you, there is nothing to be said."

Ivar pulled a red handkerchief out of the breast of his blouse and wiped his eyes and beard. "But I should not wish you to keep me if, as they say, it is against your interests, and if it is hard for you to get hands because I am here."

Alexandra made an impatient gesture, but the old man put out his hand and went on earnestly:--

"Listen, mistress, it is right that you should take these things into account. You know that my spells come from God, and that I would not harm any living creature. You believe that every one should worship God in the way revealed to him. But that is not the way of this country. The way here is for all to do alike. I am despised because I do not wear shoes, because I do not cut my hair, and because I have visions. At home, in the old country, there were many like me, who had been touched by God, or who had seen things in the graveyard at night and were different afterward. We thought nothing of it, and let them alone. But here, if a man is different in his feet or in his head, they put him in the asylum. Look at Peter Kralik; when he was a boy, drinking out of a creek, he swallowed a snake, and always after that he could eat only such food as the creature liked, for when he ate anything else, it became enraged and gnawed him. When he felt it whipping about in him, he drank alcohol to stupefy it and get some ease for himself. He could work as good as any man, and his head was clear, but they locked him up for being different in his stomach. That is the way; they have built the asylum for people who are different, and they will not even let us live in the holes with the badgers. Only your great prosperity has protected me so far. If you had had ill-fortune, they would have taken me to Hastings long ago."

As Ivar talked, his gloom lifted. Alexandra had found that she could often break his fasts and long penances by talking to him and letting him pour out the thoughts that troubled him. Sympathy always cleared his mind, and ridicule was poison to him.

"There is a great deal in what you say, Ivar. Like as not they will be wanting to take me to Hastings because I have built a silo; and then I may take you with me. But at present I need you here. Only don't come to me again telling me what people say. Let people go on talking as they like, and we will go on living as we think best. You have been with me now for twelve years, and I have gone to you for advice oftener than I have ever gone to any one. That ought to satisfy you."

Ivar bowed humbly. "Yes, mistress, I shall not trouble you with their talk again. And as for my feet, I have observed your wishes all these years, though you have never questioned me; washing them every night, even in winter."

Alexandra laughed. "Oh, never mind about your feet, Ivar. We can remember when half our neighbors went barefoot in summer. I expect old Mrs. Lee would love to slip her shoes off now sometimes, if she dared. I'm glad I'm not Lou's mother-in-law."

Ivar looked about mysteriously and lowered his voice almost to a whisper. "You know what they have over at Lou's house? A great white tub, like the stone water-troughs in the old country, to wash themselves in. When you sent me over with the strawberries, they were all in town but the old woman Lee and the baby. She took me in and showed me the thing, and she told me it was impossible to wash yourself clean in it, because, in so much water, you could not make a strong suds. So when they fill it up and send her in there, she pretends, and makes a splashing noise. Then, when they are all asleep, she washes herself in a little wooden tub she keeps under her bed."

Alexandra shook with laughter. "Poor old Mrs. Lee! They won't let her wear nightcaps, either. Never mind; when she comes to visit me, she can do all the old things in the old way, and have as much beer as she wants. We'll start an asylum for old-time people, Ivar."

Ivar folded his big handkerchief carefully and thrust it back into his blouse. "This is always the way, mistress. I come to you sorrowing, and you send me away with a light heart. And will you be so good as to tell the Irishman that he is not to work the brown gelding until the sore on its shoulder is healed?"

"That I will. Now go and put Emil's mare to the cart. I am going to drive up to the north quarter to meet the man from town who is to buy my alfalfa hay."

III

Alexandra was to hear more of Ivar's case, however. On Sunday her married brothers came to dinner. She had asked them for that day because Emil, who hated family parties, would be absent, dancing at Amedee Chevalier's wedding, up in the French country. The table was set for company in the dining-room, where highly varnished wood and colored glass and useless pieces of china were conspicuous enough to satisfy the standards of the new prosperity. Alexandra had put herself into the hands of the Hanover furniture dealer, and he had conscientiously done his best to make her dining-room look like his display window. She said frankly that she knew nothing about such things, and she was willing to be governed by the general conviction that the more useless and utterly unusable objects were, the greater their virtue as ornament. That seemed reasonable enough. Since she liked plain things herself, it was all the more necessary to have jars and punchbowls and candlesticks in the company rooms for people who did appreciate them. Her guests liked to see about them these reassuring emblems of prosperity.

The family party was complete except for Emil, and Oscar's wife who, in the country phrase, "was not going anywhere just now." Oscar sat at the foot of the table and his four tow-headed little boys, aged from twelve to five, were ranged at one side. Neither Oscar nor Lou has changed much; they have simply, as Alexandra said of them long ago, grown to be more and more like themselves. Lou now looks the older of the two; his face is thin and shrewd and wrinkled about the eyes, while Oscar's is thick and dull. For all his dullness, however, Oscar makes more money than his brother, which adds to Lou's sharpness and uneasiness and tempts him to make a show. The trouble with Lou is that he is tricky, and his neighbors have found out that, as Ivar says, he has not a fox's face for nothing. Politics being the natural field for such talents, he neglects his farm to attend conventions and to run for county offices.

Lou's wife, formerly Annie Lee, has grown to look curiously like her husband. Her face has become longer, sharper, more aggressive. She wears her yellow hair in a high pompadour, and is bedecked with rings and chains and "beauty pins." Her tight, high-heeled shoes give her an awkward walk, and she is always more or less preoccupied with her clothes. As she sat at the table, she kept telling her youngest daughter to "be careful now, and not drop anything on mother."

The conversation at the table was all in English. Oscar's wife, from the malaria district of Missouri, was ashamed of marrying a foreigner, and his boys do not understand a word of Swedish. Annie and Lou sometimes speak Swedish at home, but Annie is almost as much afraid of being "caught" at it as ever her mother was of being caught barefoot. Oscar still has a thick accent, but Lou speaks like anybody from Iowa.

"When I was in Hastings to attend the convention," he was saying, "I saw the superintendent of the asylum, and I was telling him about Ivar's symptoms. He says Ivar's case is one of the most dangerous kind, and it's a wonder he hasn't done something violent before this."

Alexandra laughed good-humoredly. "Oh, nonsense, Lou! The doctors would have us all crazy if they could. Ivar's queer, certainly, but he has more sense than half the hands I hire."

Lou flew at his fried chicken. "Oh, I guess the doctor knows his business, Alexandra. He was very much surprised when I told him how you'd put up with Ivar. He says he's likely to set fire to the barn any night, or to take after you and the girls with an axe."

Little Signa, who was waiting on the table, giggled and fled to the kitchen. Alexandra's eyes twinkled. "That was too much for Signa, Lou. We all know that Ivar's perfectly harmless. The girls would as soon expect me to chase them with an axe."

Lou flushed and signaled to his wife. "All the same, the neighbors will be having a say about it before long. He may burn anybody's barn. It's only necessary for one property-owner in the township to make complaint, and he'll be taken up by force. You'd better send him yourself and not have any hard feelings."

Alexandra helped one of her little nephews to gravy. "Well, Lou, if any of the neighbors try that, I'll have myself appointed Ivar's guardian and take the case to court, that's all. I am perfectly satisfied with him."

"Pass the preserves, Lou," said Annie in a warning tone. She had reasons for not wishing her husband to cross Alexandra too openly. "But don't you sort of hate to have people see him around here, Alexandra?" she went on with persuasive smoothness. "He IS a disgraceful object, and you're fixed up so nice now. It sort of makes people distant with you, when they never know when they'll hear him scratching about. My girls are afraid as death of him, aren't you, Milly, dear?"

Milly was fifteen, fat and jolly and pompadoured, with a creamy complexion, square white teeth, and a short upper lip. She looked like her grandmother Bergson, and had her comfortable and comfort-loving nature. She grinned at her aunt, with whom she was a great deal more at ease than she was with her mother. Alexandra winked a reply.

"Milly needn't be afraid of Ivar. She's an especial favorite of his. In my opinion Ivar has just as much right to his own way of dressing and thinking as we have. But I'll see that he doesn't bother other people. I'll keep him at home, so don't trouble any more about him, Lou. I've been wanting to ask you about your new bathtub. How does it work?"

Annie came to the fore to give Lou time to recover himself. "Oh, it works something grand! I can't keep him out of it. He washes himself all over three times a week now, and uses all the hot water. I think it's weakening to stay in as long as he does. You ought to have one, Alexandra."

"I'm thinking of it. I might have one put in the barn for Ivar, if it will ease people's minds. But before I get a bathtub, I'm going to get a piano for Milly."

Oscar, at the end of the table, looked up from his plate. "What does Milly want of a pianny? What's the matter with her organ? She can make some use of that, and play in church."

Annie looked flustered. She had begged Alexandra not to say anything about this plan before Oscar, who was apt to be jealous of what his sister did for Lou's children. Alexandra did not get on with Oscar's wife at all. "Milly can play in church just the same, and she'll still play on the organ. But practising on it so much spoils her touch. Her teacher says so," Annie brought out with spirit.

Oscar rolled his eyes. "Well, Milly must have got on pretty good if she's got past the organ. I know plenty of grown folks that ain't," he said bluntly.

Annie threw up her chin. "She has got on good, and she's going to play for her commencement when she graduates in town next year."

"Yes," said Alexandra firmly, "I think Milly deserves a piano. All the girls around here have been taking lessons for years, but Milly is the only one of them who can ever play anything when you ask her. I'll tell you when I first thought I would like to give you a piano, Milly, and that was when you learned that book of old Swedish songs that your grandfather used to sing. He had a sweet tenor voice, and when he was a young man he loved to sing. I can remember hearing him singing with the sailors down in the shipyard, when I was no bigger than Stella here," pointing to Annie's younger daughter.

Milly and Stella both looked through the door into the sitting-room, where a crayon portrait of John Bergson hung on the wall. Alexandra had had it made from a little photograph, taken for his friends just before he left Sweden; a slender man of thirty-five, with soft hair curling about his high forehead, a drooping mustache, and wondering, sad eyes that looked forward into the distance, as if they already beheld the New World.

After dinner Lou and Oscar went to the orchard to pick cherries--they had neither of them had the patience to grow an orchard of their own--and Annie went down to gossip with Alexandra's kitchen girls while they washed the dishes. She could always find out more about Alexandra's domestic economy from the prattling maids than from Alexandra herself, and what she discovered she used to her own advantage with Lou. On the Divide, farmers' daughters no longer went out into service, so Alexandra got her girls from Sweden, by paying their fare over. They stayed with her until they married, and were replaced by sisters or cousins from the old country.

Alexandra took her three nieces into the flower garden. She was fond of the little girls, especially of Milly, who came to spend a week with her aunt now and then, and read aloud to her from the old books about the house, or listened to stories about the early days on the Divide. While they were walking among the flower beds, a buggy drove up the hill and stopped in front of the gate. A man got out and stood talking to the driver. The little girls were delighted at the advent of a stranger, some one from very far away, they knew by his clothes, his gloves, and the sharp, pointed cut of his dark beard. The girls fell behind their aunt and peeped out at him from among the castor beans. The stranger came up to the gate and stood holding his hat in his hand, smiling, while Alexandra advanced slowly to meet him. As she approached he spoke in a low, pleasant voice.

"Don't you know me, Alexandra? I would have known you, anywhere."

Alexandra shaded her eyes with her hand. Suddenly she took a quick step forward. "Can it be!" she exclaimed with feeling; "can it be that it is Carl Linstrum? Why, Carl, it is!" She threw out both her hands and caught his across the gate. "Sadie, Milly, run tell your father and Uncle Oscar that our old friend Carl Linstrum is here. Be quick! Why, Carl, how did it happen? I can't believe this!" Alexandra shook the tears from her eyes and laughed.

The stranger nodded to his driver, dropped his suitcase inside the fence, and opened the gate. "Then you are glad to see me, and you can put me up overnight? I couldn't go through this country without stopping off to have a look at you. How little you have changed! Do you know, I was sure it would be like that. You simply couldn't be different. How fine you are!" He stepped back and looked at her admiringly.

Alexandra blushed and laughed again. "But you yourself, Carl--with that beard--how could I have known you? You went away a little boy." She reached for his suitcase and when he intercepted her she threw up her hands. "You see, I give myself away. I have only women come to visit me, and I do not know how to behave. Where is your trunk?"

"It's in Hanover. I can stay only a few days. I am on my way to the coast."

They started up the path. "A few days? After all these years!" Alexandra shook her finger at him. "See this, you have walked into a trap. You do not get away so easy." She put her hand affectionately on his shoulder. "You owe me a visit for the sake of old times. Why must you go to the coast at all?"

"Oh, I must! I am a fortune hunter. From Seattle I go on to Alaska."

"Alaska?" She looked at him in astonishment. "Are you going to paint the Indians?"

"Paint?" the young man frowned. "Oh! I'm not a painter, Alexandra. I'm an engraver. I have nothing to do with painting."

"But on my parlor wall I have the paintings--"

He interrupted nervously. "Oh, water-color sketches--done for amusement. I sent them to remind you of me, not because they were good. What a wonderful place you have made of this, Alexandra." He turned and looked back at the wide, map-like prospect of field and hedge and pasture. "I would never have believed it could be done. I'm disappointed in my own eye, in my imagination."

At this moment Lou and Oscar came up the hill from the orchard. They did not quicken their pace when they saw Carl; indeed, they did not openly look in his direction. They advanced distrustfully, and as if they wished the distance were longer.

Alexandra beckoned to them. "They think I am trying to fool them. Come, boys, it's Carl Linstrum, our old Carl!"

Lou gave the visitor a quick, sidelong glance and thrust out his hand. "Glad to see you."

Oscar followed with "How d' do." Carl could not tell whether their offishness came from unfriendliness or from embarrassment. He and Alexandra led the way to the porch.

"Carl," Alexandra explained, "is on his way to Seattle. He is going to Alaska."

Oscar studied the visitor's yellow shoes. "Got business there?" he asked.

Carl laughed. "Yes, very pressing business. I'm going there to get rich. Engraving's a very interesting profession, but a man never makes any money at it. So I'm going to try the goldfields."

Alexandra felt that this was a tactful speech, and Lou looked up with some interest. "Ever done anything in that line before?"

"No, but I'm going to join a friend of mine who went out from New York and has done well. He has offered to break me in."

"Turrible cold winters, there, I hear," remarked Oscar. "I thought people went up there in the spring."

"They do. But my friend is going to spend the winter in Seattle and I am to stay with him there and learn something about prospecting before we start north next year."

Lou looked skeptical. "Let's see, how long have you been away from here?"

"Sixteen years. You ought to remember that, Lou, for you were married just after we went away."

"Going to stay with us some time?" Oscar asked.

"A few days, if Alexandra can keep me."

"I expect you'll be wanting to see your old place," Lou observed more cordially. "You won't hardly know it. But there's a few chunks of your old sod house left. Alexandra wouldn't never let Frank Shabata plough over it."

Annie Lee, who, ever since the visitor was announced, had been touching up her hair and settling her lace and wishing she had worn another dress, now emerged with her three daughters and introduced them. She was greatly impressed by Carl's urban appearance, and in her excitement talked very loud and threw her head about. "And you ain't married yet? At your age, now! Think of that! You'll have to wait for Milly. Yes, we've got a boy, too. The youngest. He's at home with his grandma. You must come over to see mother and hear Milly play. She's the musician of the family. She does pyrography, too. That's burnt wood, you know. You wouldn't believe what she can do with her poker. Yes, she goes to school in town, and she is the youngest in her class by two years."

Milly looked uncomfortable and Carl took her hand again. He liked her creamy skin and happy, innocent eyes, and he could see that her mother's way of talking distressed her. "I'm sure she's a clever little girl," he murmured, looking at her thoughtfully. "Let me see-- Ah, it's your mother that she looks like, Alexandra. Mrs. Bergson must have looked just like this when she was a little girl. Does Milly run about over the country as you and Alexandra used to, Annie?"

Milly's mother protested. "Oh, my, no! Things has changed since we was girls. Milly has it very different. We are going to rent the place and move into town as soon as the girls are old enough to go out into company. A good many are doing that here now. Lou is going into business."

Lou grinned. "That's what she says. You better go get your things on. Ivar's hitching up," he added, turning to Annie.

Young farmers seldom address their wives by name. It is always "you," or "she."

Having got his wife out of the way, Lou sat down on the step and began to whittle. "Well, what do folks in New York think of William Jennings Bryan?" Lou began to bluster, as he always did when he talked politics. "We gave Wall Street a scare in ninety-six, all right, and we're fixing another to hand them. Silver wasn't the only issue," he nodded mysteriously. "There's a good many things got to be changed. The West is going to make itself heard."

Carl laughed. "But, surely, it did do that, if nothing else."

Lou's thin face reddened up to the roots of his bristly hair. "Oh, we've only begun. We're waking up to a sense of our responsibilities, out here, and we ain't afraid, neither. You fellows back there must be a tame lot. If you had any nerve you'd get together and march down to Wall Street and blow it up. Dynamite it, I mean," with a threatening nod.

He was so much in earnest that Carl scarcely knew how to answer him. "That would be a waste of powder. The same business would go on in another street. The street doesn't matter. But what have you fellows out here got to kick about? You have the only safe place there is. Morgan himself couldn't touch you. One only has to drive through this country to see that you're all as rich as barons."

"We have a good deal more to say than we had when we were poor," said Lou threateningly. "We're getting on to a whole lot of things."

As Ivar drove a double carriage up to the gate, Annie came out in a hat that looked like the model of a battleship. Carl rose and took her down to the carriage, while Lou lingered for a word with his sister.

"What do you suppose he's come for?" he asked, jerking his head toward the gate.

"Why, to pay us a visit. I've been begging him to for years."

Oscar looked at Alexandra. "He didn't let you know he was coming?"

"No. Why should he? I told him to come at any time."

Lou shrugged his shoulders. "He doesn't seem to have done much for himself. Wandering around this way!"

Oscar spoke solemnly, as from the depths of a cavern. "He never was much account."

Alexandra left them and hurried down to the gate where Annie was rattling on to Carl about her new dining-room furniture. "You must bring Mr. Linstrum over real soon, only be sure to telephone me first," she called back, as Carl helped her into the carriage. Old Ivar, his white head bare, stood holding the horses. Lou came down the path and climbed into the front seat, took up the reins, and drove off without saying anything further to any one. Oscar picked up his youngest boy and trudged off down the road, the other three trotting after him. Carl, holding the gate open for Alexandra, began to laugh. "Up and coming on the Divide, eh, Alexandra?" he cried gayly.

IV

Carl had changed, Alexandra felt, much less than one might have expected. He had not become a trim, self-satisfied city man. There was still something homely and wayward and definitely personal about him. Even his clothes, his Norfolk coat and his very high collars, were a little unconventional. He seemed to shrink into himself as he used to do; to hold himself away from things, as if he were afraid of being hurt. In short, he was more self-con-scious than a man of thirty-five is expected to be. He looked older than his years and not very strong. His black hair, which still hung in a triangle over his pale forehead, was thin at the crown, and there were fine, relentless lines about his eyes. His back, with its high, sharp shoulders, looked like the back of an over-worked German professor off on his holiday. His face was intelligent, sensitive, unhappy.

That evening after supper, Carl and Alexandra were sitting by the clump of castor beans in the middle of the flower garden. The gravel paths glittered in the moonlight, and below them the fields lay white and still.

"Do you know, Alexandra," he was saying, "I've been thinking how strangely things work out. I've been away engraving other men's pictures, and you've stayed at home and made your own." He pointed with his cigar toward the sleeping landscape. "How in the world have you done it? How have your neighbors done it?"

"We hadn't any of us much to do with it, Carl. The land did it. It had its little joke. It pretended to be poor because nobody knew how to work it right; and then, all at once, it worked itself. It woke up out of its sleep and stretched itself, and it was so big, so rich, that we suddenly found we were rich, just from sitting still. As for me, you remember when I began to buy land. For years after that I was always squeezing and borrowing until I was ashamed to show my face in the banks. And then, all at once, men began to come to me offering to lend me money--and I didn't need it! Then I went ahead and built this house. I really built it for Emil. I want you to see Emil, Carl. He is so different from the rest of us!"

"How different?"

"Oh, you'll see! I'm sure it was to have sons like Emil, and to give them a chance, that father left the old country. It's curious, too; on the outside Emil is just like an American boy,--he graduated from the State University in June, you know,--but underneath he is more Swedish than any of us. Sometimes he is so like father that he frightens me; he is so violent in his feelings like that."

"Is he going to farm here with you?"

"He shall do whatever he wants to," Alexandra declared warmly. "He is going to have a chance, a whole chance; that's what I've worked for. Sometimes he talks about studying law, and sometimes, just lately, he's been talking about going out into the sand hills and taking up more land. He has his sad times, like father. But I hope he won't do that. We have land enough, at last!" Alexandra laughed.

"How about Lou and Oscar? They've done well, haven't they?"

"Yes, very well; but they are different, and now that they have farms of their own I do not see so much of them. We divided the land equally when Lou married. They have their own way of doing things, and they do not altogether like my way, I am afraid. Perhaps they think me too independent. But I have had to think for myself a good many years and am not likely to change. On the whole, though, we take as much comfort in each other as most brothers and sisters do. And I am very fond of Lou's oldest daughter."

"I think I liked the old Lou and Oscar better, and they probably feel the same about me. I even, if you can keep a secret,"--Carl leaned forward and touched her arm, smiling,--"I even think I liked the old country better. This is all very splendid in its way, but there was something about this country when it was a wild old beast that has haunted me all these years. Now, when I come back to all this milk and honey, I feel like the old German song, 'Wo bist du, wo bist du, mein geliebtest Land?'-- Do you ever feel like that, I wonder?"

"Yes, sometimes, when I think about father and mother and those who are gone; so many of our old neighbors." Alexandra paused and looked up thoughtfully at the stars. "We can remember the graveyard when it was wild prairie, Carl, and now--"

"And now the old story has begun to write itself over there," said Carl softly. "Isn't it queer: there are only two or three human stories, and they go on repeating themselves as fiercely as if they had never happened before; like the larks in this country, that have been singing the same five notes over for thousands of years."

"Oh, yes! The young people, they live so hard. And yet I sometimes envy them. There is my little neighbor, now; the people who bought your old place. I wouldn't have sold it to any one else, but I was always fond of that girl. You must remember her, little Marie Tovesky, from Omaha, who used to visit here? When she was eighteen she ran away from the convent school and got married, crazy child! She came out here a bride, with her father and husband. He had nothing, and the old man was willing to buy them a place and set them up. Your farm took her fancy, and I was glad to have her so near me. I've never been sorry, either. I even try to get along with Frank on her account."

"Is Frank her husband?"

"Yes. He's one of these wild fellows. Most Bohemians are good-natured, but Frank thinks we don't appreciate him here, I guess. He's jealous about everything, his farm and his horses and his pretty wife. Everybody likes her, just the same as when she was little. Sometimes I go up to the Catholic church with Emil, and it's funny to see Marie standing there laughing and shaking hands with people, looking so excited and gay, with Frank sulking behind her as if he could eat everybody alive. Frank's not a bad neighbor, but to get on with him you've got to make a fuss over him and act as if you thought he was a very important person all the time, and different from other people. I find it hard to keep that up from one year's end to another."

"I shouldn't think you'd be very successful at that kind of thing, Alexandra." Carl seemed to find the idea amusing.

"Well," said Alexandra firmly, "I do the best I can, on Marie's account. She has it hard enough, anyway. She's too young and pretty for this sort of life. We're all ever so much older and slower. But she's the kind that won't be downed easily. She'll work all day and go to a Bohemian wedding and dance all night, and drive the hay wagon for a cross man next morning. I could stay by a job, but I never had the go in me that she has, when I was going my best. I'll have to take you over to see her to-morrow."

Carl dropped the end of his cigar softly among the castor beans and sighed. "Yes, I suppose I must see the old place. I'm cowardly about things that remind me of myself. It took courage to come at all, Alexandra. I wouldn't have, if I hadn't wanted to see you very, very much."

Alexandra looked at him with her calm, deliberate eyes. "Why do you dread things like that, Carl?" she asked earnestly. "Why are you dissatisfied with yourself?"

Her visitor winced. "How direct you are, Alexandra! Just like you used to be. Do I give myself away so quickly? Well, you see, for one thing, there's nothing to look forward to in my profession. Wood-engraving is the only thing I care about, and that had gone out before I began. Everything's cheap metal work nowadays, touching up miserable photographs, forcing up poor drawings, and spoiling good ones. I'm absolutely sick of it all." Carl frowned. "Alexandra, all the way out from New York I've been planning how I could deceive you and make you think me a very enviable fellow, and here I am telling you the truth the first night. I waste a lot of time pretending to people, and the joke of it is, I don't think I ever deceive any one. There are too many of my kind; people know us on sight."

Carl paused. Alexandra pushed her hair back from her brow with a puzzled, thoughtful gesture. "You see," he went on calmly, "measured by your standards here, I'm a failure. I couldn't buy even one of your cornfields. I've enjoyed a great many things, but I've got nothing to show for it all."

"But you show for it yourself, Carl. I'd rather have had your freedom than my land."

Carl shook his head mournfully. "Freedom so often means that one isn't needed anywhere. Here you are an individual, you have a background of your own, you would be missed. But off there in the cities there are thousands of rolling stones like me. We are all alike; we have no ties, we know nobody, we own nothing. When one of us dies, they scarcely know where to bury him. Our landlady and the delicatessen man are our mourners, and we leave nothing behind us but a frock-coat and a fiddle, or an easel, or a typewriter, or whatever tool we got our living by. All we have ever managed to do is to pay our rent, the exorbitant rent that one has to pay for a few square feet of space near the heart of things. We have no house, no place, no people of our own. We live in the streets, in the parks, in the theatres. We sit in restaurants and concert halls and look about at the hundreds of our own kind and shudder."

Alexandra was silent. She sat looking at the silver spot the moon made on the surface of the pond down in the pasture. He knew that she understood what he meant. At last she said slowly, "And yet I would rather have Emil grow up like that than like his two brothers. We pay a high rent, too, though we pay differently. We grow hard and heavy here. We don't move lightly and easily as you do, and our minds get stiff. If the world were no wider than my cornfields, if there were not something beside this, I wouldn't feel that it was much worth while to work. No, I would rather have Emil like you than like them. I felt that as soon as you came."

"I wonder why you feel like that?" Carl mused.

"I don't know. Perhaps I am like Carrie Jensen, the sister of one of my hired men. She had never been out of the cornfields, and a few years ago she got despondent and said life was just the same thing over and over, and she didn't see the use of it. After she had tried to kill herself once or twice, her folks got worried and sent her over to Iowa to visit some relations. Ever since she's come back she's been perfectly cheerful, and she says she's contented to live and work in a world that's so big and interesting. She said that anything as big as the bridges over the Platte and the Missouri reconciled her. And it's what goes on in the world that reconciles me."

V

Alexandra did not find time to go to her neighbor's the next day, nor the next. It was a busy season on the farm, with the corn-plowing going on, and even Emil was in the field with a team and cultivator. Carl went about over the farms with Alexandra in the morning, and in the afternoon and evening they found a great deal to talk about. Emil, for all his track practice, did not stand up under farmwork very well, and by night he was too tired to talk or even to practise on his cornet.

On Wednesday morning Carl got up before it was light, and stole downstairs and out of the kitchen door just as old Ivar was making his morning ablutions at the pump. Carl nodded to him and hurried up the draw, past the garden, and into the pasture where the milking cows used to be kept.

The dawn in the east looked like the light from some great fire that was burning under the edge of the world. The color was reflected in the globules of dew that sheathed the short gray pasture grass. Carl walked rapidly until he came to the crest of the second hill, where the Bergson pasture joined the one that had belonged to his father. There he sat down and waited for the sun to rise. It was just there that he and Alexandra used to do their milking together, he on his side of the fence, she on hers. He could remember exactly how she looked when she came over the close-cropped grass, her skirts pinned up, her head bare, a bright tin pail in either hand, and the milky light of the early morning all about her. Even as a boy he used to feel, when he saw her coming with her free step, her upright head and calm shoulders, that she looked as if she had walked straight out of the morning itself. Since then, when he had happened to see the sun come up in the country or on the water, he had often remembered the young Swedish girl and her milking pails.

Carl sat musing until the sun leaped above the prairie, and in the grass about him all the small creatures of day began to tune their tiny instruments. Birds and insects without number began to chirp, to twitter, to snap and whistle, to make all manner of fresh shrill noises. The pasture was flooded with light; every clump of ironweed and snow-on-the-mountain threw a long shadow, and the golden light seemed to be rippling through the curly grass like the tide racing in.

He crossed the fence into the pasture that was now the Shabatas' and continued his walk toward the pond. He had not gone far, however, when he discovered that he was not the only person abroad. In the draw below, his gun in his hands, was Emil, advancing cautiously, with a young woman beside him. They were moving softly, keeping close together, and Carl knew that they expected to find ducks on the pond. At the moment when they came in sight of the bright spot of water, he heard a whirr of wings and the ducks shot up into the air. There was a sharp crack from the gun, and five of the birds fell to the ground. Emil and his companion laughed delightedly, and Emil ran to pick them up. When he came back, dangling the ducks by their feet, Marie held her apron and he dropped them into it. As she stood looking down at them, her face changed. She took up one of the birds, a rumpled ball of feathers with the blood dripping slowly from its mouth, and looked at the live color that still burned on its plumage.

As she let it fall, she cried in distress, "Oh, Emil, why did you?"

"I like that!" the boy exclaimed indignantly. "Why, Marie, you asked me to come yourself."

":Yes, yes, I know," she said tearfully, "but I didn't think. I hate to see them when they are first shot. They were having such a good time, and we've spoiled it all for them."

Emil gave a rather sore laugh. "I should say we had! I'm not going hunting with you any more. You're as bad as Ivar. Here, let me take them." He snatched the ducks out of her apron.

"Don't be cross, Emil. Only--Ivar's right about wild things. They're too happy to kill. You can tell just how they felt when they flew up. They were scared, but they didn't really think anything could hurt them. No, we won't do that any more."

"All right," Emil assented. "I'm sorry I made you feel bad." As he looked down into her tearful eyes, there was a curious, sharp young bitterness in his own.

Carl watched them as they moved slowly down the draw. They had not seen him at all. He had not overheard much of their dialogue, but he felt the import of it. It made him, somehow, unreasonably mournful to find two young things abroad in the pasture in the early morning. He decided that he needed his breakfast.

VI

At dinner that day Alexandra said she thought they must really manage to go over to the Shabatas' that afternoon. "It's not often I let three days go by without seeing Marie. She will think I have forsaken her, now that my old friend has come back."

After the men had gone back to work, Alexandra put on a white dress and her sun-hat, and she and Carl set forth across the fields. "You see we have kept up the old path, Carl. It has been so nice for me to feel that there was a friend at the other end of it again."

Carl smiled a little ruefully. "All the same, I hope it hasn't been QUITE the same."

Alexandra looked at him with surprise. "Why, no, of course not. Not the same. She could not very well take your place, if that's what you mean. I'm friendly with all my neighbors, I hope. But Marie is really a companion, some one I can talk to quite frankly. You wouldn't want me to be more lonely than I have been, would you?"

Carl laughed and pushed back the triangular lock of hair with the edge of his hat. "Of course I don't. I ought to be thankful that this path hasn't been worn by--well, by friends with more pressing errands than your little Bohemian is likely to have." He paused to give Alexandra his hand as she stepped over the stile. "Are you the least bit disappointed in our coming together again?" he asked abruptly. "Is it the way you hoped it would be?"

Alexandra smiled at this. "Only better. When I've thought about your coming, I've sometimes been a little afraid of it. You have lived where things move so fast, and everything is slow here; the people slowest of all. Our lives are like the years, all made up of weather and crops and cows. How you hated cows!" She shook her head and laughed to herself.

"I didn't when we milked together. I walked up to the pasture corners this morning. I wonder whether I shall ever be able to tell you all that I was thinking about up there. It's a strange thing, Alexandra; I find it easy to be frank with you about everything under the sun except--yourself!"

"You are afraid of hurting my feelings, perhaps." Alexandra looked at him thoughtfully.

"No, I'm afraid of giving you a shock. You've seen yourself for so long in the dull minds of the people about you, that if I were to tell you how you seem to me, it would startle you. But you must see that you astonish me. You must feel when people admire you."

Alexandra blushed and laughed with some confusion. "I felt that you were pleased with me, if you mean that."

"And you've felt when other people were pleased with you?" he insisted.

"Well, sometimes. The men in town, at the banks and the county offices, seem glad to see me. I think, myself, it is more pleasant to do business with people who are clean and healthy-looking," she admitted blandly.

Carl gave a little chuckle as he opened the Shabatas' gate for her. "Oh, do you?" he asked dryly.

There was no sign of life about the Shabatas' house except a big yellow cat, sunning itself on the kitchen doorstep.

Alexandra took the path that led to the orchard. "She often sits there and sews. I didn't telephone her we were coming, because I didn't want her to go to work and bake cake and freeze ice-cream. She'll always make a party if you give her the least excuse. Do you recognize the apple trees, Carl?"

Linstrum looked about him. "I wish I had a dollar for every bucket of water I've carried for those trees. Poor father, he was an easy man, but he was perfectly merciless when it came to watering the orchard."

"That's one thing I like about Germans; they make an orchard grow if they can't make anything else. I'm so glad these trees belong to some one who takes comfort in them. When I rented this place, the tenants never kept the orchard up, and Emil and I used to come over and take care of it ourselves. It needs mowing now. There she is, down in the corner. Maria-a-a!" she called.

A recumbent figure started up from the grass and came running toward them through the flickering screen of light and shade.

"Look at her! Isn't she like a little brown rabbit?" Alexandra laughed.

Maria ran up panting and threw her arms about Alexandra. "Oh, I had begun to think you were not coming at all, maybe. I knew you were so busy. Yes, Emil told me about Mr. Linstrum being here. Won't you come up to the house?"

"Why not sit down there in your corner? Carl wants to see the orchard. He kept all these trees alive for years, watering them with his own back."

Marie turned to Carl. "Then I'm thankful to you, Mr. Linstrum. We'd never have bought the place if it hadn't been for this orchard, and then I wouldn't have had Alexandra, either." She gave Alexandra's arm a little squeeze as she walked beside her. "How nice your dress smells, Alexandra; you put rosemary leaves in your chest, like I told you."

She led them to the northwest corner of the orchard, sheltered on one side by a thick mulberry hedge and bordered on the other by a wheatfield, just beginning to yellow. In this corner the ground dipped a little, and the blue-grass, which the weeds had driven out in the upper part of the orchard, grew thick and luxuriant. Wild roses were flaming in the tufts of bunchgrass along the fence. Under a white mulberry tree there was an old wagon-seat. Beside it lay a book and a workbasket.

"You must have the seat, Alexandra. The grass would stain your dress," the hostess insisted. She dropped down on the ground at Alexandra's side and tucked her feet under her. Carl sat at a little distance from the two women, his back to the wheatfield, and watched them. Alexandra took off her shade-hat and threw it on the ground. Marie picked it up and played with the white ribbons, twisting them about her brown fingers as she talked. They made a pretty picture in the strong sunlight, the leafy pattern surrounding them like a net; the Swedish woman so white and gold, kindly and amused, but armored in calm, and the alert brown one, her full lips parted, points of yellow light dancing in her eyes as she laughed and chattered. Carl had never forgotten little Marie Tovesky's eyes, and he was glad to have an opportunity to study them. The brown iris, he found, was curiously slashed with yellow, the color of sunflower honey, or of old amber. In each eye one of these streaks must have been larger than the others, for the effect was that of two dancing points of light, two little yellow bubbles, such as rise in a glass of champagne. Sometimes they seemed like the sparks from a forge. She seemed so easily excited, to kindle with a fierce little flame if one but breathed upon her. "What a waste," Carl reflected. "She ought to be doing all that for a sweetheart. How awkwardly things come about!"

It was not very long before Marie sprang up out of the grass again. "Wait a moment. I want to show you something." She ran away and disappeared behind the low-growing apple trees.

"What a charming creature," Carl murmured. "I don't wonder that her husband is jealous. But can't she walk? does she always run?"

Alexandra nodded. "Always. I don't see many people, but I don't believe there are many like her, anywhere."

Marie came back with a branch she had broken from an apricot tree, laden with pale yellow, pink-cheeked fruit. She dropped it beside Carl. "Did you plant those, too? They are such beautiful little trees."

Carl fingered the blue-green leaves, porous like blotting-paper and shaped like birch leaves, hung on waxen red stems. "Yes, I think I did. Are these the circus trees, Alexandra?"

"Shall I tell her about them?" Alexandra asked. "Sit down like a good girl, Marie, and don't ruin my poor hat, and I'll tell you a story. A long time ago, when Carl and I were, say, sixteen and twelve, a circus came to Hanover and we went to town in our wagon, with Lou and Oscar, to see the parade. We hadn't money enough to go to the circus. We followed the parade out to the circus grounds and hung around until the show began and the crowd went inside the tent. Then Lou was afraid we looked foolish standing outside in the pasture, so we went back to Hanover feeling very sad. There was a man in the streets selling apricots, and we had never seen any before. He had driven down from somewhere up in the French country, and he was selling them twenty-five cents a peck. We had a little money our fathers had given us for candy, and I bought two pecks and Carl bought one. They cheered us a good deal, and we saved all the seeds and planted them. Up to the time Carl went away, they hadn't borne at all."

"And now he's come back to eat them," cried Marie, nodding at Carl. "That IS a good story. I can remember you a little, Mr. Linstrum. I used to see you in Hanover sometimes, when Uncle Joe took me to town. I remember you because you were always buying pencils and tubes of paint at the drug store. Once, when my uncle left me at the store, you drew a lot of little birds and flowers for me on a piece of wrapping-paper. I kept them for a long while. I thought you were very romantic because you could draw and had such black eyes."

Carl smiled. "Yes, I remember that time. Your uncle bought you some kind of a mechanical toy, a Turkish lady sitting on an ottoman and smoking a hookah, wasn't it? And she turned her head backwards and forwards."

"Oh, yes! Wasn't she splendid! I knew well enough I ought not to tell Uncle Joe I wanted it, for he had just come back from the saloon and was feeling good. You remember how he laughed? She tickled him, too. But when we got home, my aunt scolded him for buying toys when she needed so many things. We wound our lady up every night, and when she began to move her head my aunt used to laugh as hard as any of us. It was a music-box, you know, and the Turkish lady played a tune while she smoked. That was how she made you feel so jolly. As I remember her, she was lovely, and had a gold crescent on her turban."

Half an hour later, as they were leaving the house, Carl and Alexandra were met in the path by a strapping fellow in overalls and a blue shirt. He was breathing hard, as if he had been running, and was muttering to himself.

Marie ran forward, and, taking him by the arm, gave him a little push toward her guests. "Frank, this is Mr. Linstrum."

Frank took off his broad straw hat and nodded to Alexandra. When he spoke to Carl, he showed a fine set of white teeth. He was burned a dull red down to his neckband, and there was a heavy three-days' stubble on his face. Even in his agitation he was handsome, but he looked a rash and violent man.

Barely saluting the callers, he turned at once to his wife and began, in an outraged tone, "I have to leave my team to drive the old woman Hiller's hogs out-a my wheat. I go to take dat old woman to de court if she ain't careful, I tell you!"

His wife spoke soothingly. "But, Frank, she has only her lame boy to help her. She does the best she can."

Alexandra looked at the excited man and offered a suggestion. "Why don't you go over there some afternoon and hog-tight her fences? You'd save time for yourself in the end."

Frank's neck stiffened. "Not-a-much, I won't. I keep my hogs home. Other peoples can do like me. See? If that Louis can mend shoes, he can mend fence."

"Maybe," said Alexandra placidly; "but I've found it sometimes pays to mend other people's fences. Good-bye, Marie. Come to see me soon."

Alexandra walked firmly down the path and Carl followed her.

Frank went into the house and threw himself on the sofa, his face to the wall, his clenched fist on his hip. Marie, having seen her guests off, came in and put her hand coaxingly on his shoulder.

"Poor Frank! You've run until you've made your head ache, now haven't you? Let me make you some coffee."

"What else am I to do?" he cried hotly in Bohemian. "Am I to let any old woman's hogs root up my wheat? Is that what I work myself to death for?"

"Don't worry about it, Frank. I'll speak to Mrs. Hiller again. But, really, she almost cried last time they got out, she was so sorry."

Frank bounced over on his other side. "That's it; you always side with them against me. They all know it. Anybody here feels free to borrow the mower and break it, or turn their hogs in on me. They know you won't care!"

Marie hurried away to make his coffee. When she came back, he was fast asleep. She sat down and looked at him for a long while, very thoughtfully. When the kitchen clock struck six she went out to get supper, closing the door gently behind her. She was always sorry for Frank when he worked himself into one of these rages, and she was sorry to have him rough and quarrelsome with his neighbors. She was perfectly aware that the neighbors had a good deal to put up with, and that they bore with Frank for her sake.

VII

Marie's father, Albert Tovesky, was one of the more intelligent Bohemians who came West in the early seventies. He settled in Omaha and became a leader and adviser among his people there. Marie was his youngest child, by a second wife, and was the apple of his eye. She was barely sixteen, and was in the graduating class of the Omaha High School, when Frank Shabata arrived from the old country and set all the Bohemian girls in a flutter. He was easily the buck of the beer-gardens, and on Sunday he was a sight to see, with his silk hat and tucked shirt and blue frock-coat, wearing gloves and carrying a little wisp of a yellow cane. He was tall and fair, with splendid teeth and close-cropped yellow curls, and he wore a slightly disdainful expression, proper for a young man with high connections, whose mother had a big farm in the Elbe valley. There was often an interesting discontent in his blue eyes, and every Bohemian girl he met imagined herself the cause of that unsatisfied expression. He had a way of drawing out his cambric handkerchief slowly, by one corner, from his breast-pocket, that was melancholy and romantic in the extreme. He took a little flight with each of the more eligible Bohemian girls, but it was when he was with little Marie Tovesky that he drew his handkerchief out most slowly, and, after he had lit a fresh cigar, dropped the match most despairingly. Any one could see, with half an eye, that his proud heart was bleeding for somebody.

One Sunday, late in the summer after Marie's graduation, she met Frank at a Bohemian picnic down the river and went rowing with him all the afternoon. When she got home that evening she went straight to her father's room and told him that she was engaged to Shabata. Old Tovesky was having a comfortable pipe before he went to bed. When he heard his daughter's announcement, he first prudently corked his beer bottle and then leaped to his feet and had a turn of temper. He characterized Frank Shabata by a Bohemian expression which is the equivalent of stuffed shirt.

"Why don't he go to work like the rest of us did? His farm in the Elbe valley, indeed! Ain't he got plenty brothers and sisters? It's his mother's farm, and why don't he stay at home and help her? Haven't I seen his mother out in the morning at five o'clock with her ladle and her big bucket on wheels, putting liquid manure on the cabbages? Don't I know the look of old Eva Shabata's hands? Like an old horse's hoofs they are--and this fellow wearing gloves and rings! Engaged, indeed! You aren't fit to be out of school, and that's what's the matter with you. I will send you off to the Sisters of the Sacred Heart in St. Louis, and they will teach you some sense, ~I~ guess!"

Accordingly, the very next week, Albert Tovesky took his daughter, pale and tearful, down the river to the convent. But the way to make Frank want anything was to tell him he couldn't have it. He managed to have an interview with Marie before she went away, and whereas he had been only half in love with her before, he now persuaded himself that he would not stop at anything. Marie took with her to the convent, under the canvas lining of her trunk, the results of a laborious and satisfying morning on Frank's part; no less than a dozen photographs of himself, taken in a dozen different love-lorn attitudes. There was a little round photograph for her watch-case, photographs for her wall and dresser, and even long narrow ones to be used as bookmarks. More than once the handsome gentleman was torn to pieces before the French class by an indignant nun.

Marie pined in the convent for a year, until her eighteenth birthday was passed. Then she met Frank Shabata in the Union Station in St. Louis and ran away with him. Old Tovesky forgave his daughter because there was nothing else to do, and bought her a farm in the country that she had loved so well as a child. Since then her story had been a part of the history of the Divide. She and Frank had been living there for five years when Carl Linstrum came back to pay his long deferred visit to Alexandra. Frank had, on the whole, done better than one might have expected. He had flung himself at the soil with savage energy. Once a year he went to Hastings or to Omaha, on a spree. He stayed away for a week or two, and then came home and worked like a demon. He did work; if he felt sorry for himself, that was his own affair.

VIII

On the evening of the day of Alexandra's call at the Shabatas', a heavy rain set in. Frank sat up until a late hour reading the Sunday newspapers. One of the Goulds was getting a divorce, and Frank took it as a personal affront. In printing the story of the young man's marital troubles, the knowing editor gave a sufficiently colored account of his career, stating the amount of his income and the manner in which he was supposed to spend it. Frank read English slowly, and the more he read about this divorce case, the angrier he grew. At last he threw down the page with a snort. He turned to his farm-hand who was reading the other half of the paper.

"By God! if I have that young feller in de hayfield once, I show him someting. Listen here what he do wit his money." And Frank began the catalogue of the young man's reputed extravagances.

Marie sighed. She thought it hard that the Goulds, for whom she had nothing but good will, should make her so much trouble. She hated to see the Sunday newspapers come into the house. Frank was always reading about the doings of rich people and feeling outraged. He had an inexhaustible stock of stories about their crimes and follies, how they bribed the courts and shot down their butlers with impunity whenever they chose. Frank and Lou Bergson had very similar ideas, and they were two of the political agitators of the county.

The next morning broke clear and brilliant, but Frank said the ground was too wet to plough, so he took the cart and drove over to Sainte-Agnes to spend the day at Moses Marcel's saloon. After he was gone, Marie went out to the back porch to begin her butter-making. A brisk wind had come up and was driving puffy white clouds across the sky. The orchard was sparkling and rippling in the sun. Marie stood looking toward it wistfully, her hand on the lid of the churn, when she heard a sharp ring in the air, the merry sound of the whetstone on the scythe. That invitation decided her. She ran into the house, put on a short skirt and a pair of her husband's boots, caught up a tin pail and started for the orchard. Emil had already begun work and was mowing vigorously. When he saw her coming, he stopped and wiped his brow. His yellow canvas leggings and khaki trousers were splashed to the knees.

"Don't let me disturb you, Emil. I'm going to pick cherries. Isn't everything beautiful after the rain? Oh, but I'm glad to get this place mowed! When I heard it raining in the night, I thought maybe you would come and do it for me to-day. The wind wakened me. Didn't it blow dreadfully? Just smell the wild roses! They are always so spicy after a rain. We never had so many of them in here before. I suppose it's the wet season. Will you have to cut them, too?"

"If I cut the grass, I will," Emil said teasingly. "What's the matter with you? What makes you so flighty?"

"Am I flighty? I suppose that's the wet season, too, then. It's exciting to see everything growing so fast,--and to get the grass cut! Please leave the roses till last, if you must cut them. Oh, I don't mean all of them, I mean that low place down by my tree, where there are so many. Aren't you splashed! Look at the spider-webs all over the grass. Good-bye. I'll call you if I see a snake."

She tripped away and Emil stood looking after her. In a few moments he heard the cherries dropping smartly into the pail, and he began to swing his scythe with that long, even stroke that few American boys ever learn. Marie picked cherries and sang softly to herself, stripping one glittering branch after another, shivering when she caught a shower of raindrops on her neck and hair. And Emil mowed his way slowly down toward the cherry trees.

That summer the rains had been so many and opportune that it was almost more than Shabata and his man could do to keep up with the corn; the orchard was a neglected wilderness. All sorts of weeds and herbs and flowers had grown up there; splotches of wild larkspur, pale green-and-white spikes of hoarhound, plantations of wild cotton, tangles of foxtail and wild wheat. South of the apricot trees, cornering on the wheatfield, was Frank's alfalfa, where myriads of white and yellow butterflies were always fluttering above the purple blossoms. When Emil reached the lower corner by the hedge, Marie was sitting under her white mulberry tree, the pailful of cherries beside her, looking off at the gentle, tireless swelling of the wheat.

"Emil," she said suddenly--he was mowing quietly about under the tree so as not to disturb her--"what religion did the Swedes have away back, before they were Christians?"

Emil paused and straightened his back. "I don't know. About like the Germans', wasn't it?"

Marie went on as if she had not heard him. "The Bohemians, you know, were tree worshipers before the missionaries came. Father says the people in the mountains still do queer things, sometimes,--they believe that trees bring good or bad luck."

Emil looked superior. "Do they? Well, which are the lucky trees? I'd like to know."

"I don't know all of them, but I know lindens are. The old people in the mountains plant lindens to purify the forest, and to do away with the spells that come from the old trees they say have lasted from heathen times. I'm a good Catholic, but I think I could get along with caring for trees, if I hadn't anything else."

"That's a poor saying," said Emil, stooping over to wipe his hands in the wet grass.

"Why is it? If I feel that way, I feel that way. I like trees because they seem more resigned to the way they have to live than other things do. I feel as if this tree knows everything I ever think of when I sit here. When I come back to it, I never have to remind it of anything; I begin just where I left off."

Emil had nothing to say to this. He reached up among the branches and began to pick the sweet, insipid fruit,--long ivory-colored berries, tipped with faint pink, like white coral, that fall to the ground unheeded all summer through. He dropped a handful into her lap.

"Do you like Mr. Linstrum?" Marie asked suddenly.

"Yes. Don't you?"

"Oh, ever so much; only he seems kind of staid and school-teachery. But, of course, he is older than Frank, even. I'm sure I don't want to live to be more than thirty, do you? Do you think Alexandra likes him very much?"

"I suppose so. They were old friends."

"Oh, Emil, you know what I mean!" Marie tossed her head impatiently. "Does she really care about him? When she used to tell me about him, I always wondered whether she wasn't a little in love with him."

"Who, Alexandra?" Emil laughed and thrust his hands into his trousers pockets. "Alexandra's never been in love, you crazy!" He laughed again. "She wouldn't know how to go about it. The idea!"

Marie shrugged her shoulders. "Oh, you don't know Alexandra as well as you think you do! If you had any eyes, you would see that she is very fond of him. It would serve you all right if she walked off with Carl. I like him because he appreciates her more than you do."

Emil frowned. "What are you talking about, Marie? Alexandra's all right. She and I have always been good friends. What more do you want? I like to talk to Carl about New York and what a fellow can do there."

"Oh, Emil! Surely you are not thinking of going off there?"

"Why not? I must go somewhere, mustn't I?" The young man took up his scythe and leaned on it. "Would you rather I went off in the sand hills and lived like Ivar?"

Marie's face fell under his brooding gaze. She looked down at his wet leggings. "I'm sure Alexandra hopes you will stay on here," she murmured.

"Then Alexandra will be disappointed," the young man said roughly. "What do I want to hang around here for? Alexandra can run the farm all right, without me. I don't want to stand around and look on. I want to be doing something on my own account."

"That's so," Marie sighed. "There are so many, many things you can do. Almost anything you choose."

"And there are so many, many things I can't do." Emil echoed her tone sarcastically. "Sometimes I don't want to do anything at all, and sometimes I want to pull the four corners of the Divide together,"--he threw out his arm and brought it back with a jerk,--"so, like a table-cloth. I get tired of seeing men and horses going up and down, up and down."

Marie looked up at his defiant figure and her face clouded. "I wish you weren't so restless, and didn't get so worked up over things," she said sadly.

"Thank you," he returned shortly.

She sighed despondently. "Everything I say makes you cross, don't it? And you never used to be cross to me."

Emil took a step nearer and stood frowning down at her bent head. He stood in an attitude of self-defense, his feet well apart, his hands clenched and drawn up at his sides, so that the cords stood out on his bare arms. "I can't play with you like a little boy any more," he said slowly. "That's what you miss, Marie. You'll have to get some other little boy to play with." He stopped and took a deep breath. Then he went on in a low tone, so intense that it was almost threatening: "Sometimes you seem to understand perfectly, and then sometimes you pretend you don't. You don't help things any by pretending. It's then that I want to pull the corners of the Divide together. If you WON'T understand, you know, I could make you!"

Marie clasped her hands and started up from her seat. She had grown very pale and her eyes were shining with excitement and distress. "But, Emil, if I understand, then all our good times are over, we can never do nice things together any more. We shall have to behave like Mr. Linstrum. And, anyhow, there's nothing to understand!" She struck the ground with her little foot fiercely. "That won't last. It will go away, and things will be just as they used to. I wish you were a Catholic. The Church helps people, indeed it does. I pray for you, but that's not the same as if you prayed yourself."

She spoke rapidly and pleadingly, looked entreatingly into his face. Emil stood defiant, gazing down at her.

"I can't pray to have the things I want," he said slowly, "and I won't pray not to have them, not if I'm damned for it."

Marie turned away, wringing her hands. "Oh, Emil, you won't try! Then all our good times are over."

"Yes; over. I never expect to have any more."

Emil gripped the hand-holds of his scythe and began to mow. Marie took up her cherries and went slowly toward the house, crying bitterly.

IX

On Sunday afternoon, a month after Carl Linstrum's arrival, he rode with Emil up into the French country to attend a Catholic fair. He sat for most of the afternoon in the basement of the church, where the fair was held, talking to Marie Shabata, or strolled about the gravel terrace, thrown up on the hillside in front of the basement doors, where the French boys were jumping and wrestling and throwing the discus. Some of the boys were in their white baseball suits; they had just come up from a Sunday practice game down in the ballgrounds. Amedee, the newly married, Emil's best friend, was their pitcher, renowned among the country towns for his dash and skill. Amedee was a little fellow, a year younger than Emil and much more boyish in appearance; very lithe and active and neatly made, with a clear brown and white skin, and flashing white teeth. The Sainte-Agnes boys were to play the Hastings nine in a fortnight, and Amedee's lightning balls were the hope of his team. The little Frenchman seemed to get every ounce there was in him behind the ball as it left his hand.

"You'd have made the battery at the University for sure, 'Medee," Emil said as they were walking from the ball-grounds back to the church on the hill. "You're pitching better than you did in the spring."

Amedee grinned. "Sure! A married man don't lose his head no more." He slapped Emil on the back as he caught step with him. "Oh, Emil, you wanna get married right off quick! It's the greatest thing ever!"

Emil laughed. "How am I going to get married without any girl?"

Amedee took his arm. "Pooh! There are plenty girls will have you. You wanna get some nice French girl, now. She treat you well; always be jolly. See,"--he began checking off on his fingers,--"there is Severine, and Alphosen, and Josephine, and Hectorine, and Louise, and Malvina--why, I could love any of them girls! Why don't you get after them? Are you stuck up, Emil, or is anything the matter with you? I never did know a boy twenty-two years old before that didn't have no girl. You wanna be a priest, maybe? Not-a for me!" Amedee swaggered. "I bring many good Catholics into this world, I hope, and that's a way I help the Church."

Emil looked down and patted him on the shoulder. "Now you're windy, 'Medee. You Frenchies like to brag."

But Amedee had the zeal of the newly married, and he was not to be lightly shaken off. "Honest and true, Emil, don't you want ANY girl? Maybe there's some young lady in Lincoln, now, very grand,"--Amedee waved his hand languidly before his face to denote the fan of heartless beauty,--"and you lost your heart up there. Is that it?"

"Maybe," said Emil.

But Amedee saw no appropriate glow in his friend's face. "Bah!" he exclaimed in disgust. "I tell all the French girls to keep 'way from you. You gotta rock in there," thumping Emil on the ribs.

When they reached the terrace at the side of the church, Amedee, who was excited by his success on the ball-grounds, challenged Emil to a jumping-match, though he knew he would be beaten. They belted themselves up, and Raoul Marcel, the choir tenor and Father Duchesne's pet, and Jean Bordelau, held the string over which they vaulted. All the French boys stood round, cheering and humping themselves up when Emil or Amedee went over the wire, as if they were helping in the lift. Emil stopped at five-feet-five, declaring that he would spoil his appetite for supper if he jumped any more.

Angelique, Amedee's pretty bride, as blonde and fair as her name, who had come out to watch the match, tossed her head at Emil and said:--

"'Medee could jump much higher than you if he were as tall. And anyhow, he is much more graceful. He goes over like a bird, and you have to hump yourself all up."

"Oh, I do, do I?" Emil caught her and kissed her saucy mouth squarely, while she laughed and struggled and called, "'Medee! 'Medee!"

"There, you see your 'Medee isn't even big enough to get you away from me. I could run away with you right now and he could only sit down and cry about it. I'll show you whether I have to hump myself!" Laughing and panting, he picked Angelique up in his arms and began running about the rectangle with her. Not until he saw Marie Shabata's tiger eyes flashing from the gloom of the basement doorway did he hand the disheveled bride over to her husband. "There, go to your graceful; I haven't the heart to take you away from him."

Angelique clung to her husband and made faces at Emil over the white shoulder of Amedee's ball-shirt. Emil was greatly amused at her air of proprietorship and at Amedee's shameless submission to it. He was delighted with his friend's good fortune. He liked to see and to think about Amedee's sunny, natural, happy love.

He and Amedee had ridden and wrestled and larked together since they were lads of twelve. On Sundays and holidays they were always arm in arm. It seemed strange that now he should have to hide the thing that Amedee was so proud of, that the feeling which gave one of them such happiness should bring the other such despair. It was like that when Alexandra tested her seed-corn in the spring, he mused. From two ears that had grown side by side, the grains of one shot up joyfully into the light, projecting themselves into the future, and the grains from the other lay still in the earth and rotted; and nobody knew why.

X

While Emil and Carl were amusing themselves at the fair, Alexandra was at home, busy with her account-books, which had been neglected of late. She was almost through with her figures when she heard a cart drive up to the gate, and looking out of the window she saw her two older brothers. They had seemed to avoid her ever since Carl Linstrum's arrival, four weeks ago that day, and she hurried to the door to welcome them. She saw at once that they had come with some very definite purpose. They followed her stiffly into the sitting-room. Oscar sat down, but Lou walked over to the window and remained standing, his hands behind him.

"You are by yourself?" he asked, looking toward the doorway into the parlor.

"Yes. Carl and Emil went up to the Catholic fair."

For a few moments neither of the men spoke.

Then Lou came out sharply. "How soon does he intend to go away from here?"

"I don't know, Lou. Not for some time, I hope." Alexandra spoke in an even, quiet tone that often exasperated her brothers. They felt that she was trying to be superior with them.

Oscar spoke up grimly. "We thought we ought to tell you that people have begun to talk," he said meaningly.

Alexandra looked at him. "What about?"

Oscar met her eyes blankly. "About you, keeping him here so long. It looks bad for him to be hanging on to a woman this way. People think you're getting taken in."

Alexandra shut her account-book firmly. "Boys," she said seriously, "don't let's go on with this. We won't come out anywhere. I can't take advice on such a matter. I know you mean well, but you must not feel responsible for me in things of this sort. If we go on with this talk it will only make hard feeling."

Lou whipped about from the window. "You ought to think a little about your family. You're making us all ridiculous."

"How am I?"

"People are beginning to say you want to marry the fellow."

"Well, and what is ridiculous about that?"

Lou and Oscar exchanged outraged looks. "Alexandra! Can't you see he's just a tramp and he's after your money? He wants to be taken care of, he does!"

"Well, suppose I want to take care of him? Whose business is it but my own?"

"Don't you know he'd get hold of your property?"

"He'd get hold of what I wished to give him, certainly."

Oscar sat up suddenly and Lou clutched at his bristly hair.

"Give him?" Lou shouted. "Our property, our homestead?"

"I don't know about the homestead," said Alexandra quietly. "I know you and Oscar have always expected that it would be left to your children, and I'm not sure but what you're right. But I'll do exactly as I please with the rest of my land, boys."

"The rest of your land!" cried Lou, growing more excited every minute. "Didn't all the land come out of the homestead? It was bought with money borrowed on the homestead, and Oscar and me worked ourselves to the bone paying interest on it."

"Yes, you paid the interest. But when you married we made a division of the land, and you were satisfied. I've made more on my farms since I've been alone than when we all worked together."

"Everything you've made has come out of the original land that us boys worked for, hasn't it? The farms and all that comes out of them belongs to us as a family."

Alexandra waved her hand impatiently. "Come now, Lou. Stick to the facts. You are talking nonsense. Go to the county clerk and ask him who owns my land, and whether my titles are good."

Lou turned to his brother. "This is what comes of letting a woman meddle in business," he said bitterly. "We ought to have taken things in our own hands years ago. But she liked to run things, and we humored her. We thought you had good sense, Alexandra. We never thought you'd do anything foolish."

Alexandra rapped impatiently on her desk with her knuckles. "Listen, Lou. Don't talk wild. You say you ought to have taken things into your own hands years ago. I suppose you mean before you left home. But how could you take hold of what wasn't there? I've got most of what I have now since we divided the property; I've built it up myself, and it has nothing to do with you."

Oscar spoke up solemnly. "The property of a family really belongs to the men of the family, no matter about the title. If anything goes wrong, it's the men that are held responsible."

"Yes, of course," Lou broke in. "Everybody knows that. Oscar and me have always been easy-going and we've never made any fuss. We were willing you should hold the land and have the good of it, but you got no right to part with any of it. We worked in the fields to pay for the first land you bought, and whatever's come out of it has got to be kept in the family."

Oscar reinforced his brother, his mind fixed on the one point he could see. "The property of a family belongs to the men of the family, because they are held responsible, and because they do the work."

Alexandra looked from one to the other, her eyes full of indignation. She had been impatient before, but now she was beginning to feel angry. "And what about my work?" she asked in an unsteady voice.

Lou looked at the carpet. "Oh, now, Alexandra, you always took it pretty easy! Of course we wanted you to. You liked to manage round, and we always humored you. We realize you were a great deal of help to us. There's no woman anywhere around that knows as much about business as you do, and we've always been proud of that, and thought you were pretty smart. But, of course, the real work always fell on us. Good advice is all right, but it don't get the weeds out of the corn."

"Maybe not, but it sometimes puts in the crop, and it sometimes keeps the fields for corn to grow in," said Alexandra dryly. "Why, Lou, I can remember when you and Oscar wanted to sell this homestead and all the improvements to old preacher Ericson for two thousand dollars. If I'd consented, you'd have gone down to the river and scraped along on poor farms for the rest of your lives. When I put in our first field of alfalfa you both opposed me, just because I first heard about it from a young man who had been to the University. You said I was being taken in then, and all the neighbors said so. You know as well as I do that alfalfa has been the salvation of this country. You all laughed at me when I said our land here was about ready for wheat, and I had to raise three big wheat crops before the neighbors quit putting all their land in corn. Why, I remember you cried, Lou, when we put in the first big wheat-planting, and said everybody was laughing at us."

Lou turned to Oscar. "That's the woman of it; if she tells you to put in a crop, she thinks she's put it in. It makes women conceited to meddle in business. I shouldn't think you'd want to remind us how hard you were on us, Alexandra, after the way you baby Emil."

"Hard on you? I never meant to be hard. Conditions were hard. Maybe I would never have been very soft, anyhow; but I certainly didn't choose to be the kind of girl I was. If you take even a vine and cut it back again and again, it grows hard, like a tree."

Lou felt that they were wandering from the point, and that in digression Alexandra might unnerve him. He wiped his forehead with a jerk of his handkerchief. "We never doubted you, Alexandra. We never questioned anything you did.

You've always had your own way. But you can't expect us to sit like stumps and see you done out of the property by any loafer who happens along, and making yourself ridiculous into the bargain."

Oscar rose. "Yes," he broke in, "everybody's laughing to see you get took in; at your age, too. Everybody knows he's nearly five years younger than you, and is after your money. Why, Alexandra, you are forty years old!"

"All that doesn't concern anybody but Carl and me. Go to town and ask your lawyers what you can do to restrain me from disposing of my own property. And I advise you to do what they tell you; for the authority you can exert by law is the only influence you will ever have over me again." Alexandra rose. "I think I would rather not have lived to find out what I have to-day," she said quietly, closing her desk.

Lou and Oscar looked at each other questioningly. There seemed to be nothing to do but to go, and they walked out.

"You can't do business with women," Oscar said heavily as he clambered into the cart. "But anyhow, we've had our say, at last."

Lou scratched his head. "Talk of that kind might come too high, you know; but she's apt to be sensible. You hadn't ought to said that about her age, though, Oscar. I'm afraid that hurt her feelings; and the worst thing we can do is to make her sore at us. She'd marry him out of contrariness."

"I only meant," said Oscar, "that she is old enough to know better, and she is. If she was going to marry, she ought to done it long ago, and not go making a fool of herself now."

Lou looked anxious, nevertheless. "Of course," he reflected hopefully and inconsistently, "Alexandra ain't much like other women-folks. Maybe it won't make her sore. Maybe she'd as soon be forty as not!"

XI

Emil came home at about half-past seven o'clock that evening. Old Ivar met him at the windmill and took his horse, and the young man went directly into the house. He called to his sister and she answered from her bedroom, behind the sitting-room, saying that she was lying down.

Emil went to her door.

"Can I see you for a minute?" he asked. "I want to talk to you about something before Carl comes."

Alexandra rose quickly and came to the door. "Where is Carl?"

"Lou and Oscar met us and said they wanted to talk to him, so he rode over to Oscar's with them. Are you coming out?" Emil asked impatiently.

"Yes, sit down. I'll be dressed in a moment."

Alexandra closed her door, and Emil sank down on the old slat lounge and sat with his head in his hands. When his sister came out, he looked up, not knowing whether the interval had been short or long, and he was surprised to see that the room had grown quite dark. That was just as well; it would be easier to talk if he were not under the gaze of those clear, deliberate eyes, that saw so far in some directions and were so blind in others. Alexandra, too, was glad of the dusk. Her face was swollen from crying.

Emil started up and then sat down again. "Alexandra," he said slowly, in his deep young baritone, "I don't want to go away to law school this fall. Let me put it off another year. I want to take a year off and look around. It's awfully easy to rush into a profession you don't really like, and awfully hard to get out of it. Linstrum and I have been talking about that."

"Very well, Emil. Only don't go off looking for land." She came up and put her hand on his shoulder. "I've been wishing you could stay with me this winter."

"That's just what I don't want to do, Alexandra. I'm restless. I want to go to a new place. I want to go down to the City of Mexico to join one of the University fellows who's at the head of an electrical plant. He wrote me he could give me a little job, enough to pay my way, and I could look around and see what I want to do. I want to go as soon as harvest is over. I guess Lou and Oscar will be sore about it."

"I suppose they will." Alexandra sat down on the lounge beside him. "They are very angry with me, Emil. We have had a quarrel. They will not come here again."

Emil scarcely heard what she was saying; he did not notice the sadness of her tone. He was thinking about the reckless life he meant to live in Mexico.

"What about?" he asked absently.

"About Carl Linstrum. They are afraid I am going to marry him, and that some of my property will get away from them."

Emil shrugged his shoulders. "What nonsense!" he murmured. "Just like them."

Alexandra drew back. "Why nonsense, Emil?"

"Why, you've never thought of such a thing, have you? They always have to have something to fuss about."

"Emil," said his sister slowly, "you ought not to take things for granted. Do you agree with them that I have no right to change my way of living?"

Emil looked at the outline of his sister's head in the dim light. They were sitting close together and he somehow felt that she could hear his thoughts. He was silent for a moment, and then said in an embarrassed tone, "Why, no, certainly not. You ought to do whatever you want to. I'll always back you."

"But it would seem a little bit ridiculous to you if I married Carl?"

Emil fidgeted. The issue seemed to him too far-fetched to warrant discussion. "Why, no. I should be surprised if you wanted to. I can't see exactly why. But that's none of my business. You ought to do as you please. Certainly you ought not to pay any attention to what the boys say."

Alexandra sighed. "I had hoped you might understand, a little, why I do want to. But I suppose that's too much to expect. I've had a pretty lonely life, Emil. Besides Marie, Carl is the only friend I have ever had."

Emil was awake now; a name in her last sentence roused him. He put out his hand and took his sister's awkwardly. "You ought to do just as you wish, and I think Carl's a fine fellow. He and I would always get on. I don't believe any of the things the boys say about him, honest I don't. They are suspicious of him because he's intelligent. You know their way. They've been sore at me ever since you let me go away to college. They're always trying to catch me up. If I were you, I wouldn't pay any attention to them. There's nothing to get upset about. Carl's a sensible fellow. He won't mind them."

"I don't know. If they talk to him the way they did to me, I think he'll go away."

Emil grew more and more uneasy. "Think so? Well, Marie said it would serve us all right if you walked off with him."

"Did she? Bless her little heart! SHE would." Alexandra's voice broke.

Emil began unlacing his leggings. "Why don't you talk to her about it? There's Carl, I hear his horse. I guess I'll go upstairs and get my boots off. No, I don't want any supper. We had supper at five o'clock, at the fair."

Emil was glad to escape and get to his own room. He was a little ashamed for his sister, though he had tried not to show it. He felt that there was something indecorous in her proposal, and she did seem to him somewhat ridiculous. There was trouble enough in the world, he reflected, as he threw himself upon his bed, without people who were forty years old imagining they wanted to get married. In the darkness and silence Emil was not likely to think long about Alexandra. Every image slipped away but one. He had seen Marie in the crowd that afternoon. She sold candy at the fair. WHY had she ever run away with Frank Shabata, and how could she go on laughing and working and taking an interest in things? Why did she like so many people, and why had she seemed pleased when all the French and Bohemian boys, and the priest himself, crowded round her candy stand? Why did she care about any one but him? Why could he never, never find the thing he looked for in her playful, affectionate eyes?

Then he fell to imagining that he looked once more and found it there, and what it would be like if she loved him,-- she who, as Alexandra said, could give her whole heart. In that dream he could lie for hours, as if in a trance. His spirit went out of his body and crossed the fields to Marie Shabata.

At the University dances the girls had often looked wonderingly at the tall young Swede with the fine head, leaning against the wall and frowning, his arms folded, his eyes fixed on the ceiling or the floor. All the girls were a little afraid of him. He was distinguished-looking, and not the jollying kind. They felt that he was too intense and preoccupied. There was something queer about him. Emil's fraternity rather prided itself upon its dances, and sometimes he did his duty and danced every dance. But whether he was on the floor or brooding in a corner, he was always thinking about Marie Shabata. For two years the storm had been gathering in him.

XII

Carl came into the sitting-room while Alexandra was lighting the lamp. She looked up at him as she adjusted the shade. His sharp shoulders stooped as if he were very tired, his face was pale, and there were bluish shadows under his dark eyes. His anger had burned itself out and left him sick and disgusted.

"You have seen Lou and Oscar?" Alexandra asked.

"Yes." His eyes avoided hers.

Alexandra took a deep breath. "And now you are going away. I thought so."

Carl threw himself into a chair and pushed the dark lock back from his forehead with his white, nervous hand. "What a hopeless position you are in, Alexandra!" he exclaimed feverishly. "It is your fate to be always surrounded by little men. And I am no better than the rest. I am too little to face the criticism of even such men as Lou and Oscar. Yes, I am going away; to-morrow. I cannot even ask you to give me a promise until I have something to offer you. I thought, perhaps, I could do that; but I find I can't."

"What good comes of offering people things they don't need?" Alexandra asked sadly. "I don't need money. But I have needed you for a great many years. I wonder why I have been permitted to prosper, if it is only to take my friends away from me."

"I don't deceive myself," Carl said frankly. "I know that I am going away on my own account. I must make the usual effort. I must have something to show for myself. To take what you would give me, I should have to be either a very large man or a very small one, and I am only in the middle class."

Alexandra sighed. "I have a feeling that if you go away, you will not come back. Something will happen to one of us, or to both. People have to snatch at happiness when they can, in this world. It is always easier to lose than to find. What I have is yours, if you care enough about me to take it."

Carl rose and looked up at the picture of John Bergson. "But I can't, my dear, I can't! I will go North at once. Instead of idling about in California all winter, I shall be getting my bearings up there. I won't waste another week. Be patient with me, Alexandra. Give me a year!"

"As you will," said Alexandra wearily. "All at once, in a single day, I lose everything; and I do not know why. Emil, too, is going away." Carl was still studying John Bergson's face and Alexandra's eyes followed his. "Yes," she said, "if he could have seen all that would come of the task he gave me, he would have been sorry. I hope he does not see me now. I hope that he is among the old people of his blood and country, and that tidings do not reach him from the New World."

PART III. WINTER MEMORIES

I

Winter has settled down over the Divide again; the season in which Nature recuperates, in which she sinks to sleep between the fruitfulness of autumn and the passion of spring. The birds have gone. The teeming life that goes on down in the long grass is exterminated. The prairie-dog keeps his hole. The rabbits run shivering from one frozen garden patch to another and are hard put to it to find frost-bitten cabbage-stalks. At night the coyotes roam the wintry waste, howling for food. The variegated fields are all one color now; the pastures, the stubble, the roads, the sky are the same leaden gray. The hedgerows and trees are scarcely perceptible against the bare earth, whose slaty hue they have taken on. The ground is frozen so hard that it bruises the foot to walk in the roads or in the ploughed fields. It is like an iron country, and the spirit is oppressed by its rigor and melancholy. One could easily believe that in that dead landscape the germs of life and fruitfulness were extinct forever.

Alexandra has settled back into her old routine. There are weekly letters from Emil. Lou and Oscar she has not seen since Carl went away. To avoid awkward encounters in the presence of curious spectators, she has stopped going to the Norwegian Church and drives up to the Reform Church at Hanover, or goes with Marie Shabata to the Catholic Church, locally known as "the French Church." She has not told Marie about Carl, or her differences with her brothers. She was never very communicative about her own affairs, and when she came to the point, an instinct told her that about such things she and Marie would not understand one another.

Old Mrs. Lee had been afraid that family misunderstandings might deprive her of her yearly visit to Alexandra. But on the first day of December Alexandra telephoned Annie that to-morrow she would send Ivar over for her mother, and the next day the old lady arrived with her bundles. For twelve years Mrs. Lee had always entered Alexandra's sitting-room with the same exclamation, "Now we be yust-a like old times!" She enjoyed the liberty Alexandra gave her, and hearing her own language about her all day long. Here she could wear her nightcap and sleep with all her windows shut, listen to Ivar reading the Bible, and here she could run about among the stables in a pair of Emil's old boots. Though she was bent almost double, she was as spry as a gopher. Her face was as brown as if it had been varnished, and as full of wrinkles as a washerwoman's hands. She had three jolly old teeth left in the front of her mouth, and when she grinned she looked very knowing, as if when you found out how to take it, life wasn't half bad. While she and Alexandra patched and pieced and quilted, she talked incessantly about stories she read in a Swedish family paper, telling the plots in great detail; or about her life on a dairy farm in Gottland when she was a girl. Sometimes she forgot which were the printed stories and which were the real stories, it all seemed so far away. She loved to take a little brandy, with hot water and sugar, before she went to bed, and Alexandra always had it ready for her. "It sends good dreams," she would say with a twinkle in her eye.

When Mrs. Lee had been with Alexandra for a week, Marie Shabata telephoned one morning to say that Frank had gone to town for the day, and she would like them to come over for coffee in the afternoon. Mrs. Lee hurried to wash out and iron her new cross-stitched apron, which she had finished only the night before; a checked gingham apron worked with a design ten inches broad across the bottom; a hunting scene, with fir trees and a stag and dogs and huntsmen. Mrs. Lee was firm with herself at dinner, and refused a second helping of apple dumplings. "I ta-ank I save up," she said with a giggle.

At two o'clock in the afternoon Alexandra's cart drove up to the Shabatas' gate, and Marie saw Mrs. Lee's red shawl come bobbing up the path. She ran to the door and pulled the old woman into the house with a hug, helping her to take off her wraps while Alexandra blanketed the horse outside. Mrs. Lee had put on her best black satine dress--she abominated woolen stuffs, even in winter--and a crocheted collar, fastened with a big pale gold pin, containing faded daguerreotypes of her father and mother. She had not worn her apron for fear of rumpling it, and now she shook it out and tied it round her waist with a conscious air. Marie drew back and threw up her hands, exclaiming, "Oh, what a beauty! I've never seen this one before, have I, Mrs. Lee?"

The old woman giggled and ducked her head. "No, yust las' night I ma-ake. See dis tread; verra strong, no wa-ash out, no fade. My sister send from Sveden. I yust-a ta-ank you like dis."

Marie ran to the door again. "Come in, Alexandra. I have been looking at Mrs. Lee's apron. Do stop on your way home and show it to Mrs. Hiller. She's crazy about cross-stitch."

While Alexandra removed her hat and veil, Mrs. Lee went out to the kitchen and settled herself in a wooden rocking-chair by the stove, looking with great interest at the table, set for three, with a white cloth, and a pot of pink geraniums in the middle. "My, a-an't you gotta fine plants; such-a much flower. How you keep from freeze?"

She pointed to the window-shelves, full of blooming fuchsias and geraniums.

"I keep the fire all night, Mrs. Lee, and when it's very cold I put them all on the table, in the middle of the room. Other nights I only put newspapers behind them. Frank laughs at me for fussing, but when they don't bloom he says, 'What's the matter with the darned things?'-- What do you hear from Carl, Alexandra?"

"He got to Dawson before the river froze, and now I suppose I won't hear any more until spring. Before he left California he sent me a box of orange flowers, but they didn't keep very well. I have brought a bunch of Emil's letters for you." Alexandra came out from the sitting-room and pinched Marie's cheek playfully. "You don't look as if the weather ever froze you up. Never have colds, do you? That's a good girl. She had dark red cheeks like this when she was a little girl, Mrs. Lee. She looked like some queer foreign kind of a doll. I've never forgot the first time I saw you in Mieklejohn's store, Marie, the time father was lying sick. Carl and I were talking about that before he went away."

"I remember, and Emil had his kitten along. When are you going to send Emil's Christmas box?"

"It ought to have gone before this. I'll have to send it by mail now, to get it there in time."

Marie pulled a dark purple silk necktie from her workbasket. "I knit this for him. It's a good color, don't you think? Will you please put it in with your things and tell him it's from me, to wear when he goes serenading."

Alexandra laughed. "I don't believe he goes serenading much. He says in one letter that the Mexican ladies are said to be very beautiful, but that don't seem to me very warm praise."

Marie tossed her head. "Emil can't fool me. If he's bought a guitar, he goes serenading. Who wouldn't, with all those Spanish girls dropping flowers down from their windows! I'd sing to them every night, wouldn't you, Mrs. Lee?"

The old lady chuckled. Her eyes lit up as Marie bent down and opened the oven door. A delicious hot fragrance blew out into the tidy kitchen. "My, somet'ing smell good!" She turned to Alexandra with a wink, her three yellow teeth making a brave show, "I ta-ank dat stop my yaw from ache no more!" she said contentedly.

Marie took out a pan of delicate little rolls, stuffed with stewed apricots, and began to dust them over with powdered sugar. "I hope you'll like these, Mrs. Lee; Alexandra does. The Bohemians always like them with their coffee. But if you don't, I have a coffee-cake with nuts and poppy seeds. Alexandra, will you get the cream jug? I put it in the window to keep cool."

"The Bohemians," said Alexandra, as they drew up to the table, "certainly know how to make more kinds of bread than any other people in the world. Old Mrs. Hiller told me once at the church supper that she could make seven kinds of fancy bread, but Marie could make a dozen."

Mrs. Lee held up one of the apricot rolls between her brown thumb and forefinger and weighed it critically. "Yust like-a fedders," she pronounced with satisfaction. "My, a-an't dis nice!" she exclaimed as she stirred her coffee. "I yust ta-ake a liddle yelly now, too, I ta-ank."

Alexandra and Marie laughed at her forehandedness, and fell to talking of their own affairs. "I was afraid you had a cold when I talked to you over the telephone the other night, Marie. What was the matter, had you been crying?"

"Maybe I had," Marie smiled guiltily. "Frank was out late that night. Don't you get lonely sometimes in the winter, when everybody has gone away?"

"I thought it was something like that. If I hadn't had company, I'd have run over to see for myself. If you get down-hearted, what will become of the rest of us?" Alexandra asked.

"I don't, very often. There's Mrs. Lee without any coffee!"

Later, when Mrs. Lee declared that her powers were spent, Marie and Alexandra went upstairs to look for some crochet patterns the old lady wanted to borrow. "Better put on your coat, Alexandra. It's cold up there, and I have no idea where those patterns are. I may have to look through my old trunks." Marie caught up a shawl and opened the stair door, running up the steps ahead of her guest. "While I go through the bureau drawers, you might look in those hat-boxes on the closet-shelf, over where Frank's clothes hang. There are a lot of odds and ends in them."

She began tossing over the contents of the drawers, and Alexandra went into the clothes-closet. Presently she came back, holding a slender elastic yellow stick in her hand.

"What in the world is this, Marie? You don't mean to tell me Frank ever carried such a thing?"

Marie blinked at it with astonishment and sat down on the floor. "Where did you find it? I didn't know he had kept it. I haven't seen it for years."

"It really is a cane, then?"

"Yes. One he brought from the old country. He used to carry it when I first knew him. Isn't it foolish? Poor Frank!"

Alexandra twirled the stick in her fingers and laughed. "He must have looked funny!"

Marie was thoughtful. "No, he didn't, really. It didn't seem out of place. He used to be awfully gay like that when he was a young man. I guess people always get what's hardest for them, Alexandra." Marie gathered the shawl closer about her and still looked hard at the cane. "Frank would be all right in the right place," she said reflectively. "He ought to have a different kind of wife, for one thing. Do you know, Alexandra, I could pick out exactly the right sort of woman for Frank--now. The trouble is you almost have to marry a man before you can find out the sort of wife he needs; and usually it's exactly the sort you are not. Then what are you going to do about it?" she asked candidly.

Alexandra confessed she didn't know. "However," she added, "it seems to me that you get along with Frank about as well as any woman I've ever seen or heard of could."

Marie shook her head, pursing her lips and blowing her warm breath softly out into the frosty air. "No; I was spoiled at home. I like my own way, and I have a quick tongue. When Frank brags, I say sharp things, and he never forgets. He goes over and over it in his mind; I can feel him. Then I'm too giddy. Frank's wife ought to be timid, and she ought not to care about another living thing in the world but just Frank! I didn't, when I married him, but I suppose I was too young to stay like that." Marie sighed.

Alexandra had never heard Marie speak so frankly about her husband before, and she felt that it was wiser not to encourage her. No good, she reasoned, ever came from talking about such things, and while Marie was thinking aloud, Alexandra had been steadily searching the hat-boxes. "Aren't these the patterns, Maria?"

Maria sprang up from the floor. "Sure enough, we were looking for patterns, weren't we? I'd forgot about everything but Frank's other wife. I'll put that away."

She poked the cane behind Frank's Sunday clothes, and though she laughed, Alexandra saw there were tears in her eyes.

When they went back to the kitchen, the snow had begun to fall, and Marie's visitors thought they must be getting home. She went out to the cart with them, and tucked the robes about old Mrs. Lee while Alexandra took the blanket off her horse. As they drove away, Marie turned and went slowly back to the house. She took up the package of letters Alexandra had brought, but she did not read them. She turned them over and looked at the foreign stamps, and then sat watching the flying snow while the dusk deepened in the kitchen and the stove sent out a red glow.

Marie knew perfectly well that Emil's letters were written more for her than for Alexandra. They were not the sort of letters that a young man writes to his sister. They were both more personal and more painstaking; full of descriptions of the gay life in the old Mexican capital in the days when the strong hand of Porfirio Diaz was still strong. He told about bull-fights and cock-fights, churches and FIESTAS, the flower-markets and the fountains, the music and dancing, the people of all nations he met in the Italian restaurants on San Francisco Street. In short, they were the kind of letters a young man writes to a woman when he wishes himself and his life to seem interesting to her, when he wishes to enlist her imagination in his behalf.

Marie, when she was alone or when she sat sewing in the evening, often thought about what it must be like down there where Emil was; where there were flowers and street bands everywhere, and carriages rattling up and down, and where there was a little blind boot-black in front of the cathedral who could play any tune you asked for by dropping the lids of blacking-boxes on the stone steps. When everything is done and over for one at twenty-three, it is pleasant to let the mind wander forth and follow a young adventurer who has life before him. "And if it had not been for me," she thought, "Frank might still be free like that, and having a good time making people admire him. Poor Frank, getting married wasn't very good for him either. I'm afraid I do set people against him, as he says. I seem, somehow, to give him away all the time. Perhaps he would try to be agreeable to people again, if I were not around. It seems as if I always make him just as bad as he can be."

Later in the winter, Alexandra looked back upon that afternoon as the last satisfactory visit she had had with Marie. After that day the younger woman seemed to shrink more and more into herself. When she was with Alexandra she was not spontaneous and frank as she used to be. She seemed to be brooding over something, and holding something back. The weather had a good deal to do with their seeing less of each other than usual. There had not been such snowstorms in twenty years, and the path across the fields was drifted deep from Christmas until March. When the two neighbors went to see each other, they had to go round by the wagon-road, which was twice as far. They telephoned each other almost every night, though in January there was a stretch of three weeks when the wires were down, and when the postman did not come at all.

Marie often ran in to see her nearest neighbor, old Mrs. Hiller, who was crippled with rheumatism and had only her son, the lame shoemaker, to take care of her; and she went to the French Church, whatever the weather. She was a sincerely devout girl. She prayed for herself and for Frank, and for Emil, among the temptations of that gay, corrupt old city. She found more comfort in the Church that winter than ever before. It seemed to come closer to her, and to fill an emptiness that ached in her heart. She tried to be patient with her husband. He and his hired man usually played California Jack in the evening. Marie sat sewing or crocheting and tried to take a friendly interest in the game, but she was always thinking about the wide fields outside, where the snow was drifting over the fences; and about the orchard, where the snow was falling and packing, crust over crust. When she went out into the dark kitchen to fix her plants for the night, she used to stand by the window and look out at the white fields, or watch the currents of snow whirling over the orchard. She seemed to feel the weight of all the snow that lay down there. The branches had become so hard that they wounded your hand if you but tried to break a twig. And yet, down under the frozen crusts, at the roots of the trees, the secret of life was still safe, warm as the blood in one's heart; and the spring would come again! Oh, it would come again!

II

If Alexandra had had much imagination she might have guessed what was going on in Marie's mind, and she would have seen long before what was going on in Emil's. But that, as Emil himself had more than once reflected, was Alexandra's blind side, and her life had not been of the kind to sharpen her vision. Her training had all been toward the end of making her proficient in what she had undertaken to do. Her personal life, her own realization of herself, was almost a subconscious existence; like an underground river that came to the surface only here and there, at intervals months apart, and then sank again to flow on under her own fields. Nevertheless, the underground stream was there, and it was because she had so much personality to put into her enterprises and succeeded in putting it into them so completely, that her affairs prospered better than those of her neighbors.

There were certain days in her life, outwardly uneventful, which Alexandra remembered as peculiarly happy; days when she was close to the flat, fallow world about her, and felt, as it were, in her own body the joyous germination in the soil. There were days, too, which she and Emil had spent together, upon which she loved to look back. There had been such a day when they were down on the river in the dry year, looking over the land. They had made an early start one morning and had driven a long way before noon. When Emil said he was hungry, they drew back from the road, gave Brigham his oats among the bushes, and climbed up to the top of a grassy bluff to eat their lunch under the shade of some little elm trees. The river was clear there, and shallow, since there had been no rain, and it ran in ripples over the sparkling sand. Under the overhanging willows of the opposite bank there was an inlet where the water was deeper and flowed so slowly that it seemed to sleep in the sun. In this little bay a single wild duck was swimming and diving and preening her feathers, disporting herself very happily in the flickering light and shade. They sat for a long time, watching the solitary bird take its pleasure. No living thing had ever seemed to Alexandra as beautiful as that wild duck. Emil must have felt about it as she did, for afterward, when they were at home, he used sometimes to say, "Sister, you know our duck down there--" Alexandra remembered that day as one of the happiest in her life. Years afterward she thought of the duck as still there, swimming and diving all by herself in the sunlight, a kind of enchanted bird that did not know age or change.

Most of Alexandra's happy memories were as impersonal as this one; yet to her they were very personal. Her mind was a white book, with clear writing about weather and beasts and growing things. Not many people would have cared to read it; only a happy few. She had never been in love, she had never indulged in sentimental reveries. Even as a girl she had looked upon men as work-fellows. She had grown up in serious times.

There was one fancy indeed, which persisted through her girlhood. It most often came to her on Sunday mornings, the one day in the week when she lay late abed listening to the familiar morning sounds; the windmill singing in the brisk breeze, Emil whistling as he blacked his boots down by the kitchen door. Sometimes, as she lay thus luxuriously idle, her eyes closed, she used to have an illusion of being lifted up bodily and carried lightly by some one very strong. It was a man, certainly, who carried her, but he was like no man she knew; he was much larger and stronger and swifter, and he carried her as easily as if she were a sheaf of wheat. She never saw him, but, with eyes closed, she could feel that he was yellow like the sunlight, and there was the smell of ripe cornfields about him. She could feel him approach, bend over her and lift her, and then she could feel herself being carried swiftly off across the fields. After such a reverie she would rise hastily, angry with herself, and go down to the bath-house that was partitioned off the kitchen shed. There she would stand in a tin tub and prosecute her bath with vigor, finishing it by pouring buckets of cold well-water over her gleaming white body which no man on the Divide could have carried very far.

As she grew older, this fancy more often came to her when she was tired than when she was fresh and strong. Sometimes, after she had been in the open all day, overseeing the branding of the cattle or the loading of the pigs, she would come in chilled, take a concoction of spices and warm home-made wine, and go to bed with her body actually aching with fatigue. Then, just before she went to sleep, she had the old sensation of being lifted and carried by a strong being who took from her all her bodily weariness.

PART IV.
THE WHITE MULBERRY TREE

I

The French Church, properly the Church of Sainte-Agnes, stood upon a hill. The high, narrow, red-brick building, with its tall steeple and steep roof, could be seen for miles across the wheatfields, though the little town of Sainte-Agnes was completely hidden away at the foot of the hill. The church looked powerful and triumphant there on its eminence, so high above the rest of the landscape, with miles of warm color lying at its feet, and by its position and setting it reminded one of some of the churches built long ago in the wheat-lands of middle France.

Late one June afternoon Alexandra Bergson was driving along one of the many roads that led through the rich French farming country to the big church. The sunlight was shining directly in her face, and there was a blaze of light all about the red church on the hill. Beside Alexandra lounged a strikingly exotic figure in a tall Mexican hat, a silk sash, and a black velvet jacket sewn with silver buttons. Emil had returned only the night before, and his sister was so proud of him that she decided at once to take him up to the church supper, and to make him wear the Mexican costume he had brought home in his trunk. "All the girls who have stands are going to wear fancy costumes," she argued, "and some of the boys. Marie is going to tell fortunes, and she sent to Omaha for a Bohemian dress her father brought back from a visit to the old country. If you wear those clothes, they will all be pleased. And you must take your guitar. Everybody ought to do what they can to help along, and we have never done much. We are not a talented family."

The supper was to be at six o'clock, in the basement of the church, and afterward there would be a fair, with charades and an auction. Alexandra had set out from home early, leaving the house to Signa and Nelse Jensen, who were to be married next week. Signa had shyly asked to have the wedding put off until Emil came home.

Alexandra was well satisfied with her brother. As they drove through the rolling French country toward the westering sun and the stalwart church, she was thinking of that time long ago when she and Emil drove back from the river valley to the still unconquered Divide. Yes, she told herself, it had been worth while; both Emil and the country had become what she had hoped. Out of her father's children there was one who was fit to cope with the world, who had not been tied to the plow, and who had a personality apart from the soil. And that, she reflected, was what she had worked for. She felt well satisfied with her life.

When they reached the church, a score of teams were hitched in front of the basement doors that opened from the hillside upon the sanded terrace, where the boys wrestled and had jumping-matches. Amedee Chevalier, a proud father of one week, rushed out and embraced Emil. Amedee was an only son,--hence he was a very rich young man,--but he meant to have twenty children himself, like his uncle Xavier. "Oh, Emil," he cried, hugging his old friend rapturously, "why ain't you been up to see my boy? You come to-morrow, sure? Emil, you wanna get a boy right off! It's the greatest thing ever! No, no, no! Angel not sick at all. Everything just fine. That boy he come into this world laughin', and he been laughin' ever since. You come an' see!" He pounded Emil's ribs to emphasize each announcement.

Emil caught his arms. "Stop, Amedee. You're knocking the wind out of me. I brought him cups and spoons and blankets and moccasins enough for an orphan asylum. I'm awful glad it's a boy, sure enough!"

The young men crowded round Emil to admire his costume and to tell him in a breath everything that had happened since he went away. Emil had more friends up here in the French country than down on Norway Creek. The French and Bohemian boys were spirited and jolly, liked variety, and were as much predisposed to favor anything new as the Scandinavian boys were to reject it. The Norwegian and Swedish lads were much more self-centred, apt to be egotistical and jealous. They were cautious and reserved with Emil because he had been away to college, and were prepared to take him down if he should try to put on airs with them. The French boys liked a bit of swagger, and they were always delighted to hear about anything new: new clothes, new games, new songs, new dances. Now they carried Emil off to show him the club room they had just fitted up over the post-office, down in the village. They ran down the hill in a drove, all laughing and chattering at once, some in French, some in English.

Alexandra went into the cool, whitewashed basement where the women were setting the tables. Marie was standing on a chair, building a little tent of shawls where she was to tell fortunes. She sprang down and ran toward Alexandra, stopping short and looking at her in disappointment. Alexandra nodded to her encouragingly.

"Oh, he will be here, Marie. The boys have taken him off to show him something. You won't know him. He is a man now, sure enough. I have no boy left. He smokes terrible-smelling Mexican cigarettes and talks Spanish. How pretty you look, child. Where did you get those beautiful earrings?"

"They belonged to father's mother. He always promised them to me. He sent them with the dress and said I could keep them."

Marie wore a short red skirt of stoutly woven cloth, a white bodice and kirtle, a yellow silk turban wound low over her brown curls, and long coral pendants in her ears. Her ears had been pierced against a piece of cork by her great-aunt when she was seven years old. In those germless days she had worn bits of broom-straw, plucked from the common sweeping-broom, in the lobes until the holes were healed and ready for little gold rings.

When Emil came back from the village, he lingered outside on the terrace with the boys. Marie could hear him talking and strumming on his guitar while Raoul Marcel sang falsetto. She was vexed with him for staying out there. It made her very nervous to hear him and not to see him; for, certainly, she told herself, she was not going out to look for him. When the supper bell rang and the boys came trooping in to get seats at the first table, she forgot all about her annoyance and ran to greet the tallest of the crowd, in his conspicuous attire. She didn't mind showing her embarrassment at all. She blushed and laughed excitedly as she gave Emil her hand, and looked delightedly at the black velvet coat that brought out his fair skin and fine blond head. Marie was incapable of being lukewarm about anything that pleased her. She simply did not know how to give a half-hearted response. When she was delighted, she was as likely as not to stand on her tip-toes and clap her hands. If people laughed at her, she laughed with them.

"Do the men wear clothes like that every day, in the street?" She caught Emil by his sleeve and turned him about. "Oh, I wish I lived where people wore things like that! Are the buttons real silver? Put on the hat, please. What a heavy thing! How do you ever wear it? Why don't you tell us about the bull-fights?"

She wanted to wring all his experiences from him at once, without waiting a moment. Emil smiled tolerantly and stood looking down at her with his old, brooding gaze, while the French girls fluttered about him in their white dresses and ribbons, and Alexandra watched the scene with pride. Several of the French girls, Marie knew, were hoping that Emil would take them to supper, and she was relieved when he took only his sister. Marie caught Frank's arm and dragged him to the same table, managing to get seats opposite the Bergsons, so that she could hear what they were talking about. Alexandra made Emil tell Mrs. Xavier Chevalier, the mother of the twenty, about how he had seen a famous matador killed in the bull-ring. Marie listened to every word, only taking her eyes from Emil to watch Frank's plate and keep it filled. When Emil finished his account,--bloody enough to satisfy Mrs. Xavier and to make her feel thankful that she was not a matador,--Marie broke out with a volley of questions. How did the women dress when they went to bull-fights? Did they wear mantillas? Did they never wear hats?

After supper the young people played charades for the amusement of their elders, who sat gossiping between their guesses. All the shops in Sainte-Agnes were closed at eight o'clock that night, so that the merchants and their clerks could attend the fair. The auction was the liveliest part of the entertainment, for the French boys always lost their heads when they began to bid, satisfied that their extravagance was in a good cause. After all the pincushions and sofa pillows and embroidered slippers were sold, Emil precipitated a panic by taking out one of his turquoise shirt studs, which every one had been admiring, and handing it to the auctioneer. All the French girls clamored for it, and their sweethearts bid against each other recklessly. Marie wanted it, too, and she kept making signals to Frank, which he took a sour pleasure in disregarding. He didn't see the use of making a fuss over a fellow just because he was dressed like a clown. When the turquoise went to Malvina Sauvage, the French banker's daughter, Marie shrugged her shoulders and betook herself to her little tent of shawls, where she began to shuffle her cards by the light of a tallow candle, calling out, "Fortunes, fortunes!"

The young priest, Father Duchesne, went first to have his fortune read. Marie took his long white hand, looked at it, and then began to run off her cards. "I see a long journey across water for you, Father. You will go to a town all cut up by water; built on islands, it seems to be, with rivers and green fields all about. And you will visit an old lady with a white cap and gold hoops in her ears, and you will be very happy there."

"Mais, oui," said the priest, with a melancholy smile. "C'est L'Isle-Adam, chez ma mere. Vous etes tres savante, ma fille." He patted her yellow turban, calling, "Venez donc, mes garcons! Il y a ici une veritable clairvoyante!"

Marie was clever at fortune-telling, indulging in a light irony that amused the crowd. She told old Brunot, the miser, that he would lose all his money, marry a girl of sixteen, and live happily on a crust. Sholte, the fat Russian boy, who lived for his stomach, was to be disappointed in love, grow thin, and shoot himself from despondency. Amedee was to have twenty children, and nineteen of them were to be girls. Amedee slapped Frank on the back and asked him why he didn't see what the fortune-teller would promise him. But Frank shook off his friendly hand and grunted, "She tell my fortune long ago; bad enough!" Then he withdrew to a corner and sat glowering at his wife.

Frank's case was all the more painful because he had no one in particular to fix his jealousy upon. Sometimes he could have thanked the man who would bring him evidence against his wife. He had discharged a good farm-boy, Jan Smirka, because he thought Marie was fond of him; but she had not seemed to miss Jan when he was gone, and she had been just as kind to the next boy. The farm-hands would always do anything for Marie; Frank couldn't find one so surly that he would not make an effort to please her. At the bottom of his heart Frank knew well enough that if he could once give up his grudge, his wife would come back to him. But he could never in the world do that. The grudge was fundamental. Perhaps he could not have given it up if he had tried. Perhaps he got more satisfaction out of feeling himself abused than he would have got out of being loved. If he could once have made Marie thoroughly unhappy, he might have relented and raised her from the dust. But she had never humbled herself. In the first days of their love she had been his slave; she had admired him abandonedly. But the moment he began to bully her and to be unjust, she began to draw away; at first in tearful amazement, then in quiet, unspoken disgust. The distance between them had widened and hardened. It no longer contracted and brought them suddenly together. The spark of her life went somewhere else, and he was always watching to surprise it. He knew that somewhere she must get a feeling to live upon, for she was not a woman who could live without loving. He wanted to prove to himself the wrong he felt. What did she hide in her heart? Where did it go? Even Frank had his churlish delicacies; he never reminded her of how much she had once loved him. For that Marie was grateful to him.

While Marie was chattering to the French boys, Amedee called Emil to the back of the room and whispered to him that they were going to play a joke on the girls. At eleven o'clock, Amedee was to go up to the switchboard in the vestibule and turn off the electric lights, and every boy would have a chance to kiss his sweetheart before Father Duchesne could find his way up the stairs to turn the current on again. The only difficulty was the candle in Marie's tent; perhaps, as Emil had no sweetheart, he would oblige the boys by blowing out the candle. Emil said he would undertake to do that.

At five minutes to eleven he sauntered up to Marie's booth, and the French boys dispersed to find their girls. He leaned over the card-table and gave himself up to looking at her. "Do you think you could tell my fortune?" he murmured. It was the first word he had had alone with her for almost a year. "My luck hasn't changed any. It's just the same."

Marie had often wondered whether there was anyone else who could look his thoughts to you as Emil could. To-night, when she met his steady, powerful eyes, it was impossible not to feel the sweetness of the dream he was dreaming; it reached her before she could shut it out, and hid itself in her heart. She began to shuffle her cards furiously. "I'm angry with you, Emil," she broke out with petulance. "Why did you give them that lovely blue stone to sell? You might have known Frank wouldn't buy it for me, and I wanted it awfully!"

Emil laughed shortly. "People who want such little things surely ought to have them," he said dryly. He thrust his hand into the pocket of his velvet trousers and brought out a handful of uncut turquoises, as big as marbles. Leaning over the table he dropped them into her lap. "There, will those do? Be careful, don't let any one see them. Now, I suppose you want me to go away and let you play with them?"

Marie was gazing in rapture at the soft blue color of the stones. "Oh, Emil! Is everything down there beautiful like these? How could you ever come away?"

At that instant Amedee laid hands on the switchboard. There was a shiver and a giggle, and every one looked toward the red blur that Marie's candle made in the dark. Immediately that, too, was gone. Little shrieks and currents of soft laughter ran up and down the dark hall. Marie started up,--directly into Emil's arms. In the same instant she felt his lips. The veil that had hung uncertainly between them for so long was dissolved. Before she knew what she was doing, she had committed herself to that kiss that was at once a boy's and a man's, as timid as it was tender; so like Emil and so unlike any one else in the world. Not until it was over did she realize what it meant. And Emil, who had so often imagined the shock of this first kiss, was surprised at its gentleness and naturalness. It was like a sigh which they had breathed together; almost sorrowful, as if each were afraid of wakening something in the other.

When the lights came on again, everybody was laughing and shouting, and all the French girls were rosy and shining with mirth. Only Marie, in her little tent of shawls, was pale and quiet. Under her yellow turban the red coral pendants swung against white cheeks. Frank was still staring at her, but he seemed to see nothing. Years ago, he himself had had the power to take the blood from her cheeks like that. Perhaps he did not remember--perhaps he had never noticed! Emil was already at the other end of the hall, walking about with the shoulder-motion he had acquired among the Mexicans, studying the floor with his intent, deep-set eyes. Marie began to take down and fold her shawls. She did not glance up again. The young people drifted to the other end of the hall where the guitar was sounding. In a moment she heard Emil and Raoul singing:--

"Across the Rio Grand-e There lies a sunny land-e, My bright-eyed Mexico!"

Alexandra Bergson came up to the card booth. "Let me help you, Marie. You look tired."

She placed her hand on Marie's arm and felt her shiver. Marie stiffened under that kind, calm hand. Alexandra drew back, perplexed and hurt.

There was about Alexandra something of the impervious calm of the fatalist, always disconcerting to very young people, who cannot feel that the heart lives at all unless it is still at the mercy of storms; unless its strings can scream to the touch of pain.

II

Signa's wedding supper was over. The guests, and the tiresome little Norwegian preacher who had performed the marriage ceremony, were saying good-night. Old Ivar was hitching the horses to the wagon to take the wedding presents and the bride and groom up to their new home, on Alexandra's north quarter. When Ivar drove up to the gate, Emil and Marie Shabata began to carry out the presents, and Alexandra went into her bedroom to bid Signa good-bye and to give her a few words of good counsel. She was surprised to find that the bride had changed her slippers for heavy shoes and was pinning up her skirts. At that moment Nelse appeared at the gate with the two milk cows that Alexandra had given Signa for a wedding present.

Alexandra began to laugh. "Why, Signa, you and Nelse are to ride home. I'll send Ivar over with the cows in the morning."

Signa hesitated and looked perplexed. When her husband called her, she pinned her hat on resolutely. "I ta-ank I better do yust like he say," she murmured in confusion.

Alexandra and Marie accompanied Signa to the gate and saw the party set off, old Ivar driving ahead in the wagon and the bride and groom following on foot, each leading a cow. Emil burst into a laugh before they were out of hearing.

"Those two will get on," said Alexandra as they turned back to the house. "They are not going to take any chances. They will feel safer with those cows in their own stable. Marie, I am going to send for an old woman next. As soon as I get the girls broken in, I marry them off."

"I've no patience with Signa, marrying that grumpy fellow!" Marie declared. "I wanted her to marry that nice Smirka boy who worked for us last winter. I think she liked him, too."

"Yes, I think she did," Alexandra assented, "but I suppose she was too much afraid of Nelse to marry any one else. Now that I think of it, most of my girls have married men they were afraid of. I believe there is a good deal of the cow in most Swedish girls. You high-strung Bohemian can't understand us. We're a terribly practical people, and I guess we think a cross man makes a good manager."

Marie shrugged her shoulders and turned to pin up a lock of hair that had fallen on her neck. Somehow Alexandra had irritated her of late. Everybody irritated her. She was tired of everybody. "I'm going home alone, Emil, so you needn't get your hat," she said as she wound her scarf quickly about her head. "Good-night, Alexandra," she called back in a strained voice, running down the gravel walk.

Emil followed with long strides until he overtook her. Then she began to walk slowly. It was a night of warm wind and faint starlight, and the fireflies were glimmering over the wheat.

"Marie," said Emil after they had walked for a while, "I wonder if you know how unhappy I am?"

Marie did not answer him. Her head, in its white scarf, drooped forward a little.

Emil kicked a clod from the path and went on:--

"I wonder whether you are really shallow-hearted, like you seem? Sometimes I think one boy does just as well as another for you. It never seems to make much difference whether it is me or Raoul Marcel or Jan Smirka. Are you really like that?"

"Perhaps I am. What do you want me to do? Sit round and cry all day? When I've cried until I can't cry any more, then--then I must do something else."

"Are you sorry for me?" he persisted.

"No, I'm not. If I were big and free like you, I wouldn't let anything make me unhappy. As old Napoleon Brunot said at the fair, I wouldn't go lovering after no woman. I'd take the first train and go off and have all the fun there is."

"I tried that, but it didn't do any good. Everything reminded me. The nicer the place was, the more I wanted you." They had come to the stile and Emil pointed to it persuasively. "Sit down a moment, I want to ask you something." Marie sat down on the top step and Emil drew nearer. "Would you tell me something that's none of my business if you thought it would help me out? Well, then, tell me, PLEASE tell me, why you ran away with Frank Shabata!"

Marie drew back. "Because I was in love with him," she said firmly.

"Really?" he asked incredulously.

"Yes, indeed. Very much in love with him. I think I was the one who suggested our running away. From the first it was more my fault than his."

Emil turned away his face.

"And now," Marie went on, "I've got to remember that. Frank is just the same now as he was then, only then I would see him as I wanted him to be. I would have my own way. And now I pay for it."

"You don't do all the paying."

"That's it. When one makes a mistake, there's no telling where it will stop. But you can go away; you can leave all this behind you."

"Not everything. I can't leave you behind. Will you go away with me, Marie?"

Marie started up and stepped across the stile. "Emil! How wickedly you talk! I am not that kind of a girl, and you know it. But what am I going to do if you keep tormenting me like this!" she added plaintively.

"Marie, I won't bother you any more if you will tell me just one thing. Stop a minute and look at me. No, nobody can see us. Everybody's asleep. That was only a firefly. Marie, STOP and tell me!"

Emil overtook her and catching her by the shoulders shook her gently, as if he were trying to awaken a sleepwalker.

Marie hid her face on his arm. "Don't ask me anything more. I don't know anything except how miserable I am. And I thought it would be all right when you came back. Oh, Emil," she clutched his sleeve and began to cry, "what am I to do if you don't go away? I can't go, and one of us must. Can't you see?"

Emil stood looking down at her, holding his shoulders stiff and stiffening the arm to which she clung. Her white dress looked gray in the darkness. She seemed like a troubled spirit, like some shadow out of the earth, clinging to him and entreating him to give her peace. Behind her the fireflies were weaving in and out over the wheat. He put his hand on her bent head. "On my honor, Marie, if you will say you love me, I will go away."

She lifted her face to his. "How could I help it? Didn't you know?"

Emil was the one who trembled, through all his frame. After he left Marie at her gate, he wandered about the fields all night, till morning put out the fireflies and the stars.

III

One evening, a week after Signa's wedding, Emil was kneeling before a box in the sitting-room, packing his books. From time to time he rose and wandered about the house, picking up stray volumes and bringing them listlessly back to his box. He was packing without enthusiasm. He was not very sanguine about his future. Alexandra sat sewing by the table. She had helped him pack his trunk in the afternoon. As Emil came and went by her chair with his books, he thought to himself that it had not been so hard to leave his sister since he first went away to school. He was going directly to Omaha, to read law in the office of a Swedish lawyer until October, when he would enter the law school at Ann Arbor. They had planned that Alexandra was to come to Michigan--a long journey for her--at Christmas time, and spend several weeks with him. Nevertheless, he felt that this leavetaking would be more final than his earlier ones had been; that it meant a definite break with his old home and the beginning of something new--he did not know what. His ideas about the future would not crystallize; the more he tried to think about it, the vaguer his conception of it became. But one thing was clear, he told himself; it was high time that he made good to Alexandra, and that ought to be incentive enough to begin with.

As he went about gathering up his books he felt as if he were uprooting things. At last he threw himself down on the old slat lounge where he had slept when he was little, and lay looking up at the familiar cracks in the ceiling.

"Tired, Emil?" his sister asked.

"Lazy," he murmured, turning on his side and looking at her. He studied Alexandra's face for a long time in the lamplight. It had never occurred to him that his sister was a handsome woman until Marie Shabata had told him so. Indeed, he had never thought of her as being a woman at all, only a sister. As he studied her bent head, he looked up at the picture of John Bergson above the lamp. "No," he thought to himself, "she didn't get it there. I suppose I am more like that."

"Alexandra," he said suddenly, "that old walnut secretary you use for a desk was father's, wasn't it?"

Alexandra went on stitching. "Yes. It was one of the first things he bought for the old log house. It was a great extravagance in those days. But he wrote a great many letters back to the old country. He had many friends there, and they wrote to him up to the time he died. No one ever blamed him for grandfather's disgrace. I can see him now, sitting there on Sundays, in his white shirt, writing pages and pages, so carefully. He wrote a fine, regular hand, almost like engraving. Yours is something like his, when you take pains."

"Grandfather was really crooked, was he?"

"He married an unscrupulous woman, and then--then I'm afraid he was really crooked. When we first came here father used to have dreams about making a great fortune and going back to Sweden to pay back to the poor sailors the money grandfather had lost."

Emil stirred on the lounge. "I say, that would have been worth while, wouldn't it? Father wasn't a bit like Lou or Oscar, was he? I can't remember much about him before he got sick."

"Oh, not at all!" Alexandra dropped her sewing on her knee. "He had better opportunities; not to make money, but to make something of himself. He was a quiet man, but he was very intelligent. You would have been proud of him, Emil."

Alexandra felt that he would like to know there had been a man of his kin whom he could admire. She knew that Emil was ashamed of Lou and Oscar, because they were bigoted and self-satisfied. He never said much about them, but she could feel his disgust. His brothers had shown their disapproval of him ever since he first went away to school. The only thing that would have satisfied them would have been his failure at the University. As it was, they resented every change in his speech, in his dress, in his point of view; though the latter they had to conjecture, for Emil avoided talking to them about any but family matters. All his interests they treated as affectations.

Alexandra took up her sewing again. "I can remember father when he was quite a young man. He belonged to some kind of a musical society, a male chorus, in Stockholm. I can remember going with mother to hear them sing. There must have been a hundred of them, and they all wore long black coats and white neckties. I was used to seeing father in a blue coat, a sort of jacket, and when I recognized him on the platform, I was very proud. Do you remember that Swedish song he taught you, about the ship boy?"

"Yes. I used to sing it to the Mexicans. They like anything different." Emil paused. "Father had a hard fight here, didn't he?" he added thoughtfully.

"Yes, and he died in a dark time. Still, he had hope. He believed in the land."

"And in you, I guess," Emil said to himself. There was another period of silence; that warm, friendly silence, full of perfect understanding, in which Emil and Alexandra had spent many of their happiest half-hours.

At last Emil said abruptly, "Lou and Oscar would be better off if they were poor, wouldn't they?"

Alexandra smiled. "Maybe. But their children wouldn't. I have great hopes of Milly."

Emil shivered. "I don't know. Seems to me it gets worse as it goes on. The worst of the Swedes is that they're never willing to find out how much they don't know. It was like that at the University. Always so pleased with themselves! There's no getting behind that conceited Swedish grin. The Bohemians and Germans were so different."

"Come, Emil, don't go back on your own people. Father wasn't conceited, Uncle Otto wasn't. Even Lou and Oscar weren't when they were boys."

Emil looked incredulous, but he did not dispute the point. He turned on his back and lay still for a long time, his hands locked under his head, looking up at the ceiling. Alexandra knew that he was thinking of many things. She felt no anxiety about Emil. She had always believed in him, as she had believed in the land. He had been more like himself since he got back from Mexico; seemed glad to be at home, and talked to her as he used to do. She had no doubt that his wandering fit was over, and that he would soon be settled in life.

"Alexandra," said Emil suddenly, "do you remember the wild duck we saw down on the river that time?"

His sister looked up. "I often think of her. It always seems to me she's there still, just like we saw her."

"I know. It's queer what things one remembers and what things one forgets." Emil yawned and sat up. "Well, it's time to turn in." He rose, and going over to Alexandra stooped down and kissed her lightly on the cheek. "Good-night, sister. I think you did pretty well by us."

Emil took up his lamp and went upstairs. Alexandra sat finishing his new nightshirt, that must go in the top tray of his trunk.

IV

The next morning Angelique, Amedee's wife, was in the kitchen baking pies, assisted by old Mrs. Chevalier. Between the mixing-board and the stove stood the old cradle that had been Amedee's, and in it was his black-eyed son. As

Angelique, flushed and excited, with flour on her hands, stopped to smile at the baby, Emil Bergson rode up to the kitchen door on his mare and dismounted.

"'Medee is out in the field, Emil," Angelique called as she ran across the kitchen to the oven. "He begins to cut his wheat to-day; the first wheat ready to cut anywhere about here. He bought a new header, you know, because all the wheat's so short this year. I hope he can rent it to the neighbors, it cost so much. He and his cousins bought a steam thresher on shares. You ought to go out and see that header work. I watched it an hour this morning, busy as I am with all the men to feed. He has a lot of hands, but he's the only one that knows how to drive the header or how to run the engine, so he has to be everywhere at once. He's sick, too, and ought to be in his bed."

Emil bent over Hector Baptiste, trying to make him blink his round, bead-like black eyes. "Sick? What's the matter with your daddy, kid? Been making him walk the floor with you?"

Angelique sniffed. "Not much! We don't have that kind of babies. It was his father that kept Baptiste awake. All night I had to be getting up and making mustard plasters to put on his stomach. He had an awful colic. He said he felt better this morning, but I don't think he ought to be out in the field, overheating himself."

Angelique did not speak with much anxiety, not because she was indifferent, but because she felt so secure in their good fortune. Only good things could happen to a rich, energetic, handsome young man like Amedee, with a new baby in the cradle and a new header in the field.

Emil stroked the black fuzz on Baptiste's head. "I say, Angelique, one of 'Medee's grandmothers, 'way back, must have been a squaw. This kid looks exactly like the Indian babies."

Angelique made a face at him, but old Mrs. Chevalier had been touched on a sore point, and she let out such a stream of fiery PATOIS that Emil fled from the kitchen and mounted his mare.

Opening the pasture gate from the saddle, Emil rode across the field to the clearing where the thresher stood, driven by a stationary engine and fed from the header boxes. As Amedee was not on the engine, Emil rode on to the wheatfield, where he recognized, on the header, the slight, wiry figure of his friend, coatless, his white shirt puffed out by the wind, his straw hat stuck jauntily on the side of his head. The six big work-horses that drew, or rather pushed, the header, went abreast at a rapid walk, and as they were still green at the work they required a good deal of management on Amedee's part; especially when they turned the corners, where they divided, three and three, and then swung round into line again with a movement that looked as complicated as a wheel of artillery. Emil felt a new thrill of admiration for his friend, and with it the old pang of envy at the way in which Amedee could do with his might what his hand found to do, and feel that, whatever it was, it was the most important thing in the world. "I'll have to bring Alexandra up to see this thing work," Emil thought; "it's splendid!"

When he saw Emil, Amedee waved to him and called to one of his twenty cousins to take the reins. Stepping off the header without stopping it, he ran up to Emil who had dismounted. "Come along," he called. "I have to go over to the engine for a minute. I gotta green man running it, and I gotta to keep an eye on him."

Emil thought the lad was unnaturally flushed and more excited than even the cares of managing a big farm at a critical time warranted. As they passed behind a last year's stack, Amedee clutched at his right side and sank down for a moment on the straw.

"Ouch! I got an awful pain in me, Emil. Something's the matter with my insides, for sure."

Emil felt his fiery cheek. "You ought to go straight to bed, 'Medee, and telephone for the doctor; that's what you ought to do."

Amedee staggered up with a gesture of despair. "How can I? I got no time to be sick. Three thousand dollars' worth of new machinery to manage, and the wheat so ripe it will begin to shatter next week. My wheat's short, but it's gotta grand full berries. What's he slowing down for? We haven't got header boxes enough to feed the thresher, I guess."

Amedee started hot-foot across the stubble, leaning a little to the right as he ran, and waved to the engineer not to stop the engine.

Emil saw that this was no time to talk about his own affairs. He mounted his mare and rode on to Sainte-Agnes, to bid his friends there good-bye. He went first to see Raoul Marcel, and found him innocently practising the "Gloria" for the big confirmation service on Sunday while he polished the mirrors of his father's saloon.

As Emil rode homewards at three o'clock in the afternoon, he saw Amedee staggering out of the wheatfield, supported by two of his cousins. Emil stopped and helped them put the boy to bed.

V

When Frank Shabata came in from work at five o'clock that evening, old Moses Marcel, Raoul's father, telephoned him that Amedee had had a seizure in the wheatfield, and that Doctor Paradis was going to operate on him as soon as the Hanover doctor got there to help. Frank dropped a word of this at the table, bolted his supper, and rode off to Sainte-Agnes, where there would be sympathetic discussion of Amedee's case at Marcel's saloon.

As soon as Frank was gone, Marie telephoned Alexandra. It was a comfort to hear her friend's voice. Yes, Alexandra knew what there was to be known about Amedee. Emil had been there when they carried him out of the field, and had stayed with him until the doctors operated for appendicitis at five o'clock. They were afraid it was too late to do much good; it should have been done three days ago. Amedee was in a very bad way. Emil had just come home, worn out and sick himself. She had given him some brandy and put him to bed.

Marie hung up the receiver. Poor Amedee's illness had taken on a new meaning to her, now that she knew Emil had been with him. And it might so easily have been the other way--Emil who was ill and Amedee who was sad! Marie looked about the dusky sitting-room. She had seldom felt so utterly lonely. If Emil was asleep, there was not even a chance of his coming; and she could not go to Alexandra for sympathy. She meant to tell Alexandra everything, as soon as Emil went away. Then whatever was left between them would be honest.

But she could not stay in the house this evening. Where should she go? She walked slowly down through the orchard, where the evening air was heavy with the smell of wild cotton. The fresh, salty scent of the wild roses had given way before this more powerful perfume of midsummer. Wherever those ashes-of-rose balls hung on their milky stalks, the air about them was saturated with their breath. The sky was still red in the west and the evening star hung directly over the Bergsons' wind-mill. Marie crossed the fence at the wheatfield corner, and walked slowly along the path that led to Alexandra's. She could not help feeling hurt that Emil had not come to tell her about Amedee. It seemed to her most unnatural that he should not have come. If she were in trouble, certainly he was the one person in the world she would want to see. Perhaps he wished her to understand that for her he was as good as gone already.

Marie stole slowly, flutteringly, along the path, like a white night-moth out of the fields. The years seemed to stretch before her like the land; spring, summer, autumn, winter, spring; always the same patient fields, the patient little trees, the patient lives; always the same yearning, the same pulling at the chain--until the instinct to live had torn itself and bled and weakened for the last time, until the chain secured a dead woman, who might cautiously be released. Marie walked on, her face lifted toward the remote, inaccessible evening star.

When she reached the stile she sat down and waited. How terrible it was to love people when you could not really share their lives!

Yes, in so far as she was concerned, Emil was already gone. They couldn't meet any more. There was nothing for them to say. They had spent the last penny of their small change; there was nothing left but gold. The day of love-tokens was past. They had now only their hearts to give each other. And Emil being gone, what was her life to be like? In some ways, it would be easier. She would not, at least, live in perpetual fear. If Emil were once away and settled at work, she would not have the feeling that she was spoiling his life. With the memory he left her, she could be as rash as she chose. Nobody could be the worse for it but herself; and that, surely, did not matter. Her own case was clear. When a girl had loved one man, and then loved another while that man was still alive, everybody knew what to think of her. What happened to her was of little consequence, so long as she did not drag other people down with her. Emil once away, she could let everything else go and live a new life of perfect love.

Marie left the stile reluctantly. She had, after all, thought he might come. And how glad she ought to be, she told herself, that he was asleep. She left the path and went across the pasture. The moon was almost full. An owl was hooting somewhere in the fields. She had scarcely thought about where she was going when the pond glittered before her, where Emil had shot the ducks. She stopped and looked at it. Yes, there would be a dirty way out of life, if one chose to take it. But she did not want to die. She wanted to live and dream--a hundred years, forever! As long as this sweetness welled up in her heart, as long as her breast could hold this treasure of pain! She felt as the pond must feel when it held the moon like that; when it encircled and swelled with that image of gold.

In the morning, when Emil came down-stairs, Alexandra met him in the sitting-room and put her hands on his shoulders. "Emil, I went to your room as soon as it was light, but you were sleeping so sound I hated to wake you. There was nothing you could do, so I let you sleep. They telephoned from Sainte-Agnes that Amedee died at three o'clock this morning."

VI

The Church has always held that life is for the living. On Saturday, while half the village of Sainte-Agnes was mourning for Amedee and preparing the funeral black for his burial on Monday, the other half was busy with white dresses and white veils for the great confirmation service to-morrow, when the bishop was to confirm a class of one hundred boys and girls. Father Duchesne divided his time between the living and the dead. All day Saturday the church was a scene of bustling activity, a little hushed by the thought of Amedee. The choir were busy rehearsing a mass of Rossini, which they had studied and practised for this occasion. The women were trimming the altar, the boys and girls were bringing flowers.

On Sunday morning the bishop was to drive overland to Sainte-Agnes from Hanover, and Emil Bergson had been asked to take the place of one of Amedee's cousins in the cavalcade of forty French boys who were to ride across country to meet the bishop's carriage. At six o'clock on Sunday morning the boys met at the church. As they stood holding their horses by the bridle, they talked in low tones of their dead comrade. They kept repeating that Amedee had always been a good boy, glancing toward the red brick church which had played so large a part in Amedee's life, had been the scene of his most serious moments and of his happiest hours. He had played and wrestled and sung and courted under its shadow. Only three weeks ago he had proudly carried his baby there to be christened. They could not doubt that that invisible arm was still about Amedee; that through the church on earth he had passed to the church triumphant, the goal of the hopes and faith of so many hundred years.

When the word was given to mount, the young men rode at a walk out of the village; but once out among the wheatfields in the morning sun, their horses and their own youth got the better of them. A wave of zeal and fiery enthusiasm swept over them. They longed for a Jerusalem to deliver. The thud of their galloping hoofs interrupted many a country breakfast and brought many a woman and child to the door of the farmhouses as they passed. Five miles east of Sainte-Agnes they met the bishop in his open carriage, attended by two priests. Like one man the boys swung off their hats in a broad salute, and bowed their heads as the handsome old man lifted his two fingers in the episcopal blessing. The horsemen closed about the carriage like a guard, and whenever a restless horse broke from control and shot down the road ahead of the body, the bishop laughed and rubbed his plump hands together. "What fine boys!" he said to his priests. "The Church still has her cavalry."

As the troop swept past the graveyard half a mile east of the town,--the first frame church of the parish had stood there,--old Pierre Seguin was already out with his pick and spade, digging Amedee's grave. He knelt and uncovered as the bishop passed. The boys with one accord looked away from old Pierre to the red church on the hill, with the gold cross flaming on its steeple.

Mass was at eleven. While the church was filling, Emil Bergson waited outside, watching the wagons and buggies drive up the hill. After the bell began to ring, he saw Frank Shabata ride up on horseback and tie his horse to the hitch-bar. Marie, then, was not coming. Emil turned and went into the church. Amedee's was the only empty pew, and he sat down in it. Some of Amedee's cousins were there, dressed in black and weeping. When all the pews were full, the old men and boys packed the open space at the back of the church, kneeling on the floor. There was scarcely a family in town that was not represented in the confirmation class, by a cousin, at least. The new communicants, with their clear, reverent faces, were beautiful to look upon as they entered in a body and took the front benches reserved for them. Even before the Mass began, the air was charged with feeling. The choir had never sung so well and Raoul Marcel, in the "Gloria," drew even the bishop's eyes to the organ loft. For the offertory he sang Gounod's "Ave Maria,"--always spoken of in Sainte-Agnes as "the Ave Maria."

Emil began to torture himself with questions about Marie. Was she ill? Had she quarreled with her husband? Was she too unhappy to find comfort even here? Had she, perhaps, thought that he would come to her? Was she waiting for him?

Overtaxed by excitement and sorrow as he was, the rapture of the service took hold upon his body and mind. As he listened to Raoul, he seemed to emerge from the conflicting emotions which had been whirling him about and sucking him under. He felt as if a clear light broke upon his mind, and with it a conviction that good was, after all, stronger than evil, and that good was possible to men. He seemed to discover that there was a kind of rapture in which he could love forever without faltering and without sin. He looked across the heads of the people at Frank Shabata with calmness. That rapture was for those who could feel it; for people who could not, it was non-existent. He coveted nothing that was Frank Shabata's. The spirit he had met in music was his own. Frank Shabata had never found it; would never find it if he lived beside it a thousand years; would have destroyed it if he had found it, as Herod slew the innocents, as Rome slew the martyrs.

SAN--CTA MARI-I-I-A,

wailed Raoul from the organ loft;

O--RA PRO NO-O-BIS!

And it did not occur to Emil that any one had ever reasoned thus before, that music had ever before given a man this equivocal revelation.

The confirmation service followed the Mass. When it was over, the congregation thronged about the newly confirmed. The girls, and even the boys, were kissed and embraced and wept over. All the aunts and grandmothers wept with joy. The housewives had much ado to tear themselves away from the general rejoicing and hurry back to their kitchens. The country parishioners were staying in town for dinner, and nearly every house in Sainte-Agnes entertained visitors that day. Father Duchesne, the bishop, and the visiting priests dined with Fabien Sauvage, the banker. Emil and Frank Shabata were both guests of old Moise Marcel. After dinner Frank and old Moise retired to the rear room of the saloon to play California Jack and drink their cognac, and Emil went over to the banker's with Raoul, who had been asked to sing for the bishop.

At three o'clock, Emil felt that he could stand it no longer. He slipped out under cover of "The Holy City," followed by Malvina's wistful eye, and went to the stable for his mare. He was at that height of excitement from which everything is foreshortened, from which life seems short and simple, death very near, and the soul seems to soar like an eagle. As he rode past the graveyard he looked at the brown hole in the earth where Amedee was to lie, and felt no horror. That, too, was beautiful, that simple doorway into forgetfulness. The heart, when it is too much alive, aches for that brown earth, and ecstasy has no fear of death. It is the old and the poor and the maimed who shrink from that brown hole; its wooers are found among the young, the passionate, the gallant-hearted. It was not until he had passed the graveyard that Emil realized where he was going. It was the hour for saying good-bye. It might be the last time that he would see her alone, and today he could leave her without rancor, without bitterness.

Everywhere the grain stood ripe and the hot afternoon was full of the smell of the ripe wheat, like the smell of bread baking in an oven. The breath of the wheat and the sweet clover passed him like pleasant things in a dream. He could feel nothing but the sense of diminishing distance. It seemed to him that his mare was flying, or running on wheels, like a railway train. The sunlight, flashing on the window-glass of the big red barns, drove him wild with joy. He was like an arrow shot from the bow. His life poured itself out along the road before him as he rode to the Shabata farm.

When Emil alighted at the Shabatas' gate, his horse was in a lather. He tied her in the stable and hurried to the house. It was empty. She might be at Mrs. Hiller's or with Alexandra. But anything that reminded him of her would be enough, the orchard, the mulberry tree. . . When he reached the orchard the sun was hanging low over the wheatfield. Long fingers of light reached through the apple branches as through a net; the orchard was riddled and shot with gold; light was the reality, the trees were merely interferences that reflected and refracted light. Emil went softly down between the cherry trees toward the wheatfield. When he came to the corner, he stopped short and put his hand over his mouth. Marie was lying on her side under the white mulberry tree, her face half hidden in the grass, her eyes closed, her hands lying limply where they had happened to fall. She had lived a day of her new life of perfect love, and it had left her like this. Her breast rose and fell faintly, as if she were asleep. Emil threw himself down beside her and took her in his arms. The blood came back to her cheeks, her amber eyes opened slowly, and in them Emil saw his own face and the orchard and the sun. "I was dreaming this," she whispered, hiding her face against him, "don't take my dream away!"

VII

When Frank Shabata got home that night, he found Emil's mare in his stable. Such an impertinence amazed him. Like everybody else, Frank had had an exciting day. Since noon he had been drinking too much, and he was in a bad temper. He talked bitterly to himself while he put his own horse away, and as he went up the path and saw that the house was dark he felt an added sense of injury. He approached quietly and listened on the doorstep. Hearing nothing, he opened the kitchen door and went softly from one room to another. Then he went through the house again, upstairs and down, with no better result. He sat down on the bottom step of the box stairway and tried to get his wits together. In that unnatural quiet there was no sound but his own heavy breathing. Suddenly an owl began to hoot out in the fields. Frank lifted his head. An idea flashed into his mind, and his sense of injury and outrage grew. He went into his bedroom and took his murderous 405 Winchester from the closet.

When Frank took up his gun and walked out of the house, he had not the faintest purpose of doing anything with it. He did not believe that he had any real grievance. But it gratified him to feel like a desperate man. He had got into the habit of seeing himself always in desperate straits. His unhappy temperament was like a cage; he could never get out of it; and he felt that other people, his wife in particular, must have put him there. It had never more than dimly occurred to Frank that he made his own unhappiness. Though he took up his gun with dark projects in his mind, he would have been paralyzed with fright had he known that there was the slightest probability of his ever carrying any of them out.

Frank went slowly down to the orchard gate, stopped and stood for a moment lost in thought. He retraced his steps and looked through the barn and the hayloft. Then he went out to the road, where he took the foot-path along the outside of the orchard hedge. The hedge was twice as tall as Frank himself, and so dense that one could see through it only by peering closely between the leaves. He could see the empty path a long way in the moonlight. His mind traveled ahead to the stile, which he always thought of as haunted by Emil Bergson. But why had he left his horse?

At the wheatfield corner, where the orchard hedge ended and the path led across the pasture to the Bergsons', Frank stopped. In the warm, breathless night air he heard a murmuring sound, perfectly inarticulate, as low as the sound of water coming from a spring, where there is no fall, and where there are no stones to fret it. Frank strained his ears. It ceased. He held his breath and began to tremble. Resting the butt of his gun on the ground, he parted the mulberry leaves softly with his fingers and peered through the hedge at the dark figures on the grass, in the shadow of the mulberry tree. It seemed to him that they must feel his eyes, that they must hear him breathing. But they did not. Frank, who had always wanted to see things blacker than they were, for once wanted to believe less than he saw. The woman lying in the shadow might so easily be one of the Bergsons' farm-girls. . . . Again the murmur, like water welling out of the ground. This time he heard it more distinctly, and his blood was quicker than his brain. He began to act, just as a man who falls into the fire begins to act. The gun sprang to his shoulder, he sighted mechanically and fired three times without stopping, stopped without knowing why. Either he shut his eyes or he had vertigo. He did not see anything while he was firing. He thought he heard a cry simultaneous with the second report, but he was not sure. He peered again through the hedge, at the two dark figures under the tree. They had fallen a little apart from each other, and were perfectly still-- No, not quite; in a white patch of light, where the moon shone through the branches, a man's hand was plucking spasmodically at the grass.

Suddenly the woman stirred and uttered a cry, then another, and another. She was living! She was dragging herself toward the hedge! Frank dropped his gun and ran back along the path, shaking, stumbling, gasping. He had never imagined such horror. The cries followed him. They grew fainter and thicker, as if she were choking. He dropped on his knees beside the hedge and crouched like a rabbit, listening; fainter, fainter; a sound like a whine; again--a moan--another-- silence. Frank scrambled to his feet and ran on, groaning and praying. From habit he went toward the house, where he was used to being soothed when he had worked himself into a frenzy, but at the sight of the black, open door, he started back. He knew that he had murdered somebody, that a woman was bleeding and moaning in the orchard, but he had not realized before that it was his wife. The gate stared him in the face. He threw his hands over his head. Which way to turn? He lifted his tormented face and looked at the sky. "Holy Mother of God, not to suffer! She was a good girl--not to suffer!"

Frank had been wont to see himself in dramatic situations; but now, when he stood by the windmill, in the bright space between the barn and the house, facing his own black doorway, he did not see himself at all. He stood like the hare when the dogs are approaching from all sides. And he ran like a hare, back and forth about that moonlit space, before he could make up his mind to go into the dark stable for a horse. The thought of going into a doorway was terrible to him.

He caught Emil's horse by the bit and led it out. He could not have buckled a bridle on his own. After two or three attempts, he lifted himself into the saddle and started for Hanover. If he could catch the one o'clock train, he had money enough to get as far as Omaha.

While he was thinking dully of this in some less sensitized part of his brain, his acuter faculties were going over and over the cries he had heard in the orchard. Terror was the only thing that kept him from going back to her, terror that she might still be she, that she might still be suffering. A woman, mutilated and bleeding in his orchard--it was because it was a woman that he was so afraid. It was inconceivable that he should have hurt a woman. He would rather be eaten by wild beasts than see her move on the ground as she had moved in the orchard. Why had she been so careless? She knew he was like a crazy man when he was angry. She had more than once taken that gun away from him and held it, when he was angry with other people. Once it had gone off while they were struggling over it. She was never afraid. But, when she knew him, why hadn't she been more careful? Didn't she have all summer before her to love Emil Bergson in, without taking such chances? Probably she had met the Smirka boy, too, down there in the orchard. He didn't care. She could have met all the men on the Divide there, and welcome, if only she hadn't brought this horror on him.

There was a wrench in Frank's mind. He did not honestly believe that of her. He knew that he was doing her wrong. He stopped his horse to admit this to himself the more directly, to think it out the more clearly. He knew that he was to blame. For three years he had been trying to break her spirit. She had a way of making the best of things that seemed to him a sentimental affectation. He wanted his wife to resent that he was wasting his best years among these stupid and unappreciative people; but she had seemed to find the people quite good enough. If he ever got rich he meant to buy her pretty clothes and take her to California in a Pullman car, and treat her like a lady; but in the mean time he wanted her to feel that life was as ugly and as unjust as he felt it. He had tried to make her life ugly. He had refused to share any of the little pleasures she was so plucky about making for herself. She could be gay about the least thing in the world; but she must be gay! When she first came to him, her faith in him, her adoration--Frank struck the mare with his fist. Why had Marie made him do this thing; why had she brought this upon him? He was overwhelmed by sickening misfortune. All at once he heard her cries again--he had forgotten for a moment. "Maria," he sobbed aloud, "Maria!"

When Frank was halfway to Hanover, the motion of his horse brought on a violent attack of nausea. After it had passed, he rode on again, but he could think of nothing except his physical weakness and his desire to be comforted by his wife. He wanted to get into his own bed. Had his wife been at home, he would have turned and gone back to her meekly enough.

VIII

When old Ivar climbed down from his loft at four o'clock the next morning, he came upon Emil's mare, jaded and lather-stained, her bridle broken, chewing the scattered tufts of hay outside the stable door. The old man was thrown into a fright at once. He put the mare in her stall, threw her a measure of oats, and then set out as fast as his bow-legs could carry him on the path to the nearest neighbor.

"Something is wrong with that boy. Some misfortune has come upon us. He would never have used her so, in his right senses. It is not his way to abuse his mare," the old man kept muttering, as he scuttled through the short, wet pasture grass on his bare feet.

While Ivar was hurrying across the fields, the first long rays of the sun were reaching down between the orchard boughs to those two dew-drenched figures. The story of what had happened was written plainly on the orchard grass, and on the white mulberries that had fallen in the night and were covered with dark stain. For Emil the chapter had been short. He was shot in the heart, and had rolled over on his back and died. His face was turned up to the sky and his brows were drawn in a frown, as if he had realized that something had befallen him. But for Marie Shabata it had not been so easy. One ball had torn through her right lung, another had shattered the carotid artery. She must have started up and gone toward the hedge, leaving a trail of blood. There she had fallen and bled. From that spot there was another trail, heavier than the first, where she must have dragged herself back to Emil's body. Once there, she seemed not to have struggled any more. She had lifted her head to her lover's breast, taken his hand in both her own, and bled quietly to death. She was lying on her right side in an easy and natural position, her cheek on Emil's shoulder. On her face there was a look of ineffable content. Her lips were parted a little; her eyes were lightly closed, as if in a day-dream or a light slumber. After she lay down there, she seemed not to have moved an eyelash. The hand she held was covered with dark stains, where she had kissed it.

But the stained, slippery grass, the darkened mulberries, told only half the story. Above Marie and Emil, two white butterflies from Frank's alfalfa-field were fluttering in and out among the interlacing shadows; diving and soaring, now close together, now far apart; and in the long grass by the fence the last wild roses of the year opened their pink hearts to die.

When Ivar reached the path by the hedge, he saw Shabata's rifle lying in the way. He turned and peered through the branches, falling upon his knees as if his legs had been mowed from under him. "Merciful God!" he groaned;

Alexandra, too, had risen early that morning, because of her anxiety about Emil. She was in Emil's room upstairs when, from the window, she saw Ivar coming along the path that led from the Shabatas'. He was running like a spent man, tottering and lurching from side to side. Ivar never drank, and Alexandra thought at once that one of his spells had come upon him, and that he must be in a very bad way indeed. She ran downstairs and hurried out to meet him, to hide his infirmity from the eyes of her household. The old man fell in the road at her feet and caught her hand, over which he bowed his shaggy head. "Mistress, mistress," he sobbed, "it has fallen! Sin and death for the young ones! God have mercy upon us!"

PART V. ALEXANDRA

I

Ivar was sitting at a cobbler's bench in the barn, mending harness by the light of a lantern and repeating to himself the 101st Psalm. It was only five o'clock of a mid-October day, but a storm had come up in the afternoon, bringing black clouds, a cold wind and torrents of rain. The old man wore his buffalo-skin coat, and occasionally stopped to warm his fingers at the lantern. Suddenly a woman burst into the shed, as if she had been blown in, accompanied by a shower of rain-drops. It was Signa, wrapped in a man's overcoat and wearing a pair of boots over her shoes. In time of trouble Signa had come back to stay with her mistress, for she was the only one of the maids from whom Alexandra would accept much personal service. It was three months now since the news of the terrible thing that had happened in Frank Shabata's orchard had first run like a fire over the Divide. Signa and Nelse were staying on with Alexandra until winter.

"Ivar," Signa exclaimed as she wiped the rain from her face, "do you know where she is?"

The old man put down his cobbler's knife. "Who, the mistress?"

"Yes. She went away about three o'clock. I happened to look out of the window and saw her going across the fields in her thin dress and sun-hat. And now this storm has come on. I thought she was going to Mrs. Hiller's, and I telephoned as soon as the thunder stopped, but she had not been there. I'm afraid she is out somewhere and will get her death of cold."

Ivar put on his cap and took up the lantern. "JA, JA, we will see. I will hitch the boy's mare to the cart and go."

Signa followed him across the wagon-shed to the horses' stable. She was shivering with cold and excitement. "Where do you suppose she can be, Ivar?"

The old man lifted a set of single harness carefully from its peg. "How should I know?"

"But you think she is at the graveyard, don't you?" Signa persisted. "So do I. Oh, I wish she would be more like herself! I can't believe it's Alexandra Bergson come to this, with no head about anything. I have to tell her when to eat and when to go to bed."

"Patience, patience, sister," muttered Ivar as he settled the bit in the horse's mouth. "When the eyes of the flesh are shut, the eyes of the spirit are open. She will have a message from those who are gone, and that will bring her peace. Until then we must bear with her. You and I are the only ones who have weight with her. She trusts us."

"How awful it's been these last three months." Signa held the lantern so that he could see to buckle the straps. "It don't seem right that we must all be so miserable. Why do we all have to be punished? Seems to me like good times would never come again."

Ivar expressed himself in a deep sigh, but said nothing. He stooped and took a sandburr from his toe.

"Ivar," Signa asked suddenly, "will you tell me why you go barefoot? All the time I lived here in the house I wanted to ask you. Is it for a penance, or what?"

"No, sister. It is for the indulgence of the body. From my youth up I have had a strong, rebellious body, and have been subject to every kind of temptation. Even in age my temptations are prolonged. It was necessary to make some allowances; and the feet, as I understand it, are free members. There is no divine prohibition for them in the Ten Commandments. The hands, the tongue, the eyes, the heart, all the bodily desires we are commanded to subdue; but the feet are free members. I indulge them without harm to any one, even to trampling in filth when my desires are low. They are quickly cleaned again."

Signa did not laugh. She looked thoughtful as she followed Ivar out to the wagon-shed and held the shafts up for him, while he backed in the mare and buckled the hold-backs. "You have been a good friend to the mistress, Ivar," she murmured.

"And you, God be with you," replied Ivar as he clambered into the cart and put the lantern under the oilcloth lap-cover. "Now for a ducking, my girl," he said to the mare, gathering up the reins.

As they emerged from the shed, a stream of water, running off the thatch, struck the mare on the neck. She tossed her head indignantly, then struck out bravely on the soft ground, slipping back again and again as she climbed the hill to the main road. Between the rain and the darkness Ivar could see very little, so he let Emil's mare have the rein, keeping her head in the right direction. When the ground was level, he turned her out of the dirt road upon the sod, where she was able to trot without slipping.

Before Ivar reached the graveyard, three miles from the house, the storm had spent itself, and the downpour had died into a soft, dripping rain. The sky and the land were a dark smoke color, and seemed to be coming together, like two waves. When Ivar stopped at the gate and swung out his lantern, a white figure rose from beside John Bergson's white stone.

The old man sprang to the ground and shuffled toward the gate calling, "Mistress, mistress!"

Alexandra hurried to meet him and put her hand on his shoulder. "TYST! Ivar. There's nothing to be worried about. I'm sorry if I've scared you all. I didn't notice the storm till it was on me, and I couldn't walk against it. I'm glad you've come. I am so tired I didn't know how I'd ever get home."

Ivar swung the lantern up so that it shone in her face. "GUD! You are enough to frighten us, mistress. You look like a drowned woman. How could you do such a thing!"

Groaning and mumbling he led her out of the gate and helped her into the cart, wrapping her in the dry blankets on which he had been sitting.

Alexandra smiled at his solicitude. "Not much use in that, Ivar. You will only shut the wet in. I don't feel so cold now; but I'm heavy and numb. I'm glad you came."

Ivar turned the mare and urged her into a sliding trot. Her feet sent back a continual spatter of mud.

Alexandra spoke to the old man as they jogged along through the sullen gray twilight of the storm. "Ivar, I think it has done me good to get cold clear through like this, once. I don't believe I shall suffer so much any more. When you get so near the dead, they seem more real than the living. Worldly thoughts leave one. Ever since Emil died, I've suffered so when it rained. Now that I've been out in it with him, I shan't dread it. After you once get cold clear through, the feeling of the rain on you is sweet. It seems to bring back feelings you had when you were a baby. It carries you back into the dark, before you were born; you can't see things, but they come to you, somehow, and you know them and aren't afraid of them. Maybe it's like that with the dead. If they feel anything at all, it's the old things, before they were born, that comfort people like the feeling of their own bed does when they are little."

"Mistress," said Ivar reproachfully, "those are bad thoughts. The dead are in Paradise."

Then he hung his head, for he did not believe that Emil was in Paradise.

When they got home, Signa had a fire burning in the sitting-room stove. She undressed Alexandra and gave her a hot footbath, while Ivar made ginger tea in the kitchen. When Alexandra was in bed, wrapped in hot blankets, Ivar came in with his tea and saw that she drank it. Signa asked permission to sleep on the slat lounge outside her door. Alexandra endured their attentions patiently, but she was glad when they put out the lamp and left her. As she lay alone in the dark, it occurred to her for the first time that perhaps she was actually tired of life. All the physical operations of life seemed difficult and painful. She longed to be free from her own body, which ached and was so heavy. And longing itself was heavy: she yearned to be free of that.

As she lay with her eyes closed, she had again, more vividly than for many years, the old illusion of her girlhood, of being lifted and carried lightly by some one very strong. He was with her a long while this time, and carried her very far, and in his arms she felt free from pain. When he laid her down on her bed again, she opened her eyes, and, for the first time in her life, she saw him, saw him clearly, though the room was dark, and his face was covered. He was standing in the doorway of her room. His white cloak was thrown over his face, and his head was bent a little forward. His shoulders seemed as strong as the foundations of the world. His right arm, bared from the elbow, was dark and gleaming, like bronze, and she knew at once that it was the arm of the mightiest of all lovers. She knew at last for whom it was she had waited, and where he would carry her. That, she told herself, was very well. Then she went to sleep.

Alexandra wakened in the morning with nothing worse than a hard cold and a stiff shoulder. She kept her bed for several days, and it was during that time that she formed a resolution to go to Lincoln to see Frank Shabata. Ever since she last saw him in the courtroom, Frank's haggard face and wild eyes had haunted her. The trial had lasted only three days. Frank had given himself up to the police in Omaha and pleaded guilty of killing without malice and without premeditation. The gun was, of course, against him, and the judge had given him the full sentence,--ten years. He had now been in the State Penitentiary for a month.

Frank was the only one, Alexandra told herself, for whom anything could be done. He had been less in the wrong than any of them, and he was paying the heaviest penalty. She often felt that she herself had been more to blame than poor Frank. From the time the Shabatas had first moved to the neighboring farm, she had omitted no opportunity of throwing Marie and Emil together. Because she knew Frank was surly about doing little things to help his wife, she was always sending Emil over to spade or plant or carpenter for Marie. She was glad to have Emil see as much as possible of an intelligent, city-bred girl like their neighbor; she noticed that it improved his manners. She knew that Emil was fond of Marie, but it had never occurred to her that Emil's feeling might be different from her own. She wondered at herself now, but she had never thought of danger in that direction. If Marie had been unmarried,--oh, yes! Then she would have kept her eyes open. But the mere fact that she was Shabata's wife, for Alexandra, settled everything. That she was beautiful, impulsive, barely two years older than Emil, these facts had had no weight with Alexandra. Emil was a good boy, and only bad boys ran after married women.

Now, Alexandra could in a measure realize that Marie was, after all, Marie; not merely a "married woman." Sometimes, when Alexandra thought of her, it was with an aching tenderness. The moment she had reached them in the orchard that morning, everything was clear to her. There was something about those two lying in the grass, something in the way Marie had settled her cheek on Emil's shoulder, that told her everything. She wondered then how they could have helped loving each other; how she could have helped knowing that they must. Emil's cold, frowning face, the girl's content--Alexandra had felt awe of them, even in the first shock of her grief.

The idleness of those days in bed, the relaxation of body which attended them, enabled Alexandra to think more calmly than she had done since Emil's death. She and Frank, she told herself, were left out of that group of friends who had been overwhelmed by disaster. She must certainly see Frank Shabata. Even in the courtroom her heart had grieved for him. He was in a strange country, he had no kinsmen or friends, and in a moment he had ruined his life. Being what he was, she felt, Frank could not have acted otherwise. She could understand his behavior more easily than she could understand Marie's. Yes, she must go to Lincoln to see Frank Shabata.

The day after Emil's funeral, Alexandra had written to Carl Linstrum; a single page of notepaper, a bare statement of what had happened. She was not a woman who could write much about such a thing, and about her own feelings she could never write very freely. She knew that Carl was away from post-offices, prospecting somewhere in the interior. Before he started he had written her where he expected to go, but her ideas about Alaska were vague. As the weeks went by and she heard nothing from him, it seemed to Alexandra that her heart grew hard against Carl. She began to wonder whether she would not do better to finish her life alone. What was left of life seemed unimportant.

II

Late in the afternoon of a brilliant October day, Alexandra Bergson, dressed in a black suit and traveling-hat, alighted at the Burlington depot in Lincoln. She drove to the Lindell Hotel, where she had stayed two years ago when she came up for Emil's Commencement. In spite of her usual air of sureness and self-possession, Alexandra felt ill at ease in hotels, and she was glad, when she went to the clerk's desk to register, that there were not many people in the lobby. She had her supper early, wearing her hat and black jacket down to the dining-room and carrying her handbag. After supper she went out for a walk.

It was growing dark when she reached the university campus. She did not go into the grounds, but walked slowly up and down the stone walk outside the long iron fence, looking through at the young men who were running from one building to another, at the lights shining from the armory and the library. A squad of cadets were going through their drill behind the armory, and the commands of their young officer rang out at regular intervals, so sharp and quick that Alexandra could not understand them. Two stalwart girls came down the library steps and out through one of the iron gates. As they passed her, Alexandra was pleased to hear them speaking Bohemian to each other. Every few moments a boy would come running down the flagged walk and dash out into the street as if he were rushing to announce some wonder to the world. Alexandra felt a great tenderness for them all. She wished one of them would stop and speak to her. She wished she could ask them whether they had known Emil.

As she lingered by the south gate she actually did encounter one of the boys. He had on his drill cap and was swinging his books at the end of a long strap. It was dark by this time; he did not see her and ran against her. He snatched off his cap and stood bareheaded and panting. "I'm awfully sorry," he said in a bright, clear voice, with a rising inflection, as if he expected her to say something.

"Oh, it was my fault!" said Alexandra eagerly. "Are you an old student here, may I ask?"

"No, ma'am. I'm a Freshie, just off the farm. Cherry County. Were you hunting somebody?"

"No, thank you. That is--" Alexandra wanted to detain him. "That is, I would like to find some of my brother's friends. He graduated two years ago."

"Then you'd have to try the Seniors, wouldn't you? Let's see; I don't know any of them yet, but there'll be sure to be some of them around the library. That red building, right there," he pointed.

"Thank you, I'll try there," said Alexandra lingeringly.

"Oh, that's all right! Good-night." The lad clapped his cap on his head and ran straight down Eleventh Street. Alexandra looked after him wistfully.

She walked back to her hotel unreasonably comforted. "What a nice voice that boy had, and how polite he was. I know Emil was always like that to women." And again, after she had undressed and was standing in her nightgown, brushing her long, heavy hair by the electric light, she remembered him and said to herself, "I don't think I ever heard a nicer voice than that boy had. I hope he will get on well here. Cherry County; that's where the hay is so fine, and the coyotes can scratch down to water."

At nine o'clock the next morning Alexandra presented herself at the warden's office in the State Penitentiary. The warden was a German, a ruddy, cheerful-looking man who had formerly been a harness-maker. Alexandra had a letter to him from the German banker in Hanover. As he glanced at the letter, Mr. Schwartz put away his pipe.

"That big Bohemian, is it? Sure, he's gettin' along fine," said Mr. Schwartz cheerfully.

"I am glad to hear that. I was afraid he might be quarrelsome and get himself into more trouble. Mr. Schwartz, if you have time, I would like to tell you a little about Frank Shabata, and why I am interested in him."

The warden listened genially while she told him briefly something of Frank's history and character, but he did not seem to find anything unusual in her account.

"Sure, I'll keep an eye on him. We'll take care of him all right," he said, rising. "You can talk to him here, while I go to see to things in the kitchen. I'll have him sent in. He ought to be done washing out his cell by this time. We have to keep 'em clean, you know."

The warden paused at the door, speaking back over his shoulder to a pale young man in convicts' clothes who was seated at a desk in the corner, writing in a big ledger.

"Bertie, when 1037 is brought in, you just step out and give this lady a chance to talk."

The young man bowed his head and bent over his ledger again.

When Mr. Schwartz disappeared, Alexandra thrust her black-edged handkerchief nervously into her handbag. Coming out on the streetcar she had not had the least dread of meeting Frank. But since she had been here the sounds and smells in the corridor, the look of the men in convicts' clothes who passed the glass door of the warden's office, affected her unpleasantly.

The warden's clock ticked, the young convict's pen scratched busily in the big book, and his sharp shoulders were shaken every few seconds by a loose cough which he tried to smother. It was easy to see that he was a sick man. Alexandra looked at him timidly, but he did not once raise his eyes. He wore a white shirt under his striped jacket, a high collar, and a necktie, very carefully tied. His hands were thin and white and well cared for, and he had a seal ring on his little finger. When he heard steps approaching in the corridor, he rose, blotted his book, put his pen in the rack, and left the room without raising his eyes. Through the door he opened a guard came in, bringing Frank Shabata.

"You the lady that wanted to talk to 1037? Here he is. Be on your good behavior, now. He can set down, lady," seeing that Alexandra remained standing. "Push that white button when you're through with him, and I'll come."

The guard went out and Alexandra and Frank were left alone.

Alexandra tried not to see his hideous clothes. She tried to look straight into his face, which she could scarcely believe was his. It was already bleached to a chalky gray. His lips were colorless, his fine teeth looked yellowish. He glanced at Alexandra sullenly, blinked as if he had come from a dark place, and one eyebrow twitched continually. She felt at once that this interview was a terrible ordeal to him. His shaved head, showing the conformation of his skull, gave him a criminal look which he had not had during the trial.

Alexandra held out her hand. "Frank," she said, her eyes filling suddenly, "I hope you'll let me be friendly with you. I understand how you did it. I don't feel hard toward you. They were more to blame than you."

Frank jerked a dirty blue handkerchief from his trousers pocket. He had begun to cry. He turned away from Alexandra. "I never did mean to do not'ing to dat woman," he muttered. "I never mean to do not'ing to dat boy. I ain't had not'ing ag'in' dat boy. I always like dat boy fine. An' then I find him--" He stopped. The feeling went out of his face and eyes. He dropped into a chair and sat looking stolidly at the floor, his hands hanging loosely between his knees, the handkerchief lying across his striped leg. He seemed to have stirred up in his mind a disgust that had paralyzed his faculties.

"I haven't come up here to blame you, Frank. I think they were more to blame than you." Alexandra, too, felt benumbed.

Frank looked up suddenly and stared out of the office window. "I guess dat place all go to hell what I work so hard on," he said with a slow, bitter smile. "I not care a damn." He stopped and rubbed the palm of his hand over the light bristles on his head with annoyance. "I no can t'ink without my hair," he complained. "I forget English. We not talk here, except swear."

Alexandra was bewildered. Frank seemed to have undergone a change of personality. There was scarcely anything by which she could recognize her handsome Bohemian neighbor. He seemed, somehow, not altogether human. She did not know what to say to him.

"You do not feel hard to me, Frank?" she asked at last.

Frank clenched his fist and broke out in excitement. "I not feel hard at no woman. I tell you I not that kind-a man. I never hit my wife. No, never I hurt her when she devil me something awful!" He struck his fist down on the warden's desk so hard that he afterward stroked it absently. A pale pink crept over his neck and face. "Two, t'ree years I know dat woman don' care no more 'bout me, Alexandra Bergson. I know she after some other man. I know her, oo-oo! An' I ain't never hurt her. I never would-a done dat, if I ain't had dat gun along. I don' know what in hell make me take dat gun. She always say I ain't no man to carry gun. If she been in dat house, where she ought-a been-- But das a foolish talk."

Frank rubbed his head and stopped suddenly, as he had stopped before. Alexandra felt that there was something strange in the way he chilled off, as if something came up in him that extinguished his power of feeling or thinking.

"Yes, Frank," she said kindly. "I know you never meant to hurt Marie."

Frank smiled at her queerly. His eyes filled slowly with tears. "You know, I most forgit dat woman's name. She ain't got no name for me no more. I never hate my wife, but dat woman what make me do dat-- Honest to God, but I hate her! I no man to fight. I don' want to kill no boy and no woman. I not care how many men she take under dat tree. I no care for not'ing but dat fine boy I kill, Alexandra Bergson. I guess I go crazy sure 'nough."

Alexandra remembered the little yellow cane she had found in Frank's clothes-closet. She thought of how he had come to this country a gay young fellow, so attractive that the prettiest Bohemian girl in Omaha had run away with him. It seemed unreasonable that life should have landed him in such a place as this. She blamed Marie bitterly. And why, with her happy, affectionate nature, should she have brought destruction and sorrow to all who had loved her, even to poor old Joe Tovesky, the uncle who used to carry her about so proudly when she was a little girl? That was the strangest thing of all. Was there, then, something wrong in being warm-hearted and impulsive like that? Alexandra hated to think so. But there was Emil, in the Norwegian graveyard at home, and here was Frank Shabata. Alexandra rose and took him by the hand.

"Frank Shabata, I am never going to stop trying until I get you pardoned. I'll never give the Governor any peace. I know I can get you out of this place."

Frank looked at her distrustfully, but he gathered confidence from her face. "Alexandra," he said earnestly, "if I git out-a here, I not trouble dis country no more. I go back where I come from; see my mother."

Alexandra tried to withdraw her hand, but Frank held on to it nervously. He put out his finger and absently touched a button on her black jacket. "Alexandra," he said in a low tone, looking steadily at the button, "you ain' t'ink I use dat girl awful bad before--"

"No, Frank. We won't talk about that," Alexandra said, pressing his hand. "I can't help Emil now, so I'm going to do what I can for you. You know I don't go away from home often, and I came up here on purpose to tell you this."

The warden at the glass door looked in inquiringly. Alexandra nodded, and he came in and touched the white button on his desk. The guard appeared, and with a sinking heart Alexandra saw Frank led away down the corridor. After a few words with Mr. Schwartz, she left the prison and made her way to the street-car. She had refused with horror the warden's cordial invitation to "go through the institution." As the car lurched over its uneven roadbed, back toward Lincoln, Alexandra thought of how she and Frank had been wrecked by the same storm and of how, although she could come out into the sunlight, she had not much more left in her life than he. She remembered some lines from a poem she had liked in her schooldays:--

Henceforth the world will only be   A wider prison-house to me,--

and sighed. A disgust of life weighed upon her heart; some such feeling as had twice frozen Frank Shabata's features while they talked together. She wished she were back on the Divide.

When Alexandra entered her hotel, the clerk held up one finger and beckoned to her. As she approached his desk, he handed her a telegram. Alexandra took the yellow envelope and looked at it in perplexity, then stepped into the elevator without opening it. As she walked down the corridor toward her room, she reflected that she was, in a manner, immune from evil tidings. On reaching her room she locked the door, and sitting down on a chair by the dresser, opened the telegram. It was from Hanover, and it read:--   Arrived Hanover last night. Shall wait here until you come. Please hurry. CARL LINSTRUM.

Alexandra put her head down on the dresser and burst into tears.

III

The next afternoon Carl and Alexandra were walking across the fields from Mrs. Hiller's. Alexandra had left Lincoln after midnight, and Carl had met her at the Hanover station early in the morning. After they reached home, Alexandra had gone over to Mrs. Hiller's to leave a little present she had bought for her in the city. They stayed at the old lady's door but a moment, and then came out to spend the rest of the afternoon in the sunny fields.

Alexandra had taken off her black traveling suit and put on a white dress; partly because she saw that her black clothes made Carl uncomfortable and partly because she felt oppressed by them herself. They seemed a little like the prison where she had worn them yesterday, and to be out of place in the open fields. Carl had changed very little. His cheeks were browner and fuller. He looked less like a tired scholar than when he went away a year ago, but no one, even now, would have taken him for a man of business. His soft, lustrous black eyes, his whimsical smile, would be less against him in the Klondike than on the Divide. There are always dreamers on the frontier.

Carl and Alexandra had been talking since morning. Her letter had never reached him. He had first learned of her misfortune from a San Francisco paper, four weeks old, which he had picked up in a saloon, and which contained a brief account of Frank Shabata's trial. When he put down the paper, he had already made up his mind that he could reach Alexandra as quickly as a letter could; and ever since he had been on the way; day and night, by the fastest boats and trains he could catch. His steamer had been held back two days by rough weather.

As they came out of Mrs. Hiller's garden they took up their talk again where they had left it. "But could you come away like that, Carl, without arranging things? Could you just walk off and leave your business?" Alexandra asked.

Carl laughed. "Prudent Alexandra! You see, my dear, I happen to have an honest partner. I trust him with everything. In fact, it's been his enterprise from the beginning, you know. I'm in it only because he took me in. I'll have to go back in the spring. Perhaps you will want to go with me then. We haven't turned up millions yet, but we've got a start that's worth following. But this winter I'd like to spend with you. You won't feel that we ought to wait longer, on Emil's account, will you, Alexandra?"

Alexandra shook her head. "No, Carl; I don't feel that way about it. And surely you needn't mind anything Lou and Oscar say now. They are much angrier with me about Emil, now, than about you. They say it was all my fault. That I ruined him by sending him to college."

"No, I don't care a button for Lou or Oscar. The moment I knew you were in trouble, the moment I thought you might need me, it all looked different. You've always been a triumphant kind of person." Carl hesitated, looking sidewise at her strong, full figure. "But you do need me now, Alexandra?"

She put her hand on his arm. "I needed you terribly when it happened, Carl. I cried for you at night. Then everything seemed to get hard inside of me, and I thought perhaps I should never care for you again. But when I got your telegram yesterday, then--then it was just as it used to be. You are all I have in the world, you know."

Carl pressed her hand in silence. They were passing the Shabatas' empty house now, but they avoided the orchard path and took one that led over by the pasture pond.

"Can you understand it, Carl?" Alexandra murmured. "I have had nobody but Ivar and Signa to talk to. Do talk to me. Can you understand it? Could you have believed that of Marie Tovesky? I would have been cut to pieces, little by little, before I would have betrayed her trust in me!"

Carl looked at the shining spot of water before them. "Maybe she was cut to pieces, too, Alexandra. I am sure she tried hard; they both did. That was why Emil went to Mexico, of course. And he was going away again, you tell me, though he had only been home three weeks. You remember that Sunday when I went with Emil up to the French Church fair? I thought that day there was some kind of feeling, something unusual, between them. I meant to talk to you about it. But on my way back I met Lou and Oscar and got so angry that I forgot everything else. You mustn't be hard on them, Alexandra. Sit down here by the pond a minute. I want to tell you something."

They sat down on the grass-tufted bank and Carl told her how he had seen Emil and Marie out by the pond that morning, more than a year ago, and how young and charming and full of grace they had seemed to him. "It happens like that in the world sometimes, Alexandra," he added earnestly. "I've seen it before. There are women who spread ruin around them through no fault of theirs, just by being too beautiful, too full of life and love. They can't help it. People come to them as people go to a warm fire in winter. I used to feel that in her when she was a little girl. Do you remember how all the Bohemians crowded round her in the store that day, when she gave Emil her candy? You remember those yellow sparks in her eyes?"

Alexandra sighed. "Yes. People couldn't help loving her. Poor Frank does, even now, I think; though he's got himself in such a tangle that for a long time his love has been bitterer than his hate. But if you saw there was anything wrong, you ought to have told me, Carl."

Carl took her hand and smiled patiently. "My dear, it was something one felt in the air, as you feel the spring coming, or a storm in summer. I didn't SEE anything. Simply, when I was with those two young things, I felt my blood go quicker, I felt--how shall I say it?--an acceleration of life. After I got away, it was all too delicate, too intangible, to write about."

Alexandra looked at him mournfully. "I try to be more liberal about such things than I used to be. I try to realize that we are not all made alike. Only, why couldn't it have been Raoul Marcel, or Jan Smirka? Why did it have to be my boy?"

"Because he was the best there was, I suppose. They were both the best you had here."

The sun was dropping low in the west when the two friends rose and took the path again. The straw-stacks were throwing long shadows, the owls were flying home to the prairie-dog town. When they came to the corner where the pastures joined, Alexandra's twelve young colts were galloping in a drove over the brow of the hill.

"Carl," said Alexandra, "I should like to go up there with you in the spring. I haven't been on the water since we crossed the ocean, when I was a little girl. After we first came out here I used to dream sometimes about the shipyard where father worked, and a little sort of inlet, full of masts." Alexandra paused. After a moment's thought she said, "But you would never ask me to go away for good, would you?"

"Of course not, my dearest. I think I know how you feel about this country as well as you do yourself." Carl took her hand in both his own and pressed it tenderly.

"Yes, I still feel that way, though Emil is gone. When I was on the train this morning, and we got near Hanover, I felt something like I did when I drove back with Emil from the river that time, in the dry year. I was glad to come back to it. I've lived here a long time. There is great peace here, Carl, and freedom. . . . I thought when I came out of that prison, where poor Frank is, that I should never feel free again. But I do, here." Alexandra took a deep breath and looked off into the red west.

"You belong to the land," Carl murmured, "as you have always said. Now more than ever."

"Yes, now more than ever. You remember what you once said about the graveyard, and the old story writing itself over? Only it is we who write it, with the best we have."

They paused on the last ridge of the pasture, overlooking the house and the windmill and the stables that marked the site of John Bergson's homestead. On every side the brown waves of the earth rolled away to meet the sky.

"Lou and Oscar can't see those things," said Alexandra suddenly. "Suppose I do will my land to their children, what difference will that make? The land belongs to the future, Carl; that's the way it seems to me. How many of the names on the county clerk's plat will be there in fifty years? I might as well try to will the sunset over there to my brother's children. We come and go, but the land is always here. And the people who love it and understand it are the people who own it-- for a little while."

Carl looked at her wonderingly. She was still gazing into the west, and in her face there was that exalted serenity that sometimes came to her at moments of deep feeling. The level rays of the sinking sun shone in her clear eyes.

"Why are you thinking of such things now, Alexandra?"

"I had a dream before I went to Lincoln-- But I will tell you about that afterward, after we are married. It will never come true, now, in the way I thought it might." She took Carl's arm and they walked toward the gate. "How many times we have walked this path together, Carl. How many times we will walk it again! Does it seem to you like coming back to your own place? Do you feel at peace with the world here? I think we shall be very happy. I haven't any fears. I think when friends marry, they are safe. We don't suffer like--those young ones." Alexandra ended with a sigh.

They had reached the gate. Before Carl opened it, he drew Alexandra to him and kissed her softly, on her lips and on her eyes.

She leaned heavily on his shoulder. "I am tired," she murmured. "I have been very lonely, Carl."

They went into the house together, leaving the Divide behind them, under the evening star. Fortunate country, that is one day to receive hearts like Alexandra's into its bosom, to give them out again in the yellow wheat, in the rustling corn, in the shining eyes of youth!

THE END.

BOOK THREE.
SONG OF THE LARK

PART I.
FRIENDS OF CHILDHOOD

I

Dr. Howard Archie had just come up from a game of pool with the Jewish clothier and two traveling men who happened to be staying overnight in Moonstone. His offices were in the Duke Block, over the drug store. Larry, the doctor's man, had lit the overhead light in the waiting-room and the double student's lamp on the desk in the study. The isinglass sides of the hard-coal burner were aglow, and the air in the study was so hot that as he came in the doctor opened the door into his little operating-room, where there was no stove. The waiting room was carpeted and stiffly furnished, something like a country parlor. The study had worn, unpainted floors, but there was a look of winter comfort about it. The doctor's flat-top desk was large and well made; the papers were in orderly piles, under glass weights. Behind the stove a wide bookcase, with double glass doors, reached from the floor to the ceiling. It was filled with medical books of every thickness and color. On the top shelf stood a long row of thirty or forty volumes, bound all alike in dark mottled board covers, with imitation leather backs.

As the doctor in New England villages is proverbially old, so the doctor in small Colorado towns twenty-five years ago was generally young. Dr. Archie was barely thirty. He was tall, with massive shoulders which he held stiffly, and a large, well-shaped head. He was a distinguished-looking man, for that part of the world, at least.

There was something individual in the way in which his reddish-brown hair, parted cleanly at the side, bushed over his high forehead. His nose was straight and thick, and his eyes were intelligent. He wore a curly, reddish mustache and an imperial, cut trimly, which made him look a little like the pictures of Napoleon III. His hands were large and well kept, but ruggedly formed, and the backs were shaded with crinkly reddish hair. He wore a blue suit of woolly, wide-waled serge; the traveling men had known at a glance that it was made by a Denver tailor. The doctor was always well dressed.

Dr. Archie turned up the student's lamp and sat down in the swivel chair before his desk. He sat uneasily, beating a tattoo on his knees with his fingers, and looked about him as if he were bored. He glanced at his watch, then absently took from his pocket a bunch of small keys, selected one and looked at it. A contemptuous smile, barely perceptible, played on his lips, but his eyes remained meditative. Behind the door that led into the hall, under his buffaloskin driving-coat, was a locked cupboard. This the doctor opened mechanically, kicking aside a pile of muddy overshoes. Inside, on the shelves, were whiskey glasses and decanters, lemons, sugar, and bitters. Hearing a step in the empty, echoing hall without, the doctor closed the cupboard again, snapping the Yale lock. The door of the waiting-room opened, a man entered and came on into the consulting-room.

"Good-evening, Mr. Kronborg," said the doctor carelessly. "Sit down."

His visitor was a tall, loosely built man, with a thin brown beard, streaked with gray. He wore a frock coat, a broad-brimmed black hat, a white lawn necktie, and steel rimmed spectacles. Altogether there was a pretentious and important air about him, as he lifted the skirts of his coat and sat down.

"Good-evening, doctor. Can you step around to the house with me? I think Mrs. Kronborg will need you this evening." This was said with profound gravity and, curiously enough, with a slight embarrassment.

"Any hurry?" the doctor asked over his shoulder as he went into his operating-room.

Mr. Kronborg coughed behind his hand, and contracted his brows. His face threatened at every moment to break into a smile of foolish excitement. He controlled it only by calling upon his habitual pulpit manner. "Well, I think it would be as well to go immediately. Mrs. Kronborg will be more comfortable if you are there. She has been suffering for some time."

The doctor came back and threw a black bag upon his desk. He wrote some instructions for his man on a prescription pad and then drew on his overcoat. "All ready," he announced, putting out his lamp. Mr. Kronborg rose and they tramped through the empty hall and down the stairway to the street. The drug store below was dark, and the saloon next door was just closing. Every other light on Main Street was out.

On either side of the road and at the outer edge of the board sidewalk, the snow had been shoveled into breastworks. The town looked small and black, flattened down in the snow, muffled and all but extinguished. Overhead the stars shone gloriously. It was impossible not to notice them. The air was so clear that the white sand hills to the east of Moonstone gleamed softly. Following the Reverend Mr. Kronborg along the narrow walk, past the little dark, sleeping houses, the doctor looked up at the flashing night and whistled softly. It did seem that people were stupider than they need be; as if on a night like this there ought to be something better to do than to sleep nine hours, or to assist Mrs. Kronborg in functions which she could have performed so admirably unaided. He wished he had gone down to Denver to hear Fay Templeton sing "See-Saw." Then he remembered that he had a personal interest in this family, after all. They turned into another street and saw before them lighted windows; a low story-and-a-half house, with a wing built on at the right and a kitchen addition at the back, everything a little on the slant--roofs, windows, and doors. As they approached the gate, Peter Kronborg's pace grew brisker. His nervous, ministerial cough annoyed the doctor. "Exactly as if he were going to give out a text," he thought. He drew off his glove and felt in his vest pocket. "Have a troche, Kronborg," he said, producing some. "Sent me for samples. Very good for a rough throat."

"Ah, thank you, thank you. I was in something of a hurry. I neglected to put on my overshoes. Here we are, doctor." Kronborg opened his front door--seemed delighted to be at home again.

The front hall was dark and cold; the hatrack was hung with an astonishing number of children's hats and caps and cloaks. They were even piled on the table beneath the hatrack. Under the table was a heap of rubbers and overshoes. While the doctor hung up his coat and hat, Peter Kronborg opened the door into the living-room. A glare of light greeted them, and a rush of hot, stale air, smelling of warming flannels.

At three o'clock in the morning Dr. Archie was in the parlor putting on his cuffs and coat--there was no spare bedroom in that house. Peter Kronborg's seventh child, a boy, was being soothed and cosseted by his aunt, Mrs. Kronborg was asleep, and the doctor was going home. But he wanted first to speak to Kronborg, who, coatless and fluttery, was pouring coal into the kitchen stove. As the doctor crossed the dining-room he paused and listened. From one of the wing rooms, off to the left, he heard rapid, distressed breathing. He went to the kitchen door.

"One of the children sick in there?" he asked, nodding toward the partition.

Kronborg hung up the stove-lifter and dusted his fingers. "It must be Thea. I meant to ask you to look at her. She has a croupy cold. But in my excitement--Mrs. Kronborg is doing finely, eh, doctor? Not many of your patients with such a constitution, I expect."

"Oh, yes. She's a fine mother." The doctor took up the lamp from the kitchen table and unceremoniously went into the wing room. Two chubby little boys were asleep in a double bed, with the coverlids over their noses and their feet drawn up. In a single bed, next to theirs, lay a little girl of eleven, wide awake, two yellow braids sticking up on the pillow behind her. Her face was scarlet and her eyes were blazing.

The doctor shut the door behind him. "Feel pretty sick, Thea?" he asked as he took out his thermometer. "Why didn't you call somebody?"

She looked at him with greedy affection. "I thought you were here," she spoke between quick breaths. "There is a new baby, isn't there? Which?"

"Which?" repeated the doctor.

"Brother or sister?"

He smiled and sat down on the edge of the bed. "Brother," he said, taking her hand. "Open."

"Good. Brothers are better," she murmured as he put the glass tube under her tongue.

"Now, be still, I want to count." Dr. Archie reached for her hand and took out his watch. When he put her hand back under the quilt he went over to one of the windows--they were both tight shut--and lifted it a little way. He reached up and ran his hand along the cold, unpapered wall. "Keep under the covers; I'll come back to you in a moment," he said, bending over the glass lamp with his thermometer. He winked at her from the door before he shut it.

Peter Kronborg was sitting in his wife's room, holding the bundle which contained his son. His air of cheerful importance, his beard and glasses, even his shirt-sleeves, annoyed the doctor. He beckoned Kronborg into the living-room and said sternly:--

"You've got a very sick child in there. Why didn't you call me before? It's pneumonia, and she must have been sick for several days. Put the baby down somewhere, please, and help me make up the bed-lounge here in the parlor. She's got to be in a warm room, and she's got to be quiet. You must keep the other children out. Here, this thing opens up, I see," swinging back the top of the carpet lounge. "We can lift her mattress and carry her in just as she is. I don't want to disturb her more than is necessary."

Kronborg was all concern immediately. The two men took up the mattress and carried the sick child into the parlor. "I'll have to go down to my office to get some medicine, Kronborg. The drug store won't be open. Keep the covers on her. I won't be gone long. Shake down the stove and put on a little coal, but not too much; so it'll catch quickly, I mean. Find an old sheet for me, and put it there to warm."

The doctor caught his coat and hurried out into the dark street. Nobody was stirring yet, and the cold was bitter. He was tired and hungry and in no mild humor. "The idea!" he muttered; "to be such an ass at his age, about the seventh! And to feel no responsibility about the little girl. Silly old goat! The baby would have got into the world somehow; they always do. But a nice little girl like that--she's worth the whole litter. Where she ever got it from--" He turned into the Duke Block and ran up the stairs to his office.

Thea Kronborg, meanwhile, was wondering why she happened to be in the parlor, where nobody but company-- usually visiting preachers--ever slept. She had moments of stupor when she did not see anything, and moments of excitement when she felt that something unusual and pleasant was about to happen, when she saw everything clearly in the red light from the isinglass sides of the hard-coal burner--the nickel trimmings on the stove itself, the pictures on the wall, which she thought very beautiful, the flowers on the Brussels carpet, Czerny's "Daily Studies" which stood open on the upright piano. She forgot, for the time being, all about the new baby.

When she heard the front door open, it occurred to her that the pleasant thing which was going to happen was Dr. Archie himself. He came in and warmed his hands at the stove. As he turned to her, she threw herself wearily toward him, half out of her bed. She would have tumbled to the floor had he not caught her. He gave her some medicine and went to the kitchen for something he needed. She drowsed and lost the sense of his being there. When she opened her eyes again, he was kneeling before the stove, spreading something dark and sticky on a white cloth, with a big spoon; batter, perhaps. Presently she felt him taking off her nightgown. He wrapped the hot plaster about her chest. There seemed to be straps which he pinned over her shoulders. Then he took out a thread and needle and began to sew her up in it. That, she felt, was too strange; she must be dreaming anyhow, so she succumbed to her drowsiness.

Thea had been moaning with every breath since the doctor came back, but she did not know it. She did not realize that she was suffering pain. When she was conscious at all, she seemed to be separated from her body; to be perched on top of the piano, or on the hanging lamp, watching the doctor sew her up. It was perplexing and unsatisfactory, like dreaming. She wished she could waken up and see what was going on.

The doctor thanked God that he had persuaded Peter Kronborg to keep out of the way. He could do better by the child if he had her to himself. He had no children of his own. His marriage was a very unhappy one. As he lifted and undressed Thea, he thought to himself what a beautiful thing a little girl's body was,--like a flower. It was so neatly and delicately fashioned, so soft, and so milky white. Thea must have got her hair and her silky skin from her mother. She was a little Swede, through and through. Dr. Archie could not help thinking how he would cherish a little creature like this if she were his. Her hands, so little and hot, so clever, too,--he glanced at the open exercise book on the piano. When he had stitched up the flaxseed jacket, he wiped it neatly about the edges, where the paste had worked out on the skin. He put on her the clean nightgown he had warmed before the fire, and tucked the blankets about her. As he pushed back the hair that had fuzzed down over her eyebrows, he felt her head thoughtfully with the tips of his fingers. No, he couldn't say that it was different from any other child's head, though he believed that there was something very different about her. He looked intently at her wide, flushed face, freckled nose, fierce little mouth, and her delicate, tender chin--the one soft touch in her hard little Scandinavian face, as if some fairy godmother had caressed her there and left a cryptic promise. Her brows were usually drawn together defiantly, but never when she was with Dr. Archie. Her affection for him was prettier than most of the things that went to make up the doctor's life in Moonstone.

The windows grew gray. He heard a tramping on the attic floor, on the back stairs, then cries: "Give me my shirt!" "Where's my other stocking?"

"I'll have to stay till they get off to school," he reflected, "or they'll be in here tormenting her, the whole lot of them."

II

For the next four days it seemed to Dr. Archie that his patient might slip through his hands, do what he might. But she did not. On the contrary, after that she recovered very rapidly. As her father remarked, she must have inherited the "constitution" which he was never tired of admiring in her mother.

One afternoon, when her new brother was a week old, the doctor found Thea very comfortable and happy in her bed in the parlor. The sunlight was pouring in over her shoulders, the baby was asleep on a pillow in a big rocking-chair beside her. Whenever he stirred, she put out her hand and rocked him. Nothing of him was visible but a flushed, puffy forehead and an uncompromisingly big, bald cranium. The door into her mother's room stood open, and Mrs. Kronborg was sitting up in bed darning stockings. She was a short, stalwart woman, with a short neck and a determined-looking head. Her skin was very fair, her face calm and unwrinkled, and her yellow hair, braided down her back as she lay in bed, still looked like a girl's. She was a woman whom Dr. Archie respected; active, practical, unruffled; goodhumored, but determined. Exactly the sort of woman to take care of a flighty preacher. She had brought her husband some property, too,--one fourth of her father's broad acres in Nebraska,--but this she kept in her own name. She had profound respect for her husband's erudition and eloquence. She sat under his preaching with deep humility, and was as much taken in by his stiff shirt and white neckties as if she had not ironed them herself by lamplight the night before they appeared correct and spotless in the pulpit. But for all this, she had no confidence in his administration of worldly affairs. She looked to him for morning prayers and grace at table; she expected him to name the babies and to supply whatever parental sentiment there was in the house, to remember birthdays and anniversaries, to point the children to moral and patriotic ideals. It was her work to keep their bodies, their clothes, and their conduct in some sort of order, and this she accomplished with a success that was a source of wonder to her neighbors. As she used to remark, and her husband admiringly to echo, she "had never lost one." With all his flightiness, Peter Kronborg appreciated the matter-of-fact, punctual way in which his wife got her children into the world and along in it. He believed, and he was right in believing, that the sovereign State of Colorado was much indebted to Mrs. Kronborg and women like her.

Mrs. Kronborg believed that the size of every family was decided in heaven. More modern views would not have startled her; they would simply have seemed foolish--thin chatter, like the boasts of the men who built the tower of Babel, or like Axel's plan to breed ostriches in the chicken yard. From what evidence Mrs. Kronborg formed her opinions on this and other matters, it would have been difficult to say, but once formed, they were unchangeable. She would no more have questioned her convictions than she would have questioned revelation. Calm and even tempered, naturally kind, she was capable of strong prejudices, and she never forgave.

When the doctor came in to see Thea, Mrs. Kronborg was reflecting that the washing was a week behind, and deciding what she had better do about it. The arrival of a new baby meant a revision of her entire domestic schedule, and as she drove her needle along she had been working out new sleeping arrangements and cleaning days. The doctor had entered the house without knocking, after making noise enough in the hall to prepare his patients. Thea was reading, her book propped up before her in the sunlight.

"Mustn't do that; bad for your eyes," he said, as Thea shut the book quickly and slipped it under the covers.

Mrs. Kronborg called from her bed: "Bring the baby here, doctor, and have that chair. She wanted him in there for company."

Before the doctor picked up the baby, he put a yellow paper bag down on Thea's coverlid and winked at her. They had a code of winks and grimaces. When he went in to chat with her mother, Thea opened the bag cautiously, trying to keep it from crackling. She drew out a long bunch of white grapes, with a little of the sawdust in which they had been packed still clinging to them. They were called Malaga grapes in Moonstone, and once or twice during the winter the leading grocer got a keg of them. They were used mainly for table decoration, about Christmas-time. Thea had never had more than one grape at a time before. When the doctor came back she was holding the almost transparent fruit up in the sunlight, feeling the pale-green skins softly with the tips of her fingers. She did not thank him; she only snapped her eyes at him in a special way which he understood, and, when he gave her his hand, put it quickly and shyly under her cheek, as if she were trying to do so without knowing it--and without his knowing it.

Dr. Archie sat down in the rocking-chair. "And how's Thea feeling to-day?"

He was quite as shy as his patient, especially when a third person overheard his conversation. Big and handsome and superior to his fellow townsmen as Dr. Archie was, he was seldom at his ease, and like Peter Kronborg he often dodged behind a professional manner. There was sometimes a contraction of embarrassment and self consciousness all over his big body, which made him awkward--likely to stumble, to kick up rugs, or to knock over chairs. If any one was very sick, he forgot himself, but he had a clumsy touch in convalescent gossip.

Thea curled up on her side and looked at him with pleasure. "All right. I like to be sick. I have more fun then than other times."

"How's that?"

"I don't have to go to school, and I don't have to practice. I can read all I want to, and have good things,"--she patted the grapes. "I had lots of fun that time I mashed my finger and you wouldn't let Professor Wunsch make me practice. Only I had to do left hand, even then. I think that was mean."

The doctor took her hand and examined the forefinger, where the nail had grown back a little crooked. "You mustn't trim it down close at the corner there, and then it will grow straight. You won't want it crooked when you're a big girl and wear rings and have sweethearts."

She made a mocking little face at him and looked at his new scarf-pin. "That's the prettiest one you ev-ER had. I wish you'd stay a long while and let me look at it. What is it?"

Dr. Archie laughed. "It's an opal. Spanish Johnny brought it up for me from Chihuahua in his shoe. I had it set in Denver, and I wore it to-day for your benefit."

Thea had a curious passion for jewelry. She wanted every shining stone she saw, and in summer she was always going off into the sand hills to hunt for crystals and agates and bits of pink chalcedony. She had two cigar boxes full of stones that she had found or traded for, and she imagined that they were of enormous value. She was always planning how she would have them set.

"What are you reading?" The doctor reached under the covers and pulled out a book of Byron's poems. "Do you like this?"

She looked confused, turned over a few pages rapidly, and pointed to "My native land, good-night." "That," she said sheepishly.

"How about `Maid of Athens'?"

She blushed and looked at him suspiciously. "I like 'There was a sound of revelry,'" she muttered.

The doctor laughed and closed the book. It was clumsily bound in padded leather and had been presented to the Reverend Peter Kronborg by his Sunday-School class as an ornament for his parlor table.

"Come into the office some day, and I'll lend you a nice book. You can skip the parts you don't understand. You can read it in vacation. Perhaps you'll be able to understand all of it by then."

Thea frowned and looked fretfully toward the piano. "In vacation I have to practice four hours every day, and then there'll be Thor to take care of." She pronounced it "Tor."

"Thor? Oh, you've named the baby Thor?" exclaimed the doctor.

Thea frowned again, still more fiercely, and said quickly, "That's a nice name, only maybe it's a little--old fashioned." She was very sensitive about being thought a foreigner, and was proud of the fact that, in town, her father always preached in English; very bookish English, at that, one might add.

Born in an old Scandinavian colony in Minnesota, Peter Kronborg had been sent to a small divinity school in Indiana by the women of a Swedish evangelical mission, who were convinced of his gifts and who skimped and begged and gave church suppers to get the long, lazy youth through the seminary. He could still speak enough Swedish to exhort and to bury the members of his country church out at Copper Hole, and he wielded in his Moonstone pulpit a somewhat pompous English vocabulary he had learned out of books at college. He always spoke of "the infant Saviour," "our Heavenly Father," etc. The poor man had no natural, spontaneous human speech. If he had his sincere moments, they were perforce inarticulate. Probably a good deal of his pretentiousness was due to the fact that he habitually expressed himself in a book learned language, wholly remote from anything personal, native, or homely. Mrs. Kronborg spoke Swedish to her own sisters and to her sister-in-law Tillie, and colloquial English to her neighbors. Thea, who had a rather sensitive ear, until she went to school never spoke at all, except in monosyllables, and her mother was convinced that she was tongue-tied. She was still inept in speech for a child so intelligent. Her ideas were usually clear, but she seldom attempted to explain them, even at school, where she excelled in "written work" and never did more than mutter a reply.

"Your music professor stopped me on the street to-day and asked me how you were," said the doctor, rising. "He'll be sick himself, trotting around in this slush with no overcoat or overshoes."

"He's poor," said Thea simply.

The doctor sighed. "I'm afraid he's worse than that. Is he always all right when you take your lessons? Never acts as if he'd been drinking?"

Thea looked angry and spoke excitedly. "He knows a lot. More than anybody. I don't care if he does drink; he's old and poor." Her voice shook a little.

Mrs. Kronborg spoke up from the next room. "He's a good teacher, doctor. It's good for us he does drink. He'd never be in a little place like this if he didn't have some weakness. These women that teach music around here don't know nothing. I wouldn't have my child wasting time with them. If Professor Wunsch goes away, Thea'll have nobody to take from. He's careful with his scholars; he don't use bad language. Mrs. Kohler is always present when Thea takes her lesson. It's all right." Mrs. Kronborg spoke calmly and judicially. One could see that she had thought the matter out before.

"I'm glad to hear that, Mrs. Kronborg. I wish we could get the old man off his bottle and keep him tidy. Do you suppose if I gave you an old overcoat you could get him to wear it?" The doctor went to the bedroom door and Mrs. Kronborg looked up from her darning.

"Why, yes, I guess he'd be glad of it. He'll take most anything from me. He won't buy clothes, but I guess he'd wear 'em if he had 'em. I've never had any clothes to give him, having so many to make over for."

"I'll have Larry bring the coat around to-night. You aren't cross with me, Thea?" taking her hand.

Thea grinned warmly. "Not if you give Professor Wunsch a coat--and things," she tapped the grapes significantly. The doctor bent over and kissed her.

III

Being sick was all very well, but Thea knew from experience that starting back to school again was attended by depressing difficulties. One Monday morning she got up early with Axel and Gunner, who shared her wing room, and hurried into the back living-room, between the dining-room and the kitchen. There, beside a soft-coal stove, the younger children of the family undressed at night and dressed in the morning. The older daughter, Anna, and the two big boys slept upstairs, where the rooms were theoretically warmed by stovepipes from below. The first (and the worst!) thing that confronted Thea was a suit of clean, prickly red flannel, fresh from the wash. Usually the torment of breaking in a clean suit of flannel came on Sunday, but yesterday, as she was staying in the house, she had begged off. Their winter underwear was a trial to all the children, but it was bitterest to Thea because she happened to have the most sensitive skin. While she was tugging it on, her Aunt Tillie brought in warm water from the boiler and filled the tin pitcher. Thea washed her face, brushed and braided her hair, and got into her blue cashmere dress. Over this she buttoned a long apron, with sleeves, which would not be removed until she put on her cloak to go to school. Gunner and Axel, on the soap box behind the stove, had their usual quarrel about which should wear the tightest stockings, but they exchanged reproaches in low tones, for they were wholesomely afraid of Mrs. Kronborg's rawhide whip. She did not chastise her children often, but she did it thoroughly. Only a somewhat stern system of discipline could have kept any degree of order and quiet in that overcrowded house.

Mrs. Kronborg's children were all trained to dress themselves at the earliest possible age, to make their own beds,-- the boys as well as the girls,--to take care of their clothes, to eat what was given them, and to keep out of the way. Mrs. Kronborg would have made a good chess player; she had a head for moves and positions.

Anna, the elder daughter, was her mother's lieutenant. All the children knew that they must obey Anna, who was an obstinate contender for proprieties and not always fair minded. To see the young Kronborgs headed for Sunday School was like watching a military drill. Mrs. Kronborg let her children's minds alone. She did not pry into their thoughts or nag them. She respected them as individuals, and outside of the house they had a great deal of liberty. But their communal life was definitely ordered.

In the winter the children breakfasted in the kitchen; Gus and Charley and Anna first, while the younger children were dressing. Gus was nineteen and was a clerk in a dry-goods store. Charley, eighteen months younger, worked in a feed store. They left the house by the kitchen door at seven o'clock, and then Anna helped her Aunt Tillie get the breakfast for the younger ones. Without the help of this sister-in-law, Tillie Kronborg, Mrs. Kronborg's life would have been a hard one. Mrs. Kronborg often reminded Anna that "no hired help would ever have taken the same interest."

Mr. Kronborg came of a poorer stock than his wife; from a lowly, ignorant family that had lived in a poor part of Sweden. His great-grandfather had gone to Norway to work as a farm laborer and had married a Norwegian girl. This strain of Norwegian blood came out somewhere in each generation of the Kronborgs. The intemperance of one of Peter Kronborg's uncles, and the religious mania of another, had been alike charged to the Norwegian grandmother. Both Peter Kronborg and his sister Tillie were more like the Norwegian root of the family than like the Swedish, and this same Norwegian strain was strong in Thea, though in her it took a very different character.

Tillie was a queer, addle-pated thing, as flighty as a girl at thirty-five, and overweeningly fond of gay clothes--which taste, as Mrs. Kronborg philosophically said, did nobody any harm. Tillie was always cheerful, and her tongue was still for scarcely a minute during the day. She had been cruelly overworked on her father's Minnesota farm when she was a young girl, and she had never been so happy as she was now; had never before, as she said, had such social advantages. She thought her brother the most important man in Moonstone. She never missed a church service, and, much to the embarrassment of the children, she always "spoke a piece" at the Sunday-School concerts. She had a complete set of "Standard Recitations," which she conned on Sundays. This morning, when Thea and her two younger brothers sat down to breakfast, Tillie was remonstrating with Gunner because he had not learned a recitation assigned to him for George Washington Day at school. The unmemorized text lay heavily on Gunner's conscience as he attacked his buckwheat cakes and sausage. He knew that Tillie was in the right, and that "when the day came he would be ashamed of himself."

"I don't care," he muttered, stirring his coffee; "they oughtn't to make boys speak. It's all right for girls. They like to show off."

"No showing off about it. Boys ought to like to speak up for their country. And what was the use of your father buying you a new suit, if you're not going to take part in anything?"

"That was for Sunday-School. I'd rather wear my old one, anyhow. Why didn't they give the piece to Thea?" Gunner grumbled.

Tillie was turning buckwheat cakes at the griddle. "Thea can play and sing, she don't need to speak. But you've got to know how to do something, Gunner, that you have. What are you going to do when you git big and want to git into society, if you can't do nothing? Everybody'll say, `Can you sing? Can you play? Can you speak? Then git right out of society.' An' that's what they'll say to you, Mr. Gunner."

Gunner and Alex grinned at Anna, who was preparing her mother's breakfast. They never made fun of Tillie, but they understood well enough that there were subjects upon which her ideas were rather foolish. When Tillie struck the shallows, Thea was usually prompt in turning the conversation.

"Will you and Axel let me have your sled at recess?" she asked.

"All the time?" asked Gunner dubiously.

"I'll work your examples for you to-night, if you do."

"Oh, all right. There'll be a lot of 'em."

"I don't mind, I can work 'em fast. How about yours, Axel?"

Axel was a fat little boy of seven, with pretty, lazy blue eyes. "I don't care," he murmured, buttering his last buckwheat cake without ambition; "too much trouble to copy 'em down. Jenny Smiley'll let me have hers."

The boys were to pull Thea to school on their sled, as the snow was deep. The three set off together. Anna was now in the high school, and she no longer went with the family party, but walked to school with some of the older girls who were her friends, and wore a hat, not a hood like Thea.

IV

"And it was Summer, beautiful Summer!" Those were the closing words of Thea's favorite fairy tale, and she thought of them as she ran out into the world one Saturday morning in May, her music book under her arm. She was going to the Kohlers' to take her lesson, but she was in no hurry.

It was in the summer that one really lived. Then all the little overcrowded houses were opened wide, and the wind blew through them with sweet, earthy smells of garden-planting. The town looked as if it had just been washed. People were out painting their fences. The cottonwood trees were a-flicker with sticky, yellow little leaves, and the feathery tamarisks were in pink bud. With the warm weather came freedom for everybody. People were dug up, as it were. The very old people, whom one had not seen all winter, came out and sunned themselves in the yard. The double windows were taken off the houses, the tormenting flannels in which children had been encased all winter were put away in boxes, and the youngsters felt a pleasure in the cool cotton things next their skin.

Thea had to walk more than a mile to reach the Kohlers' house, a very pleasant mile out of town toward the glittering sand hills,--yellow this morning, with lines of deep violet where the clefts and valleys were. She followed the sidewalk to the depot at the south end of the town; then took the road east to the little group of adobe houses where the Mexicans lived, then dropped into a deep ravine; a dry sand creek, across which the railroad track ran on a trestle. Beyond that gulch, on a little rise of ground that faced the open sandy plain, was the Kohlers' house, where Professor Wunsch lived. Fritz Kohler was the town tailor, one of the first settlers. He had moved there, built a little house and made a garden, when Moonstone was first marked down on the map. He had three sons, but they now worked on the railroad and were stationed in distant cities. One of them had gone to work for the Santa Fe, and lived in New Mexico.

Mrs. Kohler seldom crossed the ravine and went into the town except at Christmas-time, when she had to buy presents and Christmas cards to send to her old friends in Freeport, Illinois. As she did not go to church, she did not possess such a thing as a hat. Year after year she wore the same red hood in winter and a black sunbonnet in summer. She made her own dresses; the skirts came barely to her shoe-tops, and were gathered as full as they could possibly be to the waistband. She preferred men's shoes, and usually wore the cast-offs of one of her sons. She had never learned much English, and her plants and shrubs were her companions. She lived for her men and her garden. Beside that sand gulch, she had tried to reproduce a bit of her own village in the Rhine Valley. She hid herself behind the growth she had fostered, lived under the shade of what she had planted and watered and pruned. In the blaze of the open plain she was stupid and blind like an owl. Shade, shade; that was what she was always planning and making. Behind the high tamarisk hedge, her garden was a jungle of verdure in summer. Above the cherry trees and peach trees and golden plums stood the windmill, with its tank on stilts, which kept all this verdure alive. Outside, the sage-brush grew up to the very edge of the garden, and the sand was always drifting up to the tamarisks.

Every one in Moonstone was astonished when the Kohlers took the wandering music-teacher to live with them. In seventeen years old Fritz had never had a crony, except the harness-maker and Spanish Johnny. This Wunsch came from God knew where,--followed Spanish Johnny into town when that wanderer came back from one of his tramps. Wunsch played in the dance orchestra, tuned pianos, and gave lessons. When Mrs. Kohler rescued him, he was sleeping in a dirty, unfurnished room over one of the saloons, and he had only two shirts in the world. Once he was under her roof, the old woman went at him as she did at her garden. She sewed and washed and mended for him, and made him so clean and respectable that he was able to get a large class of pupils and to rent a piano. As soon as he had money ahead, he sent to the Narrow Gauge lodging-house, in Denver, for a trunkful of music which had been held there for unpaid board. With tears in his eyes the old man--he was not over fifty, but sadly battered--told Mrs. Kohler that he asked nothing better of God than to end his days with her, and to be buried in the garden, under her linden trees. They were not American basswood, but the European linden, which has honey-colored blooms in summer, with a fragrance that surpasses all trees and flowers and drives young people wild with joy.

Thea was reflecting as she walked along that had it not been for Professor Wunsch she might have lived on for years in Moonstone without ever knowing the Kohlers, without ever seeing their garden or the inside of their house. Besides the cuckoo clock,--which was wonderful enough, and which Mrs. Kohler said she kept for "company when she was lonesome,"--the Kohlers had in their house the most wonderful thing Thea had ever seen--but of that later.

Professor Wunsch went to the houses of his other pupils to give them their lessons, but one morning he told Mrs. Kronborg that Thea had talent, and that if she came to him he could teach her in his slippers, and that would be better. Mrs. Kronborg was a strange woman. That word "talent," which no one else in Moonstone, not even Dr. Archie, would have understood, she comprehended perfectly. To any other woman there, it would have meant that a child must have her hair curled every day and must play in public. Mrs. Kronborg knew it meant that Thea must practice four hours a day. A child with talent must be kept at the piano, just as a child with measles must be kept under the blankets. Mrs. Kronborg and her three sisters had all studied piano, and all sang well, but none of them had talent. Their father had played the oboe in an orchestra in Sweden, before he came to America to better his fortunes. He had even known Jenny Lind. A child with talent had to be kept at the piano; so twice a week in summer and once a week in winter Thea went over the gulch to the Kohlers', though the Ladies' Aid Society thought it was not proper for their preacher's daughter to go "where there was so much drinking." Not that the Kohler sons ever so much as looked at a glass of beer. They were ashamed of their old folks and got out into the world as fast as possible; had their clothes made by a Denver tailor and their necks shaved up under their hair and forgot the past. Old Fritz and Wunsch, however, indulged in a friendly bottle pretty often. The two men were like comrades; perhaps the bond between them was the glass wherein lost hopes are found; perhaps it was common memories of another country; perhaps it was the grapevine in the garden--knotty, fibrous shrub, full of homesickness and sentiment, which the Germans have carried around the world with them.

As Thea approached the house she peeped between the pink sprays of the tamarisk hedge and saw the Professor and Mrs. Kohler in the garden, spading and raking. The garden looked like a relief-map now, and gave no indication of what it would be in August; such a jungle! Pole beans and potatoes and corn and leeks and kale and red cabbage--there would even be vegetables for which there is no American name. Mrs. Kohler was always getting by mail packages of seeds from Freeport and from the old country. Then the flowers! There were big sunflowers for the canary bird, tiger lilies and phlox and zinnias and lady's-slippers and portulaca and hollyhocks,--giant hollyhocks. Beside the fruit trees there was a great umbrella-shaped catalpa, and a balm-of-Gilead, two lindens, and even a ginka,--a rigid, pointed tree with leaves shaped like butterflies, which shivered, but never bent to the wind.

This morning Thea saw to her delight that the two oleander trees, one white and one red, had been brought up from their winter quarters in the cellar. There is hardly a German family in the most arid parts of Utah, New Mexico, Arizona, but has its oleander trees. However loutish the American-born sons of the family may be, there was never one who refused to give his muscle to the back-breaking task of getting those tubbed trees down into the cellar in the fall and up into the sunlight in the spring. They may strive to avert the day, but they grapple with the tub at last.

When Thea entered the gate, her professor leaned his spade against the white post that supported the turreted dove-house, and wiped his face with his shirt-sleeve; someway he never managed to have a handkerchief about him. Wunsch was short and stocky, with something rough and bear-like about his shoulders. His face was a dark, bricky red, deeply creased rather than wrinkled, and the skin was like loose leather over his neck band--he wore a brass collar button but no collar. His hair was cropped close; iron-gray bristles on a bullet-like head. His eyes were always suffused and bloodshot. He had a coarse, scornful mouth, and irregular, yellow teeth, much worn at the edges. His hands were square and red, seldom clean, but always alive, impatient, even sympathetic.

"MORGEN," he greeted his pupil in a businesslike way, put on a black alpaca coat, and conducted her at once to the piano in Mrs. Kohler's sitting-room. He twirled the stool to the proper height, pointed to it, and sat down in a wooden chair beside Thea.

"The scale of B flat major," he directed, and then fell into an attitude of deep attention. Without a word his pupil set to work.

To Mrs. Kohler, in the garden, came the cheerful sound of effort, of vigorous striving. Unconsciously she wielded her rake more lightly. Occasionally she heard the teacher's voice. "Scale of E minor...WEITER, WEITER!...IMMER I hear the thumb, like a lame foot. WEITER...WEITER, once...SCHON! The chords, quick!"

The pupil did not open her mouth until they began the second movement of the Clementi sonata, when she remonstrated in low tones about the way he had marked the fingering of a passage.

"It makes no matter what you think," replied her teacher coldly. "There is only one right way. The thumb there. EIN, ZWEI, DREI, VIER," etc. Then for an hour there was no further interruption.

At the end of the lesson Thea turned on her stool and leaned her arm on the keyboard. They usually had a little talk after the lesson.

Herr Wunsch grinned. "How soon is it you are free from school? Then we make ahead faster, eh?"

"First week in June. Then will you give me the `Invitation to the Dance'?"

He shrugged his shoulders. "It makes no matter. If you want him, you play him out of lesson hours."

"All right." Thea fumbled in her pocket and brought out a crumpled slip of paper. "What does this mean, please? I guess it's Latin."

Wunsch blinked at the line penciled on the paper. "Wherefrom you get this?" he asked gruffly.

"Out of a book Dr. Archie gave me to read. It's all English but that. Did you ever see it before?" she asked, watching his face.

"Yes. A long time ago," he muttered, scowling. "Ovidius!" He took a stub of lead pencil from his vest pocket, steadied his hand by a visible effort, and under the words:

"LENTE CURRITE, LENTE CURRITE, NOCTIS EQUI," he wrote in a clear, elegant Gothic hand,--

"GO SLOWLY, GO SLOWLY, YE STEEDS OF THE NIGHT."

He put the pencil back in his pocket and continued to stare at the Latin. It recalled the poem, which he had read as a student, and thought very fine. There were treasures of memory which no lodging-house keeper could attach. One carried things about in one's head, long after one's linen could be smuggled out in a tuning-bag. He handed the paper back to Thea. "There is the English, quite elegant," he said, rising.

Mrs. Kohler stuck her head in at the door, and Thea slid off the stool. "Come in, Mrs. Kohler," she called, "and show me the piece-picture."

The old woman laughed, pulled off her big gardening gloves, and pushed Thea to the lounge before the object of her delight. The "piece-picture," which hung on the wall and nearly covered one whole end of the room, was the handiwork of Fritz Kohler. He had learned his trade under an old-fashioned tailor in Magdeburg who required from each of his apprentices a thesis: that is, before they left his shop, each apprentice had to copy in cloth some well known German painting, stitching bits of colored stuff together on a linen background; a kind of mosaic. The pupil was allowed to select his subject, and Fritz Kohler had chosen a popular painting of Napoleon's retreat from Moscow. The gloomy Emperor and his staff were represented as crossing a stone bridge, and behind them was the blazing city, the walls and fortresses done in gray cloth with orange tongues of flame darting about the domes and minarets. Napoleon rode his white horse; Murat, in Oriental dress, a bay charger. Thea was never tired of examining this work, of hearing how long it had taken Fritz to make it, how much it had been admired, and what narrow escapes it had had from moths and fire. Silk, Mrs. Kohler explained, would have been much easier to manage than woolen cloth, in which it was often hard to get the right shades. The reins of the horses, the wheels of the spurs, the brooding eyebrows of the Emperor, Murat's fierce mustaches, the great shakos of the Guard, were all worked out with the minutest fidelity. Thea's admiration for this picture had endeared her to Mrs. Kohler. It was now many years since she used to point out its wonders to her own little boys. As Mrs. Kohler did not go to church, she never heard any singing, except the songs that floated over from Mexican Town, and Thea often sang for her after the lesson was over. This morning Wunsch pointed to the piano.

"On Sunday, when I go by the church, I hear you sing something."

Thea obediently sat down on the stool again and began, "COME, YE DISCONSOLATE." Wunsch listened thoughtfully, his hands on his knees. Such a beautiful child's voice! Old Mrs. Kohler's face relaxed in a smile of happiness; she half closed her eyes. A big fly was darting in and out of the window; the sunlight made a golden pool on the rag carpet and bathed the faded cretonne pillows on the lounge, under the piece-picture. "EARTH HAS NO SORROW THAT HEAVEN CANNOT HEAL," the song died away.

"That is a good thing to remember," Wunsch shook himself. "You believe that?" looking quizzically at Thea.

She became confused and pecked nervously at a black key with her middle finger. "I don't know. I guess so," she murmured.

Her teacher rose abruptly. "Remember, for next time, thirds. You ought to get up earlier."

That night the air was so warm that Fritz and Herr Wunsch had their after-supper pipe in the grape arbor, smoking in silence while the sound of fiddles and guitars came across the ravine from Mexican Town. Long after Fritz and his old Paulina had gone to bed, Wunsch sat motionless in the arbor, looking up through the woolly vine leaves at the glittering machinery of heaven.

"LENTE CURRITE, NOCTIS EQUI."

That line awoke many memories. He was thinking of youth; of his own, so long gone by, and of his pupil's, just beginning. He would even have cherished hopes for her, except that he had become superstitious. He believed that whatever he hoped for was destined not to be; that his affection brought ill-fortune, especially to the young; that if he held anything in his thoughts, he harmed it. He had taught in music schools in St. Louis and Kansas City, where the shallowness and complacency of the young misses had maddened him. He had encountered bad manners and bad faith, had been the victim of sharpers of all kinds, was dogged by bad luck. He had played in orchestras that were never paid and wandering opera troupes which disbanded penniless. And there was always the old enemy, more relentless than the others. It was long since he had wished anything or desired anything beyond the necessities of the body. Now that he was tempted to hope for another, he felt alarmed and shook his head.

It was his pupil's power of application, her rugged will, that interested him. He had lived for so long among people whose sole ambition was to get something for nothing that he had learned not to look for seriousness in anything. Now that he by chance encountered it, it recalled standards, ambitions, a society long forgot. What was it she reminded him of? A yellow flower, full of sunlight, perhaps. No; a thin glass full of sweet-smelling, sparkling Moselle wine. He seemed to see such a glass before him in the arbor, to watch the bubbles rising and breaking, like the silent discharge of energy in the nerves and brain, the rapid florescence in young blood--Wunsch felt ashamed and dragged his slippers along the path to the kitchen, his eyes on the ground.

V

The children in the primary grades were sometimes required to make relief maps of Moonstone in sand. Had they used colored sands, as the Navajo medicine men do in their sand mosaics, they could easily have indicated the social classifications of Moonstone, since these conformed to certain topographical boundaries, and every child understood them perfectly.

The main business street ran, of course, through the center of the town. To the west of this street lived all the people who were, as Tillie Kronborg said, "in society." Sylvester Street, the third parallel with Main Street on the west, was the longest in town, and the best dwellings were built along it. Far out at the north end, nearly a mile from the court-house and its cottonwood grove, was Dr. Archie's house, its big yard and garden surrounded by a white paling fence. The Methodist Church was in the center of the town, facing the court-house square. The Kronborgs lived half a mile south of the church, on the long street that stretched out like an arm to the depot settlement. This was the first street west of Main, and was built up only on one side. The preacher's house faced the backs of the brick and frame store buildings and a draw full of sunflowers and scraps of old iron. The sidewalk which ran in front of the Kronborgs' house was the one continuous sidewalk to the depot, and all the train men and roundhouse employees passed the front gate every time they came uptown. Thea and Mrs. Kronborg had many friends among the railroad men, who often paused to chat across the fence, and of one of these we shall have more to say.

In the part of Moonstone that lay east of Main Street, toward the deep ravine which, farther south, wound by Mexican Town, lived all the humbler citizens, the people who voted but did not run for office. The houses were little story-and-a-half cottages, with none of the fussy architectural efforts that marked those on Sylvester Street. They nestled modestly behind their cottonwoods and Virginia creeper; their occupants had no social pretensions to keep up. There were no half-glass front doors with doorbells, or formidable parlors behind closed shutters. Here the old women washed in the back yard, and the men sat in the front doorway and smoked their pipes. The people on Sylvester Street scarcely knew that this part of the town existed. Thea liked to take Thor and her express wagon and explore these quiet, shady streets, where the people never tried to have lawns or to grow elms and pine trees, but let the native timber have its way and spread in luxuriance. She had many friends there, old women who gave her a yellow rose or a spray of trumpet vine and appeased Thor with a cooky or a doughnut. They called Thea "that preacher's girl," but the demonstrative was misplaced, for when they spoke of Mr. Kronborg they called him "the Methodist preacher."

Dr. Archie was very proud of his yard and garden, which he worked himself. He was the only man in Moonstone who was successful at growing rambler roses, and his strawberries were famous. One morning when Thea was downtown on an errand, the doctor stopped her, took her hand and went over her with a quizzical eye, as he nearly always did when they met.

"You haven't been up to my place to get any strawberries yet, Thea. They're at their best just now. Mrs. Archie doesn't know what to do with them all. Come up this afternoon. Just tell Mrs. Archie I sent you. Bring a big basket and pick till you are tired."

When she got home Thea told her mother that she didn't want to go, because she didn't like Mrs. Archie.

"She is certainly one queer woman," Mrs. Kronborg assented, "but he's asked you so often, I guess you'll have to go this time. She won't bite you."

After dinner Thea took a basket, put Thor in his baby buggy, and set out for Dr. Archie's house at the other end of town. As soon as she came within sight of the house, she slackened her pace. She approached it very slowly, stopping often to pick dandelions and sand-peas for Thor to crush up in his fist.

It was his wife's custom, as soon as Dr. Archie left the house in the morning, to shut all the doors and windows to keep the dust out, and to pull down the shades to keep the sun from fading the carpets. She thought, too, that neighbors were less likely to drop in if the house was closed up. She was one of those people who are stingy without motive or reason, even when they can gain nothing by it. She must have known that skimping the doctor in heat and food made him more extravagant than he would have been had she made him comfortable. He never came home for lunch, because she gave him such miserable scraps and shreds of food. No matter how much milk he bought, he could never get thick cream for his strawberries. Even when he watched his wife lift it from the milk in smooth, ivory-colored blankets, she managed, by some sleight-of-hand, to dilute it before it got to the breakfast table. The butcher's favorite joke was about the kind of meat he sold Mrs. Archie. She felt no interest in food herself, and she hated to prepare it. She liked nothing better than to have Dr. Archie go to Denver for a few days--he often went chiefly because he was hungry--and to be left alone to eat canned salmon and to keep the house shut up from morning until night.

Mrs. Archie would not have a servant because, she said, "they ate too much and broke too much"; she even said they knew too much. She used what mind she had in devising shifts to minimize her housework. She used to tell her neighbors that if there were no men, there would be no housework. When Mrs. Archie was first married, she had been always in a panic for fear she would have children. Now that her apprehensions on that score had grown paler, she was almost as much afraid of having dust in the house as she had once been of having children in it. If dust did not get in, it did not have to be got out, she said. She would take any amount of trouble to avoid trouble. Why, nobody knew. Certainly her husband had never been able to make her out. Such little, mean natures are among the darkest and most baffling of created things. There is no law by which they can be explained. The ordinary incentives of pain and pleasure do not account for their behavior. They live like insects, absorbed in petty activities that seem to have nothing to do with any genial aspect of human life.

Mrs. Archie, as Mrs. Kronborg said, "liked to gad." She liked to have her house clean, empty, dark, locked, and to be out of it--anywhere. A church social, a prayer meeting, a ten-cent show; she seemed to have no preference. When there was nowhere else to go, she used to sit for hours in Mrs. Smiley's millinery and notion store, listening to the talk of the women who came in, watching them while they tried on hats, blinking at them from her corner with her sharp, restless little eyes. She never talked much herself, but she knew all the gossip of the town and she had a sharp ear for racy anecdotes--"traveling men's stories," they used to be called in Moonstone. Her clicking laugh sounded like a typewriting machine in action, and, for very pointed stories, she had a little screech.

Mrs. Archie had been Mrs. Archie for only six years, and when she was Belle White she was one of the "pretty" girls in Lansing, Michigan. She had then a train of suitors. She could truly remind Archie that "the boys hung around her." They did. They thought her very spirited and were always saying, "Oh, that Belle White, she's a case!" She used to play heavy practical jokes which the young men thought very clever. Archie was considered the most promising young man in "the young crowd," so Belle selected him. She let him see, made him fully aware, that she had selected him, and Archie was the sort of boy who could not withstand such enlightenment. Belle's family were sorry for him. On his wedding day her sisters looked at the big, handsome boy--he was twenty-four--as he walked down the aisle with his bride, and then they looked at each other. His besotted confidence, his sober, radiant face, his gentle, protecting arm, made them uncomfortable. Well, they were glad that he was going West at once, to fulfill his doom where they would not be onlookers. Anyhow, they consoled themselves, they had got Belle off their hands.

More than that, Belle seemed to have got herself off her hands. Her reputed prettiness must have been entirely the result of determination, of a fierce little ambition. Once she had married, fastened herself on some one, come to port,--it vanished like the ornamental plumage which drops away from some birds after the mating season. The one aggressive action of her life was over. She began to shrink in face and stature. Of her harum-scarum spirit there was nothing left but the little screech. Within a few years she looked as small and mean as she was.

Thor's chariot crept along. Thea approached the house unwillingly. She didn't care about the strawberries, anyhow. She had come only because she did not want to hurt Dr. Archie's feelings. She not only disliked Mrs. Archie, she was a little afraid of her. While Thea was getting the heavy baby-buggy through the iron gate she heard some one call, "Wait a minute!" and Mrs. Archie came running around the house from the back door, her apron over her head. She came to help with the buggy, because she was afraid the wheels might scratch the paint off the gateposts. She was a skinny little woman with a great pile of frizzy light hair on a small head.

"Dr. Archie told me to come up and pick some strawberries," Thea muttered, wishing she had stayed at home.

Mrs. Archie led the way to the back door, squinting and shading her eyes with her hand. "Wait a minute," she said again, when Thea explained why she had come.

She went into her kitchen and Thea sat down on the porch step. When Mrs. Archie reappeared she carried in her hand a little wooden butter-basket trimmed with fringed tissue paper, which she must have brought home from some church supper. "You'll have to have something to put them in," she said, ignoring the yawning willow basket which stood empty on Thor's feet. "You can have this, and you needn't mind about returning it. You know about not trampling the vines, don't you?"

Mrs. Archie went back into the house and Thea leaned over in the sand and picked a few strawberries. As soon as she was sure that she was not going to cry, she tossed the little basket into the big one and ran Thor's buggy along the gravel walk and out of the gate as fast as she could push it. She was angry, and she was ashamed for Dr. Archie. She could not help thinking how uncomfortable he would be if he ever found out about it. Little things like that were the ones that cut him most. She slunk home by the back way, and again almost cried when she told her mother about it.

Mrs. Kronborg was frying doughnuts for her husband's supper. She laughed as she dropped a new lot into the hot grease. "It's wonderful, the way some people are made," she declared. "But I wouldn't let that upset me if I was you. Think what it would be to live with it all the time. You look in the black pocketbook inside my handbag and take a dime and go downtown and get an ice-cream soda. That'll make you feel better. Thor can have a little of the ice-cream if you feed it to him with a spoon. He likes it, don't you, son?" She stooped to wipe his chin. Thor was only six months old and inarticulate, but it was quite true that he liked ice-cream.

VI

Seen from a balloon, Moonstone would have looked like a Noah's ark town set out in the sand and lightly shaded by gray-green tamarisks and cottonwoods. A few people were trying to make soft maples grow in their turfed lawns, but the fashion of planting incongruous trees from the North Atlantic States had not become general then, and the frail, brightly painted desert town was shaded by the light-reflecting, wind-loving trees of the desert, whose roots are always seeking water and whose leaves are always talking about it, making the sound of rain. The long porous roots of the cottonwood are irrepressible. They break into the wells as rats do into granaries, and thieve the water.

The long street which connected Moonstone with the depot settlement traversed in its course a considerable stretch of rough open country, staked out in lots but not built up at all, a weedy hiatus between the town and the railroad. When you set out along this street to go to the station, you noticed that the houses became smaller and farther apart, until they ceased altogether, and the board sidewalk continued its uneven course through sunflower patches, until you reached the solitary, new brick Catholic Church. The church stood there because the land was given to the parish by the man who owned the adjoining waste lots, in the hope of making them more salable--"Farrier's Addition," this patch of prairie was called in the clerk's office. An eighth of a mile beyond the church was a washout, a deep sand-gully, where the board sidewalk became a bridge for perhaps fifty feet. Just beyond the gully was old Uncle Billy Beemer's grove,--twelve town lots set out in fine, well-grown cottonwood trees, delightful to look upon, or to listen to, as they swayed and rippled in the wind. Uncle Billy had been one of the most worthless old drunkards who ever sat on a store box and told filthy stories. One night he played hide-and-seek with a switch engine and got his sodden brains knocked out. But his grove, the one creditable thing he had ever done in his life, rustled on. Beyond this grove the houses of the depot settlement began, and the naked board walk, that had run in out of the sunflowers, again became a link between human dwellings.

One afternoon, late in the summer, Dr. Howard Archie was fighting his way back to town along this walk through a blinding sandstorm, a silk handkerchief tied over his mouth. He had been to see a sick woman down in the depot settlement, and he was walking because his ponies had been out for a hard drive that morning.

As he passed the Catholic Church he came upon Thea and Thor. Thea was sitting in a child's express wagon, her feet out behind, kicking the wagon along and steering by the tongue. Thor was on her lap and she held him with one arm. He had grown to be a big cub of a baby, with a constitutional grievance, and he had to be continually amused. Thea took him philosophically, and tugged and pulled him about, getting as much fun as she could under her encumbrance. Her hair was blowing about her face, and her eyes were squinting so intently at the uneven board sidewalk in front of her that she did not see the doctor until he spoke to her.

"Look out, Thea. You'll steer that youngster into the ditch."

The wagon stopped. Thea released the tongue, wiped her hot, sandy face, and pushed back her hair. "Oh, no, I won't! I never ran off but once, and then he didn't get anything but a bump. He likes this better than a baby buggy, and so do I."

"Are you going to kick that cart all the way home?"

"Of course. We take long trips; wherever there is a sidewalk. It's no good on the road."

"Looks to me like working pretty hard for your fun. Are you going to be busy to-night? Want to make a call with me? Spanish Johnny's come home again, all used up. His wife sent me word this morning, and I said I'd go over to see him to-night. He's an old chum of yours, isn't he?"

"Oh, I'm glad. She's been crying her eyes out. When did he come?"

"Last night, on Number Six. Paid his fare, they tell me. Too sick to beat it. There'll come a time when that boy won't get back, I'm afraid. Come around to my office about eight o'clock,--and you needn't bring that!"

Thor seemed to understand that he had been insulted, for he scowled and began to kick the side of the wagon, shouting, "Go-go, go-go!" Thea leaned forward and grabbed the wagon tongue. Dr. Archie stepped in front of her and blocked the way. "Why don't you make him wait? What do you let him boss you like that for?"

"If he gets mad he throws himself, and then I can't do anything with him. When he's mad he's lots stronger than me, aren't you, Thor?" Thea spoke with pride, and the idol was appeased. He grunted approvingly as his sister began to kick rapidly behind her, and the wagon rattled off and soon disappeared in the flying currents of sand.

That evening Dr. Archie was seated in his office, his desk chair tilted back, reading by the light of a hot coal-oil lamp. All the windows were open, but the night was breathless after the sandstorm, and his hair was moist where it hung over his forehead. He was deeply engrossed in his book and sometimes smiled thoughtfully as he read. When Thea Kronborg entered quietly and slipped into a seat, he nodded, finished his paragraph, inserted a bookmark, and rose to put the book back into the case. It was one out of the long row of uniform volumes on the top shelf.

"Nearly every time I come in, when you're alone, you're reading one of those books," Thea remarked thoughtfully. "They must be very nice."

The doctor dropped back into his swivel chair, the mottled volume still in his hand. "They aren't exactly books, Thea," he said seriously. "They're a city."

"A history, you mean?"

"Yes, and no. They're a history of a live city, not a dead one. A Frenchman undertook to write about a whole cityful of people, all the kinds he knew. And he got them nearly all in, I guess. Yes, it's very interesting. You'll like to read it some day, when you're grown up."

Thea leaned forward and made out the title on the back, "A Distinguished Provincial in Paris."

"It doesn't sound very interesting."

"Perhaps not, but it is." The doctor scrutinized her broad face, low enough to be in the direct light from under the green lamp shade. "Yes," he went on with some satisfaction, "I think you'll like them some day. You're always curious about people, and I expect this man knew more about people than anybody that ever lived."

"City people or country people?"

"Both. People are pretty much the same everywhere."

"Oh, no, they're not. The people who go through in the dining-car aren't like us."

"What makes you think they aren't, my girl? Their clothes?"

Thea shook her head. "No, it's something else. I don't know." Her eyes shifted under the doctor's searching gaze and she glanced up at the row of books. "How soon will I be old enough to read them?"

"Soon enough, soon enough, little girl." The doctor patted her hand and looked at her index finger. "The nail's coming all right, isn't it? But I think that man makes you practice too much. You have it on your mind all the time." He had noticed that when she talked to him she was always opening and shutting her hands. "It makes you nervous."

"No, he don't," Thea replied stubbornly, watching Dr. Archie return the book to its niche.

He took up a black leather case, put on his hat, and they went down the dark stairs into the street. The summer moon hung full in the sky. For the time being, it was the great fact in the world. Beyond the edge of the town the plain was so white that every clump of sage stood out distinct from the sand, and the dunes looked like a shining lake. The doctor took off his straw hat and carried it in his hand as they walked toward Mexican Town, across the sand.

North of Pueblo, Mexican settlements were rare in Colorado then. This one had come about accidentally. Spanish Johnny was the first Mexican who came to Moonstone. He was a painter and decorator, and had been working in Trinidad, when Ray Kennedy told him there was a "boom" on in Moonstone, and a good many new buildings were going up. A year after Johnny settled in Moonstone, his cousin, Famos Serrenos, came to work in the brickyard; then Serrenos' cousins came to help him. During the strike, the master mechanic put a gang of Mexicans to work in the roundhouse. The Mexicans had arrived so quietly, with their blankets and musical instruments, that before Moonstone was awake to the fact, there was a Mexican quarter; a dozen families or more.

As Thea and the doctor approached the 'dobe houses, they heard a guitar, and a rich barytone voice--that of Famos Serrenos--singing "La Golandrina." All the Mexican houses had neat little yards, with tamarisk hedges and flowers, and walks bordered with shells or whitewashed stones. Johnny's house was dark. His wife, Mrs. Tellamantez, was sitting on the doorstep, combing her long, blue-black hair. (Mexican women are like the Spartans; when they are in trouble, in love, under stress of any kind, they comb and comb their hair.) She rose without embarrassment or apology, comb in hand, and greeted the doctor.

"Good-evening; will you go in?" she asked in a low, musical voice. "He is in the back room. I will make a light." She followed them indoors, lit a candle and handed it to the doctor, pointing toward the bedroom. Then she went back and sat down on her doorstep.

Dr. Archie and Thea went into the bedroom, which was dark and quiet. There was a bed in the corner, and a man was lying on the clean sheets. On the table beside him was a glass pitcher, half-full of water. Spanish Johnny looked younger than his wife, and when he was in health he was very handsome: slender, gold-colored, with wavy black hair, a round, smooth throat, white teeth, and burning black eyes. His profile was strong and severe, like an Indian's. What was termed his "wildness" showed itself only in his feverish eyes and in the color that burned on his tawny cheeks. That night he was a coppery green, and his eyes were like black holes. He opened them when the doctor held the candle before his face.

"MI TESTA!" he muttered, "MI TESTA," doctor. "LA FIEBRE!" Seeing the doctor's companion at the foot of the bed, he attempted a smile. "MUCHACHA!" he exclaimed deprecatingly.

Dr. Archie stuck a thermometer into his mouth. "Now, Thea, you can run outside and wait for me."

Thea slipped noiselessly through the dark house and joined Mrs. Tellamantez. The somber Mexican woman did not seem inclined to talk, but her nod was friendly. Thea sat down on the warm sand, her back to the moon, facing Mrs. Tellamantez on her doorstep, and began to count the moon flowers on the vine that ran over the house. Mrs. Tellamantez was always considered a very homely woman. Her face was of a strongly marked type not sympathetic to Americans. Such long, oval faces, with a full chin, a large, mobile mouth, a high nose, are not uncommon in Spain. Mrs. Tellamantez could not write her name, and could read but little. Her strong nature lived upon itself. She was chiefly known in Moonstone for her forbearance with her incorrigible husband.

Nobody knew exactly what was the matter with Johnny, and everybody liked him. His popularity would have been unusual for a white man, for a Mexican it was unprecedented. His talents were his undoing. He had a high, uncertain tenor voice, and he played the mandolin with exceptional skill. Periodically he went crazy. There was no other way to explain his behavior. He was a clever workman, and, when he worked, as regular and faithful as a burro. Then some night he would fall in with a crowd at the saloon and begin to sing. He would go on until he had no voice left, until he wheezed and rasped. Then he would play his mandolin furiously, and drink until his eyes sank back into his head. At last, when he was put out of the saloon at closing time, and could get nobody to listen to him, he would run away--along the railroad track, straight across the desert. He always managed to get aboard a freight somewhere. Once beyond Denver, he played his way southward from saloon to saloon until he got across the border. He never wrote to his wife; but she would soon begin to get newspapers from La Junta, Albuquerque, Chihuahua, with marked paragraphs announcing that Juan Tellamantez and his wonderful mandolin could be heard at the Jack Rabbit Grill, or the Pearl of Cadiz Saloon. Mrs. Tellamantez waited and wept and combed her hair. When he was completely wrung out and burned up,--all but destroyed,--her Juan always came back to her to be taken care of,--once with an ugly knife wound in the neck, once with a finger missing from his right hand,--but he played just as well with three fingers as he had with four.

Public sentiment was lenient toward Johnny, but everybody was disgusted with Mrs. Tellamantez for putting up with him. She ought to discipline him, people said; she ought to leave him; she had no self-respect. In short, Mrs. Tellamantez got all the blame. Even Thea thought she was much too humble. To-night, as she sat with her back to the moon, looking at the moon flowers and Mrs. Tellamantez's somber face, she was thinking that there is nothing so sad in the world as that kind of patience and resignation. It was much worse than Johnny's craziness. She even wondered whether it did not help to make Johnny crazy. People had no right to be so passive and resigned. She would like to roll over and over in the sand and screech at Mrs. Tellamantez. She was glad when the doctor came out.

The Mexican woman rose and stood respectful and expectant. The doctor held his hat in his hand and looked kindly at her.

"Same old thing, Mrs. Tellamantez. He's no worse than he's been before. I've left some medicine. Don't give him anything but toast water until I see him again. You're a good nurse; you'll get him out." Dr. Archie smiled encouragingly. He glanced about the little garden and wrinkled his brows. "I can't see what makes him behave so. He's killing himself, and he's not a rowdy sort of fellow. Can't you tie him up someway? Can't you tell when these fits are coming on?"

Mrs. Tellamantez put her hand to her forehead. "The saloon, doctor, the excitement; that is what makes him. People listen to him, and it excites him."

The doctor shook his head. "Maybe. He's too much for my calculations. I don't see what he gets out of it."

"He is always fooled,"--the Mexican woman spoke rapidly and tremulously, her long under lip quivering.

"He is good at heart, but he has no head. He fools himself. You do not understand in this country, you are progressive. But he has no judgment, and he is fooled." She stooped quickly, took up one of the white conch-shells that bordered the walk, and, with an apologetic inclination of her head, held it to Dr. Archie's ear. "Listen, doctor. You hear something in there? You hear the sea; and yet the sea is very far from here. You have judgment, and you know that. But he is fooled. To him, it is the sea itself. A little thing is big to him." She bent and placed the shell in the white row, with its fellows. Thea took it up softly and pressed it to her own ear. The sound in it startled her; it was like something calling one. So that was why Johnny ran away. There was something awe-inspiring about Mrs. Tellamantez and her shell.

Thea caught Dr. Archie's hand and squeezed it hard as she skipped along beside him back toward Moonstone. She went home, and the doctor went back to his lamp and his book. He never left his office until after midnight. If he did not play whist or pool in the evening, he read. It had become a habit with him to lose himself.

VII

Thea's twelfth birthday had passed a few weeks before her memorable call upon Mrs. Tellamantez. There was a worthy man in Moonstone who was already planning to marry Thea as soon as she should be old enough. His name was

Ray Kennedy, his age was thirty, and he was conductor on a freight train, his run being from Moonstone to Denver. Ray was a big fellow, with a square, open American face, a rock chin, and features that one would never happen to remember. He was an aggressive idealist, a freethinker, and, like most railroad men, deeply sentimental. Thea liked him for reasons that had to do with the adventurous life he had led in Mexico and the Southwest, rather than for anything very personal. She liked him, too, because he was the only one of her friends who ever took her to the sand hills. The sand hills were a constant tantalization; she loved them better than anything near Moonstone, and yet she could so seldom get to them. The first dunes were accessible enough; they were only a few miles beyond the Kohlers', and she could run out there any day when she could do her practicing in the morning and get Thor off her hands for an afternoon. But the real hills--the Turquoise Hills, the Mexicans called them--were ten good miles away, and one reached them by a heavy, sandy road. Dr. Archie sometimes took Thea on his long drives, but as nobody lived in the sand hills, he never had calls to make in that direction. Ray Kennedy was her only hope of getting there.

This summer Thea had not been to the hills once, though Ray had planned several Sunday expeditions. Once Thor was sick, and once the organist in her father's church was away and Thea had to play the organ for the three Sunday services. But on the first Sunday in September, Ray drove up to the Kronborgs' front gate at nine o'clock in the morning and the party actually set off. Gunner and Axel went with Thea, and Ray had asked Spanish Johnny to come and to bring Mrs. Tellamantez and his mandolin. Ray was artlessly fond of music, especially of Mexican music. He and Mrs. Tellamantez had got up the lunch between them, and they were to make coffee in the desert.

When they left Mexican Town, Thea was on the front seat with Ray and Johnny, and Gunner and Axel sat behind with Mrs. Tellamantez. They objected to this, of course, but there were some things about which Thea would have her own way. "As stubborn as a Finn," Mrs. Kronborg sometimes said of her, quoting an old Swedish saying. When they passed the Kohlers', old Fritz and Wunsch were cutting grapes at the arbor. Thea gave them a businesslike nod. Wunsch came to the gate and looked after them. He divined Ray Kennedy's hopes, and he distrusted every expedition that led away from the piano. Unconsciously he made Thea pay for frivolousness of this sort.

As Ray Kennedy's party followed the faint road across the sagebrush, they heard behind them the sound of church bells, which gave them a sense of escape and boundless freedom. Every rabbit that shot across the path, every sage hen that flew up by the trail, was like a runaway thought, a message that one sent into the desert. As they went farther, the illusion of the mirage became more instead of less convincing; a shallow silver lake that spread for many miles, a little misty in the sunlight. Here and there one saw reflected the image of a heifer, turned loose to live upon the sparse sand-grass. They were magnified to a preposterous height and looked like mammoths, prehistoric beasts standing solitary in the waters that for many thousands of years actually washed over that desert;--the mirage itself may be the ghost of that long-vanished sea. Beyond the phantom lake lay the line of many-colored hills; rich, sun-baked yellow, glowing turquoise, lavender, purple; all the open, pastel colors of the desert.

After the first five miles the road grew heavier. The horses had to slow down to a walk and the wheels sank deep into the sand, which now lay in long ridges, like waves, where the last high wind had drifted it. Two hours brought the party to Pedro's Cup, named for a Mexican desperado who had once held the sheriff at bay there. The Cup was a great amphitheater, cut out in the hills, its floor smooth and packed hard, dotted with sagebrush and greasewood.

On either side of the Cup the yellow hills ran north and south, with winding ravines between them, full of soft sand which drained down from the crumbling banks. On the surface of this fluid sand, one could find bits of brilliant stone, crystals and agates and onyx, and petrified wood as red as blood. Dried toads and lizards were to be found there, too. Birds, decomposing more rapidly, left only feathered skeletons.

After a little reconnoitering, Mrs. Tellamantez declared that it was time for lunch, and Ray took his hatchet and began to cut greasewood, which burns fiercely in its green state. The little boys dragged the bushes to the spot that Mrs. Tellamantez had chosen for her fire. Mexican women like to cook out of doors.

After lunch Thea sent Gunner and Axel to hunt for agates. "If you see a rattlesnake, run. Don't try to kill it," she enjoined.

Gunner hesitated. "If Ray would let me take the hatchet, I could kill one all right."

Mrs. Tellamantez smiled and said something to Johnny in Spanish.

"Yes," her husband replied, translating, "they say in Mexico, kill a snake but never hurt his feelings. Down in the hot country, MUCHACHA," turning to Thea, "people keep a pet snake in the house to kill rats and mice. They call him the house snake. They keep a little mat for him by the fire, and at night he curl up there and sit with the family, just as friendly!"

Gunner sniffed with disgust. "Well, I think that's a dirty Mexican way to keep house; so there!"

Johnny shrugged his shoulders. "Perhaps," he muttered. A Mexican learns to dive below insults or soar above them, after he crosses the border.

By this time the south wall of the amphitheater cast a narrow shelf of shadow, and the party withdrew to this refuge. Ray and Johnny began to talk about the Grand Canyon and Death Valley, two places much shrouded in mystery in those days, and Thea listened intently. Mrs. Tellamantez took out her drawn-work and pinned it to her knee. Ray could talk well about the large part of the continent over which he had been knocked about, and Johnny was appreciative.

"You been all over, pretty near. Like a Spanish boy," he commented respectfully.

Ray, who had taken off his coat, whetted his pocketknife thoughtfully on the sole of his shoe. "I began to browse around early. I had a mind to see something of this world, and I ran away from home before I was twelve. Rustled for myself ever since."

"Ran away?" Johnny looked hopeful. "What for?"

"Couldn't make it go with my old man, and didn't take to farming. There were plenty of boys at home. I wasn't missed."

Thea wriggled down in the hot sand and rested her chin on her arm. "Tell Johnny about the melons, Ray, please do!"

Ray's solid, sunburned cheeks grew a shade redder, and he looked reproachfully at Thea. "You're stuck on that story, kid. You like to get the laugh on me, don't you? That was the finishing split I had with my old man, John. He had a claim along the creek, not far from Denver, and raised a little garden stuff for market. One day he had a load of melons and he decided to take 'em to town and sell 'em along the street, and he made me go along and drive for him. Denver wasn't the queen city it is now, by any means, but it seemed a terrible big place to me; and when we got there, if he didn't make me drive right up Capitol Hill! Pap got out and stopped at folkses houses to ask if they didn't want to buy any melons, and I was to drive along slow. The farther I went the madder I got, but I was trying to look unconscious, when the end-gate came loose and one of the melons fell out and squashed. Just then a swell girl, all dressed up, comes out of one of the big houses and calls out, `Hello, boy, you're losing your melons!' Some dudes on the other side of the street took their hats off to her and began to laugh. I couldn't stand it any longer. I grabbed the whip and lit into that team, and they tore up the hill like jack-rabbits, them damned melons bouncing out the back every jump, the old man cussin' an' yellin' behind and everybody laughin'. I never looked behind, but the whole of Capitol Hill must have been a mess with them squashed melons. I didn't stop the team till I got out of sight of town. Then I pulled up an' left 'em with a rancher I was acquainted with, and I never went home to get the lickin' that was waitin' for me. I expect it's waitin' for me yet."

Thea rolled over in the sand. "Oh, I wish I could have seen those melons fly, Ray! I'll never see anything as funny as that. Now, tell Johnny about your first job."

Ray had a collection of good stories. He was observant, truthful, and kindly--perhaps the chief requisites in a good story-teller. Occasionally he used newspaper phrases, conscientiously learned in his efforts at self-instruction, but when he talked naturally he was always worth listening to. Never having had any schooling to speak of, he had, almost from the time he first ran away, tried to make good his loss. As a sheep-herder he had worried an old grammar to tatters, and read instructive books with the help of a pocket dictionary. By the light of many camp-fires he had pondered upon Prescott's histories, and the works of Washington Irving, which he bought at a high price from a book-agent. Mathematics and physics were easy for him, but general culture came hard, and he was determined to get it. Ray was a freethinker, and inconsistently believed himself damned for being one. When he was braking, down on the Santa Fe, at the end of his run he used to climb into the upper bunk of the caboose, while a noisy gang played poker about the stove below him, and by the roof-lamp read Robert Ingersoll's speeches and "The Age of Reason."

Ray was a loyal-hearted fellow, and it had cost him a great deal to give up his God. He was one of the stepchildren of Fortune, and he had very little to show for all his hard work; the other fellow always got the best of it. He had come in too late, or too early, on several schemes that had made money. He brought with him from all his wanderings a good deal of information (more or less correct in itself, but unrelated, and therefore misleading), a high standard of personal honor, a sentimental veneration for all women, bad as well as good, and a bitter hatred of Englishmen. Thea often thought that the nicest thing about Ray was his love for Mexico and the Mexicans, who had been kind to him when he drifted, a homeless boy, over the border. In Mexico, Ray was Senor Ken-ay-dy, and when he answered to that name he was somehow a different fellow. He spoke Spanish fluently, and the sunny warmth of that tongue kept him from being quite as hard as his chin, or as narrow as his popular science.

While Ray was smoking his cigar, he and Johnny fell to talking about the great fortunes that had been made in the Southwest, and about fellows they knew who had "struck it rich."

"I guess you been in on some big deals down there?" Johnny asked trustfully.

Ray smiled and shook his head. "I've been out on some, John. I've never been exactly in on any. So far, I've either held on too long or let go too soon. But mine's coming to me, all right." Ray looked reflective. He leaned back in the shadow and dug out a rest for his elbow in the sand. "The narrowest escape I ever had, was in the Bridal Chamber. If I hadn't let go there, it would have made me rich. That was a close call."

Johnny looked delighted. "You don' say! She was silver mine, I guess?"

"I guess she was! Down at Lake Valley. I put up a few hundred for the prospector, and he gave me a bunch of stock. Before we'd got anything out of it, my brother-in-law died of the fever in Cuba. My sister was beside herself to get his body back to Colorado to bury him. Seemed foolish to me, but she's the only sister I got. It's expensive for dead folks to travel, and I had to sell my stock in the mine to raise the money to get Elmer on the move. Two months afterward, the boys struck that big pocket in the rock, full of virgin silver. They named her the Bridal Chamber. It wasn't ore, you remember. It was pure, soft metal you could have melted right down into dollars. The boys cut it out with chisels. If old Elmer hadn't played that trick on me, I'd have been in for about fifty thousand. That was a close call, Spanish."

"I recollec'. When the pocket gone, the town go bust."

"You bet. Higher'n a kite. There was no vein, just a pocket in the rock that had sometime or another got filled up with molten silver. You'd think there would be more somewhere about, but NADA. There's fools digging holes in that mountain yet."

When Ray had finished his cigar, Johnny took his mandolin and began Kennedy's favorite, "Ultimo Amor." It was now three o'clock in the afternoon, the hottest hour in the day. The narrow shelf of shadow had widened until the floor of the amphitheater was marked off in two halves, one glittering yellow, and one purple. The little boys had come back and were making a robbers' cave to enact the bold deeds of Pedro the bandit. Johnny, stretched gracefully on the sand, passed from "Ultimo Amor" to "Fluvia de Oro," and then to "Noches de Algeria," playing languidly.

Every one was busy with his own thoughts. Mrs. Tellamantez was thinking of the square in the little town in which she was born; of the white church steps, with people genuflecting as they passed, and the round-topped acacia trees, and the band playing in the plaza. Ray Kennedy was thinking of the future, dreaming the large Western dream of easy money, of a fortune kicked up somewhere in the hills,--an oil well, a gold mine, a ledge of copper. He always told himself, when he accepted a cigar from a newly married railroad man, that he knew enough not to marry until he had found his ideal, and could keep her like a queen. He believed that in the yellow head over there in the sand he had found his ideal, and that by the time she was old enough to marry, he would be able to keep her like a queen. He would kick it up from somewhere, when he got loose from the railroad.

Thea, stirred by tales of adventure, of the Grand Canyon and Death Valley, was recalling a great adventure of her own. Early in the summer her father had been invited to conduct a reunion of old frontiersmen, up in Wyoming, near Laramie, and he took Thea along with him to play the organ and sing patriotic songs. There they stayed at the house of an old ranchman who told them about a ridge up in the hills called Laramie Plain, where the wagon-trails of the Forty-niners and the Mormons were still visible. The old man even volunteered to take Mr. Kronborg up into the hills to see this place, though it was a very long drive to make in one day. Thea had begged frantically to go along, and the old rancher, flattered by her rapt attention to his stories, had interceded for her.

They set out from Laramie before daylight, behind a strong team of mules. All the way there was much talk of the Forty-niners. The old rancher had been a teamster in a freight train that used to crawl back and forth across the plains between Omaha and Cherry Creek, as Denver was then called, and he had met many a wagon train bound for California. He told of Indians and buffalo, thirst and slaughter, wanderings in snowstorms, and lonely graves in the desert.

The road they followed was a wild and beautiful one. It led up and up, by granite rocks and stunted pines, around deep ravines and echoing gorges. The top of the ridge, when they reached it, was a great flat plain, strewn with white boulders, with the wind howling over it. There was not one trail, as Thea had expected; there were a score; deep furrows, cut in the earth by heavy wagon wheels, and now grown over with dry, whitish grass. The furrows ran side by side; when one trail had been worn too deep, the next party had abandoned it and made a new trail to the right or left. They were, indeed, only old wagon ruts, running east and west, and grown over with grass. But as Thea ran about among the white stones, her skirts blowing this way and that, the wind brought to her eyes tears that might have come anyway. The old rancher picked up an iron ox-shoe from one of the furrows and gave it to her for a keepsake. To the west one could see range after range of blue mountains, and at last the snowy range, with its white, windy peaks, the clouds caught here and there on their spurs. Again and again Thea had to hide her face from the cold for a moment. The wind never slept on this plain, the old man said. Every little while eagles flew over.

Coming up from Laramie, the old man had told them that he was in Brownsville, Nebraska, when the first telegraph wires were put across the Missouri River, and that the first message that ever crossed the river was "Westward the course of Empire takes its way." He had been in the room when the instrument began to click, and all the men there had, without thinking what they were doing, taken off their hats, waiting bareheaded to hear the message translated. Thea remembered that message when she sighted down the wagon tracks toward the blue mountains. She told herself she would never, never forget it. The spirit of human courage seemed to live up there with the eagles. For long after, when she was moved by a Fourth-of-July oration, or a band, or a circus parade, she was apt to remember that windy ridge.

To-day she went to sleep while she was thinking about it. When Ray wakened her, the horses were hitched to the wagon and Gunner and Axel were begging for a place on the front seat. The air had cooled, the sun was setting, and the desert was on fire. Thea contentedly took the back seat with Mrs. Tellamantez. As they drove homeward the stars began to come out, pale yellow in a yellow sky, and Ray and Johnny began to sing one of those railroad ditties that are usually born on the Southern Pacific and run the length of the Santa Fe and the "Q" system before they die to give place to a new one. This was a song about a Greaser dance, the refrain being something like this:--

"Pedro, Pedro, swing high, swing low, And it's allamand left again; For there's boys that's bold and there's some that's cold, But the gold boys come from Spain, Oh, the gold boys come from Spain!"

VIII

Winter was long in coming that year. Throughout October the days were bathed in sunlight and the air was clear as crystal. The town kept its cheerful summer aspect, the desert glistened with light, the sand hills every day went through magical changes of color. The scarlet sage bloomed late in the front yards, the cottonwood leaves were bright gold long before they fell, and it was not until November that the green on the tamarisks began to cloud and fade. There was a flurry of snow about Thanksgiving, and then December came on warm and clear.

Thea had three music pupils now, little girls whose mothers declared that Professor Wunsch was "much too severe." They took their lessons on Saturday, and this, of course, cut down her time for play. She did not really mind this because she was allowed to use the money--her pupils paid her twenty-five cents a lesson--to fit up a little room for herself upstairs in the half-story. It was the end room of the wing, and was not plastered, but was snugly lined with soft pine. The ceiling was so low that a grown person could reach it with the palm of the hand, and it sloped down on either side. There was only one window, but it was a double one and went to the floor. In October, while the days were still warm, Thea and Tillie papered the room, walls and ceiling in the same paper, small red and brown roses on a yellowish ground. Thea bought a brown cotton carpet, and her big brother, Gus, put it down for her one Sunday. She made white cheesecloth curtains and hung them on a tape. Her mother gave her an old walnut dresser with a broken mirror, and she had her own dumpy walnut single bed, and a blue washbowl and pitcher which she had drawn at a church fair lottery. At the head of her bed she had a tall round wooden hat-crate, from the clothing store. This, standing on end and draped with cretonne, made a fairly steady table for her lantern. She was not allowed to take a lamp upstairs, so Ray Kennedy gave her a railroad lantern by which she could read at night.

In winter this loft room of Thea's was bitterly cold, but against her mother's advice--and Tillie's--she always left her window open a little way. Mrs. Kronborg declared that she "had no patience with American physiology," though the lessons about the injurious effects of alcohol and tobacco were well enough for the boys. Thea asked Dr. Archie about the window, and he told her that a girl who sang must always have plenty of fresh air, or her voice would get husky, and that the cold would harden her throat. The important thing, he said, was to keep your feet warm. On very cold nights Thea always put a brick in the oven after supper, and when she went upstairs she wrapped it in an old flannel petticoat and put it in her bed. The boys, who would never heat bricks for themselves, sometimes carried off Thea's, and thought it a good joke to get ahead of her.

When Thea first plunged in between her red blankets, the cold sometimes kept her awake for a good while, and she comforted herself by remembering all she could of "Polar Explorations," a fat, calf-bound volume her father had bought from a book-agent, and by thinking about the members of Greely's party: how they lay in their frozen sleeping-bags, each man hoarding the warmth of his own body and trying to make it last as long as possible against the on-coming cold that would be everlasting. After half an hour or so, a warm wave crept over her body and round, sturdy legs; she glowed like a little stove with the warmth of her own blood, and the heavy quilts and red blankets grew warm wherever they touched her, though her breath sometimes froze on the coverlid. Before daylight, her internal fires went down a little, and she often wakened to find herself drawn up into a tight ball, somewhat stiff in the legs. But that made it all the easier to get up.

The acquisition of this room was the beginning of a new era in Thea's life. It was one of the most important things that ever happened to her. Hitherto, except in summer, when she could be out of doors, she had lived in constant turmoil; the family, the day school, the Sunday-School. The clamor about her drowned the voice within herself. In the end of the wing, separated from the other upstairs sleeping-rooms by a long, cold, unfinished lumber room, her mind worked better. She thought things out more clearly. Pleasant plans and ideas occurred to her which had never come before. She had certain thoughts which were like companions, ideas which were like older and wiser friends. She left them there in the morning, when she finished dressing in the cold, and at night, when she came up with her lantern and shut the door after a busy day, she found them awaiting her. There was no possible way of heating the room, but that was fortunate, for otherwise it would have been occupied by one of her older brothers.

From the time when she moved up into the wing, Thea began to live a double life. During the day, when the hours were full of tasks, she was one of the Kronborg children, but at night she was a different person. On Friday and Saturday nights she always read for a long while after she was in bed. She had no clock, and there was no one to nag her.

Ray Kennedy, on his way from the depot to his boardinghouse, often looked up and saw Thea's light burning when the rest of the house was dark, and felt cheered as by a friendly greeting. He was a faithful soul, and many disappointments had not changed his nature. He was still, at heart, the same boy who, when he was sixteen, had settled down to freeze with his sheep in a Wyoming blizzard, and had been rescued only to play the losing game of fidelity to other charges.

Ray had no very clear idea of what might be going on in Thea's head, but he knew that something was. He used to remark to Spanish Johnny, "That girl is developing something fine." Thea was patient with Ray, even in regard to the liberties he took with her name. Outside the family, every one in Moonstone, except Wunsch and Dr. Archie, called her "Thee-a," but this seemed cold and distant to Ray, so he called her "Thee." Once, in a moment of exasperation, Thea asked him why he did this, and he explained that he once had a chum, Theodore, whose name was always abbreviated thus, and that since he was killed down on the Santa Fe, it seemed natural to call somebody "Thee." Thea sighed and submitted. She was always helpless before homely sentiment and usually changed the subject.

It was the custom for each of the different Sunday Schools in Moonstone to give a concert on Christmas Eve. But this year all the churches were to unite and give, as was announced from the pulpits, "a semi-sacred concert of picked talent" at the opera house. The Moonstone Orchestra, under the direction of Professor Wunsch, was to play, and the most talented members of each Sunday School were to take part in the programme. Thea was put down by the committee "for instrumental." This made her indignant, for the vocal numbers were always more popular. Thea went to the president of the committee and demanded hotly if her rival, Lily Fisher, were going to sing. The president was a big, florid, powdered woman, a fierce W.C.T.U. worker, one of Thea's natural enemies. Her name was Johnson; her husband kept the livery stable, and she was called Mrs. Livery Johnson, to distinguish her from other families of the same surname. Mrs. Johnson was a prominent Baptist, and Lily Fisher was the Baptist prodigy. There was a not very Christian rivalry between the Baptist Church and Mr. Kronborg's church.

When Thea asked Mrs. Johnson whether her rival was to be allowed to sing, Mrs. Johnson, with an eagerness which told how she had waited for this moment, replied that "Lily was going to recite to be obliging, and to give other children a chance to sing." As she delivered this thrust, her eyes glittered more than the Ancient Mariner's, Thea thought. Mrs. Johnson disapproved of the way in which Thea was being brought up, of a child whose chosen associates were Mexicans and sinners, and who was, as she pointedly put it, "bold with men." She so enjoyed an opportunity to rebuke Thea, that, tightly corseted as she was, she could scarcely control her breathing, and her lace and her gold watch chain rose and fell "with short, uneasy motion." Frowning, Thea turned away and walked slowly homeward. She suspected guile. Lily Fisher was the most stuck-up doll in the world, and it was certainly not like her to recite to be obliging. Nobody who could sing ever recited, because the warmest applause always went to the singers.

However, when the programme was printed in the Moonstone GLEAM, there it was: "Instrumental solo, Thea Kronborg. Recitation, Lily Fisher."

Because his orchestra was to play for the concert, Mr. Wunsch imagined that he had been put in charge of the music, and he became arrogant. He insisted that Thea should play a "Ballade" by Reinecke. When Thea consulted her mother, Mrs. Kronborg agreed with her that the "Ballade" would "never take" with a Moonstone audience. She advised Thea to play "something with variations," or, at least, "The Invitation to the Dance."

"It makes no matter what they like," Wunsch replied to Thea's entreaties. "It is time already that they learn something."

Thea's fighting powers had been impaired by an ulcerated tooth and consequent loss of sleep, so she gave in. She finally had the molar pulled, though it was a second tooth and should have been saved. The dentist was a clumsy, ignorant country boy, and Mr. Kronborg would not hear of Dr. Archie's taking Thea to a dentist in Denver, though Ray Kennedy said he could get a pass for her. What with the pain of the tooth, and family discussions about it, with trying to make Christmas presents and to keep up her school work and practicing, and giving lessons on Saturdays, Thea was fairly worn out.

On Christmas Eve she was nervous and excited. It was the first time she had ever played in the opera house, and she had never before had to face so many people. Wunsch would not let her play with her notes, and she was afraid of forgetting. Before the concert began, all the participants had to assemble on the stage and sit there to be looked at. Thea wore her white summer dress and a blue sash, but Lily Fisher had a new pink silk, trimmed with white swansdown.

The hall was packed. It seemed as if every one in Moonstone was there, even Mrs. Kohler, in her hood, and old Fritz. The seats were wooden kitchen chairs, numbered, and nailed to long planks which held them together in rows. As the floor was not raised, the chairs were all on the same level. The more interested persons in the audience peered over the heads of the people in front of them to get a good view of the stage. From the platform Thea picked out many friendly faces. There was Dr. Archie, who never went to church entertainments; there was the friendly jeweler who ordered her music for her,--he sold accordions and guitars as well as watches,--and the druggist who often lent her books, and her favorite teacher from the school. There was Ray Kennedy, with a party of freshly barbered railroad men he had brought along with him. There was Mrs. Kronborg with all the children, even Thor, who had been brought out in a new white plush coat. At the back of the hall sat a little group of Mexicans, and among them Thea caught the gleam of Spanish Johnny's white teeth, and of Mrs. Tellamantez's lustrous, smoothly coiled black hair.

After the orchestra played "Selections from Erminie," and the Baptist preacher made a long prayer, Tillie Kronborg came on with a highly colored recitation, "The Polish Boy." When it was over every one breathed more freely. No committee had the courage to leave Tillie off a programme. She was accepted as a trying feature of every entertainment. The Progressive Euchre Club was the only social organization in the town that entirely escaped Tillie. After Tillie sat down, the Ladies' Quartette sang, "Beloved, it is Night," and then it was Thea's turn.

The "Ballade" took ten minutes, which was five minutes too long. The audience grew restive and fell to whispering. Thea could hear Mrs. Livery Johnson's bracelets jangling as she fanned herself, and she could hear her father's nervous, ministerial cough. Thor behaved better than any one else. When Thea bowed and returned to her seat at the back of the stage there was the usual applause, but it was vigorous only from the back of the house where the Mexicans sat, and from Ray Kennedy's CLAQUEURS. Any one could see that a good-natured audience had been bored.

Because Mr. Kronborg's sister was on the programme, it had also been necessary to ask the Baptist preacher's wife's cousin to sing. She was a "deep alto" from McCook, and she sang, "Thy Sentinel Am I." After her came Lily Fisher. Thea's rival was also a blonde, but her hair was much heavier than Thea's, and fell in long round curls over her shoulders. She was the angel-child of the Baptists, and looked exactly like the beautiful children on soap calendars. Her pink-and-white face, her set smile of innocence, were surely born of a color-press. She had long, drooping eyelashes, a little pursed-up mouth, and narrow, pointed teeth, like a squirrel's.

Lily began:--

"ROCK OF AGES, CLEFT FOR ME, carelessly the maiden sang."

Thea drew a long breath. That was the game; it was a recitation and a song in one. Lily trailed the hymn through half a dozen verses with great effect. The Baptist preacher had announced at the beginning of the concert that "owing to the length of the programme, there would be no encores." But the applause which followed Lily to her seat was such an unmistakable expression of enthusiasm that Thea had to admit Lily was justified in going back. She was attended this time by Mrs. Livery Johnson herself, crimson with triumph and gleaming-eyed, nervously rolling and unrolling a sheet of music. She took off her bracelets and played Lily's accompaniment. Lily had the effrontery to come out with, "She sang the song of Home, Sweet Home, the song that touched my heart." But this did not surprise Thea; as Ray said later in the evening, "the cards had been stacked against her from the beginning." The next issue of the GLEAM correctly stated that "unquestionably the honors of the evening must be accorded to Miss Lily Fisher." The Baptists had everything their own way.

After the concert Ray Kennedy joined the Kronborgs' party and walked home with them. Thea was grateful for his silent sympathy, even while it irritated her. She inwardly vowed that she would never take another lesson from old Wunsch. She wished that her father would not keep cheerfully singing, "When Shepherds Watched," as he marched ahead, carrying Thor. She felt that silence would become the Kronborgs for a while. As a family, they somehow seemed a little ridiculous, trooping along in the starlight. There were so many of them, for one thing. Then Tillie was so absurd. She was giggling and talking to Anna just as if she had not made, as even Mrs. Kronborg admitted, an exhibition of herself.

When they got home, Ray took a box from his overcoat pocket and slipped it into Thea's hand as he said goodnight. They all hurried in to the glowing stove in the parlor. The sleepy children were sent to bed. Mrs. Kronborg and Anna stayed up to fill the stockings.

"I guess you're tired, Thea. You needn't stay up." Mrs. Kronborg's clear and seemingly indifferent eye usually measured Thea pretty accurately.

Thea hesitated. She glanced at the presents laid out on the dining-room table, but they looked unattractive. Even the brown plush monkey she had bought for Thor with such enthusiasm seemed to have lost his wise and humorous expression. She murmured, "All right," to her mother, lit her lantern, and went upstairs.

Ray's box contained a hand-painted white satin fan, with pond lilies--an unfortunate reminder. Thea smiled grimly and tossed it into her upper drawer. She was not to be consoled by toys. She undressed quickly and stood for some time in the cold, frowning in the broken looking glass at her flaxen pig-tails, at her white neck and arms. Her own broad, resolute face set its chin at her, her eyes flashed into her own defiantly. Lily Fisher was pretty, and she was willing to be just as big a fool as people wanted her to be. Very well; Thea Kronborg wasn't. She would rather be hated than be stupid, any day. She popped into bed and read stubbornly at a queer paper book the drug-store man had given her because he couldn't sell it. She had trained herself to put her mind on what she was doing, otherwise she would have come to grief with her complicated daily schedule. She read, as intently as if she had not been flushed with anger, the strange "Musical Memories" of the Reverend H. R. Haweis. At last she blew out the lantern and went to sleep. She had many curious dreams that night. In one of them Mrs. Tellamantez held her shell to Thea's ear, and she heard the roaring, as before, and distant voices calling, "Lily Fisher! Lily Fisher!"

IX

Mr. Kronborg considered Thea a remarkable child; but so were all his children remarkable. If one of the business men downtown remarked to him that he "had a mighty bright little girl, there," he admitted it, and at once began to explain what a "long head for business" his son Gus had, or that Charley was "a natural electrician," and had put in a telephone from the house to the preacher's study behind the church.

Mrs. Kronborg watched her daughter thoughtfully. She found her more interesting than her other children, and she took her more seriously, without thinking much about why she did so. The other children had to be guided, directed, kept from conflicting with one another. Charley and Gus were likely to want the same thing, and to quarrel about it. Anna often demanded unreasonable service from her older brothers; that they should sit up until after midnight to bring her home from parties when she did not like the youth who had offered himself as her escort; or that they should drive twelve miles into the country, on a winter night, to take her to a ranch dance, after they had been working hard all day. Gunner often got bored with his own clothes or stilts or sled, and wanted Axel's. But Thea, from the time she was a little thing, had her own routine. She kept out of every one's way, and was hard to manage only when the other children interfered with her. Then there was trouble indeed: bursts of temper which used to alarm Mrs. Kronborg. "You ought to know enough to let Thea alone. She lets you alone," she often said to the other children.

One may have staunch friends in one's own family, but one seldom has admirers. Thea, however, had one in the person of her addle-pated aunt, Tillie Kronborg. In older countries, where dress and opinions and manners are not so thoroughly standardized as in our own West, there is a belief that people who are foolish about the more obvious things of life are apt to have peculiar insight into what lies beyond the obvious. The old woman who can never learn not to put the kerosene can on the stove, may yet be able to tell fortunes, to persuade a backward child to grow, to cure warts, or to tell people what to do with a young girl who has gone melancholy. Tillie's mind was a curious machine; when she was awake it went round like a wheel when the belt has slipped off, and when she was asleep she dreamed follies. But she had intuitions. She knew, for instance, that Thea was different from the other Kronborgs, worthy though they all were. Her romantic imagination found possibilities in her niece. When she was sweeping or ironing, or turning the ice-cream freezer at a furious rate, she often built up brilliant futures for Thea, adapting freely the latest novel she had read.

Tillie made enemies for her niece among the church people because, at sewing societies and church suppers, she sometimes spoke vauntingly, with a toss of her head, just as if Thea's "wonderfulness" were an accepted fact in Moonstone, like Mrs. Archie's stinginess, or Mrs. Livery Johnson's duplicity. People declared that, on this subject, Tillie made them tired.

Tillie belonged to a dramatic club that once a year performed in the Moonstone Opera House such plays as "Among the Breakers," and "The Veteran of 1812." Tillie played character parts, the flirtatious old maid or the spiteful INTRIGANTE. She used to study her parts up in the attic at home. While she was committing the lines, she got Gunner or Anna to hold the book for her, but when she began "to bring out the expression," as she said, she used, very timorously, to ask Thea to hold the book. Thea was usually--not always--agreeable about it. Her mother had told her that, since she had some influence with Tillie, it would be a good thing for them all if she could tone her down a shade and "keep her from taking on any worse than need be." Thea would sit on the foot of Tillie's bed, her feet tucked under her, and stare at the silly text. "I wouldn't make so much fuss, there, Tillie," she would remark occasionally; "I don't see the point in it"; or, "What do you pitch your voice so high for? It don't carry half as well."

"I don't see how it comes Thea is so patient with Tillie," Mrs. Kronborg more than once remarked to her husband. "She ain't patient with most people, but it seems like she's got a peculiar patience for Tillie."

Tillie always coaxed Thea to go "behind the scenes" with her when the club presented a play, and help her with her make-up. Thea hated it, but she always went. She felt as if she had to do it. There was something in Tillie's adoration of her that compelled her. There was no family impropriety that Thea was so much ashamed of as Tillie's "acting" and yet she was always being dragged in to assist her. Tillie simply had her, there. She didn't know why, but it was so. There was a string in her somewhere that Tillie could pull; a sense of obligation to Tillie's misguided aspirations. The saloon-keepers had some such feeling of responsibility toward Spanish Johnny.

The dramatic club was the pride of Tillie's heart, and her enthusiasm was the principal factor in keeping it together. Sick or well, Tillie always attended rehearsals, and was always urging the young people, who took rehearsals lightly, to "stop fooling and begin now." The young men --bank clerks, grocery clerks, insurance agents--played tricks, laughed at Tillie, and "put it up on each other" about seeing her home; but they often went to tiresome rehearsals just to oblige her. They were good-natured young fellows. Their trainer and stage-manager was young Upping, the jeweler who ordered Thea's music for her.

Though barely thirty, he had followed half a dozen professions, and had once been a violinist in the orchestra of the Andrews Opera Company, then well known in little towns throughout Colorado and Nebraska.

By one amazing indiscretion Tillie very nearly lost her hold upon the Moonstone Drama Club. The club had decided to put on "The Drummer Boy of Shiloh," a very ambitious undertaking because of the many supers needed and the scenic difficulties of the act which took place in Andersonville Prison. The members of the club consulted together in Tillie's absence as to who should play the part of the drummer boy. It must be taken by a very young person, and village boys of that age are self-conscious and are not apt at memorizing. The part was a long one, and clearly it must be given to a girl. Some members of the club suggested Thea Kronborg, others advocated Lily Fisher. Lily's partisans urged that she was much prettier than Thea, and had a much "sweeter disposition." Nobody denied these facts. But there was nothing in the least boyish about Lily, and she sang all songs and played all parts alike. Lily's simper was popular, but it seemed not quite the right thing for the heroic drummer boy.

Upping, the trainer, talked to one and another: "Lily's all right for girl parts," he insisted, "but you've got to get a girl with some ginger in her for this. Thea's got the voice, too. When she sings, `Just Before the Battle, Mother,' she'll bring down the house."

When all the members of the club had been privately consulted, they announced their decision to Tillie at the first regular meeting that was called to cast the parts. They expected Tillie to be overcome with joy, but, on the contrary, she seemed embarrassed. "I'm afraid Thea hasn't got time for that," she said jerkily. "She is always so busy with her music. Guess you'll have to get somebody else."

The club lifted its eyebrows. Several of Lily Fisher's friends coughed. Mr. Upping flushed. The stout woman who always played the injured wife called Tillie's attention to the fact that this would be a fine opportunity for her niece to show what she could do. Her tone was condescending.

Tillie threw up her head and laughed; there was something sharp and wild about Tillie's laugh--when it was not a giggle. "Oh, I guess Thea hasn't got time to do any showing off. Her time to show off ain't come yet. I expect she'll make us all sit up when it does. No use asking her to take the part. She'd turn her nose up at it. I guess they'd be glad to get her in the Denver Dramatics, if they could."

The company broke up into groups and expressed their amazement. Of course all Swedes were conceited, but they would never have believed that all the conceit of all the Swedes put together would reach such a pitch as this. They confided to each other that Tillie was "just a little off, on the subject of her niece," and agreed that it would be as well not to excite her further. Tillie got a cold reception at rehearsals for a long while afterward, and Thea had a crop of new enemies without even knowing it.

X

Wunsch and old Fritz and Spanish Johnny celebrated Christmas together, so riotously that Wunsch was unable to give Thea her lesson the next day. In the middle of the vacation week Thea went to the Kohlers' through a soft, beautiful snowstorm. The air was a tender blue-gray, like the color on the doves that flew in and out of the white dove-house on the post in the Kohlers' garden. The sand hills looked dim and sleepy. The tamarisk hedge was full of snow, like a foam of blossoms drifted over it. When Thea opened the gate, old Mrs. Kohler was just coming in from the chicken yard, with five fresh eggs in her apron and a pair of old top-boots on her feet. She called Thea to come and look at a bantam egg, which she held up proudly. Her bantam hens were remiss in zeal, and she was always delighted when they accomplished anything. She took Thea into the sitting-room, very warm and smelling of food, and brought her a plateful of little Christmas cakes, made according to old and hallowed formulae, and put them before her while she warmed her feet. Then she went to the door of the kitchen stairs and called: "Herr Wunsch, Herr Wunsch!"

Wunsch came down wearing an old wadded jacket, with a velvet collar. The brown silk was so worn that the wadding stuck out almost everywhere. He avoided Thea's eyes when he came in, nodded without speaking, and pointed directly to the piano stool. He was not so insistent upon the scales as usual, and throughout the little sonata of Mozart's she was studying, he remained languid and absent-minded. His eyes looked very heavy, and he kept wiping them with one of the new silk handkerchiefs Mrs. Kohler had given him for Christmas. When the lesson was over he did not seem inclined to talk. Thea, loitering on the stool, reached for a tattered book she had taken off the music-rest when she sat down. It was a very old Leipsic edition of the piano score of Gluck's "Orpheus." She turned over the pages curiously.

"Is it nice?" she asked.

"It is the most beautiful opera ever made," Wunsch declared solemnly. "You know the story, eh? How, when she die, Orpheus went down below for his wife?"

"Oh, yes, I know. I didn't know there was an opera about it, though. Do people sing this now?"

"ABER JA! What else? You like to try? See." He drew her from the stool and sat down at the piano. Turning over the leaves to the third act, he handed the score to Thea. "Listen, I play it through and you get the RHYTHMUS. EINS, ZWEI, DREI, VIER." He played through Orpheus' lament, then pushed back his cuffs with awakening interest and nodded at Thea. "Now, VOM BLATT, MIT MIR."

"ACH, ICH HABE SIE VERLOREN, ALL' MEIN GLUCK IST NUN DAHIN."

Wunsch sang the aria with much feeling. It was evidently one that was very dear to him.

"NOCH EINMAL, alone, yourself." He played the introductory measures, then nodded at her vehemently, and she began:--

"ACH, ICH HABE SIE VERLOREN."

When she finished, Wunsch nodded again. "SCHON," he muttered as he finished the accompaniment softly. He dropped his hands on his knees and looked up at Thea. "That is very fine, eh? There is no such beautiful melody in the world. You can take the book for one week and learn something, to pass the time. It is good to know--always. EURIDICE, EU--RI--DI--CE, WEH DASS ICH AUF ERDEN BIN!" he sang softly, playing the melody with his right hand.

Thea, who was turning over the pages of the third act, stopped and scowled at a passage. The old German's blurred eyes watched her curiously.

"For what do you look so, IMMER?" puckering up his own face. "You see something a little difficult, may-be, and you make such a face like it was an enemy."

Thea laughed, disconcerted. "Well, difficult things are enemies, aren't they? When you have to get them?"

Wunsch lowered his head and threw it up as if he were butting something. "Not at all! By no means." He took the book from her and looked at it. "Yes, that is not so easy, there. This is an old book. They do not print it so now any more, I think. They leave it out, may-be. Only one woman could sing that good."

Thea looked at him in perplexity.

Wunsch went on. "It is written for alto, you see. A woman sings the part, and there was only one to sing that good in there. You understand? Only one!" He glanced at her quickly and lifted his red forefinger upright before her eyes.

Thea looked at the finger as if she were hypnotized. "Only one?" she asked breathlessly; her hands, hanging at her sides, were opening and shutting rapidly.

Wunsch nodded and still held up that compelling finger. When he dropped his hands, there was a look of satisfaction in his face.

"Was she very great?"

Wunsch nodded.

"Was she beautiful?"

"ABER GAR NICHT! Not at all. She was ugly; big mouth, big teeth, no figure, nothing at all," indicating a luxuriant bosom by sweeping his hands over his chest. "A pole, a post! But for the voice--ACH! She have something in there, behind the eyes," tapping his temples.

Thea followed all his gesticulations intently. "Was she German?"

"No, SPANISCH." He looked down and frowned for a moment. "ACH, I tell you, she look like the Frau Tellamantez, some-thing. Long face, long chin, and ugly al-so."

"Did she die a long while ago?"

"Die? I think not. I never hear, anyhow. I guess she is alive somewhere in the world; Paris, may-be. But old, of course. I hear her when I was a youth. She is too old to sing now any more."

"Was she the greatest singer you ever heard?"

Wunsch nodded gravely. "Quite so. She was the most--" he hunted for an English word, lifted his hand over his head and snapped his fingers noiselessly in the air, enunciating fiercely, "KUNST-LER-ISCH!" The word seemed to glitter in his uplifted hand, his voice was so full of emotion.

Wunsch rose from the stool and began to button his wadded jacket, preparing to return to his half-heated room in the loft. Thea regretfully put on her cloak and hood and set out for home.

When Wunsch looked for his score late that afternoon, he found that Thea had not forgotten to take it with her. He smiled his loose, sarcastic smile, and thoughtfully rubbed his stubbly chin with his red fingers. When Fritz came home in the early blue twilight the snow was flying faster, Mrs. Kohler was cooking HASENPFEFFER in the kitchen, and the professor was seated at the piano, playing the Gluck, which he knew by heart. Old Fritz took off his shoes quietly behind the stove and lay down on the lounge before his masterpiece, where the firelight was playing over the walls of Moscow. He listened, while the room grew darker and the windows duller. Wunsch always came back to the same thing:--

"ACH, ICH HABE SIE VERLOREN,...EURIDICE, EURIDICE!"

From time to time Fritz sighed softly. He, too, had lost a Euridice.

XI

One Saturday, late in June, Thea arrived early for her lesson. As she perched herself upon the piano stool,--a wobbly, old-fashioned thing that worked on a creaky screw,--she gave Wunsch a side glance, smiling. "You must not be cross to me to-day. This is my birthday."

"So?" he pointed to the keyboard.

After the lesson they went out to join Mrs. Kohler, who had asked Thea to come early, so that she could stay and smell the linden bloom. It was one of those still days of intense light, when every particle of mica in the soil flashed like a little mirror, and the glare from the plain below seemed more intense than the rays from above. The sand ridges ran glittering gold out to where the mirage licked them up, shining and steaming like a lake in the tropics. The sky looked like blue lava, forever incapable of clouds,--a turquoise bowl that was the lid of the desert. And yet within Mrs. Kohler's green patch the water dripped, the beds had all been hosed, and the air was fresh with rapidly evaporating moisture.

The two symmetrical linden trees were the proudest things in the garden. Their sweetness embalmed all the air. At every turn of the paths,--whether one went to see the hollyhocks or the bleeding heart, or to look at the purple morning-glories that ran over the bean-poles,--wherever one went, the sweetness of the lindens struck one afresh and one always came back to them. Under the round leaves, where the waxen yellow blossoms hung, bevies of wild bees were buzzing. The tamarisks were still pink, and the flower-beds were doing their best in honor of the linden festival. The white dove-house was shining with a fresh coat of paint, and the pigeons were crooning contentedly, flying down often to drink at the drip from the water tank. Mrs. Kohler, who was transplanting pansies, came up with her trowel and told Thea it was lucky to have your birthday when the lindens were in bloom, and that she must go and look at the sweet peas. Wunsch accompanied her, and as they walked between the flower-beds he took Thea's hand.

"ES FLUSTERN UND SPRECHEN DIE BLUMEN,"--he muttered. "You know that von Heine? IM LEUCHTENDEN SOMMERMORGEN?" He looked down at Thea and softly pressed her hand.

"No, I don't know it. What does FLUSTERN mean?"

"FLUSTERN?--to whisper. You must begin now to know such things. That is necessary. How many birthdays?"

"Thirteen. I'm in my 'teens now. But how can I know words like that? I only know what you say at my lessons. They don't teach German at school. How can I learn?"

"It is always possible to learn when one likes," said Wunsch. His words were peremptory, as usual, but his tone was mild, even confidential. "There is always a way. And if some day you are going to sing, it is necessary to know well the German language."

Thea stooped over to pick a leaf of rosemary. How did Wunsch know that, when the very roses on her wall-paper had never heard it? "But am I going to?" she asked, still stooping.

"That is for you to say," returned Wunsch coldly. "You would better marry some JACOB here and keep the house for him, may-be? That is as one desires."

Thea flashed up at him a clear, laughing look. "No, I don't want to do that. You know," she brushed his coat sleeve quickly with her yellow head. "Only how can I learn anything here? It's so far from Denver."

Wunsch's loose lower lip curled in amusement. Then, as if he suddenly remembered something, he spoke seriously. "Nothing is far and nothing is near, if one desires. The world is little, people are little, human life is little. There is only one big thing--desire. And before it, when it is big, all is little. It brought Columbus across the sea in a little boat, UND SO WEITER." Wunsch made a grimace, took his pupil's hand and drew her toward the grape arbor. "Hereafter I will more speak to you in German. Now, sit down and I will teach you for your birthday that little song. Ask me the words you do not know already. Now: IM LEUCHTENDEN SOMMERMORGEN."

Thea memorized quickly because she had the power of listening intently. In a few moments she could repeat the eight lines for him. Wunsch nodded encouragingly and they went out of the arbor into the sunlight again. As they went up and down the gravel paths between the flowerbeds, the white and yellow butterflies kept darting before them, and the pigeons were washing their pink feet at the drip and crooning in their husky bass. Over and over again Wunsch made her say the lines to him. "You see it is nothing. If you learn a great many of the LIEDER, you will know the German language already. WEITER, NUN." He would incline his head gravely and listen.

"IM LEUCHTENDEN SOMMERMORGEN GEH' ICH IM GARTEN HERUM; ES FLUSTERN UND SPRECHEN DIE BLUMEN, ICH ABER, ICH WANDTE STUMM.

"ES FLUSTERN UND SPRECHEN DIE BLUMEN UND SCHAU'N MITLEIDIG MICH AN: `SEI UNSERER SCHWESTER NICHT BOSE, DU TRAURIGER, BLASSER MANN!'"

(In the soft-shining summer morning I wandered the garden within. The flowers they whispered and murmured, But I, I wandered dumb.

The flowers they whisper and murmur, And me with compassion they scan: "Oh, be not harsh to our sister, Thou sorrowful, death-pale man!")

Wunsch had noticed before that when his pupil read anything in verse the character of her voice changed altogether; it was no longer the voice which spoke the speech of Moonstone. It was a soft, rich contralto, and she read quietly; the feeling was in the voice itself, not indicated by emphasis or change of pitch. She repeated the little verses musically, like a song, and the entreaty of the flowers was even softer than the rest, as the shy speech of flowers might be, and she ended with the voice suspended, almost with a rising inflection. It was a nature-voice, Wunsch told himself, breathed from the creature and apart from language, like the sound of the wind in the trees, or the murmur of water.

"What is it the flowers mean when they ask him not to be harsh to their sister, eh?" he asked, looking down at her curiously and wrinkling his dull red forehead.

Thea glanced at him in surprise. "I suppose he thinks they are asking him not to be harsh to his sweetheart--or some girl they remind him of."

"And why TRAURIGER, BLASSER MANN?"

They had come back to the grape arbor, and Thea picked out a sunny place on the bench, where a tortoise-shell cat was stretched at full length. She sat down, bending over the cat and teasing his whiskers. "Because he had been awake all night, thinking about her, wasn't it? Maybe that was why he was up so early."

Wunsch shrugged his shoulders. "If he think about her all night already, why do you say the flowers remind him?"

Thea looked up at him in perplexity. A flash of comprehension lit her face and she smiled eagerly. "Oh, I didn't mean `remind' in that way! I didn't mean they brought her to his mind! I meant it was only when he came out in the morning, that she seemed to him like that,--like one of the flowers."

"And before he came out, how did she seem?"

This time it was Thea who shrugged her shoulders. The warm smile left her face. She lifted her eyebrows in annoyance and looked off at the sand hills.

Wunsch persisted. "Why you not answer me?"

"Because it would be silly. You are just trying to make me say things. It spoils things to ask questions."

Wunsch bowed mockingly; his smile was disagreeable. Suddenly his face grew grave, grew fierce, indeed. He pulled himself up from his clumsy stoop and folded his arms. "But it is necessary to know if you know some things. Some things cannot be taught. If you not know in the beginning, you not know in the end. For a singer there must be something in the inside from the beginning. I shall not be long in this place, may-be, and I like to know. Yes,"--he ground his heel in the gravel,--"yes, when you are barely six, you must know that already. That is the beginning of all things; DER GEIST, DIE PHANTASIE. It must be in the baby, when it makes its first cry, like DER RHYTHMUS, or it is not to be. You have some voice already, and if in the beginning, when you are with things-to-play, you know that what you will not tell me, then you can learn to sing, may-be."

Wunsch began to pace the arbor, rubbing his hands together. The dark flush of his face had spread up under the iron-gray bristles on his head. He was talking to himself, not to Thea. Insidious power of the linden bloom! "Oh, much you can learn! ABER NICHT DIE AMERICANISCHEN FRAULEIN. They have nothing inside them," striking his chest with both fists. "They are like the ones in the MARCHEN, a grinning face and hollow in the insides. Something they can learn, oh, yes, may-be! But the secret--what make the rose to red, the sky to blue, the man to love --IN DER BRUST, IN DER BRUST it is, UND OHNE DIESES GIEBT ES KEINE KUNST, GIEBT ES KEINE KUNST!" He threw up his square hand and shook it, all the fingers apart and wagging. Purple and breathless he went out of the arbor and into the house, without saying good-bye. These outbursts frightened Wunsch. They were always harbingers of ill.

Thea got her music-book and stole quietly out of the garden. She did not go home, but wandered off into the sand dunes, where the prickly pear was in blossom and the green lizards were racing each other in the glittering light. She was shaken by a passionate excitement. She did not altogether understand what Wunsch was talking about; and yet, in a way she knew. She knew, of course, that there was something about her that was different. But it was more like a friendly spirit than like anything that was a part of herself. She thought everything to it, and it answered her; happiness consisted of that backward and forward movement of herself. The something came and went, she never knew how. Sometimes she hunted for it and could not find it; again, she lifted her eyes from a book, or stepped out of doors, or wakened in the morning, and it was there,--under her cheek, it usually seemed to be, or over her breast,--a kind of warm sureness. And when it was there, everything was more interesting and beautiful, even people. When this companion was with her, she could get the most wonderful things out of Spanish Johnny, or Wunsch, or Dr. Archie.

On her thirteenth birthday she wandered for a long while about the sand ridges, picking up crystals and looking into the yellow prickly-pear blossoms with their thousand stamens. She looked at the sand hills until she wished she WERE a sand hill. And yet she knew that she was going to leave them all behind some day. They would be changing all day long, yellow and purple and lavender, and she would not be there. From that day on, she felt there was a secret between her and Wunsch. Together they had lifted a lid, pulled out a drawer, and looked at something. They hid it away and never spoke of what they had seen; but neither of them forgot it.

XII

One July night, when the moon was full, Dr. Archie was coming up from the depot, restless and discontented, wishing there were something to do. He carried his straw hat in his hand, and kept brushing his hair back from his forehead with a purposeless, unsatisfied gesture. After he passed Uncle Billy Beemer's cottonwood grove, the sidewalk ran out of the shadow into the white moonlight and crossed the sand gully on high posts, like a bridge. As the doctor approached this trestle, he saw a white figure, and recognized Thea Kronborg. He quickened his pace and she came to meet him.

"What are you doing out so late, my girl?" he asked as he took her hand.

"Oh, I don't know. What do people go to bed so early for? I'd like to run along before the houses and screech at them. Isn't it glorious out here?"

The young doctor gave a melancholy laugh and pressed her hand.

"Think of it," Thea snorted impatiently. "Nobody up but us and the rabbits! I've started up half a dozen of 'em. Look at that little one down there now,"--she stooped and pointed. In the gully below them there was, indeed, a little rabbit with a white spot of a tail, crouching down on the sand, quite motionless. It seemed to be lapping up the moonlight like cream. On the other side of the walk, down in the ditch, there was a patch of tall, rank sunflowers, their shaggy leaves white with dust. The moon stood over the cottonwood grove. There was no wind, and no sound but the wheezing of an engine down on the tracks.

"Well, we may as well watch the rabbits." Dr. Archie sat down on the sidewalk and let his feet hang over the edge. He pulled out a smooth linen handkerchief that smelled of German cologne water. "Well, how goes it? Working hard? You must know about all Wunsch can teach you by this time."

Thea shook her head. "Oh, no, I don't, Dr. Archie. He's hard to get at, but he's been a real musician in his time. Mother says she believes he's forgotten more than the music-teachers down in Denver ever knew."

"I'm afraid he won't be around here much longer," said Dr. Archie. "He's been making a tank of himself lately. He'll be pulling his freight one of these days. That's the way they do, you know. I'll be sorry on your account." He paused and ran his fresh handkerchief over his face. "What the deuce are we all here for anyway, Thea?" he said abruptly.

"On earth, you mean?" Thea asked in a low voice.

"Well, primarily, yes. But secondarily, why are we in Moonstone? It isn't as if we'd been born here. You were, but Wunsch wasn't, and I wasn't. I suppose I'm here because I married as soon as I got out of medical school and had to get a practice quick. If you hurry things, you always get left in the end. I don't learn anything here, and as for the people--In my own town in Michigan, now, there were people who liked me on my father's account, who had even known my grandfather. That meant something. But here it's all like the sand: blows north one day and south the next. We're all a lot of gamblers without much nerve, playing for small stakes. The railroad is the one real fact in this country. That has to be; the world has to be got back and forth. But the rest of us are here just because it's the end of a run and the engine has to have a drink. Some day I'll get up and find my hair turning gray, and I'll have nothing to show for it."

Thea slid closer to him and caught his arm. "No, no. I won't let you get gray. You've got to stay young for me. I'm getting young now, too."

Archie laughed. "Getting?"

"Yes. People aren't young when they're children. Look at Thor, now; he's just a little old man. But Gus has a sweetheart, and he's young!"

"Something in that!" Dr. Archie patted her head, and then felt the shape of her skull gently, with the tips of his fingers. "When you were little, Thea, I used always to be curious about the shape of your head. You seemed to have more inside it than most youngsters. I haven't examined it for a long time. Seems to be the usual shape, but uncommonly hard, some how. What are you going to do with yourself, anyway?"

"I don't know."

"Honest, now?" He lifted her chin and looked into her eyes.

Thea laughed and edged away from him.

"You've got something up your sleeve, haven't you? Anything you like; only don't marry and settle down here without giving yourself a chance, will you?"

"Not much. See, there's another rabbit!"

"That's all right about the rabbits, but I don't want you to get tied up. Remember that."

Thea nodded. "Be nice to Wunsch, then. I don't know what I'd do if he went away."

"You've got older friends than Wunsch here, Thea."

"I know." Thea spoke seriously and looked up at the moon, propping her chin on her hand. "But Wunsch is the only one that can teach me what I want to know. I've got to learn to do something well, and that's the thing I can do best."

"Do you want to be a music-teacher?"

"Maybe, but I want to be a good one. I'd like to go to Germany to study, some day. Wunsch says that's the best place,--the only place you can really learn." Thea hesitated and then went on nervously, "I've got a book that says so, too. It's

189

called `My Musical Memories.' It made me want to go to Germany even before Wunsch said anything. Of course it's a secret. You're the first one I've told."

Dr. Archie smiled indulgently. "That's a long way off. Is that what you've got in your hard noddle?" He put his hand on her hair, but this time she shook him off.

"No, I don't think much about it. But you talk about going, and a body has to have something to go TO!"

"That's so." Dr. Archie sighed. "You're lucky if you have. Poor Wunsch, now, he hasn't. What do such fellows come out here for? He's been asking me about my mining stock, and about mining towns. What would he do in a mining town? He wouldn't know a piece of ore if he saw one. He's got nothing to sell that a mining town wants to buy. Why don't those old fellows stay at home? We won't need them for another hundred years. An engine wiper can get a job, but a piano player! Such people can't make good."

"My grandfather Alstrom was a musician, and he made good."

Dr. Archie chuckled. "Oh, a Swede can make good anywhere, at anything! You've got that in your favor, miss. Come, you must be getting home."

Thea rose. "Yes, I used to be ashamed of being a Swede, but I'm not any more. Swedes are kind of common, but I think it's better to be SOMETHING."

"It surely is! How tall you are getting. You come above my shoulder now."

"I'll keep on growing, don't you think? I particularly want to be tall. Yes, I guess I must go home. I wish there'd be a fire."

"A fire?"

"Yes, so the fire-bell would ring and the roundhouse whistle would blow, and everybody would come running out. Sometime I'm going to ring the fire-bell myself and stir them all up."

"You'd be arrested."

"Well, that would be better than going to bed."

"I'll have to lend you some more books."

Thea shook herself impatiently. "I can't read every night."

Dr. Archie gave one of his low, sympathetic chuckles as he opened the gate for her. "You're beginning to grow up, that's what's the matter with you. I'll have to keep an eye on you. Now you'll have to say good-night to the moon."

"No, I won't. I sleep on the floor now, right in the moonlight. My window comes down to the floor, and I can look at the sky all night."

She shot round the house to the kitchen door, and Dr. Archie watched her disappear with a sigh. He thought of the hard, mean, frizzy little woman who kept his house for him; once the belle of a Michigan town, now dry and withered up at thirty. "If I had a daughter like Thea to watch," he reflected, "I wouldn't mind anything. I wonder if all of my life's going to be a mistake just because I made a big one then? Hardly seems fair."

Howard Archie was "respected" rather than popular in Moonstone. Everyone recognized that he was a good physician, and a progressive Western town likes to be able to point to a handsome, well-set-up, well-dressed man among its citizens. But a great many people thought Archie "distant," and they were right. He had the uneasy manner of a man who is not among his own kind, and who has not seen enough of the world to feel that all people are in some sense his own kind. He knew that every one was curious about his wife, that she played a sort of character part in Moonstone, and that people made fun of her, not very delicately. Her own friends--most of them women who were distasteful to Archie--liked to ask her to contribute to church charities, just to see how mean she could be. The little, lop-sided cake at the church supper, the cheapest pincushion, the skimpiest apron at the bazaar, were always Mrs. Archie's contribution.

All this hurt the doctor's pride. But if there was one thing he had learned, it was that there was no changing Belle's nature. He had married a mean woman; and he must accept the consequences. Even in Colorado he would have had no pretext for divorce, and, to do him justice, he had never thought of such a thing. The tenets of the Presbyterian Church in which he had grown up, though he had long ceased to believe in them, still influenced his conduct and his conception of propriety. To him there was something vulgar about divorce. A divorced man was a disgraced man; at least, he had exhibited his hurt, and made it a matter for common gossip. Respectability was so necessary to Archie that he was willing to pay a high price for it. As long as he could keep up a decent exterior, he could manage to get on; and if he could have concealed his wife's littleness from all his friends, he would scarcely have complained. He was more afraid of pity than he was of any unhappiness. Had there been another woman for whom he cared greatly, he might have had plenty of courage; but he was not likely to meet such a woman in Moonstone.

There was a puzzling timidity in Archie's make-up. The thing that held his shoulders stiff, that made him resort to a mirthless little laugh when he was talking to dull people, that made him sometimes stumble over rugs and carpets, had its counterpart in his mind. He had not the courage to be an honest thinker. He could comfort himself by evasions and compromises. He consoled himself for his own marriage by telling himself that other people's were not much better. In his work he saw pretty deeply into marital relations in Moonstone, and he could honestly say that there were not many of his friends whom he envied. Their wives seemed to suit them well enough, but they would never have suited him.

Although Dr. Archie could not bring himself to regard marriage merely as a social contract, but looked upon it as somehow made sacred by a church in which he did not believe,--as a physician he knew that a young man whose marriage is merely nominal must yet go on living his life. When he went to Denver or to Chicago, he drifted about in careless company where gayety and good-humor can be bought, not because he had any taste for such society, but because he honestly believed that anything was better than divorce. He often told himself that "hanging and wiving go by destiny." If wiving went badly with a man,--and it did oftener than not,--then he must do the best he could to keep up appearances and help the tradition of domestic happiness along. The Moonstone gossips, assembled in Mrs. Smiley's millinery and notion store, often discussed Dr. Archie's politeness to his wife, and his pleasant manner of speaking about her. "Nobody has ever got a thing out of him yet," they agreed. And it was certainly not because no one had ever tried.

When he was down in Denver, feeling a little jolly, Archie could forget how unhappy he was at home, and could even make himself believe that he missed his wife. He always bought her presents, and would have liked to send her flowers if she had not repeatedly told him never to send her anything but bulbs,--which did not appeal to him in his expansive moments. At the Denver Athletic Club banquets, or at dinner with his colleagues at the Brown Palace Hotel, he sometimes spoke sentimentally about "little Mrs. Archie," and he always drank the toast "to our wives, God bless them!" with gusto.

The determining factor about Dr. Archie was that he was romantic. He had married Belle White because he was romantic--too romantic to know anything about women, except what he wished them to be, or to repulse a pretty girl who had set her cap for him. At medical school, though he was a rather wild boy in behavior, he had always disliked coarse jokes and vulgar stories. In his old Flint's Physiology there was still a poem he had pasted there when he was a student; some verses by Dr. Oliver Wendell Holmes about the ideals of the medical profession. After so much and such disillusioning experience with it, he still had a romantic feeling about the human body; a sense that finer things dwelt in it than could be explained by anatomy. He never jested about birth or death or marriage, and did not like to hear other doctors do it. He was a good nurse, and had a reverence for the bodies of women and children. When he was tending them, one saw him at his best. Then his constraint and self-consciousness fell away from him. He was easy, gentle, competent, master of himself and of other people. Then the idealist in him was not afraid of being discovered and ridiculed.

In his tastes, too, the doctor was romantic. Though he read Balzac all the year through, he still enjoyed the Waverley Novels as much as when he had first come upon them, in thick leather-bound volumes, in his grandfather's library. He nearly always read Scott on Christmas and holidays, because it brought back the pleasures of his boyhood so vividly. He liked Scott's women. Constance de Beverley and the minstrel girl in "The Fair Maid of Perth," not the Duchesse de Langeais, were his heroines. But better than anything that ever got from the heart of a man into printer's ink, he loved the poetry of Robert Burns. "Death and Dr. Hornbook" and "The Jolly Beggars," Burns's "Reply to his Tailor," he often read aloud to himself in his office, late at night, after a glass of hot toddy. He used to read "Tam o'Shanter" to Thea Kronborg, and he got her some of the songs, set to the old airs for which they were written. He loved to hear her sing them. Sometimes when she sang, "Oh, wert thou in the cauld blast," the doctor and even Mr. Kronborg joined in. Thea never minded if people could not sing; she directed them with her head and somehow carried them along. When her father got off the pitch she let her own voice out and covered him.

XIII

At the beginning of June, when school closed, Thea had told Wunsch that she didn't know how much practicing she could get in this summer because Thor had his worst teeth still to cut.

"My God! all last summer he was doing that!" Wunsch exclaimed furiously.

"I know, but it takes them two years, and Thor is slow," Thea answered reprovingly.

The summer went well beyond her hopes, however. She told herself that it was the best summer of her life, so far. Nobody was sick at home, and her lessons were uninterrupted. Now that she had four pupils of her own and made a dollar a week, her practicing was regarded more seriously by the household. Her mother had always arranged things so that she could have the parlor four hours a day in summer. Thor proved a friendly ally. He behaved handsomely about his molars, and never objected to being pulled off into remote places in his cart. When Thea dragged him over the hill and made a camp under the shade of a bush or a bank, he would waddle about and play with his blocks, or bury his monkey in the sand and dig him up again. Sometimes he got into the cactus and set up a howl, but usually he let his sister read peacefully, while he coated his hands and face, first with an all-day sucker and then with gravel.

Life was pleasant and uneventful until the first of September, when Wunsch began to drink so hard that he was unable to appear when Thea went to take her mid-week lesson, and Mrs. Kohler had to send her home after a tearful apology. On Saturday morning she set out for the Kohlers' again, but on her way, when she was crossing the ravine, she noticed a woman sitting at the bottom of the gulch, under the railroad trestle. She turned from her path and saw that it was Mrs. Tellamantez, and she seemed to be doing drawn-work. Then Thea noticed that there was something beside her, covered up with a purple and yellow Mexican blanket. She ran up the gulch and called to Mrs. Tellamantez. The Mexican woman held up a warning finger. Thea glanced at the blanket and recognized a square red hand which protruded. The middle finger twitched slightly.

"Is he hurt?" she gasped.

Mrs. Tellamantez shook her head. "No; very sick. He knows nothing," she said quietly, folding her hands over her drawn-work.

Thea learned that Wunsch had been out all night, that this morning Mrs. Kohler had gone to look for him and found him under the trestle covered with dirt and cinders. Probably he had been trying to get home and had lost his way. Mrs. Tellamantez was watching beside the unconscious man while Mrs. Kohler and Johnny went to get help.

"You better go home now, I think," said Mrs. Tellamantez, in closing her narration.

Thea hung her head and looked wistfully toward the blanket.

"Couldn't I just stay till they come?" she asked. "I'd like to know if he's very bad."

"Bad enough," sighed Mrs. Tellamantez, taking up her work again.

Thea sat down under the narrow shade of one of the trestle posts and listened to the locusts rasping in the hot sand while she watched Mrs. Tellamantez evenly draw her threads. The blanket looked as if it were over a heap of bricks.

"I don't see him breathing any," she said anxiously.

"Yes, he breathes," said Mrs. Tellamantez, not lifting her eyes.

It seemed to Thea that they waited for hours. At last they heard voices, and a party of men came down the hill and up the gulch. Dr. Archie and Fritz Kohler came first; behind were Johnny and Ray, and several men from the roundhouse. Ray had the canvas litter that was kept at the depot for accidents on the road. Behind them trailed half a dozen boys who had been hanging round the depot.

When Ray saw Thea, he dropped his canvas roll and hurried forward. "Better run along home, Thee. This is ugly business." Ray was indignant that anybody who gave Thea music lessons should behave in such a manner.

Thea resented both his proprietary tone and his superior virtue. "I won't. I want to know how bad he is. I'm not a baby!" she exclaimed indignantly, stamping her foot into the sand.

Dr. Archie, who had been kneeling by the blanket, got up and came toward Thea, dusting his knees. He smiled and nodded confidentially. "He'll be all right when we get him home. But he wouldn't want you to see him like this, poor old chap! Understand? Now, skip!"

Thea ran down the gulch and looked back only once, to see them lifting the canvas litter with Wunsch upon it, still covered with the blanket.

The men carried Wunsch up the hill and down the road to the Kohlers'. Mrs. Kohler had gone home and made up a bed in the sitting-room, as she knew the litter could not be got round the turn in the narrow stairway. Wunsch was like a dead man. He lay unconscious all day. Ray Kennedy stayed with him till two o'clock in the afternoon, when he had to go out on his run. It was the first time he had ever been inside the Kohlers' house, and he was so much impressed by Napoleon that the piece-picture formed a new bond between him and Thea.

Dr. Archie went back at six o'clock, and found Mrs. Kohler and Spanish Johnny with Wunsch, who was in a high fever, muttering and groaning.

"There ought to be some one here to look after him to-night, Mrs. Kohler," he said. "I'm on a confinement case, and I can't be here, but there ought to be somebody. He may get violent."

Mrs. Kohler insisted that she could always do anything with Wunsch, but the doctor shook his head and Spanish Johnny grinned. He said he would stay. The doctor laughed at him. "Ten fellows like you couldn't hold him, Spanish, if he got obstreperous; an Irishman would have his hands full. Guess I'd better put the soft pedal on him." He pulled out his hypodermic.

Spanish Johnny stayed, however, and the Kohlers went to bed. At about two o'clock in the morning Wunsch rose from his ignominious cot. Johnny, who was dozing on the lounge, awoke to find the German standing in the middle of the room in his undershirt and drawers, his arms bare, his heavy body seeming twice its natural girth. His face was snarling and savage, and his eyes were crazy. He had risen to avenge himself, to wipe out his shame, to destroy his enemy. One look was enough for Johnny. Wunsch raised a chair threateningly, and Johnny, with the lightness of a PICADOR, darted under the missile and out of the open window. He shot across the gully to get help, meanwhile leaving the Kohlers to their fate.

Fritz, upstairs, heard the chair crash upon the stove. Then he heard doors opening and shutting, and some one stumbling about in the shrubbery of the garden. He and Paulina sat up in bed and held a consultation. Fritz slipped from under the covers, and going cautiously over to the window, poked out his head. Then he rushed to the door and bolted it.

"MEIN GOTT, Paulina," he gasped, "he has the axe, he will kill us!"

"The dresser," cried Mrs. Kohler; "push the dresser before the door. ACH, if you had your rabbit gun, now!"

"It is in the barn," said Fritz sadly. "It would do no good; he would not be afraid of anything now. Stay you in the bed, Paulina." The dresser had lost its casters years ago, but he managed to drag it in front of the door. "He is in the garden. He makes nothing. He will get sick again, may-be."

Fritz went back to bed and his wife pulled the quilt over him and made him lie down. They heard stumbling in the garden again, then a smash of glass.

"ACH, DAS MISTBEET!" gasped Paulina, hearing her hotbed shivered. "The poor soul, Fritz, he will cut himself. ACH! what is that?" They both sat up in bed. "WIEDER! ACH, What is he doing?"

The noise came steadily, a sound of chopping. Paulina tore off her night-cap. "DIE BAUME, DIE BAUME! He is cutting our trees, Fritz!" Before her husband could prevent her, she had sprung from the bed and rushed to the window. "DER TAUBENSCHLAG! GERECHTER HIMMEL, he is chopping the dove-house down!"

Fritz reached her side before she had got her breath again, and poked his head out beside hers. There, in the faint starlight, they saw a bulky man, barefoot, half dressed, chopping away at the white post that formed the pedestal of the dove-house. The startled pigeons were croaking and flying about his head, even beating their wings in his face, so that he struck at them furiously with the axe. In a few seconds there was a crash, and Wunsch had actually felled the dove-house.

"Oh, if only it is not the trees next!" prayed Paulina. "The dove-house you can make new again, but not DIE BAUME."

They watched breathlessly. In the garden below Wunsch stood in the attitude of a woodman, contemplating the fallen cote. Suddenly he threw the axe over his shoulder and went out of the front gate toward the town.

"The poor soul, he will meet his death!" Mrs. Kohler wailed. She ran back to her feather bed and hid her face in the pillow.

Fritz kept watch at the window. "No, no, Paulina," he called presently; "I see lanterns coming. Johnny must have gone for somebody. Yes, four lanterns, coming along the gulch. They stop; they must have seen him already. Now they are under the hill and I cannot see them, but I think they have him. They will bring him back. I must dress and go down." He caught his trousers and began pulling them on by the window. "Yes, here they come, half a dozen men. And they have tied him with a rope, Paulina!"

"ACH, the poor man! To be led like a cow," groaned Mrs. Kohler. "Oh, it is good that he has no wife!" She was reproaching herself for nagging Fritz when he drank himself into foolish pleasantry or mild sulks, and felt that she had never before appreciated her blessings.

Wunsch was in bed for ten days, during which time he was gossiped about and even preached about in Moonstone. The Baptist preacher took a shot at the fallen man from his pulpit, Mrs. Livery Johnson nodding approvingly from her pew. The mothers of Wunsch's pupils sent him notes informing him that their daughters would discontinue their music-lessons. The old maid who had rented him her piano sent the town dray for her contaminated instrument, and ever afterward declared that Wunsch had ruined its tone and scarred its glossy finish. The Kohlers were unremitting in their kindness to their friend. Mrs. Kohler made him soups and broths without stint, and Fritz repaired the dove-house and mounted it on a new post, lest it might be a sad reminder.

As soon as Wunsch was strong enough to sit about in his slippers and wadded jacket, he told Fritz to bring him some stout thread from the shop. When Fritz asked what he was going to sew, he produced the tattered score of "Orpheus" and said he would like to fix it up for a little present. Fritz carried it over to the shop and stitched it into pasteboards, covered with dark suiting-cloth. Over the stitches he glued a strip of thin red leather which he got from his friend, the harness-maker. After Paulina had cleaned the pages with fresh bread, Wunsch was amazed to see what a fine book he had. It opened stiffly, but that was no matter.

Sitting in the arbor one morning, under the ripe grapes and the brown, curling leaves, with a pen and ink on the bench beside him and the Gluck score on his knee, Wunsch pondered for a long while. Several times he dipped the pen in the ink, and then put it back again in the cigar box in which Mrs. Kohler kept her writing utensils. His thoughts wandered over a wide territory; over many countries and many years. There was no order or logical sequence in his ideas. Pictures came and went without reason. Faces, mountains, rivers, autumn days in other vineyards far away. He thought of a FUSZREISE he had made through the Hartz Mountains in his student days; of the innkeeper's pretty daughter who had lighted his pipe for him in the garden one summer evening, of the woods above Wiesbaden, haymakers on an island in the river. The roundhouse whistle woke him from his reveries. Ah, yes, he was in Moonstone, Colorado. He frowned for a moment and looked at the book on his knee. He had thought of a great many appropriate things to write in it, but suddenly he rejected all of them, opened the book, and at the top of the much-engraved title-page he wrote rapidly in purple ink:--

EINST, O WUNDER!--

A. WUNSCH. MOONSTONE, COLO. SEPTEMBER 30, 18--

Nobody in Moonstone ever found what Wunsch's first name was. That "A" may have stood for Adam, or August, or even Amadeus; he got very angry if any one asked him.

He remained A. Wunsch to the end of his chapter there. When he presented this score to Thea, he told her that in ten years she would either know what the inscription meant, or she would not have the least idea, in which case it would not matter.

When Wunsch began to pack his trunk, both the Kohlers were very unhappy. He said he was coming back some day, but that for the present, since he had lost all his pupils, it would be better for him to try some "new town." Mrs. Kohler darned and mended all his clothes, and gave him two new shirts she had made for Fritz. Fritz made him a new pair of trousers and would have made him an overcoat but for the fact that overcoats were so easy to pawn.

Wunsch would not go across the ravine to the town until he went to take the morning train for Denver. He said that after he got to Denver he would "look around." He left Moonstone one bright October morning, without telling any one good-bye. He bought his ticket and went directly into the smoking-car. When the train was beginning to pull out, he heard his name called frantically, and looking out of the window he saw Thea Kronborg standing on the siding, bareheaded and panting. Some boys had brought word to school that they saw Wunsch's trunk going over to the station, and Thea had run away from school. She was at the end of the station platform, her hair in two braids, her blue gingham dress wet to the knees because she had run across lots through the weeds. It had rained during the night, and the tall sunflowers behind her were fresh and shining.

"Good-bye, Herr Wunsch, good-bye!" she called waving to him.

He thrust his head out at the car window and called back, "LEBEN SIE WOHL, LEBEN SIE WOHL, MEIN KIND!" He watched her until the train swept around the curve beyond the roundhouse, and then sank back into his seat, muttering, "She had been running. Ah, she will run a long way; they cannot stop her!"

What was it about the child that one believed in? Was it her dogged industry, so unusual in this free-and-easy country? Was it her imagination? More likely it was because she had both imagination and a stubborn will, curiously balancing and interpenetrating each other. There was something unconscious and unawakened about her, that tempted curiosity. She had a kind of seriousness that he had not met with in a pupil before. She hated difficult things, and yet she could never pass one by. They seemed to challenge her; she had no peace until she mastered them. She had the power to make a great effort, to lift a weight heavier than herself. Wunsch hoped he would always remember her as she stood by the track, looking up at him; her broad eager face, so fair in color, with its high cheek-bones, yellow eyebrows and greenishhazel eyes. It was a face full of light and energy, of the unquestioning hopefulness of first youth. Yes, she was like a flower full of sun, but not the soft German flowers of his childhood. He had it now, the comparison he had absently reached for before: she was like the yellow prickly pear blossoms that open there in the desert; thornier and sturdier than the maiden flowers he remembered; not so sweet, but wonderful.

That night Mrs. Kohler brushed away many a tear as she got supper and set the table for two. When they sat down, Fritz was more silent than usual. People who have lived long together need a third at table: they know each other's thoughts so well that they have nothing left to say. Mrs. Kohler stirred and stirred her coffee and clattered the spoon, but she had no heart for her supper. She felt, for the first time in years, that she was tired of her own cooking. She looked across the glass lamp at her husband and asked him if the butcher liked his new overcoat, and whether he had got the shoulders right in a ready-made suit he was patching over for Ray Kennedy. After supper Fritz offered to wipe the dishes for her, but she told him to go about his business, and not to act as if she were sick or getting helpless.

When her work in the kitchen was all done, she went out to cover the oleanders against frost, and to take a last look at her chickens. As she came back from the hen-house she stopped by one of the linden trees and stood resting her hand on the trunk. He would never come back, the poor man; she knew that. He would drift on from new town to new town, from catastrophe to catastrophe. He would hardly find a good home for himself again. He would die at last in some rough place, and be buried in the desert or on the wild prairie, far enough from any linden tree!

Fritz, smoking his pipe on the kitchen doorstep, watched his Paulina and guessed her thoughts. He, too, was sorry to lose his friend. But Fritz was getting old; he had lived a long while and had learned to lose without struggle.

XIV

"Mother," said Peter Kronborg to his wife one morning about two weeks after Wunsch's departure, "how would you like to drive out to Copper Hole with me to-day?"

Mrs. Kronborg said she thought she would enjoy the drive. She put on her gray cashmere dress and gold watch and chain, as befitted a minister's wife, and while her husband was dressing she packed a black oilcloth satchel with such clothing as she and Thor would need overnight.

Copper Hole was a settlement fifteen miles northwest of Moonstone where Mr. Kronborg preached every Friday evening. There was a big spring there and a creek and a few irrigating ditches. It was a community of discouraged agriculturists who had disastrously experimented with dry farming. Mr. Kronborg always drove out one day and back the next, spending the night with one of his parishioners. Often, when the weather was fine, his wife accompanied him. To-day they set out from home after the midday meal, leaving Tillie in charge of the house. Mrs. Kronborg's maternal feeling was always garnered up in the baby, whoever the baby happened to be. If she had the baby with her, the others could look out for themselves. Thor, of course, was not, accurately speaking, a baby any longer. In the matter of nourishment he was quite independent of his mother, though this independence had not been won without a struggle. Thor was conservative in all things, and the whole family had anguished with him when he was being weaned. Being the youngest, he was still the baby for Mrs. Kronborg, though he was nearly four years old and sat up boldly on her lap this afternoon, holding on to the ends of the lines and shouting "'mup, 'mup, horsey." His father watched him affectionately and hummed hymn tunes in the jovial way that was sometimes such a trial to Thea.

Mrs. Kronborg was enjoying the sunshine and the brilliant sky and all the faintly marked features of the dazzling, monotonous landscape. She had a rather unusual capacity for getting the flavor of places and of people. Although she was so enmeshed in family cares most of the time, she could emerge serene when she was away from them. For a mother of seven, she had a singularly unprejudiced point of view. She was, moreover, a fatalist, and as she did not attempt to direct things beyond her control, she found a good deal of time to enjoy the ways of man and nature.

When they were well upon their road, out where the first lean pasture lands began and the sand grass made a faint showing between the sagebrushes, Mr. Kronborg dropped his tune and turned to his wife. "Mother, I've been thinking about something."

"I guessed you had. What is it?" She shifted Thor to her left knee, where he would be more out of the way.

"Well, it's about Thea. Mr. Follansbee came to my study at the church the other day and said they would like to have their two girls take lessons of Thea. Then I sounded Miss Meyers" (Miss Meyers was the organist in Mr. Kronborg's church) "and she said there was a good deal of talk about whether Thea wouldn't take over Wunsch's pupils. She said if Thea stopped school she wouldn't wonder if she could get pretty much all Wunsch's class. People think Thea knows about all Wunsch could teach."

Mrs. Kronborg looked thoughtful. "Do you think we ought to take her out of school so young?"

"She is young, but next year would be her last year anyway. She's far along for her age. And she can't learn much under the principal we've got now, can she?"

"No, I'm afraid she can't," his wife admitted. "She frets a good deal and says that man always has to look in the back of the book for the answers. She hates all that diagramming they have to do, and I think myself it's a waste of time."

Mr. Kronborg settled himself back into the seat and slowed the mare to a walk. "You see, it occurs to me that we might raise Thea's prices, so it would be worth her while. Seventy-five cents for hour lessons, fifty cents for half-hour lessons. If she got, say two thirds of Wunsch's class, that would bring her in upwards of ten dollars a week. Better pay than teaching a country school, and there would be more work in vacation than in winter. Steady work twelve months in the year; that's an advantage. And she'd be living at home, with no expenses."

"There'd be talk if you raised her prices," said Mrs. Kronborg dubiously.

"At first there would. But Thea is so much the best musician in town that they'd all come into line after a while. A good many people in Moonstone have been making money lately, and have bought new pianos. There were ten new pianos shipped in here from Denver in the last year. People ain't going to let them stand idle; too much money invested. I believe Thea can have as many scholars as she can handle, if we set her up a little."

"How set her up, do you mean?" Mrs. Kronborg felt a certain reluctance about accepting this plan, though she had not yet had time to think out her reasons.

"Well, I've been thinking for some time we could make good use of another room. We couldn't give up the parlor to her all the time. If we built another room on the ell and put the piano in there, she could give lessons all day long and it wouldn't bother us. We could build a clothes-press in it, and put in a bed-lounge and a dresser and let Anna have it for her sleeping-room. She needs a place of her own, now that she's beginning to be dressy."

"Seems like Thea ought to have the choice of the room, herself," said Mrs. Kronborg.

"But, my dear, she don't want it. Won't have it. I sounded her coming home from church on Sunday; asked her if she would like to sleep in a new room, if we built on. She fired up like a little wild-cat and said she'd made her own room all herself, and she didn't think anybody ought to take it away from her."

"She don't mean to be impertinent, father. She's made decided that way, like my father." Mrs. Kronborg spoke warmly. "I never have any trouble with the child. I remember my father's ways and go at her carefully. Thea's all right."

Mr. Kronborg laughed indulgently and pinched Thor's full cheek. "Oh, I didn't mean anything against your girl, mother! She's all right, but she's a little wild-cat, just the same. I think Ray Kennedy's planning to spoil a born old maid."

"Huh! She'll get something a good sight better than Ray Kennedy, you see! Thea's an awful smart girl. I've seen a good many girls take music lessons in my time, but I ain't seen one that took to it so. Wunsch said so, too. She's got the making of something in her."

"I don't deny that, and the sooner she gets at it in a businesslike way, the better. She's the kind that takes responsibility, and it'll be good for her."

Mrs. Kronborg was thoughtful. "In some ways it will, maybe. But there's a good deal of strain about teaching youngsters, and she's always worked so hard with the scholars she has. I've often listened to her pounding it into 'em. I don't want to work her too hard. She's so serious that she's never had what you might call any real childhood. Seems like she ought to have the next few years sort of free and easy. She'll be tied down with responsibilities soon enough."

Mr. Kronborg patted his wife's arm. "Don't you believe it, mother. Thea is not the marrying kind. I've watched 'em. Anna will marry before long and make a good wife, but I don't see Thea bringing up a family. She's got a good deal of her mother in her, but she hasn't got all. She's too peppery and too fond of having her own way. Then she's always got to be ahead in everything. That kind make good church-workers and missionaries and school teachers, but they don't make good wives. They fret all their energy away, like colts, and get cut on the wire."

Mrs. Kronborg laughed. "Give me the graham crackers I put in your pocket for Thor. He's hungry. You're a funny man, Peter. A body wouldn't think, to hear you, you was talking about your own daughters. I guess you see through 'em. Still, even if Thea ain't apt to have children of her own, I don't know as that's a good reason why she should wear herself out on other people's."

"That's just the point, mother. A girl with all that energy has got to do something, same as a boy, to keep her out of mischief. If you don't want her to marry Ray, let her do something to make herself independent."

"Well, I'm not against it. It might be the best thing for her. I wish I felt sure she wouldn't worry. She takes things hard. She nearly cried herself sick about Wunsch's going away. She's the smartest child of 'em all, Peter, by a long ways."

Peter Kronborg smiled. "There you go, Anna. That's you all over again. Now, I have no favorites; they all have their good points. But you," with a twinkle, "always did go in for brains."

Mrs. Kronborg chuckled as she wiped the cracker crumbs from Thor's chin and fists. "Well, you're mighty conceited, Peter! But I don't know as I ever regretted it. I prefer having a family of my own to fussing with other folks' children, that's the truth."

Before the Kronborgs reached Copper Hole, Thea's destiny was pretty well mapped out for her. Mr. Kronborg was always delighted to have an excuse for enlarging the house.

Mrs. Kronborg was quite right in her conjecture that there would be unfriendly comment in Moonstone when Thea raised her prices for music-lessons. People said she was getting too conceited for anything. Mrs. Livery Johnson put on a new bonnet and paid up all her back calls to have the pleasure of announcing in each parlor she entered that her daughters, at least, would "never pay professional prices to Thea Kronborg."

Thea raised no objection to quitting school. She was now in the "high room," as it was called, in next to the highest class, and was studying geometry and beginning Caesar. She no longer recited her lessons to the teacher she liked, but to the Principal, a man who belonged, like Mrs. Livery Johnson, to the camp of Thea's natural enemies. He taught school because he was too lazy to work among grown-up people, and he made an easy job of it. He got out of real work by inventing useless activities for his pupils, such as the "tree-diagramming system." Thea had spent hours making trees out of "Thanatopsis," Hamlet's soliloquy, Cato on "Immortality." She agonized under this waste of time, and was only too glad to accept her father's offer of liberty.

So Thea left school the first of November. By the first of January she had eight one-hour pupils and ten half-hour pupils, and there would be more in the summer. She spent her earnings generously. She bought a new Brussels carpet for the parlor, and a rifle for Gunner and Axel, and an imitation tiger-skin coat and cap for Thor. She enjoyed being able to add to the family possessions, and thought Thor looked quite as handsome in his spots as the rich children she had seen in Denver. Thor was most complacent in his conspicuous apparel. He could walk anywhere by this time--though he always preferred to sit, or to be pulled in his cart. He was a blissfully lazy child, and had a number of long, dull plays, such as making nests for his china duck and waiting for her to lay him an egg. Thea thought him very intelligent, and she was proud that he was so big and burly. She found him restful, loved to hear him call her "sitter," and really liked his companionship, especially when she was tired. On Saturday, for instance, when she taught from nine in the morning until five in the afternoon, she liked to get off in a corner with Thor after supper, away from all the bathing and dressing and joking and talking that went on in the house, and ask him about his duck, or hear him tell one of his rambling stories.

XV

By the time Thea's fifteenth birthday came round, she was established as a music teacher in Moonstone. The new room had been added to the house early in the spring, and Thea had been giving her lessons there since the middle of May. She liked the personal independence which was accorded her as a wage-earner. The family questioned her comings and goings very little. She could go buggy-riding with Ray Kennedy, for instance, without taking Gunner or Axel. She could go to Spanish Johnny's and sing part songs with the Mexicans, and nobody objected.

Thea was still under the first excitement of teaching, and was terribly in earnest about it. If a pupil did not get on well, she fumed and fretted. She counted until she was hoarse. She listened to scales in her sleep. Wunsch had taught only one pupil seriously, but Thea taught twenty. The duller they were, the more furiously she poked and prodded them. With the little girls she was nearly always patient, but with pupils older than herself, she sometimes lost her temper. One of her mistakes was to let herself in for a calling-down from Mrs. Livery Johnson. That lady appeared at the Kronborgs' one morning and announced that she would allow no girl to stamp her foot at her daughter Grace. She added that Thea's bad manners with the older girls were being talked about all over town, and that if her temper did not speedily improve she would lose all her advanced pupils. Thea was frightened. She felt she could never bear the disgrace, if such a thing happened. Besides, what would her father say, after he had gone to the expense of building an addition to the house? Mrs. Johnson demanded an apology to Grace. Thea said she was willing to make it. Mrs. Johnson said that hereafter, since she had taken lessons of the best piano teacher in Grinnell, Iowa, she herself would decide what pieces Grace should study. Thea readily consented to that, and Mrs. Johnson rustled away to tell a neighbor woman that Thea Kronborg could be meek enough when you went at her right.

Thea was telling Ray about this unpleasant encounter as they were driving out to the sand hills the next Sunday.

"She was stuffing you, all right, Thee," Ray reassured her. "There's no general dissatisfaction among your scholars. She just wanted to get in a knock. I talked to the piano tuner the last time he was here, and he said all the people he tuned for expressed themselves very favorably about your teaching. I wish you didn't take so much pains with them, myself."

"But I have to, Ray. They're all so dumb. They've got no ambition," Thea exclaimed irritably. "Jenny Smiley is the only one who isn't stupid. She can read pretty well, and she has such good hands. But she don't care a rap about it. She has no pride."

Ray's face was full of complacent satisfaction as he glanced sidewise at Thea, but she was looking off intently into the mirage, at one of those mammoth cattle that are nearly always reflected there. "Do you find it easier to teach in your new room?" he asked.

"Yes; I'm not interrupted so much. Of course, if I ever happen to want to practice at night, that's always the night Anna chooses to go to bed early."

"It's a darned shame, Thee, you didn't cop that room for yourself. I'm sore at the PADRE about that. He ought to give you that room. You could fix it up so pretty."

"I didn't want it, honest I didn't. Father would have let me have it. I like my own room better. Somehow I can think better in a little room. Besides, up there I am away from everybody, and I can read as late as I please and nobody nags me."

"A growing girl needs lots of sleep," Ray providently remarked.

Thea moved restlessly on the buggy cushions. "They need other things more," she muttered. "Oh, I forgot. I brought something to show you. Look here, it came on my birthday. Wasn't it nice of him to remember?" She took from her pocket a postcard, bent in the middle and folded, and handed it to Ray. On it was a white dove, perched on a wreath of very blue forget-me-nots, and "Birthday Greetings" in gold letters. Under this was written, "From A. Wunsch."

Ray turned the card over, examined the postmark, and then began to laugh.

"Concord, Kansas. He has my sympathy!"

"Why, is that a poor town?"

"It's the jumping-off place, no town at all. Some houses dumped down in the middle of a cornfield. You get lost in the corn. Not even a saloon to keep things going; sell whiskey without a license at the butcher shop, beer on ice with the liver and beefsteak. I wouldn't stay there over Sunday for a ten-dollar bill."

"Oh, dear! What do you suppose he's doing there? Maybe he just stopped off there a few days to tune pianos," Thea suggested hopefully.

Ray gave her back the card. "He's headed in the wrong direction. What does he want to get back into a grass country for? Now, there are lots of good live towns down on the Santa Fe, and everybody down there is musical. He could always get a job playing in saloons if he was dead broke. I've figured out that I've got no years of my life to waste in a Methodist country where they raise pork."

"We must stop on our way back and show this card to Mrs. Kohler. She misses him so."

"By the way, Thee, I hear the old woman goes to church every Sunday to hear you sing. Fritz tells me he has to wait till two o'clock for his Sunday dinner these days. The church people ought to give you credit for that, when they go for you."

Thea shook her head and spoke in a tone of resignation. "They'll always go for me, just as they did for Wunsch. It wasn't because he drank they went for him; not really. It was something else."

"You want to salt your money down, Thee, and go to Chicago and take some lessons. Then you come back, and wear a long feather and high heels and put on a few airs, and that'll fix 'em. That's what they like."

"I'll never have money enough to go to Chicago. Mother meant to lend me some, I think, but now they've got hard times back in Nebraska, and her farm don't bring her in anything. Takes all the tenant can raise to pay the taxes. Don't let's talk about that. You promised to tell me about the play you went to see in Denver."

Any one would have liked to hear Ray's simple and clear account of the performance he had seen at the Tabor Grand Opera House--Maggie Mitchell in LITTLE BAREFOOT--and any one would have liked to watch his kind face. Ray looked his best out of doors, when his thick red hands were covered by gloves, and the dull red of his sunburned face somehow seemed right in the light and wind. He looked better, too, with his hat on; his hair was thin and dry, with no particular color or character, "regular Willy-boy hair," as he himself described it. His eyes were pale beside the reddish bronze of his skin. They had the faded look often seen in the eyes of men who have lived much in the sun and wind and who have been accustomed to train their vision upon distant objects.

Ray realized that Thea's life was dull and exacting, and that she missed Wunsch. He knew she worked hard, that she put up with a great many little annoyances, and that her duties as a teacher separated her more than ever from the boys and girls of her own age. He did everything he could to provide recreation for her. He brought her candy and magazines and pineapples--of which she was very fond--from Denver, and kept his eyes and ears open for anything that might interest her. He was, of course, living for Thea. He had thought it all out carefully and had made up his mind just when he would speak to her. When she was seventeen, then he would tell her his plan and ask her to marry him. He would be willing to wait two, or even three years, until she was twenty, if she thought best. By that time he would surely have got in on something: copper, oil, gold, silver, sheep,--something.

Meanwhile, it was pleasure enough to feel that she depended on him more and more, that she leaned upon his steady kindness. He never broke faith with himself about her; he never hinted to her of his hopes for the future, never suggested that she might be more intimately confidential with him, or talked to her of the thing he thought about so constantly. He had the chivalry which is perhaps the proudest possession of his race. He had never embarrassed her by so much as a glance. Sometimes, when they drove out to the sand hills, he let his left arm lie along the back of the buggy seat, but it never came any nearer to Thea than that, never touched her. He often turned to her a face full of pride, and frank admiration, but his glance was never so intimate or so penetrating as Dr. Archie's. His blue eyes were clear and shallow, friendly, uninquiring. He rested Thea because he was so different; because, though he often told her interesting things, he never set lively fancies going in her head; because he never misunderstood her, and because he never, by any chance, for a single instant, understood her! Yes, with Ray she was safe; by him she would never be discovered!

XVI

The pleasantest experience Thea had that summer was a trip that she and her mother made to Denver in Ray Kennedy's caboose. Mrs. Kronborg had been looking forward to this excursion for a long while, but as Ray never knew at what hour his freight would leave Moonstone, it was difficult to arrange. The call-boy was as likely to summon him to start on his run at twelve o'clock midnight as at twelve o'clock noon. The first week in June started out with all the scheduled trains running on time, and a light freight business. Tuesday evening Ray, after consulting with the dispatcher, stopped at the Kronborgs' front gate to tell Mrs. Kronborg--who was helping Tillie water the flowers--that if she and Thea could be at the depot at eight o'clock the next morning, he thought he could promise them a pleasant ride and get them into Denver before nine o'clock in the evening. Mrs. Kronborg told him cheerfully, across the fence, that she would "take him up on it," and Ray hurried back to the yards to scrub out his car.

The one complaint Ray's brakemen had to make of him was that he was too fussy about his caboose. His former brakeman had asked to be transferred because, he said, "Kennedy was as fussy about his car as an old maid about her bird-cage." Joe Giddy, who was braking with Ray now, called him "the bride," because he kept the caboose and bunks so clean.

It was properly the brakeman's business to keep the car clean, but when Ray got back to the depot, Giddy was nowhere to be found. Muttering that all his brakemen seemed to consider him "easy," Ray went down to his car alone. He built a fire in the stove and put water on to heat while he got into his overalls and jumper. Then he set to work with a scrubbing-brush and plenty of soap and "cleaner." He scrubbed the floor and seats, blacked the stove, put clean sheets on the bunks, and then began to demolish Giddy's picture gallery. Ray found that his brakemen were likely to have what he termed "a taste for the nude in art," and Giddy was no exception. Ray took down half a dozen girls in tights and ballet skirts,--premiums for cigarette coupons,--and some racy calendars advertising saloons and sporting clubs, which had cost Giddy both time and trouble; he even removed Giddy's particular pet, a naked girl lying on a couch with her knee carelessly poised in the air. Underneath the picture was printed the title, "The Odalisque." Giddy was under the happy delusion that this title meant something wicked,--there was a wicked look about the consonants,--but Ray, of course, had looked it up, and Giddy was indebted to the dictionary for the privilege of keeping his lady. If "odalisque" had been what Ray called an objectionable word, he would have thrown the picture out in the first place. Ray even took down a picture of Mrs. Langtry in evening dress, because it was entitled the "Jersey Lily," and because there was a small head of Edward VII, then Prince of Wales, in one corner. Albert Edward's conduct was a popular subject of discussion among railroad men in those days, and as Ray pulled the tacks out of this lithograph he felt more indignant with the English than ever. He deposited all these pictures under the mattress of Giddy's bunk, and stood admiring his clean car in the lamplight; the walls now exhibited only a wheatfield, advertising agricultural implements, a map of Colorado, and some pictures of race-horses and hunting-dogs. At this moment Giddy, freshly shaved and shampooed, his shirt shining with the highest polish known to Chinese laundrymen, his straw hat tipped over his right eye, thrust his head in at the door.

"What in hell--" he brought out furiously. His good humored, sunburned face seemed fairly to swell with amazement and anger.

"That's all right, Giddy," Ray called in a conciliatory tone. "Nothing injured. I'll put 'em all up again as I found 'em. Going to take some ladies down in the car to-morrow."

Giddy scowled. He did not dispute the propriety of Ray's measures, if there were to be ladies on board, but he felt injured. "I suppose you'll expect me to behave like a Y.M.C.A. secretary," he growled. "I can't do my work and serve tea at the same time."

"No need to have a tea-party," said Ray with determined cheerfulness. "Mrs. Kronborg will bring the lunch, and it will be a darned good one."

Giddy lounged against the car, holding his cigar between two thick fingers. "Then I guess she'll get it," he observed knowingly. "I don't think your musical friend is much on the grub-box. Has to keep her hands white to tickle the ivories." Giddy had nothing against Thea, but he felt cantankerous and wanted to get a rise out of Kennedy.

"Every man to his own job," Ray replied agreeably, pulling his white shirt on over his head.

Giddy emitted smoke disdainfully. "I suppose so. The man that gets her will have to wear an apron and bake the pancakes. Well, some men like to mess about the kitchen." He paused, but Ray was intent on getting into his clothes as quickly as possible. Giddy thought he could go a little further. "Of course, I don't dispute your right to haul women in this car if you want to; but personally, so far as I'm concerned, I'd a good deal rather drink a can of tomatoes and do without the women AND their lunch. I was never much enslaved to hard-boiled eggs, anyhow."

"You'll eat 'em to-morrow, all the same." Ray's tone had a steely glitter as he jumped out of the car, and Giddy stood aside to let him pass. He knew that Kennedy's next reply would be delivered by hand. He had once seen Ray beat up a nasty fellow for insulting a Mexican woman who helped about the grub-car in the work train, and his fists had worked like two steel hammers. Giddy wasn't looking for trouble.

At eight o'clock the next morning Ray greeted his ladies and helped them into the car. Giddy had put on a clean shirt and yellow pig-skin gloves and was whistling his best. He considered Kennedy a fluke as a ladies' man, and if there was to be a party, the honors had to be done by some one who wasn't a blacksmith at small-talk. Giddy had, as Ray sarcastically admitted, "a local reputation as a jollier," and he was fluent in gallant speeches of a not too-veiled nature. He insisted that Thea should take his seat in the cupola, opposite Ray's, where she could look out over the country. Thea told him, as she clambered up, that she cared a good deal more about riding in that seat than about going to Denver. Ray was never so companionable and easy as when he sat chatting in the lookout of his little house on wheels. Good stories came to him, and interesting recollections. Thea had a great respect for the reports he had to write out, and for the telegrams that were handed to him at stations; for all the knowledge and experience it must take to run a freight train.

Giddy, down in the car, in the pauses of his work, made himself agreeable to Mrs. Kronborg.

"It's a great rest to be where my family can't get at me, Mr. Giddy," she told him. "I thought you and Ray might have some housework here for me to look after, but I couldn't improve any on this car."

"Oh, we like to keep her neat," returned Giddy glibly, winking up at Ray's expressive back. "If you want to see a clean ice-box, look at this one. Yes, Kennedy always carries fresh cream to eat on his oatmeal. I'm not particular. The tin cow's good enough for me."

"Most of you boys smoke so much that all victuals taste alike to you," said Mrs. Kronborg. "I've got no religious scruples against smoking, but I couldn't take as much interest cooking for a man that used tobacco. I guess it's all right for bachelors who have to eat round."

Mrs. Kronborg took off her hat and veil and made herself comfortable. She seldom had an opportunity to be idle, and she enjoyed it. She could sit for hours and watch the sage-hens fly up and the jack-rabbits dart away from the track, without being bored. She wore a tan bombazine dress, made very plainly, and carried a roomy, worn, mother-of-the-family handbag.

Ray Kennedy always insisted that Mrs. Kronborg was "a fine-looking lady," but this was not the common opinion in Moonstone. Ray had lived long enough among the Mexicans to dislike fussiness, to feel that there was something more attractive in ease of manner than in absentminded concern about hairpins and dabs of lace. He had learned to think that the way a woman stood, moved, sat in her chair, looked at you, was more important than the absence of wrinkles from her skirt. Ray had, indeed, such unusual perceptions in some directions, that one could not help wondering what he would have been if he had ever, as he said, had "half a chance."

He was right; Mrs. Kronborg was a fine-looking woman. She was short and square, but her head was a real head, not a mere jerky termination of the body. It had some individuality apart from hats and hairpins. Her hair, Moonstone women admitted, would have been very pretty "on anybody else." Frizzy bangs were worn then, but Mrs. Kronborg always dressed her hair in the same way, parted in the middle, brushed smoothly back from her low, white forehead, pinned loosely on the back of her head in two thick braids. It was growing gray about the temples, but after the manner of yellow hair it seemed only to have grown paler there, and had taken on a color like that of English primroses. Her eyes were clear and untroubled; her face smooth and calm, and, as Ray said, "strong."

Thea and Ray, up in the sunny cupola, were laughing and talking. Ray got great pleasure out of seeing her face there in the little box where he so often imagined it. They were crossing a plateau where great red sandstone boulders lay about, most of them much wider at the top than at the base, so that they looked like great toadstools.

"The sand has been blowing against them for a good many hundred years," Ray explained, directing Thea's eyes with his gloved hand. "You see the sand blows low, being so heavy, and cuts them out underneath. Wind and sand are pretty high-class architects. That's the principle of most of the Cliff-Dweller remains down at Canyon de Chelly. The sandstorms had dug out big depressions in the face of a cliff, and the Indians built their houses back in that depression."

"You told me that before, Ray, and of course you know. But the geography says their houses were cut out of the face of the living rock, and I like that better."

Ray sniffed. "What nonsense does get printed! It's enough to give a man disrespect for learning. How could them Indians cut houses out of the living rock, when they knew nothing about the art of forging metals?" Ray leaned back in his chair, swung his foot, and looked thoughtful and happy. He was in one of his favorite fields of speculation, and nothing gave him more pleasure than talking these things over with Thea Kronborg. "I'll tell you, Thee, if those old fellows had learned to work metals once, your ancient Egyptians and Assyrians wouldn't have beat them very much. Whatever they did do, they did well. Their masonry's standing there to-day, the corners as true as the Denver Capitol. They were clever at most everything but metals; and that one failure kept them from getting across. It was the quicksand that swallowed 'em up, as a race. I guess civilization proper began when men mastered metals."

Ray was not vain about his bookish phrases. He did not use them to show off, but because they seemed to him more adequate than colloquial speech. He felt strongly about these things, and groped for words, as he said, "to express himself." He had the lamentable American belief that "expression" is obligatory. He still carried in his trunk, among the unrelated possessions of a railroad man, a notebook on the title-page of which was written "Impressions on First Viewing the Grand Canyon, Ray H. Kennedy." The pages of that book were like a battlefield; the laboring author had fallen back from metaphor after metaphor, abandoned position after position. He would have admitted that the art of forging metals was nothing to this treacherous business of recording impressions, in which the material you were so full of vanished mysteriously under your striving hand. "Escaping steam!" he had said to himself, the last time he tried to read that notebook.

Thea didn't mind Ray's travel-lecture expressions. She dodged them, unconsciously, as she did her father's professional palaver. The light in Ray's pale-blue eyes and the feeling in his voice more than made up for the stiffness of his language.

"Were the Cliff-Dwellers really clever with their hands, Ray, or do you always have to make allowance and say, 'That was pretty good for an Indian'?" she asked.

Ray went down into the car to give some instructions to Giddy. "Well," he said when he returned, "about the aborigines: once or twice I've been with some fellows who were cracking burial mounds. Always felt a little ashamed of it, but we did pull out some remarkable things. We got some pottery out whole; seemed pretty fine to me. I guess their women were their artists. We found lots of old shoes and sandals made out of yucca fiber, neat and strong; and feather blankets, too."

"Feather blankets? You never told me about them."

"Didn't I? The old fellows--or the squaws--wove a close netting of yucca fiber, and then tied on little bunches of down feathers, overlapping, just the way feathers grow on a bird. Some of them were feathered on both sides. You can't get anything warmer than that, now, can you?--or prettier. What I like about those old aborigines is, that they got all their ideas from nature."

Thea laughed. "That means you're going to say something about girls' wearing corsets. But some of your Indians flattened their babies' heads, and that's worse than wearing corsets."

"Give me an Indian girl's figure for beauty," Ray insisted. "And a girl with a voice like yours ought to have plenty of lung-action. But you know my sentiments on that subject. I was going to tell you about the handsomest thing we ever looted out of those burial mounds. It was on a woman, too, I regret to say. She was preserved as perfect as any mummy that ever came out of the pyramids. She had a big string of turquoises around her neck, and she was wrapped in a fox-fur cloak, lined with little yellow feathers that must have come off wild canaries. Can you beat that, now? The fellow that claimed it sold it to a Boston man for a hundred and fifty dollars."

Thea looked at him admiringly. "Oh, Ray, and didn't you get anything off her, to remember her by, even? She must have been a princess."

Ray took a wallet from the pocket of the coat that was hanging beside him, and drew from it a little lump wrapped in worn tissue paper. In a moment a stone, soft and blue as a robin's egg, lay in the hard palm of his hand. It was a turquoise, rubbed smooth in the Indian finish, which is so much more beautiful than the incongruous high polish the white man gives that tender stone. "I got this from her necklace. See the hole where the string went through? You know how the Indians drill them? Work the drill with their teeth. You like it, don't you? They're just right for you. Blue and yellow are the Swedish colors." Ray looked intently at her head, bent over his hand, and then gave his whole attention to the track.

"I'll tell you, Thee," he began after a pause, "I'm going to form a camping party one of these days and persuade your PADRE to take you and your mother down to that country, and we'll live in the rock houses--they're as comfortable as can be--and start the cook fires up in 'em once again. I'll go into the burial mounds and get you more keepsakes than any girl ever had before." Ray had planned such an expedition for his wedding journey, and it made his heart thump to see how Thea's eyes kindled when he talked about it. "I've learned more down there about what makes history," he went on, "than in all the books I've ever read. When you sit in the sun and let your heels hang out of a doorway that drops a thousand feet, ideas come to you. You begin to feel what the human race has been up against from the beginning. There's something mighty elevating about those old habitations. You feel like it's up to you to do your best, on account of those fellows having it so hard. You feel like you owed them something."

At Wassiwappa, Ray got instructions to sidetrack until Thirty-six went by. After reading the message, he turned to his guests. "I'm afraid this will hold us up about two hours, Mrs. Kronborg, and we won't get into Denver till near midnight."

"That won't trouble me," said Mrs. Kronborg contentedly. "They know me at the Y.W.C.A., and they'll let me in any time of night. I came to see the country, not to make time. I've always wanted to get out at this white place and look around, and now I'll have a chance. What makes it so white?"

"Some kind of chalky rock." Ray sprang to the ground and gave Mrs. Kronborg his hand. "You can get soil of any color in Colorado; match most any ribbon."

While Ray was getting his train on to a side track, Mrs. Kronborg strolled off to examine the post-office and station house; these, with the water tank, made up the town. The station agent "batched" and raised chickens. He ran out to meet Mrs. Kronborg, clutched at her feverishly, and began telling her at once how lonely he was and what bad luck he was having with his poultry. She went to his chicken yard with him, and prescribed for gapes.

Wassiwappa seemed a dreary place enough to people who looked for verdure, a brilliant place to people who liked color. Beside the station house there was a blue-grass plot, protected by a red plank fence, and six fly-bitten box-elder trees, not much larger than bushes, were kept alive by frequent hosings from the water plug. Over the windows some dusty morning-glory vines were trained on strings. All the country about was broken up into low chalky hills, which were so intensely white, and spotted so evenly with sage, that they looked like white leopards crouching. White dust powdered everything, and the light was so intense that the station agent usually wore blue glasses. Behind the station there was a water course, which roared in flood time, and a basin in the soft white rock where a pool of alkali water flashed in the sun like a mirror. The agent looked almost as sick as his chickens, and Mrs. Kronborg at once invited him to lunch with her party. He had, he confessed, a distaste for his own cooking, and lived mainly on soda crackers and canned beef. He laughed apologetically when Mrs. Kronborg said she guessed she'd look about for a shady place to eat lunch.

She walked up the track to the water tank, and there, in the narrow shadows cast by the uprights on which the tank stood, she found two tramps. They sat up and stared at her, heavy with sleep. When she asked them where they were going, they told her "to the coast." They rested by day and traveled by night; walked the ties unless they could steal a ride, they said; adding that "these Western roads were getting strict." Their faces were blistered, their eyes blood-shot, and their shoes looked fit only for the trash pile.

"I suppose you're hungry?" Mrs. Kronborg asked. "I suppose you both drink?" she went on thoughtfully, not censoriously.

The huskier of the two hoboes, a bushy, bearded fellow, rolled his eyes and said, "I wonder?" But the other, who was old and spare, with a sharp nose and watery eyes, sighed. "Some has one affliction, some another," he said.

Mrs. Kronborg reflected. "Well," she said at last, "you can't get liquor here, anyway. I am going to ask you to vacate, because I want to have a little picnic under this tank for the freight crew that brought me along. I wish I had lunch enough to provide you, but I ain't. The station agent says he gets his provisions over there at the post office store, and if you are hungry you can get some canned stuff there." She opened her handbag and gave each of the tramps a half-dollar.

The old man wiped his eyes with his forefinger. "Thank 'ee, ma'am. A can of tomatters will taste pretty good to me. I wasn't always walkin' ties; I had a good job in Cleveland before--"

The hairy tramp turned on him fiercely. "Aw, shut up on that, grandpaw! Ain't you got no gratitude? What do you want to hand the lady that fur?"

The old man hung his head and turned away. As he went off, his comrade looked after him and said to Mrs. Kronborg: "It's true, what he says. He had a job in the car shops; but he had bad luck." They both limped away toward the store, and Mrs. Kronborg sighed. She was not afraid of tramps. She always talked to them, and never turned one away. She hated to think how many of them there were, crawling along the tracks over that vast country.

Her reflections were cut short by Ray and Giddy and Thea, who came bringing the lunch box and water bottles. Although there was not shadow enough to accommodate all the party at once, the air under the tank was distinctly cooler than the surrounding air, and the drip made a pleasant sound in that breathless noon. The station agent ate as if he had never been fed before, apologizing every time he took another piece of fried chicken. Giddy was unabashed before the devilled eggs of which he had spoken so scornfully last night. After lunch the men lit their pipes and lay back against the uprights that supported the tank.

"This is the sunny side of railroading, all right," Giddy drawled luxuriously.

"You fellows grumble too much," said Mrs. Kronborg as she corked the pickle jar. "Your job has its drawbacks, but it don't tie you down. Of course there's the risk; but I believe a man's watched over, and he can't be hurt on the railroad or anywhere else if it's intended he shouldn't be."

Giddy laughed. "Then the trains must be operated by fellows the Lord has it in for, Mrs. Kronborg. They figure it out that a railroad man's only due to last eleven years; then it's his turn to be smashed."

"That's a dark Providence, I don't deny," Mrs. Kronborg admitted. "But there's lots of things in life that's hard to understand."

"I guess!" murmured Giddy, looking off at the spotted white hills.

Ray smoked in silence, watching Thea and her mother clear away the lunch. He was thinking that Mrs. Kronborg had in her face the same serious look that Thea had; only hers was calm and satisfied, and Thea's was intense and questioning. But in both it was a large kind of look, that was not all the time being broken up and convulsed by trivial things. They both carried their heads like Indian women, with a kind of noble unconsciousness. He got so tired of women who were always nodding and jerking; apologizing, deprecating, coaxing, insinuating with their heads.

When Ray's party set off again that afternoon the sun beat fiercely into the cupola, and Thea curled up in one of the seats at the back of the car and had a nap.

As the short twilight came on, Giddy took a turn in the cupola, and Ray came down and sat with Thea on the rear platform of the caboose and watched the darkness come in soft waves over the plain. They were now about thirty miles from Denver, and the mountains looked very near. The great toothed wall behind which the sun had gone down now separated into four distinct ranges, one behind the other. They were a very pale blue, a color scarcely stronger than wood smoke, and the sunset had left bright streaks in the snow-filled gorges. In the clear, yellowstreaked sky the stars were coming out, flickering like newly lighted lamps, growing steadier and more golden as the sky darkened and the land beneath them fell into complete shadow. It was a cool, restful darkness that was not black or forbidding, but somehow open and free; the night of high plains where there is no moistness or mistiness in the atmosphere.

Ray lit his pipe. "I never get tired of them old stars, Thee. I miss 'em up in Washington and Oregon where it's misty. Like 'em best down in Mother Mexico, where they have everything their own way. I'm not for any country where the stars are dim." Ray paused and drew on his pipe. "I don't know as I ever really noticed 'em much till that first year I herded sheep up in Wyoming. That was the year the blizzard caught me."

"And you lost all your sheep, didn't you, Ray?" Thea spoke sympathetically. "Was the man who owned them nice about it?"

"Yes, he was a good loser. But I didn't get over it for a long while. Sheep are so damned resigned. Sometimes, to this day, when I'm dog-tired, I try to save them sheep all night long. It comes kind of hard on a boy when he first finds out how little he is, and how big everything else is."

Thea moved restlessly toward him and dropped her chin on her hand, looking at a low star that seemed to rest just on the rim of the earth. "I don't see how you stood it. I don't believe I could. I don't see how people can stand it to get knocked out, anyhow!" She spoke with such fierceness that Ray glanced at her in surprise. She was sitting on the floor of the car, crouching like a little animal about to spring.

"No occasion for you to see," he said warmly. "There'll always be plenty of other people to take the knocks for you."

"That's nonsense, Ray." Thea spoke impatiently and leaned lower still, frowning at the red star. "Everybody's up against it for himself, succeeds or fails--himself."

"In one way, yes," Ray admitted, knocking the sparks from his pipe out into the soft darkness that seemed to flow like a river beside the car. "But when you look at it another way, there are a lot of halfway people in this world who help the winners win, and the failers fail. If a man stumbles, there's plenty of people to push him down. But if he's like `the youth who bore,' those same people are foreordained to help him along. They may hate to, worse than blazes, and they may do a lot of cussin' about it, but they have to help the winners and they can't dodge it. It's a natural law, like what keeps the big clock up there going, little wheels and big, and no mix-up." Ray's hand and his pipe were suddenly outlined against the sky. "Ever occur to you, Thee, that they have to be on time close enough to MAKE TIME? The Dispatcher up there must have a long head." Pleased with his similitude, Ray went back to the lookout. Going into Denver, he had to keep a sharp watch.

Giddy came down, cheerful at the prospect of getting into port, and singing a new topical ditty that had come up from the Santa Fe by way of La Junta. Nobody knows who makes these songs; they seem to follow events automatically. Mrs. Kronborg made Giddy sing the whole twelve verses of this one, and laughed until she wiped her eyes. The story was that of Katie Casey, head diningroom girl at Winslow, Arizona, who was unjustly discharged by the Harvey House manager. Her suitor, the yardmaster, took the switchmen out on a strike until she was reinstated. Freight trains from the east and the west piled up at Winslow until the yards looked like a log-jam. The division superintendent, who was in California, had to wire instructions for Katie Casey's restoration before he could get his trains running. Giddy's song told all this with much detail, both tender and technical, and after each of the dozen verses came the refrain:--

"Oh, who would think that Katie Casey owned the Santa Fe? But it really looks that way, The dispatcher's turnin' gray, All the crews is off their pay; She can hold the freight from Albuquerq' to Needles any day; The division superintendent, he come home from Monterey, Just to see if things was pleasin' Katie Ca--a--a--sey."

Thea laughed with her mother and applauded Giddy. Everything was so kindly and comfortable; Giddy and Ray, and their hospitable little house, and the easy-going country, and the stars. She curled up on the seat again with that warm, sleepy feeling of the friendliness of the world--which nobody keeps very long, and which she was to lose early and irrevocably.

XVII

The summer flew by. Thea was glad when Ray Kennedy had a Sunday in town and could take her driving. Out among the sand hills she could forget the "new room" which was the scene of wearing and fruitless labor. Dr. Archie was away from home a good deal that year. He had put all his money into mines above Colorado Springs, and he hoped for great returns from them.

In the fall of that year, Mr. Kronborg decided that Thea ought to show more interest in church work. He put it to her frankly, one night at supper, before the whole family. "How can I insist on the other girls in the congregation being active in the work, when one of my own daughters manifests so little interest?"

"But I sing every Sunday morning, and I have to give up one night a week to choir practice," Thea declared rebelliously, pushing back her plate with an angry determination to eat nothing more.

"One night a week is not enough for the pastor's daughter," her father replied. "You won't do anything in the sewing society, and you won't take part in the Christian Endeavor or the Band of Hope. Very well, you must make it up in other ways. I want some one to play the organ and lead the singing at prayer-meeting this winter. Deacon Potter told me some time ago that he thought there would be more interest in our prayer-meetings if we had the organ. Miss Meyers don't feel that she can play on Wednesday nights. And there ought to be somebody to start the hymns. Mrs. Potter is getting old, and she always starts them too high. It won't take much of your time, and it will keep people from talking."

This argument conquered Thea, though she left the table sullenly. The fear of the tongue, that terror of little towns, is usually felt more keenly by the minister's family than by other households. Whenever the Kronborgs wanted to do anything, even to buy a new carpet, they had to take counsel together as to whether people would talk. Mrs. Kronborg had her own conviction that people talked when they felt like it, and said what they chose, no matter how the minister's family conducted themselves. But she did not impart these dangerous ideas to her children. Thea was still under the belief that public opinion could be placated; that if you clucked often enough, the hens would mistake you for one of themselves.

Mrs. Kronborg did not have any particular zest for prayer-meetings, and she stayed at home whenever she had a valid excuse. Thor was too old to furnish such an excuse now, so every Wednesday night, unless one of the children was sick, she trudged off with Thea, behind Mr. Kronborg. At first Thea was terribly bored. But she got used to prayermeeting, got even to feel a mournful interest in it.

The exercises were always pretty much the same. After the first hymn her father read a passage from the Bible, usually a Psalm. Then there was another hymn, and then her father commented upon the passage he had read and, as he said, "applied the Word to our necessities." After a third hymn, the meeting was declared open, and the old men and women took turns at praying and talking. Mrs. Kronborg never spoke in meeting. She told people firmly that she had been brought up to keep silent and let the men talk, but she gave respectful attention to the others, sitting with her hands folded in her lap.

The prayer-meeting audience was always small. The young and energetic members of the congregation came only once or twice a year, "to keep people from talking." The usual Wednesday night gathering was made up of old women, with perhaps six or eight old men, and a few sickly girls who had not much interest in life; two of them, indeed, were already preparing to die. Thea accepted the mournfulness of the prayer-meetings as a kind of spiritual discipline, like funerals. She always read late after she went home and felt a stronger wish than usual to live and to be happy.

The meetings were conducted in the Sunday-School room, where there were wooden chairs instead of pews; an old map of Palestine hung on the wall, and the bracket lamps gave out only a dim light. The old women sat motionless as Indians in their shawls and bonnets; some of them wore long black mourning veils. The old men drooped in their chairs. Every back, every face, every head said "resignation." Often there were long silences, when you could hear nothing but the crackling of the soft coal in the stove and the muffled cough of one of the sick girls.

There was one nice old lady,--tall, erect, self-respecting, with a delicate white face and a soft voice. She never whined, and what she said was always cheerful, though she spoke so nervously that Thea knew she dreaded getting up, and that she made a real sacrifice to, as she said, "testify to the goodness of her Saviour." She was the mother of the girl who coughed, and Thea used to wonder how she explained things to herself. There was, indeed, only one woman who talked because she was, as Mr. Kronborg said, "tonguey." The others were somehow impressive. They told about the sweet thoughts that came to them while they were at their work; how, amid their household tasks, they were suddenly lifted by the sense of a divine Presence. Sometimes they told of their first conversion, of how in their youth that higher Power had made itself known to them. Old Mr. Carsen, the carpenter, who gave his services as janitor to the church, used often to tell how, when he was a young man and a scoffer, bent on the destruction of both body and soul, his Saviour had come to him in the Michigan woods and had stood, it seemed to him, beside the tree he was felling; and how he dropped his axe and knelt in prayer "to Him who died for us upon the tree." Thea always wanted to ask him more about it; about his mysterious wickedness, and about the vision.

Sometimes the old people would ask for prayers for their absent children. Sometimes they asked their brothers and sisters in Christ to pray that they might be stronger against temptations. One of the sick girls used to ask them to pray that she might have more faith in the times of depression that came to her, "when all the way before seemed dark." She repeated that husky phrase so often, that Thea always remembered it.

One old woman, who never missed a Wednesday night, and who nearly always took part in the meeting, came all the way up from the depot settlement. She always wore a black crocheted "fascinator" over her thin white hair, and she made long, tremulous prayers, full of railroad terminology. She had six sons in the service of different railroads, and she always prayed "for the boys on the road, who know not at what moment they may be cut off. When, in Thy divine wisdom, their hour is upon them, may they, O our Heavenly Father, see only white lights along the road to Eternity." She used to speak, too, of "the engines that race with death"; and though she looked so old and little when she was on her knees, and her voice was so shaky, her prayers had a thrill of speed and danger in them; they made one think of the deep black canyons, the slender trestles, the pounding trains. Thea liked to look at her sunken eyes that seemed full of wisdom, at her black thread gloves, much too long in the fingers and so meekly folded one over the other. Her face was brown, and worn away as rocks are worn by water. There are many ways of describing that color of age, but in reality it is not like parchment, or like any of the things it is said to be like. That brownness and that texture of skin are found only in the faces of old human creatures, who have worked hard and who have always been poor.

One bitterly cold night in December the prayer-meeting seemed to Thea longer than usual. The prayers and the talks went on and on. It was as if the old people were afraid to go out into the cold, or were stupefied by the hot air of the room. She had left a book at home that she was impatient to get back to. At last the Doxology was sung, but the old people lingered about the stove to greet each other, and Thea took her mother's arm and hurried out to the frozen sidewalk, before her father could get away. The wind was whistling up the street and whipping the naked cottonwood trees against the telegraph poles and the sides of the houses. Thin snow clouds were flying overhead, so that the sky looked gray, with a dull phosphorescence. The icy streets and the shingle roofs of the houses were gray, too. All along the street, shutters banged or windows rattled, or gates wobbled, held by their latch but shaking on loose hinges. There was not a cat or a dog in Moonstone that night that was not given a warm shelter; the cats under the kitchen stove, the dogs in barns or coal-sheds. When Thea and her mother reached home, their mufflers were covered with ice, where their breath had frozen. They hurried into the house and made a dash for the parlor and the hard-coal burner, behind which Gunner was sitting on a stool, reading his Jules Verne book. The door stood open into the dining-room, which was heated from the parlor. Mr. Kronborg always had a lunch when he came home from prayer-meeting, and his pumpkin pie and milk were set out on the dining-table. Mrs. Kronborg said she thought she felt hungry, too, and asked Thea if she didn't want something to eat.

"No, I'm not hungry, mother. I guess I'll go upstairs."

"I expect you've got some book up there," said Mrs. Kronborg, bringing out another pie. "You'd better bring it down here and read. Nobody'll disturb you, and it's terrible cold up in that loft."

Thea was always assured that no one would disturb her if she read downstairs, but the boys talked when they came in, and her father fairly delivered discourses after he had been renewed by half a pie and a pitcher of milk.

"I don't mind the cold. I'll take a hot brick up for my feet. I put one in the stove before I left, if one of the boys hasn't stolen it. Good-night, mother." Thea got her brick and lantern, and dashed upstairs through the windy loft. She undressed at top speed and got into bed with her brick. She put a pair of white knitted gloves on her hands, and pinned over her head a piece of soft flannel that had been one of Thor's long petticoats when he was a baby. Thus equipped, she was ready for business. She took from her table a thick paper-backed volume, one of the "line" of paper novels the druggist kept to sell to traveling men. She had bought it, only yesterday, because the first sentence interested her very much, and because she saw, as she glanced over the pages, the magical names of two Russian cities. The book was a poor translation of "Anna Karenina." Thea opened it at a mark, and fixed her eyes intently upon the small print. The hymns, the sick girl, the resigned black figures were forgotten. It was the night of the ball in Moscow.

Thea would have been astonished if she could have known how, years afterward, when she had need of them, those old faces were to come back to her, long after they were hidden away under the earth; that they would seem to her then as full of meaning, as mysteriously marked by Destiny, as the people who danced the mazurka under the elegant Korsunsky.

XVIII

Mr. Kronborg was too fond of his ease and too sensible to worry his children much about religion. He was more sincere than many preachers, but when he spoke to his family about matters of conduct it was usually with a regard for keeping up appearances. The church and church work were discussed in the family like the routine of any other business. Sunday was the hard day of the week with them, just as Saturday was the busy day with the merchants on Main Street. Revivals were seasons of extra work and pressure, just as threshing-time was on the farms. Visiting elders had to be lodged and cooked for, the folding-bed in the parlor was let down, and Mrs. Kronborg had to work in the kitchen all day long and attend the night meetings.

During one of these revivals Thea's sister Anna professed religion with, as Mrs. Kronborg said, "a good deal of fluster." While Anna was going up to the mourners' bench nightly and asking for the prayers of the congregation, she disseminated general gloom throughout the household, and after she joined the church she took on an air of "set-apartness" that was extremely trying to her brothers and her sister, though they realized that Anna's sanctimoniousness was perhaps a good thing for their father. A preacher ought to have one child who did more than merely acquiesce in religious observances, and Thea and the boys were glad enough that it was Anna and not one of themselves who assumed this obligation.

"Anna, she's American," Mrs. Kronborg used to say. The Scandinavian mould of countenance, more or less marked in each of the other children, was scarcely discernible in her, and she looked enough like other Moonstone girls to be thought pretty. Anna's nature was conventional, like her face. Her position as the minister's eldest daughter was important to her, and she tried to live up to it. She read sentimental religious story-books and emulated the spiritual struggles and magnanimous behavior of their persecuted heroines. Everything had to be interpreted for Anna. Her opinions about the smallest and most commonplace things were gleaned from the Denver papers, the church weeklies, from sermons and Sunday-School addresses. Scarcely anything was attractive to her in its natural state--indeed, scarcely anything was decent until it was clothed by the opinion of some authority. Her ideas about habit, character, duty, love, marriage, were grouped under heads, like a book of popular quotations, and were totally unrelated to the emergencies of human living. She discussed all these subjects with other Methodist girls of her age. They would spend hours, for instance, in deciding what they would or would not tolerate in a suitor or a husband, and the frailties of masculine nature were too often a subject of discussion among them. In her behavior Anna was a harmless girl, mild except where her prejudices were concerned, neat and industrious, with no graver fault than priggishness; but her mind had really shocking habits of classification. The wickedness of Denver and of Chicago, and even of Moonstone, occupied her thoughts too much. She had none of the delicacy that goes with a nature of warm impulses, but the kind of fishy curiosity which justifies itself by an expression of horror.

Thea, and all Thea's ways and friends, seemed indecorous to Anna. She not only felt a grave social discrimination against the Mexicans; she could not forget that Spanish Johnny was a drunkard and that "nobody knew what he did when he ran away from home." Thea pretended, of course, that she liked the Mexicans because they were fond of music; but every one knew that music was nothing very real, and that it did not matter in a girl's relations with people. What was real, then, and what did matter? Poor Anna!

Anna approved of Ray Kennedy as a young man of steady habits and blameless life, but she regretted that he was an atheist, and that he was not a passenger conductor with brass buttons on his coat. On the whole, she wondered what such an exemplary young man found to like in Thea. Dr. Archie she treated respectfully because of his position in Moonstone, but she KNEW he had kissed the Mexican barytone's pretty daughter, and she had a whole DOSSIER of evidence about his behavior in his hours of relaxation in Denver. He was "fast," and it was because he was "fast" that Thea liked him. Thea always liked that kind of people. Dr. Archie's whole manner with Thea, Anna often told her mother, was too free. He was always putting his hand on Thea's head, or holding her hand while he laughed and looked down at her. The kindlier manifestation of human nature (about which Anna sang and talked, in the interests of which she went to conventions and wore white ribbons) were never realities to her after all. She did not believe in them. It was only in attitudes of protest or reproof, clinging to the cross, that human beings could be even temporarily decent.

Preacher Kronborg's secret convictions were very much like Anna's. He believed that his wife was absolutely good, but there was not a man or woman in his congregation whom he trusted all the way.

Mrs. Kronborg, on the other hand, was likely to find something to admire in almost any human conduct that was positive and energetic. She could always be taken in by the stories of tramps and runaway boys. She went to the circus and admired the bareback riders, who were "likely good enough women in their way." She admired Dr. Archie's fine physique and well-cut clothes as much as Thea did, and said she "felt it was a privilege to be handled by such a gentleman when she was sick."

Soon after Anna became a church member she began to remonstrate with Thea about practicing--playing "secular music"--on Sunday. One Sunday the dispute in the parlor grew warm and was carried to Mrs. Kronborg in the kitchen. She listened judicially and told Anna to read the chapter about how Naaman the leper was permitted to bow down in the house of Rimmon. Thea went back to the piano, and Anna lingered to say that, since she was in the right, her mother should have supported her.

"No," said Mrs. Kronborg, rather indifferently, "I can't see it that way, Anna. I never forced you to practice, and I don't see as I should keep Thea from it. I like to hear her, and I guess your father does. You and Thea will likely follow different lines, and I don't see as I'm called upon to bring you up alike."

Anna looked meek and abused. "Of course all the church people must hear her. Ours is the only noisy house on this street. You hear what she's playing now, don't you?"

Mrs. Kronborg rose from browning her coffee. "Yes; it's the Blue Danube waltzes. I'm familiar with 'em. If any of the church people come at you, you just send 'em to me. I ain't afraid to speak out on occasion, and I wouldn't mind one bit telling the Ladies' Aid a few things about standard composers." Mrs. Kronborg smiled, and added thoughtfully, "No, I wouldn't mind that one bit."

Anna went about with a reserved and distant air for a week, and Mrs. Kronborg suspected that she held a larger place than usual in her daughter's prayers; but that was another thing she didn't mind.

Although revivals were merely a part of the year's work, like examination week at school, and although Anna's piety impressed her very little, a time came when Thea was perplexed about religion. A scourge of typhoid broke out in Moonstone and several of Thea's schoolmates died of it. She went to their funerals, saw them put into the ground, and wondered a good deal about them. But a certain grim incident, which caused the epidemic, troubled her even more than the death of her friends.

Early in July, soon after Thea's fifteenth birthday, a particularly disgusting sort of tramp came into Moonstone in an empty box car. Thea was sitting in the hammock in the front yard when he first crawled up to the town from the depot, carrying a bundle wrapped in dirty ticking under one arm, and under the other a wooden box with rusty screening nailed over one end. He had a thin, hungry face covered with black hair. It was just before suppertime when he came along, and the street smelled of fried potatoes and fried onions and coffee. Thea saw him sniffing the air greedily and walking slower and slower. He looked over the fence. She hoped he would not stop at their gate, for her mother never turned any one away, and this was the dirtiest and most utterly wretched-looking tramp she had ever seen. There was a terrible odor about him, too. She caught it even at that distance, and put her handkerchief to her nose. A moment later she was sorry, for she knew that he had noticed it. He looked away and shuffled a little faster.

A few days later Thea heard that the tramp had camped in an empty shack over on the east edge of town, beside the ravine, and was trying to give a miserable sort of show there. He told the boys who went to see what he was doing, that he had traveled with a circus. His bundle contained a filthy clown's suit, and his box held half a dozen rattlesnakes.

Saturday night, when Thea went to the butcher shop to get the chickens for Sunday, she heard the whine of an accordion and saw a crowd before one of the saloons. There she found the tramp, his bony body grotesquely attired in the clown's suit, his face shaved and painted white,--the sweat trickling through the paint and washing it away,--and his eyes wild and feverish. Pulling the accordion in and out seemed to be almost too great an effort for him, and he panted to the tune of "Marching through Georgia." After a considerable crowd had gathered, the tramp exhibited his box of snakes, announced that he would now pass the hat, and that when the onlookers had contributed the sum of one dollar, he would eat "one of these living reptiles." The crowd began to cough and murmur, and the saloon keeper rushed off for the marshal, who arrested the wretch for giving a show without a license and hurried him away to the calaboose.

The calaboose stood in a sunflower patch,--an old hut with a barred window and a padlock on the door. The tramp was utterly filthy and there was no way to give him a bath. The law made no provision to grub-stake vagrants, so after the constable had detained the tramp for twentyfour hours, he released him and told him to "get out of town, and get quick." The fellow's rattlesnakes had been killed by the saloon keeper. He hid in a box car in the freight yard, probably hoping to get a ride to the next station, but he was found and put out. After that he was seen no more. He had disappeared and left no trace except an ugly, stupid word, chalked on the black paint of the seventy-five-foot standpipe which was the reservoir for the Moonstone water-supply; the same word, in another tongue, that the French soldier shouted at Waterloo to the English officer who bade the Old Guard surrender; a comment on life which the defeated, along the hard roads of the world, sometimes bawl at the victorious.

A week after the tramp excitement had passed over, the city water began to smell and to taste. The Kronborgs had a well in their back yard and did not use city water, but they heard the complaints of their neighbors. At first people said that the town well was full of rotting cottonwood roots, but the engineer at the pumpingstation convinced the mayor that the water left the well untainted. Mayors reason slowly, but, the well being eliminated, the official mind had to travel toward the standpipe--there was no other track for it to go in. The standpipe amply rewarded investigation. The tramp had got even with Moonstone. He had climbed the standpipe by the handholds and let himself down into seventy-five feet of cold water, with his shoes and hat and roll of ticking. The city council had a mild panic and passed a new ordinance about tramps. But the fever had already broken out, and several adults and half a dozen children died of it.

Thea had always found everything that happened in Moonstone exciting, disasters particularly so. It was gratifying to read sensational Moonstone items in the Denver paper. But she wished she had not chanced to see the tramp as he came into town that evening, sniffing the supper-laden air. His face remained unpleasantly clear in her memory, and her mind struggled with the problem of his behavior as if it were a hard page in arithmetic. Even when she was practicing, the drama of the tramp kept going on in the back of her head, and she was constantly trying to make herself realize what pitch of hatred or despair could drive a man to do such a hideous thing. She kept seeing him in his bedraggled clown suit, the white paint on his roughly shaven face, playing his accordion before the saloon. She had noticed his lean body, his high, bald forehead that sloped back like a curved metal lid. How could people fall so far out of fortune? She tried to talk to Ray Kennedy about her perplexity, but Ray would not discuss things of that sort with her. It was in his sentimental conception of women that they should be deeply religious, though men were at liberty to doubt and finally to deny. A picture called "The Soul Awakened," popular in Moonstone parlors, pretty well interpreted Ray's idea of woman's spiritual nature.

One evening when she was haunted by the figure of the tramp, Thea went up to Dr. Archie's office. She found him sewing up two bad gashes in the face of a little boy who had been kicked by a mule. After the boy had been bandaged and sent away with his father, Thea helped the doctor wash and put away the surgical instruments. Then she dropped into her accustomed seat beside his desk and began to talk about the tramp. Her eyes were hard and green with excitement, the doctor noticed.

"It seems to me, Dr. Archie, that the whole town's to blame. I'm to blame, myself. I know he saw me hold my nose when he went by. Father's to blame. If he believes the Bible, he ought to have gone to the calaboose and cleaned that man up and taken care of him. That's what I can't understand; do people believe the Bible, or don't they? If the next life is all that matters, and we're put here to get ready for it, then why do we try to make money, or learn things, or have a good time? There's not one person in Moonstone that really lives the way the New Testament says. Does it matter, or don't it?"

Dr. Archie swung round in his chair and looked at her, honestly and leniently. "Well, Thea, it seems to me like this. Every people has had its religion. All religions are good, and all are pretty much alike. But I don't see how we could live up to them in the sense you mean. I've thought about it a good deal, and I can't help feeling that while we are in this world we have to live for the best things of this world, and those things are material and positive. Now, most religions are passive, and they tell us chiefly what we should not do." The doctor moved restlessly, and his eyes hunted for something along the opposite wall: "See here, my girl, take out the years of early childhood and the time we spend in sleep and dull old age, and we only have about twenty able, waking years. That's not long enough to get acquainted with half the fine things that have been done in the world, much less to do anything ourselves. I think we ought to keep the Commandments and help other people all we can; but the main thing is to live those twenty splendid years; to do all we can and enjoy all we can."

Dr. Archie met his little friend's searching gaze, the look of acute inquiry which always touched him.

"But poor fellows like that tramp--" she hesitated and wrinkled her forehead.

The doctor leaned forward and put his hand protectingly over hers, which lay clenched on the green felt desktop. "Ugly accidents happen, Thea; always have and always will. But the failures are swept back into the pile and forgotten. They don't leave any lasting scar in the world, and they don't affect the future. The things that last are the good things. The people who forge ahead and do something, they really count." He saw tears on her cheeks, and he remembered that he had never seen her cry before, not even when she crushed her finger when she was little. He rose and walked to the window, came back and sat down on the edge of his chair.

"Forget the tramp, Thea. This is a great big world, and I want you to get about and see it all. You're going to Chicago some day, and do something with that fine voice of yours. You're going to be a number one musician and make us proud of you. Take Mary Anderson, now; even the tramps are proud of her. There isn't a tramp along the 'Q' system who hasn't heard of her. We all like people who do things, even if we only see their faces on a cigar-box lid."

They had a long talk. Thea felt that Dr. Archie had never let himself out to her so much before. It was the most grown-up conversation she had ever had with him. She left his office happy, flattered and stimulated. She ran for a long while about the white, moonlit streets, looking up at the stars and the bluish night, at the quiet houses sunk in black shade, the glittering sand hills. She loved the familiar trees, and the people in those little houses, and she loved the unknown world beyond Denver. She felt as if she were being pulled in two, between the desire to go away forever and the desire to stay forever. She had only twenty years--no time to lose.

Many a night that summer she left Dr. Archie's office with a desire to run and run about those quiet streets until she wore out her shoes, or wore out the streets themselves; when her chest ached and it seemed as if her heart were spreading all over the desert. When she went home, it was not to go to sleep. She used to drag her mattress beside her low window and lie awake for a long while, vibrating with excitement, as a machine vibrates from speed. Life rushed in upon her through that window--or so it seemed. In reality, of course, life rushes from within, not from without. There is no work of art so big or so beautiful that it was not once all contained in some youthful body, like this one which lay on the floor in the moonlight, pulsing with ardor and anticipation. It was on such nights that Thea Kronborg learned the thing that old Dumas meant when he told the Romanticists that to make a drama he needed but one passion and four walls.

XIX

It is well for its peace of mind that the traveling public takes railroads so much for granted. The only men who are incurably nervous about railway travel are the railroad operatives. A railroad man never forgets that the next run may be his turn.

On a single-track road, like that upon which Ray Kennedy worked, the freight trains make their way as best they can between passenger trains. Even when there is such a thing as a freight time-schedule, it is merely a form. Along the one track dozens of fast and slow trains dash in both directions, kept from collision only by the brains in the dispatcher's office. If one passenger train is late, the whole schedule must be revised in an instant; the trains following must be warned, and those moving toward the belated train must be assigned new meeting-places.

Between the shifts and modifications of the passenger schedule, the freight trains play a game of their own. They have no right to the track at any given time, but are supposed to be on it when it is free, and to make the best time they can between passenger trains. A freight train, on a single-track road, gets anywhere at all only by stealing bases.

Ray Kennedy had stuck to the freight service, although he had had opportunities to go into the passenger service at higher pay. He always regarded railroading as a temporary makeshift, until he "got into something," and he disliked the passenger service. No brass buttons for him, he said; too much like a livery. While he was railroading he would wear a jumper, thank you!

The wreck that "caught" Ray was a very commonplace one; nothing thrilling about it, and it got only six lines in the Denver papers. It happened about daybreak one morning, only thirty-two miles from home.

At four o'clock in the morning Ray's train had stopped to take water at Saxony, having just rounded the long curve which lies south of that station. It was Joe Giddy's business to walk back along the curve about three hundred yards and put out torpedoes to warn any train which might be coming up from behind--a freight crew is not notified of trains following, and the brakeman is supposed to protect his train. Ray was so fussy about the punctilious observance of orders that almost any brakeman would take a chance once in a while, from natural perversity.

When the train stopped for water that morning, Ray was at the desk in his caboose, making out his report. Giddy took his torpedoes, swung off the rear platform, and glanced back at the curve. He decided that he would not go back to flag this time. If anything was coming up behind, he could hear it in plenty of time. So he ran forward to look after a hot journal that had been bothering him. In a general way, Giddy's reasoning was sound. If a freight train, or even a passenger train, had been coming up behind them, he could have heard it in time. But as it happened, a light engine, which made no noise at all, was coming,--ordered out to help with the freight that was piling up at the other end of the division. This engine got no warning, came round the curve, struck the caboose, went straight through it, and crashed into the heavy lumber car ahead.

The Kronborgs were just sitting down to breakfast, when the night telegraph operator dashed into the yard at a run and hammered on the front door. Gunner answered the knock, and the telegraph operator told him he wanted to see his father a minute, quick. Mr. Kronborg appeared at the door, napkin in hand. The operator was pale and panting.

"Fourteen was wrecked down at Saxony this morning," he shouted, "and Kennedy's all broke up. We're sending an engine down with the doctor, and the operator at Saxony says Kennedy wants you to come along with us and bring your girl." He stopped for breath.

Mr. Kronborg took off his glasses and began rubbing them with his napkin.

"Bring--I don't understand," he muttered. "How did this happen?"

"No time for that, sir. Getting the engine out now. Your girl, Thea. You'll surely do that for the poor chap. Everybody knows he thinks the world of her." Seeing that Mr. Kronborg showed no indication of having made up his mind, the operator turned to Gunner. "Call your sister, kid. I'm going to ask the girl herself," he blurted out.

"Yes, yes, certainly. Daughter," Mr. Kronborg called. He had somewhat recovered himself and reached to the hall hatrack for his hat.

Just as Thea came out on the front porch, before the operator had had time to explain to her, Dr. Archie's ponies came up to the gate at a brisk trot. Archie jumped out the moment his driver stopped the team and came up to the bewildered girl without so much as saying good-morning to any one. He took her hand with the sympathetic, reassuring graveness which had helped her at more than one hard time in her life. "Get your hat, my girl. Kennedy's hurt down the road, and he wants you to run down with me. They'll have a car for us. Get into my buggy, Mr. Kronborg. I'll drive you down, and Larry can come for the team."

The driver jumped out of the buggy and Mr. Kronborg and the doctor got in. Thea, still bewildered, sat on her father's knee. Dr. Archie gave his ponies a smart cut with the whip.

When they reached the depot, the engine, with one car attached, was standing on the main track. The engineer had got his steam up, and was leaning out of the cab impatiently. In a moment they were off. The run to Saxony took forty minutes. Thea sat still in her seat while Dr. Archie and her father talked about the wreck. She took no part in the conversation and asked no questions, but occasionally she looked at Dr. Archie with a frightened, inquiring glance, which he answered by an encouraging nod. Neither he nor her father said anything about how badly Ray was hurt. When the engine stopped near Saxony, the main track was already cleared. As they got out of the car, Dr. Archie pointed to a pile of ties.

"Thea, you'd better sit down here and watch the wreck crew while your father and I go up and look Kennedy over. I'll come back for you when I get him fixed up."

The two men went off up the sand gulch, and Thea sat down and looked at the pile of splintered wood and twisted iron that had lately been Ray's caboose. She was frightened and absent-minded. She felt that she ought to be thinking about Ray, but her mind kept racing off to all sorts of trivial and irrelevant things. She wondered whether Grace Johnson would be furious when she came to take her music lesson and found nobody there to give it to her; whether she had forgotten to close the piano last night and whether Thor would get into the new room and mess the keys all up with his sticky fingers; whether Tillie would go upstairs and make her bed for her. Her mind worked fast, but she could fix it upon nothing. The grasshoppers, the lizards, distracted her attention and seemed more real to her than poor Ray.

On their way to the sand bank where Ray had been carried, Dr. Archie and Mr. Kronborg met the Saxony doctor. He shook hands with them.

"Nothing you can do, doctor. I couldn't count the fractures. His back's broken, too. He wouldn't be alive now if he weren't so confoundedly strong, poor chap. No use bothering him. I've given him morphia, one and a half, in eighths."

Dr. Archie hurried on. Ray was lying on a flat canvas litter, under the shelter of a shelving bank, lightly shaded by a slender cottonwood tree. When the doctor and the preacher approached, he looked at them intently.

"Didn't--" he closed his eyes to hide his bitter disappointment.

Dr. Archie knew what was the matter. "Thea's back there, Ray. I'll bring her as soon as I've had a look at you."

Ray looked up. "You might clean me up a trifle, doc. Won't need you for anything else, thank you all the same."

However little there was left of him, that little was certainly Ray Kennedy. His personality was as positive as ever, and the blood and dirt on his face seemed merely accidental, to have nothing to do with the man himself. Dr. Archie told Mr. Kronborg to bring a pail of water, and he began to sponge Ray's face and neck. Mr. Kronborg stood by, nervously rubbing his hands together and trying to think of something to say. Serious situations always embarrassed him and made him formal, even when he felt real sympathy.

"In times like this, Ray," he brought out at last, crumpling up his handkerchief in his long fingers,--"in times like this, we don't want to forget the Friend that sticketh closer than a brother."

Ray looked up at him; a lonely, disconsolate smile played over his mouth and his square cheeks. "Never mind about all that, PADRE," he said quietly. "Christ and me fell out long ago."

There was a moment of silence. Then Ray took pity on Mr. Kronborg's embarrassment. "You go back for the little girl, PADRE. I want a word with the doc in private."

Ray talked to Dr. Archie for a few moments, then stopped suddenly, with a broad smile. Over the doctor's shoulder he saw Thea coming up the gulch, in her pink chambray dress, carrying her sun-hat by the strings. Such a yellow head! He often told himself that he "was perfectly foolish about her hair." The sight of her, coming, went through him softly, like the morphia. "There she is," he whispered. "Get the old preacher out of the way, doc. I want to have a little talk with her."

Dr. Archie looked up. Thea was hurrying and yet hanging back. She was more frightened than he had thought she would be. She had gone with him to see very sick people and had always been steady and calm. As she came up, she looked at the ground, and he could see that she had been crying.

Ray Kennedy made an unsuccessful effort to put out his hand. "Hello, little kid, nothing to be afraid of. Darned if I don't believe they've gone and scared you! Nothing to cry about. I'm the same old goods, only a little dented. Sit down on my coat there, and keep me company. I've got to lay still a bit."

Dr. Archie and Mr. Kronborg disappeared. Thea cast a timid glance after them, but she sat down resolutely and took Ray's hand.

"You ain't scared now, are you?" he asked affectionately. "You were a regular brick to come, Thee. Did you get any breakfast?"

"No, Ray, I'm not scared. Only I'm dreadful sorry you're hurt, and I can't help crying."

His broad, earnest face, languid from the opium and smiling with such simple happiness, reassured her. She drew nearer to him and lifted his hand to her knee. He looked at her with his clear, shallow blue eyes. How he loved everything about that face and head! How many nights in his cupola, looking up the track, he had seen that face in the darkness; through the sleet and snow, or in the soft blue air when the moonlight slept on the desert.

"You needn't bother to talk, Thee. The doctor's medicine makes me sort of dopey. But it's nice to have company. Kind of cozy, don't you think? Pull my coat under you more. It's a darned shame I can't wait on you."

"No, no, Ray. I'm all right. Yes, I like it here. And I guess you ought not to talk much, ought you? If you can sleep, I'll stay right here, and be awful quiet. I feel just as much at home with you as ever, now."

That simple, humble, faithful something in Ray's eyes went straight to Thea's heart. She did feel comfortable with him, and happy to give him so much happiness. It was the first time she had ever been conscious of that power to bestow intense happiness by simply being near any one. She always remembered this day as the beginning of that knowledge. She bent over him and put her lips softly to his cheek.

Ray's eyes filled with light. "Oh, do that again, kid!" he said impulsively. Thea kissed him on the forehead, blushing faintly. Ray held her hand fast and closed his eyes with a deep sigh of happiness. The morphia and the sense of her nearness filled him with content. The gold mine, the oil well, the copper ledge--all pipe dreams, he mused, and this was a dream, too. He might have known it before. It had always been like that; the things he admired had always been away out of his reach: a college education, a gentleman's manner, an Englishman's accent--things over his head. And Thea was farther out of his reach than all the rest put together. He had been a fool to imagine it, but he was glad he had been a fool. She had given him one grand dream. Every mile of his run, from Moonstone to Denver, was painted with the colors of that hope. Every cactus knew about it. But now that it was not to be, he knew the truth. Thea was never meant for any rough fellow like him--hadn't he really known that all along, he asked himself? She wasn't meant for common men. She was like wedding cake, a thing to dream on. He raised his eyelids a little. She was stroking his hand and looking off into the distance. He felt in her face that look of unconscious power that Wunsch had seen there. Yes, she was bound for the big terminals of the world; no way stations for her. His lids drooped. In the dark he could see her as she would be after a while; in a box at the Tabor Grand in Denver, with diamonds on her neck and a tiara in her yellow hair, with all the people looking at her through their opera-glasses, and a United States Senator, maybe, talking to her. "Then you'll remember me!" He opened his eyes, and they were full of tears.

Thea leaned closer. "What did you say, Ray? I couldn't hear."

"Then you'll remember me," he whispered.

The spark in his eye, which is one's very self, caught the spark in hers that was herself, and for a moment they looked into each other's natures. Thea realized how good and how great-hearted he was, and he realized about her many things. When that elusive spark of personality retreated in each of them, Thea still saw in his wet eyes her own face, very small, but much prettier than the cracked glass at home had ever shown it. It was the first time she had seen her face in that kindest mirror a woman can ever find.

Ray had felt things in that moment when he seemed to be looking into the very soul of Thea Kronborg. Yes, the gold mine, the oil well, the copper ledge, they'd all got away from him, as things will; but he'd backed a winner once in his life! With all his might he gave his faith to the broad little hand he held. He wished he could leave her the rugged strength of his body to help her through with it all. He would have liked to tell her a little about his old dream,--there seemed long years between him and it already,--but to tell her now would somehow be unfair; wouldn't be quite the straightest thing in the world. Probably she knew, anyway. He looked up quickly. "You know, don't you, Thee, that I think you are just the finest thing I've struck in this world?"

The tears ran down Thea's cheeks. "You're too good to me, Ray. You're a lot too good to me," she faltered.

"Why, kid," he murmured, "everybody in this world's going to be good to you!"

Dr. Archie came to the gulch and stood over his patient. "How's it going?"

"Can't you give me another punch with your pacifier, doc? The little girl had better run along now." Ray released Thea's hand. "See you later, Thee."

She got up and moved away aimlessly, carrying her hat by the strings. Ray looked after her with the exaltation born of bodily pain and said between his teeth, "Always look after that girl, doc. She's a queen!"

Thea and her father went back to Moonstone on the one-o'clock passenger. Dr. Archie stayed with Ray Kennedy until he died, late in the afternoon.

XX

On Monday morning, the day after Ray Kennedy's funeral, Dr. Archie called at Mr. Kronborg's study, a little room behind the church. Mr. Kronborg did not write out his sermons, but spoke from notes jotted upon small pieces of cardboard in a kind of shorthand of his own. As sermons go, they were not worse than most. His conventional rhetoric pleased the majority of his congregation, and Mr. Kronborg was generally regarded as a model preacher. He did not smoke, he never touched spirits. His indulgence in the pleasures of the table was an endearing bond between him and the women of his congregation. He ate enormously, with a zest which seemed incongruous with his spare frame.

This morning the doctor found him opening his mail and reading a pile of advertising circulars with deep attention.

"Good-morning, Mr. Kronborg," said Dr. Archie, sitting down. "I came to see you on business. Poor Kennedy asked me to look after his affairs for him. Like most railroad men he spent his wages, except for a few investments in mines which don't look to me very promising. But his life was insured for six hundred dollars in Thea's favor."

Mr. Kronborg wound his feet about the standard of his desk-chair. "I assure you, doctor, this is a complete surprise to me."

"Well, it's not very surprising to me," Dr. Archie went on. "He talked to me about it the day he was hurt. He said he wanted the money to be used in a particular way, and in no other." Dr. Archie paused meaningly.

Mr. Kronborg fidgeted. "I am sure Thea would observe his wishes in every respect."

"No doubt; but he wanted me to see that you agreed to his plan. It seems that for some time Thea has wanted to go away to study music. It was Kennedy's wish that she should take this money and go to Chicago this winter. He felt that it would be an advantage to her in a business way: that even if she came back here to teach, it would give her more authority and make her position here more comfortable."

Mr. Kronborg looked a little startled. "She is very young," he hesitated; "she is barely seventeen. Chicago is a long way from home. We would have to consider. I think, Dr. Archie, we had better consult Mrs. Kronborg."

"I think I can bring Mrs. Kronborg around, if I have your consent. I've always found her pretty level-headed. I have several old classmates practicing in Chicago. One is a throat specialist. He has a good deal to do with singers. He probably knows the best piano teachers and could recommend a boarding-house where music students stay. I think Thea needs to get among a lot of young people who are clever like herself. Here she has no companions but old fellows like me. It's not a natural life for a young girl. She'll either get warped, or wither up before her time. If it will make you and Mrs. Kronborg feel any easier, I'll be glad to take Thea to Chicago and see that she gets started right. This throat man I speak of is a big fellow in his line, and if I can get him interested, he may be able to put her in the way of a good many things. At any rate, he'll know the right teachers. Of course, six hundred dollars won't take her very far, but even half the winter there would be a great advantage. I think Kennedy sized the situation up exactly."

"Perhaps; I don't doubt it. You are very kind, Dr. Archie." Mr. Kronborg was ornamenting his desk-blotter with hieroglyphics. "I should think Denver might be better. There we could watch over her. She is very young."

Dr. Archie rose. "Kennedy didn't mention Denver. He said Chicago, repeatedly. Under the circumstances, it seems to me we ought to try to carry out his wishes exactly, if Thea is willing."

"Certainly, certainly. Thea is conscientious. She would not waste her opportunities." Mr. Kronborg paused. "If Thea were your own daughter, doctor, would you consent to such a plan, at her present age?"

"I most certainly should. In fact, if she were my daughter, I'd have sent her away before this. She's a most unusual child, and she's only wasting herself here. At her age she ought to be learning, not teaching. She'll never learn so quickly and easily as she will right now."

"Well, doctor, you had better talk it over with Mrs. Kronborg. I make it a point to defer to her wishes in such matters. She understands all her children perfectly. I may say that she has all a mother's insight, and more."

Dr. Archie smiled. "Yes, and then some. I feel quite confident about Mrs. Kronborg. We usually agree. Goodmorning."

Dr. Archie stepped out into the hot sunshine and walked rapidly toward his office, with a determined look on his face. He found his waiting-room full of patients, and it was one o'clock before he had dismissed the last one. Then he shut his door and took a drink before going over to the hotel for his lunch. He smiled as he locked his cupboard. "I feel almost as gay as if I were going to get away for a winter myself," he thought.

Afterward Thea could never remember much about that summer, or how she lived through her impatience. She was to set off with Dr. Archie on the fifteenth of October, and she gave lessons until the first of September. Then she began to get her clothes ready, and spent whole afternoons in the village dressmaker's stuffy, littered little sewing-room. Thea and her mother made a trip to Denver to buy the materials for her dresses. Ready-made clothes for girls were not to be had in those days. Miss Spencer, the dressmaker, declared that she could do handsomely by Thea if they would only let her carry out her own ideas. But Mrs. Kronborg and Thea felt that Miss Spencer's most daring productions might seem out of place in Chicago, so they restrained her with a firm hand. Tillie, who always helped Mrs. Kronborg with the family sewing, was for letting Miss Spencer challenge Chicago on Thea's person. Since Ray Kennedy's death, Thea had become more than ever one of Tillie's heroines. Tillie swore each of her friends to secrecy, and, coming home from church or leaning over the fence, told them the most touching stories about Ray's devotion, and how Thea would "never get over it."

Tillie's confidences stimulated the general discussion of Thea's venture. This discussion went on, upon front porches and in back yards, pretty much all summer. Some people approved of Thea's going to Chicago, but most people did not. There were others who changed their minds about it every day.

Tillie said she wanted Thea to have a ball dress "above all things." She bought a fashion book especially devoted to evening clothes and looked hungrily over the colored plates, picking out costumes that would be becoming to "a blonde." She wanted Thea to have all the gay clothes she herself had always longed for; clothes she often told herself she needed "to recite in."

"Tillie," Thea used to cry impatiently, "can't you see that if Miss Spencer tried to make one of those things, she'd make me look like a circus girl? Anyhow, I don't know anybody in Chicago. I won't be going to parties."

Tillie always replied with a knowing toss of her head, "You see! You'll be in society before you know it. There ain't many girls as accomplished as you."

On the morning of the fifteenth of October the Kronborg family, all of them but Gus, who couldn't leave the store, started for the station an hour before train time. Charley had taken Thea's trunk and telescope to the depot in his delivery wagon early that morning. Thea wore her new blue serge traveling-dress, chosen for its serviceable qualities. She had done her hair up carefully, and had put a pale-blue ribbon around her throat, under a little lace collar that Mrs. Kohler had crocheted for her. As they went out of the gate, Mrs. Kronborg looked her over thoughtfully. Yes, that blue ribbon went very well with the dress, and with Thea's eyes. Thea had a rather unusual touch about such things, she reflected comfortably. Tillie always said that Thea was "so indifferent to dress," but her mother noticed that she usually put her clothes on well. She felt the more at ease about letting Thea go away from home, because she had good sense about her clothes and never tried to dress up too much. Her coloring was so individual, she was so unusually fair, that in the wrong clothes she might easily have been "conspicuous."

It was a fine morning, and the family set out from the house in good spirits. Thea was quiet and calm. She had forgotten nothing, and she clung tightly to her handbag, which held her trunk-key and all of her money that was not in an envelope pinned to her chemise. Thea walked behind the others, holding Thor by the hand, and this time she did not feel that the procession was too long. Thor was uncommunicative that morning, and would only talk about how he would rather get a sand bur in his toe every day than wear shoes and stockings. As they passed the cottonwood grove where Thea often used to bring him in his cart, she asked him who would take him for nice long walks after sister went away.

"Oh, I can walk in our yard," he replied unappreciatively. "I guess I can make a pond for my duck."

Thea leaned down and looked into his face. "But you won't forget about sister, will you?" Thor shook his head. "And won't you be glad when sister comes back and can take you over to Mrs. Kohler's to see the pigeons?"

"Yes, I'll be glad. But I'm going to have a pigeon my own self."

"But you haven't got any little house for one. Maybe Axel would make you a little house."

"Oh, her can live in the barn, her can," Thor drawled indifferently.

Thea laughed and squeezed his hand. She always liked his sturdy matter-of-factness. Boys ought to be like that, she thought.

When they reached the depot, Mr. Kronborg paced the platform somewhat ceremoniously with his daughter. Any member of his flock would have gathered that he was giving her good counsel about meeting the temptations of the world. He did, indeed, begin to admonish her not to forget that talents come from our Heavenly Father and are to be used for his glory, but he cut his remarks short and looked at his watch. He believed that Thea was a religious girl, but when she looked at him with that intent, that passionately inquiring gaze which used to move even Wunsch, Mr. Kronborg suddenly felt his eloquence fail. Thea was like her mother, he reflected; you couldn't put much sentiment across with her. As a usual thing, he liked girls to be a little more responsive. He liked them to blush at his compliments; as Mrs. Kronborg candidly said, "Father could be very soft with the girls." But this morning he was thinking that hard-headedness was a reassuring quality in a daughter who was going to Chicago alone.

Mr. Kronborg believed that big cities were places where people went to lose their identity and to be wicked. He himself, when he was a student at the Seminary--he coughed and opened his watch again. He knew, of course, that a great deal of business went on in Chicago, that there was an active Board of Trade, and that hogs and cattle were slaughtered there. But when, as a young man, he had stopped over in Chicago, he had not interested himself in the commercial activities of the city. He remembered it as a place full of cheap shows and dance halls and boys from the country who were behaving disgustingly.

Dr. Archie drove up to the station about ten minutes before the train was due. His man tied the ponies and stood holding the doctor's alligator-skin bag--very elegant, Thea thought it. Mrs. Kronborg did not burden the doctor with warnings and cautions. She said again that she hoped he could get Thea a comfortable place to stay, where they had good beds, and she hoped the landlady would be a woman who'd had children of her own. "I don't go much on old maids looking after girls," she remarked as she took a pin out of her own hat and thrust it into Thea's blue turban. "You'll be sure to lose your hatpins on the train, Thea. It's better to have an extra one in case." She tucked in a little curl that had escaped from Thea's careful twist. "Don't forget to brush your dress often, and pin it up to the curtains of your berth to-night, so it won't wrinkle. If you get it wet, have a tailor press it before it draws."

She turned Thea about by the shoulders and looked her over a last time. Yes, she looked very well. She wasn't pretty, exactly,--her face was too broad and her nose was too big. But she had that lovely skin, and she looked fresh and sweet. She had always been a sweet-smelling child. Her mother had always liked to kiss her, when she happened to think of it.

The train whistled in, and Mr. Kronborg carried the canvas "telescope" into the car. Thea kissed them all good-bye. Tillie cried, but she was the only one who did. They all shouted things up at the closed window of the Pullman car, from which Thea looked down at them as from a frame, her face glowing with excitement, her turban a little tilted in spite of three hatpins. She had already taken off her new gloves to save them. Mrs. Kronborg reflected that she would never see just that same picture again, and as Thea's car slid off along the rails, she wiped a tear from her eye. "She won't come back a little girl," Mrs. Kronborg said to her husband as they turned to go home. "Anyhow, she's been a sweet one."

While the Kronborg family were trooping slowly homeward, Thea was sitting in the Pullman, her telescope in the seat beside her, her handbag tightly gripped in her fingers. Dr. Archie had gone into the smoker. He thought she might be a little tearful, and that it would be kinder to leave her alone for a while. Her eyes did fill once, when she saw the last of the sand hills and realized that she was going to leave them behind for a long while. They always made her think of Ray, too. She had had such good times with him out there.

But, of course, it was herself and her own adventure that mattered to her. If youth did not matter so much to itself, it would never have the heart to go on. Thea was surprised that she did not feel a deeper sense of loss at leaving her old life behind her. It seemed, on the contrary, as she looked out at the yellow desert speeding by, that she had left very little. Everything that was essential seemed to be right there in the car with her. She lacked nothing. She even felt more compact and confident than usual. She was all there, and something else was there, too,--in her heart, was it, or under her cheek? Anyhow, it was about her somewhere, that warm sureness, that sturdy little companion with whom she shared a secret.

When Dr. Archie came in from the smoker, she was sitting still, looking intently out of the window and smiling, her lips a little parted, her hair in a blaze of sunshine. The doctor thought she was the prettiest thing he had ever seen, and very funny, with her telescope and big handbag. She made him feel jolly, and a little mournful, too. He knew that the splendid things of life are few, after all, and so very easy to miss.

PART II.
THE SONG OF THE LARK

I

THEA and Dr. Archie had been gone from Moonstone four days. On the afternoon of the nineteenth of October they were in a street-car, riding through the depressing, unkept wastes of North Chicago, on their way to call upon the Reverend Lars Larsen, a friend to whom Mr. Kronborg had written. Thea was still staying at the rooms of the Young Women's Christian Association, and was miserable and homesick there. The housekeeper watched her in a way that made her uncomfortable. Things had not gone very well, so far. The noise and confusion of a big city tired and disheartened her. She had not had her trunk sent to the Christian Association rooms because she did not want to double cartage charges, and now she was running up a bill for storage on it. The contents of her gray telescope were becoming untidy, and it seemed impossible to keep one's face and hands clean in Chicago. She felt as if she were still on the train, traveling without enough clothes to keep clean. She wanted another nightgown, and it did not occur to her that she could buy one. There were other clothes in her trunk that she needed very much, and she seemed no nearer a place to stay than when she arrived in the rain, on that first disillusioning morning.

Dr. Archie had gone at once to his friend Hartley Evans, the throat specialist, and had asked him to tell him of a good piano teacher and direct him to a good boarding-house. Dr. Evans said he could easily tell him who was the best piano teacher in Chicago, but that most students' boarding-houses were "abominable places, where girls got poor food for body and mind." He gave Dr. Archie several addresses, however, and the doctor went to look the places over. He left Thea in her room, for she seemed tired and was not at all like herself. His inspection of boardinghouses was not encouraging. The only place that seemed to him at all desirable was full, and the mistress of the house could not give Thea a room in which she could have a piano. She said Thea might use the piano in her parlor; but when Dr. Archie went to look at the parlor he found a girl talking to a young man on one of the corner sofas. Learning that the boarders received all their callers there, he gave up that house, too, as hopeless.

So when they set out to make the acquaintance of Mr. Larsen on the afternoon he had appointed, the question of a lodging was still undecided. The Swedish Reform Church was in a sloughy, weedy district, near a group of factories. The church itself was a very neat little building. The parsonage, next door, looked clean and comfortable, and there was a well-kept yard about it, with a picket fence. Thea saw several little children playing under a swing, and wondered why ministers always had so many. When they rang at the parsonage door, a capable-looking Swedish servant girl answered the bell and told them that Mr. Larsen's study was in the church, and that he was waiting for them there.

Mr. Larsen received them very cordially. The furniture in his study was so new and the pictures were so heavily framed, that Thea thought it looked more like the waiting-room of the fashionable Denver dentist to whom Dr. Archie had taken her that summer, than like a preacher's study. There were even flowers in a glass vase on the desk. Mr. Larsen was a small, plump man, with a short, yellow beard, very white teeth, and a little turned-up nose on which he wore gold-rimmed eye-glasses. He looked about thirty-five, but he was growing bald, and his thin, hair was parted above his left ear and brought up over the bare spot on the top of his head. He looked cheerful and agreeable. He wore a blue coat and no cuffs.

After Dr. Archie and Thea sat down on a slippery leather couch, the minister asked for an outline of Thea's plans. Dr. Archie explained that she meant to study piano with Andor Harsanyi; that they had already seen him, that Thea had played for him and he said he would be glad to teach her.

Mr. Larsen lifted his pale eyebrows and rubbed his plump white hands together. "But he is a concert pianist already. He will be very expensive."

"That's why Miss Kronborg wants to get a church position if possible. She has not money enough to see her through the winter. There's no use her coming all the way from Colorado and studying with a second-rate teacher. My friends here tell me Harsanyi is the best."

"Oh, very likely! I have heard him play with Thomas. You Western people do things on a big scale. There are half a dozen teachers that I should think--However, you know what you want." Mr. Larsen showed his contempt for such extravagant standards by a shrug. He felt that Dr. Archie was trying to impress him. He had succeeded, indeed, in bringing out the doctor's stiffest manner. Mr. Larsen went on to explain that he managed the music in his church himself, and drilled his choir, though the tenor was the official choirmaster. Unfortunately there were no vacancies in his choir just now. He had his four voices, very good ones. He looked away from Dr. Archie and glanced at Thea. She looked troubled, even a little frightened when he said this, and drew in her lower lip. She, certainly, was not pretentious, if her protector was. He continued to study her. She was sitting on the lounge, her knees far apart, her gloved hands lying stiffly in her lap, like a country girl. Her turban, which seemed a little too big for her, had got tilted in the wind,--it was always windy in that part of Chicago,--and she looked tired. She wore no veil, and her hair, too, was the worse for the wind and dust. When he said he had all the voices he required, he noticed that her gloved hands shut tightly. Mr. Larsen reflected that she was not, after all, responsible for the lofty manner of her father's physician; that she was not even responsible for her father, whom he remembered as a tiresome fellow. As he watched her tired, worried face, he felt sorry for her.

"All the same, I would like to try your voice," he said, turning pointedly away from her companion. "I am interested in voices. Can you sing to the violin?"

"I guess so," Thea replied dully. "I don't know. I never tried."

Mr. Larsen took his violin out of the case and began to tighten the keys. "We might go into the lecture-room and see how it goes. I can't tell much about a voice by the organ. The violin is really the proper instrument to try a voice." He opened a door at the back of his study, pushed Thea gently through it, and looking over his shoulder to Dr. Archie said, "Excuse us, sir. We will be back soon."

Dr. Archie chuckled. All preachers were alike, officious and on their dignity; liked to deal with women and girls, but not with men. He took up a thin volume from the minister's desk. To his amusement it proved to be a book of "Devotional and Kindred Poems; by Mrs. Aurelia S. Larsen." He looked them over, thinking that the world changed very little. He could remember when the wife of his father's minister had published a volume of verses, which all the church members had to buy and all the children were encouraged to read. His grandfather had made a face at the book and said, "Puir body!" Both ladies seemed to have chosen the same subjects, too: Jephthah's Daughter, Rizpah, David's Lament for Absalom, etc. The doctor found the book very amusing.

The Reverend Lars Larsen was a reactionary Swede. His father came to Iowa in the sixties, married a Swedish girl who was ambitious, like himself, and they moved to Kansas and took up land under the Homestead Act. After that, they bought land and leased it from the Government, acquired land in every possible way. They worked like horses, both of them; indeed, they would never have used any horse-flesh they owned as they used themselves. They reared a large family and worked their sons and daughters as mercilessly as they worked themselves; all of them but Lars. Lars was the fourth son, and he was born lazy. He seemed to bear the mark of overstrain on the part of his parents. Even in his cradle he was an example of physical inertia; anything to lie still. When he was a growing boy his mother had to drag him out of bed every morning, and he had to be driven to his chores. At school he had a model "attendance record," because he found getting his lessons easier than farm work. He was the only one of the family who went through the high school, and by the time he graduated he had already made up his mind to study for the ministry, because it seemed to him the least laborious of all callings. In so far as he could see, it was the only business in which there was practically no competition, in which a man was not all the time pitted against other men who were willing to work themselves to death. His father stubbornly opposed Lars's plan, but after keeping the boy at home for a year and finding how useless he was on the farm, he sent him to a theological seminary--as much to conceal his laziness from the neighbors as because he did not know what else to do with him.

Larsen, like Peter Kronborg, got on well in the ministry, because he got on well with the women. His English was no worse than that of most young preachers of American parentage, and he made the most of his skill with the violin. He was supposed to exert a very desirable influence over young people and to stimulate their interest in church work. He married an American girl, and when his father died he got his share of the property--which was very considerable. He invested his money carefully and was that rare thing, a preacher of independent means. His white, well-kept hands were his result,--the evidence that he had worked out his life successfully in the way that pleased him. His Kansas brothers hated the sight of his hands.

Larsen liked all the softer things of life,--in so far as he knew about them. He slept late in the morning, was fussy about his food, and read a great many novels, preferring sentimental ones. He did not smoke, but he ate a great deal of candy "for his throat," and always kept a box of chocolate drops in the upper right-hand drawer of his desk. He always bought season tickets for the symphony concerts, and he played his violin for women's culture clubs. He did not wear cuffs, except on Sunday, because he believed that a free wrist facilitated his violin practice. When he drilled his choir he always held his hand with the little and index fingers curved higher than the other two, like a noted German conductor he had seen. On the whole, the Reverend Larsen was not an insincere man; he merely spent his life resting and playing, to make up for the time his forebears had wasted grubbing in the earth. He was simple-hearted and kind; he enjoyed his candy and his children and his sacred cantatas. He could work energetically at almost any form of play.

Dr. Archie was deep in "The Lament of Mary Magdalen," when Mr. Larsen and Thea came back to the study. From the minister's expression he judged that Thea had succeeded in interesting him.

Mr. Larsen seemed to have forgotten his hostility toward him, and addressed him frankly as soon as he entered. He stood holding his violin, and as Thea sat down he pointed to her with his bow:--

"I have just been telling Miss Kronborg that though I cannot promise her anything permanent, I might give her something for the next few months. My soprano is a young married woman and is temporarily indisposed. She would be glad to be excused from her duties for a while. I like Miss Kronborg's singing very much, and I think she would benefit by the instruction in my choir. Singing here might very well lead to something else. We pay our soprano only eight dollars a Sunday, but she always gets ten dollars for singing at funerals. Miss Kronborg has a sympathetic voice, and I think there would be a good deal of demand for her at funerals. Several American churches apply to me for a soloist on such occasions, and I could help her to pick up quite a little money that way."

This sounded lugubrious to Dr. Archie, who had a physician's dislike of funerals, but he tried to accept the suggestion cordially.

"Miss Kronborg tells me she is having some trouble getting located," Mr. Larsen went on with animation, still holding his violin. "I would advise her to keep away from boarding-houses altogether. Among my parishioners there are two German women, a mother and daughter. The daughter is a Swede by marriage, and clings to the Swedish Church. They live near here, and they rent some of their rooms. They have now a large room vacant, and have asked me to recommend some one. They have never taken boarders, but Mrs. Lorch, the mother, is a good cook,--at least, I am always glad to take supper with her,--and I think I could persuade her to let this young woman partake of the family table. The daughter, Mrs. Andersen, is musical, too, and sings in the Mozart Society. I think they might like to have a music student in the house. You speak German, I suppose?" he turned to Thea.

"Oh, no; a few words. I don't know the grammar," she murmured.

Dr. Archie noticed that her eyes looked alive again, not frozen as they had looked all morning. "If this fellow can help her, it's not for me to be stand-offish," he said to himself.

"Do you think you would like to stay in such a quiet place, with old-fashioned people?" Mr. Larsen asked. "I shouldn't think you could find a better place to work, if that's what you want."

"I think mother would like to have me with people like that," Thea replied. "And I'd be glad to settle down most anywhere. I'm losing time."

"Very well, there's no time like the present. Let us go to see Mrs. Lorch and Mrs. Andersen."

The minister put his violin in its case and caught up a black-and-white checked traveling-cap that he wore when he rode his high Columbia wheel. The three left the church together.

II

SO Thea did not go to a boarding-house after all. When Dr. Archie left Chicago she was comfortably settled with Mrs. Lorch, and her happy reunion with her trunk somewhat consoled her for his departure.

Mrs. Lorch and her daughter lived half a mile from the Swedish Reform Church, in an old square frame house, with a porch supported by frail pillars, set in a damp yard full of big lilac bushes. The house, which had been left over from country times, needed paint badly, and looked gloomy and despondent among its smart Queen Anne neighbors. There was a big back yard with two rows of apple trees and a grape arbor, and a warped walk, two planks wide, which led to the coal bins at the back of the lot. Thea's room was on the second floor, overlooking this back yard, and she understood that in the winter she must carry up her own coal and kindling from the bin. There was no furnace in the house, no running water except in the kitchen, and that was why the room rent was small. All the rooms were heated by stoves, and the lodgers pumped the water they needed from the cistern under the porch, or from the well at the entrance of the grape arbor. Old Mrs. Lorch could never bring herself to have costly improvements made in her house; indeed she had very little money. She preferred to keep the house just as her husband built it, and she thought her way of living good enough for plain people.

Thea's room was large enough to admit a rented upright piano without crowding. It was, the widowed daughter said, "a double room that had always before been occupied by two gentlemen"; the piano now took the place of a second occupant. There was an ingrain carpet on the floor, green ivy leaves on a red ground, and clumsy, old-fashioned walnut furniture. The bed was very wide, and the mattress thin and hard. Over the fat pillows were "shams" embroidered in Turkey red, each with a flowering scroll--one with "Gute' Nacht," the other with "Guten Morgen." The dresser was so big that Thea wondered how it had ever been got into the house and up the narrow stairs. Besides an old horsehair armchair, there were two low plush "spring-rockers," against the massive pedestals of which one was always stumbling in the dark. Thea sat in the dark a good deal those first weeks, and sometimes a painful bump against one of those brutally immovable pedestals roused her temper and pulled her out of a heavy hour. The wall-paper was brownish yellow, with blue flowers. When it was put on, the carpet, certainly, had not been consulted. There was only one picture on the wall when Thea moved in: a large colored print of a brightly lighted church in a snow-storm, on Christmas Eve, with greens hanging about the stone doorway and arched windows. There was something warm and home, like about this picture, and Thea grew fond of it. One day, on her way into town to take her lesson, she stopped at a bookstore and bought a photograph of the Naples bust of Julius Caesar. This she had framed, and hung it on the big bare wall behind her stove. It was a curious choice, but she was at the age when people do inexplicable things. She had been interested in Caesar's "Commentaries" when she left school to begin teaching, and she loved to read about great generals; but these facts would scarcely explain her wanting that grim bald head to share her daily existence. It seemed a strange freak, when she bought so few things, and when she had, as Mrs. Andersen said to Mrs. Lorch, "no pictures of the composers at all."

Both the widows were kind to her, but Thea liked the mother better. Old Mrs. Lorch was fat and jolly, with a red face, always shining as if she had just come from the stove, bright little eyes, and hair of several colors. Her own hair was one cast of iron-gray, her switch another, and her false front still another. Her clothes always smelled of savory cooking, except when she was dressed for church or KAFFEEKLATSCH, and then she smelled of bay rum or of the lemon-verbena sprig which she tucked inside her puffy black kid glove. Her cooking justified all that Mr. Larsen had said of it, and Thea had never been so well nourished before.

The daughter, Mrs. Andersen,--Irene, her mother called her,--was a different sort of woman altogether. She was perhaps forty years old, angular, big-boned, with large, thin features, light-blue eyes, and dry, yellow hair, the bang tightly frizzed. She was pale, anaemic, and sentimental. She had married the youngest son of a rich, arrogant Swedish family who were lumber merchants in St. Paul. There she dwelt during her married life. Oscar Andersen was a strong, full-blooded fellow who had counted on a long life and had been rather careless about his business affairs. He was killed by the explosion of a steam boiler in the mills, and his brothers managed to prove that he had very little stock in the big business. They had strongly disapproved of his marriage and they agreed among themselves that they were entirely justified in defrauding his widow, who, they said, "would only marry again and give some fellow a good thing of it." Mrs. Andersen would not go to law with the family that had always snubbed and wounded her--she felt the humiliation of being thrust out more than she felt her impoverishment; so she went back to Chicago to live with her widowed mother on an income of five hundred a year. This experience had given her sentimental nature an incurable hurt. Something withered away in her. Her head had a downward droop; her step was soft and apologetic, even in her mother's house, and her smile had the sickly, uncertain flicker that so often comes from a secret humiliation. She was affable and yet shrinking, like one who has come down in the world, who has known better clothes, better carpets, better people, brighter hopes. Her husband was buried in the Andersen lot in St. Paul, with a locked iron fence around it. She had to go to his eldest brother for the key when she went to say good-bye to his grave. She clung to the Swedish Church because it had been her husband's church.

As her mother had no room for her household belongings, Mrs. Andersen had brought home with her only her bedroom set, which now furnished her own room at Mrs. Lorch's. There she spent most of her time, doing fancywork or writing letters to sympathizing German friends in St. Paul, surrounded by keepsakes and photographs of the burly Oscar Andersen. Thea, when she was admitted to this room, and shown these photographs, found herself wondering, like the Andersen family, why such a lusty, gay-looking fellow ever thought he wanted this pallid, long-cheeked woman, whose manner was always that of withdrawing, and who must have been rather thin-blooded even as a girl.

Mrs. Andersen was certainly a depressing person. It sometimes annoyed Thea very much to hear her insinuating knock on the door, her flurried explanation of why she had come, as she backed toward the stairs. Mrs. Andersen admired Thea greatly. She thought it a distinction to be even a "temporary soprano"--Thea called herself so quite seriously--in the Swedish Church. She also thought it distinguished to be a pupil of Harsanyi's. She considered Thea very handsome, very Swedish, very talented. She fluttered about the upper floor when Thea was practicing. In short, she tried to make a heroine of her, just as Tillie Kronborg had always done, and Thea was conscious of something of the sort. When she was working and heard Mrs. Andersen tip-toeing past her door, she used to shrug her shoulders and wonder whether she was always to have a Tillie diving furtively about her in some disguise or other.

At the dressmaker's Mrs. Andersen recalled Tillie even more painfully. After her first Sunday in Mr. Larsen's choir, Thea saw that she must have a proper dress for morning service. Her Moonstone party dress might do to wear in the evening, but she must have one frock that could stand the light of day. She, of course, knew nothing about Chicago dressmakers, so she let Mrs. Andersen take her to a German woman whom she recommended warmly. The German dressmaker was excitable and dramatic. Concert dresses, she said, were her specialty. In her fitting-room there were photographs of singers in the dresses she had made them for this or that SANGERFEST. She and Mrs. Andersen together achieved a costume which would have warmed Tillie Kronborg's heart. It was clearly intended for a woman of forty, with violent tastes. There seemed to be a piece of every known fabric in it somewhere. When it came home, and was spread out on her huge bed, Thea looked it over and told herself candidly that it was "a horror." However, her money was gone, and there was nothing to do but make the best of the dress. She never wore it except, as she said, "to sing in," as if it were an unbecoming uniform. When Mrs. Lorch and Irene told her that she "looked like a little bird-of-Paradise in it," Thea shut her teeth and repeated to herself words she had learned from Joe Giddy and Spanish Johnny.

In these two good women Thea found faithful friends, and in their house she found the quiet and peace which helped her to support the great experiences of that winter.

III

ANDOR HARSANYI had never had a pupil in the least like Thea Kronborg. He had never had one more intelligent, and he had never had one so ignorant. When Thea sat down to take her first lesson from him, she had never heard a work by Beethoven or a composition by Chopin. She knew their names vaguely. Wunsch had been a musician once, long before he wandered into Moonstone, but when Thea awoke his interest there was not much left of him. From him Thea had learned something about the works of Gluck and Bach, and he used to play her some of the compositions of Schumann. In his trunk he had a mutilated score of the F sharp minor sonata, which he had heard Clara Schumann play at a festival in Leipsic. Though his powers of execution were at such a low ebb, he used to play at this sonata for his pupil and managed to give her some idea of its beauty. When Wunsch was a young man, it was still daring to like Schumann; enthusiasm for his work was considered an expression of youthful waywardness. Perhaps that was why Wunsch remembered him best. Thea studied some of the KINDERSZENEN with him, as well as some little sonatas by Mozart and Clementi. But for the most part Wunsch stuck to Czerny and Hummel.

Harsanyi found in Thea a pupil with sure, strong hands, one who read rapidly and intelligently, who had, he felt, a richly gifted nature. But she had been given no direction, and her ardor was unawakened. She had never heard a symphony orchestra. The literature of the piano was an undiscovered world to her. He wondered how she had been able to work so hard when she knew so little of what she was working toward. She had been taught according to the old Stuttgart method; stiff back, stiff elbows, a very formal position of the hands. The best thing about her preparation was that she had developed an unusual power of work. He noticed at once her way of charging at difficulties. She ran to meet them as if they were foes she had long been seeking, seized them as if they were destined for her and she for them. Whatever she did well, she took for granted. Her eagerness aroused all the young Hungarian's chivalry. Instinctively one went to the rescue of a creature who had so much to overcome and who struggled so hard. He used to tell his wife that Miss Kronborg's hour took more out of him than half a dozen other lessons. He usually kept her long over time; he changed her lessons about so that he could do so, and often gave her time at the end of the day, when he could talk to her afterward and play for her a little from what he happened to be studying. It was always interesting to play for her. Sometimes she was so silent that he wondered, when she left him, whether she had got anything out of it. But a week later, two weeks later, she would give back his idea again in a way that set him vibrating.

All this was very well for Harsanyi; an interesting variation in the routine of teaching. But for Thea Kronborg, that winter was almost beyond enduring. She always remembered it as the happiest and wildest and saddest of her life. Things came too fast for her; she had not had enough preparation. There were times when she came home from her lesson and lay upon her bed hating Wunsch and her family, hating a world that had let her grow up so ignorant; when she wished that she could die then and there, and be born over again to begin anew. She said something of this kind once to her teacher, in the midst of a bitter struggle. Harsanyi turned the light of his wonderful eye upon her--poor fellow, he had but one, though that was set in such a handsome head--and said slowly: "Every artist makes himself born. It is very much harder than the other time, and longer. Your mother did not bring anything into the world to play piano. That you must bring into the world yourself."

This comforted Thea temporarily, for it seemed to give her a chance. But a great deal of the time she was comfortless. Her letters to Dr. Archie were brief and businesslike. She was not apt to chatter much, even in the stimulating company of people she liked, and to chatter on paper was simply impossible for her. If she tried to write him anything definite about her work, she immediately scratched it out as being only partially true, or not true at all. Nothing that she could say about her studies seemed unqualifiedly true, once she put it down on paper.

Late one afternoon, when she was thoroughly tired and wanted to struggle on into the dusk, Harsanyi, tired too, threw up his hands and laughed at her. "Not to-day, Miss Kronborg. That sonata will keep; it won't run away. Even if you and I should not waken up to-morrow, it will be there."

Thea turned to him fiercely. "No, it isn't here unless I have it--not for me," she cried passionately. "Only what I hold in my two hands is there for me!"

Harsanyi made no reply. He took a deep breath and sat down again. "The second movement now, quietly, with the shoulders relaxed."

There were hours, too, of great exaltation; when she was at her best and became a part of what she was doing and ceased to exist in any other sense. There were other times when she was so shattered by ideas that she could do nothing worth while; when they trampled over her like an army and she felt as if she were bleeding to death under them. She sometimes came home from a late lesson so exhausted that she could eat no supper. If she tried to eat, she was ill afterward. She used to throw herself upon the bed and lie there in the dark, not thinking, not feeling, but evaporating. That same night, perhaps, she would waken up rested and calm, and as she went over her work in her mind, the passages seemed to become something of themselves, to take a sort of pattern in the darkness. She had never learned to work away from the piano until she came to Harsanyi, and it helped her more than anything had ever helped her before.

She almost never worked now with the sunny, happy contentment that had filled the hours when she worked with Wunsch--"like a fat horse turning a sorgum mill," she said bitterly to herself. Then, by sticking to it, she could always do what she set out to do. Now, everything that she really wanted was impossible; a CANTABILE like Harsanyi's, for instance, instead of her own cloudy tone. No use telling her she might have it in ten years. She wanted it now. She wondered how she had ever found other things interesting: books, "Anna Karenina"--all that seemed so unreal and on the outside of things. She was not born a musician, she decided; there was no other way of explaining it.

Sometimes she got so nervous at the piano that she left it, and snatching up her hat and cape went out and walked, hurrying through the streets like Christian fleeing from the City of Destruction. And while she walked she cried. There was scarcely a street in the neighborhood that she had not cried up and down before that winter was over. The thing that used to lie under her cheek, that sat so warmly over her heart when she glided away from the sand hills that autumn morning, was far from her. She had come to Chicago to be with it, and it had deserted her, leaving in its place a painful longing, an unresigned despair.

Harsanyi knew that his interesting pupil--"the savage blonde," one of his male students called her--was sometimes very unhappy. He saw in her discontent a curious definition of character. He would have said that a girl with so much musical feeling, so intelligent, with good training of eye and hand, would, when thus suddenly introduced to the great literature of the piano, have found boundless happiness. But he soon learned that she was not able to forget her own poverty in the richness of the world he opened to her. Often when he played to her, her face was the picture of restless misery. She would sit crouching forward, her elbows on her knees, her brows drawn together and her gray-green eyes smaller than ever, reduced to mere pin-points of cold, piercing light. Sometimes, while she listened, she would swallow hard, two or three times, and look nervously from left to right, drawing her shoulders together. "Exactly," he thought, "as if she were being watched, or as if she were naked and heard some one coming."

On the other hand, when she came several times to see Mrs. Harsanyi and the two babies, she was like a little girl, jolly and gay and eager to play with the children, who loved her. The little daughter, Tanya, liked to touch Miss Kronborg's yellow hair and pat it, saying, "Dolly, dolly," because it was of a color much oftener seen on dolls than on people. But if Harsanyi opened the piano and sat down to play, Miss Kronborg gradually drew away from the children, retreated to a corner and became sullen or troubled. Mrs. Harsanyi noticed this, also, and thought it very strange behavior.

Another thing that puzzled Harsanyi was Thea's apparent lack of curiosity. Several times he offered to give her tickets to concerts, but she said she was too tired or that it "knocked her out to be up late." Harsanyi did not know that she was singing in a choir, and had often to sing at funerals, neither did he realize how much her work with him stirred her and exhausted her. Once, just as she was leaving his studio, he called her back and told her he could give her some tickets that had been sent him for Emma Juch that evening. Thea fingered the black wool on the edge of her plush cape and replied, "Oh, thank you, Mr. Harsanyi, but I have to wash my hair to-night."

Mrs. Harsanyi liked Miss Kronborg thoroughly. She saw in her the making of a pupil who would reflect credit upon Harsanyi. She felt that the girl could be made to look strikingly handsome, and that she had the kind of personality which takes hold of audiences. Moreover, Miss Kronborg was not in the least sentimental about her husband. Sometimes from the show pupils one had to endure a good deal. "I like that girl," she used to say, when Harsanyi told her of one of Thea's GAUCHERIES. "She doesn't sigh every time the wind blows. With her one swallow doesn't make a summer."

Thea told them very little about herself. She was not naturally communicative, and she found it hard to feel confidence in new people. She did not know why, but she could not talk to Harsanyi as she could to Dr. Archie, or to Johnny and Mrs. Tellamantez. With Mr. Larsen she felt more at home, and when she was walking she sometimes stopped at his study to eat candy with him or to hear the plot of the novel he happened to be reading.

One evening toward the middle of December Thea was to dine with the Harsanyis. She arrived early, to have time to play with the children before they went to bed. Mrs. Harsanyi took her into her own room and helped her take off her country "fascinator" and her clumsy plush cape. Thea had bought this cape at a big department store and had paid $16.50 for it. As she had never paid more than ten dollars for a coat before, that seemed to her a large price. It was very heavy and not very warm, ornamented with a showy pattern in black disks, and trimmed around the collar and the edges with some kind of black wool that "crocked" badly in snow or rain. It was lined with a cotton stuff called "farmer's satin." Mrs. Harsanyi was one woman in a thousand. As she lifted this cape from Thea's shoulders and laid it on her white bed, she wished that her husband did not have to charge pupils like this one for their lessons. Thea wore her Moonstone party dress, white organdie, made with a "V" neck and elbow sleeves, and a blue sash. She looked very pretty in it, and around her throat she had a string of pink coral and tiny white shells that Ray once brought her from Los Angeles. Mrs. Harsanyi noticed that she wore high heavy shoes which needed blacking. The choir in Mr. Larsen's church stood behind a railing, so Thea did not pay much attention to her shoes.

"You have nothing to do to your hair," Mrs. Harsanyi said kindly, as Thea turned to the mirror. "However it happens to lie, it's always pretty. I admire it as much as Tanya does."

Thea glanced awkwardly away from her and looked stern, but Mrs. Harsanyi knew that she was pleased. They went into the living-room, behind the studio, where the two children were playing on the big rug before the coal grate. Andor, the boy, was six, a sturdy, handsome child, and the little girl was four. She came tripping to meet Thea, looking like a little doll in her white net dress--her mother made all her clothes. Thea picked her up and hugged her. Mrs. Harsanyi excused herself and went to the dining-room. She kept only one maid and did a good deal of the housework herself, besides cooking her husband's favorite dishes for him. She was still under thirty, a slender, graceful woman, gracious, intelligent, and capable. She adapted herself to circumstances with a well-bred ease which solved many of her husband's difficulties, and kept him, as he said, from feeling cheap and down at the heel. No musician ever had a better wife. Unfortunately her beauty was of a very frail and impressionable kind, and she was beginning to lose it. Her face was too thin now, and there were often dark circles under her eyes.

Left alone with the children, Thea sat down on Tanya's little chair--she would rather have sat on the floor, but was afraid of rumpling her dress--and helped them play "cars" with Andor's iron railway set. She showed him new ways to lay his tracks and how to make switches, set up his Noah's ark village for stations and packed the animals in the open coal cars to send them to the stockyards. They worked out their shipment so realistically that when Andor put the two little reindeer into the stock car, Tanya snatched them out and began to cry, saying she wasn't going to have all their animals killed.

Harsanyi came in, jaded and tired, and asked Thea to go on with her game, as he was not equal to talking much before dinner. He sat down and made pretense of glancing at the evening paper, but he soon dropped it. After the railroad began to grow tiresome, Thea went with the children to the lounge in the corner, and played for them the game with which she used to amuse Thor for hours together behind the parlor stove at home, making shadow pictures against the wall with her hands. Her fingers were very supple, and she could make a duck and a cow and a sheep and a fox and a rabbit and even an elephant. Harsanyi, from his low chair, watched them, smiling. The boy was on his knees, jumping up and down with the excitement of guessing the beasts, and Tanya sat with her feet tucked under her and clapped her frail little hands. Thea's profile, in the lamplight, teased his fancy. Where had he seen a head like it before?

When dinner was announced, little Andor took Thea's hand and walked to the dining-room with her. The children always had dinner with their parents and behaved very nicely at table. "Mamma," said Andor seriously as he climbed into his chair and tucked his napkin into the collar of his blouse, "Miss Kronborg's hands are every kind of animal there is."

His father laughed. "I wish somebody would say that about my hands, Andor."

When Thea dined at the Harsanyis before, she noticed that there was an intense suspense from the moment they took their places at the table until the master of the house had tasted the soup. He had a theory that if the soup went well, the dinner would go well; but if the soup was poor, all was lost. To-night he tasted his soup and smiled, and Mrs. Harsanyi sat more easily in her chair and turned her attention to Thea. Thea loved their dinner table, because it was lighted by candles in silver candle-sticks, and she had never seen a table so lighted anywhere else. There were always flowers, too. To-night there was a little orange tree, with oranges on it, that one of Harsanyi's pupils had sent him at Thanksgiving time. After Harsanyi had finished his soup and a glass of red Hungarian wine, he lost his fagged look and became cordial and witty. He persuaded Thea to drink a little wine to-night. The first time she dined with them, when he urged her to taste the glass of sherry beside her plate, she astonished them by telling them that she "never drank."

Harsanyi was then a man of thirty-two. He was to have a very brilliant career, but he did not know it then. Theodore Thomas was perhaps the only man in Chicago who felt that Harsanyi might have a great future. Harsanyi belonged to the softer Slavic type, and was more like a Pole than a Hungarian. He was tall, slender, active, with sloping, graceful shoulders and long arms. His head was very fine, strongly and delicately modelled, and, as Thea put it, "so independent." A lock of his thick brown hair usually hung over his forehead. His eye was wonderful; full of light and fire when he was interested, soft and thoughtful when he was tired or melancholy. The meaning and power of two very fine eyes must all have gone into this one--the right one, fortunately, the one next his audience when he played. He believed that the glass eye which gave one side of his face such a dull, blind look, had ruined his career, or rather had made a career impossible for him. Harsanyi lost his eye when he was twelve years old, in a Pennsylvania mining town where explosives happened to be kept too near the frame shanties in which the company packed newly arrived Hungarian families.

His father was a musician and a good one, but he had cruelly over-worked the boy; keeping him at the piano for six hours a day and making him play in cafes and dance halls for half the night. Andor ran away and crossed the ocean with an uncle, who smuggled him through the port as one of his own many children. The explosion in which Andor was hurt killed a score of people, and he was thought lucky to get off with an eye. He still had a clipping from a Pittsburg paper, giving a list of the dead and injured. He appeared as "Harsanyi, Andor, left eye and slight injuries about the head." That was his first American "notice"; and he kept it. He held no grudge against the coal company; he understood that the accident was merely one of the things that are bound to happen in the general scramble of American life, where every one comes to grab and takes his chance.

While they were eating dessert, Thea asked Harsanyi if she could change her Tuesday lesson from afternoon to morning. "I have to be at a choir rehearsal in the afternoon, to get ready for the Christmas music, and I expect it will last until late."

Harsanyi put down his fork and looked up. "A choir rehearsal? You sing in a church?"

"Yes. A little Swedish church, over on the North side."

"Why did you not tell us?"

"Oh, I'm only a temporary. The regular soprano is not well."

"How long have you been singing there?"

"Ever since I came. I had to get a position of some kind," Thea explained, flushing, "and the preacher took me on. He runs the choir himself. He knew my father, and I guess he took me to oblige."

Harsanyi tapped the tablecloth with the ends of his fingers. "But why did you never tell us? Why are you so reticent with us?"

Thea looked shyly at him from under her brows. "Well, it's certainly not very interesting. It's only a little church. I only do it for business reasons."

"What do you mean? Don't you like to sing? Don't you sing well?"

"I like it well enough, but, of course, I don't know anything about singing. I guess that's why I never said anything about it. Anybody that's got a voice can sing in a little church like that."

Harsanyi laughed softly--a little scornfully, Thea thought. "So you have a voice, have you?"

Thea hesitated, looked intently at the candles and then at Harsanyi. "Yes," she said firmly; "I have got some, anyway."

"Good girl," said Mrs. Harsanyi, nodding and smiling at Thea. "You must let us hear you sing after dinner."

This remark seemingly closed the subject, and when the coffee was brought they began to talk of other things. Harsanyi asked Thea how she happened to know so much about the way in which freight trains are operated, and she tried to give him some idea of how the people in little desert towns live by the railway and order their lives by the coming and going of the trains. When they left the diningroom the children were sent to bed and Mrs. Harsanyi took Thea into the studio. She and her husband usually sat there in the evening.

Although their apartment seemed so elegant to Thea, it was small and cramped. The studio was the only spacious room. The Harsanyis were poor, and it was due to Mrs. Harsanyi's good management that their lives, even in hard times, moved along with dignity and order. She had long ago found out that bills or debts of any kind frightened her husband and crippled his working power. He said they were like bars on the windows, and shut out the future; they meant that just so many hundred dollars' worth of his life was debilitated and exhausted before he got to it. So Mrs. Harsanyi saw to it that they never owed anything. Harsanyi was not extravagant, though he was sometimes careless about money. Quiet and order and his wife's good taste were the things that meant most to him. After these, good food, good cigars, a little good wine. He wore his clothes until they were shabby, until his wife had to ask the tailor to come to the house and measure him for new ones. His neckties she usually made herself, and when she was in shops she always kept her eye open for silks in very dull or pale shades, grays and olives, warm blacks and browns.

When they went into the studio Mrs. Harsanyi took up her embroidery and Thea sat down beside her on a low stool, her hands clasped about her knees. While his wife and his pupil talked, Harsanyi sank into a CHAISE LONGUE in which he sometimes snatched a few moments' rest between his lessons, and smoked. He sat well out of the circle of the lamplight, his feet to the fire. His feet were slender and well shaped, always elegantly shod. Much of the grace of his movements was due to the fact that his feet were almost as sure and flexible as his hands. He listened to the conversation with amusement. He admired his wife's tact and kindness with crude young people; she taught them so much without seeming to be instructing. When the clock struck nine, Thea said she must be going home.

Harsanyi rose and flung away his cigarette. "Not yet. We have just begun the evening. Now you are going to sing for us. I have been waiting for you to recover from dinner. Come, what shall it be?" he crossed to the piano.

Thea laughed and shook her head, locking her elbows still tighter about her knees. "Thank you, Mr. Harsanyi, but if you really make me sing, I'll accompany myself. You couldn't stand it to play the sort of things I have to sing."

As Harsanyi still pointed to the chair at the piano, she left her stool and went to it, while he returned to his CHAISE LONGUE. Thea looked at the keyboard uneasily for a moment, then she began "Come, ye Disconsolate," the hymn Wunsch had always liked to hear her sing. Mrs. Harsanyi glanced questioningly at her husband, but he was looking intently at the toes of his boots, shading his forehead with his long white hand. When Thea finished the hymn she did not turn around, but immediately began "The Ninety and Nine." Mrs. Harsanyi kept trying to catch her husband's eye; but his chin only sank lower on his collar.

"There were ninety and nine that safely lay In the shelter of the fold, But one was out on the hills away, Far off from the gates of gold."

Harsanyi looked at her, then back at the fire.

"Rejoice, for the Shepherd has found his sheep."

Thea turned on the chair and grinned. "That's about enough, isn't it? That song got me my job. The preacher said it was sympathetic," she minced the word, remembering Mr. Larsen's manner.

Harsanyi drew himself up in his chair, resting his elbows on the low arms. "Yes? That is better suited to your voice. Your upper tones are good, above G. I must teach you some songs. Don't you know anything--pleasant?"

Thea shook her head ruefully. "I'm afraid I don't. Let me see--Perhaps," she turned to the piano and put her hands on the keys. "I used to sing this for Mr. Wunsch a long while ago. It's for contralto, but I'll try it." She frowned at the keyboard a moment, played the few introductory measures, and began:

"ACH, ICH HABE SIE VERLOREN,"

She had not sung it for a long time, and it came back like an old friendship. When she finished, Harsanyi sprang from his chair and dropped lightly upon his toes, a kind of ENTRE-CHAT that he sometimes executed when he formed a sudden resolution, or when he was about to follow a pure intuition, against reason. His wife said that when he gave that spring he was shot from the bow of his ancestors, and now when he left his chair in that manner she knew he was intensely interested. He went quickly to the piano.

"Sing that again. There is nothing the matter with your low voice, my girl. I will play for you. Let your voice out." Without looking at her he began the accompaniment. Thea drew back her shoulders, relaxed them instinctively, and sang.

When she finished the aria, Harsanyi beckoned her nearer. "Sing AH--AH for me, as I indicate." He kept his right hand on the keyboard and put his left to her throat, placing the tips of his delicate fingers over her larynx. "Again,--until your breath is gone.--Trill between the two tones, always; good! Again; excellent!--Now up,--stay there. E and F. Not so good, is it? F is always a hard one.--Now, try the half-tone.--That's right, nothing difficult about it.--Now, pianissimo, AH--AH. Now, swell it, AH--AH.--Again, follow my hand.--Now, carry it down.--Anybody ever tell you anything about your breathing?"

"Mr. Larsen says I have an unusually long breath," Thea replied with spirit.

Harsanyi smiled. "So you have, so you have. That was what I meant. Now, once more; carry it up and then down, AH--AH." He put his hand back to her throat and sat with his head bent, his one eye closed. He loved to hear a big voice throb in a relaxed, natural throat, and he was thinking that no one had ever felt this voice vibrate before. It was like a wild bird that had flown into his studio on Middleton Street from goodness knew how far! No one knew that it had come, or even that it existed; least of all the strange, crude girl in whose throat it beat its passionate wings. What a simple thing it was, he reflected; why had he never guessed it before? Everything about her indicated it,--the big mouth, the wide jaw and chin, the strong white teeth, the deep laugh. The machine was so simple and strong, seemed to be so easily operated. She sang from the bottom of herself. Her breath came from down where her laugh came from, the deep laugh which Mrs. Harsanyi had once called "the laugh of the people." A relaxed throat, a voice that lay on the breath, that had never been forced off the breath; it rose and fell in the air-column like the little balls which are put to shine in the jet of a fountain. The voice did not thin as it went up; the upper tones were as full and rich as the lower, produced in the same way and as unconsciously, only with deeper breath.

At last Harsanyi threw back his head and rose. "You must be tired, Miss Kronborg."

When she replied, she startled him; he had forgotten how hard and full of burs her speaking voice was. "No," she said, "singing never tires me."

Harsanyi pushed back his hair with a nervous hand. "I don't know much about the voice, but I shall take liberties and teach you some good songs. I think you have a very interesting voice."

"I'm glad if you like it. Good-night, Mr. Harsanyi." Thea went with Mrs. Harsanyi to get her wraps.

When Mrs. Harsanyi came back to her husband, she found him walking restlessly up and down the room.

"Don't you think her voice wonderful, dear?" she asked.

"I scarcely know what to think. All I really know about that girl is that she tires me to death. We must not have her often. If I did not have my living to make, then--" he dropped into a chair and closed his eyes. "How tired I am. What a voice!"

IV

AFTER that evening Thea's work with Harsanyi changed somewhat. He insisted that she should study some songs with him, and after almost every lesson he gave up half an hour of his own time to practicing them with her. He did not pretend to know much about voice production, but so far, he thought, she had acquired no really injurious habits. A healthy and powerful organ had found its own method, which was not a bad one. He wished to find out a good deal before he recommended a vocal teacher. He never told Thea what he thought about her voice, and made her general ignorance of anything worth singing his pretext for the trouble he took. That was in the beginning. After the first few lessons his own pleasure and hers were pretext enough. The singing came at the end of the lesson hour, and they both treated it as a form of relaxation.

Harsanyi did not say much even to his wife about his discovery. He brooded upon it in a curious way. He found that these unscientific singing lessons stimulated him in his own study. After Miss Kronborg left him he often lay down in his studio for an hour before dinner, with his head full of musical ideas, with an effervescence in his brain which he had sometimes lost for weeks together under the grind of teaching. He had never got so much back for himself from any pupil as he did from Miss Kronborg. From the first she had stimulated him; something in her personality invariably affected him. Now that he was feeling his way toward her voice, he found her more interesting than ever before. She lifted the tedium of the winter for him, gave him curious fancies and reveries. Musically, she was sympathetic to him. Why all this was true, he never asked himself. He had learned that one must take where and when one can the mysterious mental irritant that rouses one's imagination; that it is not to be had by order. She often wearied him, but she never bored him. Under her crudeness and brusque hardness, he felt there was a nature quite different, of which he never got so much as a hint except when she was at the piano, or when she sang. It was toward this hidden creature that he was trying, for his own pleasure, to find his way. In short, Harsanyi looked forward to his hour with Thea for the same reason that poor Wunsch had sometimes dreaded his; because she stirred him more than anything she did could adequately explain.

One afternoon Harsanyi, after the lesson, was standing by the window putting some collodion on a cracked finger, and Thea was at the piano trying over "Die Lorelei" which he had given her last week to practice. It was scarcely a song which a singing master would have given her, but he had his own reasons. How she sang it mattered only to him and to her. He was playing his own game now, without interference; he suspected that he could not do so always.

When she finished the song, she looked back over her shoulder at him and spoke thoughtfully. "That wasn't right, at the end, was it?"

"No, that should be an open, flowing tone, something like this,"--he waved his fingers rapidly in the air. "You get the idea?"

"No, I don't. Seems a queer ending, after the rest."

Harsanyi corked his little bottle and dropped it into the pocket of his velvet coat. "Why so? Shipwrecks come and go, MARCHEN come and go, but the river keeps right on. There you have your open, flowing tone."

Thea looked intently at the music. "I see," she said dully. "Oh, I see!" she repeated quickly and turned to him a glowing countenance. "It is the river.--Oh, yes, I get it now!" She looked at him but long enough to catch his glance, then turned to the piano again. Harsanyi was never quite sure where the light came from when her face suddenly flashed out at him in that way. Her eyes were too small to account for it, though they glittered like green ice in the sun. At such moments her hair was yellower, her skin whiter, her cheeks pinker, as if a lamp had suddenly been turned up inside of her. She went at the song again:

"ICH WEISS NICHT, WAS SOLL ES BEDEUTEN, DAS ICH SO TRAURIG BIN."

A kind of happiness vibrated in her voice. Harsanyi noticed how much and how unhesitatingly she changed her delivery of the whole song, the first part as well as the last. He had often noticed that she could not think a thing out in passages. Until she saw it as a whole, she wandered like a blind man surrounded by torments. After she once had her "revelation," after she got the idea that to her--not always to him--explained everything, then she went forward rapidly. But she was not always easy to help. She was sometimes impervious to suggestion; she would stare at him as if she were deaf and ignore everything he told her to do. Then, all at once, something would happen in her brain and she would begin to do all that he had been for weeks telling her to do, without realizing that he had ever told her.

To-night Thea forgot Harsanyi and his finger. She finished the song only to begin it with fresh enthusiasm.

"UND DAS HAT MIT IHREM SINGEN DIE LORELEI GETHAN."

She sat there singing it until the darkening room was so flooded with it that Harsanyi threw open a window.

"You really must stop it, Miss Kronborg. I shan't be able to get it out of my head to-night."

Thea laughed tolerantly as she began to gather up her music. "Why, I thought you had gone, Mr. Harsanyi. I like that song."

That evening at dinner Harsanyi sat looking intently into a glass of heavy yellow wine; boring into it, indeed, with his one eye, when his face suddenly broke into a smile.

"What is it, Andor?" his wife asked.

He smiled again, this time at her, and took up the nutcrackers and a Brazil nut. "Do you know," he said in a tone so intimate and confidential that he might have been speaking to himself,--"do you know, I like to see Miss Kronborg get hold of an idea. In spite of being so talented, she's not quick. But when she does get an idea, it fills her up to the eyes. She had my room so reeking of a song this afternoon that I couldn't stay there."

Mrs. Harsanyi looked up quickly, "`Die Lorelei,' you mean? One couldn't think of anything else anywhere in the house. I thought she was possessed. But don't you think her voice is wonderful sometimes?"

Harsanyi tasted his wine slowly. "My dear, I've told you before that I don't know what I think about Miss Kronborg, except that I'm glad there are not two of her. I sometimes wonder whether she is not glad. Fresh as she is at it all, I've occasionally fancied that, if she knew how, she would like to--diminish." He moved his left hand out into the air as if he were suggesting a DIMINUENDO to an orchestra.

V

BY the first of February Thea had been in Chicago almost four months, and she did not know much more about the city than if she had never quitted Moonstone. She was, as Harsanyi said, incurious. Her work took most of her time, and she found that she had to sleep a good deal. It had never before been so hard to get up in the morning. She had the bother of caring for her room, and she had to build her fire and bring up her coal. Her routine was frequently interrupted by a message from Mr. Larsen summoning her to sing at a funeral. Every funeral took half a day, and the time had to be made up. When Mrs. Harsanyi asked her if it did not depress her to sing at funerals, she replied that she "had been brought up to go to funerals and didn't mind."

Thea never went into shops unless she had to, and she felt no interest in them. Indeed, she shunned them, as places where one was sure to be parted from one's money in some way. She was nervous about counting her change, and she could not accustom herself to having her purchases sent to her address. She felt much safer with her bundles under her arm.

During this first winter Thea got no city consciousness. Chicago was simply a wilderness through which one had to find one's way. She felt no interest in the general briskness and zest of the crowds. The crash and scramble of that big, rich, appetent Western city she did not take in at all, except to notice that the noise of the drays and street-cars tired her. The brilliant window displays, the splendid furs and stuffs, the gorgeous flower-shops, the gay candy-shops, she scarcely noticed. At Christmas-time she did feel some curiosity about the toy-stores, and she wished she held Thor's little mittened fist in her hand as she stood before the windows. The jewelers' windows, too, had a strong attraction for her--she had always liked bright stones. When she went into the city she used to brave the biting lake winds and stand gazing in at the displays of diamonds and pearls and emeralds; the tiaras and necklaces and earrings, on white velvet. These seemed very well worth while to her, things worth coveting.

Mrs. Lorch and Mrs. Andersen often told each other it was strange that Miss Kronborg had so little initiative about "visiting points of interest." When Thea came to live with them she had expressed a wish to see two places: Montgomery Ward and Company's big mail-order store, and the packing-houses, to which all the hogs and cattle that went through Moonstone were bound. One of Mrs. Lorch's lodgers worked in a packing-house, and Mrs. Andersen brought Thea word that she had spoken to Mr. Eckman and he would gladly take her to Packingtown. Eckman was a toughish young Swede, and he thought it would be something of a lark to take a pretty girl through the slaughter-houses. But he was disappointed. Thea neither grew faint nor clung to the arm he kept offering her. She asked innumerable questions and was impatient because he knew so little of what was going on outside of his own department. When they got off the street-car and walked back to Mrs. Lorch's house in the dusk, Eckman put her hand in his overcoat pocket--she had no muff--and kept squeezing it ardently until she said, "Don't do that; my ring cuts me." That night he told his roommate that he "could have kissed her as easy as rolling off a log, but she wasn't worth the trouble." As for Thea, she had enjoyed the afternoon very much, and wrote her father a brief but clear account of what she had seen.

One night at supper Mrs. Andersen was talking about the exhibit of students' work she had seen at the Art Institute that afternoon. Several of her friends had sketches in the exhibit. Thea, who always felt that she was behindhand in courtesy to Mrs. Andersen, thought that here was an opportunity to show interest without committing herself to anything. "Where is that, the Institute?" she asked absently.

Mrs. Andersen clasped her napkin in both hands. "The Art Institute? Our beautiful Art Institute on Michigan Avenue? Do you mean to say you have never visited it?"

"Oh, is it the place with the big lions out in front? I remember; I saw it when I went to Montgomery Ward's. Yes, I thought the lions were beautiful."

"But the pictures! Didn't you visit the galleries?"

"No. The sign outside said it was a pay-day. I've always meant to go back, but I haven't happened to be down that way since."

Mrs. Lorch and Mrs. Andersen looked at each other. The old mother spoke, fixing her shining little eyes upon Thea across the table. "Ah, but Miss Kronborg, there are old masters! Oh, many of them, such as you could not see anywhere out of Europe."

"And Corots," breathed Mrs. Andersen, tilting her head feelingly. "Such examples of the Barbizon school!" This was meaningless to Thea, who did not read the art columns of the Sunday INTER-OCEAN as Mrs. Andersen did.

"Oh, I'm going there some day," she reassured them. "I like to look at oil paintings."

One bleak day in February, when the wind was blowing clouds of dirt like a Moonstone sandstorm, dirt that filled your eyes and ears and mouth, Thea fought her way across the unprotected space in front of the Art Institute and into the doors of the building. She did not come out again until the closing hour. In the street-car, on the long cold ride home, while she sat staring at the waistcoat buttons of a fat strap-hanger, she had a serious reckoning with herself. She seldom thought about her way of life, about what she ought or ought not to do; usually there was but one obvious and important thing to be done. But that afternoon she remonstrated with herself severely. She told herself that she was missing a great deal; that she ought to be more willing to take advice and to go to see things. She was sorry that she had let months pass without going to the Art Institute. After this she would go once a week.

The Institute proved, indeed, a place of retreat, as the sand hills or the Kohlers' garden used to be; a place where she could forget Mrs. Andersen's tiresome overtures of friendship, the stout contralto in the choir whom she so unreasonably hated, and even, for a little while, the torment of her work. That building was a place in which she could relax and play, and she could hardly ever play now. On the whole, she spent more time with the casts than with the pictures. They were at once more simple and more perplexing; and some way they seemed more important, harder to overlook. It never occurred to her to buy a catalogue, so she called most of the casts by names she made up for them. Some of them she knew; the Dying Gladiator she had read about in "Childe Harold" almost as long ago as she could remember; he was strongly associated with Dr. Archie and childish illnesses. The Venus di Milo puzzled her; she could not see why people thought her so beautiful. She told herself over and over that she did not think the Apollo Belvedere "at all handsome."

Better than anything else she liked a great equestrian statue of an evil, cruel-looking general with an unpronounceable name. She used to walk round and round this terrible man and his terrible horse, frowning at him, brooding upon him, as if she had to make some momentous decision about him.

The casts, when she lingered long among them, always made her gloomy. It was with a lightening of the heart, a feeling of throwing off the old miseries and old sorrows of the world, that she ran up the wide staircase to the pictures. There she liked best the ones that told stories. There was a painting by Gerome called "The Pasha's Grief" which always made her wish for Gunner and Axel. The Pasha was seated on a rug, beside a green candle almost as big as a telegraph pole, and before him was stretched his dead tiger, a splendid beast, and there were pink roses scattered about him. She loved, too, a picture of some boys bringing in a newborn calf on a litter, the cow walking beside it and licking it. The Corot which hung next to this painting she did not like or dislike; she never saw it.

But in that same room there was a picture--oh, that was the thing she ran upstairs so fast to see! That was her picture. She imagined that nobody cared for it but herself, and that it waited for her. That was a picture indeed. She liked even the name of it, "The Song of the Lark." The flat country, the early morning light, the wet fields, the look in the girl's heavy face--well, they were all hers, anyhow, whatever was there. She told herself that picture was "right." Just what she meant by this, it would take a clever person to explain. But to her the word covered the almost boundless satisfaction she felt when she looked at the picture.

Before Thea had any idea how fast the weeks were flying, before Mr. Larsen's "permanent" soprano had returned to her duties, spring came; windy, dusty, strident, shrill; a season almost more violent in Chicago than the winter from which it releases one, or the heat to which it eventually delivers one. One sunny morning the apple trees in Mrs. Lorch's back yard burst into bloom, and for the first time in months Thea dressed without building a fire. The morning shone like a holiday, and for her it was to be a holiday. There was in the air that sudden, treacherous softness which makes the Poles who work in the packing-houses get drunk. At such times beauty is necessary, and in Packingtown there is no place to get it except at the saloons, where one can buy for a few hours the illusion of comfort, hope, love,--whatever one most longs for.

Harsanyi had given Thea a ticket for the symphony concert that afternoon, and when she looked out at the white apple trees her doubts as to whether she ought to go vanished at once. She would make her work light that morning, she told herself. She would go to the concert full of energy. When she set off, after dinner, Mrs. Lorch, who knew Chicago weather, prevailed upon her to take her cape. The old lady said that such sudden mildness, so early in April, presaged a sharp return of winter, and she was anxious about her apple trees.

The concert began at two-thirty, and Thea was in her seat in the Auditorium at ten minutes after two--a fine seat in the first row of the balcony, on the side, where she could see the house as well as the orchestra. She had been to so few concerts that the great house, the crowd of people, and the lights, all had a stimulating effect. She was surprised to see so many men in the audience, and wondered how they could leave their business in the afternoon. During the first number Thea was so much interested in the orchestra itself, in the men, the instruments, the volume of sound, that she paid little attention to what they were playing. Her excitement impaired her power of listening. She kept saying to herself, "Now I must stop this foolishness and listen; I may never hear this again"; but her mind was like a glass that is hard to focus. She was not ready to listen until the second number, Dvorak's Symphony in E minor, called on the programme, "From the New World." The first theme had scarcely been given out when her mind became clear; instant composure fell upon her, and with it came the power of concentration. This was music she could understand, music from the New World indeed! Strange how, as the first movement went on, it brought back to her that high tableland above Laramie; the grass-grown wagon trails, the far-away peaks of the snowy range, the wind and the eagles, that old man and the first telegraph message.

When the first movement ended, Thea's hands and feet were cold as ice. She was too much excited to know anything except that she wanted something desperately, and when the English horns gave out the theme of the Largo, she knew that what she wanted was exactly that. Here were the sand hills, the grasshoppers and locusts, all the things that wakened and chirped in the early morning; the reaching and reaching of high plains, the immeasurable yearning of all flat lands. There was home in it, too; first memories, first mornings long ago; the amazement of a new soul in a new world; a soul new and yet old, that had dreamed something despairing, something glorious, in the dark before it was born; a soul obsessed by what it did not know, under the cloud of a past it could not recall.

If Thea had had much experience in concert-going, and had known her own capacity, she would have left the hall when the symphony was over. But she sat still, scarcely knowing where she was, because her mind had been far away and had not yet come back to her. She was startled when the orchestra began to play again--the entry of the gods into Walhalla. She heard it as people hear things in their sleep. She knew scarcely anything about the Wagner operas. She had a vague idea that "Rhinegold" was about the strife between gods and men; she had read something about it in Mr. Haweis's book long ago. Too tired to follow the orchestra with much understanding, she crouched down in her seat and closed her eyes. The cold, stately measures of the Walhalla music rang out, far away; the rainbow bridge throbbed out into the air, under it the wailing of the Rhine daughters and the singing of the Rhine. But Thea was sunk in twilight; it was all going on in another world. So it happened that with a dull, almost listless ear she heard for the first time that troubled music, ever-darkening, ever-brightening, which was to flow through so many years of her life.

When Thea emerged from the concert hall, Mrs. Lorch's predictions had been fulfilled. A furious gale was beating over the city from Lake Michigan. The streets were full of cold, hurrying, angry people, running for street-cars and barking at each other. The sun was setting in a clear, windy sky, that flamed with red as if there were a great fire somewhere on the edge of the city. For almost the first time Thea was conscious of the city itself, of the congestion of life all about her, of the brutality and power of those streams that flowed in the streets, threatening to drive one under. People jostled her, ran into her, poked her aside with their elbows, uttering angry exclamations. She got on the wrong car and was roughly ejected by the conductor at a windy corner, in front of a saloon. She stood there dazed and shivering. The cars passed, screaming as they rounded curves, but either they were full to the doors, or were bound for places where she did not want to go. Her hands were so cold that she took off her tight kid gloves. The street lights began to gleam in the dusk. A young man came out of the saloon and stood eyeing her questioningly while he lit a cigarette. "Looking for a friend to-night?" he asked. Thea drew up the collar of her cape and walked on a few paces. The young man shrugged his shoulders and drifted away.

Thea came back to the corner and stood there irresolutely. An old man approached her. He, too, seemed to be waiting for a car. He wore an overcoat with a black fur collar, his gray mustache was waxed into little points, and his eyes were watery. He kept thrusting his face up near hers. Her hat blew off and he ran after it--a stiff, pitiful skip he had--and brought it back to her. Then, while she was pinning her hat on, her cape blew up, and he held it down for her, looking at her intently. His face worked as if he were going to cry or were frightened. He leaned over and whispered something to her. It struck her as curious that he was really quite timid, like an old beggar. "Oh, let me ALONE!" she cried miserably between her teeth. He vanished, disappeared like the Devil in a play. But in the mean time something had got away from her; she could not remember how the violins came in after the horns, just there. When her cape blew up, perhaps--Why did these men torment her? A cloud of dust blew in her face and blinded her. There was some power abroad in the world bent upon taking away from her that feeling with which she had come out of the concert hall. Everything seemed to sweep down on her to tear it out from under her cape. If one had that, the world became one's enemy; people, buildings, wagons, cars, rushed at one to crush it under, to make one let go of it. Thea glared round her at the crowds, the ugly, sprawling streets, the long lines of lights, and she was not crying now. Her eyes were brighter than even Harsanyi had ever seen them. All these things and people were no longer remote and negligible; they had to be met, they were lined up against her, they were there to take something from her. Very well; they should never have it. They might trample her to death, but they should never have it. As long as she lived that ecstasy was going to be hers. She would live for it, work for it, die for it; but she was going to have it, time after time, height after height. She could hear the crash of the orchestra again, and she rose on the brasses. She would have it, what the trumpets were singing! She would have it, have it,--it! Under the old cape she pressed her hands upon her heaving bosom, that was a little girl's no longer.

VI

ONE afternoon in April, Theodore Thomas, the conductor of the Chicago Symphony Orchestra, had turned out his desk light and was about to leave his office in the Auditorium Building, when Harsanyi appeared in the doorway. The conductor welcomed him with a hearty hand-grip and threw off the overcoat he had just put on. He pushed Harsanyi into a chair and sat down at his burdened desk, pointing to the piles of papers and railway folders upon it.

"Another tour, clear to the coast. This traveling is the part of my work that grinds me, Andor. You know what it means: bad food, dirt, noise, exhaustion for the men and for me. I'm not so young as I once was. It's time I quit the highway. This is the last tour, I swear!"

"Then I'm sorry for the `highway.' I remember when I first heard you in Pittsburg, long ago. It was a life-line you threw me. It's about one of the people along your highway that I've come to see you. Whom do you consider the best teacher for voice in Chicago?"

Mr. Thomas frowned and pulled his heavy mustache. "Let me see; I suppose on the whole Madison Bowers is the best. He's intelligent, and he had good training. I don't like him."

Harsanyi nodded. "I thought there was no one else. I don't like him, either, so I hesitated. But I suppose he must do, for the present."

"Have you found anything promising? One of your own students?"

"Yes, sir. A young Swedish girl from somewhere in Colorado. She is very talented, and she seems to me to have a remarkable voice."

"High voice?"

"I think it will be; though her low voice has a beautiful quality, very individual. She has had no instruction in voice at all, and I shrink from handing her over to anybody; her own instinct about it has been so good. It is one of those voices that manages itself easily, without thinning as it goes up; good breathing and perfect relaxation. But she must have a teacher, of course. There is a break in the middle voice, so that the voice does not all work together; an unevenness."

Thomas looked up. "So? Curious; that cleft often happens with the Swedes. Some of their best singers have had it. It always reminds me of the space you so often see between their front teeth. Is she strong physically?"

Harsanyi's eye flashed. He lifted his hand before him and clenched it. "Like a horse, like a tree! Every time I give her a lesson, I lose a pound. She goes after what she wants."

"Intelligent, you say? Musically intelligent?"

"Yes; but no cultivation whatever. She came to me like a fine young savage, a book with nothing written in it. That is why I feel the responsibility of directing her." Harsanyi paused and crushed his soft gray hat over his knee. "She would interest you, Mr. Thomas," he added slowly. "She has a quality--very individual."

"Yes; the Scandinavians are apt to have that, too. She can't go to Germany, I suppose?"

"Not now, at any rate. She is poor."

Thomas frowned again "I don't think Bowers a really first-rate man. He's too petty to be really first-rate; in his nature, I mean. But I dare say he's the best you can do, if you can't give her time enough yourself."

Harsanyi waved his hand. "Oh, the time is nothing--she may have all she wants. But I cannot teach her to sing."

"Might not come amiss if you made a musician of her, however," said Mr. Thomas dryly.

"I have done my best. But I can only play with a voice, and this is not a voice to be played with. I think she will be a musician, whatever happens. She is not quick, but she is solid, real; not like these others. My wife says that with that girl one swallow does not make a summer."

Mr. Thomas laughed. "Tell Mrs. Harsanyi that her remark conveys something to me. Don't let yourself get too much interested. Voices are so often disappointing; especially women's voices. So much chance about it, so many factors."

"Perhaps that is why they interest one. All the intelligence and talent in the world can't make a singer. The voice is a wild thing. It can't be bred in captivity. It is a sport, like the silver fox. It happens."

Mr. Thomas smiled into Harsanyi's gleaming eye. "Why haven't you brought her to sing for me?"

"I've been tempted to, but I knew you were driven to death, with this tour confronting you."

"Oh, I can always find time to listen to a girl who has a voice, if she means business. I'm sorry I'm leaving so soon. I could advise you better if I had heard her. I can sometimes give a singer suggestions. I've worked so much with them."

"You're the only conductor I know who is not snobbish about singers." Harsanyi spoke warmly.

"Dear me, why should I be? They've learned from me, and I've learned from them." As they rose, Thomas took the younger man affectionately by the arm. "Tell me about that wife of yours. Is she well, and as lovely as ever? And such fine children! Come to see me oftener, when I get back. I miss it when you don't."

The two men left the Auditorium Building together. Harsanyi walked home. Even a short talk with Thomas always stimulated him. As he walked he was recalling an evening they once spent together in Cincinnati.

Harsanyi was the soloist at one of Thomas's concerts there, and after the performance the conductor had taken him off to a RATHSKELLER where there was excellent German cooking, and where the proprietor saw to it that Thomas had the best wines procurable. Thomas had been working with the great chorus of the Festival Association and was speaking of it with enthusiasm when Harsanyi asked him how it was that he was able to feel such an interest in choral directing and in voices generally. Thomas seldom spoke of his youth or his early struggles, but that night he turned back the pages and told Harsanyi a long story.

He said he had spent the summer of his fifteenth year wandering about alone in the South, giving violin concerts in little towns. He traveled on horseback. When he came into a town, he went about all day tacking up posters announcing his concert in the evening. Before the concert, he stood at the door taking in the admission money until his audience had arrived, and then he went on the platform and played. It was a lazy, hand-to-mouth existence, and Thomas said he must have got to like that easy way of living and the relaxing Southern atmosphere. At any rate, when he got back to New York in the fall, he was rather torpid; perhaps he had been growing too fast. From this adolescent drowsiness the lad was awakened by two voices, by two women who sang in New York in 1851, --Jenny Lind and Henrietta Sontag. They were the first great artists he had ever heard, and he never forgot his debt to them.

As he said, "It was not voice and execution alone. There was a greatness about them. They were great women, great artists. They opened a new world to me." Night after night he went to hear them, striving to reproduce the quality of their tone upon his violin. From that time his idea about strings was completely changed, and on his violin he tried always for the singing, vibrating tone, instead of the loud and somewhat harsh tone then prevalent among even the best German violinists. In later years he often advised violinists to study singing, and singers to study violin. He told Harsanyi that he got his first conception of tone quality from Jenny Lind.

"But, of course," he added, "the great thing I got from Lind and Sontag was the indefinite, not the definite, thing. For an impressionable boy, their inspiration was incalculable. They gave me my first feeling for the Italian style--but I could never say how much they gave me. At that age, such influences are actually creative. I always think of my artistic consciousness as beginning then."

All his life Thomas did his best to repay what he felt he owed to the singer's art. No man could get such singing from choruses, and no man worked harder to raise the standard of singing in schools and churches and choral societies.

VII

All through the lesson Thea had felt that Harsanyi was restless and abstracted. Before the hour was over, he pushed back his chair and said resolutely, "I am not in the mood, Miss Kronborg. I have something on my mind, and I must talk to you. When do you intend to go home?"

Thea turned to him in surprise. "The first of June, about. Mr. Larsen will not need me after that, and I have not much money ahead. I shall work hard this summer, though."

"And to-day is the first of May; May-day." Harsanyi leaned forward, his elbows on his knees, his hands locked between them. "Yes, I must talk to you about something. I have asked Madison Bowers to let me bring you to him on Thursday, at your usual lesson-time. He is the best vocal teacher in Chicago, and it is time you began to work seriously with your voice."

Thea's brow wrinkled. "You mean take lessons of Bowers?"

Harsanyi nodded, without lifting his head.

"But I can't, Mr. Harsanyi. I haven't got the time, and, besides--" she blushed and drew her shoulders up stiffly-- "besides, I can't afford to pay two teachers." Thea felt that she had blurted this out in the worst possible way, and she turned back to the keyboard to hide her chagrin.

"I know that. I don't mean that you shall pay two teachers. After you go to Bowers you will not need me. I need scarcely tell you that I shan't be happy at losing you."

Thea turned to him, hurt and angry. "But I don't want to go to Bowers. I don't want to leave you. What's the matter? Don't I work hard enough? I'm sure you teach people that don't try half as hard."

Harsanyi rose to his feet. "Don't misunderstand me, Miss Kronborg. You interest me more than any pupil I have. I have been thinking for months about what you ought to do, since that night when you first sang for me." He walked over to the window, turned, and came toward her again. "I believe that your voice is worth all that you can put into it. I have not come to this decision rashly. I have studied you, and I have become more and more convinced, against my own desires. I cannot make a singer of you, so it was my business to find a man who could. I have even consulted Theodore Thomas about it."

"But suppose I don't want to be a singer? I want to study with you. What's the matter? Do you really think I've no talent? Can't I be a pianist?"

Harsanyi paced up and down the long rug in front of her. "My girl, you are very talented. You could be a pianist, a good one. But the early training of a pianist, such a pianist as you would want to be, must be something tremendous. He must have had no other life than music. At your age he must be the master of his instrument. Nothing can ever take the place of that first training. You know very well that your technique is good, but it is not remarkable. It will never overtake your intelligence. You have a fine power of work, but you are not by nature a student. You are not by nature, I think, a pianist. You would never find yourself. In the effort to do so, I'm afraid your playing would become warped, eccentric." He threw back his head and looked at his pupil intently with that one eye which sometimes seemed to see deeper than any two eyes, as if its singleness gave it privileges. "Oh, I have watched you very carefully, Miss Kronborg. Because you had had so little and had yet done so much for yourself, I had a great wish to help you. I believe that the strongest need of your nature is to find yourself, to emerge AS yourself. Until I heard you sing I wondered how you were to do this, but it has grown clearer to me every day."

Thea looked away toward the window with hard, narrow eyes. "You mean I can be a singer because I haven't brains enough to be a pianist."

"You have brains enough and talent enough. But to do what you will want to do, it takes more than these--it takes vocation. Now, I think you have vocation, but for the voice, not for the piano. If you knew,"--he stopped and sighed,-- "if you knew how fortunate I sometimes think you. With the voice the way is so much shorter, the rewards are more easily won. In your voice I think Nature herself did for you what it would take you many years to do at the piano. Perhaps you were not born in the wrong place after all. Let us talk frankly now. We have never done so before, and I have respected your reticence. What you want more than anything else in the world is to be an artist; is that true?"

She turned her face away from him and looked down at the keyboard. Her answer came in a thickened voice. "Yes, I suppose so."

"When did you first feel that you wanted to be an artist?"

"I don't know. There was always--something."

"Did you never think that you were going to sing?"

"Yes."

"How long ago was that?"

"Always, until I came to you. It was you who made me want to play piano." Her voice trembled. "Before, I tried to think I did, but I was pretending."

Harsanyi reached out and caught the hand that was hanging at her side. He pressed it as if to give her something. "Can't you see, my dear girl, that was only because I happened to be the first artist you have ever known? If I had been a trombone player, it would have been the same; you would have wanted to play trombone. But all the while you have been working with such good-will, something has been struggling against me. See, here we were, you and I and this instrument,"--he tapped the piano,--"three good friends, working so hard. But all the while there was something fighting us: your gift, and the woman you were meant to be. When you find your way to that gift and to that woman, you will be at peace. In the beginning it was an artist that you wanted to be; well, you may be an artist, always."

Thea drew a long breath. Her hands fell in her lap. "So I'm just where I began. No teacher, nothing done. No money."

Harsanyi turned away. "Feel no apprehension about the money, Miss Kronborg. Come back in the fall and we shall manage that. I shall even go to Mr. Thomas if necessary. This year will not be lost. If you but knew what an advantage this winter's study, all your study of the piano, will give you over most singers. Perhaps things have come out better for you than if we had planned them knowingly."

"You mean they have IF I can sing."

Thea spoke with a heavy irony, so heavy, indeed, that it was coarse. It grated upon Harsanyi because he felt that it was not sincere, an awkward affectation.

He wheeled toward her. "Miss Kronborg, answer me this. YOU KNOW THAT YOU CAN SING, do you not? You have always known it. While we worked here together you sometimes said to yourself, `I have something you know nothing about; I could surprise you.' Is that also true?"

Thea nodded and hung her head.

"Why were you not frank with me? Did I not deserve it?"

She shuddered. Her bent shoulders trembled. "I don't know," she muttered. "I didn't mean to be like that. I couldn't. I can't. It's different."

"You mean it is very personal?" he asked kindly.

She nodded. "Not at church or funerals, or with people like Mr. Larsen. But with you it was--personal. I'm not like you and Mrs. Harsanyi. I come of rough people. I'm rough. But I'm independent, too. It was--all I had. There is no use my talking, Mr. Harsanyi. I can't tell you."

"You needn't tell me. I know. Every artist knows." Harsanyi stood looking at his pupil's back, bent as if she were pushing something, at her lowered head. "You can sing for those people because with them you do not commit yourself. But the reality, one cannot uncover THAT until one is sure. One can fail one's self, but one must not live to see that fail; better never reveal it. Let me help you to make yourself sure of it. That I can do better than Bowers."

Thea lifted her face and threw out her hands.

Harsanyi shook his head and smiled. "Oh, promise nothing! You will have much to do. There will not be voice only, but French, German, Italian. You will have work enough. But sometimes you will need to be understood; what you never show to any one will need companionship. And then you must come to me." He peered into her face with that searching, intimate glance. "You know what I mean, the thing in you that has no business with what is little, that will have to do only with beauty and power."

Thea threw out her hands fiercely, as if to push him away. She made a sound in her throat, but it was not articulate. Harsanyi took one of her hands and kissed it lightly upon the back. His salute was one of greeting, not of farewell, and it was for some one he had never seen.

When Mrs. Harsanyi came in at six o'clock, she found her husband sitting listlessly by the window. "Tired?" she asked.

"A little. I've just got through a difficulty. I've sent Miss Kronborg away; turned her over to Bowers, for voice."

"Sent Miss Kronborg away? Andor, what is the matter with you?"

"It's nothing rash. I've known for a long while I ought to do it. She is made for a singer, not a pianist."

Mrs. Harsanyi sat down on the piano chair. She spoke a little bitterly: "How can you be sure of that? She was, at least, the best you had. I thought you meant to have her play at your students' recital next fall. I am sure she would have made an impression. I could have dressed her so that she would have been very striking. She had so much individuality."

Harsanyi bent forward, looking at the floor. "Yes, I know. I shall miss her, of course."

Mrs. Harsanyi looked at her husband's fine head against the gray window. She had never felt deeper tenderness for him than she did at that moment. Her heart ached for him. "You will never get on, Andor," she said mournfully.

Harsanyi sat motionless. "No, I shall never get on," he repeated quietly. Suddenly he sprang up with that light movement she knew so well, and stood in the window, with folded arms. "But some day I shall be able to look her in the face and laugh because I did what I could for her. I believe in her. She will do nothing common. She is uncommon, in a common, common world. That is what I get out of it. It means more to me than if she played at my concert and brought me a dozen pupils. All this drudgery will kill me if once in a while I cannot hope something, for somebody! If I cannot sometimes see a bird fly and wave my hand to it."

His tone was angry and injured. Mrs. Harsanyi understood that this was one of the times when his wife was a part of the drudgery, of the "common, common world."

He had let something he cared for go, and he felt bitterly about whatever was left. The mood would pass, and he would be sorry. She knew him. It wounded her, of course, but that hurt was not new. It was as old as her love for him. She went out and left him alone.

VIII

ONE warm damp June night the Denver Express was speeding westward across the earthy-smelling plains of Iowa. The lights in the day-coach were turned low and the ventilators were open, admitting showers of soot and dust upon the occupants of the narrow green plush chairs which were tilted at various angles of discomfort. In each of these chairs some uncomfortable human being lay drawn up, or stretched out, or writhing from one position to another. There were tired men in rumpled shirts, their necks bare and their suspenders down; old women with their heads tied up in black handkerchiefs; bedraggled young women who went to sleep while they were nursing their babies and forgot to button up their dresses; dirty boys who added to the general discomfort by taking off their boots. The brakeman, when he came through at midnight, sniffed the heavy air disdainfully and looked up at the ventilators. As he glanced down the double rows of contorted figures, he saw one pair of eyes that were wide open and bright, a yellow head that was not overcome by the stupefying heat and smell in the car. "There's a girl for you," he thought as he stopped by Thea's chair.

"Like to have the window up a little?" he asked.

Thea smiled up at him, not misunderstanding his friendliness. "The girl behind me is sick; she can't stand a draft. What time is it, please?"

He took out his open-faced watch and held it before her eyes with a knowing look. "In a hurry?" he asked. "I'll leave the end door open and air you out. Catch a wink; the time'll go faster."

Thea nodded good-night to him and settled her head back on her pillow, looking up at the oil lamps. She was going back to Moonstone for her summer vacation, and she was sitting up all night in a day-coach because that seemed such an easy way to save money. At her age discomfort was a small matter, when one made five dollars a day by it. She had confidently expected to sleep after the car got quiet, but in the two chairs behind her were a sick girl and her mother, and the girl had been coughing steadily since ten o'clock. They had come from somewhere in Pennsylvania, and this was their second night on the road. The mother said they were going to Colorado "for her daughter's lungs." The daughter was a little older than Thea, perhaps nineteen, with patient dark eyes and curly brown hair. She was pretty in spite of being so sooty and travel-stained. She had put on an ugly figured satine kimono over her loosened clothes. Thea, when she boarded the train in Chicago, happened to stop and plant her heavy telescope on this seat. She had not intended to remain there, but the sick girl had looked up at her with an eager smile and said, "Do sit there, miss. I'd so much rather not have a gentleman in front of me."

After the girl began to cough there were no empty seats left, and if there had been Thea could scarcely have changed without hurting her feelings. The mother turned on her side and went to sleep; she was used to the cough. But the girl lay wide awake, her eyes fixed on the roof of the car, as Thea's were. The two girls must have seen very different things there.

Thea fell to going over her winter in Chicago. It was only under unusual or uncomfortable conditions like these that she could keep her mind fixed upon herself or her own affairs for any length of time. The rapid motion and the vibration of the wheels under her seemed to give her thoughts rapidity and clearness. She had taken twenty very expensive lessons from Madison Bowers, but she did not yet know what he thought of her or of her ability. He was different from any man with whom she had ever had to do. With her other teachers she had felt a personal relation; but with him she did not. Bowers was a cold, bitter, avaricious man, but he knew a great deal about voices. He worked with a voice as if he were in a laboratory, conducting a series of experiments. He was conscientious and industrious, even capable of a certain cold fury when he was working with an interesting voice, but Harsanyi declared that he had the soul of a shrimp, and could no more make an artist than a throat specialist could. Thea realized that he had taught her a great deal in twenty lessons.

Although she cared so much less for Bowers than for Harsanyi, Thea was, on the whole, happier since she had been studying with him than she had been before. She had always told herself that she studied piano to fit herself to be a music teacher. But she never asked herself why she was studying voice. Her voice, more than any other part of her, had to do with that confidence, that sense of wholeness and inner well-being that she had felt at moments ever since she could remember.

Of this feeling Thea had never spoken to any human being until that day when she told Harsanyi that "there had always been--something." Hitherto she had felt but one obligation toward it--secrecy; to protect it even from herself. She had always believed that by doing all that was required of her by her family, her teachers, her pupils, she kept that part of herself from being caught up in the meshes of common things. She took it for granted that some day, when she was older, she would know a great deal more about it. It was as if she had an appointment to meet the rest of herself sometime, somewhere. It was moving to meet her and she was moving to meet it. That meeting awaited her, just as surely as, for the poor girl in the seat behind her, there awaited a hole in the earth, already dug.

For Thea, so much had begun with a hole in the earth. Yes, she reflected, this new part of her life had all begun that morning when she sat on the clay bank beside Ray Kennedy, under the flickering shade of the cottonwood tree. She remembered the way Ray had looked at her that morning. Why had he cared so much? And Wunsch, and Dr. Archie, and Spanish Johnny, why had they? It was something that had to do with her that made them care, but it was not she. It was something they believed in, but it was not she. Perhaps each of them concealed another person in himself, just as she did. Why was it that they seemed to feel and to hunt for a second person in her and not in each other? Thea frowned up at the dull lamp in the roof of the car. What if one's second self could somehow speak to all these second selves? What if one could bring them out, as whiskey did Spanish Johnny's? How deep they lay, these second persons, and how little one knew about them, except to guard them fiercely. It was to music, more than to anything else, that these hidden things in people responded. Her mother--even her mother had something of that sort which replied to music.

Thea found herself listening for the coughing behind her and not hearing it. She turned cautiously and looked back over the head-rest of her chair. The poor girl had fallen asleep. Thea looked at her intently. Why was she so afraid of men? Why did she shrink into herself and avert her face whenever a man passed her chair? Thea thought she knew; of course, she knew. How horrible to waste away like that, in the time when one ought to be growing fuller and stronger and rounder every day. Suppose there were such a dark hole open for her, between to-night and that place where she was to meet herself? Her eyes narrowed. She put her hand on her breast and felt how warm it was; and within it there was a full, powerful pulsation. She smiled--though she was ashamed of it--with the natural contempt of strength for weakness, with the sense of physical security which makes the savage merciless. Nobody could die while they felt like that inside. The springs there were wound so tight that it would be a long while before there was any slack in them. The life in there was rooted deep. She was going to have a few things before she died. She realized that there were a great many trains dashing east and west on the face of the continent that night, and that they all carried young people who meant to have things. But the difference was that SHE WAS GOING TO GET THEM! That was all. Let people try to stop her! She glowered at the rows of feckless bodies that lay sprawled in the chairs. Let them try it once! Along with the yearning that came from some deep part of her, that was selfless and exalted, Thea had a hard kind of cockiness, a determination to get ahead. Well, there are passages in life when that fierce, stubborn self-assertion will stand its ground after the nobler feeling is overwhelmed and beaten under.

Having told herself once more that she meant to grab a few things, Thea went to sleep.

She was wakened in the morning by the sunlight, which beat fiercely through the glass of the car window upon her face. She made herself as clean as she could, and while the people all about her were getting cold food out of their lunch-baskets she escaped into the dining-car. Her thrift did not go to the point of enabling her to carry a lunchbasket. At that early hour there were few people in the dining-car. The linen was white and fresh, the darkies were trim and smiling, and the sunlight gleamed pleasantly upon the silver and the glass water-bottles. On each table there was a slender vase with a single pink rose in it. When Thea sat down she looked into her rose and thought it the most beautiful thing in the world; it was wide open, recklessly offering its yellow heart, and there were drops of water on the petals. All the future was in that rose, all that one would like to be. The flower put her in an absolutely regal mood. She had a whole pot of coffee, and scrambled eggs with chopped ham, utterly disregarding the astonishing price they cost. She had faith enough in what she could do, she told herself, to have eggs if she wanted them. At the table opposite her sat a man and his wife and little boy--Thea classified them as being "from the East." They spoke in that quick, sure staccato, which Thea, like Ray

Kennedy, pretended to scorn and secretly admired. People who could use words in that confident way, and who spoke them elegantly, had a great advantage in life, she reflected. There were so many words which she could not pronounce in speech as she had to do in singing. Language was like clothes; it could be a help to one, or it could give one away. But the most important thing was that one should not pretend to be what one was not.

When she paid her check she consulted the waiter. "Waiter, do you suppose I could buy one of those roses? I'm out of the day-coach, and there is a sick girl in there. I'd like to take her a cup of coffee and one of those flowers."

The waiter liked nothing better than advising travelers less sophisticated than himself. He told Thea there were a few roses left in the icebox and he would get one. He took the flower and the coffee into the day-coach. Thea pointed out the girl, but she did not accompany him. She hated thanks and never received them gracefully. She stood outside on the platform to get some fresh air into her lungs. The train was crossing the Platte River now, and the sunlight was so intense that it seemed to quiver in little flames on the glittering sandbars, the scrub willows, and the curling, fretted shallows.

Thea felt that she was coming back to her own land. She had often heard Mrs. Kronborg say that she "believed in immigration," and so did Thea believe in it. This earth seemed to her young and fresh and kindly, a place where refugees from old, sad countries were given another chance. The mere absence of rocks gave the soil a kind of amiability and generosity, and the absence of natural boundaries gave the spirit a wider range. Wire fences might mark the end of a man's pasture, but they could not shut in his thoughts as mountains and forests can. It was over flat lands like this, stretching out to drink the sun, that the larks sang--and one's heart sang there, too. Thea was glad that this was her country, even if one did not learn to speak elegantly there. It was, somehow, an honest country, and there was a new song in that blue air which had never been sung in the world before. It was hard to tell about it, for it had nothing to do with words; it was like the light of the desert at noon, or the smell of the sagebrush after rain; intangible but powerful. She had the sense of going back to a friendly soil, whose friendship was somehow going to strengthen her; a naive, generous country that gave one its joyous force, its large-hearted, childlike power to love, just as it gave one its coarse, brilliant flowers.

As she drew in that glorious air Thea's mind went back to Ray Kennedy. He, too, had that feeling of empire; as if all the Southwest really belonged to him because he had knocked about over it so much, and knew it, as he said, "like the blisters on his own hands." That feeling, she reflected, was the real element of companionship between her and Ray. Now that she was going back to Colorado, she realized this as she had not done before.

IX

THEA reached Moonstone in the late afternoon, and all the Kronborgs were there to meet her except her two older brothers. Gus and Charley were young men now, and they had declared at noon that it would "look silly if the whole bunch went down to the train." "There's no use making a fuss over Thea just because she's been to Chicago," Charley warned his mother. "She's inclined to think pretty well of herself, anyhow, and if you go treating her like company, there'll be no living in the house with her." Mrs. Kronborg simply leveled her eyes at Charley, and he faded away, muttering. She had, as Mr. Kronborg always said with an inclination of his head, good control over her children. Anna, too, wished to absent herself from the party, but in the end her curiosity got the better of her. So when Thea stepped down from the porter's stool, a very creditable Kronborg representation was grouped on the platform to greet her. After they had all kissed her (Gunner and Axel shyly), Mr. Kronborg hurried his flock into the hotel omnibus, in which they were to be driven ceremoniously home, with the neighbors looking out of their windows to see them go by.

All the family talked to her at once, except Thor,--impressive in new trousers,--who was gravely silent and who refused to sit on Thea's lap. One of the first things Anna told her was that Maggie Evans, the girl who used to cough in prayer meeting, died yesterday, and had made a request that Thea sing at her funeral.

Thea's smile froze. "I'm not going to sing at all this summer, except my exercises. Bowers says I taxed my voice last winter, singing at funerals so much. If I begin the first day after I get home, there'll be no end to it. You can tell them I caught cold on the train, or something."

Thea saw Anna glance at their mother. Thea remembered having seen that look on Anna's face often before, but she had never thought anything about it because she was used to it. Now she realized that the look was distinctly spiteful, even vindictive. She suddenly realized that Anna had always disliked her.

Mrs. Kronborg seemed to notice nothing, and changed the trend of the conversation, telling Thea that Dr. Archie and Mr. Upping, the jeweler, were both coming in to see her that evening, and that she had asked Spanish Johnny to come, because he had behaved well all winter and ought to be encouraged.

The next morning Thea wakened early in her own room up under the eaves and lay watching the sunlight shine on the roses of her wall-paper. She wondered whether she would ever like a plastered room as well as this one lined with scantlings. It was snug and tight, like the cabin of a little boat. Her bed faced the window and stood against the wall, under the slant of the ceiling. When she went away she could just touch the ceiling with the tips of her fingers; now she could touch it with the palm of her hand. It was so little that it was like a sunny cave, with roses running all over the roof. Through the low window, as she lay there, she could watch people going by on the farther side of the street; men, going downtown to open their stores. Thor was over there, rattling his express wagon along the sidewalk. Tillie had put a bunch of French pinks in a tumbler of water on her dresser, and they gave out a pleasant perfume. The blue jays were fighting and screeching in the cottonwood tree outside her window, as they always did, and she could hear the old Baptist deacon across the street calling his chickens, as she had heard him do every summer morning since she could remember. It was pleasant to waken up in that bed, in that room, and to feel the brightness of the morning, while light quivered about the low, papered ceiling in golden spots, refracted by the broken mirror and the glass of water that held the pinks. "IM LEUCHTENDEN SOMMERMORGEN"; those lines, and the face of her old teacher, came back to Thea, floated to her out of sleep, perhaps. She had been dreaming something pleasant, but she could not remember what. She would go to call upon Mrs. Kohler to-day, and see the pigeons washing their pink feet in the drip under the water tank, and flying about their house that was sure to have a fresh coat of white paint on it for summer. On the way home she would stop to see Mrs. Tellamantez. On Sunday she would coax Gunner to take her out to the sand hills. She had missed them in Chicago; had been homesick for their brilliant morning gold and for their soft colors at evening. The Lake, somehow, had never taken their place.

While she lay planning, relaxed in warm drowsiness, she heard a knock at her door. She supposed it was Tillie, who sometimes fluttered in on her before she was out of bed to offer some service which the family would have ridiculed. But instead, Mrs. Kronborg herself came in, carrying a tray with Thea's breakfast set out on one of the best white napkins. Thea sat up with some embarrassment and pulled her nightgown together across her chest. Mrs. Kronborg was always busy downstairs in the morning, and Thea could not remember when her mother had come to her room before.

"I thought you'd be tired, after traveling, and might like to take it easy for once." Mrs. Kronborg put the tray on the edge of the bed. "I took some thick cream for you before the boys got at it. They raised a howl." She chuckled and sat down in the big wooden rocking chair. Her visit made Thea feel grown-up, and, somehow, important.

Mrs. Kronborg asked her about Bowers and the Harsanyis. She felt a great change in Thea, in her face and in her manner. Mr. Kronborg had noticed it, too, and had spoken of it to his wife with great satisfaction while they were undressing last night. Mrs. Kronborg sat looking at her daughter, who lay on her side, supporting herself on her elbow and lazily drinking her coffee from the tray before her. Her short-sleeved nightgown had come open at the throat again, and Mrs. Kronborg noticed how white her arms and shoulders were, as if they had been dipped in new milk. Her chest was fuller than when she went away, her breasts rounder and firmer, and though she was so white where she was uncovered, they looked rosy through the thin muslin. Her body had the elasticity that comes of being highly charged with the desire to live. Her hair, hanging in two loose braids, one by either cheek, was just enough disordered to catch the light in all its curly ends.

Thea always woke with a pink flush on her cheeks, and this morning her mother thought she had never seen her eyes so wide-open and bright; like clear green springs in the wood, when the early sunlight sparkles in them. She would make a very handsome woman, Mrs. Kronborg said to herself, if she would only get rid of that fierce look she had sometimes. Mrs. Kronborg took great pleasure in good looks, wherever she found them. She still remembered that, as a baby, Thea had been the "best-formed" of any of her children.

"I'll have to get you a longer bed," she remarked, as she put the tray on the table. "You're getting too long for that one."

Thea looked up at her mother and laughed, dropping back on her pillow with a magnificent stretch of her whole body. Mrs. Kronborg sat down again.

"I don't like to press you, Thea, but I think you'd better sing at that funeral to-morrow. I'm afraid you'll always be sorry if you don't. Sometimes a little thing like that, that seems nothing at the time, comes back on one afterward and troubles one a good deal. I don't mean the church shall run you to death this summer, like they used to. I've spoken my mind to your father about that, and he's very reasonable. But Maggie talked a good deal about you to people this winter; always asked what word we'd had, and said how she missed your singing and all. I guess you ought to do that much for her."

"All right, mother, if you think so." Thea lay looking at her mother with intensely bright eyes.

"That's right, daughter." Mrs. Kronborg rose and went over to get the tray, stopping to put her hand on Thea's chest. "You're filling out nice," she said, feeling about. "No, I wouldn't bother about the buttons. Leave 'em stay off. This is a good time to harden your chest."

Thea lay still and heard her mother's firm step receding along the bare floor of the trunk loft. There was no sham about her mother, she reflected. Her mother knew a great many things of which she never talked, and all the church people were forever chattering about things of which they knew nothing. She liked her mother.

Now for Mexican Town and the Kohlers! She meant to run in on the old woman without warning, and hug her.

X

SPANISH JOHNNY had no shop of his own, but he kept a table and an order-book in one corner of the drug store where paints and wall-paper were sold, and he was sometimes to be found there for an hour or so about noon. Thea had gone into the drug store to have a friendly chat with the proprietor, who used to lend her books from his shelves. She found Johnny there, trimming rolls of wall-paper for the parlor of Banker Smith's new house. She sat down on the top of his table and watched him.

"Johnny," she said suddenly, "I want you to write down the words of that Mexican serenade you used to sing; you know, `ROSA DE NOCHE.' It's an unusual song. I'm going to study it. I know enough Spanish for that."

Johnny looked up from his roller with his bright, affable smile. "SI, but it is low for you, I think; VOZ CONTRALTO. It is low for me."

"Nonsense. I can do more with my low voice than I used to. I'll show you. Sit down and write it out for me, please." Thea beckoned him with the short yellow pencil tied to his order-book.

Johnny ran his fingers through his curly black hair. "If you wish. I do not know if that SERENATA all right for young ladies. Down there it is more for married ladies. They sing it for husbands--or somebody else, may-bee." Johnny's eyes twinkled and he apologized gracefully with his shoulders. He sat down at the table, and while Thea looked over his arm, began to write the song down in a long, slanting script, with highly ornamental capitals. Presently he looked up. "This-a song not exactly Mexican," he said thoughtfully. "It come from farther down; Brazil, Venezuela, may-bee. I learn it from some fellow down there, and he learn it from another fellow. It is-a most like Mexican, but not quite." Thea did not release him, but pointed to the paper. There were three verses of the song in all, and when Johnny had written them down, he sat looking at them meditatively, his head on one side. "I don' think for a high voice, SENORITA," he objected with polite persistence. "How you accompany with piano?"

"Oh, that will be easy enough."

"For you, may-bee!" Johnny smiled and drummed on the table with the tips of his agile brown fingers. "You know something? Listen, I tell you." He rose and sat down on the table beside her, putting his foot on the chair. He loved to talk at the hour of noon. "When you was a little girl, no bigger than that, you come to my house one day 'bout noon, like this, and I was in the door, playing guitar. You was barehead, barefoot; you run away from home. You stand there and make a frown at me an' listen. By 'n by you say for me to sing. I sing some lil' ting, and then I say for you to sing with me. You don' know no words, of course, but you take the air and you sing it justa beauti-ful! I never see a child do that, outside Mexico. You was, oh, I do' know--seven year, may-bee. By 'n by the preacher come look for you and begin for scold. I say, `Don' scold, Meester Kronborg. She come for hear guitar. She gotta some music in her, that child. Where she get?' Then he tell me 'bout your gran'papa play oboe in the old country. I never forgetta that time." Johnny chuckled softly.

Thea nodded. "I remember that day, too. I liked your music better than the church music. When are you going to have a dance over there, Johnny?"

Johnny tilted his head. "Well, Saturday night the Spanish boys have a lil' party, some DANZA. You know Miguel Ramas? He have some young cousins, two boys, very nice-a, come from Torreon. They going to Salt Lake for some job-a, and stay off with him two-three days, and he mus' have a party. You like to come?"

That was how Thea came to go to the Mexican ball. Mexican Town had been increased by half a dozen new families during the last few years, and the Mexicans had put up an adobe dance-hall, that looked exactly like one of their own dwellings, except that it was a little longer, and was so unpretentious that nobody in Moonstone knew of its existence. The "Spanish boys" are reticent about their own affairs. Ray Kennedy used to know about all their little doings, but since his death there was no one whom the Mexicans considered SIMPATICO.

On Saturday evening after supper Thea told her mother that she was going over to Mrs. Tellamantez's to watch the Mexicans dance for a while, and that Johnny would bring her home.

Mrs. Kronborg smiled. She noticed that Thea had put on a white dress and had done her hair up with unusual care, and that she carried her best blue scarf. "Maybe you'll take a turn yourself, eh? I wouldn't mind watching them Mexicans. They're lovely dancers."

Thea made a feeble suggestion that her mother might go with her, but Mrs. Kronborg was too wise for that. She knew that Thea would have a better time if she went alone, and she watched her daughter go out of the gate and down the sidewalk that led to the depot.

Thea walked slowly. It was a soft, rosy evening. The sand hills were lavender. The sun had gone down a glowing copper disk, and the fleecy clouds in the east were a burning rose-color, flecked with gold. Thea passed the cottonwood grove and then the depot, where she left the sidewalk and took the sandy path toward Mexican Town. She could hear the scraping of violins being tuned, the tinkle of mandolins, and the growl of a double bass. Where had they got a double bass? She did not know there was one in Moonstone. She found later that it was the property of one of Ramas's young cousins, who was taking it to Utah with him to cheer him at his "job-a."

The Mexicans never wait until it is dark to begin to dance, and Thea had no difficulty in finding the new hall, because every other house in the town was deserted. Even the babies had gone to the ball; a neighbor was always willing to hold the baby while the mother danced. Mrs. Tellamantez came out to meet Thea and led her in. Johnny bowed to her from the platform at the end of the room, where he was playing the mandolin along with two fiddles and the bass. The hall was a long low room, with whitewashed walls, a fairly tight plank floor, wooden benches along the sides, and a few bracket lamps screwed to the frame timbers. There must have been fifty people there, counting the children. The Mexican dances were very much family affairs. The fathers always danced again and again with their little daughters, as well as with their wives. One of the girls came up to greet Thea, her dark cheeks glowing with pleasure and cordiality, and introduced her brother, with whom she had just been dancing. "You better take him every time he asks you," she whispered. "He's the best dancer here, except Johnny."

Thea soon decided that the poorest dancer was herself. Even Mrs. Tellamantez, who always held her shoulders so stiffly, danced better than she did. The musicians did not remain long at their post. When one of them felt like dancing, he called some other boy to take his instrument, put on his coat, and went down on the floor. Johnny, who wore a blousy white silk shirt, did not even put on his coat.

The dances the railroad men gave in Firemen's Hall were the only dances Thea had ever been allowed to go to, and they were very different from this. The boys played rough jokes and thought it smart to be clumsy and to run into each other on the floor. For the square dances there was always the bawling voice of the caller, who was also the county auctioneer.

This Mexican dance was soft and quiet. There was no calling, the conversation was very low, the rhythm of the music was smooth and engaging, the men were graceful and courteous. Some of them Thea had never before seen out of their working clothes, smeared with grease from the round-house or clay from the brickyard. Sometimes, when the music happened to be a popular Mexican waltz song, the dancers sang it softly as they moved. There were three little girls under twelve, in their first communion dresses, and one of them had an orange marigold in her black hair, just over her ear. They danced with the men and with each other. There was an atmosphere of ease and friendly pleasure in the low, dimly lit room, and Thea could not help wondering whether the Mexicans had no jealousies or neighborly grudges as the people in Moonstone had. There was no constraint of any kind there to-night, but a kind of natural harmony about their movements, their greetings, their low conversation, their smiles.

Ramas brought up his two young cousins, Silvo and Felipe, and presented them. They were handsome, smiling youths, of eighteen and twenty, with pale-gold skins, smooth cheeks, aquiline features, and wavy black hair, like Johnny's. They were dressed alike, in black velvet jackets and soft silk shirts, with opal shirt-buttons and flowing black ties looped through gold rings. They had charming manners, and low, guitar-like voices. They knew almost no English, but a Mexican boy can pay a great many compliments with a very limited vocabulary. The Ramas boys thought Thea dazzlingly beautiful. They had never seen a Scandinavian girl before, and her hair and fair skin bewitched them. "BLANCO Y ORO, SEMEJANTE LA PASCUA!" (White and gold, like Easter!) they exclaimed to each other. Silvo, the younger, declared that he could never go on to Utah; that he and his double bass had reached their ultimate destination. The elder was more crafty; he asked Miguel Ramas whether there would be "plenty more girls like that _A_ Salt Lake, maybee?"

Silvo, overhearing, gave his brother a contemptuous glance. "Plenty more A PARAISO may-bee!" he retorted. When they were not dancing with her, their eyes followed her, over the coiffures of their other partners. That was not difficult; one blonde head moving among so many dark ones.

Thea had not meant to dance much, but the Ramas boys danced so well and were so handsome and adoring that she yielded to their entreaties. When she sat out a dance with them, they talked to her about their family at home, and told her how their mother had once punned upon their name. RAMA, in Spanish, meant a branch, they explained. Once when they were little lads their mother took them along when she went to help the women decorate the church for Easter. Some one asked her whether she had brought any flowers, and she replied that she had brought her "ramas." This was evidently a cherished family story.

When it was nearly midnight, Johnny announced that every one was going to his house to have "some lil' icecream and some lil' MUSICA." He began to put out the lights and Mrs. Tellamantez led the way across the square to her CASA. The Ramas brothers escorted Thea, and as they stepped out of the door, Silvo exclaimed, "HACE FRIO!" and threw his velvet coat about her shoulders.

Most of the company followed Mrs. Tellamantez, and they sat about on the gravel in her little yard while she and Johnny and Mrs. Miguel Ramas served the ice-cream. Thea sat on Felipe's coat, since Silvo's was already about her shoulders. The youths lay down on the shining gravel beside her, one on her right and one on her left. Johnny already called them "LOS ACOLITOS," the altar-boys. The talk all about them was low, and indolent. One of the girls was playing on Johnny's guitar, another was picking lightly at a mandolin. The moonlight was so bright that one could see every glance and smile, and the flash of their teeth. The moonflowers over Mrs. Tellamantez's door were wide open and of an unearthly white. The moon itself looked like a great pale flower in the sky.

After all the ice-cream was gone, Johnny approached Thea, his guitar under his arm, and the elder Ramas boy politely gave up his place. Johnny sat down, took a long breath, struck a fierce chord, and then hushed it with his other hand. "Now we have some lil' SERENATA, eh? You wan' a try?"

When Thea began to sing, instant silence fell upon the company. She felt all those dark eyes fix themselves upon her intently. She could see them shine. The faces came out of the shadow like the white flowers over the door. Felipe leaned his head upon his hand. Silvo dropped on his back and lay looking at the moon, under the impression that he was still looking at Thea. When she finished the first verse, Thea whispered to Johnny, "Again, I can do it better than that."

She had sung for churches and funerals and teachers, but she had never before sung for a really musical people, and this was the first time she had ever felt the response that such a people can give. They turned themselves and all they had over to her. For the moment they cared about nothing in the world but what she was doing. Their faces confronted her, open, eager, unprotected. She felt as if all these warm-blooded people debouched into her. Mrs. Tellamantez's fateful resignation, Johnny's madness, the adoration of the boy who lay still in the sand; in an instant these things seemed to be within her instead of without, as if they had come from her in the first place.

When she finished, her listeners broke into excited murmur. The men began hunting feverishly for cigarettes. Famos Serranos the barytone bricklayer, touched Johnny's arm, gave him a questioning look, then heaved a deep sigh. Johnny dropped on his elbow, wiping his face and neck and hands with his handkerchief. "SENORITA," he panted, "if you sing like that once in the City of Mexico, they just-a go crazy. In the City of Mexico they ain't-a sit like stumps when they hear that, not-a much! When they like, they just-a give you the town."

Thea laughed. She, too, was excited. "Think so, Johnny? Come, sing something with me. EL PARRENO; I haven't sung that for a long time."

Johnny laughed and hugged his guitar. "You not-a forget him?" He began teasing his strings. "Come!" He threw back his head, "ANOCHE-E-E--"

"ANOCHE ME CONFESSE CON UN PADRE CARMELITE, Y ME DIO PENITENCIA QUE BESARAS TU BOQUITA."

(Last night I made confession With a Carmelite father, And he gave me absolution For the kisses you imprinted.)

Johnny had almost every fault that a tenor can have. His voice was thin, unsteady, husky in the middle tones. But it was distinctly a voice, and sometimes he managed to get something very sweet out of it. Certainly it made him happy to sing. Thea kept glancing down at him as he lay there on his elbow. His eyes seemed twice as large as usual and had lights in them like those the moonlight makes on black, running water. Thea remembered the old stories about his "spells." She had never seen him when his madness was on him, but she felt something tonight at her elbow that gave her an idea of what it might be like. For the first time she fully understood the cryptic explanation that Mrs. Tellamantez had made to Dr. Archie, long ago. There were the same shells along the walk; she believed she could pick out the very one. There was the same moon up yonder, and panting at her elbow was the same Johnny--fooled by the same old things!

When they had finished, Famos, the barytone, murmured something to Johnny; who replied, "Sure we can sing `Trovatore.' We have no alto, but all the girls can sing alto and make some noise."

The women laughed. Mexican women of the poorer class do not sing like the men. Perhaps they are too indolent. In the evening, when the men are singing their throats dry on the doorstep, or around the camp-fire beside the work-train, the women usually sit and comb their hair.

While Johnny was gesticulating and telling everybody what to sing and how to sing it, Thea put out her foot and touched the corpse of Silvo with the toe of her slipper. "Aren't you going to sing, Silvo?" she asked teasingly.

The boy turned on his side and raised himself on his elbow for a moment. "Not this night, SENORITA," he pleaded softly, "not this night!" He dropped back again, and lay with his cheek on his right arm, the hand lying passive on the sand above his head.

"How does he flatten himself into the ground like that?" Thea asked herself. "I wish I knew. It's very effective, somehow."

Across the gulch the Kohlers' little house slept among its trees, a dark spot on the white face of the desert. The windows of their upstairs bedroom were open, and Paulina had listened to the dance music for a long while before she drowsed off. She was a light sleeper, and when she woke again, after midnight, Johnny's concert was at its height. She lay still until she could bear it no longer. Then she wakened Fritz and they went over to the window and leaned out. They could hear clearly there.

"DIE THEA," whispered Mrs. Kohler; "it must be. ACH, WUNDERSCHON!"

Fritz was not so wide awake as his wife. He grunted and scratched on the floor with his bare foot. They were listening to a Mexican part-song; the tenor, then the soprano, then both together; the barytone joins them, rages, is extinguished; the tenor expires in sobs, and the soprano finishes alone. When the soprano's last note died away, Fritz nodded to his wife. "JA," he said; "SCHON."

There was silence for a few moments. Then the guitar sounded fiercely, and several male voices began the sextette from "Lucia." Johnny's reedy tenor they knew well, and the bricklayer's big, opaque barytone; the others might be anybody over there--just Mexican voices. Then at the appointed, at the acute, moment, the soprano voice, like a fountain jet, shot up into the light. "HORCH! HORCH!" the old people whispered, both at once. How it leaped from among those dusky male voices! How it played in and about and around and over them, like a goldfish darting among creek minnows, like a yellow butterfly soaring above a swarm of dark ones. "Ah," said Mrs. Kohler softly, "the dear man; if he could hear her now!"

XI

MRS. KRONBORG had said that Thea was not to be disturbed on Sunday morning, and she slept until noon. When she came downstairs the family were just sitting down to dinner, Mr. Kronborg at one end of the long table, Mrs. Kronborg at the other. Anna, stiff and ceremonious, in her summer silk, sat at her father's right, and the boys were strung along on either side of the table. There was a place left for Thea between her mother and Thor. During the silence which preceded the blessing, Thea felt something uncomfortable in the air. Anna and her older brothers had lowered their eyes when she came in. Mrs. Kronborg nodded cheerfully, and after the blessing, as she began to pour the coffee, turned to her.

"I expect you had a good time at that dance, Thea. I hope you got your sleep out."

"High society, that," remarked Charley, giving the mashed potatoes a vicious swat. Anna's mouth and eyebrows became half-moons.

Thea looked across the table at the uncompromising countenances of her older brothers. "Why, what's the matter with the Mexicans?" she asked, flushing. "They don't trouble anybody, and they are kind to their families and have good manners."

"Nice clean people; got some style about them. Do you really like that kind, Thea, or do you just pretend to? That's what I'd like to know." Gus looked at her with pained inquiry. But he at least looked at her.

"They're just as clean as white people, and they have a perfect right to their own ways. Of course I like 'em. I don't pretend things."

"Everybody according to their own taste," remarked Charley bitterly. "Quit crumbing your bread up, Thor. Ain't you learned how to eat yet?"

"Children, children!" said Mr. Kronborg nervously, looking up from the chicken he was dismembering. He glanced at his wife, whom he expected to maintain harmony in the family.

"That's all right, Charley. Drop it there," said Mrs. Kronborg. "No use spoiling your Sunday dinner with race prejudices. The Mexicans suit me and Thea very well. They are a useful people. Now you can just talk about something else."

Conversation, however, did not flourish at that dinner. Everybody ate as fast as possible. Charley and Gus said they had engagements and left the table as soon as they finished their apple pie. Anna sat primly and ate with great elegance. When she spoke at all she spoke to her father, about church matters, and always in a commiserating tone, as if he had met with some misfortune. Mr. Kronborg, quite innocent of her intentions, replied kindly and absent-mindedly. After the dessert he went to take his usual Sunday afternoon nap, and Mrs. Kronborg carried some dinner to a sick neighbor. Thea and Anna began to clear the table.

"I should think you would show more consideration for father's position, Thea," Anna began as soon as she and her sister were alone.

Thea gave her a sidelong glance. "Why, what have I done to father?"

"Everybody at Sunday-School was talking about you going over there and singing with the Mexicans all night, when you won't sing for the church. Somebody heard you, and told it all over town. Of course, we all get the blame for it."

"Anything disgraceful about singing?" Thea asked with a provoking yawn.

"I must say you choose your company! You always had that streak in you, Thea. We all hoped that going away would improve you. Of course, it reflects on father when you are scarcely polite to the nice people here and make up to the rowdies."

"Oh, it's my singing with the Mexicans you object to?" Thea put down a tray full of dishes. "Well, I like to sing over there, and I don't like to over here. I'll sing for them any time they ask me to. They know something about what I'm doing. They're a talented people."

"Talented!" Anna made the word sound like escaping steam. "I suppose you think it's smart to come home and throw that at your family!"

Thea picked up the tray. By this time she was as white as the Sunday tablecloth. "Well," she replied in a cold, even tone, "I'll have to throw it at them sooner or later. It's just a question of when, and it might as well be now as any time." She carried the tray blindly into the kitchen.

Tillie, who was always listening and looking out for her, took the dishes from her with a furtive, frightened glance at her stony face. Thea went slowly up the back stairs to her loft. Her legs seemed as heavy as lead as she climbed the stairs, and she felt as if everything inside her had solidified and grown hard.

After shutting her door and locking it, she sat down on the edge of her bed. This place had always been her refuge, but there was a hostility in the house now which this door could not shut out. This would be her last summer in that room. Its services were over; its time was done. She rose and put her hand on the low ceiling. Two tears ran down her cheeks, as if they came from ice that melted slowly. She was not ready to leave her little shell. She was being pulled out too soon. She would never be able to think anywhere else as well as here. She would never sleep so well or have such dreams in any other bed; even last night, such sweet, breathless dreams--Thea hid her face in the pillow. Wherever she went she would like to take that little bed with her. When she went away from it for good, she would leave something that she could never recover; memories of pleasant excitement, of happy adventures in her mind; of warm sleep on howling winter nights, and joyous awakenings on summer mornings. There were certain dreams that might refuse to come to her at all except in a little morning cave, facing the sun--where they came to her so powerfully, where they beat a triumph in her!

The room was hot as an oven. The sun was beating fiercely on the shingles behind the board ceiling. She undressed, and before she threw herself upon her bed in her chemise, she frowned at herself for a long while in her looking-glass. Yes, she and It must fight it out together. The thing that looked at her out of her own eyes was the only friend she could count on. Oh, she would make these people sorry enough! There would come a time when they would want to make it up with her. But, never again! She had no little vanities, only one big one, and she would never forgive.

Her mother was all right, but her mother was a part of the family, and she was not. In the nature of things, her mother had to be on both sides. Thea felt that she had been betrayed. A truce had been broken behind her back. She had never had much individual affection for any of her brothers except Thor, but she had never been disloyal, never felt scorn or held grudges. As a little girl she had always been good friends with Gunner and Axel, whenever she had time to play. Even before she got her own room, when they were all sleeping and dressing together, like little cubs, and breakfasting in the kitchen, she had led an absorbing personal life of her own. But she had a cub loyalty to the other cubs. She thought them nice boys and tried to make them get their lessons. She once fought a bully who "picked on" Axel at school. She never made fun of Anna's crimpings and curlings and beauty-rites.

Thea had always taken it for granted that her sister and brothers recognized that she had special abilities, and that they were proud of it. She had done them the honor, she told herself bitterly, to believe that though they had no particular endowments, THEY WERE OF HER KIND, and not of the Moonstone kind. Now they had all grown up and become persons. They faced each other as individuals, and she saw that Anna and Gus and Charley were among the people whom she had always recognized as her natural enemies. Their ambitions and sacred proprieties were meaningless to her. She had neglected to congratulate Charley upon having been promoted from the grocery department of Commings's store to the drygoods department. Her mother had reproved her for this omission. And how was she to know, Thea asked herself, that Anna expected to be teased because Bert Rice now came and sat in the hammock with her every night? No, it was all clear enough. Nothing that she would ever do in the world would seem important to them, and nothing they would ever do would seem important to her.

Thea lay thinking intently all through the stifling afternoon. Tillie whispered something outside her door once, but she did not answer. She lay on her bed until the second church bell rang, and she saw the family go trooping up the sidewalk on the opposite side of the street, Anna and her father in the lead. Anna seemed to have taken on a very story-book attitude toward her father; patronizing and condescending, it seemed to Thea. The older boys were not in the family band. They now took their girls to church. Tillie had stayed at home to get supper. Thea got up, washed her hot face and arms, and put on the white organdie dress she had worn last night; it was getting too small for her, and she might as well wear it out. After she was dressed she unlocked her door and went cautiously downstairs. She felt as if chilling hostilities might be awaiting her in the trunk loft, on the stairway, almost anywhere. In the dining-room she found Tillie, sitting by the open window, reading the dramatic news in a Denver Sunday paper. Tillie kept a scrapbook in which she pasted clippings about actors and actresses.

"Come look at this picture of Pauline Hall in tights, Thea," she called. "Ain't she cute? It's too bad you didn't go to the theater more when you was in Chicago; such a good chance! Didn't you even get to see Clara Morris or Modjeska?"

"No; I didn't have time. Besides, it costs money, Tillie," Thea replied wearily, glancing at the paper Tillie held out to her.

Tillie looked up at her niece. "Don't you go and be upset about any of Anna's notions. She's one of these narrow kind. Your father and mother don't pay any attention to what she says. Anna's fussy; she is with me, but I don't mind her."

"Oh, I don't mind her. That's all right, Tillie. I guess I'll take a walk."

Thea knew that Tillie hoped she would stay and talk to her for a while, and she would have liked to please her. But in a house as small as that one, everything was too intimate and mixed up together. The family was the family, an integral thing. One couldn't discuss Anna there. She felt differently toward the house and everything in it, as if the battered old furniture that seemed so kindly, and the old carpets on which she had played, had been nourishing a secret grudge against her and were not to be trusted any more.

She went aimlessly out of the front gate, not knowing what to do with herself. Mexican Town, somehow, was spoiled for her just then, and she felt that she would hide if she saw Silvo or Felipe coming toward her. She walked down through the empty main street. All the stores were closed, their blinds down. On the steps of the bank some idle boys were sitting, telling disgusting stories because there was nothing else to do. Several of them had gone to school with Thea, but when she nodded to them they hung their heads and did not speak. Thea's body was often curiously expressive of what was going on in her mind, and to-night there was something in her walk and carriage that made these boys feel that she was "stuck up." If she had stopped and talked to them, they would have thawed out on the instant and would have been friendly and grateful. But Thea was hurt afresh, and walked on, holding her chin higher than ever. As she passed the Duke Block, she saw a light in Dr. Archie's office, and she went up the stairs and opened the door into his study. She found him with a pile of papers and accountbooks before him. He pointed her to her old chair at the end of his desk and leaned back in his own, looking at her with satisfaction. How handsome she was growing!

"I'm still chasing the elusive metal, Thea,"--he pointed to the papers before him,--"I'm up to my neck in mines, and I'm going to be a rich man some day."

"I hope you will; awfully rich. That's the only thing that counts." She looked restlessly about the consultingroom. "To do any of the things one wants to do, one has to have lots and lots of money."

Dr. Archie was direct. "What's the matter? Do you need some?"

Thea shrugged. "Oh, I can get along, in a little way." She looked intently out of the window at the arc streetlamp that was just beginning to sputter. "But it's silly to live at all for little things," she added quietly. "Living's too much trouble unless one can get something big out of it."

Dr. Archie rested his elbows on the arms of his chair, dropped his chin on his clasped hands and looked at her. "Living is no trouble for little people, believe me!" he exclaimed. "What do you want to get out of it?"

"Oh--so many things!" Thea shivered.

"But what? Money? You mentioned that. Well, you can make money, if you care about that more than anything else." He nodded prophetically above his interlacing fingers.

"But I don't. That's only one thing. Anyhow, I couldn't if I did." She pulled her dress lower at the neck as if she were suffocating. "I only want impossible things," she said roughly. "The others don't interest me."

Dr. Archie watched her contemplatively, as if she were a beaker full of chemicals working. A few years ago, when she used to sit there, the light from under his green lampshade used to fall full upon her broad face and yellow pigtails. Now her face was in the shadow and the line of light fell below her bare throat, directly across her bosom. The shrunken white organdie rose and fell as if she were struggling to be free and to break out of it altogether. He felt that her heart must be laboring heavily in there, but he was afraid to touch her; he was, indeed. He had never seen her like this before. Her hair, piled high on her head, gave her a commanding look, and her eyes, that used to be so inquisitive, were stormy.

"Thea," he said slowly, "I won't say that you can have everything you want--that means having nothing, in reality. But if you decide what it is you want most, YOU CAN GET IT." His eye caught hers for a moment. "Not everybody can, but you can. Only, if you want a big thing, you've got to have nerve enough to cut out all that's easy, everything that's to be had cheap." Dr. Archie paused. He picked up a paper-cutter and, feeling the edge of it softly with his fingers, he added slowly, as if to himself:--

"He either fears his fate too much, Or his deserts are small, Who dares not put it to the touch To win...or lose it all."

Thea's lips parted; she looked at him from under a frown, searching his face. "Do you mean to break loose, too, and--do something?" she asked in a low voice.

"I mean to get rich, if you call that doing anything. I've found what I can do without. You make such bargains in your mind, first."

Thea sprang up and took the paper-cutter he had put down, twisting it in her hands. "A long while first, sometimes," she said with a short laugh. "But suppose one can never get out what they've got in them? Suppose they make a mess of it in the end; then what?" She threw the paper-cutter on the desk and took a step toward the doctor, until her dress touched him. She stood looking down at him. "Oh, it's easy to fail!" She was breathing through her mouth and her throat was throbbing with excitement.

As he looked up at her, Dr. Archie's hands tightened on the arms of his chair. He had thought he knew Thea Kronborg pretty well, but he did not know the girl who was standing there. She was beautiful, as his little Swede had never been, but she frightened him. Her pale cheeks, her parted lips, her flashing eyes, seemed suddenly to mean one thing--he did not know what. A light seemed to break upon her from far away--or perhaps from far within. She seemed to grow taller, like a scarf drawn out long; looked as if she were pursued and fleeing, and--yes, she looked tormented. "It's easy to fail," he heard her say again, "and if I fail, you'd better forget about me, for I'll be one of the worst women that ever lived. I'll be an awful woman!"

In the shadowy light above the lampshade he caught her glance again and held it for a moment. Wild as her eyes were, that yellow gleam at the back of them was as hard as a diamond drill-point. He rose with a nervous laugh and dropped his hand lightly on her shoulder. "No, you won't. You'll be a splendid one!"

She shook him off before he could say anything more, and went out of his door with a kind of bound. She left so quickly and so lightly that he could not even hear her footstep in the hallway outside. Archie dropped back into his chair and sat motionless for a long while.

So it went; one loved a quaint little girl, cheerful, industrious, always on the run and hustling through her tasks; and suddenly one lost her. He had thought he knew that child like the glove on his hand. But about this tall girl who threw up her head and glittered like that all over, he knew nothing. She was goaded by desires, ambitions, revulsions that were dark to him. One thing he knew: the old highroad of life, worn safe and easy, hugging the sunny slopes, would scarcely hold her again.

After that night Thea could have asked pretty much anything of him. He could have refused her nothing. Years ago a crafty little bunch of hair and smiles had shown him what she wanted, and he had promptly married her. To-night a very different sort of girl--driven wild by doubts and youth, by poverty and riches--had let him see the fierceness of her nature. She went out still distraught, not knowing or caring what she had shown him. But to Archie knowledge of that sort was obligation. Oh, he was the same old Howard Archie!

That Sunday in July was the turning-point; Thea's peace of mind did not come back. She found it hard even to practice at home. There was something in the air there that froze her throat. In the morning, she walked as far as she could walk. In the hot afternoons she lay on her bed in her nightgown, planning fiercely. She haunted the post-office. She must have worn a path in the sidewalk that led to the post-office, that summer. She was there the moment the mail-sacks came up from the depot, morning and evening, and while the letters were being sorted and distributed she paced up and down outside, under the cottonwood trees, listening to the thump, thump, thump of Mr. Thompson's stamp. She hung upon any sort of word from Chicago; a card from Bowers, a letter from Mrs. Harsanyi, from Mr. Larsen, from her landlady,--anything to reassure her that Chicago was still there. She began to feel the same restlessness that had tortured her the last spring when she was teaching in Moonstone. Suppose she never got away again, after all? Suppose one broke a leg and had to lie in bed at home for weeks, or had pneumonia and died there. The desert was so big and thirsty; if one's foot slipped, it could drink one up like a drop of water.

This time, when Thea left Moonstone to go back to Chicago, she went alone. As the train pulled out, she looked back at her mother and father and Thor. They were calm and cheerful; they did not know, they did not understand. Something pulled in her--and broke. She cried all the way to Denver, and that night, in her berth, she kept sobbing and waking herself. But when the sun rose in the morning, she was far away. It was all behind her, and she knew that she would never cry like that again. People live through such pain only once; pain comes again, but it finds a tougher surface. Thea remembered how she had gone away the first time, with what confidence in everything, and what pitiful ignorance. Such a silly! She felt resentful toward that stupid, good-natured child. How much older she was now, and how much harder! She was going away to fight, and she was going away forever.

PART III. STUPID FACES

I

So many grinning, stupid faces! Thea was sitting by the window in Bowers's studio, waiting for him to come back from lunch. On her knee was the latest number of an illustrated musical journal in which musicians great and little stridently advertised their wares. Every afternoon she played accompaniments for people who looked and smiled like these. She was getting tired of the human countenance.

Thea had been in Chicago for two months. She had a small church position which partly paid her living expenses, and she paid for her singing lessons by playing Bowers's accompaniments every afternoon from two until six. She had been compelled to leave her old friends Mrs. Lorch and Mrs. Andersen, because the long ride from North Chicago to Bowers's studio on Michigan Avenue took too much time--an hour in the morning, and at night, when the cars were crowded, an hour and a half. For the first month she had clung to her old room, but the bad air in the cars, at the end of a long day's work, fatigued her greatly and was bad for her voice. Since she left Mrs. Lorch, she had been staying at a students' club to which she was introduced by Miss Adler, Bowers's morning accompanist, an intelligent Jewish girl from Evanston.

Thea took her lesson from Bowers every day from eleven-thirty until twelve. Then she went out to lunch with an Italian grammar under her arm, and came back to the studio to begin her work at two. In the afternoon Bowers coached professionals and taught his advanced pupils. It was his theory that Thea ought to be able to learn a great deal by keeping her ears open while she played for him.

The concert-going public of Chicago still remembers the long, sallow, discontented face of Madison Bowers. He seldom missed an evening concert, and was usually to be seen lounging somewhere at the back of the concert hall, reading a newspaper or review, and conspicuously ignoring the efforts of the performers. At the end of a number he looked up from his paper long enough to sweep the applauding audience with a contemptuous eye. His face was intelligent, with a narrow lower jaw, a thin nose, faded gray eyes, and a close-cut brown mustache. His hair was iron-gray, thin and dead-looking. He went to concerts chiefly to satisfy himself as to how badly things were done and how gullible the public was. He hated the whole race of artists; the work they did, the wages they got, and the way they spent their money. His father, old Hiram Bowers, was still alive and at work, a genial old choirmaster in Boston, full of enthusiasm at seventy. But Madison was of the colder stuff of his grandfathers, a long line of New Hampshire farmers; hard workers, close traders, with good minds, mean natures, and flinty eyes. As a boy Madison had a fine barytone voice, and his father made great sacrifices for him, sending him to Germany at an early age and keeping him abroad at his studies for years. Madison worked under the best teachers, and afterward sang in England in oratorio. His cold nature and academic methods were against him. His audiences were always aware of the contempt he felt for them. A dozen poorer singers succeeded, but Bowers did not.

Bowers had all the qualities which go to make a good teacher--except generosity and warmth. His intelligence was of a high order, his taste never at fault. He seldom worked with a voice without improving it, and in teaching the delivery of oratorio he was without a rival. Singers came from far and near to study Bach and Handel with him. Even the fashionable sopranos and contraltos of Chicago, St. Paul, and St. Louis (they were usually ladies with very rich husbands, and Bowers called them the "pampered jades of Asia") humbly endured his sardonic humor for the sake of what he could do for them. He was not at all above helping a very lame singer across, if her husband's check-book warranted it. He had a whole bag of tricks for stupid people, "life-preservers," he called them. "Cheap repairs for a cheap 'un," he used to say, but the husbands never found the repairs very cheap. Those were the days when lumbermen's daughters and brewers' wives contended in song; studied in Germany and then floated from SANGERFEST to SANGERFEST. Choral societies flourished in all the rich lake cities and river cities. The soloists came to Chicago to coach with Bowers, and he often took long journeys to hear and instruct a chorus. He was intensely avaricious, and from these semi-professionals he reaped a golden harvest. They fed his pockets and they fed his ever-hungry contempt, his scorn of himself and his accomplices. The more money he made, the more parsimonious he became. His wife was so shabby that she never went anywhere with him, which suited him exactly. Because his clients were luxurious and extravagant, he took a revengeful pleasure in having his shoes halfsoled a second time, and in getting the last wear out of a broken collar. He had first been interested in Thea Kronborg because of her bluntness, her country roughness, and her manifest carefulness about money. The mention of Harsanyi's name always made him pull a wry face. For the first time Thea had a friend who, in his own cool and guarded way, liked her for whatever was least admirable in her.

Thea was still looking at the musical paper, her grammar unopened on the window-sill, when Bowers sauntered in a little before two o'clock. He was smoking a cheap cigarette and wore the same soft felt hat he had worn all last winter. He never carried a cane or wore gloves.

Thea followed him from the reception-room into the studio. "I may cut my lesson out to-morrow, Mr. Bowers. I have to hunt a new boarding-place."

Bowers looked up languidly from his desk where he had begun to go over a pile of letters. "What's the matter with the Studio Club? Been fighting with them again?"

"The Club's all right for people who like to live that way. I don't."

Bowers lifted his eyebrows. "Why so tempery?" he asked as he drew a check from an envelope postmarked "Minneapolis."

"I can't work with a lot of girls around. They're too familiar. I never could get along with girls of my own age. It's all too chummy. Gets on my nerves. I didn't come here to play kindergarten games." Thea began energetically to arrange the scattered music on the piano.

Bowers grimaced good-humoredly at her over the three checks he was pinning together. He liked to play at a rough game of banter with her. He flattered himself that he had made her harsher than she was when she first came to him; that he had got off a little of the sugar-coating Harsanyi always put on his pupils.

"The art of making yourself agreeable never comes amiss, Miss Kronborg. I should say you rather need a little practice along that line. When you come to marketing your wares in the world, a little smoothness goes farther than a great deal of talent sometimes. If you happen to be cursed with a real talent, then you've got to be very smooth indeed, or you'll never get your money back." Bowers snapped the elastic band around his bank-book.

Thea gave him a sharp, recognizing glance. "Well, that's the money I'll have to go without," she replied.

"Just what do you mean?"

"I mean the money people have to grin for. I used to know a railroad man who said there was money in every profession that you couldn't take. He'd tried a good many jobs," Thea added musingly; "perhaps he was too particular about the kind he could take, for he never picked up much. He was proud, but I liked him for that."

Bowers rose and closed his desk. "Mrs. Priest is late again. By the way, Miss Kronborg, remember not to frown when you are playing for Mrs. Priest. You did not remember yesterday."

"You mean when she hits a tone with her breath like that? Why do you let her? You wouldn't let me."

"I certainly would not. But that is a mannerism of Mrs. Priest's. The public like it, and they pay a great deal of money for the pleasure of hearing her do it. There she is. Remember!"

Bowers opened the door of the reception-room and a tall, imposing woman rustled in, bringing with her a glow of animation which pervaded the room as if half a dozen persons, all talking gayly, had come in instead of one. She was large, handsome, expansive, uncontrolled; one felt this the moment she crossed the threshold. She shone with care and cleanliness, mature vigor, unchallenged authority, gracious good-humor, and absolute confidence in her person, her powers, her position, and her way of life; a glowing, overwhelming self-satisfaction, only to be found where human society is young and strong and without yesterdays. Her face had a kind of heavy, thoughtless beauty, like a pink peony just at the point of beginning to fade. Her brown hair was waved in front and done up behind in a great twist, held by a tortoiseshell comb with gold filigree. She wore a beautiful little green hat with three long green feathers sticking straight up in front, a little cape made of velvet and fur with a yellow satin rose on it. Her gloves, her shoes, her veil, somehow made themselves felt. She gave the impression of wearing a cargo of splendid merchandise.

Mrs. Priest nodded graciously to Thea, coquettishly to Bowers, and asked him to untie her veil for her. She threw her splendid wrap on a chair, the yellow lining out. Thea was already at the piano. Mrs. Priest stood behind her.

"'Rejoice Greatly' first, please. And please don't hurry it in there," she put her arm over Thea's shoulder, and indicated the passage by a sweep of her white glove. She threw out her chest, clasped her hands over her abdomen, lifted her chin, worked the muscles of her cheeks back and forth for a moment, and then began with conviction, "Re-jo-oice! Re-jo-oice!"

Bowers paced the room with his catlike tread. When he checked Mrs. Priest's vehemence at all, he handled her roughly; poked and hammered her massive person with cold satisfaction, almost as if he were taking out a grudge on this splendid creation. Such treatment the imposing lady did not at all resent. She tried harder and harder, her eyes growing all the while more lustrous and her lips redder. Thea played on as she was told, ignoring the singer's struggles.

When she first heard Mrs. Priest sing in church, Thea admired her. Since she had found out how dull the goodnatured soprano really was, she felt a deep contempt for her. She felt that Mrs. Priest ought to be reproved and even punished for her shortcomings; that she ought to be exposed,--at least to herself,--and not be permitted to live and shine in happy ignorance of what a poor thing it was she brought across so radiantly. Thea's cold looks of reproof were lost upon Mrs. Priest; although the lady did murmur one day when she took Bowers home in her carriage, "How handsome your afternoon girl would be if she did not have that unfortunate squint; it gives her that vacant Swede look, like an animal." That amused Bowers. He liked to watch the germination and growth of antipathies.

One of the first disappointments Thea had to face when she returned to Chicago that fall, was the news that the Harsanyis were not coming back. They had spent the summer in a camp in the Adirondacks and were moving to New York. An old teacher and friend of Harsanyi's, one of the best-known piano teachers in New York, was about to retire because of failing health and had arranged to turn his pupils over to Harsanyi. Andor was to give two recitals in New York in November, to devote himself to his new students until spring, and then to go on a short concert tour. The Harsanyis had taken a furnished apartment in New York, as they would not attempt to settle a place of their own until Andor's recitals were over. The first of December, however, Thea received a note from Mrs. Harsanyi, asking her to call at the old studio, where she was packing their goods for shipment.

The morning after this invitation reached her, Thea climbed the stairs and knocked at the familiar door. Mrs. Harsanyi herself opened it, and embraced her visitor warmly. Taking Thea into the studio, which was littered with excelsior and packing-cases, she stood holding her hand and looking at her in the strong light from the big window before she allowed her to sit down. Her quick eye saw many changes. The girl was taller, her figure had become definite, her carriage positive. She had got used to living in the body of a young woman, and she no longer tried to ignore it and behave as if she were a little girl. With that increased independence of body there had come a change in her face; an indifference, something hard and skeptical. Her clothes, too, were different, like the attire of a shopgirl who tries to follow the fashions; a purple suit, a piece of cheap fur, a three-cornered purple hat with a pompon sticking up in front. The queer country clothes she used to wear suited her much better, Mrs. Harsanyi thought. But such trifles, after all, were accidental and remediable. She put her hand on the girl's strong shoulder.

"How much the summer has done for you! Yes, you are a young lady at last. Andor will be so glad to hear about you."

Thea looked about at the disorder of the familiar room. The pictures were piled in a corner, the piano and the CHAISE LONGUE were gone. "I suppose I ought to be glad you have gone away," she said, "but I'm not. It's a fine thing for Mr. Harsanyi, I suppose."

Mrs. Harsanyi gave her a quick glance that said more than words. "If you knew how long I have wanted to get him away from here, Miss Kronborg! He is never tired, never discouraged, now."

Thea sighed. "I'm glad for that, then." Her eyes traveled over the faint discolorations on the walls where the pictures had hung. "I may run away myself. I don't know whether I can stand it here without you."

"We hope that you can come to New York to study before very long. We have thought of that. And you must tell me how you are getting on with Bowers. Andor will want to know all about it."

"I guess I get on more or less. But I don't like my work very well. It never seems serious as my work with Mr. Harsanyi did. I play Bowers's accompaniments in the afternoons, you know. I thought I would learn a good deal from the people who work with him, but I don't think I get much."

Mrs. Harsanyi looked at her inquiringly. Thea took out a carefully folded handkerchief from the bosom of her dress and began to draw the corners apart. "Singing doesn't seem to be a very brainy profession, Mrs. Harsanyi," she said slowly. "The people I see now are not a bit like the ones I used to meet here. Mr. Harsanyi's pupils, even the dumb ones, had more--well, more of everything, it seems to me. The people I have to play accompaniments for are discouraging. The professionals, like Katharine Priest and Miles Murdstone, are worst of all. If I have to play `The Messiah' much longer for Mrs. Priest, I'll go out of my mind!" Thea brought her foot down sharply on the bare floor.

Mrs. Harsanyi looked down at the foot in perplexity. "You mustn't wear such high heels, my dear. They will spoil your walk and make you mince along. Can't you at least learn to avoid what you dislike in these singers? I was never able to care for Mrs. Priest's singing."

Thea was sitting with her chin lowered. Without moving her head she looked up at Mrs. Harsanyi and smiled; a smile much too cold and desperate to be seen on a young face, Mrs. Harsanyi felt. "Mrs. Harsanyi, it seems to me that what I learn is just TO DISLIKE. I dislike so much and so hard that it tires me out. I've got no heart for anything." She threw up her head suddenly and sat in defiance, her hand clenched on the arm of the chair. "Mr. Harsanyi couldn't stand these people an hour, I know he couldn't. He'd put them right out of the window there, frizzes and feathers and all. Now, take that new soprano they're all making such a fuss about, Jessie Darcey. She's going on tour with a symphony orchestra and she's working up her repertory with Bowers. She's singing some Schumann songs Mr. Harsanyi used to go over with me. Well, I don't know what he WOULD do if he heard her."

"But if your own work goes well, and you know these people are wrong, why do you let them discourage you?"

Thea shook her head. "That's just what I don't understand myself. Only, after I've heard them all afternoon, I come out frozen up. Somehow it takes the shine off of everything. People want Jessie Darcey and the kind of thing she does; so what's the use?"

Mrs. Harsanyi smiled. "That stile you must simply vault over. You must not begin to fret about the successes of cheap people. After all, what have they to do with you?"

"Well, if I had somebody like Mr. Harsanyi, perhaps I wouldn't fret about them. He was the teacher for me. Please tell him so."

Thea rose and Mrs. Harsanyi took her hand again. "I am sorry you have to go through this time of discouragement. I wish Andor could talk to you, he would understand it so well. But I feel like urging you to keep clear of Mrs. Priest and Jessie Darcey and all their works."

Thea laughed discordantly. "No use urging me. I don't get on with them AT ALL. My spine gets like a steel rail when they come near me. I liked them at first, you know. Their clothes and their manners were so fine, and Mrs. Priest IS handsome. But now I keep wanting to tell them how stupid they are. Seems like they ought to be informed, don't you think so?" There was a flash of the shrewd grin that Mrs. Harsanyi remembered. Thea pressed her hand. "I must go now. I had to give my lesson hour this morning to a Duluth woman who has come on to coach, and I must go and play `On Mighty Pens' for her. Please tell Mr. Harsanyi that I think oratorio is a great chance for bluffers."

Mrs. Harsanyi detained her. "But he will want to know much more than that about you. You are free at seven? Come back this evening, then, and we will go to dinner somewhere, to some cheerful place. I think you need a party."

Thea brightened. "Oh, I do! I'll love to come; that will be like old times. You see," she lingered a moment, softening, "I wouldn't mind if there were only ONE of them I could really admire."

"How about Bowers?" Mrs. Harsanyi asked as they were approaching the stairway.

"Well, there's nothing he loves like a good fakir, and nothing he hates like a good artist. I always remember something Mr. Harsanyi said about him. He said Bowers was the cold muffin that had been left on the plate."

Mrs. Harsanyi stopped short at the head of the stairs and said decidedly: "I think Andor made a mistake. I can't believe that is the right atmosphere for you. It would hurt you more than most people. It's all wrong."

"Something's wrong," Thea called back as she clattered down the stairs in her high heels.

II

DURING that winter Thea lived in so many places that sometimes at night when she left Bowers's studio and emerged into the street she had to stop and think for a moment to remember where she was living now and what was the best way to get there.

When she moved into a new place her eyes challenged the beds, the carpets, the food, the mistress of the house. The boarding-houses were wretchedly conducted and Thea's complaints sometimes took an insulting form. She quarreled with one landlady after another and moved on. When she moved into a new room, she was almost sure to hate it on sight and to begin planning to hunt another place before she unpacked her trunk. She was moody and contemptuous toward her fellow boarders, except toward the young men, whom she treated with a careless familiarity which they usually misunderstood. They liked her, however, and when she left the house after a storm, they helped her to move her things and came to see her after she got settled in a new place. But she moved so often that they soon ceased to follow her. They could see no reason for keeping up with a girl who, under her jocularity, was cold, self-centered, and unimpressionable. They soon felt that she did not admire them.

Thea used to waken up in the night and wonder why she was so unhappy. She would have been amazed if she had known how much the people whom she met in Bowers's studio had to do with her low spirits. She had never been conscious of those instinctive standards which are called ideals, and she did not know that she was suffering for them. She often found herself sneering when she was on a street-car, or when she was brushing out her hair before her mirror, as some inane remark or too familiar mannerism flitted across her mind.

She felt no creature kindness, no tolerant good-will for Mrs. Priest or Jessie Darcey. After one of Jessie Darcey's concerts the glowing press notices, and the admiring comments that floated about Bowers's studio, caused Thea bitter unhappiness. It was not the torment of personal jealousy. She had never thought of herself as even a possible rival of Miss Darcey. She was a poor music student, and Jessie Darcey was a popular and petted professional. Mrs. Priest, whatever one held against her, had a fine, big, showy voice and an impressive presence. She read indifferently, was inaccurate, and was always putting other people wrong, but she at least had the material out of which singers can be made. But people seemed to like Jessie Darcey exactly because she could not sing; because, as they put it, she was "so natural and unprofessional." Her singing was pronounced "artless," her voice "birdlike." Miss Darcey was thin and awkward in person, with a sharp, sallow face. Thea noticed that her plainness was accounted to her credit, and that people spoke of it affectionately. Miss Darcey was singing everywhere just then; one could not help hearing about her. She was backed by some of the packing-house people and by the Chicago Northwestern Railroad. Only one critic raised his voice against her. Thea went to several of Jessie Darcey's concerts. It was the first time she had had an opportunity to observe the whims of the public which singers live by interesting. She saw that people liked in Miss Darcey every quality a singer ought not to have, and especially the nervous complacency that stamped her as a commonplace young woman. They seemed to have a warmer feeling for Jessie than for Mrs. Priest, an affectionate and cherishing regard. Chicago was not so very different from Moonstone, after all, and Jessie Darcey was only Lily Fisher under another name.

Thea particularly hated to accompany for Miss Darcey because she sang off pitch and didn't mind it in the least. It was excruciating to sit there day after day and hear her; there was something shameless and indecent about not singing true.

One morning Miss Darcey came by appointment to go over the programme for her Peoria concert. She was such a frail-looking girl that Thea ought to have felt sorry for her. True, she had an arch, sprightly little manner, and a flash of salmon-pink on either brown cheek. But a narrow upper jaw gave her face a pinched look, and her eyelids were heavy and relaxed. By the morning light, the purplish brown circles under her eyes were pathetic enough, and foretold no long or brilliant future. A singer with a poor digestion and low vitality; she needed no seer to cast her horoscope. If Thea had ever taken the pains to study her, she would have seen that, under all her smiles and archness, poor Miss Darcey was really frightened to death. She could not understand her success any more than Thea could; she kept catching her breath and lifting her eyebrows and trying to believe that it was true. Her loquacity was not natural, she forced herself to it, and when she confided to you how many defects she could overcome by her unusual command of head resonance, she was not so much trying to persuade you as to persuade herself.

When she took a note that was high for her, Miss Darcey always put her right hand out into the air, as if she were indicating height, or giving an exact measurement. Some early teacher had told her that she could "place" a tone more surely by the help of such a gesture, and she firmly believed that it was of great assistance to her. (Even when she was singing in public, she kept her right hand down with difficulty, nervously clasping her white kid fingers together when she took a high note. Thea could always see her elbows stiffen.) She unvaryingly executed this gesture with a smile of gracious confidence, as if she were actually putting her finger on the tone: "There it is, friends!"

This morning, in Gounod's "Ave Maria," as Miss Darcey approached her B natural:--

DANS--NOS--A--LAR--MES!

Out went the hand, with the sure airy gesture, though it was little above A she got with her voice, whatever she touched with her finger. Often Bowers let such things pass--with the right people--but this morning he snapped his jaws together and muttered, "God!" Miss Darcey tried again, with the same gesture as of putting the crowning touch, tilting her head and smiling radiantly at Bowers, as if to say, "It is for you I do all this!"

DANS--NOS A--LAR------MES!

This time she made B flat, and went on in the happy belief that she had done well enough, when she suddenly found that her accompanist was not going on with her, and this put her out completely.

She turned to Thea, whose hands had fallen in her lap. "Oh why did you stop just there! It IS too trying! Now we'd better go back to that other CRESCENDO and try it from there."

"I beg your pardon," Thea muttered. "I thought you wanted to get that B natural." She began again, as Miss Darcey indicated.

After the singer was gone, Bowers walked up to Thea and asked languidly, "Why do you hate Jessie so? Her little variations from pitch are between her and her public; they don't hurt you. Has she ever done anything to you except be very agreeable?"

"Yes, she has done things to me," Thea retorted hotly.

Bowers looked interested. "What, for example?"

"I can't explain, but I've got it in for her."

Bowers laughed. "No doubt about that. I'll have to suggest that you conceal it a little more effectually. That is-- necessary, Miss Kronborg," he added, looking back over the shoulder of the overcoat he was putting on.

He went out to lunch and Thea thought the subject closed. But late in the afternoon, when he was taking his dyspepsia tablet and a glass of water between lessons, he looked up and said in a voice ironically coaxing:--

"Miss Kronborg, I wish you would tell me why you hate Jessie."

Taken by surprise Thea put down the score she was reading and answered before she knew what she was saying, "I hate her for the sake of what I used to think a singer might be."

Bowers balanced the tablet on the end of his long forefinger and whistled softly. "And how did you form your conception of what a singer ought to be?" he asked.

"I don't know." Thea flushed and spoke under her breath; "but I suppose I got most of it from Harsanyi."

Bowers made no comment upon this reply, but opened the door for the next pupil, who was waiting in the reception-room.

It was dark when Thea left the studio that night. She knew she had offended Bowers. Somehow she had hurt herself, too. She felt unequal to the boarding-house table, the sneaking divinity student who sat next her and had tried to kiss her on the stairs last night. She went over to the waterside of Michigan Avenue and walked along beside the lake. It was a clear, frosty winter night. The great empty space over the water was restful and spoke of freedom. If she had any money at all, she would go away. The stars glittered over the wide black water. She looked up at them wearily and shook her head. She believed that what she felt was despair, but it was only one of the forms of hope. She felt, indeed, as if she were bidding the stars good-bye; but she was renewing a promise. Though their challenge is universal and eternal, the stars get no answer but that,--the brief light flashed back to them from the eyes of the young who unaccountably aspire.

The rich, noisy, city, fat with food and drink, is a spent thing; its chief concern is its digestion and its little game of hide-and-seek with the undertaker. Money and office and success are the consolations of impotence. Fortune turns kind to such solid people and lets them suck their bone in peace. She flecks her whip upon flesh that is more alive, upon that stream of hungry boys and girls who tramp the streets of every city, recognizable by their pride and discontent, who are the Future, and who possess the treasure of creative power.

III

WHILE her living arrangements were so casual and fortuitous, Bowers's studio was the one fixed thing in Thea's life. She went out from it to uncertainties, and hastened to it from nebulous confusion. She was more influenced by

Bowers than she knew. Unconsciously she began to take on something of his dry contempt, and to share his grudge without understanding exactly what it was about. His cynicism seemed to her honest, and the amiability of his pupils artificial. She admired his drastic treatment of his dull pupils. The stupid deserved all they got, and more. Bowers knew that she thought him a very clever man.

One afternoon when Bowers came in from lunch Thea handed him a card on which he read the name, "Mr. Philip Frederick Ottenburg."

"He said he would be in again to-morrow and that he wanted some time. Who is he? I like him better than the others."

Bowers nodded. "So do I. He's not a singer. He's a beer prince: son of the big brewer in St. Louis. He's been in Germany with his mother. I didn't know he was back."

"Does he take lessons?"

"Now and again. He sings rather well. He's at the head of the Chicago branch of the Ottenburg business, but he can't stick to work and is always running away. He has great ideas in beer, people tell me. He's what they call an imaginative business man; goes over to Bayreuth and seems to do nothing but give parties and spend money, and brings back more good notions for the brewery than the fellows who sit tight dig out in five years. I was born too long ago to be much taken in by these chesty boys with flowered vests, but I like Fred, all the same."

"So do I," said Thea positively.

Bowers made a sound between a cough and a laugh. "Oh, he's a lady-killer, all right! The girls in here are always making eyes at him. You won't be the first." He threw some sheets of music on the piano. "Better look that over; accompaniment's a little tricky. It's for that new woman from Detroit. And Mrs. Priest will be in this afternoon."

Thea sighed. "`I Know that my Redeemer Liveth'?"

"The same. She starts on her concert tour next week, and we'll have a rest. Until then, I suppose we'll have to be going over her programme."

The next day Thea hurried through her luncheon at a German bakery and got back to the studio at ten minutes past one. She felt sure that the young brewer would come early, before it was time for Bowers to arrive. He had not said he would, but yesterday, when he opened the door to go, he had glanced about the room and at her, and something in his eye had conveyed that suggestion.

Sure enough, at twenty minutes past one the door of the reception-room opened, and a tall, robust young man with a cane and an English hat and ulster looked in expectantly. "Ah--ha!" he exclaimed, "I thought if I came early I might have good luck. And how are you to-day, Miss Kronborg?"

Thea was sitting in the window chair. At her left elbow there was a table, and upon this table the young man sat down, holding his hat and cane in his hand, loosening his long coat so that it fell back from his shoulders. He was a gleaming, florid young fellow. His hair, thick and yellow, was cut very short, and he wore a closely trimmed beard, long enough on the chin to curl a little. Even his eyebrows were thick and yellow, like fleece. He had lively blue eyes--Thea looked up at them with great interest as he sat chatting and swinging his foot rhythmically. He was easily familiar, and frankly so. Wherever people met young Ottenburg, in his office, on shipboard, in a foreign hotel or railway compartment, they always felt (and usually liked) that artless presumption which seemed to say, "In this case we may waive formalities. We really haven't time. This is to-day, but it will soon be to-morrow, and then we may be very different people, and in some other country." He had a way of floating people out of dull or awkward situations, out of their own torpor or constraint or discouragement. It was a marked personal talent, of almost incalculable value in the representative of a great business founded on social amenities. Thea had liked him yesterday for the way in which he had picked her up out of herself and her German grammar for a few exciting moments.

"By the way, will you tell me your first name, please? Thea? Oh, then you ARE a Swede, sure enough! I thought so. Let me call you Miss Thea, after the German fashion. You won't mind? Of course not!" He usually made his assumption of a special understanding seem a tribute to the other person and not to himself.

"How long have you been with Bowers here? Do you like the old grouch? So do I. I've come to tell him about a new soprano I heard at Bayreuth. He'll pretend not to care, but he does. Do you warble with him? Have you anything of a voice? Honest? You look it, you know. What are you going in for, something big? Opera?"

Thea blushed crimson. "Oh, I'm not going in for anything. I'm trying to learn to sing at funerals."

Ottenburg leaned forward. His eyes twinkled. "I'll engage you to sing at mine. You can't fool me, Miss Thea. May I hear you take your lesson this afternoon?"

"No, you may not. I took it this morning."

He picked up a roll of music that lay behind him on the table. "Is this yours? Let me see what you are doing."

He snapped back the clasp and began turning over the songs. "All very fine, but tame. What's he got you at this Mozart stuff for? I shouldn't think it would suit your voice. Oh, I can make a pretty good guess at what will suit you! This from `Gioconda' is more in your line. What's this Grieg? It looks interesting. TAK FOR DITT ROD. What does that mean?"

"`Thanks for your Advice.' Don't you know it?"

"No; not at all. Let's try it." He rose, pushed open the door into the music-room, and motioned Thea to enter before him. She hung back.

"I couldn't give you much of an idea of it. It's a big song."

Ottenburg took her gently by the elbow and pushed her into the other room. He sat down carelessly at the piano and looked over the music for a moment. "I think I can get you through it. But how stupid not to have the German words. Can you really sing the Norwegian? What an infernal language to sing. Translate the text for me." He handed her the music.

Thea looked at it, then at him, and shook her head. "I can't. The truth is I don't know either English or Swedish very well, and Norwegian's still worse," she said confidentially. She not infrequently refused to do what she was asked to do, but it was not like her to explain her refusal, even when she had a good reason.

"I understand. We immigrants never speak any language well. But you know what it means, don't you?"

"Of course I do!"

"Then don't frown at me like that, but tell me."

Thea continued to frown, but she also smiled. She was confused, but not embarrassed. She was not afraid of Ottenburg. He was not one of those people who made her spine like a steel rail. On the contrary, he made one venturesome.

"Well, it goes something like this: Thanks for your advice! But I prefer to steer my boat into the din of roaring breakers. Even if the journey is my last, I may find what I have never found before. Onward must I go, for I yearn for the wild sea. I long to fight my way through the angry waves, and to see how far, and how long I can make them carry me."

Ottenburg took the music and began: "Wait a moment. Is that too fast? How do you take it? That right?" He pulled up his cuffs and began the accompaniment again. He had become entirely serious, and he played with fine enthusiasm and with understanding.

Fred's talent was worth almost as much to old Otto Ottenburg as the steady industry of his older sons. When Fred sang the Prize Song at an interstate meet of the TURNVEREIN, ten thousand TURNERS went forth pledged to Ottenburg beer.

As Thea finished the song Fred turned back to the first page, without looking up from the music. "Now, once more," he called. They began again, and did not hear Bowers when he came in and stood in the doorway. He stood still, blinking like an owl at their two heads shining in the sun. He could not see their faces, but there was something about his girl's back that he had not noticed before: a very slight and yet very free motion, from the toes up. Her whole back seemed plastic, seemed to be moulding itself to the galloping rhythm of the song. Bowers perceived such things sometimes-- unwillingly. He had known to-day that there was something afoot. The river of sound which had its source in his pupil had caught him two flights down. He had stopped and listened with a kind of sneering admiration. From the door he watched her with a half-incredulous, half-malicious smile.

When he had struck the keys for the last time, Ottenburg dropped his hands on his knees and looked up with a quick breath. "I got you through. What a stunning song! Did I play it right?"

Thea studied his excited face. There was a good deal of meaning in it, and there was a good deal in her own as she answered him. "You suited me," she said ungrudgingly.

After Ottenburg was gone, Thea noticed that Bowers was more agreeable than usual. She had heard the young brewer ask Bowers to dine with him at his club that evening, and she saw that he looked forward to the dinner with pleasure. He dropped a remark to the effect that Fred knew as much about food and wines as any man in Chicago. He said this boastfully.

"If he's such a grand business man, how does he have time to run around listening to singing-lessons?" Thea asked suspiciously.

As she went home to her boarding-house through the February slush, she wished she were going to dine with them. At nine o'clock she looked up from her grammar to wonder what Bowers and Ottenburg were having to eat. At that moment they were talking of her.

IV

THEA noticed that Bowers took rather more pains with her now that Fred Ottenburg often dropped in at eleven-thirty to hear her lesson. After the lesson the young man took Bowers off to lunch with him, and Bowers liked good food when another man paid for it. He encouraged Fred's visits, and Thea soon saw that Fred knew exactly why.

One morning, after her lesson, Ottenburg turned to Bowers. "If you'll lend me Miss Thea, I think I have an engagement for her. Mrs. Henry Nathanmeyer is going to give three musical evenings in April, first three Saturdays, and she has consulted me about soloists. For the first evening she has a young violinist, and she would be charmed to have Miss Kronborg. She will pay fifty dollars. Not much, but Miss Thea would meet some people there who might be useful. What do you say?"

Bowers passed the question on to Thea. "I guess you could use the fifty, couldn't you, Miss Kronborg? You can easily work up some songs."

Thea was perplexed. "I need the money awfully," she said frankly; "but I haven't got the right clothes for that sort of thing. I suppose I'd better try to get some."

Ottenburg spoke up quickly, "Oh, you'd make nothing out of it if you went to buying evening clothes. I've thought of that. Mrs. Nathanmeyer has a troop of daughters, a perfect seraglio, all ages and sizes. She'll be glad to fit you out, if you aren't sensitive about wearing kosher clothes. Let me take you to see her, and you'll find that she'll arrange that easily enough. I told her she must produce something nice, blue or yellow, and properly cut. I brought half a dozen Worth gowns through the customs for her two weeks ago, and she's not ungrateful. When can we go to see her?"

"I haven't any time free, except at night," Thea replied in some confusion.

"To-morrow evening, then? I shall call for you at eight. Bring all your songs along; she will want us to give her a little rehearsal, perhaps. I'll play your accompaniments, if you've no objection. That will save money for you and for Mrs. Nathanmeyer. She needs it." Ottenburg chuckled as he took down the number of Thea's boarding-house.

The Nathanmeyers were so rich and great that even Thea had heard of them, and this seemed a very remarkable opportunity. Ottenburg had brought it about by merely lifting a finger, apparently. He was a beer prince sure enough, as Bowers had said.

The next evening at a quarter to eight Thea was dressed and waiting in the boarding-house parlor. She was nervous and fidgety and found it difficult to sit still on the hard, convex upholstery of the chairs. She tried them one after another, moving about the dimly lighted, musty room, where the gas always leaked gently and sang in the burners. There was no one in the parlor but the medical student, who was playing one of Sousa's marches so vigorously that the china ornaments on the top of the piano rattled. In a few moments some of the pension-office girls would come in and begin to two-step. Thea wished that Ottenburg would come and let her escape. She glanced at herself in the long, somber mirror. She was wearing her pale-blue broadcloth church dress, which was not unbecoming but was certainly too heavy to wear to anybody's house in the evening. Her slippers were run over at the heel and she had not had time to have them mended, and her white gloves were not so clean as they should be. However, she knew that she would forget these annoying things as soon as Ottenburg came.

Mary, the Hungarian chambermaid, came to the door, stood between the plush portieres, beckoned to Thea, and made an inarticulate sound in her throat. Thea jumped up and ran into the hall, where Ottenburg stood smiling, his caped cloak open, his silk hat in his white-kid hand. The Hungarian girl stood like a monument on her flat heels, staring at the pink carnation in Ottenburg's coat. Her broad, pockmarked face wore the only expression of which it was capable, a kind of animal wonder. As the young man followed Thea out, he glanced back over his shoulder through the crack of the door; the Hun clapped her hands over her stomach, opened her mouth, and made another raucous sound in her throat.

"Isn't she awful?" Thea exclaimed. "I think she's half-witted. Can you understand her?"

Ottenburg laughed as he helped her into the carriage. "Oh, yes; I can understand her!" He settled himself on the front seat opposite Thea. "Now, I want to tell you about the people we are going to see. We may have a musical public in this country some day, but as yet there are only the Germans and the Jews. All the other people go to hear Jessie Darcey sing, `O, Promise Me!' The Nathanmeyers are the finest kind of Jews. If you do anything for Mrs. Henry Nathanmeyer, you must put yourself into her hands. Whatever she says about music, about clothes, about life, will be correct. And you may feel at ease with her. She expects nothing of people; she has lived in Chicago twenty years. If you were to behave like the Magyar who was so interested in my buttonhole, she would not be surprised. If you were to sing like Jessie Darcey, she would not be surprised; but she would manage not to hear you again."

"Would she? Well, that's the kind of people I want to find." Thea felt herself growing bolder.

"You will be all right with her so long as you do not try to be anything that you are not. Her standards have nothing to do with Chicago. Her perceptions--or her grandmother's, which is the same thing--were keen when all this was an Indian village. So merely be yourself, and you will like her. She will like you because the Jews always sense talent, and," he added ironically, "they admire certain qualities of feeling that are found only in the whiteskinned races."

Thea looked into the young man's face as the light of a street lamp flashed into the carriage. His somewhat academic manner amused her.

"What makes you take such an interest in singers?" she asked curiously. "You seem to have a perfect passion for hearing music-lessons. I wish I could trade jobs with you!"

"I'm not interested in singers." His tone was offended. "I am interested in talent. There are only two interesting things in the world, anyhow; and talent is one of them."

"What's the other?" The question came meekly from the figure opposite him. Another arc-light flashed in at the window.

Fred saw her face and broke into a laugh. "Why, you're guying me, you little wretch! You won't let me behave properly." He dropped his gloved hand lightly on her knee, took it away and let it hang between his own. "Do you know," he said confidentially, "I believe I'm more in earnest about all this than you are."

"About all what?"

"All you've got in your throat there."

"Oh! I'm in earnest all right; only I never was much good at talking. Jessie Darcey is the smooth talker. `You notice the effect I get there--' If she only got 'em, she'd be a wonder, you know!"

Mr. and Mrs. Nathanmeyer were alone in their great library. Their three unmarried daughters had departed in successive carriages, one to a dinner, one to a Nietzsche club, one to a ball given for the girls employed in the big department stores. When Ottenburg and Thea entered, Henry Nathanmeyer and his wife were sitting at a table at the farther end of the long room, with a reading-lamp and a tray of cigarettes and cordial-glasses between them. The overhead lights were too soft to bring out the colors of the big rugs, and none of the picture lights were on. One could merely see that there were pictures there. Fred whispered that they were Rousseaus and Corots, very fine ones which the old banker had bought long ago for next to nothing. In the hall Ottenburg had stopped Thea before a painting of a woman eating grapes out of a paper bag, and had told her gravely that there was the most beautiful Manet in the world. He made her take off her hat and gloves in the hall, and looked her over a little before he took her in. But once they were in the library he seemed perfectly satisfied with her and led her down the long room to their hostess.

Mrs. Nathanmeyer was a heavy, powerful old Jewess, with a great pompadour of white hair, a swarthy complexion, an eagle nose, and sharp, glittering eyes. She wore a black velvet dress with a long train, and a diamond necklace and earrings. She took Thea to the other side of the table and presented her to Mr. Nathanmeyer, who apologized for not rising, pointing to a slippered foot on a cushion; he said that he suffered from gout. He had a very soft voice and spoke with an accent which would have been heavy if it had not been so caressing. He kept Thea standing beside him for some time. He noticed that she stood easily, looked straight down into his face, and was not embarrassed. Even when Mrs. Nathanmeyer told Ottenburg to bring a chair for Thea, the old man did not release her hand, and she did not sit down. He admired her just as she was, as she happened to be standing, and she felt it. He was much handsomer than his wife, Thea thought. His forehead was high, his hair soft and white, his skin pink, a little puffy under his clear blue eyes. She noticed how warm and delicate his hands were, pleasant to touch and beautiful to look at. Ottenburg had told her that Mr. Nathanmeyer had a very fine collection of medals and cameos, and his fingers looked as if they had never touched anything but delicately cut surfaces.

He asked Thea where Moonstone was; how many inhabitants it had; what her father's business was; from what part of Sweden her grandfather came; and whether she spoke Swedish as a child. He was interested to hear that her mother's mother was still living, and that her grandfather had played the oboe. Thea felt at home standing there beside him; she felt that he was very wise, and that he some way took one's life up and looked it over kindly, as if it were a story. She was sorry when they left him to go into the music-room.

As they reached the door of the music-room, Mrs. Nathanmeyer turned a switch that threw on many lights. The room was even larger than the library, all glittering surfaces, with two Steinway pianos.

Mrs. Nathanmeyer rang for her own maid. "Selma will take you upstairs, Miss Kronborg, and you will find some dresses on the bed. Try several of them, and take the one you like best. Selma will help you. She has a great deal of taste. When you are dressed, come down and let us go over some of your songs with Mr. Ottenburg."

After Thea went away with the maid, Ottenburg came up to Mrs. Nathanmeyer and stood beside her, resting his hand on the high back of her chair.

"Well, GNADIGE FRAU, do you like her?"

"I think so. I liked her when she talked to father. She will always get on better with men."

Ottenburg leaned over her chair. "Prophetess! Do you see what I meant?"

"About her beauty? She has great possibilities, but you can never tell about those Northern women. They look so strong, but they are easily battered. The face falls so early under those wide cheek-bones. A single idea--hate or greed, or even love--can tear them to shreds. She is nineteen? Well, in ten years she may have quite a regal beauty, or she may have a heavy, discontented face, all dug out in channels. That will depend upon the kind of ideas she lives with."

"Or the kind of people?" Ottenburg suggested.

The old Jewess folded her arms over her massive chest, drew back her shoulders, and looked up at the young man. "With that hard glint in her eye? The people won't matter much, I fancy. They will come and go. She is very much interested in herself--as she should be."

Ottenburg frowned. "Wait until you hear her sing. Her eyes are different then. That gleam that comes in them is curious, isn't it? As you say, it's impersonal."

The object of this discussion came in, smiling. She had chosen neither the blue nor the yellow gown, but a pale rose-color, with silver butterflies. Mrs. Nathanmeyer lifted her lorgnette and studied her as she approached. She caught the characteristic things at once: the free, strong walk, the calm carriage of the head, the milky whiteness of the girl's arms and shoulders.

"Yes, that color is good for you," she said approvingly. "The yellow one probably killed your hair? Yes; this does very well indeed, so we need think no more about it."

Thea glanced questioningly at Ottenburg. He smiled and bowed, seemed perfectly satisfied. He asked her to stand in the elbow of the piano, in front of him, instead of behind him as she had been taught to do.

"Yes," said the hostess with feeling. "That other position is barbarous."

Thea sang an aria from `Gioconda,' some songs by Schumann which she had studied with Harsanyi, and the "TAK FOR DIT ROD," which Ottenburg liked.

"That you must do again," he declared when they finished this song. "You did it much better the other day. You accented it more, like a dance or a galop. How did you do it?"

Thea laughed, glancing sidewise at Mrs. Nathanmeyer. "You want it rough-house, do you? Bowers likes me to sing it more seriously, but it always makes me think about a story my grandmother used to tell."

Fred pointed to the chair behind her. "Won't you rest a moment and tell us about it? I thought you had some notion about it when you first sang it for me."

Thea sat down. "In Norway my grandmother knew a girl who was awfully in love with a young fellow. She went into service on a big dairy farm to make enough money for her outfit. They were married at Christmastime, and everybody was glad, because they'd been sighing around about each other for so long. That very summer, the day before St. John's Day, her husband caught her carrying on with another farm-hand. The next night all the farm people had a bonfire and a big dance up on the mountain, and everybody was dancing and singing. I guess they were all a little drunk, for they got to seeing how near they could make the girls dance to the edge of the cliff. Ole--he was the girl's husband--seemed the jolliest and the drunkest of anybody. He danced his wife nearer and nearer the edge of the rock, and his wife began to scream so that the others stopped dancing and the music stopped; but Ole went right on singing, and he danced her over the edge of the cliff and they fell hundreds of feet and were all smashed to pieces."

Ottenburg turned back to the piano. "That's the idea! Now, come Miss Thea. Let it go!"

Thea took her place. She laughed and drew herself up out of her corsets, threw her shoulders high and let them drop again. She had never sung in a low dress before, and she found it comfortable. Ottenburg jerked his head and they began the song. The accompaniment sounded more than ever like the thumping and scraping of heavy feet.

When they stopped, they heard a sympathetic tapping at the end of the room. Old Mr. Nathanmeyer had come to the door and was sitting back in the shadow, just inside the library, applauding with his cane. Thea threw him a bright smile. He continued to sit there, his slippered foot on a low chair, his cane between his fingers, and she glanced at him from time to time. The doorway made a frame for him, and he looked like a man in a picture, with the long, shadowy room behind him.

Mrs. Nathanmeyer summoned the maid again. "Selma will pack that gown in a box for you, and you can take it home in Mr. Ottenburg's carriage."

Thea turned to follow the maid, but hesitated. "Shall I wear gloves?" she asked, turning again to Mrs. Nathanmeyer.

"No, I think not. Your arms are good, and you will feel freer without. You will need light slippers, pink--or white, if you have them, will do quite as well."

Thea went upstairs with the maid and Mrs. Nathanmeyer rose, took Ottenburg's arm, and walked toward her husband. "That's the first real voice I have heard in Chicago," she said decidedly. "I don't count that stupid Priest woman. What do you say, father?"

Mr. Nathanmeyer shook his white head and smiled softly, as if he were thinking about something very agreeable. "SVENSK SOMMAR," he murmured. "She is like a Swedish summer. I spent nearly a year there when I was a young man," he explained to Ottenburg.

When Ottenburg got Thea and her big box into the carriage, it occurred to him that she must be hungry, after singing so much. When he asked her, she admitted that she was very hungry, indeed.

He took out his watch. "Would you mind stopping somewhere with me? It's only eleven."

"Mind? Of course, I wouldn't mind. I wasn't brought up like that. I can take care of myself."

Ottenburg laughed. "And I can take care of myself, so we can do lots of jolly things together." He opened the carriage door and spoke to the driver. "I'm stuck on the way you sing that Grieg song," he declared.

When Thea got into bed that night she told herself that this was the happiest evening she had had in Chicago. She had enjoyed the Nathanmeyers and their grand house, her new dress, and Ottenburg, her first real carriage ride, and the good supper when she was so hungry. And Ottenburg WAS jolly! He made you want to come back at him. You weren't always being caught up and mystified. When you started in with him, you went; you cut the breeze, as Ray used to say. He had some go in him.

Philip Frederick Ottenburg was the third son of the great brewer. His mother was Katarina Furst, the daughter and heiress of a brewing business older and richer than Otto Ottenburg's. As a young woman she had been a conspicuous figure in German-American society in New York, and not untouched by scandal. She was a handsome, headstrong girl, a rebellious and violent force in a provincial society. She was brutally sentimental and heavily romantic. Her free speech, her Continental ideas, and her proclivity for championing new causes, even when she did not know much about them, made her an object of suspicion. She was always going abroad to seek out intellectual affinities, and was one of the group of young women who followed Wagner about in his old age, keeping at a respectful distance, but receiving now and then a gracious acknowledgment that he appreciated their homage. When the composer died, Katarina, then a matron with a family, took to her bed and saw no one for a week.

After having been engaged to an American actor, a Welsh socialist agitator, and a German army officer, Fraulein Furst at last placed herself and her great brewery interests into the trustworthy hands of Otto Ottenburg, who had been her suitor ever since he was a clerk, learning his business in her father's office.

Her first two sons were exactly like their father. Even as children they were industrious, earnest little tradesmen. As Frau Ottenburg said, "she had to wait for her Fred, but she got him at last," the first man who had altogether pleased her. Frederick entered Harvard when he was eighteen. When his mother went to Boston to visit him, she not only got him everything he wished for, but she made handsome and often embarrassing presents to all his friends. She gave dinners and supper parties for the Glee Club, made the crew break training, and was a generally disturbing influence. In his third year Fred left the university because of a serious escapade which had somewhat hampered his life ever since. He went at once into his father's business, where, in his own way, he had made himself very useful.

Fred Ottenburg was now twenty-eight, and people could only say of him that he had been less hurt by his mother's indulgence than most boys would have been. He had never wanted anything that he could not have it, and he might have had a great many things that he had never wanted. He was extravagant, but not prodigal. He turned most of the money his mother gave him into the business, and lived on his generous salary.

Fred had never been bored for a whole day in his life. When he was in Chicago or St. Louis, he went to ballgames, prize-fights, and horse-races. When he was in Germany, he went to concerts and to the opera. He belonged to a long list of sporting-clubs and huntingclubs, and was a good boxer. He had so many natural interests that he had no affectations. At Harvard he kept away from the aesthetic circle that had already discovered Francis Thompson. He liked no poetry but German poetry. Physical energy was the thing he was full to the brim of, and music was one of its natural forms of expression. He had a healthy love of sport and art, of eating and drinking. When he was in Germany, he scarcely knew where the soup ended and the symphony began.

V

MARCH began badly for Thea. She had a cold during the first week, and after she got through her church duties on Sunday she had to go to bed with tonsilitis. She was still in the boarding-house at which young Ottenburg had called when he took her to see Mrs. Nathanmeyer. She had stayed on there because her room, although it was inconvenient and very small, was at the corner of the house and got the sunlight.

Since she left Mrs. Lorch, this was the first place where she had got away from a north light. Her rooms had all been as damp and mouldy as they were dark, with deep foundations of dirt under the carpets, and dirty walls. In her present room there was no running water and no clothes closet, and she had to have the dresser moved out to make room for her piano. But there were two windows, one on the south and one on the west, a light wall-paper with morning-glory vines, and on the floor a clean matting. The landlady had tried to make the room look cheerful, because it was hard to let. It was so small that Thea could keep it clean herself, after the Hun had done her worst. She hung her dresses on the door under a sheet, used the washstand for a dresser, slept on a cot, and opened both the windows when she practiced. She felt less walled in than she had in the other houses.

Wednesday was her third day in bed. The medical student who lived in the house had been in to see her, had left some tablets and a foamy gargle, and told her that she could probably go back to work on Monday. The landlady stuck her head in once a day, but Thea did not encourage her visits. The Hungarian chambermaid brought her soup and toast. She made a sloppy pretense of putting the room in order, but she was such a dirty creature that Thea would not let her touch her cot; she got up every morning and turned the mattress and made the bed herself. The exertion made her feel miserably ill, but at least she could lie still contentedly for a long while afterward. She hated the poisoned feeling in her throat, and no matter how often she gargled she felt unclean and disgusting. Still, if she had to be ill, she was almost glad that she had a contagious illness. Otherwise she would have been at the mercy of the people in the house. She knew that they disliked her, yet now that she was ill, they took it upon themselves to tap at her door, send her messages, books, even a miserable flower or two. Thea knew that their sympathy was an expression of self-righteousness, and she hated them for it. The divinity student, who was always whispering soft things to her, sent her "The Kreutzer Sonata."

The medical student had been kind to her: he knew that she did not want to pay a doctor. His gargle had helped her, and he gave her things to make her sleep at night. But he had been a cheat, too. He had exceeded his rights. She had no soreness in her chest, and had told him so clearly. All this thumping of her back, and listening to her breathing, was done to satisfy personal curiosity. She had watched him with a contemptuous smile. She was too sick to care; if it amused him- -She made him wash his hands before he touched her; he was never very clean. All the same, it wounded her and made her feel that the world was a pretty disgusting place. "The Kreutzer Sonata" did not make her feel any more cheerful. She threw it aside with hatred. She could not believe it was written by the same man who wrote the novel that had thrilled her.

Her cot was beside the south window, and on Wednesday afternoon she lay thinking about the Harsanyis, about old Mr. Nathanmeyer, and about how she was missing Fred Ottenburg's visits to the studio. That was much the worst thing about being sick. If she were going to the studio every day, she might be having pleasant encounters with Fred. He was always running away, Bowers said, and he might be planning to go away as soon as Mrs. Nathanmeyer's evenings were over. And here she was losing all this time!

After a while she heard the Hun's clumsy trot in the hall, and then a pound on the door. Mary came in, making her usual uncouth sounds, carrying a long box and a big basket. Thea sat up in bed and tore off the strings and paper. The basket was full of fruit, with a big Hawaiian pineapple in the middle, and in the box there were layers of pink roses with long, woody stems and dark-green leaves. They filled the room with a cool smell that made another air to breathe. Mary stood with her apron full of paper and cardboard. When she saw Thea take an envelope out from under the flowers, she uttered an exclamation, pointed to the roses, and then to the bosom of her own dress, on the left side. Thea laughed and nodded. She understood that Mary associated the color with Ottenburg's BOUTONNIERE. She pointed to the water pitcher,--she had nothing else big enough to hold the flowers,--and made Mary put it on the window sill beside her.

After Mary was gone Thea locked the door. When the landlady knocked, she pretended that she was asleep. She lay still all afternoon and with drowsy eyes watched the roses open. They were the first hothouse flowers she had ever had. The cool fragrance they released was soothing, and as the pink petals curled back, they were the only things between her and the gray sky. She lay on her side, putting the room and the boarding-house behind her. Fred knew where all the pleasant things in the world were, she reflected, and knew the road to them. He had keys to all the nice places in his pocket, and seemed to jingle them from time to time. And then, he was young; and her friends had always been old. Her mind went back over them. They had all been teachers; wonderfully kind, but still teachers. Ray Kennedy, she knew, had wanted to marry her, but he was the most protecting and teacher-like of them all. She moved impatiently in her cot and threw her braids away from her hot neck, over her pillow. "I don't want him for a teacher," she thought, frowning petulantly out of the window. "I've had such a string of them. I want him for a sweetheart."

VI

"THEA," said Fred Ottenburg one drizzly afternoon in April, while they sat waiting for their tea at a restaurant in the Pullman Building, overlooking the lake, "what are you going to do this summer?"

"I don't know. Work, I suppose."

"With Bowers, you mean? Even Bowers goes fishing for a month. Chicago's no place to work, in the summer. Haven't you made any plans?"

Thea shrugged her shoulders. "No use having any plans when you haven't any money. They are unbecoming."

"Aren't you going home?"

She shook her head. "No. It won't be comfortable there till I've got something to show for myself. I'm not getting on at all, you know. This year has been mostly wasted."

"You're stale; that's what's the matter with you. And just now you're dead tired. You'll talk more rationally after you've had some tea. Rest your throat until it comes." They were sitting by a window. As Ottenburg looked at her in the gray light, he remembered what Mrs. Nathanmeyer had said about the Swedish face "breaking early." Thea was as gray as the weather. Her skin looked sick. Her hair, too, though on a damp day it curled charmingly about her face, looked pale.

Fred beckoned the waiter and increased his order for food. Thea did not hear him. She was staring out of the window, down at the roof of the Art Institute and the green lions, dripping in the rain. The lake was all rolling mist, with a soft shimmer of robin's-egg blue in the gray. A lumber boat, with two very tall masts, was emerging gaunt and black out of the fog. When the tea came Thea ate hungrily, and Fred watched her. He thought her eyes became a little less bleak. The kettle sang cheerfully over the spirit lamp, and she seemed to concentrate her attention upon that pleasant sound. She kept looking toward it listlessly and indulgently, in a way that gave him a realization of her loneliness. Fred lit a cigarette and smoked thoughtfully. He and Thea were alone in the quiet, dusky room full of white tables. In those days Chicago people never stopped for tea. "Come," he said at last, "what would you do this summer, if you could do whatever you wished?"

"I'd go a long way from here! West, I think. Maybe I could get some of my spring back. All this cold, cloudy weather,"--she looked out at the lake and shivered,--"I don't know, it does things to me," she ended abruptly.

Fred nodded. "I know. You've been going down ever since you had tonsilitis. I've seen it. What you need is to sit in the sun and bake for three months. You've got the right idea. I remember once when we were having dinner somewhere you kept asking me about the Cliff-Dweller ruins. Do they still interest you?"

"Of course they do. I've always wanted to go down there--long before I ever got in for this."

"I don't think I told you, but my father owns a whole canyon full of Cliff-Dweller ruins. He has a big worthless ranch down in Arizona, near a Navajo reservation, and there's a canyon on the place they call Panther Canyon, chock full of that sort of thing. I often go down there to hunt. Henry Biltmer and his wife live there and keep a tidy place. He's an old German who worked in the brewery until he lost his health. Now he runs a few cattle. Henry likes to do me a favor. I've done a few for him." Fred drowned his cigarette in his saucer and studied Thea's expression, which was wistful and intent, envious and admiring. He continued with satisfaction: "If you went down there and stayed with them for two or three months, they wouldn't let you pay anything. I might send Henry a new gun, but even I couldn't offer him money for putting up a friend of mine. I'll get you transportation. It would make a new girl of you. Let me write to Henry, and you pack your trunk. That's all that's necessary. No red tape about it. What do you say, Thea?"

She bit her lip, and sighed as if she were waking up.

Fred crumpled his napkin impatiently. "Well, isn't it easy enough?"

"That's the trouble; it's TOO easy. Doesn't sound probable. I'm not used to getting things for nothing."

Ottenburg laughed. "Oh, if that's all, I'll show you how to begin. You won't get this for nothing, quite. I'll ask you to let me stop off and see you on my way to California. Perhaps by that time you will be glad to see me. Better let me break the news to Bowers. I can manage him. He needs a little transportation himself now and then. You must get corduroy riding-things and leather leggings. There are a few snakes about. Why do you keep frowning?"

"Well, I don't exactly see why you take the trouble. What do you get out of it? You haven't liked me so well the last two or three weeks."

Fred dropped his third cigarette and looked at his watch. "If you don't see that, it's because you need a tonic. I'll show you what I'll get out of it. Now I'm going to get a cab and take you home. You are too tired to walk a step. You'd better get to bed as soon as you get there. Of course, I don't like you so well when you're half anaesthetized all the time. What have you been doing to yourself?"

Thea rose. "I don't know. Being bored eats the heart out of me, I guess." She walked meekly in front of him to the elevator. Fred noticed for the hundredth time how vehemently her body proclaimed her state of feeling. He remembered how remarkably brilliant and beautiful she had been when she sang at Mrs. Nathanmeyer's: flushed and gleaming, round and supple, something that couldn't be dimmed or downed. And now she seemed a moving figure of discouragement. The very waiters glanced at her apprehensively. It was not that she made a fuss, but her back was most extraordinarily vocal. One never needed to see her face to know what she was full of that day. Yet she was certainly not mercurial. Her flesh seemed to take a mood and to "set," like plaster. As he put her into the cab, Fred reflected once more that he "gave her up." He would attack her when his lance was brighter.

PART IV. THE ANCIENT PEOPLE

I

THE San Francisco Mountain lies in Northern Arizona, above Flagstaff, and its blue slopes and snowy summit entice the eye for a hundred miles across the desert. About its base lie the pine forests of the Navajos, where the great red-trunked trees live out their peaceful centuries in that sparkling air. The PINONS and scrub begin only where the forest ends, where the country breaks into open, stony clearings and the surface of the earth cracks into deep canyons. The great pines stand at a considerable distance from each other. Each tree grows alone, murmurs alone, thinks alone. They do not intrude upon each other. The Navajos are not much in the habit of giving or of asking help. Their language is not a communicative one, and they never attempt an interchange of personality in speech. Over their forests there is the same inexorable reserve. Each tree has its exalted power to bear.

That was the first thing Thea Kronborg felt about the forest, as she drove through it one May morning in Henry Biltmer's democrat wagon--and it was the first great forest she had ever seen. She had got off the train at Flagstaff that morning, rolled off into the high, chill air when all the pines on the mountain were fired by sunrise, so that she seemed to fall from sleep directly into the forest.

Old Biltmer followed a faint wagon trail which ran southeast, and which, as they traveled, continually dipped lower, falling away from the high plateau on the slope of which Flagstaff sits. The white peak of the mountain, the snow gorges above the timber, now disappeared from time to time as the road dropped and dropped, and the forest closed behind the wagon. More than the mountain disappeared as the forest closed thus. Thea seemed to be taking very little through the wood with her. The personality of which she was so tired seemed to let go of her. The high, sparkling air drank it up like blotting-paper. It was lost in the thrilling blue of the new sky and the song of the thin wind in the PINONS. The old, fretted lines which marked one off, which defined her,--made her Thea Kronborg, Bowers's accompanist, a soprano with a faulty middle voice,--were all erased.

So far she had failed. Her two years in Chicago had not resulted in anything. She had failed with Harsanyi, and she had made no great progress with her voice. She had come to believe that whatever Bowers had taught her was of secondary importance, and that in the essential things she had made no advance. Her student life closed behind her, like the forest, and she doubted whether she could go back to it if she tried. Probably she would teach music in little country towns all her life. Failure was not so tragic as she would have supposed; she was tired enough not to care.

She was getting back to the earliest sources of gladness that she could remember. She had loved the sun, and the brilliant solitudes of sand and sun, long before these other things had come along to fasten themselves upon her and torment her. That night, when she clambered into her big German feather bed, she felt completely released from the enslaving desire to get on in the world. Darkness had once again the sweet wonder that it had in childhood.

II

THEA'S life at the Ottenburg ranch was simple and full of light, like the days themselves. She awoke every morning when the first fierce shafts of sunlight darted through the curtainless windows of her room at the ranch house. After breakfast she took her lunch-basket and went down to the canyon. Usually she did not return until sunset.

Panther Canyon was like a thousand others--one of those abrupt fissures with which the earth in the Southwest is riddled; so abrupt that you might walk over the edge of any one of them on a dark night and never know what had happened to you. This canyon headed on the Ottenburg ranch, about a mile from the ranch house, and it was accessible only at its head. The canyon walls, for the first two hundred feet below the surface, were perpendicular cliffs, striped with even-running strata of rock. From there on to the bottom the sides were less abrupt, were shelving, and lightly fringed with PINONS and dwarf cedars. The effect was that of a gentler canyon within a wilder one. The dead city lay at the point where the perpendicular outer wall ceased and the V-shaped inner gorge began. There a stratum of rock, softer than those above, had been hollowed out by the action of time until it was like a deep groove running along the sides of the canyon. In this hollow (like a great fold in the rock) the Ancient People had built their houses of yellowish stone and mortar. The over-hanging cliff above made a roof two hundred feet thick. The hard stratum below was an everlasting floor. The houses stood along in a row, like the buildings in a city block, or like a barracks.

In both walls of the canyon the same streak of soft rock had been washed out, and the long horizontal groove had been built up with houses. The dead city had thus two streets, one set in either cliff, facing each other across the ravine, with a river of blue air between them.

The canyon twisted and wound like a snake, and these two streets went on for four miles or more, interrupted by the abrupt turnings of the gorge, but beginning again within each turn. The canyon had a dozen of these false endings near its head. Beyond, the windings were larger and less perceptible, and it went on for a hundred miles, too narrow, precipitous, and terrible for man to follow it. The Cliff Dwellers liked wide canyons, where the great cliffs caught the sun. Panther Canyon had been deserted for hundreds of years when the first Spanish missionaries came into Arizona, but the masonry of the houses was still wonderfully firm; had crumbled only where a landslide or a rolling boulder had torn it.

All the houses in the canyon were clean with the cleanness of sun-baked, wind-swept places, and they all smelled of the tough little cedars that twisted themselves into the very doorways. One of these rock-rooms Thea took for her own. Fred had told her how to make it comfortable. The day after she came old Henry brought over on one of the pack-ponies a roll of Navajo blankets that belonged to Fred, and Thea lined her cave with them. The room was not more than eight by ten feet, and she could touch the stone roof with her finger-tips. This was her old idea: a nest in a high cliff, full of sun. All morning long the sun beat upon her cliff, while the ruins on the opposite side of the canyon were in shadow. In the afternoon, when she had the shade of two hundred feet of rock wall, the ruins on the other side of the gulf stood out in the blazing sunlight. Before her door ran the narrow, winding path that had been the street of the Ancient People. The yucca and niggerhead cactus grew everywhere. From her doorstep she looked out on the ocher-colored slope that ran down several hundred feet to the stream, and this hot rock was sparsely grown with dwarf trees. Their colors were so pale that the shadows of the little trees on the rock stood out sharper than the trees themselves. When Thea first came, the chokecherry bushes were in blossom, and the scent of them was almost sickeningly sweet after a shower. At the very bottom of the canyon, along the stream, there was a thread of bright, flickering, golden-green,--cottonwood seedlings. They made a living, chattering screen behind which she took her bath every morning.

Thea went down to the stream by the Indian water trail. She had found a bathing-pool with a sand bottom, where the creek was damned by fallen trees. The climb back was long and steep, and when she reached her little house in the cliff she always felt fresh delight in its comfort and inaccessibility. By the time she got there, the woolly red-and-gray blankets were saturated with sunlight, and she sometimes fell asleep as soon as she stretched her body on their warm surfaces. She used to wonder at her own inactivity. She could lie there hour after hour in the sun and listen to the strident whir of the big locusts, and to the light, ironical laughter of the quaking asps. All her life she had been hurrying and sputtering, as if she had been born behind time and had been trying to catch up. Now, she reflected, as she drew herself out long upon the rugs, it was as if she were waiting for something to catch up with her. She had got to a place where she was out of the stream of meaningless activity and undirected effort.

Here she could lie for half a day undistracted, holding pleasant and incomplete conceptions in her mind--almost in her hands. They were scarcely clear enough to be called ideas. They had something to do with fragrance and color and sound, but almost nothing to do with words. She was singing very little now, but a song would go through her head all morning, as a spring keeps welling up, and it was like a pleasant sensation indefinitely prolonged. It was much more like a sensation than like an idea, or an act of remembering. Music had never come to her in that sensuous form before. It had always been a thing to be struggled with, had always brought anxiety and exaltation and chagrin--never content and indolence. Thea began to wonder whether people could not utterly lose the power to work, as they can lose their voice or their memory. She had always been a little drudge, hurrying from one task to another--as if it mattered! And now her power to think seemed converted into a power of sustained sensation. She could become a mere receptacle for heat, or become a color, like the bright lizards that darted about on the hot stones outside her door; or she could become a continuous repetition of sound, like the cicadas.

III

THE faculty of observation was never highly developed in Thea Kronborg. A great deal escaped her eye as she passed through the world. But the things which were for her, she saw; she experienced them physically and remembered them as if they had once been a part of herself. The roses she used to see in the florists' shops in Chicago were merely roses. But when she thought of the moonflowers that grew over Mrs. Tellamantez's door, it was as if she had been that vine and had opened up in white flowers every night. There were memories of light on the sand hills, of masses of prickly-pear blossoms she had found in the desert in early childhood, of the late afternoon sun pouring through the grape leaves and the mint bed in Mrs. Kohler's garden, which she would never lose. These recollections were a part of her mind and personality. In Chicago she had got almost nothing that went into her subconscious self and took root there. But here, in Panther Canyon, there were again things which seemed destined for her.

Panther Canyon was the home of innumerable swallows. They built nests in the wall far above the hollow groove in which Thea's own rock chamber lay. They seldom ventured above the rim of the canyon, to the flat, wind-swept tableland. Their world was the blue air-river between the canyon walls. In that blue gulf the arrow-shaped birds swam all day long, with only an occasional movement of the wings. The only sad thing about them was their timidity; the way in which they lived their lives between the echoing cliffs and never dared to rise out of the shadow of the canyon walls. As they swam past her door, Thea often felt how easy it would be to dream one's life out in some cleft in the world.

From the ancient dwelling there came always a dignified, unobtrusive sadness; now stronger, now fainter,--like the aromatic smell which the dwarf cedars gave out in the sun,--but always present, a part of the air one breathed. At night, when Thea dreamed about the canyon,--or in the early morning when she hurried toward it, anticipating it,--her conception of it was of yellow rocks baking in sunlight, the swallows, the cedar smell, and that peculiar sadness--a voice out of the past, not very loud, that went on saying a few simple things to the solitude eternally.

Standing up in her lodge, Thea could with her thumb nail dislodge flakes of carbon from the rock roof--the cooking-smoke of the Ancient People. They were that near! A timid, nest-building folk, like the swallows. How often Thea remembered Ray Kennedy's moralizing about the cliff cities. He used to say that he never felt the hardness of the human struggle or the sadness of history as he felt it among those ruins. He used to say, too, that it made one feel an obligation to do one's best. On the first day that Thea climbed the water trail she began to have intuitions about the women who had worn the path, and who had spent so great a part of their lives going up and down it. She found herself trying to walk as they must have walked, with a feeling in her feet and knees and loins which she had never known before,--which must have come up to her out of the accustomed dust of that rocky trail. She could feel the weight of an Indian baby hanging to her back as she climbed.

The empty houses, among which she wandered in the afternoon, the blanketed one in which she lay all morning, were haunted by certain fears and desires; feelings about warmth and cold and water and physical strength. It seemed to Thea that a certain understanding of those old people came up to her out of the rock shelf on which she lay; that certain feelings were transmitted to her, suggestions that were simple, insistent, and monotonous, like the beating of Indian drums. They were not expressible in words, but seemed rather to translate themselves into attitudes of body, into degrees of muscular tension or relaxation; the naked strength of youth, sharp as the sunshafts; the crouching timorousness of age, the sullenness of women who waited for their captors. At the first turning of the canyon there was a half-ruined tower of yellow masonry, a watch-tower upon which the young men used to entice eagles and snare them with nets. Sometimes for a whole morning Thea could see the coppery breast and shoulders of an Indian youth there against the sky; see him throw the net, and watch the struggle with the eagle.

Old Henry Biltmer, at the ranch, had been a great deal among the Pueblo Indians who are the descendants of the Cliff-Dwellers. After supper he used to sit and smoke his pipe by the kitchen stove and talk to Thea about them. He had never found any one before who was interested in his ruins. Every Sunday the old man prowled about in the canyon, and he had come to know a good deal more about it than he could account for. He had gathered up a whole chestful of Cliff-Dweller relics which he meant to take back to Germany with him some day. He taught Thea how to find things among the ruins: grinding-stones, and drills and needles made of turkey-bones. There were fragments of pottery everywhere. Old Henry explained to her that the Ancient People had developed masonry and pottery far beyond any other crafts. After they had made houses for themselves, the next thing was to house the precious water. He explained to her how all their customs and ceremonies and their religion went back to water. The men provided the food, but water was the care of the women. The stupid women carried water for most of their lives; the cleverer ones made the vessels to hold it. Their pottery was their most direct appeal to water, the envelope and sheath of the precious element itself. The strongest Indian need was expressed in those graceful jars, fashioned slowly by hand, without the aid of a wheel.

When Thea took her bath at the bottom of the canyon, in the sunny pool behind the screen of cottonwoods, she sometimes felt as if the water must have sovereign qualities, from having been the object of so much service and desire. That stream was the only living thing left of the drama that had been played out in the canyon centuries ago. In the rapid, restless heart of it, flowing swifter than the rest, there was a continuity of life that reached back into the old time. The glittering thread of current had a kind of lightly worn, loosely knit personality, graceful and laughing. Thea's bath came to have a ceremonial gravity. The atmosphere of the canyon was ritualistic.

One morning, as she was standing upright in the pool, splashing water between her shoulder-blades with a big sponge, something flashed through her mind that made her draw herself up and stand still until the water had quite dried upon her flushed skin. The stream and the broken pottery: what was any art but an effort to make a sheath, a mould in which to imprison for a moment the shining, elusive element which is life itself,--life hurrying past us and running away, too strong to stop, too sweet to lose? The Indian women had held it in their jars. In the sculpture she had seen in the Art Institute, it had been caught in a flash of arrested motion. In singing, one made a vessel of one's throat and nostrils and held it on one's breath, caught the stream in a scale of natural intervals.

IV

THEA had a superstitious feeling about the potsherds, and liked better to leave them in the dwellings where she found them. If she took a few bits back to her own lodge and hid them under the blankets, she did it guiltily, as if she were being watched. She was a guest in these houses, and ought to behave as such. Nearly every afternoon she went to the chambers which contained the most interesting fragments of pottery, sat and looked at them for a while. Some of them were beautifully decorated. This care, expended upon vessels that could not hold food or water any better for the additional labor put upon them, made her heart go out to those ancient potters. They had not only expressed their desire, but they had expressed it as beautifully as they could. Food, fire, water, and something else--even here, in this crack in the world, so far back in the night of the past! Down here at the beginning that painful thing was already stirring; the seed of sorrow, and of so much delight.

There were jars done in a delicate overlay, like pine cones; and there were many patterns in a low relief, like basket-work. Some of the pottery was decorated in color, red and brown, black and white, in graceful geometrical patterns. One day, on a fragment of a shallow bowl, she found a crested serpent's head, painted in red on terra-cotta. Again she found half a bowl with a broad band of white cliff-houses painted on a black ground. They were scarcely conventionalized at all; there they were in the black border, just as they stood in the rock before her. It brought her centuries nearer to these people to find that they saw their houses exactly as she saw them.

Yes, Ray Kennedy was right. All these things made one feel that one ought to do one's best, and help to fulfill some desire of the dust that slept there. A dream had been dreamed there long ago, in the night of ages, and the wind had whispered some promise to the sadness of the savage. In their own way, those people had felt the beginnings of what was to come. These potsherds were like fetters that bound one to a long chain of human endeavor.

Not only did the world seem older and richer to Thea now, but she herself seemed older. She had never been alone for so long before, or thought so much. Nothing had ever engrossed her so deeply as the daily contemplation of that line of pale-yellow houses tucked into the wrinkle of the cliff. Moonstone and Chicago had become vague. Here everything was simple and definite, as things had been in childhood. Her mind was like a ragbag into which she had been frantically thrusting whatever she could grab. And here she must throw this lumber away. The things that were really hers separated themselves from the rest. Her ideas were simplified, became sharper and clearer. She felt united and strong.

When Thea had been at the Ottenburg ranch for two months, she got a letter from Fred announcing that he "might be along at almost any time now." The letter came at night, and the next morning she took it down into the canyon with her. She was delighted that he was coming soon. She had never felt so grateful to any one, and she wanted to tell him everything that had happened to her since she had been there--more than had happened in all her life before. Certainly she liked Fred better than any one else in the world. There was Harsanyi, of course--but Harsanyi was always tired. Just now, and here, she wanted some one who had never been tired, who could catch an idea and run with it.

She was ashamed to think what an apprehensive drudge she must always have seemed to Fred, and she wondered why he had concerned himself about her at all. Perhaps she would never be so happy or so good-looking again, and she would like Fred to see her, for once, at her best. She had not been singing much, but she knew that her voice was more

268

interesting than it had ever been before. She had begun to understand that--with her, at least--voice was, first of all, vitality; a lightness in the body and a driving power in the blood. If she had that, she could sing. When she felt so keenly alive, lying on that insensible shelf of stone, when her body bounded like a rubber ball away from its hardness, then she could sing. This, too, she could explain to Fred. He would know what she meant.

Another week passed. Thea did the same things as before, felt the same influences, went over the same ideas; but there was a livelier movement in her thoughts, and a freshening of sensation, like the brightness which came over the underbrush after a shower. A persistent affirmation--or denial--was going on in her, like the tapping of the woodpecker in the one tall pine tree across the chasm. Musical phrases drove each other rapidly through her mind, and the song of the cicada was now too long and too sharp. Everything seemed suddenly to take the form of a desire for action.

It was while she was in this abstracted state, waiting for the clock to strike, that Thea at last made up her mind what she was going to try to do in the world, and that she was going to Germany to study without further loss of time. Only by the merest chance had she ever got to Panther Canyon. There was certainly no kindly Providence that directed one's life; and one's parents did not in the least care what became of one, so long as one did not misbehave and endanger their comfort. One's life was at the mercy of blind chance. She had better take it in her own hands and lose everything than meekly draw the plough under the rod of parental guidance. She had seen it when she was at home last summer,--the hostility of comfortable, selfsatisfied people toward any serious effort. Even to her father it seemed indecorous. Whenever she spoke seriously, he looked apologetic. Yet she had clung fast to whatever was left of Moonstone in her mind. No more of that! The Cliff-Dwellers had lengthened her past. She had older and higher obligations.

V

ONE Sunday afternoon late in July old Henry Biltmer was rheumatically descending into the head of the canyon. The Sunday before had been one of those cloudy days--fortunately rare--when the life goes out of that country and it becomes a gray ghost, an empty, shivering uncertainty. Henry had spent the day in the barn; his canyon was a reality only when it was flooded with the light of its great lamp, when the yellow rocks cast purple shadows, and the resin was fairly cooking in the corkscrew cedars. The yuccas were in blossom now. Out of each clump of sharp bayonet leaves rose a tall stalk hung with greenish-white bells with thick, fleshy petals. The niggerhead cactus was thrusting its crimson blooms up out of every crevice in the rocks.

Henry had come out on the pretext of hunting a spade and pick-axe that young Ottenburg had borrowed, but he was keeping his eyes open. He was really very curious about the new occupants of the canyon, and what they found to do there all day long. He let his eye travel along the gulf for a mile or so to the first turning, where the fissure zigzagged out and then receded behind a stone promontory on which stood the yellowish, crumbling ruin of the old watch-tower.

From the base of this tower, which now threw its shadow forward, bits of rock kept flying out into the open gulf--skating upon the air until they lost their momentum, then falling like chips until they rang upon the ledges at the bottom of the gorge or splashed into the stream. Biltmer shaded his eyes with his hand. There on the promontory, against the cream-colored cliff, were two figures nimbly moving in the light, both slender and agile, entirely absorbed in their game. They looked like two boys. Both were hatless and both wore white shirts.

Henry forgot his pick-axe and followed the trail before the cliff-houses toward the tower. Behind the tower, as he well knew, were heaps of stones, large and small, piled against the face of the cliff. He had always believed that the Indian watchmen piled them there for ammunition. Thea and Fred had come upon these missiles and were throwing them for distance. As Biltmer approached he could hear them laughing, and he caught Thea's voice, high and excited, with a ring of vexation in it. Fred was teaching her to throw a heavy stone like a discus. When it was Fred's turn, he sent a triangular-shaped stone out into the air with considerable skill. Thea watched it enviously, standing in a half-defiant posture, her sleeves rolled above her elbows and her face flushed with heat and excitement. After Fred's third missile had rung upon the rocks below, she snatched up a stone and stepped impatiently out on the ledge in front of him. He caught her by the elbows and pulled her back.

"Not so close, you silly! You'll spin yourself off in a minute."

"You went that close. There's your heel-mark," she retorted.

"Well, I know how. That makes a difference." He drew a mark in the dust with his toe. "There, that's right. Don't step over that. Pivot yourself on your spine, and make a half turn. When you've swung your length, let it go."

Thea settled the flat piece of rock between her wrist and fingers, faced the cliff wall, stretched her arm in position, whirled round on her left foot to the full stretch of her body, and let the missile spin out over the gulf. She hung expectantly in the air, forgetting to draw back her arm, her eyes following the stone as if it carried her fortunes with it. Her comrade watched her; there weren't many girls who could show a line like that from the toe to the thigh, from the shoulder to the tip of the outstretched hand. The stone spent itself and began to fall. Thea drew back and struck her knee furiously with her palm.

"There it goes again! Not nearly so far as yours. What IS the matter with me? Give me another." She faced the cliff and whirled again. The stone spun out, not quite so far as before.

Ottenburg laughed. "Why do you keep on working AFTER you've thrown it? You can't help it along then."

Without replying, Thea stooped and selected another stone, took a deep breath and made another turn. Fred watched the disk, exclaiming, "Good girl! You got past the pine that time. That's a good throw."

She took out her handkerchief and wiped her glowing face and throat, pausing to feel her right shoulder with her left hand.

"Ah--ha, you've made yourself sore, haven't you? What did I tell you? You go at things too hard. I'll tell you what I'm going to do, Thea," Fred dusted his hands and began tucking in the blouse of his shirt, "I'm going to make some single-sticks and teach you to fence. You'd be all right there. You're light and quick and you've got lots of drive in you. I'd like to have you come at me with foils; you'd look so fierce," he chuckled.

She turned away from him and stubbornly sent out another stone, hanging in the air after its flight. Her fury amused Fred, who took all games lightly and played them well. She was breathing hard, and little beads of moisture had gathered on her upper lip. He slipped his arm about her. "If you will look as pretty as that--" he bent his head and kissed her. Thea was startled, gave him an angry push, drove at him with her free hand in a manner quite hostile. Fred was on his mettle in an instant. He pinned both her arms down and kissed her resolutely.

When he released her, she turned away and spoke over her shoulder. "That was mean of you, but I suppose I deserved what I got."

"I should say you did deserve it," Fred panted, "turning savage on me like that! I should say you did deserve it!"

He saw her shoulders harden. "Well, I just said I deserved it, didn't I? What more do you want?"

"I want you to tell me why you flew at me like that! You weren't playing; you looked as if you'd like to murder me."

She brushed back her hair impatiently. "I didn't mean anything, really. You interrupted me when I was watching the stone. I can't jump from one thing to another. I pushed you without thinking."

Fred thought her back expressed contrition. He went up to her, stood behind her with his chin above her shoulder, and said something in her ear. Thea laughed and turned toward him. They left the stone-pile carelessly, as if they had never been interested in it, rounded the yellow tower, and disappeared into the second turn of the canyon, where the dead city, interrupted by the jutting promontory, began again.

Old Biltmer had been somewhat embarrassed by the turn the game had taken. He had not heard their conversation, but the pantomime against the rocks was clear enough. When the two young people disappeared, their host retreated rapidly toward the head of the canyon.

"I guess that young lady can take care of herself," he chuckled. "Young Fred, though, he has quite a way with them."

VI

DAY was breaking over Panther Canyon. The gulf was cold and full of heavy, purplish twilight. The wood smoke which drifted from one of the cliff-houses hung in a blue scarf across the chasm, until the draft caught it and whirled it away. Thea was crouching in the doorway of her rock house, while Ottenburg looked after the crackling fire in the next cave. He was waiting for it to burn down to coals before he put the coffee on to boil.

They had left the ranch house that morning a little after three o'clock, having packed their camp equipment the day before, and had crossed the open pasture land with their lantern while the stars were still bright. During the descent into

270

the canyon by lantern-light, they were chilled through their coats and sweaters. The lantern crept slowly along the rock trail, where the heavy air seemed to offer resistance. The voice of the stream at the bottom of the gorge was hollow and threatening, much louder and deeper than it ever was by day--another voice altogether. The sullenness of the place seemed to say that the world could get on very well without people, red or white; that under the human world there was a geological world, conducting its silent, immense operations which were indifferent to man. Thea had often seen the desert sunrise,--a lighthearted affair, where the sun springs out of bed and the world is golden in an instant. But this canyon seemed to waken like an old man, with rheum and stiffness of the joints, with heaviness, and a dull, malignant mind. She crouched against the wall while the stars faded, and thought what courage the early races must have had to endure so much for the little they got out of life.

At last a kind of hopefulness broke in the air. In a moment the pine trees up on the edge of the rim were flashing with coppery fire. The thin red clouds which hung above their pointed tops began to boil and move rapidly, weaving in and out like smoke. The swallows darted out of their rock houses as at a signal, and flew upward, toward the rim. Little brown birds began to chirp in the bushes along the watercourse down at the bottom of the ravine, where everything was still dusky and pale. At first the golden light seemed to hang like a wave upon the rim of the canyon; the trees and bushes up there, which one scarcely noticed at noon, stood out magnified by the slanting rays. Long, thin streaks of light began to reach quiveringly down into the canyon. The red sun rose rapidly above the tops of the blazing pines, and its glow burst into the gulf, about the very doorstep on which Thea sat. It bored into the wet, dark underbrush. The dripping cherry bushes, the pale aspens, and the frosty PINONS were glittering and trembling, swimming in the liquid gold. All the pale, dusty little herbs of the bean family, never seen by any one but a botanist, became for a moment individual and important, their silky leaves quite beautiful with dew and light. The arch of sky overhead, heavy as lead a little while before, lifted, became more and more transparent, and one could look up into depths of pearly blue.

The savor of coffee and bacon mingled with the smell of wet cedars drying, and Fred called to Thea that he was ready for her. They sat down in the doorway of his kitchen, with the warmth of the live coals behind them and the sunlight on their faces, and began their breakfast, Mrs. Biltmer's thick coffee cups and the cream bottle between them, the coffee-pot and frying-pan conveniently keeping hot among the embers.

"I thought you were going back on the whole proposition, Thea, when you were crawling along with that lantern. I couldn't get a word out of you."

"I know. I was cold and hungry, and I didn't believe there was going to be any morning, anyway. Didn't you feel queer, at all?"

Fred squinted above his smoking cup. "Well, I am never strong for getting up before the sun. The world looks unfurnished. When I first lit the fire and had a square look at you, I thought I'd got the wrong girl. Pale, grim--you were a sight!"

Thea leaned back into the shadow of the rock room and warmed her hands over the coals. "It was dismal enough. How warm these walls are, all the way round; and your breakfast is so good. I'm all right now, Fred."

"Yes, you're all right now." Fred lit a cigarette and looked at her critically as her head emerged into the sun again. "You get up every morning just a little bit handsomer than you were the day before. I'd love you just as much if you were not turning into one of the loveliest women I've ever seen; but you are, and that's a fact to be reckoned with." He watched her across the thin line of smoke he blew from his lips. "What are you going to do with all that beauty and all that talent, Miss Kronborg?"

She turned away to the fire again. "I don't know what you're talking about," she muttered with an awkwardness which did not conceal her pleasure.

Ottenburg laughed softly. "Oh, yes, you do! Nobody better! You're a close one, but you give yourself away sometimes, like everybody else. Do you know, I've decided that you never do a single thing without an ulterior motive." He threw away his cigarette, took out his tobacco-pouch and began to fill his pipe. "You ride and fence and walk and climb, but I know that all the while you're getting somewhere in your mind. All these things are instruments; and I, too, am an instrument." He looked up in time to intercept a quick, startled glance from Thea. "Oh, I don't mind," he chuckled; "not a bit. Every woman, every interesting woman, has ulterior motives, many of 'em less creditable than yours. It's your constancy that amuses me. You must have been doing it ever since you were two feet high."

Thea looked slowly up at her companion's good-humored face. His eyes, sometimes too restless and sympathetic in town, had grown steadier and clearer in the open air. His short curly beard and yellow hair had reddened in the sun and wind. The pleasant vigor of his person was always delightful to her, something to signal to and laugh with in a world of negative people. With Fred she was never becalmed. There was always life in the air, always something coming and going, a rhythm of feeling and action,--stronger than the natural accord of youth. As she looked at him, leaning against the sunny wall, she felt a desire to be frank with him. She was not willfully holding anything back. But, on the other hand, she could not force things that held themselves back. "Yes, it was like that when I was little," she said at last. "I had to be close, as you call it, or go under. But I didn't know I had been like that since you came. I've had nothing to be close about. I haven't thought about anything but having a good time with you. I've just drifted."

Fred blew a trail of smoke out into the breeze and looked knowing. "Yes, you drift like a rifle ball, my dear. It's your--your direction that I like best of all. Most fellows wouldn't, you know. I'm unusual."

They both laughed, but Thea frowned questioningly. "Why wouldn't most fellows? Other fellows have liked me."

"Yes, serious fellows. You told me yourself they were all old, or solemn. But jolly fellows want to be the whole target. They would say you were all brain and muscle; that you have no feeling."

She glanced at him sidewise. "Oh, they would, would they?"

"Of course they would," Fred continued blandly. "Jolly fellows have no imagination. They want to be the animating force. When they are not around, they want a girl to be--extinct," he waved his hand. "Old fellows like Mr. Nathanmeyer understand your kind; but among the young ones, you are rather lucky to have found me. Even I wasn't always so wise. I've had my time of thinking it would not bore me to be the Apollo of a homey flat, and I've paid out a trifle to learn better. All those things get very tedious unless they are hooked up with an idea of some sort. It's because we DON'T come out here only to look at each other and drink coffee that it's so pleasant to--look at each other." Fred drew on his pipe for a while, studying Thea's abstraction. She was staring up at the far wall of the canyon with a troubled expression that drew her eyes narrow and her mouth hard. Her hands lay in her lap, one over the other, the fingers interlacing. "Suppose," Fred came out at length,--"suppose I were to offer you what most of the young men I know would offer a girl they'd been sitting up nights about: a comfortable flat in Chicago, a summer camp up in the woods, musical evenings, and a family to bring up. Would it look attractive to you?"

Thea sat up straight and stared at him in alarm, glared into his eyes. "Perfectly hideous!" she exclaimed.

Fred dropped back against the old stonework and laughed deep in his chest. "Well, don't be frightened. I won't offer them. You're not a nest-building bird. You know I always liked your song, `Me for the jolt of the breakers!' I understand."

She rose impatiently and walked to the edge of the cliff. "It's not that so much. It's waking up every morning with the feeling that your life is your own, and your strength is your own, and your talent is your own; that you're all there, and there's no sag in you." She stood for a moment as if she were tortured by uncertainty, then turned suddenly back to him. "Don't talk about these things any more now," she entreated. "It isn't that I want to keep anything from you. The trouble is that I've got nothing to keep--except (you know as well as I) that feeling. I told you about it in Chicago once. But it always makes me unhappy to talk about it. It will spoil the day. Will you go for a climb with me?" She held out her hands with a smile so eager that it made Ottenburg feel how much she needed to get away from herself.

He sprang up and caught the hands she put out so cordially, and stood swinging them back and forth. "I won't tease you. A word's enough to me. But I love it, all the same. Understand?" He pressed her hands and dropped them. "Now, where are you going to drag me?"

"I want you to drag me. Over there, to the other houses. They are more interesting than these." She pointed across the gorge to the row of white houses in the other cliff. "The trail is broken away, but I got up there once. It's possible. You have to go to the bottom of the canyon, cross the creek, and then go up hand-over-hand."

Ottenburg, lounging against the sunny wall, his hands in the pockets of his jacket, looked across at the distant dwellings. "It's an awful climb," he sighed, "when I could be perfectly happy here with my pipe. However--" He took up his stick and hat and followed Thea down the water trail. "Do you climb this path every day? You surely earn your bath. I went down and had a look at your pool the other afternoon. Neat place, with all those little cottonwoods. Must be very becoming."

"Think so?" Thea said over her shoulder, as she swung round a turn.

"Yes, and so do you, evidently. I'm becoming expert at reading your meaning in your back. I'm behind you so much on these single-foot trails. You don't wear stays, do you?"

"Not here."

"I wouldn't, anywhere, if I were you. They will make you less elastic. The side muscles get flabby. If you go in for opera, there's a fortune in a flexible body. Most of the German singers are clumsy, even when they're well set up."

Thea switched a PINON branch back at him. "Oh, I'll never get fat! That I can promise you."

Fred smiled, looking after her. "Keep that promise, no matter how many others you break," he drawled.

The upward climb, after they had crossed the stream, was at first a breathless scramble through underbrush. When they reached the big boulders, Ottenburg went first because he had the longer leg-reach, and gave Thea a hand when the step was quite beyond her, swinging her up until she could get a foothold. At last they reached a little platform among the rocks, with only a hundred feet of jagged, sloping wall between them and the cliff-houses.

Ottenburg lay down under a pine tree and declared that he was going to have a pipe before he went any farther. "It's a good thing to know when to stop, Thea," he said meaningly.

"I'm not going to stop now until I get there," Thea insisted. "I'll go on alone."

Fred settled his shoulder against the tree-trunk. "Go on if you like, but I'm here to enjoy myself. If you meet a rattler on the way, have it out with him."

She hesitated, fanning herself with her felt hat. "I never have met one."

"There's reasoning for you," Fred murmured languidly.

Thea turned away resolutely and began to go up the wall, using an irregular cleft in the rock for a path. The cliff, which looked almost perpendicular from the bottom, was really made up of ledges and boulders, and behind these she soon disappeared. For a long while Fred smoked with half-closed eyes, smiling to himself now and again. Occasionally he lifted an eyebrow as he heard the rattle of small stones among the rocks above. "In a temper," he concluded; "do her good." Then he subsided into warm drowsiness and listened to the locusts in the yuccas, and the tap-tap of the old woodpecker that was never weary of assaulting the big pine.

Fred had finished his pipe and was wondering whether he wanted another, when he heard a call from the cliff far above him. Looking up, he saw Thea standing on the edge of a projecting crag. She waved to him and threw her arm over her head, as if she were snapping her fingers in the air.

As he saw her there between the sky and the gulf, with that great wash of air and the morning light about her, Fred recalled the brilliant figure at Mrs. Nathanmeyer's. Thea was one of those people who emerge, unexpectedly, larger than we are accustomed to see them. Even at this distance one got the impression of muscular energy and audacity,--a kind of brilliancy of motion,--of a personality that carried across big spaces and expanded among big things. Lying still, with his hands under his head, Ottenburg rhetorically addressed the figure in the air. "You are the sort that used to run wild in Germany, dressed in their hair and a piece of skin. Soldiers caught 'em in nets. Old Nathanmeyer," he mused, "would like a peep at her now. Knowing old fellow. Always buying those Zorn etchings of peasant girls bathing. No sag in them either. Must be the cold climate." He sat up. "She'll begin to pitch rocks on me if I don't move." In response to another impatient gesture from the crag, he rose and began swinging slowly up the trail.

It was the afternoon of that long day. Thea was lying on a blanket in the door of her rock house. She and Ottenburg had come back from their climb and had lunch, and he had gone off for a nap in one of the cliff-houses farther down the path. He was sleeping peacefully, his coat under his head and his face turned toward the wall.

Thea, too, was drowsy, and lay looking through halfclosed eyes up at the blazing blue arch over the rim of the canyon. She was thinking of nothing at all. Her mind, like her body, was full of warmth, lassitude, physical content. Suddenly an eagle, tawny and of great size, sailed over the cleft in which she lay, across the arch of sky. He dropped for a moment into the gulf between the walls, then wheeled, and mounted until his plumage was so steeped in light that he looked like a golden bird. He swept on, following the course of the canyon a little way and then disappearing beyond the rim. Thea sprang to her feet as if she had been thrown up from the rock by volcanic action. She stood rigid on the edge of the stone shelf, straining her eyes after that strong, tawny flight. O eagle of eagles! Endeavor, achievement, desire, glorious striving of human art! From a cleft in the heart of the world she saluted it...It had come all the way; when men lived in caves, it was there. A vanished race; but along the trails, in the stream, under the spreading cactus, there still glittered in the sun the bits of their frail clay vessels, fragments of their desire.

VII

FROM the day of Fred's arrival, he and Thea were unceasingly active. They took long rides into the Navajo pine forests, bought turquoises and silver bracelets from the wandering Indian herdsmen, and rode twenty miles to Flagstaff upon the slightest pretext. Thea had never felt this pleasant excitement about any man before, and she found herself trying very hard to please young Ottenburg. She was never tired, never dull. There was a zest about waking up in the morning and dressing, about walking, riding, even about sleep.

One morning when Thea came out from her room at seven o'clock, she found Henry and Fred on the porch, looking up at the sky. The day was already hot and there was no breeze. The sun was shining, but heavy brown clouds were hanging in the west, like the smoke of a forest fire. She and Fred had meant to ride to Flagstaff that morning, but Biltmer advised against it, foretelling a storm. After breakfast they lingered about the house, waiting for the weather to make up its mind. Fred had brought his guitar, and as they had the dining-room to themselves, he made Thea go over some songs with him. They got interested and kept it up until Mrs. Biltmer came to set the table for dinner. Ottenburg knew some of the Mexican things Spanish Johnny used to sing. Thea had never before happened to tell him about Spanish Johnny, and he seemed more interested in Johnny than in Dr. Archie or Wunsch.

After dinner they were too restless to endure the ranch house any longer, and ran away to the canyon to practice with single-sticks. Fred carried a slicker and a sweater, and he made Thea wear one of the rubber hats that hung in Biltmer's gun-room. As they crossed the pasture land the clumsy slicker kept catching in the lacings of his leggings.

"Why don't you drop that thing?" Thea asked. "I won't mind a shower. I've been wet before."

"No use taking chances."

From the canyon they were unable to watch the sky, since only a strip of the zenith was visible. The flat ledge about the watch-tower was the only level spot large enough for single-stick exercise, and they were still practicing there when, at about four o'clock, a tremendous roll of thunder echoed between the cliffs and the atmosphere suddenly became thick.

Fred thrust the sticks in a cleft in the rock. "We're in for it, Thea. Better make for your cave where there are blankets." He caught her elbow and hurried her along the path before the cliff-houses. They made the half-mile at a quick trot, and as they ran the rocks and the sky and the air between the cliffs turned a turbid green, like the color in a moss agate. When they reached the blanketed rock room, they looked at each other and laughed. Their faces had taken on a greenish pallor. Thea's hair, even, was green.

"Dark as pitch in here," Fred exclaimed as they hurried over the old rock doorstep. "But it's warm. The rocks hold the heat. It's going to be terribly cold outside, all right." He was interrupted by a deafening peal of thunder. "Lord, what an echo! Lucky you don't mind. It's worth watching out there. We needn't come in yet."

The green light grew murkier and murkier. The smaller vegetation was blotted out. The yuccas, the cedars, and PINONS stood dark and rigid, like bronze. The swallows flew up with sharp, terrified twitterings. Even the quaking asps were still. While Fred and Thea watched from the doorway, the light changed to purple. Clouds of dark vapor, like chlorine gas, began to float down from the head of the canyon and hung between them and the cliff-houses in the opposite wall. Before they knew it, the wall itself had disappeared. The air was positively venomous-looking, and grew colder every minute. The thunder seemed to crash against one cliff, then against the other, and to go shrieking off into the inner canyon.

The moment the rain broke, it beat the vapors down. In the gulf before them the water fell in spouts, and dashed from the high cliffs overhead. It tore aspens and chokecherry bushes out of the ground and left the yuccas hanging by their tough roots. Only the little cedars stood black and unmoved in the torrents that fell from so far above. The rock chamber was full of fine spray from the streams of water that shot over the doorway. Thea crept to the back wall and rolled herself in a blanket, and Fred threw the heavier blankets over her. The wool of the Navajo sheep was soon kindled by the warmth of her body, and was impenetrable to dampness. Her hair, where it hung below the rubber hat, gathered the moisture like a sponge. Fred put on the slicker, tied the sweater about his neck, and settled himself cross-legged beside her. The chamber was so dark that, although he could see the outline of her head and shoulders, he could not see her face. He struck a wax match to light his pipe. As he sheltered it between his hands, it sizzled and sputtered, throwing a yellow flicker over Thea and her blankets.

"You look like a gypsy," he said as he dropped the match. "Any one you'd rather be shut up with than me? No? Sure about that?"

"I think I am. Aren't you cold?"

"Not especially." Fred smoked in silence, listening to the roar of the water outside. "We may not get away from here right away," he remarked.

"I shan't mind. Shall you?"

He laughed grimly and pulled on his pipe. "Do you know where you're at, Miss Thea Kronborg?" he said at last. "You've got me going pretty hard, I suppose you know. I've had a lot of sweethearts, but I've never been so much-- engrossed before. What are you going to do about it?" He heard nothing from the blankets. "Are you going to play fair, or is it about my cue to cut away?"

"I'll play fair. I don't see why you want to go."

"What do you want me around for?--to play with?"

Thea struggled up among the blankets. "I want you for everything. I don't know whether I'm what people call in love with you or not. In Moonstone that meant sitting in a hammock with somebody. I don't want to sit in a hammock with you, but I want to do almost everything else. Oh, hundreds of things!"

"If I run away, will you go with me?"

"I don't know. I'll have to think about that. Maybe I would." She freed herself from her wrappings and stood up. "It's not raining so hard now. Hadn't we better start this minute? It will be night before we get to Biltmer's."

Fred struck another match. "It's seven. I don't know how much of the path may be washed away. I don't even know whether I ought to let you try it without a lantern."

Thea went to the doorway and looked out. "There's nothing else to do. The sweater and the slicker will keep me dry, and this will be my chance to find out whether these shoes are really water-tight. They cost a week's salary." She retreated to the back of the cave. "It's getting blacker every minute."

Ottenburg took a brandy flask from his coat pocket. "Better have some of this before we start. Can you take it without water?"

Thea lifted it obediently to her lips. She put on the sweater and Fred helped her to get the clumsy slicker on over it. He buttoned it and fastened the high collar. She could feel that his hands were hurried and clumsy. The coat was too big, and he took off his necktie and belted it in at the waist. While she tucked her hair more securely under the rubber hat he stood in front of her, between her and the gray doorway, without moving.

"Are you ready to go?" she asked carelessly.

"If you are," he spoke quietly, without moving, except to bend his head forward a little.

Thea laughed and put her hands on his shoulders. "You know how to handle me, don't you?" she whispered. For the first time, she kissed him without constraint or embarrassment.

"Thea, Thea, Thea!" Fred whispered her name three times, shaking her a little as if to waken her. It was too dark to see, but he could feel that she was smiling.

When she kissed him she had not hidden her face on his shoulder,--she had risen a little on her toes, and stood straight and free. In that moment when he came close to her actual personality, he felt in her the same expansion that he had noticed at Mrs. Nathanmeyer's. She became freer and stronger under impulses. When she rose to meet him like that, he felt her flash into everything that she had ever suggested to him, as if she filled out her own shadow.

She pushed him away and shot past him out into the rain. "Now for it, Fred," she called back exultantly. The rain was pouring steadily down through the dying gray twilight, and muddy streams were spouting and foaming over the cliff.

Fred caught her and held her back. "Keep behind me, Thea. I don't know about the path. It may be gone altogether. Can't tell what there is under this water."

But the path was older than the white man's Arizona. The rush of water had washed away the dust and stones that lay on the surface, but the rock skeleton of the Indian trail was there, ready for the foot. Where the streams poured down through gullies, there was always a cedar or a PINON to cling to. By wading and slipping and climbing, they got along. As they neared the head of the canyon, where the path lifted and rose in steep loops to the surface of the plateau, the climb was more difficult. The earth above had broken away and washed down over the trail, bringing rocks and bushes and even young trees with it. The last ghost of daylight was dying and there was no time to lose. The canyon behind them was already black.

"We've got to go right through the top of this pine tree, Thea. No time to hunt a way around. Give me your hand." After they had crashed through the mass of branches, Fred stopped abruptly. "Gosh, what a hole! Can you jump it? Wait a minute."

He cleared the washout, slipped on the wet rock at the farther side, and caught himself just in time to escape a tumble. "If I could only find something to hold to, I could give you a hand. It's so cursed dark, and there are no trees here where they're needed. Here's something; it's a root. It will hold all right." He braced himself on the rock, gripped the crooked root with one hand and swung himself across toward Thea, holding out his arm. "Good jump! I must say you don't lose your nerve in a tight place. Can you keep at it a little longer? We're almost out. Have to make that next ledge. Put your foot on my knee and catch something to pull by."

Thea went up over his shoulder. "It's hard ground up here," she panted. "Did I wrench your arm when I slipped then? It was a cactus I grabbed, and it startled me."

"Now, one more pull and we're on the level."

They emerged gasping upon the black plateau. In the last five minutes the darkness had solidified and it seemed as if the skies were pouring black water. They could not see where the sky ended or the plain began. The light at the ranch house burned a steady spark through the rain. Fred drew Thea's arm through his and they struck off toward the light. They could not see each other, and the rain at their backs seemed to drive them along. They kept laughing as they stumbled over tufts of grass or stepped into slippery pools. They were delighted with each other and with the adventure which lay behind them.

"I can't even see the whites of your eyes, Thea. But I'd know who was here stepping out with me, anywhere. Part coyote you are, by the feel of you. When you make up your mind to jump, you jump! My gracious, what's the matter with your hand?"

"Cactus spines. Didn't I tell you when I grabbed the cactus? I thought it was a root. Are we going straight?"

"I don't know. Somewhere near it, I think. I'm very comfortable, aren't you? You're warm, except your cheeks. How funny they are when they're wet. Still, you always feel like you. I like this. I could walk to Flagstaff. It's fun, not being able to see anything. I feel surer of you when I can't see you. Will you run away with me?"

Thea laughed. "I won't run far to-night. I'll think about it. Look, Fred, there's somebody coming."

"Henry, with his lantern. Good enough! Halloo! Hallo--o--o!" Fred shouted.

The moving light bobbed toward them. In half an hour Thea was in her big feather bed, drinking hot lentil soup, and almost before the soup was swallowed she was asleep.

VIII

ON the first day of September Fred Ottenburg and Thea Kronborg left Flagstaff by the east-bound express. As the bright morning advanced, they sat alone on the rear platform of the observation car, watching the yellow miles unfold and disappear. With complete content they saw the brilliant, empty country flash by. They were tired of the desert and the dead races, of a world without change or ideas. Fred said he was glad to sit back and let the Santa Fe do the work for a while.

"And where are we going, anyhow?" he added.

"To Chicago, I suppose. Where else would we be going?" Thea hunted for a handkerchief in her handbag.

"I wasn't sure, so I had the trunks checked to Albuquerque. We can recheck there to Chicago, if you like. Why Chicago? You'll never go back to Bowers. Why wouldn't this be a good time to make a run for it? We could take the southern branch at Albuquerque, down to El Paso, and then over into Mexico. We are exceptionally free. Nobody waiting for us anywhere."

Thea sighted along the steel rails that quivered in the light behind them. "I don't see why I couldn't marry you in Chicago, as well as any place," she brought out with some embarrassment.

Fred took the handbag out of her nervous clasp and swung it about on his finger. "You've no particular love for that spot, have you? Besides, as I've told you, my family would make a row. They are an excitable lot. They discuss and argue everlastingly. The only way I can ever put anything through is to go ahead, and convince them afterward."

"Yes; I understand. I don't mind that. I don't want to marry your family. I'm sure you wouldn't want to marry mine. But I don't see why we have to go so far."

"When we get to Winslow, you look about the freight yards and you'll probably see several yellow cars with my name on them. That's why, my dear. When your visiting-card is on every beer bottle, you can't do things quietly. Things get into the papers." As he watched her troubled expression, he grew anxious. He leaned forward on his camp-chair, and kept twirling the handbag between his knees. "Here's a suggestion, Thea," he said presently. "Dismiss it if you don't like it: suppose we go down to Mexico on the chance. You've never seen anything like Mexico City; it will be a lark for you, anyhow. If you change your mind, and don't want to marry me, you can go back to Chicago, and I'll take a steamer from Vera Cruz and go up to New York. When I get to Chicago, you'll be at work, and nobody will ever be the wiser. No reason why we shouldn't both travel in Mexico, is there? You'll be traveling alone. I'll merely tell you the right places to stop, and come to take you driving. I won't put any pressure on you. Have I ever?" He swung the bag toward her and looked up under her hat.

"No, you haven't," she murmured. She was thinking that her own position might be less difficult if he had used what he called pressure. He clearly wished her to take the responsibility.

"You have your own future in the back of your mind all the time," Fred began, "and I have it in mine. I'm not going to try to carry you off, as I might another girl. If you wanted to quit me, I couldn't hold you, no matter how many times you had married me. I don't want to overpersuade you. But I'd like mighty well to get you down to that jolly old city, where everything would please you, and give myself a chance. Then, if you thought you could have a better time with me than without me, I'd try to grab you before you changed your mind. You are not a sentimental person."

Thea drew her veil down over her face. "I think I am, a little; about you," she said quietly. Fred's irony somehow hurt her.

"What's at the bottom of your mind, Thea?" he asked hurriedly. "I can't tell. Why do you consider it at all, if you're not sure? Why are you here with me now?"

Her face was half-averted. He was thinking that it looked older and more firm--almost hard--under a veil.

"Isn't it possible to do things without having any very clear reason?" she asked slowly. "I have no plan in the back of my mind. Now that I'm with you, I want to be with you; that's all. I can't settle down to being alone again. I am here to-day because I want to be with you to-day." She paused. "One thing, though; if I gave you my word, I'd keep it. And you could hold me, though you don't seem to think so. Maybe I'm not sentimental, but I'm not very light, either. If I went off with you like this, it wouldn't be to amuse myself."

Ottenburg's eyes fell. His lips worked nervously for a moment. "Do you mean that you really care for me, Thea Kronborg?" he asked unsteadily.

"I guess so. It's like anything else. It takes hold of you and you've got to go through with it, even if you're afraid. I was afraid to leave Moonstone, and afraid to leave Harsanyi. But I had to go through with it."

"And are you afraid now?" Fred asked slowly.

"Yes; more than I've ever been. But I don't think I could go back. The past closes up behind one, somehow. One would rather have a new kind of misery. The old kind seems like death or unconsciousness. You can't force your life back into that mould again. No, one can't go back." She rose and stood by the back grating of the platform, her hand on the brass rail.

Fred went to her side. She pushed up her veil and turned her most glowing face to him. Her eyes were wet and there were tears on her lashes, but she was smiling the rare, whole-hearted smile he had seen once or twice before. He looked at her shining eyes, her parted lips, her chin a little lifted. It was as if they were colored by a sunrise he could not see. He put his hand over hers and clasped it with a strength she felt. Her eyelashes trembled, her mouth softened, but her eyes were still brilliant.

"Will you always be like you were down there, if I go with you?" she asked under her breath.

His fingers tightened on hers. "By God, I will!" he muttered.

"That's the only promise I'll ask you for. Now go away for a while and let me think about it. Come back at lunchtime and I'll tell you. Will that do?"

"Anything will do, Thea, if you'll only let me keep an eye on you. The rest of the world doesn't interest me much. You've got me in deep."

Fred dropped her hand and turned away. As he glanced back from the front end of the observation car, he saw that she was still standing there, and any one would have known that she was brooding over something. The earnestness of her head and shoulders had a certain nobility. He stood looking at her for a moment.

When he reached the forward smoking-car, Fred took a seat at the end, where he could shut the other passengers from his sight. He put on his traveling-cap and sat down wearily, keeping his head near the window. "In any case, I shall help her more than I shall hurt her," he kept saying to himself. He admitted that this was not the only motive which impelled him, but it was one of them. "I'll make it my business in life to get her on. There's nothing else I care about so much as seeing her have her chance. She hasn't touched her real force yet. She isn't even aware of it. Lord, don't I know something about them? There isn't one of them that has such a depth to draw from. She'll be one of the great artists of our time. Playing accompaniments for that cheese-faced sneak! I'll get her off to Germany this winter, or take her. She hasn't got any time to waste now. I'll make it up to her, all right."

Ottenburg certainly meant to make it up to her, in so far as he could. His feeling was as generous as strong human feelings are likely to be. The only trouble was, that he was married already, and had been since he was twenty.

His older friends in Chicago, people who had been friends of his family, knew of the unfortunate state of his personal affairs; but they were people whom in the natural course of things Thea Kronborg would scarcely meet. Mrs. Frederick Ottenburg lived in California, at Santa Barbara, where her health was supposed to be better than elsewhere, and her husband lived in Chicago. He visited his wife every winter to reinforce her position, and his devoted mother, although her hatred for her daughter-inlaw was scarcely approachable in words, went to Santa Barbara every year to make things look better and to relieve her son.

When Frederick Ottenburg was beginning his junior year at Harvard, he got a letter from Dick Brisbane, a Kansas City boy he knew, telling him that his FIANCEE, Miss Edith Beers, was going to New York to buy her trousseau. She would be at the Holland House, with her aunt and a girl from Kansas City who was to be a bridesmaid, for two weeks or more. If Ottenburg happened to be going down to New York, would he call upon Miss Beers and "show her a good time"?

Fred did happen to be going to New York. He was going down from New Haven, after the Thanksgiving game. He called on Miss Beers and found her, as he that night telegraphed Brisbane, a "ripping beauty, no mistake." He took her and her aunt and her uninteresting friend to the theater and to the opera, and he asked them to lunch with him at the Waldorf. He took no little pains in arranging the luncheon with the head waiter. Miss Beers was the sort of girl with whom a young man liked to seem experienced. She was dark and slender and fiery. She was witty and slangy; said daring things and carried them off with NONCHALANCE. Her childish extravagance and contempt for all the serious facts of life could be charged to her father's generosity and his long packing-house purse. Freaks that would have been vulgar and ostentatious in a more simpleminded girl, in Miss Beers seemed whimsical and picturesque. She darted about in magnificent furs and pumps and close-clinging gowns, though that was the day of full skirts. Her hats were large and floppy. When she wriggled out of her moleskin coat at luncheon, she looked like a slim black weasel. Her satin dress was a mere sheath, so conspicuous by its severity and scantness that every one in the dining-room stared. She ate nothing but alligator-pear salad and hothouse grapes, drank a little champagne, and took cognac in her coffee. She ridiculed, in the raciest slang, the singers they had heard at the opera the night before, and when her aunt pretended to reprove her, she murmured indifferently, "What's the matter with you, old sport?" She rattled on with a subdued loquaciousness, always keeping her voice low and monotonous, always looking out of the corner of her eye and speaking, as it were, in asides, out of the corner of her mouth. She was scornful of everything,--which became her eyebrows. Her face was mobile and discontented, her eyes quick and black. There was a sort of smouldering fire about her, young Ottenburg thought. She entertained him prodigiously.

After luncheon Miss Beers said she was going uptown to be fitted, and that she would go alone because her aunt made her nervous. When Fred held her coat for her, she murmured, "Thank you, Alphonse," as if she were addressing the waiter. As she stepped into a hansom, with a long stretch of thin silk stocking, she said negligently, over her fur collar, "Better let me take you along and drop you somewhere." He sprang in after her, and she told the driver to go to the Park.

It was a bright winter day, and bitterly cold. Miss Beers asked Fred to tell her about the game at New Haven, and when he did so paid no attention to what he said. She sank back into the hansom and held her muff before her face, lowering it occasionally to utter laconic remarks about the people in the carriages they passed, interrupting Fred's narrative in a disconcerting manner. As they entered the Park he happened to glance under her wide black hat at her black eyes and hair--the muff hid everything else--and discovered that she was crying. To his solicitous inquiry she replied that it "was enough to make you damp, to go and try on dresses to marry a man you weren't keen about."

Further explanations followed. She had thought she was "perfectly cracked" about Brisbane, until she met Fred at the Holland House three days ago. Then she knew she would scratch Brisbane's eyes out if she married him. What was she going to do?

Fred told the driver to keep going. What did she want to do? Well, she didn't know. One had to marry somebody, after all the machinery had been put in motion. Perhaps she might as well scratch Brisbane as anybody else; for scratch she would, if she didn't get what she wanted.

Of course, Fred agreed, one had to marry somebody. And certainly this girl beat anything he had ever been up against before. Again he told the driver to go ahead. Did she mean that she would think of marrying him, by any chance? Of course she did, Alphonse. Hadn't he seen that all over her face three days ago? If he hadn't, he was a snowball.

By this time Fred was beginning to feel sorry for the driver. Miss Beers, however, was compassionless. After a few more turns, Fred suggested tea at the Casino. He was very cold himself, and remembering the shining silk hose and pumps, he wondered that the girl was not frozen. As they got out of the hansom, he slipped the driver a bill and told him to have something hot while he waited.

At the tea-table, in a snug glass enclosure, with the steam sputtering in the pipes beside them and a brilliant winter sunset without, they developed their plan. Miss Beers had with her plenty of money, destined for tradesmen, which she was quite willing to divert into other channels--the first excitement of buying a trousseau had worn off, anyway. It was very much like any other shopping. Fred had his allowance and a few hundred he had won on the game. She would meet him to-morrow morning at the Jersey ferry. They could take one of the west-bound Pennsylvania trains and go--anywhere, some place where the laws weren't too fussy.--Fred had not even thought about the laws!--It would be all right with her father; he knew Fred's family.

Now that they were engaged, she thought she would like to drive a little more. They were jerked about in the cab for another hour through the deserted Park. Miss Beers, having removed her hat, reclined upon Fred's shoulder.

The next morning they left Jersey City by the latest fast train out. They had some misadventures, crossed several States before they found a justice obliging enough to marry two persons whose names automatically instigated inquiry. The bride's family were rather pleased with her originality; besides, any one of the Ottenburg boys was clearly a better match than young Brisbane. With Otto Ottenburg, however, the affair went down hard, and to his wife, the once proud Katarina Furst, such a disappointment was almost unbearable. Her sons had always been clay in her hands, and now the GELIEBTER SOHN had escaped her.

Beers, the packer, gave his daughter a house in St. Louis, and Fred went into his father's business. At the end of a year, he was mutely appealing to his mother for sympathy. At the end of two, he was drinking and in open rebellion. He had learned to detest his wife. Her wastefulness and cruelty revolted him. The ignorance and the fatuous conceit which lay behind her grimacing mask of slang and ridicule humiliated him so deeply that he became absolutely reckless. Her grace was only an uneasy wriggle, her audacity was the result of insolence and envy, and her wit was restless spite. As her personal mannerisms grew more and more odious to him, he began to dull his perceptions with champagne. He had it for tea, he drank it with dinner, and during the evening he took enough to insure that he would be well insulated when he got home. This behavior spread alarm among his friends. It was scandalous, and it did not occur among brewers. He was violating the NOBLESSE OBLIGE of his guild. His father and his father's partners looked alarmed.

When Fred's mother went to him and with clasped hands entreated an explanation, he told her that the only trouble was that he couldn't hold enough wine to make life endurable, so he was going to get out from under and enlist in the navy. He didn't want anything but the shirt on his back and clean salt air. His mother could look out; he was going to make a scandal.

Mrs. Otto Ottenburg went to Kansas City to see Mr. Beers, and had the satisfaction of telling him that he had brought up his daughter like a savage, EINE UNGEBILDETE. All the Ottenburgs and all the Beers, and many of their friends, were drawn into the quarrel. It was to public opinion, however and not to his mother's activities, that Fred owed his partial escape from bondage. The cosmopolitan brewing world of St. Louis had conservative standards. The Ottenburgs' friends were not predisposed in favor of the plunging Kansas City set, and they disliked young Fred's wife from the day that she was brought among them. They found her ignorant and ill-bred and insufferably impertinent. When they became aware of how matters were going between her and Fred, they omitted no opportunity to snub her. Young Fred had always been popular, and St. Louis people took up his cause with warmth. Even the younger men, among whom Mrs. Fred tried to draft a following, at first avoided and then ignored her. Her defeat was so conspicuous, her life became such a desert, that she at last consented to accept the house in Santa Barbara which Mrs. Otto Ottenburg had long owned and cherished. This villa, with its luxuriant gardens, was the price of Fred's furlough. His mother was only too glad to offer it in his behalf. As soon as his wife was established in California, Fred was transferred from St. Louis to Chicago.

A divorce was the one thing Edith would never, never, give him. She told him so, and she told his family so, and her father stood behind her. She would enter into no arrangement that might eventually lead to divorce. She had insulted her husband before guests and servants, had scratched his face, thrown hand-mirrors and hairbrushes and nail-scissors at him often enough, but she knew that Fred was hardly the fellow who would go into court and offer that sort of evidence. In her behavior with other men she was discreet.

After Fred went to Chicago, his mother visited him often, and dropped a word to her old friends there, who were already kindly disposed toward the young man. They gossiped as little as was compatible with the interest they felt, undertook to make life agreeable for Fred, and told his story only where they felt it would do good: to girls who seemed to find the young brewer attractive. So far, he had behaved well, and had kept out of entanglements.

Since he was transferred to Chicago, Fred had been abroad several times, and had fallen more and more into the way of going about among young artists,--people with whom personal relations were incidental. With women, and even girls, who had careers to follow, a young man might have pleasant friendships without being regarded as a prospective suitor or lover. Among artists his position was not irregular, because with them his marriageableness was not an issue. His tastes, his enthusiasm, and his agreeable personality made him welcome.

With Thea Kronborg he had allowed himself more liberty than he usually did in his friendships or gallantries with young artists, because she seemed to him distinctly not the marrying kind. She impressed him as equipped to be an artist, and to be nothing else; already directed, concentrated, formed as to mental habit. He was generous and sympathetic, and she was lonely and needed friendship; needed cheerfulness. She had not much power of reaching out toward useful people or useful experiences, did not see opportunities. She had no tact about going after good positions or enlisting the interest of influential persons. She antagonized people rather than conciliated them. He discovered at once that she had a merry side, a robust humor that was deep and hearty, like her laugh, but it slept most of the time under her own doubts and the dullness of her life. She had not what is called a "sense of humor." That is, she had no intellectual humor; no power to enjoy the absurdities of people, no relish of their pretentiousness and inconsistencies--which only depressed her. But her joviality, Fred felt, was an asset, and ought to be developed. He discovered that she was more receptive and more effective under a pleasant stimulus than she was under the gray grind which she considered her salvation. She was still Methodist enough to believe that if a thing were hard and irksome, it must be good for her. And yet, whatever she did well was spontaneous. Under the least glow of excitement, as at Mrs. Nathanmeyer's, he had seen the apprehensive, frowning drudge of Bowers's studio flash into a resourceful and consciously beautiful woman.

His interest in Thea was serious, almost from the first, and so sincere that he felt no distrust of himself. He believed that he knew a great deal more about her possibilities than Bowers knew, and he liked to think that he had given her a stronger hold on life. She had never seen herself or known herself as she did at Mrs. Nathanmeyer's musical evenings.

She had been a different girl ever since. He had not anticipated that she would grow more fond of him than his immediate usefulness warranted. He thought he knew the ways of artists, and, as he said, she must have been "at it from her cradle." He had imagined, perhaps, but never really believed, that he would find her waiting for him sometime as he found her waiting on the day he reached the Biltmer ranch. Once he found her so--well, he did not pretend to be anything more or less than a reasonably well-intentioned young man. A lovesick girl or a flirtatious woman he could have handled easily enough. But a personality like that, unconsciously revealing itself for the first time under the exaltation of a personal feeling,--what could one do but watch it? As he used to say to himself, in reckless moments back there in the canyon, "You can't put out a sunrise." He had to watch it, and then he had to share it.

Besides, was he really going to do her any harm? The Lord knew he would marry her if he could! Marriage would be an incident, not an end with her; he was sure of that. If it were not he, it would be some one else; some one who would be a weight about her neck, probably; who would hold her back and beat her down and divert her from the first plunge for which he felt she was gathering all her energies. He meant to help her, and he could not think of another man who would. He went over his unmarried friends, East and West, and he could not think of one who would know what she was driving at--or care. The clever ones were selfish, the kindly ones were stupid.

"Damn it, if she's going to fall in love with somebody, it had better be me than any of the others--of the sort she'd find. Get her tied up with some conceited ass who'd try to make her over, train her like a puppy! Give one of 'em a big nature like that, and he'd be horrified. He wouldn't show his face in the clubs until he'd gone after her and combed her down to conform to some fool idea in his own head--put there by some other woman, too, his first sweetheart or his grandmother or a maiden aunt. At least, I understand her. I know what she needs and where she's bound, and I mean to see that she has a fighting chance."

His own conduct looked crooked, he admitted; but he asked himself whether, between men and women, all ways were not more or less crooked. He believed those which are called straight were the most dangerous of all. They seemed to him, for the most part, to lie between windowless stone walls, and their rectitude had been achieved at the expense of light and air. In their unquestioned regularity lurked every sort of human cruelty and meanness, and every kind of humiliation and suffering. He would rather have any woman he cared for wounded than crushed. He would deceive her not once, he told himself fiercely, but a hundred times, to keep her free.

When Fred went back to the observation car at one o'clock, after the luncheon call, it was empty, and he found Thea alone on the platform. She put out her hand, and met his eyes.

"It's as I said. Things have closed behind me. I can't go back, so I am going on--to Mexico?" She lifted her face with an eager, questioning smile.

Fred met it with a sinking heart. Had he really hoped she would give him another answer? He would have given pretty much anything--But there, that did no good. He could give only what he had. Things were never complete in this world; you had to snatch at them as they came or go without. Nobody could look into her face and draw back, nobody who had any courage. She had courage enough for anything--look at her mouth and chin and eyes! Where did it come from, that light? How could a face, a familiar face, become so the picture of hope, be painted with the very colors of youth's exaltation? She was right; she was not one of those who draw back. Some people get on by avoiding dangers, others by riding through them.

They stood by the railing looking back at the sand levels, both feeling that the train was steaming ahead very fast. Fred's mind was a confusion of images and ideas. Only two things were clear to him: the force of her determination, and the belief that, handicapped as he was, he could do better by her than another man would do. He knew he would always remember her, standing there with that expectant, forward-looking smile, enough to turn the future into summer.

PART V. DR. ARCHIE'S VENTURE

I

DR. HOWARD ARCHIE had come down to Denver for a meeting of the stockholders in the San Felipe silver mine. It was not absolutely necessary for him to come, but he had no very pressing cases at home. Winter was closing down in Moonstone, and he dreaded the dullness of it. On the 10th day of January, therefore, he was registered at the Brown Palace Hotel. On the morning of the 11th he came down to breakfast to find the streets white and the air thick with snow. A wild northwester was blowing down from the mountains, one of those beautiful storms that wrap Denver in dry, furry snow, and make the city a loadstone to thousands of men in the mountains and on the plains. The brakemen out on their box-cars, the miners up in their diggings, the lonely homesteaders in the sand hills of Yucca and Kit Carson Counties, begin to think of Denver, muffled in snow, full of food and drink and good cheer, and to yearn for her with that admiration which makes her, more than other American cities, an object of sentiment.

Howard Archie was glad he had got in before the storm came. He felt as cheerful as if he had received a legacy that morning, and he greeted the clerk with even greater friendliness than usual when he stopped at the desk for his mail. In the dining-room he found several old friends seated here and there before substantial breakfasts: cattlemen and mining engineers from odd corners of the State, all looking fresh and well pleased with themselves. He had a word with one and another before he sat down at the little table by a window, where the Austrian head waiter stood attentively behind a chair. After his breakfast was put before him, the doctor began to run over his letters. There was one directed in Thea Kronborg's handwriting, forwarded from Moonstone. He saw with astonishment, as he put another lump of sugar into his cup, that this letter bore a New York postmark. He had known that Thea was in Mexico, traveling with some Chicago people, but New York, to a Denver man, seems much farther away than Mexico City. He put the letter behind his plate, upright against the stem of his water goblet, and looked at it thoughtfully while he drank his second cup of coffee. He had been a little anxious about Thea; she had not written to him for a long while.

As he never got good coffee at home, the doctor always drank three cups for breakfast when he was in Denver. Oscar knew just when to bring him a second pot, fresh and smoking. "And more cream, Oscar, please. You know I like lots of cream," the doctor murmured, as he opened the square envelope, marked in the upper right-hand corner, "Everett House, Union Square." The text of the letter was as follows:--

DEAR DOCTOR ARCHIE:--

I have not written to you for a long time, but it has not been unintentional. I could not write you frankly, and so I would not write at all. I can be frank with you now, but not by letter. It is a great deal to ask, but I wonder if you could come to New York to help me out? I have got into difficulties, and I need your advice. I need your friendship. I am afraid I must even ask you to lend me money, if you can without serious inconvenience. I have to go to Germany to study, and it can't be put off any longer. My voice is ready. Needless to say, I don't want any word of this to reach my family. They are the last people I would turn to, though I love my mother dearly. If you can come, please telegraph me at this hotel. Don't despair of me. I'll make it up to you yet.

Your old friend, THEA KRONBORG.

This in a bold, jagged handwriting with a Gothic turn to the letters,--something between a highly sophisticated hand and a very unsophisticated one,--not in the least smooth or flowing.

The doctor bit off the end of a cigar nervously and read the letter through again, fumbling distractedly in his pockets for matches, while the waiter kept trying to call his attention to the box he had just placed before him. At last Oscar came out, as if the idea had just struck him, "Matches, sir?"

"Yes, thank you." The doctor slipped a coin into his palm and rose, crumpling Thea's letter in his hand and thrusting the others into his pocket unopened. He went back to the desk in the lobby and beckoned to the clerk, upon whose kindness he threw himself apologetically.

"Harry, I've got to pull out unexpectedly. Call up the Burlington, will you, and ask them to route me to New York the quickest way, and to let us know. Ask for the hour I'll get in. I have to wire."

"Certainly, Dr. Archie. Have it for you in a minute." The young man's pallid, clean-scraped face was all sympathetic interest as he reached for the telephone. Dr. Archie put out his hand and stopped him.

"Wait a minute. Tell me, first, is Captain Harris down yet?"

"No, sir. The Captain hasn't come down yet this morning."

"I'll wait here for him. If I don't happen to catch him, nail him and get me. Thank you, Harry."

The doctor spoke gratefully and turned away. He began to pace the lobby, his hands behind him, watching the bronze elevator doors like a hawk. At last Captain Harris issued from one of them, tall and imposing, wearing a Stetson and fierce mustaches, a fur coat on his arm, a solitaire glittering upon his little finger and another in his black satin ascot. He was one of the grand old bluffers of those good old days. As gullible as a schoolboy, he had managed, with his sharp eye and knowing air and twisted blond mustaches, to pass himself off for an astute financier, and the Denver papers respectfully referred to him as the Rothschild of Cripple Creek.

Dr. Archie stopped the Captain on his way to breakfast. "Must see you a minute, Captain. Can't wait. Want to sell you some shares in the San Felipe. Got to raise money."

The Captain grandly bestowed his hat upon an eager porter who had already lifted his fur coat tenderly from his arm and stood nursing it. In removing his hat, the Captain exposed a bald, flushed dome, thatched about the ears with yellowish gray hair. "Bad time to sell, doctor. You want to hold on to San Felipe, and buy more. What have you got to raise?"

"Oh, not a great sum. Five or six thousand. I've been buying up close and have run short."

"I see, I see. Well, doctor, you'll have to let me get through that door. I was out last night, and I'm going to get my bacon, if you lose your mine." He clapped Archie on the shoulder and pushed him along in front of him. "Come ahead with me, and we'll talk business."

Dr. Archie attended the Captain and waited while he gave his order, taking the seat the old promoter indicated.

"Now, sir," the Captain turned to him, "you don't want to sell anything. You must be under the impression that I'm one of these damned New England sharks that get their pound of flesh off the widow and orphan. If you're a little short, sign a note and I'll write a check. That's the way gentlemen do business. If you want to put up some San Felipe as collateral, let her go, but I shan't touch a share of it. Pens and ink, please, Oscar,"--he lifted a large forefinger to the Austrian.

The Captain took out his checkbook and a book of blank notes, and adjusted his nose-nippers. He wrote a few words in one book and Archie wrote a few in the other. Then they each tore across perforations and exchanged slips of paper.

"That's the way. Saves office rent," the Captain commented with satisfaction, returning the books to his pocket. "And now, Archie, where are you off to?"

"Got to go East to-night. A deal waiting for me in New York." Dr. Archie rose.

The Captain's face brightened as he saw Oscar approaching with a tray, and he began tucking the corner of his napkin inside his collar, over his ascot. "Don't let them unload anything on you back there, doctor," he said genially, "and don't let them relieve you of anything, either. Don't let them get any Cripple stuff off you. We can manage our own silver out here, and we're going to take it out by the ton, sir!"

The doctor left the dining-room, and after another consultation with the clerk, he wrote his first telegram to Thea:--

Miss Thea Kronborg, Everett House, New York.

Will call at your hotel eleven o'clock Friday morning. Glad to come. Thank you. ARCHIE

He stood and heard the message actually clicked off on the wire, with the feeling that she was hearing the click at the other end. Then he sat down in the lobby and wrote a note to his wife and one to the other doctor in Moonstone. When he at last issued out into the storm, it was with a feeling of elation rather than of anxiety. Whatever was wrong, he could make it right. Her letter had practically said so.

He tramped about the snowy streets, from the bank to the Union Station, where he shoved his money under the grating of the ticket window as if he could not get rid of it fast enough. He had never been in New York, never been farther east than Buffalo. "That's rather a shame," he reflected boyishly as he put the long tickets in his pocket, "for a man nearly forty years old." However, he thought as he walked up toward the club, he was on the whole glad that his first trip had a human interest, that he was going for something, and because he was wanted. He loved holidays. He felt as if he were going to Germany himself. "Queer,"--he went over it with the snow blowing in his face,--"but that sort of thing is more interesting than mines and making your daily bread. It's worth paying out to be in on it,--for a fellow like me. And when it's Thea--Oh, I back her!" he laughed aloud as he burst in at the door of the Athletic Club, powdered with snow.

Archie sat down before the New York papers and ran over the advertisements of hotels, but he was too restless to read. Probably he had better get a new overcoat, and he was not sure about the shape of his collars. "I don't want to look different to her from everybody else there," he mused. "I guess I'll go down and have Van look me over. He'll put me right."

So he plunged out into the snow again and started for his tailor's. When he passed a florist's shop he stopped and looked in at the window, smiling; how naturally pleasant things recalled one another. At the tailor's he kept whistling, "Flow gently, Sweet Afton," while Van Dusen advised him, until that resourceful tailor and haberdasher exclaimed, "You must have a date back there, doctor; you behave like a bridegroom," and made him remember that he wasn't one.

Before he let him go, Van put his finger on the Masonic pin in his client's lapel. "Mustn't wear that, doctor. Very bad form back there."

II

FRED OTTENBURG, smartly dressed for the afternoon, with a long black coat and gaiters was sitting in the dusty parlor of the Everett House. His manner was not in accord with his personal freshness, the good lines of his clothes, and the shining smoothness of his hair. His attitude was one of deep dejection, and his face, though it had the cool, unimpeachable fairness possible only to a very blond young man, was by no means happy. A page shuffled into the room and looked about. When he made out the dark figure in a shadowy corner, tracing over the carpet pattern with a cane, he droned, "The lady says you can come up, sir."

Fred picked up his hat and gloves and followed the creature, who seemed an aged boy in uniform, through dark corridors that smelled of old carpets. The page knocked at the door of Thea's sitting-room, and then wandered away. Thea came to the door with a telegram in her hand. She asked Ottenburg to come in and pointed to one of the clumsy, sullen-looking chairs that were as thick as they were high. The room was brown with time, dark in spite of two windows that opened on Union Square, with dull curtains and carpet, and heavy, respectable-looking furniture in somber colors. The place was saved from utter dismalness by a coal fire under the black marble mantelpiece,--brilliantly reflected in a long mirror that hung between the two windows. This was the first time Fred had seen the room, and he took it in quickly, as he put down his hat and gloves.

Thea seated herself at the walnut writing-desk, still holding the slip of yellow paper. "Dr. Archie is coming," she said. "He will be here Friday morning."

"Well, that's good, at any rate," her visitor replied with a determined effort at cheerfulness. Then, turning to the fire, he added blankly, "If you want him."

"Of course I want him. I would never have asked such a thing of him if I hadn't wanted him a great deal. It's a very expensive trip." Thea spoke severely. Then she went on, in a milder tone. "He doesn't say anything about the money, but I think his coming means that he can let me have it."

Fred was standing before the mantel, rubbing his hands together nervously. "Probably. You are still determined to call on him?" He sat down tentatively in the chair Thea had indicated. "I don't see why you won't borrow from me, and let him sign with you, for instance. That would constitute a perfectly regular business transaction. I could bring suit against either of you for my money."

Thea turned toward him from the desk. "We won't take that up again, Fred. I should have a different feeling about it if I went on your money. In a way I shall feel freer on Dr. Archie's, and in another way I shall feel more bound. I shall try even harder." She paused. "He is almost like my father," she added irrelevantly.

"Still, he isn't, you know," Fred persisted. "It wouldn't be anything new. I've loaned money to students before, and got it back, too."

"Yes; I know you're generous," Thea hurried over it, "but this will be the best way. He will be here on Friday did I tell you?"

"I think you mentioned it. That's rather soon. May I smoke?" he took out a small cigarette case. "I suppose you'll be off next week?" he asked as he struck a match.

"Just as soon as I can," she replied with a restless movement of her arms, as if her dark-blue dress were too tight for her. "It seems as if I'd been here forever."

"And yet," the young man mused, "we got in only four days ago. Facts really don't count for much, do they? It's all in the way people feel: even in little things."

Thea winced, but she did not answer him. She put the telegram back in its envelope and placed it carefully in one of the pigeonholes of the desk.

"I suppose," Fred brought out with effort, "that your friend is in your confidence?"

"He always has been. I shall have to tell him about myself. I wish I could without dragging you in."

Fred shook himself. "Don't bother about where you drag me, please," he put in, flushing. "I don't give--" he subsided suddenly.

"I'm afraid," Thea went on gravely, "that he won't understand. He'll be hard on you."

Fred studied the white ash of his cigarette before he flicked it off. "You mean he'll see me as even worse than I am. Yes, I suppose I shall look very low to him: a fifthrate scoundrel. But that only matters in so far as it hurts his feelings."

Thea sighed. "We'll both look pretty low. And after all, we must really be just about as we shall look to him."

Ottenburg started up and threw his cigarette into the grate. "That I deny. Have you ever been really frank with this preceptor of your childhood, even when you WERE a child? Think a minute, have you? Of course not! From your cradle, as I once told you, you've been `doing it' on the side, living your own life, admitting to yourself things that would horrify him. You've always deceived him to the extent of letting him think you different from what you are. He couldn't understand then, he can't understand now. So why not spare yourself and him?"

She shook her head. "Of course, I've had my own thoughts. Maybe he has had his, too. But I've never done anything before that he would much mind. I must put myself right with him,--as right as I can,--to begin over. He'll make allowances for me. He always has. But I'm afraid he won't for you."

"Leave that to him and me. I take it you want me to see him?" Fred sat down again and began absently to trace the carpet pattern with his cane. "At the worst," he spoke wanderingly, "I thought you'd perhaps let me go in on the business end of it and invest along with you. You'd put in your talent and ambition and hard work, and I'd put in the money and--well, nobody's good wishes are to be scorned, not even mine. Then, when the thing panned out big, we could share together. Your doctor friend hasn't cared half so much about your future as I have."

"He's cared a good deal. He doesn't know as much about such things as you do. Of course you've been a great deal more help to me than any one else ever has," Thea said quietly. The black clock on the mantel began to strike. She listened to the five strokes and then said, "I'd have liked your helping me eight months ago. But now, you'd simply be keeping me."

"You weren't ready for it eight months ago." Fred leaned back at last in his chair. "You simply weren't ready for it. You were too tired. You were too timid. Your whole tone was too low. You couldn't rise from a chair like that,"--she had started up apprehensively and gone toward the window.--"You were fumbling and awkward. Since then you've come into your personality. You were always locking horns with it before. You were a sullen little drudge eight months ago, afraid of being caught at either looking or moving like yourself. Nobody could tell anything about you. A voice is not an instrument that's found ready-made. A voice is personality. It can be as big as a circus and as common as dirt.--There's good money in that kind, too, but I don't happen to be interested in them.--Nobody could tell much about what you might be able to do, last winter. I divined more than anybody else."

"Yes, I know you did." Thea walked over to the oldfashioned mantel and held her hands down to the glow of the fire. "I owe so much to you, and that's what makes things hard. That's why I have to get away from you altogether. I depend on you for so many things. Oh, I did even last winter, in Chicago!" She knelt down by the grate and held her hands closer to the coals. "And one thing leads to another."

Ottenburg watched her as she bent toward the fire. His glance brightened a little. "Anyhow, you couldn't look as you do now, before you knew me. You WERE clumsy. And whatever you do now, you do splendidly. And you can't cry enough to spoil your face for more than ten minutes. It comes right back, in spite of you. It's only since you've known me that you've let yourself be beautiful."

Without rising she turned her face away. Fred went on impetuously. "Oh, you can turn it away from me, Thea; you can take it away from me! All the same--" his spurt died and he fell back. "How can you turn on me so, after all!" he sighed.

"I haven't. But when you arranged with yourself to take me in like that, you couldn't have been thinking very kindly of me. I can't understand how you carried it through, when I was so easy, and all the circumstances were so easy."

Her crouching position by the fire became threatening. Fred got up, and Thea also rose.

"No," he said, "I can't make you see that now. Some time later, perhaps, you will understand better. For one thing, I honestly could not imagine that words, names, meant so much to you." Fred was talking with the desperation of a man who has put himself in the wrong and who yet feels that there was an idea of truth in his conduct. "Suppose that you had married your brakeman and lived with him year after year, caring for him even less than you do for your doctor, or for Harsanyi. I suppose you would have felt quite all right about it, because that relation has a name in good standing. To me, that seems--sickening!" He took a rapid turn about the room and then as Thea remained standing, he rolled one of the elephantine chairs up to the hearth for her.

"Sit down and listen to me for a moment, Thea." He began pacing from the hearthrug to the window and back again, while she sat down compliantly. "Don't you know most of the people in the world are not individuals at all? They never have an individual idea or experience. A lot of girls go to boarding-school together, come out the same season, dance at the same parties, are married off in groups, have their babies at about the same time, send their children to school together, and so the human crop renews itself. Such women know as much about the reality of the forms they go through as they know about the wars they learn the dates of. They get their most personal experiences out of novels and plays. Everything is second-hand with them. Why, you COULDN'T live like that."

Thea sat looking toward the mantel, her eyes half closed, her chin level, her head set as if she were enduring something. Her hands, very white, lay passive on her dark gown. From the window corner Fred looked at them and at her. He shook his head and flashed an angry, tormented look out into the blue twilight over the Square, through which muffled cries and calls and the clang of car bells came up from the street. He turned again and began to pace the floor, his hands in his pockets.

"Say what you will, Thea Kronborg, you are not that sort of person. You will never sit alone with a pacifier and a novel. You won't subsist on what the old ladies have put into the bottle for you. You will always break through into the realities. That was the first thing Harsanyi found out about you; that you couldn't be kept on the outside. If you'd lived in Moonstone all your life and got on with the discreet brakeman, you'd have had just the same nature. Your children would have been the realities then, probably. If they'd been commonplace, you'd have killed them with driving. You'd have managed some way to live twenty times as much as the people around you."

Fred paused. He sought along the shadowy ceiling and heavy mouldings for words. When he began again, his voice was lower, and at first he spoke with less conviction, though again it grew on him. "Now I knew all this--oh, knew it better than I can ever make you understand! You've been running a handicap. You had no time to lose. I wanted you to have what you need and to get on fast--get through with me, if need be; I counted on that. You've no time to sit round and analyze your conduct or your feelings. Other women give their whole lives to it. They've nothing else to do. Helping a man to get his divorce is a career for them; just the sort of intellectual exercise they like."

Fred dived fiercely into his pockets as if he would rip them out and scatter their contents to the winds. Stopping before her, he took a deep breath and went on again, this time slowly. "All that sort of thing is foreign to you. You'd be nowhere at it. You haven't that kind of mind. The grammatical niceties of conduct are dark to you. You're simple--and poetic." Fred's voice seemed to be wandering about in the thickening dusk. "You won't play much. You won't, perhaps, love many times." He paused. "And you did love me, you know. Your railroad friend would have understood me. I COULD have thrown you back. The reverse was there,--it stared me in the face,--but I couldn't pull it. I let you drive ahead." He threw out his hands. What Thea noticed, oddly enough, was the flash of the firelight on his cuff link. He turned again. "And you'll always drive ahead," he muttered. "It's your way."

There was a long silence. Fred had dropped into a chair. He seemed, after such an explosion, not to have a word left in him. Thea put her hand to the back of her neck and pressed it, as if the muscles there were aching.

"Well," she said at last, "I at least overlook more in you than I do in myself. I am always excusing you to myself. I don't do much else."

"Then why, in Heaven's name, won't you let me be your friend? You make a scoundrel of me, borrowing money from another man to get out of my clutches."

"If I borrow from him, it's to study. Anything I took from you would be different. As I said before, you'd be keeping me."

"Keeping! I like your language. It's pure Moonstone, Thea,--like your point of view. I wonder how long you'll be a Methodist." He turned away bitterly.

"Well, I've never said I wasn't Moonstone, have I? I am, and that's why I want Dr. Archie. I can't see anything so funny about Moonstone, you know." She pushed her chair back a little from the hearth and clasped her hands over her knee, still looking thoughtfully into the red coals. "We always come back to the same thing, Fred. The name, as you call it, makes a difference to me how I feel about myself. You would have acted very differently with a girl of your own kind, and that's why I can't take anything from you now. You've made everything impossible. Being married is one thing and not being married is the other thing, and that's all there is to it. I can't see how you reasoned with yourself, if you took the trouble to reason. You say I was too much alone, and yet what you did was to cut me off more than I ever had been. Now I'm going to try to make good to my friends out there. That's all there is left for me."

"Make good to your friends!" Fred burst out. "What one of them cares as I care, or believes as I believe? I've told you I'll never ask a gracious word from you until I can ask it with all the churches in Christendom at my back."

Thea looked up, and when she saw Fred's face, she thought sadly that he, too, looked as if things were spoiled for him. "If you know me as well as you say you do, Fred," she said slowly, "then you are not being honest with yourself. You know that I can't do things halfway. If you kept me at all--you'd keep me." She dropped her head wearily on her hand and sat with her forehead resting on her fingers.

Fred leaned over her and said just above his breath, "Then, when I get that divorce, you'll take it up with me again? You'll at least let me know, warn me, before there is a serious question of anybody else?"

Without lifting her head, Thea answered him. "Oh, I don't think there will ever be a question of anybody else. Not if I can help it. I suppose I've given you every reason to think there will be,--at once, on shipboard, any time."

Ottenburg drew himself up like a shot. "Stop it, Thea!" he said sharply. "That's one thing you've never done. That's like any common woman." He saw her shoulders lift a little and grow calm. Then he went to the other side of the room and took up his hat and gloves from the sofa. He came back cheerfully. "I didn't drop in to bully you this afternoon. I came to coax you to go out for tea with me somewhere." He waited, but she did not look up or lift her head, still sunk on her hand.

Her handkerchief had fallen. Fred picked it up and put it on her knee, pressing her fingers over it. "Good-night, dear and wonderful," he whispered,--"wonderful and dear! How can you ever get away from me when I will always follow you, through every wall, through every door, wherever you go." He looked down at her bent head, and the curve of her neck that was so sad. He stooped, and with his lips just touched her hair where the firelight made it ruddiest. "I didn't know I had it in me, Thea. I thought it was all a fairy tale. I don't know myself any more." He closed his eyes and breathed deeply. "The salt's all gone out of your hair. It's full of sun and wind again. I believe it has memories." Again she heard him take a deep breath. "I could do without you for a lifetime, if that would give you to yourself. A woman like you doesn't find herself, alone."

She thrust her free hand up to him. He kissed it softly, as if she were asleep and he were afraid of waking her.

From the door he turned back irrelevantly. "As to your old friend, Thea, if he's to be here on Friday, why,"--he snatched out his watch and held it down to catch the light from the grate,--"he's on the train now! That ought to cheer you. Good-night." She heard the door close.

III

ON Friday afternoon Thea Kronborg was walking excitedly up and down her sitting-room, which at that hour was flooded by thin, clear sunshine. Both windows were open, and the fire in the grate was low, for the day was one of those false springs that sometimes blow into New York from the sea in the middle of winter, soft, warm, with a persuasive salty moisture in the air and a relaxing thaw under foot. Thea was flushed and animated, and she seemed as restless as the sooty sparrows that chirped and cheeped distractingly about the windows. She kept looking at the black clock, and then down into the Square. The room was full of flowers, and she stopped now and then to arrange them or to move them into the sunlight. After the bellboy came to announce a visitor, she took some Roman hyacinths from a glass and stuck them in the front of her dark-blue dress.

When at last Fred Ottenburg appeared in the doorway, she met him with an exclamation of pleasure. "I am glad you've come, Fred. I was afraid you might not get my note, and I wanted to see you before you see Dr. Archie. He's so nice!" She brought her hands together to emphasize her statement.

"Is he? I'm glad. You see I'm quite out of breath. I didn't wait for the elevator, but ran upstairs. I was so pleased at being sent for." He dropped his hat and overcoat. "Yes, I should say he is nice! I don't seem to recognize all of these," waving his handkerchief about at the flowers.

"Yes, he brought them himself, in a big box. He brought lots with him besides flowers. Oh, lots of things! The old Moonstone feeling,"--Thea moved her hand back and forth in the air, fluttering her fingers,--"the feeling of starting out, early in the morning, to take my lesson."

"And you've had everything out with him?"

"No, I haven't."

"Haven't?" He looked up in consternation.

"No, I haven't!" Thea spoke excitedly, moving about over the sunny patches on the grimy carpet. "I've lied to him, just as you said I had always lied to him, and that's why I'm so happy. I've let him think what he likes to think. Oh, I couldn't do anything else, Fred,"--she shook her head emphatically. "If you'd seen him when he came in, so pleased and excited! You see this is a great adventure for him. From the moment I began to talk to him, he entreated me not to say too much, not to spoil his notion of me. Not in so many words, of course. But if you'd seen his eyes, his face, his kind hands! Oh, no! I couldn't." She took a deep breath, as if with a renewed sense of her narrow escape.

"Then, what did you tell him?" Fred demanded.

Thea sat down on the edge of the sofa and began shutting and opening her hands nervously. "Well, I told him enough, and not too much. I told him all about how good you were to me last winter, getting me engagements and things, and how you had helped me with my work more than anybody. Then I told him about how you sent me down to the ranch when I had no money or anything." She paused and wrinkled her forehead. "And I told him that I wanted to marry you and ran away to Mexico with you, and that I was awfully happy until you told me that you couldn't marry me because-- well, I told him why." Thea dropped her eyes and moved the toe of her shoe about restlessly on the carpet.

"And he took it from you, like that?" Fred asked, almost with awe.

"Yes, just like that, and asked no questions. He was hurt; he had some wretched moments. I could see him squirming and squirming and trying to get past it. He kept shutting his eyes and rubbing his forehead. But when I told him that I absolutely knew you wanted to marry me, that you would whenever you could, that seemed to help him a good deal."

"And that satisfied him?" Fred asked wonderingly. He could not quite imagine what kind of person Dr. Archie might be.

"He took me by the shoulders once and asked, oh, in such a frightened way, `Thea, was he GOOD to you, this young man?' When I told him you were, he looked at me again: `And you care for him a great deal, you believe in him?' Then he seemed satisfied." Thea paused. "You see, he's just tremendously good, and tremendously afraid of things--of some things. Otherwise he would have got rid of Mrs. Archie." She looked up suddenly: "You were right, though; one can't tell people about things they don't know already."

Fred stood in the window, his back to the sunlight, fingering the jonquils. "Yes, you can, my dear. But you must tell it in such a way that they don't know you're telling it, and that they don't know they're hearing it."

Thea smiled past him, out into the air. "I see. It's a secret. Like the sound in the shell."

"What's that?" Fred was watching her and thinking how moving that faraway expression, in her, happened to be. "What did you say?"

She came back. "Oh, something old and Moonstony! I have almost forgotten it myself. But I feel better than I thought I ever could again. I can't wait to be off. Oh, Fred," she sprang up, "I want to get at it!"

As she broke out with this, she threw up her head and lifted herself a little on her toes. Fred colored and looked at her fearfully, hesitatingly. Her eyes, which looked out through the window, were bright--they had no memories. No, she did not remember. That momentary elevation had no associations for her. It was unconscious.

He looked her up and down and laughed and shook his head. "You are just all I want you to be--and that is,--not for me! Don't worry, you'll get at it. You are at it. My God! have you ever, for one moment, been at anything else?"

Thea did not answer him, and clearly she had not heard him. She was watching something out in the thin light of the false spring and its treacherously soft air.

Fred waited a moment. "Are you going to dine with your friend to-night?"

"Yes. He has never been in New York before. He wants to go about. Where shall I tell him to go?"

"Wouldn't it be a better plan, since you wish me to meet him, for you both to dine with me? It would seem only natural and friendly. You'll have to live up a little to his notion of us." Thea seemed to consider the suggestion favorably. "If you wish him to be easy in his mind," Fred went on, "that would help. I think, myself, that we are rather nice together. Put on one of the new dresses you got down there, and let him see how lovely you can be. You owe him some pleasure, after all the trouble he has taken."

Thea laughed, and seemed to find the idea exciting and pleasant. "Oh, very well! I'll do my best. Only don't wear a dress coat, please. He hasn't one, and he's nervous about it."

Fred looked at his watch. "Your monument up there is fast. I'll be here with a cab at eight. I'm anxious to meet him. You've given me the strangest idea of his callow innocence and aged indifference."

She shook her head. "No, he's none of that. He's very good, and he won't admit things. I love him for it. Now, as I look back on it, I see that I've always, even when I was little, shielded him."

As she laughed, Fred caught the bright spark in her eye that he knew so well, and held it for a happy instant. Then he blew her a kiss with his finger-tips and fled.

IV

AT nine o'clock that evening our three friends were seated in the balcony of a French restaurant, much gayer and more intimate than any that exists in New York to-day. This old restaurant was built by a lover of pleasure, who knew that to dine gayly human beings must have the reassurance of certain limitations of space and of a certain definite style; that the walls must be near enough to suggest shelter, the ceiling high enough to give the chandeliers a setting. The place was crowded with the kind of people who dine late and well, and Dr. Archie, as he watched the animated groups in the long room below the balcony, found this much the most festive scene he had ever looked out upon. He said to himself, in a jovial mood somewhat sustained by the cheer of the board, that this evening alone was worth his long journey. He followed attentively the orchestra, ensconced at the farther end of the balcony, and told Thea it made him feel "quite musical" to recognize "The Invitation to the Dance" or "The Blue Danube," and that he could remember just what kind of day it was when he heard her practicing them at home, and lingered at the gate to listen.

For the first few moments, when he was introduced to young Ottenburg in the parlor of the Everett House, the doctor had been awkward and unbending. But Fred, as his father had often observed, "was not a good mixer for nothing." He had brought Dr. Archie around during the short cab ride, and in an hour they had become old friends.

From the moment when the doctor lifted his glass and, looking consciously at Thea, said, "To your success," Fred liked him. He felt his quality; understood his courage in some directions and what Thea called his timidity in others, his unspent and miraculously preserved youthfulness. Men could never impose upon the doctor, he guessed, but women always could. Fred liked, too, the doctor's manner with Thea, his bashful admiration and the little hesitancy by which he betrayed his consciousness of the change in her. It was just this change that, at present, interested Fred more than anything else. That, he felt, was his "created value," and it was his best chance for any peace of mind. If that were not real, obvious to an old friend like Archie, then he cut a very poor figure, indeed.

Fred got a good deal, too, out of their talk about Moonstone. From her questions and the doctor's answers he was able to form some conception of the little world that was almost the measure of Thea's experience, the one bit of the human drama that she had followed with sympathy and understanding. As the two ran over the list of their friends, the mere sound of a name seemed to recall volumes to each of them, to indicate mines of knowledge and observation they had in common. At some names they laughed delightedly, at some indulgently and even tenderly.

"You two young people must come out to Moonstone when Thea gets back," the doctor said hospitably.

"Oh, we shall!" Fred caught it up. "I'm keen to know all these people. It is very tantalizing to hear only their names."

"Would they interest an outsider very much, do you think, Dr. Archie?" Thea leaned toward him. "Isn't it only because we've known them since I was little?"

The doctor glanced at her deferentially. Fred had noticed that he seemed a little afraid to look at her squarely--perhaps a trifle embarrassed by a mode of dress to which he was unaccustomed. "Well, you are practically an outsider yourself, Thea, now," he observed smiling. "Oh, I know," he went on quickly in response to her gesture of protest,--"I know you don't change toward your old friends, but you can see us all from a distance now. It's all to your advantage that you can still take your old interest, isn't it, Mr. Ottenburg?"

"That's exactly one of her advantages, Dr. Archie. Nobody can ever take that away from her, and none of us who came later can ever hope to rival Moonstone in the impression we make. Her scale of values will always be the Moonstone scale. And, with an artist, that IS an advantage." Fred nodded.

Dr. Archie looked at him seriously. "You mean it keeps them from getting affected?"

"Yes; keeps them from getting off the track generally."

While the waiter filled the glasses, Fred pointed out to Thea a big black French barytone who was eating anchovies by their tails at one of the tables below, and the doctor looked about and studied his fellow diners.

"Do you know, Mr. Ottenburg," he said deeply, "these people all look happier to me than our Western people do. Is it simply good manners on their part, or do they get more out of life?"

Fred laughed to Thea above the glass he had just lifted. "Some of them are getting a good deal out of it now, doctor. This is the hour when bench-joy brightens."

Thea chuckled and darted him a quick glance. "Benchjoy! Where did you get that slang?"

"That happens to be very old slang, my dear. Older than Moonstone or the sovereign State of Colorado. Our old friend Mr. Nathanmeyer could tell us why it happens to hit you." He leaned forward and touched Thea's wrist, "See that fur coat just coming in, Thea. It's D'Albert. He's just back from his Western tour. Fine head, hasn't he?"

"To go back," said Dr. Archie; "I insist that people do look happier here. I've noticed it even on the street, and especially in the hotels."

Fred turned to him cheerfully. "New York people live a good deal in the fourth dimension, Dr. Archie. It's that you notice in their faces."

The doctor was interested. "The fourth dimension," he repeated slowly; "and is that slang, too?"

"No,"--Fred shook his head,--"that's merely a figure. I mean that life is not quite so personal here as it is in your part of the world. People are more taken up by hobbies, interests that are less subject to reverses than their personal affairs. If you're interested in Thea's voice, for instance, or in voices in general, that interest is just the same, even if your mining stocks go down."

The doctor looked at him narrowly. "You think that's about the principal difference between country people and city people, don't you?"

Fred was a little disconcerted at being followed up so resolutely, and he attempted to dismiss it with a pleasantry. "I've never thought much about it, doctor. But I should say, on the spur of the moment, that that is one of the principal differences between people anywhere. It's the consolation of fellows like me who don't accomplish much. The fourth dimension is not good for business, but we think we have a better time."

Dr. Archie leaned back in his chair. His heavy shoulders were contemplative. "And she," he said slowly; "should you say that she is one of the kind you refer to?" He inclined his head toward the shimmer of the pale-green dress beside him. Thea was leaning, just then, over the balcony rail, her head in the light from the chandeliers below.

"Never, never!" Fred protested. "She's as hard-headed as the worst of you--with a difference."

The doctor sighed. "Yes, with a difference; something that makes a good many revolutions to the second. When she was little I used to feel her head to try to locate it."

Fred laughed. "Did you, though? So you were on the track of it? Oh, it's there! We can't get round it, miss," as Thea looked back inquiringly. "Dr. Archie, there's a fellow townsman of yours I feel a real kinship for." He pressed a cigar upon Dr. Archie and struck a match for him. "Tell me about Spanish Johnny."

The doctor smiled benignantly through the first waves of smoke. "Well, Johnny's an old patient of mine, and he's an old admirer of Thea's. She was born a cosmopolitan, and I expect she learned a good deal from Johnny when she used to run away and go to Mexican Town. We thought it a queer freak then."

The doctor launched into a long story, in which he was often eagerly interrupted or joyously confirmed by Thea, who was drinking her coffee and forcing open the petals of the roses with an ardent and rather rude hand. Fred settled down into enjoying his comprehension of his guests. Thea, watching Dr. Archie and interested in his presentation, was unconsciously impersonating her suave, goldtinted friend. It was delightful to see her so radiant and responsive again. She had kept her promise about looking her best; when one could so easily get together the colors of an apple branch in early spring, that was not hard to do. Even Dr. Archie felt, each time he looked at her, a fresh consciousness. He recognized the fine texture of her mother's skin, with the difference that, when she reached across the table to give him a bunch of grapes, her arm was not only white, but somehow a little dazzling. She seemed to him taller, and freer in all her movements. She had now a way of taking a deep breath when she was interested, that made her seem very strong, somehow, and brought her at one quite overpoweringly. If he seemed shy, it was not that he was intimidated by her worldly clothes, but that her greater positiveness, her whole augmented self, made him feel that his accustomed manner toward her was inadequate.

Fred, on his part, was reflecting that the awkward position in which he had placed her would not confine or chafe her long. She looked about at other people, at other women, curiously. She was not quite sure of herself, but she was not in the least afraid or apologetic. She seemed to sit there on the edge, emerging from one world into another, taking her bearings, getting an idea of the concerted movement about her, but with absolute self-confidence. So far from shrinking, she expanded. The mere kindly effort to please Dr. Archie was enough to bring her out.

There was much talk of aurae at that time, and Fred mused that every beautiful, every compellingly beautiful woman, had an aura, whether other people did or no. There was, certainly, about the woman he had brought up from Mexico, such an emanation. She existed in more space than she occupied by measurement. The enveloping air about her head and shoulders was subsidized--was more moving than she herself, for in it lived the awakenings, all the first sweetness that life kills in people. One felt in her such a wealth of JUGENDZEIT, all those flowers of the mind and the blood that bloom and perish by the myriad in the few exhaustless years when the imagination first kindles. It was in watching her as she emerged like this, in being near and not too near, that one got, for a moment, so much that one had lost; among other legendary things the legendary theme of the absolutely magical power of a beautiful woman.

After they had left Thea at her hotel, Dr. Archie admitted to Fred, as they walked up Broadway through the rapidly chilling air, that once before he had seen their young friend flash up into a more potent self, but in a darker mood. It was in his office one night, when she was at home the summer before last. "And then I got the idea," he added simply, "that she would not live like other people: that, for better or worse, she had uncommon gifts."

"Oh, we'll see that it's for better, you and I," Fred reassured him. "Won't you come up to my hotel with me? I think we ought to have a long talk."

"Yes, indeed," said Dr. Archie gratefully; "I think we ought."

V

THEA was to sail on Tuesday, at noon, and on Saturday Fred Ottenburg arranged for her passage, while she and Dr. Archie went shopping. With rugs and sea-clothes she was already provided; Fred had got everything of that sort she needed for the voyage up from Vera Cruz. On Sunday afternoon Thea went to see the Harsanyis. When she returned to her hotel, she found a note from Ottenburg, saying that he had called and would come again to-morrow.

On Monday morning, while she was at breakfast, Fred came in. She knew by his hurried, distracted air as he entered the dining-room that something had gone wrong. He had just got a telegram from home. His mother had been thrown from her carriage and hurt; a concussion of some sort, and she was unconscious. He was leaving for St. Louis that night on the eleven o'clock train. He had a great deal to attend to during the day. He would come that evening, if he might, and stay with her until train time, while she was doing her packing. Scarcely waiting for her consent, he hurried away.

All day Thea was somewhat cast down. She was sorry for Fred, and she missed the feeling that she was the one person in his mind. He had scarcely looked at her when they exchanged words at the breakfast-table. She felt as if she were set aside, and she did not seem so important even to herself as she had yesterday. Certainly, she reflected, it was high time that she began to take care of herself again. Dr. Archie came for dinner, but she sent him away early, telling him that she would be ready to go to the boat with him at half-past ten the next morning. When she went upstairs, she looked gloomily at the open trunk in her sitting-room, and at the trays piled on the sofa. She stood at the window and watched a quiet snowstorm spending itself over the city. More than anything else, falling snow always made her think of Moonstone; of the Kohlers' garden, of Thor's sled, of dressing by lamplight and starting off to school before the paths were broken.

When Fred came, he looked tired, and he took her hand almost without seeing her.

"I'm so sorry, Fred. Have you had any more word?"

"She was still unconscious at four this afternoon. It doesn't look very encouraging." He approached the fire and warmed his hands. He seemed to have contracted, and he had not at all his habitual ease of manner. "Poor mother!" he exclaimed; "nothing like this should have happened to her. She has so much pride of person. She's not at all an old woman, you know. She's never got beyond vigorous and rather dashing middle age." He turned abruptly to Thea and for the first time really looked at her. "How badly things come out! She'd have liked you for a daughter-in-law. Oh, you'd have fought like the devil, but you'd have respected each other." He sank into a chair and thrust his feet out to the fire. "Still," he went on thoughtfully, seeming to address the ceiling, "it might have been bad for you. Our big German houses, our good German cooking--you might have got lost in the upholstery. That substantial comfort might take the temper out of you, dull your edge. Yes," he sighed, "I guess you were meant for the jolt of the breakers."

"I guess I'll get plenty of jolt," Thea murmured, turning to her trunk.

"I'm rather glad I'm not staying over until to-morrow," Fred reflected. "I think it's easier for me to glide out like this. I feel now as if everything were rather casual, anyhow. A thing like that dulls one's feelings."

Thea, standing by her trunk, made no reply. Presently he shook himself and rose. "Want me to put those trays in for you?"

"No, thank you. I'm not ready for them yet."

Fred strolled over to the sofa, lifted a scarf from one of the trays and stood abstractedly drawing it through his fingers. "You've been so kind these last few days, Thea, that I began to hope you might soften a little; that you might ask me to come over and see you this summer."

"If you thought that, you were mistaken," she said slowly. "I've hardened, if anything. But I shan't carry any grudge away with me, if you mean that."

He dropped the scarf. "And there's nothing--nothing at all you'll let me do?"

"Yes, there is one thing, and it's a good deal to ask. If I get knocked out, or never get on, I'd like you to see that Dr. Archie gets his money back. I'm taking three thousand dollars of his."

"Why, of course I shall. You may dismiss that from your mind. How fussy you are about money, Thea. You make such a point of it." He turned sharply and walked to the windows.

Thea sat down in the chair he had quitted. "It's only poor people who feel that way about money, and who are really honest," she said gravely. "Sometimes I think that to be really honest, you must have been so poor that you've been tempted to steal."

"To what?"

"To steal. I used to be, when I first went to Chicago and saw all the things in the big stores there. Never anything big, but little things, the kind I'd never seen before and could never afford. I did take something once, before I knew it."

Fred came toward her. For the first time she had his whole attention, in the degree to which she was accustomed to having it. "Did you? What was it?" he asked with interest.

"A sachet. A little blue silk bag of orris-root powder. There was a whole counterful of them, marked down to fifty cents. I'd never seen any before, and they seemed irresistible. I took one up and wandered about the store with it. Nobody seemed to notice, so I carried it off."

Fred laughed. "Crazy child! Why, your things always smell of orris; is it a penance?"

"No, I love it. But I saw that the firm didn't lose anything by me. I went back and bought it there whenever I had a quarter to spend. I got a lot to take to Arizona. I made it up to them."

"I'll bet you did!" Fred took her hand. "Why didn't I find you that first winter? I'd have loved you just as you came!"

Thea shook her head. "No, you wouldn't, but you might have found me amusing. The Harsanyis said yesterday afternoon that I wore such a funny cape and that my shoes always squeaked. They think I've improved. I told them it was your doing if I had, and then they looked scared."

"Did you sing for Harsanyi?"

"Yes. He thinks I've improved there, too. He said nice things to me. Oh, he was very nice! He agrees with you about my going to Lehmann, if she'll take me. He came out to the elevator with me, after we had said good-bye. He said something nice out there, too, but he seemed sad."

"What was it that he said?"

"He said, `When people, serious people, believe in you, they give you some of their best, so--take care of it, Miss Kronborg.' Then he waved his hands and went back."

"If you sang, I wish you had taken me along. Did you sing well?" Fred turned from her and went back to the window. "I wonder when I shall hear you sing again." He picked up a bunch of violets and smelled them. "You know, your leaving me like this--well, it's almost inhuman to be able to do it so kindly and unconditionally."

"I suppose it is. It was almost inhuman to be able to leave home, too,--the last time, when I knew it was for good. But all the same, I cared a great deal more than anybody else did. I lived through it. I have no choice now. No matter how much it breaks me up, I have to go. Do I seem to enjoy it?"

Fred bent over her trunk and picked up something which proved to be a score, clumsily bound. "What's this? Did you ever try to sing this?" He opened it and on the engraved title-page read Wunsch's inscription, "EINST, O WUNDER!" He looked up sharply at Thea.

"Wunsch gave me that when he went away. I've told you about him, my old teacher in Moonstone. He loved that opera."

Fred went toward the fireplace, the book under his arm, singing softly:--

"EINST, O WUNDER, ENTBLUHT AUF MEINEM GRABE, EINE BLUME DER ASCHE MEINES HERZENS;"

"You have no idea at all where he is, Thea?" He leaned against the mantel and looked down at her.

"No, I wish I had. He may be dead by this time. That was five years ago, and he used himself hard. Mrs. Kohler was always afraid he would die off alone somewhere and be stuck under the prairie. When we last heard of him, he was in Kansas."

"If he were to be found, I'd like to do something for him. I seem to get a good deal of him from this." He opened the book again, where he kept the place with his finger, and scrutinized the purple ink. "How like a German! Had he ever sung the song for you?"

"No. I didn't know where the words were from until once, when Harsanyi sang it for me, I recognized them."

Fred closed the book. "Let me see, what was your noble brakeman's name?"

Thea looked up with surprise. "Ray, Ray Kennedy."

"Ray Kennedy!" he laughed. "It couldn't well have been better! Wunsch and Dr. Archie, and Ray, and I,"--he told them off on his fingers,--"your whistling-posts! You haven't done so badly. We've backed you as we could, some in our weakness and some in our might. In your dark hours--and you'll have them--you may like to remember us." He smiled whimsically and dropped the score into the trunk. "You are taking that with you?"

"Surely I am. I haven't so many keepsakes that I can afford to leave that. I haven't got many that I value so highly."

"That you value so highly?" Fred echoed her gravity playfully. "You are delicious when you fall into your vernacular." He laughed half to himself.

"What's the matter with that? Isn't it perfectly good English?"

"Perfectly good Moonstone, my dear. Like the readymade clothes that hang in the windows, made to fit everybody and fit nobody, a phrase that can be used on all occasions. Oh,"--he started across the room again,--"that's one of the fine things about your going! You'll be with the right sort of people and you'll learn a good, live, warm German, that will be like yourself. You'll get a new speech full of shades and color like your voice; alive, like your mind. It will be almost like being born again, Thea."

She was not offended. Fred had said such things to her before, and she wanted to learn. In the natural course of things she would never have loved a man from whom she could not learn a great deal.

"Harsanyi said once," she remarked thoughtfully, "that if one became an artist one had to be born again, and that one owed nothing to anybody."

"Exactly. And when I see you again I shall not see you, but your daughter. May I?" He held up his cigarette case questioningly and then began to smoke, taking up again the song which ran in his head:--

"DEUTLICH SCHIMMERT AUF JEDEM, PURPURBLÄTTCHEN, ADELAIDE!"

"I have half an hour with you yet, and then, exit Fred." He walked about the room, smoking and singing the words under his breath. "You'll like the voyage," he said abruptly. "That first approach to a foreign shore, stealing up on it and finding it--there's nothing like it. It wakes up everything that's asleep in you. You won't mind my writing to some people in Berlin? They'll be nice to you."

"I wish you would." Thea gave a deep sigh. "I wish one could look ahead and see what is coming to one."

"Oh, no!" Fred was smoking nervously; "that would never do. It's the uncertainty that makes one try. You've never had any sort of chance, and now I fancy you'll make it up to yourself. You'll find the way to let yourself out in one long flight."

Thea put her hand on her heart. "And then drop like the rocks we used to throw--anywhere." She left the chair and went over to the sofa, hunting for something in the trunk trays. When she came back she found Fred sitting in her place. "Here are some handkerchiefs of yours. I've kept one or two. They're larger than mine and useful if one has a headache."

"Thank you. How nicely they smell of your things!" He looked at the white squares for a moment and then put them in his pocket. He kept the low chair, and as she stood beside him he took her hands and sat looking intently at them, as if he were examining them for some special purpose, tracing the long round fingers with the tips of his own. "Ordinarily, you know, there are reefs that a man catches to and keeps his nose above water. But this is a case by itself. There seems to be no limit as to how much I can be in love with you. I keep going." He did not lift his eyes from her fingers, which he continued to study with the same fervor. "Every kind of stringed instrument there is plays in your hands, Thea," he whispered, pressing them to his face.

She dropped beside him and slipped into his arms, shutting her eyes and lifting her cheek to his. "Tell me one thing," Fred whispered. "You said that night on the boat, when I first told you, that if you could you would crush it all up in your hands and throw it into the sea. Would you, all those weeks?"

She shook her head.

"Answer me, would you?"

"No, I was angry then. I'm not now. I'd never give them up. Don't make me pay too much." In that embrace they lived over again all the others. When Thea drew away from him, she dropped her face in her hands. "You are good to me," she breathed, "you are!"

Rising to his feet, he put his hands under her elbows and lifted her gently. He drew her toward the door with him. "Get all you can. Be generous with yourself. Don't stop short of splendid things. I want them for you more than I want anything else, more than I want one splendid thing for myself. I can't help feeling that you'll gain, somehow, by my losing so much. That you'll gain the very thing I lose. Take care of her, as Harsanyi said. She's wonderful!" He kissed her and went out of the door without looking back, just as if he were coming again to-morrow.

Thea went quickly into her bedroom. She brought out an armful of muslin things, knelt down, and began to lay them in the trays. Suddenly she stopped, dropped forward and leaned against the open trunk, her head on her arms. The tears fell down on the dark old carpet. It came over her how many people must have said good-bye and been unhappy in that room. Other people, before her time, had hired this room to cry in. Strange rooms and strange streets and faces, how sick at heart they made one! Why was she going so far, when what she wanted was some familiar place to hide in?--the rock house, her little room in Moonstone, her own bed. Oh, how good it would be to lie down in that little bed, to cut the nerve that kept one struggling, that pulled one on and on, to sink into peace there, with all the family safe and happy downstairs. After all, she was a Moonstone girl, one of the preacher's children. Everything else was in Fred's imagination. Why was she called upon to take such chances? Any safe, humdrum work that did not compromise her would be better. But if she failed now, she would lose her soul. There was nowhere to fall, after one took that step, except into abysses of wretchedness. She knew what abysses, for she could still hear the old man playing in the snowstorm, it was released in her like a passion of longing. Every nerve in her body thrilled to it. It brought her to her feet, carried her somehow to bed and into troubled sleep.

That night she taught in Moonstone again: she beat her pupils in hideous rages, she kept on beating them. She sang at funerals, and struggled at the piano with Harsanyi. In one dream she was looking into a hand-glass and thinking that she was getting better-looking, when the glass began to grow smaller and smaller and her own reflection to shrink, until she realized that she was looking into Ray Kennedy's eyes, seeing her face in that look of his which she could never forget. All at once the eyes were Fred Ottenburg's, and not Ray's. All night she heard the shrieking of trains, whistling in and out of Moonstone, as she used to hear them in her sleep when they blew shrill in the winter air. But to-night they were terrifying,--the spectral, fated trains that "raced with death," about which the old woman from the depot used to pray.

In the morning she wakened breathless after a struggle with Mrs. Livery Johnson's daughter. She started up with a bound, threw the blankets back and sat on the edge of the bed, her night-dress open, her long braids hanging over her bosom, blinking at the daylight. After all, it was not too late. She was only twenty years old, and the boat sailed at noon. There was still time!

PART VI. KRONBORG

I

It is a glorious winter day. Denver, standing on her high plateau under a thrilling green-blue sky, is masked in snow and glittering with sunlight. The Capitol building is actually in armor, and throws off the shafts of the sun until the beholder is dazzled and the outlines of the building are lost in a blaze of reflected light. The stone terrace is a white field over which fiery reflections dance, and the trees and bushes are faithfully repeated in snow--on every black twig a soft, blurred line of white. From the terrace one looks directly over to where the mountains break in their sharp, familiar lines against the sky. Snow fills the gorges, hangs in scarfs on the great slopes, and on the peaks the fiery sunshine is gathered up as by a burning-glass.

Howard Archie is standing at the window of his private room in the offices of the San Felipe Mining Company, on the sixth floor of the Raton Building, looking off at the mountain glories of his State while he gives dictation to his secretary. He is ten years older than when we saw him last, and emphatically ten years more prosperous. A decade of coming into things has not so much aged him as it has fortified, smoothed, and assured him. His sandy hair and imperial conceal whatever gray they harbor. He has not grown heavier, but more flexible, and his massive shoulders carry fifty years and the control of his great mining interests more lightly than they carried forty years and a country practice. In short, he is one of the friends to whom we feel grateful for having got on in the world, for helping to keep up the general temperature and our own confidence in life. He is an acquaintance that one would hurry to overtake and greet among a hundred. In his warm handshake and generous smile there is the stimulating cordiality of good fellows come into good fortune and eager to pass it on; something that makes one think better of the lottery of life and resolve to try again.

When Archie had finished his morning mail, he turned away from the window and faced his secretary. "Did anything come up yesterday afternoon while I was away, T. B.?"

Thomas Burk turned over the leaf of his calendar. "Governor Alden sent down to say that he wanted to see you before he sends his letter to the Board of Pardons. Asked if you could go over to the State House this morning."

Archie shrugged his shoulders. "I'll think about it."

The young man grinned.

"Anything else?" his chief continued.

T. B. swung round in his chair with a look of interest on his shrewd, clean-shaven face. "Old Jasper Flight was in, Dr. Archie. I never expected to see him alive again. Seems he's tucked away for the winter with a sister who's a housekeeper at the Oxford. He's all crippled up with rheumatism, but as fierce after it as ever. Wants to know if you or the company won't grub-stake him again. Says he's sure of it this time; had located something when the snow shut down on him in December. He wants to crawl out at the first break in the weather, with that same old burro with the split ear. He got somebody to winter the beast for him. He's superstitious about that burro, too; thinks it's divinely guided. You ought to hear the line of talk he put up here yesterday; said when he rode in his carriage, that burro was a-going to ride along with him."

Archie laughed. "Did he leave you his address?"

"He didn't neglect anything," replied the clerk cynically.

"Well, send him a line and tell him to come in again. I like to hear him. Of all the crazy prospectors I've ever known, he's the most interesting, because he's really crazy. It's a religious conviction with him, and with most of 'em it's a gambling fever or pure vagrancy. But Jasper Flight believes that the Almighty keeps the secret of the silver deposits in these hills, and gives it away to the deserving. He's a downright noble figure. Of course I'll stake him! As long as he can crawl out in the spring. He and that burro are a sight together. The beast is nearly as white as Jasper; must be twenty years old."

"If you stake him this time, you won't have to again," said T. B. knowingly. "He'll croak up there, mark my word. Says he never ties the burro at night now, for fear he might be called sudden, and the beast would starve. I guess that animal could eat a lariat rope, all right, and enjoy it."

"I guess if we knew the things those two have eaten, and haven't eaten, in their time, T. B., it would make us vegetarians." The doctor sat down and looked thoughtful. "That's the way for the old man to go. It would be pretty hard luck if he had to die in a hospital. I wish he could turn up something before he cashes in. But his kind seldom do; they're bewitched. Still, there was Stratton. I've been meeting Jasper Flight, and his side meat and tin pans, up in the mountains for years, and I'd miss him. I always halfway believe the fairy tales he spins me. Old Jasper Flight," Archie murmured, as if he liked the name or the picture it called up.

A clerk came in from the outer office and handed Archie a card. He sprang up and exclaimed, "Mr. Ottenburg? Bring him in."

Fred Ottenburg entered, clad in a long, fur-lined coat, holding a checked-cloth hat in his hand, his cheeks and eyes bright with the outdoor cold. The two men met before Archie's desk and their handclasp was longer than friendship prompts except in regions where the blood warms and quickens to meet the dry cold. Under the general keying-up of the altitude, manners take on a heartiness, a vivacity, that is one expression of the half-unconscious excitement which Colorado people miss when they drop into lower strata of air. The heart, we are told, wears out early in that high atmosphere, but while it pumps it sends out no sluggish stream. Our two friends stood gripping each other by the hand and smiling.

"When did you get in, Fred? And what have you come for?" Archie gave him a quizzical glance.

"I've come to find out what you think you're doing out here," the younger man declared emphatically. "I want to get next, I do. When can you see me?"

"Anything on to-night? Then suppose you dine with me. Where can I pick you up at five-thirty?"

"Bixby's office, general freight agent of the Burlington." Ottenburg began to button his overcoat and drew on his gloves. "I've got to have one shot at you before I go, Archie. Didn't I tell you Pinky Alden was a cheap squirt?"

Alden's backer laughed and shook his head. "Oh, he's worse than that, Fred. It isn't polite to mention what he is, outside of the Arabian Nights. I guessed you'd come to rub it into me."

Ottenburg paused, his hand on the doorknob, his high color challenging the doctor's calm. "I'm disgusted with you, Archie, for training with such a pup. A man of your experience!"

"Well, he's been an experience," Archie muttered. "I'm not coy about admitting it, am I?"

Ottenburg flung open the door. "Small credit to you. Even the women are out for capital and corruption, I hear. Your Governor's done more for the United Breweries in six months than I've been able to do in six years. He's the lily-livered sort we're looking for. Good-morning."

That afternoon at five o'clock Dr. Archie emerged from the State House after his talk with Governor Alden, and crossed the terrace under a saffron sky. The snow, beaten hard, was blue in the dusk; a day of blinding sunlight had not even started a thaw. The lights of the city twinkled pale below him in the quivering violet air, and the dome of the State House behind him was still red with the light from the west. Before he got into his car, the doctor paused to look about him at the scene of which he never tired. Archie lived in his own house on Colfax Avenue, where he had roomy grounds and a rose garden and a conservatory. His housekeeping was done by three Japanese boys, devoted and resourceful, who were able to manage Archie's dinner parties, to see that he kept his engagements, and to make visitors who stayed at the house so comfortable that they were always loath to go away.

Archie had never known what comfort was until he became a widower, though with characteristic delicacy, or dishonesty, he insisted upon accrediting his peace of mind to the San Felipe, to Time, to anything but his release from Mrs. Archie.

Mrs. Archie died just before her husband left Moonstone and came to Denver to live, six years ago. The poor woman's fight against dust was her undoing at last. One summer day when she was rubbing the parlor upholstery with gasoline,-- the doctor had often forbidden her to use it on any account, so that was one of the pleasures she seized upon in his absence,--an explosion occurred. Nobody ever knew exactly how it happened, for Mrs. Archie was dead when the neighbors rushed in to save her from the burning house. She must have inhaled the burning gas and died instantly.

Moonstone severity relented toward her somewhat after her death. But even while her old cronies at Mrs. Smiley's millinery store said that it was a terrible thing, they added that nothing but a powerful explosive COULD have killed Mrs. Archie, and that it was only right the doctor should have a chance.

Archie's past was literally destroyed when his wife died. The house burned to the ground, and all those material reminders which have such power over people disappeared in an hour. His mining interests now took him to Denver so often that it seemed better to make his headquarters there. He gave up his practice and left Moonstone for good. Six months afterward, while Dr. Archie was living at the Brown Palace Hotel, the San Felipe mine began to give up that silver hoard which old Captain Harris had always accused it of concealing, and San Felipe headed the list of mining quotations in every daily paper, East and West. In a few years Dr. Archie was a very rich man. His mine was such an important item in the mineral output of the State, and Archie had a hand in so many of the new industries of Colorado and New Mexico, that his political influence was considerable. He had thrown it all, two years ago, to the new reform party, and had brought about the election of a governor of whose conduct he was now heartily ashamed. His friends believed that Archie himself had ambitious political plans.

II

WHEN Ottenburg and his host reached the house on Colfax Avenue, they went directly to the library, a long double room on the second floor which Archie had arranged exactly to his own taste. It was full of books and mounted specimens of wild game, with a big writing-table at either end, stiff, old-fashioned engravings, heavy hangings and deep upholstery.

When one of the Japanese boys brought the cocktails, Fred turned from the fine specimen of peccoray he had been examining and said, "A man is an owl to live in such a place alone, Archie. Why don't you marry? As for me, just because I can't marry, I find the world full of charming, unattached women, any one of whom I could fit up a house for with alacrity."

"You're more knowing than I." Archie spoke politely. "I'm not very wide awake about women. I'd be likely to pick out one of the uncomfortable ones--and there are a few of them, you know." He drank his cocktail and rubbed his hands together in a friendly way. "My friends here have charming wives, and they don't give me a chance to get lonely. They are very kind to me, and I have a great many pleasant friendships."

Fred put down his glass. "Yes, I've always noticed that women have confidence in you. You have the doctor's way of getting next. And you enjoy that kind of thing?"

"The friendship of attractive women? Oh, dear, yes! I depend upon it a great deal."

The butler announced dinner, and the two men went downstairs to the dining-room. Dr. Archie's dinners were always good and well served, and his wines were excellent.

"I saw the Fuel and Iron people to-day," Ottenburg said, looking up from his soup. "Their heart is in the right place. I can't see why in the mischief you ever got mixed up with that reform gang, Archie. You've got nothing to reform out here. The situation has always been as simple as two and two in Colorado; mostly a matter of a friendly understanding."

"Well,"--Archie spoke tolerantly,--"some of the young fellows seemed to have red-hot convictions, and I thought it was better to let them try their ideas out."

Ottenburg shrugged his shoulders. "A few dull young men who haven't ability enough to play the old game the old way, so they want to put on a new game which doesn't take so much brains and gives away more advertising that's what your anti-saloon league and vice commission amounts to. They provide notoriety for the fellows who can't distinguish themselves at running a business or practicing law or developing an industry. Here you have a mediocre lawyer with no brains and no practice, trying to get a look-in on something. He comes up with the novel proposition that the prostitute has a hard time of it, puts his picture in the paper, and the first thing you know, he's a celebrity. He gets the rake-off and she's just where she was before. How could you fall for a mouse-trap like Pink Alden, Archie?"

Dr. Archie laughed as he began to carve. "Pink seems to get under your skin. He's not worth talking about. He's gone his limit. People won't read about his blameless life any more. I knew those interviews he gave out would cook him. They were a last resort. I could have stopped him, but by that time I'd come to the conclusion that I'd let the reformers down. I'm not against a general shaking-up, but the trouble with Pinky's crowd is they never get beyond a general writing-up. We gave them a chance to do something, and they just kept on writing about each other and what temptations they had overcome."

While Archie and his friend were busy with Colorado politics, the impeccable Japanese attended swiftly and intelligently to his duties, and the dinner, as Ottenburg at last remarked, was worthy of more profitable conversation.

"So it is," the doctor admitted. "Well, we'll go upstairs for our coffee and cut this out. Bring up some cognac and arak, Tai," he added as he rose from the table.

They stopped to examine a moose's head on the stairway, and when they reached the library the pine logs in the fireplace had been lighted, and the coffee was bubbling before the hearth. Tai placed two chairs before the fire and brought a tray of cigarettes.

"Bring the cigars in my lower desk drawer, boy," the doctor directed. "Too much light in here, isn't there, Fred? Light the lamp there on my desk, Tai." He turned off the electric glare and settled himself deep into the chair opposite Ottenburg's.

"To go back to our conversation, doctor," Fred began while he waited for the first steam to blow off his coffee; "why don't you make up your mind to go to Washington? There'd be no fight made against you. I needn't say the United Breweries would back you. There'd be some KUDOS coming to us, too; backing a reform candidate."

Dr. Archie measured his length in his chair and thrust his large boots toward the crackling pitch-pine. He drank his coffee and lit a big black cigar while his guest looked over the assortment of cigarettes on the tray. "You say why don't I," the doctor spoke with the deliberation of a man in the position of having several courses to choose from, "but, on the other hand, why should I?" He puffed away and seemed, through his half-closed eyes, to look down several long roads with the intention of luxuriously rejecting all of them and remaining where he was. "I'm sick of politics. I'm disillusioned about serving my crowd, and I don't particularly want to serve yours. Nothing in it that I particularly want; and a man's not effective in politics unless he wants something for himself, and wants it hard. I can reach my ends by straighter roads. There are plenty of things to keep me busy. We haven't begun to develop our resources in this State; we haven't had a look in on them yet. That's the only thing that isn't fake--making men and machines go, and actually turning out a product."

The doctor poured himself some white cordial and looked over the little glass into the fire with an expression which led Ottenburg to believe that he was getting at something in his own mind. Fred lit a cigarette and let his friend grope for his idea.

"My boys, here," Archie went on, "have got me rather interested in Japan. Think I'll go out there in the spring, and come back the other way, through Siberia. I've always wanted to go to Russia." His eyes still hunted for something in his big fireplace. With a slow turn of his head he brought them back to his guest and fixed them upon him. "Just now, I'm thinking of running on to New York for a few weeks," he ended abruptly.

Ottenburg lifted his chin. "Ah!" he exclaimed, as if he began to see Archie's drift. "Shall you see Thea?"

"Yes." The doctor replenished his cordial glass. "In fact, I suspect I am going exactly TO see her. I'm getting stale on things here, Fred. Best people in the world and always doing things for me. I'm fond of them, too, but I've been with them too much. I'm getting ill-tempered, and the first thing I know I'll be hurting people's feelings. I snapped Mrs. Dandridge up over the telephone this afternoon when she asked me to go out to Colorado Springs on Sunday to meet some English people who are staying at the Antlers. Very nice of her to want me, and I was as sour as if she'd been trying to work me for something. I've got to get out for a while, to save my reputation."

To this explanation Ottenburg had not paid much attention. He seemed to be looking at a fixed point: the yellow glass eyes of a fine wildcat over one of the bookcases. "You've never heard her at all, have you?" he asked reflectively. "Curious, when this is her second season in New York."

"I was going on last March. Had everything arranged. And then old Cap Harris thought he could drive his car and me through a lamp-post and I was laid up with a compound fracture for two months. So I didn't get to see Thea."

Ottenburg studied the red end of his cigarette attentively. "She might have come out to see you. I remember you covered the distance like a streak when she wanted you."

Archie moved uneasily. "Oh, she couldn't do that. She had to get back to Vienna to work on some new parts for this year. She sailed two days after the New York season closed."

"Well, then she couldn't, of course." Fred smoked his cigarette close and tossed the end into the fire. "I'm tremendously glad you're going now. If you're stale, she'll jack you up. That's one of her specialties. She got a rise out of me last December that lasted me all winter."

"Of course," the doctor apologized, "you know so much more about such things. I'm afraid it will be rather wasted on me. I'm no judge of music."

"Never mind that." The younger man pulled himself up in his chair. "She gets it across to people who aren't judges. That's just what she does." He relapsed into his former lassitude. "If you were stone deaf, it wouldn't all be wasted. It's a great deal to watch her. Incidentally, you know, she is very beautiful. Photographs give you no idea."

Dr. Archie clasped his large hands under his chin. "Oh, I'm counting on that. I don't suppose her voice will sound natural to me. Probably I wouldn't know it."

Ottenburg smiled. "You'll know it, if you ever knew it. It's the same voice, only more so. You'll know it."

"Did you, in Germany that time, when you wrote me? Seven years ago, now. That must have been at the very beginning."

"Yes, somewhere near the beginning. She sang one of the Rhine daughters." Fred paused and drew himself up again. "Sure, I knew it from the first note. I'd heard a good many young voices come up out of the Rhine, but, by gracious, I hadn't heard one like that!" He fumbled for another cigarette. "Mahler was conducting that night. I met him as he was leaving the house and had a word with him. `Interesting voice you tried out this evening,' I said. He stopped and smiled. `Miss Kronborg, you mean? Yes, very. She seems to sing for the idea. Unusual in a young singer.' I'd never heard him admit before that a singer could have an idea. She not only had it, but she got it across. The Rhine music, that I'd known since I was a boy, was fresh to me, vocalized for the first time. You realized that she was beginning that long story, adequately, with the end in view. Every phrase she sang was basic. She simply WAS the idea of the Rhine music." Ottenburg rose and stood with his back to the fire. "And at the end, where you don't see the maidens at all, the same thing again: two pretty voices AND the Rhine voice." Fred snapped his fingers and dropped his hand.

The doctor looked up at him enviously. "You see, all that would be lost on me," he said modestly. "I don't know the dream nor the interpretation thereof. I'm out of it. It's too bad that so few of her old friends can appreciate her."

"Take a try at it," Fred encouraged him. "You'll get in deeper than you can explain to yourself. People with no personal interest do that."

"I suppose," said Archie diffidently, "that college German, gone to seed, wouldn't help me out much. I used to be able to make my German patients understand me."

"Sure it would!" cried Ottenburg heartily. "Don't be above knowing your libretto. That's all very well for musicians, but common mortals like you and me have got to know what she's singing about. Get out your dictionary and go at it as you would at any other proposition. Her diction is beautiful, and if you know the text you'll get a great deal. So long as you're going to hear her, get all that's coming to you. You bet in Germany people know their librettos by heart! You Americans are so afraid of stooping to learn anything."

"I AM a little ashamed," Archie admitted. "I guess that's the way we mask our general ignorance. However, I'll stoop this time; I'm more ashamed not to be able to follow her. The papers always say she's such a fine actress." He took up the tongs and began to rearrange the logs that had burned through and fallen apart. "I suppose she has changed a great deal?" he asked absently.

"We've all changed, my dear Archie,--she more than most of us. Yes, and no. She's all there, only there's a great deal more of her. I've had only a few words with her in several years. It's better not, when I'm tied up this way. The laws are barbarous, Archie."

"Your wife is--still the same?" the doctor asked sympathetically.

"Absolutely. Hasn't been out of a sanitarium for seven years now. No prospect of her ever being out, and as long as she's there I'm tied hand and foot. What does society get out of such a state of things, I'd like to know, except a tangle of irregularities? If you want to reform, there's an opening for you!"

"It's bad, oh, very bad; I agree with you!" Dr. Archie shook his head. "But there would be complications under another system, too. The whole question of a young man's marrying has looked pretty grave to me for a long while. How have they the courage to keep on doing it? It depresses me now to buy wedding presents." For some time the doctor watched his guest, who was sunk in bitter reflections. "Such things used to go better than they do now, I believe. Seems to me all the married people I knew when I was a boy were happy enough." He paused again and bit the end off a fresh cigar. "You never saw Thea's mother, did you, Ottenburg? That's a pity. Mrs. Kronborg was a fine woman. I've always been afraid Thea made a mistake, not coming home when Mrs. Kronborg was ill, no matter what it cost her."

Ottenburg moved about restlessly. "She couldn't, Archie, she positively couldn't. I felt you never understood that, but I was in Dresden at the time, and though I wasn't seeing much of her, I could size up the situation for myself. It was by just a lucky chance that she got to sing ELIZABETH that time at the Dresden Opera, a complication of circumstances. If she'd run away, for any reason, she might have waited years for such a chance to come again. She gave a wonderful performance and made a great impression. They offered her certain terms; she had to take them and follow it up then and there. In that game you can't lose a single trick. She was ill herself, but she sang. Her mother was ill, and she sang. No, you mustn't hold that against her, Archie. She did the right thing there." Ottenburg drew out his watch. "Hello! I must be traveling. You hear from her regularly?"

"More or less regularly. She was never much of a letterwriter. She tells me about her engagements and contracts, but I know so little about that business that it doesn't mean much to me beyond the figures, which seem very impressive. We've had a good deal of business correspondence, about putting up a stone to her father and mother, and, lately, about her youngest brother, Thor. He is with me now; he drives my car. To-day he's up at the mine."

Ottenburg, who had picked up his overcoat, dropped it. "Drives your car?" he asked incredulously.

"Yes. Thea and I have had a good deal of bother about Thor. We tried a business college, and an engineering school, but it was no good. Thor was born a chauffeur before there were cars to drive. He was never good for anything else; lay around home and collected postage stamps and took bicycles to pieces, waiting for the automobile to be invented. He's just as much a part of a car as the steering-gear. I can't find out whether he likes his job with me or not, or whether he feels any curiosity about his sister. You can't find anything out from a Kronborg nowadays. The mother was different."

Fred plunged into his coat. "Well, it's a queer world, Archie. But you'll think better of it, if you go to New York. Wish I were going with you. I'll drop in on you in the morning at about eleven. I want a word with you about this Interstate Commerce Bill. Good-night."

Dr. Archie saw his guest to the motor which was waiting below, and then went back to his library, where he replenished the fire and sat down for a long smoke. A man of Archie's modest and rather credulous nature develops late, and makes his largest gain between forty and fifty. At thirty, indeed, as we have seen, Archie was a soft-hearted boy under a manly exterior, still whistling to keep up his courage. Prosperity and large responsibilities--above all, getting free of poor Mrs. Archie--had brought out a good deal more than he knew was in him. He was thinking tonight as he sat before the fire, in the comfort he liked so well, that but for lucky chances, and lucky holes in the ground, he would still be a country practitioner, reading his old books by his office lamp. And yet, he was not so fresh and energetic as he ought to be. He was tired of business and of politics. Worse than that, he was tired of the men with whom he had to do and of the women who, as he said, had been kind to him. He felt as if he were still hunting for something, like old Jasper Flight. He knew that this was an unbecoming and ungrateful state of mind, and he reproached himself for it. But he could not help wondering why it was that life, even when it gave so much, after all gave so little. What was it that he had expected and missed? Why was he, more than he was anything else, disappointed?

He fell to looking back over his life and asking himself which years of it he would like to live over again,--just as they had been,--and they were not many. His college years he would live again, gladly. After them there was nothing he would care to repeat until he came to Thea Kronborg. There had been something stirring about those years in Moonstone, when he was a restless young man on the verge of breaking into larger enterprises, and when she was a restless child on the verge of growing up into something unknown. He realized now that she had counted for a great deal more to him than he knew at the time. It was a continuous sort of relationship. He was always on the lookout for her as he went about the town, always vaguely expecting her as he sat in his office at night. He had never asked himself then if it was strange that he should find a child of twelve the most interesting and companionable person in Moonstone. It had seemed a pleasant, natural kind of solicitude. He explained it then by the fact that he had no children of his own. But now, as he looked back at those years, the other interests were faded and inanimate. The thought of them was heavy. But wherever his life had touched Thea Kronborg's, there was still a little warmth left, a little sparkle. Their friendship seemed to run over those discontented years like a leafy pattern, still bright and fresh when the other patterns had faded into the dull background. Their walks and drives and confidences, the night they watched the rabbit in the moonlight,--why were these things stirring to remember? Whenever he thought of them, they were distinctly different from the other memories of his life;

always seemed humorous, gay, with a little thrill of anticipation and mystery about them. They came nearer to being tender secrets than any others he possessed. Nearer than anything else they corresponded to what he had hoped to find in the world, and had not found. It came over him now that the unexpected favors of fortune, no matter how dazzling, do not mean very much to us. They may excite or divert us for a time, but when we look back, the only things we cherish are those which in some way met our original want; the desire which formed in us in early youth, undirected, and of its own accord.

III

FOR the first four years after Thea went to Germany things went on as usual with the Kronborg family. Mrs. Kronborg's land in Nebraska increased in value and brought her in a good rental. The family drifted into an easier way of living, half without realizing it, as families will. Then Mr. Kronborg, who had never been ill, died suddenly of cancer of the liver, and after his death Mrs. Kronborg went, as her neighbors said, into a decline. Hearing discouraging reports of her from the physician who had taken over his practice, Dr. Archie went up from Denver to see her. He found her in bed, in the room where he had more than once attended her, a handsome woman of sixty with a body still firm and white, her hair, faded now to a very pale primrose, in two thick braids down her back, her eyes clear and calm. When the doctor arrived, she was sitting up in her bed, knitting. He felt at once how glad she was to see him, but he soon gathered that she had made no determination to get well. She told him, indeed, that she could not very well get along without Mr. Kronborg. The doctor looked at her with astonishment. Was it possible that she could miss the foolish old man so much? He reminded her of her children.

"Yes," she replied; "the children are all very well, but they are not father. We were married young."

The doctor watched her wonderingly as she went on knitting, thinking how much she looked like Thea. The difference was one of degree rather than of kind. The daughter had a compelling enthusiasm, the mother had none. But their framework, their foundation, was very much the same.

In a moment Mrs. Kronborg spoke again. "Have you heard anything from Thea lately?"

During his talk with her, the doctor gathered that what Mrs. Kronborg really wanted was to see her daughter Thea. Lying there day after day, she wanted it calmly and continuously. He told her that, since she felt so, he thought they might ask Thea to come home.

"I've thought a good deal about it," said Mrs. Kronborg slowly. "I hate to interrupt her, now that she's begun to get advancement. I expect she's seen some pretty hard times, though she was never one to complain. Perhaps she'd feel that she would like to come. It would be hard, losing both of us while she's off there."

When Dr. Archie got back to Denver he wrote a long letter to Thea, explaining her mother's condition and how much she wished to see her, and asking Thea to come, if only for a few weeks. Thea had repaid the money she had borrowed from him, and he assured her that if she happened to be short of funds for the journey, she had only to cable him.

A month later he got a frantic sort of reply from Thea. Complications in the opera at Dresden had given her an unhoped-for opportunity to go on in a big part. Before this letter reached the doctor, she would have made her debut as ELIZABETH, in "Tannhauser." She wanted to go to her mother more than she wanted anything else in the world, but, unless she failed,--which she would not,--she absolutely could not leave Dresden for six months. It was not that she chose to stay; she had to stay--or lose everything. The next few months would put her five years ahead, or would put her back so far that it would be of no use to struggle further. As soon as she was free, she would go to Moonstone and take her mother back to Germany with her. Her mother, she was sure, could live for years yet, and she would like German people and German ways, and could be hearing music all the time. Thea said she was writing her mother and begging her to help her one last time; to get strength and to wait for her six months, and then she (Thea) would do everything. Her mother would never have to make an effort again.

Dr. Archie went up to Moonstone at once. He had great confidence in Mrs. Kronborg's power of will, and if Thea's appeal took hold of her enough, he believed she might get better. But when he was shown into the familiar room off the parlor, his heart sank. Mrs. Kronborg was lying serene and fateful on her pillows. On the dresser at the foot of her bed there was a large photograph of Thea in the character in which she was to make her debut. Mrs. Kronborg pointed to it.

"Isn't she lovely, doctor? It's nice that she hasn't changed much. I've seen her look like that many a time."

They talked for a while about Thea's good fortune. Mrs. Kronborg had had a cablegram saying, "First performance well received. Great relief." In her letter Thea said; "If you'll only get better, dear mother, there's nothing I can't do. I will make a really great success, if you'll try with me. You shall have everything you want, and we will always be together. I have a little house all picked out where we are to live."

"Bringing up a family is not all it's cracked up to be," said Mrs. Kronborg with a flicker of irony, as she tucked the letter back under her pillow. "The children you don't especially need, you have always with you, like the poor. But the bright ones get away from you. They have their own way to make in the world. Seems like the brighter they are, the farther they go. I used to feel sorry that you had no family, doctor, but maybe you're as well off."

"Thea's plan seems sound to me, Mrs. Kronborg. There's no reason I can see why you shouldn't pull up and live for years yet, under proper care. You'd have the best doctors in the world over there, and it would be wonderful to live with anybody who looks like that." He nodded at the photograph of the young woman who must have been singing "DICH, THEURE HALLE, GRUSS' ICH WIEDER," her eyes looking up, her beautiful hands outspread with pleasure.

Mrs. Kronborg laughed quite cheerfully. "Yes, wouldn't it? If father were here, I might rouse myself. But sometimes it's hard to come back. Or if she were in trouble, maybe I could rouse myself."

"But, dear Mrs. Kronborg, she is in trouble," her old friend expostulated. "As she says, she's never needed you as she needs you now. I make my guess that she's never begged anybody to help her before."

Mrs. Kronborg smiled. "Yes, it's pretty of her. But that will pass. When these things happen far away they don't make such a mark; especially if your hands are full and you've duties of your own to think about. My own father died in Nebraska when Gunner was born,--we were living in Iowa then,--and I was sorry, but the baby made it up to me. I was father's favorite, too. That's the way it goes, you see."

The doctor took out Thea's letter to him, and read it over to Mrs. Kronborg. She seemed to listen, and not to listen.

When he finished, she said thoughtfully: "I'd counted on hearing her sing again. But I always took my pleasures as they come. I always enjoyed her singing when she was here about the house. While she was practicing I often used to leave my work and sit down in a rocker and give myself up to it, the same as if I'd been at an entertainment. I was never one of these housekeepers that let their work drive them to death. And when she had the Mexicans over here, I always took it in. First and last,"--she glanced judicially at the photograph,--"I guess I got about as much out of Thea's voice as anybody will ever get."

"I guess you did!" the doctor assented heartily; "and I got a good deal myself. You remember how she used to sing those Scotch songs for me, and lead us with her head, her hair bobbing?"

"'Flow Gently, Sweet Afton,'--I can hear it now," said Mrs. Kronborg; "and poor father never knew when he sang sharp! He used to say, 'Mother, how do you always know when they make mistakes practicing?'" Mrs. Kronborg chuckled.

Dr. Archie took her hand, still firm like the hand of a young woman. "It was lucky for her that you did know. I always thought she got more from you than from any of her teachers."

"Except Wunsch; he was a real musician," said Mrs. Kronborg respectfully. "I gave her what chance I could, in a crowded house. I kept the other children out of the parlor for her. That was about all I could do. If she wasn't disturbed, she needed no watching. She went after it like a terrier after rats from the first, poor child. She was downright afraid of it. That's why I always encouraged her taking Thor off to outlandish places. When she was out of the house, then she was rid of it."

After they had recalled many pleasant memories together, Mrs. Kronborg said suddenly: "I always understood about her going off without coming to see us that time. Oh, I know! You had to keep your own counsel. You were a good friend to her. I've never forgot that." She patted the doctor's sleeve and went on absently. "There was something she didn't want to tell me, and that's why she didn't come. Something happened when she was with those people in Mexico. I worried for a good while, but I guess she's come out of it all right. She'd had a pretty hard time, scratching along alone like that when she was so young, and my farms in Nebraska were down so low that I couldn't help her none. That's no way to send a girl out. But I guess, whatever there was, she wouldn't be afraid to tell me now." Mrs. Kronborg looked up at the photograph with a smile. "She doesn't look like she was beholding to anybody, does she?"

"She isn't, Mrs. Kronborg. She never has been. That was why she borrowed the money from me."

"Oh, I knew she'd never have sent for you if she'd done anything to shame us. She was always proud." Mrs. Kronborg paused and turned a little on her side. "It's been quite a satisfaction to you and me, doctor, having her voice turn out so fine. The things you hope for don't always turn out like that, by a long sight. As long as old Mrs. Kohler lived, she used always to translate what it said about Thea in the German papers she sent. I could make some of it out myself,--it's not very different from Swedish,--but it pleased the old lady. She left Thea her piece-picture of the burning of Moscow. I've got it put away in moth-balls for her, along with the oboe her grandfather brought from Sweden. I want her to take father's oboe back there some day." Mrs. Kronborg paused a moment and compressed her lips. "But I guess she'll take a finer instrument than that with her, back to Sweden!" she added.

Her tone fairly startled the doctor, it was so vibrating with a fierce, defiant kind of pride he had heard often in Thea's voice. He looked down wonderingly at his old friend and patient. After all, one never knew people to the core. Did she, within her, hide some of that still passion of which her daughter was all-compact?

"That last summer at home wasn't very nice for her," Mrs. Kronborg began as placidly as if the fire had never leaped up in her. "The other children were acting-up because they thought I might make a fuss over her and give her the big-head. We gave her the dare, somehow, the lot of us, because we couldn't understand her changing teachers and all that. That's the trouble about giving the dare to them quiet, unboastful children; you never know how far it'll take 'em. Well, we ought not to complain, doctor; she's given us a good deal to think about."

The next time Dr. Archie came to Moonstone, he came to be a pall-bearer at Mrs. Kronborg's funeral. When he last looked at her, she was so serene and queenly that he went back to Denver feeling almost as if he had helped to bury Thea Kronborg herself. The handsome head in the coffin seemed to him much more really Thea than did the radiant young woman in the picture, looking about at the Gothic vaultings and greeting the Hall of Song.

IV

ONE bright morning late in February Dr. Archie was breakfasting comfortably at the Waldorf. He had got into Jersey City on an early train, and a red, windy sunrise over the North River had given him a good appetite. He consulted the morning paper while he drank his coffee and saw that "Lohengrin" was to be sung at the opera that evening. In the list of the artists who would appear was the name "Kronborg." Such abruptness rather startled him. "Kronborg": it was impressive and yet, somehow, disrespectful; somewhat rude and brazen, on the back page of the morning paper. After breakfast he went to the hotel ticket office and asked the girl if she could give him something for "Lohengrin," "near the front." His manner was a trifle awkward and he wondered whether the girl noticed it. Even if she did, of course, she could scarcely suspect. Before the ticket stand he saw a bunch of blue posters announcing the opera casts for the week. There was "Lohengrin," and under it he saw:--

ELSA VON BRABANT...Thea Kronborg.

That looked better. The girl gave him a ticket for a seat which she said was excellent. He paid for it and went out to the cabstand. He mentioned to the driver a number on Riverside Drive and got into a taxi. It would not, of course, be the right thing to call upon Thea when she was going to sing in the evening. He knew that much, thank goodness! Fred Ottenburg had hinted to him that, more than almost anything else, that would put one in wrong.

When he reached the number to which he directed his letters, he dismissed the cab and got out for a walk. The house in which Thea lived was as impersonal as the Waldorf, and quite as large. It was above 116th Street, where the Drive narrows, and in front of it the shelving bank dropped to the North River. As Archie strolled about the paths which traversed this slope, below the street level, the fourteen stories of the apartment hotel rose above him like a perpendicular cliff. He had no idea on which floor Thea lived, but he reflected, as his eye ran over the many windows, that the outlook would be fine from any floor. The forbidding hugeness of the house made him feel as if he had expected to meet Thea in a crowd and had missed her. He did not really believe that she was hidden away behind any of those glittering windows, or that he was to hear her this evening. His walk was curiously uninspiring and unsuggestive. Presently remembering that Ottenburg had encouraged him to study his lesson, he went down to the opera house and bought a libretto. He had even brought his old "Adler's German and English" in his trunk, and after luncheon he settled down in his gilded suite at the Waldorf with a big cigar and the text of "Lohengrin."

The opera was announced for seven-forty-five, but at half-past seven Archie took his seat in the right front of the orchestra circle. He had never been inside the Metropolitan Opera House before, and the height of the audience room, the rich color, and the sweep of the balconies were not without their effect upon him. He watched the house fill with a growing feeling of expectation. When the steel curtain rose and the men of the orchestra took their places, he felt distinctly nervous. The burst of applause which greeted the conductor keyed him still higher. He found that he had taken off his gloves and twisted them to a string. When the lights went down and the violins began the overture, the place looked larger than ever; a great pit, shadowy and solemn. The whole atmosphere, he reflected, was somehow more serious than he had anticipated.

After the curtains were drawn back upon the scene beside the Scheldt, he got readily into the swing of the story. He was so much interested in the bass who sang KING HENRY that he had almost forgotten for what he was waiting so nervously, when the HERALD began in stentorian tones to summon ELSA VON BRABANT. Then he began to realize that he was rather frightened. There was a flutter of white at the back of the stage, and women began to come in: two, four, six, eight, but not the right one. It flashed across him that this was something like buck-fever, the paralyzing moment that comes upon a man when his first elk looks at him through the bushes, under its great antlers; the moment when a man's mind is so full of shooting that he forgets the gun in his hand until the buck nods adieu to him from a distant hill.

All at once, before the buck had left him, she was there. Yes, unquestionably it was she. Her eyes were downcast, but the head, the cheeks, the chin--there could be no mistake; she advanced slowly, as if she were walking in her sleep. Some one spoke to her; she only inclined her head. He spoke again, and she bowed her head still lower. Archie had forgotten his libretto, and he had not counted upon these long pauses. He had expected her to appear and sing and reassure him. They seemed to be waiting for her. Did she ever forget? Why in thunder didn't she--She made a sound, a faint one. The people on the stage whispered together and seemed confounded. His nervousness was absurd. She must have done this often before; she knew her bearings. She made another sound, but he could make nothing of it. Then the King sang to her, and Archie began to remember where they were in the story. She came to the front of the stage, lifted her eyes for the first time, clasped her hands and began, "EINSAM IN TRUBEN TAGEN."

Yes, it was exactly like buck-fever. Her face was there, toward the house now, before his eyes, and he positively could not see it. She was singing, at last, and he positively could not hear her. He was conscious of nothing but an uncomfortable dread and a sense of crushing disappointment. He had, after all, missed her. Whatever was there, she was not there--for him.

The King interrupted her. She began again, "IN LICHTER WAFFEN SCHEINE." Archie did not know when his buckfever passed, but presently he found that he was sitting quietly in a darkened house, not listening to but dreaming upon a river of silver sound. He felt apart from the others, drifting alone on the melody, as if he had been alone with it for a long while and had known it all before. His power of attention was not great just then, but in so far as it went he seemed to be looking through an exalted calmness at a beautiful woman from far away, from another sort of life and feeling and understanding than his own, who had in her face something he had known long ago, much brightened and beautified. As a lad he used to believe that the faces of people who died were like that in the next world; the same faces, but shining with the light of a new understanding. No, Ottenburg had not prepared him!

What he felt was admiration and estrangement. The homely reunion, that he had somehow expected, now seemed foolish. Instead of feeling proud that he knew her better than all these people about him, he felt chagrined at his own ingenuousness. For he did not know her better. This woman he had never known; she had somehow devoured his little friend, as the wolf ate up Red Ridinghood. Beautiful, radiant, tender as she was, she chilled his old affection; that sort of feeling was not appropriate. She seemed much, much farther away from him than she had seemed all those years when she was in Germany. The ocean he could cross, but there was something here he could not cross. There was a moment, when she turned to the King and smiled that rare, sunrise smile of her childhood, when he thought she was coming back to him. After the HERALD'S second call for her champion, when she knelt in her impassioned prayer, there was again something familiar, a kind of wild wonder that she had had the power to call up long ago. But she merely reminded him of Thea; this was not the girl herself.

After the tenor came on, the doctor ceased trying to make the woman before him fit into any of his cherished recollections. He took her, in so far as he could, for what she was then and there. When the knight raised the kneeling girl and put his mailed hand on her hair, when she lifted to him a face full of worship and passionate humility, Archie gave up his last reservation. He knew no more about her than did the hundreds around him, who sat in the shadow and looked on, as he looked, some with more understanding, some with less. He knew as much about ORTRUDE or LOHENGRIN as he knew about ELSA--more, because she went further than they, she sustained the legendary beauty of her conception more consistently. Even he could see that. Attitudes, movements, her face, her white arms and fingers, everything was suffused with a rosy tenderness, a warm humility, a gracious and yet--to him--wholly estranging beauty.

During the balcony singing in the second act the doctor's thoughts were as far away from Moonstone as the singer's doubtless were. He had begun, indeed, to feel the exhilaration of getting free from personalities, of being released from his own past as well as from Thea Kronborg's. It was very much, he told himself, like a military funeral, exalting and impersonal. Something old died in one, and out of it something new was born. During the duet with ORTRUDE, and the splendors of the wedding processional, this new feeling grew and grew. At the end of the act there were many curtain calls and ELSA acknowledged them, brilliant, gracious, spirited, with her far-breaking smile; but on the whole she was harder and more self-contained before the curtain than she was in the scene behind it. Archie did his part in the applause that greeted her, but it was the new and wonderful he applauded, not the old and dear. His personal, proprietary pride in her was frozen out.

He walked about the house during the ENTR'ACTE, and here and there among the people in the foyer he caught the name "Kronborg." On the staircase, in front of the coffeeroom, a long-haired youth with a fat face was discoursing to a group of old women about "die Kronborg." Dr. Archie gathered that he had crossed on the boat with her.

After the performance was over, Archie took a taxi and started for Riverside Drive. He meant to see it through to-night. When he entered the reception hall of the hotel before which he had strolled that morning, the hall porter challenged him. He said he was waiting for Miss Kronborg. The porter looked at him suspiciously and asked whether he had an appointment. He answered brazenly that he had. He was not used to being questioned by hall boys. Archie sat first in one tapestry chair and then in another, keeping a sharp eye on the people who came in and went up in the elevators. He walked about and looked at his watch. An hour dragged by. No one had come in from the street now for about twenty minutes, when two women entered, carrying a great many flowers and followed by a tall young man in chauffeur's uniform. Archie advanced toward the taller of the two women, who was veiled and carried her head very firmly. He confronted her just as she reached the elevator. Although he did not stand directly in her way, something in his attitude compelled her to stop. She gave him a piercing, defiant glance through the white scarf that covered her face. Then she lifted her hand and brushed the scarf back from her head. There was still black on her brows and lashes. She was very pale and her face was drawn and deeply lined. She looked, the doctor told himself with a sinking heart, forty years old. Her suspicious, mystified stare cleared slowly.

"Pardon me," the doctor murmured, not knowing just how to address her here before the porters, "I came up from the opera. I merely wanted to say good-night to you."

Without speaking, still looking incredulous, she pushed him into the elevator. She kept her hand on his arm while the cage shot up, and she looked away from him, frowning, as if she were trying to remember or realize something. When the cage stopped, she pushed him out of the elevator through another door, which a maid opened, into a square hall. There she sank down on a chair and looked up at him.

"Why didn't you let me know?" she asked in a hoarse voice.

Archie heard himself laughing the old, embarrassed laugh that seldom happened to him now. "Oh, I wanted to take my chance with you, like anybody else. It's been so long, now!"

She took his hand through her thick glove and her head dropped forward. "Yes, it has been long," she said in the same husky voice, "and so much has happened."

"And you are so tired, and I am a clumsy old fellow to break in on you to-night," the doctor added sympathetically. "Forgive me, this time." He bent over and put his hand soothingly on her shoulder. He felt a strong shudder run through her from head to foot.

Still bundled in her fur coat as she was, she threw both arms about him and hugged him. "Oh, Dr. Archie, DR. ARCHIE,"--she shook him,--"don't let me go. Hold on, now you're here," she laughed, breaking away from him at the same moment and sliding out of her fur coat. She left it for the maid to pick up and pushed the doctor into the sitting-room, where she turned on the lights. "Let me LOOK at you. Yes; hands, feet, head, shoulders--just the same. You've grown no older. You can't say as much for me, can you?"

She was standing in the middle of the room, in a white silk shirtwaist and a short black velvet skirt, which somehow suggested that they had `cut off her petticoats all round about.' She looked distinctly clipped and plucked. Her hair was parted in the middle and done very close to her head, as she had worn it under the wig. She looked like a fugitive, who had escaped from something in clothes caught up at hazard. It flashed across Dr. Archie that she was running away from the other woman down at the opera house, who had used her hardly.

He took a step toward her. "I can't tell a thing in the world about you, Thea--if I may still call you that."

She took hold of the collar of his overcoat. "Yes, call me that. Do: I like to hear it. You frighten me a little, but I expect I frighten you more. I'm always a scarecrow after I sing a long part like that--so high, too." She absently pulled out the handkerchief that protruded from his breast pocket and began to wipe the black paint off her eyebrows and lashes. "I can't take you in much to-night, but I must see you for a little while." She pushed him to a chair. "I shall be more recognizable to-morrow. You mustn't think of me as you see me to-night. Come at four to-morrow afternoon and have tea with me. Can you? That's good."

She sat down in a low chair beside him and leaned forward, drawing her shoulders together. She seemed to him inappropriately young and inappropriately old, shorn of her long tresses at one end and of her long robes at the other.

"How do you happen to be here?" she asked abruptly. "How can you leave a silver mine? I couldn't! Sure nobody'll cheat you? But you can explain everything tomorrow." She paused. "You remember how you sewed me up in a poultice, once? I wish you could to-night. I need a poultice, from top to toe. Something very disagreeable happened down there. You said you were out front? Oh, don't say anything about it. I always know exactly how it goes, unfortunately. I was rotten in the balcony. I never get that. You didn't notice it? Probably not, but I did."

Here the maid appeared at the door and her mistress rose. "My supper? Very well, I'll come. I'd ask you to stay, doctor, but there wouldn't be enough for two. They seldom send up enough for one,"--she spoke bitterly. "I haven't got a sense of you yet,"--turning directly to Archie again. "You haven't been here. You've only announced yourself, and told me you are coming to-morrow. You haven't seen me, either. This is not I. But I'll be here waiting for you to-morrow, my whole works! Goodnight, till then." She patted him absently on the sleeve and gave him a little shove toward the door.

V

WHEN Archie got back to his hotel at two o'clock in the morning, he found Fred Ottenburg's card under his door, with a message scribbled across the top: "When you come in, please call up room 811, this hotel." A moment later Fred's voice reached him over the telephone.

"That you, Archie? Won't you come up? I'm having some supper and I'd like company. Late? What does that matter? I won't keep you long."

Archie dropped his overcoat and set out for room 811. He found Ottenburg in the act of touching a match to a chafing-dish, at a table laid for two in his sitting-room. "I'm catering here," he announced cheerfully. "I let the waiter off at midnight, after he'd set me up. You'll have to account for yourself, Archie."

The doctor laughed, pointing to three wine-coolers under the table. "Are you expecting guests?"

"Yes, two." Ottenburg held up two fingers,--"you, and my higher self. He's a thirsty boy, and I don't invite him often. He has been known to give me a headache. Now, where have you been, Archie, until this shocking hour?"

"Bah, you've been banting!" the doctor exclaimed, pulling out his white gloves as he searched for his handkerchief and throwing them into a chair. Ottenburg was in evening clothes and very pointed dress shoes. His white waistcoat, upon which the doctor had fixed a challenging eye, went down straight from the top button, and he wore a camelia. He was conspicuously brushed and trimmed and polished. His smoothly controlled excitement was wholly different from his usual easy cordiality, though he had his face, as well as his figure, well in hand. On the serving-table there was an empty champagne pint and a glass. He had been having a little starter, the doctor told himself, and would probably be running on high gear before he got through. There was even now an air of speed about him.

"Been, Freddy?"--the doctor at last took up his question. "I expect I've been exactly where you have. Why didn't you tell me you were coming on?"

"I wasn't, Archie." Fred lifted the cover of the chafingdish and stirred the contents. He stood behind the table, holding the lid with his handkerchief. "I had never thought of such a thing. But Landry, a young chap who plays her accompaniments and who keeps an eye out for me, telegraphed me that Madame Rheinecker had gone to Atlantic City with a bad throat, and Thea might have a chance to sing ELSA. She has sung it only twice here before, and I missed it in Dresden. So I came on. I got in at four this afternoon and saw you registered, but I thought I wouldn't butt in. How lucky you got here just when she was coming on for this. You couldn't have hit a better time." Ottenburg stirred the contents of the dish faster and put in more sherry. "And where have you been since twelve o'clock, may I ask?"

Archie looked rather self-conscious, as he sat down on a fragile gilt chair that rocked under him, and stretched out his long legs. "Well, if you'll believe me, I had the brutality to go to see her. I wanted to identify her. Couldn't wait."

Ottenburg placed the cover quickly on the chafing-dish and took a step backward. "You did, old sport? My word! None but the brave deserve the fair. Well,"--he stooped to turn the wine,--"and how was she?"

"She seemed rather dazed, and pretty well used up. She seemed disappointed in herself, and said she hadn't done herself justice in the balcony scene."

"Well, if she didn't, she's not the first. Beastly stuff to sing right in there; lies just on the `break' in the voice." Fred pulled a bottle out of the ice and drew the cork. Lifting his glass he looked meaningly at Archie. "You know who, doctor. Here goes!" He drank off his glass with a sigh of satisfaction. After he had turned the lamp low under the chafing-dish, he remained standing, looking pensively down at the food on the table. "Well, she rather pulled it off! As a backer, you're a winner, Archie. I congratulate you." Fred poured himself another glass. "Now you must eat something, and so must I. Here, get off that bird cage and find a steady chair. This stuff ought to be rather good; head waiter's suggestion. Smells all right." He bent over the chafing-dish and began to serve the contents. "Perfectly innocuous: mushrooms and truffles and a little crab-meat. And now, on the level, Archie, how did it hit you?"

Archie turned a frank smile to his friend and shook his head. "It was all miles beyond me, of course, but it gave me a pulse. The general excitement got hold of me, I suppose. I like your wine, Freddy." He put down his glass. "It goes to the spot to-night. She WAS all right, then? You weren't disappointed?"

"Disappointed? My dear Archie, that's the high voice we dream of; so pure and yet so virile and human. That combination hardly ever happens with sopranos." Ottenburg sat down and turned to the doctor, speaking calmly and trying to dispel his friend's manifest bewilderment. "You see, Archie, there's the voice itself, so beautiful and individual, and then there's something else; the thing in it which responds to every shade of thought and feeling, spontaneously, almost unconsciously. That color has to be born in a singer, it can't be acquired; lots of beautiful voices haven't a vestige of it. It's almost like another gift--the rarest of all. The voice simply is the mind and is the heart. It can't go wrong in interpretation, because it has in it the thing that makes all interpretation. That's why you feel so sure of her. After you've listened to her for an hour or so, you aren't afraid of anything. All the little dreads you have with other artists vanish. You lean back and you say to yourself, `No, THAT voice will never betray.' TREULICH GEFUHRT, TREULICH BEWACHT."

Archie looked envyingly at Fred's excited, triumphant face. How satisfactory it must be, he thought, to really know what she was doing and not to have to take it on hearsay. He took up his glass with a sigh. "I seem to need a good deal of cooling off to-night. I'd just as lief forget the Reform Party for once.

"Yes, Fred," he went on seriously; "I thought it sounded very beautiful, and I thought she was very beautiful, too. I never imagined she could be as beautiful as that."

"Wasn't she? Every attitude a picture, and always the right kind of picture, full of that legendary, supernatural thing she gets into it. I never heard the prayer sung like that before. That look that came in her eyes; it went right out through the back of the roof. Of course, you get an ELSA who can look through walls like that, and visions and Grail-knights happen naturally. She becomes an abbess, that girl, after LOHENGRIN leaves her. She's made to live with ideas and enthusiasms, not with a husband." Fred folded his arms, leaned back in his chair, and began to sing softly:--

"Ein Ritter nahte da."

"Doesn't she die, then, at the end?" the doctor asked guardedly.

Fred smiled, reaching under the table. "Some ELSAS do; she didn't. She left me with the distinct impression that she was just beginning. Now, doctor, here's a cold one." He twirled a napkin smoothly about the green glass, the cork gave and slipped out with a soft explosion. "And now we must have another toast. It's up to you, this time."

The doctor watched the agitation in his glass. "The same," he said without lifting his eyes. "That's good enough. I can't raise you."

Fred leaned forward, and looked sharply into his face. "That's the point; how COULD you raise me? Once again!"

"Once again, and always the same!" The doctor put down his glass. "This doesn't seem to produce any symptoms in me to-night." He lit a cigar. "Seriously, Freddy, I wish I knew more about what she's driving at. It makes me jealous, when you are so in it and I'm not."

"In it?" Fred started up. "My God, haven't you seen her this blessed night?--when she'd have kicked any other man down the elevator shaft, if I know her. Leave me something; at least what I can pay my five bucks for."

"Seems to me you get a good deal for your five bucks," said Archie ruefully. "And that, after all, is what she cares about,--what people get."

Fred lit a cigarette, took a puff or two, and then threw it away. He was lounging back in his chair, and his face was pale and drawn hard by that mood of intense concentration which lurks under the sunny shallows of the vineyard. In his voice there was a longer perspective than usual, a slight remoteness. "You see, Archie, it's all very simple, a natural development. It's exactly what Mahler said back there in the beginning, when she sang WOGLINDE. It's the idea, the basic idea, pulsing behind every bar she sings. She simplifies a character down to the musical idea it's built on, and makes everything conform to that. The people who chatter about her being a great actress don't seem to get the notion of where SHE gets the notion. It all goes back to her original endowment, her tremendous musical talent. Instead of inventing a lot of business and expedients to suggest character, she knows the thing at the root, and lets the musical pattern take care of her. The score pours her into all those lovely postures, makes the light and shadow go over her face, lifts her and drops her. She lies on it, the way she used to lie on the Rhine music. Talk about rhythm!"

The doctor frowned dubiously as a third bottle made its appearance above the cloth. "Aren't you going in rather strong?"

Fred laughed. "No, I'm becoming too sober. You see this is breakfast now; kind of wedding breakfast. I feel rather weddingish. I don't mind. You know," he went on as the wine gurgled out, "I was thinking to-night when they sprung the wedding music, how any fool can have that stuff played over him when he walks up the aisle with some dough-faced little hussy who's hooked him. But it isn't every fellow who can see--well, what we saw tonight. There are compensations in life, Dr. Howard Archie, though they come in disguise. Did you notice her when she came down the stairs? Wonder where she gets that brightand-morning star look? Carries to the last row of the family circle. I moved about all over the house. I'll tell you a secret, Archie: that carrying power was one of the first things that put me wise. Noticed it down there in Arizona, in the open. That, I said, belongs only to the big ones." Fred got up and began to move rhythmically about the room, his hands in his pockets. The doctor was astonished at his ease and steadiness, for there were slight lapses in his speech. "You see, Archie, ELSA isn't a part that's particularly suited to Thea's voice at all, as I see her voice. It's over-lyrical for her. She makes it, but there's nothing in it that fits her like a glove, except, maybe, that long duet in the third act. There, of course,"--he held out his hands as if he were measuring something,--"we know exactly where we are. But wait until they give her a chance at something that lies properly in her voice, and you'll see me rosier than I am to-night."

Archie smoothed the tablecloth with his hand. "I am sure I don't want to see you any rosier, Fred."

Ottenburg threw back his head and laughed. "It's enthusiasm, doctor. It's not the wine. I've got as much inflated as this for a dozen trashy things: brewers' dinners and political orgies. You, too, have your extravagances, Archie. And what I like best in you is this particular enthusiasm, which is not at all practical or sensible, which is downright Quixotic. You are not altogether what you seem, and you have your reservations. Living among the wolves, you have not become one. LUPIBUS VIVENDI NON LUPUS SUM."

The doctor seemed embarrassed. "I was just thinking how tired she looked, plucked of all her fine feathers, while we get all the fun. Instead of sitting here carousing, we ought to go solemnly to bed."

"I get your idea." Ottenburg crossed to the window and threw it open. "Fine night outside; a hag of a moon just setting. It begins to smell like morning. After all, Archie, think of the lonely and rather solemn hours we've spent waiting for all this, while she's been--reveling."

Archie lifted his brows. "I somehow didn't get the idea to-night that she revels much."

"I don't mean this sort of thing." Fred turned toward the light and stood with his back to the window. "That," with a nod toward the wine-cooler, "is only a cheap imitation, that any poor stiff-fingered fool can buy and feel his shell grow thinner. But take it from me, no matter what she pays, or how much she may see fit to lie about it, the real, the master revel is hers." He leaned back against the window sill and crossed his arms. "Anybody with all that voice and all that talent and all that beauty, has her hour. Her hour," he went on deliberately, "when she can say, 'there it is, at last, WIE IM TRAUM ICH. As in my dream I dreamed it, as in my will it was.'"

He stood silent a moment, twisting the flower from his coat by the stem and staring at the blank wall with haggard abstraction. "Even I can say to-night, Archie," he brought out slowly, "'As in my dream I dreamed it, as in my will it was.' Now, doctor, you may leave me. I'm beautifully drunk, but not with anything that ever grew in France."

The doctor rose. Fred tossed his flower out of the window behind him and came toward the door. "I say," he called, "have you a date with anybody?"

The doctor paused, his hand on the knob. "With Thea, you mean? Yes. I'm to go to her at four this afternoon--if you haven't paralyzed me."

"Well, you won't eat me, will you, if I break in and send up my card? She'll probably turn me down cold, but that won't hurt my feelings. If she ducks me, you tell her for me, that to spite me now she'd have to cut off more than she can spare. Good-night, Archie."

VI

IT was late on the morning after the night she sang ELSA, when Thea Kronborg stirred uneasily in her bed. The room was darkened by two sets of window shades, and the day outside was thick and cloudy. She turned and tried to recapture unconsciousness, knowing that she would not be able to do so. She dreaded waking stale and disappointed after a great effort. The first thing that came was always the sense of the futility of such endeavor, and of the absurdity of trying too hard. Up to a certain point, say eighty degrees, artistic endeavor could be fat and comfortable, methodical and prudent. But if you went further than that, if you drew yourself up toward ninety degrees, you parted with your defenses and left yourself exposed to mischance. The legend was that in those upper reaches you might be divine; but you were much likelier to be ridiculous. Your public wanted just about eighty degrees; if you gave it more it blew its nose and put a crimp in you. In the morning, especially, it seemed to her very probable that whatever struggled above the good average was not quite sound. Certainly very little of that superfluous ardor, which cost so dear, ever got across the footlights. These misgivings waited to pounce upon her when she wakened. They hovered about her bed like vultures.

She reached under her pillow for her handkerchief, without opening her eyes. She had a shadowy memory that there was to be something unusual, that this day held more disquieting possibilities than days commonly held. There was something she dreaded; what was it? Oh, yes, Dr. Archie was to come at four.

A reality like Dr. Archie, poking up out of the past, reminded one of disappointments and losses, of a freedom that was no more: reminded her of blue, golden mornings long ago, when she used to waken with a burst of joy at recovering her precious self and her precious world; when she never lay on her pillows at eleven o'clock like something the waves had washed up. After all, why had he come? It had been so long, and so much had happened. The things she had lost, he would miss readily enough. What she had gained, he would scarcely perceive. He, and all that he recalled, lived for her as memories. In sleep, and in hours of illness or exhaustion, she went back to them and held them to her heart. But they were better as memories. They had nothing to do with the struggle that made up her actual life. She felt drearily that she was not flexible enough to be the person her old friend expected her to be, the person she herself wished to be with him.

Thea reached for the bell and rang twice,--a signal to her maid to order her breakfast. She rose and ran up the window shades and turned on the water in her bathroom, glancing into the mirror apprehensively as she passed it. Her bath usually cheered her, even on low mornings like this. Her white bathroom, almost as large as her sleepingroom, she regarded as a refuge. When she turned the key behind her, she left care and vexation on the other side of the door. Neither her maid nor the management nor her letters nor her accompanist could get at her now.

When she pinned her braids about her head, dropped her nightgown and stepped out to begin her Swedish movements, she was a natural creature again, and it was so that she liked herself best. She slid into the tub with anticipation and splashed and tumbled about a good deal. Whatever else she hurried, she never hurried her bath. She used her brushes and sponges and soaps like toys, fairly playing in the water. Her own body was always a cheering sight to her. When she was careworn, when her mind felt old and tired, the freshness of her physical self, her long, firm lines, the smoothness of her skin, reassured her. This morning, because of awakened memories, she looked at herself more carefully than usual, and was not discouraged. While she was in the tub she began to whistle softly the tenor aria, "AH! FUYEZ, DOUCE IMAGE," somehow appropriate to the bath. After a noisy moment under the cold shower, she stepped out on the rug flushed and glowing, threw her arms above her head, and rose on her toes, keeping the elevation as long as she could. When she dropped back on her heels and began to rub herself with the towels, she took up the aria again, and felt quite in the humor for seeing Dr. Archie. After she had returned to her bed, the maid brought her letters and the morning papers with her breakfast.

"Telephone Mr. Landry and ask him if he can come at half-past three, Theresa, and order tea to be brought up at five."

When Howard Archie was admitted to Thea's apartment that afternoon, he was shown into the music-room back of the little reception room. Thea was sitting in a davenport behind the piano, talking to a young man whom she later introduced as her friend Mr. Landry. As she rose, and came to meet him, Archie felt a deep relief, a sudden thankfulness. She no longer looked clipped and plucked, or dazed and fleeing.

Dr. Archie neglected to take account of the young man to whom he was presented. He kept Thea's hands and held her where he met her, taking in the light, lively sweep of her hair, her clear green eyes and her throat that came up strong and dazzlingly white from her green velvet gown. The chin was as lovely as ever, the cheeks as smooth. All the lines of last night had disappeared. Only at the outer corners of her eyes, between the eye and the temple, were the faintest indications of a future attack--mere kitten scratches that playfully hinted where one day the cat would claw her. He studied her without any embarrassment. Last night everything had been awkward; but now, as he held her hands, a kind of harmony came between them, a reestablishment of confidence.

"After all, Thea,--in spite of all, I still know you," he murmured.

She took his arm and led him up to the young man who was standing beside the piano. "Mr. Landry knows all about you, Dr. Archie. He has known about you for many years." While the two men shook hands she stood between them, drawing them together by her presence and her glances. "When I first went to Germany, Landry was studying there. He used to be good enough to work with me when I could not afford to have an accompanist for more than two hours a day. We got into the way of working together. He is a singer, too, and has his own career to look after, but he still manages to give me some time. I want you to be friends." She smiled from one to the other.

The rooms, Archie noticed, full of last night's flowers, were furnished in light colors, the hotel bleakness of them a little softened by a magnificent Steinway piano, white bookshelves full of books and scores, some drawings of ballet dancers, and the very deep sofa behind the piano.

"Of course," Archie asked apologetically, "you have seen the papers?"

"Very cordial, aren't they? They evidently did not expect as much as I did. ELSA is not really in my voice. I can sing the music, but I have to go after it."

"That is exactly," the doctor came out boldly, "what Fred Ottenburg said this morning."

They had remained standing, the three of them, by the piano, where the gray afternoon light was strongest. Thea turned to the doctor with interest. "Is Fred in town? They were from him, then--some flowers that came last night without a card." She indicated the white lilacs on the window sill. "Yes, he would know, certainly," she said thoughtfully. "Why don't we sit down? There will be some tea for you in a minute, Landry. He's very dependent upon it," disapprovingly to Archie. "Now tell me, Doctor, did you really have a good time last night, or were you uncomfortable? Did you feel as if I were trying to hold my hat on by my eyebrows?"

He smiled. "I had all kinds of a time. But I had no feeling of that sort. I couldn't be quite sure that it was you at all. That was why I came up here last night. I felt as if I'd lost you."

She leaned toward him and brushed his sleeve reassuringly. "Then I didn't give you an impression of painful struggle? Landry was singing at Weber and Fields' last night. He didn't get in until the performance was half over. But I see the TRIBUNE man felt that I was working pretty hard. Did you see that notice, Oliver?"

Dr. Archie looked closely at the red-headed young man for the first time, and met his lively brown eyes, full of a droll, confiding sort of humor. Mr. Landry was not prepossessing. He was undersized and clumsily made, with a red, shiny face and a sharp little nose that looked as if it had been whittled out of wood and was always in the air, on the scent of something. Yet it was this queer little beak, with his eyes, that made his countenance anything of a face at all. From a distance he looked like the groceryman's delivery boy in a small town. His dress seemed an acknowledgment of his grotesqueness: a short coat, like a little boys' roundabout, and a vest fantastically sprigged and dotted, over a lavender shirt.

At the sound of a muffled buzz, Mr. Landry sprang up.

"May I answer the telephone for you?" He went to the writing-table and took up the receiver. "Mr. Ottenburg is downstairs," he said, turning to Thea and holding the mouthpiece against his coat.

"Tell him to come up," she replied without hesitation. "How long are you going to be in town, Dr. Archie?"

"Oh, several weeks, if you'll let me stay. I won't hang around and be a burden to you, but I want to try to get educated up to you, though I expect it's late to begin."

Thea rose and touched him lightly on the shoulder. "Well, you'll never be any younger, will you?"

"I'm not so sure about that," the doctor replied gallantly.

The maid appeared at the door and announced Mr. Frederick Ottenburg. Fred came in, very much got up, the doctor reflected, as he watched him bending over Thea's hand. He was still pale and looked somewhat chastened, and the lock of hair that hung down over his forehead was distinctly moist. But his black afternoon coat, his gray tie and gaiters were of a correctness that Dr. Archie could never attain for all the efforts of his faithful slave, Van Deusen, the Denver haberdasher. To be properly up to those tricks, the doctor supposed, you had to learn them young. If he were to buy a silk hat that was the twin of Ottenburg's, it would be shaggy in a week, and he could never carry it as Fred held his.

Ottenburg had greeted Thea in German, and as she replied in the same language, Archie joined Mr. Landry at the window. "You know Mr. Ottenburg, he tells me?"

Mr. Landry's eyes twinkled. "Yes, I regularly follow him about, when he's in town. I would, even if he didn't send me such wonderful Christmas presents: Russian vodka by the half-dozen!"

Thea called to them, "Come, Mr. Ottenburg is calling on all of us. Here's the tea."

The maid opened the door and two waiters from downstairs appeared with covered trays. The tea-table was in the parlor. Thea drew Ottenburg with her and went to inspect it. "Where's the rum? Oh, yes, in that thing! Everything seems to be here, but send up some currant preserves and cream cheese for Mr. Ottenburg. And in about fifteen minutes, bring some fresh toast. That's all, thank you."

For the next few minutes there was a clatter of teacups and responses about sugar. "Landry always takes rum. I'm glad the rest of you don't. I'm sure it's bad." Thea poured the tea standing and got through with it as quickly as possible, as if it were a refreshment snatched between trains. The tea-table and the little room in which it stood seemed to be out of scale with her long step, her long reach, and the energy of her movements. Dr. Archie, standing near her, was pleasantly aware of the animation of her figure. Under the clinging velvet, her body seemed independent and unsubdued.

They drifted, with their plates and cups, back to the music-room. When Thea followed them, Ottenburg put down his tea suddenly. "Aren't you taking anything? Please let me." He started back to the table.

"No, thank you, nothing. I'm going to run over that aria for you presently, to convince you that I can do it. How did the duet go, with Schlag?"

She was standing in the doorway and Fred came up to her: "That you'll never do any better. You've worked your voice into it perfectly. Every NUANCE--wonderful!"

"Think so?" She gave him a sidelong glance and spoke with a certain gruff shyness which did not deceive anybody, and was not meant to deceive. The tone was equivalent to "Keep it up. I like it, but I'm awkward with it."

Fred held her by the door and did keep it up, furiously, for full five minutes. She took it with some confusion, seeming all the while to be hesitating, to be arrested in her course and trying to pass him. But she did not really try to pass, and her color deepened. Fred spoke in German, and Archie caught from her an occasional JA? SO? muttered rather than spoken.

When they rejoined Landry and Dr. Archie, Fred took up his tea again. "I see you're singing VENUS Saturday night. Will they never let you have a chance at ELIZABETH?"

She shrugged her shoulders. "Not here. There are so many singers here, and they try us out in such a stingy way. Think of it, last year I came over in October, and it was the first of December before I went on at all! I'm often sorry I left Dresden."

"Still," Fred argued, "Dresden is limited."

"Just so, and I've begun to sigh for those very limitations. In New York everything is impersonal. Your audience never knows its own mind, and its mind is never twice the same. I'd rather sing where the people are pig-headed and throw carrots at you if you don't do it the way they like it. The house here is splendid, and the night audiences are exciting. I hate the matinees; like singing at a KAFFEKLATSCH." She rose and turned on the lights.

"Ah!" Fred exclaimed, "why do you do that? That is a signal that tea is over." He got up and drew out his gloves.

"Not at all. Shall you be here Saturday night?" She sat down on the piano bench and leaned her elbow back on the keyboard. "Necker sings ELIZABETH. Make Dr. Archie go. Everything she sings is worth hearing."

"But she's failing so. The last time I heard her she had no voice at all. She IS a poor vocalist!"

Thea cut him off. "She's a great artist, whether she's in voice or not, and she's the only one here. If you want a big voice, you can take my ORTRUDE of last night; that's big enough, and vulgar enough."

Fred laughed and turned away, this time with decision. "I don't want her!" he protested energetically. "I only wanted to get a rise out of you. I like Necker's ELIZABETH well enough. I like your VENUS well enough, too."

"It's a beautiful part, and it's often dreadfully sung. It's very hard to sing, of course."

Ottenburg bent over the hand she held out to him. "For an uninvited guest, I've fared very well. You were nice to let me come up. I'd have been terribly cut up if you'd sent me away. May I?" He kissed her hand lightly and backed toward the door, still smiling, and promising to keep an eye on Archie. "He can't be trusted at all, Thea. One of the waiters at Martin's worked a Tourainian hare off on him at luncheon yesterday, for seven twenty-five."

Thea broke into a laugh, the deep one he recognized. "Did he have a ribbon on, this hare? Did they bring him in a gilt cage?"

"No,"--Archie spoke up for himself,--"they brought him in a brown sauce, which was very good. He didn't taste very different from any rabbit."

"Probably came from a push-cart on the East Side." Thea looked at her old friend commiseratingly. "Yes, DO keep an eye on him, Fred. I had no idea," shaking her head. "Yes, I'll be obliged to you."

"Count on me!" Their eyes met in a gay smile, and Fred bowed himself out.

VII

ON Saturday night Dr. Archie went with Fred Ottenburg to hear "Tannhauser." Thea had a rehearsal on Sunday afternoon, but as she was not on the bill again until Wednesday, she promised to dine with Archie and Ottenburg on Monday, if they could make the dinner early.

At a little after eight on Monday evening, the three friends returned to Thea's apartment and seated themselves for an hour of quiet talk.

"I'm sorry we couldn't have had Landry with us tonight," Thea said, "but he's on at Weber and Fields' every night now. You ought to hear him, Dr. Archie. He often sings the old Scotch airs you used to love."

"Why not go down this evening?" Fred suggested hopefully, glancing at his watch. "That is, if you'd like to go. I can telephone and find what time he comes on."

Thea hesitated. "No, I think not. I took a long walk this afternoon and I'm rather tired. I think I can get to sleep early and be so much ahead. I don't mean at once, however," seeing Dr. Archie's disappointed look. "I always like to hear Landry," she added. "He never had much voice, and it's worn, but there's a sweetness about it, and he sings with such taste."

"Yes, doesn't he? May I?" Fred took out his cigarette case. "It really doesn't bother your throat?"

"A little doesn't. But cigar smoke does. Poor Dr. Archie! Can you do with one of those?"

"I'm learning to like them," the doctor declared, taking one from the case Fred proffered him.

"Landry's the only fellow I know in this country who can do that sort of thing," Fred went on. "Like the best English ballad singers. He can sing even popular stuff by higher lights, as it were."

Thea nodded. "Yes; sometimes I make him sing his most foolish things for me. It's restful, as he does it. That's when I'm homesick, Dr. Archie."

"You knew him in Germany, Thea?" Dr. Archie had quietly abandoned his cigarette as a comfortless article. "When you first went over?"

"Yes. He was a good friend to a green girl. He helped me with my German and my music and my general discouragement. Seemed to care more about my getting on than about himself. He had no money, either. An old aunt had loaned him a little to study on.--Will you answer that, Fred?"

Fred caught up the telephone and stopped the buzz while Thea went on talking to Dr. Archie about Landry. Telling some one to hold the wire, he presently put down the instrument and approached Thea with a startled expression on his face.

"It's the management," he said quietly. "Gloeckler has broken down: fainting fits. Madame Rheinecker is in Atlantic City and Schramm is singing in Philadelphia tonight. They want to know whether you can come down and finish SIEGLINDE."

"What time is it?"

"Eight fifty-five. The first act is just over. They can hold the curtain twenty-five minutes."

Thea did not move. "Twenty-five and thirty-five makes sixty," she muttered. "Tell them I'll come if they hold the curtain till I am in the dressing-room. Say I'll have to wear her costumes, and the dresser must have everything ready. Then call a taxi, please."

Thea had not changed her position since he first interrupted her, but she had grown pale and was opening and shutting her hands rapidly. She looked, Fred thought, terrified. He half turned toward the telephone, but hung on one foot.

"Have you ever sung the part?" he asked.

"No, but I've rehearsed it. That's all right. Get the cab." Still she made no move. She merely turned perfectly blank eyes to Dr. Archie and said absently, "It's curious, but just at this minute I can't remember a bar of 'Walkure' after the first act. And I let my maid go out." She sprang up and beckoned Archie without so much, he felt sure, as knowing who he was. "Come with me." She went quickly into her sleeping-chamber and threw open a door into a trunk-room. "See that white trunk? It's not locked. It's full of wigs, in boxes. Look until you find one marked `Ring 2.' Bring it quick!" While she directed him, she threw open a square trunk and began tossing out shoes of every shape and color.

Ottenburg appeared at the door. "Can I help you?"

She threw him some white sandals with long laces and silk stockings pinned to them. "Put those in something, and then go to the piano and give me a few measures in there--you know." She was behaving somewhat like a cyclone now, and while she wrenched open drawers and closet doors, Ottenburg got to the piano as quickly as possible and began to herald the reappearance of the Volsung pair, trusting to memory.

In a few moments Thea came out enveloped in her long fur coat with a scarf over her head and knitted woolen gloves on her hands. Her glassy eye took in the fact that Fred was playing from memory, and even in her distracted state, a faint smile flickered over her colorless lips. She stretched out a woolly hand, "The score, please. Behind you, there."

Dr. Archie followed with a canvas box and a satchel. As they went through the hall, the men caught up their hats and coats. They left the music-room, Fred noticed, just seven minutes after he got the telephone message. In the elevator Thea said in that husky whisper which had so perplexed Dr. Archie when he first heard it, "Tell the driver he must do it in twenty minutes, less if he can. He must leave the light on in the cab. I can do a good deal in twenty minutes. If only you hadn't made me eat--Damn that duck!" she broke out bitterly; "why did you?"

"Wish I had it back! But it won't bother you, to-night. You need strength," he pleaded consolingly.

But she only muttered angrily under her breath, "Idiot, idiot!"

Ottenburg shot ahead and instructed the driver, while the doctor put Thea into the cab and shut the door. She did not speak to either of them again. As the driver scrambled into his seat she opened the score and fixed her eyes upon it. Her face, in the white light, looked as bleak as a stone quarry.

As her cab slid away, Ottenburg shoved Archie into a second taxi that waited by the curb. "We'd better trail her," he explained. "There might be a hold-up of some kind." As the cab whizzed off he broke into an eruption of profanity.

"What's the matter, Fred?" the doctor asked. He was a good deal dazed by the rapid evolutions of the last ten minutes.

"Matter enough!" Fred growled, buttoning his overcoat with a shiver. "What a way to sing a part for the first time! That duck really is on my conscience. It will be a wonder if she can do anything but quack! Scrambling on in the middle of a performance like this, with no rehearsal! The stuff she has to sing in there is a fright--rhythm, pitch,--and terribly difficult intervals."

"She looked frightened," Dr. Archie said thoughtfully, "but I thought she looked--determined."

Fred sniffed. "Oh, determined! That's the kind of rough deal that makes savages of singers. Here's a part she's worked on and got ready for for years, and now they give her a chance to go on and butcher it. Goodness knows when she's looked at the score last, or whether she can use the business she's studied with this cast. Necker's singing BRUNNHILDE; she may help her, if it's not one of her sore nights."

"Is she sore at Thea?" Dr. Archie asked wonderingly.

"My dear man, Necker's sore at everything. She's breaking up; too early; just when she ought to be at her best. There's one story that she is struggling under some serious malady, another that she learned a bad method at the Prague Conservatory and has ruined her organ. She's the sorest thing in the world. If she weathers this winter through, it'll be her last. She's paying for it with the last rags of her voice. And then--" Fred whistled softly.

"Well, what then?"

"Then our girl may come in for some of it. It's dog eat dog, in this game as in every other."

The cab stopped and Fred and Dr. Archie hurried to the box office. The Monday-night house was sold out. They bought standing room and entered the auditorium just as the press representative of the house was thanking the audience for their patience and telling them that although Madame Gloeckler was too ill to sing, Miss Kronborg had kindly consented to finish her part. This announcement was met with vehement applause from the upper circles of the house.

"She has her--constituents," Dr. Archie murmured.

"Yes, up there, where they're young and hungry. These people down here have dined too well. They won't mind, however. They like fires and accidents and DIVERTISSEMENTS. Two SIEGLINDES are more unusual than one, so they'll be satisfied."

After the final disappearance of the mother of Siegfried, Ottenburg and the doctor slipped out through the crowd and left the house. Near the stage entrance Fred found the driver who had brought Thea down. He dismissed him and got a larger car. He and Archie waited on the sidewalk, and when Kronborg came out alone they gathered her into the cab and sprang in after her.

Thea sank back into a corner of the back seat and yawned. "Well, I got through, eh?" Her tone was reassuring. "On the whole, I think I've given you gentlemen a pretty lively evening, for one who has no social accomplishments."

"Rather! There was something like a popular uprising at the end of the second act. Archie and I couldn't keep it up as long as the rest of them did. A howl like that ought to show the management which way the wind is blowing. You probably know you were magnificent."

"I thought it went pretty well," she spoke impartially. "I was rather smart to catch his tempo there, at the beginning of the first recitative, when he came in too soon, don't you think? It's tricky in there, without a rehearsal. Oh, I was all right! He took that syncopation too fast in the beginning. Some singers take it fast there--think it sounds more impassioned. That's one way!" She sniffed, and Fred shot a mirthful glance at Archie. Her boastfulness would have been childish in a schoolboy. In the light of what she had done, of the strain they had lived through during the last two hours, it made one laugh,--almost cry. She went on, robustly: "And I didn't feel my dinner, really, Fred. I am hungry again, I'm ashamed to say,--and I forgot to order anything at my hotel."

Fred put his hand on the door. "Where to? You must have food."

"Do you know any quiet place, where I won't be stared at? I've still got make-up on."

"I do. Nice English chop-house on Forty-fourth Street. Nobody there at night but theater people after the show, and a few bachelors." He opened the door and spoke to the driver.

As the car turned, Thea reached across to the front seat and drew Dr. Archie's handkerchief out of his breast pocket.

"This comes to me naturally," she said, rubbing her cheeks and eyebrows. "When I was little I always loved your handkerchiefs because they were silk and smelled of Cologne water. I think they must have been the only really clean handkerchiefs in Moonstone. You were always wiping my face with them, when you met me out in the dust, I remember. Did I never have any?"

"I think you'd nearly always used yours up on your baby brother."

Thea sighed. "Yes, Thor had such a way of getting messy. You say he's a good chauffeur?" She closed her eyes for a moment as if they were tired. Suddenly she looked up. "Isn't it funny, how we travel in circles? Here you are, still getting me clean, and Fred is still feeding me. I would have died of starvation at that boarding-house on Indiana Avenue if he hadn't taken me out to the Buckingham and filled me up once in a while. What a cavern I was to fill, too. The waiters used to look astonished. I'm still singing on that food."

Fred alighted and gave Thea his arm as they crossed the icy sidewalk. They were taken upstairs in an antiquated lift and found the cheerful chop-room half full of supper parties. An English company playing at the Empire had just come in. The waiters, in red waistcoats, were hurrying about. Fred got a table at the back of the room, in a corner, and urged his waiter to get the oysters on at once.

"Takes a few minutes to open them, sir," the man expostulated.

"Yes, but make it as few as possible, and bring the lady's first. Then grilled chops with kidneys, and salad."

Thea began eating celery stalks at once, from the base to the foliage. "Necker said something nice to me tonight. You might have thought the management would say something, but not they." She looked at Fred from under her blackened lashes. "It WAS a stunt, to jump in and sing that second act without rehearsal. It doesn't sing itself."

Ottenburg was watching her brilliant eyes and her face. She was much handsomer than she had been early in the evening. Excitement of this sort enriched her. It was only under such excitement, he reflected, that she was entirely illuminated, or wholly present. At other times there was something a little cold and empty, like a big room with no people in it. Even in her most genial moods there was a shadow of restlessness, as if she were waiting for something and were exercising the virtue of patience. During dinner she had been as kind as she knew how to be, to him and to Archie, and had given them as much of herself as she could. But, clearly, she knew only one way of being really kind, from the core of her heart out; and there was but one way in which she could give herself to people largely and gladly, spontaneously. Even as a girl she had been at her best in vigorous effort, he remembered; physical effort, when there was no other kind at hand. She could be expansive only in explosions. Old Nathanmeyer had seen it. In the very first song Fred had ever heard her sing, she had unconsciously declared it.

Thea Kronborg turned suddenly from her talk with Archie and peered suspiciously into the corner where Ottenburg sat with folded arms, observing her. "What's the matter with you, Fred? I'm afraid of you when you're quiet,--fortunately you almost never are. What are you thinking about?"

"I was wondering how you got right with the orchestra so quickly, there at first. I had a flash of terror," he replied easily.

She bolted her last oyster and ducked her head. "So had I! I don't know how I did catch it. Desperation, I suppose; same way the Indian babies swim when they're thrown into the river. I HAD to. Now it's over, I'm glad I had to. I learned a whole lot to-night."

Archie, who usually felt that it behooved him to be silent during such discussions, was encouraged by her geniality to venture, "I don't see how you can learn anything in such a turmoil; or how you can keep your mind on it, for that matter."

Thea glanced about the room and suddenly put her hand up to her hair. "Mercy, I've no hat on! Why didn't you tell me? And I seem to be wearing a rumpled dinner dress, with all this paint on my face! I must look like something you picked up on Second Avenue. I hope there are no Colorado reformers about, Dr. Archie. What a dreadful old pair these people must be thinking you! Well, I had to eat." She sniffed the savor of the grill as the waiter uncovered it. "Yes, draught beer, please. No, thank you, Fred, NO champagne.--To go back to your question, Dr. Archie, you can believe I keep my mind on it. That's the whole trick, in so far as stage experience goes; keeping right there every second. If I think of anything else for a flash, I'm gone, done for. But at the same time, one can take things in--with another part of your brain, maybe. It's different from what you get in study, more practical and conclusive. There are some things you learn best in calm, and some in storm. You learn the delivery of a part only before an audience."

"Heaven help us," gasped Ottenburg. "Weren't you hungry, though! It's beautiful to see you eat."

"Glad you like it. Of course I'm hungry. Are you staying over for `Rheingold' Friday afternoon?"

"My dear Thea,"--Fred lit a cigarette,--"I'm a serious business man now. I have to sell beer. I'm due in Chicago on Wednesday. I'd come back to hear you, but FRICKA is not an alluring part."

"Then you've never heard it well done." She spoke up hotly. "Fat German woman scolding her husband, eh? That's not my idea. Wait till you hear my FRICKA. It's a beautiful part." Thea leaned forward on the table and touched Archie's arm. "You remember, Dr. Archie, how my mother always wore her hair, parted in the middle and done low on her neck behind, so you got the shape of her head and such a calm, white forehead? I wear mine like that for FRICKA. A little more coronet effect, built up a little higher at the sides, but the idea's the same. I think you'll notice it." She turned to Ottenburg reproachfully: "It's noble music, Fred, from the first measure. There's nothing lovelier than the WONNIGER HAUSRATH. It's all such comprehensive sort of music--fateful. Of course, FRICKA KNOWS," Thea ended quietly.

Fred sighed. "There, you've spoiled my itinerary. Now I'll have to come back, of course. Archie, you'd better get busy about seats to-morrow."

"I can get you box seats, somewhere. I know nobody here, and I never ask for any." Thea began hunting among her wraps. "Oh, how funny! I've only these short woolen gloves, and no sleeves. Put on my coat first. Those English people can't make out where you got your lady, she's so made up of contradictions." She rose laughing and plunged her arms into the coat Dr. Archie held for her. As she settled herself into it and buttoned it under her chin, she gave him an old signal with her eyelid. "I'd like to sing another part to-night. This is the sort of evening I fancy, when there's something to do. Let me see: I have to sing in `Trovatore' Wednesday night, and there are rehearsals for the `Ring' every day this week. Consider me dead until Saturday, Dr. Archie. I invite you both to dine with me on Saturday night, the day after `Rheingold.' And Fred must leave early, for I want to talk to you alone. You've been here nearly a week, and I haven't had a serious word with you. TAK FOR MAD, Fred, as the Norwegians say."

VIII

THE "Ring of the Niebelungs" was to be given at the Metropolitan on four successive Friday afternoons. After the first of these performances, Fred Ottenburg went home with Landry for tea. Landry was one of the few public entertainers who own real estate in New York. He lived in a little three-story brick house on Jane Street, in Greenwich Village, which had been left to him by the same aunt who paid for his musical education.

Landry was born, and spent the first fifteen years of his life, on a rocky Connecticut farm not far from Cos Cob. His father was an ignorant, violent man, a bungling farmer and a brutal husband. The farmhouse, dilapidated and damp, stood in a hollow beside a marshy pond. Oliver had worked hard while he lived at home, although he was never clean or warm in winter and had wretched food all the year round. His spare, dry figure, his prominent larynx, and the peculiar red of his face and hands belonged to the choreboy he had never outgrown. It was as if the farm, knowing he would escape from it as early as he could, had ground its mark on him deep. When he was fifteen Oliver ran away and went to live with his Catholic aunt, on Jane Street, whom his mother was never allowed to visit. The priest of St. Joseph's Parish discovered that he had a voice.

Landry had an affection for the house on Jane Street, where he had first learned what cleanliness and order and courtesy were. When his aunt died he had the place done over, got an Irish housekeeper, and lived there with a great many beautiful things he had collected. His living expenses were never large, but he could not restrain himself from buying graceful and useless objects. He was a collector for much the same reason that he was a Catholic, and he was a Catholic chiefly because his father used to sit in the kitchen and read aloud to his hired men disgusting "exposures" of the Roman Church, enjoying equally the hideous stories and the outrage to his wife's feelings.

At first Landry bought books; then rugs, drawings, china. He had a beautiful collection of old French and Spanish fans. He kept them in an escritoire he had brought from Spain, but there were always a few of them lying about in his sitting-room.

While Landry and his guest were waiting for the tea to be brought, Ottenburg took up one of these fans from the low marble mantel-shelf and opened it in the firelight. One side was painted with a pearly sky and floating clouds. On the other was a formal garden where an elegant shepherdess with a mask and crook was fleeing on high heels from a satin-coated shepherd.

"You ought not to keep these things about, like this, Oliver. The dust from your grate must get at them."

"It does, but I get them to enjoy them, not to have them. They're pleasant to glance at and to play with at odd times like this, when one is waiting for tea or something."

Fred smiled. The idea of Landry stretched out before his fire playing with his fans, amused him. Mrs. McGinnis brought the tea and put it before the hearth: old teacups that were velvety to the touch and a pot-bellied silver cream pitcher of an Early Georgian pattern, which was always brought, though Landry took rum.

Fred drank his tea walking about, examining Landry's sumptuous writing-table in the alcove and the Boucher drawing in red chalk over the mantel. "I don't see how you can stand this place without a heroine. It would give me a raging thirst for gallantries."

Landry was helping himself to a second cup of tea. "Works quite the other way with me. It consoles me for the lack of her. It's just feminine enough to be pleasant to return to. Not any more tea? Then sit down and play for me. I'm always playing for other people, and I never have a chance to sit here quietly and listen."

Ottenburg opened the piano and began softly to boom forth the shadowy introduction to the opera they had just heard. "Will that do?" he asked jokingly. "I can't seem to get it out of my head."

"Oh, excellently! Thea told me it was quite wonderful, the way you can do Wagner scores on the piano. So few people can give one any idea of the music. Go ahead, as long as you like. I can smoke, too." Landry flattened himself out on his cushions and abandoned himself to ease with the circumstance of one who has never grown quite accustomed to ease.

Ottenburg played on, as he happened to remember. He understood now why Thea wished him to hear her in "Rheingold." It had been clear to him as soon as FRICKA rose from sleep and looked out over the young world, stretching one white arm toward the new Gotterburg shining on the heights. "WOTAN! GEMAHL! ERWACHE!" She was pure Scandinavian, this FRICKA: "Swedish summer"! he remembered old Mr. Nathanmeyer's phrase. She had wished him to see her because she had a distinct kind of loveliness for this part, a shining beauty like the light of sunset on distant sails. She seemed to take on the look of immortal loveliness, the youth of the golden apples, the shining body and the shining mind. FRICKA had been a jealous spouse to him for so long that he had forgot she meant wisdom before she meant domestic order, and that, in any event, she was always a goddess. The FRICKA of that afternoon was so clear and sunny, so nobly conceived, that she made a whole atmosphere about herself and quite redeemed from shabbiness the helplessness and unscrupulousness of the gods. Her reproaches to WOTAN were the pleadings of a tempered mind, a consistent sense of beauty. In the long silences of her part, her shining presence was a visible complement to the discussion of the orchestra. As the themes which were to help in weaving the drama to its end first came vaguely upon the ear, one saw their import and tendency in the face of this clearest-visioned of the gods.

In the scene between FRICKA and WOTAN, Ottenburg stopped. "I can't seem to get the voices, in there."

Landry chuckled. "Don't try. I know it well enough. I expect I've been over that with her a thousand times. I was playing for her almost every day when she was first working on it. When she begins with a part she's hard to work with:

so slow you'd think she was stupid if you didn't know her. Of course she blames it all on her accompanist. It goes on like that for weeks sometimes. This did. She kept shaking her head and staring and looking gloomy. All at once, she got her line--it usually comes suddenly, after stretches of not getting anywhere at all--and after that it kept changing and clearing. As she worked her voice into it, it got more and more of that `gold' quality that makes her FRICKA so different."

Fred began FRICKA'S first aria again. "It's certainly different. Curious how she does it. Such a beautiful idea, out of a part that's always been so ungrateful. She's a lovely thing, but she was never so beautiful as that, really. Nobody is." He repeated the loveliest phrase. "How does she manage it, Landry? You've worked with her."

Landry drew cherishingly on the last cigarette he meant to permit himself before singing. "Oh, it's a question of a big personality--and all that goes with it. Brains, of course. Imagination, of course. But the important thing is that she was born full of color, with a rich personality. That's a gift of the gods, like a fine nose. You have it, or you haven't. Against it, intelligence and musicianship and habits of industry don't count at all. Singers are a conventional race. When Thea was studying in Berlin the other girls were mortally afraid of her. She has a pretty rough hand with women, dull ones, and she could be rude, too! The girls used to call her DIE WOLFIN."

Fred thrust his hands into his pockets and leaned back against the piano. "Of course, even a stupid woman could get effects with such machinery: such a voice and body and face. But they couldn't possibly belong to a stupid woman, could they?"

Landry shook his head. "It's personality; that's as near as you can come to it. That's what constitutes real equipment. What she does is interesting because she does it. Even the things she discards are suggestive. I regret some of them. Her conceptions are colored in so many different ways. You've heard her ELIZABETH? Wonderful, isn't it? She was working on that part years ago when her mother was ill. I could see her anxiety and grief getting more and more into the part. The last act is heart-breaking. It's as homely as a country prayer meeting: might be any lonely woman getting ready to die. It's full of the thing every plain creature finds out for himself, but that never gets written down. It's unconscious memory, maybe; inherited memory, like folk-music. I call it personality."

Fred laughed, and turning to the piano began coaxing the FRICKA music again. "Call it anything you like, my boy. I have a name for it myself, but I shan't tell you." He looked over his shoulder at Landry, stretched out by the fire. "You have a great time watching her, don't you?"

"Oh, yes!" replied Landry simply. "I'm not interested in much that goes on in New York. Now, if you'll excuse me, I'll amuse myself here. I don't often get a chance at a good piano when I'm away from home. You haven't had this one long, have you? Action's a bit stiff. I say," he stopped Landry in the doorway, "has Thea ever been down here?"

Landry turned back. "Yes. She came several times when I had erysipelas. I was a nice mess, with two nurses. She brought down some inside window-boxes, planted with crocuses and things. Very cheering, only I couldn't see them or her."

"Didn't she like your place?"

"She thought she did, but I fancy it was a good deal cluttered up for her taste. I could hear her pacing about like something in a cage. She pushed the piano back against the wall and the chairs into corners, and she broke my amber elephant." Landry took a yellow object some four inches high from one of his low bookcases. "You can see where his leg is glued on,--a souvenir. Yes, he's lemon amber, very fine."

Landry disappeared behind the curtains and in a moment Fred heard the wheeze of an atomizer. He put the amber elephant on the piano beside him and seemed to get a great deal of amusement out of the beast.

IX

WHEN Archie and Ottenburg dined with Thea on Saturday evening, they were served downstairs in the hotel dining-room, but they were to have their coffee in her own apartment. As they were going up in the elevator after dinner, Fred turned suddenly to Thea. "And why, please, did you break Landry's amber elephant?"

She looked guilty and began to laugh. "Hasn't he got over that yet? I didn't really mean to break it. I was perhaps careless. His things are so over-petted that I was tempted to be careless with a lot of them."

"How can you be so heartless, when they're all he has in the world?"

"He has me. I'm a great deal of diversion for him; all he needs. There," she said as she opened the door into her own hall, "I shouldn't have said that before the elevator boy."

"Even an elevator boy couldn't make a scandal about Oliver. He's such a catnip man."

Dr. Archie laughed, but Thea, who seemed suddenly to have thought of something annoying, repeated blankly, "Catnip man?"

"Yes, he lives on catnip, and rum tea. But he's not the only one. You are like an eccentric old woman I know in Boston, who goes about in the spring feeding catnip to street cats. You dispense it to a lot of fellows. Your pull seems to be more with men than with women, you know; with seasoned men, about my age, or older. Even on Friday afternoon I kept running into them, old boys I hadn't seen for years, thin at the part and thick at the girth, until I stood still in the draft and held my hair on. They're always there; I hear them talking about you in the smoking room. Probably we don't get to the point of apprehending anything good until we're about forty. Then, in the light of what is going, and of what, God help us! is coming, we arrive at understanding."

"I don't see why people go to the opera, anyway,--serious people." She spoke discontentedly. "I suppose they get something, or think they do. Here's the coffee. There, please," she directed the waiter. Going to the table she began to pour the coffee, standing. She wore a white dress trimmed with crystals which had rattled a good deal during dinner, as all her movements had been impatient and nervous, and she had twisted the dark velvet rose at her girdle until it looked rumpled and weary. She poured the coffee as if it were a ceremony in which she did not believe. "Can you make anything of Fred's nonsense, Dr. Archie?" she asked, as he came to take his cup.

Fred approached her. "My nonsense is all right. The same brand has gone with you before. It's you who won't be jollied. What's the matter? You have something on your mind."

"I've a good deal. Too much to be an agreeable hostess." She turned quickly away from the coffee and sat down on the piano bench, facing the two men. "For one thing, there's a change in the cast for Friday afternoon. They're going to let me sing SIEGLINDE." Her frown did not conceal the pleasure with which she made this announcement.

"Are you going to keep us dangling about here forever, Thea? Archie and I are supposed to have other things to do." Fred looked at her with an excitement quite as apparent as her own.

"Here I've been ready to sing SIEGLINDE for two years, kept in torment, and now it comes off within two weeks, just when I want to be seeing something of Dr. Archie. I don't know what their plans are down there. After Friday they may let me cool for several weeks, and they may rush me. I suppose it depends somewhat on how things go Friday afternoon."

"Oh, they'll go fast enough! That's better suited to your voice than anything you've sung here. That gives you every opportunity I've waited for." Ottenburg crossed the room and standing beside her began to play "DU BIST DER LENZ."

With a violent movement Thea caught his wrists and pushed his hands away from the keys.

"Fred, can't you be serious? A thousand things may happen between this and Friday to put me out. Something will happen. If that part were sung well, as well as it ought to be, it would be one of the most beautiful things in the world. That's why it never is sung right, and never will be." She clenched her hands and opened them despairingly, looking out of the open window. "It's inaccessibly beautiful!" she brought out sharply.

Fred and Dr. Archie watched her. In a moment she turned back to them. "It's impossible to sing a part like that well for the first time, except for the sort who will never sing it any better. Everything hangs on that first night, and that's bound to be bad. There you are," she shrugged impatiently. "For one thing, they change the cast at the eleventh hour and then rehearse the life out of me."

Ottenburg put down his cup with exaggerated care. "Still, you really want to do it, you know."

"Want to?" she repeated indignantly; "of course I want to! If this were only next Thursday night--But between now and Friday I'll do nothing but fret away my strength. Oh, I'm not saying I don't need the rehearsals! But I don't need them strung out through a week. That system's well enough for phlegmatic singers; it only drains me. Every single feature of operatic routine is detrimental to me. I usually go on like a horse that's been fixed to lose a race. I have to work hard to do my worst, let alone my best. I wish you could hear me sing well, once," she turned to Fred defiantly; "I have, a few times in my life, when there was nothing to gain by it."

Fred approached her again and held out his hand. "I recall my instructions, and now I'll leave you to fight it out with Archie. He can't possibly represent managerial stupidity to you as I seem to have a gift for doing."

As he smiled down at her, his good humor, his good wishes, his understanding, embarrassed her and recalled her to herself. She kept her seat, still holding his hand. "All the same, Fred, isn't it too bad, that there are so many things--" She broke off with a shake of the head.

"My dear girl, if I could bridge over the agony between now and Friday for you--But you know the rules of the game; why torment yourself? You saw the other night that you had the part under your thumb. Now walk, sleep, play with Archie, keep your tiger hungry, and she'll spring all right on Friday. I'll be there to see her, and there'll be more than I, I suspect. Harsanyi's on the Wilhelm der Grosse; gets in on Thursday."

"Harsanyi?" Thea's eye lighted. "I haven't seen him for years. We always miss each other." She paused, hesitating. "Yes, I should like that. But he'll be busy, maybe?"

"He gives his first concert at Carnegie Hall, week after next. Better send him a box if you can."

"Yes, I'll manage it." Thea took his hand again. "Oh, I should like that, Fred!" she added impulsively. "Even if I were put out, he'd get the idea,"--she threw back her head,--"for there is an idea!"

"Which won't penetrate here," he tapped his brow and began to laugh. "You are an ungrateful huzzy, COMME LES AUTRES!"

Thea detained him as he turned away. She pulled a flower out of a bouquet on the piano and absently drew the stem through the lapel of his coat. "I shall be walking in the Park to-morrow afternoon, on the reservoir path, between four and five, if you care to join me. You know that after Harsanyi I'd rather please you than anyone else. You know a lot, but he knows even more than you."

"Thank you. Don't try to analyze it. SCHLAFEN SIE WOHL!" he kissed her fingers and waved from the door, closing it behind him.

"He's the right sort, Thea." Dr. Archie looked warmly after his disappearing friend. "I've always hoped you'd make it up with Fred."

"Well, haven't I? Oh, marry him, you mean! Perhaps it may come about, some day. Just at present he's not in the marriage market any more than I am, is he?"

"No, I suppose not. It's a damned shame that a man like Ottenburg should be tied up as he is, wasting all the best years of his life. A woman with general paresis ought to be legally dead."

"Don't let us talk about Fred's wife, please. He had no business to get into such a mess, and he had no business to stay in it. He's always been a softy where women were concerned."

"Most of us are, I'm afraid," Dr. Archie admitted meekly.

"Too much light in here, isn't there? Tires one's eyes. The stage lights are hard on mine." Thea began turning them out. "We'll leave the little one, over the piano." She sank down by Archie on the deep sofa. "We two have so much to talk about that we keep away from it altogether; have you noticed? We don't even nibble the edges. I wish we had Landry here to-night to play for us. He's very comforting."

"I'm afraid you don't have enough personal life, outside your work, Thea." The doctor looked at her anxiously.

She smiled at him with her eyes half closed. "My dear doctor, I don't have any. Your work becomes your personal life. You are not much good until it does. It's like being woven into a big web. You can't pull away, because all your little tendrils are woven into the picture. It takes you up, and uses you, and spins you out; and that is your life. Not much else can happen to you."

"Didn't you think of marrying, several years ago?"

"You mean Nordquist? Yes; but I changed my mind. We had been singing a good deal together. He's a splendid creature."

"Were you much in love with him, Thea?" the doctor asked hopefully.

She smiled again. "I don't think I know just what that expression means. I've never been able to find out. I think I was in love with you when I was little, but not with any one since then. There are a great many ways of caring for people. It's not, after all, a simple state, like measles or tonsilitis. Nordquist is a taking sort of man. He and I were out in a rowboat once in a terrible storm. The lake was fed by glaciers,--ice water,--and we couldn't have swum a stroke if the boat had filled. If we hadn't both been strong and kept our heads, we'd have gone down. We pulled for every ounce there was in us, and we just got off with our lives. We were always being thrown together like that, under some kind of pressure. Yes, for a while I thought he would make everything right." She paused and sank back, resting her head on a cushion, pressing her eyelids down with her fingers. "You see," she went on abruptly, "he had a wife and two children. He hadn't lived with her for several years, but when she heard that he wanted to marry again, she began to make trouble. He earned a good deal of money, but he was careless and always wretchedly in debt. He came to me one day and told me he thought his wife would settle for a hundred thousand marks and consent to a divorce. I got very angry and sent him away. Next day he came back and said he thought she'd take fifty thousand."

Dr. Archie drew away from her, to the end of the sofa.

"Good God, Thea,"--He ran his handkerchief over his forehead. "What sort of people--" He stopped and shook his head.

Thea rose and stood beside him, her hand on his shoulder. "That's exactly how it struck me," she said quietly. "Oh, we have things in common, things that go away back, under everything. You understand, of course. Nordquist didn't. He thought I wasn't willing to part with the money. I couldn't let myself buy him from Fru Nordquist, and he couldn't see why. He had always thought I was close about money, so he attributed it to that. I am careful,"--she ran her arm through Archie's and when he rose began to walk about the room with him. "I can't be careless with money. I began the world on six hundred dollars, and it was the price of a man's life. Ray Kennedy had worked hard and been sober and denied himself, and when he died he had six hundred dollars to show for it. I always measure things by that six hundred dollars, just as I measure high buildings by the Moonstone standpipe. There are standards we can't get away from."

Dr. Archie took her hand. "I don't believe we should be any happier if we did get away from them. I think it gives you some of your poise, having that anchor. You look," glancing down at her head and shoulders, "sometimes so like your mother."

"Thank you. You couldn't say anything nicer to me than that. On Friday afternoon, didn't you think?"

"Yes, but at other times, too. I love to see it. Do you know what I thought about that first night when I heard you sing? I kept remembering the night I took care of you when you had pneumonia, when you were ten years old. You were a terribly sick child, and I was a country doctor without much experience. There were no oxygen tanks about then. You pretty nearly slipped away from me. If you had--"

Thea dropped her head on his shoulder. "I'd have saved myself and you a lot of trouble, wouldn't I? Dear Dr. Archie!" she murmured.

"As for me, life would have been a pretty bleak stretch, with you left out." The doctor took one of the crystal pendants that hung from her shoulder and looked into it thoughtfully. "I guess I'm a romantic old fellow, underneath. And you've always been my romance. Those years when you were growing up were my happiest. When I dream about you, I always see you as a little girl."

They paused by the open window. "Do you? Nearly all my dreams, except those about breaking down on the stage or missing trains, are about Moonstone. You tell me the old house has been pulled down, but it stands in my mind, every stick and timber. In my sleep I go all about it, and look in the right drawers and cupboards for everything. I often dream that I'm hunting for my rubbers in that pile of overshoes that was always under the hatrack in the hall. I pick up every overshoe and know whose it is, but I can't find my own. Then the school bell begins to ring and I begin to cry. That's the house I rest in when I'm tired. All the old furniture and the worn spots in the carpet--it rests my mind to go over them."

They were looking out of the window. Thea kept his arm. Down on the river four battleships were anchored in line, brilliantly lighted, and launches were coming and going, bringing the men ashore. A searchlight from one of the ironclads was playing on the great headland up the river, where it makes its first resolute turn. Overhead the night-blue sky was intense and clear.

"There's so much that I want to tell you," she said at last, "and it's hard to explain. My life is full of jealousies and disappointments, you know. You get to hating people who do contemptible work and who get on just as well as you do. There are many disappointments in my profession, and bitter, bitter contempts!" Her face hardened, and looked much older. "If you love the good thing vitally, enough to give up for it all that one must give up for it, then you must hate the cheap thing just as hard. I tell you, there is such a thing as creative hate! A contempt that drives you through fire, makes you risk everything and lose everything, makes you a long sight better than you ever knew you could be." As she glanced at Dr. Archie's face, Thea stopped short and turned her own face away. Her eyes followed the path of the searchlight up the river and rested upon the illumined headland.

"You see," she went on more calmly, "voices are accidental things. You find plenty of good voices in common women, with common minds and common hearts. Look at that woman who sang ORTRUDE with me last week. She's new here and the people are wild about her. `Such a beautiful volume of tone!' they say. I give you my word she's as stupid as an owl and as coarse as a pig, and any one who knows anything about singing would see that in an instant. Yet she's quite as popular as Necker, who's a great artist. How can I get much satisfaction out of the enthusiasm of a house that likes her atrociously bad performance at the same time that it pretends to like mine? If they like her, then they ought to hiss me off the stage. We stand for things that are irreconcilable, absolutely. You can't try to do things right and not despise the people who do them wrong. How can I be indifferent? If that doesn't matter, then nothing matters. Well, sometimes I've come home as I did the other night when you first saw me, so full of bitterness that it was as if my mind were full of daggers. And I've gone to sleep and wakened up in the Kohlers' garden, with the pigeons and the white rabbits, so happy! And that saves me." She sat down on the piano bench. Archie thought she had forgotten all about him, until she called his name. Her voice was soft now, and wonderfully sweet. It seemed to come from somewhere deep within her, there were such strong vibrations in it. "You see, Dr. Archie, what one really strives for in art is not the sort of thing you are likely to find when you drop in for a performance at the opera. What one strives for is so far away, so deep, so beautiful"--she lifted her shoulders with a long breath, folded her hands in her lap and sat looking at him with a resignation that made her face noble,--"that there's nothing one can say about it, Dr. Archie."

Without knowing very well what it was all about, Archie was passionately stirred for her. "I've always believed in you, Thea; always believed," he muttered.

She smiled and closed her eyes. "They save me: the old things, things like the Kohlers' garden. They are in everything I do."

"In what you sing, you mean?"

"Yes. Not in any direct way,"--she spoke hurriedly,--"the light, the color, the feeling. Most of all the feeling. It comes in when I'm working on a part, like the smell of a garden coming in at the window. I try all the new things, and then go back to the old. Perhaps my feelings were stronger then. A child's attitude toward everything is an artist's attitude. I am more or less of an artist now, but then I was nothing else. When I went with you to Chicago that first time, I carried with me the essentials, the foundation of all I do now. The point to which I could go was scratched in me then. I haven't reached it yet, by a long way."

Archie had a swift flash of memory. Pictures passed before him. "You mean," he asked wonderingly, "that you knew then that you were so gifted?"

Thea looked up at him and smiled. "Oh, I didn't know anything! Not enough to ask you for my trunk when I needed it. But you see, when I set out from Moonstone with you, I had had a rich, romantic past. I had lived a long, eventful life, and an artist's life, every hour of it. Wagner says, in his most beautiful opera, that art is only a way of remembering youth. And the older we grow the more precious it seems to us, and the more richly we can present that memory. When we've got it all out,--the last, the finest thrill of it, the brightest hope of it,"--she lifted her hand above her head and dropped it,--"then we stop. We do nothing but repeat after that. The stream has reached the level of its source. That's our measure."

There was a long, warm silence. Thea was looking hard at the floor, as if she were seeing down through years and years, and her old friend stood watching her bent head. His look was one with which he used to watch her long ago, and which, even in thinking about her, had become a habit of his face. It was full of solicitude, and a kind of secret gratitude, as if to thank her for some inexpressible pleasure of the heart. Thea turned presently toward the piano and began softly to waken an old air:--

"Ca' the yowes to the knowes, Ca' them where the heather grows, Ca' them where the burnie rowes, My bonnie dear-ie."

Archie sat down and shaded his eyes with his hand. She turned her head and spoke to him over her shoulder. "Come on, you know the words better than I. That's right."

"We'll gae down by Clouden's side, Through the hazels spreading wide, O'er the waves that sweetly glide, To the moon sae clearly. Ghaist nor bogle shalt thou fear, Thou'rt to love and Heav'n sae dear, Nocht of ill may come thee near, My bonnie dear-ie!"

"We can get on without Landry. Let's try it again, I have all the words now. Then we'll have `Sweet Afton.' Come: `CA' THE YOWES TO THE KNOWES'--"

X

OTTENBURG dismissed his taxicab at the 91st Street entrance of the Park and floundered across the drive through a wild spring snowstorm. When he reached the reservoir path he saw Thea ahead of him, walking rapidly against the wind. Except for that one figure, the path was deserted. A flock of gulls were hovering over the reservoir, seeming bewildered by the driving currents of snow that whirled above the black water and then disappeared within it. When he had almost overtaken Thea, Fred called to her, and she turned and waited for him with her back to the wind. Her hair and furs were powdered with snowflakes, and she looked like some rich-pelted animal, with warm blood, that had run in out of the woods. Fred laughed as he took her hand.

"No use asking how you do. You surely needn't feel much anxiety about Friday, when you can look like this."

She moved close to the iron fence to make room for him beside her, and faced the wind again. "Oh, I'm WELL enough, in so far as that goes. But I'm not lucky about stage appearances. I'm easily upset, and the most perverse things happen."

"What's the matter? Do you still get nervous?"

"Of course I do. I don't mind nerves so much as getting numbed," Thea muttered, sheltering her face for a moment with her muff. "I'm under a spell, you know, hoodooed. It's the thing I WANT to do that I can never do. Any other effects I can get easily enough."

"Yes, you get effects, and not only with your voice. That's where you have it over all the rest of them; you're as much at home on the stage as you were down in Panther Canyon--as if you'd just been let out of a cage. Didn't you get some of your ideas down there?"

Thea nodded. "Oh, yes! For heroic parts, at least. Out of the rocks, out of the dead people. You mean the idea of standing up under things, don't you, meeting catastrophe? No fussiness. Seems to me they must have been a reserved, somber people, with only a muscular language, all their movements for a purpose; simple, strong, as if they were dealing with fate bare-handed." She put her gloved fingers on Fred's arm. "I don't know how I can ever thank you enough. I don't know if I'd ever have got anywhere without Panther Canyon. How did you know that was the one thing to do for me? It's the sort of thing nobody ever helps one to, in this world. One can learn how to sing, but no singing teacher can give anybody what I got down there. How did you know?"

"I didn't know. Anything else would have done as well. It was your creative hour. I knew you were getting a lot, but I didn't realize how much."

Thea walked on in silence. She seemed to be thinking.

"Do you know what they really taught me?" she came out suddenly. "They taught me the inevitable hardness of human life. No artist gets far who doesn't know that. And you can't know it with your mind. You have to realize it in your body, somehow; deep. It's an animal sort of feeling. I sometimes think it's the strongest of all. Do you know what I'm driving at?"

"I think so. Even your audiences feel it, vaguely: that you've sometime or other faced things that make you different."

Thea turned her back to the wind, wiping away the snow that clung to her brows and lashes. "Ugh!" she exclaimed; "no matter how long a breath you have, the storm has a longer. I haven't signed for next season, yet, Fred. I'm holding out for a big contract: forty performances. Necker won't be able to do much next winter. It's going to be one of those between seasons; the old singers are too old, and the new ones are too new. They might as well risk me as anybody. So I want good terms. The next five or six years are going to be my best."

"You'll get what you demand, if you are uncompromising. I'm safe in congratulating you now."

Thea laughed. "It's a little early. I may not get it at all. They don't seem to be breaking their necks to meet me. I can go back to Dresden."

As they turned the curve and walked westward they got the wind from the side, and talking was easier.

Fred lowered his collar and shook the snow from his shoulders. "Oh, I don't mean on the contract particularly. I congratulate you on what you can do, Thea, and on all that lies behind what you do. On the life that's led up to it, and on being able to care so much. That, after all, is the unusual thing."

She looked at him sharply, with a certain apprehension. "Care? Why shouldn't I care? If I didn't, I'd be in a bad way. What else have I got?" She stopped with a challenging interrogation, but Ottenburg did not reply. "You mean," she persisted, "that you don't care as much as you used to?"

"I care about your success, of course." Fred fell into a slower pace. Thea felt at once that he was talking seriously and had dropped the tone of half-ironical exaggeration he had used with her of late years. "And I'm grateful to you for what you demand from yourself, when you might get off so easily. You demand more and more all the time, and you'll do more and more. One is grateful to anybody for that; it makes life in general a little less sordid. But as a matter of fact, I'm not much interested in how anybody sings anything."

"That's too bad of you, when I'm just beginning to see what is worth doing, and how I want to do it!" Thea spoke in an injured tone.

"That's what I congratulate you on. That's the great difference between your kind and the rest of us. It's how long you're able to keep it up that tells the story. When you needed enthusiasm from the outside, I was able to give it to you. Now you must let me withdraw."

"I'm not tying you, am I?" she flashed out. "But withdraw to what? What do you want?"

Fred shrugged. "I might ask you, What have I got? I want things that wouldn't interest you; that you probably wouldn't understand. For one thing, I want a son to bring up."

"I can understand that. It seems to me reasonable. Have you also found somebody you want to marry?"

"Not particularly." They turned another curve, which brought the wind to their backs, and they walked on in comparative calm, with the snow blowing past them. "It's not your fault, Thea, but I've had you too much in my mind. I've not given myself a fair chance in other directions. I was in Rome when you and Nordquist were there. If that had kept up, it might have cured me."

"It might have cured a good many things," remarked Thea grimly.

Fred nodded sympathetically and went on. "In my library in St. Louis, over the fireplace, I have a property spear I had copied from one in Venice,--oh, years ago, after you first went abroad, while you were studying. You'll probably be singing BRUNNHILDE pretty soon now, and I'll send it on to you, if I may. You can take it and its history for what they're worth. But I'm nearly forty years old, and I've served my turn. You've done what I hoped for you, what I was honestly willing to lose you for--then. I'm older now, and I think I was an ass. I wouldn't do it again if I had the chance, not much! But I'm not sorry. It takes a great many people to make one--BRUNNHILDE."

Thea stopped by the fence and looked over into the black choppiness on which the snowflakes fell and disappeared with magical rapidity. Her face was both angry and troubled. "So you really feel I've been ungrateful. I thought you sent me out to get something. I didn't know you wanted me to bring in something easy. I thought you wanted something--" She took a deep breath and shrugged her shoulders. "But there! nobody on God's earth wants it, REALLY! If one other person wanted it,"--she thrust her hand out before him and clenched it,--"my God, what I could do!"

Fred laughed dismally. "Even in my ashes I feel myself pushing you! How can anybody help it? My dear girl, can't you see that anybody else who wanted it as you do would be your rival, your deadliest danger? Can't you see that it's your great good fortune that other people can't care about it so much?"

But Thea seemed not to take in his protest at all. She went on vindicating herself. "It's taken me a long while to do anything, of course, and I've only begun to see daylight. But anything good is--expensive. It hasn't seemed long. I've always felt responsible to you."

Fred looked at her face intently, through the veil of snowflakes, and shook his head. "To me? You are a truthful woman, and you don't mean to lie to me. But after the one responsibility you do feel, I doubt if you've enough left to feel responsible to God! Still, if you've ever in an idle hour fooled yourself with thinking I had anything to do with it, Heaven knows I'm grateful."

"Even if I'd married Nordquist," Thea went on, turning down the path again, "there would have been something left out. There always is. In a way, I've always been married to you. I'm not very flexible; never was and never shall be. You caught me young. I could never have that over again. One can't, after one begins to know anything. But I look back on it. My life hasn't been a gay one, any more than yours. If I shut things out from you, you shut them out from me. We've been a help and a hindrance to each other. I guess it's always that way, the good and the bad all mixed up. There's only one thing that's all beautiful--and always beautiful! That's why my interest keeps up."

"Yes, I know." Fred looked sidewise at the outline of her head against the thickening atmosphere. "And you give one the impression that that is enough. I've gradually, gradually given you up."

"See, the lights are coming out." Thea pointed to where they flickered, flashes of violet through the gray tree-tops. Lower down the globes along the drives were becoming a pale lemon color. "Yes, I don't see why anybody wants to marry an artist, anyhow. I remember Ray Kennedy used to say he didn't see how any woman could marry a gambler, for she would only be marrying what the game left." She shook her shoulders impatiently. "Who marries who is a small matter, after all. But I hope I can bring back your interest in my work. You've cared longer and more than anybody else, and I'd like to have somebody human to make a report to once in a while. You can send me your spear. I'll do my best. If you're not interested, I'll do my best anyhow. I've only a few friends, but I can lose every one of them, if it has to be. I learned how to lose when my mother died.--We must hurry now. My taxi must be waiting."

The blue light about them was growing deeper and darker, and the falling snow and the faint trees had become violet. To the south, over Broadway, there was an orange reflection in the clouds. Motors and carriage lights flashed by on the drive below the reservoir path, and the air was strident with horns and shrieks from the whistles of the mounted policemen.

Fred gave Thea his arm as they descended from the embankment. "I guess you'll never manage to lose me or Archie, Thea. You do pick up queer ones. But loving you is a heroic discipline. It wears a man out. Tell me one thing: could I have kept you, once, if I'd put on every screw?"

Thea hurried him along, talking rapidly, as if to get it over. "You might have kept me in misery for a while, perhaps. I don't know. I have to think well of myself, to work. You could have made it hard. I'm not ungrateful. I was a difficult proposition to deal with. I understand now, of course. Since you didn't tell me the truth in the beginning, you couldn't very well turn back after I'd set my head. At least, if you'd been the sort who could, you wouldn't have had to,--for I'd not have cared a button for that sort, even then." She stopped beside a car that waited at the curb and gave him her hand. "There. We part friends?"

Fred looked at her. "You know. Ten years."

"I'm not ungrateful," Thea repeated as she got into her cab.

"Yes," she reflected, as the taxi cut into the Park carriage road, "we don't get fairy tales in this world, and he has, after all, cared more and longer than anybody else." It was dark outside now, and the light from the lamps along the drive flashed into the cab. The snowflakes hovered like swarms of white bees about the globes.

Thea sat motionless in one corner staring out of the window at the cab lights that wove in and out among the trees, all seeming to be bent upon joyous courses. Taxicabs were still new in New York, and the theme of popular minstrelsy. Landry had sung her a ditty he heard in some theater on Third Avenue, about:

"But there passed him a bright-eyed taxi With the girl of his heart inside."

Almost inaudibly Thea began to hum the air, though she was thinking of something serious, something that had touched her deeply. At the beginning of the season, when she was not singing often, she had gone one afternoon to hear Paderewski's recital. In front of her sat an old German couple, evidently poor people who had made sacrifices to pay for their excellent seats. Their intelligent enjoyment of the music, and their friendliness with each other, had interested her more than anything on the programme. When the pianist began a lovely melody in the first movement of the Beethoven D minor sonata, the old lady put out her plump hand and touched her husband's sleeve and they looked at each other in recognition. They both wore glasses, but such a look! Like forget-menots, and so full of happy recollections. Thea wanted to put her arms around them and ask them how they had been able to keep a feeling like that, like a nosegay in a glass of water.

XI

DR. ARCHIE saw nothing of Thea during the following week. After several fruitless efforts, he succeeded in getting a word with her over the telephone, but she sounded so distracted and driven that he was glad to say good-night and hang up the instrument. There were, she told him, rehearsals not only for "Walkure," but also for "Gotterdammerung," in which she was to sing WALTRAUTE two weeks later.

On Thursday afternoon Thea got home late, after an exhausting rehearsal. She was in no happy frame of mind. Madame Necker, who had been very gracious to her that night when she went on to complete Gloeckler's performance of SIEGLINDE, had, since Thea was cast to sing the part instead of Gloeckler in the production of the "Ring," been chilly and disapproving, distinctly hostile. Thea had always felt that she and Necker stood for the same sort of endeavor, and that Necker recognized it and had a cordial feeling for her. In Germany she had several times sung BRANGAENA to Necker's ISOLDE, and the older artist had let her know that she thought she sang it beautifully. It was a bitter disappointment to find that the approval of so honest an artist as Necker could not stand the test of any significant recognition by the management. Madame Necker was forty, and her voice was failing just when her powers were at their height. Every fresh young voice was an enemy, and this one was accompanied by gifts which she could not fail to recognize.

Thea had her dinner sent up to her apartment, and it was a very poor one. She tasted the soup and then indignantly put on her wraps to go out and hunt a dinner. As she was going to the elevator, she had to admit that she was behaving foolishly. She took off her hat and coat and ordered another dinner. When it arrived, it was no better than the first. There was even a burnt match under the milk toast. She had a sore throat, which made swallowing painful and boded ill for the morrow. Although she had been speaking in whispers all day to save her throat, she now perversely summoned the housekeeper and demanded an account of some laundry that had been lost. The housekeeper was indifferent and impertinent, and Thea got angry and scolded violently. She knew it was very bad for her to get into a rage just before bedtime, and after the housekeeper left she realized that for ten dollars' worth of underclothing she had been unfitting herself for a performance which might eventually mean many thousands. The best thing now was to stop reproaching herself for her lack of sense, but she was too tired to control her thoughts.

While she was undressing--Therese was brushing out her SIEGLINDE wig in the trunk-room--she went on chiding herself bitterly. "And how am I ever going to get to sleep in this state?" she kept asking herself. "If I don't sleep, I'll be perfectly worthless to-morrow. I'll go down there to-morrow and make a fool of myself. If I'd let that laundry alone with whatever nigger has stolen it--WHY did I undertake to reform the management of this hotel to-night? After to-morrow I could pack up and leave the place. There's the Phillamon--I liked the rooms there better, anyhow--and the Umberto--" She began going over the advantages and disadvantages of different apartment hotels. Suddenly she checked herself. "What AM I doing this for? I can't move into another hotel to-night. I'll keep this up till morning. I shan't sleep a wink."

Should she take a hot bath, or shouldn't she? Sometimes it relaxed her, and sometimes it roused her and fairly put her beside herself. Between the conviction that she must sleep and the fear that she couldn't, she hung paralyzed. When she looked at her bed, she shrank from it in every nerve. She was much more afraid of it than she had ever been of the stage of any opera house. It yawned before her like the sunken road at Waterloo.

She rushed into her bathroom and locked the door. She would risk the bath, and defer the encounter with the bed a little longer. She lay in the bath half an hour. The warmth of the water penetrated to her bones, induced pleasant reflections and a feeling of well-being. It was very nice to have Dr. Archie in New York, after all, and to see him get so much satisfaction out of the little companionship she was able to give him. She liked people who got on, and who became more interesting as they grew older. There was Fred; he was much more interesting now than he had been at thirty. He was intelligent about music, and he must be very intelligent in his business, or he would not be at the head of the Brewers'

Trust. She respected that kind of intelligence and success. Any success was good. She herself had made a good start, at any rate, and now, if she could get to sleep--Yes, they were all more interesting than they used to be. Look at Harsanyi, who had been so long retarded; what a place he had made for himself in Vienna. If she could get to sleep, she would show him something to-morrow that he would understand.

She got quickly into bed and moved about freely between the sheets. Yes, she was warm all over. A cold, dry breeze was coming in from the river, thank goodness! She tried to think about her little rock house and the Arizona sun and the blue sky. But that led to memories which were still too disturbing. She turned on her side, closed her eyes, and tried an old device.

She entered her father's front door, hung her hat and coat on the rack, and stopped in the parlor to warm her hands at the stove. Then she went out through the diningroom, where the boys were getting their lessons at the long table; through the sitting-room, where Thor was asleep in his cot bed, his dress and stocking hanging on a chair. In the kitchen she stopped for her lantern and her hot brick. She hurried up the back stairs and through the windy loft to her own glacial room. The illusion was marred only by the consciousness that she ought to brush her teeth before she went to bed, and that she never used to do it. Why--? The water was frozen solid in the pitcher, so she got over that. Once between the red blankets there was a short, fierce battle with the cold; then, warmer--warmer. She could hear her father shaking down the hard-coal burner for the night, and the wind rushing and banging down the village street. The boughs of the cottonwood, hard as bone, rattled against her gable. The bed grew softer and warmer. Everybody was warm and well downstairs. The sprawling old house had gathered them all in, like a hen, and had settled down over its brood. They were all warm in her father's house. Softer and softer. She was asleep. She slept ten hours without turning over. From sleep like that, one awakes in shining armor.

On Friday afternoon there was an inspiring audience; there was not an empty chair in the house. Ottenburg and Dr. Archie had seats in the orchestra circle, got from a ticket broker. Landry had not been able to get a seat, so he roamed about in the back of the house, where he usually stood when he dropped in after his own turn in vaudeville was over. He was there so often and at such irregular hours that the ushers thought he was a singer's husband, or had something to do with the electrical plant.

Harsanyi and his wife were in a box, near the stage, in the second circle. Mrs. Harsanyi's hair was noticeably gray, but her face was fuller and handsomer than in those early years of struggle, and she was beautifully dressed. Harsanyi himself had changed very little. He had put on his best afternoon coat in honor of his pupil, and wore a pearl in his black ascot. His hair was longer and more bushy than he used to wear it, and there was now one gray lock on the right side. He had always been an elegant figure, even when he went about in shabby clothes and was crushed with work. Before the curtain rose he was restless and nervous, and kept looking at his watch and wishing he had got a few more letters off before he left his hotel. He had not been in New York since the advent of the taxicab, and had allowed himself too much time. His wife knew that he was afraid of being disappointed this afternoon. He did not often go to the opera because the stupid things that singers did vexed him so, and it always put him in a rage if the conductor held the tempo or in any way accommodated the score to the singer.

When the lights went out and the violins began to quaver their long D against the rude figure of the basses, Mrs. Harsanyi saw her husband's fingers fluttering on his knee in a rapid tattoo. At the moment when SIEGLINDE entered from the side door, she leaned toward him and whispered in his ear, "Oh, the lovely creature!" But he made no response, either by voice or gesture. Throughout the first scene he sat sunk in his chair, his head forward and his one yellow eye rolling restlessly and shining like a tiger's in the dark. His eye followed SIEGLINDE about the stage like a satellite, and as she sat at the table listening to SIEGMUND'S long narrative, it never left her. When she prepared the sleeping draught and disappeared after HUNDING, Harsanyi bowed his head still lower and put his hand over his eye to rest it. The tenor,--a young man who sang with great vigor, went on:--

"WALSE! WALSE! WO IST DEIN SCHWERT?"

Harsanyi smiled, but he did not look forth again until SIEGLINDE reappeared. She went through the story of her shameful bridal feast and into the Walhall' music, which she always sang so nobly, and the entrance of the oneeyed stranger:--

"MIR ALLEIN WECKTE DAS AUGE."

Mrs. Harsanyi glanced at her husband, wondering whether the singer on the stage could not feel his commanding glance. On came the CRESCENDO:--

"WAS JE ICH VERLOR, WAS JE ICH BEWEINT WAR' MIR GEWONNEN."

(All that I have lost, All that I have mourned, Would I then have won.)

Harsanyi touched his wife's arm softly.

Seated in the moonlight, the VOLSUNG pair began their loving inspection of each other's beauties, and the music born of murmuring sound passed into her face, as the old poet said,--and into her body as well. Into one lovely attitude after another the music swept her, love impelled her. And the voice gave out all that was best in it. Like the spring, indeed, it blossomed into memories and prophecies, it recounted and it foretold, as she sang the story of her friendless life, and of how the thing which was truly herself, "bright as the day, rose to the surface" when in the hostile world she for the first time beheld her Friend. Fervently she rose into the hardier feeling of action and daring, the pride in hero-strength and hero-blood, until in a splendid burst, tall and shining like a Victory, she christened him:--

"SIEGMUND--SO NENN ICH DICH!"

Her impatience for the sword swelled with her anticipation of his act, and throwing her arms above her head, she fairly tore a sword out of the empty air for him, before NOTHUNG had left the tree. IN HOCHSTER TRUNKENHEIT, indeed, she burst out with the flaming cry of their kinship: "If you are SIEGMUND, I am SIEGLINDE!" Laughing, singing, bounding, exulting,--with their passion and their sword,--the VOLSUNGS ran out into the spring night.

As the curtain fell, Harsanyi turned to his wife. "At last," he sighed, "somebody with ENOUGH! Enough voice and talent and beauty, enough physical power. And such a noble, noble style!"

"I can scarcely believe it, Andor. I can see her now, that clumsy girl, hunched up over your piano. I can see her shoulders. She always seemed to labor so with her back. And I shall never forget that night when you found her voice."

The audience kept up its clamor until, after many reappearances with the tenor, Kronborg came before the curtain alone. The house met her with a roar, a greeting that was almost savage in its fierceness. The singer's eyes, sweeping the house, rested for a moment on Harsanyi, and she waved her long sleeve toward his box.

"She OUGHT to be pleased that you are here," said Mrs. Harsanyi. "I wonder if she knows how much she owes to you."

"She owes me nothing," replied her husband quickly. "She paid her way. She always gave something back, even then."

"I remember you said once that she would do nothing common," said Mrs. Harsanyi thoughtfully.

"Just so. She might fail, die, get lost in the pack. But if she achieved, it would be nothing common. There are people whom one can trust for that. There is one way in which they will never fail." Harsanyi retired into his own reflections.

After the second act Fred Ottenburg brought Archie to the Harsanyis' box and introduced him as an old friend of Miss Kronborg. The head of a musical publishing house joined them, bringing with him a journalist and the president of a German singing society. The conversation was chiefly about the new SIEGLINDE. Mrs. Harsanyi was gracious and enthusiastic, her husband nervous and uncommunicative. He smiled mechanically, and politely answered questions addressed to him. "Yes, quite so." "Oh, certainly." Every one, of course, said very usual things with great conviction. Mrs. Harsanyi was used to hearing and uttering the commonplaces which such occasions demanded. When her husband withdrew into the shadow, she covered his retreat by her sympathy and cordiality. In reply to a direct question from Ottenburg, Harsanyi said, flinching, "ISOLDE? Yes, why not? She will sing all the great roles, I should think."

The chorus director said something about "dramatic temperament." The journalist insisted that it was "explosive force," "projecting power."

Ottenburg turned to Harsanyi. "What is it, Mr. Harsanyi? Miss Kronborg says if there is anything in her, you are the man who can say what it is."

The journalist scented copy and was eager. "Yes, Harsanyi. You know all about her. What's her secret?"

Harsanyi rumpled his hair irritably and shrugged his shoulders. "Her secret? It is every artist's secret,"--he waved his hand,--"passion. That is all. It is an open secret, and perfectly safe. Like heroism, it is inimitable in cheap materials."

The lights went out. Fred and Archie left the box as the second act came on.

Artistic growth is, more than it is anything else, a refining of the sense of truthfulness. The stupid believe that to be truthful is easy; only the artist, the great artist, knows how difficult it is. That afternoon nothing new came to Thea Kronborg, no enlightenment, no inspiration. She merely came into full possession of things she had been refining and perfecting for so long. Her inhibitions chanced to be fewer than usual, and, within herself, she entered into the inheritance that she herself had laid up, into the fullness of the faith she had kept before she knew its name or its meaning.

Often when she sang, the best she had was unavailable; she could not break through to it, and every sort of distraction and mischance came between it and her. But this afternoon the closed roads opened, the gates dropped. What she had so often tried to reach, lay under her hand. She had only to touch an idea to make it live.

While she was on the stage she was conscious that every movement was the right movement, that her body was absolutely the instrument of her idea. Not for nothing had she kept it so severely, kept it filled with such energy and fire. All that deep-rooted vitality flowered in her voice, her face, in her very finger-tips. She felt like a tree bursting into bloom. And her voice was as flexible as her body; equal to any demand, capable of every NUANCE. With the sense of its perfect companionship, its entire trustworthiness, she had been able to throw herself into the dramatic exigencies of the part, everything in her at its best and everything working together.

The third act came on, and the afternoon slipped by. Thea Kronborg's friends, old and new, seated about the house on different floors and levels, enjoyed her triumph according to their natures. There was one there, whom nobody knew, who perhaps got greater pleasure out of that afternoon than Harsanyi himself. Up in the top gallery a gray-haired little Mexican, withered and bright as a string of peppers beside a'dobe door, kept praying and cursing under his breath, beating on the brass railing and shouting "Bravo! Bravo!" until he was repressed by his neighbors.

He happened to be there because a Mexican band was to be a feature of Barnum and Bailey's circus that year. One of the managers of the show had traveled about the Southwest, signing up a lot of Mexican musicians at low wages, and had brought them to New York. Among them was Spanish Johnny. After Mrs. Tellamantez died, Johnny abandoned his trade and went out with his mandolin to pick up a living for one. His irregularities had become his regular mode of life.

When Thea Kronborg came out of the stage entrance on Fortieth Street, the sky was still flaming with the last rays of the sun that was sinking off behind the North River. A little crowd of people was lingering about the door--musicians from the orchestra who were waiting for their comrades, curious young men, and some poorly dressed girls who were hoping to get a glimpse of the singer. She bowed graciously to the group, through her veil, but she did not look to the right or left as she crossed the sidewalk to her cab. Had she lifted her eyes an instant and glanced out through her white scarf, she must have seen the only man in the crowd who had removed his hat when she emerged, and who stood with it crushed up in his hand. And she would have known him, changed as he was. His lustrous black hair was full of gray, and his face was a good deal worn by the EXTASI, so that it seemed to have shrunk away from his shining eyes and teeth and left them too prominent. But she would have known him. She passed so near that he could have touched her, and he did not put on his hat until her taxi had snorted away. Then he walked down Broadway with his hands in his overcoat pockets, wearing a smile which embraced all the stream of life that passed him and the lighted towers that rose into the limpid blue of the evening sky. If the singer, going home exhausted in her cab, was wondering what was the good of it all, that smile, could she have seen it, would have answered her. It is the only commensurate answer.

Here we must leave Thea Kronborg. From this time on the story of her life is the story of her achievement. The growth of an artist is an intellectual and spiritual development which can scarcely be followed in a personal narrative. This story attempts to deal only with the simple and concrete beginnings which color and accent an artist's work, and to give some account of how a Moonstone girl found her way out of a vague, easy-going world into a life of disciplined endeavor. Any account of the loyalty of young hearts to some exalted ideal, and the passion with which they strive, will always, in some of us, rekindle generous emotions.

EPILOGUE

MOONSTONE again, in the year 1909. The Methodists are giving an ice-cream sociable in the grove about the new court-house. It is a warm summer night of full moon. The paper lanterns which hang among the trees are foolish toys, only dimming, in little lurid circles, the great softness of the lunar light that floods the blue heavens and the high plateau. To the east the sand hills shine white as of old, but the empire of the sand is gradually diminishing. The grass grows thicker over the dunes than it used to, and the streets of the town are harder and firmer than they were twenty-five years ago. The old inhabitants will tell you that sandstorms are infrequent now, that the wind blows less persistently in the spring and plays a milder tune. Cultivation has modified the soil and the climate, as it modifies human life.

The people seated about under the cottonwoods are much smarter than the Methodists we used to know. The interior of the new Methodist Church looks like a theater, with a sloping floor, and as the congregation proudly say, "opera chairs." The matrons who attend to serving the refreshments to-night look younger for their years than did the women of Mrs. Kronborg's time, and the children all look like city children. The little boys wear "Buster Browns" and the little girls Russian blouses. The country child, in made-overs and cut-downs, seems to have vanished from the face of the earth.

At one of the tables, with her Dutch-cut twin boys, sits a fair-haired, dimpled matron who was once Lily Fisher. Her husband is president of the new bank, and she "goes East for her summers," a practice which causes envy and discontent among her neighbors. The twins are well-behaved children, biddable, meek, neat about their clothes, and always mindful of the proprieties they have learned at summer hotels. While they are eating their icecream and trying not to twist the spoon in their mouths, a little shriek of laughter breaks from an adjacent table. The twins look up. There sits a spry little old spinster whom they know well. She has a long chin, a long nose, and she is dressed like a young girl, with a pink sash and a lace garden hat with pink rosebuds. She is surrounded by a crowd of boys,--loose and lanky, short and thick,--who are joking with her roughly, but not unkindly.

"Mamma," one of the twins comes out in a shrill treble, "why is Tillie Kronborg always talking about a thousand dollars?"

The boys, hearing this question, break into a roar of laughter, the women titter behind their paper napkins, and even from Tillie there is a little shriek of appreciation. The observing child's remark had made every one suddenly realize that Tillie never stopped talking about that particular sum of money. In the spring, when she went to buy early strawberries, and was told that they were thirty cents a box, she was sure to remind the grocer that though her name was Kronborg she didn't get a thousand dollars a night. In the autumn, when she went to buy her coal for the winter, she expressed amazement at the price quoted her, and told the dealer he must have got her mixed up with her niece to think she could pay such a sum. When she was making her Christmas presents, she never failed to ask the women who came into her shop what you COULD make for anybody who got a thousand dollars a night. When the Denver papers announced that Thea Kronborg had married Frederick Ottenburg, the head of the Brewers' Trust, Moonstone people expected that Tillie's vain-gloriousness would take another form. But Tillie had hoped that Thea would marry a title, and she did not boast much about Ottenburg,--at least not until after her memorable trip to Kansas City to hear Thea sing.

Tillie is the last Kronborg left in Moonstone. She lives alone in a little house with a green yard, and keeps a fancywork and millinery store. Her business methods are informal, and she would never come out even at the end of the year, if she did not receive a draft for a good round sum from her niece at Christmas time. The arrival of this draft always renews the discussion as to what Thea would do for her aunt if she really did the right thing. Most of the Moonstone people think Thea ought to take Tillie to New York and keep her as a companion. While they are feeling sorry for Tillie because she does not live at the Plaza, Tillie is trying not to hurt their feelings by showing too plainly how much she realizes the superiority of her position. She tries to be modest when she complains to the postmaster that her New York paper is more than three days late. It means enough, surely, on the face of it, that she is the only person in Moonstone who takes a New York paper or who has any reason for taking one. A foolish young girl, Tillie lived in the splendid sorrows of "Wanda" and "Strathmore"; a foolish old girl, she lives in her niece's triumphs. As she often says, she just missed going on the stage herself.

That night after the sociable, as Tillie tripped home with a crowd of noisy boys and girls, she was perhaps a shade troubled. The twin's question rather lingered in her ears. Did she, perhaps, insist too much on that thousand dollars? Surely, people didn't for a minute think it was the money she cared about? As for that, Tillie tossed her head, she didn't care a rap. They must understand that this money was different.

When the laughing little group that brought her home had gone weaving down the sidewalk through the leafy shadows and had disappeared, Tillie brought out a rocking chair and sat down on her porch. On glorious, soft summer nights like this, when the moon is opulent and full, the day submerged and forgotten, she loves to sit there behind her rose-vine and let her fancy wander where it will. If you chanced to be passing down that Moonstone street and saw that alert white figure rocking there behind the screen of roses and lingering late into the night, you might feel sorry for her, and how mistaken you would be! Tillie lives in a little magic world, full of secret satisfactions. Thea Kronborg has given much noble pleasure to a world that needs all it can get, but to no individual has she given more than to her queer old aunt in Moonstone. The legend of Kronborg, the artist, fills Tillie's life; she feels rich and exalted in it. What delightful things happen in her mind as she sits there rocking! She goes back to those early days of sand and sun, when Thea was a child and Tillie was herself, so it seems to her, "young." When she used to hurry to church to hear Mr. Kronborg's wonderful sermons, and when Thea used to stand up by the organ of a bright Sunday morning and sing "Come, Ye Disconsolate." Or she thinks about that wonderful time when the Metropolitan Opera Company sang a week's engagement in Kansas City, and Thea sent for her and had her stay with her at the Coates House and go to every performance at Convention Hall. Thea let Tillie go through her costume trunks and try on her wigs and jewels. And the kindness of Mr. Ottenburg! When Thea dined in her own room, he went down to dinner with Tillie, and never looked bored or absent-minded when she chattered. He took her to the hall the first time Thea sang there, and sat in the box with her and helped her through "Lohengrin." After the first act, when Tillie turned tearful eyes to him and burst out, "I don't care, she always seemed grand like that, even when she was a girl. I expect I'm crazy, but she just seems to me full of all them old times!"-- Ottenburg was so sympathetic and patted her hand and said, "But that's just what she is, full of the old times, and you are a wise woman to see it." Yes, he said that to her. Tillie often wondered how she had been able to bear it when Thea came down the stairs in the wedding robe embroidered in silver, with a train so long it took six women to carry it.

Tillie had lived fifty-odd years for that week, but she got it, and no miracle was ever more miraculous than that. When she used to be working in the fields on her father's Minnesota farm, she couldn't help believing that she would some day have to do with the "wonderful," though her chances for it had then looked so slender.

The morning after the sociable, Tillie, curled up in bed, was roused by the rattle of the milk cart down the street. Then a neighbor boy came down the sidewalk outside her window, singing "Casey Jones" as if he hadn't a care in the world. By this time Tillie was wide awake. The twin's question, and the subsequent laughter, came back with a faint twinge. Tillie knew she was short-sighted about facts, but this time--Why, there were her scrapbooks, full of newspaper and magazine articles about Thea, and half-tone cuts, snap-shots of her on land and sea, and photographs of her in all her parts. There, in her parlor, was the phonograph that had come from Mr. Ottenburg last June, on Thea's birthday; she had only to go in there and turn it on, and let Thea speak for herself. Tillie finished brushing her white hair and laughed as she gave it a smart turn and brought it into her usual French twist. If Moonstone doubted, she had evidence enough: in black and white, in figures and photographs, evidence in hair lines on metal disks. For one who had so often seen two and two as making six, who had so often stretched a point, added a touch, in the good game of trying to make the world brighter than it is, there was positive bliss in having such deep foundations of support. She need never tremble in secret lest she might sometime stretch a point in Thea's favor.--Oh, the comfort, to a soul too zealous, of having at last a rose so red it could not be further painted, a lily so truly auriferous that no amount of gilding could exceed the fact!

Tillie hurried from her bedroom, threw open the doors and windows, and let the morning breeze blow through her little house.

In two minutes a cob fire was roaring in her kitchen stove, in five she had set the table. At her household work Tillie was always bursting out with shrill snatches of song, and as suddenly stopping, right in the middle of a phrase, as if she had been struck dumb. She emerged upon the back porch with one of these bursts, and bent down to get her butter and cream out of the ice-box. The cat was purring on the bench and the morning-glories were thrusting their purple trumpets in through the lattice-work in a friendly way. They reminded Tillie that while she was waiting for the coffee to boil she could get some flowers for her breakfast table. She looked out uncertainly at a bush of sweet-briar that grew at the edge of her yard, off across the long grass and the tomato vines. The front porch, to be sure, was dripping with crimson ramblers that ought to be cut for the good of the vines; but never the rose in the hand for Tillie! She caught up the kitchen shears and off she dashed through grass and drenching dew. Snip, snip; the short-stemmed sweet-briars, salmon-pink and golden-hearted, with their unique and inimitable woody perfume, fell into her apron.

After she put the eggs and toast on the table, Tillie took last Sunday's New York paper from the rack beside the cupboard and sat down, with it for company. In the Sunday paper there was always a page about singers, even in summer, and that week the musical page began with a sympathetic account of Madame Kronborg's first performance of ISOLDE in London. At the end of the notice, there was a short paragraph about her having sung for the King at Buckingham Palace and having been presented with a jewel by His Majesty.

Singing for the King; but Goodness! she was always doing things like that! Tillie tossed her head. All through breakfast she kept sticking her sharp nose down into the glass of sweet-briar, with the old incredible lightness of heart, like a child's balloon tugging at its string. She had always insisted, against all evidence, that life was full of fairy tales, and it was! She had been feeling a little down, perhaps, and Thea had answered her, from so far. From a common person, now, if you were troubled, you might get a letter. But Thea almost never wrote letters. She answered every one, friends and foes alike, in one way, her own way, her only way. Once more Tillie has to remind herself that it is all true, and is not something she has "made up." Like all romancers, she is a little terrified at seeing one of her wildest conceits admitted by the hardheaded world. If our dream comes true, we are almost afraid to believe it; for that is the best of all good fortune, and nothing better can happen to any of us.

When the people on Sylvester Street tire of Tillie's stories, she goes over to the east part of town, where her legends are always welcome. The humbler people of Moonstone still live there. The same little houses sit under the cottonwoods; the men smoke their pipes in the front doorways, and the women do their washing in the back yard. The older women remember Thea, and how she used to come kicking her express wagon along the sidewalk, steering by the tongue and holding Thor in her lap. Not much happens in that part of town, and the people have long memories. A boy grew up on one of those streets who went to Omaha and built up a great business, and is now very rich. Moonstone people always speak of him and Thea together, as examples of Moonstone enterprise. They do, however, talk oftener of Thea. A voice has even a wider appeal than a fortune. It is the one gift that all creatures would possess if they could. Dreary Maggie Evans, dead nearly twenty years, is still remembered because Thea sang at her funeral "after she had studied in Chicago."

However much they may smile at her, the old inhabitants would miss Tillie. Her stories give them something to talk about and to conjecture about, cut off as they are from the restless currents of the world. The many naked little sandbars which lie between Venice and the mainland, in the seemingly stagnant water of the lagoons, are made habitable and wholesome only because, every night, a foot and a half of tide creeps in from the sea and winds its fresh brine up through all that network of shining waterways. So, into all the little settlements of quiet people, tidings of what their boys and girls are doing in the world bring real refreshment; bring to the old, memories, and to the young, dreams.

THE END

BOOK FOUR.
MY ÁNTONIA

TO CARRIE AND IRENE MINER

In memory of affections old and true

Optima dies ... prima fugit VIRGIL

INTRODUCTION

LAST summer I happened to be crossing the plains of Iowa in a season of intense heat, and it was my good fortune to have for a traveling companion James Quayle Burden--Jim Burden, as we still call him in the West. He and I are old friends--we grew up together in the same Nebraska town--and we had much to say to each other. While the train flashed through never-ending miles of ripe wheat, by country towns and bright-flowered pastures and oak groves wilting in the sun, we sat in the observation car, where the woodwork was hot to the touch and red dust lay deep over everything. The dust and heat, the burning wind, reminded us of many things. We were talking about what it is like to spend one's childhood in little towns like these, buried in wheat and corn, under stimulating extremes of climate: burning summers when the world lies green and billowy beneath a brilliant sky, when one is fairly stifled in vegetation, in the color and smell of strong weeds and heavy harvests; blustery winters with little snow, when the whole country is stripped bare and gray as sheet-iron. We agreed that no one who had not grown up in a little prairie town could know anything about it. It was a kind of freemasonry, we said.

Although Jim Burden and I both live in New York, and are old friends, I do not see much of him there. He is legal counsel for one of the great Western railways, and is sometimes away from his New York office for weeks together. That is one reason why we do not often meet. Another is that I do not like his wife.

When Jim was still an obscure young lawyer, struggling to make his way in New York, his career was suddenly advanced by a brilliant marriage. Genevieve Whitney was the only daughter of a distinguished man. Her marriage with young Burden was the subject of sharp comment at the time. It was said she had been brutally jilted by her cousin, Rutland Whitney, and that she married this unknown man from the West out of bravado. She was a restless, headstrong girl, even then, who liked to astonish her friends. Later, when I knew her, she was always doing something unexpected. She gave one of her town houses for a Suffrage headquarters, produced one of her own plays at the Princess Theater, was arrested for picketing during a garment-makers' strike, etc. I am never able to believe that she has much feeling for the causes to which she lends her name and her fleeting interest. She is handsome, energetic, executive, but to me she seems unimpressionable and temperamentally incapable of enthusiasm. Her husband's quiet tastes irritate her, I think, and she finds it worth while to play the patroness to a group of young poets and painters of advanced ideas and mediocre ability. She has her own fortune and lives her own life. For some reason, she wishes to remain Mrs. James Burden.

As for Jim, no disappointments have been severe enough to chill his naturally romantic and ardent disposition. This disposition, though it often made him seem very funny when he was a boy, has been one of the strongest elements in his success. He loves with a personal passion the great country through which his railway runs and branches. His faith in it and his knowledge of it have played an important part in its development. He is always able to raise capital for new enterprises in Wyoming or Montana, and has helped young men out there to do remarkable things in mines and timber and oil. If a young man with an idea can once get Jim Burden's attention, can manage to accompany him when he goes off into the wilds hunting for lost parks or exploring new canyons, then the money which means action is usually forthcoming. Jim is still able to lose himself in those big Western dreams. Though he is over forty now, he meets new people and new enterprises with the impulsiveness by which his boyhood friends remember him. He never seems to me to grow older. His fresh color and sandy hair and quick-changing blue eyes are those of a young man, and his sympathetic, solicitous interest in women is as youthful as it is Western and American.

During that burning day when we were crossing Iowa, our talk kept returning to a central figure, a Bohemian girl whom we had known long ago and whom both of us admired. More than any other person we remembered, this girl seemed to mean to us the country, the conditions, the whole adventure of our childhood. To speak her name was to call up pictures of people and places, to set a quiet drama going in one's brain. I had lost sight of her altogether, but Jim had found her again after long years, had renewed a friendship that meant a great deal to him, and out of his busy life had set apart time enough to enjoy that friendship. His mind was full of her that day. He made me see her again, feel her presence, revived all my old affection for her.

"I can't see," he said impetuously, "why you have never written anything about Antonia."

I told him I had always felt that other people--he himself, for one knew her much better than I. I was ready, however, to make an agreement with him; I would set down on paper all that I remembered of Antonia if he would do the same. We might, in this way, get a picture of her.

He rumpled his hair with a quick, excited gesture, which with him often announces a new determination, and I could see that my suggestion took hold of him. "Maybe I will, maybe I will!" he declared. He stared out of the window for a few moments, and when he turned to me again his eyes had the sudden clearness that comes from something the mind itself sees. "Of course," he said, "I should have to do it in a direct way, and say a great deal about myself. It's through myself that I knew and felt her, and I've had no practice in any other form of presentation."

I told him that how he knew her and felt her was exactly what I most wanted to know about Antonia. He had had opportunities that I, as a little girl who watched her come and go, had not.

Months afterward Jim Burden arrived at my apartment one stormy winter afternoon, with a bulging legal portfolio sheltered under his fur overcoat. He brought it into the sitting-room with him and tapped it with some pride as he stood warming his hands.

"I finished it last night--the thing about Antonia," he said. "Now, what about yours?"

I had to confess that mine had not gone beyond a few straggling notes.

"Notes? I didn't make any." He drank his tea all at once and put down the cup. "I didn't arrange or rearrange. I simply wrote down what of herself and myself and other people Antonia's name recalls to me. I suppose it hasn't any form. It hasn't any title, either." He went into the next room, sat down at my desk and wrote on the pinkish face of the portfolio the word, "Antonia." He frowned at this a moment, then prefixed another word, making it "My Antonia." That seemed to satisfy him.

"Read it as soon as you can," he said, rising, "but don't let it influence your own story."

My own story was never written, but the following narrative is Jim's manuscript, substantially as he brought it to me.

NOTES: [1] The Bohemian name Antonia is strongly accented on the first syllable, like the English name Anthony, and the `i' is, of course, given the sound of long `e'. The name is pronounced An'-ton-ee-ah.

PART I. THE SHIMERDAS

I

I FIRST HEARD OF Antonia on what seemed to me an interminable journey across the great midland plain of North America. I was ten years old then; I had lost both my father and mother within a year, and my Virginia relatives were sending me out to my grandparents, who lived in Nebraska. I travelled in the care of a mountain boy, Jake Marpole, one of the `hands' on my father's old farm under the Blue Ridge, who was now going West to work for my grandfather. Jake's experience of the world was not much wider than mine. He had never been in a railway train until the morning when we set out together to try our fortunes in a new world.

We went all the way in day-coaches, becoming more sticky and grimy with each stage of the journey. Jake bought everything the newsboys offered him: candy, oranges, brass collar buttons, a watch-charm, and for me a `Life of Jesse James,' which I remember as one of the most satisfactory books I have ever read. Beyond Chicago we were under the protection of a friendly passenger conductor, who knew all about the country to which we were going and gave us a great deal of advice in exchange for our confidence. He seemed to us an experienced and worldly man who had been almost everywhere; in his conversation he threw out lightly the names of distant states and cities. He wore the rings and pins and badges of different fraternal orders to which he belonged. Even his cuff-buttons were engraved with hieroglyphics, and he was more inscribed than an Egyptian obelisk.

Once when he sat down to chat, he told us that in the immigrant car ahead there was a family from `across the water' whose destination was the same as ours.

`They can't any of them speak English, except one little girl, and all she can say is "We go Black Hawk, Nebraska." She's not much older than you, twelve or thirteen, maybe, and she's as bright as a new dollar. Don't you want to go ahead and see her, Jimmy? She's got the pretty brown eyes, too!'

This last remark made me bashful, and I shook my head and settled down to `Jesse James.' Jake nodded at me approvingly and said you were likely to get diseases from foreigners.

I do not remember crossing the Missouri River, or anything about the long day's journey through Nebraska. Probably by that time I had crossed so many rivers that I was dull to them. The only thing very noticeable about Nebraska was that it was still, all day long, Nebraska.

I had been sleeping, curled up in a red plush seat, for a long while when we reached Black Hawk. Jake roused me and took me by the hand. We stumbled down from the train to a wooden siding, where men were running about with lanterns. I couldn't see any town, or even distant lights; we were surrounded by utter darkness. The engine was panting heavily after its long run. In the red glow from the fire-box, a group of people stood huddled together on the platform, encumbered by bundles and boxes. I knew this must be the immigrant family the conductor had told us about. The woman wore a fringed shawl tied over her head, and she carried a little tin trunk in her arms, hugging it as if it were a baby. There was an old man, tall and stooped. Two half-grown boys and a girl stood holding oilcloth bundles, and a little girl clung to her mother's skirts. Presently a man with a lantern approached them and began to talk, shouting and exclaiming. I pricked up my ears, for it was positively the first time I had ever heard a foreign tongue.

Another lantern came along. A bantering voice called out: `Hello, are you Mr. Burden's folks? If you are, it's me you're looking for. I'm Otto Fuchs. I'm Mr. Burden's hired man, and I'm to drive you out. Hello, Jimmy, ain't you scared to come so far west?'

I looked up with interest at the new face in the lantern-light. He might have stepped out of the pages of `Jesse James.' He wore a sombrero hat, with a wide leather band and a bright buckle, and the ends of his moustache were twisted up stiffly, like little horns. He looked lively and ferocious, I thought, and as if he had a history. A long scar ran across one cheek and drew the corner of his mouth up in a sinister curl. The top of his left ear was gone, and his skin was brown as an Indian's. Surely this was the face of a desperado. As he walked about the platform in his high-heeled boots, looking for our trunks, I saw that he was a rather slight man, quick and wiry, and light on his feet. He told us we had a long night drive ahead of us, and had better be on the hike. He led us to a hitching-bar where two farm-wagons were tied, and I saw the foreign family crowding into one of them. The other was for us. Jake got on the front seat with Otto Fuchs, and I rode on the straw in the bottom of the wagon-box, covered up with a buffalo hide. The immigrants rumbled off into the empty darkness, and we followed them.

I tried to go to sleep, but the jolting made me bite my tongue, and I soon began to ache all over. When the straw settled down, I had a hard bed. Cautiously I slipped from under the buffalo hide, got up on my knees and peered over the side of the wagon. There seemed to be nothing to see; no fences, no creeks or trees, no hills or fields. If there was a road, I could not make it out in the faint starlight. There was nothing but land: not a country at all, but the material out of which countries are made. No, there was nothing but land--slightly undulating, I knew, because often our wheels ground against the brake as we went down into a hollow and lurched up again on the other side. I had the feeling that the world was left behind, that we had got over the edge of it, and were outside man's jurisdiction. I had never before looked up at the sky when there was not a familiar mountain ridge against it. But this was the complete dome of heaven, all there was of it. I did not believe that my dead father and mother were watching me from up there; they would still be looking for me at the sheep-fold down by the creek, or along the white road that led to the mountain pastures. I had left even their spirits behind me. The wagon jolted on, carrying me I knew not whither. I don't think I was homesick. If we never arrived anywhere, it did not matter. Between that earth and that sky I felt erased, blotted out. I did not say my prayers that night: here, I felt, what would be would be.

II

I DO NOT REMEMBER our arrival at my grandfather's farm sometime before daybreak, after a drive of nearly twenty miles with heavy work-horses. When I awoke, it was afternoon. I was lying in a little room, scarcely larger than the bed that held me, and the window-shade at my head was flapping softly in a warm wind. A tall woman, with wrinkled brown skin and black hair, stood looking down at me; I knew that she must be my grandmother. She had been crying, I could see, but when I opened my eyes she smiled, peered at me anxiously, and sat down on the foot of my bed.

`Had a good sleep, Jimmy?' she asked briskly. Then in a very different tone she said, as if to herself, `My, how you do look like your father!' I remembered that my father had been her little boy; she must often have come to wake him like this when he overslept. `Here are your clean clothes,' she went on, stroking my coverlid with her brown hand as she talked. `But first you come down to the kitchen with me, and have a nice warm bath behind the stove. Bring your things; there's nobody about.'

`Down to the kitchen' struck me as curious; it was always `out in the kitchen' at home. I picked up my shoes and stockings and followed her through the living-room and down a flight of stairs into a basement. This basement was divided into a dining-room at the right of the stairs and a kitchen at the left. Both rooms were plastered and whitewashed--the plaster laid directly upon the earth walls, as it used to be in dugouts. The floor was of hard cement. Up under the wooden ceiling there were little half-windows with white curtains, and pots of geraniums and wandering Jew in the deep sills. As I entered the kitchen, I sniffed a pleasant smell of gingerbread baking. The stove was very large, with bright nickel trimmings, and behind it there was a long wooden bench against the wall, and a tin washtub, into which grandmother poured hot and cold water. When she brought the soap and towels, I told her that I was used to taking my bath without help. `Can you do your ears, Jimmy? Are you sure? Well, now, I call you a right smart little boy.'

It was pleasant there in the kitchen. The sun shone into my bath-water through the west half-window, and a big Maltese cat came up and rubbed himself against the tub, watching me curiously. While I scrubbed, my grandmother busied herself in the dining-room until I called anxiously, `Grandmother, I'm afraid the cakes are burning!' Then she came laughing, waving her apron before her as if she were shooing chickens.

She was a spare, tall woman, a little stooped, and she was apt to carry her head thrust forward in an attitude of attention, as if she were looking at something, or listening to something, far away. As I grew older, I came to believe that it was only because she was so often thinking of things that were far away. She was quick-footed and energetic in all her movements. Her voice was high and rather shrill, and she often spoke with an anxious inflection, for she was exceedingly desirous that everything should go with due order and decorum. Her laugh, too, was high, and perhaps a little strident, but there was a lively intelligence in it. She was then fifty-five years old, a strong woman, of unusual endurance.

After I was dressed, I explored the long cellar next the kitchen. It was dug out under the wing of the house, was plastered and cemented, with a stairway and an outside door by which the men came and went. Under one of the windows there was a place for them to wash when they came in from work.

While my grandmother was busy about supper, I settled myself on the wooden bench behind the stove and got acquainted with the cat--he caught not only rats and mice, but gophers, I was told. The patch of yellow sunlight on the floor travelled back toward the stairway, and grandmother and I talked about my journey, and about the arrival of the new Bohemian family; she said they were to be our nearest neighbours. We did not talk about the farm in Virginia, which had been her home for so many years. But after the men came in from the fields, and we were all seated at the supper table, then she asked Jake about the old place and about our friends and neighbours there.

My grandfather said little. When he first came in he kissed me and spoke kindly to me, but he was not demonstrative. I felt at once his deliberateness and personal dignity, and was a little in awe of him. The thing one immediately noticed about him was his beautiful, crinkly, snow-white beard. I once heard a missionary say it was like the beard of an Arabian sheik. His bald crown only made it more impressive.

Grandfather's eyes were not at all like those of an old man; they were bright blue, and had a fresh, frosty sparkle. His teeth were white and regular--so sound that he had never been to a dentist in his life. He had a delicate skin, easily roughened by sun and wind. When he was a young man his hair and beard were red; his eyebrows were still coppery.

As we sat at the table, Otto Fuchs and I kept stealing covert glances at each other. Grandmother had told me while she was getting supper that he was an Austrian who came to this country a young boy and had led an adventurous life in the Far West among mining-camps and cow outfits. His iron constitution was somewhat broken by mountain pneumonia, and he had drifted back to live in a milder country for a while. He had relatives in Bismarck, a German settlement to the north of us, but for a year now he had been working for grandfather.

The minute supper was over, Otto took me into the kitchen to whisper to me about a pony down in the barn that had been bought for me at a sale; he had been riding him to find out whether he had any bad tricks, but he was a `perfect gentleman,' and his name was Dude. Fuchs told me everything I wanted to know: how he had lost his ear in a Wyoming blizzard when he was a stage-driver, and how to throw a lasso. He promised to rope a steer for me before sundown next day. He got out his `chaps' and silver spurs to show them to Jake and me, and his best cowboy boots, with tops stitched in bold design--roses, and true-lover's knots, and undraped female figures. These, he solemnly explained, were angels.

Before we went to bed, Jake and Otto were called up to the living-room for prayers. Grandfather put on silver-rimmed spectacles and read several Psalms. His voice was so sympathetic and he read so interestingly that I wished he had chosen one of my favourite chapters in the Book of Kings. I was awed by his intonation of the word `Selah.' `He shall choose our inheritance for us, the excellency of Jacob whom He loved. Selah.' I had no idea what the word meant; perhaps he had not. But, as he uttered it, it became oracular, the most sacred of words.

Early the next morning I ran out-of-doors to look about me. I had been told that ours was the only wooden house west of Black Hawk--until you came to the Norwegian settlement, where there were several. Our neighbours lived in sod houses and dugouts--comfortable, but not very roomy. Our white frame house, with a storey and half-storey above the basement, stood at the east end of what I might call the farmyard, with the windmill close by the kitchen door. From the windmill the ground sloped westward, down to the barns and granaries and pig-yards. This slope was trampled hard and bare, and washed out in winding gullies by the rain. Beyond the corncribs, at the bottom of the shallow draw, was a muddy little pond, with rusty willow bushes growing about it. The road from the post-office came directly by our door, crossed the farmyard, and curved round this little pond, beyond which it began to climb the gentle swell of unbroken prairie to the west. There, along the western sky-line it skirted a great cornfield, much larger than any field I had ever seen. This cornfield, and the sorghum patch behind the barn, were the only broken land in sight. Everywhere, as far as the eye could reach, there was nothing but rough, shaggy, red grass, most of it as tall as I.

North of the house, inside the ploughed fire-breaks, grew a thick-set strip of box-elder trees, low and bushy, their leaves already turning yellow. This hedge was nearly a quarter of a mile long, but I had to look very hard to see it at all. The little trees were insignificant against the grass. It seemed as if the grass were about to run over them, and over the plum-patch behind the sod chicken-house.

As I looked about me I felt that the grass was the country, as the water is the sea. The red of the grass made all the great prairie the colour of winestains, or of certain seaweeds when they are first washed up. And there was so much motion in it; the whole country seemed, somehow, to be running.

I had almost forgotten that I had a grandmother, when she came out, her sunbonnet on her head, a grain-sack in her hand, and asked me if I did not want to go to the garden with her to dig potatoes for dinner.

The garden, curiously enough, was a quarter of a mile from the house, and the way to it led up a shallow draw past the cattle corral. Grandmother called my attention to a stout hickory cane, tipped with copper, which hung by a leather thong from her belt. This, she said, was her rattlesnake cane. I must never go to the garden without a heavy stick or a corn-knife; she had killed a good many rattlers on her way back and forth. A little girl who lived on the Black Hawk road was bitten on the ankle and had been sick all summer.

I can remember exactly how the country looked to me as I walked beside my grandmother along the faint wagon-tracks on that early September morning. Perhaps the glide of long railway travel was still with me, for more than anything else I felt motion in the landscape; in the fresh, easy-blowing morning wind, and in the earth itself, as if the shaggy grass were a sort of loose hide, and underneath it herds of wild buffalo were galloping, galloping ...

Alone, I should never have found the garden--except, perhaps, for the big yellow pumpkins that lay about unprotected by their withering vines--and I felt very little interest in it when I got there. I wanted to walk straight on through the red grass and over the edge of the world, which could not be very far away. The light air about me told me that the world ended here: only the ground and sun and sky were left, and if one went a little farther there would be only sun and sky, and one would float off into them, like the tawny hawks which sailed over our heads making slow shadows on the grass. While grandmother took the pitchfork we found standing in one of the rows and dug potatoes, while I picked them up out of the soft brown earth and put them into the bag, I kept looking up at the hawks that were doing what I might so easily do.

When grandmother was ready to go, I said I would like to stay up there in the garden awhile.

She peered down at me from under her sunbonnet. `Aren't you afraid of snakes?'

`A little,' I admitted, `but I'd like to stay, anyhow.'

`Well, if you see one, don't have anything to do with him. The big yellow and brown ones won't hurt you; they're bull-snakes and help to keep the gophers down. Don't be scared if you see anything look out of that hole in the bank over there. That's a badger hole. He's about as big as a big 'possum, and his face is striped, black and white. He takes a chicken once in a while, but I won't let the men harm him. In a new country a body feels friendly to the animals. I like to have him come out and watch me when I'm at work.'

Grandmother swung the bag of potatoes over her shoulder and went down the path, leaning forward a little. The road followed the windings of the draw; when she came to the first bend, she waved at me and disappeared. I was left alone with this new feeling of lightness and content.

I sat down in the middle of the garden, where snakes could scarcely approach unseen, and leaned my back against a warm yellow pumpkin. There were some ground-cherry bushes growing along the furrows, full of fruit. I turned back the papery triangular sheaths that protected the berries and ate a few. All about me giant grasshoppers, twice as big as any I had ever seen, were doing acrobatic feats among the dried vines. The gophers scurried up and down the ploughed ground. There in the sheltered draw-bottom the wind did not blow very hard, but I could hear it singing its humming tune up on the level, and I could see the tall grasses wave. The earth was warm under me, and warm as I crumbled it through my fingers. Queer little red bugs came out and moved in slow squadrons around me. Their backs were polished vermilion, with black spots. I kept as still as I could. Nothing happened. I did not expect anything to happen. I was something that lay under the sun and felt it, like the pumpkins, and I did not want to be anything more. I was entirely happy. Perhaps we feel like that when we die and become a part of something entire, whether it is sun and air, or goodness and knowledge. At any rate, that is happiness; to be dissolved into something complete and great. When it comes to one, it comes as naturally as sleep.

III

ON SUNDAY MORNING Otto Fuchs was to drive us over to make the acquaintance of our new Bohemian neighbours. We were taking them some provisions, as they had come to live on a wild place where there was no garden or chicken-house, and very little broken land. Fuchs brought up a sack of potatoes and a piece of cured pork from the cellar, and grandmother packed some loaves of Saturday's bread, a jar of butter, and several pumpkin pies in the straw of the wagon-box. We clambered up to the front seat and jolted off past the little pond and along the road that climbed to the big cornfield.

I could hardly wait to see what lay beyond that cornfield; but there was only red grass like ours, and nothing else, though from the high wagon-seat one could look off a long way. The road ran about like a wild thing, avoiding the deep draws, crossing them where they were wide and shallow. And all along it, wherever it looped or ran, the sunflowers grew; some of them were as big as little trees, with great rough leaves and many branches which bore dozens of blossoms. They made a gold ribbon across the prairie. Occasionally one of the horses would tear off with his teeth a plant full of blossoms, and walk along munching it, the flowers nodding in time to his bites as he ate down toward them.

The Bohemian family, grandmother told me as we drove along, had bought the homestead of a fellow countryman, Peter Krajiek, and had paid him more than it was worth. Their agreement with him was made before they left the old country, through a cousin of his, who was also a relative of Mrs. Shimerda. The Shimerdas were the first Bohemian family to come to this part of the county. Krajiek was their only interpreter, and could tell them anything he chose. They could not speak enough English to ask for advice, or even to make their most pressing wants known. One son, Fuchs said, was well-grown, and strong enough to work the land; but the father was old and frail and knew nothing about farming. He was a weaver by trade; had been a skilled workman on tapestries and upholstery materials. He had brought his fiddle with him, which wouldn't be of much use here, though he used to pick up money by it at home.

`If they're nice people, I hate to think of them spending the winter in that cave of Krajiek's,' said grandmother. `It's no better than a badger hole; no proper dugout at all. And I hear he's made them pay twenty dollars for his old cookstove that ain't worth ten.'

`Yes'm,' said Otto; `and he's sold 'em his oxen and his two bony old horses for the price of good workteams. I'd have interfered about the horses--the old man can understand some German--if I'd I a' thought it would do any good. But Bohemians has a natural distrust of Austrians.'

Grandmother looked interested. `Now, why is that, Otto?'

Fuchs wrinkled his brow and nose. `Well, ma'm, it's politics. It would take me a long while to explain.'

The land was growing rougher; I was told that we were approaching Squaw Creek, which cut up the west half of the Shimerdas' place and made the land of little value for farming. Soon we could see the broken, grassy clay cliffs which indicated the windings of the stream, and the glittering tops of the cottonwoods and ash trees that grew down in the ravine. Some of the cottonwoods had already turned, and the yellow leaves and shining white bark made them look like the gold and silver trees in fairy tales.

As we approached the Shimerdas' dwelling, I could still see nothing but rough red hillocks, and draws with shelving banks and long roots hanging out where the earth had crumbled away. Presently, against one of those banks, I saw a sort of shed, thatched with the same wine-coloured grass that grew everywhere. Near it tilted a shattered windmill frame, that had no wheel. We drove up to this skeleton to tie our horses, and then I saw a door and window sunk deep in the drawbank. The door stood open, and a woman and a girl of fourteen ran out and looked up at us hopefully. A little girl trailed along behind them. The woman had on her head the same embroidered shawl with silk fringes that she wore when she had alighted from the train at Black Hawk. She was not old, but she was certainly not young. Her face was alert and lively, with a sharp chin and shrewd little eyes. She shook grandmother's hand energetically.

`Very glad, very glad!' she ejaculated. Immediately she pointed to the bank out of which she had emerged and said, `House no good, house no good!'

Grandmother nodded consolingly. `You'll get fixed up comfortable after while, Mrs. Shimerda; make good house.'

My grandmother always spoke in a very loud tone to foreigners, as if they were deaf. She made Mrs. Shimerda understand the friendly intention of our visit, and the Bohemian woman handled the loaves of bread and even smelled them, and examined the pies with lively curiosity, exclaiming, `Much good, much thank!'--and again she wrung grandmother's hand.

The oldest son, Ambroz--they called it Ambrosch--came out of the cave and stood beside his mother. He was nineteen years old, short and broad-backed, with a close-cropped, flat head, and a wide, flat face. His hazel eyes were little and shrewd, like his mother's, but more sly and suspicious; they fairly snapped at the food. The family had been living on corncakes and sorghum molasses for three days.

The little girl was pretty, but Antonia--they accented the name thus, strongly, when they spoke to her--was still prettier. I remembered what the conductor had said about her eyes. They were big and warm and full of light, like the sun shining on brown pools in the wood. Her skin was brown, too, and in her cheeks she had a glow of rich, dark colour. Her brown hair was curly and wild-looking. The little sister, whom they called Yulka (Julka), was fair, and seemed mild and obedient. While I stood awkwardly confronting the two girls, Krajiek came up from the barn to see what was going on. With him was another Shimerda son. Even from a distance one could see that there was something strange about this boy. As he approached us, he began to make uncouth noises, and held up his hands to show us his fingers, which were webbed to the first knuckle, like a duck's foot. When he saw me draw back, he began to crow delightedly, `Hoo, hoo-hoo, hoo-hoo!' like a rooster. His mother scowled and said sternly, `Marek!' then spoke rapidly to Krajiek in Bohemian.

`She wants me to tell you he won't hurt nobody, Mrs. Burden. He was born like that. The others are smart. Ambrosch, he make good farmer.' He struck Ambrosch on the back, and the boy smiled knowingly.

At that moment the father came out of the hole in the bank. He wore no hat, and his thick, iron-grey hair was brushed straight back from his forehead. It was so long that it bushed out behind his ears, and made him look like the old portraits I remembered in Virginia. He was tall and slender, and his thin shoulders stooped. He looked at us understandingly, then took grandmother's hand and bent over it. I noticed how white and well-shaped his own hands were. They looked calm, somehow, and skilled. His eyes were melancholy, and were set back deep under his brow. His face was ruggedly formed, but it looked like ashes--like something from which all the warmth and light had died out. Everything about this old man was in keeping with his dignified manner. He was neatly dressed. Under his coat he wore a knitted grey vest, and, instead of a collar, a silk scarf of a dark bronze-green, carefully crossed and held together by a red coral pin. While Krajiek was translating for Mr. Shimerda, Antonia came up to me and held out her hand coaxingly. In a moment we were running up the steep drawside together, Yulka trotting after us.

When we reached the level and could see the gold tree-tops, I pointed toward them, and Antonia laughed and squeezed my hand as if to tell me how glad she was I had come. We raced off toward Squaw Creek and did not stop until the ground itself stopped--fell away before us so abruptly that the next step would have been out into the tree-tops. We stood panting on the edge of the ravine, looking down at the trees and bushes that grew below us. The wind was so strong that I had to hold my hat on, and the girls' skirts were blown out before them. Antonia seemed to like it; she held her little sister by the hand and chattered away in that language which seemed to me spoken so much more rapidly than mine. She looked at me, her eyes fairly blazing with things she could not say.

`Name? What name?' she asked, touching me on the shoulder. I told her my name, and she repeated it after me and made Yulka say it. She pointed into the gold cottonwood tree behind whose top we stood and said again, `What name?'

We sat down and made a nest in the long red grass. Yulka curled up like a baby rabbit and played with a grasshopper. Antonia pointed up to the sky and questioned me with her glance. I gave her the word, but she was not satisfied and pointed to my eyes. I told her, and she repeated the word, making it sound like `ice.' She pointed up to the sky, then to my eyes, then back to the sky, with movements so quick and impulsive that she distracted me, and I had no idea what she wanted. She got up on her knees and wrung her hands. She pointed to her own eyes and shook her head, then to mine and to the sky, nodding violently.

`Oh,' I exclaimed, `blue; blue sky.'

She clapped her hands and murmured, `Blue sky, blue eyes,' as if it amused her. While we snuggled down there out of the wind, she learned a score of words. She was alive, and very eager. We were so deep in the grass that we could see nothing but the blue sky over us and the gold tree in front of us. It was wonderfully pleasant. After Antonia had said the new words over and over, she wanted to give me a little chased silver ring she wore on her middle finger. When she coaxed and insisted, I repulsed her quite sternly. I didn't want her ring, and I felt there was something reckless and extravagant about her wishing to give it away to a boy she had never seen before. No wonder Krajiek got the better of these people, if this was how they behaved.

While we were disputing `about the ring, I heard a mournful voice calling, `Antonia, Antonia!' She sprang up like a hare. "Tatinek! Tatinek!' she shouted, and we ran to meet the old man who was coming toward us. Antonia reached him first, took his hand and kissed it. When I came up, he touched my shoulder and looked searchingly down into my face for several seconds. I became somewhat embarrassed, for I was used to being taken for granted by my elders.

We went with Mr. Shimerda back to the dugout, where grandmother was waiting for me. Before I got into the wagon, he took a book out of his pocket, opened it, and showed me a page with two alphabets, one English and the other

Bohemian. He placed this book in my grandmother's hands, looked at her entreatingly, and said, with an earnestness which I shall never forget, `Te-e-ach, te-e-ach my Antonia!'

IV

ON THE AFTERNOON of that same Sunday I took my first long ride on my pony, under Otto's direction. After that Dude and I went twice a week to the post-office, six miles east of us, and I saved the men a good deal of time by riding on errands to our neighbours. When we had to borrow anything, or to send about word that there would be preaching at the sod schoolhouse, I was always the messenger. Formerly Fuchs attended to such things after working hours.

All the years that have passed have not dimmed my memory of that first glorious autumn. The new country lay open before me: there were no fences in those days, and I could choose my own way over the grass uplands, trusting the pony to get me home again. Sometimes I followed the sunflower-bordered roads. Fuchs told me that the sunflowers were introduced into that country by the Mormons; that at the time of the persecution, when they left Missouri and struck out into the wilderness to find a place where they could worship God in their own way, the members of the first exploring party, crossing the plains to Utah, scattered sunflower seed as they went. The next summer, when the long trains of wagons came through with all the women and children, they had the sunflower trail to follow. I believe that botanists do not confirm Fuchs's story, but insist that the sunflower was native to those plains. Nevertheless, that legend has stuck in my mind, and sunflower-bordered roads always seem to me the roads to freedom.

I used to love to drift along the pale-yellow cornfields, looking for the damp spots one sometimes found at their edges, where the smartweed soon turned a rich copper colour and the narrow brown leaves hung curled like cocoons about the swollen joints of the stem. Sometimes I went south to visit our German neighbours and to admire their catalpa grove, or to see the big elm tree that grew up out of a deep crack in the earth and had a hawk's nest in its branches. Trees were so rare in that country, and they had to make such a hard fight to grow, that we used to feel anxious about them, and visit them as if they were persons. It must have been the scarcity of detail in that tawny landscape that made detail so precious.

Sometimes I rode north to the big prairie-dog town to watch the brown earth-owls fly home in the late afternoon and go down to their nests underground with the dogs. Antonia Shimerda liked to go with me, and we used to wonder a great deal about these birds of subterranean habit. We had to be on our guard there, for rattlesnakes were always lurking about. They came to pick up an easy living among the dogs and owls, which were quite defenceless against them; took possession of their comfortable houses and ate the eggs and puppies. We felt sorry for the owls. It was always mournful to see them come flying home at sunset and disappear under the earth. But, after all, we felt, winged things who would live like that must be rather degraded creatures. The dog-town was a long way from any pond or creek. Otto Fuchs said he had seen populous dog-towns in the desert where there was no surface water for fifty miles; he insisted that some of the holes must go down to water--nearly two hundred feet, hereabouts. Antonia said she didn't believe it; that the dogs probably lapped up the dew in the early morning, like the rabbits.

Antonia had opinions about everything, and she was soon able to make them known. Almost every day she came running across the prairie to have her reading lesson with me. Mrs. Shimerda grumbled, but realized it was important that one member of the family should learn English. When the lesson was over, we used to go up to the watermelon patch behind the garden. I split the melons with an old corn-knife, and we lifted out the hearts and ate them with the juice trickling through our fingers. The white Christmas melons we did not touch, but we watched them with curiosity. They were to be picked late, when the hard frosts had set in, and put away for winter use. After weeks on the ocean, the Shimerdas were famished for fruit. The two girls would wander for miles along the edge of the cornfields, hunting for ground-cherries.

Antonia loved to help grandmother in the kitchen and to learn about cooking and housekeeping. She would stand beside her, watching her every movement. We were willing to believe that Mrs. Shimerda was a good housewife in her own country, but she managed poorly under new conditions: the conditions were bad enough, certainly!

I remember how horrified we were at the sour, ashy-grey bread she gave her family to eat. She mixed her dough, we discovered, in an old tin peck-measure that Krajiek had used about the barn. When she took the paste out to bake it, she left smears of dough sticking to the sides of the measure, put the measure on the shelf behind the stove, and let this residue ferment. The next time she made bread, she scraped this sour stuff down into the fresh dough to serve as yeast.

During those first months the Shimerdas never went to town. Krajiek encouraged them in the belief that in Black Hawk they would somehow be mysteriously separated from their money. They hated Krajiek, but they clung to him because he was the only human being with whom they could talk or from whom they could get information. He slept with the old man and the two boys in the dugout barn, along with the oxen. They kept him in their hole and fed him for the same reason that the prairie-dogs and the brown owls house the rattlesnakes--because they did not know how to get rid of him.

V

WE KNEW THAT THINGS were hard for our Bohemian neighbours, but the two girls were lighthearted and never complained. They were always ready to forget their troubles at home, and to run away with me over the prairie, scaring rabbits or starting up flocks of quail.

I remember Antonia's excitement when she came into our kitchen one afternoon and announced: `My papa find friends up north, with Russian mans. Last night he take me for see, and I can understand very much talk. Nice mans, Mrs. Burden. One is fat and all the time laugh. Everybody laugh. The first time I see my papa laugh in this kawntree. Oh, very nice!'

I asked her if she meant the two Russians who lived up by the big dog-town. I had often been tempted to go to see them when I was riding in that direction, but one of them was a wild-looking fellow and I was a little afraid of him. Russia seemed to me more remote than any other country-- farther away than China, almost as far as the North Pole. Of all the strange, uprooted people among the first settlers, those two men were the strangest and the most aloof. Their last names were unpronounceable, so they were called Pavel and Peter. They went about making signs to people, and until the Shimerdas came they had no friends. Krajiek could understand them a little, but he had cheated them in a trade, so they avoided him. Pavel, the tall one, was said to be an anarchist; since he had no means of imparting his opinions, probably his wild gesticulations and his generally excited and rebellious manner gave rise to this supposition. He must once have been a very strong man, but now his great frame, with big, knotty joints, had a wasted look, and the skin was drawn tight over his high cheekbones. His breathing was hoarse, and he always had a cough.

Peter, his companion, was a very different sort of fellow; short, bow-legged, and as fat as butter. He always seemed pleased when he met people on the road, smiled and took off his cap to everyone, men as well as women. At a distance, on his wagon, he looked like an old man; his hair and beard were of such a pale flaxen colour that they seemed white in the sun. They were as thick and curly as carded wool. His rosy face, with its snub nose, set in this fleece, was like a melon among its leaves. He was usually called `Curly Peter,' or `Rooshian Peter.'

The two Russians made good farm-hands, and in summer they worked out together. I had heard our neighbours laughing when they told how Peter always had to go home at night to milk his cow. Other bachelor homesteaders used canned milk, to save trouble. Sometimes Peter came to church at the sod schoolhouse. It was there I first saw him, sitting on a low bench by the door, his plush cap in his hands, his bare feet tucked apologetically under the seat.

After Mr. Shimerda discovered the Russians, he went to see them almost every evening, and sometimes took Antonia with him. She said they came from a part of Russia where the language was not very different from Bohemian, and if I wanted to go to their place, she could talk to them for me. One afternoon, before the heavy frosts began, we rode up there together on my pony.

The Russians had a neat log house built on a grassy slope, with a windlass well beside the door. As we rode up the draw, we skirted a big melon patch, and a garden where squashes and yellow cucumbers lay about on the sod. We found Peter out behind his kitchen, bending over a washtub. He was working so hard that he did not hear us coming. His whole body moved up and down as he rubbed, and he was a funny sight from the rear, with his shaggy head and bandy legs. When he straightened himself up to greet us, drops of perspiration were rolling from his thick nose down onto his curly beard. Peter dried his hands and seemed glad to leave his washing. He took us down to see his chickens, and his cow that was grazing on the hillside. He told Antonia that in his country only rich people had cows, but here any man could have one who would take care of her. The milk was good for Pavel, who was often sick, and he could make butter by beating sour cream with a wooden spoon. Peter was very fond of his cow. He patted her flanks and talked to her in Russian while he pulled up her lariat pin and set it in a new place.

After he had shown us his garden, Peter trundled a load of watermelons up the hill in his wheelbarrow. Pavel was not at home. He was off somewhere helping to dig a well. The house I thought very comfortable for two men who were `batching.' Besides the kitchen, there was a living-room, with a wide double bed built against the wall, properly made up with blue gingham sheets and pillows. There was a little storeroom, too, with a window, where they kept guns and saddles and tools, and old coats and boots. That day the floor was covered with garden things, drying for winter; corn and beans and fat yellow cucumbers. There were no screens or window-blinds in the house, and all the doors and windows stood wide open, letting in flies and sunshine alike.

Peter put the melons in a row on the oilcloth-covered table and stood over them, brandishing a butcher knife. Before the blade got fairly into them, they split of their own ripeness, with a delicious sound. He gave us knives, but no plates, and the top of the table was soon swimming with juice and seeds. I had never seen anyone eat so many melons as Peter ate. He assured us that they were good for one--better than medicine; in his country people lived on them at this time of year. He was very hospitable and jolly. Once, while he was looking at Antonia, he sighed and told us that if he had stayed at home in Russia perhaps by this time he would have had a pretty daughter of his own to cook and keep house for him. He said he had left his country because of a `great trouble.'

When we got up to go, Peter looked about in perplexity for something that would entertain us. He ran into the storeroom and brought out a gaudily painted harmonica, sat down on a bench, and spreading his fat legs apart began to play like a whole band. The tunes were either very lively or very doleful, and he sang words to some of them.

Before we left, Peter put ripe cucumbers into a sack for Mrs. Shimerda and gave us a lard-pail full of milk to cook them in. I had never heard of cooking cucumbers, but Antonia assured me they were very good. We had to walk the pony all the way home to keep from spilling the milk.

VI

ONE AFTERNOON WE WERE having our reading lesson on the warm, grassy bank where the badger lived. It was a day of amber sunlight, but there was a shiver of coming winter in the air. I had seen ice on the little horsepond that morning, and as we went through the garden we found the tall asparagus, with its red berries, lying on the ground, a mass of slimy green.

Tony was barefooted, and she shivered in her cotton dress and was comfortable only when we were tucked down on the baked earth, in the full blaze of the sun. She could talk to me about almost anything by this time. That afternoon she was telling me how highly esteemed our friend the badger was in her part of the world, and how men kept a special kind of dog, with very short legs, to hunt him. Those dogs, she said, went down into the hole after the badger and killed him there in a terrific struggle underground; you could hear the barks and yelps outside. Then the dog dragged himself back, covered with bites and scratches, to be rewarded and petted by his master. She knew a dog who had a star on his collar for every badger he had killed.

The rabbits were unusually spry that afternoon. They kept starting up all about us, and dashing off down the draw as if they were playing a game of some kind. But the little buzzing things that lived in the grass were all dead--all but one. While we were lying there against the warm bank, a little insect of the palest, frailest green hopped painfully out of the buffalo grass and tried to leap into a bunch of bluestem. He missed it, fell back, and sat with his head sunk between his long legs, his antennae quivering, as if he were waiting for something to come and finish him. Tony made a warm nest for him in her hands; talked to him gaily and indulgently in Bohemian. Presently he began to sing for us--a thin, rusty little chirp. She held him close to her ear and laughed, but a moment afterward I saw there were tears in her eyes. She told me that in her village at home there was an old beggar woman who went about selling herbs and roots she had dug up in the forest. If you took her in and gave her a warm place by the fire, she sang old songs to the children in a cracked voice, like this. Old Hata, she was called, and the children loved to see her coming and saved their cakes and sweets for her.

When the bank on the other side of the draw began to throw a narrow shelf of shadow, we knew we ought to be starting homeward; the chill came on quickly when the sun got low, and Antonia's dress was thin. What were we to do with the frail little creature we had lured back to life by false pretences? I offered my pockets, but Tony shook her head and carefully put the green insect in her hair, tying her big handkerchief down loosely over her curls. I said I would go with her until we could see Squaw Creek, and then turn and run home. We drifted along lazily, very happy, through the magical light of the late afternoon.

All those fall afternoons were the same, but I never got used to them. As far as we could see, the miles of copper-red grass were drenched in sunlight that was stronger and fiercer than at any other time of the day. The blond cornfields were red gold, the haystacks turned rosy and threw long shadows. The whole prairie was like the bush that burned with fire and was not consumed. That hour always had the exultation of victory, of triumphant ending, like a hero's death--heroes who died young and gloriously. It was a sudden transfiguration, a lifting-up of day.

How many an afternoon Antonia and I have trailed along the prairie under that magnificence! And always two long black shadows flitted before us or followed after, dark spots on the ruddy grass.

We had been silent a long time, and the edge of the sun sank nearer and nearer the prairie floor, when we saw a figure moving on the edge of the upland, a gun over his shoulder. He was walking slowly, dragging his feet along as if he had no purpose. We broke into a run to overtake him.

`My papa sick all the time,' Tony panted as we flew. `He not look good, Jim.'

As we neared Mr. Shimerda she shouted, and he lifted his head and peered about. Tony ran up to him, caught his hand and pressed it against her cheek. She was the only one of his family who could rouse the old man from the torpor in which he seemed to live. He took the bag from his belt and showed us three rabbits he had shot, looked at Antonia with a wintry flicker of a smile and began to tell her something. She turned to me.

`My tatinek make me little hat with the skins, little hat for winter!' she exclaimed joyfully. `Meat for eat, skin for hat'--she told off these benefits on her fingers.

Her father put his hand on her hair, but she caught his wrist and lifted it carefully away, talking to him rapidly. I heard the name of old Hata. He untied the handkerchief, separated her hair with his fingers, and stood looking down at the green insect. When it began to chirp faintly, he listened as if it were a beautiful sound.

I picked up the gun he had dropped; a queer piece from the old country, short and heavy, with a stag's head on the cock. When he saw me examining it, he turned to me with his far-away look that always made me feel as if I were down at the bottom of a well. He spoke kindly and gravely, and Antonia translated:

`My tatinek say when you are big boy, he give you his gun. Very fine, from Bohemie. It was belong to a great man, very rich, like what you not got here; many fields, many forests, many big house. My papa play for his wedding, and he give my papa fine gun, and my papa give you.'

I was glad that this project was one of futurity. There never were such people as the Shimerdas for wanting to give away everything they had. Even the mother was always offering me things, though I knew she expected substantial presents in return. We stood there in friendly silence, while the feeble minstrel sheltered in Antonia's hair went on with its scratchy chirp. The old man's smile, as he listened, was so full of sadness, of pity for things, that I never afterward forgot it. As the sun sank there came a sudden coolness and the strong smell of earth and drying grass. Antonia and her father went off hand in hand, and I buttoned up my jacket and raced my shadow home.

VII

MUCH AS I LIKED Antonia, I hated a superior tone that she sometimes took with me. She was four years older than I, to be sure, and had seen more of the world; but I was a boy and she was a girl, and I resented her protecting manner. Before the autumn was over, she began to treat me more like an equal and to defer to me in other things than reading lessons. This change came about from an adventure we had together.

One day when I rode over to the Shimerdas' I found Antonia starting off on foot for Russian Peter's house, to borrow a spade Ambrosch needed. I offered to take her on the pony, and she got up behind me. There had been another black frost the night before, and the air was clear and heady as wine. Within a week all the blooming roads had been despoiled, hundreds of miles of yellow sunflowers had been transformed into brown, rattling, burry stalks.

We found Russian Peter digging his potatoes. We were glad to go in and get warm by his kitchen stove and to see his squashes and Christmas melons, heaped in the storeroom for winter. As we rode away with the spade, Antonia suggested that we stop at the prairie-dog-town and dig into one of the holes. We could find out whether they ran straight down, or were horizontal, like mole-holes; whether they had underground connections; whether the owls had nests down there, lined with feathers. We might get some puppies, or owl eggs, or snakeskins.

The dog-town was spread out over perhaps ten acres. The grass had been nibbled short and even, so this stretch was not shaggy and red like the surrounding country, but grey and velvety. The holes were several yards apart, and were disposed with a good deal of regularity, almost as if the town had been laid out in streets and avenues. One always felt that an orderly and very sociable kind of life was going on there. I picketed Dude down in a draw, and we went wandering about, looking for a hole that would be easy to dig. The dogs were out, as usual, dozens of them, sitting up on their hind legs over the doors of their houses. As we approached, they barked, shook their tails at us, and scurried underground. Before the mouths of the holes were little patches of sand and gravel, scratched up, we supposed, from a long way below the surface. Here and there, in the town, we came on larger gravel patches, several yards away from any hole. If the dogs had scratched the sand up in excavating, how had they carried it so far? It was on one of these gravel beds that I met my adventure.

We were examining a big hole with two entrances. The burrow sloped into the ground at a gentle angle, so that we could see where the two corridors united, and the floor was dusty from use, like a little highway over which much travel went. I was walking backward, in a crouching position, when I heard Antonia scream. She was standing opposite me, pointing behind me and shouting something in Bohemian. I whirled round, and there, on one of those dry gravel beds, was the biggest snake I had ever seen. He was sunning himself, after the cold night, and he must have been asleep when Antonia screamed. When I turned, he was lying in long loose waves, like a letter `W.' He twitched and began to coil slowly. He was not merely a big snake, I thought--he was a circus monstrosity. His abominable muscularity, his loathsome, fluid motion, somehow made me sick. He was as thick as my leg, and looked as if millstones couldn't crush the disgusting vitality out of him. He lifted his hideous little head, and rattled. I didn't run because I didn't think of it--if my back had been against a stone wall I couldn't have felt more cornered. I saw his coils tighten--now he would spring, spring his length, I remembered. I ran up and drove at his head with my spade, struck him fairly across the neck, and in a minute he was all about my feet in wavy loops. I struck now from hate. Antonia, barefooted as she was, ran up behind me. Even after I had pounded his ugly head flat, his body kept on coiling and winding, doubling and falling back on itself. I walked away and turned my back. I felt seasick.

Antonia came after me, crying, `O Jimmy, he not bite you? You sure? Why you not run when I say?'

`What did you jabber Bohunk for? You might have told me there was a snake behind me!' I said petulantly.

`I know I am just awful, Jim, I was so scared.' She took my handkerchief from my pocket and tried to wipe my face with it, but I snatched it away from her. I suppose I looked as sick as I felt.

`I never know you was so brave, Jim,' she went on comfortingly. `You is just like big mans; you wait for him lift his head and then you go for him. Ain't you feel scared a bit? Now we take that snake home and show everybody. Nobody ain't seen in this kawntree so big snake like you kill.'

She went on in this strain until I began to think that I had longed for this opportunity, and had hailed it with joy. Cautiously we went back to the snake; he was still groping with his tail, turning up his ugly belly in the light. A faint, fetid smell came from him, and a thread of green liquid oozed from his crushed head.

`Look, Tony, that's his poison,' I said.

I took a long piece of string from my pocket, and she lifted his head with the spade while I tied a noose around it. We pulled him out straight and measured him by my riding-quirt; he was about five and a half feet long. He had twelve rattles, but they were broken off before they began to taper, so I insisted that he must once have had twenty-four. I explained to Antonia how this meant that he was twenty-four years old, that he must have been there when white men first came, left on from buffalo and Indian times. As I turned him over, I began to feel proud of him, to have a kind of respect for his age and size. He seemed like the ancient, eldest Evil. Certainly his kind have left horrible unconscious memories in all warm-blooded life. When we dragged him down into the draw, Dude sprang off to the end of his tether and shivered all over--wouldn't let us come near him.

We decided that Antonia should ride Dude home, and I would walk. As she rode along slowly, her bare legs swinging against the pony's sides, she kept shouting back to me about how astonished everybody would be. I followed with the spade over my shoulder, dragging my snake. Her exultation was contagious. The great land had never looked to me so big and free. If the red grass were full of rattlers, I was equal to them all. Nevertheless, I stole furtive glances behind me now and then to see that no avenging mate, older and bigger than my quarry, was racing up from the rear.

The sun had set when we reached our garden and went down the draw toward the house. Otto Fuchs was the first one we met. He was sitting on the edge of the cattle-pond, having a quiet pipe before supper. Antonia called him to come quick and look. He did not say anything for a minute, but scratched his head and turned the snake over with his boot.

`Where did you run onto that beauty, Jim?'

`Up at the dog-town,' I answered laconically.

`Kill him yourself? How come you to have a weepon?'

`We'd been up to Russian Peter's, to borrow a spade for Ambrosch.'

Otto shook the ashes out of his pipe and squatted down to count the rattles. `It was just luck you had a tool,' he said cautiously. `Gosh! I wouldn't want to do any business with that fellow myself, unless I had a fence-post along. Your grandmother's snake-cane wouldn't more than tickle him. He could stand right up and talk to you, he could. Did he fight hard?'

Antonia broke in: `He fight something awful! He is all over Jimmy's boots. I scream for him to run, but he just hit and hit that snake like he was crazy.'

Otto winked at me. After Antonia rode on he said: `Got him in the head first crack, didn't you? That was just as well.'

We hung him up to the windmill, and when I went down to the kitchen, I found Antonia standing in the middle of the floor, telling the story with a great deal of colour.

Subsequent experiences with rattlesnakes taught me that my first encounter was fortunate in circumstance. My big rattler was old, and had led too easy a life; there was not much fight in him. He had probably lived there for years, with a fat prairie-dog for breakfast whenever he felt like it, a sheltered home, even an owl-feather bed, perhaps, and he had forgot that the world doesn't owe rattlers a living. A snake of his size, in fighting trim, would be more than any boy could handle. So in reality it was a mock adventure; the game was fixed for me by chance, as it probably was for many a dragon-slayer. I had been adequately armed by Russian Peter; the snake was old and lazy; and I had Antonia beside me, to appreciate and admire.

That snake hung on our corral fence for several days; some of the neighbours came to see it and agreed that it was the biggest rattler ever killed in those parts. This was enough for Antonia. She liked me better from that time on, and she never took a supercilious air with me again. I had killed a big snake--I was now a big fellow.

VIII

WHILE THE AUTUMN COLOUR was growing pale on the grass and cornfields, things went badly with our friends the Russians. Peter told his troubles to Mr. Shimerda: he was unable to meet a note which fell due on the first of November; had to pay an exorbitant bonus on renewing it, and to give a mortgage on his pigs and horses and even his milk cow. His creditor was Wick Cutter, the merciless Black Hawk money-lender, a man of evil name throughout the county, of whom I shall have more to say later. Peter could give no very clear account of his transactions with Cutter. He only knew that he had first borrowed two hundred dollars, then another hundred, then fifty--that each time a bonus was added to the principal, and the debt grew faster than any crop he planted. Now everything was plastered with mortgages.

Soon after Peter renewed his note, Pavel strained himself lifting timbers for a new barn, and fell over among the shavings with such a gush of blood from the lungs that his fellow workmen thought he would die on the spot. They hauled him home and put him into his bed, and there he lay, very ill indeed. Misfortune seemed to settle like an evil bird on the roof of the log house, and to flap its wings there, warning human beings away. The Russians had such bad luck that people were afraid of them and liked to put them out of mind.

One afternoon Antonia and her father came over to our house to get buttermilk, and lingered, as they usually did, until the sun was low. Just as they were leaving, Russian Peter drove up. Pavel was very bad, he said, and wanted to talk to Mr. Shimerda and his daughter; he had come to fetch them. When Antonia and her father got into the wagon, I entreated grandmother to let me go with them: I would gladly go without my supper, I would sleep in the Shimerdas' barn and run home in the morning. My plan must have seemed very foolish to her, but she was often large-minded about humouring the desires of other people. She asked Peter to wait a moment, and when she came back from the kitchen she brought a bag of sandwiches and doughnuts for us.

Mr. Shimerda and Peter were on the front seat; Antonia and I sat in the straw behind and ate our lunch as we bumped along. After the sun sank, a cold wind sprang up and moaned over the prairie. If this turn in the weather had come sooner, I should not have got away. We burrowed down in the straw and curled up close together, watching the angry red die out of the west and the stars begin to shine in the clear, windy sky. Peter kept sighing and groaning. Tony whispered to me that he was afraid Pavel would never get well. We lay still and did not talk. Up there the stars grew magnificently bright. Though we had come from such different parts of the world, in both of us there was some dusky superstition that those shining groups have their influence upon what is and what is not to be. Perhaps Russian Peter, come from farther away than any of us, had brought from his land, too, some such belief.

The little house on the hillside was so much the colour of the night that we could not see it as we came up the draw. The ruddy windows guided us--the light from the kitchen stove, for there was no lamp burning.

We entered softly. The man in the wide bed seemed to be asleep. Tony and I sat down on the bench by the wall and leaned our arms on the table in front of us. The firelight flickered on the hewn logs that supported the thatch overhead. Pavel made a rasping sound when he breathed, and he kept moaning. We waited. The wind shook the doors and windows impatiently, then swept on again, singing through the big spaces. Each gust, as it bore down, rattled the panes, and swelled off like the others. They made me think of defeated armies, retreating; or of ghosts who were trying desperately to get in for shelter, and then went moaning on. Presently, in one of those sobbing intervals between the blasts, the coyotes tuned up with their whining howl; one, two, three, then all together--to tell us that winter was coming. This sound brought an answer from the bed--a long complaining cry--as if Pavel were having bad dreams or were waking to some old misery. Peter listened, but did not stir. He was sitting on the floor by the kitchen stove. The coyotes broke out again; yap, yap, yap--then the high whine. Pavel called for something and struggled up on his elbow.

`He is scared of the wolves,' Antonia whispered to me. `In his country there are very many, and they eat men and women.' We slid closer together along the bench.

I could not take my eyes off the man in the bed. His shirt was hanging open, and his emaciated chest, covered with yellow bristle, rose and fell horribly. He began to cough. Peter shuffled to his feet, caught up the teakettle and mixed him some hot water and whiskey. The sharp smell of spirits went through the room.

Pavel snatched the cup and drank, then made Peter give him the bottle and slipped it under his pillow, grinning disagreeably, as if he had outwitted someone. His eyes followed Peter about the room with a contemptuous, unfriendly expression. It seemed to me that he despised him for being so simple and docile.

Presently Pavel began to talk to Mr. Shimerda, scarcely above a whisper. He was telling a long story, and as he went on, Antonia took my hand under the table and held it tight. She leaned forward and strained her ears to hear him. He grew more and more excited, and kept pointing all around his bed, as if there were things there and he wanted Mr. Shimerda to see them.

`It's wolves, Jimmy,' Antonia whispered. `It's awful, what he says!'

The sick man raged and shook his fist. He seemed to be cursing people who had wronged him. Mr. Shimerda caught him by the shoulders, but could hardly hold him in bed. At last he was shut off by a coughing fit which fairly choked him. He pulled a cloth from under his pillow and held it to his mouth. Quickly it was covered with bright red spots--I thought I had never seen any blood so bright. When he lay down and turned his face to the wall, all the rage had gone out of him. He lay patiently fighting for breath, like a child with croup. Antonia's father uncovered one of his long bony legs and rubbed it rhythmically. From our bench we could see what a hollow case his body was. His spine and shoulder-blades stood out like the bones under the hide of a dead steer left in the fields. That sharp backbone must have hurt him when he lay on it.

Gradually, relief came to all of us. Whatever it was, the worst was over. Mr. Shimerda signed to us that Pavel was asleep. Without a word Peter got up and lit his lantern. He was going out to get his team to drive us home. Mr. Shimerda went with him. We sat and watched the long bowed back under the blue sheet, scarcely daring to breathe.

On the way home, when we were lying in the straw, under the jolting and rattling Antonia told me as much of the story as she could. What she did not tell me then, she told later; we talked of nothing else for days afterward.

When Pavel and Peter were young men, living at home in Russia, they were asked to be groomsmen for a friend who was to marry the belle of another village. It was in the dead of winter and the groom's party went over to the wedding in sledges. Peter and Pavel drove in the groom's sledge, and six sledges followed with all his relatives and friends.

After the ceremony at the church, the party went to a dinner given by the parents of the bride. The dinner lasted all afternoon; then it became a supper and continued far into the night. There was much dancing and drinking. At midnight the parents of the bride said good-bye to her and blessed her. The groom took her up in his arms and carried her out to his sledge and tucked her under the blankets. He sprang in beside her, and Pavel and Peter (our Pavel and Peter!) took the front seat. Pavel drove. The party set out with singing and the jingle of sleigh-bells, the groom's sledge going first. All the drivers were more or less the worse for merry-making, and the groom was absorbed in his bride.

The wolves were bad that winter, and everyone knew it, yet when they heard the first wolf-cry, the drivers were not much alarmed. They had too much good food and drink inside them. The first howls were taken up and echoed and with quickening repetitions. The wolves were coming together. There was no moon, but the starlight was clear on the snow. A black drove came up over the hill behind the wedding party. The wolves ran like streaks of shadow; they looked no bigger than dogs, but there were hundreds of them.

Something happened to the hindmost sledge: the driver lost control--he was probably very drunk--the horses left the road, the sledge was caught in a clump of trees, and overturned. The occupants rolled out over the snow, and the fleetest of the wolves sprang upon them. The shrieks that followed made everybody sober. The drivers stood up and lashed their horses. The groom had the best team and his sledge was lightest--all the others carried from six to a dozen people.

Another driver lost control. The screams of the horses were more terrible to hear than the cries of the men and women. Nothing seemed to check the wolves. It was hard to tell what was happening in the rear; the people who were falling behind shrieked as piteously as those who were already lost. The little bride hid her face on the groom's shoulder and sobbed. Pavel sat still and watched his horses. The road was clear and white, and the groom's three blacks went like the wind. It was only necessary to be calm and to guide them carefully.

At length, as they breasted a long hill, Peter rose cautiously and looked back. `There are only three sledges left,' he whispered.

`And the wolves?' Pavel asked.

`Enough! Enough for all of us.'

Pavel reached the brow of the hill, but only two sledges followed him down the other side. In that moment on the hilltop, they saw behind them a whirling black group on the snow. Presently the groom screamed. He saw his father's sledge overturned, with his mother and sisters. He sprang up as if he meant to jump, but the girl shrieked and held him back. It was even then too late. The black ground-shadows were already crowding over the heap in the road, and one horse ran out across the fields, his harness hanging to him, wolves at his heels. But the groom's movement had given Pavel an idea.

They were within a few miles of their village now. The only sledge left out of six was not very far behind them, and Pavel's middle horse was failing. Beside a frozen pond something happened to the other sledge; Peter saw it plainly. Three big wolves got abreast of the horses, and the horses went crazy. They tried to jump over each other, got tangled up in the harness, and overturned the sledge.

When the shrieking behind them died away, Pavel realized that he was alone upon the familiar road. `They still come?' he asked Peter.

`Yes.'

`How many?'

`Twenty, thirty--enough.'

Now his middle horse was being almost dragged by the other two. Pavel gave Peter the reins and stepped carefully into the back of the sledge. He called to the groom that they must lighten--and pointed to the bride. The young man cursed him and held her tighter. Pavel tried to drag her away. In the struggle, the groom rose. Pavel knocked him over the side of the sledge and threw the girl after him. He said he never remembered exactly how he did it, or what happened afterward. Peter, crouching in the front seat, saw nothing. The first thing either of them noticed was a new sound that broke into the clear air, louder than they had ever heard it before--the bell of the monastery of their own village, ringing for early prayers.

Pavel and Peter drove into the village alone, and they had been alone ever since. They were run out of their village. Pavel's own mother would not look at him. They went away to strange towns, but when people learned where they came from, they were always asked if they knew the two men who had fed the bride to the wolves. Wherever they went, the story followed them. It took them five years to save money enough to come to America. They worked in Chicago, Des Moines, Fort Wayne, but they were always unfortunate. When Pavel's health grew so bad, they decided to try farming.

Pavel died a few days after he unburdened his mind to Mr. Shimerda, and was buried in the Norwegian graveyard. Peter sold off everything, and left the country--went to be cook in a railway construction camp where gangs of Russians were employed.

At his sale we bought Peter's wheelbarrow and some of his harness. During the auction he went about with his head down, and never lifted his eyes. He seemed not to care about anything. The Black Hawk money-lender who held mortgages on Peter's livestock was there, and he bought in the sale notes at about fifty cents on the dollar. Everyone said Peter kissed the cow before she was led away by her new owner. I did not see him do it, but this I know: after all his furniture and his cookstove and pots and pans had been hauled off by the purchasers, when his house was stripped and bare, he sat down on the floor with his clasp-knife and ate all the melons that he had put away for winter. When Mr. Shimerda and Krajiek drove up in their wagon to take Peter to the train, they found him with a dripping beard, surrounded by heaps of melon rinds.

The loss of his two friends had a depressing effect upon old Mr. Shimerda. When he was out hunting, he used to go into the empty log house and sit there, brooding. This cabin was his hermitage until the winter snows penned him in his cave. For Antonia and me, the story of the wedding party was never at an end. We did not tell Pavel's secret to anyone, but guarded it jealously--as if the wolves of the Ukraine had gathered that night long ago, and the wedding party been sacrificed, to give us a painful and peculiar pleasure. At night, before I went to sleep, I often found myself in a sledge drawn by three horses, dashing through a country that looked something like Nebraska and something like Virginia.

IX

THE FIRST SNOWFALL came early in December. I remember how the world looked from our sitting-room window as I dressed behind the stove that morning: the low sky was like a sheet of metal; the blond cornfields had faded out into ghostliness at last; the little pond was frozen under its stiff willow bushes. Big white flakes were whirling over everything and disappearing in the red grass.

Beyond the pond, on the slope that climbed to the cornfield, there was, faintly marked in the grass, a great circle where the Indians used to ride. Jake and Otto were sure that when they galloped round that ring the Indians tortured prisoners, bound to a stake in the centre; but grandfather thought they merely ran races or trained horses there. Whenever one looked at this slope against the setting sun, the circle showed like a pattern in the grass; and this morning, when the first light spray of snow lay over it, it came out with wonderful distinctness, like strokes of Chinese white on canvas. The old figure stirred me as it had never done before and seemed a good omen for the winter.

As soon as the snow had packed hard, I began to drive about the country in a clumsy sleigh that Otto Fuchs made for me by fastening a wooden goods-box on bobs. Fuchs had been apprenticed to a cabinetmaker in the old country and was very handy with tools. He would have done a better job if I hadn't hurried him. My first trip was to the post-office, and the next day I went over to take Yulka and Antonia for a sleigh-ride.

It was a bright, cold day. I piled straw and buffalo robes into the box, and took two hot bricks wrapped in old blankets. When I got to the Shimerdas', I did not go up to the house, but sat in my sleigh at the bottom of the draw and called. Antonia and Yulka came running out, wearing little rabbit-skin hats their father had made for them. They had heard about my sledge from Ambrosch and knew why I had come. They tumbled in beside me and we set off toward the north, along a road that happened to be broken.

The sky was brilliantly blue, and the sunlight on the glittering white stretches of prairie was almost blinding. As Antonia said, the whole world was changed by the snow; we kept looking in vain for familiar landmarks. The deep arroyo through which Squaw Creek wound was now only a cleft between snowdrifts--very blue when one looked down into it. The tree-tops that had been gold all the autumn were dwarfed and twisted, as if they would never have any life in them again. The few little cedars, which were so dull and dingy before, now stood out a strong, dusky green. The wind had the burning taste of fresh snow; my throat and nostrils smarted as if someone had opened a hartshorn bottle. The cold stung, and at the same time delighted one. My horse's breath rose like steam, and whenever we stopped he smoked all over. The cornfields got back a little of their colour under the dazzling light, and stood the palest possible gold in the sun and snow. All about us the snow was crusted in shallow terraces, with tracings like ripple-marks at the edges, curly waves that were the actual impression of the stinging lash in the wind.

The girls had on cotton dresses under their shawls; they kept shivering beneath the buffalo robes and hugging each other for warmth. But they were so glad to get away from their ugly cave and their mother's scolding that they begged me to go on and on, as far as Russian Peter's house. The great fresh open, after the stupefying warmth indoors, made them behave like wild things. They laughed and shouted, and said they never wanted to go home again. Couldn't we settle down and live in Russian Peter's house, Yulka asked, and couldn't I go to town and buy things for us to keep house with?

All the way to Russian Peter's we were extravagantly happy, but when we turned back--it must have been about four o'clock--the east wind grew stronger and began to howl; the sun lost its heartening power and the sky became grey and sombre. I took off my long woollen comforter and wound it around Yulka's throat. She got so cold that we made her hide her head under the buffalo robe. Antonia and I sat erect, but I held the reins clumsily, and my eyes were blinded by the wind a good deal of the time. It was growing dark when we got to their house, but I refused to go in with them and get warm. I knew my hands would ache terribly if I went near a fire. Yulka forgot to give me back my comforter, and I had to drive home directly against the wind. The next day I came down with an attack of quinsy, which kept me in the house for nearly two weeks.

The basement kitchen seemed heavenly safe and warm in those days--like a tight little boat in a winter sea. The men were out in the fields all day, husking corn, and when they came in at noon, with long caps pulled down over their ears and their feet in red-lined overshoes, I used to think they were like Arctic explorers. In the afternoons, when grandmother sat upstairs darning, or making husking-gloves, I read `The Swiss Family Robinson' aloud to her, and I felt that the Swiss family had no advantages over us in the way of an adventurous life. I was convinced that man's strongest antagonist is the cold. I admired the cheerful zest with which grandmother went about keeping us warm and comfortable and well-fed. She often reminded me, when she was preparing for the return of the hungry men, that this country was not like Virginia; and that here a cook had, as she said, `very little to do with.' On Sundays she gave us as much chicken as we could eat, and on other days we had ham or bacon or sausage meat. She baked either pies or cake for us every day, unless, for a change, she made my favourite pudding, striped with currants and boiled in a bag.

Next to getting warm and keeping warm, dinner and supper were the most interesting things we had to think about. Our lives centred around warmth and food and the return of the men at nightfall. I used to wonder, when they came in tired from the fields, their feet numb and their hands cracked and sore, how they could do all the chores so conscientiously: feed and water and bed the horses, milk the cows, and look after the pigs. When supper was over, it took them a long while to get the cold out of their bones. While grandmother and I washed the dishes and grandfather read his paper upstairs, Jake and Otto sat on the long bench behind the stove, `easing' their inside boots, or rubbing mutton tallow into their cracked hands.

Every Saturday night we popped corn or made taffy, and Otto Fuchs used to sing, `For I Am a Cowboy and Know I've Done Wrong,' or, `Bury Me Not on the Lone Prairie.' He had a good baritone voice and always led the singing when we went to church services at the sod schoolhouse.

I can still see those two men sitting on the bench; Otto's close-clipped head and Jake's shaggy hair slicked flat in front by a wet comb. I can see the sag of their tired shoulders against the whitewashed wall. What good fellows they were, how much they knew, and how many things they had kept faith with!

Fuchs had been a cowboy, a stage-driver, a bartender, a miner; had wandered all over that great Western country and done hard work everywhere, though, as grandmother said, he had nothing to show for it. Jake was duller than Otto. He could scarcely read, wrote even his name with difficulty, and he had a violent temper which sometimes made him behave like a crazy man--tore him all to pieces and actually made him ill. But he was so soft-hearted that anyone could impose upon him. If he, as he said, `forgot himself' and swore before grandmother, he went about depressed and shamefaced all day. They were both of them jovial about the cold in winter and the heat in summer, always ready to work overtime and to meet emergencies. It was a matter of pride with them not to spare themselves. Yet they were the sort of men who never get on, somehow, or do anything but work hard for a dollar or two a day.

On those bitter, starlit nights, as we sat around the old stove that fed us and warmed us and kept us cheerful, we could hear the coyotes howling down by the corrals, and their hungry, wintry cry used to remind the boys of wonderful animal stories; about grey wolves and bears in the Rockies, wildcats and panthers in the Virginia mountains. Sometimes Fuchs could be persuaded to talk about the outlaws and desperate characters he had known. I remember one funny story about himself that made grandmother, who was working her bread on the bread-board, laugh until she wiped her eyes with her bare arm, her hands being floury. It was like this:

When Otto left Austria to come to America, he was asked by one of his relatives to look after a woman who was crossing on the same boat, to join her husband in Chicago. The woman started off with two children, but it was clear that her family might grow larger on the journey. Fuchs said he `got on fine with the kids,' and liked the mother, though she played a sorry trick on him. In mid-ocean she proceeded to have not one baby, but three! This event made Fuchs the object of undeserved notoriety, since he was travelling with her. The steerage stewardess was indignant with him, the doctor regarded him with suspicion. The first-cabin passengers, who made up a purse for the woman, took an embarrassing interest in Otto, and often enquired of him about his charge. When the triplets were taken ashore at New York, he had, as he said, `to carry some of them.' The trip to Chicago was even worse than the ocean voyage. On the train it was very difficult to get milk for the babies and to keep their bottles clean. The mother did her best, but no woman, out of her natural resources, could feed three babies. The husband, in Chicago, was working in a furniture factory for modest wages, and when he met his family at the station he was rather crushed by the size of it. He, too, seemed to consider Fuchs in some fashion to blame. `I was sure glad,' Otto concluded, `that he didn't take his hard feeling out on that poor woman; but he had a sullen eye for me, all right! Now, did you ever hear of a young feller's having such hard luck, Mrs. Burden?'

Grandmother told him she was sure the Lord had remembered these things to his credit, and had helped him out of many a scrape when he didn't realize that he was being protected by Providence.

X

FOR SEVERAL WEEKS after my sleigh-ride, we heard nothing from the Shimerdas. My sore throat kept me indoors, and grandmother had a cold which made the housework heavy for her. When Sunday came she was glad to have a day of rest. One night at supper Fuchs told us he had seen Mr. Shimerda out hunting.

`He's made himself a rabbit-skin cap, Jim, and a rabbit-skin collar that he buttons on outside his coat. They ain't got but one overcoat among 'em over there, and they take turns wearing it. They seem awful scared of cold, and stick in that hole in the bank like badgers.'

`All but the crazy boy,' Jake put in. `He never wears the coat. Krajiek says he's turrible strong and can stand anything. I guess rabbits must be getting scarce in this locality. Ambrosch come along by the cornfield yesterday where I was at work and showed me three prairie dogs he'd shot. He asked me if they was good to eat. I spit and made a face and took on, to scare him, but he just looked like he was smarter'n me and put 'em back in his sack and walked off.'

Grandmother looked up in alarm and spoke to grandfather. `Josiah, you don't suppose Krajiek would let them poor creatures eat prairie dogs, do you?'

`You had better go over and see our neighbours tomorrow, Emmaline,' he replied gravely.

Fuchs put in a cheerful word and said prairie dogs were clean beasts and ought to be good for food, but their family connections were against them. I asked what he meant, and he grinned and said they belonged to the rat family.

When I went downstairs in the morning, I found grandmother and Jake packing a hamper basket in the kitchen.

`Now, Jake,' grandmother was saying, `if you can find that old rooster that got his comb froze, just give his neck a twist, and we'll take him along. There's no good reason why Mrs. Shimerda couldn't have got hens from her neighbours last fall and had a hen-house going by now. I reckon she was confused and didn't know where to begin. I've come strange to a new country myself, but I never forgot hens are a good thing to have, no matter what you don't have.

`Just as you say, ma'm,' said Jake, `but I hate to think of Krajiek getting a leg of that old rooster.' He tramped out through the long cellar and dropped the heavy door behind him.

After breakfast grandmother and Jake and I bundled ourselves up and climbed into the cold front wagon-seat. As we approached the Shimerdas', we heard the frosty whine of the pump and saw Antonia, her head tied up and her cotton dress blown about her, throwing all her weight on the pump-handle as it went up and down. She heard our wagon, looked back over her shoulder, and, catching up her pail of water, started at a run for the hole in the bank.

Jake helped grandmother to the ground, saying he would bring the provisions after he had blanketed his horses. We went slowly up the icy path toward the door sunk in the drawside. Blue puffs of smoke came from the stovepipe that stuck out through the grass and snow, but the wind whisked them roughly away.

Mrs. Shimerda opened the door before we knocked and seized grandmother's hand. She did not say `How do!' as usual, but at once began to cry, talking very fast in her own language, pointing to her feet which were tied up in rags, and looking about accusingly at everyone.

The old man was sitting on a stump behind the stove, crouching over as if he were trying to hide from us. Yulka was on the floor at his feet, her kitten in her lap. She peeped out at me and smiled, but, glancing up at her mother, hid again. Antonia was washing pans and dishes in a dark corner. The crazy boy lay under the only window, stretched on a gunny-sack stuffed with straw. As soon as we entered, he threw a grain-sack over the crack at the bottom of the door. The air in the cave was stifling, and it was very dark, too. A lighted lantern, hung over the stove, threw out a feeble yellow glimmer.

Mrs. Shimerda snatched off the covers of two barrels behind the door, and made us look into them. In one there were some potatoes that had been frozen and were rotting, in the other was a little pile of flour. Grandmother murmured something in embarrassment, but the Bohemian woman laughed scornfully, a kind of whinny-laugh, and, catching up an empty coffee-pot from the shelf, shook it at us with a look positively vindictive.

Grandmother went on talking in her polite Virginia way, not admitting their stark need or her own remissness, until Jake arrived with the hamper, as if in direct answer to Mrs. Shimerda's reproaches. Then the poor woman broke down. She dropped on the floor beside her crazy son, hid her face on her knees, and sat crying bitterly. Grandmother paid no heed to her, but called Antonia to come and help empty the basket. Tony left her corner reluctantly. I had never seen her crushed like this before.

`You not mind my poor mamenka, Mrs. Burden. She is so sad,' she whispered, as she wiped her wet hands on her skirt and took the things grandmother handed her.

The crazy boy, seeing the food, began to make soft, gurgling noises and stroked his stomach. Jake came in again, this time with a sack of potatoes. Grandmother looked about in perplexity.

`Haven't you got any sort of cave or cellar outside, Antonia? This is no place to keep vegetables. How did your potatoes get frozen?'

`We get from Mr. Bushy, at the post-office what he throw out. We got no potatoes, Mrs. Burden,' Tony admitted mournfully.

When Jake went out, Marek crawled along the floor and stuffed up the door-crack again. Then, quietly as a shadow, Mr. Shimerda came out from behind the stove. He stood brushing his hand over his smooth grey hair, as if he were trying to clear away a fog about his head. He was clean and neat as usual, with his green neckcloth and his coral pin. He took grandmother's arm and led her behind the stove, to the back of the room. In the rear wall was another little cave; a round hole, not much bigger than an oil barrel, scooped out in the black earth. When I got up on one of the stools and peered into it, I saw some quilts and a pile of straw. The old man held the lantern. `Yulka,' he said in a low, despairing voice, `Yulka; my Antonia!'

Grandmother drew back. `You mean they sleep in there--your girls?' He bowed his head.

Tony slipped under his arm. `It is very cold on the floor, and this is warm like the badger hole. I like for sleep there,' she insisted eagerly. `My mamenka have nice bed, with pillows from our own geese in Bohemie. See, Jim?' She pointed to the narrow bunk which Krajiek had built against the wall for himself before the Shimerdas came.

Grandmother sighed. `Sure enough, where WOULD you sleep, dear! I don't doubt you're warm there. You'll have a better house after while, Antonia, and then you will forget these hard times.'

Mr. Shimerda made grandmother sit down on the only chair and pointed his wife to a stool beside her. Standing before them with his hand on Antonia's shoulder, he talked in a low tone, and his daughter translated. He wanted us to know that they were not beggars in the old country; he made good wages, and his family were respected there. He left Bohemia with more than a thousand dollars in savings, after their passage money was paid. He had in some way lost on exchange in New York, and the railway fare to Nebraska was more than they had expected. By the time they paid Krajiek for the land, and bought his horses and oxen and some old farm machinery, they had very little money left. He wished grandmother to know, however, that he still had some money. If they could get through until spring came, they would buy a cow and chickens and plant a garden, and would then do very well. Ambrosch and Antonia were both old enough to work in the fields, and they were willing to work. But the snow and the bitter weather had disheartened them all.

Antonia explained that her father meant to build a new house for them in the spring; he and Ambrosch had already split the logs for it, but the logs were all buried in the snow, along the creek where they had been felled.

While grandmother encouraged and gave them advice, I sat down on the floor with Yulka and let her show me her kitten. Marek slid cautiously toward us and began to exhibit his webbed fingers. I knew he wanted to make his queer noises for me--to bark like a dog or whinny like a horse--but he did not dare in the presence of his elders. Marek was always trying to be agreeable, poor fellow, as if he had it on his mind that he must make up for his deficiencies.

Mrs. Shimerda grew more calm and reasonable before our visit was over, and, while Antonia translated, put in a word now and then on her own account. The woman had a quick ear, and caught up phrases whenever she heard English spoken. As we rose to go, she opened her wooden chest and brought out a bag made of bed-ticking, about as long as a flour sack and half as wide, stuffed full of something. At sight of it, the crazy boy began to smack his lips. When Mrs. Shimerda opened the bag and stirred the contents with her hand, it gave out a salty, earthy smell, very pungent, even among the other odours of that cave. She measured a teacup full, tied it up in a bit of sacking, and presented it ceremoniously to grandmother.

`For cook,' she announced. `Little now; be very much when cook,' spreading out her hands as if to indicate that the pint would swell to a gallon. `Very good. You no have in this country. All things for eat better in my country.'

`Maybe so, Mrs. Shimerda,' grandmother said dryly. `I can't say but I prefer our bread to yours, myself.'

Antonia undertook to explain. `This very good, Mrs. Burden'--she clasped her hands as if she could not express how good--'it make very much when you cook, like what my mama say. Cook with rabbit, cook with chicken, in the gravy-- oh, so good!'

All the way home grandmother and Jake talked about how easily good Christian people could forget they were their brothers' keepers.

`I will say, Jake, some of our brothers and sisters are hard to keep. Where's a body to begin, with these people? They're wanting in everything, and most of all in horse-sense. Nobody can give 'em that, I guess. Jimmy, here, is about as able to take over a homestead as they are. Do you reckon that boy Ambrosch has any real push in him?'

`He's a worker, all right, ma'm, and he's got some ketch-on about him; but he's a mean one. Folks can be mean enough to get on in this world; and then, ag'in, they can be too mean.'

That night, while grandmother was getting supper, we opened the package Mrs. Shimerda had given her. It was full of little brown chips that looked like the shavings of some root. They were as light as feathers, and the most noticeable thing about them was their penetrating, earthy odour. We could not determine whether they were animal or vegetable.

`They might be dried meat from some queer beast, Jim. They ain't dried fish, and they never grew on stalk or vine. I'm afraid of 'em. Anyhow, I shouldn't want to eat anything that had been shut up for months with old clothes and goose pillows.'

She threw the package into the stove, but I bit off a corner of one of the chips I held in my hand, and chewed it tentatively. I never forgot the strange taste; though it was many years before I knew that those little brown shavings, which the Shimerdas had brought so far and treasured so jealously, were dried mushrooms. They had been gathered, probably, in some deep Bohemian forest....

XI

DURING THE WEEK before Christmas, Jake was the most important person of our household, for he was to go to town and do all our Christmas shopping. But on the twenty-first of December, the snow began to fall. The flakes came down so thickly that from the sitting-room windows I could not see beyond the windmill--its frame looked dim and grey, unsubstantial like a shadow. The snow did not stop falling all day, or during the night that followed. The cold was not severe, but the storm was quiet and resistless. The men could not go farther than the barns and corral. They sat about the house most of the day as if it were Sunday; greasing their boots, mending their suspenders, plaiting whiplashes.

On the morning of the twenty-second, grandfather announced at breakfast that it would be impossible to go to Black Hawk for Christmas purchases. Jake was sure he could get through on horseback, and bring home our things in saddle-bags; but grandfather told him the roads would be obliterated, and a newcomer in the country would be lost ten times over. Anyway, he would never allow one of his horses to be put to such a strain.

We decided to have a country Christmas, without any help from town. I had wanted to get some picture books for Yulka and Antonia; even Yulka was able to read a little now. Grandmother took me into the ice-cold storeroom, where she had some bolts of gingham and sheeting. She cut squares of cotton cloth and we sewed them together into a book. We bound it between pasteboards, which I covered with brilliant calico, representing scenes from a circus. For two days I sat at the dining-room table, pasting this book full of pictures for Yulka. We had files of those good old family magazines which used to publish coloured lithographs of popular paintings, and I was allowed to use some of these. I took `Napoleon Announcing the Divorce to Josephine' for my frontispiece. On the white pages I grouped Sunday-School cards and advertising cards which I had brought from my `old country.' Fuchs got out the old candle-moulds and made tallow candles. Grandmother hunted up her fancy cake-cutters and baked gingerbread men and roosters, which we decorated with burnt sugar and red cinnamon drops.

On the day before Christmas, Jake packed the things we were sending to the Shimerdas in his saddle-bags and set off on grandfather's grey gelding. When he mounted his horse at the door, I saw that he had a hatchet slung to his belt, and he gave grandmother a meaning look which told me he was planning a surprise for me. That afternoon I watched long and eagerly from the sitting-room window. At last I saw a dark spot moving on the west hill, beside the half-buried cornfield, where the sky was taking on a coppery flush from the sun that did not quite break through. I put on my cap and ran out to meet Jake. When I got to the pond, I could see that he was bringing in a little cedar tree across his pommel. He used to help my father cut Christmas trees for me in Virginia, and he had not forgotten how much I liked them.

By the time we had placed the cold, fresh-smelling little tree in a corner of the sitting-room, it was already Christmas Eve. After supper we all gathered there, and even grandfather, reading his paper by the table, looked up with friendly interest now and then. The cedar was about five feet high and very shapely. We hung it with the gingerbread animals, strings of popcorn, and bits of candle which Fuchs had fitted into pasteboard sockets. Its real splendours, however, came from the most unlikely place in the world--from Otto's cowboy trunk. I had never seen anything in that trunk but old boots and spurs and pistols, and a fascinating mixture of yellow leather thongs, cartridges, and shoemaker's wax. From under the lining he now produced a collection of brilliantly coloured paper figures, several inches high and stiff enough to stand alone. They had been sent to him year after year, by his old mother in Austria. There was a bleeding heart, in tufts of paper lace; there were the three kings, gorgeously apparelled, and the ox and the ass and the shepherds; there was the Baby in the manger, and a group of angels, singing; there were camels and leopards, held by the black slaves of the three kings. Our tree became the talking tree of the fairy tale; legends and stories nestled like birds in its branches. Grandmother said it reminded her of the Tree of Knowledge. We put sheets of cotton wool under it for a snow-field, and Jake's pocket-mirror for a frozen lake.

I can see them now, exactly as they looked, working about the table in the lamplight: Jake with his heavy features, so rudely moulded that his face seemed, somehow, unfinished; Otto with his half-ear and the savage scar that made his upper lip curl so ferociously under his twisted moustache. As I remember them, what unprotected faces they were; their very roughness and violence made them defenceless. These boys had no practised manner behind which they could retreat and hold people at a distance. They had only their hard fists to batter at the world with. Otto was already one of those drifting, case-hardened labourers who never marry or have children of their own. Yet he was so fond of children!

XII

ON CHRISTMAS MORNING, when I got down to the kitchen, the men were just coming in from their morning chores--the horses and pigs always had their breakfast before we did. Jake and Otto shouted `Merry Christmas!' to me, and winked at each other when they saw the waffle-irons on the stove. Grandfather came down, wearing a white shirt and his Sunday coat. Morning prayers were longer than usual. He read the chapters from Saint Matthew about the birth of Christ, and as we listened, it all seemed like something that had happened lately, and near at hand. In his prayer he thanked the Lord for the first Christmas, and for all that it had meant to the world ever since. He gave thanks for our food and comfort, and prayed for the poor and destitute in great cities, where the struggle for life was harder than it was here with us. Grandfather's prayers were often very interesting. He had the gift of simple and moving expression. Because he talked so little, his words had a peculiar force; they were not worn dull from constant use. His prayers reflected what he was thinking about at the time, and it was chiefly through them that we got to know his feelings and his views about things.

After we sat down to our waffles and sausage, Jake told us how pleased the Shimerdas had been with their presents; even Ambrosch was friendly and went to the creek with him to cut the Christmas tree. It was a soft grey day outside, with heavy clouds working across the sky, and occasional squalls of snow. There were always odd jobs to be done about the barn on holidays, and the men were busy until afternoon. Then Jake and I played dominoes, while Otto wrote a long letter home to his mother. He always wrote to her on Christmas Day, he said, no matter where he was, and no matter how long it had been since his last letter. All afternoon he sat in the dining-room. He would write for a while, then sit idle, his clenched fist lying on the table, his eyes following the pattern of the oilcloth. He spoke and wrote his own language so seldom that it came to him awkwardly. His effort to remember entirely absorbed him.

At about four o'clock a visitor appeared: Mr. Shimerda, wearing his rabbit-skin cap and collar, and new mittens his wife had knitted. He had come to thank us for the presents, and for all grandmother's kindness to his family. Jake and Otto joined us from the basement and we sat about the stove, enjoying the deepening grey of the winter afternoon and the atmosphere of comfort and security in my grandfather's house. This feeling seemed completely to take possession of Mr. Shimerda. I suppose, in the crowded clutter of their cave, the old man had come to believe that peace and order had vanished from the earth, or existed only in the old world he had left so far behind. He sat still and passive, his head resting against the back of the wooden rocking-chair, his hands relaxed upon the arms. His face had a look of weariness and pleasure, like that of sick people when they feel relief from pain. Grandmother insisted on his drinking a glass of Virginia apple-brandy after his long walk in the cold, and when a faint flush came up in his cheeks, his features might have been cut out of a shell, they were so transparent. He said almost nothing, and smiled rarely; but as he rested there we all had a sense of his utter content.

As it grew dark, I asked whether I might light the Christmas tree before the lamp was brought. When the candle-ends sent up their conical yellow flames, all the coloured figures from Austria stood out clear and full of meaning against the green boughs. Mr. Shimerda rose, crossed himself, and quietly knelt down before the tree, his head sunk forward. His long body formed a letter `S.' I saw grandmother look apprehensively at grandfather. He was rather narrow in religious matters, and sometimes spoke out and hurt people's feelings. There had been nothing strange about the tree before, but now, with some one kneeling before it--images, candles ... Grandfather merely put his finger-tips to his brow and bowed his venerable head, thus Protestantizing the atmosphere.

We persuaded our guest to stay for supper with us. He needed little urging. As we sat down to the table, it occurred to me that he liked to look at us, and that our faces were open books to him. When his deep-seeing eyes rested on me, I felt as if he were looking far ahead into the future for me, down the road I would have to travel.

At nine o'clock Mr. Shimerda lighted one of our lanterns and put on his overcoat and fur collar. He stood in the little entry hall, the lantern and his fur cap under his arm, shaking hands with us. When he took grandmother's hand, he bent over it as he always did, and said slowly, `Good woman!' He made the sign of the cross over me, put on his cap and went off in the dark. As we turned back to the sitting-room, grandfather looked at me searchingly. `The prayers of all good people are good,' he said quietly.

XIII

THE WEEK FOLLOWING Christmas brought in a thaw, and by New Year's Day all the world about us was a broth of grey slush, and the guttered slope between the windmill and the barn was running black water. The soft black earth stood out in patches along the roadsides. I resumed all my chores, carried in the cobs and wood and water, and spent the afternoons at the barn, watching Jake shell corn with a hand-sheller.

One morning, during this interval of fine weather, Antonia and her mother rode over on one of their shaggy old horses to pay us a visit. It was the first time Mrs. Shimerda had been to our house, and she ran about examining our carpets and curtains and furniture, all the while commenting upon them to her daughter in an envious, complaining tone. In the kitchen she caught up an iron pot that stood on the back of the stove and said: `You got many, Shimerdas no got.' I thought it weak-minded of grandmother to give the pot to her.

After dinner, when she was helping to wash the dishes, she said, tossing her head: `You got many things for cook. If I got all things like you, I make much better.'

She was a conceited, boastful old thing, and even misfortune could not humble her. I was so annoyed that I felt coldly even toward Antonia and listened unsympathetically when she told me her father was not well.

`My papa sad for the old country. He not look good. He never make music any more. At home he play violin all the time; for weddings and for dance. Here never. When I beg him for play, he shake his head no. Some days he take his violin out of his box and make with his fingers on the strings, like this, but never he make the music. He don't like this kawntree.'

`People who don't like this country ought to stay at home,' I said severely. `We don't make them come here.'

`He not want to come, never!' she burst out. `My mamenka make him come. All the time she say: "America big country; much money, much land for my boys, much husband for my girls." My papa, he cry for leave his old friends what make music with him. He love very much the man what play the long horn like this'--she indicated a slide trombone. "They go to school together and are friends from boys. But my mama, she want Ambrosch for be rich, with many cattle."'

`Your mama,' I said angrily, `wants other people's things.'

"Your grandfather is rich," she retorted fiercely. `Why he not help my papa? Ambrosch be rich, too, after while, and he pay back. He is very smart boy. For Ambrosch my mama come here.'

Ambrosch was considered the important person in the family. Mrs. Shimerda and Antonia always deferred to him, though he was often surly with them and contemptuous toward his father. Ambrosch and his mother had everything their own way. Though Antonia loved her father more than she did anyone else, she stood in awe of her elder brother.

After I watched Antonia and her mother go over the hill on their miserable horse, carrying our iron pot with them, I turned to grandmother, who had taken up her darning, and said I hoped that snooping old woman wouldn't come to see us any more.

Grandmother chuckled and drove her bright needle across a hole in Otto's sock. `She's not old, Jim, though I expect she seems old to you. No, I wouldn't mourn if she never came again. But, you see, a body never knows what traits poverty might bring out in 'em. It makes a woman grasping to see her children want for things. Now read me a chapter in "The Prince of the House of David." Let's forget the Bohemians.'

We had three weeks of this mild, open weather. The cattle in the corral ate corn almost as fast as the men could shell it for them, and we hoped they would be ready for an early market. One morning the two big bulls, Gladstone and Brigham Young, thought spring had come, and they began to tease and butt at each other across the barbed wire that separated them. Soon they got angry. They bellowed and pawed up the soft earth with their hoofs, rolling their eyes and tossing their heads. Each withdrew to a far corner of his own corral, and then they made for each other at a gallop. Thud, thud, we could hear the impact of their great heads, and their bellowing shook the pans on the kitchen shelves. Had they not been dehorned, they would have torn each other to pieces. Pretty soon the fat steers took it up and began butting and horning each other. Clearly, the affair had to be stopped. We all stood by and watched admiringly while Fuchs rode into the corral with a pitchfork and prodded the bulls again and again, finally driving them apart.

The big storm of the winter began on my eleventh birthday, the twentieth of January. When I went down to breakfast that morning, Jake and Otto came in white as snow-men, beating their hands and stamping their feet. They began to laugh boisterously when they saw me, calling:

`You've got a birthday present this time, Jim, and no mistake. They was a full-grown blizzard ordered for you.'

All day the storm went on. The snow did not fall this time, it simply spilled out of heaven, like thousands of featherbeds being emptied. That afternoon the kitchen was a carpenter-shop; the men brought in their tools and made two great wooden shovels with long handles. Neither grandmother nor I could go out in the storm, so Jake fed the chickens and brought in a pitiful contribution of eggs.

Next day our men had to shovel until noon to reach the barn--and the snow was still falling! There had not been such a storm in the ten years my grandfather had lived in Nebraska. He said at dinner that we would not try to reach the cattle--they were fat enough to go without their corn for a day or two; but tomorrow we must feed them and thaw out their water-tap so that they could drink. We could not so much as see the corrals, but we knew the steers were over there, huddled together under the north bank. Our ferocious bulls, subdued enough by this time, were probably warming each other's backs. `This'll take the bile out of 'em!' Fuchs remarked gleefully.

At noon that day the hens had not been heard from. After dinner Jake and Otto, their damp clothes now dried on them, stretched their stiff arms and plunged again into the drifts. They made a tunnel through the snow to the hen-house, with walls so solid that grandmother and I could walk back and forth in it. We found the chickens asleep; perhaps they thought night had come to stay. One old rooster was stirring about, pecking at the solid lump of ice in their water-tin. When we flashed the lantern in their eyes, the hens set up a great cackling and flew about clumsily, scattering down-feathers. The mottled, pin-headed guinea-hens, always resentful of captivity, ran screeching out into the tunnel and tried to poke their ugly, painted faces through the snow walls. By five o'clock the chores were done just when it was time to begin them all over again! That was a strange, unnatural sort of day.

XIV

ON THE MORNING of the twenty-second I wakened with a start. Before I opened my eyes, I seemed to know that something had happened. I heard excited voices in the kitchen--grandmother's was so shrill that I knew she must be almost beside herself. I looked forward to any new crisis with delight. What could it be, I wondered, as I hurried into my clothes. Perhaps the barn had burned; perhaps the cattle had frozen to death; perhaps a neighbour was lost in the storm.

Down in the kitchen grandfather was standing before the stove with his hands behind him. Jake and Otto had taken off their boots and were rubbing their woollen socks. Their clothes and boots were steaming, and they both looked exhausted. On the bench behind the stove lay a man, covered up with a blanket. Grandmother motioned me to the dining-room. I obeyed reluctantly. I watched her as she came and went, carrying dishes. Her lips were tightly compressed and she kept whispering to herself: `Oh, dear Saviour!' `Lord, Thou knowest!'

Presently grandfather came in and spoke to me: `Jimmy, we will not have prayers this morning, because we have a great deal to do. Old Mr. Shimerda is dead, and his family are in great distress. Ambrosch came over here in the middle of the night, and Jake and Otto went back with him. The boys have had a hard night, and you must not bother them with questions. That is Ambrosch, asleep on the bench. Come in to breakfast, boys.'

After Jake and Otto had swallowed their first cup of coffee, they began to talk excitedly, disregarding grandmother's warning glances. I held my tongue, but I listened with all my ears.

`No, sir,' Fuchs said in answer to a question from grandfather, `nobody heard the gun go off. Ambrosch was out with the ox-team, trying to break a road, and the women-folks was shut up tight in their cave. When Ambrosch come in, it was dark and he didn't see nothing, but the oxen acted kind of queer. One of 'em ripped around and got away from him--bolted clean out of the stable. His hands is blistered where the rope run through. He got a lantern and went back and found the old man, just as we seen him.'

`Poor soul, poor soul!' grandmother groaned. `I'd like to think he never done it. He was always considerate and un-wishful to give trouble. How could he forget himself and bring this on us!'

`I don't think he was out of his head for a minute, Mrs. Burden,' Fuchs declared. `He done everything natural. You know he was always sort of fixy, and fixy he was to the last. He shaved after dinner, and washed hisself all over after the girls had done the dishes. Antonia heated the water for him. Then he put on a clean shirt and clean socks, and after he was dressed he kissed her and the little one and took his gun and said he was going out to hunt rabbits. He must have gone right down to the barn and done it then. He layed down on that bunk-bed, close to the ox stalls, where he always slept. When we found him, everything was decent except'--Fuchs wrinkled his brow and hesitated--'except what he couldn't nowise foresee. His coat was hung on a peg, and his boots was under the bed. He'd took off that silk neckcloth he always wore, and folded it smooth and stuck his pin through it. He turned back his shirt at the neck and rolled up his sleeves.'

`I don't see how he could do it!' grandmother kept saying.

Otto misunderstood her. `Why, ma'am, it was simple enough; he pulled the trigger with his big toe. He layed over on his side and put the end of the barrel in his mouth, then he drew up one foot and felt for the trigger. He found it all right!'

`Maybe he did,' said Jake grimly. `There's something mighty queer about it.'

`Now what do you mean, Jake?' grandmother asked sharply.

`Well, ma'm, I found Krajiek's axe under the manger, and I picks it up and carries it over to the corpse, and I take my oath it just fit the gash in the front of the old man's face. That there Krajiek had been sneakin' round, pale and quiet, and when he seen me examinin' the axe, he begun whimperin', "My God, man, don't do that!" "I reckon I'm a-goin' to look into this," says I. Then he begun to squeal like a rat and run about wringin' his hands. "They'll hang me!" says he. "My God, they'll hang me sure!"'

Fuchs spoke up impatiently. `Krajiek's gone silly, Jake, and so have you. The old man wouldn't have made all them preparations for Krajiek to murder him, would he? It don't hang together. The gun was right beside him when Ambrosch found him.'

`Krajiek could 'a' put it there, couldn't he?' Jake demanded.

Grandmother broke in excitedly: `See here, Jake Marpole, don't you go trying to add murder to suicide. We're deep enough in trouble. Otto reads you too many of them detective stories.'

`It will be easy to decide all that, Emmaline,' said grandfather quietly. `If he shot himself in the way they think, the gash will be torn from the inside outward.'

`Just so it is, Mr. Burden,' Otto affirmed. `I seen bunches of hair and stuff sticking to the poles and straw along the roof. They was blown up there by gunshot, no question.'

Grandmother told grandfather she meant to go over to the Shimerdas' with him.

`There is nothing you can do,' he said doubtfully. `The body can't be touched until we get the coroner here from Black Hawk, and that will be a matter of several days, this weather.'

`Well, I can take them some victuals, anyway, and say a word of comfort to them poor little girls. The oldest one was his darling, and was like a right hand to him. He might have thought of her. He's left her alone in a hard world.' She glanced distrustfully at Ambrosch, who was now eating his breakfast at the kitchen table.

Fuchs, although he had been up in the cold nearly all night, was going to make the long ride to Black Hawk to fetch the priest and the coroner. On the grey gelding, our best horse, he would try to pick his way across the country with no roads to guide him.

`Don't you worry about me, Mrs. Burden,' he said cheerfully, as he put on a second pair of socks. `I've got a good nose for directions, and I never did need much sleep. It's the grey I'm worried about. I'll save him what I can, but it'll strain him, as sure as I'm telling you!'

`This is no time to be over-considerate of animals, Otto; do the best you can for yourself. Stop at the Widow Steavens's for dinner. She's a good woman, and she'll do well by you.'

After Fuchs rode away, I was left with Ambrosch. I saw a side of him I had not seen before. He was deeply, even slavishly, devout. He did not say a word all morning, but sat with his rosary in his hands, praying, now silently, now aloud. He never looked away from his beads, nor lifted his hands except to cross himself. Several times the poor boy fell asleep where he sat, wakened with a start, and began to pray again.

No wagon could be got to the Shimerdas' until a road was broken, and that would be a day's job. Grandfather came from the barn on one of our big black horses, and Jake lifted grandmother up behind him. She wore her black hood and was bundled up in shawls. Grandfather tucked his bushy white beard inside his overcoat. They looked very Biblical as they set off, I thought. Jake and Ambrosch followed them, riding the other black and my pony, carrying bundles of clothes that we had got together for Mrs. Shimerda. I watched them go past the pond and over the hill by the drifted cornfield. Then, for the first time, I realized that I was alone in the house.

I felt a considerable extension of power and authority, and was anxious to acquit myself creditably. I carried in cobs and wood from the long cellar, and filled both the stoves. I remembered that in the hurry and excitement of the morning nobody had thought of the chickens, and the eggs had not been gathered. Going out through the tunnel, I gave the hens their corn, emptied the ice from their drinking-pan, and filled it with water. After the cat had had his milk, I could think of nothing else to do, and I sat down to get warm. The quiet was delightful, and the ticking clock was the most pleasant of companions. I got `Robinson Crusoe' and tried to read, but his life on the island seemed dull compared with ours. Presently, as I looked with satisfaction about our comfortable sitting-room, it flashed upon me that if Mr. Shimerda's soul were lingering about in this world at all, it would be here, in our house, which had been more to his liking than any other in the neighbourhood. I remembered his contented face when he was with us on Christmas Day. If he could have lived with us, this terrible thing would never have happened.

I knew it was homesickness that had killed Mr. Shimerda, and I wondered whether his released spirit would not eventually find its way back to his own country. I thought of how far it was to Chicago, and then to Virginia, to Baltimore--and then the great wintry ocean. No, he would not at once set out upon that long journey. Surely, his exhausted spirit, so tired of cold and crowding and the struggle with the ever-falling snow, was resting now in this quiet house.

I was not frightened, but I made no noise. I did not wish to disturb him. I went softly down to the kitchen which, tucked away so snugly underground, always seemed to me the heart and centre of the house. There, on the bench behind the stove, I thought and thought about Mr. Shimerda. Outside I could hear the wind singing over hundreds of miles of snow. It was as if I had let the old man in out of the tormenting winter, and were sitting there with him. I went over all that Ántonia had ever told me about his life before he came to this country; how he used to play the fiddle at weddings and dances. I thought about the friends he had mourned to leave, the trombone-player, the great forest full of game--belonging, as Ántonia said, to the `nobles'--from which she and her mother used to steal wood on moonlight nights. There was a white hart that lived in that forest, and if anyone killed it, he would be hanged, she said. Such vivid pictures came to me that they might have been Mr. Shimerda's memories, not yet faded out from the air in which they had haunted him.

It had begun to grow dark when my household returned, and grandmother was so tired that she went at once to bed. Jake and I got supper, and while we were washing the dishes he told me in loud whispers about the state of things over at the Shimerdas'. Nobody could touch the body until the coroner came. If anyone did, something terrible would happen, apparently. The dead man was frozen through, `just as stiff as a dressed turkey you hang out to freeze,' Jake said. The horses and oxen would not go into the barn until he was frozen so hard that there was no longer any smell of blood. They were stabled there now, with the dead man, because there was no other place to keep them. A lighted lantern was kept hanging over Mr. Shimerda's head. Ántonia and Ambrosch and the mother took turns going down to pray beside him. The crazy boy went with them, because he did not feel the cold. I believed he felt cold as much as anyone else, but he liked to be thought insensible to it. He was always coveting distinction, poor Marek!

Ambrosch, Jake said, showed more human feeling than he would have supposed him capable of, but he was chiefly concerned about getting a priest, and about his father's soul, which he believed was in a place of torment and would remain there until his family and the priest had prayed a great deal for him. `As I understand it,' Jake concluded, `it will be a matter of years to pray his soul out of Purgatory, and right now he's in torment.'

`I don't believe it,' I said stoutly. `I almost know it isn't true.' I did not, of course, say that I believed he had been in that very kitchen all afternoon, on his way back to his own country. Nevertheless, after I went to bed, this idea of punishment and Purgatory came back on me crushingly. I remembered the account of Dives in torment, and shuddered. But Mr. Shimerda had not been rich and selfish: he had only been so unhappy that he could not live any longer.

XV

OTTO FUCHS GOT back from Black Hawk at noon the next day. He reported that the coroner would reach the Shimerdas' sometime that afternoon, but the missionary priest was at the other end of his parish, a hundred miles away, and the trains were not running. Fuchs had got a few hours' sleep at the livery barn in town, but he was afraid the grey gelding had strained himself. Indeed, he was never the same horse afterward. That long trip through the deep snow had taken all the endurance out of him.

Fuchs brought home with him a stranger, a young Bohemian who had taken a homestead near Black Hawk, and who came on his only horse to help his fellow countrymen in their trouble. That was the first time I ever saw Anton Jelinek. He was a strapping young fellow in the early twenties then, handsome, warm-hearted, and full of life, and he came to us like a miracle in the midst of that grim business. I remember exactly how he strode into our kitchen in his felt boots and long wolfskin coat, his eyes and cheeks bright with the cold. At sight of grandmother, he snatched off his fur cap, greeting her in a deep, rolling voice which seemed older than he.

`I want to thank you very much, Mrs. Burden, for that you are so kind to poor strangers from my kawntree.'

He did not hesitate like a farmer boy, but looked one eagerly in the eye when he spoke. Everything about him was warm and spontaneous. He said he would have come to see the Shimerdas before, but he had hired out to husk corn all the fall, and since winter began he had been going to the school by the mill, to learn English, along with the little children. He told me he had a nice `lady-teacher' and that he liked to go to school.

At dinner grandfather talked to Jelinek more than he usually did to strangers.

`Will they be much disappointed because we cannot get a priest?' he asked.

Jelinek looked serious.

`Yes, sir, that is very bad for them. Their father has done a great sin'--he looked straight at grandfather. `Our Lord has said that.'

Grandfather seemed to like his frankness.

`We believe that, too, Jelinek. But we believe that Mr. Shimerda's soul will come to its Creator as well off without a priest. We believe that Christ is our only intercessor.'

The young man shook his head. `I know how you think. My teacher at the school has explain. But I have seen too much. I believe in prayer for the dead. I have seen too much.'

We asked him what he meant.

He glanced around the table. `You want I shall tell you? When I was a little boy like this one, I begin to help the priest at the altar. I make my first communion very young; what the Church teach seem plain to me. By 'n' by war-times come, when the Prussians fight us. We have very many soldiers in camp near my village, and the cholera break out in that camp, and the men die like flies. All day long our priest go about there to give the Sacrament to dying men, and I go with him to carry the vessels with the Holy Sacrament. Everybody that go near that camp catch the sickness but me and the priest. But we have no sickness, we have no fear, because we carry that blood and that body of Christ, and it preserve us.' He paused, looking at grandfather. `That I know, Mr. Burden, for it happened to myself. All the soldiers know, too. When we walk along the road, the old priest and me, we meet all the time soldiers marching and officers on horse. All those officers, when they see what I carry under the cloth, pull up their horses and kneel down on the ground in the road until we pass. So I feel very bad for my kawntree-man to die without the Sacrament, and to die in a bad way for his soul, and I feel sad for his family.'

We had listened attentively. It was impossible not to admire his frank, manly faith.

`I am always glad to meet a young man who thinks seriously about these things,' said grandfather, `and I would never be the one to say you were not in God's care when you were among the soldiers.' After dinner it was decided that young Jelinek should hook our two strong black farm-horses to the scraper and break a road through to the Shimerdas', so that a wagon could go when it was necessary. Fuchs, who was the only cabinetmaker in the neighbourhood was set to work on a coffin.

Jelinek put on his long wolfskin coat, and when we admired it, he told us that he had shot and skinned the coyotes, and the young man who `batched' with him, Jan Bouska, who had been a fur-worker in Vienna, made the coat. From the windmill I watched Jelinek come out of the barn with the blacks, and work his way up the hillside toward the cornfield. Sometimes he was completely hidden by the clouds of snow that rose about him; then he and the horses would emerge black and shining.

Our heavy carpenter's bench had to be brought from the barn and carried down into the kitchen. Fuchs selected boards from a pile of planks grandfather had hauled out from town in the fall to make a new floor for the oats-bin. When at last the lumber and tools were assembled, and the doors were closed again and the cold draughts shut out, grandfather rode away to meet the coroner at the Shimerdas', and Fuchs took off his coat and settled down to work. I sat on his worktable and watched him. He did not touch his tools at first, but figured for a long while on a piece of paper, and measured the planks and made marks on them. While he was thus engaged, he whistled softly to himself, or teasingly pulled at his half-ear. Grandmother moved about quietly, so as not to disturb him. At last he folded his ruler and turned a cheerful face to us.

`The hardest part of my job's done,' he announced. `It's the head end of it that comes hard with me, especially when I'm out of practice. The last time I made one of these, Mrs. Burden,' he continued, as he sorted and tried his chisels, `was for a fellow in the Black Tiger Mine, up above Silverton, Colorado. The mouth of that mine goes right into the face of the cliff, and they used to put us in a bucket and run us over on a trolley and shoot us into the shaft. The bucket travelled across a box canon three hundred feet deep, and about a third full of water. Two Swedes had fell out of that bucket once, and hit the water, feet down. If you'll believe it, they went to work the next day. You can't kill a Swede. But in my time a little Eyetalian tried the high dive, and it turned out different with him. We was snowed in then, like we are now, and I happened to be the only man in camp that could make a coffin for him. It's a handy thing to know, when you knock about like I've done.'

`We'd be hard put to it now, if you didn't know, Otto,' grandmother said.

`Yes, 'm,' Fuchs admitted with modest pride. `So few folks does know how to make a good tight box that'll turn water. I sometimes wonder if there'll be anybody about to do it for me. However, I'm not at all particular that way.'

All afternoon, wherever one went in the house, one could hear the panting wheeze of the saw or the pleasant purring of the plane. They were such cheerful noises, seeming to promise new things for living people: it was a pity that those freshly planed pine boards were to be put underground so soon. The lumber was hard to work because it was full of frost, and the boards gave off a sweet smell of pine woods, as the heap of yellow shavings grew higher and higher. I wondered why Fuchs had not stuck to cabinet-work, he settled down to it with such ease and content. He handled the tools as if he liked the feel of them; and when he planed, his hands went back and forth over the boards in an eager, beneficent way as if he were blessing them. He broke out now and then into German hymns, as if this occupation brought back old times to him.

At four o'clock Mr. Bushy, the postmaster, with another neighbour who lived east of us, stopped in to get warm. They were on their way to the Shimerdas'. The news of what had happened over there had somehow got abroad through the snow-blocked country. Grandmother gave the visitors sugar-cakes and hot coffee. Before these callers were gone, the brother of the Widow Steavens, who lived on the Black Hawk road, drew up at our door, and after him came the father of the German family, our nearest neighbours on the south. They dismounted and joined us in the dining-room. They were all eager for any details about the suicide, and they were greatly concerned as to where Mr. Shimerda would be buried. The nearest Catholic cemetery was at Black Hawk, and it might be weeks before a wagon could get so far. Besides,

Mr. Bushy and grandmother were sure that a man who had killed himself could not be buried in a Catholic graveyard. There was a burying-ground over by the Norwegian church, west of Squaw Creek; perhaps the Norwegians would take Mr. Shimerda in.

After our visitors rode away in single file over the hill, we returned to the kitchen. Grandmother began to make the icing for a chocolate cake, and Otto again filled the house with the exciting, expectant song of the plane. One pleasant thing about this time was that everybody talked more than usual. I had never heard the postmaster say anything but `Only papers, to-day,' or, `I've got a sackful of mail for ye,' until this afternoon. Grandmother always talked, dear woman: to herself or to the Lord, if there was no one else to listen; but grandfather was naturally taciturn, and Jake and Otto were often so tired after supper that I used to feel as if I were surrounded by a wall of silence. Now everyone seemed eager to talk. That afternoon Fuchs told me story after story: about the Black Tiger Mine, and about violent deaths and casual buryings, and the queer fancies of dying men. You never really knew a man, he said, until you saw him die. Most men were game, and went without a grudge.

The postmaster, going home, stopped to say that grandfather would bring the coroner back with him to spend the night. The officers of the Norwegian church, he told us, had held a meeting and decided that the Norwegian graveyard could not extend its hospitality to Mr. Shimerda.

Grandmother was indignant. `If these foreigners are so clannish, Mr. Bushy, we'll have to have an American graveyard that will be more liberal-minded. I'll get right after Josiah to start one in the spring. If anything was to happen to me, I don't want the Norwegians holding inquisitions over me to see whether I'm good enough to be laid amongst 'em.'

Soon grandfather returned, bringing with him Anton Jelinek, and that important person, the coroner. He was a mild, flurried old man, a Civil War veteran, with one sleeve hanging empty. He seemed to find this case very perplexing, and said if it had not been for grandfather he would have sworn out a warrant against Krajiek. `The way he acted, and the way his axe fit the wound, was enough to convict any man.'

Although it was perfectly clear that Mr. Shimerda had killed himself, Jake and the coroner thought something ought to be done to Krajiek because he behaved like a guilty man. He was badly frightened, certainly, and perhaps he even felt some stirrings of remorse for his indifference to the old man's misery and loneliness.

At supper the men ate like vikings, and the chocolate cake, which I had hoped would linger on until tomorrow in a mutilated condition, disappeared on the second round. They talked excitedly about where they should bury Mr. Shimerda; I gathered that the neighbours were all disturbed and shocked about something. It developed that Mrs. Shimerda and Ambrosch wanted the old man buried on the southwest corner of their own land; indeed, under the very stake that marked the corner. Grandfather had explained to Ambrosch that some day, when the country was put under fence and the roads were confined to section lines, two roads would cross exactly on that corner. But Ambrosch only said, `It makes no matter.'

Grandfather asked Jelinek whether in the old country there was some superstition to the effect that a suicide must be buried at the cross-roads.

Jelinek said he didn't know; he seemed to remember hearing there had once been such a custom in Bohemia. `Mrs. Shimerda is made up her mind,' he added. `I try to persuade her, and say it looks bad for her to all the neighbours; but she say so it must be. "There I will bury him, if I dig the grave myself," she say. I have to promise her I help Ambrosch make the grave tomorrow.'

Grandfather smoothed his beard and looked judicial. `I don't know whose wish should decide the matter, if not hers. But if she thinks she will live to see the people of this country ride over that old man's head, she is mistaken.'

XVI

MR. SHIMERDA LAY DEAD in the barn four days, and on the fifth they buried him. All day Friday Jelinek was off with Ambrosch digging the grave, chopping out the frozen earth with old axes. On Saturday we breakfasted before daylight and got into the wagon with the coffin. Jake and Jelinek went ahead on horseback to cut the body loose from the pool of blood in which it was frozen fast to the ground.

When grandmother and I went into the Shimerdas' house, we found the womenfolk alone; Ambrosch and Marek were at the barn. Mrs. Shimerda sat crouching by the stove, Antonia was washing dishes. When she saw me, she ran out of her dark corner and threw her arms around me. `Oh, Jimmy,' she sobbed, `what you tink for my lovely papa!' It seemed to me that I could feel her heart breaking as she clung to me.

Mrs. Shimerda, sitting on the stump by the stove, kept looking over her shoulder toward the door while the neighbours were arriving. They came on horseback, all except the postmaster, who brought his family in a wagon over the only broken wagon-trail. The Widow Steavens rode up from her farm eight miles down the Black Hawk road. The cold drove the women into the cave-house, and it was soon crowded. A fine, sleety snow was beginning to fall, and everyone was afraid of another storm and anxious to have the burial over with.

Grandfather and Jelinek came to tell Mrs. Shimerda that it was time to start. After bundling her mother up in clothes the neighbours had brought, Antonia put on an old cape from our house and the rabbit-skin hat her father had made for her. Four men carried Mr. Shimerda's box up the hill; Krajiek slunk along behind them. The coffin was too wide for the door, so it was put down on the slope outside. I slipped out from the cave and looked at Mr. Shimerda. He was lying on his side, with his knees drawn up. His body was draped in a black shawl, and his head was bandaged in white muslin, like a mummy's; one of his long, shapely hands lay out on the black cloth; that was all one could see of him.

Mrs. Shimerda came out and placed an open prayer-book against the body, making the sign of the cross on the bandaged head with her fingers. Ambrosch knelt down and made the same gesture, and after him Antonia and Marek. Yulka hung back. Her mother pushed her forward, and kept saying something to her over and over. Yulka knelt down, shut her eyes, and put out her hand a little way, but she drew it back and began to cry wildly. She was afraid to touch the bandage. Mrs. Shimerda caught her by the shoulders and pushed her toward the coffin, but grandmother interfered.

`No, Mrs. Shimerda,' she said firmly, `I won't stand by and see that child frightened into spasms. She is too little to understand what you want of her. Let her alone.'

At a look from grandfather, Fuchs and Jelinek placed the lid on the box, and began to nail it down over Mr. Shimerda. I was afraid to look at Antonia. She put her arms round Yulka and held the little girl close to her.

The coffin was put into the wagon. We drove slowly away, against the fine, icy snow which cut our faces like a sandblast. When we reached the grave, it looked a very little spot in that snow-covered waste. The men took the coffin to the edge of the hole and lowered it with ropes. We stood about watching them, and the powdery snow lay without melting on the caps and shoulders of the men and the shawls of the women. Jelinek spoke in a persuasive tone to Mrs. Shimerda, and then turned to grandfather.

`She says, Mr. Burden, she is very glad if you can make some prayer for him here in English, for the neighbours to understand.'

Grandmother looked anxiously at grandfather. He took off his hat, and the other men did likewise. I thought his prayer remarkable. I still remember it. He began, `Oh, great and just God, no man among us knows what the sleeper knows, nor is it for us to judge what lies between him and Thee.' He prayed that if any man there had been remiss toward the stranger come to a far country, God would forgive him and soften his heart. He recalled the promises to the widow and the fatherless, and asked God to smooth the way before this widow and her children, and to `incline the hearts of men to deal justly with her.' In closing, he said we were leaving Mr. Shimerda at `Thy judgment seat, which is also Thy mercy seat.'

All the time he was praying, grandmother watched him through the black fingers of her glove, and when he said `Amen,' I thought she looked satisfied with him. She turned to Otto and whispered, `Can't you start a hymn, Fuchs? It would seem less heathenish.'

Fuchs glanced about to see if there was general approval of her suggestion, then began, `Jesus, Lover of my Soul,' and all the men and women took it up after him. Whenever I have heard the hymn since, it has made me remember that white waste and the little group of people; and the bluish air, full of fine, eddying snow, like long veils flying:

`While the nearer waters roll,   While the tempest still is high.'

Years afterward, when the open-grazing days were over, and the red grass had been ploughed under and under until it had almost disappeared from the prairie; when all the fields were under fence, and the roads no longer ran about like wild things, but followed the surveyed section-lines, Mr. Shimerda's grave was still there, with a sagging wire fence around it, and an unpainted wooden cross. As grandfather had predicted, Mrs. Shimerda never saw the roads going over his head. The road from the north curved a little to the east just there, and the road from the west swung out a little to the south;

so that the grave, with its tall red grass that was never mowed, was like a little island; and at twilight, under a new moon or the clear evening star, the dusty roads used to look like soft grey rivers flowing past it. I never came upon the place without emotion, and in all that country it was the spot most dear to me. I loved the dim superstition, the propitiatory intent, that had put the grave there; and still more I loved the spirit that could not carry out the sentence--the error from the surveyed lines, the clemency of the soft earth roads along which the home-coming wagons rattled after sunset. Never a tired driver passed the wooden cross, I am sure, without wishing well to the sleeper.

XVII

WHEN SPRING CAME, AFTER that hard winter, one could not get enough of the nimble air. Every morning I wakened with a fresh consciousness that winter was over. There were none of the signs of spring for which I used to watch in Virginia, no budding woods or blooming gardens. There was only--spring itself; the throb of it, the light restlessness, the vital essence of it everywhere: in the sky, in the swift clouds, in the pale sunshine, and in the warm, high wind--rising suddenly, sinking suddenly, impulsive and playful like a big puppy that pawed you and then lay down to be petted. If I had been tossed down blindfold on that red prairie, I should have known that it was spring.

Everywhere now there was the smell of burning grass. Our neighbours burned off their pasture before the new grass made a start, so that the fresh growth would not be mixed with the dead stand of last year. Those light, swift fires, running about the country, seemed a part of the same kindling that was in the air.

The Shimerdas were in their new log house by then. The neighbours had helped them to build it in March. It stood directly in front of their old cave, which they used as a cellar. The family were now fairly equipped to begin their struggle with the soil. They had four comfortable rooms to live in, a new windmill--bought on credit--a chicken-house and poultry. Mrs. Shimerda had paid grandfather ten dollars for a milk cow, and was to give him fifteen more as soon as they harvested their first crop.

When I rode up to the Shimerdas' one bright windy afternoon in April, Yulka ran out to meet me. It was to her, now, that I gave reading lessons; Antonia was busy with other things. I tied my pony and went into the kitchen where Mrs. Shimerda was baking bread, chewing poppy seeds as she worked. By this time she could speak enough English to ask me a great many questions about what our men were doing in the fields. She seemed to think that my elders withheld helpful information, and that from me she might get valuable secrets. On this occasion she asked me very craftily when grandfather expected to begin planting corn. I told her, adding that he thought we should have a dry spring and that the corn would not be held back by too much rain, as it had been last year.

She gave me a shrewd glance. `He not Jesus,' she blustered; `he not know about the wet and the dry.

I did not answer her; what was the use? As I sat waiting for the hour when Ambrosch and Antonia would return from the fields, I watched Mrs. Shimerda at her work. She took from the oven a coffee-cake which she wanted to keep warm for supper, and wrapped it in a quilt stuffed with feathers. I have seen her put even a roast goose in this quilt to keep it hot. When the neighbours were there building the new house, they saw her do this, and the story got abroad that the Shimerdas kept their food in their featherbeds.

When the sun was dropping low, Antonia came up the big south draw with her team. How much older she had grown in eight months! She had come to us a child, and now she was a tall, strong young girl, although her fifteenth birthday had just slipped by. I ran out and met her as she brought her horses up to the windmill to water them. She wore the boots her father had so thoughtfully taken off before he shot himself, and his old fur cap. Her outgrown cotton dress switched about her calves, over the boot-tops. She kept her sleeves rolled up all day, and her arms and throat were burned as brown as a sailor's. Her neck came up strongly out of her shoulders, like the bole of a tree out of the turf. One sees that draught-horse neck among the peasant women in all old countries.

She greeted me gaily, and began at once to tell me how much ploughing she had done that day. Ambrosch, she said, was on the north quarter, breaking sod with the oxen.

`Jim, you ask Jake how much he ploughed to-day. I don't want that Jake get more done in one day than me. I want we have very much corn this fall.'

While the horses drew in the water, and nosed each other, and then drank again, Antonia sat down on the windmill step and rested her head on her hand.

`You see the big prairie fire from your place last night? I hope your grandpa ain't lose no stacks?'

`No, we didn't. I came to ask you something, Tony. Grandmother wants to know if you can't go to the term of school that begins next week over at the sod schoolhouse. She says there's a good teacher, and you'd learn a lot.'

Antonia stood up, lifting and dropping her shoulders as if they were stiff. `I ain't got time to learn. I can work like mans now. My mother can't say no more how Ambrosch do all and nobody to help him. I can work as much as him. School is all right for little boys. I help make this land one good farm.'

She clucked to her team and started for the barn. I walked beside her, feeling vexed. Was she going to grow up boastful like her mother, I wondered? Before we reached the stable, I felt something tense in her silence, and glancing up I saw that she was crying. She turned her face from me and looked off at the red streak of dying light, over the dark prairie.

I climbed up into the loft and threw down the hay for her, while she unharnessed her team. We walked slowly back toward the house. Ambrosch had come in from the north quarter, and was watering his oxen at the tank.

Antonia took my hand. `Sometime you will tell me all those nice things you learn at the school, won't you, Jimmy?' she asked with a sudden rush of feeling in her voice. `My father, he went much to school. He know a great deal; how to make the fine cloth like what you not got here. He play horn and violin, and he read so many books that the priests in Bohemie come to talk to him. You won't forget my father, Jim?' `No,' I said, `I will never forget him.'

Mrs. Shimerda asked me to stay for supper. After Ambrosch and Antonia had washed the field dust from their hands and faces at the wash-basin by the kitchen door, we sat down at the oilcloth-covered table. Mrs. Shimerda ladled meal mush out of an iron pot and poured milk on it. After the mush we had fresh bread and sorghum molasses, and coffee with the cake that had been kept warm in the feathers. Antonia and Ambrosch were talking in Bohemian; disputing about which of them had done more ploughing that day. Mrs. Shimerda egged them on, chuckling while she gobbled her food.

Presently Ambrosch said sullenly in English: `You take them ox tomorrow and try the sod plough. Then you not be so smart.'

His sister laughed. `Don't be mad. I know it's awful hard work for break sod. I milk the cow for you tomorrow, if you want.'

Mrs. Shimerda turned quickly to me. `That cow not give so much milk like what your grandpa say. If he make talk about fifteen dollars, I send him back the cow.'

`He doesn't talk about the fifteen dollars,' I exclaimed indignantly. `He doesn't find fault with people.'

`He say I break his saw when we build, and I never,' grumbled Ambrosch.

I knew he had broken the saw, and then hid it and lied about it. I began to wish I had not stayed for supper. Everything was disagreeable to me. Antonia ate so noisily now, like a man, and she yawned often at the table and kept stretching her arms over her head, as if they ached. Grandmother had said, `Heavy field work'll spoil that girl. She'll lose all her nice ways and get rough ones.' She had lost them already.

After supper I rode home through the sad, soft spring twilight. Since winter I had seen very little of Antonia. She was out in the fields from sunup until sundown. If I rode over to see her where she was ploughing, she stopped at the end of a row to chat for a moment, then gripped her plough-handles, clucked to her team, and waded on down the furrow, making me feel that she was now grown up and had no time for me. On Sundays she helped her mother make garden or sewed all day. Grandfather was pleased with Antonia. When we complained of her, he only smiled and said, `She will help some fellow get ahead in the world.'

Nowadays Tony could talk of nothing but the prices of things, or how much she could lift and endure. She was too proud of her strength. I knew, too, that Ambrosch put upon her some chores a girl ought not to do, and that the farm-hands around the country joked in a nasty way about it. Whenever I saw her come up the furrow, shouting to her beasts, sunburned, sweaty, her dress open at the neck, and her throat and chest dust-plastered, I used to think of the tone in which poor Mr. Shimerda, who could say so little, yet managed to say so much when he exclaimed, `My Antonia!'

XVIII

AFTER I BEGAN TO go to the country school, I saw less of the Bohemians. We were sixteen pupils at the sod schoolhouse, and we all came on horseback and brought our dinner. My schoolmates were none of them very interesting, but I somehow felt that, by making comrades of them, I was getting even with Antonia for her indifference. Since the father's death, Ambrosch was more than ever the head of the house, and he seemed to direct the feelings as well as the fortunes of his womenfolk. Antonia often quoted his opinions to me, and she let me see that she admired him, while she thought of me only as a little boy. Before the spring was over, there was a distinct coldness between us and the Shimerdas. It came about in this way.

One Sunday I rode over there with Jake to get a horse-collar which Ambrosch had borrowed from him and had not returned. It was a beautiful blue morning. The buffalo-peas were blooming in pink and purple masses along the roadside, and the larks, perched on last year's dried sunflower stalks, were singing straight at the sun, their heads thrown back and their yellow breasts a-quiver. The wind blew about us in warm, sweet gusts. We rode slowly, with a pleasant sense of Sunday indolence.

We found the Shimerdas working just as if it were a week-day. Marek was cleaning out the stable, and Antonia and her mother were making garden, off across the pond in the draw-head. Ambrosch was up on the windmill tower, oiling the wheel. He came down, not very cordially. When Jake asked for the collar, he grunted and scratched his head. The collar belonged to grandfather, of course, and Jake, feeling responsible for it, flared up. `Now, don't you say you haven't got it, Ambrosch, because I know you have, and if you ain't a-going to look for it, I will.'

Ambrosch shrugged his shoulders and sauntered down the hill toward the stable. I could see that it was one of his mean days. Presently he returned, carrying a collar that had been badly used--trampled in the dirt and gnawed by rats until the hair was sticking out of it.

`This what you want?' he asked surlily.

Jake jumped off his horse. I saw a wave of red come up under the rough stubble on his face. `That ain't the piece of harness I loaned you, Ambrosch; or, if it is, you've used it shameful. I ain't a-going to carry such a looking thing back to Mr. Burden.'

Ambrosch dropped the collar on the ground. `All right,' he said coolly, took up his oil-can, and began to climb the mill. Jake caught him by the belt of his trousers and yanked him back. Ambrosch's feet had scarcely touched the ground when he lunged out with a vicious kick at Jake's stomach. Fortunately, Jake was in such a position that he could dodge it. This was not the sort of thing country boys did when they played at fisticuffs, and Jake was furious. He landed Ambrosch a blow on the head--it sounded like the crack of an axe on a cow-pumpkin. Ambrosch dropped over, stunned.

We heard squeals, and looking up saw Antonia and her mother coming on the run. They did not take the path around the pond, but plunged through the muddy water, without even lifting their skirts. They came on, screaming and clawing the air. By this time Ambrosch had come to his senses and was sputtering with nosebleed.

Jake sprang into his saddle. `Let's get out of this, Jim,' he called.

Mrs. Shimerda threw her hands over her head and clutched as if she were going to pull down lightning. `Law, law!' she shrieked after us. `Law for knock my Ambrosch down!'

`I never like you no more, Jake and Jim Burden,' Antonia panted. `No friends any more!'

Jake stopped and turned his horse for a second. `Well, you're a damned ungrateful lot, the whole pack of you,' he shouted back. `I guess the Burdens can get along without you. You've been a sight of trouble to them, anyhow!'

We rode away, feeling so outraged that the fine morning was spoiled for us. I hadn't a word to say, and poor Jake was white as paper and trembling all over. It made him sick to get so angry.

`They ain't the same, Jimmy,' he kept saying in a hurt tone. `These foreigners ain't the same. You can't trust 'em to be fair. It's dirty to kick a feller. You heard how the women turned on you--and after all we went through on account of 'em last winter! They ain't to be trusted. I don't want to see you get too thick with any of 'em.'

`I'll never be friends with them again, Jake,' I declared hotly. `I believe they are all like Krajiek and Ambrosch underneath.'

Grandfather heard our story with a twinkle in his eye. He advised Jake to ride to town tomorrow, go to a justice of the peace, tell him he had knocked young Shimerda down, and pay his fine. Then if Mrs. Shimerda was inclined to make trouble--her son was still under age--she would be forestalled. Jake said he might as well take the wagon and haul to market the pig he had been fattening. On Monday, about an hour after Jake had started, we saw Mrs. Shimerda and her Ambrosch proudly driving by, looking neither to the right nor left. As they rattled out of sight down the Black Hawk road, grandfather chuckled, saying he had rather expected she would follow the matter up.

Jake paid his fine with a ten-dollar bill grandfather had given him for that purpose. But when the Shimerdas found that Jake sold his pig in town that day, Ambrosch worked it out in his shrewd head that Jake had to sell his pig to pay his fine. This theory afforded the Shimerdas great satisfaction, apparently. For weeks afterward, whenever Jake and I met Antonia on her way to the post-office, or going along the road with her work-team, she would clap her hands and call to us in a spiteful, crowing voice:

`Jake-y, Jake-y, sell the pig and pay the slap!'

Otto pretended not to be surprised at Antonia's behaviour. He only lifted his brows and said, `You can't tell me anything new about a Czech; I'm an Austrian.'

Grandfather was never a party to what Jake called our feud with the Shimerdas. Ambrosch and Antonia always greeted him respectfully, and he asked them about their affairs and gave them advice as usual. He thought the future looked hopeful for them. Ambrosch was a far-seeing fellow; he soon realized that his oxen were too heavy for any work except breaking sod, and he succeeded in selling them to a newly arrived German. With the money he bought another team of horses, which grandfather selected for him. Marek was strong, and Ambrosch worked him hard; but he could never teach him to cultivate corn, I remember. The one idea that had ever got through poor Marek's thick head was that all exertion was meritorious. He always bore down on the handles of the cultivator and drove the blades so deep into the earth that the horses were soon exhausted.

In June, Ambrosch went to work at Mr. Bushy's for a week, and took Marek with him at full wages. Mrs. Shimerda then drove the second cultivator; she and Antonia worked in the fields all day and did the chores at night. While the two women were running the place alone, one of the new horses got colic and gave them a terrible fright.

Antonia had gone down to the barn one night to see that all was well before she went to bed, and she noticed that one of the roans was swollen about the middle and stood with its head hanging. She mounted another horse, without waiting to saddle him, and hammered on our door just as we were going to bed. Grandfather answered her knock. He did not send one of his men, but rode back with her himself, taking a syringe and an old piece of carpet he kept for hot applications when our horses were sick. He found Mrs. Shimerda sitting by the horse with her lantern, groaning and wringing her hands. It took but a few moments to release the gases pent up in the poor beast, and the two women heard the rush of wind and saw the roan visibly diminish in girth.

`If I lose that horse, Mr. Burden,' Antonia exclaimed, `I never stay here till Ambrosch come home! I go drown myself in the pond before morning.'

When Ambrosch came back from Mr. Bushy's, we learned that he had given Marek's wages to the priest at Black Hawk, for Masses for their father's soul. Grandmother thought Antonia needed shoes more than Mr. Shimerda needed prayers, but grandfather said tolerantly, `If he can spare six dollars, pinched as he is, it shows he believes what he professes.'

It was grandfather who brought about a reconciliation with the Shimerdas. One morning he told us that the small grain was coming on so well, he thought he would begin to cut his wheat on the first of July. He would need more men, and if it were agreeable to everyone he would engage Ambrosch for the reaping and threshing, as the Shimerdas had no small grain of their own.

`I think, Emmaline,' he concluded, `I will ask Antonia to come over and help you in the kitchen. She will be glad to earn something, and it will be a good time to end misunderstandings. I may as well ride over this morning and make arrangements. Do you want to go with me, Jim?' His tone told me that he had already decided for me.

After breakfast we set off together. When Mrs. Shimerda saw us coming, she ran from her door down into the draw behind the stable, as if she did not want to meet us. Grandfather smiled to himself while he tied his horse, and we followed her.

Behind the barn we came upon a funny sight. The cow had evidently been grazing somewhere in the draw. Mrs. Shimerda had run to the animal, pulled up the lariat pin, and, when we came upon her, she was trying to hide the cow in an old cave in the bank. As the hole was narrow and dark, the cow held back, and the old woman was slapping and pushing at her hind quarters, trying to spank her into the drawside.

Grandfather ignored her singular occupation and greeted her politely. `Good morning, Mrs. Shimerda. Can you tell me where I will find Ambrosch? Which field?'

`He with the sod corn.' She pointed toward the north, still standing in front of the cow as if she hoped to conceal it.

`His sod corn will be good for fodder this winter,' said grandfather encouragingly. `And where is Antonia?'

`She go with.' Mrs. Shimerda kept wiggling her bare feet about nervously in the dust.

`Very well. I will ride up there. I want them to come over and help me cut my oats and wheat next month. I will pay them wages. Good morning. By the way, Mrs. Shimerda,' he said as he turned up the path, `I think we may as well call it square about the cow.'

She started and clutched the rope tighter. Seeing that she did not understand, grandfather turned back. `You need not pay me anything more; no more money. The cow is yours.'

`Pay no more, keep cow?' she asked in a bewildered tone, her narrow eyes snapping at us in the sunlight.

`Exactly. Pay no more, keep cow.' He nodded.

Mrs. Shimerda dropped the rope, ran after us, and, crouching down beside grandfather, she took his hand and kissed it. I doubt if he had ever been so much embarrassed before. I was a little startled, too. Somehow, that seemed to bring the Old World very close.

We rode away laughing, and grandfather said: `I expect she thought we had come to take the cow away for certain, Jim. I wonder if she wouldn't have scratched a little if we'd laid hold of that lariat rope!'

Our neighbours seemed glad to make peace with us. The next Sunday Mrs. Shimerda came over and brought Jake a pair of socks she had knitted. She presented them with an air of great magnanimity, saying, `Now you not come any more for knock my Ambrosch down?'

Jake laughed sheepishly. `I don't want to have no trouble with Ambrosch. If he'll let me alone, I'll let him alone.'

`If he slap you, we ain't got no pig for pay the fine,' she said insinuatingly.

Jake was not at all disconcerted. `Have the last word ma'm,' he said cheerfully. `It's a lady's privilege.'

XIX

JULY CAME ON with that breathless, brilliant heat which makes the plains of Kansas and Nebraska the best corn country in the world. It seemed as if we could hear the corn growing in the night; under the stars one caught a faint crackling in the dewy, heavy-odoured cornfields where the feathered stalks stood so juicy and green. If all the great plain from the Missouri to the Rocky Mountains had been under glass, and the heat regulated by a thermometer, it could not have been better for the yellow tassels that were ripening and fertilizing the silk day by day. The cornfields were far apart in those times, with miles of wild grazing land between. It took a clear, meditative eye like my grandfather's to foresee that they would enlarge and multiply until they would be, not the Shimerdas' cornfields, or Mr. Bushy's, but the world's cornfields; that their yield would be one of the great economic facts, like the wheat crop of Russia, which underlie all the activities of men, in peace or war.

The burning sun of those few weeks, with occasional rains at night, secured the corn. After the milky ears were once formed, we had little to fear from dry weather. The men were working so hard in the wheatfields that they did not notice the heat--though I was kept busy carrying water for them--and grandmother and Antonia had so much to do in the kitchen that they could not have told whether one day was hotter than another. Each morning, while the dew was still on the grass, Antonia went with me up to the garden to get early vegetables for dinner. Grandmother made her wear a sunbonnet, but as soon as we reached the garden she threw it on the grass and let her hair fly in the breeze. I remember how, as we bent over the pea-vines, beads of perspiration used to gather on her upper lip like a little moustache.

`Oh, better I like to work out-of-doors than in a house!' she used to sing joyfully. `I not care that your grandmother say it makes me like a man. I like to be like a man.' She would toss her head and ask me to feel the muscles swell in her brown arm.

We were glad to have her in the house. She was so gay and responsive that one did not mind her heavy, running step, or her clattery way with pans. Grandmother was in high spirits during the weeks that Antonia worked for us.

All the nights were close and hot during that harvest season. The harvesters slept in the hayloft because it was cooler there than in the house. I used to lie in my bed by the open window, watching the heat lightning play softly along the horizon, or looking up at the gaunt frame of the windmill against the blue night sky. One night there was a beautiful electric storm, though not enough rain fell to damage the cut grain. The men went down to the barn immediately after supper, and when the dishes were washed, Antonia and I climbed up on the slanting roof of the chicken-house to watch the clouds. The thunder was loud and metallic, like the rattle of sheet iron, and the lightning broke in great zigzags across the heavens, making everything stand out and come close to us for a moment. Half the sky was chequered with black thunderheads, but all the west was luminous and clear: in the lightning flashes it looked like deep blue water, with the sheen of moonlight on it; and the mottled part of the sky was like marble pavement, like the quay of some splendid seacoast city, doomed to destruction. Great warm splashes of rain fell on our upturned faces. One black cloud, no bigger than a little boat, drifted out into the clear space unattended, and kept moving westward. All about us we could hear the felty beat of the raindrops on the soft dust of the farmyard. Grandmother came to the door and said it was late, and we would get wet out there.

`In a minute we come,' Antonia called back to her. `I like your grandmother, and all things here,' she sighed. `I wish my papa live to see this summer. I wish no winter ever come again.'

`It will be summer a long while yet,' I reassured her. `Why aren't you always nice like this, Tony?'

`How nice?'

`Why, just like this; like yourself. Why do you all the time try to be like Ambrosch?'

She put her arms under her head and lay back, looking up at the sky. `If I live here, like you, that is different. Things will be easy for you. But they will be hard for us.'

PART II. THE HIRED GIRLS

I

I HAD BEEN LIVING with my grandfather for nearly three years when he decided to move to Black Hawk. He and grandmother were getting old for the heavy work of a farm, and as I was now thirteen they thought I ought to be going to school. Accordingly our homestead was rented to `that good woman, the Widow Steavens,' and her bachelor brother, and we bought Preacher White's house, at the north end of Black Hawk. This was the first town house one passed driving in from the farm, a landmark which told country people their long ride was over.

We were to move to Black Hawk in March, and as soon as grandfather had fixed the date he let Jake and Otto know of his intention. Otto said he would not be likely to find another place that suited him so well; that he was tired of farming and thought he would go back to what he called the `wild West.' Jake Marpole, lured by Otto's stories of adventure, decided to go with him. We did our best to dissuade Jake. He was so handicapped by illiteracy and by his trusting disposition that he would be an easy prey to sharpers. Grandmother begged him to stay among kindly, Christian people, where he was known; but there was no reasoning with him. He wanted to be a prospector. He thought a silver mine was waiting for him in Colorado.

Jake and Otto served us to the last. They moved us into town, put down the carpets in our new house, made shelves and cupboards for grandmother's kitchen, and seemed loath to leave us. But at last they went, without warning. Those two fellows had been faithful to us through sun and storm, had given us things that cannot be bought in any market in the world. With me they had been like older brothers; had restrained their speech and manners out of care for me, and given me so much good comradeship. Now they got on the westbound train one morning, in their Sunday clothes, with their oilcloth valises--and I never saw them again. Months afterward we got a card from Otto, saying that Jake had been down with mountain fever, but now they were both working in the Yankee Girl Mine, and were doing well. I wrote to them at that address, but my letter was returned to me, `Unclaimed.' After that we never heard from them.

Black Hawk, the new world in which we had come to live, was a clean, well-planted little prairie town, with white fences and good green yards about the dwellings, wide, dusty streets, and shapely little trees growing along the wooden sidewalks. In the centre of the town there were two rows of new brick `store' buildings, a brick schoolhouse, the court-house, and four white churches. Our own house looked down over the town, and from our upstairs windows we could see the winding line of the river bluffs, two miles south of us. That river was to be my compensation for the lost freedom of the farming country.

We came to Black Hawk in March, and by the end of April we felt like town people. Grandfather was a deacon in the new Baptist Church, grandmother was busy with church suppers and missionary societies, and I was quite another boy, or thought I was. Suddenly put down among boys of my own age, I found I had a great deal to learn. Before the spring term of school was over, I could fight, play `keeps,' tease the little girls, and use forbidden words as well as any boy in my class. I was restrained from utter savagery only by the fact that Mrs. Harling, our nearest neighbour, kept an eye on me, and if my behaviour went beyond certain bounds I was not permitted to come into her yard or to play with her jolly children.

We saw more of our country neighbours now than when we lived on the farm. Our house was a convenient stopping-place for them. We had a big barn where the farmers could put up their teams, and their womenfolk more often accompanied them, now that they could stay with us for dinner, and rest and set their bonnets right before they went shopping. The more our house was like a country hotel, the better I liked it. I was glad, when I came home from school at noon, to see a farm-wagon standing in the back yard, and I was always ready to run downtown to get beefsteak or baker's bread for unexpected company. All through that first spring and summer I kept hoping that Ambrosch would bring Antonia and Yulka to see our new house. I wanted to show them our red plush furniture, and the trumpet-blowing cherubs the German paperhanger had put on our parlour ceiling.

When Ambrosch came to town, however, he came alone, and though he put his horses in our barn, he would never stay for dinner, or tell us anything about his mother and sisters. If we ran out and questioned him as he was slipping through the yard, he would merely work his shoulders about in his coat and say, `They all right, I guess.'

Mrs. Steavens, who now lived on our farm, grew as fond of Antonia as we had been, and always brought us news of her. All through the wheat season, she told us, Ambrosch hired his sister out like a man, and she went from farm to farm, binding sheaves or working with the threshers. The farmers liked her and were kind to her; said they would rather have her for a hand than Ambrosch. When fall came she was to husk corn for the neighbours until Christmas, as she had done the year before; but grandmother saved her from this by getting her a place to work with our neighbours, the Harlings.

II

GRANDMOTHER OFTEN SAID THAT if she had to live in town, she thanked God she lived next the Harlings. They had been farming people, like ourselves, and their place was like a little farm, with a big barn and a garden, and an orchard and grazing lots--even a windmill. The Harlings were Norwegians, and Mrs. Harling had lived in Christiania until she was ten years old. Her husband was born in Minnesota. He was a grain merchant and cattle-buyer, and was generally considered the most enterprising business man in our county. He controlled a line of grain elevators in the little towns along the railroad to the west of us, and was away from home a great deal. In his absence his wife was the head of the household.

Mrs. Harling was short and square and sturdy-looking, like her house. Every inch of her was charged with an energy that made itself felt the moment she entered a room. Her face was rosy and solid, with bright, twinkling eyes and a stubborn little chin. She was quick to anger, quick to laughter, and jolly from the depths of her soul. How well I remember her laugh; it had in it the same sudden recognition that flashed into her eyes, was a burst of humour, short and intelligent. Her rapid footsteps shook her own floors, and she routed lassitude and indifference wherever she came. She could not be negative or perfunctory about anything. Her enthusiasm, and her violent likes and dislikes, asserted themselves in all the everyday occupations of life. Wash-day was interesting, never dreary, at the Harlings'. Preserving-time was a prolonged festival, and house-cleaning was like a revolution. When Mrs. Harling made garden that spring, we could feel the stir of her undertaking through the willow hedge that separated our place from hers.

Three of the Harling children were near me in age. Charley, the only son-- they had lost an older boy--was sixteen; Julia, who was known as the musical one, was fourteen when I was; and Sally, the tomboy with short hair, was a year younger. She was nearly as strong as I, and uncannily clever at all boys' sports. Sally was a wild thing, with sunburned yellow hair, bobbed about her ears, and a brown skin, for she never wore a hat. She raced all over town on one roller skate, often cheated at `keeps,' but was such a quick shot one couldn't catch her at it.

The grown-up daughter, Frances, was a very important person in our world. She was her father's chief clerk, and virtually managed his Black Hawk office during his frequent absences. Because of her unusual business ability, he was stern and exacting with her. He paid her a good salary, but she had few holidays and never got away from her responsibilities. Even on Sundays she went to the office to open the mail and read the markets. With Charley, who was not interested in business, but was already preparing for Annapolis, Mr. Harling was very indulgent; bought him guns and tools and electric batteries, and never asked what he did with them.

Frances was dark, like her father, and quite as tall. In winter she wore a sealskin coat and cap, and she and Mr. Harling used to walk home together in the evening, talking about grain-cars and cattle, like two men. Sometimes she came over to see grandfather after supper, and her visits flattered him. More than once they put their wits together to rescue some unfortunate farmer from the clutches of Wick Cutter, the Black Hawk money-lender. Grandfather said Frances Harling was as good a judge of credits as any banker in the county. The two or three men who had tried to take advantage of her in a deal acquired celebrity by their defeat. She knew every farmer for miles about: how much land he had under cultivation, how many cattle he was feeding, what his liabilities were. Her interest in these people was more than a business interest. She carried them all in her mind as if they were characters in a book or a play.

When Frances drove out into the country on business, she would go miles out of her way to call on some of the old people, or to see the women who seldom got to town. She was quick at understanding the grandmothers who spoke no English, and the most reticent and distrustful of them would tell her their story without realizing they were doing so. She went to country funerals and weddings in all weathers. A farmer's daughter who was to be married could count on a wedding present from Frances Harling.

In August the Harlings' Danish cook had to leave them. Grandmother entreated them to try Antonia. She cornered Ambrosch the next time he came to town, and pointed out to him that any connection with Christian Harling would strengthen his credit and be of advantage to him. One Sunday Mrs. Harling took the long ride out to the Shimerdas' with Frances. She said she wanted to see `what the girl came from' and to have a clear understanding with her mother. I was in our yard when they came driving home, just before sunset. They laughed and waved to me as they passed, and I could see they were in great good humour. After supper, when grandfather set off to church, grandmother and I took my short cut through the willow hedge and went over to hear about the visit to the Shimerdas'.

We found Mrs. Harling with Charley and Sally on the front porch, resting after her hard drive. Julia was in the hammock--she was fond of repose--and Frances was at the piano, playing without a light and talking to her mother through the open window.

Mrs. Harling laughed when she saw us coming. `I expect you left your dishes on the table tonight, Mrs. Burden,' she called. Frances shut the piano and came out to join us.

They had liked Antonia from their first glimpse of her; felt they knew exactly what kind of girl she was. As for Mrs. Shimerda, they found her very amusing. Mrs. Harling chuckled whenever she spoke of her. `I expect I am more at home with that sort of bird than you are, Mrs. Burden. They're a pair, Ambrosch and that old woman!'

They had had a long argument with Ambrosch about Antonia's allowance for clothes and pocket-money. It was his plan that every cent of his sister's wages should be paid over to him each month, and he would provide her with such clothing as he thought necessary. When Mrs. Harling told him firmly that she would keep fifty dollars a year for Antonia's own use, he declared they wanted to take his sister to town and dress her up and make a fool of her. Mrs. Harling gave us a lively account of Ambrosch's behaviour throughout the interview; how he kept jumping up and putting on his cap as if he were through with the whole business, and how his mother tweaked his coat-tail and prompted him in Bohemian. Mrs. Harling finally agreed to pay three dollars a week for Antonia's services--good wages in those days--and to keep her in shoes. There had been hot dispute about the shoes, Mrs. Shimerda finally saying persuasively that she would send Mrs. Harling three fat geese every year to `make even.' Ambrosch was to bring his sister to town next Saturday.

`She'll be awkward and rough at first, like enough,' grandmother said anxiously, `but unless she's been spoiled by the hard life she's led, she has it in her to be a real helpful girl.'

Mrs. Harling laughed her quick, decided laugh. `Oh, I'm not worrying, Mrs. Burden! I can bring something out of that girl. She's barely seventeen, not too old to learn new ways. She's good-looking, too!' she added warmly.

Frances turned to grandmother. `Oh, yes, Mrs. Burden, you didn't tell us that! She was working in the garden when we got there, barefoot and ragged. But she has such fine brown legs and arms, and splendid colour in her cheeks--like those big dark red plums.'

We were pleased at this praise. Grandmother spoke feelingly. `When she first came to this country, Frances, and had that genteel old man to watch over her, she was as pretty a girl as ever I saw. But, dear me, what a life she's led, out in the fields with those rough threshers! Things would have been very different with poor Antonia if her father had lived.'

The Harlings begged us to tell them about Mr. Shimerda's death and the big snowstorm. By the time we saw grandfather coming home from church, we had told them pretty much all we knew of the Shimerdas.

`The girl will be happy here, and she'll forget those things,' said Mrs. Harling confidently, as we rose to take our leave.

III

ON SATURDAY AMBROSCH drove up to the back gate, and Antonia jumped down from the wagon and ran into our kitchen just as she used to do. She was wearing shoes and stockings, and was breathless and excited. She gave me a playful shake by the shoulders. `You ain't forget about me, Jim?'

Grandmother kissed her. `God bless you, child! Now you've come, you must try to do right and be a credit to us.'

Antonia looked eagerly about the house and admired everything. `Maybe I be the kind of girl you like better; now I come to town,' she suggested hopefully.

How good it was to have Antonia near us again; to see her every day and almost every night! Her greatest fault, Mrs. Harling found, was that she so often stopped her work and fell to playing with the children. She would race about the orchard with us, or take sides in our hay-fights in the barn, or be the old bear that came down from the mountain and carried off Nina. Tony learned English so quickly that by the time school began she could speak as well as any of us.

I was jealous of Tony's admiration for Charley Harling. Because he was always first in his classes at school, and could mend the water-pipes or the doorbell and take the clock to pieces, she seemed to think him a sort of prince. Nothing that Charley wanted was too much trouble for her. She loved to put up lunches for him when he went hunting, to mend his ball-gloves and sew buttons on his shooting-coat, baked the kind of nut-cake he liked, and fed his setter dog when he was away on trips with his father. Antonia had made herself cloth working-slippers out of Mr. Harling's old coats, and in these she went padding about after Charley, fairly panting with eagerness to please him.

Next to Charley, I think she loved Nina best. Nina was only six, and she was rather more complex than the other children. She was fanciful, had all sorts of unspoken preferences, and was easily offended. At the slightest disappointment or displeasure, her velvety brown eyes filled with tears, and she would lift her chin and walk silently away. If we ran after her and tried to appease her, it did no good. She walked on unmollified. I used to think that no eyes in the world could grow so large or hold so many tears as Nina's. Mrs. Harling and Antonia invariably took her part. We were never given a chance to explain. The charge was simply: `You have made Nina cry. Now, Jimmy can go home, and Sally must get her arithmetic.' I liked Nina, too; she was so quaint and unexpected, and her eyes were lovely; but I often wanted to shake her.

We had jolly evenings at the Harlings' when the father was away. If he was at home, the children had to go to bed early, or they came over to my house to play. Mr. Harling not only demanded a quiet house, he demanded all his wife's attention. He used to take her away to their room in the west ell, and talk over his business with her all evening. Though we did not realize it then, Mrs. Harling was our audience when we played, and we always looked to her for suggestions. Nothing flattered one like her quick laugh.

Mr. Harling had a desk in his bedroom, and his own easy-chair by the window, in which no one else ever sat. On the nights when he was at home, I could see his shadow on the blind, and it seemed to me an arrogant shadow. Mrs. Harling paid no heed to anyone else if he was there. Before he went to bed she always got him a lunch of smoked salmon or anchovies and beer. He kept an alcohol lamp in his room, and a French coffee-pot, and his wife made coffee for him at any hour of the night he happened to want it.

Most Black Hawk fathers had no personal habits outside their domestic ones; they paid the bills, pushed the baby-carriage after office hours, moved the sprinkler about over the lawn, and took the family driving on Sunday. Mr. Harling, therefore, seemed to me autocratic and imperial in his ways. He walked, talked, put on his gloves, shook hands, like a man who felt that he had power. He was not tall, but he carried his head so haughtily that he looked a commanding figure, and there was something daring and challenging in his eyes. I used to imagine that the 'nobles' of whom Antonia was always talking probably looked very much like Christian Harling, wore caped overcoats like his, and just such a glittering diamond upon the little finger.

Except when the father was at home, the Harling house was never quiet. Mrs. Harling and Nina and Antonia made as much noise as a houseful of children, and there was usually somebody at the piano. Julia was the only one who was held down to regular hours of practising, but they all played. When Frances came home at noon, she played until dinner was ready. When Sally got back from school, she sat down in her hat and coat and drummed the plantation melodies that Negro minstrel troupes brought to town. Even Nina played the Swedish Wedding March.

Mrs. Harling had studied the piano under a good teacher, and somehow she managed to practise every day. I soon learned that if I were sent over on an errand and found Mrs. Harling at the piano, I must sit down and wait quietly until she turned to me. I can see her at this moment: her short, square person planted firmly on the stool, her little fat hands moving quickly and neatly over the keys, her eyes fixed on the music with intelligent concentration.

IV

`I won't have none of your weevily wheat, and I won't have none of your barley, But I'll take a measure of fine white flour, to make a cake for Charley.'

WE WERE SINGING rhymes to tease Antonia while she was beating up one of Charley's favourite cakes in her big mixing-bowl.

It was a crisp autumn evening, just cold enough to make one glad to quit playing tag in the yard, and retreat into the kitchen. We had begun to roll popcorn balls with syrup when we heard a knock at the back door, and Tony dropped her spoon and went to open it.

A plump, fair-skinned girl was standing in the doorway. She looked demure and pretty, and made a graceful picture in her blue cashmere dress and little blue hat, with a plaid shawl drawn neatly about her shoulders and a clumsy pocket-book in her hand.

`Hello, Tony. Don't you know me?' she asked in a smooth, low voice, looking in at us archly.

Antonia gasped and stepped back.

`Why, it's Lena! Of course I didn't know you, so dressed up!'

Lena Lingard laughed, as if this pleased her. I had not recognized her for a moment, either. I had never seen her before with a hat on her head--or with shoes and stockings on her feet, for that matter. And here she was, brushed and smoothed and dressed like a town girl, smiling at us with perfect composure.

`Hello, Jim,' she said carelessly as she walked into the kitchen and looked about her. `I've come to town to work, too, Tony.'

`Have you, now? Well, ain't that funny!' Antonia stood ill at ease, and didn't seem to know just what to do with her visitor.

The door was open into the dining-room, where Mrs. Harling sat crocheting and Frances was reading. Frances asked Lena to come in and join them.

`You are Lena Lingard, aren't you? I've been to see your mother, but you were off herding cattle that day. Mama, this is Chris Lingard's oldest girl.'

Mrs. Harling dropped her worsted and examined the visitor with quick, keen eyes. Lena was not at all disconcerted. She sat down in the chair Frances pointed out, carefully arranging her pocket-book and grey cotton gloves on her lap. We followed with our popcorn, but Antonia hung back--said she had to get her cake into the oven.

`So you have come to town,' said Mrs. Harling, her eyes still fixed on Lena. `Where are you working?'

`For Mrs. Thomas, the dressmaker. She is going to teach me to sew. She says I have quite a knack. I'm through with the farm. There ain't any end to the work on a farm, and always so much trouble happens. I'm going to be a dressmaker.'

`Well, there have to be dressmakers. It's a good trade. But I wouldn't run down the farm, if I were you,' said Mrs. Harling rather severely. `How is your mother?'

`Oh, mother's never very well; she has too much to do. She'd get away from the farm, too, if she could. She was willing for me to come. After I learn to do sewing, I can make money and help her.'

`See that you don't forget to,' said Mrs. Harling sceptically, as she took up her crocheting again and sent the hook in and out with nimble fingers.

`No, 'm, I won't,' said Lena blandly. She took a few grains of the popcorn we pressed upon her, eating them discreetly and taking care not to get her fingers sticky.

Frances drew her chair up nearer to the visitor. `I thought you were going to be married, Lena,' she said teasingly. `Didn't I hear that Nick Svendsen was rushing you pretty hard?'

Lena looked up with her curiously innocent smile. `He did go with me quite a while. But his father made a fuss about it and said he wouldn't give Nick any land if he married me, so he's going to marry Annie Iverson. I wouldn't like to be her; Nick's awful sullen, and he'll take it out on her. He ain't spoke to his father since he promised.'

Frances laughed. `And how do you feel about it?'

`I don't want to marry Nick, or any other man,' Lena murmured. `I've seen a good deal of married life, and I don't care for it. I want to be so I can help my mother and the children at home, and not have to ask lief of anybody.'

`That's right,' said Frances. `And Mrs. Thomas thinks you can learn dressmaking?'

`Yes, 'm. I've always liked to sew, but I never had much to do with. Mrs. Thomas makes lovely things for all the town ladies. Did you know Mrs. Gardener is having a purple velvet made? The velvet came from Omaha. My, but it's lovely!' Lena sighed softly and stroked her cashmere folds. `Tony knows I never did like out-of-door work,' she added.

Mrs. Harling glanced at her. `I expect you'll learn to sew all right, Lena, if you'll only keep your head and not go gadding about to dances all the time and neglect your work, the way some country girls do.'

`Yes, 'm. Tiny Soderball is coming to town, too. She's going to work at the Boys' Home Hotel. She'll see lots of strangers,' Lena added wistfully.

`Too many, like enough,' said Mrs. Harling. `I don't think a hotel is a good place for a girl; though I guess Mrs. Gardener keeps an eye on her waitresses.'

Lena's candid eyes, that always looked a little sleepy under their long lashes, kept straying about the cheerful rooms with naive admiration. Presently she drew on her cotton gloves. `I guess I must be leaving,' she said irresolutely.

Frances told her to come again, whenever she was lonesome or wanted advice about anything. Lena replied that she didn't believe she would ever get lonesome in Black Hawk.

She lingered at the kitchen door and begged Antonia to come and see her often. `I've got a room of my own at Mrs. Thomas's, with a carpet.'

Tony shuffled uneasily in her cloth slippers. `I'll come sometime, but Mrs. Harling don't like to have me run much,' she said evasively.

`You can do what you please when you go out, can't you?' Lena asked in a guarded whisper. `Ain't you crazy about town, Tony? I don't care what anybody says, I'm done with the farm!' She glanced back over her shoulder toward the dining-room, where Mrs. Harling sat.

When Lena was gone, Frances asked Antonia why she hadn't been a little more cordial to her.

`I didn't know if your mother would like her coming here,' said Antonia, looking troubled. `She was kind of talked about, out there.'

'Yes, I know. But mother won't hold it against her if she behaves well here. You needn't say anything about that to the children. I guess Jim has heard all that gossip?'

When I nodded, she pulled my hair and told me I knew too much, anyhow. We were good friends, Frances and I.

I ran home to tell grandmother that Lena Lingard had come to town. We were glad of it, for she had a hard life on the farm.

Lena lived in the Norwegian settlement west of Squaw Creek, and she used to herd her father's cattle in the open country between his place and the Shimerdas'. Whenever we rode over in that direction we saw her out among her cattle, bareheaded and barefooted, scantily dressed in tattered clothing, always knitting as she watched her herd. Before I knew Lena, I thought of her as something wild, that always lived on the prairie, because I had never seen her under a roof. Her yellow hair was burned to a ruddy thatch on her head; but her legs and arms, curiously enough, in spite of constant exposure to the sun, kept a miraculous whiteness which somehow made her seem more undressed than other girls who went scantily clad. The first time I stopped to talk to her, I was astonished at her soft voice and easy, gentle ways. The girls out there usually got rough and mannish after they went to herding. But Lena asked Jake and me to get off our horses and stay awhile, and behaved exactly as if she were in a house and were accustomed to having visitors. She was not embarrassed by her ragged clothes, and treated us as if we were old acquaintances. Even then I noticed the unusual colour of her eyes--a shade of deep violet--and their soft, confiding expression.

Chris Lingard was not a very successful farmer, and he had a large family. Lena was always knitting stockings for little brothers and sisters, and even the Norwegian women, who disapproved of her, admitted that she was a good daughter to her mother. As Tony said, she had been talked about. She was accused of making Ole Benson lose the little sense he had--and that at an age when she should still have been in pinafores.

Ole lived in a leaky dugout somewhere at the edge of the settlement. He was fat and lazy and discouraged, and bad luck had become a habit with him. After he had had every other kind of misfortune, his wife, `Crazy Mary,' tried to set a neighbour's barn on fire, and was sent to the asylum at Lincoln. She was kept there for a few months, then escaped and walked all the way home, nearly two hundred miles, travelling by night and hiding in barns and haystacks by day. When she got back to the Norwegian settlement, her poor feet were as hard as hoofs. She promised to be good, and was allowed to stay at home--though everyone realized she was as crazy as ever, and she still ran about barefooted through the snow, telling her domestic troubles to her neighbours.

Not long after Mary came back from the asylum, I heard a young Dane, who was helping us to thresh, tell Jake and Otto that Chris Lingard's oldest girl had put Ole Benson out of his head, until he had no more sense than his crazy wife. When Ole was cultivating his corn that summer, he used to get discouraged in the field, tie up his team, and wander off to wherever Lena Lingard was herding. There he would sit down on the drawside and help her watch her cattle. All the settlement was talking about it. The Norwegian preacher's wife went to Lena and told her she ought not to allow this; she begged Lena to come to church on Sundays. Lena said she hadn't a dress in the world any less ragged than the one on her back. Then the minister's wife went through her old trunks and found some things she had worn before her marriage.

The next Sunday Lena appeared at church, a little late, with her hair done up neatly on her head, like a young woman, wearing shoes and stockings, and the new dress, which she had made over for herself very becomingly. The congregation stared at her. Until that morning no one--unless it were Ole--had realized how pretty she was, or that she was growing up. The swelling lines of her figure had been hidden under the shapeless rags she wore in the fields. After the last hymn had been sung, and the congregation was dismissed, Ole slipped out to the hitch-bar and lifted Lena on her horse. That, in itself, was shocking; a married man was not expected to do such things. But it was nothing to the scene that followed. Crazy Mary darted out from the group of women at the church door, and ran down the road after Lena, shouting horrible threats.

`Look out, you Lena Lingard, look out! I'll come over with a corn-knife one day and trim some of that shape off you. Then you won't sail round so fine, making eyes at the men!...'

The Norwegian women didn't know where to look. They were formal housewives, most of them, with a severe sense of decorum. But Lena Lingard only laughed her lazy, good-natured laugh and rode on, gazing back over her shoulder at Ole's infuriated wife.

The time came, however, when Lena didn't laugh. More than once Crazy Mary chased her across the prairie and round and round the Shimerdas' cornfield. Lena never told her father; perhaps she was ashamed; perhaps she was more afraid of his anger than of the corn-knife. I was at the Shimerdas' one afternoon when Lena came bounding through the red grass as fast as her white legs could carry her. She ran straight into the house and hid in Antonia's feather-bed. Mary was not far behind: she came right up to the door and made us feel how sharp her blade was, showing us very graphically just what she meant to do to Lena. Mrs. Shimerda, leaning out of the window, enjoyed the situation keenly, and was sorry when Antonia sent Mary away, mollified by an apronful of bottle-tomatoes. Lena came out from Tony's room behind the kitchen, very pink from the heat of the feathers, but otherwise calm. She begged Antonia and me to go with her, and help get her cattle together; they were scattered and might be gorging themselves in somebody's cornfield.

`Maybe you lose a steer and learn not to make somethings with your eyes at married men,' Mrs. Shimerda told her hectoringly.

Lena only smiled her sleepy smile. `I never made anything to him with my eyes. I can't help it if he hangs around, and I can't order him off. It ain't my prairie.'

V

AFTER LENA CAME To Black Hawk, I often met her downtown, where she would be matching sewing silk or buying `findings' for Mrs. Thomas. If I happened to walk home with her, she told me all about the dresses she was helping to make, or about what she saw and heard when she was with Tiny Soderball at the hotel on Saturday nights.

The Boys' Home was the best hotel on our branch of the Burlington, and all the commercial travellers in that territory tried to get into Black Hawk for Sunday. They used to assemble in the parlour after supper on Saturday nights. Marshall Field's man, Anson Kirkpatrick, played the piano and sang all the latest sentimental songs. After Tiny had helped the cook wash the dishes, she and Lena sat on the other side of the double doors between the parlour and the dining-room, listening to the music and giggling at the jokes and stories. Lena often said she hoped I would be a travelling man when I grew up. They had a gay life of it; nothing to do but ride about on trains all day and go to theatres when they were in big cities. Behind the hotel there was an old store building, where the salesmen opened their big trunks and spread out their samples on the counters. The Black Hawk merchants went to look at these things and order goods, and Mrs. Thomas, though she was I retail trade,' was permitted to see them and to `get ideas.' They were all generous, these travelling men; they gave Tiny Soderball handkerchiefs and gloves and ribbons and striped stockings, and so many bottles of perfume and cakes of scented soap that she bestowed some of them on Lena.

One afternoon in the week before Christmas, I came upon Lena and her funny, square-headed little brother Chris, standing before the drugstore, gazing in at the wax dolls and blocks and Noah's Arks arranged in the frosty show window. The boy had come to town with a neighbour to do his Christmas shopping, for he had money of his own this year. He was only twelve, but that winter he had got the job of sweeping out the Norwegian church and making the fire in it every Sunday morning. A cold job it must have been, too!

We went into Duckford's dry-goods store, and Chris unwrapped all his presents and showed them to me something for each of the six younger than himself, even a rubber pig for the baby. Lena had given him one of Tiny Soderball's bottles of perfume for his mother, and he thought he would get some handkerchiefs to go with it. They were cheap, and he hadn't much money left. We found a tableful of handkerchiefs spread out for view at Duckford's. Chris wanted those with initial letters in the corner, because he had never seen any before. He studied them seriously, while Lena looked over his shoulder, telling him she thought the red letters would hold their colour best. He seemed so perplexed that I thought perhaps he hadn't enough money, after all. Presently he said gravely:

`Sister, you know mother's name is Berthe. I don't know if I ought to get B for Berthe, or M for Mother.'

Lena patted his bristly head. `I'd get the B, Chrissy. It will please her for you to think about her name. Nobody ever calls her by it now.'

That satisfied him. His face cleared at once, and he took three reds and three blues. When the neighbour came in to say that it was time to start, Lena wound Chris's comforter about his neck and turned up his jacket collar--he had no overcoat--and we watched him climb into the wagon and start on his long, cold drive. As we walked together up the windy street, Lena wiped her eyes with the back of her woollen glove. `I get awful homesick for them, all the same,' she murmured, as if she were answering some remembered reproach.

VI

WINTER COMES DOWN SAVAGELY over a little town on the prairie. The wind that sweeps in from the open country strips away all the leafy screens that hide one yard from another in summer, and the houses seem to draw closer together. The roofs, that looked so far away across the green tree-tops, now stare you in the face, and they are so much uglier than when their angles were softened by vines and shrubs.

In the morning, when I was fighting my way to school against the wind, I couldn't see anything but the road in front of me; but in the late afternoon, when I was coming home, the town looked bleak and desolate to me. The pale, cold light of the winter sunset did not beautify--it was like the light of truth itself. When the smoky clouds hung low in the west and the red sun went down behind them, leaving a pink flush on the snowy roofs and the blue drifts, then the wind sprang up afresh, with a kind of bitter song, as if it said: `This is reality, whether you like it or not. All those frivolities of summer, the light and shadow, the living mask of green that trembled over everything, they were lies, and this is what was underneath. This is the truth.' It was as if we were being punished for loving the loveliness of summer.

If I loitered on the playground after school, or went to the post-office for the mail and lingered to hear the gossip about the cigar-stand, it would be growing dark by the time I came home. The sun was gone; the frozen streets stretched long and blue before me; the lights were shining pale in kitchen windows, and I could smell the suppers cooking as I passed. Few people were abroad, and each one of them was hurrying toward a fire. The glowing stoves in the houses were like magnets. When one passed an old man, one could see nothing of his face but a red nose sticking out between a frosted beard and a long plush cap. The young men capered along with their hands in their pockets, and sometimes tried a slide on the icy sidewalk. The children, in their bright hoods and comforters, never walked, but always ran from the moment they left their door, beating their mittens against their sides. When I got as far as the Methodist Church, I was about halfway home. I can remember how glad I was when there happened to be a light in the church, and the painted glass window shone out at us as we came along the frozen street. In the winter bleakness a hunger for colour came over people, like the Laplander's craving for fats and sugar. Without knowing why, we used to linger on the sidewalk outside the church when the lamps were lighted early for choir practice or prayer-meeting, shivering and talking until our feet were like lumps of ice. The crude reds and greens and blues of that coloured glass held us there.

On winter nights, the lights in the Harlings' windows drew me like the painted glass. Inside that warm, roomy house there was colour, too. After supper I used to catch up my cap, stick my hands in my pockets, and dive through the willow hedge as if witches were after me. Of course, if Mr. Harling was at home, if his shadow stood out on the blind of the west room, I did not go in, but turned and walked home by the long way, through the street, wondering what book I should read as I sat down with the two old people.

Such disappointments only gave greater zest to the nights when we acted charades, or had a costume ball in the back parlour, with Sally always dressed like a boy. Frances taught us to dance that winter, and she said, from the first lesson, that Antonia would make the best dancer among us. On Saturday nights, Mrs. Harling used to play the old operas for us--'Martha,' `Norma,' `Rigoletto'--telling us the story while she played. Every Saturday night was like a party. The parlour, the back parlour, and the dining-room were warm and brightly lighted, with comfortable chairs and sofas, and gay pictures on the walls. One always felt at ease there. Antonia brought her sewing and sat with us--she was already beginning to make pretty clothes for herself. After the long winter evenings on the prairie, with Ambrosch's sullen silences and her mother's complaints, the Harlings' house seemed, as she said, `like Heaven' to her. She was never too tired to make taffy or chocolate cookies for us. If Sally whispered in her ear, or Charley gave her three winks, Tony would rush into the kitchen and build a fire in the range on which she had already cooked three meals that day.

While we sat in the kitchen waiting for the cookies to bake or the taffy to cool, Nina used to coax Antonia to tell her stories--about the calf that broke its leg, or how Yulka saved her little turkeys from drowning in the freshet, or about old Christmases and weddings in Bohemia. Nina interpreted the stories about the creche fancifully, and in spite of our derision she cherished a belief that Christ was born in Bohemia a short time before the Shimerdas left that country. We all liked Tony's stories. Her voice had a peculiarly engaging quality; it was deep, a little husky, and one always heard the breath vibrating behind it. Everything she said seemed to come right out of her heart.

One evening when we were picking out kernels for walnut taffy, Tony told us a new story.

`Mrs. Harling, did you ever hear about what happened up in the Norwegian settlement last summer, when I was threshing there? We were at Iversons', and I was driving one of the grain-wagons.'

Mrs. Harling came out and sat down among us. `Could you throw the wheat into the bin yourself, Tony?' She knew what heavy work it was.

`Yes, ma'm, I did. I could shovel just as fast as that fat Andern boy that drove the other wagon. One day it was just awful hot. When we got back to the field from dinner, we took things kind of easy. The men put in the horses and got the machine going, and Ole Iverson was up on the deck, cutting bands. I was sitting against a straw-stack, trying to get some shade. My wagon wasn't going out first, and somehow I felt the heat awful that day. The sun was so hot like it was going to burn the world up. After a while I see a man coming across the stubble, and when he got close I see it was a tramp. His toes stuck out of his shoes, and he hadn't shaved for a long while, and his eyes was awful red and wild, like he had some sickness. He comes right up and begins to talk like he knows me already. He says: `The ponds in this country is done got so low a man couldn't drownd himself in one of 'em.'

`I told him nobody wanted to drownd themselves, but if we didn't have rain soon we'd have to pump water for the cattle.

`"Oh, cattle," he says, "you'll all take care of your cattle! Ain't you got no beer here?" I told him he'd have to go to the Bohemians for beer; the Norwegians didn't have none when they threshed. "My God!" he says, "so it's Norwegians now, is it? I thought this was Americy."

`Then he goes up to the machine and yells out to Ole Iverson, "Hello, partner, let me up there. I can cut bands, and I'm tired of trampin'. I won't go no farther."

`I tried to make signs to Ole, 'cause I thought that man was crazy and might get the machine stopped up. But Ole, he was glad to get down out of the sun and chaff--it gets down your neck and sticks to you something awful when it's hot like that. So Ole jumped down and crawled under one of the wagons for shade, and the tramp got on the machine. He cut bands all right for a few minutes, and then, Mrs. Harling, he waved his hand to me and jumped head-first right into the threshing machine after the wheat.

`I begun to scream, and the men run to stop the horses, but the belt had sucked him down, and by the time they got her stopped, he was all beat and cut to pieces. He was wedged in so tight it was a hard job to get him out, and the machine ain't never worked right since.'

`Was he clear dead, Tony?' we cried.

`Was he dead? Well, I guess so! There, now, Nina's all upset. We won't talk about it. Don't you cry, Nina. No old tramp won't get you while Tony's here.'

Mrs. Harling spoke up sternly. `Stop crying, Nina, or I'll always send you upstairs when Antonia tells us about the country. Did they never find out where he came from, Antonia?'

`Never, ma'm. He hadn't been seen nowhere except in a little town they call Conway. He tried to get beer there, but there wasn't any saloon. Maybe he came in on a freight, but the brakeman hadn't seen him. They couldn't find no letters nor nothing on him; nothing but an old penknife in his pocket and the wishbone of a chicken wrapped up in a piece of paper, and some poetry.'

`Some poetry?' we exclaimed.

`I remember,' said Frances. `It was "The Old Oaken Bucket," cut out of a newspaper and nearly worn out. Ole Iverson brought it into the office and showed it to me.'

`Now, wasn't that strange, Miss Frances?' Tony asked thoughtfully. `What would anybody want to kill themselves in summer for? In threshing time, too! It's nice everywhere then.'

`So it is, Antonia,' said Mrs. Harling heartily. `Maybe I'll go home and help you thresh next summer. Isn't that taffy nearly ready to eat? I've been smelling it a long while.'

There was a basic harmony between Antonia and her mistress. They had strong, independent natures, both of them. They knew what they liked, and were not always trying to imitate other people. They loved children and animals and music, and rough play and digging in the earth. They liked to prepare rich, hearty food and to see people eat it; to make up soft white beds and to see youngsters asleep in them. They ridiculed conceited people and were quick to help unfortunate ones. Deep down in each of them there was a kind of hearty joviality, a relish of life, not over-delicate, but very invigorating. I never tried to define it, but I was distinctly conscious of it. I could not imagine Antonia's living for a week in any other house in Black Hawk than the Harlings'.

VII

WINTER LIES TOO LONG in country towns; hangs on until it is stale and shabby, old and sullen. On the farm the weather was the great fact, and men's affairs went on underneath it, as the streams creep under the ice. But in Black Hawk the scene of human life was spread out shrunken and pinched, frozen down to the bare stalk.

Through January and February I went to the river with the Harlings on clear nights, and we skated up to the big island and made bonfires on the frozen sand. But by March the ice was rough and choppy, and the snow on the river bluffs was grey and mournful-looking. I was tired of school, tired of winter clothes, of the rutted streets, of the dirty drifts and the piles of cinders that had lain in the yards so long. There was only one break in the dreary monotony of that month: when Blind d'Arnault, the Negro pianist, came to town. He gave a concert at the Opera House on Monday night, and he and his manager spent Saturday and Sunday at our comfortable hotel. Mrs. Harling had known d'Arnault for years. She told Antonia she had better go to see Tiny that Saturday evening, as there would certainly be music at the Boys' Home.

Saturday night after supper I ran downtown to the hotel and slipped quietly into the parlour. The chairs and sofas were already occupied, and the air smelled pleasantly of cigar smoke. The parlour had once been two rooms, and the floor was swaybacked where the partition had been cut away. The wind from without made waves in the long carpet. A coal stove glowed at either end of the room, and the grand piano in the middle stood open.

There was an atmosphere of unusual freedom about the house that night, for Mrs. Gardener had gone to Omaha for a week. Johnnie had been having drinks with the guests until he was rather absent-minded. It was Mrs. Gardener who ran the business and looked after everything. Her husband stood at the desk and welcomed incoming travellers. He was a popular fellow, but no manager.

Mrs. Gardener was admittedly the best-dressed woman in Black Hawk, drove the best horse, and had a smart trap and a little white-and-gold sleigh. She seemed indifferent to her possessions, was not half so solicitous about them as her friends were. She was tall, dark, severe, with something Indian-like in the rigid immobility of her face. Her manner was cold, and she talked little. Guests felt that they were receiving, not conferring, a favour when they stayed at her house. Even the smartest travelling men were flattered when Mrs. Gardener stopped to chat with them for a moment. The patrons of the hotel were divided into two classes: those who had seen Mrs. Gardener's diamonds, and those who had not.

When I stole into the parlour, Anson Kirkpatrick, Marshall Field's man, was at the piano, playing airs from a musical comedy then running in Chicago. He was a dapper little Irishman, very vain, homely as a monkey, with friends everywhere, and a sweetheart in every port, like a sailor. I did not know all the men who were sitting about, but I recognized a furniture salesman from Kansas City, a drug man, and Willy O'Reilly, who travelled for a jewellery house and sold musical instruments. The talk was all about good and bad hotels, actors and actresses and musical prodigies. I learned that Mrs. Gardener had gone to Omaha to hear Booth and Barrett, who were to play there next week, and that Mary Anderson was having a great success in `A Winter's Tale,' in London.

The door from the office opened, and Johnnie Gardener came in, directing Blind d'Arnault--he would never consent to be led. He was a heavy, bulky mulatto, on short legs, and he came tapping the floor in front of him with his gold-headed cane. His yellow face was lifted in the light, with a show of white teeth, all grinning, and his shrunken, papery eyelids lay motionless over his blind eyes.

`Good evening, gentlemen. No ladies here? Good evening, gentlemen. We going to have a little music? Some of you gentlemen going to play for me this evening?' It was the soft, amiable Negro voice, like those I remembered from early childhood, with the note of docile subservience in it. He had the Negro head, too; almost no head at all; nothing behind the ears but folds of neck under close-clipped wool. He would have been repulsive if his face had not been so kindly and happy. It was the happiest face I had seen since I left Virginia.

He felt his way directly to the piano. The moment he sat down, I noticed the nervous infirmity of which Mrs. Harling had told me. When he was sitting, or standing still, he swayed back and forth incessantly, like a rocking toy. At the piano, he swayed in time to the music, and when he was not playing, his body kept up this motion, like an empty mill grinding on. He found the pedals and tried them, ran his yellow hands up and down the keys a few times, tinkling off scales, then turned to the company.

'She seems all right, gentlemen. Nothing happened to her since the last time I was here. Mrs. Gardener, she always has this piano tuned up before I come. Now gentlemen, I expect you've all got grand voices. Seems like we might have some good old plantation songs tonight.'

The men gathered round him, as he began to play 'My Old Kentucky Home.' They sang one Negro melody after another, while the mulatto sat rocking himself, his head thrown back, his yellow face lifted, his shrivelled eyelids never fluttering.

He was born in the Far South, on the d'Arnault plantation, where the spirit if not the fact of slavery persisted. When he was three weeks old, he had an illness which left him totally blind. As soon as he was old enough to sit up alone and toddle about, another affliction, the nervous motion of his body, became apparent. His mother, a buxom young Negro wench who was laundress for the d'Arnaults, concluded that her blind baby was 'not right' in his head, and she was ashamed of him. She loved him devotedly, but he was so ugly, with his sunken eyes and his 'fidgets,' that she hid him away from people. All the dainties she brought down from the Big House were for the blind child, and she beat and cuffed her other children whenever she found them teasing him or trying to get his chicken-bone away from him. He began to talk early, remembered everything he heard, and his mammy said he 'wasn't all wrong.' She named him Samson, because he was blind, but on the plantation he was known as 'yellow Martha's simple child.' He was docile and obedient, but when he was six years old he began to run away from home, always taking the same direction. He felt his way through the lilacs, along the boxwood hedge, up to the south wing of the Big House, where Miss Nellie d'Arnault practised the piano every morning. This angered his mother more than anything else he could have done; she was so ashamed of his ugliness that she couldn't bear to have white folks see him. Whenever she caught him slipping away from the cabin, she whipped him unmercifully, and told him what dreadful things old Mr. d'Arnault would do to him if he ever found him near the Big House. But the next time Samson had a chance, he ran away again. If Miss d'Arnault stopped practising for a moment and went toward the window, she saw this hideous little pickaninny, dressed in an old piece of sacking, standing in the open space between the hollyhock rows, his body rocking automatically, his blind face lifted to the sun and wearing an expression of idiotic rapture. Often she was tempted to tell Martha that the child must be kept at home, but somehow the memory of his foolish, happy face deterred her. She remembered that his sense of hearing was nearly all he had-- though it did not occur to her that he might have more of it than other children.

One day Samson was standing thus while Miss Nellie was playing her lesson to her music-teacher. The windows were open. He heard them get up from the piano, talk a little while, and then leave the room. He heard the door close after them. He crept up to the front windows and stuck his head in: there was no one there. He could always detect the presence of anyone in a room. He put one foot over the window-sill and straddled it.

His mother had told him over and over how his master would give him to the big mastiff if he ever found him 'meddling.' Samson had got too near the mastiff's kennel once, and had felt his terrible breath in his face. He thought about that, but he pulled in his other foot.

Through the dark he found his way to the Thing, to its mouth. He touched it softly, and it answered softly, kindly. He shivered and stood still. Then he began to feel it all over, ran his finger-tips along the slippery sides, embraced the carved legs, tried to get some conception of its shape and size, of the space it occupied in primeval night. It was cold and hard, and like nothing else in his black universe. He went back to its mouth, began at one end of the keyboard and felt his way down into the mellow thunder, as far as he could go. He seemed to know that it must be done with the fingers, not with the fists or the feet. He approached this highly artificial instrument through a mere instinct, and coupled himself to it, as if he knew it was to piece him out and make a whole creature of him. After he had tried over all the sounds, he began to finger out passages from things Miss Nellie had been practising, passages that were already his, that lay under the bone of his pinched, conical little skull, definite as animal desires.

The door opened; Miss Nellie and her music-master stood behind it, but blind Samson, who was so sensitive to presences, did not know they were there. He was feeling out the pattern that lay all ready-made on the big and little keys.

When he paused for a moment, because the sound was wrong and he wanted another, Miss Nellie spoke softly. He whirled about in a spasm of terror, leaped forward in the dark, struck his head on the open window, and fell screaming and bleeding to the floor. He had what his mother called a fit. The doctor came and gave him opium.

When Samson was well again, his young mistress led him back to the piano. Several teachers experimented with him. They found he had absolute pitch, and a remarkable memory. As a very young child he could repeat, after a fashion, any composition that was played for him. No matter how many wrong notes he struck, he never lost the intention of a passage, he brought the substance of it across by irregular and astonishing means. He wore his teachers out. He could never learn like other people, never acquired any finish. He was always a Negro prodigy who played barbarously and wonderfully. As piano-playing, it was perhaps abominable, but as music it was something real, vitalized by a sense of rhythm that was stronger than his other physical senses--that not only filled his dark mind, but worried his body incessantly. To hear him, to watch him, was to see a Negro enjoying himself as only a Negro can. It was as if all the agreeable sensations possible to creatures of flesh and blood were heaped up on those black-and-white keys, and he were gloating over them and trickling them through his yellow fingers.

In the middle of a crashing waltz, d'Arnault suddenly began to play softly, and, turning to one of the men who stood behind him, whispered, `Somebody dancing in there.' He jerked his bullet-head toward the dining-room. `I hear little feet--girls, I spect.'

Anson Kirkpatrick mounted a chair and peeped over the transom. Springing down, he wrenched open the doors and ran out into the dining-room. Tiny and Lena, Antonia and Mary Dusak, were waltzing in the middle of the floor. They separated and fled toward the kitchen, giggling.

Kirkpatrick caught Tiny by the elbows. `What's the matter with you girls? Dancing out here by yourselves, when there's a roomful of lonesome men on the other side of the partition! Introduce me to your friends, Tiny.'

The girls, still laughing, were trying to escape. Tiny looked alarmed. `Mrs. Gardener wouldn't like it,' she protested. `She'd be awful mad if you was to come out here and dance with us.'

`Mrs. Gardener's in Omaha, girl. Now, you're Lena, are you?--and you're Tony and you're Mary. Have I got you all straight?'

O'Reilly and the others began to pile the chairs on the tables. Johnnie Gardener ran in from the office.

`Easy, boys, easy!' he entreated them. `You'll wake the cook, and there'll be the devil to pay for me. She won't hear the music, but she'll be down the minute anything's moved in the dining-room.'

`Oh, what do you care, Johnnie? Fire the cook and wire Molly to bring another. Come along, nobody'll tell tales.'

Johnnie shook his head. `'S a fact, boys,' he said confidentially. `If I take a drink in Black Hawk, Molly knows it in Omaha!'

His guests laughed and slapped him on the shoulder. `Oh, we'll make it all right with Molly. Get your back up, Johnnie.'

Molly was Mrs. Gardener's name, of course. `Molly Bawn' was painted in large blue letters on the glossy white sides of the hotel bus, and `Molly' was engraved inside Johnnie's ring and on his watch-case--doubtless on his heart, too. He was an affectionate little man, and he thought his wife a wonderful woman; he knew that without her he would hardly be more than a clerk in some other man's hotel.

At a word from Kirkpatrick, d'Arnault spread himself out over the piano, and began to draw the dance music out of it, while the perspiration shone on his short wool and on his uplifted face. He looked like some glistening African god of pleasure, full of strong, savage blood. Whenever the dancers paused to change partners or to catch breath, he would boom out softly, `Who's that goin' back on me? One of these city gentlemen, I bet! Now, you girls, you ain't goin' to let that floor get cold?'

Antonia seemed frightened at first, and kept looking questioningly at Lena and Tiny over Willy O'Reilly's shoulder. Tiny Soderball was trim and slender, with lively little feet and pretty ankles--she wore her dresses very short. She was quicker in speech, lighter in movement and manner than the other girls. Mary Dusak was broad and brown of countenance, slightly marked by smallpox, but handsome for all that. She had beautiful chestnut hair, coils of it; her forehead was low and smooth, and her commanding dark eyes regarded the world indifferently and fearlessly. She looked bold and resourceful and unscrupulous, and she was all of these. They were handsome girls, had the fresh colour of their country upbringing, and in their eyes that brilliancy which is called--by no metaphor, alas!--'the light of youth.'

D'Arnault played until his manager came and shut the piano. Before he left us, he showed us his gold watch which struck the hours, and a topaz ring, given him by some Russian nobleman who delighted in Negro melodies, and had heard d'Arnault play in New Orleans. At last he tapped his way upstairs, after bowing to everybody, docile and happy. I walked home with Antonia. We were so excited that we dreaded to go to bed. We lingered a long while at the Harlings' gate, whispering in the cold until the restlessness was slowly chilled out of us.

VIII

THE HARLING CHILDREN and I were never happier, never felt more contented and secure, than in the weeks of spring which broke that long winter. We were out all day in the thin sunshine, helping Mrs. Harling and Tony break the ground and plant the garden, dig around the orchard trees, tie up vines and clip the hedges. Every morning, before I was up, I could hear Tony singing in the garden rows. After the apple and cherry trees broke into bloom, we ran about under them, hunting for the new nests the birds were building, throwing clods at each other, and playing hide-and-seek with Nina. Yet the summer which was to change everything was coming nearer every day. When boys and girls are growing up, life can't stand still, not even in the quietest of country towns; and they have to grow up, whether they will or no. That is what their elders are always forgetting.

It must have been in June, for Mrs. Harling and Antonia were preserving cherries, when I stopped one morning to tell them that a dancing pavilion had come to town. I had seen two drays hauling the canvas and painted poles up from the depot.

That afternoon three cheerful-looking Italians strolled about Black Hawk, looking at everything, and with them was a dark, stout woman who wore a long gold watch-chain about her neck and carried a black lace parasol. They seemed especially interested in children and vacant lots. When I overtook them and stopped to say a word, I found them affable and confiding. They told me they worked in Kansas City in the winter, and in summer they went out among the farming towns with their tent and taught dancing. When business fell off in one place, they moved on to another.

The dancing pavilion was put up near the Danish laundry, on a vacant lot surrounded by tall, arched cottonwood trees. It was very much like a merry-go-round tent, with open sides and gay flags flying from the poles. Before the week was over, all the ambitious mothers were sending their children to the afternoon dancing class. At three o'clock one met little girls in white dresses and little boys in the round-collared shirts of the time, hurrying along the sidewalk on their way to the tent. Mrs. Vanni received them at the entrance, always dressed in lavender with a great deal of black lace, her important watch-chain lying on her bosom. She wore her hair on the top of her head, built up in a black tower, with red coral combs. When she smiled, she showed two rows of strong, crooked yellow teeth. She taught the little children herself, and her husband, the harpist, taught the older ones.

Often the mothers brought their fancywork and sat on the shady side of the tent during the lesson. The popcorn man wheeled his glass wagon under the big cottonwood by the door, and lounged in the sun, sure of a good trade when the dancing was over. Mr. Jensen, the Danish laundryman, used to bring a chair from his porch and sit out in the grass plot. Some ragged little boys from the depot sold pop and iced lemonade under a white umbrella at the corner, and made faces at the spruce youngsters who came to dance. That vacant lot soon became the most cheerful place in town. Even on the hottest afternoons the cottonwoods made a rustling shade, and the air smelled of popcorn and melted butter, and Bouncing Bets wilting in the sun. Those hardy flowers had run away from the laundryman's garden, and the grass in the middle of the lot was pink with them.

The Vannis kept exemplary order, and closed every evening at the hour suggested by the city council. When Mrs. Vanni gave the signal, and the harp struck up 'Home, Sweet Home,' all Black Hawk knew it was ten o'clock. You could set your watch by that tune as confidently as by the roundhouse whistle.

At last there was something to do in those long, empty summer evenings, when the married people sat like images on their front porches, and the boys and girls tramped and tramped the board sidewalks--northward to the edge of the open prairie, south to the depot, then back again to the post-office, the ice-cream parlour, the butcher shop. Now there was a place where the girls could wear their new dresses, and where one could laugh aloud without being reproved by the ensuing silence. That silence seemed to ooze out of the ground, to hang under the foliage of the black maple trees with the bats and shadows. Now it was broken by lighthearted sounds. First the deep purring of Mr. Vanni's harp came in silvery ripples through the blackness of the dusty-smelling night; then the violins fell in--one of them was almost like a flute. They called so archly, so seductively, that our feet hurried toward the tent of themselves. Why hadn't we had a tent before?

Dancing became popular now, just as roller skating had been the summer before. The Progressive Euchre Club arranged with the Vannis for the exclusive use of the floor on Tuesday and Friday nights. At other times anyone could dance who paid his money and was orderly; the railroad men, the roundhouse mechanics, the delivery boys, the iceman, the farm-hands who lived near enough to ride into town after their day's work was over.

I never missed a Saturday night dance. The tent was open until midnight then. The country boys came in from farms eight and ten miles away, and all the country girls were on the floor--Antonia and Lena and Tiny, and the Danish laundry girls and their friends. I was not the only boy who found these dances gayer than the others. The young men who belonged to the Progressive Euchre Club used to drop in late and risk a tiff with their sweethearts and general condemnation for a waltz with `the hired girls.'

IX

THERE WAS A CURIOUS social situation in Black Hawk. All the young men felt the attraction of the fine, well-set-up country girls who had come to town to earn a living, and, in nearly every case, to help the father struggle out of debt, or to make it possible for the younger children of the family to go to school.

Those girls had grown up in the first bitter-hard times, and had got little schooling themselves. But the younger brothers and sisters, for whom they made such sacrifices and who have had `advantages,' never seem to me, when I meet them now, half as interesting or as well educated. The older girls, who helped to break up the wild sod, learned so much from life, from poverty, from their mothers and grandmothers; they had all, like Antonia, been early awakened and made observant by coming at a tender age from an old country to a new.

I can remember a score of these country girls who were in service in Black Hawk during the few years I lived there, and I can remember something unusual and engaging about each of them. Physically they were almost a race apart, and out-of-door work had given them a vigour which, when they got over their first shyness on coming to town, developed into a positive carriage and freedom of movement, and made them conspicuous among Black Hawk women.

That was before the day of high-school athletics. Girls who had to walk more than half a mile to school were pitied. There was not a tennis-court in the town; physical exercise was thought rather inelegant for the daughters of well-to-do families. Some of the high-school girls were jolly and pretty, but they stayed indoors in winter because of the cold, and in summer because of the heat. When one danced with them, their bodies never moved inside their clothes; their muscles seemed to ask but one thing--not to be disturbed. I remember those girls merely as faces in the schoolroom, gay and rosy, or listless and dull, cut off below the shoulders, like cherubs, by the ink-smeared tops of the high desks that were surely put there to make us round-shouldered and hollow-chested.

The daughters of Black Hawk merchants had a confident, unenquiring belief that they were `refined,' and that the country girls, who `worked out,' were not. The American farmers in our county were quite as hard-pressed as their neighbours from other countries. All alike had come to Nebraska with little capital and no knowledge of the soil they must subdue. All had borrowed money on their land. But no matter in what straits the Pennsylvanian or Virginian found himself, he would not let his daughters go out into service. Unless his girls could teach a country school, they sat at home in poverty.

The Bohemian and Scandinavian girls could not get positions as teachers, because they had had no opportunity to learn the language. Determined to help in the struggle to clear the homestead from debt, they had no alternative but to go into service. Some of them, after they came to town, remained as serious and as discreet in behaviour as they had been when they ploughed and herded on their father's farm. Others, like the three Bohemian Marys, tried to make up for the years of youth they had lost. But every one of them did what she had set out to do, and sent home those hard-earned dollars. The girls I knew were always helping to pay for ploughs and reapers, brood-sows, or steers to fatten.

One result of this family solidarity was that the foreign farmers in our county were the first to become prosperous. After the fathers were out of debt, the daughters married the sons of neighbours--usually of like nationality--and the girls who once worked in Black Hawk kitchens are to-day managing big farms and fine families of their own; their children are better off than the children of the town women they used to serve.

I thought the attitude of the town people toward these girls very stupid. If I told my schoolmates that Lena Lingard's grandfather was a clergyman, and much respected in Norway, they looked at me blankly. What did it matter? All foreigners were ignorant people who couldn't speak English. There was not a man in Black Hawk who had the intelligence or cultivation, much less the personal distinction, of Antonia's father. Yet people saw no difference between her and the three Marys; they were all Bohemians, all `hired girls.'

I always knew I should live long enough to see my country girls come into their own, and I have. To-day the best that a harassed Black Hawk merchant can hope for is to sell provisions and farm machinery and automobiles to the rich farms where that first crop of stalwart Bohemian and Scandinavian girls are now the mistresses.

The Black Hawk boys looked forward to marrying Black Hawk girls, and living in a brand-new little house with best chairs that must not be sat upon, and hand-painted china that must not be used. But sometimes a young fellow would look up from his ledger, or out through the grating of his father's bank, and let his eyes follow Lena Lingard, as she passed the window with her slow, undulating walk, or Tiny Soderball, tripping by in her short skirt and striped stockings.

The country girls were considered a menace to the social order. Their beauty shone out too boldly against a conventional background. But anxious mothers need have felt no alarm. They mistook the mettle of their sons. The respect for respectability was stronger than any desire in Black Hawk youth.

Our young man of position was like the son of a royal house; the boy who swept out his office or drove his delivery wagon might frolic with the jolly country girls, but he himself must sit all evening in a plush parlour where conversation dragged so perceptibly that the father often came in and made blundering efforts to warm up the atmosphere. On his way home from his dull call, he would perhaps meet Tony and Lena, coming along the sidewalk whispering to each other, or the three Bohemian Marys in their long plush coats and caps, comporting themselves with a dignity that only made their eventful histories the more piquant. If he went to the hotel to see a travelling man on business, there was Tiny, arching her shoulders at him like a kitten. If he went into the laundry to get his collars, there were the four Danish girls, smiling up from their ironing-boards, with their white throats and their pink cheeks.

The three Marys were the heroines of a cycle of scandalous stories, which the old men were fond of relating as they sat about the cigar-stand in the drugstore. Mary Dusak had been housekeeper for a bachelor rancher from Boston, and after several years in his service she was forced to retire from the world for a short time. Later she came back to town to take the place of her friend, Mary Svoboda, who was similarly embarrassed. The three Marys were considered as dangerous as high explosives to have about the kitchen, yet they were such good cooks and such admirable housekeepers that they never had to look for a place.

The Vannis' tent brought the town boys and the country girls together on neutral ground. Sylvester Lovett, who was cashier in his father's bank, always found his way to the tent on Saturday night. He took all the dances Lena Lingard would give him, and even grew bold enough to walk home with her. If his sisters or their friends happened to be among the onlookers on `popular nights,' Sylvester stood back in the shadow under the cottonwood trees, smoking and watching Lena with a harassed expression. Several times I stumbled upon him there in the dark, and I felt rather sorry for him. He reminded me of Ole Benson, who used to sit on the drawside and watch Lena herd her cattle. Later in the summer, when Lena went home for a week to visit her mother, I heard from Antonia that young Lovett drove all the way out there to see her, and took her buggy-riding. In my ingenuousness I hoped that Sylvester would marry Lena, and thus give all the country girls a better position in the town.

Sylvester dallied about Lena until he began to make mistakes in his work; had to stay at the bank until after dark to make his books balance. He was daft about her, and everyone knew it. To escape from his predicament he ran away with a widow six years older than himself, who owned a half-section. This remedy worked, apparently. He never looked at Lena again, nor lifted his eyes as he ceremoniously tipped his hat when he happened to meet her on the sidewalk.

So that was what they were like, I thought, these white-handed, high-collared clerks and bookkeepers! I used to glare at young Lovett from a distance and only wished I had some way of showing my contempt for him.

X

IT WAS AT THE Vannis' tent that Antonia was discovered. Hitherto she had been looked upon more as a ward of the Harlings than as one of the `hired girls.' She had lived in their house and yard and garden; her thoughts never seemed to stray outside that little kingdom. But after the tent came to town she began to go about with Tiny and Lena and their friends. The Vannis often said that Antonia was the best dancer of them all. I sometimes heard murmurs in the crowd outside the pavilion that Mrs. Harling would soon have her hands full with that girl. The young men began to joke with each other about `the Harlings' Tony' as they did about `the Marshalls' Anna' or `the Gardeners' Tiny.'

Antonia talked and thought of nothing but the tent. She hummed the dance tunes all day. When supper was late, she hurried with her dishes, dropped and smashed them in her excitement. At the first call of the music, she became irresponsible. If she hadn't time to dress, she merely flung off her apron and shot out of the kitchen door. Sometimes I went with her; the moment the lighted tent came into view she would break into a run, like a boy. There were always partners waiting for her; she began to dance before she got her breath.

Antonia's success at the tent had its consequences. The iceman lingered too long now, when he came into the covered porch to fill the refrigerator. The delivery boys hung about the kitchen when they brought the groceries. Young farmers who were in town for Saturday came tramping through the yard to the back door to engage dances, or to invite Tony to parties and picnics. Lena and Norwegian Anna dropped in to help her with her work, so that she could get away early. The boys who brought her home after the dances sometimes laughed at the back gate and wakened Mr. Harling from his first sleep. A crisis was inevitable.

One Saturday night Mr. Harling had gone down to the cellar for beer. As he came up the stairs in the dark, he heard scuffling on the back porch, and then the sound of a vigorous slap. He looked out through the side door in time to see a pair of long legs vaulting over the picket fence. Antonia was standing there, angry and excited. Young Harry Paine, who was to marry his employer's daughter on Monday, had come to the tent with a crowd of friends and danced all evening. Afterward, he begged Antonia to let him walk home with her. She said she supposed he was a nice young man, as he was one of Miss Frances's friends, and she didn't mind. On the back porch he tried to kiss her, and when she protested-- because he was going to be married on Monday--he caught her and kissed her until she got one hand free and slapped him.

Mr. Harling put his beer-bottles down on the table. `This is what I've been expecting, Antonia. You've been going with girls who have a reputation for being free and easy, and now you've got the same reputation. I won't have this and that fellow tramping about my back yard all the time. This is the end of it, tonight. It stops, short. You can quit going to these dances, or you can hunt another place. Think it over.'

The next morning when Mrs. Harling and Frances tried to reason with Antonia, they found her agitated but determined. `Stop going to the tent?' she panted. `I wouldn't think of it for a minute! My own father couldn't make me stop! Mr. Harling ain't my boss outside my work. I won't give up my friends, either. The boys I go with are nice fellows. I thought Mr. Paine was all right, too, because he used to come here. I guess I gave him a red face for his wedding, all right!' she blazed out indignantly.

`You'll have to do one thing or the other, Antonia,' Mrs. Harling told her decidedly. `I can't go back on what Mr. Harling has said. This is his house.'

`Then I'll just leave, Mrs. Harling. Lena's been wanting me to get a place closer to her for a long while. Mary Svoboda's going away from the Cutters' to work at the hotel, and I can have her place.'

Mrs. Harling rose from her chair. `Antonia, if you go to the Cutters' to work, you cannot come back to this house again. You know what that man is. It will be the ruin of you.'

Tony snatched up the teakettle and began to pour boiling water over the glasses, laughing excitedly. `Oh, I can take care of myself! I'm a lot stronger than Cutter is. They pay four dollars there, and there's no children. The work's nothing; I can have every evening, and be out a lot in the afternoons.'

`I thought you liked children. Tony, what's come over you?'

`I don't know, something has.' Antonia tossed her head and set her jaw. `A girl like me has got to take her good times when she can. Maybe there won't be any tent next year. I guess I want to have my fling, like the other girls.'

Mrs. Harling gave a short, harsh laugh. `If you go to work for the Cutters, you're likely to have a fling that you won't get up from in a hurry.'

Frances said, when she told grandmother and me about this scene, that every pan and plate and cup on the shelves trembled when her mother walked out of the kitchen. Mrs. Harling declared bitterly that she wished she had never let herself get fond of Antonia.

XI

WICK CUTTER WAS the money-lender who had fleeced poor Russian Peter. When a farmer once got into the habit of going to Cutter, it was like gambling or the lottery; in an hour of discouragement he went back.

Cutter's first name was Wycliffe, and he liked to talk about his pious bringing-up. He contributed regularly to the Protestant churches, `for sentiment's sake,' as he said with a flourish of the hand. He came from a town in Iowa where there were a great many Swedes, and could speak a little Swedish, which gave him a great advantage with the early Scandinavian settlers.

In every frontier settlement there are men who have come there to escape restraint. Cutter was one of the `fast set' of Black Hawk business men. He was an inveterate gambler, though a poor loser. When we saw a light burning in his office late at night, we knew that a game of poker was going on. Cutter boasted that he never drank anything stronger than sherry, and he said he got his start in life by saving the money that other young men spent for cigars. He was full of moral maxims for boys. When he came to our house on business, he quoted `Poor Richard's Almanack' to me, and told me he was delighted to find a town boy who could milk a cow. He was particularly affable to grandmother, and whenever they met he would begin at once to talk about `the good old times' and simple living. I detested his pink, bald head, and his yellow whiskers, always soft and glistening. It was said he brushed them every night, as a woman does her hair. His white teeth looked factory-made. His skin was red and rough, as if from perpetual sunburn; he often went away to hot springs to take mud baths. He was notoriously dissolute with women. Two Swedish girls who had lived in his house were the worse for the experience. One of them he had taken to Omaha and established in the business for which he had fitted her. He still visited her.

Cutter lived in a state of perpetual warfare with his wife, and yet, apparently, they never thought of separating. They dwelt in a fussy, scroll-work house, painted white and buried in thick evergreens, with a fussy white fence and barn. Cutter thought he knew a great deal about horses, and usually had a colt which he was training for the track. On Sunday mornings one could see him out at the fair grounds, speeding around the race-course in his trotting-buggy, wearing yellow gloves and a black-and-white-check travelling cap, his whiskers blowing back in the breeze. If there were any boys about, Cutter would offer one of them a quarter to hold the stop-watch, and then drive off, saying he had no change and would `fix it up next time.' No one could cut his lawn or wash his buggy to suit him. He was so fastidious and prim about his place that a boy would go to a good deal of trouble to throw a dead cat into his back yard, or to dump a sackful of tin cans in his alley. It was a peculiar combination of old-maidishness and licentiousness that made Cutter seem so despicable.

He had certainly met his match when he married Mrs. Cutter. She was a terrifying-looking person; almost a giantess in height, raw-boned, with iron-grey hair, a face always flushed, and prominent, hysterical eyes. When she meant to be entertaining and agreeable, she nodded her head incessantly and snapped her eyes at one. Her teeth were long and curved, like a horse's; people said babies always cried if she smiled at them. Her face had a kind of fascination for me: it was the very colour and shape of anger. There was a gleam of something akin to insanity in her full, intense eyes. She was formal in manner, and made calls in rustling, steel-grey brocades and a tall bonnet with bristling aigrettes.

Mrs. Cutter painted china so assiduously that even her wash-bowls and pitchers, and her husband's shaving-mug, were covered with violets and lilies. Once, when Cutter was exhibiting some of his wife's china to a caller, he dropped a piece. Mrs. Cutter put her handkerchief to her lips as if she were going to faint and said grandly: `Mr. Cutter, you have broken all the Commandments--spare the finger-bowls!'

They quarrelled from the moment Cutter came into the house until they went to bed at night, and their hired girls reported these scenes to the town at large. Mrs. Cutter had several times cut paragraphs about unfaithful husbands out of the newspapers and mailed them to Cutter in a disguised handwriting. Cutter would come home at noon, find the mutilated journal in the paper-rack, and triumphantly fit the clipping into the space from which it had been cut. Those two could quarrel all morning about whether he ought to put on his heavy or his light underwear, and all evening about whether he had taken cold or not.

The Cutters had major as well as minor subjects for dispute. The chief of these was the question of inheritance: Mrs. Cutter told her husband it was plainly his fault they had no children. He insisted that Mrs. Cutter had purposely remained childless, with the determination to outlive him and to share his property with her `people,' whom he detested. To this she would reply that unless he changed his mode of life, she would certainly outlive him. After listening to her insinuations about his physical soundness, Cutter would resume his dumb-bell practice for a month, or rise daily at the hour when his wife most liked to sleep, dress noisily, and drive out to the track with his trotting-horse.

Once when they had quarrelled about household expenses, Mrs. Cutter put on her brocade and went among their friends soliciting orders for painted china, saying that Mr. Cutter had compelled her `to live by her brush.' Cutter wasn't shamed as she had expected; he was delighted!

Cutter often threatened to chop down the cedar trees which half-buried the house. His wife declared she would leave him if she were stripped of the `privacy' which she felt these trees afforded her. That was his opportunity, surely; but he never cut down the trees. The Cutters seemed to find their relations to each other interesting and stimulating, and certainly the rest of us found them so. Wick Cutter was different from any other rascal I have ever known, but I have found Mrs. Cutters all over the world; sometimes founding new religions, sometimes being forcibly fed--easily recognizable, even when superficially tamed.

XII

AFTER ANTONIA WENT TO live with the Cutters, she seemed to care about nothing but picnics and parties and having a good time. When she was not going to a dance, she sewed until midnight. Her new clothes were the subject of caustic comment. Under Lena's direction she copied Mrs. Gardener's new party dress and Mrs. Smith's street costume so ingeniously in cheap materials that those ladies were greatly annoyed, and Mrs. Cutter, who was jealous of them, was secretly pleased.

Tony wore gloves now, and high-heeled shoes and feathered bonnets, and she went downtown nearly every afternoon with Tiny and Lena and the Marshalls' Norwegian Anna. We high-school boys used to linger on the playground at the afternoon recess to watch them as they came tripping down the hill along the board sidewalk, two and two. They were growing prettier every day, but as they passed us, I used to think with pride that Antonia, like Snow-White in the fairy tale, was still `fairest of them all.'

Being a senior now, I got away from school early. Sometimes I overtook the girls downtown and coaxed them into the ice-cream parlour, where they would sit chattering and laughing, telling me all the news from the country.

I remember how angry Tiny Soderball made me one afternoon. She declared she had heard grandmother was going to make a Baptist preacher of me. `I guess you'll have to stop dancing and wear a white necktie then. Won't he look funny, girls?'

Lena laughed. `You'll have to hurry up, Jim. If you're going to be a preacher, I want you to marry me. You must promise to marry us all, and then baptize the babies.'

Norwegian Anna, always dignified, looked at her reprovingly.

`Baptists don't believe in christening babies, do they, Jim?'

I told her I didn't know what they believed, and didn't care, and that I certainly wasn't going to be a preacher.

`That's too bad,' Tiny simpered. She was in a teasing mood. `You'd make such a good one. You're so studious. Maybe you'd like to be a professor. You used to teach Tony, didn't you?'

Antonia broke in. `I've set my heart on Jim being a doctor. You'd be good with sick people, Jim. Your grandmother's trained you up so nice. My papa always said you were an awful smart boy.'

I said I was going to be whatever I pleased. `Won't you be surprised, Miss Tiny, if I turn out to be a regular devil of a fellow?'

They laughed until a glance from Norwegian Anna checked them; the high-school principal had just come into the front part of the shop to buy bread for supper. Anna knew the whisper was going about that I was a sly one. People said there must be something queer about a boy who showed no interest in girls of his own age, but who could be lively enough when he was with Tony and Lena or the three Marys.

The enthusiasm for the dance, which the Vannis had kindled, did not at once die out. After the tent left town, the Euchre Club became the Owl Club, and gave dances in the Masonic Hall once a week. I was invited to join, but declined. I was moody and restless that winter, and tired of the people I saw every day. Charley Harling was already at Annapolis, while I was still sitting in Black Hawk, answering to my name at roll-call every morning, rising from my desk at the sound of a bell and marching out like the grammar-school children. Mrs. Harling was a little cool toward me, because I continued to champion Antonia. What was there for me to do after supper? Usually I had learned next day's lessons by the time I left the school building, and I couldn't sit still and read forever.

In the evening I used to prowl about, hunting for diversion. There lay the familiar streets, frozen with snow or liquid with mud. They led to the houses of good people who were putting the babies to bed, or simply sitting still before the parlour stove, digesting their supper. Black Hawk had two saloons. One of them was admitted, even by the church people, to be as respectable as a saloon could be. Handsome Anton Jelinek, who had rented his homestead and come to town, was the proprietor. In his saloon there were long tables where the Bohemian and German farmers could eat the lunches they brought from home while they drank their beer. Jelinek kept rye bread on hand and smoked fish and strong imported cheeses to please the foreign palate. I liked to drop into his bar-room and listen to the talk. But one day he overtook me on the street and clapped me on the shoulder.

`Jim,' he said, `I am good friends with you and I always like to see you. But you know how the church people think about saloons. Your grandpa has always treated me fine, and I don't like to have you come into my place, because I know he don't like it, and it puts me in bad with him.'

So I was shut out of that.

One could hang about the drugstore; and listen to the old men who sat there every evening, talking politics and telling raw stories. One could go to the cigar factory and chat with the old German who raised canaries for sale, and look at his stuffed birds. But whatever you began with him, the talk went back to taxidermy. There was the depot, of course; I often went down to see the night train come in, and afterward sat awhile with the disconsolate telegrapher who was always hoping to be transferred to Omaha or Denver, `where there was some life.' He was sure to bring out his pictures of actresses and dancers. He got them with cigarette coupons, and nearly smoked himself to death to possess these desired forms and faces. For a change, one could talk to the station agent; but he was another malcontent; spent all his spare time writing letters to officials requesting a transfer. He wanted to get back to Wyoming where he could go trout-fishing on Sundays. He used to say `there was nothing in life for him but trout streams, ever since he'd lost his twins.'

These were the distractions I had to choose from. There were no other lights burning downtown after nine o'clock. On starlight nights I used to pace up and down those long, cold streets, scowling at the little, sleeping houses on either side, with their storm-windows and covered back porches. They were flimsy shelters, most of them poorly built of light wood, with spindle porch-posts horribly mutilated by the turning-lathe. Yet for all their frailness, how much jealousy and envy and unhappiness some of them managed to contain! The life that went on in them seemed to me made up of evasions and negations; shifts to save cooking, to save washing and cleaning, devices to propitiate the tongue of gossip. This guarded mode of existence was like living under a tyranny. People's speech, their voices, their very glances, became furtive and repressed. Every individual taste, every natural appetite, was bridled by caution. The people asleep in those houses, I thought, tried to live like the mice in their own kitchens; to make no noise, to leave no trace, to slip over the surface of things in the dark. The growing piles of ashes and cinders in the back yards were the only evidence that the wasteful, consuming process of life went on at all. On Tuesday nights the Owl Club danced; then there was a little stir in the streets, and here and there one could see a lighted window until midnight. But the next night all was dark again.

After I refused to join `the Owls,' as they were called, I made a bold resolve to go to the Saturday night dances at Firemen's Hall. I knew it would be useless to acquaint my elders with any such plan. Grandfather didn't approve of dancing, anyway; he would only say that if I wanted to dance I could go to the Masonic Hall, among `the people we knew.' It was just my point that I saw altogether too much of the people we knew.

My bedroom was on the ground floor, and as I studied there, I had a stove in it. I used to retire to my room early on Saturday night, change my shirt and collar and put on my Sunday coat. I waited until all was quiet and the old people were asleep, then raised my window, climbed out, and went softly through the yard. The first time I deceived my grandparents I felt rather shabby, perhaps even the second time, but I soon ceased to think about it.

The dance at the Firemen's Hall was the one thing I looked forward to all the week. There I met the same people I used to see at the Vannis' tent. Sometimes there were Bohemians from Wilber, or German boys who came down on the afternoon freight from Bismarck. Tony and Lena and Tiny were always there, and the three Bohemian Marys, and the Danish laundry girls.

The four Danish girls lived with the laundryman and his wife in their house behind the laundry, with a big garden where the clothes were hung out to dry. The laundryman was a kind, wise old fellow, who paid his girls well, looked out for them, and gave them a good home. He told me once that his own daughter died just as she was getting old enough to help her mother, and that he had been `trying to make up for it ever since.' On summer afternoons he used to sit for hours on the sidewalk in front of his laundry, his newspaper lying on his knee, watching his girls through the big open window while they ironed and talked in Danish. The clouds of white dust that blew up the street, the gusts of hot wind that withered his vegetable garden, never disturbed his calm. His droll expression seemed to say that he had found the secret of contentment. Morning and evening he drove about in his spring wagon, distributing freshly ironed clothes, and collecting bags of linen that cried out for his suds and sunny drying-lines. His girls never looked so pretty at the dances as they did standing by the ironing-board, or over the tubs, washing the fine pieces, their white arms and throats bare, their cheeks bright as the brightest wild roses, their gold hair moist with the steam or the heat and curling in little damp spirals about their ears. They had not learned much English, and were not so ambitious as Tony or Lena; but they were kind, simple girls and they were always happy. When one danced with them, one smelled their clean, freshly ironed clothes that had been put away with rosemary leaves from Mr. Jensen's garden.

There were never girls enough to go round at those dances, but everyone wanted a turn with Tony and Lena.

Lena moved without exertion, rather indolently, and her hand often accented the rhythm softly on her partner's shoulder. She smiled if one spoke to her, but seldom answered. The music seemed to put her into a soft, waking dream, and her violet-coloured eyes looked sleepily and confidingly at one from under her long lashes. When she sighed she exhaled a heavy perfume of sachet powder. To dance `Home, Sweet Home,' with Lena was like coming in with the tide. She danced every dance like a waltz, and it was always the same waltz--the waltz of coming home to something, of inevitable, fated return. After a while one got restless under it, as one does under the heat of a soft, sultry summer day.

When you spun out into the floor with Tony, you didn't return to anything. You set out every time upon a new adventure. I liked to schottische with her; she had so much spring and variety, and was always putting in new steps and slides. She taught me to dance against and around the hard-and-fast beat of the music. If, instead of going to the end of the railroad, old Mr. Shimerda had stayed in New York and picked up a living with his fiddle, how different Antonia's life might have been!

Antonia often went to the dances with Larry Donovan, a passenger conductor who was a kind of professional ladies' man, as we said. I remember how admiringly all the boys looked at her the night she first wore her velveteen dress, made like Mrs. Gardener's black velvet. She was lovely to see, with her eyes shining, and her lips always a little parted when she danced. That constant, dark colour in her cheeks never changed.

One evening when Donovan was out on his run, Antonia came to the hall with Norwegian Anna and her young man, and that night I took her home. When we were in the Cutters' yard, sheltered by the evergreens, I told her she must kiss me good night.

`Why, sure, Jim.' A moment later she drew her face away and whispered indignantly, `Why, Jim! You know you ain't right to kiss me like that. I'll tell your grandmother on you!'

`Lena Lingard lets me kiss her,' I retorted, `and I'm not half as fond of her as I am of you.'

`Lena does?' Tony gasped. `If she's up to any of her nonsense with you, I'll scratch her eyes out!' She took my arm again and we walked out of the gate and up and down the sidewalk. `Now, don't you go and be a fool like some of these town boys. You're not going to sit around here and whittle store-boxes and tell stories all your life. You are going away to school and make something of yourself. I'm just awful proud of you. You won't go and get mixed up with the Swedes, will you?'

`I don't care anything about any of them but you,' I said. `And you'll always treat me like a kid, suppose.'

She laughed and threw her arms around me. `I expect I will, but you're a kid I'm awful fond of, anyhow! You can like me all you want to, but if I see you hanging round with Lena much, I'll go to your grandmother, as sure as your name's Jim Burden! Lena's all right, only--well, you know yourself she's soft that way. She can't help it. It's natural to her.'

If she was proud of me, I was so proud of her that I carried my head high as I emerged from the dark cedars and shut the Cutters' gate softly behind me. Her warm, sweet face, her kind arms, and the true heart in her; she was, oh, she was still my Antonia! I looked with contempt at the dark, silent little houses about me as I walked home, and thought of the stupid young men who were asleep in some of them. I knew where the real women were, though I was only a boy; and I would not be afraid of them, either!

I hated to enter the still house when I went home from the dances, and it was long before I could get to sleep. Toward morning I used to have pleasant dreams: sometimes Tony and I were out in the country, sliding down straw-stacks as we used to do; climbing up the yellow mountains over and over, and slipping down the smooth sides into soft piles of chaff.

One dream I dreamed a great many times, and it was always the same. I was in a harvest-field full of shocks, and I was lying against one of them. Lena Lingard came across the stubble barefoot, in a short skirt, with a curved reaping-hook in her hand, and she was flushed like the dawn, with a kind of luminous rosiness all about her. She sat down beside me, turned to me with a soft sigh and said, `Now they are all gone, and I can kiss you as much as I like.'

I used to wish I could have this flattering dream about Antonia, but I never did.

XIII

I NOTICED ONE AFTERNOON that grandmother had been crying. Her feet seemed to drag as she moved about the house, and I got up from the table where I was studying and went to her, asking if she didn't feel well, and if I couldn't help her with her work.

`No, thank you, Jim. I'm troubled, but I guess I'm well enough. Getting a little rusty in the bones, maybe,' she added bitterly.

I stood hesitating. `What are you fretting about, grandmother? Has grandfather lost any money?'

`No, it ain't money. I wish it was. But I've heard things. You must 'a' known it would come back to me sometime.' She dropped into a chair, and, covering her face with her apron, began to cry. `Jim,' she said, `I was never one that claimed old folks could bring up their grandchildren. But it came about so; there wasn't any other way for you, it seemed like.'

I put my arms around her. I couldn't bear to see her cry.

`What is it, grandmother? Is it the Firemen's dances?'

She nodded.

`I'm sorry I sneaked off like that. But there's nothing wrong about the dances, and I haven't done anything wrong. I like all those country girls, and I like to dance with them. That's all there is to it.'

`But it ain't right to deceive us, son, and it brings blame on us. People say you are growing up to be a bad boy, and that ain't just to us.'

`I don't care what they say about me, but if it hurts you, that settles it. I won't go to the Firemen's Hall again.'

I kept my promise, of course, but I found the spring months dull enough. I sat at home with the old people in the evenings now, reading Latin that was not in our high-school course. I had made up my mind to do a lot of college requirement work in the summer, and to enter the freshman class at the university without conditions in the fall. I wanted to get away as soon as possible.

Disapprobation hurt me, I found--even that of people whom I did not admire. As the spring came on, I grew more and more lonely, and fell back on the telegrapher and the cigar-maker and his canaries for companionship. I remember I took a melancholy pleasure in hanging a May-basket for Nina Harling that spring. I bought the flowers from an old German woman who always had more window plants than anyone else, and spent an afternoon trimming a little workbasket. When dusk came on, and the new moon hung in the sky, I went quietly to the Harlings' front door with my offering, rang the bell, and then ran away as was the custom. Through the willow hedge I could hear Nina's cries of delight, and I felt comforted.

On those warm, soft spring evenings I often lingered downtown to walk home with Frances, and talked to her about my plans and about the reading I was doing. One evening she said she thought Mrs. Harling was not seriously offended with me.

`Mama is as broad-minded as mothers ever are, I guess. But you know she was hurt about Antonia, and she can't understand why you like to be with Tiny and Lena better than with the girls of your own set.'

`Can you?' I asked bluntly.

Frances laughed. `Yes, I think I can. You knew them in the country, and you like to take sides. In some ways you're older than boys of your age. It will be all right with mama after you pass your college examinations and she sees you're in earnest.'

`If you were a boy,' I persisted, `you wouldn't belong to the Owl Club, either. You'd be just like me.'

She shook her head. `I would and I wouldn't. I expect I know the country girls better than you do. You always put a kind of glamour over them. The trouble with you, Jim, is that you're romantic. Mama's going to your Commencement. She asked me the other day if I knew what your oration is to be about. She wants you to do well.'

I thought my oration very good. It stated with fervour a great many things I had lately discovered. Mrs. Harling came to the Opera House to hear the Commencement exercises, and I looked at her most of the time while I made my speech. Her keen, intelligent eyes never left my face. Afterward she came back to the dressing-room where we stood, with our diplomas in our hands, walked up to me, and said heartily: `You surprised me, Jim. I didn't believe you could do as well as that. You didn't get that speech out of books.' Among my graduation presents there was a silk umbrella from Mrs. Harling, with my name on the handle.

I walked home from the Opera House alone. As I passed the Methodist Church, I saw three white figures ahead of me, pacing up and down under the arching maple trees, where the moonlight filtered through the lush June foliage. They hurried toward me; they were waiting for me--Lena and Tony and Anna Hansen.

`Oh, Jim, it was splendid!' Tony was breathing hard, as she always did when her feelings outran her language. `There ain't a lawyer in Black Hawk could make a speech like that. I just stopped your grandpa and said so to him. He won't tell you, but he told us he was awful surprised himself, didn't he, girls?'

Lena sidled up to me and said teasingly, `What made you so solemn? I thought you were scared. I was sure you'd forget.'

Anna spoke wistfully.

`It must make you very happy, Jim, to have fine thoughts like that in your mind all the time, and to have words to put them in. I always wanted to go to school, you know.'

`Oh, I just sat there and wished my papa could hear you! Jim'--Antonia took hold of my coat lapels--'there was something in your speech that made me think so about my papa!'

`I thought about your papa when I wrote my speech, Tony,' I said. `I dedicated it to him.'

She threw her arms around me, and her dear face was all wet with tears.

I stood watching their white dresses glimmer smaller and smaller down the sidewalk as they went away. I have had no other success that pulled at my heartstrings like that one.

XIV

THE DAY AFTER COMMENCEMENT I moved my books and desk upstairs, to an empty room where I should be undisturbed, and I fell to studying in earnest. I worked off a year's trigonometry that summer, and began Virgil alone. Morning after morning I used to pace up and down my sunny little room, looking off at the distant river bluffs and the roll of the blond pastures between, scanning the `Aeneid' aloud and committing long passages to memory. Sometimes in the evening Mrs. Harling called to me as I passed her gate, and asked me to come in and let her play for me. She was lonely for Charley, she said, and liked to have a boy about. Whenever my grandparents had misgivings, and began to wonder whether I was not too young to go off to college alone, Mrs. Harling took up my cause vigorously. Grandfather had such respect for her judgment that I knew he would not go against her.

I had only one holiday that summer. It was in July. I met Antonia downtown on Saturday afternoon, and learned that she and Tiny and Lena were going to the river next day with Anna Hansen--the elder was all in bloom now, and Anna wanted to make elderblow wine.

`Anna's to drive us down in the Marshalls' delivery wagon, and we'll take a nice lunch and have a picnic. Just us; nobody else. Couldn't you happen along, Jim? It would be like old times.'

I considered a moment. `Maybe I can, if I won't be in the way.'

On Sunday morning I rose early and got out of Black Hawk while the dew was still heavy on the long meadow grasses. It was the high season for summer flowers. The pink bee-bush stood tall along the sandy roadsides, and the cone-flowers and rose mallow grew everywhere. Across the wire fence, in the long grass, I saw a clump of flaming orange-coloured milkweed, rare in that part of the state. I left the road and went around through a stretch of pasture that was always cropped short in summer, where the gaillardia came up year after year and matted over the ground with the deep, velvety red that is in Bokhara carpets. The country was empty and solitary except for the larks that Sunday morning, and it seemed to lift itself up to me and to come very close.

The river was running strong for midsummer; heavy rains to the west of us had kept it full. I crossed the bridge and went upstream along the wooded shore to a pleasant dressing-room I knew among the dogwood bushes, all overgrown with wild grapevines. I began to undress for a swim. The girls would not be along yet. For the first time it occurred to me that I should be homesick for that river after I left it. The sandbars, with their clean white beaches and their little groves of willows and cottonwood seedlings, were a sort of No Man's Land, little newly created worlds that belonged to the Black Hawk boys. Charley Harling and I had hunted through these woods, fished from the fallen logs, until I knew every inch of the river shores and had a friendly feeling for every bar and shallow.

After my swim, while I was playing about indolently in the water, I heard the sound of hoofs and wheels on the bridge. I struck downstream and shouted, as the open spring wagon came into view on the middle span. They stopped the horse, and the two girls in the bottom of the cart stood up, steadying themselves by the shoulders of the two in front, so that they could see me better. They were charming up there, huddled together in the cart and peering down at me like curious deer when they come out of the thicket to drink. I found bottom near the bridge and stood up, waving to them.

`How pretty you look!' I called.

`So do you!' they shouted altogether, and broke into peals of laughter. Anna Hansen shook the reins and they drove on, while I zigzagged back to my inlet and clambered up behind an overhanging elm. I dried myself in the sun, and dressed slowly, reluctant to leave that green enclosure where the sunlight flickered so bright through the grapevine leaves and the woodpecker hammered away in the crooked elm that trailed out over the water. As I went along the road back to the bridge, I kept picking off little pieces of scaly chalk from the dried water gullies, and breaking them up in my hands.

When I came upon the Marshalls' delivery horse, tied in the shade, the girls had already taken their baskets and gone down the east road which wound through the sand and scrub. I could hear them calling to each other. The elder bushes did not grow back in the shady ravines between the bluffs, but in the hot, sandy bottoms along the stream, where their roots were always in moisture and their tops in the sun. The blossoms were unusually luxuriant and beautiful that summer.

I followed a cattle path through the thick under-brush until I came to a slope that fell away abruptly to the water's edge. A great chunk of the shore had been bitten out by some spring freshet, and the scar was masked by elder bushes, growing down to the water in flowery terraces. I did not touch them. I was overcome by content and drowsiness and by the warm silence about me. There was no sound but the high, singsong buzz of wild bees and the sunny gurgle of the water underneath. I peeped over the edge of the bank to see the little stream that made the noise; it flowed along perfectly clear over the sand and gravel, cut off from the muddy main current by a long sandbar. Down there, on the lower shelf of the bank, I saw Antonia, seated alone under the pagoda-like elders. She looked up when she heard me, and smiled, but I saw that she had been crying. I slid down into the soft sand beside her and asked her what was the matter.

`It makes me homesick, Jimmy, this flower, this smell,' she said softly. `We have this flower very much at home, in the old country. It always grew in our yard and my papa had a green bench and a table under the bushes. In summer, when they were in bloom, he used to sit there with his friend that played the trombone. When I was little I used to go down there to hear them talk--beautiful talk, like what I never hear in this country.'

`What did they talk about?' I asked her.

She sighed and shook her head. `Oh, I don't know! About music, and the woods, and about God, and when they were young.' She turned to me suddenly and looked into my eyes. `You think, Jimmy, that maybe my father's spirit can go back to those old places?'

I told her about the feeling of her father's presence I had on that winter day when my grandparents had gone over to see his dead body and I was left alone in the house. I said I felt sure then that he was on his way back to his own country, and that even now, when I passed his grave, I always thought of him as being among the woods and fields that were so dear to him.

Antonia had the most trusting, responsive eyes in the world; love and credulousness seemed to look out of them with open faces.

`Why didn't you ever tell me that before? It makes me feel more sure for him.' After a while she said: `You know, Jim, my father was different from my mother. He did not have to marry my mother, and all his brothers quarrelled with him because he did. I used to hear the old people at home whisper about it. They said he could have paid my mother money, and not married her. But he was older than she was, and he was too kind to treat her like that. He lived in his mother's house, and she was a poor girl come in to do the work. After my father married her, my grandmother never let my mother come into her house again. When I went to my grandmother's funeral was the only time I was ever in my grandmother's house. Don't that seem strange?'

While she talked, I lay back in the hot sand and looked up at the blue sky between the flat bouquets of elder. I could hear the bees humming and singing, but they stayed up in the sun above the flowers and did not come down into the shadow of the leaves. Antonia seemed to me that day exactly like the little girl who used to come to our house with Mr. Shimerda.

`Some day, Tony, I am going over to your country, and I am going to the little town where you lived. Do you remember all about it?'

`Jim,' she said earnestly, `if I was put down there in the middle of the night, I could find my way all over that little town; and along the river to the next town, where my grandmother lived. My feet remember all the little paths through the woods, and where the big roots stick out to trip you. I ain't never forgot my own country.'

There was a crackling in the branches above us, and Lena Lingard peered down over the edge of the bank.

`You lazy things!' she cried. `All this elder, and you two lying there! Didn't you hear us calling you?' Almost as flushed as she had been in my dream, she leaned over the edge of the bank and began to demolish our flowery pagoda. I had never seen her so energetic; she was panting with zeal, and the perspiration stood in drops on her short, yielding upper lip. I sprang to my feet and ran up the bank.

It was noon now, and so hot that the dogwoods and scrub-oaks began to turn up the silvery underside of their leaves, and all the foliage looked soft and wilted. I carried the lunch-basket to the top of one of the chalk bluffs, where even on the calmest days there was always a breeze. The flat-topped, twisted little oaks threw light shadows on the grass. Below us we could see the windings of the river, and Black Hawk, grouped among its trees, and, beyond, the rolling country, swelling gently until it met the sky. We could recognize familiar farm-houses and windmills. Each of the girls pointed out to me the direction in which her father's farm lay, and told me how many acres were in wheat that year and how many in corn.

`My old folks,' said Tiny Soderball, `have put in twenty acres of rye. They get it ground at the mill, and it makes nice bread. It seems like my mother ain't been so homesick, ever since father's raised rye flour for her.'

`It must have been a trial for our mothers,' said Lena, `coming out here and having to do everything different. My mother had always lived in town. She says she started behind in farm-work, and never has caught up.'

`Yes, a new country's hard on the old ones, sometimes,' said Anna thoughtfully. `My grandmother's getting feeble now, and her mind wanders. She's forgot about this country, and thinks she's at home in Norway. She keeps asking mother to take her down to the waterside and the fish market. She craves fish all the time. Whenever I go home I take her canned salmon and mackerel.'

`Mercy, it's hot!' Lena yawned. She was supine under a little oak, resting after the fury of her elder-hunting, and had taken off the high-heeled slippers she had been silly enough to wear. `Come here, Jim. You never got the sand out of your hair.' She began to draw her fingers slowly through my hair.

Antonia pushed her away. `You'll never get it out like that,' she said sharply. She gave my head a rough touzling and finished me off with something like a box on the ear. `Lena, you oughtn't to try to wear those slippers any more. They're too small for your feet. You'd better give them to me for Yulka.'

`All right,' said Lena good-naturedly, tucking her white stockings under her skirt. `You get all Yulka's things, don't you? I wish father didn't have such bad luck with his farm machinery; then I could buy more things for my sisters. I'm going to get Mary a new coat this fall, if the sulky plough's never paid for!'

Tiny asked her why she didn't wait until after Christmas, when coats would be cheaper. `What do you think of poor me?' she added; `with six at home, younger than I am? And they all think I'm rich, because when I go back to the country I'm dressed so fine!' She shrugged her shoulders. `But, you know, my weakness is playthings. I like to buy them playthings better than what they need.'

`I know how that is,' said Anna. `When we first came here, and I was little, we were too poor to buy toys. I never got over the loss of a doll somebody gave me before we left Norway. A boy on the boat broke her and I still hate him for it.'

`I guess after you got here you had plenty of live dolls to nurse, like me!' Lena remarked cynically.

`Yes, the babies came along pretty fast, to be sure. But I never minded. I was fond of them all. The youngest one, that we didn't any of us want, is the one we love best now.'

Lena sighed. `Oh, the babies are all right; if only they don't come in winter. Ours nearly always did. I don't see how mother stood it. I tell you what, girls'--she sat up with sudden energy--'I'm going to get my mother out of that old sod house where she's lived so many years. The men will never do it. Johnnie, that's my oldest brother, he's wanting to get married now, and build a house for his girl instead of his mother. Mrs. Thomas says she thinks I can move to some other town pretty soon, and go into business for myself. If I don't get into business, I'll maybe marry a rich gambler.'

`That would be a poor way to get on,' said Anna sarcastically. `I wish I could teach school, like Selma Kronn. Just think! She'll be the first Scandinavian girl to get a position in the high school. We ought to be proud of her.'

Selma was a studious girl, who had not much tolerance for giddy things like Tiny and Lena; but they always spoke of her with admiration.

Tiny moved about restlessly, fanning herself with her straw hat. `If I was smart like her, I'd be at my books day and night. But she was born smart--and look how her father's trained her! He was something high up in the old country.'

`So was my mother's father,' murmured Lena, `but that's all the good it does us! My father's father was smart, too, but he was wild. He married a Lapp. I guess that's what's the matter with me; they say Lapp blood will out.'

`A real Lapp, Lena?' I exclaimed. `The kind that wear skins?'

`I don't know if she wore skins, but she was a Lapps all right, and his folks felt dreadful about it. He was sent up North on some government job he had, and fell in with her. He would marry her.'

`But I thought Lapland women were fat and ugly, and had squint eyes, like Chinese?' I objected.

`I don't know, maybe. There must be something mighty taking about the Lapp girls, though; mother says the Norwegians up North are always afraid their boys will run after them.'

In the afternoon, when the heat was less oppressive, we had a lively game of `Pussy Wants a Corner,' on the flat bluff-top, with the little trees for bases. Lena was Pussy so often that she finally said she wouldn't play any more. We threw ourselves down on the grass, out of breath.

`Jim,' Antonia said dreamily, `I want you to tell the girls about how the Spanish first came here, like you and Charley Harling used to talk about. I've tried to tell them, but I leave out so much.'

They sat under a little oak, Tony resting against the trunk and the other girls leaning against her and each other, and listened to the little I was able to tell them about Coronado and his search for the Seven Golden Cities. At school we were taught that he had not got so far north as Nebraska, but had given up his quest and turned back somewhere in Kansas. But Charley Harling and I had a strong belief that he had been along this very river. A farmer in the county north of ours, when he was breaking sod, had turned up a metal stirrup of fine workmanship, and a sword with a Spanish inscription on the blade. He lent these relics to Mr. Harling, who brought them home with him. Charley and I scoured them, and they were on exhibition in the Harling office all summer. Father Kelly, the priest, had found the name of the Spanish maker on the sword and an abbreviation that stood for the city of Cordova.

`And that I saw with my own eyes,' Antonia put in triumphantly. `So Jim and Charley were right, and the teachers were wrong!'

The girls began to wonder among themselves. Why had the Spaniards come so far? What must this country have been like, then? Why had Coronado never gone back to Spain, to his riches and his castles and his king? I couldn't tell them. I only knew the schoolbooks said he `died in the wilderness, of a broken heart.'

`More than him has done that,' said Antonia sadly, and the girls murmured assent.

We sat looking off across the country, watching the sun go down. The curly grass about us was on fire now. The bark of the oaks turned red as copper. There was a shimmer of gold on the brown river. Out in the stream the sandbars glittered like glass, and the light trembled in the willow thickets as if little flames were leaping among them. The breeze sank to stillness. In the ravine a ringdove mourned plaintively, and somewhere off in the bushes an owl hooted. The girls sat listless, leaning against each other. The long fingers of the sun touched their foreheads.

Presently we saw a curious thing: There were no clouds, the sun was going down in a limpid, gold-washed sky. Just as the lower edge of the red disk rested on the high fields against the horizon, a great black figure suddenly appeared on the face of the sun. We sprang to our feet, straining our eyes toward it. In a moment we realized what it was. On some upland farm, a plough had been left standing in the field. The sun was sinking just behind it. Magnified across the distance by the horizontal light, it stood out against the sun, was exactly contained within the circle of the disk; the handles, the tongue, the share--black against the molten red. There it was, heroic in size, a picture writing on the sun.

Even while we whispered about it, our vision disappeared; the ball dropped and dropped until the red tip went beneath the earth. The fields below us were dark, the sky was growing pale, and that forgotten plough had sunk back to its own littleness somewhere on the prairie.

XV

LATE IN AUGUST the Cutters went to Omaha for a few days, leaving Antonia in charge of the house. Since the scandal about the Swedish girl, Wick Cutter could never get his wife to stir out of Black Hawk without him.

The day after the Cutters left, Antonia came over to see us. Grandmother noticed that she seemed troubled and distracted. `You've got something on your mind, Antonia,' she said anxiously.

`Yes, Mrs. Burden. I couldn't sleep much last night.' She hesitated, and then told us how strangely Mr. Cutter had behaved before he went away. He put all the silver in a basket and placed it under her bed, and with it a box of papers which he told her were valuable. He made her promise that she would not sleep away from the house, or be out late in the evening, while he was gone. He strictly forbade her to ask any of the girls she knew to stay with her at night. She would be perfectly safe, he said, as he had just put a new Yale lock on the front door.

Cutter had been so insistent in regard to these details that now she felt uncomfortable about staying there alone. She hadn't liked the way he kept coming into the kitchen to instruct her, or the way he looked at her. `I feel as if he is up to some of his tricks again, and is going to try to scare me, somehow.'

Grandmother was apprehensive at once. `I don't think it's right for you to stay there, feeling that way. I suppose it wouldn't be right for you to leave the place alone, either, after giving your word. Maybe Jim would be willing to go over there and sleep, and you could come here nights. I'd feel safer, knowing you were under my own roof. I guess Jim could take care of their silver and old usury notes as well as you could.'

Antonia turned to me eagerly. `Oh, would you, Jim? I'd make up my bed nice and fresh for you. It's a real cool room, and the bed's right next the window. I was afraid to leave the window open last night.'

I liked my own room, and I didn't like the Cutters' house under any circumstances; but Tony looked so troubled that I consented to try this arrangement. I found that I slept there as well as anywhere, and when I got home in the morning, Tony had a good breakfast waiting for me. After prayers she sat down at the table with us, and it was like old times in the country.

The third night I spent at the Cutters', I awoke suddenly with the impression that I had heard a door open and shut. Everything was still, however, and I must have gone to sleep again immediately.

The next thing I knew, I felt someone sit down on the edge of the bed. I was only half awake, but I decided that he might take the Cutters' silver, whoever he was. Perhaps if I did not move, he would find it and get out without troubling me. I held my breath and lay absolutely still. A hand closed softly on my shoulder, and at the same moment I felt something hairy and cologne-scented brushing my face. If the room had suddenly been flooded with electric light, I couldn't have seen more clearly the detestable bearded countenance that I knew was bending over me. I caught a handful of whiskers and pulled, shouting something. The hand that held my shoulder was instantly at my throat. The man became insane; he stood over me, choking me with one fist and beating me in the face with the other, hissing and chuckling and letting out a flood of abuse.

`So this is what she's up to when I'm away, is it? Where is she, you nasty whelp, where is she? Under the bed, are you, hussy? I know your tricks! Wait till I get at you! I'll fix this rat you've got in here. He's caught, all right!'

So long as Cutter had me by the throat, there was no chance for me at all. I got hold of his thumb and bent it back, until he let go with a yell. In a bound, I was on my feet, and easily sent him sprawling to the floor. Then I made a dive for the open window, struck the wire screen, knocked it out, and tumbled after it into the yard.

Suddenly I found myself running across the north end of Black Hawk in my night-shirt, just as one sometimes finds one's self behaving in bad dreams. When I got home, I climbed in at the kitchen window. I was covered with blood from my nose and lip, but I was too sick to do anything about it. I found a shawl and an overcoat on the hat-rack, lay down on the parlour sofa, and in spite of my hurts, went to sleep.

Grandmother found me there in the morning. Her cry of fright awakened me. Truly, I was a battered object. As she helped me to my room, I caught a glimpse of myself in the mirror. My lip was cut and stood out like a snout. My nose looked like a big blue plum, and one eye was swollen shut and hideously discoloured. Grandmother said we must have the doctor at once, but I implored her, as I had never begged for anything before, not to send for him. I could stand anything, I told her, so long as nobody saw me or knew what had happened to me. I entreated her not to let grandfather, even, come into my room. She seemed to understand, though I was too faint and miserable to go into explanations. When she took off my night-shirt, she found such bruises on my chest and shoulders that she began to cry. She spent the whole morning bathing and poulticing me, and rubbing me with arnica. I heard Antonia sobbing outside my door, but I asked grandmother to send her away. I felt that I never wanted to see her again. I hated her almost as much as I hated Cutter. She had let me in for all this disgustingness. Grandmother kept saying how thankful we ought to be that I had been there instead of Antonia. But I lay with my disfigured face to the wall and felt no particular gratitude. My one concern was that grandmother should keep everyone away from me. If the story once got abroad, I would never hear the last of it. I could well imagine what the old men down at the drugstore would do with such a theme.

While grandmother was trying to make me comfortable, grandfather went to the depot and learned that Wick Cutter had come home on the night express from the east, and had left again on the six o'clock train for Denver that morning. The agent said his face was striped with court-plaster, and he carried his left hand in a sling. He looked so used up, that the agent asked him what had happened to him since ten o'clock the night before; whereat Cutter began to swear at him and said he would have him discharged for incivility.

That afternoon, while I was asleep, Antonia took grandmother with her, and went over to the Cutters' to pack her trunk. They found the place locked up, and they had to break the window to get into Antonia's bedroom. There everything was in shocking disorder. Her clothes had been taken out of her closet, thrown into the middle of the room, and trampled and torn. My own garments had been treated so badly that I never saw them again; grandmother burned them in the Cutters' kitchen range.

While Antonia was packing her trunk and putting her room in order, to leave it, the front doorbell rang violently. There stood Mrs. Cutter--locked out, for she had no key to the new lock--her head trembling with rage. `I advised her to control herself, or she would have a stroke,' grandmother said afterward.

Grandmother would not let her see Antonia at all, but made her sit down in the parlour while she related to her just what had occurred the night before. Antonia was frightened, and was going home to stay for a while, she told Mrs. Cutter; it would be useless to interrogate the girl, for she knew nothing of what had happened.

Then Mrs. Cutter told her story. She and her husband had started home from Omaha together the morning before. They had to stop over several hours at Waymore Junction to catch the Black Hawk train. During the wait, Cutter left her at the depot and went to the Waymore bank to attend to some business. When he returned, he told her that he would have to stay overnight there, but she could go on home. He bought her ticket and put her on the train. She saw him slip a twenty-dollar bill into her handbag with her ticket. That bill, she said, should have aroused her suspicions at once--but did not.

The trains are never called at little junction towns; everybody knows when they come in. Mr. Cutter showed his wife's ticket to the conductor, and settled her in her seat before the train moved off. It was not until nearly nightfall that she discovered she was on the express bound for Kansas City, that her ticket was made out to that point, and that Cutter must have planned it so. The conductor told her the Black Hawk train was due at Waymore twelve minutes after the Kansas City train left. She saw at once that her husband had played this trick in order to get back to Black Hawk without her. She had no choice but to go on to Kansas City and take the first fast train for home.

Cutter could have got home a day earlier than his wife by any one of a dozen simpler devices; he could have left her in the Omaha hotel, and said he was going on to Chicago for a few days. But apparently it was part of his fun to outrage her feelings as much as possible.

`Mr. Cutter will pay for this, Mrs. Burden. He will pay!' Mrs. Cutter avouched, nodding her horse-like head and rolling her eyes.

Grandmother said she hadn't a doubt of it.

Certainly Cutter liked to have his wife think him a devil. In some way he depended upon the excitement He could arouse in her hysterical nature. Perhaps he got the feeling of being a rake more from his wife's rage and amazement than from any experiences of his own. His zest in debauchery might wane, but never Mrs. Cutter's belief in it. The reckoning with his wife at the end of an escapade was something he counted on--like the last powerful liqueur after a long dinner. The one excitement he really couldn't do without was quarrelling with Mrs. Cutter!

PART III. LENA LINGARD

I

AT THE UNIVERSITY I had the good fortune to come immediately under the influence of a brilliant and inspiring young scholar. Gaston Cleric had arrived in Lincoln only a few weeks earlier than I, to begin his work as head of the Latin Department. He came West at the suggestion of his physicians, his health having been enfeebled by a long illness in Italy. When I took my entrance examinations, he was my examiner, and my course was arranged under his supervision.

I did not go home for my first summer vacation, but stayed in Lincoln, working off a year's Greek, which had been my only condition on entering the freshman class. Cleric's doctor advised against his going back to New England, and, except for a few weeks in Colorado, he, too, was in Lincoln all that summer. We played tennis, read, and took long walks together. I shall always look back on that time of mental awakening as one of the happiest in my life. Gaston Cleric introduced me to the world of ideas; when one first enters that world everything else fades for a time, and all that went before is as if it had not been. Yet I found curious survivals; some of the figures of my old life seemed to be waiting for me in the new.

In those days there were many serious young men among the students who had come up to the university from the farms and the little towns scattered over the thinly settled state. Some of those boys came straight from the cornfields with only a summer's wages in their pockets, hung on through the four years, shabby and underfed, and completed the course by really heroic self-sacrifice. Our instructors were oddly assorted; wandering pioneer school-teachers, stranded ministers of the Gospel, a few enthusiastic young men just out of graduate schools. There was an atmosphere of endeavour, of expectancy and bright hopefulness about the young college that had lifted its head from the prairie only a few years before.

Our personal life was as free as that of our instructors. There were no college dormitories; we lived where we could and as we could. I took rooms with an old couple, early settlers in Lincoln, who had married off their children and now lived quietly in their house at the edge of town, near the open country. The house was inconveniently situated for students, and on that account I got two rooms for the price of one. My bedroom, originally a linen-closet, was unheated and was barely large enough to contain my cot-bed, but it enabled me to call the other room my study. The dresser, and the great walnut wardrobe which held all my clothes, even my hats and shoes, I had pushed out of the way, and I considered them non-existent, as children eliminate incongruous objects when they are playing house. I worked at a commodious green-topped table placed directly in front of the west window which looked out over the prairie. In the corner at my right were all my books, in shelves I had made and painted myself. On the blank wall at my left the dark, old-fashioned wall-paper was covered by a large map of ancient Rome, the work of some German scholar. Cleric had ordered it for me when he was sending for books from abroad. Over the bookcase hung a photograph of the Tragic Theatre at Pompeii, which he had given me from his collection.

When I sat at work I half-faced a deep, upholstered chair which stood at the end of my table, its high back against the wall. I had bought it with great care. My instructor sometimes looked in upon me when he was out for an evening tramp, and I noticed that he was more likely to linger and become talkative if I had a comfortable chair for him to sit in, and if he found a bottle of Benedictine and plenty of the kind of cigarettes he liked, at his elbow. He was, I had discovered, parsimonious about small expenditures--a trait absolutely inconsistent with his general character. Sometimes when he came he was silent and moody, and after a few sarcastic remarks went away again, to tramp the streets of Lincoln, which were almost as quiet and oppressively domestic as those of Black Hawk. Again, he would sit until nearly midnight, talking about Latin and English poetry, or telling me about his long stay in Italy.

I can give no idea of the peculiar charm and vividness of his talk. In a crowd he was nearly always silent. Even for his classroom he had no platitudes, no stock of professorial anecdotes. When he was tired, his lectures were clouded, obscure, elliptical; but when he was interested they were wonderful. I believe that Gaston Cleric narrowly missed being a great poet, and I have sometimes thought that his bursts of imaginative talk were fatal to his poetic gift. He squandered too much in the heat of personal communication. How often I have seen him draw his dark brows together, fix his eyes upon some object on the wall or a figure in the carpet, and then flash into the lamplight the very image that was in his brain. He could bring the drama of antique life before one out of the shadows--white figures against blue backgrounds. I shall never forget his face as it looked one night when he told me about the solitary day he spent among the sea temples at Paestum: the soft wind blowing through the roofless columns, the birds flying low over the flowering marsh grasses, the changing lights on the silver, cloud-hung mountains. He had wilfully stayed the short summer night there, wrapped in his coat and rug, watching the constellations on their path down the sky until `the bride of old Tithonus' rose out of the sea, and the mountains stood sharp in the dawn. It was there he caught the fever which held him back on the eve of his departure for Greece and of which he lay ill so long in Naples. He was still, indeed, doing penance for it.

I remember vividly another evening, when something led us to talk of Dante's veneration for Virgil. Cleric went through canto after canto of the `Commedia,' repeating the discourse between Dante and his `sweet teacher,' while his cigarette burned itself out unheeded between his long fingers. I can hear him now, speaking the lines of the poet Statius, who spoke for Dante: `I was famous on earth with the name which endures longest and honours most. The seeds of my ardour were the sparks from that divine flame whereby more than a thousand have kindled; I speak of the "Aeneid," mother to me and nurse to me in poetry.'

Although I admired scholarship so much in Cleric, I was not deceived about myself; I knew that I should never be a scholar. I could never lose myself for long among impersonal things. Mental excitement was apt to send me with a rush back to my own naked land and the figures scattered upon it. While I was in the very act of yearning toward the new forms that Cleric brought up before me, my mind plunged away from me, and I suddenly found myself thinking of the places and people of my own infinitesimal past. They stood out strengthened and simplified now, like the image of the plough against the sun. They were all I had for an answer to the new appeal. I begrudged the room that Jake and Otto and Russian Peter took up in my memory, which I wanted to crowd with other things. But whenever my consciousness was quickened, all those early friends were quickened within it, and in some strange way they accompanied me through all my new experiences. They were so much alive in me that I scarcely stopped to wonder whether they were alive anywhere else, or how.

II

ONE MARCH EVENING in my sophomore year I was sitting alone in my room after supper. There had been a warm thaw all day, with mushy yards and little streams of dark water gurgling cheerfully into the streets out of old snowbanks. My window was open, and the earthy wind blowing through made me indolent. On the edge of the prairie, where the sun had gone down, the sky was turquoise blue, like a lake, with gold light throbbing in it. Higher up, in the utter clarity of the western slope, the evening star hung like a lamp suspended by silver chains--like the lamp engraved upon the title-page of old Latin texts, which is always appearing in new heavens, and waking new desires in men. It reminded me, at any rate, to shut my window and light my wick in answer. I did so regretfully, and the dim objects in the room emerged from the shadows and took their place about me with the helpfulness which custom breeds.

I propped my book open and stared listlessly at the page of the `Georgics' where tomorrow's lesson began. It opened with the melancholy reflection that, in the lives of mortals the best days are the first to flee. 'Optima dies ... prima fugit.' I turned back to the beginning of the third book, which we had read in class that morning. 'Primus ego in patriam mecum ... deducam Musas'; `for I shall be the first, if I live, to bring the Muse into my country.' Cleric had explained to us that `patria' here meant, not a nation or even a province, but the little rural neighbourhood on the Mincio where the poet was born. This was not a boast, but a hope, at once bold and devoutly humble, that he might bring the Muse (but lately come to Italy from her cloudy Grecian mountains), not to the capital, the palatia Romana, but to his own little I country'; to his father's fields, `sloping down to the river and to the old beech trees with broken tops.'

Cleric said he thought Virgil, when he was dying at Brindisi, must have remembered that passage. After he had faced the bitter fact that he was to leave the `Aeneid' unfinished, and had decreed that the great canvas, crowded with figures of gods and men, should be burned rather than survive him unperfected, then his mind must have gone back to the perfect utterance of the `Georgics,' where the pen was fitted to the matter as the plough is to the furrow; and he must have said to himself, with the thankfulness of a good man, `I was the first to bring the Muse into my country.'

We left the classroom quietly, conscious that we had been brushed by the wing of a great feeling, though perhaps I alone knew Cleric intimately enough to guess what that feeling was. In the evening, as I sat staring at my book, the fervour of his voice stirred through the quantities on the page before me. I was wondering whether that particular rocky strip of New England coast about which he had so often told me was Cleric's patria. Before I had got far with my reading, I was disturbed by a knock. I hurried to the door and when I opened it saw a woman standing in the dark hall.

`I expect you hardly know me, Jim.'

The voice seemed familiar, but I did not recognize her until she stepped into the light of my doorway and I beheld-- Lena Lingard! She was so quietly conventionalized by city clothes that I might have passed her on the street without seeing her. Her black suit fitted her figure smoothly, and a black lace hat, with pale-blue forget-me-nots, sat demurely on her yellow hair.

I led her toward Cleric's chair, the only comfortable one I had, questioning her confusedly.

She was not disconcerted by my embarrassment. She looked about her with the naive curiosity I remembered so well. `You are quite comfortable here, aren't you? I live in Lincoln now, too, Jim. I'm in business for myself. I have a dressmaking shop in the Raleigh Block, out on O Street. I've made a real good start.'

`But, Lena, when did you come?'

`Oh, I've been here all winter. Didn't your grandmother ever write you? I've thought about looking you up lots of times. But we've all heard what a studious young man you've got to be, and I felt bashful. I didn't know whether you'd be glad to see me.' She laughed her mellow, easy laugh, that was either very artless or very comprehending, one never quite knew which. `You seem the same, though--except you're a young man, now, of course. Do you think I've changed?'

`Maybe you're prettier--though you were always pretty enough. Perhaps it's your clothes that make a difference.'

`You like my new suit? I have to dress pretty well in my business.'

She took off her jacket and sat more at ease in her blouse, of some soft, flimsy silk. She was already at home in my place, had slipped quietly into it, as she did into everything. She told me her business was going well, and she had saved a little money.

`This summer I'm going to build the house for mother I've talked about so long. I won't be able to pay up on it at first, but I want her to have it before she is too old to enjoy it. Next summer I'll take her down new furniture and carpets, so she'll have something to look forward to all winter.'

I watched Lena sitting there so smooth and sunny and well-cared-for, and thought of how she used to run barefoot over the prairie until after the snow began to fly, and how Crazy Mary chased her round and round the cornfields. It seemed to me wonderful that she should have got on so well in the world. Certainly she had no one but herself to thank for it.

`You must feel proud of yourself, Lena,' I said heartily. `Look at me; I've never earned a dollar, and I don't know that I'll ever be able to.'

`Tony says you're going to be richer than Mr. Harling some day. She's always bragging about you, you know.'

`Tell me, how IS Tony?'

`She's fine. She works for Mrs. Gardener at the hotel now. She's housekeeper. Mrs. Gardener's health isn't what it was, and she can't see after everything like she used to. She has great confidence in Tony. Tony's made it up with the Harlings, too. Little Nina is so fond of her that Mrs. Harling kind of overlooked things.'

`Is she still going with Larry Donovan?'

`Oh, that's on, worse than ever! I guess they're engaged. Tony talks about him like he was president of the railroad. Everybody laughs about it, because she was never a girl to be soft. She won't hear a word against him. She's so sort of innocent.'

I said I didn't like Larry, and never would.

Lena's face dimpled. `Some of us could tell her things, but it wouldn't do any good. She'd always believe him. That's Antonia's failing, you know; if she once likes people, she won't hear anything against them.'

`I think I'd better go home and look after Antonia,' I said.

`I think you had.' Lena looked up at me in frank amusement. `It's a good thing the Harlings are friendly with her again. Larry's afraid of them. They ship so much grain, they have influence with the railroad people. What are you studying?' She leaned her elbows on the table and drew my book toward her. I caught a faint odour of violet sachet. `So that's Latin, is it? It looks hard. You do go to the theatre sometimes, though, for I've seen you there. Don't you just love a good play, Jim? I can't stay at home in the evening if there's one in town. I'd be willing to work like a slave, it seems to me, to live in a place where there are theatres.'

`Let's go to a show together sometime. You are going to let me come to see you, aren't you?'

`Would you like to? I'd be ever so pleased. I'm never busy after six o'clock, and I let my sewing girls go at half-past five. I board, to save time, but sometimes I cook a chop for myself, and I'd be glad to cook one for you. Well'--she began to put on her white gloves--'it's been awful good to see you, Jim.'

`You needn't hurry, need you? You've hardly told me anything yet.'

`We can talk when you come to see me. I expect you don't often have lady visitors. The old woman downstairs didn't want to let me come up very much. I told her I was from your home town, and had promised your grandmother to come and see you. How surprised Mrs. Burden would be!' Lena laughed softly as she rose.

When I caught up my hat, she shook her head. `No, I don't want you to go with me. I'm to meet some Swedes at the drugstore. You wouldn't care for them. I wanted to see your room so I could write Tony all about it, but I must tell her how I left you right here with your books. She's always so afraid someone will run off with you!' Lena slipped her silk sleeves into the jacket I held for her, smoothed it over her person, and buttoned it slowly. I walked with her to the door. `Come and see me sometimes when you're lonesome. But maybe you have all the friends you want. Have you?' She turned her soft cheek to me. `Have you?' she whispered teasingly in my ear. In a moment I watched her fade down the dusky stairway.

When I turned back to my room the place seemed much pleasanter than before. Lena had left something warm and friendly in the lamplight. How I loved to hear her laugh again! It was so soft and unexcited and appreciative gave a favourable interpretation to everything. When I closed my eyes I could hear them all laughing--the Danish laundry girls and the three Bohemian Marys. Lena had brought them all back to me. It came over me, as it had never done before, the relation between girls like those and the poetry of Virgil. If there were no girls like them in the world, there would be no poetry. I understood that clearly, for the first time. This revelation seemed to me inestimably precious. I clung to it as if it might suddenly vanish.

As I sat down to my book at last, my old dream about Lena coming across the harvest-field in her short skirt seemed to me like the memory of an actual experience. It floated before me on the page like a picture, and underneath it stood the mournful line: 'Optima dies ... prima fugit.'

III

IN LINCOLN THE BEST part of the theatrical season came late, when the good companies stopped off there for one-night stands, after their long runs in New York and Chicago. That spring Lena went with me to see Joseph Jefferson in `Rip Van Winkle,' and to a war play called `Shenandoah.' She was inflexible about paying for her own seat; said she was in business now, and she wouldn't have a schoolboy spending his money on her. I liked to watch a play with Lena; everything was wonderful to her, and everything was true. It was like going to revival meetings with someone who was always being converted. She handed her feelings over to the actors with a kind of fatalistic resignation. Accessories of costume and scene meant much more to her than to me. She sat entranced through `Robin Hood' and hung upon the lips of the contralto who sang, `Oh, Promise Me!'

Toward the end of April, the billboards, which I watched anxiously in those days, bloomed out one morning with gleaming white posters on which two names were impressively printed in blue Gothic letters: the name of an actress of whom I had often heard, and the name `Camille.'

I called at the Raleigh Block for Lena on Saturday evening, and we walked down to the theatre. The weather was warm and sultry and put us both in a holiday humour. We arrived early, because Lena liked to watch the people come in. There was a note on the programme, saying that the `incidental music' would be from the opera `Traviata,' which was made from the same story as the play. We had neither of us read the play, and we did not know what it was about--though I seemed to remember having heard it was a piece in which great actresses shone. `The Count of Monte Cristo,' which I had seen James O'Neill play that winter, was by the only Alexandre Dumas I knew. This play, I saw, was by his son, and I expected a family resemblance. A couple of jack-rabbits, run in off the prairie, could not have been more innocent of what awaited them than were Lena and I.

Our excitement began with the rise of the curtain, when the moody Varville, seated before the fire, interrogated Nanine. Decidedly, there was a new tang about this dialogue. I had never heard in the theatre lines that were alive, that presupposed and took for granted, like those which passed between Varville and Marguerite in the brief encounter before her friends entered. This introduced the most brilliant, worldly, the most enchantingly gay scene I had ever looked upon. I had never seen champagne bottles opened on the stage before--indeed, I had never seen them opened anywhere. The memory of that supper makes me hungry now; the sight of it then, when I had only a students' boarding-house dinner behind me, was delicate torment. I seem to remember gilded chairs and tables (arranged hurriedly by footmen in white gloves and stockings), linen of dazzling whiteness, glittering glass, silver dishes, a great bowl of fruit, and the reddest of roses. The room was invaded by beautiful women and dashing young men, laughing and talking together. The men were dressed more or less after the period in which the play was written; the women were not. I saw no inconsistency. Their talk seemed to open to one the brilliant world in which they lived; every sentence made one older and wiser, every pleasantry enlarged one's horizon. One could experience excess and satiety without the inconvenience of learning what to do with one's hands in a drawing-room! When the characters all spoke at once and I missed some of the phrases they flashed at each other, I was in misery. I strained my ears and eyes to catch every exclamation.

The actress who played Marguerite was even then old-fashioned, though historic. She had been a member of Daly's famous New York company, and afterward a `star' under his direction. She was a woman who could not be taught, it is said, though she had a crude natural force which carried with people whose feelings were accessible and whose taste was not squeamish. She was already old, with a ravaged countenance and a physique curiously hard and stiff. She moved with difficulty--I think she was lame--I seem to remember some story about a malady of the spine. Her Armand was disproportionately young and slight, a handsome youth, perplexed in the extreme. But what did it matter? I believed devoutly in her power to fascinate him, in her dazzling loveliness. I believed her young, ardent, reckless, disillusioned, under sentence, feverish, avid of pleasure. I wanted to cross the footlights and help the slim-waisted Armand in the frilled shirt to convince her that there was still loyalty and devotion in the world. Her sudden illness, when the gaiety was at its height, her pallor, the handkerchief she crushed against her lips, the cough she smothered under the laughter while Gaston kept playing the piano lightly--it all wrung my heart. But not so much as her cynicism in the long dialogue with her lover which followed. How far was I from questioning her unbelief! While the charmingly sincere young man pleaded with her--accompanied by the orchestra in the old `Traviata' duet, 'misterioso, misterios' altero!'--she maintained her bitter scepticism, and the curtain fell on her dancing recklessly with the others, after Armand had been sent away with his flower.

Between the acts we had no time to forget. The orchestra kept sawing away at the `Traviata' music, so joyous and sad, so thin and far-away, so clap-trap and yet so heart-breaking. After the second act I left Lena in tearful contemplation of the ceiling, and went out into the lobby to smoke. As I walked about there I congratulated myself that I had not brought some Lincoln girl who would talk during the waits about the junior dances, or whether the cadets would camp at Plattsmouth. Lena was at least a woman, and I was a man.

Through the scene between Marguerite and the elder Duval, Lena wept unceasingly, and I sat helpless to prevent the closing of that chapter of idyllic love, dreading the return of the young man whose ineffable happiness was only to be the measure of his fall.

I suppose no woman could have been further in person, voice, and temperament from Dumas' appealing heroine than the veteran actress who first acquainted me with her. Her conception of the character was as heavy and uncompromising as her diction; she bore hard on the idea and on the consonants. At all times she was highly tragic, devoured by remorse. Lightness of stress or behaviour was far from her. Her voice was heavy and deep: `Ar-r-r-mond!' she would begin, as if she were summoning him to the bar of Judgment. But the lines were enough. She had only to utter them. They created the character in spite of her.

The heartless world which Marguerite re-entered with Varville had never been so glittering and reckless as on the night when it gathered in Olympe's salon for the fourth act. There were chandeliers hung from the ceiling, I remember, many servants in livery, gaming-tables where the men played with piles of gold, and a staircase down which the guests made their entrance. After all the others had gathered round the card-tables and young Duval had been warned by Prudence, Marguerite descended the staircase with Varville; such a cloak, such a fan, such jewels--and her face! One knew at a glance how it was with her. When Armand, with the terrible words, `Look, all of you, I owe this woman nothing!' flung the gold and bank-notes at the half-swooning Marguerite, Lena cowered beside me and covered her face with her hands.

The curtain rose on the bedroom scene. By this time there wasn't a nerve in me that hadn't been twisted. Nanine alone could have made me cry. I loved Nanine tenderly; and Gaston, how one clung to that good fellow! The New Year's presents were not too much; nothing could be too much now. I wept unrestrainedly. Even the handkerchief in my breast-pocket, worn for elegance and not at all for use, was wet through by the time that moribund woman sank for the last time into the arms of her lover.

When we reached the door of the theatre, the streets were shining with rain. I had prudently brought along Mrs. Harling's useful Commencement present, and I took Lena home under its shelter. After leaving her, I walked slowly out into the country part of the town where I lived. The lilacs were all blooming in the yards, and the smell of them after the rain, of the new leaves and the blossoms together, blew into my face with a sort of bitter sweetness. I tramped through the puddles and under the showery trees, mourning for Marguerite Gauthier as if she had died only yesterday, sighing with the spirit of 1840, which had sighed so much, and which had reached me only that night, across long years and several languages, through the person of an infirm old actress. The idea is one that no circumstances can frustrate. Wherever and whenever that piece is put on, it is April.

IV

HOW WELL I REMEMBER the stiff little parlour where I used to wait for Lena: the hard horsehair furniture, bought at some auction sale, the long mirror, the fashion-plates on the wall. If I sat down even for a moment, I was sure to find threads and bits of coloured silk clinging to my clothes after I went away. Lena's success puzzled me. She was so easygoing; had none of the push and self-assertiveness that get people ahead in business. She had come to Lincoln, a country girl, with no introductions except to some cousins of Mrs. Thomas who lived there, and she was already making clothes for the women of `the young married set.' Evidently she had great natural aptitude for her work. She knew, as she said, `what people looked well in.' She never tired of poring over fashion-books. Sometimes in the evening I would find her alone in her work-room, draping folds of satin on a wire figure, with a quite blissful expression of countenance. I couldn't help thinking that the years when Lena literally hadn't enough clothes to cover herself might have something to do with her untiring interest in dressing the human figure. Her clients said that Lena `had style,' and overlooked her habitual inaccuracies. She never, I discovered, finished anything by the time she had promised, and she frequently spent more money on materials than her customer had authorized. Once, when I arrived at six o'clock, Lena was ushering out a fidgety mother and her awkward, overgrown daughter. The woman detained Lena at the door to say apologetically:

`You'll try to keep it under fifty for me, won't you, Miss Lingard? You see, she's really too young to come to an expensive dressmaker, but I knew you could do more with her than anybody else.'

`Oh, that will be all right, Mrs. Herron. I think we'll manage to get a good effect,' Lena replied blandly.

I thought her manner with her customers very good, and wondered where she had learned such self-possession.

Sometimes after my morning classes were over, I used to encounter Lena downtown, in her velvet suit and a little black hat, with a veil tied smoothly over her face, looking as fresh as the spring morning. Maybe she would be carrying home a bunch of jonquils or a hyacinth plant. When we passed a candy store her footsteps would hesitate and linger. `Don't let me go in,' she would murmur. `Get me by if you can.' She was very fond of sweets, and was afraid of growing too plump.

We had delightful Sunday breakfasts together at Lena's. At the back of her long work-room was a bay-window, large enough to hold a box-couch and a reading-table. We breakfasted in this recess, after drawing the curtains that shut out the long room, with cutting-tables and wire women and sheet-draped garments on the walls. The sunlight poured in, making everything on the table shine and glitter and the flame of the alcohol lamp disappear altogether. Lena's curly black water-spaniel, Prince, breakfasted with us. He sat beside her on the couch and behaved very well until the Polish violin-teacher across the hall began to practise, when Prince would growl and sniff the air with disgust. Lena's landlord, old Colonel Raleigh, had given her the dog, and at first she was not at all pleased. She had spent too much of her life taking care of animals to have much sentiment about them. But Prince was a knowing little beast, and she grew fond of him. After breakfast I made him do his lessons; play dead dog, shake hands, stand up like a soldier. We used to put my cadet cap on his head--I had to take military drill at the university--and give him a yard-measure to hold with his front leg. His gravity made us laugh immoderately.

Lena's talk always amused me. Antonia had never talked like the people about her. Even after she learned to speak English readily, there was always something impulsive and foreign in her speech. But Lena had picked up all the conventional expressions she heard at Mrs. Thomas's dressmaking shop. Those formal phrases, the very flower of small-town proprieties, and the flat commonplaces, nearly all hypocritical in their origin, became very funny, very engaging, when they were uttered in Lena's soft voice, with her caressing intonation and arch naivete. Nothing could be more diverting than to hear Lena, who was almost as candid as Nature, call a leg a `limb' or a house a `home.'

We used to linger a long while over our coffee in that sunny corner. Lena was never so pretty as in the morning; she wakened fresh with the world every day, and her eyes had a deeper colour then, like the blue flowers that are never so blue as when they first open. I could sit idle all through a Sunday morning and look at her. Ole Benson's behaviour was now no mystery to me.

`There was never any harm in Ole,' she said once. `People needn't have troubled themselves. He just liked to come over and sit on the drawside and forget about his bad luck. I liked to have him. Any company's welcome when you're off with cattle all the time.'

`But wasn't he always glum?' I asked. `People said he never talked at all.'

`Sure he talked, in Norwegian. He'd been a sailor on an English boat and had seen lots of queer places. He had wonderful tattoos. We used to sit and look at them for hours; there wasn't much to look at out there. He was like a picture book. He had a ship and a strawberry girl on one arm, and on the other a girl standing before a little house, with a fence and gate and all, waiting for her sweetheart. Farther up his arm, her sailor had come back and was kissing her. "The Sailor's Return," he called it.'

I admitted it was no wonder Ole liked to look at a pretty girl once in a while, with such a fright at home.

`You know,' Lena said confidentially, `he married Mary because he thought she was strong-minded and would keep him straight. He never could keep straight on shore. The last time he landed in Liverpool he'd been out on a two years' voyage. He was paid off one morning, and by the next he hadn't a cent left, and his watch and compass were gone. He'd got with some women, and they'd taken everything. He worked his way to this country on a little passenger boat. Mary was a stewardess, and she tried to convert him on the way over. He thought she was just the one to keep him steady. Poor Ole! He used to bring me candy from town, hidden in his feed-bag. He couldn't refuse anything to a girl. He'd have given away his tattoos long ago, if he could. He's one of the people I'm sorriest for.'

If I happened to spend an evening with Lena and stayed late, the Polish violin-teacher across the hall used to come out and watch me descend the stairs, muttering so threateningly that it would have been easy to fall into a quarrel with him. Lena had told him once that she liked to hear him practise, so he always left his door open, and watched who came and went.

There was a coolness between the Pole and Lena's landlord on her account. Old Colonel Raleigh had come to Lincoln from Kentucky and invested an inherited fortune in real estate, at the time of inflated prices. Now he sat day after day in his office in the Raleigh Block, trying to discover where his money had gone and how he could get some of it back. He was a widower, and found very little congenial companionship in this casual Western city. Lena's good looks and gentle manners appealed to him. He said her voice reminded him of Southern voices, and he found as many opportunities of hearing it as possible. He painted and papered her rooms for her that spring, and put in a porcelain bathtub in place of the tin one that had satisfied the former tenant. While these repairs were being made, the old gentleman often dropped in to consult Lena's preferences. She told me with amusement how Ordinsky, the Pole, had presented himself at her door one evening, and said that if the landlord was annoying her by his attentions, he would promptly put a stop to it.

`I don't exactly know what to do about him,' she said, shaking her head, `he's so sort of wild all the time. I wouldn't like to have him say anything rough to that nice old man. The colonel is long-winded, but then I expect he's lonesome. I don't think he cares much for Ordinsky, either. He said once that if I had any complaints to make of my neighbours, I mustn't hesitate.'

One Saturday evening when I was having supper with Lena, we heard a knock at her parlour door, and there stood the Pole, coatless, in a dress shirt and collar. Prince dropped on his paws and began to growl like a mastiff, while the visitor apologized, saying that he could not possibly come in thus attired, but he begged Lena to lend him some safety pins.

`Oh, you'll have to come in, Mr. Ordinsky, and let me see what's the matter.' She closed the door behind him. `Jim, won't you make Prince behave?'

I rapped Prince on the nose, while Ordinsky explained that he had not had his dress clothes on for a long time, and tonight, when he was going to play for a concert, his waistcoat had split down the back. He thought he could pin it together until he got it to a tailor.

Lena took him by the elbow and turned him round. She laughed when she saw the long gap in the satin. `You could never pin that, Mr. Ordinsky. You've kept it folded too long, and the goods is all gone along the crease. Take it off. I can put a new piece of lining-silk in there for you in ten minutes.' She disappeared into her work-room with the vest, leaving me to confront the Pole, who stood against the door like a wooden figure. He folded his arms and glared at me with his excitable, slanting brown eyes. His head was the shape of a chocolate drop, and was covered with dry, straw-coloured hair that fuzzed up about his pointed crown. He had never done more than mutter at me as I passed him, and I was surprised when he now addressed me. `Miss Lingard,' he said haughtily, `is a young woman for whom I have the utmost, the utmost respect.'

`So have I,' I said coldly.

He paid no heed to my remark, but began to do rapid finger-exercises on his shirt-sleeves, as he stood with tightly folded arms.

`Kindness of heart,' he went on, staring at the ceiling, `sentiment, are not understood in a place like this. The noblest qualities are ridiculed. Grinning college boys, ignorant and conceited, what do they know of delicacy!'

I controlled my features and tried to speak seriously.

`If you mean me, Mr. Ordinsky, I have known Miss Lingard a long time, and I think I appreciate her kindness. We come from the same town, and we grew up together.'

His gaze travelled slowly down from the ceiling and rested on me. `Am I to understand that you have this young woman's interests at heart? That you do not wish to compromise her?'

`That's a word we don't use much here, Mr. Ordinsky. A girl who makes her own living can ask a college boy to supper without being talked about. We take some things for granted.'

`Then I have misjudged you, and I ask your pardon'--he bowed gravely. `Miss Lingard,' he went on, `is an absolutely trustful heart. She has not learned the hard lessons of life. As for you and me, noblesse oblige'--he watched me narrowly.

Lena returned with the vest. `Come in and let us look at you as you go out, Mr. Ordinsky. I've never seen you in your dress suit,' she said as she opened the door for him.

A few moments later he reappeared with his violin-case a heavy muffler about his neck and thick woollen gloves on his bony hands. Lena spoke encouragingly to him, and he went off with such an important professional air that we fell to laughing as soon as we had shut the door. `Poor fellow,' Lena said indulgently, `he takes everything so hard.'

After that Ordinsky was friendly to me, and behaved as if there were some deep understanding between us. He wrote a furious article, attacking the musical taste of the town, and asked me to do him a great service by taking it to the editor of the morning paper. If the editor refused to print it, I was to tell him that he would be answerable to Ordinsky `in person.' He declared that he would never retract one word, and that he was quite prepared to lose all his pupils. In spite of the fact that nobody ever mentioned his article to him after it appeared--full of typographical errors which he thought intentional--he got a certain satisfaction from believing that the citizens of Lincoln had meekly accepted the epithet `coarse barbarians.' `You see how it is,' he said to me, `where there is no chivalry, there is no amour-propre.' When I met him on his rounds now, I thought he carried his head more disdainfully than ever, and strode up the steps of front porches and rang doorbells with more assurance. He told Lena he would never forget how I had stood by him when he was `under fire.'

All this time, of course, I was drifting. Lena had broken up my serious mood. I wasn't interested in my classes. I played with Lena and Prince, I played with the Pole, I went buggy-riding with the old colonel, who had taken a fancy to me and used to talk to me about Lena and the `great beauties' he had known in his youth. We were all three in love with Lena.

Before the first of June, Gaston Cleric was offered an instructorship at Harvard College, and accepted it. He suggested that I should follow him in the fall, and complete my course at Harvard. He had found out about Lena--not from me--and he talked to me seriously.

`You won't do anything here now. You should either quit school and go to work, or change your college and begin again in earnest. You won't recover yourself while you are playing about with this handsome Norwegian. Yes, I've seen her with you at the theatre. She's very pretty, and perfectly irresponsible, I should judge.'

Cleric wrote my grandfather that he would like to take me East with him. To my astonishment, grandfather replied that I might go if I wished. I was both glad and sorry on the day when the letter came. I stayed in my room all evening and thought things over. I even tried to persuade myself that I was standing in Lena's way--it is so necessary to be a little noble!--and that if she had not me to play with, she would probably marry and secure her future.

The next evening I went to call on Lena. I found her propped up on the couch in her bay-window, with her foot in a big slipper. An awkward little Russian girl whom she had taken into her work-room had dropped a flat-iron on Lena's toe. On the table beside her there was a basket of early summer flowers which the Pole had left after he heard of the accident. He always managed to know what went on in Lena's apartment.

Lena was telling me some amusing piece of gossip about one of her clients, when I interrupted her and picked up the flower basket.

`This old chap will be proposing to you some day, Lena.'

`Oh, he has--often!' she murmured.

`What! After you've refused him?'

`He doesn't mind that. It seems to cheer him to mention the subject. Old men are like that, you know. It makes them feel important to think they're in love with somebody.'

`The colonel would marry you in a minute. I hope you won't marry some old fellow; not even a rich one.' Lena shifted her pillows and looked up at me in surprise.

`Why, I'm not going to marry anybody. Didn't you know that?'

`Nonsense, Lena. That's what girls say, but you know better. Every handsome girl like you marries, of course.'

She shook her head. `Not me.'

`But why not? What makes you say that?' I persisted.

Lena laughed.

`Well, it's mainly because I don't want a husband. Men are all right for friends, but as soon as you marry them they turn into cranky old fathers, even the wild ones. They begin to tell you what's sensible and what's foolish, and want you to stick at home all the time. I prefer to be foolish when I feel like it, and be accountable to nobody.'

`But you'll be lonesome. You'll get tired of this sort of life, and you'll want a family.'

`Not me. I like to be lonesome. When I went to work for Mrs. Thomas I was nineteen years old, and I had never slept a night in my life when there weren't three in the bed. I never had a minute to myself except when I was off with the cattle.'

Usually, when Lena referred to her life in the country at all, she dismissed it with a single remark, humorous or mildly cynical. But tonight her mind seemed to dwell on those early years. She told me she couldn't remember a time when she was so little that she wasn't lugging a heavy baby about, helping to wash for babies, trying to keep their little chapped hands and faces clean. She remembered home as a place where there were always too many children, a cross man and work piling up around a sick woman.

`It wasn't mother's fault. She would have made us comfortable if she could. But that was no life for a girl! After I began to herd and milk, I could never get the smell of the cattle off me. The few underclothes I had I kept in a cracker-box. On Saturday nights, after everybody was in bed, then I could take a bath if I wasn't too tired. I could make two trips to the windmill to carry water, and heat it in the wash-boiler on the stove. While the water was heating, I could bring in a washtub out of the cave, and take my bath in the kitchen. Then I could put on a clean night-gown and get into bed with two others, who likely hadn't had a bath unless I'd given it to them. You can't tell me anything about family life. I've had plenty to last me.'

`But it's not all like that,' I objected.

`Near enough. It's all being under somebody's thumb. What's on your mind, Jim? Are you afraid I'll want you to marry me some day?'

Then I told her I was going away.

`What makes you want to go away, Jim? Haven't I been nice to you?'

`You've been just awfully good to me, Lena,' I blurted. `I don't think about much else. I never shall think about much else while I'm with you. I'll never settle down and grind if I stay here. You know that.'

I dropped down beside her and sat looking at the floor. I seemed to have forgotten all my reasonable explanations.

Lena drew close to me, and the little hesitation in her voice that had hurt me was not there when she spoke again.

`I oughtn't to have begun it, ought I?' she murmured. `I oughtn't to have gone to see you that first time. But I did want to. I guess I've always been a little foolish about you. I don't know what first put it into my head, unless it was Antonia, always telling me I mustn't be up to any of my nonsense with you. I let you alone for a long while, though, didn't I?'

She was a sweet creature to those she loved, that Lena Lingard!

At last she sent me away with her soft, slow, renunciatory kiss.

`You aren't sorry I came to see you that time?' she whispered. `It seemed so natural. I used to think I'd like to be your first sweetheart. You were such a funny kid!'

She always kissed one as if she were sadly and wisely sending one away forever.

We said many good-byes before I left Lincoln, but she never tried to hinder me or hold me back. `You are going, but you haven't gone yet, have you?' she used to say.

My Lincoln chapter closed abruptly. I went home to my grandparents for a few weeks, and afterward visited my relatives in Virginia until I joined Cleric in Boston. I was then nineteen years old.

PART IV.
THE PIONEER WOMAN'S STORY

I

TWO YEARS AFTER I left Lincoln, I completed my academic course at Harvard. Before I entered the Law School I went home for the summer vacation. On the night of my arrival, Mrs. Harling and Frances and Sally came over to greet me. Everything seemed just as it used to be. My grandparents looked very little older. Frances Harling was married now, and she and her husband managed the Harling interests in Black Hawk. When we gathered in grandmother's parlour, I could hardly believe that I had been away at all. One subject, however, we avoided all evening.

When I was walking home with Frances, after we had left Mrs. Harling at her gate, she said simply, `You know, of course, about poor Antonia.'

Poor Antonia! Everyone would be saying that now, I thought bitterly. I replied that grandmother had written me how Antonia went away to marry Larry Donovan at some place where he was working; that he had deserted her, and that there was now a baby. This was all I knew.

`He never married her,' Frances said. `I haven't seen her since she came back. She lives at home, on the farm, and almost never comes to town. She brought the baby in to show it to mama once. I'm afraid she's settled down to be Ambrosch's drudge for good.'

I tried to shut Antonia out of my mind. I was bitterly disappointed in her. I could not forgive her for becoming an object of pity, while Lena Lingard, for whom people had always foretold trouble, was now the leading dressmaker of Lincoln, much respected in Black Hawk. Lena gave her heart away when she felt like it, but she kept her head for her business and had got on in the world.

Just then it was the fashion to speak indulgently of Lena and severely of Tiny Soderball, who had quietly gone West to try her fortune the year before. A Black Hawk boy, just back from Seattle, brought the news that Tiny had not gone to the coast on a venture, as she had allowed people to think, but with very definite plans. One of the roving promoters that used to stop at Mrs. Gardener's hotel owned idle property along the waterfront in Seattle, and he had offered to set Tiny up in business in one of his empty buildings. She was now conducting a sailors' lodging-house. This, everyone said, would be the end of Tiny. Even if she had begun by running a decent place, she couldn't keep it up; all sailors' boarding-houses were alike.

When I thought about it, I discovered that I had never known Tiny as well as I knew the other girls. I remembered her tripping briskly about the dining-room on her high heels, carrying a big trayful of dishes, glancing rather pertly at the spruce travelling men, and contemptuously at the scrubby ones--who were so afraid of her that they didn't dare to ask for two kinds of pie. Now it occurred to me that perhaps the sailors, too, might be afraid of Tiny. How astonished we should have been, as we sat talking about her on Frances Harling's front porch, if we could have known what her future was really to be! Of all the girls and boys who grew up together in Black Hawk, Tiny Soderball was to lead the most adventurous life and to achieve the most solid worldly success.

This is what actually happened to Tiny: While she was running her lodging-house in Seattle, gold was discovered in Alaska. Miners and sailors came back from the North with wonderful stories and pouches of gold. Tiny saw it and weighed it in her hands. That daring, which nobody had ever suspected in her, awoke. She sold her business and set out for Circle City, in company with a carpenter and his wife whom she had persuaded to go along with her. They reached Skaguay in a snowstorm, went in dog-sledges over the Chilkoot Pass, and shot the Yukon in flatboats. They reached Circle City on the very day when some Siwash Indians came into the settlement with the report that there had been a rich gold strike farther up the river, on a certain Klondike Creek. Two days later Tiny and her friends, and nearly everyone else in Circle City, started for the Klondike fields on the last steamer that went up the Yukon before it froze for the winter. That boatload of people founded Dawson City. Within a few weeks there were fifteen hundred homeless men in camp. Tiny and the carpenter's wife began to cook for them, in a tent. The miners gave her a building lot, and the carpenter put up a log hotel for her. There she sometimes fed a hundred and fifty men a day. Miners came in on snowshoes from their placer claims twenty miles away to buy fresh bread from her, and paid for it in gold.

That winter Tiny kept in her hotel a Swede whose legs had been frozen one night in a storm when he was trying to find his way back to his cabin. The poor fellow thought it great good fortune to be cared for by a woman, and a woman who spoke his own tongue. When he was told that his feet must be amputated, he said he hoped he would not get well; what could a working-man do in this hard world without feet? He did, in fact, die from the operation, but not before he had deeded Tiny Soderball his claim on Hunker Creek. Tiny sold her hotel, invested half her money in Dawson building lots, and with the rest she developed her claim. She went off into the wilds and lived on the claim. She bought other claims from discouraged miners, traded or sold them on percentages.

After nearly ten years in the Klondike, Tiny returned, with a considerable fortune, to live in San Francisco. I met her in Salt Lake City in 1908. She was a thin, hard-faced woman, very well-dressed, very reserved in manner. Curiously enough, she reminded me of Mrs. Gardener, for whom she had worked in Black Hawk so long ago. She told me about some of the desperate chances she had taken in the gold country, but the thrill of them was quite gone. She said frankly that nothing interested her much now but making money. The only two human beings of whom she spoke with any feeling were the Swede, Johnson, who had given her his claim, and Lena Lingard. She had persuaded Lena to come to San Francisco and go into business there.

`Lincoln was never any place for her,' Tiny remarked. `In a town of that size Lena would always be gossiped about. Frisco's the right field for her. She has a fine class of trade. Oh, she's just the same as she always was! She's careless, but she's level-headed. She's the only person I know who never gets any older. It's fine for me to have her there; somebody who enjoys things like that. She keeps an eye on me and won't let me be shabby. When she thinks I need a new dress, she makes it and sends it home with a bill that's long enough, I can tell you!'

Tiny limped slightly when she walked. The claim on Hunker Creek took toll from its possessors. Tiny had been caught in a sudden turn of weather, like poor Johnson. She lost three toes from one of those pretty little feet that used to trip about Black Hawk in pointed slippers and striped stockings. Tiny mentioned this mutilation quite casually--didn't seem sensitive about it. She was satisfied with her success, but not elated. She was like someone in whom the faculty of becoming interested is worn out.

II

SOON AFTER I GOT home that summer, I persuaded my grandparents to have their photographs taken, and one morning I went into the photographer's shop to arrange for sittings. While I was waiting for him to come out of his developing-room, I walked about trying to recognize the likenesses on his walls: girls in Commencement dresses, country brides and grooms holding hands, family groups of three generations. I noticed, in a heavy frame, one of those depressing `crayon enlargements' often seen in farm-house parlours, the subject being a round-eyed baby in short dresses. The photographer came out and gave a constrained, apologetic laugh.

`That's Tony Shimerda's baby. You remember her; she used to be the Harlings' Tony. Too bad! She seems proud of the baby, though; wouldn't hear to a cheap frame for the picture. I expect her brother will be in for it Saturday.'

I went away feeling that I must see Antonia again. Another girl would have kept her baby out of sight, but Tony, of course, must have its picture on exhibition at the town photographer's, in a great gilt frame. How like her! I could forgive her, I told myself, if she hadn't thrown herself away on such a cheap sort of fellow.

Larry Donovan was a passenger conductor, one of those train-crew aristocrats who are always afraid that someone may ask them to put up a car-window, and who, if requested to perform such a menial service, silently point to the button that calls the porter. Larry wore this air of official aloofness even on the street, where there were no car-windows to compromise his dignity. At the end of his run he stepped indifferently from the train along with the passengers, his street hat on his head and his conductor's cap in an alligator-skin bag, went directly into the station and changed his clothes. It was a matter of the utmost importance to him never to be seen in his blue trousers away from his train. He was usually cold and distant with men, but with all women he had a silent, grave familiarity, a special handshake, accompanied by a significant, deliberate look. He took women, married or single, into his confidence; walked them up and down in the moonlight, telling them what a mistake he had made by not entering the office branch of the service, and how much better fitted he was to fill the post of General Passenger Agent in Denver than the rough-shod man who then bore that title. His unappreciated worth was the tender secret Larry shared with his sweethearts, and he was always able to make some foolish heart ache over it.

As I drew near home that morning, I saw Mrs. Harling out in her yard, digging round her mountain-ash tree. It was a dry summer, and she had now no boy to help her. Charley was off in his battleship, cruising somewhere on the Caribbean sea. I turned in at the gate it was with a feeling of pleasure that I opened and shut that gate in those days; I liked the feel of it under my hand. I took the spade away from Mrs. Harling, and while I loosened the earth around the tree, she sat down on the steps and talked about the oriole family that had a nest in its branches.

`Mrs. Harling,' I said presently, `I wish I could find out exactly how Antonia's marriage fell through.'

`Why don't you go out and see your grandfather's tenant, the Widow Steavens? She knows more about it than anybody else. She helped Antonia get ready to be married, and she was there when Antonia came back. She took care of her when the baby was born. She could tell you everything. Besides, the Widow Steavens is a good talker, and she has a remarkable memory.'

III

ON THE FIRST OR second day of August I got a horse and cart and set out for the high country, to visit the Widow Steavens. The wheat harvest was over, and here and there along the horizon I could see black puffs of smoke from the steam threshing-machines. The old pasture land was now being broken up into wheatfields and cornfields, the red grass was disappearing, and the whole face of the country was changing. There were wooden houses where the old sod dwellings used to be, and little orchards, and big red barns; all this meant happy children, contented women, and men who saw their lives coming to a fortunate issue. The windy springs and the blazing summers, one after another, had enriched and mellowed that flat tableland; all the human effort that had gone into it was coming back in long, sweeping lines of fertility. The changes seemed beautiful and harmonious to me; it was like watching the growth of a great man or of a great idea. I recognized every tree and sandbank and rugged draw. I found that I remembered the conformation of the land as one remembers the modelling of human faces.

When I drew up to our old windmill, the Widow Steavens came out to meet me. She was brown as an Indian woman, tall, and very strong. When I was little, her massive head had always seemed to me like a Roman senator's. I told her at once why I had come.

`You'll stay the night with us, Jimmy? I'll talk to you after supper. I can take more interest when my work is off my mind. You've no prejudice against hot biscuit for supper? Some have, these days.'

While I was putting my horse away, I heard a rooster squawking. I looked at my watch and sighed; it was three o'clock, and I knew that I must eat him at six.

After supper Mrs. Steavens and I went upstairs to the old sitting-room, while her grave, silent brother remained in the basement to read his farm papers. All the windows were open. The white summer moon was shining outside, the windmill was pumping lazily in the light breeze. My hostess put the lamp on a stand in the corner, and turned it low because of the heat. She sat down in her favourite rocking-chair and settled a little stool comfortably under her tired feet. `I'm troubled with calluses, Jim; getting old,' she sighed cheerfully. She crossed her hands in her lap and sat as if she were at a meeting of some kind.

`Now, it's about that dear Antonia you want to know? Well, you've come to the right person. I've watched her like she'd been my own daughter.

`When she came home to do her sewing that summer before she was to be married, she was over here about every day. They've never had a sewing-machine at the Shimerdas', and she made all her things here. I taught her hemstitching, and I helped her to cut and fit. She used to sit there at that machine by the window, pedalling the life out of it--she was so strong--and always singing them queer Bohemian songs, like she was the happiest thing in the world.

`"Antonia," I used to say, "don't run that machine so fast. You won't hasten the day none that way."

`Then she'd laugh and slow down for a little, but she'd soon forget and begin to pedal and sing again. I never saw a girl work harder to go to housekeeping right and well-prepared. Lovely table-linen the Harlings had given her, and Lena Lingard had sent her nice things from Lincoln. We hemstitched all the tablecloths and pillow-cases, and some of the sheets. Old Mrs. Shimerda knit yards and yards of lace for her underclothes. Tony told me just how she meant to have everything in her house. She'd even bought silver spoons and forks, and kept them in her trunk. She was always coaxing brother to go to the post-office. Her young man did write her real often, from the different towns along his run.

`The first thing that troubled her was when he wrote that his run had been changed, and they would likely have to live in Denver. "I'm a country girl," she said, "and I doubt if I'll be able to manage so well for him in a city. I was counting on keeping chickens, and maybe a cow." She soon cheered up, though.

`At last she got the letter telling her when to come. She was shaken by it; she broke the seal and read it in this room. I suspected then that she'd begun to get faint-hearted, waiting; though she'd never let me see it.

`Then there was a great time of packing. It was in March, if I remember rightly, and a terrible muddy, raw spell, with the roads bad for hauling her things to town. And here let me say, Ambrosch did the right thing. He went to Black Hawk and bought her a set of plated silver in a purple velvet box, good enough for her station. He gave her three hundred dollars in money; I saw the cheque. He'd collected her wages all those first years she worked out, and it was but right. I shook him by the hand in this room. "You're behaving like a man, Ambrosch," I said, "and I'm glad to see it, son."

`'Twas a cold, raw day he drove her and her three trunks into Black Hawk to take the night train for Denver--the boxes had been shipped before. He stopped the wagon here, and she ran in to tell me good-bye. She threw her arms around me and kissed me, and thanked me for all I'd done for her. She was so happy she was crying and laughing at the same time, and her red cheeks was all wet with rain.

`"You're surely handsome enough for any man," I said, looking her over.

`She laughed kind of flighty like, and whispered, "Good-bye, dear house!" and then ran out to the wagon. I expect she meant that for you and your grandmother, as much as for me, so I'm particular to tell you. This house had always been a refuge to her.

`Well, in a few days we had a letter saying she got to Denver safe, and he was there to meet her. They were to be married in a few days. He was trying to get his promotion before he married, she said. I didn't like that, but I said nothing. The next week Yulka got a postal card, saying she was "well and happy." After that we heard nothing. A month went by, and old Mrs. Shimerda began to get fretful. Ambrosch was as sulky with me as if I'd picked out the man and arranged the match.

`One night brother William came in and said that on his way back from the fields he had passed a livery team from town, driving fast out the west road. There was a trunk on the front seat with the driver, and another behind. In the back seat there was a woman all bundled up; but for all her veils, he thought `twas Antonia Shimerda, or Antonia Donovan, as her name ought now to be.

`The next morning I got brother to drive me over. I can walk still, but my feet ain't what they used to be, and I try to save myself. The lines outside the Shimerdas' house was full of washing, though it was the middle of the week. As we got nearer, I saw a sight that made my heart sink--all those underclothes we'd put so much work on, out there swinging in the wind. Yulka came bringing a dishpanful of wrung clothes, but she darted back into the house like she was loath to see us. When I went in, Antonia was standing over the tubs, just finishing up a big washing. Mrs. Shimerda was going about her work, talking and scolding to herself. She didn't so much as raise her eyes. Tony wiped her hand on her apron and held it out to me, looking at me steady but mournful. When I took her in my arms she drew away. "Don't, Mrs. Steavens," she says, "you'll make me cry, and I don't want to."

`I whispered and asked her to come out-of-doors with me. I knew she couldn't talk free before her mother. She went out with me, bareheaded, and we walked up toward the garden.

`"I'm not married, Mrs. Steavens," she says to me very quiet and natural-like, "and I ought to be."

`"Oh, my child," says I, "what's happened to you? Don't be afraid to tell me!"

`She sat down on the drawside, out of sight of the house. "He's run away from me," she said. "I don't know if he ever meant to marry me."

`"You mean he's thrown up his job and quit the country?" says I.

`"He didn't have any job. He'd been fired; blacklisted for knocking down fares. I didn't know. I thought he hadn't been treated right. He was sick when I got there. He'd just come out of the hospital. He lived with me till my money gave

412

out, and afterward I found he hadn't really been hunting work at all. Then he just didn't come back. One nice fellow at the station told me, when I kept going to look for him, to give it up. He said he was afraid Larry'd gone bad and wouldn't come back any more. I guess he's gone to Old Mexico. The conductors get rich down there, collecting half-fares off the natives and robbing the company. He was always talking about fellows who had got ahead that way."

`I asked her, of course, why she didn't insist on a civil marriage at once--that would have given her some hold on him. She leaned her head on her hands, poor child, and said, "I just don't know, Mrs. Steavens. I guess my patience was wore out, waiting so long. I thought if he saw how well I could do for him, he'd want to stay with me."

`Jimmy, I sat right down on that bank beside her and made lament. I cried like a young thing. I couldn't help it. I was just about heart-broke. It was one of them lovely warm May days, and the wind was blowing and the colts jumping around in the pastures; but I felt bowed with despair. My Antonia, that had so much good in her, had come home disgraced. And that Lena Lingard, that was always a bad one, say what you will, had turned out so well, and was coming home here every summer in her silks and her satins, and doing so much for her mother. I give credit where credit is due, but you know well enough, Jim Burden, there is a great difference in the principles of those two girls. And here it was the good one that had come to grief! I was poor comfort to her. I marvelled at her calm. As we went back to the house, she stopped to feel of her clothes to see if they was drying well, and seemed to take pride in their whiteness--she said she'd been living in a brick block, where she didn't have proper conveniences to wash them.

`The next time I saw Antonia, she was out in the fields ploughing corn. All that spring and summer she did the work of a man on the farm; it seemed to be an understood thing. Ambrosch didn't get any other hand to help him. Poor Marek had got violent and been sent away to an institution a good while back. We never even saw any of Tony's pretty dresses. She didn't take them out of her trunks. She was quiet and steady. Folks respected her industry and tried to treat her as if nothing had happened. They talked, to be sure; but not like they would if she'd put on airs. She was so crushed and quiet that nobody seemed to want to humble her. She never went anywhere. All that summer she never once came to see me. At first I was hurt, but I got to feel that it was because this house reminded her of too much. I went over there when I could, but the times when she was in from the fields were the times when I was busiest here. She talked about the grain and the weather as if she'd never had another interest, and if I went over at night she always looked dead weary. She was afflicted with toothache; one tooth after another ulcerated, and she went about with her face swollen half the time. She wouldn't go to Black Hawk to a dentist for fear of meeting people she knew. Ambrosch had got over his good spell long ago, and was always surly. Once I told him he ought not to let Antonia work so hard and pull herself down. He said, "If you put that in her head, you better stay home." And after that I did.

`Antonia worked on through harvest and threshing, though she was too modest to go out threshing for the neighbours, like when she was young and free. I didn't see much of her until late that fall when she begun to herd Ambrosch's cattle in the open ground north of here, up toward the big dog-town. Sometimes she used to bring them over the west hill, there, and I would run to meet her and walk north a piece with her. She had thirty cattle in her bunch; it had been dry, and the pasture was short, or she wouldn't have brought them so far.

`It was a fine open fall, and she liked to be alone. While the steers grazed, she used to sit on them grassy banks along the draws and sun herself for hours. Sometimes I slipped up to visit with her, when she hadn't gone too far.

`"It does seem like I ought to make lace, or knit like Lena used to," she said one day, "but if I start to work, I look around and forget to go on. It seems such a little while ago when Jim Burden and I was playing all over this country. Up here I can pick out the very places where my father used to stand. Sometimes I feel like I'm not going to live very long, so I'm just enjoying every day of this fall."

`After the winter begun she wore a man's long overcoat and boots, and a man's felt hat with a wide brim. I used to watch her coming and going, and I could see that her steps were getting heavier. One day in December, the snow began to fall. Late in the afternoon I saw Antonia driving her cattle homeward across the hill. The snow was flying round her and she bent to face it, looking more lonesome-like to me than usual. "Deary me," I says to myself, "the girl's stayed out too late. It'll be dark before she gets them cattle put into the corral." I seemed to sense she'd been feeling too miserable to get up and drive them.

`That very night, it happened. She got her cattle home, turned them into the corral, and went into the house, into her room behind the kitchen, and shut the door. There, without calling to anybody, without a groan, she lay down on the bed and bore her child.

`I was lifting supper when old Mrs. Shimerda came running down the basement stairs, out of breath and screeching:

`"Baby come, baby come!" she says. "Ambrosch much like devil!"

`Brother William is surely a patient man. He was just ready to sit down to a hot supper after a long day in the fields. Without a word he rose and went down to the barn and hooked up his team. He got us over there as quick as it was humanly possible. I went right in, and began to do for Antonia; but she laid there with her eyes shut and took no account of me. The old woman got a tubful of warm water to wash the baby. I overlooked what she was doing and I said out loud: "Mrs. Shimerda, don't you put that strong yellow soap near that baby. You'll blister its little skin." I was indignant.

`"Mrs. Steavens," Antonia said from the bed, "if you'll look in the top tray of my trunk, you'll see some fine soap." That was the first word she spoke.

`After I'd dressed the baby, I took it out to show it to Ambrosch. He was muttering behind the stove and wouldn't look at it.

`"You'd better put it out in the rain-barrel," he says.

`"Now, see here, Ambrosch," says I, "there's a law in this land, don't forget that. I stand here a witness that this baby has come into the world sound and strong, and I intend to keep an eye on what befalls it." I pride myself I cowed him.

`Well I expect you're not much interested in babies, but Antonia's got on fine. She loved it from the first as dearly as if she'd had a ring on her finger, and was never ashamed of it. It's a year and eight months old now, and no baby was ever better cared-for. Antonia is a natural-born mother. I wish she could marry and raise a family, but I don't know as there's much chance now.'

I slept that night in the room I used to have when I was a little boy, with the summer wind blowing in at the windows, bringing the smell of the ripe fields. I lay awake and watched the moonlight shining over the barn and the stacks and the pond, and the windmill making its old dark shadow against the blue sky.

IV

THE NEXT AFTERNOON I walked over to the Shimerdas'. Yulka showed me the baby and told me that Antonia was shocking wheat on the southwest quarter. I went down across the fields, and Tony saw me from a long way off. She stood still by her shocks, leaning on her pitchfork, watching me as I came. We met like the people in the old song, in silence, if not in tears. Her warm hand clasped mine.

`I thought you'd come, Jim. I heard you were at Mrs. Steavens's last night. I've been looking for you all day.'

She was thinner than I had ever seen her, and looked as Mrs. Steavens said, `worked down,' but there was a new kind of strength in the gravity of her face, and her colour still gave her that look of deep-seated health and ardour. Still? Why, it flashed across me that though so much had happened in her life and in mine, she was barely twenty-four years old.

Antonia stuck her fork in the ground, and instinctively we walked toward that unploughed patch at the crossing of the roads as the fittest place to talk to each other. We sat down outside the sagging wire fence that shut Mr. Shimerda's plot off from the rest of the world. The tall red grass had never been cut there. It had died down in winter and come up again in the spring until it was as thick and shrubby as some tropical garden-grass. I found myself telling her everything: why I had decided to study law and to go into the law office of one of my mother's relatives in New York City; about Gaston Cleric's death from pneumonia last winter, and the difference it had made in my life. She wanted to know about my friends, and my way of living, and my dearest hopes.

`Of course it means you are going away from us for good,' she said with a sigh. `But that don't mean I'll lose you. Look at my papa here; he's been dead all these years, and yet he is more real to me than almost anybody else. He never goes out of my life. I talk to him and consult him all the time. The older I grow, the better I know him and the more I understand him.'

She asked me whether I had learned to like big cities. `I'd always be miserable in a city. I'd die of lonesomeness. I like to be where I know every stack and tree, and where all the ground is friendly. I want to live and die here. Father Kelly says everybody's put into this world for something, and I know what I've got to do. I'm going to see that my little girl has a better chance than ever I had. I'm going to take care of that girl, Jim.'

I told her I knew she would. `Do you know, Antonia, since I've been away, I think of you more often than of anyone else in this part of the world. I'd have liked to have you for a sweetheart, or a wife, or my mother or my sister--anything that a woman can be to a man. The idea of you is a part of my mind; you influence my likes and dislikes, all my tastes, hundreds of times when I don't realize it. You really are a part of me.'

She turned her bright, believing eyes to me, and the tears came up in them slowly, `How can it be like that, when you know so many people, and when I've disappointed you so? Ain't it wonderful, Jim, how much people can mean to each other? I'm so glad we had each other when we were little. I can't wait till my little girl's old enough to tell her about all the things we used to do. You'll always remember me when you think about old times, won't you? And I guess everybody thinks about old times, even the happiest people.'

As we walked homeward across the fields, the sun dropped and lay like a great golden globe in the low west. While it hung there, the moon rose in the east, as big as a cart-wheel, pale silver and streaked with rose colour, thin as a bubble or a ghost-moon. For five, perhaps ten minutes, the two luminaries confronted each other across the level land, resting on opposite edges of the world.

In that singular light every little tree and shock of wheat, every sunflower stalk and clump of snow-on-the-mountain, drew itself up high and pointed; the very clods and furrows in the fields seemed to stand up sharply. I felt the old pull of the earth, the solemn magic that comes out of those fields at nightfall. I wished I could be a little boy again, and that my way could end there.

We reached the edge of the field, where our ways parted. I took her hands and held them against my breast, feeling once more how strong and warm and good they were, those brown hands, and remembering how many kind things they had done for me. I held them now a long while, over my heart. About us it was growing darker and darker, and I had to look hard to see her face, which I meant always to carry with me; the closest, realest face, under all the shadows of women's faces, at the very bottom of my memory.

`I'll come back,' I said earnestly, through the soft, intrusive darkness.

`Perhaps you will'--I felt rather than saw her smile. `But even if you don't, you're here, like my father. So I won't be lonesome.'

As I went back alone over that familiar road, I could almost believe that a boy and girl ran along beside me, as our shadows used to do, laughing and whispering to each other in the grass.

PART V. CUZAK'S BOYS

I

I TOLD ANTONIA I would come back, but life intervened, and it was twenty years before I kept my promise. I heard of her from time to time; that she married, very soon after I last saw her, a young Bohemian, a cousin of Anton Jelinek; that they were poor, and had a large family. Once when I was abroad I went into Bohemia, and from Prague I sent Antonia some photographs of her native village. Months afterward came a letter from her, telling me the names and ages of her many children, but little else; signed, `Your old friend, Antonia Cuzak.' When I met Tiny Soderball in Salt Lake, she told me that Antonia had not `done very well'; that her husband was not a man of much force, and she had had a hard life. Perhaps it was cowardice that kept me away so long. My business took me West several times every year, and it was always in the back of my mind that I would stop in Nebraska some day and go to see Antonia. But I kept putting it off until the next trip. I did not want to find her aged and broken; I really dreaded it. In the course of twenty crowded years one parts with many illusions. I did not wish to lose the early ones. Some memories are realities, and are better than anything that can ever happen to one again.

I owe it to Lena Lingard that I went to see Antonia at last. I was in San Francisco two summers ago when both Lena and Tiny Soderball were in town. Tiny lives in a house of her own, and Lena's shop is in an apartment house just around the corner. It interested me, after so many years, to see the two women together. Tiny audits Lena's accounts occasionally, and invests her money for her; and Lena, apparently, takes care that Tiny doesn't grow too miserly. `If there's anything I can't stand,' she said to me in Tiny's presence, `it's a shabby rich woman.' Tiny smiled grimly and assured me that Lena would never be either shabby or rich. `And I don't want to be,' the other agreed complacently.

Lena gave me a cheerful account of Antonia and urged me to make her a visit.

`You really ought to go, Jim. It would be such a satisfaction to her. Never mind what Tiny says. There's nothing the matter with Cuzak. You'd like him. He isn't a hustler, but a rough man would never have suited Tony. Tony has nice children--ten or eleven of them by this time, I guess. I shouldn't care for a family of that size myself, but somehow it's just right for Tony. She'd love to show them to you.'

On my way East I broke my journey at Hastings, in Nebraska, and set off with an open buggy and a fairly good livery team to find the Cuzak farm. At a little past midday, I knew I must be nearing my destination. Set back on a swell of land at my right, I saw a wide farm-house, with a red barn and an ash grove, and cattle-yards in front that sloped down to the highroad. I drew up my horses and was wondering whether I should drive in here, when I heard low voices. Ahead of me, in a plum thicket beside the road, I saw two boys bending over a dead dog. The little one, not more than four or five, was on his knees, his hands folded, and his close-clipped, bare head drooping forward in deep dejection. The other stood beside him, a hand on his shoulder, and was comforting him in a language I had not heard for a long while. When I stopped my horses opposite them, the older boy took his brother by the hand and came toward me. He, too, looked grave. This was evidently a sad afternoon for them.

`Are you Mrs. Cuzak's boys?' I asked.

The younger one did not look up; he was submerged in his own feelings, but his brother met me with intelligent grey eyes. `Yes, sir.'

`Does she live up there on the hill? I am going to see her. Get in and ride up with me.'

He glanced at his reluctant little brother. `I guess we'd better walk. But we'll open the gate for you.'

I drove along the side-road and they followed slowly behind. When I pulled up at the windmill, another boy, barefooted and curly-headed, ran out of the barn to tie my team for me. He was a handsome one, this chap, fair-skinned and freckled, with red cheeks and a ruddy pelt as thick as a lamb's wool, growing down on his neck in little tufts. He tied my team with two flourishes of his hands, and nodded when I asked him if his mother was at home. As he glanced at me, his face dimpled with a seizure of irrelevant merriment, and he shot up the windmill tower with a lightness that struck me as disdainful. I knew he was peering down at me as I walked toward the house.

Ducks and geese ran quacking across my path. White cats were sunning themselves among yellow pumpkins on the porch steps. I looked through the wire screen into a big, light kitchen with a white floor. I saw a long table, rows of wooden chairs against the wall, and a shining range in one corner. Two girls were washing dishes at the sink, laughing and chattering, and a little one, in a short pinafore, sat on a stool playing with a rag baby. When I asked for their mother, one of the girls dropped her towel, ran across the floor with noiseless bare feet, and disappeared. The older one, who wore shoes and stockings, came to the door to admit me. She was a buxom girl with dark hair and eyes, calm and self-possessed.

`Won't you come in? Mother will be here in a minute.'

Before I could sit down in the chair she offered me, the miracle happened; one of those quiet moments that clutch the heart, and take more courage than the noisy, excited passages in life. Antonia came in and stood before me; a stalwart, brown woman, flat-chested, her curly brown hair a little grizzled. It was a shock, of course. It always is, to meet people after long years, especially if they have lived as much and as hard as this woman had. We stood looking at each other. The eyes that peered anxiously at me were--simply Antonia's eyes. I had seen no others like them since I looked into them last, though I had looked at so many thousands of human faces. As I confronted her, the changes grew less apparent to me, her identity stronger. She was there, in the full vigour of her personality, battered but not diminished, looking at me, speaking to me in the husky, breathy voice I remembered so well.

`My husband's not at home, sir. Can I do anything?'

`Don't you remember me, Antonia? Have I changed so much?'

She frowned into the slanting sunlight that made her brown hair look redder than it was. Suddenly her eyes widened, her whole face seemed to grow broader. She caught her breath and put out two hard-worked hands.

`Why, it's Jim! Anna, Yulka, it's Jim Burden!' She had no sooner caught my hands than she looked alarmed. `What's happened? Is anybody dead?'

I patted her arm.

`No. I didn't come to a funeral this time. I got off the train at Hastings and drove down to see you and your family.'

She dropped my hand and began rushing about. `Anton, Yulka, Nina, where are you all? Run, Anna, and hunt for the boys. They're off looking for that dog, somewhere. And call Leo. Where is that Leo!' She pulled them out of corners and came bringing them like a mother cat bringing in her kittens. `You don't have to go right off, Jim? My oldest boy's not here. He's gone with papa to the street fair at Wilber. I won't let you go! You've got to stay and see Rudolph and our papa.' She looked at me imploringly, panting with excitement.

While I reassured her and told her there would be plenty of time, the barefooted boys from outside were slipping into the kitchen and gathering about her.

`Now, tell me their names, and how old they are.'

As she told them off in turn, she made several mistakes about ages, and they roared with laughter. When she came to my light-footed friend of the windmill, she said, `This is Leo, and he's old enough to be better than he is.'

He ran up to her and butted her playfully with his curly head, like a little ram, but his voice was quite desperate. `You've forgot! You always forget mine. It's mean! Please tell him, mother!' He clenched his fists in vexation and looked up at her impetuously.

She wound her forefinger in his yellow fleece and pulled it, watching him. `Well, how old are you?'

`I'm twelve,' he panted, looking not at me but at her; `I'm twelve years old, and I was born on Easter Day!'

She nodded to me. `It's true. He was an Easter baby.'

The children all looked at me, as if they expected me to exhibit astonishment or delight at this information. Clearly, they were proud of each other, and of being so many. When they had all been introduced, Anna, the eldest daughter, who had met me at the door, scattered them gently, and came bringing a white apron which she tied round her mother's waist.

`Now, mother, sit down and talk to Mr. Burden. We'll finish the dishes quietly and not disturb you.'

Antonia looked about, quite distracted. `Yes, child, but why don't we take him into the parlour, now that we've got a nice parlour for company?'

The daughter laughed indulgently, and took my hat from me. `Well, you're here, now, mother, and if you talk here, Yulka and I can listen, too. You can show him the parlour after while.' She smiled at me, and went back to the dishes, with her sister. The little girl with the rag doll found a place on the bottom step of an enclosed back stairway, and sat with her toes curled up, looking out at us expectantly.

`She's Nina, after Nina Harling,' Antonia explained. `Ain't her eyes like Nina's? I declare, Jim, I loved you children almost as much as I love my own. These children know all about you and Charley and Sally, like as if they'd grown up with you. I can't think of what I want to say, you've got me so stirred up. And then, I've forgot my English so. I don't often talk it any more. I tell the children I used to speak real well.' She said they always spoke Bohemian at home. The little ones could not speak English at all--didn't learn it until they went to school.

`I can't believe it's you, sitting here, in my own kitchen. You wouldn't have known me, would you, Jim? You've kept so young, yourself. But it's easier for a man. I can't see how my Anton looks any older than the day I married him. His teeth have kept so nice. I haven't got many left. But I feel just as young as I used to, and I can do as much work. Oh, we don't have to work so hard now! We've got plenty to help us, papa and me. And how many have you got, Jim?'

When I told her I had no children, she seemed embarrassed. `Oh, ain't that too bad! Maybe you could take one of my bad ones, now? That Leo; he's the worst of all.' She leaned toward me with a smile. `And I love him the best,' she whispered.

`Mother!' the two girls murmured reproachfully from the dishes.

Antonia threw up her head and laughed. `I can't help it. You know I do. Maybe it's because he came on Easter Day, I don't know. And he's never out of mischief one minute!'

I was thinking, as I watched her, how little it mattered--about her teeth, for instance. I know so many women who have kept all the things that she had lost, but whose inner glow has faded. Whatever else was gone, Antonia had not lost the fire of life. Her skin, so brown and hardened, had not that look of flabbiness, as if the sap beneath it had been secretly drawn away.

While we were talking, the little boy whom they called Jan came in and sat down on the step beside Nina, under the hood of the stairway. He wore a funny long gingham apron, like a smock, over his trousers, and his hair was clipped so short that his head looked white and naked. He watched us out of his big, sorrowful grey eyes.

`He wants to tell you about the dog, mother. They found it dead,' Anna said, as she passed us on her way to the cupboard.

Antonia beckoned the boy to her. He stood by her chair, leaning his elbows on her knees and twisting her apron strings in his slender fingers, while he told her his story softly in Bohemian, and the tears brimmed over and hung on his long lashes. His mother listened, spoke soothingly to him and in a whisper promised him something that made him give her a quick, teary smile. He slipped away and whispered his secret to Nina, sitting close to her and talking behind his hand.

When Anna finished her work and had washed her hands, she came and stood behind her mother's chair. `Why don't we show Mr. Burden our new fruit cave?' she asked.

We started off across the yard with the children at our heels. The boys were standing by the windmill, talking about the dog; some of them ran ahead to open the cellar door. When we descended, they all came down after us, and seemed quite as proud of the cave as the girls were.

Ambrosch, the thoughtful-looking one who had directed me down by the plum bushes, called my attention to the stout brick walls and the cement floor. `Yes, it is a good way from the house,' he admitted. `But, you see, in winter there are nearly always some of us around to come out and get things.'

Anna and Yulka showed me three small barrels; one full of dill pickles, one full of chopped pickles, and one full of pickled watermelon rinds.

`You wouldn't believe, Jim, what it takes to feed them all!' their mother exclaimed. `You ought to see the bread we bake on Wednesdays and Saturdays! It's no wonder their poor papa can't get rich, he has to buy so much sugar for us to preserve with. We have our own wheat ground for flour--but then there's that much less to sell.'

Nina and Jan, and a little girl named Lucie, kept shyly pointing out to me the shelves of glass jars. They said nothing, but, glancing at me, traced on the glass with their finger-tips the outline of the cherries and strawberries and crabapples within, trying by a blissful expression of countenance to give me some idea of their deliciousness.

`Show him the spiced plums, mother. Americans don't have those,' said one of the older boys. `Mother uses them to make kolaches,' he added.

Leo, in a low voice, tossed off some scornful remark in Bohemian.

I turned to him. `You think I don't know what kolaches are, eh? You're mistaken, young man. I've eaten your mother's kolaches long before that Easter Day when you were born.'

`Always too fresh, Leo,' Ambrosch remarked with a shrug.

Leo dived behind his mother and grinned out at me.

We turned to leave the cave; Antonia and I went up the stairs first, and the children waited. We were standing outside talking, when they all came running up the steps together, big and little, tow heads and gold heads and brown, and flashing little naked legs; a veritable explosion of life out of the dark cave into the sunlight. It made me dizzy for a moment.

The boys escorted us to the front of the house, which I hadn't yet seen; in farm-houses, somehow, life comes and goes by the back door. The roof was so steep that the eaves were not much above the forest of tall hollyhocks, now brown and in seed. Through July, Antonia said, the house was buried in them; the Bohemians, I remembered, always planted hollyhocks. The front yard was enclosed by a thorny locust hedge, and at the gate grew two silvery, mothlike trees of the mimosa family. From here one looked down over the cattle-yards, with their two long ponds, and over a wide stretch of stubble which they told me was a ryefield in summer.

At some distance behind the house were an ash grove and two orchards: a cherry orchard, with gooseberry and currant bushes between the rows, and an apple orchard, sheltered by a high hedge from the hot winds. The older children turned back when we reached the hedge, but Jan and Nina and Lucie crept through it by a hole known only to themselves and hid under the low-branching mulberry bushes.

As we walked through the apple orchard, grown up in tall bluegrass, Antonia kept stopping to tell me about one tree and another. `I love them as if they were people,' she said, rubbing her hand over the bark. `There wasn't a tree here when we first came. We planted every one, and used to carry water for them, too--after we'd been working in the fields all day. Anton, he was a city man, and he used to get discouraged. But I couldn't feel so tired that I wouldn't fret about these trees when there was a dry time. They were on my mind like children. Many a night after he was asleep I've got up and come out and carried water to the poor things. And now, you see, we have the good of them. My man worked in the orange groves in Florida, and he knows all about grafting. There ain't one of our neighbours has an orchard that bears like ours.'

In the middle of the orchard we came upon a grape arbour, with seats built along the sides and a warped plank table. The three children were waiting for us there. They looked up at me bashfully and made some request of their mother.

`They want me to tell you how the teacher has the school picnic here every year. These don't go to school yet, so they think it's all like the picnic.'

After I had admired the arbour sufficiently, the youngsters ran away to an open place where there was a rough jungle of French pinks, and squatted down among them, crawling about and measuring with a string.

`Jan wants to bury his dog there,' Antonia explained. `I had to tell him he could. He's kind of like Nina Harling; you remember how hard she used to take little things? He has funny notions, like her.'

We sat down and watched them. Antonia leaned her elbows on the table. There was the deepest peace in that orchard. It was surrounded by a triple enclosure; the wire fence, then the hedge of thorny locusts, then the mulberry hedge which kept out the hot winds of summer and held fast to the protecting snows of winter. The hedges were so tall that we could see nothing but the blue sky above them, neither the barn roof nor the windmill. The afternoon sun poured down on us through the drying grape leaves. The orchard seemed full of sun, like a cup, and we could smell the ripe apples on the trees. The crabs hung on the branches as thick as beads on a string, purple-red, with a thin silvery glaze over them. Some hens and ducks had crept through the hedge and were pecking at the fallen apples. The drakes were handsome fellows, with pinkish grey bodies, their heads and necks covered with iridescent green feathers which grew close and full, changing to blue like a peacock's neck. Antonia said they always reminded her of soldiers--some uniform she had seen in the old country, when she was a child.

`Are there any quail left now?' I asked. I reminded her how she used to go hunting with me the last summer before we moved to town. `You weren't a bad shot, Tony. Do you remember how you used to want to run away and go for ducks with Charley Harling and me?'

`I know, but I'm afraid to look at a gun now.' She picked up one of the drakes and ruffled his green capote with her fingers. `Ever since I've had children, I don't like to kill anything. It makes me kind of faint to wring an old goose's neck. Ain't that strange, Jim?'

`I don't know. The young Queen of Italy said the same thing once, to a friend of mine. She used to be a great huntswoman, but now she feels as you do, and only shoots clay pigeons.'

`Then I'm sure she's a good mother,' Antonia said warmly.

She told me how she and her husband had come out to this new country when the farm-land was cheap and could be had on easy payments. The first ten years were a hard struggle. Her husband knew very little about farming and often grew discouraged. `We'd never have got through if I hadn't been so strong. I've always had good health, thank God, and I was able to help him in the fields until right up to the time before my babies came. Our children were good about taking care of each other. Martha, the one you saw when she was a baby, was such a help to me, and she trained Anna to be just like her. My Martha's married now, and has a baby of her own. Think of that, Jim!

`No, I never got down-hearted. Anton's a good man, and I loved my children and always believed they would turn out well. I belong on a farm. I'm never lonesome here like I used to be in town. You remember what sad spells I used to have, when I didn't know what was the matter with me? I've never had them out here. And I don't mind work a bit, if I don't have to put up with sadness.' She leaned her chin on her hand and looked down through the orchard, where the sunlight was growing more and more golden.

`You ought never to have gone to town, Tony,' I said, wondering at her.

She turned to me eagerly.

`Oh, I'm glad I went! I'd never have known anything about cooking or housekeeping if I hadn't. I learned nice ways at the Harlings', and I've been able to bring my children up so much better. Don't you think they are pretty well-behaved for country children? If it hadn't been for what Mrs. Harling taught me, I expect I'd have brought them up like wild rabbits. No, I'm glad I had a chance to learn; but I'm thankful none of my daughters will ever have to work out. The trouble with me was, Jim, I never could believe harm of anybody I loved.'

While we were talking, Antonia assured me that she could keep me for the night. `We've plenty of room. Two of the boys sleep in the haymow till cold weather comes, but there's no need for it. Leo always begs to sleep there, and Ambrosch goes along to look after him.'

I told her I would like to sleep in the haymow, with the boys.

`You can do just as you want to. The chest is full of clean blankets, put away for winter. Now I must go, or my girls will be doing all the work, and I want to cook your supper myself.'

As we went toward the house, we met Ambrosch and Anton, starting off with their milking-pails to hunt the cows. I joined them, and Leo accompanied us at some distance, running ahead and starting up at us out of clumps of ironweed, calling, `I'm a jack rabbit,' or, `I'm a big bull-snake.'

I walked between the two older boys--straight, well-made fellows, with good heads and clear eyes. They talked about their school and the new teacher, told me about the crops and the harvest, and how many steers they would feed that winter. They were easy and confidential with me, as if I were an old friend of the family--and not too old. I felt like a boy in their company, and all manner of forgotten interests revived in me. It seemed, after all, so natural to be walking along a barbed-wire fence beside the sunset, toward a red pond, and to see my shadow moving along at my right, over the close-cropped grass.

`Has mother shown you the pictures you sent her from the old country?' Ambrosch asked. `We've had them framed and they're hung up in the parlour. She was so glad to get them. I don't believe I ever saw her so pleased about anything.' There was a note of simple gratitude in his voice that made me wish I had given more occasion for it.

I put my hand on his shoulder. `Your mother, you know, was very much loved by all of us. She was a beautiful girl.'

`Oh, we know!' They both spoke together; seemed a little surprised that I should think it necessary to mention this. `Everybody liked her, didn't they? The Harlings and your grandmother, and all the town people.'

`Sometimes,' I ventured, `it doesn't occur to boys that their mother was ever young and pretty.'

`Oh, we know!' they said again, warmly. `She's not very old now,' Ambrosch added. `Not much older than you.'

`Well,' I said, `if you weren't nice to her, I think I'd take a club and go for the whole lot of you. I couldn't stand it if you boys were inconsiderate, or thought of her as if she were just somebody who looked after you. You see I was very much in love with your mother once, and I know there's nobody like her.'

The boys laughed and seemed pleased and embarrassed.

`She never told us that,' said Anton. `But she's always talked lots about you, and about what good times you used to have. She has a picture of you that she cut out of the Chicago paper once, and Leo says he recognized you when you drove up to the windmill. You can't tell about Leo, though; sometimes he likes to be smart.'

We brought the cows home to the corner nearest the barn, and the boys milked them while night came on. Everything was as it should be: the strong smell of sunflowers and ironweed in the dew, the clear blue and gold of the sky, the evening star, the purr of the milk into the pails, the grunts and squeals of the pigs fighting over their supper. I began to feel the loneliness of the farm-boy at evening, when the chores seem everlastingly the same, and the world so far away.

What a tableful we were at supper: two long rows of restless heads in the lamplight, and so many eyes fastened excitedly upon Antonia as she sat at the head of the table, filling the plates and starting the dishes on their way. The children were seated according to a system; a little one next an older one, who was to watch over his behaviour and to see that he got his food. Anna and Yulka left their chairs from time to time to bring fresh plates of kolaches and pitchers of milk.

After supper we went into the parlour, so that Yulka and Leo could play for me. Antonia went first, carrying the lamp. There were not nearly chairs enough to go round, so the younger children sat down on the bare floor. Little Lucie whispered to me that they were going to have a parlour carpet if they got ninety cents for their wheat. Leo, with a good deal of fussing, got out his violin. It was old Mr. Shimerda's instrument, which Antonia had always kept, and it was too big for him. But he played very well for a self-taught boy. Poor Yulka's efforts were not so successful. While they were playing, little Nina got up from her corner, came out into the middle of the floor, and began to do a pretty little dance on the boards with her bare feet. No one paid the least attention to her, and when she was through she stole back and sat down by her brother.

Antonia spoke to Leo in Bohemian. He frowned and wrinkled up his face. He seemed to be trying to pout, but his attempt only brought out dimples in unusual places. After twisting and screwing the keys, he played some Bohemian airs, without the organ to hold him back, and that went better. The boy was so restless that I had not had a chance to look at his face before. My first impression was right; he really was faun-like. He hadn't much head behind his ears, and his tawny fleece grew down thick to the back of his neck. His eyes were not frank and wide apart like those of the other boys, but were deep-set, gold-green in colour, and seemed sensitive to the light. His mother said he got hurt oftener than all the others put together. He was always trying to ride the colts before they were broken, teasing the turkey gobbler, seeing just how much red the bull would stand for, or how sharp the new axe was.

After the concert was over, Antonia brought out a big boxful of photographs: she and Anton in their wedding clothes, holding hands; her brother Ambrosch and his very fat wife, who had a farm of her own, and who bossed her husband, I was delighted to hear; the three Bohemian Marys and their large families.

`You wouldn't believe how steady those girls have turned out,' Antonia remarked. `Mary Svoboda's the best butter-maker in all this country, and a fine manager. Her children will have a grand chance.'

As Antonia turned over the pictures the young Cuzaks stood behind her chair, looking over her shoulder with interested faces. Nina and Jan, after trying to see round the taller ones, quietly brought a chair, climbed up on it, and stood close together, looking. The little boy forgot his shyness and grinned delightedly when familiar faces came into view. In the group about Antonia I was conscious of a kind of physical harmony. They leaned this way and that, and were not afraid to touch each other. They contemplated the photographs with pleased recognition; looked at some admiringly, as if these characters in their mother's girlhood had been remarkable people. The little children, who could not speak English, murmured comments to each other in their rich old language.

Antonia held out a photograph of Lena that had come from San Francisco last Christmas. `Does she still look like that? She hasn't been home for six years now.' Yes, it was exactly like Lena, I told her; a comely woman, a trifle too plump, in a hat a trifle too large, but with the old lazy eyes, and the old dimpled ingenuousness still lurking at the corners of her mouth.

There was a picture of Frances Harling in a befrogged riding costume that I remembered well. `Isn't she fine!' the girls murmured. They all assented. One could see that Frances had come down as a heroine in the family legend. Only Leo was unmoved.

`And there's Mr. Harling, in his grand fur coat. He was awfully rich, wasn't he, mother?'

`He wasn't any Rockefeller,' put in Master Leo, in a very low tone, which reminded me of the way in which Mrs. Shimerda had once said that my grandfather `wasn't Jesus.' His habitual scepticism was like a direct inheritance from that old woman.

`None of your smart speeches,' said Ambrosch severely.

Leo poked out a supple red tongue at him, but a moment later broke into a giggle at a tintype of two men, uncomfortably seated, with an awkward-looking boy in baggy clothes standing between them: Jake and Otto and I! We had it taken, I remembered, when we went to Black Hawk on the first Fourth of July I spent in Nebraska. I was glad to see Jake's grin again, and Otto's ferocious moustaches. The young Cuzaks knew all about them. `He made grandfather's coffin, didn't he?' Anton asked.

`Wasn't they good fellows, Jim?' Antonia's eyes filled. `To this day I'm ashamed because I quarrelled with Jake that way. I was saucy and impertinent to him, Leo, like you are with people sometimes, and I wish somebody had made me behave.'

`We aren't through with you, yet,' they warned me. They produced a photograph taken just before I went away to college: a tall youth in striped trousers and a straw hat, trying to look easy and jaunty.

`Tell us, Mr. Burden,' said Charley, `about the rattler you killed at the dog-town. How long was he? Sometimes mother says six feet and sometimes she says five.'

These children seemed to be upon very much the same terms with Antonia as the Harling children had been so many years before. They seemed to feel the same pride in her, and to look to her for stories and entertainment as we used to do.

It was eleven o'clock when I at last took my bag and some blankets and started for the barn with the boys. Their mother came to the door with us, and we tarried for a moment to look out at the white slope of the corral and the two ponds asleep in the moonlight, and the long sweep of the pasture under the star-sprinkled sky.

The boys told me to choose my own place in the haymow, and I lay down before a big window, left open in warm weather, that looked out into the stars. Ambrosch and Leo cuddled up in a hay-cave, back under the eaves, and lay giggling and whispering. They tickled each other and tossed and tumbled in the hay; and then, all at once, as if they had been shot, they were still. There was hardly a minute between giggles and bland slumber.

I lay awake for a long while, until the slow-moving moon passed my window on its way up the heavens. I was thinking about Antonia and her children; about Anna's solicitude for her, Ambrosch's grave affection, Leo's jealous, animal little love. That moment, when they all came tumbling out of the cave into the light, was a sight any man might have come far to see. Antonia had always been one to leave images in the mind that did not fade--that grew stronger with time. In my memory there was a succession of such pictures, fixed there like the old woodcuts of one's first primer: Antonia kicking her bare legs against the sides of my pony when we came home in triumph with our snake; Antonia in her black shawl and fur cap, as she stood by her father's grave in the snowstorm; Antonia coming in with her work-team along the evening sky-line. She lent herself to immemorial human attitudes which we recognize by instinct as universal and true. I had not been mistaken. She was a battered woman now, not a lovely girl; but she still had that something which fires the imagination, could still stop one's breath for a moment by a look or gesture that somehow revealed the meaning in common things. She had only to stand in the orchard, to put her hand on a little crab tree and look up at the apples, to make you feel the goodness of planting and tending and harvesting at last. All the strong things of her heart came out in her body, that had been so tireless in serving generous emotions.

It was no wonder that her sons stood tall and straight. She was a rich mine of life, like the founders of early races.

II

WHEN I AWOKE IN THE morning, long bands of sunshine were coming in at the window and reaching back under the eaves where the two boys lay. Leo was wide awake and was tickling his brother's leg with a dried cone-flower he had pulled out of the hay. Ambrosch kicked at him and turned over. I closed my eyes and pretended to be asleep. Leo lay on his back, elevated one foot, and began exercising his toes. He picked up dried flowers with his toes and brandished them in the belt of sunlight. After he had amused himself thus for some time, he rose on one elbow and began to look at me, cautiously, then critically, blinking his eyes in the light. His expression was droll; it dismissed me lightly. `This old fellow is no different from other people. He doesn't know my secret.' He seemed conscious of possessing a keener power of enjoyment than other people; his quick recognitions made him frantically impatient of deliberate judgments. He always knew what he wanted without thinking.

After dressing in the hay, I washed my face in cold water at the windmill. Breakfast was ready when I entered the kitchen, and Yulka was baking griddle-cakes. The three older boys set off for the fields early. Leo and Yulka were to drive to town to meet their father, who would return from Wilber on the noon train.

`We'll only have a lunch at noon,' Antonia said, and cook the geese for supper, when our papa will be here. I wish my Martha could come down to see you. They have a Ford car now, and she don't seem so far away from me as she used to. But her husband's crazy about his farm and about having everything just right, and they almost never get away except on Sundays. He's a handsome boy, and he'll be rich some day. Everything he takes hold of turns out well. When they bring that baby in here, and unwrap him, he looks like a little prince; Martha takes care of him so beautiful. I'm reconciled to her being away from me now, but at first I cried like I was putting her into her coffin.'

We were alone in the kitchen, except for Anna, who was pouring cream into the churn. She looked up at me. `Yes, she did. We were just ashamed of mother. She went round crying, when Martha was so happy, and the rest of us were all glad. Joe certainly was patient with you, mother.'

Antonia nodded and smiled at herself. `I know it was silly, but I couldn't help it. I wanted her right here. She'd never been away from me a night since she was born. If Anton had made trouble about her when she was a baby, or wanted me to leave her with my mother, I wouldn't have married him. I couldn't. But he always loved her like she was his own.'

`I didn't even know Martha wasn't my full sister until after she was engaged to Joe,' Anna told me.

Toward the middle of the afternoon, the wagon drove in, with the father and the eldest son. I was smoking in the orchard, and as I went out to meet them, Antonia came running down from the house and hugged the two men as if they had been away for months.

`Papa,' interested me, from my first glimpse of him. He was shorter than his older sons; a crumpled little man, with run-over boot-heels, and he carried one shoulder higher than the other. But he moved very quickly, and there was an air of jaunty liveliness about him. He had a strong, ruddy colour, thick black hair, a little grizzled, a curly moustache, and red lips. His smile showed the strong teeth of which his wife was so proud, and as he saw me his lively, quizzical eyes told me that he knew all about me. He looked like a humorous philosopher who had hitched up one shoulder under the burdens of life, and gone on his way having a good time when he could. He advanced to meet me and gave me a hard hand, burned red on the back and heavily coated with hair. He wore his Sunday clothes, very thick and hot for the weather, an unstarched white shirt, and a blue necktie with big white dots, like a little boy's, tied in a flowing bow. Cuzak began at once to talk about his holiday--from politeness he spoke in English.

`Mama, I wish you had see the lady dance on the slack-wire in the street at night. They throw a bright light on her and she float through the air something beautiful, like a bird! They have a dancing bear, like in the old country, and two-three merry-go-around, and people in balloons, and what you call the big wheel, Rudolph?'

`A Ferris wheel,' Rudolph entered the conversation in a deep baritone voice. He was six foot two, and had a chest like a young blacksmith. `We went to the big dance in the hall behind the saloon last night, mother, and I danced with all the girls, and so did father. I never saw so many pretty girls. It was a Bohunk crowd, for sure. We didn't hear a word of English on the street, except from the show people, did we, papa?'

Cuzak nodded. `And very many send word to you, Antonia. You will excuse'--turning to me--`if I tell her.' While we walked toward the house he related incidents and delivered messages in the tongue he spoke fluently, and I dropped a little behind, curious to know what their relations had become--or remained. The two seemed to be on terms of easy friendliness, touched with humour. Clearly, she was the impulse, and he the corrective. As they went up the hill he kept glancing at her sidewise, to see whether she got his point, or how she received it. I noticed later that he always looked at people sidewise, as a work-horse does at its yokemate. Even when he sat opposite me in the kitchen, talking, he would turn his head a little toward the clock or the stove and look at me from the side, but with frankness and good nature. This trick did not suggest duplicity or secretiveness, but merely long habit, as with the horse.

He had brought a tintype of himself and Rudolph for Antonia's collection, and several paper bags of candy for the children. He looked a little disappointed when his wife showed him a big box of candy I had got in Denver--she hadn't let the children touch it the night before. He put his candy away in the cupboard, `for when she rains,' and glanced at the box, chuckling. `I guess you must have hear about how my family ain't so small,' he said.

Cuzak sat down behind the stove and watched his womenfolk and the little children with equal amusement. He thought they were nice, and he thought they were funny, evidently. He had been off dancing with the girls and forgetting that he was an old fellow, and now his family rather surprised him; he seemed to think it a joke that all these children should belong to him. As the younger ones slipped up to him in his retreat, he kept taking things out of his pockets; penny dolls, a wooden clown, a balloon pig that was inflated by a whistle. He beckoned to the little boy they called Jan, whispered to him, and presented him with a paper snake, gently, so as not to startle him. Looking over the boy's head he said to me, `This one is bashful. He gets left.'

Cuzak had brought home with him a roll of illustrated Bohemian papers. He opened them and began to tell his wife the news, much of which seemed to relate to one person. I heard the name Vasakova, Vasakova, repeated several times with lively interest, and presently I asked him whether he were talking about the singer, Maria Vasak.

`You know? You have heard, maybe?' he asked incredulously. When I assured him that I had heard her, he pointed out her picture and told me that Vasak had broken her leg, climbing in the Austrian Alps, and would not be able to fill her engagements. He seemed delighted to find that I had heard her sing in London and in Vienna; got out his pipe and lit it to enjoy our talk the better. She came from his part of Prague. His father used to mend her shoes for her when she was a student. Cuzak questioned me about her looks, her popularity, her voice; but he particularly wanted to know whether I had noticed her tiny feet, and whether I thought she had saved much money. She was extravagant, of course, but he hoped she wouldn't squander everything, and have nothing left when she was old. As a young man, working in Wienn, he had seen a good many artists who were old and poor, making one glass of beer last all evening, and `it was not very nice, that.'

When the boys came in from milking and feeding, the long table was laid, and two brown geese, stuffed with apples, were put down sizzling before Antonia. She began to carve, and Rudolph, who sat next his mother, started the plates on their way. When everybody was served, he looked across the table at me.

`Have you been to Black Hawk lately, Mr. Burden? Then I wonder if you've heard about the Cutters?'

No, I had heard nothing at all about them.

`Then you must tell him, son, though it's a terrible thing to talk about at supper. Now, all you children be quiet, Rudolph is going to tell about the murder.'

`Hurrah! The murder!' the children murmured, looking pleased and interested.

Rudolph told his story in great detail, with occasional promptings from his mother or father.

Wick Cutter and his wife had gone on living in the house that Antonia and I knew so well, and in the way we knew so well. They grew to be very old people. He shrivelled up, Antonia said, until he looked like a little old yellow monkey, for his beard and his fringe of hair never changed colour. Mrs. Cutter remained flushed and wild-eyed as we had known her, but as the years passed she became afflicted with a shaking palsy which made her nervous nod continuous instead of occasional. Her hands were so uncertain that she could no longer disfigure china, poor woman! As the couple grew older, they quarrelled more and more often about the ultimate disposition of their `property.' A new law was passed in the state, securing the surviving wife a third of her husband's estate under all conditions. Cutter was tormented by the fear that Mrs. Cutter would live longer than he, and that eventually her `people,' whom he had always hated so violently, would inherit. Their quarrels on this subject passed the boundary of the close-growing cedars, and were heard in the street by whoever wished to loiter and listen.

One morning, two years ago, Cutter went into the hardware store and bought a pistol, saying he was going to shoot a dog, and adding that he `thought he would take a shot at an old cat while he was about it.' (Here the children interrupted Rudolph's narrative by smothered giggles.)

Cutter went out behind the hardware store, put up a target, practised for an hour or so, and then went home. At six o'clock that evening, when several men were passing the Cutter house on their way home to supper, they heard a pistol shot. They paused and were looking doubtfully at one another, when another shot came crashing through an upstairs window. They ran into the house and found Wick Cutter lying on a sofa in his upstairs bedroom, with his throat torn open, bleeding on a roll of sheets he had placed beside his head.

`Walk in, gentlemen,' he said weakly. `I am alive, you see, and competent. You are witnesses that I have survived my wife. You will find her in her own room. Please make your examination at once, so that there will be no mistake.'

One of the neighbours telephoned for a doctor, while the others went into Mrs. Cutter's room. She was lying on her bed, in her night-gown and wrapper, shot through the heart. Her husband must have come in while she was taking her afternoon nap and shot her, holding the revolver near her breast. Her night-gown was burned from the powder.

The horrified neighbours rushed back to Cutter. He opened his eyes and said distinctly, `Mrs. Cutter is quite dead, gentlemen, and I am conscious. My affairs are in order.' Then, Rudolph said, `he let go and died.'

On his desk the coroner found a letter, dated at five o'clock that afternoon. It stated that he had just shot his wife; that any will she might secretly have made would be invalid, as he survived her. He meant to shoot himself at six o'clock and would, if he had strength, fire a shot through the window in the hope that passersby might come in and see him `before life was extinct,' as he wrote.

`Now, would you have thought that man had such a cruel heart?' Antonia turned to me after the story was told. `To go and do that poor woman out of any comfort she might have from his money after he was gone!'

`Did you ever hear of anybody else that killed himself for spite, Mr. Burden?' asked Rudolph.

I admitted that I hadn't. Every lawyer learns over and over how strong a motive hate can be, but in my collection of legal anecdotes I had nothing to match this one. When I asked how much the estate amounted to, Rudolph said it was a little over a hundred thousand dollars.

Cuzak gave me a twinkling, sidelong glance. `The lawyers, they got a good deal of it, sure,' he said merrily.

A hundred thousand dollars; so that was the fortune that had been scraped together by such hard dealing, and that Cutter himself had died for in the end!

After supper Cuzak and I took a stroll in the orchard and sat down by the windmill to smoke. He told me his story as if it were my business to know it.

His father was a shoemaker, his uncle a furrier, and he, being a younger son, was apprenticed to the latter's trade. You never got anywhere working for your relatives, he said, so when he was a journeyman he went to Vienna and worked in a big fur shop, earning good money. But a young fellow who liked a good time didn't save anything in Vienna; there were too many pleasant ways of spending every night what he'd made in the day. After three years there, he came to New York. He was badly advised and went to work on furs during a strike, when the factories were offering big wages. The strikers won, and Cuzak was blacklisted. As he had a few hundred dollars ahead, he decided to go to Florida and raise oranges. He had always thought he would like to raise oranges! The second year a hard frost killed his young grove, and he fell ill with malaria. He came to Nebraska to visit his cousin, Anton Jelinek, and to look about. When he began to look about, he saw Antonia, and she was exactly the kind of girl he had always been hunting for. They were married at once, though he had to borrow money from his cousin to buy the wedding ring.

`It was a pretty hard job, breaking up this place and making the first crops grow,' he said, pushing back his hat and scratching his grizzled hair. `Sometimes I git awful sore on this place and want to quit, but my wife she always say we better stick it out. The babies come along pretty fast, so it look like it be hard to move, anyhow. I guess she was right, all right. We got this place clear now. We pay only twenty dollars an acre then, and I been offered a hundred. We bought another quarter ten years ago, and we got it most paid for. We got plenty boys; we can work a lot of land. Yes, she is a good wife for a poor man. She ain't always so strict with me, neither. Sometimes maybe I drink a little too much beer in town, and when I come home she don't say nothing. She don't ask me no questions. We always get along fine, her and me, like at first. The children don't make trouble between us, like sometimes happens.' He lit another pipe and pulled on it contentedly.

I found Cuzak a most companionable fellow. He asked me a great many questions about my trip through Bohemia, about Vienna and the Ringstrasse and the theatres.

`Gee! I like to go back there once, when the boys is big enough to farm the place. Sometimes when I read the papers from the old country, I pretty near run away,' he confessed with a little laugh. `I never did think how I would be a settled man like this.'

He was still, as Antonia said, a city man. He liked theatres and lighted streets and music and a game of dominoes after the day's work was over. His sociability was stronger than his acquisitive instinct. He liked to live day by day and night by night, sharing in the excitement of the crowd.--Yet his wife had managed to hold him here on a farm, in one of the loneliest countries in the world.

I could see the little chap, sitting here every evening by the windmill, nursing his pipe and listening to the silence; the wheeze of the pump, the grunting of the pigs, an occasional squawking when the hens were disturbed by a rat. It did rather seem to me that Cuzak had been made the instrument of Antonia's special mission. This was a fine life, certainly, but it wasn't the kind of life he had wanted to live. I wondered whether the life that was right for one was ever right for two!

I asked Cuzak if he didn't find it hard to do without the gay company he had always been used to. He knocked out his pipe against an upright, sighed, and dropped it into his pocket.

`At first I near go crazy with lonesomeness,' he said frankly, `but my woman is got such a warm heart. She always make it as good for me as she could. Now it ain't so bad; I can begin to have some fun with my boys, already!'

As we walked toward the house, Cuzak cocked his hat jauntily over one ear and looked up at the moon. `Gee!' he said in a hushed voice, as if he had just wakened up, `it don't seem like I am away from there twenty-six year!'

III

AFTER DINNER THE NEXT day I said good-bye and drove back to Hastings to take the train for Black Hawk. Antonia and her children gathered round my buggy before I started, and even the little ones looked up at me with friendly faces. Leo and Ambrosch ran ahead to open the lane gate. When I reached the bottom of the hill, I glanced back. The group was still there by the windmill. Antonia was waving her apron.

At the gate Ambrosch lingered beside my buggy, resting his arm on the wheel-rim. Leo slipped through the fence and ran off into the pasture.

`That's like him,' his brother said with a shrug. `He's a crazy kid. Maybe he's sorry to have you go, and maybe he's jealous. He's jealous of anybody mother makes a fuss over, even the priest.'

I found I hated to leave this boy, with his pleasant voice and his fine head and eyes. He looked very manly as he stood there without a hat, the wind rippling his shirt about his brown neck and shoulders.

`Don't forget that you and Rudolph are going hunting with me up on the Niobrara next summer,' I said. `Your father's agreed to let you off after harvest.'

He smiled. `I won't likely forget. I've never had such a nice thing offered to me before. I don't know what makes you so nice to us boys,' he added, blushing.

`Oh, yes, you do!' I said, gathering up my reins.

He made no answer to this, except to smile at me with unabashed pleasure and affection as I drove away.

My day in Black Hawk was disappointing. Most of my old friends were dead or had moved away. Strange children, who meant nothing to me, were playing in the Harlings' big yard when I passed; the mountain ash had been cut down, and only a sprouting stump was left of the tall Lombardy poplar that used to guard the gate. I hurried on. The rest of the morning I spent with Anton Jelinek, under a shady cottonwood tree in the yard behind his saloon. While I was having my midday dinner at the hotel, I met one of the old lawyers who was still in practice, and he took me up to his office and talked over the Cutter case with me. After that, I scarcely knew how to put in the time until the night express was due.

I took a long walk north of the town, out into the pastures where the land was so rough that it had never been ploughed up, and the long red grass of early times still grew shaggy over the draws and hillocks. Out there I felt at home again. Overhead the sky was that indescribable blue of autumn; bright and shadowless, hard as enamel. To the south I could see the dun-shaded river bluffs that used to look so big to me, and all about stretched drying cornfields, of the pale-gold colour, I remembered so well. Russian thistles were blowing across the uplands and piling against the wire fences like barricades. Along the cattle-paths the plumes of goldenrod were already fading into sun-warmed velvet, grey with gold threads in it. I had escaped from the curious depression that hangs over little towns, and my mind was full of pleasant things; trips I meant to take with the Cuzak boys, in the Bad Lands and up on the Stinking Water. There were enough Cuzaks to play with for a long while yet. Even after the boys grew up, there would always be Cuzak himself! I meant to tramp along a few miles of lighted streets with Cuzak.

As I wandered over those rough pastures, I had the good luck to stumble upon a bit of the first road that went from Black Hawk out to the north country; to my grandfather's farm, then on to the Shimerdas' and to the Norwegian settlement. Everywhere else it had been ploughed under when the highways were surveyed; this half-mile or so within the pasture fence was all that was left of that old road which used to run like a wild thing across the open prairie, clinging to the high places and circling and doubling like a rabbit before the hounds.

On the level land the tracks had almost disappeared--were mere shadings in the grass, and a stranger would not have noticed them. But wherever the road had crossed a draw, it was easy to find. The rains had made channels of the wheel-ruts and washed them so deeply that the sod had never healed over them. They looked like gashes torn by a grizzly's claws, on the slopes where the farm-wagons used to lurch up out of the hollows with a pull that brought curling muscles on the smooth hips of the horses. I sat down and watched the haystacks turn rosy in the slanting sunlight.

This was the road over which Antonia and I came on that night when we got off the train at Black Hawk and were bedded down in the straw, wondering children, being taken we knew not whither. I had only to close my eyes to hear the rumbling of the wagons in the dark, and to be again overcome by that obliterating strangeness. The feelings of that night were so near that I could reach out and touch them with my hand. I had the sense of coming home to myself, and of having found out what a little circle man's experience is. For Antonia and for me, this had been the road of Destiny; had taken us to those early accidents of fortune which predetermined for us all that we can ever be. Now I understood that the same road was to bring us together again. Whatever we had missed, we possessed together the precious, the incommunicable past.

THE END

Premium
Classic Books

Our mission is to provide you with the best classic books in history. Most of our books have been rescued and converted from their physical edition to a digital format. Many of these pieces have been found in different libraries worldwide and, in some cases, may contain spelling mistakes due to their antiquity.

We apologize in advance and we would appreciate your cooperation. If you find any spelling errors, please send us an email with the word and the page number, so that our team of collaborators can correct it immediately.

In exchange for your valuable collaboration we will send you the corrected e-book for free.

Our vision is to improve every day and provide a better service. Thank you very much for your understanding and valuable collaboration.

®2019 premiumclassicbooks@gmail.com

Made in the USA
Middletown, DE
16 October 2023

40943793R00255